Hailed as "the publishing event of the decade" (*Publishers Weekly*), THE SHELTERS OF STONE is the fifth in the bestselling Earth's Children® series, following:

THE CLAN OF THE CAVE BEAR
"Our nomination for the year's great escape."
—*Playboy*

"Imaginative, exciting."
—*The New York Times Book Review*

THE VALLEY OF HORSES
"A powerful story . . . Auel is a highly imaginative writer. She humanizes prehistory and gives it immediacy and clarity."
—*The New York Times Book Review*

"Auel may be creating one of the most believable characters in English fiction—one to rank with Sherlock Holmes, Scarlett O'Hara, and a handful of others."
—UPI

THE MAMMOTH HUNTERS
"A compelling, pulse-quickening tale of adventure, love, and survival during a period of human history that has seldom been drawn upon by other fiction writers."
—*Chicago Tribune Book World*

"Storytelling in the grand tradition . . . From the violent panorama of spring on the steppes to musicians jamming on a mammoth-bone marimba, Auel's books are a stunning example of world building."
—*Vogue*

THE PLAINS OF PASSAGE
"Pure entertainment at its sublime, wholly exhilarating best."
—*Los Angeles Times*

"Thrilling . . . This magical book is rich in details of all kinds . . . but it is the depth of the characters' emotional lives . . . that gives the novel such a stranglehold."
—*Cosmopolitan*

BY JEAN M. AUEL

The Land of Painted Caves
The Shelters of Stone
The Plains of Passage
The Mammoth Hunters
The Valley of Horses
The Clan of the Cave Bear

THE SHELTERS OF STONE

THE SHELTERS OF STONE

JEAN M. AUEL

EARTH'S CHILDREN®

BANTAM BOOKS TRADE PAPERBACKS
NEW YORK

2011 Bantam Books Trade Paperback Edition

Copyright © 2002 by Jean M. Auel
Map and illustrations by Radica Prato
Inset map copyright © Palacios after Auel
Excerpt from *The Land of Painted Caves* © 2011 by Jean M. Auel
Reading group guide copyright © 2011 by Random House, Inc.

EARTH'S CHILDREN is a trademark of Jean M. Auel

Published in the United States by Bantam Books, an imprint of
The Random House Publishing Group, a division of Random House, Inc., New York.

BANTAM BOOKS and the rooster colophon are registered trademarks of
Random House, Inc.

Originally published in hardcover in the United States by
Crown Publishers, a division of Random House, Inc., in 2002.

ISBN 978-0-553-38261-7
eBook ISBN 978-0-307-76764-6

This book contains an excerpt from the forthcoming title
The Land of Painted Caves by Jean M. Auel. This excerpt has been set for this
edition only and may not reflect the final content of the forthcoming edition.

PRINTED IN THE UNITED STATES OF AMERICA

www.bantamdell.com

6   8   9   7

For KENDALL,

who knows more about what's to come than almost anyone

... except his mother,

and for CHRISTY,

the mother of his boys,

and for FORREST, SKYLAR, and SLADE,

three of the best,

with love

I am more grateful than I can say for the assistance of many people who have helped me to learn about the ancient world of the people who lived when glaciers advanced far south of today's margins and covered a quarter of the earth's surface. However, there are some details which I have chosen to use, particularly with regard to certain theories and the timing of certain sites and events, which may not be accepted by the majority of the professional community at this time. Some may be oversights but others were chosen deliberately, usually because it felt more accurate to this subjective novelist who must write about people with an understanding of human nature and logical motivation for their actions.

Most especially, I want to thank Dr. Jean-Philippe Rigaud, whom I met on my first research trip to Europe at his archeological excavation named *Flageolet* in southwest France, once a hunting camp on a hillside that overlooked a broad grassy plain and the migrating Ice Age animals it supported. Though I was just an unknown American novelist, he took the time to explain some of the discoveries of that site, and he helped to arrange a visit to Lascaux Cave. I was brought to tears when I saw that sanctuary of prehistoric splendor painted by those early modern humans of Upper Paleolithic Europe, the Cro Magnons—work that can still stand against the finest of today.

Later, when we met again at La Micoque, a very early Neanderthal site, I began to get more of a sense of the unique time at the beginning of our prehistory when the first anatomically modern humans arrived in Europe and encountered the Neanderthals who had been living there since long before the last Ice Age. Because I wanted to understand the process that is used to learn about our ancient ancestors, my husband and I worked for a short time at Dr. Rigaud's more recent excavation, *Grotte Seize.* He also gave me many insights into the rich and expansive living site, which today is named *Laugerie Haute,* but that I have called the Ninth Cave of the Zelandonii.

Dr. Rigaud has been of help throughout the series, but I appreciate his assistance with this book in particular. Before I started writing

The Shelters of Stone, I took all the information I had gathered about the region and the way it was then and wrote the entire background setting in terms of the story, giving the sites my own names and describing the landscape so that when I needed the information it was easily available in my own words. I have asked many scientists and other specialists uncountable questions, but I never asked anyone to check my work before it was published. I have always taken full responsibility for the choices I made in selecting the details that were used in my books, for the way I decided to use them, and the imagination I added to them—and I still do. But because the setting for this novel is so well known, not only to archeologists and other professionals, but to the many people who have visited the region, I needed to be sure that my background details were as accurate as I could make them, so I did something I had never done before. I asked Dr. Rigaud, who knows the region and understands the archeology, to check over those many, many pages of background material for obvious errors. I didn't fully realize what a huge job I had asked of him, and I thank him profoundly for his time and efforts. He paid me the compliment of saying that the information was reasonably accurate, but he also told me some things I didn't know or hadn't understood, which I was able to correct and incorporate. Any mistakes remaining are entirely mine.

I am deeply grateful to another French archeologist, Dr. Jean Clottes, whom I met through his colleague, Dr. Rigaud. In Montignac, at the celebration for the fiftieth anniversary of the discovery of Lascaux Cave, he was kind enough to translate for me in quiet tones the gist of some of the presentations given in French at the conference that was held in conjunction with the Lascaux event. Over the years since then we have met on both sides of the Atlantic, and I cannot thank him enough for his kindness and exceptional generosity with his time and assistance. He has guided me through many painted and engraved caves, especially in the region near the Pyrenees Mountains. Besides the fabulous caves on Count Begouen's property, I was particularly impressed with Gargas, which has so much more than the handprints for which it is so well known. I also appreciated more than I can say my second visit deep into Niaux Cave with him, which lasted about six hours and was a wonderful revelation partly because by then I had learned much more about the painted caves than I knew the first time. Though these places are not yet included in the story, the many discussions with him about concepts and ideas, especially regarding the reasons that the Cro Magnons may have had for decorating their caves and living sites, have been enlightening.

I made my first visit to the cave of Niaux in the foothills of the Pyrenees in 1982, for which I must thank Dr. Jean-Michel Belamy. I was indelibly impressed with Niaux, the animals painted on the walls of the Black Salon, the children's footprints, the beautifully painted horses deep inside the extensive cavern beyond the small lake, and much more. I was moved beyond words, for Dr. Belamy's more recent gift of the exceptional first edition of the first book about the cave of Niaux.

I feel gratitude beyond measure to Count Robert Begouen, who has protected and preserved the remarkable caves on his land, L'Enlene, Tuc d'Audoubert, and Trois Frères, and established a unique museum for the artifacts that have been so carefully excavated from them. I was overwhelmed with the two caves I saw, and am deeply grateful to him, and Dr. Clottes, for guiding my visits.

I also want to thank Dr. David Lewis-Williams, a gentle man with strong convictions, whose work with the Bushmen in Africa and the remarkable rock paintings of their ancestors has engendered profound and fascinating ideas and several books, one co-written with Dr. Clottes, *The Shamans of Prehistory*, which suggests that the ancient French cave painters may have had similar reasons for decorating the rock walls of their caves.

Thanks are also owed to Dr. Roy Larick for his helpfulness and especially for unlocking the protective metal door and showing me the beautiful horse head carved in deep relief on the wall in the lower cave at Commarque.

I am also grateful to Dr. Paul Bahn for helping me to understand some of the conference presentations at the Lascaux anniversary meeting by translating them for me. Through his efforts, I had the honor of meeting three of the men who as boys discovered the beautiful cave of Lascaux in the 1940's. The site brought me to tears when I saw its white walls filled with such remarkable polychrome paintings, I can only imagine the impression it must have made on the four boys who followed a dog into a hole and saw the cave for the first time since its entrance collapsed 15,000 years ago. Dr. Bahn has been of great assistance to me, both through discussions and his books about the intriguing prehistoric era that are the subject of this series of novels.

I feel great warmth and gratitude to Dr. Jan Jelinek for continued discussions about the Upper Paleolithic Era. His insights about the people who lived during the time when anatomically modern humans arrived and settled in Europe and met the Neanderthals who were living there are always valuable. I also want to thank him for his assistance to the Czech publishers in their translations of the previous books in this series.

I read the books of Dr. Alexander Marshack, who pioneered the technique of examining carved artifacts under a microscope, long before I met him and I appreciate the efforts he has made into the understanding of Cro Magnons and Neanderthals, and the papers he sends me. I have been impressed with his cogent and thoughtful theories based on his careful studies, and continue to read his work for his penetrating and intelligent perceptions about the people who lived during the last Ice Age.

During the three months I lived near Les Eyzies de Tayac in southwest France doing research for this book, I visited Font-de-Guame Cave many times. I owe special thanks to Paulette Daubisse, who was the director and in charge of the people who guided the visitors to that beautifully painted ancient cave, for her kindness, and particularly for giving me a special private tour. She lived with that very singular site for many years, and knew it as though it were her own home. She showed me many formations and paintings that are not usually presented to the casual visitor—it would make the tours far too long—and I am more grateful than she can know for the unique insights that were revealed.

I also want to thank M. Renaud Bombard of Presse de la Cité, my French publisher, for his willingness to help me find whatever I needed, whenever I was in France doing research. Whether it was a place to make copies of a large manuscript not too far from where I was staying with someone there who could speak English so I could explain what I needed, or a good hotel in the region during the off-season when most hotels were closed, or a fabulous restaurant in the Loire valley where we could celebrate the anniversary of dear friends, or late reservations in a popular resort area on the Mediterranean which happened to be on the way to a site I wanted to see. Whatever it was, M. Bombard always managed to make it happen, and I am truly grateful.

In order to write this book, I had to learn about more than archeology and paleoanthropology and there are several other people who were of great assistance. A sincere thank-you to Dr. Ronald Naito, doctor of internal medicine in Portland, Oregon, and my personal physician for many years, who was willing to call me after his office hours and answer my questions about the symptoms and progression of certain illnesses and injuries. I also want to thank Dr. Brett Bolhofner, doctor of orthopaedic medicine in St. Petersburg, Florida, for his information about bone trauma and injuries, but even more for putting my son's shattered hip and pelvis back together after his automobile accident. Thanks also to Joseph J. Pica, orthopaedic surgery and trauma, and physician assistant to Dr. Bolhofner, for his cogent explanation of internal injuries, and his excellent care of my son. I also appreciated the discussion with Rick Frye, volunteer emergency paramedic in Washington State, about what to do first in medical emergencies.

Thanks also to Dr. John Kallas, Portland, Oregon, expert in the collection of wild foods, who continually experiments with processing and cooking them, for sharing his extensive knowledge not only of wild plant foods, but also of clams, mussels and vegetables from the sea. I had no idea there were so many different kinds of edible seaweed.

And special thanks to Lenette Stroebel of Prineville, Oregon, who has been breeding back from wild horses to the original Tarpan, and turning up some interesting characteristics. For example, they have hooves so hard they don't need horseshoes even on rocky ground, they have a stand-up mane, and they have markings similar to the horses painted on some cave walls, such as the dark legs and tail, and sometimes stripes on the flanks. And they have a beautiful gray color called gruya. She not only allowed me to see the horses, but she told me a great deal about them, and then sent a wonderful series of photographs of one of her mares giving birth, which gave me the basis for the birth of Whinney's foal.

I am grateful to Claudine Fisher, professor of French at Portland State University and Honorary French Counsel for Oregon, for French translations of research material and correspondence, and for advice and insights about this and other manuscripts, and additional things French.

To early readers, Karen Auel-Feuer, Kendall Auel, Cathy Humble, Deanna Sterett, Claudine Fisher and Ray Auel, who hurriedly read a first finished draft and offered some good constructive suggestions, thank you.

I am deeply indebted to Betty Prashker, my sharp, smart and savvy editor. Her suggestions are always helpful and her insights invaluable.

Thanks beyond measure to my literary agent, Jean Naggar, who flew here to read the first finished draft, and along with her husband, Serge Naggar, made some suggestions, but told me it worked. She has been there from the beginning, performing miracles with this series. Thanks also to Jennifer Weltz of the Jean V. Naggar Literary Agency, who is working with Jean to perform further miracles especially with foreign rights.

With great regret, I offer gratitude *in memoriam*, to David Abrams, professor of anthropology and archeology in Sacramento, California. In 1982, David and his research assistant and future wife, Diane Kelly, took Ray and me on my first research trip to Europe— France, Austria, Czechoslovakia, and Ukraine (then Russia)—to visit for the first time some of the sites where the books in the Earth's Children® series took place, some 30,000 years ago. I was able to get a sense of the localities, which helped me tremendously. We became friends with David and Diane, and saw each other several times over the years, both here and in Europe. It was a shock to learn that he was so ill—he was too young to go—but he held on with perseverance for much longer than anyone predicted, always keeping a wonderfully positive attitude. I miss him.

I must thank another dear friend, *in memoriam*, Richard Ausman, who helped me to write these books by designing comfortable places where I could live and work. "Oz" had a special genius for creating beautiful and efficient homes, but more than that, he had been a good friend to both Ray and me for years. He thought they had caught the cancer in time, and married Paula hoping for many more years with her and her children, but it was not to be. I feel great sadness that he is no longer with us.

There are many others I probably should thank for insights and assistance, but this is too long already, so I will end with the one who counts the most. I am grateful to Ray, for his love, support and encouragement, for helping to provide the time and space for me to work in spite of my strange hours, and for being there.

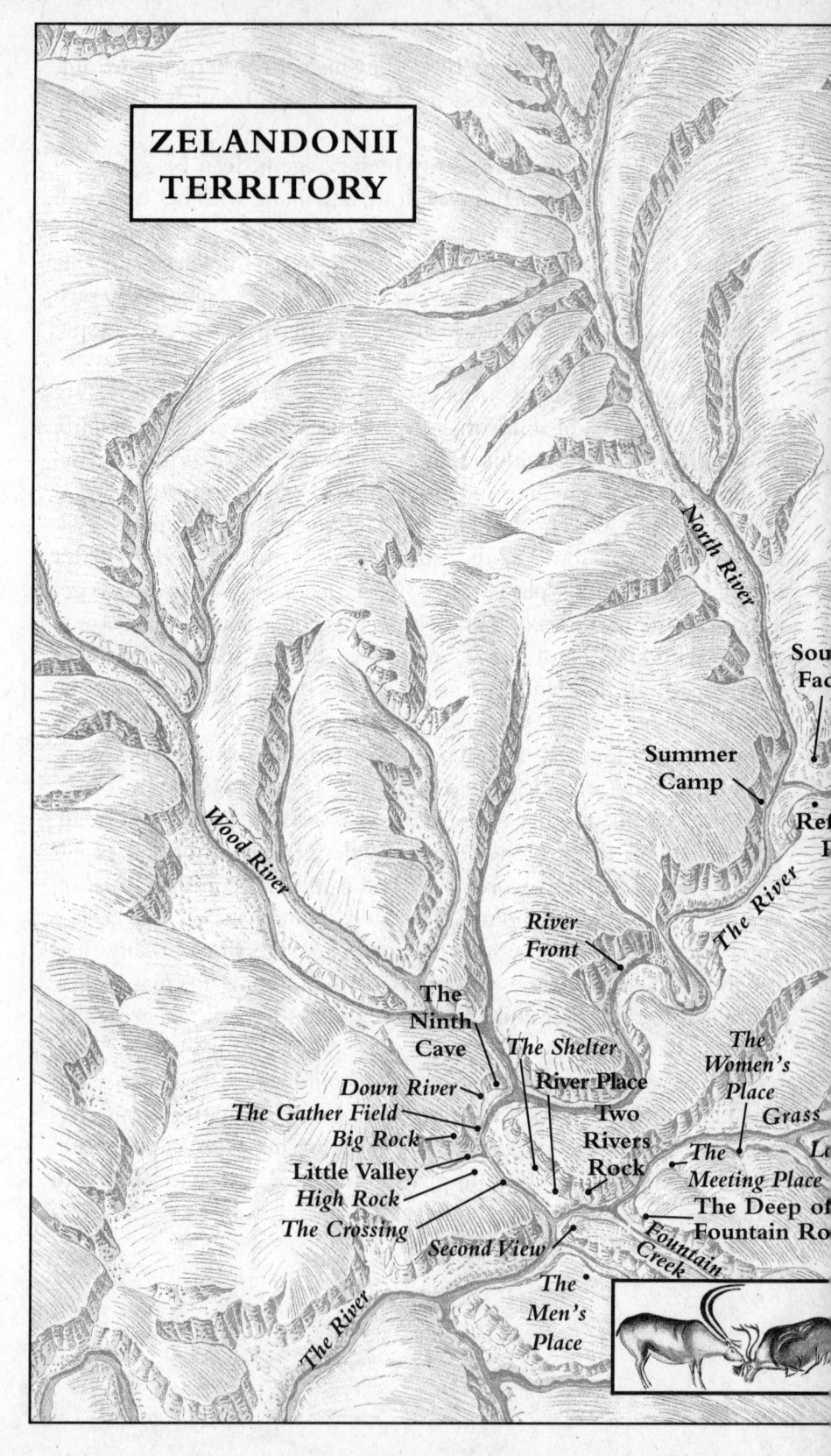

ZELANDONII TERRITORY

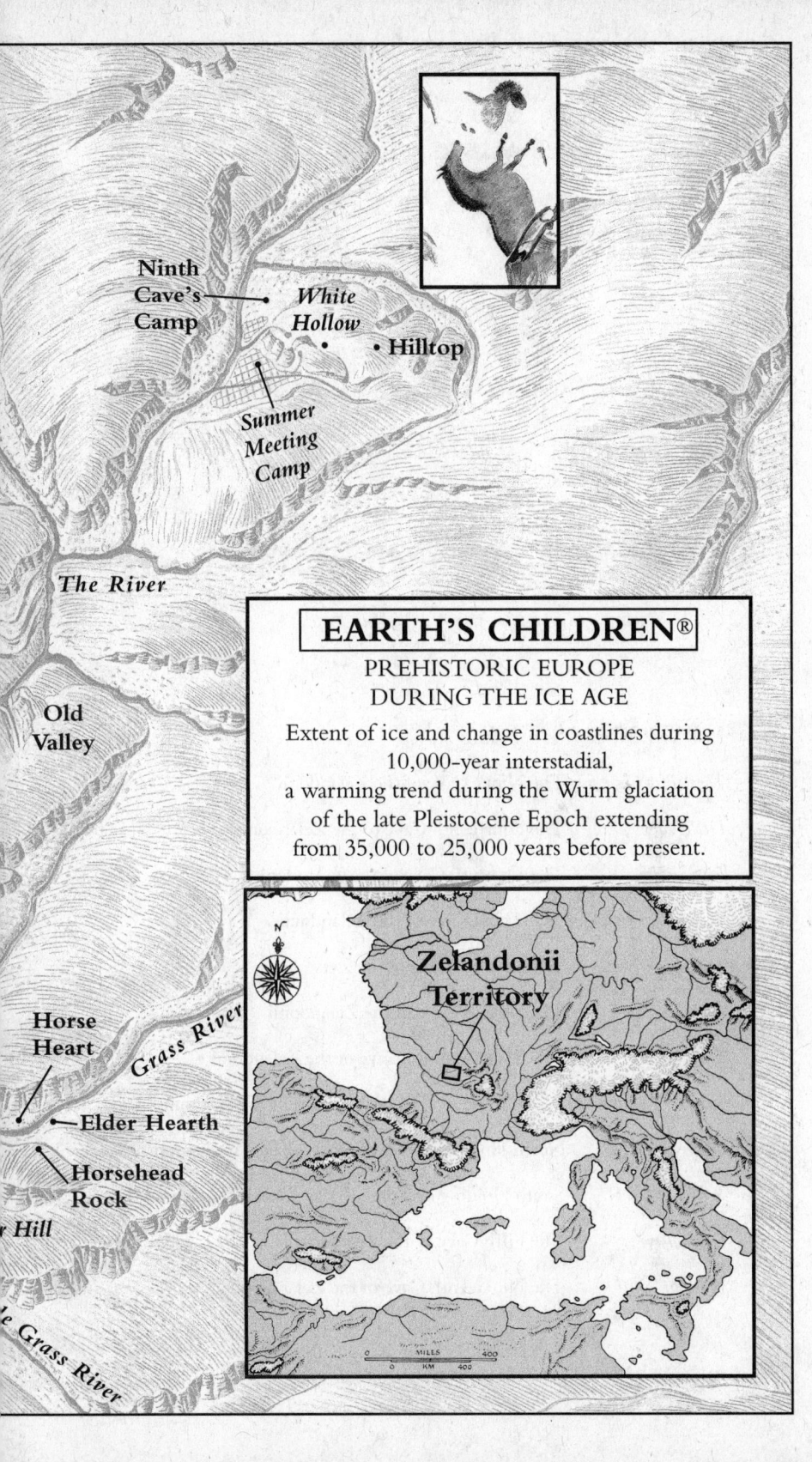

Ninth Cave's Camp

White Hollow

• Hilltop

Summer Meeting Camp

The River

Old Valley

Horse Heart

Grass River

—Elder Hearth

Horsehead Rock

Hill

le Grass River

EARTH'S CHILDREN®

PREHISTORIC EUROPE
DURING THE ICE AGE

Extent of ice and change in coastlines during
10,000-year interstadial,
a warming trend during the Wurm glaciation
of the late Pleistocene Epoch extending
from 35,000 to 25,000 years before present.

Zelandonii Territory

MILES 400
KM 400

LIVING SITES

The Ninth Cave	The Ninth Cave of the Zelandonii
Little Valley	The Fourteenth Cave of the Zelandonii
River Place	The Eleventh Cave of the Zelandonii
Two Rivers Rock	The Third Cave of the Zelandonii
Horsehead Rock	The Seventh Cave of the Zelandonii
Elder Hearth	The Second Cave of the Zelandonii
Three Rocks	The Twenty-ninth Cave of the Zelandonii
Summer Camp	West Holding of Three Rocks, The Twenty-ninth Cave
South Face	North Holding of Three Rocks, The Twenty-ninth Cave
Reflection Rock	South Holding of Three Rocks, The Twenty-ninth Cave
Old Valley	The Fifth Cave of the Zelandonii
Hilltop	The Nineteenth Cave of the Zelandonii

THE SHELTERS OF STONE

eople were gathering on the limestone ledge, looking down at them warily. No one made a gesture of welcome, and some held spears in positions of readiness if not actual threat. The young woman could almost feel their edgy fear. She watched from the bottom of the path as more people crowded together on the ledge, staring down, many more than she thought there would be. She had seen that reluctance to greet them from other people they had met on their Journey. It's not just them, she told herself, it's always that way in the beginning, but she felt uneasy.

The tall man jumped down from the back of the young stallion. He was neither reluctant nor uneasy, but he hesitated for a moment, holding the stallion's halter rope. He turned around and noticed that she was hanging back. "Ayla, will you hold Racer's rope? He seems nervous," he said, then looked up at the ledge. "I guess they do too."

She nodded, lifted her leg over, slid down from the mare's back, and took the rope. In addition to the tension of seeing strange people, the young brown horse was still agitated around his dam. She was no longer in heat, but residual odors from her encounter with the herd stallion still clung. Ayla held the halter rope of the brown male close, but gave the dun-yellow mare a long lead, and stood between them. She considered giving Whinney her head; her horse was more accustomed to large groups of strangers now, and was not usually high-strung, but she seemed nervous too. That throng of people would make anyone nervous.

When the wolf appeared, Ayla heard sounds of agitation and alarm from the ledge in front of the cave—if it could be called a cave. She'd never seen one quite like it. Wolf pressed against the side of her leg and moved somewhat in front of her, suspiciously defensive; she could feel the vibration of his barely audible growl. He was much more guarded around strangers now than he had been when they began their long Journey a year ago, but he had been little more than a puppy then, and he had become more protective of her after some perilous experiences.

As the man strode up the incline toward the apprehensive people, he showed no fear, but the woman was glad for the opportunity to wait behind and observe them before she had to meet them. She'd been expecting—dreading—this moment for more than a year, and first impressions were important . . . on both sides.

Though others held back, a young woman rushed toward him. Jondalar recognized his younger sister immediately, though the pretty girl had blossomed into a beautiful young woman during the five years of his absence.

"Jondalar! I knew it was you!" she said, flinging herself at him. "You finally came home!"

He gave her a big hug, then picked her up and swung her around in his enthusiasm. "Folara, I am so happy to see you!" When he put her down, he looked at her at arm's length. "But you've grown. You were just a girl when I left, now you're a beautiful woman . . . just as I always knew you'd be," he said, with slightly more than a brotherly glint in his eye.

She smiled at him, looked into his unbelievably vivid blue eyes and was drawn by their magnetism. She felt herself flush, not from his compliment, although that's what those standing nearby thought, but from the rush of attraction she felt for the man, brother or not, whom she had not seen for many years. She had heard stories of her handsome big brother with the unusual eyes, who could charm any woman, but her memory was of a tall adoring playmate who was willing to go along with any game or activity she wanted to play. This was the first time as a young woman that she was exposed to the full effect of his unconscious charisma. Jondalar noticed her reaction and smiled warmly at her sweet confusion.

She glanced away toward the bottom of the path near the small river. "Who is that woman, Jondé?" she asked. "And where did the animals come from? Animals run away from people, why don't those animals run away from her? Is she a Zelandoni? Has she Called them?" Then she frowned. "Where's Thonolan?" She took a sharp intake of breath at the look of pain that tightened Jondalar's brow.

"Thonolan travels the next world now, Folara," he said, "and I wouldn't be here if it weren't for that woman."

"Oh, Jondé! What happened?"

"It's a long story, and this is not the time to tell it," he said, but he had to smile at the name she called him. It was her personal nickname for him. "I haven't heard that name since I left. Now I know I'm home. How is everyone, Folara? Is mother all right? And Willamar?"

"They're both fine. Mother gave us a scare a couple of years ago. But Zelandoni worked her special magic, and she seems fine now. Come and see for yourself," she said, taking his hand and starting to lead him the rest of the way up the path.

Jondalar turned and waved at Ayla, trying to let her know that he would be back soon. He hated leaving her there alone with the animals, but he needed to see his mother, to see for himself that she was all right. That "scare" bothered him, and he needed to talk to people about the animals. They had both come to realize how strange and frightening it was to most people to see animals that did not run away from them.

People knew animals. All the people they had met on their Journey hunted them, and most honored or paid homage to them or their spirits in one way or another. Animals had been observed carefully for as long as anyone could remember. People knew the environments they favored and the foods they liked, their migration patterns and seasonal movements, their birthing periods and rutting schedules. But no one had ever tried to touch a living breathing animal in a friendly way. No one had ever tried to tie a rope around the head of any animal and lead it around. No one had ever tried to tame an animal, or even imagined that one could be.

As pleased as these people were to see a kinsman return from a long Journey—especially one that few ever expected to see again—the tame animals were such an unknown phenomenon, their first reaction was fear. It was so strange, so inexplicable, so far beyond their experience or imagination, it could not be natural. It had to be unnatural, supernatural. The only thing that kept many of them from running and hiding, or attempting to kill the fearsome animals, was that Jondalar, whom they knew, had arrived with them, and he was striding up the path from Wood River with his sister looking perfectly normal under the bright light of the sun.

Folara had shown some courage rushing forward the way she had, but she was young and had the fearlessness of youth. And she was so pleased to see her brother, who had always been a special favorite, she couldn't wait. Jondalar would never do anything to harm her and he didn't fear the animals.

Ayla watched from the foot of the path while people surrounded him, welcoming him with smiles, hugs, kisses, pats, handshakes using both hands, and many words. She noticed a hugely fat woman, a brown-haired man whom Jondalar hugged, and an older woman that he greeted warmly and then kept his arm around. Probably his mother, she thought, and wondered what the woman would think of her.

These people were his family, his kin, his friends, people he had grown up with. She was a stranger, a disturbing stranger who brought animals and who knew what other threatening foreign ways and outrageous ideas. Would they accept her? What if they didn't? She couldn't go back, her people lived more than a year's travel to the east. Jondalar had promised that he would leave with her if she wanted—or was forced—to go, but that was before he saw everyone, before he was greeted so warmly. How would he feel now?

She felt a nudge behind her and reached up to stroke Whinney's sturdy neck, grateful that her friend had reminded her that she was not alone. When she lived in the valley, after she left the Clan, for a long time the horse had been her only companion. She hadn't noticed the slack in Whinney's rope as the horse moved closer to her, but she gave Racer a bit more lead. The mare and her offspring usually found friendship and comfort in each other, but when the mare came into season it had disturbed their usual pattern.

More people—how could there be so many?—were looking in her direction, and Jondalar was talking earnestly with the brown-haired man, then he waved at her, and smiled. When he started back down, he was followed by the young woman, the brown-haired man, and a few others. Ayla took a deep breath and waited.

As they approached, the wolf's growl became louder. She reached down to keep him close to her. "It's all right, Wolf. It's just Jondalar's kin," she said. Her calming touch was a signal to him to stop growling, not to appear too threatening. The signal had been difficult to teach him, but worth the effort, especially now, she thought. She wished she knew of a touch that would calm her.

The group with Jondalar stopped a little distance back, trying not to show their trepidation, or to stare at the animals that openly stared at them and held their place even when strange people approached them. Jondalar stepped into the breach.

"I think we should start with formal introductions, Joharran," he said, looking at the brown-haired man.

As Ayla dropped both halter ropes in preparation for a formal introduction, which required contact with both hands, the horses stepped back, but the wolf stayed. She noticed the glint of fear in the man's eye, although she doubted that this man was afraid of much, and glanced at Jondalar, wondering if he had a reason for wanting formal introductions immediately. She looked closely at the unfamiliar man and was suddenly reminded of Brun, the leader of the clan that she grew up with. Powerful, proud, intelligent, competent, he had feared little—except the world of the spirits.

"Ayla, this is Joharran, Leader of the Ninth Cave of the Zelandonii, son of Marthona, former Leader of the Ninth Cave, born to the hearth of Joconan, former Leader of the Ninth Cave," the tall blond man said with seriousness, then grinned, "not to mention Brother of Jondalar, Traveler to Distant Lands."

There were a few quick smiles. His comment relieved the tension somewhat. Strictly, in a formal introduction, a person could give the entire list of their names and ties to validate their status—all their own designations, titles, and accomplishments, and all their kin and their relationships, along with their titles and accomplishments—and some did. But as a matter of practice, except in the most ceremonial of circumstances, just the primary ones were mentioned. It was not uncommon, however, for young people, especially brothers, to make jocular additions to the long and sometimes tedious recitation of one's kinships, and Jondalar was reminding him of past years, before he was burdened with the responsibilities of leadership.

"Joharran, this is Ayla of the Mamutoi, Member of the Lion Camp, Daughter of the Mammoth Hearth, Chosen by the Spirit of the Cave Lion, and Protected by the Cave Bear."

The brown-haired man crossed the distance between himself and the young woman, and held out both hands, palms up, in the understood gesture of welcome and open-handed friendship. He did not recognize any of her ties, and he wasn't entirely sure which were most important.

"In the name of Doni, the Great Earth Mother, I welcome you, Ayla of the Mamutoi, Daughter of the Mammoth Hearth," he said.

Ayla took both his hands. "In the name of Mut, Great Mother of All, I greet you, Joharran, Leader of the Ninth Cave of the Zelandonii," then she smiled, "and Brother of the Traveler, Jondalar."

Joharran noticed, first, that she spoke his language well, but with an unusual accent, then he became conscious of her strange clothing and her foreign look, but when she smiled, he smiled back. Partly because she had showed her understanding of Jondalar's remark and let Joharran know that his brother was important to her, but mostly because he could not resist her smile.

Ayla was an attractive woman by anyone's standards: she was tall, had a firm well-shaped body, long dark blond hair that tended to wave, clear blue-gray eyes, and fine features, though of a slightly different character from those of Zelandonii women. But when she smiled, it was as if the sun had cast a special beam on her that lit each feature from within. She seemed to glow with such stunning beauty, Joharran caught his breath. Jondalar had always said her smile was remarkable, and he grinned, seeing that his brother was not immune to it.

Then Joharran noticed the stallion prance nervously toward Jondalar, and he eyed the wolf. "Jondalar tells me we need to make some . . . ah . . . accommodation for these animals . . . somewhere nearby, I presume." Not too near, he thought.

"The horses just need a field with grass, near water, but we need to tell people that they shouldn't try to get close to them in the beginning unless Jondalar or I am with them. Whinney and Racer are nervous around people until they get used to them," Ayla said.

"I don't think that will be a problem," Joharran said, catching the movement of Whinney's tail, and eyeing her. "They can stay here, if this small valley is appropriate."

"This will be fine," Jondalar said. "Though we may move them upstream, out of the way a little."

"Wolf is accustomed to sleeping near me," Ayla continued. She noticed Joharran's frown. "He's become quite protective and might cause a commotion if he can't be close by."

She could see his resemblance to Jondalar, particularly in his forehead knotted with worry, and wanted to smile. But Joharran was seriously concerned. This was not a time for smiles, even if his expression gave her a feeling of warm familiarity.

Jondalar, too, had seen his brother's worried frown. "I think this would be a good time to introduce Joharran to Wolf," he said.

Joharran's eyes flew open in near panic, but before he could object, she reached for his hand as she bent down beside the meat-eater. She put her arm around the large wolf's neck to settle an incipient growl—even she could smell the man's fear; she was sure Wolf could.

"Let him smell your hand first," she said. "That's Wolf's formal introduction." The wolf had learned from previous experience that it was important to Ayla for him to accept within his pack of humans the people she introduced to him in this way. He didn't like the smell of fear, but sniffed the man to become familiar with him.

"Have you ever really felt the fur of a living wolf, Joharran?" she asked, looking up at him. "If you notice, it's a little coarse," she said, leading his hand to feel the animal's rather shaggy neck fur. "He's still shedding and itchy, and he loves to be scratched behind the ears," she continued, showing him how.

Joharran felt the fur, but was more aware of the warmth, and suddenly realized this was a living wolf! And he didn't seem to mind being touched.

Ayla observed that his hand was not as stiff, and that he actually attempted to rub the place she indicated. "Let him smell your hand again."

When Joharran brought his hand around toward the wolf's nose, he widened his eyes again, with surprise. "That wolf licked me!" he said, not sure if it was in preparation for something better—or worse. Then he saw Wolf lick Ayla's face, and she seemed very pleased about it.

"Yes, you were good, Wolf," she said, smiling, as she fondled him and roughed up his mane. Then she stood up and patted the front of her shoulders. The wolf jumped up, put his paws on the place she had indicated, and as she exposed her throat, he licked her neck, and then took her chin and jaw in his mouth with a rumbling growl, but great gentleness.

Jondalar noticed the gasps of astonishment from Joharran and the others, and realized how frightening the familiar act of wolfish affection must seem to people who didn't understand. His brother looked at him, his expression both fearful and amazed. "What's he doing to her?"

"Are you sure that's all right?" Folara asked at nearly the same time. She could no longer keep still. The other people were making indecisive nervous movements as well.

Jondalar smiled. "Yes, Ayla is fine. He loves her, he would never hurt her. That's how wolves show affection. It took me a while to get used to it, too, and I've known Wolf as long as she has, ever since he was a fuzzy little cub."

"That's no cub! That's a big wolf! That's the biggest wolf I ever saw!" Joharran said. "He could tear her throat out!"

"Yes. He could tear her throat out. I've seen him tear a woman's throat out . . . a woman who was trying to kill Ayla," Jondalar said. "Wolf protects her."

The Zelandonii who were watching breathed a collective sigh of relief when the wolf got down, and stood by her side again with his mouth open and his tongue hanging out the side, showing his teeth. Wolf had that look that Jondalar thought of as his wolf grin, as though he was pleased with himself.

"Does he do that all the time?" Folara asked. "To . . . anyone?"

"No," Jondalar said. "Only to Ayla, and sometimes me, if he's feeling particularly happy, and only if we allow it. He's well behaved, he won't harm anyone . . . unless Ayla is threatened."

"What about children?" Folara asked. "Wolves often go after the weak and the young."

At the mention of children, looks of concern appeared on the faces of the people standing nearby.

"Wolf loves children," Ayla quickly explained, "and he is very protective toward them, particularly very young or weak ones. He was raised with the children of the Lion Camp."

"There was a very weak and sickly boy, who belonged to the Lion Hearth," Jondalar contributed. "You should have seen them play together. Wolf was always careful around him."

"That's a very unusual animal," another man said. "It's hard to believe a wolf could behave so . . . unwolflike."

"You're right, Solaban," Jondalar said. "He does behave in ways that seem very unwolflike to people, but if we were wolves we wouldn't think so. He was raised with people and Ayla says he thinks of people as his pack. He treats people as though they were wolves."

"Does he hunt?" the man Jondalar had called Solaban wanted to know.

"Yes," Ayla said. "Sometimes he hunts alone, for himself, and sometimes he helps us hunt."

"How does he know what he should hunt and what he shouldn't?" Folara asked. "Like those horses."

Ayla smiled. "The horses are part of his pack, too. You notice they are not afraid of him. And he never hunts people. Otherwise, he can hunt any animal he wants, unless I tell him not to."

8

"And if you say no, he doesn't?" another man asked.

"That's right, Rushemar," Jondalar affirmed.

The man shook his head in wonder. It was hard to believe anyone could have such control over a powerful hunting animal.

"Well, Joharran," Jondalar said. "Do you think it's safe enough to bring Ayla and Wolf up?"

The man thought for a moment, then nodded. "However, if there is any trouble . . ."

"There won't be, Joharran," Jondalar stated, then turned to Ayla. "My mother has invited us to stay with her. Folara still lives with her, but she has her own room, and so does Marthona and Willamar. He's gone on a trading mission now. She has offered her central living space to us. Of course, we could stay with Zelandoni at the visitors hearth, if you'd rather."

"I would be pleased to stay with your mother, Jondalar," Ayla said.

"Good! Mother also suggested that we wait with most formal introductions until we get settled in. It isn't as though I need to be introduced, and there's no point in repeating everything to each one when we can do it all at once."

"We're already planning a welcoming feast for tonight," Folara said. "And probably another one later, for all the nearby Caves."

"I appreciate your mother's thoughtfulness, Jondalar. It would be easier to meet everyone at once, but you might introduce me to this young woman," Ayla said.

Folara smiled.

"Of course, I was planning to," Jondalar said. "Ayla, this is my sister, Folara, Blessed of Doni, of the Ninth Cave of the Zelandonii; Daughter of Marthona, former Leader of the Ninth Cave; born to the hearth of Willamar, Traveler and Trade Master; Sister of Joharran, Leader of the Ninth Cave; Sister of Jondalar . . ."

"She knows about you, Jondalar, and I've already heard her names and ties," Folara said, impatient with the formalities, then held out both hands toward Ayla. "In the name of Doni, the Great Earth Mother, I welcome you, Ayla of the Mamutoi, Friend of horses and wolves."

The crowd of people standing on the sunny stone porch quickly moved back when they saw the woman and the wolf start up the path along with Jondalar and the small group accompanying them. One or two took a step closer while others craned their necks around them. When they reached the stone ledge Ayla got her first view of the living space of the Ninth Cave of the Zelandonii. The sight surprised her.

Though she knew the word "Cave" in the name of Jondalar's home did not refer to a place, but to the group of people who lived there, the formation she saw was not a cave, not as she had thought of one. A cave was a dark chamber or series of them within a rock face or cliff or underground with an opening to the outside. The living space of these people was the area beneath a huge overhanging shelf jutting out of the limestone cliff, an abri, that provided protection from rain or snow, but was open to daylight.

The high cliffs of the region were once the floor beneath the surface of an ancient sea. As the calcareous shells of crustaceans who lived in the sea were discarded, they built up on the floor and eventually became calcium carbonate—limestone. During certain periods of time, for a variety of reasons, some of the deposited shells created thick layers of limestone that were harder than others. When the earth shifted and exposed the sea floor to eventually become cliffs, the weathering processes of wind and water cut into the relatively softer stone more easily, gouging out deep spaces, and leaving ledges of the harder stone between.

Although the cliffs were also riddled with caves, which was common for limestone, these unusual shelflike formations created shelters of stone that made exceptionally good living sites and had been used as such for a great many thousands of years.

Jondalar led Ayla toward the older woman she had seen from the foot of the path. The woman was tall and dignified in her bearing as she waited patiently for them. Her hair, more gray than light brown, was pulled back from her face into one long braid, which was coiled at the back of her head. Her clear direct appraising eyes were also gray.

When they reached her, Jondalar began the formal introduction. "Ayla, this is Marthona, former Leader of the Ninth Cave of the Zelandonii; Daughter of Jemara; born to the hearth of Rabanar; mated to Willamar, Trade Master of the Ninth Cave; Mother of Joharran, Leader of the Ninth Cave; Mother of Folara, Blessed of Doni; Mother of . . ." He started to say "Thonolan," hesitated, then quickly filled in, "Jondalar, Returned Traveler." Then he turned to his mother.

"Marthona, this is Ayla of the Lion Camp of the Mamutoi,

Daughter of the Mammoth Hearth, Chosen by the Spirit of the Cave Lion, Protected by the Spirit of the Cave Bear."

Marthona held out her two hands. "In the name of Doni, the Great Earth Mother, I welcome you, Ayla of the Mamutoi."

"In the name of Mut, Great Mother of All, I greet you, Marthona of the Ninth Cave of the Zelandonii, and Mother of Jondalar," Ayla said, as they joined hands.

Marthona heard Ayla's words, wondered at her strange speech mannerism, noted how well she spoke in spite of it, and thought it was either a minor speech defect or the accent of a completely unfamiliar language from a very distant place. She smiled. "You have come a long way, Ayla, left all you knew and loved behind. If you had not, I don't think I would have Jondalar back home. I am grateful to you for that. I hope you will soon feel at home here, and I will do all I can to help you."

Ayla knew Jondalar's mother was sincere. Her directness and honesty were genuine; she was glad to have her son back. Ayla was relieved and touched by Marthona's welcome. "I have looked forward to meeting you since Jondalar first spoke of you . . . but I have been a little afraid, too," she replied with a similar directness and honesty.

"I don't blame you. I would have found it very difficult in your place. Come, let me show you where you can put your things. You must be tired and would like to rest before the welcoming celebration tonight," Marthona said, starting to lead them toward the area under the overhang. Suddenly Wolf started whining, yelped a little "puppy bark," and stretched his front paws out with his back end and tail up in a playful posture.

Jondalar was startled. "What is he doing?"

Ayla looked at Wolf, rather surprised as well. The animal repeated his gestures, and suddenly she smiled. "I think he's trying to get Marthona's attention," she said. "He thinks she didn't notice him, and I think he wants to be introduced."

"And I want to meet him, too," Marthona said.

"You don't fear him!" Ayla said. "And he knows it!"

"I watched. I didn't see anything to fear," she said, extending her hand toward the wolf. He sniffed her hand, licked it, and whined again.

"I think Wolf wants you to touch him; he does love attention from people he likes," Ayla said.

"You do like that, don't you?" the older woman said as she stroked him. "Wolf? Is that what you called him?"

"Yes. It's just the Mamutoi word for 'wolf.' It seemed like the right name for him," Ayla explained.

"But, I've never seen him take to anyone so fast," Jondalar said, looking at his mother with awe.

"Nor have I," Ayla said, watching Marthona with the wolf. "Maybe he's just happy to meet someone who's not afraid of him."

As they walked into the shade of the overhanging stone, Ayla felt an immediate cooling of temperature. For a heartbeat, she shivered with a chill of fear, and glanced up at the huge shelf of stone jutting out of the cliff wall, wondering if it could collapse. But when her eyes grew accustomed to the dimmer light, she was astonished by more than the physical formation of Jondalar's home. The space under the rock shelter was huge, much larger than she had imagined.

She had seen similar overhangs in the cliffs along this river on their way here, some obviously inhabited, though none seemed quite as sizable as this one. Everyone in the entire region knew of the immense rock shelter and the great number of people it housed. The Ninth Cave was the largest of all the communities that called themselves Zelandonii.

Clustered together at the eastern end of the protected space, along the back wall and freestanding in the middle, were individual structures, many quite large, made partly of stone and partly of wooden frames covered with hides. The hides were decorated with beautifully rendered pictures of animals and various abstract symbols painted in black and many vivid shades of red, yellow, and brown. The structures were arranged in a west-facing curve around an open space near the center of the area covered by the overhanging stone shelf, which was filled with a confusion of objects and people.

As Ayla looked more closely, what at first had struck her all at once as a mélange of rich clutter was resolving itself into areas dedicated to different tasks, often near to related tasks. It only seemed confusing initially because so many activities were going on.

She saw hides being cured in frames, and long shafts of spears, apparently in the process of being straightened, leaning against a crosspiece supported by two posts. Baskets in different stages of completion were stacked in another place, and thongs were drying stretched between pairs of bone posts. Long skeins of cordage hung from pegs pounded into crossbeams above unfinished nets stretched across a frame, and loosely woven netting in bundles on the ground. Skins, some dyed various colors including many shades of red, were cut into pieces and nearby, partially assembled articles of clothing were hanging.

She recognized most of the crafts, but near the clothing was an activity that was entirely unfamiliar. A frame held many strands of thin cord vertically, with a design partially formed from the material woven horizontally across them. She wanted to go over and look closer, and promised herself she would, later. Pieces of wood, stone, bone, antler, and mammoth ivory were in other places, carved into implements—ladles, spoons, bowls, tongs, weapons—most of them with carved and sometimes painted decorations. There were also small sculptures and carvings that were not implements or tools. They seemed to be made for themselves or some purpose of which she wasn't aware.

She saw vegetables and herbs hanging high from large frames with many crosspieces, and lower to the ground, meat drying on racks. Somewhat away from other activities was an area scattered with sharp stone chips; for people like Jondalar she thought, flint-knappers who made tools, knives, and spear points.

And everywhere she looked, she saw people. The community that lived under the spacious rock shelter was of a size to match the space. Ayla had grown up in a clan of less than thirty people; at the Clan Gathering, which occurred once every seven years, two hundred people came together for a short period, a huge assembly to her then. Though the Mamutoi Summer Meeting drew a much greater number, the Ninth Cave of the Zelandonii, alone, comprised of over two hundred individuals living together at this one place, was larger than the entire Clan Gathering!

Ayla didn't know how many people were standing around watching them, but she was reminded of the time she had walked with Brun's clan into that congregation of clans and felt all of them looking at her. They had tried to be unobtrusive, but the people who were staring as Marthona led Jondalar, Ayla, and a wolf to her living place weren't even polite about it. They didn't try to look down or glance away. She wondered if she would ever get used to living with so many people living close by all the time; she wondered if she wanted to.

2

The huge woman glanced up at the movement of the leather drape stretched across the entrance, then quickly looked down as the young blond stranger emerged from Marthona's dwelling. She was sitting in her accustomed place, a seat carved out of a solid block of limestone, strong enough to support her massive bulk. The leather-padded stone seat had been made especially for her, and was located exactly where she wanted it: toward the back of the large open area under the enormous overhanging cliff that protected the settlement, but within sight of almost the entire communal living space.

The woman appeared to be meditating, but it wasn't the first time she had used the place to quietly observe some person or activity. The people had learned not to intrude upon her meditations, unless it was an emergency, especially when she wore her ivory chest plaque with the plain, undecorated side facing out. When the side that was carved with symbols and animals was showing, anyone was free to approach her, but when she reversed the plaque to the blank side, it became a symbol of silence and meant that she did not wish to speak and did not want to be disturbed.

The Cave had grown so accustomed to her being there, they almost didn't see her, for all her usually commanding presence. She had cultivated that effect carefully and had no compunctions about it. As spiritual leader of the Ninth Cave of the Zelandonii, she considered the welfare of the people her responsibility and used every means her fertile brain could devise to carry out her duty.

She watched the younger woman leave the rock shelter and head toward the path that led to the valley, and noticed the unmistakably foreign look of her leather tunic. The old donier was also aware that she moved with the resilience of health and strength, and a confidence that belied her youth and the fact that she was among complete strangers in their living place.

Zelandoni got up and walked toward the structure, one of the many such dwelling places of various sizes scattered within the limestone abri. At the entrance to the dwelling that divided the private living space from the open public area, she tapped on the stiff rawhide panel next to the drape-closed entry and heard the padded strides of soft leather footwear approaching. The tall, fair-haired, surprisingly handsome man pulled back the drape. Eyes of an unusually vivid shade of blue looked surprised, then warmed with pleasure.

"Zelandoni! How nice to see you," he said, "but mother isn't here right now."

"What makes you think I'm here to see Marthona? You're the one who's been gone five years." Her tone was sharp.

He was suddenly flustered and at a loss for words.

"Well, are you going to leave me standing out here, Jondalar?"

"Oh. . . . Come in, of course," he said, his brow knotting into a habitual frown, erasing the warm smile. He stepped back, holding the drape aside as she entered.

They studied each other in silence for a time. When he'd left, she had just become First Among Those Who Served The Mother; she'd had five years to grow into the position and she had grown into it. The woman he knew had become immensely fat. She was two or three times the size of most women, with huge breasts and broad buttocks. She had a soft full face crowded by three chins, but her piercing blue eyes seemed to miss nothing. She had always been tall and strong, and she carried her great size with grace, and a demeanor that asserted her prestige and authority. She had a presence, an aura of power about her that commanded respect.

They both spoke at once. "Can I get you . . ." Jondalar started.
"You've changed. . . ."

"I'm sorry . . ." he apologized for what seemed like an interruption, feeling oddly constrained. Then he noticed just the slightest hint of a smile, and a familiar look in her eye, and he felt himself relax.

"I am glad to see you . . . Zolena," he said. His brow smoothed out and his smile returned as he focused his compelling eyes full of warmth and love on her.

"You haven't changed that much," she said, feeling herself respond to his charisma and the memories it evoked. "No one has called me Zolena for a long time." She appraised him again carefully, "You have changed, though. Grown up some. You're more handsome than ever. . . ."

He started to protest, but she shook her head at him. "Don't make objections, Jondalar. You know it's true. But there's a difference. You look . . . how can I say it . . . you don't have that hungry look, that need that every woman wanted to satisfy. I think you have found what you've been searching for. You are happy in a way that you have never been."

"I never could keep anything from you," he said, smiling with an excited, almost childlike delight. "It's Ayla. We plan to mate at this summer's Matrimonial. I suppose we could have had a mating ceremony before we left, or along the way, but I wanted to wait until we got home so you could slip that thong over our wrists and tie the knot for us."

Just talking about her had changed his expression, and Zelandoni had a momentary sense of the almost obsessive love he felt for this woman called Ayla. It concerned her, raised all the protective instincts she felt for her people—particularly this person—as the voice, surrogate, and instrument of the Great Earth Mother. She knew the powerful emotions he had struggled with growing up, and finally learned to keep under control. But a woman he loved that much could hurt him terribly, perhaps even destroy him. Her eyes narrowed. She wanted to know more about this young woman who had captivated him so completely. Just what kind of hold did she have on him?

"How can you be so sure she's right for you? Where did you meet her? How much do you really know about her?"

Jondalar sensed her concern, but something else, too, something that worried him. Zelandoni was the highest ranked spiritual leader of all the zelandonia, and she was not First for nothing. She was a powerful woman and he didn't want her turning against Ayla. The greatest concern he—and, he knew, Ayla, too—had had during their long and difficult Journey to his home was whether or not she would be accepted by his people. For all her exceptional qualities, there were some things about her that he wished she would keep secret, though he doubted that she would. She could have enough difficulties—and probably would have from some people—without incurring the enmity of this particular woman. Quite the opposite, more than anyone Ayla needed the support of Zelandoni.

He reached out and held the shoulders of the woman, needing to persuade her, somehow, not only to accept Ayla but to help her, but he wasn't sure how. Looking into her eyes, he couldn't help remembering the love they once had shared, and suddenly he knew that, as difficult as it might be for him, only complete honesty would work . . . if anything would.

Jondalar was a private man about his personal feelings; it was the way he'd learned to control his powerful emotions, to keep them to himself. It was not easy for him to talk about them to anyone, not even someone who knew him as well as she did.

"Zelandoni . . ." His voice softened. "Zolena . . . you know it was you that spoiled me for other women. I was hardly more than a boy, and you were the most exciting woman any man could hope for. I wasn't alone in wetting my dreams with thoughts of you, but you made mine come true. I burned for you, and when you came to me, became my donii-woman, I couldn't get enough of you. My first manhood was filled with you, but you know it didn't end there. I wanted more and as much as you fought it, you did, too. Even though it was forbidden, I loved you, and you loved me. I still love you. I will always love you.

"Even afterwards, after all the trouble we caused everyone, and mother sending me to live with Dalanar, when I came back, no one ever came close to you. I hungered for you lying spent beside another woman, and I hungered for more than your body. I wanted to share a hearth with you. I didn't care about the difference in age, or that no man was supposed to fall in love with his donii-woman. I wanted to spend my life with you."

"And look what you would have gotten, Jondalar," Zolena said. She was moved, more than she imagined she could be anymore. "Have you taken a good look? I'm not just older than you. I'm so fat, I'm starting to have trouble getting around. I'm still strong or I'd have more, and will as time goes on. You are young, and so good to look at, women ache for you. The Mother chose me. She must have known I would grow to look like her. That's fine for Zelandoni, but at your hearth, I would have been just a fat old woman, and you would still be a handsome young man."

"Do you think I would have cared? Zolena, I had to travel beyond the end of the Great Mother River before I found a woman who could compare with you—you can't imagine how far that is. I would do it again, and more. I thank the Great Mother that I found Ayla. I love her, as I would have loved you. Be good to her, Zolena . . . Zelandoni. Don't hurt her."

"That's just it. If she's right for you, if she 'compares,' I couldn't hurt her, and she wouldn't hurt you, could not. That's what I need to know, Jondalar."

They both looked up as the drape over the entrance was moved aside. Ayla came into the dwelling carrying traveling packs, and saw Jondalar holding the shoulders of an enormously fat woman. He pulled his hands away, looking disconcerted, almost ashamed, as though he was doing something wrong.

What was it about the way Jondalar was looking at the woman, about the way his hands had held her shoulders? And the woman? In spite of her size, there was a seductive quality to the way she held her body. But another characteristic quickly asserted itself. As she turned to look at Ayla, she moved with a sense of assurance and composure that was a manifest sign of her authority.

Observing small details of expression and posture for meaning was second nature to the young woman. The Clan, the people who raised her, did not speak primarily with words. They communicated with signs, gestures, and nuances of facial expression and stance. When she lived with the Mamutoi, her ability to interpret body language had evolved and expanded to include understanding the unconscious signals and gestures of those who used spoken language. Suddenly Ayla knew who the woman was, and realized something important had transpired between the man and the woman that involved her. She sensed she was facing a critical test, but she didn't hesitate.

"She's the one, isn't she, Jondalar?" Ayla said, approaching them.

"I'm the one what?" Zelandoni said, glaring at the stranger.

Ayla stared back at the woman without flinching. "You're the one I must thank," she said. "Until I met Jondalar, I didn't understand about the Mother's Gifts, especially Her Gift of Pleasure. I had only known pain and anger, but he was patient and gentle, and I learned to know the joy. He told me about the woman who taught him. I thank you, Zelandoni, for teaching Jondalar so he could give me Her Gift. But I am grateful to you for something much more important . . . and more difficult for you. Thank you for giving him up so he could find me."

Zelandoni was surprised, though she showed little sign of it. Ayla's words were not at all what she expected to hear. Their eyes locked as the woman studied Ayla, searching for a sense of her depth, a perception of her feelings, an insight to the truth. The older woman's comprehension of unconscious signals and body language was not dissimilar to Ayla's, though more intuitive. Her ability had developed through subliminal observation and instinctive analysis, not the expanded application of a language learned as a child, but was no less astute. Zelandoni didn't know how she knew, she just knew.

It took a moment before she became aware of something curious. Though the young woman seemed to be entirely fluent in Zelandonii—her command of the language was so good, she used it like one born to it—there could be no doubt she was a foreigner.

The One Who Served was not unfamiliar with visitors who spoke with the accent of another language, but Ayla's speech had a strangely exotic quality, unlike anything she'd ever heard. Her voice was not unpleasant, somewhat low-pitched, but a little throaty, and she had trouble with certain sounds. She recalled Jondalar's remark about how far he had gone on his Journey, and a thought crossed Zelandoni's mind in the few heartbeats that the two women stood confronting each other: this woman had been willing to travel a great distance to come home with him.

Only then did she notice that the young woman's face had a distinctly foreign look and tried to identify the difference. Ayla was attractive, but one expected that of any woman Jondalar would bring home. Her face was somewhat broader and shorter than that of Zelandonii women, but nicely proportioned, with a well-defined jaw. She was a shade taller than the older woman, and her rather dark blond hair was enhanced with sun-lightened streaks. Her clear gray-blue eyes held secrets, a strong will, but no hint of malice.

Zelandoni nodded, and turned to Jondalar. "She'll do."

He let out a breath, then looked from one to the other. "How did you know this was Zelandoni, Ayla? You haven't been introduced yet, have you?"

"It was not hard. You still love her, and she loves you."

"But . . . but . . . how . . . ?" he sputtered.

"Don't you know I've seen that look in your eyes? Don't you think I understand how a woman who loves you feels inside?" Ayla said.

"Some people would be jealous if they saw someone they loved looking at someone else with love," he said.

Zelandoni suspected that the "some people" he was thinking of was himself. "Don't you think she can see a handsome young man and a fat old woman, Jondalar? It's what anyone would see. Your love for me is no threat to her. If your memory still blinds you, I am grateful enough."

She turned to Ayla. "I wasn't sure about you. If I had felt you weren't right for him, it would not matter how far you have traveled, you would never mate him."

"Nothing you could do would stop it," Ayla said.

"See?" Zelandoni said, turning to look at Jondalar. "I told you if she was right for you, I couldn't hurt her."

"Did you think Marona was right for me, Zelandoni?" Jondalar said with a touch of irritation, beginning to feel as though between them, he had no right to make up his own mind. "You never objected when I was promised to her."

"That didn't matter. You didn't love her. She couldn't hurt you."

Both women were looking at him, and though they bore no resemblance to each other, their expressions were so similar, they seemed to look alike. Suddenly Jondalar laughed. "Well, I'm glad to know the two loves of my life are going to be friends," he said.

Zelandoni raised an eyebrow and gave him a stern look. "Whatever makes you think we are going to be friends?" she said, but she smiled to herself as she left.

Jondalar felt a strange set of mixed emotions as he watched Zelandoni leave, but he was pleased that the powerful woman appeared willing to accept Ayla. His sister had been friendly toward her, too, and his mother. All the women that he really cared about seemed ready to welcome her—at least for now, he thought. His mother had even told her she would do whatever she could to make Ayla feel at home.

The leather drape across the entrance moved and Jondalar felt a tingle of surprise when he saw his mother, since he had just been thinking about her. Marthona entered, carrying the preserved stomach of some middle-size animal full of a liquid that had seeped through the nearly waterproof container enough to stain it a deep purple. Jondalar's face lit up with a grin.

"Mother, you brought out some of your wine!" he said. "Ayla, do you remember the drink that we had when we stayed with the Sharamudoi? The bilberry wine? Now you'll get a chance to taste Marthona's wine. She's known for it. No matter what fruit most people use, their juice often turns sour, but mother has a way with it." He smiled at her and added, "Maybe someday she'll tell me her secret."

Marthona smiled back at the tall man, but made no comment. From her expression, Ayla sensed that she did have a secret technique, and that she was good at keeping secrets, not only her own. She probably knew many. There were layers and hidden depths to the woman, for all that she was forthright and honest in what she said. And for all that she was friendly and welcoming, Ayla knew that Jondalar's mother would reserve judgment before fully accepting her.

Suddenly Ayla was reminded of Iza, the woman of the Clan who had been like a mother to her. Iza also knew many secrets, yet, like the rest of the Clan, she didn't lie. With a language of gestures, and nuances conveyed by postures and expressions, they couldn't lie. It would be known immediately. But they could refrain from mentioning. Though it might be understood that something was held back, it was allowed, for the sake of privacy.

This was not the first time she had been reminded of the Clan recently, she realized. The Ninth Cave's leader, Jondalar's brother Joharran, had reminded her of Brun, her clan's leader. Why did Jondalar's kin remind her of the Clan? she wondered.

"You must be hungry," Marthona said, including both of them in her glance.

Jondalar smiled. "Yes, I am hungry! We haven't eaten since early this morning. I was in such a hurry to get here, and we were so close, I didn't want to stop."

"If you've brought all your things in, sit and rest while I prepare some food for you." Marthona led them to a low table, indicated cushions for them to sit on, and poured some of the deep red liquid into cups for each of them. She looked around. "I don't see your wolf-animal, Ayla. I know you brought him in. Does he also need food? What does he eat?"

"I usually feed him whatever we eat, but he also hunts for himself. I brought him in so he would know where his place is, but he came with me the first time I went back down to the valley where the horses are, and decided to stay. He comes and goes on his own, unless I want him," Ayla said.

"How does he know when you want him?"

"She has a special whistle to call him," Jondalar said. "We call the horses with whistles, too." He picked up his cup, tasted, then smiled and sighed with appreciation. "Now I know I'm home." He tasted again, then closed his eyes and savored. "What fruit is this made from, mother?"

"Mostly from those round berries that grow in clusters on long vines only on protected south-facing slopes," Marthona explained for Ayla's benefit. "There's an area several miles southeast of here that I always check. Some years it doesn't grow well at all, but we had a fairly warm winter a few years back, and the following autumn the clusters were huge, very fruity, sweet but not too sweet. I added a little elderberry, and some blackberry juice, but not much. This wine was a favorite. It's a little stronger than usual. I don't have much left."

Ayla sniffed the aroma of fruit as she held the cup to her lips to taste. The liquid was tart and tangy, dry, not the sweet taste she had expected from the fruity smell. She sensed the alcoholic character she had first tasted in the birch beer made by Talut, the Lion Camp's headman, but this was more like the fermented bilberry juice made by the Sharamudoi, except that that had been sweeter, as she recalled.

She hadn't liked the harsh bite of alcohol when she first experienced it, but the rest of the Lion Camp seemed to enjoy the birch beer so much, and she wanted to fit in and be like them, so she made herself drink it. After a time, she got more used to it, though she suspected that the reason people liked it was not as much for its taste as for the heady, if disorienting, feeling it caused. Too much usually made her feel giddy and too friendly, but some people became sad, or angry, or even violent.

This beverage had something more, however. Elusive complexities altered the simple character of the fruit juice in an extraordinary way. It was a drink she could learn to enjoy.

"This is very good," Ayla said. "I not ever tasted anything . . . I never tasted anything quite like it," she corrected herself, feeling slightly embarrassed. She was completely comfortable in Zelandonii; it was the first spoken language she had learned after living with the Clan. Jondalar had taught her while he was recovering from the wounds of the lion mauling. Though she did have difficulty with certain sounds—no matter how hard she tried, she couldn't get them quite right—she seldom made mistakes in phrasing like that anymore. She glanced at Jondalar and Marthona, but they hadn't seemed to notice. She relaxed and looked around.

Though she had been in and out of Marthona's dwelling several times, she had not really looked at it closely. She took the time to observe more carefully, and was surprised and delighted at every turn. The construction was interesting, similar but not the same as the dwellings inside the Losadunai cave, where they had stopped to visit before crossing the glacier on the high plateau.

The first two or three feet of the outside walls of each dwelling were constructed of limestone. Fairly large blocks were roughly trimmed and placed on either side of the entry, but stone tools were not suitable for finely shaping building stone easily or quickly. The rest of the low walls were made up of limestone as it was found, or roughly shaped with a hammerstone. Various pieces, generally close to the same size—perhaps two or three inches wide, not quite as deep, and three or four times longer than they were wide—but some larger and some smaller pieces—were ingeniously fitted together so that they interlocked into a tight compressive structure.

The roughly lozenge-shaped pieces were selected and graded for size, then arranged side by side lengthwise so that the width of the walls was equivalent to the length of the stones. The thick walls were constructed in layers so that each stone was placed in the dip where the two stones under it came together. Occasionally smaller stones were used to fill in gaps, especially around the larger blocks near the entry.

As they were layered up they were corbeled inward slightly, cantilevered in such a way that each successive layer overhung the layer below by a little. Careful selection and placement were done so that any irregularities in the stone contributed to the runoff of moisture on the outside, whether it was rainwater blown in, accumulated condensation, or ice melt.

No mortar or mud was needed to plug holes or add support. The rough limestone offered purchase enough to prevent sliding or slipping, and the mass of stones was held by its own weight and could even take the thrust of a beam of juniper or pine inserted into the walls to support other building elements or shelving structures. The stones were so cunningly fitted together that no chink of light showed through, and no errant blasts of winter wind could find an opening. The effect was also quite attractive, with a pleasing texture, especially seen from outside.

Inside, the stone windbreak wall was all but hidden by a second wall made of panels of rawhide—untreated leather that dried stiff and hard—attached to wooden posts sunk into the dirt floor. The panels began at ground level but extended above the stone walls vertically to a height of eight or nine feet. Ayla recalled that the upper panels were lavishly decorated on the outside. Many of the panels were also painted with animals and enigmatic marks on the inside, but the colors seemed less bright because it was darker inside. Because Marthona's structure was built against the slightly sloping back of the cliff, underneath the overhanging shelf, one wall of the dwelling was solid limestone.

Ayla looked up. There was no ceiling except the underside of the stone ledge some distance above. With the exception of occasional downdrafts, smoke from fires rose over the wall panels and drifted out along the lofty stone, leaving the air essentially clear. The cliff overhang protected them from inclement weather, and with warm clothing the dwellings could be quite comfortable even when it was cold. They were fairly large, not like some of the cozy, easy to heat, fully enclosed, but often smoke-filled little living spaces she had seen.

While the wood and leather walls offered protection from wind and rain that might blow in, they were designed more to define an area of personal space and provide some measure of privacy, at least from eyes if not ears. Some of the upper sections of the panels could be opened to admit light and neighborly conversations, if desired, but when the window panels were closed, it was considered courteous for visitors to use the entry and ask for admittance, not just call out from outside or walk in.

Ayla examined the floor more closely when her eye caught sight of stones fitted together. The limestone of the huge cliffs in the region could be broken and often sheared off naturally, along the lines of its crystal structure, into large rather flat fragments. The dirt floor inside the dwelling was paved with irregular sections of the flat stones, then covered with mats woven out of grasses and reeds, and rugs of soft fur.

Ayla turned her attention back to the conversation between Jondalar and his mother. Taking a sip of the wine, she noticed the cup in her hand. It was made of a hollow horn, bison, she thought, probably a section cut off not too far from the tip since it was rather narrow in diameter. She lifted it up to look underneath; the bottom was wood, shaped to fit the smaller, slightly lopsided, circular end, and wedged in tight. She saw scratch marks on the side, but when she looked more closely, she was surprised to find that it was a picture of a horse from side view, perfectly and delicately engraved.

She put the cup down, then inspected the low platform around which they were seated. It was a thin slab of limestone resting on a supporting bentwood frame with legs, all lashed together with thongs. The top was covered with a mat of some kind of rather fine fiber, woven with intricate designs that suggested animals and various abstract lines and shapes, in gradations of an earthy reddish color. Several pillows made of various materials were arranged around it. The leather ones were of a similar shade of red.

Two stone lamps rested on the stone table. One was beautifully carved and shaped into a shallow bowl with a decorated handle, the other was a rough equivalent with a depression that had been quickly pecked out of the center of a hunk of limestone. Both held melted tallow—animal fat that had been rendered in boiling water—and burning wicks. The roughly made lamp had two wicks, and the finished one, three. Each wick shed the same amount of light. Ayla had the feeling that the rougher one had been made recently for quick additional lighting in the dimly lit dwelling space at the back of the abri, and would see only temporary use.

The interior space, divided into four areas by movable partitions, was orderly and uncluttered, and lighted by several more stone lamps. The dividing screens, most colored or decorated in some way, also had wood frames, some with opaque panels, usually the stiff rawhide of uncured leather. But a few were translucent, probably made of some large animal's intestines that had been cut open and dried flat, Ayla thought.

At the left end of the back stone wall, adjacent to an exterior panel, was an especially beautiful screen that appeared to be made of the shadow skin—the parchmentlike material that could be removed in large sections from the inner side of animal hides if it was left to dry without scraping. A horse and some enigmatic designs, which included lines, dots, and squares, had been drawn on it in black and shades of yellow and red. Ayla recalled that the Mamut of the Lion Camp had used a similar screen during ceremonies, although the animals and markings on his were painted only in black. His had come from the shadow skin of a white mammoth, and was his most sacred possession.

On the floor in front of the screen was a grayish fur that Ayla was sure came from the hide of a horse in thick winter coat. The glow of a small fire, which seemed to come from a niche in the wall behind it, lighted the horse screen, emphasizing its decorations.

Shelves, made of thinner segments of limestone than the paving and spaced at various intervals, lined the stone wall to the right of the screen and held an array of objects and implements. Vague shapes could be seen on the floor in a storage area below the lowest shelf, where the slope of the wall was deepest. Ayla recognized the functional use of many of the things, but some had been carved and colored with such skill, they were objects of beauty as well.

To the right of the shelves, a leather-paneled screen jutting out from the stone wall marked the corner of the room and the beginning of another room. The screens only suggested a division between the rooms, and through an opening Ayla could see a raised platform piled high with soft furs. Someone's sleeping space, she thought. Another sleeping space was loosely defined by screens, dividing it from the room they occupied and from the first sleeping room.

The draped entrance was part of the wall of wood-framed hide panels opposite the stone wall, and on the side across from the sleeping spaces was a fourth room, where Marthona was preparing food. Along the entry wall near the cooking room, freestanding wooden shelves held artfully arranged baskets and bowls, beautifully decorated with carved, woven, or painted geometric designs and realistic depictions of animals. Larger containers were on the floor next to the wall, some with lids while others openly revealed their contents: vegetables, fruits, grains, dried meats.

There were four sides to the roughly rectangular dwelling, though the outside walls were not perfectly straight nor the spaces entirely symmetrical. They curved somewhat unevenly, tending to follow the contours of the space under the overhanging shelf, and made allowances for other dwellings.

"You've changed things around, mother," Jondalar said. "It seems roomier than I remember."

"It is roomier, Jondalar. There's only three of us here now. Folara sleeps in there," Marthona said, indicating the second sleeping space. "Willamar and I sleep in the other room." She motioned toward the room against the stone wall. "You and Ayla may use the main room. We can move the table closer to the wall to make room for a bed platform, if you like."

To Ayla, the place seemed quite roomy. The dwelling was much larger than the individual living spaces of each hearth—each family—in the semisubterranean longhouse of the Lion Camp, although not as big as her small cave in the valley, where she had lived alone. But, unlike this living area, the Mamutoi lodge was not a natural formation; the people of the Lion Camp had made it themselves.

Her attention was drawn to the nearby partition that separated the cooking space from the main room. It bent in the middle, and she realized it was two translucent screens connected in an unusual way. The wooden poles that made up the inside of the frame and legs of both panels were inserted in circles of transversely cut hollow bison horn. The rings formed a kind of hinge near the bottom and top that allowed the double screen to fold back. She wondered if other screens were made the same way.

She looked into the cooking space, curious about the facilities. Marthona was kneeling on a mat beside a hearth circled with stones of similar size; the paving stones around it were swept clean. Behind the woman in a darker corner lit by a single stone lamp were more shelves that held cups, bowls, platters, and implements. She noticed dried herbs and vegetables hanging and then saw the end of a frame with crosspieces to which they were tied. On a work platform beside the hearth were bowls, baskets, and a large bone platter with pieces of fresh red meat cut into chunks.

Ayla wondered if she should offer to help, but she didn't know where anything was kept, or what Marthona was making. It was less than helpful to get in someone's way. Better to wait, she thought.

She watched Marthona skewer the meat on four pointed sticks and place them over hot coals between two upright stones, notched to hold several skewers at once. Then, with a ladle carved out of an ibex horn, the woman scooped liquid out of a tightly woven basket into wooden bowls. With a pair of springy tongs made of wood bent all the way around, she fished a couple of smooth stones out of the cooking basket and added another hot one from the fire, then brought the two bowls to Ayla and Jondalar.

Ayla noticed the round globes of small onions and some other root vegetables in the rich broth, and realized how hungry she was, but she waited and watched to see what Jondalar did. He took out his eating knife, a small, pointed, flint blade inserted into an antler handle, and speared a small root vegetable. He put it in his mouth and chewed a moment, then took a drink of the broth from the bowl. Ayla took out her eating knife and did the same.

The soup had a delicious and flavorful meaty broth, but there was no meat in it, only vegetables, an unusual combination of herbs, to her taste, and something else, but she didn't know what. It surprised her because she could almost always distinguish the ingredients in food. The meat, browned over the fire on skewers, was soon brought to them. It also had an unusual and delicious flavor. She wanted to ask, but held her tongue.

"Aren't you eating, mother? This is good," Jondalar said, spearing another piece of vegetable.

"Folara and I ate earlier. I made a lot because I keep expecting

Willamar. Now I'm glad I did," she smiled. "I only had to heat the soup for you, and cook the aurochs meat. I had it soaking in wine."

That was the taste, Ayla thought, as she took another sip of the red liquid. It was in the soup, too.

"When is Willamar coming back?" Jondalar asked. "I'm looking forward to seeing him."

"Soon," Marthona said. "He went on a trading mission, west, to the Great Waters, to get salt and whatever else he could trade for, but he knows when we plan to leave for the Summer Meeting. He'll certainly be back before then, unless something delays him, but I expect him any time now."

"Laduni of the Losadunai told me they trade with a Cave that digs salt from a mountain. They call it Salt Mountain," Jondalar said.

"A mountain of salt? I never knew there was salt in mountains, Jondalar. I think you are going to have stories to tell for a long time, and no one will know what is Story-Telling and what is true," Marthona said.

Jondalar grinned, but Ayla had the distinct feeling that his mother doubted what she had been told, without actually saying so.

"I didn't see it myself, but I rather think this story is true," he said. "They did have salt, and they live quite far from salt water. If they had to trade or travel a great distance for it, I don't think they would have been so liberal with it."

Jondalar's grin grew wider, as though he'd thought of something funny. "Speaking of traveling great distances, I have a message for you, mother, from someone we met on our Journey, someone you know."

"From Dalanar, or Jerika?" she asked.

"We have a message from them, too. They are coming to the Summer Meeting. Dalanar is going to try to persuade some young zelandoni to go back with them. The First Cave of the Lanzadonii is growing. I wouldn't be surprised if they start a second Cave soon," Jondalar said.

"I don't think it will be difficult to find someone," Marthona commented. "It would be quite an honor. Whoever goes would truly be First, the first and only Lanzadoni."

"But, since they don't have One Who Serves yet, Dalanar wants Joplaya and Echozar to be joined at the Zelandonii Matrimonial," Jondalar continued.

A quick frown flickered across Marthona's face. "Your close cousin is such a beautiful young woman, unusual, but beautiful. None of the young men can keep his eyes away from her when she comes to the Zelandonii Meetings. Why would she choose Echozar when she could have any man she wanted?"

"No, not any man," Ayla said. Marthona looked at her and saw a glint of defensive heat. She flushed slightly, and looked away. "And she told me she'd never find anyone who would love her as much as Echozar."

"You're right, Ayla," Marthona said, paused a moment, then, looking directly at her, added, "There are some men she can't have." The older woman's eyes glanced fleetingly at her son. "But she and Echozar do seem ... mismatched. Joplaya is stunningly beautiful, and he is ... not. But appearances don't count for everything; sometimes they don't count for much at all. And Echozar does seem to be a kind and caring man."

Though she hadn't really said it, Ayla knew Marthona had quickly understood the reason Joplaya had made the choice she did; Jondalar's "close cousin," the daughter of Dalanar's mate, loved a man she could never have. No one else mattered, so she chose the one that she knew truly loved her. And Ayla understood that Marthona's objection was minor, prompted by a personal sense of aesthetics, not some outraged sense of propriety, as she had feared. Jondalar's mother loved beautiful things, and it seemed appropriate for a beautiful woman to join with a man who matched her, but she understood that beauty of character was more important.

Jondalar didn't seem to notice the slight tension between the two women, he was too delighted with himself for remembering the words he was asked to pass on to his mother, from someone he had never heard her mention. "The message I have for you is not from the Lanzadonii. We stayed with some people on our Journey, stayed longer than we planned, though I hadn't planned to stay at all ... but that's another story. When we left, their One Who Serves said, 'When you see Marthona, tell her Bodoa sends her love.'"

Jondalar had hoped to get a reaction from his self-possessed and dignified mother by mentioning a name from her past that she had probably forgotten. He meant it as playful banter in their friendly game of words and implied meanings, saying without saying, but he didn't expect the reaction he got.

Marthona's eyes opened wide and her face blanched. "Bodoa! Oh, Great Mother! Bodoa?" She put her hand on her chest, and seemed to have trouble catching her breath.

"Mother! Are you all right?" Jondalar said, jumping up and hovering over her. "I'm sorry, I didn't mean to shock you like that. Should I get Zelandoni?"

"No, no, I'm fine," Marthona said, taking a deep breath. "But I was surprised. I didn't think I'd ever hear that name again. I didn't even know she was still alive. Did you . . . come to know her well?"

"She said she was almost a co-mate with you and Joconan, but I thought she was probably overstating, perhaps not remembering accurately," Jondalar said. "How come you never mentioned her?" Ayla gave him a quizzical look. She didn't know he hadn't quite believed the S'Armuna.

"It was too painful, Jondalar. Bodoa was like a sister. I would have been happy to co-mate with her, but our Zelandoni talked against it. He said they had promised her uncle that she'd return after her training. You said she is One Who Serves? Perhaps it was for the best, but she was so angry when she left. I pleaded with her to wait for the season to change before trying to cross the glacier, but she wouldn't listen. I'm happy to know she survived the crossing, and glad to know she sends her love. Do you think she really meant it?"

"Yes, I'm sure she did, mother. But she wouldn't have had to go back to her home," Jondalar said. "Her uncle had already left this world, and her mother as well. She did become S'Armuna, but her anger caused her to misuse her calling. She helped an evil woman to become leader, though she didn't know how evil Attaroa would become. S'Armuna is making up for it, now. I think she has found affirmation of her calling in helping her Cave overcome the bad years, though she may have to become their leader until someone can grow into it, like you did, mother. Bodoa was remarkable, she even discovered a way to turn mud into stone."

"Mud into stone? Jondalar, you do sound like a traveling Story-Teller," Marthona said. "How can I know what to believe if you are going to tell such incredible tales?"

"Believe me. I'm telling the truth," Jondalar said with perfect seriousness and no subtle word games. "I have not become a traveling Story-Teller who goes from Cave to Cave embellishing legends and histories to make them exciting, but I have made a long Journey and seen many things." He glanced at Ayla. "If you had not seen it, would you have believed people could ride on the backs of horses or make friends with a wolf? I have more things to tell you that you will find hard to believe, and some things to show you that will make you doubt your own eyes."

"All right, Jondalar. You have convinced me. I will not question you again . . . even if I do find what you say hard to believe," she said, and then smiled, with a mischievous charm that Ayla had not seen before. For a moment, the woman looked years younger, and Ayla understood where Jondalar got his smile.

Marthona picked up her cup of wine and sipped it slowly, encouraging them to finish eating. When they were done, she took the bowls and skewers away, gave them a soft, damp, absorbent skin to wipe their personal eating knives before they put them away, and poured them more wine.

"You've been gone a long time, Jondalar," she said to her son. Ayla had the feeling she was choosing her words carefully. "I understand you must have many stories to tell about your long Journey. You, too, Ayla," she said, looking at the young woman. "It will take a long time to tell them all, I would think. I hope you do plan to stay . . . for some time." She looked significantly at Jondalar. "You may stay here as long as you like, though it may feel crowded . . . after a while. Perhaps you will be wanting a place of your own . . . nearby . . . sometime. . . ."

Jondalar grinned. "Yes, mother, we will. Don't worry, I'm not leaving again. This is home. I'm planning to stay, we both are, unless someone objects. Is that the story you want to hear? Ayla and I are not mated yet, but we will be. I already told Zelandoni—she was here just before you came in with the wine. I wanted to wait until we got home so we could be joined here and have her tie the knot, at the Matrimonial this summer. I'm tired of traveling," he added with vehemence.

Marthona smiled her happiness. "It would be nice to see a child born to your hearth, perhaps even of your spirit, Jondalar," she said.

He looked at Ayla and smiled. "I feel the same way," he said.

Marthona hoped he was implying what it seemed, but she didn't want to ask. He should be the one to tell her. She just wished he wouldn't try to be so evasive about as important a matter as the possibility of children born to her son's hearth.

"You might be pleased to know," Jondalar continued, "Thonolan left a child of his spirit, if not his hearth, with at least one Cave, maybe more. A Losadunai woman named Filonia, one who found him pleasing, discovered she had been blessed soon after we stopped. She's mated now and has two children. Laduna told me that when word got around that she was pregnant, every eligible Losadunai man found a reason to visit. She had her pick, but she named her first, a daughter, Thonolia. I saw the little girl. She looks a lot like Folara used to, when she was little.

"Too bad they live so far away, and across a glacier. That's a long way to travel, although on the way back, it seemed close to home." He paused thoughtfully. "I never did like traveling that much. I would never have traveled as far as I did, if it hadn't been for Thonolan. . . ." Suddenly he noticed his mother's expression, and when he realized whom he had been talking about, his smile faded.

"Thonolan was born to Willamar's hearth," Marthona said, "born of his spirit, too, I'm certain. He always wanted to keep moving, even when he was a baby. Is he still traveling?"

Ayla noticed again an indirectness to the questions Marthona asked, or sometimes didn't ask but made clear nonetheless. Then she recalled that Jondalar had always been a little disconcerted by the directness and frank curiosity of the Mamutoi, and she had a sudden insight. The people who called themselves the Mammoth Hunters, the people who had adopted her and whose ways she had struggled so hard to learn, were not the same as Jondalar's people. Although the Clan referred to all the people who looked like her as the Others, the Zelandonii were not the Mamutoi and it was not only the language that was different. She would have to pay attention to differences in the way the Zelandonii did things, if she wanted to fit in here.

Jondalar took a deep breath, realizing this was the time to tell his mother about his brother. He reached over and took both of his mother's hands in his. "I'm sorry, mother. Thonolan travels in the next world now."

Marthona's clear, direct eyes showed the depth of her sudden grief and sadness over the loss of her youngest son; her shoulders seemed to collapse from the heavy burden. She had suffered the loss of loved ones before, but she had never lost a child. It seemed harder to lose one that she had raised to adulthood, who still should have had the fullness of life before him. She closed her eyes, trying to master her emotions, then straightened her shoulders and looked at the son who had returned to her.

"Were you with him, Jondalar?"

"Yes," he said, reliving the time, and feeling his grief afresh. "It was a cave lion . . . Thonolan followed it into a canyon. . . . I tried to stop him, but he wouldn't listen."

Jondalar was fighting for control, and Ayla remembered that night in her valley when his grief overwhelmed him while she held him and rocked him like a child. She didn't even know his language then, but no language is needed to understand grief. She reached over and touched his arm, to let him know she was there for him without interfering in the moment between mother and son. It was not lost on Marthona that Ayla's touch seemed to help. He took a breath.

"I have something for you, mother," he said, getting up and going to his traveling pack. He took out a wrapped packet, then, thinking about it, took out another.

"Thonolan found a woman and fell in love. Her people called themselves Sharamudoi. They lived near the end of the Great Mother River, where the river was so big, you understand why she was named for the Great Mother. The Sharamudoi were really two people. The Shamudoi half lived on the land and hunted chamois in the mountains, and the Ramudoi lived on the water and hunted giant sturgeon in the river. In the winter, the Ramudoi moved in with the Shamudoi, each family of one group had a family of the other they were tied to, mated in a way. They seemed to be two different people, but there were a lot of close connections between them that made them each a half of one people." Jondalar found it difficult to explain the unique and complex culture.

"Thonolan was so much in love, he was willing to become one of them. He became part of the Shamudoi half, when he mated with Jetamio."

"What a beautiful name," Marthona said.

"She was beautiful. You would have loved her."

"Was?"

"She died trying to give birth to a baby who would have been the son of his hearth. Thonolan couldn't stand losing her. I think he wanted to follow her to the next world."

"He was always so happy, so carefree. . . ."

"I know, but when Jetamio died, he changed. He wasn't happy and carefree anymore, just reckless. He couldn't stay with the Shara- mudoi anymore. I tried to persuade him to go home with me, but he insisted on going east. I couldn't let him go alone. The Ramudoi gave us one of their boats—they make exceptional boats—and we went downstream, but we lost everything in the great delta at the end of the Great Mother River, where it empties into Beran Sea. I got hurt, and Thonolan almost got sucked into quicksand, but a Camp of Mamutoi rescued us."

"Is that where you met Ayla?"

Jondalar looked at Ayla, then back at his mother. "No," he said, pausing for a moment, "after we left Willow Camp, Thonolan decided he wanted to go north and hunt mammoth with them during their Summer Meeting, but I don't think he really cared. He just wanted to keep going." Jondalar closed his eyes and breathed deep again.

"We were hunting a deer," he picked up the story again, "but we didn't know the same deer was being stalked by a lioness. She pounced about the same time that we threw spears. The spears landed first, but the lioness took the kill. Thonolan decided to go after it; he said it was his, not hers. I told him not to argue with a lioness, let her have it, but he insisted on following her back to her den. We waited a while, and when the lioness left, Thonolan decided to go into the canyon and take a piece of the meat. The lioness had a mate, and he wasn't going to let go of that kill. The lion killed him, and mauled me pretty bad, too."

Marthona frowned in concern. "You were mauled by a lion?"

"If it hadn't been for Ayla, I'd be dead," Jondalar said. "She saved my life. She got me away from that lion, and treated my wounds, too. She's a healer."

Marthona looked at Ayla, then back at Jondalar with surprise. "She got you away from a lion?"

"Whinney helped me, and I couldn't have done it if it was just any lion," Ayla tried to explain.

Jondalar understood his mother's confusion. And he knew the explanation wasn't going to make it any easier to believe. "You've seen how Wolf and the horses mind her. . . ."

"You're not telling me . . ."

"You tell her, Ayla," Jondalar said.

"The lion was one I found when he was a cub," Ayla began. "He'd been trampled by deer and his mother had left him for dead. He almost was. I was the one who had chased those deer, trying to get one to fall into my pit-trap. I did get one, and on the way back to the valley, I found the cub and took him back, too. Whinney wasn't too happy about it, the lion scent scared her, but I got both the deer and the lion cub back to my cave. I treated him, and he recovered, but he couldn't take care of himself alone, so I had to be his mother. Whinney learned to take care of him, too." Ayla smiled, remembering. "It was so funny to watch them together when he was little."

Marthona looked at the young woman and gained a new understanding. "Is that how you do it?" she said. "The wolf. And the horses, too?"

Now it was Ayla's turn to stare in surprise. No one had ever made the connection so quickly before. She was so pleased that Marthona was able to understand, she beamed. "Yes! Of course! That's what I've tried to tell everyone! If you find an animal very young, and feed him and raise him as though he were your own child, he becomes attached to you, and you to him. The lion that killed Thonolan, and mauled Jondalar, was the lion I raised. He was like a son to me."

"But by then he was a full-grown lion, wasn't he? Living with a mate? How could you get him away from Jondalar?" Marthona asked. She was incredulous.

"We hunted together. When he was little, I shared my kills with him, and when he got bigger, I made him share his with me. He always did what I asked. I was his mother. Lions are used to minding their mothers," Ayla said.

"I don't understand it, either," Jondalar said, seeing his mother's expression. "That lion was the biggest lion I have ever seen, but Ayla stopped him in his tracks, just short of attacking me a second time. I saw her ride on his back, more than once. The whole Mamutoi Summer Meeting saw her ride that lion. I've seen it, and I still have trouble believing it."

"I am only sorry that I wasn't able to save Thonolan," Ayla said. "I heard a man's scream, but by the time I got there, Thonolan was already dead."

Ayla's words reminded Marthona of her grief, and they were all wrapped in their own feelings for a while, but Marthona wanted to know more, wanted to understand. "I'm glad to know he found someone to love," she said.

Jondalar picked up the first package he had taken from his traveling pack. "On the day that Thonolan and Jetamio were mated, he told me you knew he would never return, but he made me promise him that someday I would. And he told me when I did to bring you something beautiful, the way Willamar always does. When Ayla and

I stopped to visit the Sharamudoi on our way back, Roshario gave this to me for you—Roshario was the woman who raised Jetamio, after her mother died. She said it was Jetamio's favorite," Jondalar said, giving the package to his mother.

Jondalar cut the cord that tied the leather-wrapped package. At first, Marthona thought the gift was the soft chamois skin itself, it was so beautiful, but when she opened it, she caught her breath at the sight of a beautiful necklace. It was made of chamois teeth, the perfect white canines of young animals, pierced through the root, graduated in size and symmetrically matched, each one separated by graduated segments of the backbones of small sturgeons, with a shimmering, iridescent mother-of-pearl pendant that resembled a boat hanging from the middle.

"It represents the people that Thonolan chose to join, the Sharamudoi, both sides of them. The chamois of the land for the Shamudoi, and the sturgeon of the river for the Ramudoi, and the shell boat for both of them. Roshario wanted you to have something that belonged to Thonolan's chosen woman," Jondalar said.

Tears traced their way down Marthona's face as she looked at the beautiful gift. "Jondalar, what made him think I knew he wasn't coming back?" she asked.

"He said you told him 'Good Journey' when he left, not 'Until you return,'" he said.

A new freshet of tears welled up and overflowed. "He was right. I didn't think he'd be back. As much as I denied it to myself, I was sure when he left that I would never see him again. And when I learned that you had gone with him, I thought I had lost two sons. Jondalar, I wish Thonolan had come home with you, but I'm so happy that at least you are back," she said, reaching for him.

Ayla couldn't help shedding her own tears watching Jondalar and his mother embrace. She began to understand now why Jondalar couldn't stay with the Sharamudoi when Tholie and Markeno had wanted them to. She knew how it felt to lose a son. She knew that she would never see her son again, but she wished she knew how he was, what happened to him, what kind of life he lived.

The drape at the entrance moved aside again. "Guess who's home?" Folara cried, rushing in. She was followed more calmly by Willamar.

3

Marthona hurried to greet the man who had just returned, and they embraced warmly.

"Well! I see that tall son of yours is back, Marthona! I never thought he would turn out to be a traveler. Maybe he should have become a trader instead of a knapper," Willamar said, slipping out of his backpack. Then he gave Jondalar a hearty hug. "You haven't shrunk any, I notice," the older man said with a big grin, looking up at the full six-foot-six-inch height of the yellow-haired man.

Jondalar grinned back. It was the way the man had always greeted him, with jokes about his height. At well over six feet, Willamar, who had been as much the man of his hearth as Dalanar, was not exactly short himself, but Jondalar matched the size of the man to whom Marthona had been mated when he was born, before they severed the tie.

"Where's your other son, Marthona?" Willamar asked, still grinning. Then he noticed her tearstained face and realized how distraught she was. When he saw her pain reflected in Jondalar, his grin faded.

"Thonolan travels the next world now," Jondalar said. "I was just telling mother . . ." He saw the man blanch, then stagger as though struck a physical blow.

"But . . . but he can't be in the next world," Willamar said with shocked disbelief. "He's too young. He hasn't found a woman to make a hearth with." His voice rose in pitch with each statement. "He . . . he hasn't come home yet. . . ." The last objection was almost a keening wail.

Willamar had always been fond of all of Marthona's children, but when they mated, Joharran, the child she had borne to Joconan's hearth, was nearly ready for his donii-woman, almost a man; that relationship was one of friendship. And though he had quickly grown to love Jondalar, who was a toddler and still nursing, it was Thonolan, and Folara, who were the children of his hearth. He was convinced Thonolan was the son of his spirit, too, because the boy was like him in so many ways, but in particular because he liked to travel and always wanted to see new places. He knew that in her heart, Marthona had feared that she would never see him again, or Jondalar either when she learned that he had gone with his brother. But Willamar thought that was just a mother's worry. Willamar had expected Thonolan to return, just as he himself always did.

The man seemed dazed, disoriented. Marthona poured a cup of liquid from the red flask, while Jondalar and Folara urged him to sit down on the cushions by the low table.

"Have some wine," Marthona said, sitting beside him. He felt numb, unable to comprehend the tragedy. He picked up the cup and drank it down, without seeming to know that he did, then sat staring at the cup.

Ayla wished there was something she could do. She thought of getting her medicine bag and making a soothing and relaxing drink for him. But he didn't know her, and she knew he was getting the best kind of care he could at this time: the attention and concern of people who loved him. She thought about how she would feel if she suddenly found out Durc was dead. It was one thing to know she would never see her son again, but she could still imagine him growing up, with Uba to love and take care of him.

"Thonolan did find a woman to love," Marthona said, trying to comfort him. Seeing her man's heartache and need had pulled her out of her own distress to help him. "Jondalar brought me something that belonged to her." She picked up the necklace to show him. He seemed to be staring into space, unaware of anything around him, then he gave a shudder and closed his eyes. After a time, he turned to look at Marthona, seeming to remember that she had spoken to him, though he could not recall what she said. "This belonged to Thonolan's mate," she said, holding it out to him. "Jondalar said it represents her people. They lived near a big river ... the Great Mother River."

"He did get that far, then," Willamar said, his voice hollow with anguish.

"Even farther," Jondalar said. "We reached the end of the Great Mother River, went all the way to Beran Sea, and beyond. Thonolan wanted to go north from there and hunt mammoth with the Mamutoi." Willamar looked up at him, his expression pained and puzzled, as though he wasn't quite understanding what was said. "And I have something of his," Jondalar said, trying to think of a way to help the man. He picked up the other wrapped package from the table. "Markeno gave it to me. Markeno was his cross-mate, part of his Ramudoi family."

Jondalar opened the leather-wrapped package and showed Willamar and Marthona an implement made out of an antler of a red deer—a variety of elk—with the tines above the first fork detached. A hole about an inch and a half in diameter had been made in the wide space just below the first fork. The tool was Thonolan's shaft straightener.

Thonolan's craft had been the knowledge of how to apply stress to wood, usually heated with hot stones or steam. The tool was used to gain better control and leverage when exerting pressure to straighten bends or kinks out of the shafts so the spears he made would fly true. It was particularly useful near the end of a long branch where a hand grip was not possible. When the end was inserted through the hole, additional leverage was gained, making it possible to straighten the tips. Though it was called a straightener, the tool could be used to bend wood around, to make a snowshoe, or tongs, or any other object that required bent wood. They were different aspects of the same skill.

The sturdy, foot-long handle of the tool was carved with symbols and with the animals and plants of spring. The carvings represented many things, depending on the context; carvings and paintings were always much more complex than they seemed. All such depictions honored the Great Earth Mother, and in that sense the designs on Thonolan's straightener were made so that She would allow the spirits of the animals to be drawn to the spears made with the tool. There was also a seasonal element represented that was part of an esoteric spiritual aspect. The beautifully made depictions were not simply representations, but, Jondalar knew, his brother had liked the carvings because they were beautiful.

Willamar seemed to focus on the pierced antler tool, then he reached for it. "This was Thonolan's," he said.

"Yes," Marthona said. "Do you remember when Thonolan bent the wood to make the support for this table with that tool?" She touched the low, stone-slab platform in front of her.

"Thonolan was good at his craft," Willamar said, his voice still strange, distant.

"Yes, he was," Jondalar said. "I think part of the reason he felt so comfortable with the Sharamudoi was that they did things with wood that he never imagined could be done. They bent wood to make boats. They would shape and hollow out a log to make a canoe, a kind of boat, then bend the sides to widen it. They could make it bigger by adding strakes—long planks—along the sides, bending them to follow the shape of the boat, and fastening them together. The Ramudoi were very skilled at handling boats in the water, but both the Shamudoi and Ramudoi worked together to make them.

"I considered staying with them. They are wonderful people. When Ayla and I stopped to visit with them on the way back, they wanted both of us to stay. If I had, I think I would have chosen the Ramudoi half. And there was a youngster there that was really interested in learning flint-knapping."

Jondalar knew he was babbling, but he was at a loss of what to do or say, and was trying to fill the emptiness. He had never seen Willamar so shaken.

There was a tapping at the entrance, but without waiting for an invitation, Zelandoni pushed the drape aside and came in. Folara followed her, and Ayla realized the young woman had slipped out and summoned the woman. She nodded approval to herself; it was the right thing to do. Jondalar's sister was a wise young woman.

It had worried Folara to see Willamar so upset. She had no idea what to do except to get help. And Zelandoni was the donier: the giver of Doni's Gifts, the one who acted as the intermediary of the Great Earth Mother to Her children, the dispenser of assistance and medication, the one you went to for help.

Folara had told the powerful woman the essence of the problem; Zelandoni glanced around and took in the situation quickly. She turned and spoke quietly to the young woman, who immediately headed for the cooking area and started blowing on the coals in the fireplace to get them started again. But the fire was dead. Marthona had spread the embers to cook the meat evenly and hadn't gotten back to rekindle and bank the fire to keep it alive.

Here was something Ayla could do to help. She left the scene of grief and quickly went to her pack near the entrance. She knew exactly where her tinder kit was, and as she snatched it and headed for the cooking area, she thought of Barzec, the Mamutoi man who made it for her after she had given each hearth of the Lion Camp a firestone.

"Let me help you make a fire," she said.

Folara smiled. She knew how to make fire, but it was upsetting to see the man of her hearth so distressed, and she was pleased to have someone there with her. Willamar had always been so strong, so steady, so self-possessed.

"If you get some kindling, I'll start it," Ayla said.

"The fire-starting sticks are over here," Folara said, turning toward the back shelf.

"That's all right. I don't need them," Ayla said, opening her tinder kit. It had several compartments and small pouches. She opened one and poured out crushed, dried horse dung, from another she pulled out fluffy fireweed fibers and arranged them on top of the dung, and from a third she poured out some shaved slivers of wood beside the first pile.

Folara watched. During the long Journey, Ayla obviously had learned to have fire-making materials easily at hand, but the younger woman looked puzzled when Ayla next took out a couple of stones. Leaning close to the tinder, the woman her brother had brought home with him struck the two stones together and blew at the tinder, and it burst into flame. It was uncanny!

"How did you do that?" Folara asked, completely astonished.

"I'll show you later," Ayla said. "Right now, let's keep this fire going so we can get some water boiling for Zelandoni."

Folara felt a rush of something like fear. "How did you know what I was going to do?"

Ayla glanced at her, then looked again. Folara's face showed her consternation. With one brother's return after a long absence, bringing tame animals and a unknown woman with him, then learning of the death of the other brother, and seeing Willamar's unexpected and disturbing reaction, it had been a tense, exciting, and anxious day. After the stranger appeared to create fire by magic and then seemed to know something that no one had told her, Folara began to wonder if all the speculation and gossip about Jondalar's woman having supernatural powers could be true. Ayla could see she was overwrought and was fairly sure she knew why.

"I met Zelandoni. I know she's your healer. That's why you went to get her, isn't it?" Ayla asked.

"Yes, she's the donier," the young woman said.

"Healers usually like to make a tea or a drink to help calm someone who is upset. I assumed that she asked you to boil water for her to make it with," Ayla carefully explained.

Folara visibly relaxed; it was perfectly reasonable.

"And I promise I'll show you how to make fire like that. Anyone can do it . . . with the right stones."

"Anyone?"

"Yes, even you," Ayla said, smiling.

The young woman smiled, too. She had been dying of curiosity about the woman and had so many questions she wanted to ask, but she hadn't wanted to be impolite. Now she had even more questions, but the foreign woman did not feel so unapproachable. In fact, she seemed rather nice.

"Would you tell me about the horses, too?"

Ayla gave her big pleased grin. She suddenly realized that although Folara might be every inch a tall and beautiful young woman, she hadn't been one for too long. She'd have to ask Jondalar how many years Folara counted, but Ayla suspected that she was still quite young, probably close in age to Latie, the daughter of Nezzie, who was the mate of the Mamutoi Lion Camp's headman.

"Of course. I'll even take you down to meet them," she glanced toward the low table where everyone was gathered, "maybe tomorrow, after everything is calmed down. You can go down and look at them any time you want, but don't get too close by yourself until the horses get to know you."

"Oh, I won't," Folara said.

Recalling Latie's fascination with the horses, Ayla smiled and asked, "Would you like to ride on Whinney's back sometime?"

"Oh! Could I?" Folara asked, breathless, her eyes open wide. At that moment, Ayla could almost see Latie in Jondalar's sister. She had developed such a passion for the horses that Ayla had wondered if she might try to get a baby horse of her own someday.

Ayla went back to her fire-making as Folara reached for the waterbag—the waterproof stomach of some large animal. "I need to get more water. This is almost empty," the young woman said.

The coal was still glowing, barely alive. Ayla blew on it a little more, added shavings, then the small kindling that Folara had given her, and finally a few of the larger pieces of wood. She saw the cooking stones and put several into the fire to heat. When Folara returned, the waterbag was bulging and seemed quite heavy, but the young woman was obviously used to lifting it and filled a deep wooden bowl with water, likely the one that Marthona used for making tea. Then she gave Ayla the wooden tongs with the slightly charred ends. When she felt they were hot enough, Ayla used the tongs to pick up a hot stone. It sizzled and sent up a cloud of steam when she dropped it in the water. She added a second, then fished out the first one and replaced it with a third, and then more.

Folara went to tell Zelandoni the water was nearly ready. Ayla knew she must have told her something else as well from the way the older woman's head jerked up to look at her. Ayla watched the woman haul herself up from the low cushions, and thought of Creb, the Clan Mog-ur. He'd had a lame leg and it made it difficult for him to get up from low seats. His favorite place to relax had been a bent old tree with a low branch that was just the right height to sit on and get up from easily.

The woman came into the cooking room. "I understand the water is hot." Ayla nodded toward the steaming bowl. "And did I hear Folara correctly? She said you were going to show her how to start a fire with stones. What kind of trick is that?"

"Yes. I have some firestones. Jondalar has some, too. The only trick is learning how to use them, and it's not hard. I'll be happy to show you any time you would like. We had planned to, anyway." Zelandoni looked back toward Willamar. Ayla knew she was pulled two ways.

"Not now," the woman said under her breath, shaking her head. She measured some dried herbs into the palm of her hand from a pouch tied to a belt around her ample waist, then dropped them into the steaming water. "I wish I had brought some yarrow," she mumbled to herself.

"I have some, if you'd like," Ayla said.

"What?" Zelandoni said. She was concentrating on what she was doing and hadn't really paid attention.

"I said I have some yarrow, if you want it. You said you wished you had brought some."

"Did I? I was thinking it, but why would you have yarrow?"

"I am a medicine woman . . . a healer. I always have some basic medicines with me. Yarrow is one. It's good for stomachaches, it relaxes, and it helps wounds heal clean and fast," she said.

Zelandoni's jaw would have dropped open if she hadn't caught it halfway down. "You're a healer? The woman Jondalar brought home is a healer?" She almost laughed, then closed her eyes and shook her head. "I think we are going to have to have a long talk, Ayla."

"I would be happy to talk to you anytime," she said, "but do you want the yarrow?"

Zelandoni thought for a moment. *She can't be One Who Serves. If she was, she would never leave her people to follow some man to his home, even if she did choose to mate. But she may know a little about herbs. A lot of people learn something about them. If she has some yarrow, why not use it? It has a distinctive enough odor so I can tell if it's right.* "Yes. I think it would be helpful, if you have some handy."

Ayla hurried to her traveling pack, reached into a side pocket, and took out her otterskin medicine bag. *This is getting very worn,* she thought as she carried it back. *I'm going to have to replace it soon.* When she got to the cooking room, Zelandoni looked with interest at the strange container. It appeared to be made of the entire animal. She had never seen one like it, but there was something about it that seemed authentic.

The younger woman lifted the otter head flap, loosened the drawstring tie around the neck, then looked inside and withdrew a small pouch. She knew what it contained from the shade of color of the leather, the fiber of the drawstring closure, and the number and arrangement of the knots on the dangling ends. She untied the knot that closed it—it was a kind of knot that was easy to loosen if you knew how—and handed the pouch to the woman.

Zelandoni wondered how Ayla knew that she had the correct herb without smelling it, but when she brought it to her nose, she knew it was right. The donier poured a little into her palm, looked it over carefully to see if it was just leaves, or leaves and flowers, and if there was anything else in it. It appeared to be pure yarrow leaf. She added a few pinches to the wooden bowl.

"Should I add another cooking stone?" Ayla asked, wondering if she wanted an infusion or a decoction—steeped or boiled.

"No," the donier said. "I don't want anything too strong. He only needs a mild infusion. He's almost over the shock. Willamar is a strong man. He's worried about Marthona now, and I want to give some to her. I need to be careful with her medicine."

Ayla thought she must be giving Jondalar's mother regular doses of some medicine that she was watching carefully. "Would you like me to make some tea for everyone?" she asked.

"I'm not sure. What kind?" the older healer asked.

"Just something mild that tastes good. Some mint, or chamomile. I even have some linden flowers to sweeten it."

"Yes, why don't you. Some chamomile with the linden flowers would be nice, gently calming," Zelandoni said as she turned to go.

Ayla was smiling as she removed more pouches from her medicine bag. Healing magic, she knows it! I haven't lived near anyone who knows medicines and healing magic since I left the Clan! It's going to be wonderful to have someone to talk to about it.

Ayla had originally learned healing—at least herbal medicine and treatments, if not matters of the spirit world—from Iza, her Clan mother, who was recognized as a worthy descendant of the foremost line of medicine women. She had learned additional details from the other medicine women at the Clan Gathering to which she had gone with Brun's clan. Later, at the Summer Meeting of the Mamutoi, she had spent a considerable amount of time with the mamutii.

She discovered that all Those Who Served The Mother were conversant with both medicines and spirits, but not equally skilled. It often depended on an individual's own interests. Some mamutii were particularly knowledgeable about medications, some were more interested in healing practices, some in people generally and why certain ones would recover from the same illness or injury and others would not. And some cared only about things of the spirit world and the mind, and were not much interested in healing at all.

Ayla wanted to know everything. She tried to absorb it all—ideas about the spirit world, knowledge and uses of counting words, memorizing legends and histories—but she was particularly and endlessly fascinated with anything related to healing: medicines, practices, treatments, and causes. She had experimented with different plants and herbs on herself the way Iza had taught her, using knowledge and care, and learned whatever she could from healers she had met on their Journey. She thought of herself as someone with knowledge, but who was still learning. She didn't fully realize how much she knew or how highly skilled she was. But the one thing she had missed more than anything since leaving the Clan was having someone with whom to discuss it all, a colleague.

Folara helped her make the tea and showed her where things were. They both carried steaming cups out for everyone. Willamar was obviously in a better state of mind and asking Jondalar the details of Thonolan's death. He had just begun to retell the circumstances of the cave lion attack when they all looked up at the tapping sound from the entrance.

"Come in," Marthona called.

Joharran moved aside the drape and looked a little surprised to see everyone gathered together inside, including Zelandoni. "I came to see Willamar. I'd like to know how the trading went. I saw Tivonan and you drop a big pack, but with all the excitement and the feast tonight, I thought we should wait until tomorrow to have a meet . . . ," he was saying as he approached. Then he noticed that something seemed wrong. He looked from one to the other, and finally to Zelandoni.

"Jondalar was just telling us about the cave lion that . . . attacked Thonolan," she said, and, seeing his horrified look, realized that he didn't know about the death of his youngest brother. It wasn't going to be easy on him, either. Thonolan had been well loved. "Sit down, Joharran. I think everyone should hear about it all together. Shared grief is easier to bear, and I doubt that Jondalar wants to repeat this too many times."

Ayla caught Zelandoni's eye, tilted her head toward the first calming drink that the woman had prepared, then toward the second tea that she had made. Zelandoni nodded at the second, then watched as Ayla silently poured a cup and unobtrusively handed it to Joharran. He took it without even noticing as he listened to Jondalar summarize the incidents leading up to Thonolan's death. Zelandoni was becoming more intrigued by the young woman. She had something, perhaps something more than a little knowledge of herbs.

"What happened after the lion attacked him, Jondalar?" Joharran asked.

"He attacked me."

"How did you get away?"

"That's Ayla's story to tell," Jondalar said. All eyes suddenly turned to her.

The first time Jondalar had done that, told a story up to a point and then turned it over to her without warning, she had been very disconcerted. She was more used to it now, but these people were his kin, his family. She was going to have to talk about the death of one of their own, a man she never knew, who obviously had been very dear to them. She felt her nervousness in the pit of her stomach.

"I was riding on Whinney's back," she began. "Her belly was full with Racer, but she needed exercise, so I rode her a little every day. We usually went east, because it was easier, but I was tired of going the same way all the time, so for a change I thought I'd go west. We went to the far end of the valley where the cliff wall began to level out. We crossed the little river, and I almost changed my mind about going in that direction. Whinney was pulling the pole drag and it was a steep slope, but she's surefooted and climbed up without too much trouble."

"What's a pole drag?" Folara asked.

"It's just two poles attached at one end to Whinney's back, with the other ends dragging the ground, and a sturdy carrier between the poles behind her. That's how Whinney helped me carry things back to my cave, like the animals I hunted," Ayla said, trying to explain the travois she devised.

"Why didn't you just get some people to help you?" Folara wanted to know.

"There were no people to help me. I lived alone in the valley," Ayla said.

The assembled group looked at each other in surprise, but before someone else could ask another question, Zelandoni interjected, "I'm sure we could all ask many questions of Ayla, but we can do that later. Why don't we let her finish telling us about Thonolan and Jondalar now."

There were nods of agreement, as they all turned their attention back to the stranger.

"As we were going past a canyon, I heard the roar of a lion, and then a scream, the scream of a man in pain," Ayla continued. They were hanging on her every word, and Folara couldn't be quiet.

"What did you do?"

"I didn't know what to do at first, but I had to go find out who had screamed. I had to try to help, if I could. Whinney took me to the canyon. I got down behind a rock and slowly tried to look in. Then I saw the lion, and heard him. It was Baby. I wasn't afraid anymore and went in. I knew he wouldn't hurt us," she said.

This time it was Zelandoni who couldn't keep still. "You recognized a lion's roar? Went right into the canyon of a roaring lion?"

"It wasn't just any lion. It was Baby. My lion. The one I raised," Ayla said, trying to make an important distinction. She glanced at Jondalar, and he was grinning in spite of the seriousness of the events she was relating. He couldn't help it.

"They already told me about this lion," Marthona said. "Apparently Ayla has a way with other animals, not just horses and wolves. Jondalar says he saw her ride the back of this lion, just like the horses. He claims others have seen it, too. Please continue, Ayla."

Zelandoni thought she'd have to look into this connection with animals. She had seen the horses by The River, and knew Ayla had a wolf with her, but she'd been seeing to a sick child in one of the other dwellings when Marthona led them to her place. They weren't in evidence at the moment, and she had put them out of her mind for the time being.

"When I got to the back end of the canyon," Ayla continued, "I saw Baby up on a ledge with two men. I thought both of them were dead, but when I climbed up and looked, I realized only one was dead. The other was still alive, but without help, he wouldn't be for very long. I managed to get Jondalar down off the ledge and tied him to the pole drag."

"What about the lion?" Joharran asked. "Cave lions don't usually let anything come between them and something they've killed."

"No, they don't, but this was Baby. I told him to go away." Ayla saw his look of stunned disbelief. "Just like I used to when we hunted together. I don't think he was hungry anyway, his lioness had just brought him a deer. And he didn't hunt people. I raised him. I was his mother. People were his family . . . his pride. I think the only reason he attacked the two men was that they had encroached on his den, his territory.

"But I didn't want to leave the other man there. The lioness wouldn't think people were family. There wasn't room for him on the pole drag, and no time for a burial. I was afraid Jondalar would die, too, if I didn't get him back to my cave. I noticed a steep scree slope at the back of the ledge, with a rock holding it back. I dragged the body there and used my spear—I used big thick Clan spears then—to pry the rock out of the way so the gravel would cover him. I hated to leave him like that, without even a message to the Spirit World. I'm not a mog-ur, but I used Creb's ritual and asked the spirit of the Great Cave Bear to help guide him to the Land of the Spirits. Then Whinney and I brought Jondalar home."

There were so many questions Zelandoni wanted to ask. Who or what was a "grrrub," which was what the name Creb sounded like to her. And why the spirit of a cave bear instead of the Great Earth Mother? She hadn't understood half of what Ayla said, and found the other half hard to believe. "Well, it's a good thing Jondalar wasn't hurt as bad as you thought," the older healer said.

Ayla shook her head. What did she mean? Jondalar was nearly dead. She still wasn't sure how she saved him.

Jondalar could guess what Ayla was thinking from her expression. It was obvious Zelandoni had made some assumptions that needed to be corrected. He stood up. "I think you need to know how badly I was mauled," he said, lifting his tunic and untying the waist thong of his summer leggings.

Although men seldom went entirely naked, even on the hottest days of summer, and neither did women, showing one's bare body was not a concern. People often saw each other when they went swimming or took sweat baths. It wasn't his exposed manhood that people stared at when Jondalar bared himself, it was the massive scarring on his upper thigh and groin.

The wounds had healed well; there was evidence that Ayla had actually sewn pieces of his skin together in places, Zelandoni noted. She had made seven individual stitches in his leg: four knots along the deepest wound and three more to hold torn muscles in place. No one had ever taught her, it was the only way she could think of to keep the gaping gashes closed.

Jondalar had given no hint that he had sustained such a serious injury. There was no limping or favoring of that leg, and except for the scars themselves, the muscle tissue underneath appeared fairly normal. There were other scars and marks on his body around his right shoulder and chest from the scratches and gashes made by the lion, and another apparently unrelated scar on his rib. It was evident that his long Journey had not left him unscathed.

They all understood now how severely Jondalar had been hurt, and why he had to be tended to immediately, but only Zelandoni had any idea how close to death he was. She flushed to think how seriously she had underrated Ayla's ability as a healer and was embarrassed to think of her rather offhand remark.

"I am sorry, Ayla. I had no idea you were so skilled. I think the Ninth Cave of the Zelandonii is fortunate that Jondalar has brought such a well-trained healer with him," she said, noticing Jondalar's smile as he covered himself again, and a small sigh of relief from Ayla.

Zelandoni was even more determined to learn more about this stranger. This animal association had to mean something, and someone that skilled as a healer had to be brought within the authority and influence of the zelandonia. A stranger like that could wreak havoc within the orderly life of her people without some control and supervision. But since it was Jondalar who brought her, she would have to take it slowly. There was much to learn about this woman first.

"It seems I have you to thank for the return of at least one of my sons, Ayla," Marthona said. "I am happy to have him and grateful to you."

"If only Thonolan could have returned, it would indeed be a joyful occasion. But Marthona knew when he left that he would not return," Willamar said, then, looking at his hearth mate, "I didn't want to believe you, but I should have known. He wanted to see everything, and go everyplace. That alone would have kept him traveling. Even as a small child his curiosity was too great."

The comment reminded Jondalar of a deep concern he had long felt. Perhaps now was the appropriate time.

"Zelandoni, I need to ask you, is it possible for his spirit to find his own way to the spirit world?" Jondalar's habitual worried frown matched Joharran's. "After the woman he mated died, Thonolan wasn't himself, and he did not go to the next world with the proper assistance. His bones are still under that pile of gravel on the eastern steppes, he had no proper burial. What if his spirit is lost, wandering in the next world with no one to show him the way?"

The large woman frowned. It was a serious question, and one that had to be handled with delicacy, especially for the sake of Thonolan's grieving family. "Didn't you say something about some hurried ritual you performed, Ayla? Tell me about it."

"There's not much to tell," she said. "It was the ritual Creb always used when a person died and their spirit left this world. I was more concerned about the man who was living, but I wanted to do something to help the other one to find his way."

"She took me to the place later," Jondalar added, "and gave me some powdered red ochre to sprinkle over the rocks of his grave. When we left the valley for the last time, we went back to the canyon where Thonolan and I were attacked. I found a very special stone that came from the pile that buried him. I brought it with me. I hoped it might help you to find his spirit if it still wanders, so you could help him find his way. It's in my pack, I'll get it."

Jondalar got up, went to his pack, and quickly returned with a simple leather pouch attached to a length of thong so that it could be worn around the neck, although it showed little sign of such usage. He opened it and shook two objects out of it into his palm. One was a small chunk of red ochre. The other appeared to be a small, sharp-edged piece of ordinary gray rock shaped somewhat like a flattened pyramid. But when he picked it up and showed the bottom unseen surface, there were gasps and looks of surprise. That facet was lined with a thin layer of milky blue opal, shimmering with fiery red highlights.

"I was standing there, thinking of Thonolan, and this rolled down the gravel slope and landed at my feet," Jondalar explained. "Ayla said that I should put it in my amulet—this pouch—and take it home with me. I don't know what it means, but it felt—it feels—as if Thonolan's spirit is somehow connected with it."

He handed the stone to Zelandoni. No one else felt inclined to touch it, and Joharran actually shuddered, Ayla noticed. The woman studied it carefully, giving herself time to think and consider what to say.

"I think you are right, Jondalar," she said. "This is connected with Thonolan's spirit. I am not sure what it means, I need to study it more, and ask the Mother for guidance, but you were wise to bring it to me." She was silent for a while, then added, "Thonolan's spirit was adventuresome. Perhaps this world was too small for him. He may still be traveling in the next world, not because he's lost, but because he may not be ready to find his place there, yet. How far east were you when his life on this world ended?"

"Beyond the inland sea at the end of the great river, the one that begins on the other side of the highland glacier."

"The one they call the Great Mother River?"

"Yes."

Zelandoni was silent again. Finally she spoke. "It may be, Jondalar, that Thonolan's quest could only be satisfied in the next world, in the land of the spirits. Perhaps Doni felt it was time to call him, and let you return home. What Ayla did may have been enough, but I don't quite understand what she did, or why she did it. I need to ask some questions."

She looked at the tall, handsome man she had once loved, still loved in her own way, and the young woman sitting beside him who had managed to astonish her more than once in the short time since she arrived. "First, who is this 'Grrrub' you speak of, and why did you appeal to the spirit of a cave bear and not the Great Earth Mother?"

She could see where Zelandoni's questions were leading, and because they were direct questions, she almost felt compelled to answer. She had learned what a lie was, and that some people could say a thing that wasn't true, but she could not. The most she could do was refrain from mentioning, and that was particularly difficult when she was asked a direct question. Ayla looked down and stared at her hands. There were black smudges on them from making the fire.

She had been sure that eventually it would all come out, but she had hoped to spend some time with Jondalar's people first, to get to know some of them. Perhaps it was just as well. If she was going to have to leave, it would be better to do it before she grew to like them.

But what about Jondalar? She loved him. What if she had to leave without him? His child was inside her. Not just the child of his hearth, or even the child of his spirit. His child. It didn't matter what anyone else believed, she was convinced, she knew it was his child, as much as hers. He had started it growing inside her when they shared Pleasures—the Gift of Pleasure given to Her children by the Great Earth Mother.

She had been afraid to look at him, avoiding it for fear of what she might see. Suddenly she looked up, directly at him. She had to know.

4

Jondalar smiled and nodded his head imperceptibly. Then he reached for her hand, gave it a little squeeze, and held it. Ayla could hardly believe it. It was all right! He understood and he was telling her it was all right. She could say whatever she wanted about the Clan. He would stay with her. He loved her. She smiled back, her big wonderful smile, full of love.

Jondalar, too, had seen where Zelandoni's questions were leading, and much to his own surprise, he didn't care. At one time he had been so concerned about what his family and his people would think of this woman, and what they might think of him for bringing her home with him, he almost gave her up, almost lost her. Now, it didn't matter. As much as he cared about them, as glad as he was to see them, if his own family wouldn't accept her along with him, then he'd leave. It was Ayla he loved. Together, they had much to offer. Several Caves had already asked them to stay and live with them, including Dalanar's Lanzadonii. He was sure they could find a home—somewhere.

The donier knew something had passed between Ayla and Jondalar, some kind of approval or affirmation. It made her curious, but she had learned that observation and patience often satisfied her curiosity better than questions.

Ayla turned to look at Zelandoni to answer. "Creb was mog-ur of Brun's clan, the one who knew the spirit world, but he was more than just mog-ur. He was like you, Zelandoni, he was First, The Mog-ur of the whole Clan. But to me, Creb was . . . man of my hearth, though I wasn't born there, and the woman he lived with, Iza, was his sibling, not his mate. Creb never had mate."

"Who or what is the Clan?" Zelandoni asked. She noticed that Ayla's accent got thicker when she spoke of them.

"The Clan is . . . I was . . . adopted by the Clan. They are the ones who took me in when I was . . . alone. Creb and Iza took care of me, raised me. Iza was mother, only mother I remember. And she was medicine woman, healer. Iza was First, too, in a way. She was most respected of all medicine women, as her mother and her grandmother had been, all the way back in unbroken line to beginning of Clan."

"Is that where you learned your healing skills?" Zelandoni asked, leaning forward on the cushions.

"Yes. Iza taught me, even though I wasn't her true daughter, and didn't have her memories like Uba did. Uba was my sister. Not a true sibling, but still my sister."

"What happened to your real mother, your family, the people you were born to?" Zelandoni wanted to know. Everyone was curious, fascinated, but they let her ask the questions.

Ayla sat back and looked up, as though trying to find an answer. Then she looked at the large woman who was regarding her so intently. "I don't know. I don't remember. I was young, Iza guessed that I could count five years . . . although they didn't have counting words like Zelandonii. The Clan named the years beginning as babies. The first was the birthing year, then the nursing year, the weaning year, and so on. I put it into counting words," she tried to explain. Then she stopped. She couldn't explain everything, tell her whole life with the Clan. It would be better to just answer the questions.

"You don't remember anything about your own people?" Zelandoni pressed.

"I only know what Iza told me. An earthquake had destroyed their cave, and Brun's clan was looking for a new one when she found me beside a river, unconscious. They had been without a home for some time, but Brun allowed her to take me with them. She said I must have been attacked by a cave lion because there were four claw marks on my leg, with the wide spacing of a cave lion, and they were . . . running, poisoned, corrupted," Ayla tried to find the right words.

"Yes, I understand," the donier said. "Festered, suppurant, perhaps to the stage of morbid corruption. Cat claws tend to do that."

"I still have the scars. That's how Creb knew the Cave Lion was my totem, even though it's usually a man's totem. I still dream sometimes of being in a small dark place and seeing a big cat claw coming," Ayla said.

"That's a powerful dream. Do you have any other dreams? About that time in your life, I mean?"

"One that's more frightening, but hard to explain. I never quite remember it. It's more a feeling, a feeling of an earthquake." The young woman shuddered. "I hate earthquakes!"

Zelandoni nodded knowingly. "Any others?"

"No . . . yes, but only once, when Jondalar was still recovering, and was teaching me to speak. . . ."

Zelandoni thought that was a peculiar way to phrase it and glanced at Marthona to see if she had noted the odd expression.

"I understood some," Ayla said. "I had learned many words, but I was having trouble putting all together, then I dreamed of my mother, my real mother. I saw her face, and she spoke to me. The learning was easier after that."

"Ahhh . . . That's a very important dream," the One Who Served commented. "It's always important when the Mother comes to you in your dreams, whatever form She takes, but particularly when She takes the form of your own mother speaking to you from the next world."

Jondalar recalled a dream he had had of the Mother when they were still in Ayla's valley. A very strange dream. I should tell Zelandoni about it sometime, he thought.

"So, if you dreamed of the Mother, why didn't you appeal to her to help Thonolan find his way in the next world? I don't understand why you called upon the spirit of a cave bear and not the Great Earth Mother."

"I didn't know about the Great Earth Mother until Jondalar told me, after I learned your language."

"You didn't know about Doni, about the Great Earth Mother?" Folara asked with amazement. None of the Zelandonii had ever heard of anyone who did not recognize the Great Mother in some name or form. They were all mystified.

"The Clan honors Ursus, the Great Cave Bear," she said. "That's why I called on Ursus to help guide the spirit of the dead man—I didn't know his name then—even though he wasn't Clan. I did ask the Spirit of the Cave Lion to help, too, since he was my totem."

"Well, if you didn't know Her, then you did what you could, under the circumstances. I'm sure it helped," Zelandoni said, but she was more concerned than she showed. How could any of Her children not know the Mother?

"I have a totem, too," Willamar said. "Mine is the Golden Eagle." He sat up a little straighter. "My mother told me that when I was an infant, an eagle picked me up and tried to carry me away, but she grabbed me and held on. I still show the scars. The zelandoni told her that the Golden Eagle spirit recognized me as one of his own kind. Not many people have personal totems, not among the Zelandonii, but if you have one, it is thought to be lucky."

"Well, you were lucky enough to get away," Joharran said.

"I guess I was lucky enough to get away from the cave lion that marked me," Ayla said, "and so was Jondalar. I think his totem is the Cave Lion, too. What do you think, Zelandoni?"

Ayla had been telling Jondalar that the Cave Lion spirit had chosen him ever since she could talk to him, but he had always avoided any comment about it. It seemed that individual totems weren't as important to his people as they were to the Clan, but it was important to her. She didn't want to take any chances.

The Clan believed that a man's totem had to be stronger than a woman's totem, for her to have children. That was why her strong male totem had upset Iza so. In spite of her powerful totem, Ayla did have a son, but there had been difficulties, beginning in pregnancy, during his birth and, many believed, afterward. They were sure he was unlucky—that his mother had no mate, no man to raise him properly, confirmed it. The difficulties and misfortune were blamed on the fact that she was a woman with a male totem. Now that she was pregnant again, she wanted no problems for this child that Jondalar had started, not for her or the baby. Though she had learned a great deal about the Mother, she had not forgotten Clan teachings, and if Jondalar's totem was a Cave Lion like hers, then, she was sure, it would be strong enough for her to have a healthy baby, who would have a normal life.

Something in Ayla's tone of voice caught Zelandoni's attention. She looked closely at the young woman. She wants Jondalar to have a Cave Lion totem, the woman realized, it is very important to her, this totem. Totem spirits must have greater significance to these Clan people who raised her. It probably is true that the Cave Lion is his totem now, and it won't hurt him if people think he's lucky. He probably is to have gotten back at all!

"I believe you're right, Ayla," the donier said. "Jondalar can claim the Cave Lion as his totem, and claim the luck. He was very lucky you were there when he needed you."

"I told you, Jondalar!" Ayla said, looking relieved.

Why does she or this Clan put so much importance on the Spirit of the Cave Lion? Or the Cave Bear? Zelandoni wondered. All the spirits are important, those of animals, even those of plants, or insects, everything, but it is the Great Mother who gave birth to them all. Who are these people? This Clan?

"You did say you lived alone in a valley, didn't you? Where was this Clan that raised you, Ayla?" the donier asked.

"Yes, I'd like to know, too. Didn't Jondalar introduce you as Ayla of the Mamutoi?" Joharran said.

"You said you didn't know the Mother, but you greeted us with a welcome from 'The Great Mother of All,' which is one of the names we give Doni," Folara added.

Ayla looked from one to the other, then at Jondalar, feeling a touch of panic. There was a hint of a grin on his face, as though he was rather enjoying the way Ayla's truthful answers baffled everyone. He squeezed her hand again, but didn't say anything. He was interested in how she would respond. She relaxed a bit.

"My clan lived at the south end of the land that extended far into Beran Sea. Iza told me just before she died that I should look for my own people. She said they lived north, on the mainland, but when I finally did look for them, I couldn't find anyone. The summer was half over before I found the valley, and I was afraid that the cold season would come and I wouldn't be prepared for it. The valley was a good place, protected from winds, a small river, lots of plants and animals, even a small cave. I decided to stay for the winter, and ended up staying for three years, with only Whinney and Baby for company. Maybe I was waiting for Jondalar," she said, smiling at the man.

"I found him in late spring; it was near the end of summer before Jondalar was well enough to travel. We decided to make a small trek, explore the region. We made camp each night in a different place, going farther from the valley than I had gone before. Then we met Talut, the headman of the Lion Camp, and he invited us to visit. We stayed with them until the beginning of the next summer, and while I was there, they adopted me. They wanted Jondalar to stay, too, and become one of them, but even then, he was planning to return."

"Well, I'm glad he did," Marthona said.

"It seems you are very lucky, to have people so willing to adopt you," Zelandoni said. She couldn't help but wonder at the strange story Ayla was telling. She wasn't alone in her reservations. It all seemed rather farfetched, and she still had more questions than answers.

"At first, I'm sure it was Nezzie's idea—she was Talut's mate. I think she convinced him because I helped Rydag when he had a bad . . . problem. Rydag was weak in . . ." Ayla didn't know the correct words and was frustrated. Jondalar had never taught them to her. He could have given her precise words for various kinds of flint, and specific words for the processes of shaping it into tools and weapons, but medicinal and healing terminology was not a part of his normal vocabulary. She turned to him and spoke to him in Mamutoi. "What is your word for foxglove? That plant I always collected for Rydag?"

He told her, but even before Ayla could repeat it and attempt to explain, Zelandoni was sure she understood what had happened. As soon as she heard Jondalar say the word, she knew not only the plant, but its uses. She had a good idea that the person Ayla was talking about had an internal weakness with the organ that pumped blood, the heart, that could be helped by the proper extraction of elements from foxglove. It also made her realize why someone would want to adopt a healer who was skilled enough to know how to use something as beneficial, though potentially dangerous, as that plant. And if that someone was in a position of authority, as a headman's mate would be, she could understand how Ayla might be adopted so quickly. After listening to Ayla tell essentially what she had guessed, she made another assumption.

"This person, Rydag, was a child?" she asked, to confirm her final speculation.

"Yes," Ayla replied, feeling a moment of sadness.

Zelandoni felt she understood about Ayla and the Mamutoi, but the Clan still left her perplexed. She decided to try a different approach. "I know you are very skilled in the healing ways, Ayla, but often those who become knowledgeable have a mark of some kind so people will recognize them. Like this one," she said, touching a tattoo on her forehead above her left temple. "I see no mark on you."

Ayla looked closely at the tattoo. It was a rectangle divided into six smaller rectangles, almost squares, in two rows of three each, with four legs above that, if connected, would have made a third row of squares. The outline of the rectangles was dark, but three of the squares were filled in with shades of red, and one with yellow.

Although it was a unique mark, several of the people she had seen had tattooed markings of one kind or another, including Marthona, Joharran, and Willamar. She didn't know if the marks meant something in particular, but after Zelandoni had explained the meaning of hers, Ayla suspected they might.

"Mamut had a mark on his cheek," Ayla said, touching the place on her cheek. "All the mamutii did. Some had other marks, too. I might have been given one, if I had stayed. Mamut started training me soon after he adopted me, but I was not fully trained before I left, so I was never marked."

"But didn't you say you were adopted by the woman who was the mate of the headman?"

"I thought Nezzie was going to adopt me, and she did, too, but at the ceremony, Mamut said Mammoth Hearth, not Lion Hearth. He adopted me instead."

"This Mamut is One Who Serves The Mother?" Zelandoni asked, thinking, so she was training to be One Who Serves.

"Yes, like you. The Mammoth Hearth was his, and for Those Who Serve The Mother. Most people choose the Mammoth Hearth, or feel they have been chosen. Mamut said I was born to it." She flushed a little and looked aside, feeling rather embarrassed to be talking about something that had been given, which she hadn't earned. It made her think of Iza and how carefully the woman had tried to train her to be a good Clan woman.

"I think your Mamut was a wise man," Zelandoni said. "But you said you learned your healing skills from a woman of the people who raised you, this Clan. Don't they do anything to mark their healers, to give them status and recognition?"

"I was given a certain black stone, a special sign to keep in my amulet when I was accepted as a medicine woman of the Clan," Ayla said. "But they don't make a mark like a tattoo for medicine woman, only for totem, when a boy becomes a man."

"How do people recognize one when they need to call upon a healer for help?"

Ayla hadn't thought about that before. She paused to consider it. "Medicine women don't have to be marked. People know. A medicine woman has status in her own right. Her position is always recognized. Iza was the highest ranked woman in the clan, even higher than Brun's mate."

Zelandoni shook her head. Ayla obviously thought she had explained something, but the woman didn't understand. "I'm sure that's true, but how do people know?"

"By her position," Ayla repeated, then tried to clarify. "By the position she takes when the clan goes somewhere, the place she stands when she eats, by the signs she uses when she . . . talks, by the signals that are made to her when she's addressed."

"Isn't that all so awkward? This cumbersome use of positions and signs?" Zelandoni asked.

"Not for them. That's the way people of the Clan talk. With signs. They don't talk with words as we do," Ayla said.

"But, why not?" Marthona wanted to know.

"They can't. They can't make all the sounds we do. They can make some, but not all. They talk with their hands and their bodies," Ayla tried to explain.

Jondalar could see the bewilderment of his mother and kin growing, and Ayla getting more frustrated. He decided it was time to cut the confusion.

"Ayla was raised by flatheads, mother," he said.

There was a stunned silence.

"Flatheads! Flatheads are animals!" Joharran said.

"No, they're not," Jondalar said.

"Of course they are," Folara said. "They can't talk!"

"They can talk, they just don't talk the way you do," Jondalar said. "I can even talk their language a little, but of course Ayla is much better. When she said I taught her to speak, she meant it." He glanced at Zelandoni; he'd noted her earlier expression. "She forgot how to speak whatever language she knew when she was a child, she could only speak the Clan way. The Clan are flatheads, flatheads call themselves the Clan."

"How could they call themselves anything, if they talk with their hands?" Folara asked.

"They do have some words," Ayla repeated, "they just can't say everything. They don't even hear all the sounds we make. They could understand, if they started young, but they're not used to hearing them." She thought about Rydag. He could understand everything that was said, even if he couldn't say it.

"Well, I didn't know they called themselves by any name," Marthona said, then she thought of something else. "How did you and Ayla communicate, Jondalar?"

"We didn't, at first," he said. "In the beginning, of course, we didn't need to. Ayla knew what to do. I was hurt and she took care of me."

"Are you telling me, Jondalar, that she learned from flatheads how to heal that cave lion mauling?" Zelandoni said.

Ayla answered instead. "I told you, Iza came from the most respected line of medicine women in the Clan. She taught me."

"I find all this about intelligent flatheads very difficult to believe," Zelandoni said.

"I don't," Willamar said.

Everybody turned to look at the Trade Master.

"I don't think they are animals at all. I haven't for a long time. I've seen too many in my travels."

"Why haven't you said something before?" Joharran asked.

"It never came up," Willamar said. "No one ever asked and I never thought about it that much."

"What changed your mind about them, Willamar?" Zelandoni asked. This brought out a new aspect. She was going to have to put some thought into this startling idea Jondalar and the foreign woman had presented.

"Let me think. The first time I began to doubt they were animals was many years ago," Willamar began. "I was south and west of here, traveling alone. The weather had changed quickly, a sudden cold snap, and I was in a hurry to get home. I kept going until it was almost dark, and camped beside a small stream. I planned to cross in the morning. When I woke up, I discovered I had stopped right across from a party of flatheads. I was actually afraid of them—you know what you hear—so I watched them closely, to be prepared in case they decided to come after me."

"What did they do?" Joharran asked.

"Nothing, except break camp just like anyone would," Willamar said. "They knew I was there, of course, but I was alone, so I couldn't give them much trouble, and they didn't seem in a big hurry. They boiled some water and made something hot to drink, rolled up their tents—different from ours, lower to the ground and harder to see—but they packed them on their backs, and left at a fast jog."

"Could you tell if any were women?" Ayla asked.

"It was pretty cold, they were all covered. They do wear clothes. You don't notice it in summer because they don't wear much, and you seldom see them in winter. We don't tend to travel much then, or very far, and they probably don't, either."

"You're right, they don't like to go too far from home when it's cold or snowy," Ayla commented.

"Most had beards, I'm not sure if they all did," Willamar said.

"Young men don't have beards. Did you notice if any of them carried a basket on her back?"

"I don't think so," he said.

"Clan women don't hunt, but if the men go on a long trek, women often go along to dry the meat and carry it back, so it was probably a short-range hunting party, just men," Ayla said.

"Did you do that?" Folara asked. "Go along on long hunting trips?"

"Yes, I even went along once when they hunted a mammoth," Ayla said, "but not to hunt."

Jondalar noticed that everyone seemed more curious than closed-minded. Though he was sure many people would be more intolerant, at least his kin seemed interested in learning about flatheads . . . the Clan.

"Joharran," Jondalar said, "I'm glad this came up now, because I was planning to talk to you anyway. There's something you need to know. We met a Clan couple on our way here, just before we started over that plateau glacier to the east. They told us that several clans are planning to get together to talk about us, and the problems they've been having with us. They call us the Others."

"I'm having trouble believing they can call us anything," the man said, "much less have meetings to talk about us."

"Well, believe it, because if you don't, we could be in some trouble."

Several voices spoke at once.

"What do you mean?" "What kind of trouble?"

"I know of one situation in the Losadunai region. A gang of young ruffians from several Caves started baiting flatheads—Clan men. I understand they started out several years ago by picking on just one, like running a rhino down? But Clan men are nothing to fool with. They're smart and they're strong. A couple of those young men found that out when one or two got caught, so they started picking on the women. Clan women don't fight, usually, so it wasn't as much fun, no challenge. To make it more interesting, they started forcing Clan women to . . . well, I wouldn't call it Pleasures."

"What?" Joharran said.

"You heard me right," Jondalar affirmed.

"Great Mother!" Zelandoni blurted.

"That's terrible!" Marthona said at the same time.

"How awful!" Folara cried, wrinkling her nose with disgust.

"Despicable!" Willamar spat.

"They think so, too," Jondalar said. "They are not going to put up with it much longer, and once they realize they can do something about it, they are not going to put up with much from us at all. Aren't there rumors that these caves used to belong to them? What if they want them back?"

"Those are rumors, Jondalar. There's nothing in the Histories or the Elder Legends to confirm it," Zelandoni said. "Only bears are mentioned."

Ayla didn't say anything, but she thought the rumors might be true.

"In any case, they aren't getting them," Joharran said. "This is our home, Zelandonii territory."

"But there's something else you should know that could work in our favor. According to Guban—that was the man's name . . ."

"They have names?" Joharran said.

"Of course they have names," Ayla said, "just like the people in my clan. His name is Guban, hers is Yorga." Ayla gave the names the true Clan pronunciation, with the full throaty, deep, guttural sounds. Jondalar smiled. She did that on purpose, he thought.

If that's how they speak, I certainly know where her accent comes from, Zelandoni thought. She must be telling the truth. She was raised by them. But did she really learn her medicine from them?

"What I was trying to say, Joharran, is that Guban . . ." his pronunciation was much easier to understand ". . . told me that some people, I don't know which Caves, have approached some clans with the idea of establishing trading relations."

"Trading! With flatheads!" Joharran said.

"Why not?" Willamar said. "I think it could be interesting. Depends what they have to trade, of course."

"Sounds like the Trade Master talking," Jondalar said.

"Speaking of trading, what are the Losadunai doing about those young men?" Willamar wanted to know. "We trade with them. I'd hate to have some trading party come down off the other side of that glacier and walk into a party of flatheads with revenge on their minds."

"When we . . . I first heard about it, five years ago, they weren't doing much," Jondalar said, trying to avoid making reference to

Thonolan. "They knew it was going on, some of the men were still calling it 'high spirits,' but Laduni became really upset, just talking about it. Then it got worse. We stopped to visit the Losadunai on our way back. The Clan men had started going out with their women when they were gathering food, guarding them, and those 'high-spirited' young men weren't going to provoke the Clan men by going after the women then, so they went after a young woman of Laduni's Cave—all of them—forced a young woman . . . before First Rites."

"Oh, no! How could they, Jondé?" Folara said, bursting into tears.

"Great Mother's Underground!" Joharran thundered.

"That's just where they should be sent!" Willamar said.

"They are abominations! I can't even imagine a strong enough punishment!" Zelandoni fumed.

Marthona, unable to say anything, had her hand on her chest and looked appalled.

Ayla had felt deeply for the young woman who had been assaulted and had tried to ease her anguish, but she couldn't help but notice how much more strongly Jondalar's kin had reacted to the news of a young woman of the Others being attacked by the gang than they had when they learned of the attacks on Clan women. When it was Clan women, they were offended, but when it was one of their own, they were outraged.

That, more than anything that had been said or done, made her understand the extent of the chasm that separated the two peoples. Then she wondered what their reactions would have been—inconceivable as the idea was to her—if it had been a gang of Clan men . . . flatheads that had committed such an abominable act on Zelandonii women?

"You can be sure the Losadunai are doing something about those young men, now," Jondalar said. "The young woman's mother was crying for blood retribution against the Cave of the leader of those degenerate men."

"Ahhh, that's bad news. What a difficult situation for the leaders," Marthona said.

"It's her right!" Folara proclaimed.

"Yes, of course, it's her right," Marthona said, "but then some kin or another, or the whole Cave, will resist and that could lead to fighting, maybe someone getting killed, and then someone wants revenge for that. Who knows where it would end up? What are they going to do, Jondalar?"

"Several Cave leaders sent runners with messages, and many of them got together and talked. They've agreed to send out trackers, find the young men, separate them to break up the gang, and then each Cave is going to deal with their own member individually. They will be severely punished, I imagine, but they'll be given a chance to make restitution," Jondalar explained.

"I'd say that's a good plan, especially if they all agree to it, including the Cave of the instigator," Joharran said, "and if the young men come peaceably, once they've been found . . ."

"I'm not sure about the leader, but I think the rest of them want to go home, and would agree to anything to be allowed back. They looked hungry, cold, and dirty, and not too happy," Jondalar said.

"You saw them?" Marthona asked.

"That's how we met the Clan couple. The gang had gone after the woman, they didn't see the man around. But he had climbed up on a high rock to scout game and jumped down when they attacked his woman. Broke his leg, but it didn't stop him from trying to fight them off. We happened upon them then; it was not far from the glacier we were getting ready to cross." Jondalar smiled. "Between Ayla, Wolf, and me, not to mention the two Clan people, we chased them off in a hurry. There's not much fight left in those boys. And with Wolf and the horses, and the fact that we knew who they were, when they had never seen us before, well, I think we put a scare in them."

"Yes," Zelandoni said thoughtfully. "I can see how it would."

"You would have scared me," Joharran said with a wry smile.

"Then Ayla convinced the Clan man to let her set his broken leg," Jondalar continued. "We camped together for a couple of days. I made him a couple of sticks to lean on and help him walk, and he decided to go home. I was able to talk to him a little, though Ayla did most of it. I think I became something like a brother to him," he said.

"It occurs to me," Marthona said, "that if there is a possibility of trouble with—what do they call themselves? Clan people?—and they can communicate enough to negotiate, it could be very helpful to have someone like Ayla around who can talk to them, Joharran."

"I've been thinking the same thing," Zelandoni added. She had also been thinking about what Jondalar had said of the fearful effect Ayla's animals had on people, though she didn't mention it. It could be useful.

"That's true, of course, mother, but it's going to be hard to get used to the idea of talking to flatheads, or calling them something else, and I'm not the only one who's going to have trouble," Joharran said. He paused, then shook his head as if to himself. "If they talk with their hands, how do you know they're really talking and not just waving their arms around?"

Everyone looked at Ayla. She turned to Jondalar.

"I think you should show them," he said, "and maybe you could talk at the same time, the way you did when you were talking to Guban and translating for me."

"What should I say?"

"Why not just greet them, as if you were speaking for Guban?" he said.

Ayla thought for a time. She couldn't really greet them the way Guban would. He was a man, and a woman would never greet anyone the same way a man would. She could make a greeting sign, that gesture was always the same, but one never made only a greeting sign. It was always modified depending on who was making it and to whom it was being made. And there really was no sign for a person of the Clan to greet one of the Others. It had never been done before, not in a formal, acknowledged way. Perhaps she could think of how it would be done if they ever had to. She stood up and backed into the clear area in the middle of the main room.

"This woman would greet you, People of the Others," Ayla began, then paused. "Or perhaps one should say People of the Mother," she said, trying to think of how the Clan might make the signs.

"Try Children of the Mother, or Children of the Great Earth Mother," Jondalar suggested.

She nodded and started over. "This woman . . . called Ayla, would greet you, Children of Doni, the Great Earth Mother." She said her own name and that of the Mother in verbal sounds, but with the inflection and tonal quality of the Clan. The rest was communicated with signs in formal Clan language and spoken in Zelandonii.

"This woman would hope that at some time you would be greeted by one of the Clan of the Cave Bear, and that the greeting would be returned. The Mog-ur told this woman the Clan is ancient, the memories go deep. The Clan was here when the new ones came. They named the new ones, the Others, the ones who were not Clan.

The Clan chose to go their own way, to avoid the Others. That is the Clan way and Clan traditions change slowly, yet some of the Clan would begin to change, would make new traditions. If that is to be, this woman would hope that the change would harm neither Clan nor Others."

Her Zelandoni translation was spoken in a soft-voiced monotone, with as much precision and as little accent as she could. The words told them what she was saying, but they could see that she was not making random hand wavings. The purposeful gestures, the subtle motion of the body indicating a movement, lifting the head in pride, bowing in acquiescence, even raising an eyebrow, all flowed together smoothly with graceful intention. Though the significance of each motion was not clear, that her movements had meaning was.

The total effect was startling, and beautiful; it sent a shiver down Marthona's back. She glanced at Zelandoni, who caught her quick look and nodded. She, too, had felt something profound. Jondalar noticed the discreet byplay; he was watching those who were watching Ayla and could see the impression she was making. Joharran was staring in rapt attention with a frown creasing his forehead; Willamar had a slight smile and was nodding approval; Folara's smile was unabashed. She was so delighted, he had to smile, too.

When she was done, Ayla sat down at the table again, lowering herself to a cross-legged position with an elegant ease that was more noticeable after her performance. There was an uneasy silence around the table. No one knew quite what to say, and each felt they needed time to think. Finally Folara felt compelled to fill the void.

"That was wonderful, Ayla! Beautiful, almost like a dance," she said.

"It's hard for me to think of it that way. It's the way they talk. Although I remember that I used to love to watch the storytellers," Ayla said.

"It was very expressive," Marthona said, then looked at her son. "You can do that, too, Jondalar?"

"Not like Ayla can. She taught the people of Lion Camp so they could communicate with Rydag. They had some fun at their Summer Meeting with it because they could talk to each other without anyone else knowing it," he said.

"Rydag, wasn't that the child with the bad heart?" Zelandoni asked. "Why couldn't he talk like everyone else?"

Jondalar and Ayla looked at each other. "Rydag was half Clan, and had the same difficulty making sounds that they do," Ayla said. "So I taught him and the Lion Camp his language."

"Half Clan?" Joharran said. "You mean half flathead? A half flathead abomination!"

"He was a child!" Ayla said, glaring at him in anger. "Just like any other child. No child is an abomination!"

Joharran was surprised at her reaction, then recalled that she had been raised by them and understood why she would feel offended. He tried to stutter an apology. "I . . . I . . . I'm sorry. It's what everyone thinks."

Zelandoni stepped in to calm the situation. "Ayla, you must remember, we haven't had time to consider everything you have said. We have always thought of your Clan people as animals, and something half human and half animal as an abomination. I'm sure you must be correct, this . . . Rydag was a child."

She's right, Ayla said to herself, and it isn't as if you didn't know how the Zelandonii felt. Jondalar made that clear the first time you mentioned Durc. She tried to compose herself.

"But, I'd like to understand something," Zelandoni continued, searching for a way to ask her questions without offending the stranger. "The person named Nezzie was the mate of the headman of the Lion Camp, is that correct?"

"Yes." Ayla could see where she was leading and glanced at Jondalar. She felt sure he was trying to repress a smile. It made her feel better; he knew, too, and was taking some perverse delight in the discomfiture of the powerful donier.

"This child, this Rydag, was hers?"

Jondalar almost wished Ayla would say yes, just to make them think. It had taken a lot for him to overcome the beliefs of his people, bred into him since childhood, practically with his mother's milk. If they thought a woman who had given birth to an "abomination" could become the mate of a headman, it might shake that belief a bit, and the more he thought about it, the more he was convinced that for their own good, for their own safety, his people had to change, had to accept the fact that the Clan were people, too.

"She nursed him," Ayla explained, "along with her own daughter. He was the son of a Clan woman who was alone and died shortly after his birth. Nezzie adopted him, just as Iza adopted me when I had no one to take care of me."

It was still a shock, and in some ways even more startling because the headman's mate had voluntarily chosen to care for the newborn who could have been left to die with its mother. A silence descended upon the group as each one paused to consider what had just been learned.

Wolf had stayed behind in the valley where the horses were grazing to explore the new territory. After a time that was appropriate to him and for his own reasons, he decided to return to the place that Ayla had made him understand was home, the place he should go when he wanted to find her. Like all of his kind, the wolf moved with efficient speed and such effortless grace, he seemed to be floating as he loped through the wooded landscape. Several people were in Wood River Valley picking berries. One man caught a glimpse of Wolf moving like a silent wraith between the trees.

"That wolf is coming! And he's by himself!" the man shouted. He scrambled out of the way as fast as he could.

"Where's my baby?" a woman cried in a panic. She looked around, saw her toddler, and ran to pick her up and carry her away.

When Wolf reached the path that led to the ledge, he ran up it with the same supple, fast-moving pace.

"There's that wolf! I don't like the idea of a wolf coming up here, right onto our ledge," another woman said.

"Joharran said we should allow him to come and go as he wants, but I'm going to get my spear," a man said. "Maybe he won't hurt anyone, but I don't trust that animal."

People backed out of the way to give him a wide berth when Wolf reached the ledge at the top of the path and headed directly for Marthona's dwelling. One man knocked over several spear shafts when he bumped into them in his hurry to put plenty of clearance between himself and the efficient, four-legged hunter. The wolf sensed the fear of the people around him and didn't like it, but he continued toward the location Ayla had indicated he was to go.

The silence within Marthona's dwelling was shattered when Willamar, catching sight of the entrance drape moving, suddenly jumped up and shouted. "There's a wolf! Great Mother, how did that wolf get here?"

"It's all right, Willamar," Marthona said, trying to calm him. "He's allowed in here." Folara caught her eldest brother's eye and smiled, and though Joharran was still nervous around the animal, he could give her a knowing smile back.

"That's Ayla's wolf," Jondalar said, getting up to ward off any hasty reactions as Ayla rushed to the entrance to settle the animal, who had been more scared than Willamar to be greeted by such loud, frantic noise in the place he had been shown to come. Wolf's tail was between his legs, his hackles were raised, and his teeth were bared.

If Zelandoni could have, she would have jumped up just as fast as Willamar. A loud, menacing growl seemed to be directed specifically at her, and she shook with fear. Even though she had heard about Ayla's animals and seen them from a distance, she was terrified by the huge predator that had entered the dwelling. She had never been so close to a wolf; in the wild wolves usually ran away from groups of people.

She watched with amazement as Ayla fearlessly hurried toward Wolf, stooped down, put her arms around him, and held him, speaking words, only some of which she understood, seeking to calm the animal. The wolf first became excited, and licked the neck and face of the woman while she fondled him, then did indeed calm down. It was the most unbelievable demonstration of supernatural powers she had ever witnessed. Just what kind of mysterious ability did this woman possess to command that kind of control over such an animal? She felt gooseflesh raise at the thought.

Willamar had calmed down as well, with the encouragement of Marthona and Jondalar, and after seeing Ayla with the wolf.

"I think Willamar should meet Wolf, don't you, Ayla?" Marthona said.

"Especially since they are going to be sharing the same dwelling," Jondalar said. Willamar gaped at him with an amazed look of disbelief.

Ayla stood up and walked toward them, signaling Wolf to follow closely. "The way Wolf gets acquainted is to become familiar with your scent. If you hold out your hand to let him smell it . . . ," she started to say, reaching for his hand.

The man pulled it away. "Are you sure about this?" he said, looking at Marthona.

His mate smiled, then held out her hand toward the wolf. He smelled her hand, then licked it. "You gave some of us quite a fright, Wolf, coming in unannounced before you had met everyone," she said.

Willamar was still a bit hesitant, but he could hardly do less than Marthona had, and put his hand forward. Ayla introduced Wolf in the usual manner, saying for the man's benefit, as the wolf took in his scent, "Wolf, this is Willamar. He lives here with Marthona." The wolf licked him, then gave a little yip.

"Why did he do that?" Willamar asked, drawing his hand back quickly.

"I'm not sure, but perhaps he smelled Marthona on you, and he warmed to her very quickly," Ayla suggested. "Try petting or scratching him." As though Willamar's tentative scratching only tickled, Wolf suddenly curled up and vigorously scratched behind his own ear, bringing smiles and chuckles at his rather undignified posture. When he was through, he went straight to Zelandoni.

She eyed him warily, but stood her ground. She had been terrified when the wolf appeared at the entrance of the dwelling. Jondalar was more aware of her reaction than the others. He had seen her petrified fear. They had been concerned about Willamar, who had jumped up and shouted, and hadn't noticed the quiet terror of the woman. She was just as glad they hadn't. One Who Served The Mother was thought of as fearless, and in fact, that was generally true. She couldn't remember the last time she had felt such alarm.

"I think he knows he hasn't met you, Zelandoni," Jondalar said. "And since he's going to be living here, I think you should be introduced to each other, too." From the way he looked at her, she guessed that Jondalar knew how frightened she had been, and acknowledged it with a nod.

"I think you're right. What is it that I'm supposed to do, give him my hand?" she said, thrusting it toward the wolf. He sniffed, then licked, then, with no warning, took her hand with his teeth and held it in his mouth with a low growl.

"What's he doing?" Folara said. She hadn't officially met him, either. "He only used his teeth with Ayla, before."

"I'm not sure," Jondalar said with a note of concern.

Zelandoni looked sternly at Wolf, and he let go.

"Did he hurt you?" Folara asked. "Why did he do that?"

"No, of course he didn't hurt me. He did it to let me know that I have nothing to fear from him," Zelandoni said, making no attempt to scratch him. "We understand each other." Then she contemplated Ayla, who returned her gaze. "And we have a lot to learn about each other."

"Yes, we do. I'm looking forward to it," she replied.

"And Wolf still needs to meet Folara," Jondalar said. "Come here, Wolf, come and meet my little sister."

Responding to the playfulness in his voice, Wolf bounded toward him. "This is Folara, Wolf," he said. The young woman quickly discovered how much fun it was to pet and scratch and handle the wolf.

"Now it's my turn," Ayla said. "I would like to be introduced to Willamar," she said, then, turning to the donier, "and Zelandoni, although I already feel that I know you both."

Marthona stepped forward. "Of course. I had forgotten that you haven't formally met them. Ayla, this is Willamar, Renowned Traveler and Trade Master of the Ninth Cave of the Zelandonii, Mated to Marthona, Man of the Hearth to Folara, Blessed of Doni." Then she looked at the man. "Willamar, please welcome Ayla of the Lion Camp of the Mamutoi, Daughter of the Mammoth Hearth, Chosen by the Spirit of the Cave Lion, Protected by the Cave Bear," she smiled at the animal, "and Friend of Wolf, and two horses," she added.

After the incidents and stories that Ayla had just told, Jondalar's kin understood the meanings of her names and ties more and felt they knew her better. It made her seem less of a stranger. Willamar and Ayla grasped both hands and greeted each other in the name of the Mother with the phrases of the formal introduction, except that Willamar referred to her as "mother" rather than "friend of Wolf." Ayla had noticed that people seldom repeated introductions exactly, often adding their own variation.

"I look forward to meeting the horses, and I think I'm going to add 'Chosen by the Golden Eagle' to my names. After all, it is my totem," he said with a warm smile, and squeezed her hands before he let go. She smiled back, a big, dazzling smile. I am happy to see Jondalar after all this time, he thought, and how wonderful for Marthona that he brought a woman back to mate. It means he plans to stay. And such a beautiful woman. If they are of his spirit, imagine what her children will look like.

Jondalar decided that he should be the one to formally introduce Ayla and Zelandoni. "Ayla, this is Zelandoni, First Among Those Who Serve The Great Earth Mother, the Voice of Doni, Surrogate of She Who Blesses, the Donier, Giver of Help and Healing, Instrument of the Original Ancestor, Spiritual Leader of the Ninth Cave of the Zelandonii, and Friend of Jondalar once known as Zolena." He said the last with a smile. It was not one of her usual titles.

"Zelandoni, this is Ayla of the Mamutoi," he began, and at the end added "soon to be mated to Jondalar, I hope."

It's a good thing he said "I hope," Zelandoni said to herself as she stepped forward with both hands extended. This mating hasn't been approved yet. "As the Voice of Doni, Great Earth Mother, I welcome you, Ayla of the Mamutoi, Daughter of the Mammoth Hearth," she said, taking both of Ayla's hands in hers and naming what to her were the most important titles.

"In the name of Mut, Mother of All, who is also Doni, I greet you, Zelandoni, First Among Those Who Serve The Great Earth Mother," Ayla said. As the two women faced each other, Jondalar fervently hoped that they would become good friends. He would never want either as an enemy.

"And now I must go. I hadn't planned to stay so long," Zelandoni said.

"I have to go, too," Joharran said, leaning over to brush his mother's cheek with his, then getting up. "There's a lot to do before the feast tonight. And, Willamar, tomorrow I want to hear how the trading went."

After Zelandoni and Joharran left, Marthona asked Ayla if she wanted to rest before the celebration.

"I feel so dirty and hot from traveling. There is nothing I'd like better right now than to go for a swim, to cool off, and wash. Does soaproot grow nearby?"

"It does," Marthona said. "Jondalar, behind the big rock upstream along The River a short distance from Wood River Valley. You know where that is, don't you?"

"Yes, I know. Wood River Valley is where the horses are, Ayla. I'll show you the place. A swim does sound good." Jondalar put an arm around Marthona. "And it's good to be home, mother. I really don't think I want to travel again for a long time."

5

I want to get my comb and I think I still have some dried ceanothus flowers left, to wash my hair," Ayla said, opening her traveling packs. "And the chamois skin from Roshario to dry off with," she added, pulling it out.

Wolf was bounding toward the entry and back to them again, as though urging them to hurry.

"I think Wolf knows we're going swimming," Jondalar said. "I sometimes think that animal can understand language, even if he can't speak it."

"I'll take my change of clothes so I have something clean to put on, and why don't we spread out the sleeping furs before we go," Ayla said, putting down her towel and other things, and pulling loose the ties of another bundle.

They quickly made a sleeping place and set out the few other possessions they had with them, then Ayla shook out the tunic and short pants she had been keeping aside. She examined the outfit closely. It was made of soft, supple buckskin, cut in a simple Mamutoi style, but was undecorated, and though clean, it was stained. Even with washing, it was difficult to get stains out of the velvety-textured nap of the leather, but it was the only thing she had to wear to the feast. Traveling limited the amount one could take, even with horses to help with transport, and she had wanted to bring other things that were more important to her than changes of clothing.

Ayla noticed that Marthona was watching her and said, "This is all I have to wear tonight. I hope it will be all right. I couldn't bring much with me. Roshario gave me a beautiful decorated outfit made in the Sharamudoi style out of that wonderful leather they make, but I gave it to Madenia, that young Losadunai woman who was attacked so brutally."

"That was kind of you," the woman said.

"I had to lighten my load anyway, and Madenia seemed so pleased, but now I wish I had one like it. It would be nice to dress for the feast tonight in something a little less worn. Once we get settled, I'll have to make some clothes." She smiled at the woman and looked around. "It's still hard to believe we're finally here."

"It's hard for me to believe, too," Marthona said, then after a pause, "I would like to help you make some clothes, if you wouldn't object."

"No, I wouldn't object at all. I'd appreciate it." Ayla smiled. "Everything you have here is so beautiful, Marthona, and I don't know what is appropriate for Zelandoni women to wear."

"Can I help, too?" Folara added. "Mother's ideas about clothes are not always what younger women like."

"I'd love to have help from both of you, but this will have to do for now," Ayla said, holding up her worn outfit.

"It will certainly be fine for tonight," Marthona said. Then she nodded to herself, as though making a decision. "I have something I would like to give you, Ayla. It's in my sleeping room."

Ayla followed Marthona into her room. "I have been saving this for you for a long time," the woman said as she opened a covered wooden box.

"But you just met me!" Ayla exclaimed.

"For the woman Jondalar would someday choose for a mate. It belonged to Dalanar's mother." She held out a necklace.

Ayla caught her breath with surprise, and with some hesitation took the proffered necklace. She examined it cautiously. It was made of matched shells, perfect deer teeth, and finely carved heads of female deer made from ivory. A lustrous yellowish orange pendant hung at the center.

"It is beautiful," Ayla breathed. She felt particularly drawn to the pendant, and she looked at it carefully. It was shiny, polished from being worn and handled. "This is amber, isn't it?"

"Yes. That stone has been in the family for many generations. Dalanar's mother made it into this necklace. She gave it to me when Jondalar was born and told me to give it to the woman he chose."

"Amber is not cold like other stones," Ayla said, holding the pendant in her hand. "It feels warm, as though it has a living spirit."

"How interesting that you should say that. Dalanar's mother always said this piece had life," Marthona said. "Try it on. See how it looks on you."

Marthona guided Ayla toward the limestone wall of her sleeping room. A hole had been dug out of it, and wedged into the hole was the round end that grew out of the horn core of a megaceros, then extended and flattened out into the typical palmate antler. The tines of the projecting antler had been broken off, leaving a slightly uneven shelf with a concave scalloped edge. Resting on top and leaning against the somewhat forward sloping wall, but nearly perpendicular to the floor, was a small plank of wood with a very smooth surface.

As Ayla approached, she noticed that it reflected with surprising clarity the wooden and wickerware containers across the room, and the flame burning in a stone oil lamp near them. Then she stopped in amazement.

"I can see myself!" Ayla said. She reached out to touch the surface. The wood had been rubbed smooth with sandstone, dyed a deep black with oxides of manganese, and polished with fat to a high sheen.

"Haven't you ever seen a reflector?" Folara asked. She was standing just inside the room, near the panel at the entrance, dying of curiosity to see the gift her mother was giving to Ayla.

"Not like this. I've looked in a still pool of water on a sunny day," Ayla said, "but this is right here, in your sleeping room!"

"Don't the Mamutoi have reflectors? To see how they look when they dress for some important occasion?" Folara asked. "How do they know if everything is right?"

Ayla frowned in thought for a moment. "They look at each other. Nezzie always made sure Talut had everything on right before ceremonies, and when Deegie—she was my friend—arranged my hair, everyone made nice comments," Ayla explained.

"Well, let's see how the necklace looks on you, Ayla," Marthona said, putting it around her neck and holding the back closed.

Ayla admired the necklace, noting how well it lay on her chest, and then she found herself studying the reflection of her face. She seldom saw herself, and her own features were more unfamiliar than those of the people around her whom she had met only recently. Though the reflecting surface was reasonably good, the lighting inside the room was dim, and her image was somewhat dark. She appeared rather drab, colorless, and flat-faced to herself.

Ayla had grown up among the Clan thinking of herself as big and ugly because, although she was thinner-boned than the women of the Clan, she was taller than the men, and she looked different, both in their eyes and her own. She was more accustomed to judging beauty in terms of the stronger features of the Clan, with their long broad faces and sloped-back foreheads, heavy overhanging browridges, sharp prominent noses, and large, richly colored brown eyes. Her own blue-gray eyes seemed faded in comparison.

After she had lived among the Others for a while, she didn't feel that she looked so strange anymore, but she still could not see herself as beautiful, though Jondalar had told her often enough that she was. She knew what was considered attractive to the Clan; she didn't quite know how to define beauty in terms of the Others. To her, Jondalar, with his masculine and therefore stronger features and vivid blue eyes was far more beautiful than she.

"I think it suits her," Willamar said. He had strolled over to add his opinion. Even he hadn't known Marthona had the necklace. It was her dwelling that he had moved into; she had made room for him and his possessions, and she made him comfortable. He liked the way she ordered and arranged things, and he had no desire to poke into every nook and cranny or bother her belongings.

Jondalar was standing behind him, looking over his shoulder, grinning. "You never told me grandam gave that to you when I was born, mother."

"She didn't give it to me for you. It was meant for the woman you would mate. The one with whom you would make a hearth, to which she could bring her children—with the blessing of the Mother," she replied, taking the necklace from around Ayla's neck and putting it into her hands.

"Well, you've given it to the right person," he said. "Are you going to wear it tonight, Ayla?"

She looked at it, frowning slightly. "No. All I have is that old outfit and this is too beautiful to wear with that. I think I'll wait until I have something appropriate to wear with it."

Marthona smiled and nodded slightly in approval.

As they were leaving the sleeping room, Ayla could see another hole cut into the limestone wall above the sleeping platform. It was somewhat larger and seemed to go into the wall rather deeply. A small stone lamp burned in front, and in the light behind it she could make out from her view a part of the full rounded figurine of an amply endowed woman. It was a donii, Ayla knew, a representation of Doni, the Great Earth Mother, and, when She chose, a receptacle for Her Spirit.

Above the niche, she noticed on the stone wall above the sleeping place, another of those mats, similar to the one on the table, made with fine fibers woven into an intricate pattern. She wished she could examine it closely, find out how it was made. Then she realized that she probably could. They weren't traveling anymore. This was going to be her home.

Folara rushed out of the dwelling after Ayla and Jondalar left and hurried to another one nearby. She had almost asked if she could go with them, then she caught her mother's eye and the bare shake of her head, and it made her realize that they might want to be alone. Besides, she knew her friends would be full of questions for her. She scratched on the panel of the next structure. "Ramila? It's me, Folara."

A moment later a plump, attractive, brown-haired young woman pulled back the drape. "Folara! We were waiting for you, but then Galeya had to go. She said to meet her by the stump."

They both walked out from under the overhang, talking animatedly together. As they approached the tall stump of a lightning-struck juniper tree they saw a thin, wiry young woman with red hair hurrying toward it from another direction, struggling to carry two wet and bulging, fairly large waterbags.

"Galeya, did you just get here?" Ramila asked.

"Yes, have you been waiting long?" Galeya said.

"No, Folara came for me only a few moments ago. We were just walking here when we saw you," Ramila said, taking one of the bags as they started back.

"Let me carry your waterbag the rest of the way, Galeya," Folara said, relieving her of the other bag. "Is this for the feast tonight?"

"What else? I feel like I've done nothing but carry things all day, but it will be fun to have an unplanned gather. I think it's going to be bigger than they thought, though. We may end up in the Gather Field. I've heard that several of the nearby Caves have sent runners offering food for the feast. You know that means most of their Cave want to come," Galeya said. Then, stopping and turning to look at Folara, she said, "Well, aren't you going to tell us about her?"

"I don't know much yet. We're just starting to get acquainted. She is going to live with us. She and Jondalar are promised, they're going to tie the knot at the Summer Matrimonial. She's kind of like a zelandoni. Not exactly, she doesn't have a mark or anything, but she knows spirits, and she's a healer. She saved Jondalar's life. Thonolan was already traveling the next world when she found them. They had been attacked by a cave lion! You won't believe the stories they have to tell," Folara chattered on excitedly as they walked back along the stone front porch of the community.

Many people were busy with various activities related to the feast, but several stopped to watch the young women, especially Folara, knowing she had spent some time with the stranger and the returned Zelandonii man. And some were listening to her, in particular an attractive woman with very light blond hair and dark gray eyes. She was carrying a bone tray of fresh meat and affecting not to notice the young women, but she was walking in the same direction and staying close enough to hear. She had originally intended to go another way entirely, until she heard Folara talking.

"What's she like?" Ramila asked.

"I think she's nice. She talks a little funny, but she comes from very far away. Even her clothes are different . . . what little she has. She only has one extra outfit. It's very plain, but she has nothing for dressing up, so she's going to wear it tonight. She said she wants some Zelandonii clothes, but she doesn't know what's appropriate, and she wants to dress right. Mother and I are going to help her make some. She's going to take me down to meet the horses tomorrow. I might even ride one. She and Jondalar just went down there, to go swimming and bathing in The River."

"Are you really going to get on the back of a horse, Folara?" Ramila asked.

The woman who had been listening didn't wait to hear the answer. She had stopped for a moment, then, with a malicious smile, hurried away.

Wolf ran ahead, stopping now and then to make sure the woman and man were still following him. The sloping path down from the northeast end of the front terrace led to a meadow on the right bank of a small river that was nearing its confluence with the main stream. The level grassy lea was surrounded by open, mixed woodland that grew more dense farther upstream.

When they reached the meadow, Whinney whickered a greeting and some people who were watching from a distance shook their heads in amazement when the wolf ran straight to the mare and they touched noses. Then the canine struck a playful pose with his tail and back end up and his front end down, and yipped a puppy bark at the young stallion. Racer lifted his head in a neigh and pawed the ground, returning the playful gesture.

The horses seemed particularly happy to see them. The mare approached and put her head across Ayla's shoulder, while the woman hugged the sturdy neck. They leaned against each other in a familiar posture of comfort and reassurance. Jondalar patted and stroked the young stallion, rubbing and scratching the itchy places Racer presented. The dark brown horse took a few paces forward, then nuzzled Ayla, wanting contact with her, too. Then they all crowded close together, including the wolf, welcoming each other's familiar presence in this place of so many strangers.

"I feel like going for a ride," Ayla said. She looked up at the position of the sun in the afternoon sky. "We have time for a short one, don't we?"

"We should have. No one will gather for the feast until it's almost dark." Jondalar smiled. "Let's go! We can swim afterward," he said. "I feel as though someone is watching me all the time."

"Someone is," Ayla said. "I know it's just natural curiosity, but it would be nice to get away for a while."

Several more people had gathered to watch from some distance. They saw the woman leap with ease onto the back of the dun-yellow mare, and the tall man seem to do little more than step up to mount the brown stallion. They left at a fast pace, the wolf following along with ease.

Jondalar led the way, first upstream a short distance to a shallow crossing of the tributary, then continuing upstream along the opposite bank of the small river a little farther until they saw a gorgelike narrow valley on their right. They rode north away from the stream and up the length of the confined vale along a rocky dry streambed that became a runoff creek in wet weather. At the end of the gorge was a steep but climbable trail that eventually opened out onto a high windy plateau that overlooked the waterways and countryside below. They stopped to take in the commanding view.

At an elevation of some six hundred fifty feet, the plateau was one of the highest in the immediate area and afforded a breathtaking panorama, not only of the rivers and valley floodplains, but across to the landscape of rolling hills of the highlands on the other side. The limestone Causses above the river valleys were not level plateaus.

Limestone is soluble in water, given enough time and the right acidic content. Over the long ages rivers and accumulated groundwater had cut down through the limestone base of the region, carving the once flat floor of the ancient sea into hills and valleys. The existing rivers created the deepest valleys and the steepest cliffs, but though the stone walls that reared up and constrained the valleys often had a uniformity of height in any one section, they varied in elevation from place to place, following the pattern of hills above.

At a cursory glance, the vegetation of the dry, windy, high Causses on both sides of the primary river all seemed the same, similar to the open plains of the continental steppes to the east. Grass was most prevalent, with stunted junipers, pines, and spruces clinging to exposed areas near streams and ponds, and brush and small trees growing in the dips and dells.

But depending on where it grew, the plant life could be surprisingly different. The sparse tops and north-facing sides of the hills favored a more arctic herbage that flourished where it was cold and dry, while the south-facing slopes were greener and richer in lower-latitude boreal and temperate-climate plants.

The broad valley of the main river below was more lush, with deciduous trees and evergreens lining the banks. Showing a paler shade of green than they would later in the season, the freshly leafed-out trees were mostly the small-leaved varieties like silver birches and willows, but even conifers such as spruces and pines showed light-colored needles of new growth at the tips. The junipers, and occasional evergreen oaks, were more mottled with their spring color appearing at the ends of branches and twigs.

At times along its course, the waterway meandered through the middle of verdant meadows in the level floodplains, with the tall grass of early summer turning to gold. In other places the curves and loops of The River's course narrowed the stream and forced it to flow against the stone walls, closer to the cliffs on first one side and then the other.

In places where the conditions were just right, the floodplains of some rivers, especially tributaries, supported small mixed forests. In protected areas, especially on south-facing slopes away from the wind, chestnut, walnut, hazelnut, and apple trees grew, many stunted, and nonbearing in some years, but providing a welcome bounty in others. Along with the trees were a variety of fruit-bearing vines, bushes, and plants, including strawberries, raspberries, and currants, with some grapes, gooseberries, and blackberries, a few raspberrylike yellow cloudberries, and several varieties of round blueberries.

At even higher elevations, fragile tundra vegetation prevailed, especially the high massif to the north, which was cloaked with glacial ice, though it brandished several active volcanoes—Ayla and Jondalar had found hot springs in the region when they traveled through it several days before they arrived. Lichens clung to rocks, herbs hovered only inches above the ground, and dwarfed shrubs lay prostrate across the frigid land over a base of permanently frozen subsoil. Mosses in variegated colors of green and gray softened the landscape in wetter regions, along with reeds, rushes, and certain grasses. The diversity of vegetation throughout the region made for a richness of variety and choice, and encouraged a like richness of animal life.

They continued along a trail that turned northeast across the elevated field to the edge of a steep cliff that overlooked The River, which was now flowing almost precisely from north to south as it washed against the wall of limestone below. On relatively level ground the path crossed over a small stream, then took a northwestern turn. The creek continued to the edge and dropped down the face of the scarp. They drew to a halt when the trail began a gradual descent down the other side and turned back. On the way back they urged the horses to a gallop and raced across the high open field until the animals slowed of their own accord. When they came to the small stream again, they stopped to let the horses water, along with Wolf, and got down to get a drink themselves.

Ayla had not felt so wonderfully free riding the horse since she first climbed on the back of the mare. There were no encumbrances, no travois or traveling packs, not a saddle blanket or even a halter. Just her bare legs against the horse's back, the way she had originally learned to ride, transmitting signals to Whinney's sensitive skin— unconsciously at first—to guide the animal in the direction she wanted to go.

Racer had a rope halter; it was the way Jondalar had trained the stallion, though he'd had to invent both the device to hold the stallion's head and the signals to tell the horse where he wanted to go. He also felt free in a way that he hadn't for a long time. It had been a long Journey, and the responsibility of getting them home safely had weighed heavily on him. That weight was gone, along with his traveling packs, and riding the horse was nothing short of fun. They both felt exhilarated, excited, unaccountably pleased with themselves, and they showed it with their delighted smiles as they walked along the stream a few paces.

"That was a good idea, Ayla, going for a ride," Jondalar said, grinning at her.

"I think so, too," she said, smiling back the way that he always loved.

"Oh, woman, you are so beautiful," he said, putting his arms around her waist and looking down at her with his intensely blue and vibrant eyes showing all his love and happiness. The only place she had ever seen a color to match his eyes was on top of a glacier in the deep wells of meltwater.

"You are beautiful, Jondalar. I know you say that men are not called beautiful, but you are to me, you know." She put her arms around his neck, feeling the full force of the natural charisma that few could resist.

"You can call me anything you want," he said as he bent down to kiss her, and suddenly hoped it would not stop there. They had grown accustomed to their privacy, to being alone in the middle of the open landscape, away from curious eyes. He was going to have to get used to being around so many people again . . . but not just now.

His tongue gently prodded her mouth open, then reached for the softness and warmth inside. She explored his in return, closing her eyes to let herself feel the sensations he was already beginning to arouse. He held her close, enjoying the feel of her body next to his. And soon, he was thinking, they would have the ceremony to join together and form a hearth to which she would bring her children, the children of his hearth, perhaps the children of his spirit, and, if she was right, even more than that. They might even be his children, the children of his body, started with his essence. The same essence he could feel rising in him now.

He pulled back and looked at her, then with more urgency kissed her neck, tasted the salt on her skin, and reached for her breast. It was fuller, he could feel the difference already; soon it would be full of milk. He untied the belt around her waist, reached inside to hold the firm round weight, and felt the hard erect nipple in his palm.

He lifted her top and she helped him pull it off, and then she stepped out of her short pants. For a moment, he just looked at her standing in the sun, and filled his eyes with the womanliness of her: the beauty of her smiling face, the firm muscularity of her body, the large, high breasts and proud nipples, the slight rounding of her stomach, the dark blond hair of her mound. He loved her so much, wanted her so much, tears came to his eyes.

Quickly, he unfastened his own clothing and laid them out on the grass. She took a few paces toward him, and when he stood up, she reached for him as he enfolded her in his arms. She closed her eyes as he kissed her mouth, and her neck and throat, and when he filled his hands with her breasts, she filled hers with his rearing manhood. He dropped to his knees, tasting the salt of the skin of her neck and running his tongue from her throat to her cleavage, holding both breasts, and then as she bent over slightly, he took a nipple in his mouth.

She held her breath, feeling the jolt of excitement reach all the way to her place of Pleasures inside, and another when he changed to the other nipple and suckled hard, while he massaged the first with his knowing fingers. Then he pressed her breasts together to get both in his mouth at once. She moaned and gave herself up to the sensations.

He traced each hard, eager nipple again and dropped lower, to her navel, then to her mound, flicked his warm tongue into her slit, and tickled the small knob within. Fierce sensations raced through her as she arced toward him and a cry escaped her lips. With his arms wrapped around her rounded bottom, he pulled her toward him pushing his tongue in and out of her slit over her hard nodule.

Standing there, her hands on his arms, her breath coming in short moaning gasps as she felt every warm stroke, she felt the tide rise inside her, pressing against her until suddenly it released with a spasm, and another, and another of delight. He felt the warmth and wetness, and savored the taste that was distinctly Ayla.

She opened her eyes and looked down at his mischievous smile. "You caught me by surprise," she said.

"I know," he said, grinning.

"It's my turn now," she said with a laugh, giving him a little shove that toppled him over. She covered him with herself and kissed him, noting the slight taste of herself. Then she nibbled his ear and kissed his neck and his throat, while he smiled with delight. He loved it when she had fun with him and joined him in playfulness when they felt in that mood.

She was kissing his chest and his nipples, and running her tongue through his hair and to his navel, and then lower still until she found his full, ready member. He closed his eyes when he felt her warm mouth cover him, letting the feeling fill him as she moved up and down, creating suction along the way. He had taught her, as he had been taught, the ways to please each other. For a moment he thought of Zelandoni, when she was young and known as Zolena, remembering when he thought he'd never find a woman like her. But he had, and suddenly he was so overwhelmed, he sent a thought of gratitude to the Great Earth Mother. What would he do if he ever lost Ayla?

His mood suddenly changed. He had enjoyed being playful, but now he wanted the woman. He sat up, pulled her up on her knees to face him, and sat her on his lap with her legs on either side of him. He took her in his arms and kissed her with an intensity that surprised her, then held her tight. She didn't know what had changed his mood, but her love for him was as strong and she responded in kind.

Then he was kissing her shoulders and neck, and caressing her breasts. She felt his need upon him so hard, it almost raised her up. He was nuzzling her breasts, trying to find her nipples. She lifted up a bit, arched her back, and felt the sensations race through her as he suckled and nibbled. She felt his hard, fiery rod under her and raised up a little higher, and without thinking, she found herself guiding him into her.

It was almost more than he could bear as she lowered herself on him, taking him into her warm, wet, eager embrace. She lifted again, leaned back, while he held her close with one arm to keep one nipple in his mouth while he massaged her other one, as though he couldn't quite get enough of her full womanness.

She was guiding herself on him, feeling the Pleasure fill her with every stroke, breathing hard and crying out. Suddenly the need was stronger upon him, building with each lift and plunge. He let go of her breasts, leaned back on his hands, and raised up, lowered, and raised again. Both cried out as waves of intense Pleasure grew with each thrust, until with a glorious flood of shuddering release, they peaked in a culmination of delight.

A few more strokes and he lay back on the grass, felt a small stone under his shoulder and ignored it. Ayla lay forward, on top of him, her head resting on his chest, and stayed there for a while. Finally she sat up again. He smiled at her as she rose up and disengaged. He would have liked to stay close longer, but they did have to get back. She walked the few feet to the small stream and squatted down to rinse off. Jondalar rinsed off as well.

"We are going to be swimming and washing as soon as we get there," he said.

"I know. That's why I'm not being too careful."

For Ayla, cleansing herself, if it was at all possible, was a ritual taught to her by Iza, her Clan mother, though the woman had wondered if her strange daughter, so tall and unattractive, would ever have reason to use it. Because Ayla was so meticulous about it, even using freezing icy streams, it had become a habit for Jondalar as well, though he hadn't always been so fastidious.

When she went to get her clothes, Wolf approached her, head lowered and tail wagging. When he was young, she'd had to train him to stay away from them when they shared Pleasures on their Journey. It had annoyed Jondalar to have the wolf bother them, and she hadn't liked being interrupted, either. When it wasn't enough to tell Wolf, quite forcefully, to go away when he came sniffing around to see what they were doing, Ayla had been required to tie a rope around his neck to keep him away, sometimes quite a distance away. Eventually he had learned, but he always approached her cautiously afterward until she signaled him that it was all right.

The horses, patiently grazing nearby, came at their whistles. They rode to the edge of the plateau and stopped again to look down at the valleys of the primary river and its tributary, and the complement of limestone cliffs that paralleled their courses. From the high field they could see the confluence of the small river flowing from the northwest and the main stream as it approached from the east. The smaller river flowed into the primary just before the larger river turned south, while it was still moving down a west-flowing section of its course. To the south, at the end of a series of cliffs, they saw the geologic block of limestone that contained the tremendous overhanging ledge of the Ninth Cave, with its long front terrace. But as Ayla looked down at the home of the Ninth Cave, it was not the remarkable size of its overhanging shelter that held her attention, but another most unusual formation.

Long before, during a formative orogeny, a period of mountain building when impressive peaks were folded and raised at the leisurely pace of geologic time, a pillar of igneous rock broke away from the place of its volcanic birth and fell into a stream. The wall of stone from which the pillar had come had taken the shape of its crystal structure as fiery magma cooled into basalt, forming itself into great columns with flat sides meeting at angles.

As the rock that broke loose was moved along, pushed by torrential floods and dragged by glacial ice, the columnar piece of basalt, though bashed and battered, retained its basic shape. The pillar of stone was eventually deposited on the floor of an inland sea, along with deep layers of accumulated sediments of marine life that were creating limestone. Later earth movements raised the sea floor, which eventually became a land of rounded hills and cliffs along river valleys. As water, weather, and wind eroded the great faces of vertical limestone into the shelters and caves used by the Zelandonii, they also exposed the erratic, the battered piece of basalt from a distant location shaped like a column.

As if its sheer size weren't enough to make the site unique, the huge abri was made even more unusual by the strange long stone embedded near the top and jutting out of the front of the huge limestone overhang. Though buried deeply into the cliff at one end, it was weathering out at such an angle that it seemed about to fall, making a distinctive landmark that added a striking element to the extraordinary rock shelter of the Ninth Cave. Ayla had seen it when she first arrived and, with a shiver of recognition, felt she had seen it before.

"Does that stone have a name?" she asked, pointing to it.

"It's called the Falling Stone," Jondalar said.

"That's a good name for it," she said. "And didn't your mother mention names for those rivers?"

"The main river doesn't really have a name," Jondalar said. "Everyone just calls it The River. Most people think of it as the most important river in the region, even though it's not the biggest. It flows into a much larger one south of here—in fact, we call that one Big River—but many of the Zelandonii Caves live near this one, and everyone knows it's the one that's meant when someone says The River.

"The little tributary down there is called Wood River," Jondalar continued. "Many trees grow near it, and there is more wood in that valley than in most. It's not used by hunters much." Ayla nodded in tacit understanding.

The valley of the feeder stream, flanked on the right by limestone cliffs and on the left by steep hills, was not like most of the open grassy valleys of the main river and its other nearby tributaries. It was dense with trees and vegetation, especially upstream. Unlike more open areas, woodlands were not prized by hunters, because hunting was more difficult. Animals were harder to see with trees and brush to hide behind and use for camouflage, and those that migrated in large herds tended to prefer valleys with sizable fields of grass. On the other hand, the valley did provide wood, for constructions, and implements, and for fire. Fruits and nuts were also collected, and several other plants that were gathered for food and other uses, along with smaller animals that fell to snares and traps. In a land of relatively few trees, no one disdained the value of Wood River Valley's contributions.

At the northeastern edge of the Ninth Cave's terrace below, which also offered a view of the two river valleys, Ayla saw the obvious remains of a good-size fire. She hadn't noticed it when she was there, she had been more concerned with following the trail down to the horse's meadow in Wood River Valley.

"Why is there such a large hearth at the edge of the terrace, Jondalar? It can't be for warmth; is it used for cooking?"

"That's a signal fire," he said, then continued when he noticed her puzzled expression. "A big balefire can be seen for quite a distance from that spot. We send messages to other Caves with the fires, and they pass the messages on with their signal fires."

"What kind of messages?"

"Oh, many kinds. They are used a lot when herds are moving, letting hunters know what's been seen. They are sometimes used to announce events or gathers, or some other kind of meeting."

"But how does someone know what the fire means?"

"It's usually arranged in advance, especially when it's the season for certain herds to move and a hunt is planned. And there are certain fire signals that mean someone needs help. Any time that people see a fire burning there, they know to take notice. If they don't know what it means, they will send a runner to find out."

"That's a very clever idea," she said, then added a thought. "It's something like the Clan signs and signals, isn't it? Communicating without words."

"I never thought of it that way, but I suppose you're right," he said.

Jondalar went back a different way from the one they had come. He headed toward The River Valley along a switchback trail that traversed a zigzag down the steeper incline near the top, then turned right through grass and brush on the more gradual slope. It came out along the edge of the flat lowlands of the right bank of The River and cut directly across Wood River Valley to the horse's meadow.

On the way back, Ayla felt relaxed, but she didn't have the exhilarating sense of freedom that she'd had on the ride out. Though she liked everyone she had met so far, there was still the big feast, and she was not anticipating meeting the rest of the Ninth Cave of the Zelandonii tonight. She wasn't used to so many people all at once.

They left Whinney and Racer in the grassy lea and found the place where the soap plant grew, but Jondalar had to point it out. It was one Ayla was not familiar with. She studied it carefully, noted similarities and differences, and made sure she would know it in the future, then got her pouch of dried ceanothus flowers.

Wolf jumped into The River with them but didn't stay in long after they stopped paying attention to him. After a long swim to soak away the dust and grime of traveling, they crushed the root of the plant and some water in a depression of a flat rock with a rounded stone to release the saponin-rich foam. They rubbed it on themselves and, laughing, on each other, then dove under to rinse off. She gave some ceanothus to Jondalar, then applied some directly to her wet hair. The plant was not as soapy, foaming up only a little, but it smelled sweet and fresh. By the time she rinsed again, the young woman was ready to get out.

After drying with the soft skins, they spread them out and sat on them, sunning themselves. Ayla picked up the comb with four long teeth that had been carved out of mammoth ivory, which was a gift from her Mamutoi friend, Deegie, but when she started combing her hair, Jondalar stopped her.

"Let me do that for you," he said, taking the comb. He had developed a fondness for combing her hair after she washed it, taking pleasurable delight in feeling the thick mass of wet hair dry into soft, springy tresses. And it made her feel unaccustomedly pampered.

"I like your mother and your sister," Ayla said, sitting with her back to him while he combed, "and Willamar, too."

"They like you, too."

"And Joharran seems like a good leader. Do you know you and your brother have the same frown lines?" she asked. "I had to like him, he looks so familiar."

"He was smitten by that beautiful smile of yours," Jondalar said. "Just as I am."

Ayla was quiet for a time, then showed the direction her thoughts had taken with her next comment. "You didn't tell me there were so many people in your Cave. It's like a whole Clan Gathering lives here," she said. "And you seem to know them all. I'm not sure if I ever will."

"Don't worry. You will. It won't take you long," he said, trying to work out a particularly irksome tangle. "Oh, sorry, did I pull too hard?"

"No, it's fine. I'm glad I finally met your Zelandoni. She knows medicine; it will be wonderful to have someone to talk with about it."

"She's a powerful woman, Ayla."

"That's obvious. How long has she been Zelandoni?"

"Let me think," he answered. "Not long after I left to live with Dalanar, I think. I still thought of her as Zolena then. She was beautiful. Voluptuous. I don't think she was ever thin, but she is growing to look more and more like the Great Mother. I think she likes you." He stopped combing for a moment, paused, then started to laugh.

"What's so funny?" Ayla asked.

"I was listening to you tell her how you found me, and about Baby and all. She'll be asking you more questions, you can be sure. I was watching her expression. Every time you answered a question, she probably wanted to ask you three more. You just made her more curious. You do it every time. You are a mystery, even to me. Do you know just how remarkable you are, woman?"

She had turned around, and he was looking at her with loving eyes.

"Give me a little time and I'll show you how remarkable *you* can be," she answered, a lazy, sensuous smile spreading across her face. Jondalar reached over to kiss her.

They heard a laugh and they both jerked around.

"Oh, did we interrupt anything?" said a woman. It was the attractive light-haired, dark-eyed woman who had listened to Folara tell her friends about the newly arrived travelers. Two other women were with her.

"Marona!" Jondalar said, frowning slightly. "No, you are not interrupting anything. I'm just surprised to see you."

"Why should you be surprised to see me? Did you think I had left on an unexpected Journey?" Marona said.

Jondalar squirmed and glanced at Ayla, who was looking at the women. "No. Of course not. I guess I'm just surprised."

"We were just out taking a walk when we happened to see you there, and I admit, Jondalar, I couldn't resist wanting to make you feel a little uncomfortable. After all, we were Promised."

They hadn't been formally Promised, but he didn't argue with her. He knew he had certainly given her the impression that they were.

"I didn't know that you would still be living here. I thought you might have mated someone from another Cave," Jondalar said.

"I did," she said. "It didn't last, so I came back." She had been eyeing his hard, tanned, naked body in a way that was familiar to him. "You haven't changed much in five years, Jondalar. Except for a few nasty scars." She turned her gaze to Ayla. "But we really didn't come here to talk to you. We came to meet your friend," Marona said.

"She'll be formally introduced to everyone tonight," he said, feeling protective of Ayla.

"That's what we heard, but we don't need a formal introduction. We just wanted to greet her and make her welcome."

He could hardly refuse to introduce them. "Ayla, of the Lion Camp of the Mamutoi, this is Marona of the Ninth Cave of the Zelandonii, and her friends," he looked more closely, "Portula? Of the Fifth Cave? Is it you?" Jondalar asked.

The woman smiled and blushed with pleasure to be remembered. Marona frowned at her. "Yes, I'm Portula, but I'm Third Cave now." She certainly remembered him. He had been chosen for her First Rites.

But he recalled that she had been one of those young women who had followed him around afterward, trying to get him alone, even though they were forbidden to associate for at least a year after First Rites. Her persistence had spoiled somewhat his memory of a ceremony that usually left him with a warm glow of fondness for the young woman involved.

"I don't think I know your other friend, Marona," Jondalar said. She seemed to be a little younger than the other two.

"I am Lorava, Portula's sister," the young woman said.

"We all became acquainted when I was mated to a man from the Fifth Cave," Marona said. "They came to visit me." She turned to Ayla. "Greetings, Ayla of the Mamutoi."

Ayla stood up to return the greetings. Although it normally wouldn't have bothered her, she found herself feeling slightly disconcerted to be greeting unfamiliar women with no clothes on, and wrapped her drying skin around her, tucking it in at the waist, and put her amulet back around her neck.

"Grrreetings, Marrrona, of the Ninth Cave of the Zelandonyee,"

Ayla said, her slightly rolled r's and peculiar throaty accent marking her immediately as a stranger. "Grrreetings, Porrrtula of the Fifth Cave, and Grrreetings to her Sister, Lorrrava," she continued.

The younger woman tittered at Ayla's funny way of talking and then tried to hide it, and Jondalar thought he noticed a trace of a smirk on Marona's face. His brow wrinkled in a frown.

"I wanted to do more than greet you, Ayla," Marona said. "I don't know if Jondalar ever mentioned it, but as you know by now, we were Promised before he decided to leave on this great Journey he suddenly had to make. As I'm sure you must know, I wasn't very pleased about it."

Jondalar was trying to think of something to say to ward off what he felt sure was coming, Marona letting Ayla know that she was very unhappy by giving her an earful of his faults, but she surprised him.

"But that was in the past," Marona said. "To be honest, I haven't thought about him in years, until you arrived today. Other people may not have forgotten, however, and some of them like to talk. I wanted to give them something else to talk about, to show them that I can greet you appropriately." She motioned toward her friends to include them. "We were going to go to my room to get ready for your Welcome Feast tonight, and we thought you might like to join us, Ayla. My cousin Wylopa is there already—you remember Wylopa, don't you, Jondalar? I thought it would give you a chance to get acquainted with some women before all the formal meetings tonight."

Ayla noticed some tension, particularly between Jondalar and Marona, but under the circumstances that wouldn't be unusual. Jondalar had mentioned Marona, and that they had been almost Promised before he left, and Ayla could imagine how she would feel in the woman's place. But Marona had been straightforward about it, and Ayla did want to get to know some of the women better.

She missed women friends. She had known so few women her own age when she was growing up. Uba, Iza's true daughter, had been like a sister to her, but Uba was much younger, and while Ayla had grown to care for all the women of Brun's clan, there were differences. No matter how hard she tried to be a good Clan woman, some things she could not change. It wasn't until she went to live with the Mamutoi and met Deegie that she came to appreciate the fun of having someone her own age to talk to. She missed Deegie, and Tholie of the Sharamudoi, too, who had quickly become a friend that Ayla would always remember.

"Thank you, Marona. I would like to join you. This is all I have to wear," she said, quickly putting on her simple, travel-strained outfit, "but Marthona and Folara are going to help me make some clothes. I'd like to see what you wear."

"Perhaps we can give you a few things, as a welcoming gift," Marona said.

"Would you take this drying skin back with you, Jondalar?" Ayla said.

"Of course," he said. He held her close for a heartbeat and brushed her cheek with his, then she left with the three women.

As Jondalar watched them go, his troubled frown deepened. Though he hadn't formally asked Marona to be his mate, he had led her to believe they would be joined at the Matrimonial of the upcoming Summer Meeting before he left, and she had been making plans. Instead he left with his brother on a Journey and just hadn't shown up. It must have been difficult for her.

It wasn't that he had loved her. There was no doubt she was beautiful. Most men considered her to be the most beautiful and desirable woman at the Summer Meetings. And though he didn't entirely agree, she certainly had her ways when it came to sharing Doni's Gift of Pleasure. She just wasn't the one he desired most. But people said they were perfect for each other, they looked so good together, and everyone had expected them to tie the knot. He more or less did, too. He knew he wanted to share a hearth with a woman and her children someday, and since he couldn't have Zolena, the one woman he wanted, it might as well be Marona.

He had not really admitted it to himself, but he had felt relieved when he decided to go with Thonolan on a Journey. At the time, it seemed the easiest way to extricate himself from his involvement with her. He had been sure she would find someone else while he was gone. She said she had, but it hadn't lasted. He had expected to find her with a hearth full of children. She didn't say anything about children at all. It was surprising.

He had no idea he would find her unmated when he returned. She was still a beautiful woman, but she did have a temper and a vicious streak. She could be very spiteful and vindictive. Jondalar's forehead knotted with concern as he watched Ayla and the three women walking toward the Ninth Cave.

6

Wolf saw Ayla walking along the path through the horse meadow with the three women and raced toward her. Lorava squealed at the sight of the large carnivore, Portula gasped and looked around in panic for a place to run, and Marona blanched in fear. Ayla glanced at the women as soon as she saw the wolf and, noting their reactions, quickly signaled him to stay.

"Stop, Wolf!" she voiced aloud, more for the benefit of the women than to halt the animal, although it did reinforce her signal. Wolf stopped in his tracks and watched Ayla, alert for a sign that he could approach her. "Would you like to meet Wolf?" she said, then, seeing that the women still showed fear, she added, "He won't hurt you."

"Why would I want to meet an animal?" Marona said.

The tone of her voice made Ayla look more closely at the light-haired woman. She noted fear but, surprisingly, an inflection of disgust and even anger. Ayla could understand the fear, but the rest of Marona's reaction seemed inappropriate. It was certainly not the response she was used to seeing the animal evoke. The other two women looked at Marona, then seemed to follow her lead, showing no indication that they wanted to get close to the wolf.

Wolf's stance had become more wary, Ayla saw. He must sense something, too, she thought. "Wolf, go find Jondalar," she said, giving him a signal to go. He stayed a moment longer, watching her, then bounded away as she turned to walk up the path toward the enormous stone shelter of the Ninth Cave with the three women.

They passed by several people on the path, and each one showed an immediate reaction to seeing her with the women. Some cast speculative glances or bemused smiles, some seemed surprised, even startled. Only young children seemed to pay no attention to them. Ayla could not help but notice, and it put her a bit on edge.

She studied Marona and the other women, though not obviously, using the techniques of women of the Clan. No one could be more inconspicuous than Clan women. They could quietly fade into the background and seem to disappear, and they gave the impression that they were not aware of anything around them, but that was misleading.

From the time they were very young, girls were taught never to stare or even look directly at a man, to be unobtrusive, and yet they were expected to know when one needed or wanted her attention. As a consequence, Clan women learned to focus carefully and precisely, and with a glance absorb significant information from posture, movement, and expression very quickly. And they missed little.

Ayla was as adept as any of them, though she wasn't as aware of this legacy of her years with the Clan as she was of her ability to read body language. Her observations of the women put her on guard and made her think again about Marona's motives, but she didn't want to make any assumptions.

Once they were under the stone ledge they headed in a different direction from the one she had gone before and entered a large dwelling more toward the middle of the space. Marona led them in and they were greeted by another woman who seemed to be waiting for them.

"Ayla, this is my cousin, Wylopa," Marona said on their way through the main room and into a side sleeping room. "Wylopa, this is Ayla."

"Greetings," Wylopa said.

After the rather formal introductions Ayla had had to all of Jondalar's close kin, this offhand presentation to Marona's cousin, with no welcome though it was her first time in this dwelling, struck Ayla as odd. It was not consistent with the behavior she had already come to expect from the Zelandonii.

"Grrreetings, Wylopa," Ayla said. "This dwelling, is it yourrrs?"

Wylopa was surprised at Ayla's unusual enunciation and was so unused to hearing any language other than her own, she had some trouble understanding the stranger.

"No," Marona interjected. "This is the home of my brother and his mate, and their three children. Wylopa and I live here with them. We share this room."

Ayla glanced quickly around at the space set off by panels, similar to the way Marthona's dwelling was divided.

"We were going to fix our hair and faces for the celebration tonight," Portula said. She glanced at Marona with an ingratiating smile, which became a smirk when she looked back at Ayla. "We thought you might like to get ready with us."

"Thank you for asking me. I would like to see what you do," Ayla said. "I don't know Zelandonii ways. My friend Deegie used to fix my hair sometimes, but she is Mamutoi, and lives very far away. I know I will never see her again, and I miss her. It's nice to have women friends."

Portula was surprised and touched by the newcomer's honest and friendly response; her smirk warmed to a real smile.

"Since it's a feast to welcome you," Marona said, "we thought we would give you something to wear, too. I asked my cousin to gather some clothes for you to try on, Ayla." Marona looked at clothing that had been placed around. "You've found a good selection, Wylopa." Lorava giggled. Portula looked away.

Ayla noticed several outfits spread out on the bed and floor, primarily leggings and long-sleeved shirts or tunics. Then she looked at the clothing the four women were wearing.

Wylopa, who seemed older than Marona, was wearing an outfit similar to the ones laid out, worn quite loose, Ayla noticed. Lorava, who was rather young, had on a short sleeveless leather tunic, belted around the hips, cut somewhat differently from the ones spread out. Portula, who was fairly plump, wore a full skirt made of some kind of fibrous material and a loose-fitting top with a long fringe that hung over the skirt. Marona, who was thin but shapely, had on a very short sleeveless top, open in front, profusely decorated with beads and feathers, with a reddish fringe around the bottom that stopped just below her waist, and a loincloth skirt, similar to the kind Ayla had worn on hot days on her Journey.

Jondalar had shown her how to take a rectangular strip of soft leather, pull it up between her legs, and tie it on with a thong around her waist. Letting the long ends hang down both front and back, and pulling them together at the sides, made the loincloth resemble a short skirt. Marona's, she noticed, was fringed on both front and back ends. She had left an open space on both sides, showing a long, bare, shapely leg, and tied the thong low, barely over her hips, causing the fringe in front and back to sway when she walked. Ayla thought Marona's clothes—the very short top that did not meet in front and could never be closed, and the skimpy loincloth skirt—looked small for her, as though they had been made for a child, not a woman. Yet she was certain that the light-haired woman chose her clothing purposefully and with great care.

"Go ahead, pick something out," Marona said, "and then we'll fix your hair. We want this to be a special night for you."

"All these things look so big, and heavy," Ayla said. "Won't they be too warm?"

"It cools off at night," Wylopa said, "and these clothes are supposed to be worn loose. Like this." She lifted her arms and showed the loose blousy fit.

"Here, try this on," Marona said, picking up a tunic. "We'll show you how it's supposed to be worn."

Ayla removed her own tunic, then her amulet bag from around her neck and put it on a shelf, and let the women slip the other tunic over her head. Even though she was taller than any of the four women, it hung down to her knees and the long sleeves fell below her fingertips.

"This is too big," Ayla said. She didn't see Lorava, but she thought she heard a muffled sound behind her.

"No, it's not," Wylopa said, smiling broadly. "You just need a belt, and you're supposed to roll up the sleeves. Like I did, see? Portula, bring that belt, so I can show her."

The plump woman brought a belt, but she wasn't smiling anymore, unlike Marona and her cousin, who smiled excessively. Marona took the belt and wrapped it around Ayla. "You tie it low, like this, around your hips, and let it blouse out, and then the fringe hangs down. See?"

Ayla still felt there was far too much material. "No, I don't think this one fits right. It really is too big. And look at these leggings," she said, taking the pair that was beside the tunic and holding them in front of herself. "The waist comes up much too high." She pulled the tunic off over her head.

"You're right," Marona said. "Try on another one." They picked out another outfit, slightly smaller and very intricately decorated with ivory beads and shells.

"This is very beautiful," Ayla said, looking down at the front of the tunic. "Almost too beautiful. . . ."

Lorava snorted strangely, and Ayla turned to look at her, but she was facing away.

"But it's really very heavy, and still too big," Ayla continued, taking off the second tunic.

"I suppose you might think it's too big if you're not used to

Zelandonii clothes," Marona said, frowning, then she brightened with a self-satisfied smile. "But perhaps you are right. Wait here. I think I know something that would be just perfect, and it was just made." She left the sleeping room and went into another part of the dwelling. After a while, she returned with another outfit.

This one was much smaller and lighter in weight. Ayla tried it on. The tight leggings came halfway down her calf but fit correctly at the waist, where the front overlapped and tied with a sturdy flexible thong. The top was a sleeveless tunic, with a deep V cut down the front, laced together with thin leather thongs. It was a little small, and Ayla could not lace it together tightly, but with the thongs loosened, it wasn't bad. Unlike the others, it was a simple, undecorated outfit, made of a soft leather that felt nice against her skin.

"This is very comfortable," Ayla said.

"And I have just the thing to set it off," Marona said, showing her a belt woven out of various colored fibers into an intricate pattern.

"This is beautifully made and very interesting," Ayla said as Marona tied it low around her waist. She felt satisfied with the outfit. "This one will do," she said. "I thank you for your gift." She put on her amulet and folded her other clothes.

Lorava choked and coughed. "I need some water," she said, and dashed from the room.

"Now, you must let me fix your hair," Wylopa said, still smiling broadly.

"I promise to do your face after I do Portula's," Marona said.

"And you said you'd fix my hair, Wylopa," Portula said.

"You promised to do me, too," Lorava said from the entrance to the room.

"If you are over your coughing spell," Marona said, giving the young woman a hard look.

While Wylopa combed and fussed with her hair, Ayla watched with interest as Marona decorated the faces of the two other women. She used solidified fats mixed with finely powdered red and yellow ochres to add color to mouths, cheeks, and forehead, and mixed with black charcoal to emphasize the eyes. Then she used more intense shades of the same colors to add carefully drawn designs of dots, curved lines, and various other shapes to their faces in a way that reminded Ayla of the tattoos she had seen on some people.

"Let me do your face now, Ayla," Marona said. "I think Wylopa is done with your hair."

"Oh, yes!" Wylopa said. "I'm finished. Let Marona do your face."

While the face decorations of the women were interesting, Ayla felt uncomfortable with the idea. In Marthona's dwelling, there was a subtle use of color and design that was very pleasing, but Ayla wasn't sure she liked the way the women looked. It seemed too much, somehow.

"No . . . I don't think so," Ayla said.

"But you have to!" Lorava said, looking dismayed.

"Everyone does it," Marona said. "You would be the only one without it."

"Yes! Go on. Let Marona do it. It's what all the women do," Wylopa said.

"You really should," Lorava urged. "Everyone always wants Marona to paint her face. You're lucky she's willing."

They were pressing her so hard, it made Ayla want to resist. Marthona had not said anything to her about having to get her face painted. She wanted to take the time to find her way and not be pushed into customs she was not familiar with.

"No, not this time. Perhaps later," Ayla said.

"Oh, go ahead and do it. Don't spoil everything," Lorava said.

"No! I don't want to have my face painted," Ayla said with such firm resolve, they finally stopped pressing her.

She watched them dress each other's hair in intricate plaits and coils, placing decorated combs and pins attractively. Finally, they added facial ornaments. Ayla hadn't really noticed the holes at strategic locations in their faces until they put earrings into their earlobes and pluglike ornaments into their noses, cheeks, and under the lower lips, but she saw that some of the painted decorations now accentuated the ornaments that had been added.

"Don't you have any piercings?" Lorava asked. "You'll just have to get some. Too bad we can't do them now."

Ayla wasn't sure if she wanted to be pierced, except perhaps in the earlobes so she could wear the earrings she had brought with her all the way from the Summer Meeting of the Mammoth Hunters. She watched the women add beads and pendants around their necks and bracelets on their arms.

She noticed that the women glanced from time to time at something behind a dividing panel. Finally, a little bored with all the combing and decorating, she got up and wandered over to see what they were looking at. She heard Lorava gasp when she saw the piece of blackened shiny wood, similar to the reflector in Marthona's dwelling, and looked at herself.

Ayla was not happy with the reflection she saw. Her hair had been dressed into braids and coils, but they seemed to be in odd unattractive placements, not in the pleasing symmetrical order of the other women. She saw Wylopa and Marona looking at each other, then look away. When she tried to catch the eye of one of the women, they avoided her. Something strange was going on, and she didn't think she liked it. She certainly did not like what had been done to her hair.

"I think I'll wear my hair loose," Ayla said as she began to take out the combs, pins, and bindings. "Jondalar likes it that way." When she had removed all the paraphernalia, she picked up the comb and pulled it through her long, thick, dark blond hair, springy with a fresh-washed natural wave.

She adjusted her amulet around her neck—she never liked to be without it, though she often wore it under her clothes—then looked at herself in the reflector. Maybe someday she'd learn to fix her own hair, but for now she liked it much better the way it fell naturally. She glanced at Wylopa and wondered why the woman hadn't seen how peculiar her hair had looked.

Ayla noticed her leather amulet bag in the reflector and tried to see it the way someone else might. It was lumpy with the objects it contained, and the color was much darker from sweat and wear than it had been. The small decorated bag had originally been intended as a sewing kit. Now, only dark quill-shafts remained of what had once been white feathers decorating the rounded bottom edge, but the ivory-beaded design was still intact and added an interesting look with the simple leather tunic. She decided to let it show.

She remembered that it was her friend Deegie who had persuaded her to use it as her amulet when she saw the plain and grimy pouch Ayla had worn before. Now this one was old and worn. She thought she ought to make a new one soon to replace it, but she would not throw this one away. It held too many memories.

She could hear activity outside and was getting very tired of watching the women adding insignificant little finishing touches to each other's face or hair that had no visible effect that she could discern. Finally there was a scratch on the rawhide panel beside the opening of the living structure.

"Everyone's waiting for Ayla," a voice called. It sounded like Folara.

"Tell them she'll be out soon," Marona answered. "Are you sure you won't let me paint your face a little, Ayla? After all, it is a celebration for you."

"No, I really don't want to."

"Well, since they're waiting for you, maybe you should go ahead. We'll be along in a while," Marona said. "We still have to change."

"I think I will," Ayla said, glad to have an excuse to leave. They had been inside for a long time, it seemed to her. "Thank you for your gifts," she remembered to say. "This is really a very comfortable outfit." She picked up her worn tunic and short pants and went out.

She saw no one under the overhanging shelter; Folara had gone ahead without waiting for her. Ayla quickly veered toward Marthona's dwelling and left her old clothing inside the entrance. Then she walked rapidly toward the crowd of people she saw outside, beyond the shadow of the high stone shelf that protected the structures nestled beneath it.

As she came out into the light of the late afternoon sun, a few people nearby noticed her and stopped talking to gape. Then a few more noticed her and stared, jostling their neighbors to look, too. Ayla slowed down and then stopped, looking back at the people who were looking at her. Soon all the talking stopped. Suddenly, into the stillness, someone let out a stifled guffaw. Then another person laughed, and another. Soon everyone was laughing.

Why were they laughing? Were they laughing at her? Was something wrong? Her face reddened with embarrassment. Had she committed some terrible blunder? She looked around, wanting to run away but not knowing which way to turn.

She saw Jondalar striding toward her, his face an angry scowl. Marthona was hurrying toward her, too, from another direction.

"Jondalar!" Ayla called out as he approached. "Why is everyone laughing at me? What's wrong? What have I done?" She was speaking in Mamutoi and didn't realize it.

"You are wearing a boy's winter underwear. Your belt is one that is worn by a young man during his puberty initiation, to let people know he is ready for his donii-woman," Jondalar said in the same language she had spoken. He was furious that Ayla had been made the butt of such a cruel joke on her first day with his people.

"Where did you get those clothes?" Marthona asked as she approached.

"Marona," Jondalar answered for her. "When we were at The River, she came and told Ayla that she wanted to help her dress for the celebration tonight. I should have guessed she had some vicious plan in mind to get back at me."

They all turned around and looked back under the abri toward the dwelling of Marona's brother. Standing just inside the shadows of the overhang were the four women. They were holding their sides, leaning against each other, laughing so hard at the woman they had tricked into wearing completely inappropriate boys' clothing, that tears were streaming down their faces, smearing their careful makeup with red and black streaks. Ayla realized they were taking great pleasure in her discomfort and embarrassment.

As she watched the women, she felt a flush of anger rise within her. This was the gift they wanted to give her? To welcome her? They wanted people to laugh at her like this? She understood then that everything they had laid out for her was inappropriate for a woman. It was obvious to her now that it all had been men's clothing. But it wasn't only the clothes, she realized. Was that why they had made her hair look so peculiar? So people would laugh at her? And had they planned to paint her face to make her look laughable, too?

Ayla had always rejoiced in laughter. When she lived with the Clan, she was the only one who laughed with pleasure, until her son was born. When people of the Clan made a grimace that resembled a smile, it was not a sign of happiness. It was an expression of nervousness, or fearfulness, or it signaled a threat of possible aggression. Her son was the only baby who smiled and laughed as she did, and though it made them uneasy, she had loved Durc's happy giggles.

When she had lived in the valley, she had laughed with delight at the antics of Whinney and Baby when they were young. Jondalar's ready smile and rare uninhibited laughter had made her know she had met her own kind in him, had made her love him more. And it had been Talut's welcoming smile and hearty bellow that encouraged her to visit the Lion Camp the first time they met. She had met many people in their travels, and had laughed with them many times, but she had never been laughed at before. She had never learned that laughter could be used to hurt. This was the first time laughter had caused her pain and not joy.

Marthona, too, was not happy with the nasty trick that had been played on the visitor, the guest of the Ninth Cave of the Zelandonii, whom her son had brought home to mate with him and become one of them.

"Come with me, Ayla," Marthona said. "Let me get you something more appropriate. I'm sure we can find something of mine that you can wear."

"Or something of mine," Folara said. She had seen the whole incident and had come to help.

Ayla started to go with them, then stopped. "No," she said.

Those women had given her the wrong clothes as "gifts of welcome" because they wanted to make her look outlandish, different, to show she didn't belong. Well, she had thanked them for their "gifts" and she was going to wear them! It was not the first time she had been the object of stares. She had always been the odd one, the ugly one, the strange one, among the people of the Clan. They had never laughed at her—they didn't know how to laugh like that—but they had all stared at her when she arrived at the Clan Gathering.

If she had been able to stand being the only one who was different, who did not belong, the only one who was not Clan at the entire Clan Gathering, she could certainly stand up to the Zelandonii. At least they looked the same. Ayla straightened her back, clamped her jaw shut, jutted out her chin, and glared at the laughing throng.

"Thank you, Marthona. And you, too, Folara. But this outfit will do just fine. It was given to me as a gift of welcome. I would not be so discourteous as to cast it aside."

She glanced behind her and noticed that Marona and the others were gone. They had returned to Marona's room. Ayla turned back to face the large gathering of people who had assembled and started walking toward them. Marthona and Folara looked at Jondalar, stunned, when she passed by, but he could only shrug and shake his head.

Ayla caught a familiar movement out of the corner of her eye as she proceeded. Wolf had appeared at the head of the path and was running toward her. When he reached her, she patted herself and he jumped up and put his paws on the front of her shoulders, then licked her throat and took it gently in his jaws. There was an audible commotion from the crowd. Ayla signaled him down, then indicated that he should follow her, closely, the way she had taught him at the Mamutoi Summer Meeting.

As Ayla moved through the group, there was something about the way she walked, something about her determination, something about her defiant look in the face of those who laughed, and something about Wolf walking at her side, that silenced them. Soon, no one felt like laughing anymore.

She walked into the midst of a group of people whom she had met before. Willamar, Joharran, and Zelandoni greeted her. She turned around to find Jondalar right behind her, followed by Marthona and Folara.

"I have not yet met some of the people here. Would you introduce me, Jondalar?" Ayla said.

Joharran stepped forward instead. "Ayla of the Mamutoi, Member of the Lion Camp, Daughter of the Mammoth Hearth, Chosen by the Spirit of the Cave Lion, and Protected by the Spirit of the Cave Bear . . . and Friend of horses and a wolf, this is my mate, Proleva of the Ninth Cave of the Zelandonii, Daughter of . . ."

Willamar grinned as formal introductions were made to close kin and friends, but his expression was in no way derisive. Marthona, more and more amazed, observed with greater interest the young woman her son had brought home with him. She caught Zelandoni's eye, and a knowing glance passed between them; they would discuss this later.

Many people looked at her more than once—especially men, who began to notice how well the garments and belt fit the person wearing them, in spite of what they meant to them. She had been traveling for the past year, walking or riding a horse, and her muscles were firm. The close-fitting boy's winter undergarment emphasized her lean, muscular, well-formed body. Since she hadn't been able to lace the thongs together in front across her firm but rather ample breasts, the opening exposed her cleavage, somehow more enticing than the more familiar naked breasts they often saw. The leggings showed off her long, shapely legs and rounded buttocks, and the cinched belt, in spite of what its design symbolized, accented her waist, only slightly thickened with the early stages of pregnancy.

On Ayla the outfit took on new meaning. Although many women did wear facial ornaments and paint, her lack of them only served to highlight her natural beauty. Her long hair, tumbling loosely in the disarray of natural waves and ringlets that caught the last rays of the setting sun, was an appealing and sensuous contrast to the well-groomed coiffures of the other women. She seemed young and reminded adult men of their own youth and their first awakening to the Great Earth Mother's Gift of Pleasure. It made them wish they were young again and that Ayla was their donii-woman.

The outlandishness of Ayla's clothing was quickly forgotten, accepted as somehow appropriate for the beautiful stranger with the low-pitched voice and exotic accent. It was certainly no more strange than her control over horses and Wolf.

Jondalar noticed people watching Ayla and heard her name mentioned in the undercurrent of conversation. Then he overheard a man say, "That's a remarkably beautiful woman Jondalar has brought home with him."

"You'd expect him to bring a beautiful woman," a woman's voice replied, "but she has courage, too, and a strong will. I'd like to get to know her better."

The comments made Jondalar look at Ayla again, and suddenly he saw the way she looked, not the incongruity of the costume. Few women could claim such an exceptional shape, especially women of her age, who usually had had a child or two to slacken youthful muscle tone. Few would choose to wear such a close-fitting outfit even if it had been appropriate. Most would prefer looser, more concealing, and for them more comfortable clothes. And he did love her hair worn loose like that. She is a beautiful woman, he thought, and courageous. He relaxed and smiled, remembering their afternoon ride and the stop on the high field, thinking how lucky he was.

Marona and her three confederates had returned, still laughing, to her room to repair the damage to their face paint. They had planned to make their appearance later, dressed in their best and most suitable clothing, expecting to make a grand entrance.

Marona had exchanged the loincloth skirt for a long graceful one of very soft pliable leather with a long fringed overskirt, which she wrapped around her waist and hips and tied, but she wore the same decorated short top. Portula had been wearing her favorite skirt and top. Lorava had only the short tunic dress with her, but the other women had loaned her a long fringed overskirt and several extra necklaces and bracelets, and fixed her hair and painted her face much more elaborately than she had ever worn it before. Wylopa, laughing as she removed the decorated shirt and trousers made for a man, had changed into her own highly decorated trousers, dyed an orangy shade of red, and more deeply colored tunic with a dark fringe.

When they were ready, they left the dwelling and walked together to the open front terrace, but when people noticed Marona and her friends, they pointedly turned their backs on them and ignored them. The Zelandonii were not a cruel people. They had laughed at the stranger only because they were startled by the idea of a grown woman wearing a boy's winter underwear and puberty belt. But most of them were not pleased about the crude prank. It had reflected badly on all of them, made them seem to be discourteous and inhospitable. Ayla was their guest and would very likely soon be one of their own. And besides, she had carried it off so well, it showed her mettle, made them proud of her.

The four women saw a large group crowded around someone, and when several people left, they could see Ayla at the center, still wearing the clothes they had given her. She hadn't even changed! Marona was shocked. She had been sure one of Jondalar's kin would have given the newcomer something more appropriate to wear—that is, if she dared to show her face again. But her plans to show up the strange woman that Jondalar had brought back with him, after leaving her in the lurch with nothing but an empty promise, had instead shown what a spiteful and mean-spirited person she was.

Marona's cruel joke had turned back on her, and she was fuming. She had coaxed and cajoled her friends into joining her, promising them they would be the center of attention, telling them how much they would shine. Instead, everyone seemed to be talking about Jondalar's woman. Even her strange accent, at which Lorava had nearly laughed out loud, and Wylopa had had difficulty understanding, was called exotic and charming.

Ayla was the one getting all the attention, and Marona's three friends were sorry they had allowed themselves to be persuaded. Portula, in particular, had been reluctant. She had agreed only because Marona had promised to paint her face, and Marona was known for her intricate facial designs. Ayla had not seemed so bad. She was friendly, and now she definitely was making friends . . . with everyone else.

Why hadn't they seen how the boy's outfit showed off the newcomer's beauty when she put it on? But the women had seen what they expected to see, the symbolism, not the reality. None of them could have imagined wearing such garments in public, but they didn't matter to Ayla. She had no emotional or cultural sensitivity toward them or what they represented. If she thought about them at all, it was only to notice how comfortable they were. Once the shock of the laughter had subsided, she forgot about it. And because she did, everyone else did, too.

A large block of limestone with a fairly flat top surface occupied a space on the terrace in front of the great abri. It had broken off the end of the overhanging shelf so long before, no one remembered a time when it wasn't there. It was often used when someone wanted to get the attention of people who had gathered in the area, because when a person stood on it, it raised them a few feet above the level of the crowd.

As Joharran jumped up onto the Speaking Stone, an expectant hush began to descend on the gathering. He held his hand out to Ayla, to help her up, then to Jondalar to invite him to stand beside her. Wolf jumped up without an invitation and stood between the woman and man of the only pack he had ever known. Standing together on the rock elevated above the others, the tall handsome man, the beautiful exotic woman, and the huge magnificent wolf made a stunning scene. Marthona and Zelandoni, who were standing side by side, looked at the trio, and then at each other for a moment, each filled with her own thoughts that would have been hard to put into words.

Joharran stood, waiting until the crowd noticed them and quieted. Looking out at the people, he was sure the entire Ninth Cave was looking back at him. Not a single person seemed to be missing. Then he recognized several people from nearby Caves, and then several more. He realized the gathering was much larger than he had anticipated.

Most of the Third Cave were on the left, and the Fourteenth Cave were beside them. Toward the back on the right were many people from the Eleventh. There were even a few from the Second Cave and some from their kin across the valley that separated them, the Seventh Cave. Interspersed among the others he noted a few people from the Twenty-ninth, and even a couple from the Fifth. Every Cave in the neighboring vicinity was represented, and some had come quite a distance.

Word has spread fast, he thought, runners must have gone out. We might not need to have a second gathering for the larger community. Everyone seems to be here. I should have realized they would be. And all the Caves upriver along the way must have seen them, too. After all, Jondalar and Ayla traveled south sitting on the backs of horses. There may be a lot more people at the Summer Meeting this year. Maybe we should plan a big hunt before we leave, to help with provisions.

When he had everyone's attention, he waited a beat more while he collected his thoughts. Finally, he began.

"As leader of the Ninth Cave of the Zelandonii, I, Joharran, wish to speak." The last few voices stilled. "I see that we have many visitors tonight, and in the name of Doni, the Great Earth Mother, I am pleased to welcome all of you to this gathering to celebrate the return of my brother Jondalar, from his long Journey. We are grateful that the Mother watched over his steps as he walked in strange lands, and thankful that She guided his wandering feet back home again."

Voices of concurrence called out. Joharran paused, and Ayla noticed his brow furrow in that same familiar way that Jondalar's so often did. She felt the same warm glow of affection for him that she had the first time she noticed that likeness.

"As most of you may know already," Joharran continued, "the brother who started out with Jondalar will not return. Thonolan walks the next world now. The Mother called a favorite back to Her." He looked down at his feet for a moment.

There was that reference again, Ayla thought. It was not necessarily considered lucky to have too many talents, too many Gifts, to be loved so much that one was considered favored of the Mother. She sometimes missed Her favorites and called them back to Her early, when they were still young.

"But Jondalar did not return alone," Joharran continued, then he smiled at Ayla. "I don't think many people would be surprised to learn that my brother met a woman on his Journey." There was a titter of laughter and many knowing smiles from the crowd. "But I must admit that I didn't expect even Jondalar to find someone quite so remarkable."

Ayla felt her face redden when Joharran's words became clear. This time her embarrassment was not because of ridiculing laughter, but the result of his praise.

"Proper introductions to each individual here could take days, especially if everyone decided to include all their names and ties." Joharran smiled again and many people responded with nods and knowing looks. "And our guest would never remember everyone, so we decided to introduce our visitor to all of you, and let each of you introduce yourselves as you have the opportunity."

Joharran turned and smiled at the woman standing on the raised stone with him, but then he looked at the tall blond man and his expression became more serious. "Jondalar of the Ninth Cave of the Zelandonii, Master Flint-Knapper; Son of Marthona, former Leader of the Ninth Cave; born to the Hearth of Dalanar, Leader and Founder of the Lanzadonii; Brother of Joharran, Leader of the Ninth Cave, has returned after five years from a long and difficult Journey. He has brought with him a woman from a land so distant, it took a full year just to make the Journey back."

The leader of the Ninth Cave took both of Ayla's hands in his. "In the name of Doni, the Great Earth Mother, I present to all the Zelandonii, Ayla of the Mamutoi, Member of the Lion Camp, Daughter of the Mammoth Hearth, Chosen by the Spirit of the Cave Lion, and Protected by the Spirit of the Cave Bear," then he smiled, "and as we have seen, Friend of horses and this wolf." Jondalar was convinced the wolf smiled, as though he knew he had been introduced.

Ayla of the Mamutoi, she thought, remembering when she was Ayla of No People and feeling a great swelling of gratitude toward Talut and Nezzie and the rest of the Lion Camp for giving her a place to claim. She struggled to hold back the tears that threatened. She missed them all.

Joharran dropped one of Ayla's hands, but, holding up the other, faced out toward the assembled Caves. "Please welcome this woman who traveled so far with Jondalar, welcome her to this land of the Zelandonii, the Great Mother Earth's Children. Show this woman the hospitality and respect with which the Zelandonii honor all their guests, especially one of the Blessed of Doni. Let her know we value our visitors."

There were sidelong glances in the direction of Marona and her friends. The joke wasn't at all funny anymore. It was their turn to feel embarrassed, and Portula, at least, turned crimson when she looked up at the foreign woman standing on the Speaking Stone wearing a Zelandonii boy's underwear and puberty belt. She hadn't known the clothing she was given was inappropriate. It didn't matter. The way she wore it made it entirely proper.

Then Ayla, feeling a need to do something, took a small step forward. "In the name of Mut, Great Mother of All, whom you know as Doni, I greet you Zelandonii, Children of this beautiful land, Children of the Great Earth Mother, and thank you for welcoming me.

I thank you, too, for accepting my animal friends into your midst; for allowing Wolf to stay with me inside a dwelling." Wolf looked up at her at the sound of his name. "And for providing a place for the horses, Whinney and Racer."

The immediate reaction of the crowd was startled surprise. Though her accent was quite noticeable, it wasn't the way she spoke that astonished the people. In the spirit of the formality of the introductions, Ayla said the name of her mare the way she had originally given it to Whinney, and they were stunned by the sound that had come out of her mouth. Ayla had made such a perfect horse's whinny that for a moment, they thought it was a horse. It was not the first time she had surprised people with her ability to imitate the sound of an animal—a horse was not the only animal she could mimic.

Ayla had no memory of the language she had known as a child; she could not remember anything about her life before the Clan, except a few vague dreams and a mortal fear of earthquakes. But Ayla's kind had an inherent compulsion, a genetic drive nearly as strong as hunger, for verbal speech. When she was living alone in the valley after she left the Clan and before she had learned to speak again from Jondalar, she developed verbalizations for herself to which she attributed meaning, a language only she, and Whinney and Racer to some extent, could understand.

Ayla had a natural aptitude for reproducing sounds, but having no verbal language and living alone, hearing only the sounds made by animals, she began to mimic them. The personal language she devised was a combination of the baby sounds her son had begun to make before she was forced to leave him, the few words spoken by the Clan, and onomatopoeic mimicking of the sounds made by animals, including bird whistles. Time and practice had made her so proficient at imitating their sounds, even the animals could not tell the difference.

Many people could imitate animals, it was a useful hunting strategy if the mimic was good enough, but she was so good, it was uncanny. That was what caused the moment of consternation, but the people, who were used to a certain element of banter from speakers when the occasion wasn't entirely serious, became convinced she had made the sound as a gesture of humor. The initial shock gave way to smiles and chuckles as they relaxed.

Ayla, who had been a bit apprehensive at their first reaction, noticed the easing of tension and relaxed in turn. When they smiled at her, she could not help but smile back, one of her glorious, beautiful smiles that seemed to make her glow.

"Jondalar, with a filly like that, how are you going to keep the young stallions away?" a voice called out. It was the first open acknowledgment of her beauty and appeal.

The yellow-haired man smiled. "I'll have to take her out riding often, keep her busy," he said. "You know that I learned how to ride while I was gone, don't you?"

"Jondalar, you knew how to 'ride' before you left!"

There was a burst of laughter; this time, Ayla realized, the laughter was meant in fun.

Joharran spoke up when it settled down. "I have only one more thing to say," he said. "I want to invite all the Zelandonii who have come from neighboring Caves to join the Ninth Cave in the feast we have prepared to welcome Jondalar and Ayla home."

7

Marvelous aromas had been emanating from community cooking areas at the unoccupied far southwestern end of the abri all day, stimulating everyone's appetite, and a number of people had been busy with last minute preparations before Joharran began to speak. After the introductions, as the throng pressed toward the far end, Jondalar and Ayla were urged ahead, although the crowd was careful to allow space around the wolf, who followed a step behind the woman.

The food was attractively arranged on platters and in bowls of shaped bone, woven grass and fiber, and carved wood and displayed on long, low tables made of blocks and slabs of limestone. Bent wood tongs, carved horn spoons, and large flint knives were conveniently nearby, ready to be used as serving implements. Most people brought their own eating dishes, though there were extras for those who needed them.

Ayla stopped to admire the display for a moment. There were whole roasted haunches of young reindeer, plump grouse, platters of trout and pike, and, even more prized during the early summer season, servings of still scarce vegetables: young roots, fresh greens, new shoots, and tightly coiled young ferns. Edible sweet milkweed flowers added a pleasing decoration to many of the dishes. There were also nuts and dried fruits from the previous autumn's harvest, and containers of rich broth with chunks of reconstituted dried aurochs meat, roots, and mushrooms.

The thought struck Ayla that if they still had such prized food left after living through the rigors of the long winter, it spoke well, indeed, for their ability to organize the collection, preservation, storage, and distribution of adequate provisions to maintain the several Caves of Zelandonii throughout the cold season. The two hundred or so people of the Ninth Cave alone would have been too large a community for a less productive region to sustain year-round, but the exceptionally rich environment, as well as the large number of unusually convenient and serviceable natural shelters, encouraged the growing population of several Caves.

The home of the Ninth Cave of the Zelandonii was a high limestone cliff whose face was carved by weather and wear into an enormous, overhanging shelf that went from slightly south of due east to almost southwest in a long, shallow, south-facing curve that followed The River. The jutting overhang sheltered an area six hundred fifty feet in length and almost one hundred fifty feet in depth, offering nearly one hundred thousand square feet of covered living space. The stone floor of the abri beneath, layered with centuries of packed dirt and stone rubble, extended as a terrace or front porch somewhat beyond the edge of the huge rock ledge.

With so much space available, the members of the Ninth Cave did not fill up the entire protected area with living structures. No one made a purposeful decision to do so, but perhaps intuitively to lay claim and declare boundaries distinct from the adjacent area where the craftspeople of the vicinity tended to congregate, the residential dwellings of the Ninth Cave were clustered at the eastern end of the abri. Since they had plenty of room to spread out, the site immediately to the west of the dwellings was used for the community workplaces. Southwest of that, and continuing toward the end, was a large unoccupied space for children to play and for people to gather outside of their dwellings yet still be protected from inclement weather.

Though none of the others approached the size of the Ninth Cave, there were many other Zelandonii Caves along The River and its tributaries, most of them living, at least in winter, in similar sheltered limestone abris with capacious front porches of the same material. Though the people didn't know it, and their descendants wouldn't even think in such terms for many millennia, the location of the land of the Zelandonii was halfway between the North Pole and the equator. They didn't need to know it to understand the benefits of their middle-latitude position. They had lived there for many generations and had learned from experience, passed down through example and lore, that the territory had advantages in all seasons, if one knew how to utilize them.

In summer, people tended to travel around the larger region that they thought of as Zelandonii land, usually living in the open in tents or lodges constructed of natural materials, especially when gathering together into larger groups and often when visiting or hunting or harvesting quantities of vegetable produce. But when they could, they were always happy to find a south-facing stone shelter to use temporarily, or to share the shelters of friends and kin, because of their distinct advantages.

Even during the Ice Age, when the leading edge of the nearest mass of ice was only a few hundred miles to the north, clear days could get quite hot at middle latitudes in the warm season. As the sun passed overhead, seeming to circle the great mother planet, it rode high in the southwest sky. The great protective overhanging cliff of the Ninth Cave, and others that faced south or southwest, cast a shadow beneath it in the heat of midday, offering a respite of enticing cool shade.

And when the weather began to chill, heralding the severe season of intense cold in periglacial territories, they welcomed their more permanent and protected homes. During the glacial winters, though sharp winds and temperatures well below freezing prevailed, the bitter cold days were often dry and clear. The shining orb hung low in the sky then, and the long rays of the afternoon sun could penetrate deep into a south-facing shelter to lay a kiss of solar warmth on the receptive stone. The great limestone abri cherished its precious gift, holding it until evening, when the nip of frost bit deeper, then it gave back its warmth to the protected space.

Proper clothing and fire were essential to survival on the northern continents when glaciers covered nearly a quarter of the earth's surface, but in the land of the Zelandonii passive solar heat made a significant contribution toward warming their living space. The huge cliffs with their protective shelters were a significant reason the region was among the most heavily populated in all that cold ancient world.

Ayla smiled at the woman responsible for organizing the feast. "It looks so beautiful, Proleva. If the wonderful smells hadn't made me so hungry, I would just like to look at it."

Proleva smiled back, pleased.

"That is her specialty," Marthona said. Ayla turned, somewhat surprised to see Jondalar's mother; she had looked for her before she stepped down from the Speaking Stone but couldn't find her. "No one can put together a feast or a gathering like Proleva. She's a good cook, too, but it's her skill at organizing the contributions of food and help from other people that makes her such an asset to Joharran and the Ninth Cave."

"I learned from you, Marthona," Proleva said, obviously delighted at the high praise from the mother of her mate.

"You have more than outdone me. I was never as good at making feasts as you have become," Marthona said.

Ayla noticed the very specific reference to making feasts and recalled that Marthona's "specialty" had not been organizing feasts and gatherings. Her organizing skills had been utilized as the leader of the Ninth Cave before Joharran.

"I hope you let me help you next time, Proleva," Ayla said. "I would like to learn from you."

"I'd be happy to have your help next time, but since this feast is for you, and people are waiting for you to start, can I serve you some of this young reindeer roast?"

"What about your wolf-animal?" Marthona asked. "Would he like some meat?"

"He would, but he doesn't need tender young meat. He would probably be happy with a bone, if there is one with a little meat left on it that isn't needed for soup," Ayla said.

"There are several by the cooking fires over there," Proleva said, "but do take a slice of this reindeer and some daylily buds for yourself first."

Ayla held out her eating bowl to accept the piece of meat and ladle of hot green vegetables, then Proleva called another woman to come and serve the food and walked with Ayla toward the cooking hearths, staying on her left side, away from Wolf. She led them to the bones piled to one side of a large hearth and helped Ayla pick out a broken long bone with a shiny knob at one end. The marrow had been extracted, but pieces of brownish drying raw meat were still clinging to it.

"This will do fine," Ayla said, while the wolf eyed her with tongue-lolling anticipation. "Would you like to give it to him, Proleva?"

Proleva frowned nervously. She didn't want to be impolite to Ayla, especially after Marona's trick, but she wasn't eager to give a bone to a wolf.

"I would," Marthona said, knowing it would make everyone less fearful to see her do it. "What should I do?"

"You can hold it out to him, or you can toss it to him," Ayla said. She noticed that several people, including Jondalar, had joined them. He had an amused smile on his face.

Marthona took the bone and held it out toward the animal as he approached, then with a change of mind, she tossed it in the general direction of the wolf. He jumped up and grabbed it in the air with his teeth, a trick that drew appreciative comments, then he looked at Ayla expectantly.

"Take it over there, Wolf," she said, signaling him as well, indicating the big charred stump at the edge of the terrace. The wolf carried the bone like a prized possession, settled himself near the stump, and began to gnaw on it.

When they went back to the serving tables, everyone wanted to give Ayla and Jondalar samples of special treats, which she noticed had a different variety of tastes from the ones she had known in her childhood. One thing she had learned on her travels, however, was that whatever foods the people of a region liked best, while they might be unusual, they generally tasted good.

A man, somewhat older than Jondalar, approached the group that surrounded Ayla. Though Ayla thought he appeared rather slovenly—his unwashed blond hair was dark with grease, and his clothing was grimy and needed repair—many people smiled at him, particularly the young men. He carried a container, similar to a waterbag, over his shoulder. It had been made from the nearly waterproof stomach of an animal and was full of liquid, which distended its shape.

By the size of it, Ayla guessed the container had probably come from the stomach of a horse; it did not appear to have the distinctive contours of a waterbag made from a ruminant with a multiple-chambered stomach. And by the smell, she knew it did not contain water. Rather, the odor reminded her of Talut's bouza, the fermented drink that the headman of the Lion Camp made out of birch sap and other ingredients—which he liked to keep secret but usually included grains of some kind.

A young man who had been hovering near Ayla looked up and smiled broadly. "Laramar!" he said. "Have you brought some of your barma?"

Jondalar was glad to see him distracted. He didn't know him, but had learned the man's name was Charezal. He was a new member of the Ninth Cave who had come from a rather distant group of Zelandonii, and quite young. He probably hadn't even met his first donii-woman when I left, Jondalar thought, but he had been fluttering around Ayla like a gnat.

"Yes. I thought I would make a contribution to the Welcome Feast for this young woman," Laramar said, smiling at Ayla.

His smile seemed insincere, which aroused her Clan sensitivity. She paid closer attention to the language his body spoke and quickly decided this was not a man to be trusted.

"A contribution?" one of the women asked with a hint of sarcasm. Ayla thought it was Salova, the mate of Rushemar, one of the two men whom she regarded as Joharran's seconds in command, as Grod had been Brun's in the Clan. Leaders needed someone they could rely on, she had decided.

"I thought it was the least I could do," Laramar said. "It isn't often that a Cave can welcome someone from so far away."

As he lifted the heavy bag from his shoulder and turned to put it down on a nearby stone table, Ayla overheard the woman mutter under her breath, "And even less often that Laramar contributes anything. I wonder what he wants."

It seemed obvious to Ayla that she was not alone in mistrusting the man. Others did not trust him, either. It made her curious about him. People with cups in hand were already gathering around him, but he made a point of singling out Ayla and Jondalar.

"I think the returned traveler and the woman he brought with him should get the first drinks," Laramar said.

"They can hardly refuse such a great honor," Salova murmured.

Ayla barely heard the scornful comment and wondered if anyone else did. But the woman was right. They could not refuse. Ayla looked at Jondalar, who pointedly emptied the water from his cup and nodded toward the man. She emptied her cup as they walked up to Laramar.

"Thank you," Jondalar said, smiling. Ayla thought his smile was as insincere as Laramar's. "This is very thoughtful of you. Everyone knows your barma is the best, Laramar. Have you met Ayla yet?"

"Along with everyone else," he said, "but I haven't really been introduced."

"Ayla, of the Mamutoi, this is Laramar of the Ninth Cave of the Zelandonii. It is true. No one makes barma better than his," Jondalar said.

Ayla thought it seemed a rather limited formal introduction, but the man smiled at the praise. She handed Jondalar her cup to free both of her hands and held them out to the man. "In the name of the Great Earth Mother I greet you, Laramar of the Ninth Cave of the Zelandonii," she said.

"And I welcome you," he said, taking her hands, but holding them only briefly, almost as if he was embarrassed. "Rather than a formal one, let me offer you a better welcome."

Laramar proceeded to open the container. First he unwrapped a waterproof piece of cleaned intestine from a pouring spout that had been made of a single vertebra from the backbone of an aurochs. Extraneous material around the tubular bone had been carved away and a groove cut around the outside. Then it had been inserted into a natural opening of the stomach and a strong cord tied around the skin that encircled the bone so that it was pulled into the groove, to hold it in place and make a watertight connection. Then he pulled out the stopper, a thin leather thong that had been knotted several times at one end until it was big enough to plug the central hole. It was much easier to control the flow of liquid from the flexible bag through the natural hole in the center of the solid section of spine.

Ayla had retrieved her cup from Jondalar and held it out. Laramar filled it somewhat more than half-full. Then he poured some for Jondalar. Ayla took a small sip. "This is good," she said, smiling. "When I lived with the Mamutoi, the headman, Talut, used to make a drink similar to this out of birch sap and grains and other ingredients, but I must admit, this is better."

Laramar looked around at the people nearby with a smirk of satisfaction.

"What is this made of?" Ayla asked, trying to get the taste.

"I don't always make it the same way. It depends on what's available. Sometimes I use birch sap and grains," Laramar said, being evasive. "Can you guess what's in it?"

She tasted again. It was harder to guess ingredients when they were fermented. "I think there are grains, perhaps birch sap or sap from some other tree, and maybe fruit, but something else, something sweet. I can't tell the proportions, though, how much of each is used," Ayla said.

"You have a good sense of taste," he said, evidently impressed. "This batch does have fruit, apples that were left on a tree through a frost, which makes them a little more sweet, but the sweet you are tasting is honey."

"Of course! Now that you mention it, I can taste honey," Ayla said.

"I can't always get honey, but when I can, it makes the barma better, and stronger," Laramar said, this time with a smile that was genuine. There were not many with whom he could discuss the making of his brew.

Most people had a craft, something in which they developed the skill to excel. Laramar knew that he could make barma better than anyone. He considered it his craft, the one thing he could do well, but he felt that few gave him the credit he thought he deserved.

Many foods fermented naturally, some on the vine or tree on which they grew; even animals who ate them were sometimes affected. And many people made fermented beverages, as least occasionally, but they were inconsistent and their product often turned sour. Marthona was often cited for making an excellent wine, but it was considered by many a minor thing, and of course, it wasn't her only skill.

Laramar could always be counted on to make a fermented brew that became alcoholic, not vinegary, and his was often very good. He knew that it wasn't a minor thing, it took skill and knowledge to do it well, but most people cared only about his end product. It didn't help that he was known to drink a lot of it himself and was often too "sick" in the mornings to go hunting or to participate in some cooperative, sometimes unpleasant, but usually necessary activity that needed to be done for the Cave.

Shortly after he poured the barma for the guests of honor, a woman appeared at Laramar's side. A toddler was hanging on her leg that she seemed to be ignoring. She had a cup in her hand which she held toward Laramar. A flicker of displeasure danced across his features for a moment, but he held his expression carefully neutral as he poured her some barma.

"Aren't you going to introduce her to your mate?" she said, obviously directing her question to Laramar, but looking at Ayla.

"Ayla, this is my mate, Tremeda, and the one hanging on her is her youngest boy," Laramar said, complying with her request minimally, and somewhat reluctantly, Ayla thought.

"Tremeda, this is Ayla of the . . . Matumo."

"In the name of the Mother, I greet you, Tremeda of . . . ," Ayla started, putting down her cup so she could use both hands in the formal greeting.

"I welcome you, Ayla," Tremeda said, then took a drink, not bothering with trying to free her hands for greetings.

Two more children had crowded around her. The clothing on all the children was so ragged, stained, and dirty, it was hard to see the minor differences that Ayla had observed between young Zelandonii girls and boys, and Tremeda, herself, looked little better. Her hair was uncombed, her clothes stained and dirty. Ayla suspected that Tremeda indulged too heavily in her mate's brew. The eldest of the children, a boy, Ayla thought, was looking at her with an unpleasant expression.

"Why does she talk so funny?" he said, looking up at his mother. "And why is she wearing boy's underwear?"

"I don't know. Why don't you ask her?" Tremeda said, drinking the last of the liquid in her cup.

Ayla glanced at Laramar and noticed that he was fuming with anger. He looked ready to hit the youngster. Before he could, Ayla spoke to the boy. "The reason I have a different way of speaking is that I come from far away and grew up with people who don't talk the same way as the Zelandonii. Jondalar taught me to speak your language after I was already grown. As for these clothes, they were given to me as a gift earlier today."

The youngster seemed surprised that she had answered him, but he didn't hesitate to ask another question. "Why would someone give you boys' clothes?" the boy said.

"I don't know," she said. "Perhaps they meant it as a joke, but I rather like them. They are very comfortable. Don't you think so?"

"I guess so. I never had any as good as those," the boy said.

"Then perhaps we can make some for you. I'd be willing if you will help me," Ayla said.

His eyes lit up. "Do you mean it?"

"Yes, I mean it. Will you tell me your name?"

"I'm Bologan," he said.

Ayla held out both her hands. Bologan looked at her in surprise. He had not expected a full formal greeting and wasn't sure what to do. He didn't think he had a formal designation. He had never heard his mother or the man of his hearth greet anyone using their names and ties. Ayla reached down and took both his grimy hands in hers.

"I am Ayla of the Mamutoi, Member of the Lion Camp," she began, and continued with her full formal designation. When he didn't respond with his, she did it for him. "In the name of Mut, the Great Earth Mother, also known as Doni, I greet you, Bologan of the Ninth Cave of the Zelandonii; Son of Tremeda, Blessed of Doni, mated to Laramar, Maker of the Most Excellent Barma."

The way she said it made it sound as if he really did have names and ties to be proud of, like everyone else. He looked up at his mother and her mate. Laramar was not angry anymore. They were smiling and seemed rather pleased at the way she had named them.

Ayla noticed Marthona and Salova had joined them. "I would like some of that Most Excellent Barma," Salova said. Laramar seemed more than pleased to oblige.

"And me too," Charezal said, getting his request in first as other people started crowding around Laramar, holding out their cups.

Ayla noticed that Tremeda got another cupful, too, before she moved off, followed by the children. Bologan looked at her as they were moving away. She smiled at him and was pleased to see him smile back.

"I think you've made a friend of that young man," Marthona said.

"A rather rowdy young man," Salova added. "Are you really going to make him some winter underwear?"

"Why not? I would like to learn how this is made," Ayla said, indicating the clothing she had on. "I may have a son someday. And I might like to make another outfit for myself."

"Make one for yourself! You mean you are going to wear that?" Salova said.

"With a few variations, like a slightly better-fitting top. Have you ever tried one on? It is very comfortable. And besides, it was given to me as a gift of welcome. I'm going to show how much I appreciate it," Ayla said, a touch of her anger and pride showing.

Salova's eyes opened wide as she looked at the stranger Jondalar had brought home, suddenly conscious of her unusual enunciation again. This woman is not someone to anger, she thought. Marona may have tried to embarrass Ayla, but Ayla has turned it back on her. Marona will be the one who ends up being humiliated. She'll cringe every time she sees her wearing that outfit. I don't think I would want Ayla mad at me!

"I'm sure Bologan could use something warm to wear this winter," Marthona said. She had not missed a bit of the subtle communication between the two younger women. It's probably just as well for Ayla to begin establishing her place right away, she thought. People need to know she cannot be taken advantage of easily. After all, she will be mating a man who was born and raised among the people who are the responsible leaders of the Zelandonii.

"He could use something to wear anytime," Salova said. "Has he ever had anything decent? The only reason those children have anything at all is that people take pity on them and give them their castoffs. As much as he drinks, have you noticed that Laramar always manages to have enough barma to trade for whatever he wants, especially to make more barma, but not enough to feed his mate and her brood? And he's never around when something needs to be done, like spreading rock powder on the trenches, or even to go hunting.

"And Tremeda doesn't help," Salova continued. "They are too much alike. She's always too 'sick' to help with food gathering or community projects, though it doesn't seem to bother her to ask for a share of someone else's efforts to feed her 'poor, hungry children.' And who can refuse? They are indeed poorly dressed, seldom clean, and often hungry."

After the meal, the gathering became more boisterous, especially after Laramar's barma appeared. As darkness came on, the revelers moved to an area closer to the middle of the space under the huge rock shelf that roofed the entire settlement, and a large fire was lit barely under the edge of the overhead shelter. Even during the hottest days of summer, nighttime brought a penetrating chill, a reminder of the great masses of glacial ice to the north.

The bonfire threw heat back under the abri, and as the rock warmed, it added to the comfort of the surroundings. So did the friendly, if constantly changing, crowd gathered around the recently arrived couple. Ayla met so many people that, in spite of her exceptional memorizing skill, she wasn't sure she would remember them all.

Wolf suddenly appeared again about the same time as Proleva, carrying a sleepy Jaradal, joined the group. The boy perked up and wanted to get down, much to his mother's obvious dismay.

"Wolf won't hurt him," Ayla said.

"He's very good with children, Proleva," Jondalar added. "He was raised with the children of the Lion Camp, and was especially protective of one boy who was weak and sickly."

The nervous mother stooped to let the boy down while keeping an arm around him. Ayla joined them, putting her arm around the animal, primarily to reassure the woman.

"Would you like to touch Wolf, Jaradal?" Ayla asked. He nodded his head up and down solemnly. She guided his hand toward Wolf's head.

"He's tickly!" Jaradal said with a smile.

"Yes, his fur is tickly. It tickles him, too. He's shedding; that means some of his hair is coming out," Ayla said.

"Does it hurt?" Jaradal asked.

"No. It just tickles. That's why he especially likes to be scratched now."

"Why is his hair coming out?"

"Because it's getting warmer. In winter, when it's cold, he grows a lot of hair to keep warm, but it's too hot in summer," Ayla explained.

"Why doesn't he put a coat on when it's cold?" Jaradal pressed.

The answer came from another source. "It's hard for wolves to make coats, so the Mother makes one for them every winter," Zelandoni said. She had joined the group shortly after Proleva. "In summer, when it gets warm, the Mother takes their coats off. When Wolf sheds his fur, it's Doni's way of taking off his coat, Jaradal."

Ayla was surprised at the gentleness in the woman's voice as she talked to the small boy, and the look of tenderness in her eyes. It made her wonder if Zelandoni had ever wanted children. With her knowledge of medicine, Ayla was sure the donier would know how to dislodge a pregnancy, but it was more difficult to know how to start one or to prevent a miscarriage. I wonder how she thinks new life starts, Ayla thought, or if she knows how to prevent it.

When Proleva picked up the boy to take him to their dwelling, Wolf started to follow. Ayla called him back. "I think you should go to Marthona's dwelling, Wolf," she said, giving him a "go home" signal. His home was anyplace that Ayla had laid her furs.

As the chill darkness overwhelmed the region beyond the palliative of firelight, many people left the main celebration area. Some, especially families with young children, retired to personal dwellings. Others, mostly young couples but older people as well and occasionally more than two, were in the shadows around the edges of the fire, involved with each other in more private ways, sometimes talking, sometimes embracing. It was not uncommon to share partners at such events, and as long as all the parties were agreeable, no ill will resulted.

The occasion reminded Ayla of a celebration to Honor the Mother, and if it honored Her to share Her Gift of Pleasure, She seemed to be well honored that evening. The Zelandonii were not so different from the Mamutoi, Ayla thought, or the Sharamudoi, or the Losadunai, and even the language was the same as the Lanzadonii.

Several men tried to entice the beautiful stranger into sharing the Great Mother's pleasurable Gift. Ayla enjoyed the attention, but she made it plain that she had no desire for anyone except Jondalar.

He had mixed feelings about all the interest she was getting. He was pleased that she was so well received by his people, and proud that so many men admired the woman he had brought home, but he wished that they would not be so openly eager to take her to their furs—especially that stranger called Charezal—and he was glad that she showed no inclination for anyone else.

Jealousy was not well tolerated by the Zelandonii. It could lead to discord and strife, even fighting, and as a community, they valued harmony and cooperation above all else. In a land that was little more than a frozen waste for a large part of the year, willing mutual assistance was essential for survival. Most of their customs and practices were aimed at maintaining goodwill and discouraging anything, such as jealousy, that might jeopardize their amicable relations.

Jondalar knew he would have trouble hiding his jealousy if Ayla chose someone else. He did not want to share her with anyone. Perhaps, after they had been mated for many years and the comfort of habit occasionally gave way to the excitement of someone new, it would be different, but not yet, and in his heart he doubted if he could ever willingly share her.

Some people had started singing and dancing, and Ayla was trying to move in their direction, but everyone around her crowded in close, wanting to talk. One man in particular, who had been hovering around the edge of the group most of the evening, now seemed determined to speak to her. Ayla thought she had noticed someone unusual earlier, but when she tried to focus on him, someone else would ask her a question or make a comment that distracted her.

She looked up as a man handed her another cup of the barma. Though the drink reminded her of Talut's bouza, this was stronger. She was feeling a bit giddy and decided it was time to stop. She was familiar with the effects such fermented drinks could have on her, and she did not want to get too "friendly" the first time she met Jondalar's people.

She smiled at the man who had given her the cup in anticipation of politely refusing him, but the shock of seeing him froze the smile on her face for a moment. It quickly became an expression of genuine warmth and friendliness.

"I am Brukeval," he said. He seemed hesitant and shy. "I'm a cousin of Jondalar." His voice was quite low-pitched, but rich and resonant, very pleasing.

"Greetings! I am called Ayla of the Mamutoi," she said, intrigued by more than his voice or demeanor.

He did not quite resemble the rest of the Zelandonii she had met. Rather than the usual blue or gray eyes, his large eyes were quite dark. Ayla thought they might be brown, but it was hard to be sure in firelight. More startling than his eyes, however, was his general appearance. He had a look that was familiar to her. His features had the cast of the Clan!

He's a mixture, both Clan and Others. I'm sure of it, she thought. She studied him, but only with glances. He seemed to bring out her Clan woman training and she found herself being careful not to stare too directly. She didn't think he was an equal mixture of half Clan, half Others, like Echozar, to whom Joplaya was Promised . . . or her own son.

The look of the Others was stronger in this man; his forehead was essentially high and straight, sloping back only a little, and when he turned she could see that while his head was long, the back of it was round and lacked the protruding bony occipital bun. But his browridges, which overhung his large deep-set eyes, were his most distinctive feature, not quite as imposing as men of the Clan, but definitely prominent. His nose was quite big, too, and though more finely modeled than Clan men, it had the same general shape.

She thought he probably had a receding chin. His dark brown beard made it hard to tell, but the beard itself made the man seem similar to the men she had known as a child. The first time Jondalar had shaved, which he usually did in summer, it had been a shock to her, and it had made him appear very young, preadolescent. She had never seen a grown man without a beard before that. This man was somewhat shorter than average, slightly shorter than her, though he was powerfully built, burly with heavy muscles and a deep barrel chest.

Brukeval had all the masculine qualities of the men she had grown up with, and she thought he was quite handsome in a comfortable way. She even felt a slight tingle of attraction. She was also feeling tipsy—definitely no more cups of barma for her.

Ayla's warm smile communicated her feeling, but Brukeval thought there was an engaging shyness about her, too, in the way she glanced aside and looked down. He was not used to women reacting to him with such warmth, especially beautiful women who were with his tall, charismatic cousin.

"I thought you might want a cup of Laramar's barma," Brukeval said. "There have been so many people around you, all wanting to talk, but no one seemed to think you might be thirsty."

"Thank you. I actually am thirsty, but I don't dare have any more of that," she said, indicating the cup. "I've already had so much, I'm dizzy." Then she smiled, one of her full, glowing, irresistible smiles.

Brukeval was so entranced, he forgot to breathe for a moment. He'd been wanting to meet her all evening, but had been afraid to approach her. He had been casually spurned by beautiful women before. With her golden hair gleaming in the firelight, her firm and remarkably shapely body shown off becomingly by the soft clinging leather, and the slightly foreign features giving her an exotic appeal, he thought she was the most extraordinarily beautiful woman he had ever seen.

"Can I get you something else to drink?" Brukeval finally asked, smiling with a boyish eagerness to please. He hadn't expected her to be so open and friendly to him.

"Go away, Brukeval. I was here first," said Charezal, not entirely in fun. He had seen the way she smiled at Brukeval, and he had been trying all evening to entice Ayla away, or at least extract a promise that she would meet him some other time.

Few men would have been so persistent in trying to interest a woman chosen by Jondalar, but Charezal had moved to the Ninth Cave only the year before from a distant Cave. He was several years younger than Jondalar, had not even reached manhood by the time the man and his brother left on their Journey, and was not aware of the tall man's reputation as someone who had an incomparable way with women. He had learned only that day that the leader had a brother. He had, however, heard rumors and gossip about Brukeval.

"You don't think she's going to be interested in someone whose mother was half flathead, do you?" Charezal said.

There was a gasp from the crowd and a sudden silence. No one had openly made such a reference to Brukeval in years. His face distorted with a venomous look of pure hatred as he glared at the young man in a barely controlled rage. Ayla was stunned to see the transformation. She had seen that kind of rage from a man of the Clan once before, and it frightened her.

But this was not the first time someone had poked fun at Brukeval like that. He had felt especially sensitive to Ayla's predicament when she was laughed at for wearing the clothes Marona and her friends had given to her. Brukeval had been the butt of cruel jokes, too. He had wanted to run to her, protect her, as Jondalar did, and when he saw the way she stood up to their laughter, tears had come to his eyes. As he'd watched her walk so proudly and face them all down, he had lost his heart to her.

Later, though he ached to talk to her, he suffered agonies of indecision and hesitated to introduce himself. Women didn't always respond favorably to him, and he would rather have admired her from a distance than see her look at him with the disdain some beautiful women did. But after watching her for some time, he finally decided to take a chance. And then, she had been so nice to him! She had seemed to welcome his presence. Her smile had been so warm and receptive, it made her even more beautiful.

In the silence after Charezal's remark, Brukeval watched Jondalar move up behind Ayla, hovering protectively. He envied Jondalar. He had always envied Jondalar, who was even taller than most. Though he had never taken part in the sport of name-calling, and had in fact defended him more than once, he felt that Jondalar pitied him, and that was worse. Now Jondalar had come home with this beautiful woman that everyone admired. Why were some people so favored?

But his glare at Charezal had upset Ayla more than he could know. She hadn't seen an expression like that since she left Brun's clan; it reminded her of Broud, the son of Brun's mate, who had often looked at her like that. Though Brukeval was not angry at her, she shuddered at the memory and wanted to get away.

She turned to Jondalar. "Let's go. I'm tired," she said under her breath in Mamutoi, and realized that she really was—exhausted, in fact. They had just completed a long, hard Journey, and so much had happened, it was hard to believe they had arrived only that day. There had been the anxiety of meeting Jondalar's family and the sadness of telling them about Thonolan's death; the unpleasantness of Marona's joke as well as the excitement of meeting all the people of this large Cave; and now Brukeval. It was too much.

Jondalar could see that the incident between Brukeval and Charezal had distressed her, and he had some idea why. "It has been a long day," he said. "I think it's time for us to go."

Brukeval seemed upset that they were leaving so soon after he had finally gotten up courage to talk to her. He smiled hesitantly. "Do you have to go?" he asked.

"It's late. Many people have already gone to bed, and I am tired," she said, smiling back at him. Without that malevolent expression, she could smile at him, but it lacked the earlier warmth. They said good night to the people nearby, but when she looked back, she noticed Brukeval glaring again at Charezal.

As she and Jondalar walked back toward the dwellings and Marthona's place, Ayla asked, "Did you see the way your cousin was looking at Charezal? It was filled with hate."

"I can't say I blame him for being upset at Charezal," he said. Jondalar had not exactly warmed to the man, either. "You know it's a terrible insult to call someone a flathead, and even worse to say someone's mother is one. Brukeval has been teased before, especially when he was young—children can be cruel."

Jondalar went on to explain that when Brukeval was a child, whenever someone had wanted to tease him, they called him "flathead." Though he lacked that specific characteristic of the Clan that had given rise to the epithet—the sloped-back forehead—it was the one word that was all but guaranteed to make him react with fury. And to the young orphan who had hardly known her, it was worse to refer to his mother in a way that meant the most despicable kind of abomination imaginable, half animal, half human.

Because of his predictable emotional response, with the casual cruelty of children, those who were bigger or older often teased him by calling him "flathead" or "son of an abomination" when he was young. But as he grew older, what he lacked in stature, he made up for in strength. After a few battles with boys who, though taller than him, were no match for his phenomenal muscular power, especially coupled with untempered rage, they stopped the hated taunts, at least to his face.

"I don't know why it should bother people so much, but it's probably true," Ayla said. "I think he is part Clan. He reminds me of Echozar, but Brukeval has less Clan. You can see it is not as strong—except for that look. That reminded me of the way Broud looked at me."

"I'm not so sure he's a mixture. Maybe some ancestor came from a distant place and it's only chance that he bears some superficial resemblance to f . . . Clan people," Jondalar said.

"He's your cousin, what do you know about him?"

"I don't really know much for sure, but I can tell you what I've heard," Jondalar said. "Some of the older people say that when Brukeval's grandmother was barely a young woman, she somehow got separated from her people while traveling to a Summer Meeting that was quite far away. She was supposed to have her First Rites at that meeting. By the time she was found it was the end of summer. They say she was irrational, hardly even coherent. She claimed she had been attacked by animals. They say she was never quite right again, but she didn't live long. Not long after she returned, it was discovered she had been blessed by the Mother, even though she had never had First Rites. She died shortly after giving birth to Brukeval's mother, or perhaps as the result of it."

"Where do they think she was?"

"No one knows."

Ayla frowned in thought. "She must have found food and shelter while she was gone," she said.

"I don't think she was starving," he said.

"The animals that attacked her, did she say what kind they were?"

"Not that I've heard."

"Did she have any scratch or bite marks or other injuries?" Ayla continued.

"I don't know."

Ayla stopped as they were approaching the area of the dwellings and looked at the tall man in the dim light of the crescent moon and the distant fire. "Don't the Zelandonii call the Clan animals? Did his grandmother ever say anything about the ones you call flatheads?"

"They do say she hated flatheads, and would run away screaming at the sight of one," Jondalar said.

"What about Brukeval's mother? Did you know her? What did she look like?"

"I don't recall much, I was pretty young," Jondalar said. "She was short. I remember that she had big, beautiful eyes, dark like Brukeval's, brownish, but not really dark brown, more hazel. People used to say her eyes were her best feature."

"Brownish, like Guban's eyes?" Ayla asked.

"Now that you mention it, I guess they were."

"Are you sure Brukeval's mother didn't have the look of the Clan, like Echozar . . . and Rydag?"

"I don't think she was considered very pretty, but I don't recall her having browridges, like Yorga. She never did mate. I guess men weren't too interested in her."

"How did she get pregnant?"

She could see Jondalar's smile even in the dark. "You are convinced that it takes a man, aren't you? Everyone just said the Mother Blessed her, but Zolena . . . Zelandoni once told me that she was one of those rare women who was Blessed immediately after First Rites. People always think that's too young, but it happens."

Ayla was nodding in agreement. "What happened to her?"

"I don't know. Zelandoni said she was never very healthy. I think she died when Brukeval was quite young. He was raised by Marona's mother, she was a cousin of Brukeval's mother, but I don't think she cared much for him. It was more an obligation. Marthona used to watch him sometimes. I remember playing with him when we were little. Some of the older boys picked on him even then. He has always hated it when someone called him a flathead."

"No wonder he was so furious at Charezal. At least now I understand. But that look . . ." Ayla shuddered again. "He looked just like Broud. As long as I can remember, Broud hated me. I don't know why. He just hated me and nothing I ever did could change it. For a while I tried, but I will tell you, Jondalar. I would never want Brukeval to hate me."

Wolf looked up in greeting when they entered Marthona's dwelling. He had found Ayla's sleeping furs and curled up near them when she told him to "go home." Ayla smiled when she saw his eyes glowing in the light of the one lamp Marthona had left burning. He licked her face and throat in eager welcome when she sat down. Then he welcomed Jondalar.

"He's not used to so many people," Ayla said.

When he went back to Ayla, she held his head between her hands and looked into his shining eyes. "What's the matter, Wolf? A lot of strangers to get used to? I know how you feel."

"They won't be strangers for long, Ayla," Jondalar said. "Everyone already loves you."

"Except Marona and her friends," Ayla said, sitting up and loosening the ties of the soft leather top that was meant to be winter underwear for boys.

He was still disturbed over the way Marona had treated her, and so was she, it seemed. He wished that she hadn't had to be put through such an ordeal, especially her first day here. He wanted her to be happy with his people. She would soon be one of them. But he was proud of the way she had handled it.

"You were wonderful. The way you put Marona in her place. Everyone thought so," he said.

"Why did those women want people to laugh at me? They don't know me, and they didn't even try to get acquainted."

"It's my fault, Ayla," Jondalar said, stopping in the middle of unlacing the ties around the upper portion of his footwear that was wrapped around the calf of one leg. "Marona had every right to expect me to be there for the Matrimonial that summer. I left without explanations. She must have been terribly hurt. How would you feel if you and everyone you knew expected you to mate someone who didn't show up?"

"I would be very unhappy, and angry at you, but I hope I wouldn't try to hurt someone I didn't know," Ayla said, loosening the waist ties of her leggings. "When they said they wanted to fix my hair, it made me think of Deegie, but I combed my own hair when I looked in the reflector and saw what they did. I thought you told me the Zelandonii were people who believed in courtesy and hospitality."

"They do," he said. "Most of them."

"But not everyone. Not your former women friends. Maybe you should tell me who else I should watch out for," Ayla said.

"Ayla, don't let Marona color your opinion about everyone else. Couldn't you tell how much most people liked you? Give them a chance."

"What about the ones who tease orphan boys and turn them into Brouds?"

"Most people are not like that, Ayla," he said, looking at her with a troubled expression.

She exhaled a long sigh. "No, you're right. Your mother is not like that, or your sister, or the rest of your kin. Even Brukeval was very nice to me. It's just that the last time I saw that expression was when Broud told Goov to put a death curse on me. I'm sorry, Jondalar. I'm just tired." Suddenly she reached for him, buried her face in his neck, and let out a sob. "I wanted to make a good impression on your people, and make new friends, but those women didn't want to be friends. They just pretended they did."

"You did make a good impression, Ayla. You couldn't have made a better one. Marona always did have a temper, but I was sure she would find someone else while I was gone. She is very attractive, everyone always said she was the Beauty of the Bunch, the most desirable woman at every Summer Meeting. I guess that's why everyone expected us to mate," he said.

"Because you were the most handsome and she was the most beautiful?" Ayla asked.

"I suppose," he said, feeling himself flush and glad for the faint light. "I don't know why she isn't mated now."

"She said she was, but it didn't last."

"I know. But why didn't she find someone else? It's not like she suddenly forgot how to Pleasure a man, or became less attractive and desirable."

"Maybe she did, Jondalar. If you didn't want her, maybe other men decided to look again. A woman who is willing to hurt someone she doesn't even know may be less attractive than you think," Ayla said as she pulled the leggings off one leg.

Jondalar frowned. "I hope it's not my fault. It's bad enough that I left her in such a predicament. I would hate to think I made it impossible for her to find another mate."

Ayla looked at him quizzically. "Why would you think that?"

"Didn't you say that maybe if I didn't want her, other men . . ."

"Other men might look again. If they didn't like what they saw, how is that your fault?"

"Well . . . ah . . ."

"You can blame yourself for leaving without explaining. I'm sure she was hurt and embarrassed. But she has had five years to find someone else, and you said she is considered very desirable. If she couldn't find someone else, it's not your fault, Jondalar," Ayla said.

Jondalar paused, then nodded. "You're right," he said, and continued removing his clothing. "Let's go to sleep. Things will look better in the morning."

As she crawled into her warm and comfortable sleeping furs, Ayla had another thought. "If Marona is so good at 'Pleasuring,' I wonder why she doesn't have any children?"

Jondalar chuckled. "I hope you are right about Doni's Gift making children. It would be like two Gifts . . ." He stopped as he was lifting his side of the covers. "But you're right! She doesn't have any children."

"Don't hold the cover up like that! It's cold!" she said in a loud whisper.

He quickly got into the sleeping roll and snuggled his naked body next to hers. "That could be the reason she never mated," he continued, "or at least part of it. When a man decides to mate, he usually wants a woman who can bring children to his hearth. A woman can have children, and stay at her mother's hearth, or even make her own hearth, but the only way a man can have children at his hearth is to mate a woman so she can bring her children to it. If Marona mated and didn't have any children, it could make her less desirable."

"That would be a shame," Ayla said, feeling a sudden stab of empathy. She knew how much she wanted children. She had wanted a baby of her own from the time she watched Iza give birth to Uba, and she was sure that it was Broud's hatred that had given her one. It was his hatred that had caused him to force her, and if he hadn't forced her, no new life would have started growing inside her.

She didn't know it at the time, of course, but looking closely at her son had made her understand. Brun's clan had never seen a child like hers, and since her son didn't look quite like her—like the Others—they thought he was a deformed child of the Clan; but she could see he was a mixture. He had some of her characteristics and some of theirs, and with a sudden insight, she had realized that when a man put his organ in that place where babies came from, somehow it made new life start. It wasn't what the Clan believed, and it wasn't what Jondalar's people or any of the Others believed, but Ayla was convinced it was true.

Lying next to Jondalar, knowing she was carrying his baby inside her, Ayla felt a pang of pity and sorrow for the woman who had lost him and, perhaps, could not have children. Could she really blame Marona for being upset? How would she feel if she lost Jondalar? Tears threatened at the thought, and a flush of warmth at her good fortune washed over her.

It was a nasty trick, though, and it could have turned out far worse than it did. Ayla couldn't help getting angry, and she hadn't known what they would do when she decided to face them all down. They all might have turned on her. She might feel sympathy for Marona, but she didn't have to like her. And then there was Brukeval. His Clan look had made her feel friendly toward him, but now she was wary.

Jondalar held her until he thought she was asleep, trying to stay awake until he was sure. Then he closed his eyes and slept, too. But

Ayla woke up in the middle of the night, feeling a pressure and needing to relieve herself. Wolf silently followed her to the night basket near the entrance. When she got back into bed, he curled up next to her. She felt grateful for the warmth and protection of the wolf on one side and the man on the other, but it was a long time before she fell asleep again.

8

Ayla slept late. When she sat up and looked around, Jondalar was gone, and Wolf, too. She was alone in the dwelling, but someone had left a full waterbag and a closely woven, watertight basin so she could freshen herself. A carved wooden cup nearby held a liquid. It smelled like mint tea, cold, but she was in no mood to drink anything at the moment.

She got up to use the large basket that was beside the door to relieve herself—she definitely noticed an increased frequency of need. Then she grabbed her amulet and quickly pulled it off to get it out of the way before she used the basin, not to wash herself, but to hold the results of her queasy stomach. Her nausea seemed worse than usual this morning. Laramar's barma, she thought. Morning-after sickness along with morning sickness. I think I'll forgo the drink from now on. It's probably not good for me right now anyway, or the baby.

When she had emptied her stomach, she used the mint tea to rinse out her mouth. She noticed that someone had placed the bundle of clean but stained clothes she had originally planned to wear the night before near her sleeping furs. As she put them on, she recalled leaving them just inside the entrance. She did intend to keep the outfit Marona had given her, partly because she was determined to wear the clothing again on principle, but also because it was comfortable and she really couldn't see anything wrong with wearing it. Not today, though.

She tied on the sturdy waist thong that she had worn while traveling, adjusted the knife sheath into its comfortably familiar place and arranged the rest of the dangling implements and pouches, and slipped her amulet bag back over her head. She picked up the smelly basin and carried it out with her, but she left it near the entrance, not quite sure where to dispose of its contents, and went to look for someone to ask. A woman with a child, who was approaching the dwelling, greeted her. From somewhere in the depths of her memory, Ayla came up with a name.

"Pleasant day to you . . . Ramara. Is this your son?"

"Yes. Robenan wants to play with Jaradal, and I was looking for Proleva. She wasn't at home, and I wondered if they were here."

"No one is in the dwelling. When I got up, everyone was gone. I don't know where they are. I'm feeling very lazy this morning. I slept rather late," Ayla said.

"Most people did," Ramara said. "Not many people felt like getting up early after the celebration last night. Laramar makes a potent drink. It's what he's known for—the only thing he's known for."

Ayla detected a tone of disdain in the woman's comments. It made her feel a little hesitation about asking Ramara where there was an appropriate place to dispose of her morning mess, but there was no one else nearby, and she didn't want to leave it.

"Ramara . . . I wonder if I could ask you, where can I . . . get rid of some . . . waste?"

The woman looked puzzled for a moment, then glanced in the direction that Ayla had inadvertently looked, and smiled. "You want the toilet trenches, I think. See over there, toward the eastern edge of the terrace, not out front where the signal fires are lit, but toward the back. There's a path."

"Yes, I see it," Ayla said.

"It goes uphill," Ramara continued. "Follow that a little way and you will come to a split. The left trail is steeper. It continues up and will take you to the top of this cliff. But take the right path. It curves up around the side until you can see Wood River below. A little beyond is a level open field with several trenches—you'll smell it before you get there," Ramara said. "It has been a while since we dusted it, and you can tell."

Ayla shook her head. "Dusted it?"

"Sprinkled it with cooked cliff dust. We do it all the time, but I don't suppose all people do," Ramara said, bending over and picking up Robenan, who was getting restless.

"How do you cook cliff dust? And why?" Ayla asked.

"How you do it is to start with cliff rock, pound it into dust, and heat it in a hot fire—we use the signal fire hearth—then strew it in the trenches. Why is because it takes away a lot of the smell, or covers it up. But when you pass water or add liquid, the dust tends to get hard again, and when the trenches fill up with waste and hardened rock dust, you have to dig new ones, which is a lot of work. So we don't like to dust them too often. But they need it now. We have a big Cave, and the trenches get used a lot. Just follow the path. You shouldn't have any trouble locating them."

"I'm sure I'll find them. Thank you, Ramara," Ayla said as the woman left.

She started to pick up the bowl, had another thought, and ducked inside to get the waterbag so she could rinse out the woven basin. Then she picked up the smelly thing and started for the path. Gathering and storing food for such a large Cave of people is a lot of work, she thought as she headed along the trail, but so is taking care of the waste. Brun's clan just went outside, the women in one place, the men in another, and they changed their places every so often. Ayla thought about the process Ramara had explained and was intrigued.

The heating, or calcining, of limestone to get quicklime and using it to decrease the smell of waste products was not a practice she was familiar with, but for people who lived in limestone cliffs and used fire continuously, quicklime was a natural by-product. After cleaning a hearth of ashes, which would invariably include the accidentally accumulated lime, and dumping them on a pile of other waste materials, it wouldn't take long for the deodorizing effect to be noticed.

With so many people living in one place, more or less permanently except during the summer when various groups of them were gone for periods of time, there were many tasks that required the effort and cooperation of the entire community, such as digging toilet trenches or, as she had just learned, roasting the limestone cliff rocks to make quicklime.

The sun was near its zenith before Ayla returned from the trench field. She found a sunny place near the back path to dry and air out the woven bowl, then decided to check on the horses and refill the waterbag at the same time. Several people greeted her when she reached the front terrace, some of whose names she recalled, but not all. She smiled and nodded in return, but felt a trifle embarrassed about those she couldn't remember. She took it as a failure of memory on her part and made a decision to learn who everyone was as soon as possible.

She remembered feeling the same way when members of Brun's clan let it be known that they thought she was somewhat slow because she couldn't remember as well as Clan youngsters. As a result, because she wanted to fit in with the people who had found and adopted her, she disciplined herself to remember what she was taught the first time it was explained. She didn't know that in the process of exercising her native intelligence to retain what she learned, she was training her own memorizing ability far beyond that which was normal for her own kind.

As time went on, she grew to understand that their memory worked differently from hers. Though she didn't fully understand what they were, she knew that people of the Clan had "memories" that she did not have, not in the same way. In a form of instinct that had evolved along a somewhat divergent track, the people of the Clan were born with most of the knowledge they would need to survive, information that over time had been assimilated into the genes of their individual ancestors in the same way that instinctive knowledge was acquired by any animal, including the human one.

Rather than having to learn and memorize, as Ayla did, Clan children only had to be "reminded" once in order to trigger their inherent racial memories. The people of the Clan knew a great deal about their ancient world and how to live in it, and once they learned something new, they never forgot; but unlike Ayla and her kind, they did not learn new things easily. Change was hard for them, but when the Others arrived in their land, they brought change with them.

Whinney and Racer were not where she had left them in the horse meadow, but were grazing farther up the valley, away from the more well-used area that was close to the confluence of Wood River with The River. When Whinney saw her, the mare dropped her head, flipped it up, and described a circle in the air with her nose. Then she arched her neck, lowered her head, and, with tail outstretched, ran toward the woman, eagerly happy to see her. Racer pranced alongside his dam with his neck proudly arched, ears forward and tail up, high-stepping toward her in a smooth-striding canter.

They nickered greetings. Ayla responded in kind and smiled. "What are you two so happy about?" she said, using Clan signs and the language of words she had invented for herself in her valley. It was the way she had talked to Whinney from the beginning, and the way she still talked to the horses. She knew they didn't entirely understand her, but they did recognize some of the words and certain of the signals, as well as the tone of voice that conveyed her delight in seeing them.

"You certainly are full of yourselves today. Do you know we've reached the end of our Journey and won't be traveling anymore?"

she continued. "Do you like this place? I hope so." She reached out to scratch the mare in the places she liked, and then the stallion, then she felt around Whinney's sides and belly, trying to determine if she was carrying a foal after her tryst with the stallion.

"It's too early to tell for sure, but I think you are going to have a baby, too, Whinney. Even I don't show that much yet and I've already missed my second moon time." She examined herself the same way she had checked out the mare, thinking, my waist is thicker, my belly is rounder, my breasts are sore and a little bigger. "And I get sick in the morning," she continued saying and signing, "but only a little when I first get up, not like before, when I was sick all the time. I don't think there's any doubt that I'm pregnant, but I'm feeling good right now. Good enough to go for a ride. How would you like a little exercise, Whinney?"

The horse flipped up her head again, as if in reply.

I wonder where Jondalar is? I think I'll look for him and see if he wants to ride, she said to herself. I'll get the riding blanket, too, it is more comfortable, but bareback for now.

With a practiced, fluid movement, she grabbed the end of Whinney's short, stand-up mane and leapt onto her back, then headed toward the abri. She directed the horse with the tension of her leg muscles, without thinking about it—after so long, it was second nature—but she let the mare go at her own pace and just rode. She heard Racer following behind, as he was accustomed to doing.

I wonder how long I'll be able to jump on like that? I'll need to step up on something to reach her back when I get big, Ayla thought, then she almost hugged herself with pleasure at the idea that she was going to have a baby. Her thoughts strayed back to the long Journey they had just completed, and to the day before. She had met so many people, it was hard to remember them all, but Jondalar was right: most people were not bad. I shouldn't let the few who are unpleasant—Marona, and Brukeval when he behaved like Broud—spoil good feelings toward the rest. I wonder why it's easier to remember the bad ones. Maybe because there aren't many.

The day was warm; the hot sun warmed even the steady wind. As Ayla neared a small tributary, not much more than a trickle, but quick and sparkling, she looked upstream and saw a little waterfall coming down the rock face. She felt thirsty and, remembering that she had wanted to fill the waterbag, turned toward the water glinting down the side of the cliff.

She got off her horse, and they all took a drink from the pool at the bottom of the falls, Ayla from cupped hands, then she filled the waterbag with the cold, fresh liquid. She sat there a while, feeling refreshed and still a bit indolent, picking up small pebbles and idly tossing them into the water. Her eyes scanned the unfamiliar terrain, unconsciously noting details. She picked up another stone, rolled it in her hand, feeling the texture, looking at it but not seeing it, then tossed it.

It took a while for the character of the stone to penetrate her consciousness. Then she scrambled around to find it again, and when she picked it up—or one like it—she looked at it more carefully. It was a small, grayish-gold nodule, with the sharp angles and flat sides of its inherent crystal structure. Suddenly she reached for the flint knife she carried in the sheath on her belt and struck the stone with the back of it. Sparks flew! She struck it again.

"This is a firestone!" she shouted aloud.

She hadn't seen any since she left her valley. She looked closely at the stones and pebbles on the ground in and near the streambed, and spied another piece of iron pyrite, and then another. She picked up several as her excitement grew.

She sat back on her heels, looking at her small pile of similar stones. There are firestones here! Now we won't have to be so careful with the ones we have, we can get more. She could hardly wait to show Jondalar.

She gathered them up and a few more that she noticed, then whistled for Whinney, who had strayed off toward a patch of succulent green. But just before she made ready to mount, she saw Jondalar striding in their direction, Wolf at his side.

"Jondalar!" she called out, running toward him. "Look what I found!" she said, holding out several of the pieces of iron pyrite as she ran. "Firestones! There are firestones around here. They're all over this stream!"

He hurried toward her, beaming a great smile, as much in response to her exuberant delight as for the remarkable find. "I didn't know they were so close, but then I never much paid attention to this kind of stone, I was always looking for flint. Show me where you found them."

She took him to the little pool at the foot of the waterfall, then trained her eyes on the rocks of the streambed and along the sides of the diminutive waterway. "Look!" she said triumphantly. "There's another one," pointing at a stone on the bank.

Jondalar knelt down and picked it up. "You're right! This will make a difference, Ayla. It could mean firestones for everybody. If they are here, there may be other places nearby that have them, too. No one even knows about them yet, I haven't had a chance to tell anyone."

"Folara knows, and Zelandoni," Ayla said.

"How do they know?"

"Remember the calming tea Zelandoni made for Willamar when you told him about your brother? I made Folara nervous when I used a firestone to start the fire that had gone out, so I promised her I'd show her how they worked. She told Zelandoni," Ayla said.

"So Zelandoni knows. Somehow she always ends up knowing about things first," Jondalar said. "But we'll have to come back and look for more, later. Right now, some people want to talk to you."

"About the Clan?" she guessed.

"Joharran came and got me this morning for a meeting, before I really wanted to get up, but I made him let you sleep. I've been talking about our meeting with Guban and Yorga. They're very interested, but it's hard for them to believe the Clan are people and not animals. Zelandoni has been analyzing some of the Elder Legends more closely—she's the one who knows about the history of the Zelandonii—trying to see if there are any hints about flatheads . . . the Clan . . . living around here before the Zelandonii. When Ramara said you were up, Joharran wanted me to get you," Jondalar said. "He's not the only one with a lot of questions."

Jondalar had brought Racer's rope halter with him, but the frisky young stallion balked a bit, still feeling playful. With some patience, and scratching of itchy places, the horse finally acquiesced. The man mounted and they started back through the open woodlands of the small valley.

Jondalar pulled up to ride beside Ayla and, after some hesitation, remarked, "Ramara said when she talked to you this morning, that she thought you were sick, perhaps not used to Laramar's barma. How are you feeling?"

It's going to be hard to keep secrets around here, Ayla thought. "I'm fine, Jondalar," she said.

"He does make a strong brew. You weren't feeling too well last night."

"I was tired last night," Ayla said. "And this morning, it was just a little sickness, because I'm going to have a baby." From his expression, she suspected he was concerned about more than her morning sickness.

"It was a full day. You met a lot of people."

"And I liked most of them," she said, looking at him with a little grin. "I'm just not used to so many at one time. It's like a whole Clan Gathering. I can't even remember everyone's name."

"You just met them. No one expects you to remember them all."

They dismounted in the horse meadow and left the horses at the foot of the path. As she glanced up, Ayla noticed the Falling Stone silhouetted against the clear sky, and for a moment, it seemed to emanate a strange glow; but when she blinked, it was gone. The sun is bright, she thought. I must have looked at it without shading my eyes.

Wolf appeared out of the high grass; he had followed them in a desultory way, exploring small holes and chasing interesting scents. When he saw Ayla standing still, blinking, he decided it was time to properly greet the alpha leader of his pack. The huge canine caught her off guard when he jumped up and put his paws on the front of her shoulders. She staggered a bit, but caught herself and braced to hold his weight as he licked her jaw and held it in his teeth.

"Good morning, Wolf!" she said, holding his shaggy ruff in both hands. "I think you're feeling full of yourself today, too. Just like the horses." He dropped down and followed her up the path, ignoring the gawks of those who had not seen that particular display of affection before, and the smirks of those who had and were enjoying the reaction. Ayla signaled him to stay with her.

She thought about stopping at Marthona's dwelling to leave the full waterbag, but Jondalar continued beyond the dwelling area and she walked with him. They passed by the work area toward the southwest end of the overhang. Ahead, Ayla saw several people standing and sitting near the remains of the previous night's bonfire.

"There you are!" Joharran said, getting up from a small block of limestone and coming toward them.

As they got closer, Ayla noticed a small fire burning at the edge of the large blackened ring. Nearby was a deep basket, which was filled with steaming liquid upon which floated bits of leaves and other vegetal material. It was coated with something dark, and her nose detected the scent of pine pitch, which had been used to keep it watertight.

Proleva ladled some into a cup. "Have some hot tea, Ayla," she said, extending the cup to her.

"Thank you," Ayla said, taking the cup. She took a drink. It was a nice blend of herbs, with just a hint of pine. She drank more, then realized that she would have preferred something solid. The liquid was making her stomach queasy again, and her head was aching. She noticed an unoccupied stone block and sat down, hoping her stomach would settle. Wolf lay down at her feet. She held the cup in her hand without drinking and wished she had brewed some of the special "morning after" drink she had developed for Talut, the Mamutoi headman of the Lion Camp.

Zelandoni looked at Ayla closely and thought she detected some familiar signs. "This might be an appropriate time to stop for a bite to eat. Are there any leftovers from last night?" she said to Proleva.

"That's a good idea," Marthona said. "It's after midday. Have you had anything to eat yet, Ayla?"

"No," she said, feeling rather grateful that someone thought to ask. "I slept very late, then I went to the trenches, and up Wood River Valley to check on the horses. I refilled this waterbag at a little creek." She held it up. "That's where Jondalar found me."

"Good. If you don't mind, we'll use it to make more tea, and I'll get someone to bring food for everyone," Proleva said as she headed toward the dwellings at a brisk pace.

Ayla glanced around to see who was at this meeting and immediately caught Willamar's eye. They exchanged smiles. He was talking to Marthona, Zelandoni, and Jondalar, whose back was to her at the moment. Joharran had turned his attention to Solaban and Rushemar, his close friends and advisers. Ayla recalled that Ramara, the woman with the little boy with whom she had spoken earlier, was Solaban's mate. She had met Rushemar's mate the night before, too. She closed her eyes to try to remember her name. Salova, that was it. Sitting still had helped; her nausea had quieted.

Of the others who were there, she remembered that the gray-haired man was the leader of a nearby Cave. Manvelar was his name. He was talking to another man, whom she did not think she had met. He glanced apprehensively at Wolf now and then. A tall, thin woman who carried herself with a great deal of authority was another Cave leader, Ayla recalled, but she could not remember her name. The man beside her had a tattoo similar to Zelandoni's, and Ayla guessed he was also a spiritual leader.

It occurred to her that this group of people were all leaders of one kind or another in this community. In the Clan, these people would be the ones with the highest status. Among the Mamutoi, they would be the equivalent of the Council of Sisters and Brothers. The Zelandonii did not have dual leadership of a sister and brother as headwoman-headman for each Camp as the Mamutoi did; instead some Zelandonii leaders were men and some were women.

Proleva was returning at the same brisk pace. Though she seemed to be responsible for providing food for the group—she had been the one they turned to when food was wanted, Ayla noticed—she was obviously not the one who would bring and serve it. She was returning to the meeting; she must have considered herself an active participant. It appeared that the leader's mate could be a leader, too.

In the Clan, all the people at this kind of meeting would be men. There were no women leaders; women had no status in their own right. Except for medicine women, a woman's status depended on the rank of her mate. How would they reconcile that if they ever visited each other? she wondered.

"Ramara and Salova and some others are organizing a meal for us," Proleva announced, nodding toward Solaban and Rushemar.

"Good," Joharran said, which seemed to be a signal that the meeting was back in session. Everyone stopped chatting with one another and looked at him. He turned to her. "Ayla was presented last night. Have all of you introduced yourselves?"

"I wasn't here last night," said the man who had been talking with the gray-haired leader.

"Then allow me to introduce you," Joharran said. As the man stepped forward, Ayla stood up, but signaled Wolf to stay back. "Ayla, this is Brameval, Leader of Little Valley, the Fourteenth Cave of the Zelandonii. Brameval, meet Ayla of the Lion Camp of the Mamutoi ..." Joharran paused for a moment, trying to bring to mind the rest of her unfamiliar names and ties. "Daughter of the Mammoth Hearth." That's enough, he thought.

Brameval repeated his name and his function as he held out his hands. "In the name of Doni, you are welcome," he said.

Ayla accepted his hands. "In the name of Mut, Great Mother of All, also known as Doni, I greet you," she said, smiling.

He had noticed the difference in the way she spoke before, and even more now, but he responded to her smile and held her hands a moment longer. "Little Valley is the best place to catch fish. The people of the Fourteenth Cave are known as the best fishers; we make very good fish traps. We are close neighbors, you must visit us soon."

"Thank you, I would like to visit. I like fish, and I like to catch them, but I don't know how to trap them. When I was young, I learned to catch fish with my hands." Ayla emphasized her comment by lifting hers, which were still held by Brameval.

"Now that, I would like to see," he said as he let go.

The woman leader stepped forward. "I would like to introduce our donier, the Zelandoni of River Place," she said. "He was not here last night, either." She glanced at Brameval, raised her eyebrows, and added, "The Eleventh Cave is known for making the rafts that are used to travel up and down The River. It's much easier to transport heavy loads on a raft than on the backs of people. If you are interested, you are welcome to come and visit."

"I would be most interested to learn about the way you make your floating river craft," Ayla said, trying to remember if they had been introduced and what her name was. "The Mamutoi make a kind of floating bowl out of thick hides fastened to a wooden frame, and use them to carry people and their things across rivers. On our way here, Jondalar and I made one to cross a large river, but the river was rough, and the small round boat was so light, it was hard to control. When we attached it to Whinney's pole drag, it was better."

"I don't understand 'winnies pole drag.' What does that mean?" the leader of the Eleventh Cave asked.

"Whinney is the name of one of the horses, Kareja," Jondalar said, getting up and coming forward. "The pole drag was devised by Ayla. She can tell you what it is."

Ayla described the conveyance and added, "With it Whinney could help me bring the animals I hunted back to my shelter. I'll show you sometime."

"When we reached the other side of that river," Jondalar added, "we decided to attach the bowl boat to the poles instead of the woven platform because we could put most of our things in it. That way, when we crossed rivers, the boat would float and nothing got wet, and attached to the poles, it was easier to control."

"Rafts can be a little hard to control, too," the woman leader said. "I think all watercraft must be hard to control."

"Some are easier than others. On my Journey, I stayed for a while with the Sharamudoi. They carve beautiful boats out of large tree trunks. The front and back come to points, and they use oars to steer them where they want to go. It takes practice, but the Ramudoi, the River People half of the Sharamudoi, are very good at it," Jondalar said.

"What are oars?"

"Oars look something like flattened spoons, and they use them to push the boat through the water. I helped to make one of their boats and learned to use oars."

"Do you think they would work better than the long poles we use to push the rafts through the water?"

"This talking about boats can be very interesting, Kareja," the man who had stepped forward said, interrupting. He was shorter than the woman and slight of build. "But I haven't been introduced yet. I think I'd better do it myself." Kareja flushed slightly, but made no comment. When Ayla heard her name, she recalled that they had been introduced.

"I am Zelandoni of the Eleventh Cave of the Zelandonii, also known as River Place. In the name of Doni, Great Earth Mother, I welcome you, Ayla of the Mamutoi, Daughter of the Mammoth Hearth," he said, holding out his hands.

"I greet you, Zelandoni of the Eleventh as One Who Serves She Who Is The Mother of All," Ayla said, grasping his hands. He had a powerful grip that belied his slight build, and she sensed not only his wiry strength, but an inner force and surety. She also detected something else in the way he moved that reminded her of some of the mamutii she had met at the Mamutoi Summer Meeting.

The old Mamut who had adopted her had spoken of those who carried the essence of both male and female in one body. They were thought to possess the power of both genders and were sometimes feared, but if they joined the ranks of Those Who Served The Mother, they were often believed to be especially powerful and were welcomed. As a result, he had explained, many men who found themselves drawn to men as a woman would be, or women who were attracted to women as a man, were drawn to the Mammoth Hearth. She wondered if the same was true with the zelandonia and, judging from the man who stood there, guessed it might be.

She noticed the tattoo above his temple again. Like Zelandoni Who Was First, it consisted of squares, some outlined, some colored in, but he had fewer and different ones were filled in, and some additional curved markings. It made her aware that everyone there, except for Jondalar and herself, had some kind of facial tattoo. The least conspicuous was Willamar's, the most ornate decorated the face of the woman leader, Kareja.

"Since Kareja has already bragged about the achievements of the Eleventh Cave," the donier added, turning to acknowledge the Cave's leader, "I will only add my invitation to you to visit, but I would like to ask a question. Are you also One Who Serves?"

Ayla frowned. "No," she said. "What makes you think so?"

"I have been listening to gossip." He smiled with his admission. "With your control over animals," he said, motioning toward the wolf, "many people think you must be. And I recall hearing about mammoth hunting people to the east. It was said that Those Who Serve eat only mammoth and they all live in one place, perhaps at one hearth. When you were introduced as 'of the Mammoth Hearth,' I wondered if any of that was true."

"Not quite," Ayla said, smiling. "It is true that among the Mammoth Hunters, Those Who Serve The Mother belong to the Mammoth Hearth, but that doesn't mean they all live together. It is a name, like the 'zelandonia.' There are many hearths—the Lion Hearth, the Fox Hearth, the Crane Hearth. They indicate the . . . line a person is affiliated with. One is usually born to a hearth, but can also be adopted. There are many different hearths at one Camp, which is named after the founder's hearth. Mine was called the Lion Camp because Talut was of the Lion Hearth, and he was the headman. His sister, Tulie, was headwoman—every Camp has both a sister and brother as leaders."

Everyone was listening with interest. Learning how other people organized themselves and lived was fascinating to people who primarily knew only their own way.

"Mamutoi means 'the mammoth hunters' in their language, or perhaps 'the children of the Mother who hunt mammoths,' since they also honor the Mother," Ayla continued, trying to make it clear. "The mammoth is especially sacred to them. That's why the Mammoth Hearth is reserved for Those Who Serve. People usually choose the Mammoth Hearth, or feel they are chosen, but I was adopted by the old Mamut of the Lion Camp, so I am a 'Daughter of the Mammoth Hearth.' If I were One Who Served, I would say 'Chosen by the Mammoth Hearth' or 'Called to the Mammoth Hearth.'"

The two Zelandonia were poised to ask more questions, but

Joharran interrupted. Although he was also intrigued, he was more interested at the moment in the people who had raised Ayla than the ones who had adopted her. "I'd like to hear more about the Mamutoi," he said, "but Jondalar has been telling us some interesting things about those flatheads you met on your trip back. If what he says is true, we need to start thinking about flatheads in a completely different way. To be honest, I'm afraid they may pose a greater threat than we ever thought."

"Why a threat?" Ayla asked, immediately on her guard.

"From what Jondalar tells me, they are ... thinking people. We have always thought of flatheads as animals little different from cave bears, perhaps even related to them; a smaller, somewhat more intelligent type, but an animal," Joharran said.

"We know some of the hollows and caves around here were once cave bear dens," Marthona put in. "And Zelandoni was telling us that some of the Elder Legends and Histories say that sometimes cave bears were killed or chased away so that the First People could have homes. If some of those 'cave bears' were flatheads ... well ... if they are intelligent people, anything is possible."

"If they are people, and we have treated them like animals, hostile animals," Joharran paused, "I have to say that, if I were in their place, I would be considering some way to retaliate. I would have tried to get back at us a long time ago. I think we need to be aware of the possibility that they may."

Ayla relaxed. Joharran had stated his position well. She could understand why he thought they might be a threat. He might even be right.

"I wonder if that's why people have always insisted that flatheads are animals," Willamar said. "Killing animals is one thing, if it's necessary for food or shelter, but if they were people, even a strange kind of people, that's something else. No one wants to think that their ancestors killed people and stole their homes, but if you convince yourself that they are animals, you can live with it."

Ayla thought that was a surprising insight, but Willamar had made wise and intelligent comments before. She was beginning to understand why Jondalar had always spoken of him with such affection and respect. He was an exceptional man.

"Bad feelings can lie dormant for a long time," Marthona said, "many generations, but if they have Histories and Legends, it gives them long memories, and trouble can flare up. Since you know so much more about them, I wonder if we could ask you some questions, Ayla."

She wondered if she should tell them that the Clan did have stories and legends, but they didn't need them to remember their history. They were born with long memories.

"It might be smart to attempt to make contact with them in a different way than we have in the past," Joharran continued. "Perhaps we can avoid problems before they materialize. We might consider sending a delegation to meet with them, perhaps to discuss trading."

"What do you think, Ayla?" Willamar said. "Would they be interested in trading with us?"

Ayla frowned in thought. "I don't know. The Clan I knew were aware of people like us. To them, we were the Others, but they avoided contact. For the most part, the small clan I grew up with didn't think about the Others most of the time. They knew I was one and not Clan, but I was a child, and a girl child at that. I was of little significance to Brun and the men, at least when I was young," she said. "But Brun's clan didn't live near the Others. I think that was lucky for me. Until they found me, no one in his clan had ever seen a young one of the Others; some had never seen an adult, even from a distance. They were willing to take me in and take care of me, but I'm not sure how they would have felt if they had been chased away from their homes, or harassed by a pack of rough young men."

"But Jondalar told us some people had contacted the ones you met on the way about trading," Willamar said. "If other people trade with them, why can't we?"

"Doesn't that depend on whether they really are people and not animals related to cave bears?" Brameval interjected.

"They are people, Brameval," Jondalar said. "If you ever had close contact with one, you'd know. And they're smart. I encountered more than the couple that Ayla and I met when I was on my Journey. Remind me to tell you some stories, later."

"You say you were actually raised by them, Ayla," Manvelar said. "Tell us something about them. What kind of people are they?" The gray-haired man seemed reasonable, not one to jump to conclusions without learning as much as he could.

Ayla nodded, but paused for a moment to think before she replied. "It's interesting that you think they are related to cave bears. There is a strange kind of truth in that; the Clan believe they are, too. They even live with one, sometimes."

"Hhmmmf!" Brameval snorted, as if to say, "I told you!"

Ayla directed her comments to him. "The Clan venerates Ursus, the Spirit of the Cave Bear, much the way the Others honor the Great Earth Mother. They refer to themselves as the Clan of the Cave Bear. When the Clan has their big Gathering—like a Summer Meeting, but not every year—they have a very sacred ceremony for the Cave Bear Spirit. Long before the Clan Gathering, the host clan captures a cave bear cub, who lives with them in their cave. They feed him and raise him as one of their own children, at least until he gets too big, then they build a place for him that will keep him from running away, but they still feed and pamper him.

"During the Clan Gathering," Ayla continued, "the men compete to see who will have the honor of sending Ursus to the World of the Spirits to speak for the Clan and carry their messages. The three men who have won the most competitions are chosen—it takes at least that many to send a full-grown cave bear to the next world. While it is an honor to be chosen, it is very dangerous. Often the cave bear takes one or more of the men with him to the Spirit World."

"So they communicate with the world of the spirits," said Zelandoni of the Eleventh.

"And they bury their dead with red ochre," Jondalar said, knowing his words carried a deep meaning to the man.

"This information will take some time to comprehend," the leader of the Eleventh Cave said, "and a great deal of consideration. It will mean many changes."

"You're right, of course, Kareja," said the First Among Those Who Served.

"Right now, we don't need much thought to consider stopping for a meal," said Proleva, glancing back toward the eastern end of the terrace. Everyone turned and looked in the same direction. A procession of people was coming with platters and containers of food.

The people at the meeting broke into small groups to eat. Manvelar sat beside Ayla, opposite Jondalar, with his dish of food. He had made a point of introducing himself the night before, but with the throng surrounding the newcomer, he hadn't tried to get better acquainted. His Cave was nearby, and he knew he'd have time later. "You've had several invitations, but let me add another," he said. "You must come and visit Two Rivers Rock; the Third Cave of the Zelandonii are close neighbors."

"If the Fourteenth Cave are known as the best fishers, and the Eleventh Cave for making rafts, what is the Third Cave known for?" Ayla asked.

Jondalar answered for him. "Hunting."

"Doesn't everyone hunt?" she asked.

"Of course, that's why they don't brag about it, just because everyone hunts. Some individual hunters from other Caves like to talk about their own prowess, and they may be good, but as a group, the Third Cave are the best hunters."

Manvelar smiled. "We do brag about it, in our own way, but I think the reason we have become such good hunters is our location. Our shelter is high above the confluence of two rivers, with wide grassy valleys. This one," he said, waving a hand that held a meaty bone toward The River, "and another called Grass River. Most of the animals we hunt migrate through these two valleys, and we've got the best place from which to watch for them at any time of the year. We've learned to judge when certain ones will likely appear and we usually let everyone else know, but we are often the first ones to hunt them."

"That may be true, Manvelar, but all the hunters of the Third Cave are good, not just one or two. They work hard to perfect their skill. All of them," Jondalar said. "Ayla understands that. She loves to hunt, she is amazing with a sling, but wait until we show you the new spear-thrower we developed. It throws a spear so much farther and faster, you won't believe it. Ayla is more accurate, and I can throw a little farther, but anyone can hit an animal from twice or even three times as far as you can with a spear thrown by hand."

"I would like to see that!" Manvelar said. "Joharran wants to arrange a hunt soon to add provisions for the Summer Meeting. That may be a good time to demonstrate this new weapon, Jondalar." Then, turning to Ayla, he added, "Both of you are joining the hunt, aren't you?"

"Yes, I'd like to." She paused to take a bite, then, looking at the men, she said, "I have a question. Why are Caves numbered the way they are? Is there some order or meaning to the numbers?"

"The oldest Caves have the lowest numbers," Jondalar said. "They were established first. The Third Cave was established before the Ninth, and the Ninth before the Eleventh or Fourteenth. There is no First Cave anymore. The oldest is the Second Cave of the Zelandonii, which isn't too far from here. Manvelar's Cave is the next oldest. It was established by the First People."

"When you taught me the counting words, Jondalar, they were always said in a particular order," Ayla said. "This is the Ninth Cave, and Manvelar, yours is the Third Cave. Where are the people from the Caves with numbers in between?"

The gray-haired man smiled. Ayla had picked the right person to ask for information about the Zelandonii. Manvelar had a long-standing interest in the history of his people, and had acquired quite a store of information from various members of the zelandonia, traveling Story-Tellers, and people who had heard tales that were passed down from their ancestors. Members of the zelandonia, including Zelandoni herself, sometimes asked him questions.

"Over the years since the First People established the founding Caves, many things have changed," Manvelar said. "People have moved or found mates in other Caves. Some Caves grew smaller, some bigger."

"Like the Ninth Cave, some grew unusually large," Jondalar added.

"The Histories tell of sickness that sometimes claimed many people, or bad years when people starved." Manvelar picked up the story again. "When Caves get small, sometimes two or more join together. The combined Cave usually takes the lowest number, but not always. When Caves get too big for the size of their shelter, they may break off to form a new Cave, often close by. Some time ago a group from the Second Cave broke off and moved to the other side of their valley. They are called the Seventh Cave because at that time there was a Third, Fourth, Fifth, and Sixth in existence. There is still a Third, of course, and a Fifth, up north, but no longer a Fourth or Sixth."

Ayla was delighted to learn more about the Zelandonii and smiled her gratitude for the explanation. The three of them sat companionably together for a while, eating quietly. Then Ayla had another question. "Are all Caves known for something special, like fishing or hunting or raft-making?"

"Most of them," Jondalar said.

"What is the Ninth Cave known for?"

"Their artists and craftspeople," Manvelar answered for him. "All Caves have skilled artisans, but the Ninth Cave has the best. That's partly why they are so large. It is not just the children born, but anyone who wants the best training in anything from carving to toolmaking wants to move to the Ninth Cave."

"That's mainly because of Down River," Jondalar said.

"What is 'Down River'?" Ayla asked.

"It's the next shelter just downriver from here," Jondalar explained. "It's not the home of an organized Cave, although you might think so from the number of people who are usually there. It's the place where people go to work on their projects, and to talk to other people about them. I'll take you there, maybe after this meeting—if we get away before dark."

After everyone had eaten, including the servers, the children of several of the people, and Wolf, they relaxed with cups and bowls of hot tea. Ayla was feeling much better. Her nausea was gone and so was her headache, but she noticed her increased need to pass water again. As the ones who had brought the meal were leaving with the largely empty serving dishes, Ayla noticed that Marthona was standing alone for a moment and walked over to her.

"Is there a place to pass water nearby?" she asked quietly. "Or do we have to go back to the dwellings?"

Marthona smiled. "I was thinking about the same thing. There's a path to The River near the Standing Stone, a little steep near the top, but it goes to a place near the bank that is used mainly by the women. I'll show you." Wolf followed them, watched Ayla for a while, then discovered a scent more interesting and left to explore more of the bank of The River. On the way back, they passed Kareja heading down the path. They nodded to each other in mutual understanding.

After everything was cleared away, and Joharran made sure everyone was there, he stood up. It seemed to be a signal to resume discussions. Everyone looked at the leader of the Ninth Cave.

"Ayla," Joharran said, "while we were eating, Kareja brought up a question. Jondalar says that he can communicate with flatheads, the Clan, as you call them, but not like you can. Do you know their language as well as he says?"

"Yes, I know the language," Ayla said. "I was raised by them. I didn't know any other language until I met Jondalar. At one time I must have, when I was very young, before I lost my own people, but I didn't remember it at all."

"But the place where you grew up was very far from here, a year's travel, isn't that right?" Joharran continued. Ayla nodded. "The language of people who live far away is not the same as ours. I cannot understand you when you and Jondalar speak Mamutoi. Even the

Losadunai, who live much closer, have a different language. Some words are similar, and I can grasp a little, but I can't communicate beyond simple concepts. I understand the language of these Clan people is not the same as ours, but how can you, who come from so far away, understand the language of the ones who live around here?"

"I understand your doubt," Ayla said. "I wasn't sure myself when we first met Guban and Yorga if I would be able to communicate with them. But language with words is different from the kind of language they use, not only because of the signs and signals, but because they have two languages."

"What do you mean, two languages?" asked Zelandoni Who Was First.

"They have an ordinary common language that each clan uses every day among themselves," Ayla explained. "Although they use hand signs and gestures for the most part, including postures and expressions, they also use some words, even though they can't make all of the sounds that the Others can. Some clans speak words more than others. The common everyday language and words of Guban and Yorga were different from those of my clan, and I couldn't understand them. But the Clan also has a special, formal language that they use to speak to the World of the Spirits, and to communicate with people from other clans who have a different ordinary language. It is very ancient and no words are used, except some personal names. That was the language I used."

"Let me make sure I understand this," Zelandoni said. "This Clan—we're talking about flatheads here—not only have one language, they have two, and one of them is mutually intelligible with any other flathead, even someone who lives a year's Journey away?"

"It is rather hard to believe, isn't it?" Jondalar said with a wide grin. "But it is true."

Zelandoni shook her head. The rest looked just as skeptical.

"It's a very ancient language, and people of the Clan have very long memories," Ayla tried to explain. "They don't forget anything."

"I find it difficult to believe that they can really communicate much with only gestures and signs, anyway," Brameval said.

"I feel the same way," Kareja said. "As Joharran said about the Losadunai and the Zelandonii comprehending each other's languages, perhaps we are talking about only simple concepts."

"You gave a little demonstration in my home yesterday," Marthona said. "Could you show all of us?"

"And if, as you say, Jondalar knows some of this language, perhaps he could translate for us," Manvelar added. Everyone nodded.

Ayla stood up. She paused, gathering her thoughts. Then, with the motions of the ancient formal language, she signed, "This woman would greet the man Manvelar." She spoke the name aloud, but her speech mannerism, her peculiar accent, was much stronger when she said it.

Jondalar translated. "Greetings Manvelar."

"This woman would greet the man Joharran," Ayla continued.

"And you, too, Joharran," Jondalar said. They went through a few more simple statements, but he could tell they were not getting across the full extent of the comprehensive, if silent, language. He knew she could say more, but he couldn't translate the full complexity.

"You're just giving me basic signs, aren't you, Ayla."

"I don't think you can translate more than basic signs, Jondalar. That's all I taught the Lion Camp and you. Just enough so you could communicate with Rydag. I'm afraid the full language wouldn't mean much to you," Ayla said.

"When you showed us, Ayla," Marthona said, "you did your own translation. I think that would be more clear."

"Yes, why don't you show Brameval and the others that way, by using both languages," Jondalar suggested.

"All right, but what should I say?"

"Why don't you tell us about your life with them," Zelandoni suggested. "Do you remember when they first took you in?"

Jondalar smiled at the big woman. That was a good idea. It would not only show everyone the language, it would also show the compassion of the people, that they were willing to take in an orphan child, even a strange orphan child. It would show that the Clan treated one of ours better than we treated them.

Ayla stood for a moment, gathering her thoughts; then in both the formal sign language of the Clan and the words of the Zelandonii, she began. "I don't recall much of the beginning, but Iza often told me how she found me. They were looking for a new cave. There had been an earthquake, probably the one I still dream about. It destroyed their home, falling stones inside the cave killed several of Brun's clan, and many things were damaged. They buried their dead, then left. Even if the cave was still there, it was unlucky to stay. The spirits of their totems were unhappy there and wanted them to leave. They were traveling quickly. They needed a new home soon, not just for themselves, but because their protective Spirits needed a place where they would be content."

Though Ayla kept her voice neutral and told the story with signs and movements, the people were already caught up in her tale. To them, totems were an aspect of the Mother and they understood the disasters that the Great Earth Mother could wreak when she was not happy.

"Iza told me they were following a river when they saw carrion birds circling overhead. Brun and Grod saw me first, but passed by. They were looking for food, and would have been glad if the carrion birds had spotted prey killed by a hunting animal. They might be able to keep a four-legged hunter away long enough to take some of the meat. They thought I was dead, but they don't eat people, not even one of the Others."

There was a grace and easy flow to Ayla's movements as she spoke. She made the signs and gestures with practiced ease. "When Iza saw me lying on the ground beside the river, she stopped to look. She was a medicine woman and interested. My leg had been clawed by a big cat, she thought probably a cave lion, and the wound had festered. At first, she thought I was dead, too, but then she heard me moan, so she examined me closer and discovered that I was breathing. She asked Brun, the leader, who was her sibling, if she could take me with them. He did not forbid it."

"Good!" "Yes!" came responses from the audience. Jondalar smiled to himself.

"Iza was pregnant at the time, but she picked me up and carried me until they made camp for the night. She wasn't sure if her medicine would work on the Others, but she knew of a case where it had before, so she decided to try. She made a poultice to draw out the infection. She carried me all the next day, too. I remember the first time I woke up and saw her face, I screamed, but she held me and comforted me. By the third day, I was able to walk a little, and by then, Iza decided I was meant to be her child."

Ayla stopped there. There was a profound silence. It was a moving story.

"How old were you?" Proleva finally asked.

"Iza told me later that she thought I could count about five years at the time. I was perhaps the age of Jaradal, or Robenan," she added, looking at Solaban.

"Did you say all that with the gestures, too?" Solaban asked. "Can they really say so much without words?"

"There is not a sign for every word I said, but they would have understood essentially the same story. Their language is more than just the motions of the hands. It is everything; even a flicker of an eyelid or a nod of the head can convey meaning."

"But with that kind of language," Jondalar added, "they cannot tell a lie. If they tried, an expression or posture would give them away. When I first met her, Ayla didn't even have a concept for saying something that is not true. She even had trouble understanding what I meant. Though she understands now, she still can't do it. Ayla can't lie. She never learned how. That's how she was raised."

"There may be more merit than one would realize in speaking without words," Marthona said quietly.

"I think it is obvious from watching her that this kind of sign language is a natural way of communicating for Ayla," Zelandoni said, thinking to herself that her motions would not be so smooth and graceful if she was faking. And what reason would she have to lie about it—could it be true that she can't tell a lie? She wasn't entirely convinced, but Jondalar's arguments had been persuasive.

"Tell us more about your life with them," Zelandoni of the Eleventh said. "You don't have to continue with the signs, unless you want to. It is beautiful to watch, but I think you have made your point. You said they buried their dead. I'd like to know more of their burial practices."

"Yes, they bury their dead. I was there when Iza died."

The discussion continued all afternoon. Ayla gave a moving account of the ceremony and ritual of the burial, then told them more about her childhood. People asked many questions, interrupting often to discuss and request more information.

Joharran finally noticed it was getting dark. "I think Ayla is tired, and we're all hungry again," he said. "Before we break up, I think we should talk about a hunt before the Summer Meeting."

"Jondalar was telling me they have a new hunting weapon to show us," Manvelar said. "Perhaps tomorrow or the next day would be a good day to hunt. That would give the Third Cave time to develop some plans to offer about where we should go."

"Good," Joharran said, "but now, Proleva has arranged another meal for us, if anyone is hungry."

The meeting had been intense and fascinating, but people were glad to be up and moving around. As they walked back toward the dwellings, Ayla thought about the meeting, and all the questions. She knew she had answered everything truthfully, but she also knew she hadn't volunteered much beyond what was asked. In particular, she had avoided any mention of her son. She knew that to the Zelandonii he would be thought of as an abomination, and though she could not lie, she could refrain from mentioning.

9

It was dark inside when they reached Marthona's dwelling. Folara had gone to stay with her friend Ramila, rather than wait alone for her mother, Willamar, Ayla, and Jondalar to return. They had seen her during the evening meal, but the discussions had continued on a more informal basis, and the young woman knew they were not likely to return early.

Not even a faint glow from dying coals in the fireplace could be seen when they pushed aside the entry drape.

"I'll get a lamp or a torch and get a fire start from Joharran's," Willamar said.

"I don't see any light there," Marthona said. "He was at the meeting and so was Proleva. They probably went to get Jaradal."

"How about Solaban's?" Willamar said.

"I don't see a light there, either. Ramara must be gone. Solaban was at the meeting all day, too."

"You don't have to bother getting fire," Ayla said. "I have the firestones I found today. I can have one going in a heartbeat."

"What are firestones?" Marthona and Willamar said almost in unison.

"We'll show you," Jondalar said. Though she couldn't see his face, Ayla knew he was grinning.

"I will need tinder," Ayla said. "Something to catch a spark."

"There is tinder by the hearth, but I'm not sure I can find the fireplace without stumbling over something," Marthona said. "We can get a fire start from someone."

"You'd have to go in and find a lamp or a torch in the dark, wouldn't you?" Jondalar said.

"We can borrow a lamp," Marthona said.

"I think I can make enough spark lights to find the fireplace," Ayla said, taking out her flint knife and feeling in her pouch for the firestones she had found.

She entered the dwelling first, holding the nodule of iron pyrite in front of her in her left hand and her knife in the right. For a moment she felt as though she were entering a deep cave. The darkness was so intense, it seemed to push back at her. A quick chill shook her. She struck the firestone with the back of her flint blade.

"Ooohhh," Ayla heard Marthona say as a bright spark lit up the charcoal black interior for an instant and then died.

"How did you do that?" Willamar asked. "Can you do it again?"

"I did it with my flint knife and a firestone," Ayla said, and struck the two together to show that she could, indeed, do it again. The long-lived spark allowed her to take a few steps toward the fireplace. She struck it again and moved a little closer to it. When she reached the cooking hearth, she saw that Marthona had found her way there, too.

"I keep my tinder here, on this side," Marthona said. "Where do you want it?"

"Near the edge here is fine," Ayla said. She felt Marthona's hand in the dark, and the soft, dry bits of some kind of fibrous substance it held. Ayla put the tinder on the ground, bent over close, and struck the firestone again. This time the spark jumped to the small pile of quick-burning material and made a faint red glow. Ayla blew at it gently and was rewarded with a little flame. She piled a bit more tinder on it. Marthona was ready with some small bits of wood, and then bigger kindling, and in what seemed hardly more than a heartbeat, a warm fire lit the inside of the dwelling.

"Now, I want to see this firestone," Willamar said after lighting a few lamps.

Ayla gave him the small nodule of iron pyrite. Willamar studied the grayish-gold stone, turning it over to see all sides. "It just looks like a stone, with an interesting color. How do you make fire with it?" he asked. "Can anyone do it?"

"Yes, anyone can," Jondalar said. "I'll show you. Can I have some of that tinder, mother?"

While Marthona got more tinder, Jondalar went to his traveling pack for his fire-making kit and removed the flint striker and firestone. Then he made a small pile of the soft fibers—probably cattail or fireweed fibers mixed with a bit of pitch and crumbled dry rotted wood from a dead tree, he thought. It was the tinder his mother had always preferred. Bending close to the quick-catching tinder, Jondalar struck the flint and iron pyrite together. The spark, not as easy to see next to the burning fire, still landed on the pile of starting material, singed it brown, and sent up a whiff of smoke. Jondalar blew up a small flame and added more fuel. Soon a second fire was burning in the ash-darkened circle surrounded by stones that was the hearth of the dwelling.

"Can I try it?" Marthona said.

"It does take a little practice to draw off a spark and make it land where you want, but it's not hard to do," Jondalar said, giving her the stone and the striker.

"I'd like to try, too, when you're done," Willamar said.

"You don't have to wait," Ayla said. "I'll get the flint striker from my fire-starting kit and show you. I've been using the back of my knife, but I've already chipped it and I'd rather not break the blade."

Their first attempts were tentative and awkward, but with Ayla and Jondalar showing them the technique, both Marthona and Willamar began to get a feel for it. Willamar was the first to get a fire going, but then had trouble doing it a second time. Once Marthona made a fire, she had mastered the technique, but with practice and advice from the two experts, mixed with much laughter, it wasn't long before both of them were drawing sparks from the stone and making fires with ease.

Folara came home to find all four of them smiling with delight on their knees around the hearth, which held several little fires. Wolf came in with her. He'd grown tired of staying in one place all day with Ayla, and when he found Jaradal with Folara, who encouraged him, he couldn't resist joining them. They were pleased to show off their acquaintance with the curiously friendly predator, and the association made him less threatening to the other people of the Cave.

After Wolf greeted everyone appropriately and drank some water, he went to the corner near the entrance that he had claimed as his own and curled up to rest after a wonderfully tiring day with Jaradal and some of the other children.

"What's going on?" Folara said after the excitement of greetings, when she noticed the hearth. "Why do you have so many fires in the fireplace?"

"We've been learning to make fire with stones," Willamar said.

"With Ayla's firestone?" Folara said.

"Yes. It's so easy," Marthona said.

"I promised to show you, Folara. Would you like to try now?" Ayla said.

"Have you really done it, mother?" Folara asked.

"Of course."

"And you, too, Willamar?"

"Yes. It takes some practice, but it's not hard," he said.

"Well, I guess I can't be the only one in the family who doesn't know how," Folara said.

While Ayla was showing the young woman the finer points of making a fire with stones, with advice from Jondalar and the new expert, Willamar, Marthona used the existing fires to heat cooking stones. She filled her tea-making basket with water and began to slice some cold cooked bison meat. When the cooking stones were hot, she put several in the teapot basket, bringing forth a steaming cloud, then added a couple along with a bit more water to a container made of willow withes tightly interwoven with fibers attached to a wooden base. It contained vegetables that had been cooked that morning: daylily buds, cut pieces of the green stems of poke, elder shoots, thistle stems, burdock stems, coiled baby ferns, and lily corms, flavored with wild basil, elderberry flowers, and pignut roots for added spice.

By the time Marthona had a light supper ready, Folara had added her small fire to the ones still burning in the hearth. Everyone got their own eating dishes and cups for tea and sat on cushions around the low table. After the meal, Ayla brought a bowl of leftovers and an extra piece of meat to Wolf, poured herself another cup of tea, and rejoined the others.

"I want to know more about these firestones," Willamar said. "I've never heard of people making fire like that before."

"Where did you learn to do that, Jondé?" Folara asked.

"Ayla showed me," Jondalar said.

"Where did you learn, Ayla?" Folara said.

"It wasn't anything I learned or planned or thought about, it just happened."

"But how could something like that 'just happen'?" Folara asked.

Ayla took a sip of tea and closed her eyes to recall the event. "It was one of those days when everything seemed to go wrong," she began. "My first winter in the valley was just beginning, the river was turning to ice, and my fire had gone out in the middle of the night. Whinney was still a baby and hyenas were nosing around my cave in the dark, but I couldn't find my sling. I had to chase them off by throwing cooking stones. In the morning, I was going to cut wood to make a fire, but I dropped my axe and it broke. It was the only one I had, so I had to make a new one. Luckily, I had noticed that there were flint nodules in the heap of stones and animal bones that had piled up below the cave.

"I went down to the rocky bank by the river to knap a new axe and some other tools. While I was working, I put my stone retoucher down, but my mind was on the flint and I picked up the wrong stone by mistake. It wasn't my retoucher, it was a stone like this, and when I hit the flint with it, I got a spark. It made me think of fire, and I needed to make a fire, anyway, so I decided to try to make it with a spark from the stone. After a few tries, it worked."

"You make it sound so simple," Marthona said, "but I'm not sure I would have tried to make a fire like that, even if I had seen a spark."

"I was alone in that valley, with no one to show me how to do things, or to tell me what couldn't be done," Ayla said. "I'd already hunted and killed a horse, which was against Clan traditions, and then adopted her foal, which the Clan would never have allowed. I'd done so many things I wasn't supposed to do that by then I was ready to try any idea that came to me."

"Do you have many of these firestones?" Willamar asked.

"There were a lot of firestones on that rocky beach," Jondalar answered. "Before we left the valley for the last time, we gathered as many as we could find. We gave a few away on our Journey, but I tried to save as many as I could for people here. We never found any more of them along the way."

"That's too bad," the Trade Master said. "It would have been nice to share them, perhaps even to trade them."

"But we can!" Jondalar said. "Ayla found some this morning, in Wood River Valley, just before we went to the meeting. It's the first time I've seen any since we left her valley."

"You found more? Here? Where?" Willamar asked.

"At the foot of a little waterfall," Ayla said.

"If there are some in one little place, there may be more close by," Jondalar added.

"That's true," Willamar said. "How many people have you told about these firestones?"

"I haven't had time to tell anyone, but Zelandoni knows," Jondalar said. "Folara told her."

"Who told you?" Marthona asked her.

"Ayla did, or rather I saw her use one," Folara explained. "Yesterday, when you came home, Willamar."

"But, she didn't see it herself?" Willamar asked, a grin starting.

"I don't think so," Folara said.

"This is going to be fun. I can't wait to show her!" Willamar said. "She is going to be so astounded, but she won't want to show it."

"It will be fun," Jondalar said, also grinning. "It's not easy to surprise that woman."

"That's because she knows so much," Marthona said. "But you've already impressed her more than you realize, Ayla."

"That's true," Willamar said. "They both have. Have you two got any more surprises tucked away that you haven't told us about?"

"Well, I think you're going to be amazed by the spear-thrower we're going to demonstrate tomorrow, and you can't imagine how good Ayla is with a sling," Jondalar said. "And though it might not mean too much to you, I've learned some exciting new flint-knapping techniques. Even Dalanar was impressed."

"If Dalanar was impressed, I have to be," Willamar said.

"And then there's the thread-puller," Ayla said.

"Thread-puller?" Marthona said.

"Yes, for sewing. I just couldn't learn how to pull a tiny cord or a sinew thread though a hole that was punched with an awl. Then I had an idea, but the whole Lion Camp helped to make the first one. If you like, I'll get my sewing kit and show you," Ayla said.

"Do you think it would help someone whose eyes can't see the holes as well as they once could?" Marthona asked.

"I think so," Ayla said. "Let me get it."

"Why don't you wait until tomorrow, when there's more light. It's not as easy to see in firelight as it is in sunlight," Marthona said. "But I would like to see it."

"Well, Jondalar, you have certainly caused some excitement around here," Willamar said. "Just your return would have been enough, but you brought back much more than yourself. I've always said travel opens new possibilities, advances new ideas."

"I think you're right, Willamar," Jondalar said. "But I'll tell you truthfully, I'm tired of traveling. I'm going to be content to stay home for a long time."

"You're going to the Summer Meeting, aren't you, Jondé?" Folara asked.

"Of course. We're going to be mated there, little sister," Jondalar said, putting his arm around Ayla. "Going to the Summer Meeting isn't really traveling, especially after the Journey we made. Going to the Summer Meeting is part of being home. Which reminds me, Willamar, since Joharran is planning an extra hunt before we go, do you know where we can get disguises? Ayla wants to hunt, too, and we both need them."

"I'm sure we can find something. I have an extra set of antlers, if we go after red deer. Many people have skins and other things," the Trade Master said.

"What are disguises?" Ayla asked.

"We cover ourselves with hides, and sometimes wear antlers or horns so we can get closer to a herd. Animals are leery of people, so we try to make them think we're animals," Willamar explained.

"Jondalar, maybe we could take the horses, like the time Whinney and I helped the Mamutoi hunt bison," Ayla said, then looked at Willamar. "When we're on horseback, animals don't see us, they see the horses. We get very close, and with the spear-thowers, even with just two of us, and Wolf, we've been very successful."

"Using your animals to help hunt animals? You didn't mention that when I asked if you had any more surprises tucked away. Did you think that wouldn't be amazing?" Willamar said with a smile.

"I have a feeling even they don't know all the surprises they have in store for us," Marthona commented, then, after a pause, "Would anyone like a little more chamomile tea before going to bed?" She glanced at Ayla. "I find it very soothing and relaxing, and you were put through quite an interrogation today. These Clan people have much more to them than I ever imagined."

Folara's ears pricked up at that. Everyone had been talking about the long meeting, and her friends had been after her to give them a hint, assuming she would know. She had told them that she didn't know any more than anyone else, but she managed to imply that she just couldn't say what she knew. At least now she had some idea about the subject of the meeting. She listened closely as the conversation continued.

". . . they seem to have many fine qualities," Marthona was saying. "They care for their sick, and their leader seemed to have the best interests of his people foremost. The knowledge of their medicine woman must have been quite extensive, if Zelandoni's reaction is any indication, and I have a feeling she will want to know more about their spiritual leader. I think she would have liked to ask you many more questions, Ayla, but held back. Joharran was more interested in the people and their way of life."

There was a settling in, a moment of silence. Gazing at Marthona's beautiful home in the subdued mellow light cast by the fire in the hearth and the oil-burning lamps, Ayla noticed more aesthetic details. The dwelling complemented the woman and reminded Ayla of the feeling of elegance with which Ranec had arranged his living space in the Lion Camp longhouse. He was an artist, a fine carver, and he had taken the time to explain to her his feelings and ideas about creating and appreciating beauty, for himself and in homage to the Great Earth Mother. She felt that Marthona must have some of the same feeling.

Sipping warm tea, Ayla watched Jondalar's family as they relaxed quietly around the low table, and she felt a sense of peace and contentment she hadn't known before. These were people she could understand, people like her, and at that moment it struck her that she truly was one of the Others. Then she had a sudden picture of the cave of Brun's clan where she grew up, and the contrast astounded her.

Among the Zelandonii, each family had individual dwellings with screens and walls separating the living units. Voices and sounds could be heard from within the dwellings, which by custom were ignored, but each family had visual privacy. The Mamutoi had also defined areas within the Lion Camp's earthlodge for each family, with drapes that assured visual privacy, if it was desired.

In the cave of her clan, the boundaries of each family's living space were known, even if not defined with anything more than a few strategically placed stones. Privacy was a matter of social practice; one did not look directly into the hearth of one's neighbor, did not "see" beyond the invisible boundary. The Clan was good at not seeing what they were not supposed to see. Ayla recalled with a wrenching ache the way even those who loved her had simply stopped seeing her when she was cursed with death.

The Zelandonii also defined the spaces within and outside the dwellings, with places for sleeping, cooking and eating, and various work projects. Within the Clan, areas for different activities were not as precisely located. Generally, sleeping places were made and a hearth located, but for the most part, the division of space was a matter of custom, habit, and behavior. They were mental and social divisions, not physical ones. Women avoided places where men were working, men stayed away from the women's activities, and work projects were often done where it was convenient at the time.

The Zelandonii seem to have more time to do things than the Clan, Ayla was thinking. They all seem to make so many things, and not just necessary things. Maybe it's the way they hunt that makes the difference. She was lost in thought and didn't hear a question that had been put to her.

"Ayla? . . . Ayla!" Jondalar said loudly.

"Oh! I'm sorry, Jondalar. What did you say?"

"What were you thinking about that you didn't even hear me?"

"I was thinking about the differences between the Others and the Clan, and I was wondering why the Zelandonii seem to make more things than the Clan did," Ayla said.

"Did you come up with an answer?" Marthona asked.

"I don't know, but maybe different ways of hunting might have something to do with it," Ayla said. "When Brun and his hunters went out, they usually brought back a whole animal, sometimes two. The Lion Camp could count about the same number of people as Brun's clan, but when they hunted, everyone who could went out, men, women, even some children, if only for the drive. They usually killed many animals and brought back only the best and richest parts, and saved most of the meat for winter. I don't recall a time that either starved, but by the end of winter, the clan was often left with only the leanest and least filling food, and sometimes had to hunt in spring when animals were thin. The Lion Camp ran out of some foods, and were hungry for greens, but they seemed to eat well even in late spring."

"That may be something to mention to Joharran, later," Willamar said, yawning as he got up. "But right now, I'm going to bed. We're likely to have a busy day tomorrow, too."

Marthona got up from the cushions when Willamar did and carried the serving dishes into the cooking room.

Folara stood up, stretching and yawning in a way that was so similar to Willamar, Ayla smiled at the resemblance. "I'm going to bed, too. I'll help you clean those dishes in the morning, mother," she said, wiping out her wooden eating bowl with a small piece of soft deerskin before putting it away. "I'm too tired now."

"Are you going hunting, Folara?" Jondalar asked.

"I haven't decided. I'll see how I feel later," she replied, heading for her sleeping room.

After Marthona and Willamar went into their sleeping space, Jondalar moved aside the low table and spread out their sleeping furs. As they settled into them, Wolf came to sleep beside Ayla. He didn't mind staying out of the way when people were around, but when Ayla went to bed, he felt his place was beside her.

"I really like your family, Jondalar," Ayla said. "I think I'm going to like living with the Zelandonii. I was thinking about what you said last night, and you're right. I shouldn't judge everyone by a few unpleasant people."

"Don't judge everyone by the best, either," Jondalar said. "You never know how people will react to something. I'd take them one at a time."

"I think everyone has some good and some bad," Ayla said. "Some have a little more of one than the other. I always hope people will have more good than bad, and I like to believe most do. Remember Frebec? He was really nasty in the beginning, but in the end, he turned out to be nice."

"I have to admit, he surprised me," Jondalar said, snuggling close to her and nuzzling her neck.

"You don't surprise me, though," she said, smiling as she felt his hand between her thighs. "I know what you're thinking."

"I hope you're thinking the same thing," he said. As she reached up to kiss him, she returned the gesture. "And I think maybe you are."

The kiss was long and lingering. They both felt their desire grow, but there was no rush, no need to hurry. They were home, Jondalar thought. Through all the difficulties of the long and dangerous Journey, he had brought her home with him. Now she was safe, the dangers were over. He stopped and looked down at her, and felt so much love for her, he didn't know if he could contain it.

Even in the soft light of dying fires, Ayla could see the love in blue eyes that were a rich shade of violet in the firelight, and she felt herself fill with the same emotion. When she was growing up, she never dreamed she would find a man like Jondalar, never dreamed she would be so lucky.

He felt a catch in his throat and bent down to kiss her again, and knew he had to have her, to love her, to join with her. He was grateful to know that she was there for him. She always seemed ready for him, to want him whenever he wanted her. She had never played coy games with him, the way some women did.

Marona came to his mind for a moment. She had liked to play those games, not as much with him, but with others. And suddenly he was grateful that he had gone off with his brother on an unknown adventure instead of staying and mating with Marona. If only Thonolan had lived . . .

But Ayla was alive, though he had come close to losing her more than once. Jondalar felt her mouth open to his searching tongue, felt the warmth of her breath. He kissed her neck, and nibbled her earlobe, and ran his tongue down to her throat in a warm caress.

She held herself still, resisting the tickling sensation and letting it become internal spasms of expectation. He kissed the hollow of her throat and detoured to one side toward an erect nipple, circling it, nibbling it. Her anticipation was so intense, she almost felt a sense of relief when he finally took it in his mouth and suckled. She felt the jolt of excitement in the depths of her being, and at the place of her Pleasures.

He was ready, he was so ready, but he felt himself fill even more when he heard her soft moan as he suckled and gently bit first one nipple and then the other. The urge suddenly came upon him so strongly, he wanted her that instant, but he wanted her to be as ready as he was. He knew how to bring her there.

She could feel his eager desire, and it fired her own. She would have been happy to open herself to him at that moment, but when he pushed down the top cover of their sleeping roll and moved lower, she held her breath, knowing what was coming and wanting it.

His tongue circled her navel for only a moment; he didn't want to wait, and neither did she. As she kicked off the top cover, she felt a moment's hesitation at the thought of the others in their sleeping places nearby. Ayla wasn't used to being in a dwelling with other people and felt a little constrained. Jondalar seemed to have no such compunctions.

The unease slipped from her mind as she felt him kiss her thigh, press her legs apart and kiss the other, and then kiss the soft folds of her womanhood. He savored her familiar taste, licked slowly, and then found her small, hard nodule.

Her moan was louder. She felt flashes of Pleasure like lightning blaze through her as he sucked and massaged her with his tongue. She didn't know she was so ready. It came on her quicker than she expected. Almost without warning, she was there, feeling peaks of Pleasure and a overwhelming desire for him, for his manhood.

She reached for him, pulled him up to her, and helped him to enter. He penetrated deeply. With the first stroke, he struggled to hold back, to wait a little, but she was ready, urging him, and he gave himself up to it. With joyous abandon, he plunged, fully, once more, and then again, and then he was there, as she was, feeling the waves of Pleasure mount up and spill over, again and again and again.

Jondalar rested on top of her, a moment she had always savored, but then he remembered that she was pregnant and he worried that his weight was too much. She felt an instant of disappointment when he moved away so soon.

As he rolled off to the side, he wondered again if she could be right. Was this how that baby had started inside her? Was it his baby, too, as Ayla always insisted? Had the Mother given her children not only this wondrous Gift of Pleasure, but was it Her way of Blessing a woman with new life? Could that be why men were created, to start the new life inside a woman? He wanted Ayla to be right, he wanted it to be true, but how would he ever know?

After a while, Ayla got up. From a travel pack she took a small wooden bowl and poured some water into it from the waterbag. Wolf had retreated to his chosen corner near the entrance and greeted her with his usual tentative approach after their Pleasures. She smiled at him and gave him the signal that he had done well; then, standing over the night basket, she cleaned herself as Iza had taught her when she first became a woman. Iza, I know you doubted that I would have need of the training, she thought, but you were right to teach me the cleansing rituals then.

Jondalar was half-asleep when she went back to bed. He'd been too tired to get up, but she'd air out and brush off their sleeping roll to clean it in the morning. Now that they were going to stay in one place for a while, she would even have time to wash their furs, she thought. Nezzie had shown her how to do it, but it took time and care.

Ayla rolled over on her side and Jondalar cuddled up behind her, resting on his side. They were nestled together like two spoons on edge, and he fell asleep holding her, but she was unable to nod off, although she was comfortable and satisfied. She had slept much later than usual that morning, and as she lay awake, she began thinking about the Clan and the Others again. Recollections of her life with them and her stays with various groups of Others kept coming to her mind, and she found herself making comparisons.

The same kinds of materials were at hand for both peoples, but the uses to which they had been put were not quite the same. Both hunted animals, both gathered foods that grew, and both used hides, bones, vegetal materials, and stones for clothing, shelter, implements, and weapons, but there were differences.

Perhaps the most noticeable was that while Jondalar's people decorated their environment with paintings and carvings of animals and designs, the people of the Clan did not. Though she didn't quite know how to explain it, even to herself, she did perceive that people of the Clan expressed the beginnings of such decoration. Red ochre in a burial, for example, that imparted color to the body. Their interest in unusual objects that they collected to put in their amulets. Totem scars and color markings made on the body for special purposes. But the primeval people of the Clan created no legacy of art.

Only Ayla's kind of people did; only people like the Mamutoi and the Zelandonii, and the rest of the Others they had met on their Journey. She wondered if the unknown people to whom she had been born decorated the material objects in their world, and she believed they did. It was the ones who came later, the ones who shared that cold ancient world with the Clan for a time, the ones they called the Others, who were the first to see an animal in a moving, living, breathing form and reproduce it as a drawing or a carving. It was a profound distinction.

The creation of art, the delineation of animals or purposeful markings, was an expression of the ability to make abstractions—the ability to take the essence of a thing and make of it a symbol that stands for the thing itself. The symbol for a thing has another form as well: a sound, a word. A brain that could think in terms of art was a brain capable of developing to its fullest potential another abstraction of great significance: language. And the same brain that was capable of creating a synthesis of the abstraction of art and the abstraction of language would someday form a synergism of both symbols, in effect, a memory of the words: writing.

Unlike the day before, Ayla opened her eyes very early the next morning. No red coals glowed in the fireplace and all the lamps were out, but she could discern the contours of the limestone shelf high overhead, above the dark wall panels of Marthona's dwelling, in the faint reflection of first light, the initial lightening of the sky that heralded the coming of the sun. No one else was stirring when she quietly slipped out of the furs and made her way in the not quite pitch-dark to use the night basket. Wolf lifted his head the moment she got up, whined a greeting of happiness, and followed her.

She felt a little nauseated, but not quite enough to vomit, and had an urge for something solid to calm her unsettled stomach. She went to the cooking room and started a small fire, then took a few bites of the bison meat that was left on the pelvic bone serving platter from the night before, and a few soggy vegetables from the bottom of the cooking-storage basket. She wasn't sure if she felt better or not, but she decided to see if she could make a stomach-settling tea for herself. She didn't know who had made the tea for her the day before, but wondered if it was Jondalar and thought she'd make one of his favorite morning teas as well.

She got her medicine bag from her traveling pack. Now that we're finally here, I can replenish my supply of herbs and medicines, she thought as she looked at each package and thought about its uses. Sweet rush can help an upset stomach, but no, Iza told me it could cause a miscarriage, and I don't want to do that. While she was considering the possible side effects, her mind supplied another bit from her extensive store of medicinal knowledge. Black birch bark can help prevent a miscarriage, but I don't have any. Well, I don't think I'm in danger of losing this one.

I had a much harder time with Durc. Ayla remembered when Iza went out to get fresh snakeroot so she wouldn't lose him. Iza was already sick by then, and she got cold and wet and it made her worse. I don't think she ever recovered completely, Ayla thought. I miss you, Iza. I wish you were nearby so I could tell you that I did find a man to mate. I wish you had lived to meet him. I think you would have approved.

Basil, of course! That can help prevent miscarriage, and it makes a nice drink. She put that package aside. Mint would be good. It settles nausea and helps stomachaches and tastes good. Jondalar likes it, too. She kept that pouch out, too. And hops, that's good for headaches and cramps, relaxes, she thought as she put it beside the mint. Not too much, though, hops can make you drowsy.

Milk thistle seeds might be good for me right now, but they need to be steeped a long time, Ayla thought as she continued going through the limited supply of medicinal herbs she had with her. Woodruff, yes, it smells so good. And it calms the stomach, but it's not too strong. And chamomile, I could use that instead of mint, it's good for upset stomachs, too. It might taste better with the other herbs, but mint for Jondalar. Marjoram could be good, but no, Iza always used the fresh tops for stomach problems, not dried.

What else was it that Iza liked to use fresh? Raspberry leaf! Of course! That's what I need. It's especially good for morning sickness. I don't have any leaves, but there were raspberries at the feast the other night, so they must grow nearby. It's the right season, too. It's best to pick the leaf when the berries are ripe. I should make sure I get enough for when I go into labor. Iza always used it when a woman was delivering. She told me it relaxed the mother's womb and helped the baby come out more easily.

I still have some linden flowers left; that's especially good for a nervous stomach, and the leaves are sweet and make a nice-tasting tea. The Sharamudoi had a wonderful big old linden tree nearby. I wonder if any linden trees grow around here? She saw movement out of the corner of her eye and looked up to see Marthona coming out of her sleeping area. Wolf also looked up, then stood up expectantly.

"You're up early this morning, Ayla," she said in a soft voice, so as not to disturb those who were still sleeping. She reached down to pat the wolf to acknowledge him.

"I usually am . . . if I don't stay up late the night before, feasting and drinking strong beverages," Ayla replied in an equally quiet tone and with a wry smile.

"Yes, Laramar makes a potent drink, but people seem to like it," Marthona said. "I see you have a fire going already. I usually try to bank the fire at night so I have coals to start one in the morning, but with those firestones you showed us, I could get lazy. What are you making?"

"A morning tea," Ayla said. "I like to make a wake-up tea for Jondalar in the morning, too. Can I make some for you?"

"When the water is hot, I have a tea mixture that Zelandoni wants me to take in the morning," Marthona said, starting to clean up the remains of the late supper from the night before. "Jondalar told me about your habit of making him morning tea. He was determined to make a tea for you to drink when you woke up yesterday. He said you always had a hot cup ready for him, and for once, he wanted you to wake up to tea. I suggested that he make mint, since it tastes good cold, and it seemed you might sleep late."

"I wondered if it was Jondalar who made that. But were you the one who left the basin and water?" Ayla asked. Marthona smiled and nodded.

Ayla reached for the bentwood tongs used to pick up cooking rocks, took a hot stone from the fire, and dropped it into the tightly woven tea basket full of water. It steamed and hissed and sent up a few preliminary bubbles. She added another, and after a while, she removed the stones and added more. When the water was boiling, both women infused their individual tea mixtures. Though the low table had been moved closer to the entry to make room for the extra sleeping furs, there was ample room for the two women to sit companionably around it on cushions, sipping their hot beverages.

"I've been wanting a chance to talk to you, Ayla," Marthona murmured softly. "I often wondered if Jondalar would ever find a woman he could love." She almost said "again," but caught herself. "He always had many friends, was well-liked, but he kept his real feelings to himself and few people knew him well. Thonolan was closer to him than anyone. I always thought he would mate one day, but I didn't know if he would ever allow himself to fall in love. I believe he has." She smiled at Ayla.

"It's true that he often keeps his feelings to himself. I almost mated another man before I realized that. Even though I loved Jondalar, I thought he had stopped loving me," Ayla said.

"I don't think there is any doubt. It's quite obvious that he loves you, and I'm happy he found you." Marthona took a sip of tea. "I was proud of you the other day, Ayla. It took courage to face people the way you did after Marona's trick. . . . You know she and Jondalar had talked of mating, don't you?"

"Yes, he told me."

"Though I would not have objected, of course, I will admit that I'm glad he didn't choose her. She is an attractive woman and everyone always thought she was perfect for him, but I didn't," Marthona said.

Ayla rather hoped Marthona would tell her why. The woman stopped and took a drink of her tea.

"I would like to give you something a little more appropriate to wear than the 'gift' Marona gave you," the older woman said when she finished her drink and put the cup down.

"You have already given me something beautiful to wear," Ayla said. "Dalanar's mother's necklace."

Marthona smiled as she got up and went quietly into her sleeping room. She returned with a garment draped over her arm. She held it up to show Ayla. It was a long tunic in a pale, soft color rather like the whitened stems of grass after the long winter, beautifully decorated with beads and shells, sewings of colored thread, and long fringes, but it was not made of leather. On close inspection, Ayla saw that it was made of thin cords or threads of some fiber crossed over and under each other, rather like basketry in texture, but very tightly woven. How could anyone weave such fine cords like that? It was similar to the mat on the low table, but even more fine.

"I have never seen anything like this," Ayla said. "What kind of material is it? Where does it come from?"

"I make it; I weave it on a special frame," Marthona said. "Do you know the plant called flax? A tall, thin plant with blue flowers?"

"Yes, I'm familiar with a plant like that, and I think Jondalar said it was called flax," Ayla said. "It's good for severe skin problems, like boils and open sores and rashes, even inside the mouth."

"Have you ever twined it into cordage?" Marthona asked.

"I may have, I don't recall, but I can understand how it could be. It does have long fibers."

"That's what I used to make this."

"I know that flax is useful, but I didn't know it could be used to make something as beautiful as this."

"I thought you might be able to use it for your Matrimonial. We'll be leaving for the Summer Meeting soon, at the next full moon, and you said you didn't have anything to wear for special occasions," Marthona said.

"Oh, Marthona, how nice of you," Ayla said, "but I do have a Matrimonial outfit. Nezzie made it for me, and I promised her I would wear it. I hope you don't mind. I brought it with me all the way from the Summer Meeting last year. It is made in the Mamutoi style, and they have special customs about the way it should be worn."

"I think it would be most appropriate for you to wear a Mamutoi Matrimonial outfit, Ayla. I just didn't know if you had anything to wear, and I wasn't sure if we'd have time to make something before we leave. Please keep this anyway," Marthona said, smiling as she gave it to her. Ayla thought she seemed relieved. "You may have other occasions when you will want to wear something special."

"Thank you! This is so beautiful!" Ayla said, holding it up and looking at it again, then in front of her to see how the loose garment would fit. "It must take a long time to make."

"Yes, but I enjoy it. I've worked out the process over many years. Willamar helped me to make the frame I use, and Thonolan, before he left. Most people have a special craft of some kind. We often trade the things we make, or give them as gifts. I'm getting a little old to do much of anything else now, but I don't see as well as I once did, especially the close work."

"I was going to show you the thread-puller today!" Ayla said, jumping up. "I think it would make it easier for someone who doesn't see as well to sew. I'll get it." She went to her travel packs to get her sewing kit and saw one of the special packages she had brought with her. Smiling to herself, she took it back to the table, too. "Would you like to see my Matrimonial outfit, Marthona?"

"Yes, I would, but I didn't want to ask. Some people like to keep it a secret and surprise everyone," Marthona commented.

"I have a different surprise," Ayla said as she unpacked her Matrimonial outfit. "But I think I will tell you. Life has begun inside me. I am carrying Jondalar's baby."

10

Ayla! Are you sure?" Marthona asked with a smile. She did think it was a rather strange way of saying that the Mother had Blessed her—carrying Jondalar's baby—even if it probably was the child of his spirit.

"As sure as anyone can be. I have missed two moon times, I feel a little sick in the mornings, and I'm aware of some changes in me that usually mean pregnancy," Ayla said.

"How wonderful!" Jondalar's mother said. She reached over and gave Ayla a hug. "If you are already Blessed, it brings luck to your mating, or so people claim."

Sitting at the low table, the young woman untied the leather-wrapped package and tried to shake the wrinkles out of the tunic and leggings that had been carried across a continent through every season for the past year. Marthona examined the outfit and quickly saw past the creases as she realized what magnificent garments they were. Ayla would most definitely stand out at the Mating Ceremonial wearing this.

First of all, the style was utterly unique. Both men and women of the Zelandonii, with some differences and variations related to gender, usually wore rather loosely bloused pullover tunics, belted at the hips, with various embellishments of bone, shell, feather, or fur and fringes of leather or cordage. Women's clothing, particularly the clothes they wore for special occasions, often had long hanging fringes that swayed as they walked, and a young woman quickly learned how to make the dangling decoration accentuate her movements.

Among the Zelandonii, a naked woman was an ordinary sight, but fringes were considered very provocative. It wasn't that women didn't usually wear clothing, but removing clothes to wash or change or for whatever reason in their close-knit society with relatively little privacy was hardly given a thought. On the other hand, a fringe, especially a red fringe, could give a woman an allure so tantalizing, it could drive men to extremes, on rare occasions even violence because of a particular association.

When women took on the role of donii-women—when they were making themselves available to teach young men about the Great Earth Mother's Gift of Pleasure—they wore a long red fringe dangling around their hips to denote their important ritual status. On hot days of summer, they often wore little more than the fringe.

While donii-women were protected by custom and convention from inappropriate advances and, in any case, they tended to stay in certain areas when they wore the red fringe, it was believed dangerous for a woman to wear such a fringe at any other time. Who could tell what it might drive a man to do? Though women often wore fringes of colors other than red, any fringe invariably had some erotic implications.

As a result, the word "fringe," in subtle innuendo or crude jokes, often carried the double meaning of pubic hair. When a man was so captivated by a woman that he couldn't stay away from her or stop looking at her, it was said that he was "snared by her fringe."

Zelandonii women wore other decorations or sewed them to their clothing, but they particularly liked to wear fringes that moved sensuously when they walked, whether they decorated a warm winter tunic or a naked body. And though they avoided explicitly red fringes, many women chose colors that contained a strong hint of red.

Ayla's Mamutoi outfit had no fringes, but there was no doubt that a tremendous amount of effort had been put into making it. The leather, which was of the finest quality, was a rich, earthy, golden yellow hue that almost matched the color of her hair, the result primarily of yellow ochres mixed subtly with reds and other colors. The hide had probably come from deer of some variety, or perhaps saiga antelope, Marthona thought, though it wasn't the usual velvety soft buckskin of a well-scraped hide. Instead, although it was very soft, the leather had a burnished, shiny finish that was somewhat waterproof.

But the quality of the basic garments was only the beginning; it was the exquisite decoration that made the outfit so extraordinary. The long leather tunic and the lower part of the leggings were covered with elaborate geometric designs made predominantly of ivory beads, some sections solidly filled in. The designs began with downward pointing triangles, which developed horizontally into zigzags and vertically into diamonds and chevrons, then evolved into complex geometric figures such as rectangular spirals and concentric rhomboids.

The ivory beaded designs were highlighted and defined by many small amber beads in shades both lighter and darker than the leather, but of the same tone, and with embroideries of red, brown, and black. The tunic, which fell to a downward-pointing triangle at the back, opened down the front, with the section below the hips tapering so that when it was brought together, another downward-pointing triangle was created. It was tied closed at the waist with a finger-woven sash in a similar geometric pattern made of red mammoth hair with accents of ivory mouflon wool, brown musk ox underdown, and deep reddish-black woolly rhinoceros hair.

The outfit was stunning, a magnificent work of art. The workmanship in every detail was excellent. It was evident that someone had secured the finest materials and utilized the most skillful and accomplished artisans to create the finished outfit, and no effort had been spared. The beadwork was a good example. Though Marthona saw them only as a huge number, more than three thousand ivory beads made from mammoth tusk were sewn onto the garments, and each small bead had been carved, pierced, and polished by hand.

Jondalar's mother had never seen anything like it, but she knew immediately that whoever had directed the outfit to be made commanded great respect and held a very high position within the community. It was clear that the time and labor that went into the making of it were incalculable, yet the outfit had been given to Ayla when she left. None of the benefits of the resources and work would stay within the community that made it. Ayla said she had been adopted, but whoever had adopted her obviously possessed tremendous power and prestige—in effect, wealth—and no one understood that better than Marthona.

No wonder she wants to wear her own Matrimonial outfit, Marthona thought, and she should. It won't hurt Jondalar's prestige, either. This young woman is certainly full of surprises. Without question, she is going to be the most talked about woman at the Summer Meeting this year.

"The outfit is striking, Ayla, really quite beautiful," Marthona said. "Who made it for you?"

"Nezzie did, but she had a lot of help." Ayla was pleased by the older woman's reaction.

"Yes, I'm sure she did," Marthona commented. "You've mentioned her before, but I don't recall exactly who she is."

"She's the mate of Talut, the headman of the Lion Camp, the one who was going to adopt me, but then Mamut did instead. I think it was Mamut who asked Nezzie to make it."

"And Mamut is One Who Serves the Mother?"

"I think he may have been First, like your Zelandoni. Anyway, he was certainly the oldest. I think he was the oldest Mamutoi alive. When I left, my friend Deegie was expecting, and her brother's woman was almost ready to give birth. Both children would be counted his fifth generation."

Marthona gave a knowing nod. She knew that whoever had adopted Ayla had a great deal of influence; she hadn't realized he was probably the most respected and powerful person of all his people. That explained a lot, she thought. "You said there were certain customs associated with wearing this?"

"The Mamutoi do not think it's appropriate to wear a Matrimonial outfit before the ceremony. You can show family and close friends, but you are not supposed to wear it in public," Ayla said. "Would you like to see how the tunic looks?"

Jondalar grunted and turned over in his sleep, and Marthona glanced in the direction of their sleeping furs. She lowered her voice even more. "So long as Jondalar is still asleep. We do not consider it appropriate for him to see you in your Matrimonial clothing until the ceremony."

Ayla slipped off her summer tunic and picked up the heavy, ornately decorated one. "Nezzie told me to wear it closed like this if I just want to show someone," Ayla whispered as she tied it closed with the sash. "But for the ceremony, it should be open, like this," she said, rearranging the garment and retying the sash. "Nezzie said, 'A woman proudly shows her breasts when she is joined, when she brings her hearth to form a union with a man.' I'm not really supposed to wear it open before the mating ceremony, but since you are Jondalar's mother, I think it's right for you to see."

Marthona nodded. "I am very pleased that you showed me. It is our custom to show Matrimonial clothing before the occasion only to women, intimate friends or family, but I don't think anyone else should see yours just yet. I think it would be . . . ," Marthona paused and smiled, "interesting to surprise everyone. If you like, we can hang it in my room so the creases can straighten out. A little steam would help, too."

"Thank you. I've been wondering where I could put it. Can this beautiful tunic that you gave me stay in your room, too?" Ayla paused, remembering something else. "And I have another tunic I would like to put somewhere, one I made. Would you keep that for me?"

"Yes, of course. But put your outfits away for now. We can do it after Willamar wakes up. Is there anything else you'd like me to keep?" Marthona said.

"I have necklaces and things, but they can stay in my traveling packs, since I'll be taking them with me to the Summer Meeting," Ayla said.

"Do you have much?" Marthona couldn't resist asking.

"Only two necklaces, including the one from you, an armband, two spiral shells for my ears, given to me by a woman who dances, and two matched pieces of amber that Tulie gave me when I left. She was the headwoman of the Lion Camp, Talut's sister, and Deegie's mother. She thought I should wear them on my ears at my mating, since they would match the tunic. I would like to, but my ears are not pierced," Ayla said.

"I'm sure Zelandoni would be happy to pierce them for you, if you want," Marthona said.

"I think I would. I don't want any other piercings, at least not yet, but I would like to wear the matched ambers when Jondalar and I are mated, and the outfit from Nezzie."

"This Nezzie must have been quite fond of you to have done so much for you," Marthona commented.

"I certainly was fond of her," Ayla replied. "If it hadn't been for Nezzie, I don't think I would have followed Jondalar when he left. I was supposed to mate with Ranec the next day. He was the son of her brother's hearth, although she was more like a mother to him. But Nezzie knew Jondalar loved me, and she told me that if I really loved him to go after him and tell him so. She was right. It was hard to tell Ranec I was leaving, though. I did care for him, very much, but I loved Jondalar."

"You must have, or you would not have left people who held you in such high regard to come home with him," Marthona said.

Ayla noticed Jondalar shifting around again and stood up. Marthona sipped her tea, watching the young woman as she refolded her Matrimonial outfit, then the woven tunic, and put them in her traveling pack. When she returned, she motioned toward her sewing kit, which was on the table.

"My thread-puller is in that," Ayla explained. "Perhaps we can go out in the sunlight after Jondalar's morning tea is ready, and I'll show it to you."

"Yes, I would like to see it."

Ayla went around to the cooking hearth, added wood to the fire, then some cooking stones to heat, and measured out some dried herbs in the palm of her hand for Jondalar's tea. His mother was thinking that her first impression of Ayla was right. She was attractive, but there was more to her than that. She seemed genuinely concerned about Jondalar's welfare. She would make a good mate for him.

Ayla was thinking about Marthona, admiring her quiet, self-assured dignity and regal grace. She felt that Jondalar's mother had a great depth of understanding, but Ayla was sure that the woman who had been leader could be very strong if she had to be. No wonder her people hadn't wanted her to step down after her mate died, the young woman thought. It must have been difficult for Joharran to follow after her, but he seemed comfortable in the position now, as far as she could tell.

Ayla quietly placed Jondalar's cup of hot tea near him, thinking she would have to find some of the twigs he liked to use to clean his teeth, after he chewed the ends. He liked the taste of wintergreen. She would look for the evergreen that resembled willow the first chance she had. Marthona finished her tea, Ayla picked up her sewing kit, and both women slipped quietly out of the dwelling. Wolf followed them.

It was still early when they reached the stone front terrace. The sun had just opened its brilliant eye and peeked over the edge of the eastern hills. Its bright glare gave the rock of the cliff a warm ruddy glow, but the air was refreshingly cool. Not many people were moving about yet.

Marthona led them toward the edge near the dark circle of the signal fire. They sat on some large rocks that had been arranged around it, with their backs to the blinding radiance that was climbing through the red-and-gold haze to the cloudless blue vault. Wolf left them and continued down to Wood River Valley.

Ayla untied the drawstring of her sewing kit, a small leather bag sewn together around the sides and gathered at the top. Missing ivory beads that had once formed a geometric pattern and frayed threads of embroidery betrayed the heavy use of the worn pouch. She emptied the small objects it contained into her lap. There were various sizes of cords and threads made of plant fibers, sinew, and animal hair, including several of the wool of mammoth, mouflon, musk ox, and rhino, each wound around small bone phalanges. Several small, sharp blades of flint used for cutting were tied together with sinew, as was a bundle of awls of bone and flint that were for piercing. A small square of tough mammoth hide served as a thimble. The last objects were three small tubes made of hollow bird bones.

She picked up a tube, removed a diminutive wad of leather from one end, and tipped the contents into her hand. A small tapering shaft of ivory slid out, with a point at one end—similar to an awl, but with a tiny hole at the other end. She handed it carefully to Marthona.

"Do you see the hole?" Ayla asked.

Marthona held it away from her. "I can't really see it well," she said, then brought it closer and felt the small object, first the sharp point, then along the shaft to the opposite end. "Ah! There it is! I can feel it. That's a very small hole, not much bigger than the hole of a bead."

"The Mamutoi do pierce beads, but no one at Lion Camp was a skilled bead-maker. Jondalar made the boring tool used to make the hole. I think that was the most difficult part of making this thread-puller. I didn't bring anything to sew, but I'll show you how it works," Ayla said, taking it back. She selected the bone phalange that held sinew, unwound a length, wet the end in her mouth, deftly poked it through the hole, and pulled it through. Then she handed it to Marthona.

The woman looked at the threaded needle, but saw more with her hands than with her aging eyes, which could still see objects that were far away quite well, but not nearly so well as those that were near. Her frown of concentration as she examined it suddenly brightened to a smile of understanding. "Of course!" she said. "With this I believe I could sew again!"

"On some things, you need to make a hole with an awl first. As sharp as you can make it, the ivory point won't pierce thick or tough leather very easily," Ayla explained, "but it's still better than trying to get the thread through a hole without it. I could make holes, but I just couldn't learn how to pick up the thread through the hole with the point of an awl, no matter how patient Nezzie and Deegie were."

Marthona smiled in agreement, then looked puzzled. "Most young girls have that trouble when they are learning; didn't you learn to sew when you were young?"

"The Clan doesn't sew, not in the same way. They wear wraps that are tied on. A few things are knotted together, like birch bark containers, but they have rather large holes to pull through the cords that are tied together, not like the fine little holes that Nezzie wanted me to make," Ayla said.

"I keep forgetting your childhood was ... unusual," Marthona said. "If you didn't learn to sew as a girl, I can see how it would be difficult, but this is a remarkably clever device." She looked up. "I think Proleva is coming this way. I would like to show her, if you don't mind."

"I don't mind at all," Ayla said. Glancing at the sunny terrace in front of the overhang, she saw Joharran's mate and Salova, Rushemar's mate, coming toward them, and noticed that many more people were up and moving about.

The women greeted each other, then Marthona said, "Look at this, Proleva. You, too, Salova. Ayla calls it a 'thread-puller.' She was just showing it to me. It's very clever, and I think it will help me to sew again, even if I can't see close very clearly anymore. I'll be able to do it by feel."

The two women, who had both constructed many garments in their lives, quickly grasped the concept of the new implement and were soon discussing its potential with excitement.

"Learning to use this will be easy, I think," Salova said. "But making this thread-puller must have been difficult."

"Jondalar helped with this one. He made the fine boring tool to drill the small hole," Ayla explained.

"It would take someone with his skill. Before he left, I remember that he made flint awls and some boring tools for piercing beads," Proleva said. "I think Salova's right. It might be hard to make a thread-puller like this, but I'm sure it would be worth the effort. I'd like to try one."

"I'd be happy to let you try this one, Proleva, and I have two others, of different sizes," Ayla said. "The size I choose depends on what I want to sew."

"Thank you, but I don't think I'll have time today with all the planning for the hunt. Joharran thinks this Summer Meeting is going to be especially well attended," Proleva said, then smiled at Ayla, "because of you. The news that Jondalar has returned and brought a woman back with him is already running up and down The River, and beyond. He wants to make sure that we bring enough to feed the extra people when we sponsor a feast."

"And everyone will be excited to meet you, to see if the stories about you are true," Salova said, smiling. She had felt the same way.

"By the time we get there, they won't be true," Proleva said. "Stories always grow."

"But most people know that, and don't believe half of the stories to begin with. I think Jondalar and Ayla will manage to surprise a few people this year," Marthona said.

Proleva noticed a rare expression on the face of the former leader of the Ninth Cave of the Zelandonii, a sly and rather self-satisfied smile. She wondered what Marthona knew that no one else did.

"Are you coming with us to Two Rivers Rock today, Marthona?" Proleva asked.

"Yes. I think I will. I would like to see a demonstration of this 'spear-thrower' Jondalar has been talking about. If it's as clever as this thread-pulling device," Marthona said, and recalling her fire-making experience of the night before, "and other ideas they've brought back with them, it should be interesting."

Joharran led the way around a steep section of rock that was close to The River, which made everyone walk single file. Marthona followed behind him, and as she looked at the back of her eldest son, she was feeling rather pleased to know that she not only had a son walking in front of her, but for the first time in many years, her son Jondalar was behind her. Ayla followed Jondalar, with Wolf on her heels. Other people from the Ninth Cave trailed them, but left a gap of several paces behind the wolf. More people joined them as they passed by the Fourteenth Cave.

They came to a place along The River between the shelters of the Fourteenth Cave on their side and Eleventh Cave on the other side where the waterway broadened out and foamed around rocks jutting out of the water. The River was easily fordable there, shallow enough to wade across, and the location that most people used to get to the other side. Ayla heard people refer to it as the Crossing.

Some of those who wore foot coverings sat down to take them off. Others were barefoot like Ayla, or apparently didn't care if their footwear got wet. The people from the Fourteenth Cave held back and allowed Joharran and the Ninth Cave to start across first. It was a courtesy to him, since Joharran was the one who had suggested a last hunt before they left for the Summer Meeting and was nominally the leader.

As Jondalar stepped into the cold water, he was reminded of something he had wanted to tell his brother. "Joharran, wait a moment," he called. The man stopped. Marthona was beside him. "When we went with the Lion Camp to the Summer Meeting of the Mamutoi, we had to cross a rather deep river just before we reached the place where the Meeting was held. The people of Wolf Camp, who were hosting the Meeting, had put piles of rock and gravel in the water to make stepping-stones so people could cross the river without getting wet. I know we sometimes do, too, but their river was so deep, you could fish between the stones. I thought it was a clever idea and wanted to remember to tell someone when I got back."

"This river runs fast. Wouldn't it wash the stones away?" Joharran asked.

"Their river was fast, too, and deep enough for salmon and sturgeon, other fish, too. The water flowed through the spaces between. They said the rocks washed out when it flooded, but they built new stepping-stones every year. It was good fishing off the rock piles near the middle of the river," Jondalar explained. Other people had stopped and were listening, too.

"Perhaps it's worth considering," Marthona said.

"What about the rafts? Wouldn't stepping-stones get in the way?" a man asked.

"It's not deep enough here for the rafts most of the time. People usually have to carry them and whatever is on them around the Crossing anyway," Joharran said.

As Ayla waited while the discussion continued, she observed that the water was clear enough to see rocks on the bottom and an occasional fish. Then she realized that the middle of the stream offered a unique view of the area. Looking ahead, south, on the left bank of The River, she saw a cliff with shelters that was probably the place they were going, and just beyond it, a tributary joining the mainstream. Across the smaller river was the start of a line of steep cliffs that paralleled the main river. She turned and looked the other way. Upriver, toward the north she could see more high cliffs and the huge rock shelter of the Ninth Cave situated on the right bank at the outside of a sharp bend.

Joharran started out again, leading the long line of people that were headed toward the home of the Third Cave of the Zelandonii. Ayla noticed some people waiting ahead, waving at them. She recognized Kareja and the Zelandoni of the Eleventh among them. The line lengthened as they fell in behind. As they drew near the high cliff ahead, Ayla got a better look at the huge rock wall, one of many spectacular limestone cliffs in the valley of The River.

It had been carved, by the same natural forces that had created all the rock shelters in the region, into two and in places three levels of terraces stacked one above the other. Halfway up the massive rock ahead was a shelf more than three hundred feet long in front of a sheltered opening. It was the main level for the ordinary living activities of the Third Cave, and most of the dwellings were located there. The terrace offered the protection of a rocky ceiling to the abri below, while it in turn was sheltered by a overhanging cliff above.

Jondalar noticed Ayla observing the great limestone cliff and stopped for a moment to let her catch up with him. The path wasn't as narrow and they could walk abreast. "The place where Grass River joins The River is called Two Rivers," he said. "That cliff is Two Rivers Rock because it overlooks the confluence."

"I thought it was the Third Cave," Ayla said.

"It is known as the home of the Third Cave of the Zelandonii, but its name is Two Rivers Rock, just like the home of the Fourteenth Cave of the Zelandonii is called Little Valley, and the home of the Eleventh Cave is River Place," Jondalar explained.

"Then what is the home of the Ninth Cave called?" Ayla said.

"The Ninth Cave," Jondalar said, and noticed her frown.

"Why doesn't it have another name like the others?" she asked.

"I'm not sure," Jondalar said. "It's just always been the Ninth Cave. I suppose it could have been called something like 'Two Rivers Rock,' since Wood River joins The River nearby, but the Third Cave already had that name. Or it might have been 'Big Rock,' but another place is called that."

"There are other names it could have been called. Something about the Falling Stone, maybe. No other place has such an unusual object, does it?" Ayla asked, trying to understand. It was easier to remember things if they were consistent, but there always seemed to be exceptions.

"No, not that I've ever seen," Jondalar said.

"But the Ninth Cave is just the Ninth Cave and doesn't have any other name except that," Ayla said. "I wonder why."

"Maybe it's because our shelter is unique for so many reasons. No one has seen or even heard of a single rock shelter as big, or one that has so many people. It does overlook two rivers, like some others, but Wood River Valley has more trees than most other valleys. The Eleventh Cave always asks to cut trees for their rafts from there. And then, as you said, there is the Falling Stone," Jondalar said. "Everyone knows of the Ninth Cave, even people from far away, but no single name really describes it all. I guess it just came to be known for the people who live there, the Ninth Cave."

Ayla nodded, but she was still frowning. "Well, naming it for the people does make it unique, I suppose."

As they neared the home of the Third Cave, Ayla could see a clutter of tents, lean-tos, frames, and racks in the space between the base of the cliff and The River. A random scatter of hearths—the dark circular lenses of former fires and a few with burning flames—were interspersed among the structures. It was the main working area of the Third Cave's outside activities and included a small dock along the bank of The River to secure rafts.

The territory of the Third Cave encompassed not only the cliff, but the area below the stone terraces all the way to the edge of the water of both rivers and in some places beyond. It wasn't owned by them. People, particularly from the other nearby Caves, could walk into another Cave's territory and use its resources, but it was considered polite to be invited or to ask first. Such tacit strictures were understood by adults. Children, of course, could go anywhere they wanted.

The region along The River between Wood River just beyond the Ninth Cave on the north and Grass River at Two Rivers Rock on the south was considered a cohesive community by the Zelandonii who lived there. In effect, it was an extended village, though they didn't, quite, have a concept for that kind of settlement or give a name to it. But when Jondalar was traveling and referred to the Ninth Cave of the Zelandonii as his home, it was not only the many people of that particular stone shelter that he thought of, but the entire neighboring community.

The visitors began ascending the trail toward the main level of Two Rivers Rock but stopped when they reached the lower level to wait for a person who wanted to join the meeting. While they were standing there, Ayla looked up and found herself reaching for the nearby wall to steady herself. The top of the cliff overhung so far that as the eye followed the massive stone walls up, it gave her the feeling that the cliff itself was bending over backward along with the viewer.

"That's Kimeran," Jondalar said, grinning, as the man greeted Joharran. Ayla looked at the stranger, who was blond and taller than Joharran. She was struck by the subtle body language of the two men, who seemed to regard each other as equals.

The newcomer eyed the wolf with apprehension, but made no comment as they continued up to the next level. When they finally reached the main level, Ayla had to stop again, halted this time by the spectacular view. Her breath caught in her throat. The stone front porch of the Third Cave's rock shelter commanded an expansive vista of the surrounding countryside. Somewhat upstream along Grass River, she could even see another small watercourse that joined the secondary.

"Ayla." She turned around when she heard her name. Joharran was behind her, with the man who had just joined them. "I want to introduce you to someone."

The man took a step forward and held out both hands, but his eyes glanced warily at the wolf beside her, who was looking at him with attentive curiosity. He seemed to be as tall as Jondalar and, with his blond hair, bore a superficial resemblance to him. She put her hand down to signal the animal to stay back as she moved forward to greet him.

"Kimeran, this is Ayla of the Mamutoi . . . ," Joharran began. Kimeran took both of her hands in his as the leader of the Ninth Cave continued with her names and ties. Joharran had noticed the man's anxious look and understood exactly how he felt. "Ayla, this is Kimeran, Leader of Elder Hearth, the Second Cave of the Zelandonii, Brother of Zelandoni of the Second Cave, Descendant of the Founder of the Seventh Cave of the Zelandonii."

"In the name of Doni, the Great Earth Mother, you are welcome to the land of the Zelandonii, Ayla of the Mamutoi," Kimeran said.

"In the name of Mut, Mother of All, also known as Doni and by many other names, I greet you Kimeran, Leader of Elder Hearth, the Second Cave of the Zelandonii," Ayla said, then smiled and repeated his complete introduction. Kimeran noticed her foreign accent and then her lovely smile. She was truly beautiful, he thought, but could he expect any less from Jondalar?

"Kimeran!" Jondalar said when they finished the formal words. "It's good to see you!"

"And you, Jondalar." The men grabbed each other's hands, then gave each other a rough but affectionate hug.

"So you are leader of the Second now," Jondalar said.

"Yes. For a couple of years. I wondered if you'd make it back. I heard you had returned, but I had to come and see for myself if all the stories about you are true. I think they must be," Kimeran said, smiling at Ayla, but still keeping a cautious distance from the wolf.

"Ayla, Kimeran and I have been friends for a long time. We went through our manhood ceremony together, got our belts . . . became men at the same time." Jondalar smiled and shook his head at the memory. "We were all about the same age, but I felt that I stood out because I was taller than everyone. I was so glad when I saw Kimeran coming because he was as tall as me. I wanted to stand near him so I wouldn't be so noticeable. I think he felt the same way." He turned back to the man, who was also smiling, but his expression changed at Jondalar's next words. "Kimeran, I think you should come and meet Wolf."

"Meet him?"

"Yes, Wolf won't hurt you, Ayla will introduce you. Then he'll know you as a friend."

Kimeran felt disconcerted as Jondalar walked him toward the four-legged hunter. It was the biggest wolf he'd ever seen, but the woman obviously wasn't afraid. She went down on one knee and put an arm around him, then looked up and smiled. The wolf's mouth was open, his teeth were bared, and his tongue was hanging out the side. Was that wolf sneering at him?

"Put your hand out so Wolf can smell it," Jondalar urged.

"What's that word you called him?" Kimeran said, frowning and avoiding the gesture. He wasn't at all sure he wanted to offer his hand to the animal, but people were standing around watching, and he didn't want to seem afraid, either.

"It's the name Ayla gave him, it's the Mamutoi word for 'wolf.'"

When Ayla took his right hand, Kimeran knew he was committed. He took a deep breath and allowed her to bring that important appendage close to the mouth that was full of sharp teeth.

Kimeran was surprised, as most people were, when Ayla went through the process of showing him how to touch the wolf, and he was startled when Wolf licked his hand. But when he felt Wolf's living warmth, the man wondered why the animal stood still for the touching, and once the initial wonder was over, he found himself paying more attention to the woman.

What kind of power does she have? he wondered. Is she Zelandoni? He was particularly aware of the zelandonia and their unique abilities. She speaks in perfectly clear and understandable Zelandonii, but she has a manner of speaking that is strange. It is not exactly an accent, he thought. She almost seems to swallow some of the sounds. It isn't unpleasant, but it does make you take notice of her ... not that you wouldn't anyway. She has a foreign look, you know she's a stranger, but a beautiful, exotic stranger, and the wolf is a part of it. How does she control a wolf? He took on a look of wonder, almost awe.

Ayla had been watching Kimeran's expressions and saw the look of wonder. She glanced away when she felt herself starting to smile, then she looked up at him. "I've taken care of Wolf since he was a little pup," she said. "He was raised with the children of the Lion Camp. He's used to people."

Kimeran felt a flush of surprise. It was almost as though she knew what he was thinking and gave him an answer to his questions before he even asked.

"Did you come alone?" Jondalar asked when Kimeran could finally stop looking at the wolf, and Ayla, and turned his attention back to him.

"More are coming. We got word that Joharran wanted to organize a last hunt before leaving for the Summer Meeting. Manvelar sent a runner to the Seventh, and they sent one to us, but I didn't want to wait for everyone and came ahead," he said.

"Kimeran's Cave is that way, Ayla," Jondalar said, pointing down the valley of Grass River. "Can you see that small tributary?" Ayla nodded. "That's the Little Grass River. Continue along Grass River beyond the tributary to reach the Second and the Seventh Caves. They're related, and live across a rich meadow from each other."

The two men began talking, reminiscing and catching up, but

Ayla was distracted again by the panoramic scene. The Third Cave's spacious upper terrace gave the inhabitants many advantages. It was well protected by its large overhang from unpleasant weather, yet it offered an extraordinary view.

Unlike the wooded valley near the Ninth Cave, the valleys of both the Grass and the Little Grass Rivers were rich, luxuriant grasslands, but different from the broad meadows of the floodplain of The River. A variety of trees and brush lined the banks of the primary river, but beyond the narrow gallery forest it was an open field of essentially shortgrass that was favored by ruminant grazers. Directly across The River toward the west, the broad floodplain led to a series of hills that climbed up to a grass-covered highland.

The valleys of both the Grass and the Little Grass Rivers were wetter, almost swampy at certain times of year, which supported the tallgrass varieties of grass that grew higher than a man in places, and were often mixed with herbaceous forbs. The wide variety of plants invited many different types of grazing and browsing animals that preferred specific kinds or parts of the various grasses and leafy herbs as they migrated seasonally across the landscape.

Since the main terrace of Two Rivers Rock overlooked the valleys of both The River and Grass River, it made an ideal location from which to monitor the itinerant herds. As a consequence, over time the people of the Third Cave gained not only great skill in tracking the movements of herds, but knowledge of the seasonal changes and weather patterns that signaled the appearance of the various animals. With that edge their proficiency as hunters grew. Though every Cave hunted, the spears of the hunters of the Third Cave living at Two Rivers Rock brought down more of the grazers and browsers that migrated through the grassy floodplains of the river valleys than any of the others.

The primacy of the Third Cave's hunting knowledge and skill was known by most of the Zelandonii, but especially acknowledged by their nearest neighbors. They were the ones to whom the others turned for insight and information whenever anyone planned to go hunting, particularly when a major, community-wide, group hunt was considered.

Ayla looked toward the left, south. The grassy valleys of the two rivers, which joined just below, opened out between high cliffs. Enlarged by Grass River, The River flowed southwest close against the base of the tall cliffs, around the rocks of a deep bend, and out of sight, heading for a larger river farther south and eventually to the Great Waters some distance to the west.

Then Ayla looked right, to the north, back the way they had come. The upstream valley of The River was a broad green meadow with the sparkling shimmer of sunlight reflecting off the meandering waterway glinting through the junipers, silver birches, willows, and pines, even an occasional evergreen oak, that marked its course. Upstream on the opposite bank, where The River made a sweeping turn toward the rising sun, the high cliffs and the immense overhanging shelter of the Ninth Cave could be seen.

Manvelar strode toward them, smiling in welcome. Though the gray-haired man was not young, Ayla noticed that he walked with vitality and confidence. She found it difficult to judge his age. After greetings and a few formal introductions, Manvelar led the group to an unoccupied section on the main level somewhat north of the living area.

"We're preparing a midday meal for everyone," Manvelar announced, "but if anyone is thirsty, there's water and some cups here." He indicated a couple of large wet waterbags propped up against a stone, with a few woven cups stacked nearby.

Most people accepted the offer, though many had brought their personal drinking cups. It was not uncommon to take one's own cup, bowl, and eating knife in a pouch or carryall of some kind even when going on short trips or visiting friends. Ayla brought not only her own cup, but a bowl for Wolf. People stared with fascination as the magnificent animal eagerly lapped up the water she gave him, and several smiled. It was somehow comforting to realize that the wolf, who seemed bound to the woman with an inexplicably mysterious tie, could be so ordinary as to need a drink of water.

They settled down with an air of pleasant anticipation, some people sitting on stones, some standing, waiting for things to get started. Manvelar delayed until everyone was quiet and ready, then he acknowledged a young woman who had been standing close to him.

"We've had watchers, both here and at Second View, for the past two days," he said.

"That's Second View, Ayla," Jondalar said quietly. She looked where he indicated. Across the confluence of Two Rivers and its wide floodplain was another small rock shelter jutting out sharply from an acute corner at the beginning of the line of cliffs that paralleled The River as it continued downstream. "Although it's separated by Grass River, the Third Cave considers Second View to be a part of Two Rivers Rock."

Ayla looked again toward the place called Second View, then took a few steps to look over the edge down at the water. From her perspective, she could see that at its mouth, Grass River broadened out into a small fan-shaped delta as it approached the larger waterway. On the right bank of the smaller river, at the base of Two Rivers Rock, a path heading east, upstream, forked off toward the flowing water. She noticed that the offshoot trail led to the bank of Grass River at one edge of the delta where it was wide and shallow, but back from the turbulance of the confluence of Two Rivers. It was where the Third Cave crossed Grass River.

On the other side, a path continued across the valley formed by the floodplain of both rivers for about a quarter of a mile to the jutting corner abri. Small and high, it didn't offer much shelter beneath it, but a rocky path led to the top, a stone platform from which there was an alternative view of the valleys of both rivers from the opposite side of Grass River.

". . . Thefona arrived with information just before you came," Manvelar was saying. "I think there are a couple of possibilities for a good hunt, Joharran. We've been keeping track of a mixed herd of about eight giant deer with young moving this way, and Thefona has just spotted a good-sized herd of bison."

"Either one would do, whichever we could be most assured of getting. What would you suggest?" Joharran asked.

"If it was just the Third Cave, we'd probably wait for the giant deer at The River and pick off a couple at the Crossing, but if you're looking for a substantial kill, I'd go for the bison and drive them into a surround," Manvelar said.

"We could do both," Jondalar said.

Several people smiled. "He wants them all? Was Jondalar always so eager?" someone remarked, Ayla wasn't sure who.

"Eager, yes, though not usually for hunting animals," a woman's voice retorted. A chorus of chuckles and laughter followed.

Ayla caught sight of the speaker. It was Kareja, the leader of the Eleventh Cave. Ayla recalled meeting her and being impressed, but she didn't like the tone of her comments. It seemed as if she was making fun of Jondalar, and Ayla had too recently been the object of similar-sounding laughter. She looked to see how he was reacting. A flush of color tinted his face, but he made a wry grin. He's embarrassed, Ayla thought, and trying not to show it.

"I guess that did sound a little eager, and I know it seems as if we can't do it all, but I think we can. When we were living with the Mamutoi, Ayla, on her horse, helped the Lion Camp drive bison into a surround," Jondalar tried to explain. "A horse can run faster than any person, and we can direct the horses where we want them to go. We can help drive those bison, and head them off when they try to break away. And you'll see how easy it would be to bring down a giant deer with this spear-thrower. Probably more than a couple. I think you will all be surprised at what this can do." He held up the hunting weapon as he spoke. It was a rather flat, narrow wooden shaft that seemed far too simple to do all that the returned traveler claimed for it.

"You're saying you think we can do it all?" Joharran asked.

The gathering was interrupted by people of the Third Cave bringing food. After a leisurely midday meal, further discussion revealed that the location of the bison herd was not far from a previously built surround that could be repaired and made serviceable. They planned to spend a day repairing the corral trap, and if they could get it ready, and if the bison didn't wander away, they would hunt the bison the morning after, but they would also watch the giant deer. Ayla listened carefully when the talk turned to the strategic planning of the hunt, but she did not volunteer herself and Whinney to help. She would see how things worked out.

"Well, let's see this wonderful new weapon, Jondalar," Joharran finally said.

"Yes," Manvelar said. "You've made me very curious. We can use the practice field in Grass Valley."

11

The practice field was near the foot of Two Rivers Rock and consisted of a central runway of dirt that had been trampled bare from heavy use. Even the grass around it was flattened by the many people that had been standing and walking on it. One end of the run was marked by a large section of limestone that had once been an overhanging ledge, which had fallen some unknown time before. Its formerly sharp edges were rounded with the wear of time and climbing feet. At the other end four hides were wrapped and tied around bundles of dry grass that poked through several previous spear holes. On each of the hides, the shape of a different animal was painted.

"You'll have to move those targets farther away, at least twice the distance," Jondalar said.

"Twice the distance?" Kareja asked, eyeing the wooden implement in his hands.

"At least."

The object Jondalar held had been carved from a straight piece of wood and was about the length of his forearm from the ends of his extended fingers to his elbow. It was narrow and flat, with a long groove down the center and two leather loops near the front. A backstop at the rear had a tapering prong extending from it, a hook that fit into a hole carved into the butt of a light spear.

Out of a rawhide quiver, Jondalar took a flint point that was attached to a short length of wood with sinew and glue, made of boiled hooves and scraps of hide. The rear end of the short shank tapered to a rounded point. The object appeared to be a disproportionately short spear, or perhaps a kind of knife with an unusual handle. Then he pulled out of a holder a long shaft that was fletched at one end with two feathers like a spear but had no point at the other. There was a murmur of curiosity from the crowd.

He inserted the tapered end of the shank that was attached to the flint point into a hole that had been carved into the front end of the much longer shaft, and held out a two-piece, rather graceful, spear. There was an exclamation of understanding from some, but not all.

"I've made a few changes since I first developed this spear-throwing technique," Jondalar said to the assembled group. "I keep trying out new ideas to see how they work. This detachable spear point turned out to be a good one. Rather than the long shaft splintering every time a spear lands wrong or breaking when an animal you've hit runs away, with this," he held up the spear and separated the two pieces again, "the point will pull out of the shaft and you don't have to make a whole new spear."

There was an interested murmur from the crowd in response. It took time and effort to shape a spear shaft to make it straight so that it would fly true when it was thrown, and there wasn't a hunter there who hadn't broken one at the worst possible time.

"You may notice that this spear is somewhat smaller and more lightweight than normal spears," Jondalar continued.

"That's it!" Willamar exclaimed. "I knew there was something about that spear that was different, besides the fact that it's made in two parts. It somehow seems more graceful, almost feminine. Like a 'Mother' spear."

"We discovered that a lighter spear will actually fly better," Jondalar said.

"But will it pierce?" Brameval said. "It may not go as far, but I've found that a spear needs some heft. If it's too lightweight, it bounces off a thick hide, or breaks the point."

"I think it's time for a demonstration," Jondalar said, picking up his holder and quiver and moving back toward the fallen rocks. He had brought spare shafts and additional detachable points, but they were not all the same. Some were tipped with flint, though each point had a slightly different shape, others were made of a long piece of carved bone, shaped to a sharp point with a base that was split to facilitate attaching to the shorter intermediate shaft. He fitted a few more spears together in readiness while Solaban and Rushemar dragged a target farther away.

"Is this far enough, Jondalar?" Solaban shouted.

Jondalar glanced at Ayla. The wolf had stationed himself beside her. She held her spear-thrower and had a long quiver on her back with extra spears already put together. She smiled at him and he smiled back, but it was a nervous smile. He had decided to begin with a demonstration and then explain and answer questions.

"It will do," he said. It was well within range, quite close, in fact, but it would do for his first demonstration. He could be more accurate as well. He didn't have to tell them to stand out of the way. They were all loping back, more than happy to stay clear of a spear cast with the unfamiliar implement. He waited for them to return, and while they were all looking on with expressions ranging from expectant to doubtful, he prepared to throw.

Holding the spear-thrower horizontally in his right hand, with his thumb and index fingers through the two front loops, he quickly slapped a spear into the groove. He slid it back so that the hook of the thrower, which also acted as a backstop, fit into the hole in the fletched butt end, and without hesitation he launched the spear. He did it so quickly, many people hardly noticed the way that the back end of the thrower raised up while he held on to the front with the aid of the loops, effectively adding the length of the spear-thrower to the length of his arm and thereby gaining the advantage of the additional leverage.

What they did see was a spear fly with twice the usual speed and land in the middle of the deer painted on the hide with such force that it penetrated clear through the bundle of grass. To the observers' surprise, a second spear followed the first with nearly as much force, landing close to the same hole. Ayla had followed Jondalar's cast with one of her own. There was a stunned silence, and then a babble of questions.

"Did you see that!"

"I didn't see you throw, can you do it again, Jondalar?"

"That spear nearly went through the target, how did you throw it so hard?"

"Hers went through it, too. What gives them such force?"

"Can I see that thing? What do you call it? A spear-thrower?"

The last questions came from Joharran, and Jondalar gave him the implement. His brother looked it over carefully, even turning it over and noticing the simple carving of a giant deer on the back. It made him smile. He'd seen a similar carving before.

"Not bad, for a flint-knapper," he said, indicating the carving.

"How do you know I did it?"

"I remember when you thought you might be a carver, Jondalar. I think I still have a plate you once gave me with a carving like that. But where did this come from?" he said, handing the thrower back. "And I'd like to see how you use it."

"I worked it out when I was staying with Ayla in her valley. It's really not difficult to use, but it does take practice to gain control. I can throw farther, but Ayla is more accurate than I am," Jondalar explained as he picked up another spear. "Do you see this small hole that I carved into the back end of this spear?"

Joharran and several other people crowded near to see the rounded indentation.

"What's the purpose of that?" Kareja asked.

"I'll show you. See this hooklike projection at the back of the thrower? They fit together like this," he said, inserting the point of the hook into the hole. He adjusted the spear so that it lay flat on the thrower, with the two feathers of the fletching on either side, then he put his thumb and index finger through the leather loops, and held the spear and the thrower together in a horizontal position. Everyone was crowding around, trying to see. "Ayla, why don't you show them, too." Ayla went through a similar demonstration.

"She is holding it differently," Kareja said. "She has her first two fingers through the loops, Jondalar is using his thumb and forefinger."

"You are very perceptive, Kareja," Marthona remarked.

"This works best for me," Ayla explained. "Jondalar used to hold it this way, but now he prefers to hold it his way. Either way is fine. You can hold it whatever way is most comfortable for you."

Kareja nodded, then said, "Your spears are smaller and lighter than usual, too."

"At first we used bigger spears, but Jondalar came up with these smaller ones after a while. They are easier to handle and better for accuracy," Ayla said.

Jondalar continued with the demonstration. "When you throw, notice how the back of the spear-thrower raises up, giving the spear an extra push?" With the spear and thrower in his right hand, he took hold of the spear with his left to show the movement in slow motion without letting the spear drop. "That's what gives it the extra force."

"When that spear-thrower is fully extended, it's as though your arm is half again as long," Brameval said. He hadn't said much before, and it took Ayla a moment to recall that he was the leader of the Fourteenth Cave.

"Would you throw the spear again? Show us once more how it works?" Manvelar said.

Jondalar pulled back, took aim, and let fly. The spear punched through the target again. Ayla's spear followed a heartbeat later.

Kareja looked at the woman Jondalar had brought home and smiled. She hadn't known Ayla was so accomplished. It rather surprised her. She had assumed the quite obviously attractive woman would be more like Marona, the one he had chosen before he left, but this woman might be worth getting to know better.

"Would you like to try it, Kareja?" Ayla asked, offering her spear-thrower.

"Yes, I would," the leader of the Eleventh Cave said, smiling broadly. She took the thrower and examined it while Ayla got another spear shaft with a detachable point. She noticed the bison carved on the bottom and wondered if Jondalar had made it, too. It was a decent carving, not exceptional, but adequate.

Wolf wandered off while Ayla and Jondalar showed people the techniques they would have to practice in order to effectively use the new hunting weapon. While some managed to make some good distance throws, it was obvious that accuracy would take more time. Ayla was standing back, watching, when she caught a movement out of the corner of her eye. She turned to see Wolf chasing something. When she caught a glimpse of it, she took her sling out of a pouch, along with a couple of smooth, rounded stones.

She placed the stone in the pouch of leather in the middle of the sling, and when the ptarmigan in full summer plumage flew up, she was ready. She hurled it at the plump bird and saw it drop. A second ptarmigan flew up, and a second stone from Ayla's sling brought it down. By then, Wolf had found the first one. She intercepted him as he was carrying it off and took it out of his mouth, then picked up the second and carried them both by their feet. Suddenly she realized it was the right season and started looking around in the grass. She spied the nest and, with a grin of delight, picked up several eggs as well. She would be able to cook Creb's favorite dish, ptarmigan stuffed with its own eggs.

She was pleased with herself as she walked back with Wolf at her side and didn't notice until she drew near that everyone had stopped practicing and was staring at her. Some were smiling, but most people looked surprised. Jondalar was grinning.

"Didn't I tell you about her skill with a sling?" Jondalar said. He was feeling smug, and it showed.

"But you didn't say she used the wolf to flush out game. With her sling and the wolf, why did you need to come up with this thing?" Joharran said, holding up the spear-thrower.

"In fact, it was her sling that gave me the idea for it," Jondalar said, "and she didn't have Wolf then, though she had hunted with a cave lion."

Most people thought Jondalar was joking, although looking at the woman holding a couple of dead ptarmigan, with the wolf at her side, they weren't sure what to believe.

"How did you develop this spear-thrower, Jondalar?" Joharran asked. It had been his turn to try, and he still had the thrower in his hand.

"Watching Ayla throw a stone with that sling made me wish I could throw a spear like that. In fact, my first tries were with a kind of sling, but then I realized I needed something stiffer, less flexible. Eventually, I came up with this idea," Jondalar explained. "But at that time, I didn't know what you could really do with one. It takes practice, as you can guess by now, but we have even learned to use them from horseback. Now that you've had a chance to try them, maybe we should give you a real demonstration. Too bad we didn't bring the horses, but at least I can give you a better idea of their range."

Several spears had been retrieved from the targets. Jondalar picked one up, took the thrower from Joharran, and walked back a few feet. He sighted toward the targets, but instead of aiming directly for the hay bundles, he gave it as hard a cast as he could. The spear sailed over the bundles, going more than half again the distance before landing in the distant grass. Sounds of amazement could be heard.

Ayla went next, and though she didn't have quite the power of the tall, muscular man, her spear fell only a little short of Jondalar's. Ayla's physical strength was greater than that of most women; it was the result of her upbringing. The people of the Clan were stronger and more robust than the Others. For her to keep up with them, to simply perform the ordinary work that was expected of Clan women and girls as she grew up, she had had to develop stronger bones and more muscle power than was normal for her kind.

As the spears were gathered, the people talked about the new weapon they had just seen. Casting a spear with a spear-thrower did not appear to be much different from throwing a spear by hand. The difference was in the results. It flew more than twice as far and with much greater force. That was the aspect most discussed, because it was immediately understood how much safer it would be to throw a spear from a greater distance.

Hunting accidents, while not common, were also not rare. More than one hunter had been maimed or killed by a pain-maddened, wounded animal. The question was how long and how much effort it would take to gain, if not the level of expertise displayed by Jondalar and Ayla, at least enough skill to use the spear-thrower competently. Some seemed to feel that they already had adequate techniques to hunt effectively, but some, especially the younger ones who were still learning, were more interested.

At first glance, the new weapon seemed so simple, and in fact it was. But it was based on principles that, although understood intuitively, would not be codified until much later. The spear-thrower was a handle, a unique detachable handle that utilized the mechanical advantage of leverage to add impetus to a spear, making it fly much farther and faster than a spear thrown with just an arm.

People had been using handles of various kinds for as long as they could remember, and any handle would amplify the force of muscles. For example, a sharp chip of stone—flint, jasper, chert, quartz, obsidian—was a cutting tool when held in the hand, but a handle multiplied the force that could be applied to the edge, increasing the effectiveness of the knife and giving the user more control.

But the spear-thrower was more than a new use of principles that were innately known. It was an example of an inborn characteristic of people like Jondalar and Ayla that made their survival more likely: the ability to conceive of an idea and turn it into a useful object, to take an abstract thought and make it real. That was their greatest Gift, though they didn't even recognize it for what it was.

The visitors spent the rest of the afternoon discussing strategies for the upcoming hunt. They decided to go after the herd of bison that had been sighted, since there were more animals in that group. Jondalar mentioned again that he thought they could hunt both the bison and the giant deer, but he didn't press the matter. Ayla said nothing, deciding to wait and see. The visitors were fed another meal and urged to stay the night. Some people chose to stay, but Joharran had some things he wanted to prepare before the hunt, and he had promised Kareja to stop for a short visit with the Eleventh Cave on the way back.

It was still light, though the sun was falling in the west when the Ninth Cave started down the path. When they reached the relatively flat stretch of land near the bank of The River, Ayla turned and looked up again at the multiple levels of shelflike shelters of Two Rivers Rock. Some people were waving at them with a beckoning "come-back" gesture that was used by many people. She noticed that the visitors waved back with a similar motion; theirs meant "come-and-visit."

Walking near the bank, they followed the cliff around to the right, back toward the north. As they continued upstream, the rock wall on their side of The River became less and less high. Near the lowest part at the bottom of a slope they saw a stone shelter. Slightly farther back and up the slope, perhaps one hundred twenty feet away, was a second abri, but stretching more or less continually along the same terrace level. A small cave could also be seen nearby. The two shelters, the cave, and the long terrace constituted the living site of another community in this densely populated regional settlement—the Eleventh Cave of the Zelandonii.

Kareja and the people of the Eleventh Cave had left Two Rivers Rock before the Ninth, and the leader was standing beside Zelandoni of the Eleventh as the group approached, waiting to greet them. Seeing them together, Ayla noticed that Kareja was taller than Zelandoni of the Eleventh. It was not that she was so tall, Ayla realized as they drew near, but that he was rather short. As he greeted her, she noticed again his strong grip. But she sensed something else about him. The man had certain mannerisms that had confused her when she first met him and came across quite strongly as he greeted and welcomed the visitors.

Suddenly she perceived that he did not appraise her the way most of the Zelandonii men did, whether overtly or with more subtlety, and she understood that this man did not look to women to satisfy his personal needs. When she was living with the Lion Camp, she recalled listening with much interest to a discussion about people who carried the essence of both male and female within them. Then she remembered Jondalar saying that such Zelandoni often made excellent healers, and she couldn't help but smile. Perhaps he would be another person with whom she could discuss practices and techniques of healing and medicine.

His smile in return was friendly. "Welcome to River Place, the home of the Eleventh Cave of the Zelandonii," he said. Another man, who was standing to the side and slightly behind him, was smiling at the Zelandoni in a warm and loving way. He was rather tall and had nice regular features that Ayla thought would be considered handsome, but he moved in a way that struck her as womanly.

The Zelandoni turned to look at the tall man and signaled him forward. "I'd like to introduce my friend, Marolan of the Eleventh Cave of the Zelandonii," he said, then continued the rest of the formal introduction, which seemed somewhat longer than usual, Ayla thought.

While he was speaking, Jondalar moved up beside her, which made her feel better when she was in a new situation, and she had been in many since they had returned to the land of his people. She turned to smile at him, then turned back to take both hands of the man. He was not as tall as Jondalar, she noted, but somewhat taller than her.

"In the name of the Mut, the Great Mother of All, also known as Doni, I greet you, Marolan of the Eleventh Cave of the Zelandonii," she concluded. His smile was cordial and he seemed interested in talking, but they had to step aside to make room for others that the leader and the Zelandoni of the Eleventh Cave were welcoming, and some people moved between them before they could exchange any conversational pleasantries. There would be time to talk later, she thought.

She glanced around to examine her surroundings. Although the location was higher than the bank, and somewhat back from the edge of the water, it was still rather close to The River. She commented on it to Marthona.

"Yes, they are close to The River," the woman said. "Some people think they could be subject to flooding. Zelandoni says there are some hints about it in the Elder Legends, but no one living now, not even the oldest, has any memory of floods here. They do take advantage of their location, though."

Willamar explained that because of their immediate access, the people of the Eleventh Cave made good use of The River's resources. Fishing was a principal activity, but more important, the Eleventh Cave was known for water transport. "River rafts are used to carry substantial amounts of whatever needs to be transported—food, goods, or people," he said. "The people of the Eleventh Cave are not only the most skilled at poling the rafts up and down The River, for themselves, and for neighboring Caves, but they make most of them."

"That's their skill," Jondalar added. "The Eleventh Cave specializes in making and using river rafts. Their home is known as River Place."

"Isn't that what those logs are?" she asked, pointing to several constructions made of wood and logs near the edge of the water. They weren't unfamiliar. She had seen something like them before and tried to remember where. Then it came to her. The S'Armunai women had used a raft. When she was trying to find Jondalar and following the only trail that led away from the site of his disappearance, she had come to a river and seen a small raft nearby.

"Not all of them. The one that looks like a big raft is their dock. The smaller platforms tied to it are rafts. Most Caves have a place near the water to secure rafts, some not much more than a simple piling, others have more elaborate docks, but none are quite like theirs. When somebody wants to travel or transport something, either up- or downriver, they go to the Eleventh Cave to make arrangements. They make fairly regular runs," Jondalar said. "I'm glad we're stopping here. I've been wanting to tell them about the Sharamudoi and their wonderfully maneuverable river craft that are shaped out of logs."

Joharran had overheard. "I don't think you'll have time to get into much of a discussion about river craft right now, unless you want to stay behind. I'd like to get back to the Ninth Cave before dark," he said. "I told Kareja I'd stop because she wanted to show you around, Ayla, and I'd like to make a trip upriver by raft after the hunt to meet with some of the other leaders about the Summer Meeting."

"If we had one of those small Ramudoi dugout boats, a couple of people could paddle upriver and wouldn't have to worry about poling a heavy raft," Jondalar said.

"How long would it take to make one?" Joharran asked.

"It takes a lot of work," Jondalar acknowledged. "But once it's made, it could last a while."

"That won't help me now, will it?"

"No. I was thinking of what a help it might be later."

"Perhaps, but I need to get upriver in the next few days," Joharran said, "and back again. If the Eleventh Cave is planning a trip, it would be easier, and much faster coming back, but I can walk if I have to."

"You could use the horses," Ayla said.

"You could use the horses, Ayla." Joharran gave her a wry grin. "I don't know how to make them go where I want."

"A horse can carry two people. You could ride behind me," she said.

"Or me," Jondalar said.

"Well, maybe sometime, but right now I think I'll find out if the Eleventh Cave is planning a trip upriver soon," Joharran said.

They hadn't noticed Kareja approach. "In fact, I have been thinking about making a run upriver," she said. They all looked up. "I'm going to the meeting, too, Joharran, and if the hunt is successful . . .," even if it was considered likely, no one ever presumed that any hunt would be successful; it would be bad luck, ". . . it might be a good idea to take some meat to the site of the Summer Meeting and cache it nearby beforehand. I think you are right that the Meeting will be particularly well attended this year." She turned to Ayla. "I know you can't stay long, but I wanted to show you our place and introduce you to some people." She didn't exactly ignore Jondalar, but she directed her comments to Ayla.

Jondalar looked more closely at the leader of the Eleventh Cave. She had been one of the most derisive of those who had teased him about his hunting suggestions and claims about their new hunting weapons, though now she seemed quite impressed with Ayla . . . after she had shown her skill. Maybe he should wait before bringing up the new kind of boats, and maybe Kareja wasn't the one he should talk to about them, he thought, wondering who their foremost raft-maker was now.

He tried to remember what he knew about Kareja. She'd never had many men interested in her, he recalled. Not because she wasn't attractive, but she hadn't seemed particularly interested in men and didn't encourage them. But he didn't recall her being interested in women, either. She had always lived with her mother, Dorova. Jondalar wondered if she still did.

Her mother had never chosen to live with a man, he knew. He couldn't remember who the man of her hearth was, or if anyone ever knew which man's spirit the Great Mother had chosen to make Dorova pregnant. People had wondered about the name she had chosen for her daughter, mostly because it resembled the sound of the word *courageous*. Did she think Kareja would need courage? It did take courage to be the leader of a Cave.

Ayla knew the wolf would draw attention and bent down to reassure him with strokes and words of comfort. She drew comfort from him as well. It was hard to be the focus of so much constant scrutiny, and it was not likely to diminish soon. She was not exactly looking forward to the Summer Meeting for just that reason, even though she was anticipating the Matrimonial that would make her Jondalar's mate. She took a deep breath and let out a surreptitious sigh, then straightened up. Giving Wolf a signal to stay close, she joined Kareja and walked toward the first of the living shelters.

It was similar to all the other shelters of stone in the region. Relative differences in the hardness of the limestone had caused the cliffs to erode at dissimilar rates, creating spaces in between terraces and overhanging ledges that were protected from precipitation above yet open to daylight. With the addition of structures built to block wind and fire to provide warmth, the spaces in the limestone cliffs provided very advantageous living conditions even during Ice Age winters in periglacial regions.

After meeting several people and introducing Wolf to a few, Ayla was led to the other stone shelter, the one in which Kareja lived. She met the leader's mother, Dorova, but no other relatives. Kareja did not appear to have a mate or siblings, and she made it clear that she wanted no children, saying that taking care of her Cave was responsibility enough.

Kareja paused and seemed to be studying Ayla, then she said, "Since you are so knowledgeable about horses, I want to show you something."

Jondalar was a little surprised when the leader headed toward a small cave. He knew where they were going, and people didn't usually bring unknown visitors to their sacred places on their first visit. Near the entrance of the cave's single gallery was a series of cryptic lines, and inside were several crude engravings that were rather difficult to see. On the ceiling, however, was a large, finely engraved horse, and more markings at the end.

"That is a remarkable horse," Ayla said. "Whoever made it must know horses well. Does that person live here?"

"I don't think so, though her spirit may still linger," Kareja said. "It has been here a long time. Some ancestor made it, we don't know who."

The last thing Ayla was shown was the dock with two rafts tied to it, and a working area where another raft was being built. She would have liked to stay longer and learn more, but Joharran was in a hurry and Jondalar had said he had to make some preparations as well. Ayla didn't want to stay by herself, especially on her first visit, but she did promise to return.

The party continued north upstream along The River to the foot of a small rocky escarpment where there was a small rock shelter.

Ayla noticed that rock debris tended to accumulate along the edge of the cliff overhang. The accumulation of talus created a wall of loose, sharp-edged gravel below the lip of the abri.

There was some evidence of use. Several panel screens stood behind the talus, and one that had fallen down. An old sleeping roll, so worn that most of the fur was gone, had been tossed against the back wall. The black circular remains of a few fireplaces were evident, two of them encircled by stones and one with two forked sticks planted in the ground across from each other, used, Ayla was sure, to support meat spitted for roasting.

Ayla thought she saw a few wisps of smoke coming from one hearth, and she was surprised. The place seemed to be abandoned, yet it looked as though it had been used recently.

"What Cave lives here?" she asked.

"No Cave lives here," Joharran said.

"But all of them use it," Jondalar added.

"Everyone uses this place occasionally," Willamar said. "It's a place to get out of the rain, or for a group of youngsters to gather, or for a couple to be alone at night, but no one lives here permanently. People just call it 'The Shelter.'"

After stopping at The Shelter, they continued up the valley of The River to the Crossing. Looking ahead, Ayla again saw the cliffs and distinctive overhanging shelter of the Ninth Cave on the right bank at the outside of the sharp bend. After crossing, they followed a well-worn path beside The River along the base of a slope with thinning trees and brush.

They again walked single file as the trail narrowed between The River and a sheer vertical cliff. "This is the one called 'High Rock,' isn't it?" Ayla said, slowing down to let Jondalar catch up.

"Yes," he said as they approached a fork in the path just beyond the sheer wall. The fork headed back the way they had come but angled up.

"Where does that path go?" she asked.

"To some caves that are high up in that steep wall we just passed," he said. She nodded.

After a few yards, the trail going north led to a valley oriented in an east-west direction that was enclosed by cliffs. A small stream ran down the middle of the valley into The River, which at that point was flowing almost exactly north to south. So narrow that it was very nearly a gorge, the valley nestled between two steep embankments: High Rock, the vertical cliff just passed on the south, and a second mass of rock of even more grand proportions on the north.

"Does that have a name?" Ayla asked.

"Everybody just calls it Big Rock," Jondalar said, "and the little stream is called Fish Creek."

As they looked up the path that ran beside a stream, they saw several people walking down. Brameval was leading the way, approaching them with a big smile. "Come and visit, Joharran," he said when he reached them. "We'd like to show Ayla around and introduce her to a few people."

Jondalar could tell from his expression that his brother really didn't want to stop again, though he knew it would be very impolite to refuse. Marthona, too, could read his expression and jumped in, not willing to let her son make a blunder that might antagonize a good neighbor just because he thought he had to hurry back. Whatever his plans, they weren't that important.

"Of course," she said. "We'd love to stop for a while. We can't stay long this time. We have to get ready for the hunt, and Joharran has some things he must do."

"How did he know we were passing by just now?" Ayla asked Jondalar as they walked up the path that ran beside Fish Creek and approached their settlement.

"Remember that fork in the path that headed up to caves in High Rock?" he said. "Brameval must have had a watcher up there, and when he saw us coming, he just ran down and told him."

Ayla saw a crowd of people waiting for them and noticed that the sections of the huge blocks of limestone that faced the creek held several small caves and abris and one immense rock shelter. When they reached it, Brameval turned around and held out his arms in a gesture that encompassed the entire place.

"Welcome to Little Valley, the home of the Fourteenth Cave of the Zelandonii," he said.

The spacious abri was fronted by a large terrace that was accessible from either side by means of a gradual ramp into which a narrow path of shallow steps had been carved out along the wall. A small hole in the cliff wall above had been slightly enlarged and could be used as a lookout or a smoke hole. A portion of the front opening of the stone shelter was protected from the elements by a wall of piled limestone shards.

The visitors from the Ninth Cave were invited into the primary living site of the small valley community and offered a cup of tea, which was already made. Chamomile, Ayla determined after taking a taste. Wolf was obviously curious to explore this new stone shelter—probably no more so than Ayla—but she kept him at her side. Everyone knew of the wolf who obeyed the woman, of course, and many had already seen him, but from a distance. It was obvious to her that it was more unnerving to have him inside their home.

She introduced Wolf to Brameval's sister and their Zelandoni while the others looked on. Even though the Ninth Cave were close friends with the Fourteenth, everyone knew it was the stranger, Ayla, who was the focus of attention. After the introductions, and a second round of tea, there was the uncomfortable silence of strangers not quite knowing what to do or say next. Joharran was looking with longing toward the path that led out, toward The River.

"Would you like to see the rest of Little Valley, Ayla?" Brameval said when it became apparent that Joharran was getting anxious to go.

"Yes, I would," she said.

With some relief, the visitors from the Ninth Cave and several people from the Fourteenth filed down the steps carved along the wall, as children jumped off the front. While the large shelter was the main home of the Fourteenth Cave, two other small rock shelters next to each other at the foot of the south-facing cliff were also used.

They stopped at a small shelter just a few feet away. "This is the Shelter of the Salmon," Brameval said, leading the way into a small, nearly circular enclosure about twenty feet across.

He pointed up. Ayla looked and saw sculptured in low relief on the vaulted ceiling a life-size salmon almost four feet long, carved with the hooked jaws of a male swimming upstream to spawn. It was part of a more complex scene, containing in addition a rectangle divided by seven lines, the forelegs of a horse, and other enigmatic markings and engravings, along with a negative handprint picked out of a black background. The entire vault had substantial areas of solid red and black color used to accent the engravings.

They made a rather quick tour of the rest of Little Valley. In the southwest, opposite the large rock shelter, was a rather spacious cave, and in the south a ledge opened in front of a small abri, which was extended into the cliff wall by a gallery cave some sixty-five feet long. To the right of the entrance of the cave, on a small natural terracette, two aurochs were carved with vigorous outlines, and the suggestion of a rhinoceros.

Ayla was quite impressed with all the natural sites in Little Valley and was quite open about showing it. Brameval and the Fourteenth Cave were proud of their home and were delighted to show it off to someone who demonstrated her appreciation. They were also getting accustomed to the wolf, especially since Ayla was careful to keep him under control. Several people encouraged the visitors, or at least Ayla, to stay for a meal.

"I would like to," Ayla said, "but not this time. I'd love to come back, though."

"Well, before you go, I'll show you our weir," Brameval said. "It's on the way to The River."

He led the rather large group that had gathered, including the visitors, to a permanent dammed fish trap that had been constructed in Fish Creek. The waterway that ran through the narrow valley was a salmon-spawning stream, where adult fish returned every year. By making various adaptations, the weir was an effective way to catch many of the other varieties of fish that also found the small stream tempting. But most prized were the huge salmon, up to five feet in length although four feet was more common for an adult male.

"We also make fishing nets to catch fish, especially from The River," Brameval said.

"The people I grew up with lived near an inland sea. Sometimes they went to the mouth of the river that flowed near their cave and used nets to catch sturgeon. They were happy when they caught females because they particularly liked the roe, the tiny black fish eggs," Ayla said.

"I've tasted sturgeon roe," Brameval said, "when we visited the people who live near the Great Waters of the West. It's good, but sturgeon don't often come this far upstream. Salmon do, of course, and their eggs are good, too, they're bigger and bright-colored, almost red. I prefer the fish to the eggs, though. I think salmon like red. Did you know male salmon get red when they're swimming upstream? I'm not as familiar with sturgeon. I understand they can get quite big."

"Jondalar caught one of the biggest sturgeon I've ever seen. I think it was longer than two of him," Ayla said, turning to smile at the tall man, and with a twinkle in her eye she added, "It gave him quite a ride."

"Unless you are planning to stay here, I think Jondalar will have to tell that story later," Joharran interjected.

"Yes, later," Jondalar said. The story was a little embarrassing, and he wasn't eager to tell it, anyway.

They continued talking about fishing as they walked together back toward The River. "When people like to fish by themselves, they often use a gorge. You know how it works, don't you?" Brameval asked. "You take a small piece of wood, sharpen it at both ends, and tie a fine cord in the middle," he was eagerly explaining, using his hands as he talked. "I usually attach a float and tie the other end to a pole. Fasten an earthworm around the gorge and dangle it in the water, then watch it. When you see a nibble, with luck, a quick jerk will pull the gorge so that it's horizontal across the throat or mouth with the two points stuck in either side. Even youngsters can get quite good."

Jondalar was smiling. "I know. You taught me when I was young," he said, then looked at Ayla. "Don't get Brameval started talking about fishing." The leader looked slightly embarrassed. "Ayla fishes, too, Brameval." The man smiled at the woman. "She can catch fish with her bare hands."

"Yes, she told me," Brameval said. "It must be difficult."

"It takes a lot of patience, but it's not hard," Ayla said. "I'll show you sometime."

After leaving the narrow gorge of Little Valley, Ayla noticed that the huge mass of limestone called Big Rock, which formed the north side of the Fourteenth Cave's small vale, soared up steeply, but unlike High Rock, it did not crowd close to The River. After several yards the path widened out as the tall limestone walls that lined the right bank pulled back from the edge of the water until a large field separated the stone walls from the flowing river.

"This is called the Gather Field," Jondalar said. "It's another place that's used by all the Caves around here. When we all want to get together for a gathering, like a feast or a meeting to let everyone know something, this place is big enough to hold us. We sometimes use it after a big hunt to dry the meat for winter. I suppose if there was a stone shelter here or a usable cave, it would have been claimed, but anyone can use it now. Mostly in summer, when a tent is a good enough shelter to stay in for a few days."

Ayla looked across at the limestone wall. Though there were no usable abris or deep caves, the face of the cliff was split by ledges and crevices where birds nested.

"I used to climb that wall a lot when I was young," Jondalar said. "There are all kinds of lookout perches and a spectacular view of The River Valley."

"The youngsters still do," Willamar said.

Beyond the Gather Field and just downstream from the Ninth Cave, another ridge of limestone cliffs crowded close to The River. Here, the forces that had eroded the stone of the cliff had created a rounded bulging appearance that rose to the top, and like all the limestone cliffs and overhangs, the warm yellowish natural color of the stone was streaked with shades of dark gray.

The trail climbed up a rather steep slope from The River to a sizable level terrace that extended beyond a row of substantial rock shelters, separated in places by sheer rock walls that had no protective overhangs. From the south, several simple structures of hide and wood were seen under the bulging overhang of rock shelters. They were constructed in the pattern of a longhouse, with a row of hearths down the middle paralleling the cliff wall.

Two fairly large stone shelters at the northern end of the terrace, about fifty yards apart, were almost contiguous with the enormous overhanging rock shelter of the Ninth Cave, but because of the way the cliff curved, the shelters did not face south, which Ayla felt made this place less desirable. She looked down at the southerly end of the terrace of the Ninth Cave beyond a spring-fed stream that ran off the edge of the stone porch, and she realized that this ledge was somewhat higher in elevation.

"Which Cave claims this place?" Ayla asked.

"No Cave really claims it," Jondalar said. "It's called Down River, probably because it's just downriver from the Ninth Cave. The runoff of the spring that rises out of the back wall has worn through the stone porch that makes a natural division between the Ninth Cave and Down River. We made a bridge to connect the two places. The Ninth Cave probably uses it more than any other, but all of the Caves use it."

"What do they use it for?" Ayla asked.

"For making things. It's a place to work. People come here to work on their crafts, especially crafts that use hard materials."

Ayla noticed then that the whole terrace of Down River, but especially within and around the area of the two northernmost abris, was littered with a refuse of ivory, bone, antler, wood, and stone from knapping flint and making tools, hunting weapons, and various implements.

"Jondalar, I'm going on ahead," Joharran said. "We're almost home and I know you want to stay here and tell Ayla all about Down River."

The rest of the people of the Ninth Cave went on with him. It was dusk, and would soon be dark.

"The first of these stone shelters is used mostly by those who work flint," Jondalar said. "Flint leaves a lot of sharp pieces when you work it. It's best to keep them in one place." Then he looked around and saw that the debitage of chips and flakes, left behind in the process of making knives, spear points, scrapers, the chisel-like tools called burins, and other weapons and tools out of the hard siliceous stone, was all over. "Well," he smiled, "that was the original idea."

He told her that most of the stone tools made here were taken to the second rock shelter to be attached to handles made out of other materials such as wood or bone, and many of those would then be used to make other things out of the same hard materials, but there were no hard and fast rules about what was made where. They often worked together.

For example, the worker who shaped flint into a knife blade often collaborated closely with the one who made the handle for it, perhaps chipping a bit more off the tang of the blade to fit into the handle better, or suggesting that the haft be modified or thinned for better balance. Or the shaper of a bone spear point might ask the flint-knapper to sharpen a tool or suggest a way to rework it to make it easier to use. Or the carver who decorated the handle or shaft might want a special chisel point, and only a skilled and experienced knapper could detach a burin-spall off the end of the flint implement at just the right angle to get the desired result.

Jondalar greeted a few crafters who were still around the second stone shelter at the north end of the terrace, working on some project, and introduced Ayla. They eyed the wolf warily, but went back to work after the animal and the couple passed on.

"It's getting dark," Ayla said. "Where will those people sleep?"

"They could come to the Ninth Cave, but they'll probably light a fire and stay up late, and then spend the night in one of those sleeping lodges under the first shelters we passed," he explained. "They're trying to finish before tomorrow. If you recall, there were many more crafters here earlier today. The rest have either gone home or are staying with friends at the Ninth Cave."

"Does everyone come here to work on projects?" Ayla asked.

"Every Cave has a work site like this near their living area, usually smaller, but whenever crafters have a question or an idea to work out, they come here," Jondalar said.

He went on to explain that it was also where a young person was taken who had developed an interest and wanted to learn something about a particular craft. It was a good place to discuss things, such as the quality of flint from various regions and the best uses for each variety. Or to exchange views about techniques about anything: how to cut down a tree with a flint axe, or remove suitable pieces of ivory from a mammoth tusk, or cut a tine off an antler, or bore a hole through a shell or a tooth, or shape and pierce beads, or rough out an approximate shape for a bone spear point. It was the place to discuss acquiring raw material and to plan trips or trading missions to get it.

And not least, it was a good place to just talk about who was interested in whom, who was having problems with a mate or a mate's mother, whose daughter, son, or hearth-child had taken a first step, or spoken a new word, or made a tool, or found a good patch of berries, or tracked an animal, or made a first kill. Ayla quickly got the idea that it was a place for both serious work and friendly camaraderie.

"We'd better get going before it's too dark to find our way," Jondalar said, "especially since we don't have torches. Besides, if we are going hunting tomorrow, there's a few things we will need, too, and we'll be off early."

The sun had already set, though the last glimmerings of light colored the sky overhead when they finally headed down toward the bridge over the runoff creek from the spring. They crossed over to the end of the shelter of stone that was the home of Jondalar and his people, the Ninth Cave of the Zelandonii. As the path leveled out, Ayla noticed that the light from several fires ahead was reflected off the underside of the limestone overhang. It was a welcoming sight. For all the protection of the animal Spirits that helped to define her, only people knew how to make fire.

12

It was still dark when they heard a light tap on the doorpost. "The zelandonia are preparing the hunting ceremony," a voice said.

"We'll be right there," Jondalar said quietly.

They were already awake, but not dressed. Ayla had been fighting down a bit of nausea and trying to decide what to wear, not that she had much to choose from. She would have to make herself some clothes. Perhaps she would be able to get a hide or two from their kill today. She looked again at the sleeveless tunic and calf-length leggings, the boys' underwear Marona had given to her, and made a decision. Why not? It was a comfortable outfit, and it would probably be hot later today.

Jondalar watched her put on the clothing Marona had given her, but didn't say anything. It had been given to her, after all. She could use it for anything she wanted. He looked up when he saw his mother coming out of her sleeping place.

"Mother, I hope we didn't wake you," Jondalar said.

"You didn't wake me. I still feel an edge of excitement just before a hunt, even though I haven't gone hunting for years," Marthona said. "I suppose that's why I like to be involved in the planning and the rituals. I'm going to the ceremony, too."

"We both are," Willamar said, stepping out from behind the screen that divided their sleeping room from the rest of dwelling.

"I'm coming, too," Folara said, her sleepy-eyed, tousled head looking around the edge of her screen. She yawned and rubbed her eyes. "I just need a little time to get dressed." Suddenly her eyes opened wide. "Ayla! Are you wearing that?"

Ayla looked down at herself, then stood up straight. "This was given to me as a 'gift,'" she said with a touch of defensive belligerence, "and I intend to wear it. Besides," she added with a smile, "I don't have many clothes, and this is easy to move in. If I tie a cloak or a fur around me, it will be warm in the chill of the morning, but later, when it gets hot, it will be cool and comfortable. It really is a very practical outfit."

There was a moment of awkward silence, then Willamar chuckled. "You know, she's right. I would have never thought of wearing winter underwear as summer hunting clothes, but why not?"

Marthona studied Ayla carefully, then gave her a shrewd smile. "If Ayla wears that outfit," she said, "people will talk. Older women will disapprove, but under the circumstances, some will feel she's justified, and by this time next year, half the young women will be wearing the same thing."

Jondalar visibly relaxed. "Do you really think so, mother?"

He hadn't known what to say when he saw Ayla putting on the clothes. Marona had given them to her for the sole purpose of causing her embarrassment, but it occurred to him that if his mother was right—and Marthona was seldom wrong about such things—it would be Marona who would be not only embarrassed, but not allowed to forget it. Every time she saw someone wear such an outfit, it would remind her that her spiteful trick had not pleased anyone.

Folara was looking dumbfounded, glancing from her mother to Ayla, then back to Marthona again.

"You'd better hurry if you're coming, Folara," the older woman chided. "It will be daylight soon."

Willamar lit a torch from the banked fire in the cooking room while they waited. It was one of several they had prepared after they had walked into a dark dwelling, the night Ayla taught them how to make fire with flint and iron pyrite. When Folara came out, still trying to tie her hair back with a strip of leather, they moved the leather drape aside and slipped out quietly. Ayla bent down to touch Wolf's head, a signal in the dark for him to stay close, as they walked toward several bobbing firelights in the direction of the stone front porch.

Quite a number of people were already congregated on the front ledge when the residents of Marthona's dwelling, including the wolf, appeared. Some were holding stone oil lamps, which shed just enough light in the dark for them to find their way but burned for some time; others held torches, which gave more light but burned out faster.

They waited a while longer until a few more people joined them, then the whole group started toward the south end of the abri. It was difficult to distinguish individuals or even see where they were going when they started out. The torches carried by some lighted the space around them, but made everything beyond the glow of the light seem blacker.

Ayla kept her hand on Jondalar's arm as they walked along the stone ledge, past the uninhabited section of the Ninth Cave's cliff overhang to the gully that separated the Ninth Cave from Down River. The small creek that ran through the trench—the runoff of the fresh spring welling up out of the back wall—was a handy source of water for the craftspeople when they were working, and during bad weather an extra source for the Ninth Cave as well.

The torchbearers stood at either end of the bridge that led up to the stone shelters of Down River. In the flickering light, each person walked carefully on the logs that were lashed together and laid across the small gully. Ayla thought the sky was beginning to turn from true black to the deep midnight blue of predawn, the first sign that the sun would soon be breaking. But stars still filled the night sky.

There were no fires burning in the two large shelters of Down River. The last of the crafters had long since retired to the sleeping lodges. The hunting party passed by the lodges, then continued down the steep path to the Gather Field between High Rock and The River. From quite a distance away, they could see the large balefire in the middle of the field and people around it. When they drew near, Ayla noted that, like the torches, the fire lighted the space around it, but made it difficult to see beyond. Fire was wonderful to have at night, but there were limitations.

They were met by several of the zelandonia, including the One Who Was First Among Those Who Served The Mother, the Zelandoni of the Ninth Cave. The large woman greeted them and told them where they would stand for the ceremony. As she walked away, her broad silhouette almost blocked the light from the fire, but only for a moment.

More people were arriving. Ayla recognized Brameval in the firelight and realized it was a group from the Fourteenth Cave. She glanced up and was aware that the sky had definitely become deep blue. Then another group of people carrying torches appeared, Kareja and Manvelar among them. The Eleventh and Third Caves had arrived. Manvelar motioned to Joharran, then approached him.

"I wanted to tell you, I think we should go after the giant deer today rather than the bison," Manvelar said. "When the watchers came up last evening, after you left, they said the bison have moved away from the surround trap. It won't be easy to chase them into it now."

Joharran looked disappointed for a moment, but hunting always did require flexibility. Animals roamed where they chose for their own needs, not for a hunter's convenience. A successful hunter was adaptable.

"All right, let's tell Zelandoni," he said.

At a signal, everyone moved to an area between the fire and the rear of the field, facing the back wall. The closeness of the fire and the crowd of people raised the temperature, and Ayla savored the warmth. The exercise of walking to the Gather Field, at a fairly good pace in spite of the darkness, had served to keep her warm enough, but standing around waiting had caused her to begin to feel the chill. The wolf pressed against her leg; he was not happy having so many strange people so close. Ayla knelt down to reassure him.

The reflection of the large fire behind them danced on the rough vertical surface of the rock. Suddenly a loud wailing sounded and the staccato of drums. Then she heard another sound and felt the hair rising at the nape of her neck and a shiver down her spine. She had heard a sound like that only once before . . . at the Clan Gathering! She would never forget the sound of a bullroarer. It was the sound that called in the spirits!

She knew how the sound was made. It came from a flat, oval-shaped piece of wood or bone with a hole at one end by which a cord was attached. Spinning the object around by the cord produced the eerie, wailing roar. But knowing how it was made in no way changed the effect it had; a sound like that could come only from the Spirit World. That wasn't what gave her the chill, however. What was hard to believe was that the Zelandonii would have a ceremony that called in the spirits the same way the Clan did.

Ayla crowded close to Jondalar, wanting the assurance of him near her. Then her attention was caught by a movement in the fire's reflection on the wall that was more than firelight. A shadow in the shape of a giant deer with large palmate antlers and a hump on his withers had flickered through it. She turned around and looked back but didn't see anything, and wondered if she had imagined it. She turned back to face the wall, and the antlered deer flickered through again, then a bison.

The bullroarer tapered off, but another sound had begun, at first so low that she was barely conscious of it. Then the low wailing chant increased in pitch and a heavy rhythmical booming began. The wailing interweaved in counterpoint to the swelling sound that reverberated off the back wall as both grew louder. Ayla's temples throbbed to the steady *thrum, thrum, thrum,* and her heart pounded in her ears at the same tempo and just as loud. It seemed that her limbs had turned to ice, and her legs refused to move; she was petrified. She broke out in a cold sweat. Then, abruptly, the pounding stopped and the wailing began to form words.

"O Spirit of the Giant Deer. We praise you."

"We praise you. . . ." Voices around her repeated the phrase, but they were not quite all together.

The chanting background grew louder.

"Spirit of Bison, we want you near. We praise you."

"We praise you." This time the hunters spoke in unison.

"The Mother's Children want you here. We call you."

"We call you."

"Immortal Soul, no death you fear. We praise you."

"We praise you." The voices were louder now.

"Your mortal lives are drawing near, we call you."

The tone was growing high-pitched, expectant.

"We call you." The voices were louder still.

"Give them to us and shed no tear. We praise you."

"We praise you."

"The Mother wills it, do you hear? We call you."

Now it was demanding.

"We call you. We call you. *We call you!* "

They were shouting. Ayla's voice had joined the rest, though she wasn't even aware of it. Then she noticed a large figure taking form on the rough wall. A barely visible dark figure was moving in front of the wall, somehow causing the shape of a giant deer to take form. A mature male with large antlers that seemed to breathe in the dawning light.

The hunters kept repeating in a low, monotonous drone in rhythm with the deep booming drum, "We call you. We call you. We call you. We call you."

"Give them to us! Shed no tear!"

"The Mother wills it. Hear! Hear! Hear!" the voices nearly screamed. Suddenly a light seemed to turn on, and a loud wailing cry was heard that ended in a death rattle.

"She hears!" the chanting voice said abruptly. All sound suddenly ceased. Ayla looked up, but the deer was gone. Only the first bright beam of light of the sunrise remained.

There was no sound or movement at first. Then Ayla became conscious of breathing and shuffling movements. The hunters appeared dazed and were looking around as though they had just awakened. Ayla heaved a great sigh, then knelt down again and hugged the wolf. When she looked up, Proleva was there, handing her a cup of hot tea.

Ayla murmured her thanks and sipped the tea gratefully. She was thirsty, and no longer feeling the nausea of morning sickness, she realized, though she wasn't sure when it had stopped. Perhaps on the hike to the Gather Field. She and Jondalar, with Wolf close by, walked with Joharran and his mate back to the fire, where the hot tea had been made. They were joined by Marthona and Willamar, and Folara.

"Kareja says she has a disguise for you, Ayla," Joharran said. "We can pick it up when we pass by the Eleventh Cave."

Ayla nodded, not quite sure how a disguise would be used to hunt giant deer.

Then she looked around to see who else was in the hunting party. She recognized Rushemar and Solaban and was not surprised. She would expect to see the leader's advisers, the ones Joharran always turned to for assistance. She was startled to see Brukeval, then wondered why. He was, after all, a member of the Ninth Cave. Why shouldn't he hunt with them? She was even more surprised to see Marona's friend Portula. But when the woman saw her, she flushed, stared for a moment, then turned away.

"I don't think Portula expected to see you wearing those clothes," Marthona said quietly to Ayla.

The sun was climbing the great blue vault, and the hunters set out quickly, leaving behind those who were not joining the hunt. As they headed toward The River, the warm sun dissipated the somber mood wrought by the ceremony, and the conversation, held in quiet whispers earlier in the morning, reached a more normal tone. They spoke seriously but confidently about the hunt. Their mission might not be assured, but the familiar ritual had addressed the spirit of the giant deer—and the bison, just in case—and had focused everyone's attention on the hunt, and the phantom manifestation on the back wall of the Gather Field had reinforced their spiritual bonds with the world beyond the material one.

Ayla felt a dampness in the air from a morning mist rising near the water. She glanced to the side and caught her breath at the sheer unexpected beauty of a momentary natural phenomenon. Twigs and leaves and blades of grass, highlighted by a beam of light, sparkled with the brilliance of every rainbow color, caused by the refraction of sunlight through the prisms of droplets. Even the symmetrical perfection of a spider's web, whose sticky strands were designed to capture that predator's quarry, had snared instead jeweled drops of condensed moisture along its slender threads.

"Jondalar, look," she said, calling his attention to the display. Folara stopped, too, then Willamar.

"I would take that as a favorable sign," the Trade Master said, smiling broadly before moving on.

Where The River widened, the water foamed and tumbled over its pebble-strewn bed, but parted around larger rocks, unable to entice them to join in the playful dance of whitewater and shimmering ripples. The hunters started across The River at the broad shallows, stepping from stone to stone through the deeper middle. Some of the large rocks were brought there by a more turbulent stream of a different season during past years, and some were carried there recently to fill in the gaps left by nature. As Ayla followed the others, her thoughts turned toward the upcoming hunt. Then, just as she was about to start across, she suddenly stopped.

"What's wrong, Ayla?" Jondalar asked with a concerned frown.

"Nothing's wrong," she said. "I'm going back to get the horses. I'll be able to catch up before the hunters reach Two Rivers Rock. Even if we don't use the horses for hunting, they can help carry the kill back."

Jondalar nodded. "That's a good idea. I'll come with you," he said, then turning to Willamar. "Will you tell Joharran we've gone back for the horses? It won't take long."

"Come on, Wolf," Ayla said as they headed back toward the Ninth Cave.

But the way Jondalar went was not the way they had come. After reaching the Gather Field, instead of taking the steep path up to Down River and on to the Ninth Cave across the stone ledges, he led them along a lesser-used and somewhat overgrown trail along the right bank of The River in front of the shelters of stone. Depending on the bends and turns the waterway took across its floodplain, the path was sometimes beyond a grassy field that was between the ledge and The River and sometimes close to the stone front porch.

There were several paths leading up to the shelters along the way, and one Ayla recalled using when she'd had to relieve herself after that long meeting about the Clan. The memory prompted her to use the place again; she had to pass water more frequently now that she was pregnant. Wolf sniffed her water; he seemed more interested in it lately, and she wondered if he could tell she was expecting.

A few people noticed them walking back and waved or beckoned. Jondalar was sure they were curious about why they had returned, but he didn't respond. They'd find out soon enough. When they reached the end of the line of cliffs, they turned into Wood Valley, and Ayla whistled. Wolf raced ahead.

"Do you think he knows we're going to get Whinney and Racer?" Ayla said.

"I wouldn't doubt it," Jondalar said. "I'm always amazed at what he seems to know."

"Here they come!" Ayla said, her voice full of happiness. She realized she hadn't seen them for more than a day and had missed them. Whinney nickered when she saw Ayla and went straight to her with her head held high, but she lowered it over the woman's shoulder while Ayla hugged her neck. Racer let out a loud neigh and pranced toward Jondalar with his tail high and his neck arched, then presented his favorite scratching places to the man.

"I've missed them, but I think they've missed us, too," Ayla said. After some greeting scratchings and strokings, and nose touchings with Wolf, she suggested they go up and get riding blankets and Whinney's harness for the pole drag.

"I'll go," Jondalar said. "We'd better get going if we're planning on hunting today, and everybody will be asking questions. I think it will be easier for me to say we have to hurry. If you do it, someone may take it wrong, since they don't really know you yet."

"And I don't really know them," Ayla said. "That's a good idea. I'll check the horses over and make sure they're all right. Bring the carrying baskets, too, and a water bowl for Wolf. And maybe the sleeping rolls. Who knows where we'll be staying tonight. You should probably bring Whinney's halter, too."

They caught up with the rest of the hunting party just as they were reaching Two Rivers Rock. They had ridden along The River, splashing along the edge of the left bank after crossing.

"I was beginning to wonder if you'd make it back before we started," Kareja said. "I did stop off and pick up a disguise for you, Ayla." Ayla thanked her.

At the Two Rivers confluence, the hunting party turned into Grass Valley. Kimeran and some people from the Second and Seventh Caves, who were joining them but had not gone to the ceremony at the Gather Field, had waited upstream. When the rest of the hunters reached them, they stopped for a strategy meeting. Ayla and Jondalar got down from the horses and moved closer to listen.

". . . Thefona said the bison were moving north two days ago," Manvelar was saying. "It looked as if they would be in a good position by today, but they changed direction and headed east, away from the surround. Thefona's one of our best. She can see farther than anyone, and she's been watching that herd for some time. I think they will be in a good position to chase into the trap soon, but probably not today. That's why we thought the megaceros would be a better choice. They watered upriver from here, and now they're browsing on leaf greens near the tall grass."

"How many are there?" Joharran asked.

"Three mature does, a yearling buck, four spotted young, and a stag with a good-sized rack," Thefona answered. "A typical small herd."

"I was hoping to get several animals, but I don't want to take them all. That's why I wanted the bison. They travel in bigger herds," Joharran said.

"Except for giant deer and reindeer, most deer don't travel in herds at all. They like trees and more wooded places, where it's easier to hide. You seldom see more than a few bucks, or a doe or two and the young, except during the season when the males and females come together," Thefona said.

Ayla was sure Joharran knew that, but Thefona was young and proud of the knowledge she had gained as watcher. Joharran had allowed her to recount what she had learned.

"I think we should leave the stag, and at least one of the does, and her young one if we can be sure it's hers," Joharran said.

Ayla thought that was a good decision. Again, she found herself impressed with Joharran and observed him more closely. Jondalar's brother was nearly a head shorter than him, but his stocky, powerful build left no doubt that he was the equal of most men in strength. Leadership of the large and sometimes unruly Cave sat well on his shoulders; he exuded confidence. Brun, the leader of her clan, would have understood him, she thought. He, too, had been a good leader . . . unlike Broud.

Most of the Zelandonii leaders she had met seemed well suited to their position. Caves usually chose their leaders well, but had Joharran been unable to fulfill the position, the Cave would have simply shifted toward a more adequate leader. Without formality, there were no rules needed to dispossess a leader; he simply would have lost his following.

But Broud had not been chosen, she realized. He was destined to be the next leader from the moment he was born. Since he was born to the mate of a leader, it was believed he would have the memories for it. And perhaps he did, but in different proportions. Certain qualities that could contribute to leadership, such as pride, an ability to command, and to elicit respect, were accentuated in Broud. Brun's pride had come from the achievements of his clan, which also earned him respect, and he directed well because he paid attention to others, then decided. Broud's pride was exaggerated to hubris; he liked telling people what to do but did not listen to seasoned advice, and he wanted respect for his own exploits. Though Brun had tried to help him, Broud would never be the leader Brun had been.

As the meeting was breaking up, Ayla spoke quietly to Jondalar. "I'd like to ride ahead and see if I can find the bison. Do you think Joharran would mind if I asked Thefona where she last saw them?"

"No, I don't think so, but why don't you mention it to him," Jondalar said.

They both approached the leader, and when Ayla told him her plan, he said he had been going to ask Thefona the same thing. "Do you think you can locate those bison?" he asked.

"I don't know, but they didn't seem to be very far, and Whinney can run much faster than a person can," Ayla said.

"But I thought you said you wanted to hunt the megaceros with us," Joharran said.

"I do, but I think I can scout ahead and still meet you where the deer are in time to join you," she said.

"Well, I wouldn't mind knowing where those bison are," Joharran said. "Let's go ask Thefona where they were."

"I think I'll go with Ayla," Jondalar said. "She isn't familiar with this region yet. She might not understand Thefona's directions."

"Go ahead, but I hope you make it back in time. I'd like to see those spear-throwers of yours in action," Joharran said. "If they do half of what you say they can, it could make a big difference."

After talking with Thefona, Ayla and Jondalar took off at a gallop with Wolf loping behind, while the rest of the hunters continued to follow Grass River upstream. The countryside of Zelandonii territory was a dramatic land carved in high relief, with steep cliffs, broad river valleys, rolling hills, and elevated plateaus. The rivers sometimes meandered across meadows and fields with a gallery of trees along their banks, and at other times flowed beside high rock walls. The people who lived there were accustomed to its varied landscape and moved through it comfortably, whether it meant climbing a steep hillside or scaling a nearly vertical cliff, jumping across slippery stones to cross a river or swimming upstream against its current, walking single file between a wall of rock on one side and a rushing river on the other or spreading out on an open plain.

The hunters broke up into small groups as they moved through the nearly waist-high but still green grass of the open field of the valley. Joharran kept watching for the return of his brother and his strange entourage—the foreign woman, two horses, and a wolf—hoping they would get back in time to join the hunt, though he knew it would not make much difference. With so many hunters and so few animals, there was little doubt they would be able to get the ones they wanted.

It was midmorning before the stag with prodigious antlers was sighted, and the hunters stopped to discuss deployment of those in pursuit. Joharran heard hoofbeats and turned around. With inadvertent but perfect timing, Jondalar and Ayla returned.

"We found them!" Jondalar said in an excited whisper when they had dismounted. He would have shouted if he hadn't noticed that the giant deer were very close by. "And they've changed direction again. They're heading toward the surround! I'm sure we could encourage them to move that way faster."

"But how far away are they?" Joharran asked. "We have to walk. The rest of us don't have horses to ride."

"Not very far, the surround was made by the Third Cave. It isn't that far from here. You could get there without too much trouble," Ayla said. "If you'd rather hunt bison, you can, Joharran."

"Actually, big brother, you could hunt both," Jondalar said.

"We're here now, and a deer in your sight is worth much more than two bison in a distant surround," Joharran said. "But if this doesn't take too long, we may try for the bison later. Now, do you want to join the hunt?"

"Yes," Jondalar said.

"I do," Ayla said at nearly the same time. "Let's tie the horses to that tree over there, by the stream, Jondalar. Maybe I should tie a restraint on Wolf, too. He can get excited about hunting and may want to 'help,' but that could be a problem for the other hunters, or he could get in the way if he's not sure what to do."

While the decisions were made about tactics, Ayla studied the small herd, especially the stag. Ayla remembered the first time she saw a fully developed, mature megaceros stag. This giant deer was much the same. Somewhat taller than a horse at the withers, though certainly not as big as a mammoth, they were called giant deer because they were the most imposing of all the varieties of deer. But it wasn't the size of the animal itself that made them so impressive, it was the size of their antlers. Each one of the massive, palm-shaped, deciduous horns that emerged from their heads grew larger each year and in a mature male could reach twelve feet in length.

Ayla visualized the length of one antler as two men the size of Jondalar, with one standing on the other's shoulders. The size of their antlers precluded the forested habitat that was often preferred by many of their cousins; the megaceros were deer of the open plains. Although they ate grass, especially the green tops of the tall grass varieties, and grazed more than other deer, they also browsed on young brush and trees and leafy herbaceous plants near streams when they could.

Once giant deer reached their full growth, though their bones no longer enlarged, the enormous growing antlers added to the illusion that megaceros stags increased in height and breadth with each season. Support of such huge racks required the deer to develop massive shoulder and neck muscles, which did increase slightly over time to accommodate the greater weight of the enlarging antlers, and to evolve a distinctive hump on their withers where muscles, tendons, and connective tissue bunched together. It was a genetic manifestation of the species. Even the females had a marked, though smaller, hump. Such enormous musculature, however, made the heads of the megaceros seem small, and those males that sported immense racks had heads that appeared disproportionately petite.

While the leaders were discussing tactics, the disguises were taken out, then Joharran and several others passed around skin bags of grease. Ayla crinkled her nose in distaste at the smell.

"It's made from the musk glands in the legs of the deer, and mixed with fat from just above the tail," Jondalar told her. "It covers our scent in case the wind shifts suddenly."

Ayla nodded and began smearing the greasy mixture on her arms and underarms and her legs and groin. While Jondalar was putting on his deer disguise, Ayla struggled with hers.

"Let me show you," Kareja said. She was already in hers.

Ayla smiled gratefully as the woman showed her how to wear the capelike hide covering with a deer head still attached. She picked up the antlers that were fastened to a separate headpiece, though she didn't understand what the extra wooden parts were for.

"This is heavy!" Ayla said, surprised at the weight when she put on the antler headwear.

"And they're small ones, from a young buck. You don't want that big stag to think you are competition," Kareja said.

"How does it stay balanced when you move?" Ayla said, trying to shift the antlers to a better position.

"That's what these are for," Kareja said, using the wooden supports to prop up the ungainly headdress.

"No wonder the megaceros have such big necks," Ayla said. "They need muscles just to hold these things up."

The hunters aproached with the wind blowing in their faces, which carried the human scent away from the deer's sensitive noses. They stopped when they could see the animals. The giant deer were browsing on the tender young leaves of low-growing brush.

"Watch them," Jondalar said softly. "See how they eat for a while, then look up? Then they move a few steps forward and start to feed again. We're going to copy their motions. Take a few steps toward them, then dip your head, just as though you were a deer who had just seen some juicy new leaves and stopped to take a bite. Then look up. Stand perfectly still while you are looking up. Don't look at him directly, but keep your eye on that big stag, and don't move at all when you see him looking at you.

"Now we're going to spread out in the same pattern they make. We want them think we're just another herd of deer while we get close to them. Keep your spears out of sight as much as possible. Hold them upright behind your antlers while you move, and don't move too fast," he explained.

Ayla listened intently to the instructions. This was interesting. She had spent years watching wild creatures, especially carnivores, but also animals she hunted. She had studied them closely, absorbing every detail. She taught herself to track them and finally taught herself to hunt them, but she had never pretended to be an animal before. She first watched the rest of the hunters, then carefully observed the deer.

Growing up learning to understand the gestures and movements of the Clan gave her an edge. She had a keen eye for detail, for the smallest movements made by the animals. She saw how they shook their heads to rid themselves of buzzing insects and quickly learned to imitate the movement. She unconsciously timed the movements, judging how long they kept their heads down and how long they looked around. She was excited by this new way to hunt, and intrigued. She almost felt like a deer as she moved forward with the hunters toward their quarry.

Ayla picked out the animal she planned to aim for and was slowly moving toward it. At first she thought she might try for a fat doe, but she decided she wanted antlers, so she changed her mind and chose the young buck instead. Jondalar had told her that the meat would be divided among all the people, but the hide, antlers, sinew, and whatever else might be useful belonged to the hunter who killed the animal.

When the hunters were almost in the midst of the deer, she saw Joharran give a prearranged signal. The hunters gripped their spears in readiness; Ayla and Jondalar adjusted theirs in their spear-throwers. She knew she could have cast her spear long before, but most of the hunters did not have spear-throwers, and her throw would have frightened the rest of the deer away, before the others were close enough to hurl theirs.

When Joharran saw that everyone was ready, he gave another quick signal. Almost as one, the hunters flung their spears. Several of the huge deer threw up their heads, startled into flight before they realized they were already hit. The proud stag bugled a call as a signal to run, but only one doe and her calf followed him. It was so fast, so unexpected, the rest staggered as they strained to take a step and fell to their knees as he leapt away.

The hunters went to check their kills, to humanely dispatch any animals that might still be alive, and to verify which one should be credited to whom. Each person's spears were marked with decorations that clearly identified to whom they belonged. All the hunters knew their own weapons in any case, but the distinguishing symbols left no doubt and avoided disputes. If more than one hunter's spear found the same mark, they tried to determine which one had made the kill. If it was not obvious, the kill was claimed by both and would be shared.

It was quickly acknowledged that Ayla's smaller, lighter spear had found the young buck. Some of the hunters knew that the young male had been browsing on a low bush somewhat away from the rest of the deer and on the opposite side of their approach. Not an easy target, and apparently no one else had attempted it, at least no other spear had found it. People talked about not only the long-distance weapon, but her skill with it, and wondered how much practice it would take to match her. Some were willing to try, but others looked at the successful hunt and weren't sure they needed to make the effort.

Manvelar approached Joharran and several others of the Ninth Cave, including Jondalar and Ayla. "What did you find out about the bison?" he asked.

The planning and preparations for the hunt had built up an eager anticipation, but stalking the deer and dispatching them had been so quick and efficient, it had left the hunters with a measure of excess energy that had not been used up.

"The herd was moving north again, toward the surround," Jondalar said.

"Do you really think that they might get close enough to it so we can take advantage of the surround today?" Joharran asked. "It's still early, and I wouldn't mind getting a few of those bison."

"We can make sure they do," Jondalar said.

"How?" Kareja asked. Jondalar noticed there wasn't as much sarcasm in her tone as there had been the day before.

"Manvelar, do you know where the surround is? And how long would it take the hunters to get there from here?" Jondalar said.

"Yes, but Thefona can tell you that better than I," Manvelar said. The young woman was not only a good lookout, she was a good hunter. She came forward when Manvelar mentioned her name and beckoned her. "How far is it to the surround?"

She thought for a moment, looked up at the position of the sun in the sky, then said, "If we set a good pace, we could get there not much after the sun is highest, I think. But the last time I saw them, the bison weren't that close to the surround."

"When we found them, they were heading in that direction, and I think we can speed them up, with the help of the horses and Wolf," Jondalar said. "Ayla has done it before."

"What if you can't? What if we get there, and there are no bison?" Kimeran asked. He hadn't been around Jondalar much since his return, or Ayla, and though he'd heard many stories about his friend and the woman he'd brought back with him, he hadn't been exposed to as many of the surprises they had brought with them as some of the others. He hadn't seen them ride the horses until that morning and wasn't at all sure about them.

"Then we will have nothing to show for our efforts, but it won't be the first time," Manvelar said.

Kimeran shrugged, and smiled wryly. "I suppose that's true," he said.

"Does anyone else have any objections to trying for the bison? We can just settle for the deer," Joharran said. "We need to start butchering them, anyway."

"That's not a problem," Manvelar said. "Thefona can lead you to the surround. She knows the way. I'll go back to Two Rivers Rock and organize some people to get started with the butchering, and send a runner to the other Caves to come and help. We'll need more help if you are lucky with the bison hunt."

"I'm ready to try for the bison."

"I'll go."

"Count me in."

Several people volunteered.

"All right," Joharran said. "You two go ahead and see what you can do about getting those bison started toward the surround. The rest of us will get there as fast as we can."

Ayla and Jondalar headed for the horses. Wolf was particularly glad to see them coming. He did not like being physically restrained. Ayla did not confine his movements often, and he wasn't used to it. The horses seemed to adjust to it more easily, but their activities were more often controlled. They mounted the horses and rode off at a fast pace, the wolf loping alongside them, leaving the people on foot watching as they quickly disappeared in the distance. It was true. Horses could certainly travel faster than people.

They decided to go to the surround first, so they could judge how far away the bison were from it. Ayla was fascinated with the circular trap and took a little time to inspect it. It consisted of many small trees and logs, filled in mostly with brush, but also with whatever they could find, such as bones and antlers. The surround had originally been constructed some years before, and it had moved somewhat from its original place. None of the trees from which it was made were sunk into the ground. Rather, they were lashed together, fixed firmly to each other, so that when some creature crashed into it, it wouldn't break through. The fencing had some give, some elasticity, and would instead move with the blow; sometimes, with an extremely hard thrust, the entire structure shifted.

It took a great deal of effort on the part of many people to cut down trees and branches and haul them to a logical site, especially on a largely treeless grassland, then erect a fence that could withstand the crush of heavy animals milling around inside it and the occasional assault by one maddened with fear. Each year the parts that had fallen down or rotted away were repaired or replaced. They tried to keep it sound for as long as they could. It was easier to repair than entirely rebuild, especially since there were more than one, at various strategic locations.

This surround was located in a narrow valley between a limestone cliff on one side and steep hills on the other that was a natural migration route. At one time a river had flowed through it, and a runoff stream still filled the dry bed occasionally. Hunters used it only sporadically; animals seemed to learn quickly if a particular route was consistently dangerous and tended to avoid it.

The ones who had come to repair the trap had also set up a portable fencing of panels that funneled the animals driven into the valley toward an opening in the surround. Usually hunters had time enough to establish a cadre of people to stand behind the panels to harass any animals that attempted to bolt away back toward the trap. Since this was a rather unplanned, spontaneous hunt, no one was there yet. But Ayla did notice that some scraps of leather and cloth, pieces of woven belts, and grass wands, long bunches of grass fastened to sticks, were tucked into the frames of the panels or held down with stones.

"Jondalar," she called to him. He rode up to her. She had picked up a grass wand and a piece of leather. "Anything that flutters or moves in an unexpected way tends to spook bison, especially when they're running, at least that's what happened when we were driving bison toward the Lion Camp's surround. These must be used to shake at animals heading toward the surround, to keep them from breaking away. Do you think anybody would object if we borrowed a few? They could be useful when we're trying to drive the herd this way."

"You're right. That is what they're for," Jondalar said, "and I'm sure no one would mind if we borrow some if it will help us get those bison here."

They left the valley and headed toward the place where they had last seen the herd. The trail trampled by the slowly moving animals was easy to find, and they were a little closer to the valley than they were earlier. There were about fifty bison in all, males, females, and young. They were starting to come together to form the huge migratory herd that would develop later in the season.

At certain times of the year, bison congregated in such huge numbers, it was like watching a sinuously moving river of dark brown spiked with large black horns. At other times, they broke up into smaller groupings, sometimes not much more than an extended family, but they preferred to form herds of some size. On the whole there was safety in numbers. While predators, especially cave lions and packs of wolves, often brought down a bison from a herd, it was usually one that was slow or weak, which allowed the healthy and strong to survive.

They approached the herd slowly, but the bison hardly noticed them. Horses were not animals that posed a threat, though they did give Wolf a wider berth. They were aware of him, but didn't panic; they merely avoided him, sensing that a single wolf could not take down an animal the size of a bison. Male bison were typically six feet six inches at the top of the hump on their shoulders and weighed a ton. They had long black horns and a beard that jutted forward from heavy jaws. Females were smaller, but both were quick and agile, able to climb steep slopes and leap over substantial obstacles.

They could gallop, tail up and head down, in long strides across even rocky landscapes. Bison didn't mind water and could swim well, drying off their thick fur by rolling in the sand or dirt. They tended to graze in the evening and relaxed to chew their cud during the day. Their hearing and sense of smell were acute. Full-grown bison could be violent and aggressive, and were difficult to kill with teeth and claws or with spears, but one bison provided fifteen hundred pounds of meat, plus fat, bones, skin, hair, and horns. Bison were proud and noble animals, respected by those who hunted them and admired for their strength and courage.

"What do you think would be the best way to get them started?" Jondalar said. "Usually the hunters let them go at their own pace, and try to guide them slowly toward the surround, at least until they get close."

"When we hunted on our Journey here, we usually tried to get an animal to bolt away from the herd. This time we want them all to keep going in the same direction, toward that valley," Ayla said. "I think riding up behind them and shouting would get them going, but if we wave these things at them, I think it would be a help, especially for the bison that tries to dash away. We don't want them stampeding in the wrong direction. Wolf always liked to chase them, too, and he got good at keeping them together."

She looked up at the sun and tried to estimate when they might arrive at the surround, and wondered how close the hunters were. Well, the important thing is to get them moving toward the trap, she thought.

They moved around to the side opposite the direction they wanted to start them going, then, looking at each other, they nodded and, with a loud yell, urged the horses toward the herd. Ayla was holding a grass wand in one hand and the scrap of leather in the other, both hands free because she didn't use a halter or a rein to direct Whinney.

It had been an entirely spontaneous gesture the first time she got on the back of the horse, and she made no attempt to guide her. She simply clung to the horse's mane and let the animal run. She felt a sense of freedom and excitement as though she were flying like the wind. The horse slowed and headed back to the valley on her own. It was the only home she knew. Afterward, Ayla couldn't stop riding, but in the beginning the training was unconscious. Only later did she realize that she had been using the pressure and movement of her body to signal her intent.

The first time Ayla hunted large game, by herself, after she left the Clan, she drove the herd of horses that used the valley she had found toward a pit-trap she had dug. She didn't know the horse that happened to fall into her trap was a nursing mother until she noticed some hyenas stalking the foal. She used her sling to drive the ugly creatures away, rescuing the young horse more because she hated hyenas than because she wanted to save the animal, but once she had saved it, she felt obliged to care for it. She had learned years before that a baby could eat what its mother ate, if it was softened, and cooked a broth of grains to feed the young filly.

Ayla soon came to realize that in saving the horse, she had done herself a favor. She was alone in the valley and became grateful for the company of a living being to share her lonely life. It wasn't her intention to tame the horse and she never thought of it in those terms. She looked upon the horse as her friend. Later, she became a friend who allowed the woman to ride on her back and who went where Ayla wanted her to go because she chose to.

Whinney left to live with a herd for a while, when she came into her first season, but came back to Ayla after the herd stallion died. Her foal was born not long after the woman found the wounded man, who turned out to be Jondalar. The young colt became his to name and train, finding his own means. He invented the halter to help him direct and control the young stallion. Ayla found the device useful to use on Whinney when she needed to keep her restrained to a specific area, and Jondalar used one if he needed to lead Whinney. He seldom tried to ride the mare since he didn't fully understand the signals Ayla used to guide her, and the horse didn't understand his. Ayla had a similar problem with Racer.

Ayla glanced at Jondalar, who was dashing after a bison, guiding Racer with ease, shaking a grass wand in the face of a young bull to get him stampeding along with the others. She saw a frightened cow veer off and started after her, but Wolf got there first and drove her back. She smiled at the wolf; he was having a wonderful time chasing the bison. They had all—the woman, the man, the two horses, and the wolf—learned to work together, and hunt together, on their year-long Journey following the Great Mother River in their passage across the plains from the east.

As they neared the narrow valley, Ayla noticed a man standing off to the side, waving at her, and breathed a sigh of relief. The hunters had arrived. They would keep the bison heading in the right direction once they were stampeded into the valley, but a couple of bison at the head of the herd were trying to swerve away. She leaned forward, an all but unconscious signal to Whinney to go faster. As though she knew what was in the woman's mind, the mare raced to cut off the bison reluctant to enter the narrower way. Ayla yelled as Whinney neared, shaking the grass wand and flapping the piece of leather in the canny old cow's face, and managed to turn her back. The rest of the bison followed.

The two people on horses and the wolf kept the bison stampeding together and heading in the same direction, but the valley narrowed as they approached the restricted opening of the surround, which slowed them down as they crowded each other. Ayla noticed a bull trying to bolt to get away from the press behind them.

A hunter stepped out from behind a panel and attempted to stop him with a spear. The weapon found its mark, but it wasn't a mortal wound and the momentum kept the bison going. The hunter jumped back and tried to get out of the way by ducking back behind the panel, but it was a flimsy barrier against the mighty bull. Enraged by the pain of the wound, the huge shaggy animal ignored the panel and knocked it aside. The man fell with it, and in the confusion, the bison trampled him.

Ayla, watching in horror, had her spear-thrower out and was reaching for a spear when she saw one thud into the bison. She threw her spear also, then urged Whinney forward, disregarding the danger of the other stampeding animals, and jumped off the horse's back even before she stopped. She pulled the panel out of the way and knelt beside the man who was lying on the ground not far from the fallen bison. She heard him moan. He was alive.

13

Whinney was prancing nervously, sweating heavily, as the rest of the bison swept by and into the surround. When the woman reached for her medicine bag from one of the carrier baskets, she stroked the horse for a moment to comfort her, but her mind was already focused on the man and what she might be able to do for him. She wasn't even aware when the gate to the surround was closed, trapping the bison inside, or when some of the hunters began to methodically dispatch the ones they wanted.

The wolf had enjoyed chasing the animals, but even before the gate was closed he had suddenly stopped running after them and begun searching for Ayla. He found her kneeling beside the wounded man. Some people began to form a circle around her and the man on the ground, but with the wolf there, they kept their distance. Ayla was oblivious to the people watching her as she began to examine him. He was unconscious, but she could feel a slight beating in his neck, under his jaw. She opened his clothing.

There was no blood, but a large blue-black smudge was already forming on his chest and abdomen. Carefully, she felt his chest and stomach around the darkening bruise. She pressed in once. He flinched and made a cry of pain, but did not wake up. She listened to his breathing and heard a soft gurgling, then noted that blood dribbled from the side of his mouth and knew he was injured internally.

She looked up and saw Jondalar's piercing blue eyes and his familiar frown of concern, and then a second, nearly identical frown, with a questioning look. She shook her head at Joharran.

"I'm sorry," she said. "That bison stepped on him." She looked down at the dead animal beside him. "His ribs are broken. They are piercing his lungs and I don't know what else. He is bleeding inside. I'm afraid nothing can be done. If he has a mate, someone should send for her. I'm afraid he will walk the world of the spirits before morning."

"Nooooo!" came a cry from the crowd. A young man pushed his way forward and threw himself down beside the man. "It's not true!

It can't be true! How does she know? Only a Zelandoni knows. She's not even one of us!"

"It's his brother," Joharran said.

The young man tried to hug the man on the ground, then turned the wounded man's head to try to make his brother look at him. "Wake up, Shevonar! Please wake up," the young man wailed.

"Come on, Ranokol. You're not helping him." The leader of the Ninth Cave tried to help the young man up, but was fought off and pushed away.

"It's all right, Joharran. Let him stay. A brother has a right to say farewell," Ayla said, then, noticing the man starting to stir, she added, "A brother might cause him to wake up, though, and he will be in pain."

"Don't you have some willow bark or something for pain in your medicine bag, Ayla?" Jondalar said. He knew she was never without a few basic medicinal herbs. Hunting always posed some danger, and she would have anticipated that.

"Yes, of course, but I don't think he should have anything to drink. Not with such severe injuries inside." She paused, then said, "But, maybe a poultice would help him. I could try it. First, we need to get him to someplace comfortable, and we'll need wood for a fire, and water to boil. Does he have a mate, Joharran?" she asked again. The man nodded. "Then someone should go for her, and for Zelandoni, too."

"Of course," Joharran said, suddenly aware of her strange accent, though he had all but forgotten it until then.

Manvelar stepped in. "Let's get some people looking for a place to take this man, where he can be comfortable, away from this hunting field."

"Isn't there a small cave in that cliff over there?" Thefona said.

"There's bound to be one somewhere nearby," Kimeran said.

"You're right," Manvelar said. "Thefona, why don't you get some people and go look for a place to take him."

"We'll go with her," Kimeran said, and called over the people from the Second and Seventh Caves who had joined the hunt.

"Brameval, perhaps you could organize a few people to get wood and water. And we'll have to make something to carry him. Some people brought sleeping rolls, we'll get some for him, and whatever else he needs," Manvelar continued, then he called out to the hunters, "We need a good runner, to take a message back to Two Rivers Rock."

"Let me go," Jondalar said. "I can take the message, and Racer is the best 'runner' here."

"I think you're right about that."

"Then maybe you could go on to Ninth Cave to get Relona here, and Zelandoni, too," Joharran said. "Tell Proleva what happened. She'll know how to get everything organized. Zelandoni should be the one to tell Shevonar's mate. She may want you to explain to Relona what happened, but leave it up to her."

Joharran turned to face the hunters that were still standing around the wounded man, most of them from the Ninth Cave. "Rushemar, the sun is high and getting hotter. We have paid dearly for this day's kill, let's not waste it. The bison need to be gutted and skinned. Kareja and the Eleventh Cave have started, but I'm sure she could use some help. Solaban, maybe you could take a few people and help Brameval get wood and water, and whatever else Ayla needs, and when Kimeran and Thefona find a place, you can help move Shevonar."

"Someone should go to the other Caves and let them know we need help," Brameval said.

"Jondalar, can you stop on your way back and let them know what happened?" Joharran asked.

"When you get to Two Rivers Rock, tell them to light the signal fire," Manvelar said.

"Good idea," Joharran said. "Then the Caves will know something is wrong and will be expecting a messenger." He went to the woman, the foreigner, who would likely be a member of his Cave one day, and probably a Zelandoni, and was already contributing every way she could. "Do what you can for him, Ayla. We'll get his mate and Zelandoni here as soon as we can. If there is anything you need, ask Solaban. He will get it for you."

"Thank you, Joharran," she said, then turned to Jondalar. "If you tell her what happened, I'm sure Zelandoni will know what to bring, but let me check my bag. There are a couple of herbs I'd like if she has them. And take Whinney with you. Then you can use the pole drag to bring things here, she's more used to it than Racer. Zelandoni could even ride here on it, and Shevonar's mate on Whinney's back, if they're willing."

"I don't know, Ayla. Zelandoni's pretty heavy," Jondalar said.

"I'm sure Whinney can handle it. You just have to come up with a comfortable seat." Then she looked at Jondalar with a wry expression. "But you're right, most people aren't used to using horses for traveling. I'm sure the women would rather walk, but they will need tents and supplies. The pole drag will be good for that."

Ayla removed the carrying baskets before she put the halter on Whinney and gave the rope attached to it to Jondalar. He fastened the other end of it to the back of Racer's halter with enough lead so she could follow, and started out. But the mare was not accustomed to trailing behind the stallion she had borne. He had always followed her. Even though Jondalar was sitting on Racer's back, guiding him with a rein attached to his halter, Whinney stayed slightly ahead of them, yet she seemed to sense which way the man wanted to go.

Horses were willing to do the bidding of their human friends, Ayla thought, smiling to herself as she watched them leave, so long as it didn't upset their own sense of the proper order of things. She saw Wolf was observing her when she turned around. She had signaled him to stay when the horses left, now he was waiting patiently.

Her ironic inner smile at the behavior of the horses was quickly dispelled when she looked at the man lying where he fell. "He'll need to be carried, Joharran," she said.

The leader nodded, then called on some people to help. They improvised a carrying device by first binding together a couple of spears to make a sturdy pole, then fastening pieces of clothing across two of them. By the time Thefona and Kimeran returned with news of a small shelter nearby, the man had been carefully moved to the stretcher and was ready to be carried. Ayla called Wolf to her as four men each lifted one end of a pole.

When they arrived, Ayla helped several people who had begun cleaning out the hollowed-out space at ground level in the nearby limestone wall, protected by a small overhanging ledge. The dirt floor was littered with dried leaves and debris blown in by the wind, and dried hyena droppings left sometime before by the scavenging carnivores who had used the place for a lair.

Ayla was pleased to find that water was close by. There was a smaller cave at the back of the sheltered depression and just inside it was a spring-fed pool of fresh water that ran off in a ditch that had formed along the cliff wall. She told Solaban where to set up a fireplace with the wood he and Brameval, and a few others, had brought.

When Ayla asked, several people volunteered their sleeping rolls, which were piled on top of each other to create a slightly raised bed. The injured man had awakened when they moved him onto the stretcher, but was unconscious by the time he arrived at the shelter. He moaned in pain when they moved him to the bed and awoke again, grimacing and struggling to breathe. Ayla folded another bedroll and propped him up on it to try to make him more comfortable. He tried to smile his thanks, but coughed up blood instead. She wiped his chin with a piece of soft rabbit skin, an item she usually kept with her medicinals.

Ayla went through the limited supplies in her medicine bag and tried to think if there was anything she might have forgotten that would help allay his pain. Gentian roots might help, or a wash of arnica. Both could relieve the internal pain of bruises and other aches, but she had neither with her. The fine hairs on the fruit of hops could be used as a sedative to help him relax, just by breathing the air near them, but they were not readily available. Maybe something in smoke would help, since swallowing liquid was not going to be possible. No, it would probably make him cough, which would be worse. She knew it was hopeless, it was just a matter of time, but she had to do something, at least for his pain.

Wait, she thought. Didn't I see that plant from the valerian family on the way here? The one with the aromatic roots? One of the Mamuti at that Summer Meeting called it spikenard. I don't know the name in Zelandonii. She looked up at the people around her and saw the young woman that Manvelar seemed to have a lot of respect for, the lookout from the Third Cave, Thefona.

Thefona had stayed to help clean out the small shelter she found and was still there, watching Ayla. The foreign woman intrigued her. There was something about her that made people pay attention to her, and she seemed to have gained the respect of the Ninth Cave in the short time she had been there. Thefona wondered how much the woman really knew about healing. She didn't have any kind of tattoo marks like the zelandonia did, but the people she came from might have different ways. Some people tried to fool others about what they knew, but the stranger didn't seem to be trying to impress anyone by bragging or talking big. Instead, she did things that were genuinely impressive, like the way she used that spear-throwing thing. Thefona had been thinking about Ayla, but was surprised when the woman called her name.

"Thefona, may I ask you something?" Ayla said.

"Yes," Thefona said, and thought, She does have a strange way of talking. Not her words, but the way they sound. Maybe that's why she doesn't talk much.

"Do you know much about plants?"

"Everyone knows something about plants," Thefona said.

"I'm thinking about one whose leaves resemble foxglove, but it has yellow flowers, like dandelions. The name I know it by is 'spikenard,' but that's a Mamutoi word."

"I'm sorry. I know some food plants. I don't know much about medicine plants. You would need a Zelandoni for that," Thefona said.

Ayla paused, then said, "Would you watch Shevonar, Thefona? I thought I noticed some spikenard on my way here. I'm going back the way we came and look for it. If he wakes up again, or if there is any change at all, would you send someone to find me?" Ayla said. Then she decided to add an explanation, though explaining her actions as a medicine woman was not something she usually did. "If it is what I think it is, it could be helpful. I've used the mashed roots as a poultice to help mend bone fractures, but it is easily absorbed and has soothing powers. If I mix it with a little datura and maybe some pulverized yarrow leaves, I think it might help ease his pain. I want to see if I can find it."

"Yes, of course I'll watch him," Thefona said, pleased, for some unknown reason, that the foreign woman had asked for her help.

Joharran and Manvelar were talking to Ranokol in quiet tones, but even though they were right next to her, Ayla hardly heard them. She was concentrating on the wounded man and watching the water heating—far too slowly. Wolf was lying on the ground nearby, with his head between his paws, watching her every move. When the water began to steam, she added the spikenard roots so they would soften enough to be pounded into a mash for a poultice. She had been glad to find comfrey as well. A wet dressing of the fresh crushed roots and leaves was also good for bruises and fractures, and while she didn't think it would mend Shevonar's injuries, she was willing to try anything that might ease his pain.

When it was ready, she plastered the warm mashed root directly on the almost black bruise that was spreading down his chest to his stomach. She noticed his abdomen was getting hard. His eyes opened while she was covering it with a piece of leather to keep it warm.

"Shevonar?" she said. His eyes seemed aware, but puzzled. Perhaps he didn't recognize her, she thought. "My name is Ayla. Your mate," she hesitated, then remembered her name, "Relona is on her way here." He took a breath and winced with pain. It seemed to surprise him. "You were hurt, Shevonar, by a bison. Zelandoni is on her way, too. I am trying to help until she gets here. I put a poultice on your chest to draw out some of the pain."

He nodded, but even that was an effort.

"Do you want to see your brother? He's been waiting to see you."

He nodded again, and Ayla got up and went to the men waiting nearby. "He's awake. He'd like to see you," she said to Ranokol.

The young man quickly got up and went to his brother's bed. Ayla followed, along with Joharran and Manvelar.

"How are you feeling?" Ranokol said.

Shevonar tried to smile, but it turned into a grimace of pain as an unexpected cough brought up a drool of red out of the corner of his mouth. A look of panic filled his brother's eyes, then he noticed the plaster on his brother's chest.

"What is this?" Ranokol said, his voice taut, almost a squeal.

"It is a poultice for his pain." Ayla's voice was normally rather low-pitched, and she said the words slowly and calmly. She understood the panic and fear of the man's brother.

"Who told you to do anything to him? It's probably making him worse. Get this off him!" he screamed.

"No, Ranokol," Shevonar said. The voice of the injured man could hardly be heard. "Not her fault. Helps." He tried to sit up, then collapsed, unconscious.

"Shevonar. Wake up, Shevonar! He's dead! Oh Great Mother, he's dead!" Ranokol cried, slumping down on the bed beside his brother.

Ayla checked Shevonar's pulse, while Joharran pulled Ranokol away. "No. He's not dead, yet," she said. "But he doesn't have long. I hope his mate arrives soon."

"He's not dead, Ranokol, but he could have been," Joharran said angrily. "This woman may not be zelandoni, but she knows how to help. You're the one who is making him worse. Who knows if he'll wake up again to say his last words to Relona."

"No one can make him worse, Joharran. There is no hope for him. He may go anytime. Don't blame a man grieving for his brother," Ayla said, then moved to get up. "Let me make some tea, to settle everyone."

"You don't have to, Ayla. I will. Just tell me what to make."

Ayla looked up and saw Thefona, and smiled. "If you just get some water boiling, I'll get something for all of us," she said. Then she turned back to check on Shevonar. He struggled with every difficult breath he took. She wanted to make him more comfortable, but when she tried to move him, he moaned in pain. She shook her head, surprised that he was still alive, then reached for her medicine bag to see what she had to make tea. Perhaps chamomile, she thought, with dried linden flowers or licorice root to sweeten it.

The long afternoon wore on. People came and went, but Ayla didn't notice them. Shevonar regained consciousness and asked for his mate, then slipped back into a restless sleep several times. His stomach was distended and hard, and the skin was almost black. She felt sure he was trying to hold on just to see her again.

Somewhat later, Ayla picked up her waterbag to get a drink, found it empty, then put it down and forgot about her thirst. Portula had come into the small shelter to see how things were. She still felt self-conscious about her part in Marona's trick and tried to stay out of the way, but she saw Ayla pick up the waterbag, shake it, and find it empty. Portula hurried to the pool, filled her own waterbag, and returned with the cold water.

"Would you like a drink, Ayla?" she asked, holding out her dripping waterbag.

Ayla looked up and was surprised to see the woman. "Thank you," she said, holding out her drinking cup. "I was a little thirsty."

Portula stood there for a moment after Ayla was through, looking uncomfortable. "I want to apologize to you," she finally said. "I'm sorry I let Marona talk me into playing that joke on you. It was not a very nice thing to do. I don't know what to say."

"There really isn't anything to say, is there, Portula?" Ayla said. "And I did get a warm and comfortable hunting outfit. Though I doubt that was what Marona intended, I will get use out of it, so let's just forget about it."

"Is there anything I can do to help?" Portula said.

"There isn't anything anyone can to do help. I'm surprised he is still with us. He asks for his mate when he wakes up. Joharran told him she is on her way," Ayla said. "I think he's holding on for her. I only wish I could do more to make it easier for him, but most medicines that alleviate pain have to be swallowed. I've given him a skin soaked with water to wet his mouth, but with his injury, I'm afraid if he drank anything, it would make it worse."

Joharran was out in front of the shelter looking south, the way Jondalar had gone, anxiously waiting for his return with Relona. The sun was falling low in the west, and darkness would follow soon. He had sent people to collect more wood so they could build up a large bonfire to help guide them; they were even taking some from the surround. The last time Shevonar woke, he eyes were glazed, and the leader knew death was near.

The young man had put up such a brave struggle to cling to a last shred of life, Joharran hoped his mate would arrive before he lost the battle. Finally, in the distance he saw movement, something approaching. He hurried in that direction and was relieved to see a horse. When they were closer, he went to Relona and guided the distraught woman to the stone shelter where her mate lay dying.

As she drew near, Ayla gently touched the man's arm. "Shevonar. Shevonar! Relona's here." She moved his arm again. He opened his eyes and looked at Ayla. "She's here. Relona's here," she said. Shevonar closed his eyes again and shook his head slightly, trying to make himself wake up.

"Shevonar, it's me. I came as fast as I could. Talk to me. Please talk to me." Relona's voice cracked in a sob.

The injured man opened his eyes and fought to focus on the face bending near. "Relona," he said. It was barely audible. The start of a smile was erased by an expression of pain. He looked again at the woman and watched her eyes fill with tears. "Don't cry," he whispered, then closed his eyes and struggled to breathe.

Relona's eyes were pleading when she looked up at Ayla, who looked down, then back up, and shook her head. She glanced around in panic, desperately searching out someone else who would give her another answer, but no one would return her gaze. She looked back at the man and watched him strain to take a breath, then saw blood spill from the corner of his mouth.

"Shevonar!" she cried, and reached for his hand.

"Relona . . . wanted to see you once more," he gasped, opening his eyes. "Say good-bye before I walk . . . the spirit world. If Doni allows . . . will see you there." He closed his eyes and they heard a feeble rattle as he tried to draw in a breath. Then, a low moan grew louder, and though Ayla was sure he was trying to control it, the sound increased. He stopped and tried to take a breath. Then, Ayla thought she heard a muted popping sound from inside him as he suddenly cried out in an agonizing scream. When the sound died away, he breathed no more.

"No, no. Shevonar, Shevonaaar," Relona cried. She laid her head on his chest and heaved great sobs of sorrow and grief. Ranokol was standing beside her with tears running down his cheeks, looking bewildered, dazed, at a loss. He didn't know what to do.

Suddenly they were startled by a loud and eerie howl at close quarters that sent shivers down their backs. As one, they looked at Wolf. He was standing on all four legs with his head thrown back, wailing a spine-tingling wolf song.

"What's he doing?" Ranokol said, quite upset.

"He is grieving for your brother," said the familiar voice of Zelandoni. "As we all do."

Everyone was relieved to see her. She had arrived with Relona and several others, but had stayed back to observe when Shevonar's mate rushed ahead. Relona's sobs turned to a wailing moan, a keening of her grief. Zelandoni joined her in her anguished lament, then several others. Wolf howled along with them. Finally, Ranokol broke down sobbing and threw himself across the man on the bed. An instant later he and Relona were clinging together, rocking and keening their sorrow.

Ayla thought it was good for both of them. To alleviate his pain and anger, she knew Ranokol needed to let his grief out, and Relona had helped him. When Wolf howled again, she joined him in a howl so realistic, many thought at first it was another wolf. Then, to the surprise of those who had kept a vigil for the man in the shelter, from a distance they heard another wolf howl, joining in the keening wolf song of grief.

After a while, the donier helped Relona up and led her to a fur that had been spread on the ground near the fire. Joharran helped the man's brother to a place on the other side of the hearth. The woman sat there rocking back and forth, making a low moaning sound, indifferent to everything around her. Ranokol just sat staring blankly at the fire.

The Zelandoni of the Third spoke quietly with the huge Zelandoni from the Ninth Cave, and shortly after returned with a steaming cup of liquid in each hand. The donier of the Ninth Cave took one cup from the Third and urged it on Relona, who drank it without objection, as though she didn't know, or care, what she did. The Third's other cup was brought to Ranokol, who ignored the proffered drink, but after some urging he finally drank it. Soon both of them were lying on the furs near the fire, asleep.

"I'm glad to see her quieted," Joharran said, "and him, too."

"They needed to grieve," Ayla said.

"Yes, they did, but now they need to rest," Zelandoni said. "And so do you, Ayla."

"Have something to eat first," Proleva said. Joharran's mate had come with Relona and Zelandoni and a few others from the Ninth Cave. "We roasted some bison meat, and the Third Cave brought other food."

"I'm not hungry," Ayla said.

"But you must be tired," Joharran said. "You hardly left his side for a moment."

"I wish I could have done more for him. I couldn't think of anything to help him," Ayla said, shaking her head and looking dejected.

"But you did," said the older man who was the Zelandoni of the Third. "You eased his pain. No one could have done more, and he wouldn't have held on to life without your help. I would not have used a poultice in that way. To ease aches or bruises, yes, but for internal injuries? I don't think I would have thought of it. Yet it did seem to help."

"Yes. It was a perceptive way to treat him," the Ninth's Zelandoni said. "Have you done that before?"

"No. And I wasn't sure it would help, but I had to try something," Ayla said.

"You did well," the donier said. "But now you should have something to eat, and rest."

"No, nothing to eat, but I think I will lie down for a while," Ayla said. "Where's Jondalar?"

"He went out with Rushemar and Solaban, and a couple of others to get more wood. Some went along just to hold torches, but Jondalar wanted to be sure there would be enough to last the night, and this valley doesn't have many trees. They should be back soon. Jondalar put your sleeping furs over there," Joharran said, showing her the place.

Ayla lay down, thinking to rest a while until Jondalar came back. She was asleep almost as soon as she closed her eyes. When the fuel collectors returned with the wood, nearly everyone was asleep. They put it in a pile near the fireplace, then went to the sleeping places they had chosen. Jondalar noticed the wooden bowl she usually took with her and used to heat small amounts of water with hot stones for medicinal teas. She had also constructed a makeshift framework of antlers, shed the previous season, to support a waterbag directly over a flame. Although the deer bladder held water, it seeped a little, which prevented it from catching on fire when it was used for heating water or cooking.

Joharran stopped his brother to talk for a few moments. "Jondalar, I want to learn more about those spear-throwers. I saw that bison fall from your spear, and you were farther away than most. If we'd all had that weapon, we wouldn't have had to get so close, and Shevonar might not have been trampled."

"You know I'll show anyone who wants to learn, but it does take practice," Jondalar said.

"How long did it take you? I don't mean to be as good as you are now, but to gain enough skill to really hunt with it?" Joharran asked.

"We've been using the spear-throwers for a few years now, but by the end of the first summer, we were hunting with them," Jondalar said. "It wasn't until the Journey back that we got good at hunting from the backs of the horses, though. Wolf can be a help, too."

"It's still hard to get used to the idea of using animals for anything besides meat or fur," Joharran said. "I wouldn't have believed you could if I hadn't seen it with my own eyes. But it's that spear-thrower I want to know more about. We'll talk tomorrow."

The brothers bade a good night to each other, then Jondalar went to where Ayla was sleeping and joined her. Wolf looked up. He watched her breathing quietly in the glow from the fire, then looked back at the wolf. I'm glad he's always there watching out for her, he thought, and stroked his head, then he slipped in beside her. He was sorry Shevonar had died, not only because he was a member of the Ninth Cave, but because he knew how hard it was on Ayla when someone died and there was nothing she could do. She was a healer, but there were some wounds no one could heal.

Zelandoni had been busy all morning, preparing the body of Shevonar to be carried back to the Ninth Cave. Being near someone whose spirit had left the body was very disturbing for most people, and his burial would involve more than the usual ritual. It was considered very bad luck if someone died while hunting. If they were alone, the bad luck was obvious, the misfortune had been accomplished, but a Zelandoni usually performed a cleansing ritual to ward off any possible future effects. If two or three hunters went out and one of them died, it was still considered a personal matter, and a ceremony with the survivors and family members was adequate. But when someone died on a hunt that involved not just one Cave but the whole community, that was serious. Something on a community level had to be done.

The One Who Was First was thinking about what might be needed, perhaps a prohibition on the hunting of bison for the rest of the season to assuage the ill fortune might be required. Ayla saw her relaxing with a cup of tea near the fire, sitting on a stack of several thickly stuffed pads that had been brought for her on Whinney's pole drag. She seldom sat on low cushions, finding it more and more difficult and cumbersome to get up as she grew more corpulent with each year.

Ayla approached the donier. "Zelandoni, can I talk to you?"

"Yes, of course."

"If you're too busy, it can wait. I just wanted to ask you something," Ayla said.

"I can spare a little time now," Zelandoni said. "Get a cup for tea and join me." She motioned to Ayla to sit on a mat on the ground.

"I just wanted to ask you if you know of anything more that I could have done for Shevonar. Is there any way to heal internal wounds? When I lived with the Clan, there was a man who had been accidentally stabbed with a knife. A piece broke off inside and Iza cut in and removed it, but I don't think there was a way to cut in and fix Shevonar's wounds," Ayla said.

It was obvious how much it bothered the foreign woman that she had been able to do so little for the man, and Zelandoni was moved by her concern. It was the sort of thing a good acolyte might feel.

"There is not much that can be done to help anyone who has been stepped on by a full-grown bison, Ayla," Zelandoni said. "Some lumps and swellings can be lanced to drain, or small objects cut out, slivers or that broken piece of the knife that your Clan woman removed, but that was a brave thing for her to do. It is dangerous to cut into the body. You are creating an injury that often is bigger than the one you are trying to fix. I have cut in a few times, but only when I was sure it would help and there was no other way."

"That's how I feel," Ayla said.

"It's also necessary to know something about what the inside of the body is like. There are many similarities between the inside of a human body and the inside of an animal's body, and I have often butchered an animal very carefully to see what it looks like and how they are connected. It's easy to see the tubes that carry blood from the heart, and the sinew that moves the muscles. Those things are very similar in all animals, but some things are different, an aurochs's stomach is different from a horse's, for example, and many things are arranged differently. It can be useful and quite interesting."

"I have found that to be true," Ayla said. "I've hunted and butchered many animals, and it does help to understand about people. I am sure Shevonar's ribs were broken, and splinters had penetrated his . . . breathing sacs."

"Lungs."

"His lungs, and I think his . . . other organs. In Mamutoi, I would say 'liver' and 'spleen.' I don't know the words in Zelandonii. They bleed heavily when damaged. Do you know which ones I mean?" Ayla said.

"Yes, I do," the First said.

"The blood had no place to go. I think that's why he turned black and got so hard. It filled him up inside until something burst," the young woman said.

"I examined him, and I agree with your assessment. The blood filled his stomach and some of his intestines. I believe part of the intestines burst," the donier said.

"The intestines are the long tubes that lead to the outside?"

"Yes."

"Jondalar taught me that word. They were damaged on Shevonar, too, I think, but it was the blood filling him up inside that made him die."

"Yes. The small bone in his left lower leg was also broken, and his right wrist, but those would not have been fatal, of course," Zelandoni said.

"No, and I wasn't so concerned about those breaks, I just wondered if you knew of anything else that I could have done for him," Ayla said, her earnest face full of concern.

"It bothers you that you couldn't save him, doesn't it?"

Ayla nodded and lowered her head.

"You did everything you could, Ayla. We will all walk in the world of the spirits someday. When Doni calls us, young or old, we have no choice. Not even a Zelandoni is gifted enough to stop it, or even to know when it will happen. That is a secret Doni shares with no one. She allowed the Spirit of the Bison to take Shevonar in exchange for the bison we took. It is a sacrifice She sometimes demands. Perhaps She felt we needed to be reminded that Her Gifts should not be taken for granted. We kill Her creatures so that we may live, but we need to appreciate the Gift of Life She has given us when we take the lives of Her animals. The Great Mother is not always gentle. Sometimes Her lessons are hard."

"Yes. That is what I have learned. I do not think the Spirit World is a gentle place. The lessons are hard, but valuable," Ayla said.

Zelandoni did not reply. She had found that people often kept talking to fill the gap if she did not respond immediately, and she learned more from her silence than she would have from asking questions. After a time, Ayla did continue.

"I remember when Creb told me that the Spirit of the Cave Lion had chosen me. He said the Cave Lion was a strong totem, who would offer powerful protection, but that strong totems are hard to live with. He told me if I paid attention, my totem would help me, and let me know when I've made the right decision, but he said totems test you to make sure you are worthy before they give you something. He also said the Cave Lion would not have chosen me if I was not worthy," Ayla said. "Maybe he meant able to bear it."

The donier was surprised at the depth of understanding Ayla's comments showed. Were the people that she called Clan really capable of such perception? If she had said the Great Earth Mother instead of the Spirit of the Cave Lion, the words could have come from a Zelandoni.

Finally, The One Who Was First continued. "Nothing could be done for Shevonar, except to ease his pain, and you did that. Using a poultice was an intriguing approach. Did you learn that from your Clan woman?"

"No," Ayla said, shaking her head. "I've never done that before. But he was in so much pain, and I knew with his injuries I couldn't give him anything liquid to drink. I thought of using smoke. I've burned mullein to make a smoke that alleviates certain coughs, and I know plants that are sometimes burned in sweatlodges, but I was afraid that it might make him cough, and with his damaged breathing sacs, I didn't want to do that. Then I noticed the bruising, though it was more than that, I think. The bruise on his skin turned almost black after a while, but I know that certain plants can ease the pain of bruising when put on the skin, and I happened to notice some on the way here from the hunting surround. So I went back and got some. It seemed to help a little."

"Yes, I think it did," the donier said. "I may try that sometime myself. You do seem to have a natural, inborn sense about healing,

Ayla. And I think it's telling that you feel bad. Every good healer that I know is always bothered when someone is lost. But there was nothing more you could have done. The Mother decided to call him, and no one can thwart Her will."

"You're right, of course, Zelandoni. I didn't think there was any hope, but I wanted to ask anyway. I know you have much to do, and I don't want to take any more of your time," Ayla said as she got up to leave. "Thank you for answering my questions."

Zelandoni watched the young woman as she started to walk away. "Ayla," she called. "I wonder if you would do something for me."

"Of course, anything, Zelandoni," she said.

"When we get back to the Ninth Cave, will you dig up some red ochre? There is an embankment near The River by the big rock. Do you know where that is?"

"Yes, I saw the ochre when Jondalar and I went swimming. It's very bright red, more red than most. I'll get some for you."

"I will tell you how to purify your hands, and give you a special basket for it when we get back," Zelandoni said.

14

It was a somber group of people that returned to the Ninth Cave the next day. The hunt had been eminently successful, but the cost had been too dear. As soon as they arrived, Joharran turned Shevonar's body over to the zelandonia, to prepare it for burial. It was taken to the far end of the shelter, near the bridge up to Down River, to be ritually washed and dressed in his ceremonial clothing and jewelry by Zelandoni, Relona, and several others.

"Ayla," Zelandoni called as she was walking back to Marthona's dwelling. "We're going to be needing that red ochre you said you would get for me."

"I'll go get it right away," Ayla said.

"Come with me. I'll give you a special basket and something to dig it with," the woman said. Zelandoni led her to her dwelling and held the drape aside so Ayla could enter. She had never been inside the donier's home before, and she looked around with interest. Something about it reminded her of Iza's hearth, perhaps the many drying leaves and other parts of plants that were hanging from cords strung across the back end of the main room. There were several raised beds against the wall panels in the front part, though she was sure that was not where the large woman slept. There appeared to be two other rooms partitioned off. Glancing through the opening, she saw that one of them appeared to be a cooking area. She guessed the other might be a sleeping room.

"Here's the basket and the pick for collecting the red earth," Zelandoni said, giving her a sturdy container stained red from use and an adzelike digging tool firmly attached to an antler handle.

Ayla left Zelandoni's dwelling carrying the basket and pick. Zelandoni walked out with her and started toward the south end of the shelter. Wolf had found a place where he liked to rest on the stone porch, out of the way, but where he could watch the activities. When he saw Ayla, he immediately ran to her. The donier stopped.

"I think it might be wise if you kept Wolf away from the body of

Shevonar," she said. "For his own protection. Until the man is safely buried in sacred ground, his life spirit is floating free and very confused. I know how to protect people, but I'm not sure how to defend a wolf, and I am concerned that Shevonar's elan might try to inhabit this animal. I have seen wolves go mad, and foam at the mouth. I believe they are trying to fight off something, maybe something evil or a bewildered spirit. The bite of such an animal will kill like a deadly poison."

"I will look for Folara and ask her to watch him when I bring the red ochre," Ayla said.

Wolf followed along behind her as she walked down the path toward the place where she and Jondalar had gone swimming and cleaned themselves shortly after they arrived. She filled the basket nearly full, then started back up the path. She saw Folara talking to her mother and explained Zelandoni's request. The young woman grinned, delighted to stay with the wolf. Her mother had just asked her to come and help prepare the body. It was not something she wanted to do, and she knew Marthona would not refuse Ayla's request.

"It may be best to keep him inside Marthona's dwelling. If you want to go out, I have a special rope that can be put around his neck in a way that won't choke him. Wolf doesn't like it much, but he'll put up with it. Come with me and I'll show you how to put it on him," Ayla said.

Then she walked to the far end of the ledge and gave the red ochre to the First. She stayed to help clean and dress the body of Shevonar. Jondalar's mother soon came to help as well—she had done it many times before—and told Ayla that Folara had invited several young people to their dwelling, and Wolf seemed content to be with them.

Ayla was intrigued by the clothing they put on the dead hunter, though she was reluctant to mention her interest at the time. The outfit consisted of a loose, soft tunic made of the furs of different animals, and hides tanned and colored in various shades that were sewn together into intricate patterns and accented with beads, shells, and fringes. The tunic was bloused and belted at the hips with a colorful band of woven fabric. The leggings, though less elaborate, matched the tunic, as did the calf-high foot coverings, which had a fringe and an edging of fur attached to the tops. Necklaces made of shells, beads, various animal teeth, and ivory carvings had been placed around his neck and artfully arranged.

Then the body was laid out on blocks of limestone, on top of a large, somewhat flexible blanket-size mat of grasses woven with designs that were colored with red ochre. Long cords were strung through each end, which, Marthona explained to Ayla, could be pulled together so that the mat would envelop him. The lengths of cordage would then be wrapped around the shrouded body and tied. Beneath the mat was a strong netting made of flax cordage, which could be slung from a pole like a hammock so that he could be carried to the sacred ground and lowered into the grave.

Shevonar had been a spear-maker, and his tools for making them were placed beside him, along with some finished spears and the parts of some he had been working on, which included wooden shafts, ivory and flint points, and the sinew, cords, and glue used to attach them. The sinew and cords were used to fasten the points to the shafts, and to bind sections of shorter pieces of wood together to make longer spears, which were then cemented with resinous pitch or glue.

Relona had brought the things from their dwelling, and she sobbed with grief when she placed Shevonar's favorite shaft-straightener within easy reach of his right hand. It was made of an antler of a red deer, the stem part, from the horn core at the head to the first branching tines. After the tines had been cut off, a good-size hole was bored through the wide end where the antler had begun to branch out. Ayla recognized that it was similar to the tool Jondalar had brought back with them that had belonged to his brother Thonolan.

Depictions of animals, including a stylized mountain sheep with large horns, and various symbols had been carved into the device. She recalled Jondalar saying that they lent potency to the shaft-straightener so that the spears made with it would fly straight and true, and would have a compelling attractiveness to the animal at which they were aimed, to make a clean kill. That they also added a pleasing aesthetic touch was appreciated.

While Shevonar's body was being prepared under the supervision of Zelandoni, Joharran was directing others to construct a temporary shelter with a rooflike covering made of a thin layer of thatched grasses supported by poles. When the body was ready, the shelter was placed over him, then walled with quickly made movable panels. The Zelandonia entered the shelter to perform the ritual that would keep the free-floating spirit close to the body and within the shelter.

When they finished, everyone who had touched or handled or worked close to the man whose life-force had left his body had to be ritually cleaned themselves. Water was the element that was used, and flowing water was considered best for this particular cleansing. They were all required to immerse themselves completely in The River.

Whether they undressed or were fully clothed didn't matter. They followed the path down to The River bank below the stone shelf. The Zelandonia invoked the Great Mother, then the women went upstream a ways, and the men downstream. All of the women removed their clothing, but a few of the men jumped in, clothing and all.

Jondalar had helped build the burial shelter. He and the others who had erected the shelter around the body were also required to be purified in The River. Afterward he walked with Ayla back up the path. Proleva had arranged to have a meal ready for them. Marthona sat with Jondalar and Ayla, and Zelandoni joined them after a while, leaving the grieving widow with her family. Willamar came looking for Marthona and sat with them, also. While she was with people with whom she felt comfortable, Ayla thought this would be a good time to ask about the clothing they had put on Shevonar's body.

"Does everyone who dies get dressed in such special clothes?" she asked. "It must have taken a lot of work to make Shevonar's outfit."

"Most people want to wear their best clothes for special occasions, or when they first meet people. That's why they have ceremonial clothes. They want to be recognized and make a good impression. Since people don't know what to expect when they reach the next world, they want to make the right impression there, and they want whoever they meet to know who they are," Marthona said.

"I didn't think clothes went to the next world," Ayla said. "It's the spirit that goes. The body stays here, doesn't it?"

"The body returns to the womb of the Great Earth Mother," Zelandoni said, "the life spirit, the elan, returns to Her spirit in the next world, but everything has a spirit form, rocks, trees, the food we eat, even the clothes we wear. The elan of a person doesn't want to return naked, or empty-handed. That's why Shevonar was dressed in his Ceremonial clothes, and given the tools of his craft and his hunting weapons to take with him. He will be given food, too."

Ayla nodded. She speared a rather large piece of meat, took one end in her teeth, then, holding the other end, cut off the piece in her mouth with her knife and put the rest back on her scapula bone plate. She chewed for a while with a thoughtful expression, then swallowed.

"Shevonar's clothes were beautiful. So many little pieces all sewn together into a pattern like that," she commented. "Animals and designs, it almost seemed to tell a story."

"In a way, it does," Willamar said, smiling. "That's how people are recognized, distinguished from each other. Everything on his

Ceremonial outfit means something. It has to have his elandon, and his mate's, and of course, the Zelandonii abelan."

Ayla looked puzzled. "I don't understand those words. What's an elandon? Or a Zelandonii abelan?" she asked.

Everyone looked at Ayla with surprise. They were such commonly used terms, and Ayla spoke Zelandoni so well, it was hard to believe she didn't know them.

Jondalar looked a bit chagrined. "I guess the words never came up," he said. "When you found me, Ayla, I was wearing Sharamudoi clothes, and they don't have quite the same way of showing who a person is. The Mamutoi have something similar, but not the same. A Zelandonii abelan is a . . . well . . . it's like those tattoos on the sides of Zelandoni's and Marthona's forehead," the man tried to explain.

Ayla looked at Marthona, then Zelandoni. She knew all the zelandonia and the leaders had an elaborate tattoo made up of squares and rectangles of different colors, sometimes embellished with additional lines and swirls, but she'd never heard a name for the mark.

"Perhaps I can explain the meaning of the words," Zelandoni said.

Jondalar looked relieved.

"I suppose we should start with 'elan.' You do know that word?"

"I heard you use it today," Ayla said. "It means something like spirit or life-force, I think."

"But you didn't learn this word before?" Zelandoni asked, scowling at Jondalar.

"Jondalar always said 'spirit.' Is that wrong?" Ayla said.

"No, it's not wrong. And I suppose we do tend to use 'elan' more when there is a death, or a birth, because death is the absence or end of elan, and birth is the beginning," the donier said.

"When a child is born, when a new life comes into this world, it is filled with elan, the vital force of life," the One Who Was First said. "When the child is named, a Zelandoni creates a mark that is a symbol for that spirit, that new person, and paints it or carves it on some object—a rock, a bone, a piece of wood. That mark is called an abelan. Each abelan is different and is used to designate a particular individual. It might be a design made of lines or shapes or dots, or a simplified form of an animal. Whatever comes to mind when the Zelandoni meditates about the infant."

"That's what Creb—The Mog-ur—used to do, meditate, to decide what a new baby's totem was!" Ayla said, surprised. She wasn't alone.

"You are talking about the Clan man who was the . . . Zelandoni of your clan?" the donier asked.

"Yes!" Ayla said, and nodded.

"I'll have to think on that," the large woman said, more astounded than she wanted to let on. "To continue, the Zelandoni meditates, then decides on the mark. The object with the mark on it, the symbol object, is the elandon. The Zelandoni gives it to the baby's mother to keep safe until the child is grown. When they pass into adulthood, the mother gives her children their elandons as part of their coming of age ceremony.

"But the symbol thing, the elandon, is more than just a material object with designs painted or engraved on it. It can hold the elan, the life-force, the spirit, the essence of each member of the Cave, much the way a donii can hold the Mother's spirit. The elandon has more power than any other personal item. It is so powerful that in the wrong hands it can be used against a person to create terrible afflictions and adversity. Therefore, a mother keeps her children's elandons in a place known only to her, and perhaps her mother, or her mate." Suddenly Ayla realized that she would be responsible for the elandon of the child she was carrying.

Zelandoni explained that when the elandon was given to a child who had reached adulthood, that person would hide it in a place known only to the new adult, often quite far away. But an innocuous object, like a stone, would be picked up from close by as a surrogate and given to a Zelandoni, who customarily put it in a crack in a stone wall of a sacred place, perhaps a cave, as an offering to the Great Mother. While the thing that was offered seemed insignificant, its meaning was much greater. It was understood that Doni could trace the surrogate back to the original symbol thing, and from that to the person to whom it belonged, without anyone, not even a Zelandoni, knowing where the elandon was hidden.

Willamar tactfully added that the zelandonia as a whole were highly respected and considered trustworthy and beneficial. "But they are very powerful," he said. "For many people a touch of apprehension is part of the respect they command, and any individual Zelandoni is only human. A few have been known to misuse their knowledge and abilities, and some people fear that given the opportunity, one of those might be tempted to use a powerful object like the elandon against someone they disliked, or to teach a person a lesson if they felt they had been wronged. I have never known it to happen, but people do like to embellish stories."

"If anyone disturbs a person's symbol thing, it could make a person sick, or even die. Let me tell you an Elder Legend," Marthona said. "In the past, it is said, some families used to put all their symbol things together, in the same place. Sometimes even entire Caves put them all in one place.

"There was one Cave that put all their symbol things together in a special little cave in the side of a hill near their shelter. It was considered such a sacred place that no one would dare to disturb them. One very wet spring, an avalanche washed down the slope, destroying the cave and everything in it. The people blamed each other and stopped being cooperative. Without each other's help, life became very difficult. The people scattered, and the Cave died. So people learned that if someone disturbed all the elandons, or even if they were dislodged by natural shifts caused by water, wind, or earth movements, the family or Cave had serious problems. That is why each person needs to hide her own symbol thing."

"It is all right to put surrogate stones together," Zelandoni added. "The Mother appreciates them, and She can trace them back, but they are just little tokens, not the real elandons."

Ayla was delighted with the "Legend." She had heard people talk about the Elder Legends, but she didn't realize they were stories told to help people understand things they needed to know. They reminded her of stories that old Dorv used to tell to Brun's clan in the winter.

Then the donier continued. "The abelan is a symbol or mark or pattern that always has life-force associated with it. It is used specifically to identify or characterize someone or some group. The Zelandonii abelan identifies all of us and is the most significant. It is a symbol made of squares or rectangles, often with variations and embellishments. It may be different colors, or made of different materials, or even different numbers of squares, but it must have the basic shapes. Part of this is a Zelandonii abelan," she said, pointing to the mark tattooed on the side of her forehead. Ayla noticed that three rows of three squares were part of the design.

"The squares tell anyone who sees it that my people are Zelandonii. Because one can count nine of them, the mark also identifies me as a member of the Ninth Cave. There is more to this tattoo, of course," she continued. "It also marks me as a member of the zelandonia, and declares that I am considered by the other Zelandonia as First Among Those Who Serve The Great Earth Mother. Although no longer as significant, a part of it is also my own personal abelan.

You will notice that Marthona's tattoo is different from mine, although parts of it are the same."

Ayla turned to examine the former leader's tattoo. Marthona tilted her head to show it better. "There are the nine squares," Ayla said, "but the mark is on the other side of her forehead, and there are other marks, more curved. Now that I look at it, one of them seems to have the shape of a horse, from the neck, across the back and down the hind legs."

"Yes," Marthona said. "The tattoo artist was very good and captured the essence of my abelan. Though more stylized so that it could work with the whole pattern, it is very close to the mark on my elandon, which is a horse, but simplified like that."

"Our tattoos tell you something about each of us," Zelandoni said. "You know that I Serve The Mother because mine is on the left. You know that Marthona is or was a leader of her Cave because hers is on the right side of her forehead. You know we are both Zelandonii, because of the squares, and that we are of the Ninth Cave."

"I think Manvelar's tattoo had three squares, but I don't remember if I could count up to fourteen squares on Brameval's forehead," Ayla said.

"No, you couldn't," Zelandoni said. "Caves are not always identified by the number of squares, but a person's Cave is always identified in some way. Brameval's tattoo has fourteen dots in a certain shape."

"Not everyone has tattoos," Ayla said. "Willamar has a small one on the middle of his forehead, but Jondalar doesn't have one at all."

"Only people who are leaders have tattoos on their foreheads," Jondalar said. "Zelandoni is a spiritual leader, mother was a Cave leader. Willamar is the Trade Master. It is an important position, and his advice is often asked, so he is also considered a leader."

"Though most people would rather show who they are with their clothes, like Shevonar, some people have tattoos on other places, their cheeks or chins, even hands, usually someplace that shows and is not covered up by clothes. Not much point in putting an identifying mark where no one can see it. The other tattoos often show something a person wants to be recognized for, but usually it's a personal achievement, not a primary tie relationship," Marthona said.

"Among the Mamutoi, the mamuti—that's like zelandonia—have tattoos on their cheeks, but not squares. They use chevrons," Ayla said. "They start with a diamond shape, which is like a square turned so that it points up and down, or half of that, a triangle—they particularly like downward-pointing triangles. Then they repeat the pointed

260

shape, like one point nestled inside another. Sometimes they connect them and make zigzags. All those symbols have meanings, too. Mamut was just starting to teach them to me the winter before I left."

Zelandoni and Marthona caught each other's eyes and nodded a slight acknowledgment. The donier had talked with the former leader about Ayla's abilities and suggested that she, perhaps, ought to consider affiliating with the zelandonia in some way. They both agreed that it might be better for her and everyone else.

"Then Shevonar's tunic has his mark, his abelan, and the Zelandonii abelan," Ayla stated, as though learning a lesson by rote.

"Yes. He will be recognized by everyone, including Doni. The Great Earth Mother will know that he is one of Her children who lived in the southwest region of this land," Zelandoni said. "But that is only part of the design on Shevonar's Ceremonial tunic. The entire outfit has meaning, including the necklaces. Besides the Zelandonii abelan, part of the pattern includes the nine squares that identify his Cave, and other patterns that define his lineage. There are symbol marks for the woman he mated, the abelans of her children born to his hearth. His craft, spear-making, is represented, and of course, his own symbol mark. His abelan is the most personal, and personally powerful element of all. His Ceremonial outfit, which are his burial clothes now, are, I suppose you could say, a visual display of his names and ties."

"Shevonar's Ceremonial outfit is particularly nice," Marthona said. "It was created by the old pattern-maker, who is gone now. He was very good."

Ayla had thought the clothing of the Zelandonii was very interesting, some of it quite beautiful—particularly Marthona's things—but she'd had no idea of the complexity of the meanings associated with it. Some things had seemed too ornate for her taste. She had learned to appreciate the pure form and usefulness of the things she made, just as her Clan mother did. Occasionally she varied the pattern in a basket she was weaving, or showed off the grain of the wood in a bowl or cup she carved and sanded smooth, but she had never added decorations.

Now she was beginning to understand how the clothes and jewelry that people wore, as well as their facial tattoos, characterized and identified them. Shevonar's ensemble, for all that it was highly decorated, was one that she felt had a balanced and pleasing pattern. She was surprised, however, when Marthona said that it had been created by an old man.

"Shevonar's clothes must have taken a lot of work. Why would an old man spend so much time making clothes?" Ayla asked.

Jondalar smiled. "Because the old man's craft was designing Ceremonial and burial clothing. That's what a pattern-maker does."

"The old man didn't make Shevonar's Ceremonial clothes, he planned how they would go together," Marthona said. "There are so many aspects to include, it takes a special skill and an artistic eye to put them together in a pleasing way. But he could arrange to have the clothes made. Several people had worked closely with him for many years, and the team was in great demand. Now, one of them plans the clothing, but she isn't as good, not yet."

"But why would the old man or anyone else do it for Shevonar?" Ayla asked.

"He traded for it," Jondalar said.

Ayla frowned. It was obvious she still didn't quite understand. "I thought people traded with other Camps or Caves. I didn't know they traded with people in their own Cave."

"But why not?" Willamar said. "Shevonar was a spear-maker. He was known for his well-made spears, but he couldn't arrange all the elements and symbols he wanted to show on his Ceremonial outfit in a way that pleased him. So he traded twenty of his finest spears for that outfit, and he prized it greatly."

"It was one of the last the old man made," Marthona said. "After his eyes no longer allowed him to practice his craft, he traded Shevonar's spears, one by one, for other things he wanted, but he saved the best one for himself. His bones are now buried in sacred ground, but he took that spear with him to the spirit world. It was one that had both his and Shevonar's abelans on it."

"If he is especially pleased with his handiwork," Jondalar explained, "along with the abelan of the person it is being made for, a spear-maker sometimes incorporates his own symbol mark within the design carved or painted on it."

Ayla learned during the hunt that certain marks on spears were very important. She knew that every spear carried a mark of its owner, so that there would be no doubt who had killed which animal. She didn't know that it was called an abelan, or that it was so important to the Zelandonii. She had seen one dispute resolved because of the marks. Two spears had found the same animal, but only one was imbedded in a vital organ.

Though each spear bore the owner's symbol mark, she had heard the hunters talking about the spear-makers. They always seemed to know who made which spear, whether or not it bore the mark of the one who made it. The style of the spear and the decorations on it declared the maker.

"What is your abelan, Jondalar?" she asked.

"It's not anything specific, it's just a mark. It looks like this," he said. He smoothed out the dry dirt nearby, and with his finger drew a line, then a second line that started parallel with the first line, but converged to a point at the end. A small line joined the two lines near the pointed end. "I always thought that when I was born, the Zelandoni couldn't think of anything that day," he said, then looked at the First and grinned. "Or maybe it's the tail of an ermine, white with a black tip. I always liked those little ermine tails. Do you think my abelan could be an ermine?"

"Well, your totem is a Cave Lion," Ayla said, "just like mine. I think your abelan can be anything you say it is. Why not an ermine? Ermines are feisty little weasels, but pretty in winter, all white except for their black eyes and the black tips of their tails. Actually, their brown summer coats are not bad, either." She thought for a moment, then asked, "What is Shevonar's abelan?"

"I saw one of his spears near his resting place," Jondalar said. "I'll get it and show you."

He quickly got the spear and showed her Shevonar's symbol mark. It was a stylized representation of a mouflon, a mountain sheep with large curved horns.

"I should take that with me," Zelandoni said. "We'll need it to make a copy of his abelan."

"Why do you need to make a copy?" Ayla asked.

"The same symbol that marked his spears, clothing, and other posessions will mark his grave post," Jondalar said.

As they walked back toward their dwellings, Ayla thought about the discussion and drew a few conclusions on her own. Though the symbol object, the elandon, itself was concealed, the symbol mark, the abelan, that had been made on it was known not only to the person it symbolized, but to everyone else. It did possess some power, especially for the one to whom it belonged, but not for someone who might want to misuse it. It was too well-known. Real power came from the unknown, the esoteric.

The following morning, Joharran rapped on the post beside the entrance to Marthona's dwelling. Jondalar pushed the drape aside and was surprised to see his brother.

"Aren't you going to the meeting this morning?" he asked.

"Yes, of course, but I wanted to talk to you and Ayla, first," Joharran said.

"Come in, then," Jondalar said.

Joharran stepped in and let the heavy entrance drape fall back. Marthona and Willamar came out of their sleeping room and greeted him warmly. Ayla was putting leftover food from breakfast into the wooden bowl she had designated as Wolf's. She looked up and smiled.

"Joharran told me he wanted to talk to us," Jondalar said, looking at Ayla.

"I won't take much time, but I've been thinking about those spear-throwing weapons of yours. If more of us had been able to cast a spear from the distance you did, Jondalar, we might have been able to stop that bison before it trampled Shevonar. It's too late to help him, but I want the rest of the hunters to have that safety measure. Would you, both of you, be willing to show everyone how to make one of those, and how to use it?"

Jondalar smiled. "Of course we will. That's what I was hoping all along. I could hardly wait to show how they work, so everyone could see their advantage."

All of the residents of Marthona's dwelling, except Folara, walked with Joharran to the meeting area near the south end of the huge abri. By the time they reached it, a good number of people had already arrived. Messengers had been sent to the Zelandonia of the Caves that took part in the hunt to meet and talk about the burial ceremony. Besides the spiritual leader of the Ninth, the Zelandonia of the Fourteenth Cave, the Eleventh, the Third, the Second, and the Zelandoni of the Seventh were there. Most of those to whom the people looked for leadership also made an appearance, as well as several others who were interested.

"The Spirit of the Bison has claimed one of us in return for her own," the large donier said. "It is a sacrifice we must make if she demands it." She looked at the people, who were nodding their heads in acknowledgment. Her commanding presence was never so evident as when she was with other Zelandonia. Then it became apparent that she was First Among Those Who Served The Mother.

As the meeting continued, a couple of the Zelandonia got into a small difference of opinion about a minor point, and the First was allowing the dispute to run its course. Joharran found his mind straying from the talk about Shevonar's burial to a consideration of where to set up practice targets. After talking to Ayla and Jondalar, Joharran decided to encourage his hunters to make spear-throwers and start practicing even before they left for the Summer Meeting. He wanted them to become skilled in Jondalar's new weapon as quickly as possible. But not today. He knew there would be no using of weapons this day. This was the day the spirit of Shevonar, his elan, would be guided to the next world.

Zelandoni's mind was also occupied with other thoughts, though she appeared to be seriously considering the points of view being offered. She had been thinking about Jondalar's younger brother ever since she was given the stone with the opalescent face from his grave far to the east, but she had been waiting for an appropriate time.

She knew that both Jondalar and Ayla would have to be involved in the process, and making contact with the next world was fearsome enough under any circumstances, especially for those who were not trained to deal with it—it could be dangerous even for those who were. It was safer when there were many people around during the ceremony to aid and support those who would be making the contact directly.

Since he was killed during a hunt that involved most of the nearby Caves, Shevonar's burial would have to be a major ceremony that would include and invoke the protection of the entire community. This might be a good time to make an attempt to enter more deeply into the spirit world to search for Thonolan's vital force, Zelandoni thought. She glanced at Ayla and wondered how the foreign woman would react. Ayla continually surprised the donier with her knowledge, her competence, and even her commendable attitude.

The old donier had been flattered when the young woman came to her to ask if there was anything more she could have done for Shevonar, especially considering the skill she had shown. And it was surprisingly appropriate for the young woman to suggest that Jondalar take a stone from his brother's burial place, considering that she was unfamiliar with their practices, Zelandoni thought. The stone that had presented itself to him was certainly unique. It seemed entirely ordinary, until one turned it over and saw that bluish, opalescent face with the fiery red points.

That opalescent blue is undoubtedly an aspect of clear, she thought, and red is the color of life, the most important of the Mother's Five Sacred Colors. That little stone is clearly an object of power. Something will have to be done with it after we are through with it.

She was only half listening to the disagreement, when it came to her that the unique stone from Thonolan's grave was rather like a surrogate stone. With it, the Mother could trace Thonolan's elan. The best and safest place for it would be in a crack of a sacred cave near the surrogate stones of his family. She knew where almost all of the surrogate stones of the Ninth Cave were, and many of those from other Caves. She even knew the hiding places of some actual elandons besides her own.

There had been a few unusual circumstances that had required her to step in and assume the duties of a parent and take responsibility for the elandons of some children, and she'd had to hide the symbol things for a few people who were incapable, either mentally or physically, of hiding their own. She never spoke of those, and would never for any reason try to take advantage of her knowledge. She was well aware of the dangers, to herself as well as the person the elandon represented.

Ayla's mind was beginning to wander, too. She wasn't familiar with Zelandonii burial customs, and she was quite interested, but the present discussion, which seemed rather interminable, was beyond her grasp. She didn't even know some of the esoteric words they used. Instead she was thinking about some of the things she had learned recently.

It had been explained that people were usually buried in sacred ground, though burial grounds changed after they acquired a certain number of graves. Too many lingering spirits in one place could give them too much power. Those who died at the same time might be kept together, or if they were especially close, but there was not one single burial ground. Instead, burying was done in small areas scattered throughout the landscape.

Whatever place was chosen, the burial area was marked by posts set in the ground around the graves at close intervals and at the head of each grave. The posts were carved or painted with the abelans of the people who were buried there, symbols that proclaimed the danger of entering the area. Spirits of the dead who no longer had a body to inhabit might lurk within the confines staked out, but could not go beyond the palisade. The zelandonia made the exorcistic fence so that the spirits who could not find their way to the spirit world would not be able to cross the boundary and steal the body of someone still walking in this world.

Without powerful protection, those who entered within the fenced area were in grave danger. Spirits began to gather even before a corpse was laid to rest, and they had been known to attempt to gain possession of the body of a living being and wage war with the person's own spirit for control. It was usually known by the drastic change of the person, who might do things that were out of character, or see things that were not seen by others, or cry out for no apparent reason, or become violent, or seem unable to comprehend the world around them and withdraw into themselves.

After many years, when the poles had fallen down of their own accord and rotted into the earth, and vegetation had grown over the graves and refreshed the gravesite, the sacred ground was no longer considered hallowed, no longer dangerous; the spirits were gone. It was said the Great Earth Mother had claimed Her own and given the place back to Her children.

Ayla, and the others who had been musing, immediately brought their attention back to the discussion when they heard the voice of the First. Since the disputing Zelandonia could not seem to work out their differences, the powerful donier decided it was time to step in. She made a decision that included aspects of all the points of view and explained it in a way that made it seem the only possible way. Then they went on to talk about the safeguards that would be needed for those who would be bringing Shevonar's body to the sacred burial ground so they would be protected from the lost and wandering souls.

There would be a feast to fortify everyone so that each person's own spirit had the strength to fight off the lost souls, and of course, everyone looked to Proleva to organize it. In addition, they talked about the food that would be placed in the grave, along with weapons and tools. The grave food would not be eaten, but the spirit of the food would nourish the free-floating spirit to give him strength to find his way. Everything possible was done so the departing soul would have no reason to turn back or linger too long.

Later that morning, Ayla went out with the horses, riding on Whinney with Racer and Wolf following behind. Then she combed them, while checking them over to make sure everything was well with them. She was used to spending every day with the horses, but since they had arrived, she had been with Jondalar's people most of the time, and she missed the animals. The way they greeted her, with such enthusiastic affection, she thought they probably missed her, and Jondalar, too.

She stopped by Joharran's home on the way back and asked Proleva if she knew where Jondalar was.

"He went with Joharran, Rushemar, and Solaban to dig a pit for Shevonar," the woman said. Proleva had much to do, but at the moment was waiting for some others and had a little time. She had been wanting to get to know this woman with so many talents who would soon be joined with her mate's brother, and asked, "Would you like some chamomile tea?"

Ayla hesitated. "I think I should go back to Marthona's, but I'd love to have some tea with you another time."

Wolf, who had enjoyed the outing as much as the horses, had followed Ayla in. Jaradal, spying the animal, came running toward him. The wolf poked his nose at the youngster, wanting to be petted. Jaradal chuckled delightedly and rubbed Wolf's head.

"I have to tell you, Ayla," Proleva said, "I was very concerned at first when Jaradal said he had touched your animal. It's hard to believe that a meat-eating, hunting animal like that can be so gentle with children. When Folara brought him in here and I saw Marsola crawl all over him, I couldn't believe it. She pulled his fur, poked at his eyes, even grabbed his jaw and looked inside his mouth, and Wolf just lay there like he loved it. I was absolutely amazed. Even Salova was smiling, though when she first saw her baby girl with that wolf, she was terrified."

"Wolf has a special fondness for children," Ayla explained. "He grew up playing and sleeping with them in the earthlodge of the Lion Camp. They were his litter-mates, and grown wolves are always protective and indulgent toward the young of their pack. He seems to think all young children belong to his pack."

As Ayla and Wolf made their way toward Marthona's dwelling, something about Proleva was nagging at the back of her mind. It was the way she held herself, the way she moved, the way her loose tunic fit. Suddenly it came to her, and she smiled. Proleva was pregnant! She was sure of it.

When Ayla went into Marthona's dwelling, no one was there. It made her wish she had stayed and had tea with Proleva, though she wondered where Jondalar's mother was. She wasn't with Proleva, maybe she went to see Zelandoni, Ayla thought. They seemed close, or at least respected each other. They were always talking or giving each other knowing looks. If she went to look for Marthona there, it would give her a reason to call upon the donier, whom she definitely wanted to know better.

Of course, I really don't have to find Marthona, and Zelandoni is very busy right now. Perhaps I shouldn't bother her, Ayla thought, but she had been feeling at loose ends and wanted something meaningful to do. Maybe I could help. At least I could offer.

Ayla went to the dwelling of Zelandoni and tapped lightly on the panel near the entrance drape. The woman must have been standing nearby. She pushed aside the drape within a heartbeat or two.

"Ayla," she said, looking rather surprised to see the young woman and the wolf. "Is there something I can do for you?"

"I was looking for Marthona. She isn't at home and she wasn't with Proleva. I wondered if she might have come here," Ayla said.

"No, she's not here."

"Well, I'm sorry to have bothered you. I know how busy you are. I shouldn't have taken up your time," Ayla said.

"It's perfectly all right," the donier said, then she noted that the young woman seemed tense, but eager, and somehow hopeful. "Did you want Marthona for anything special?"

"No, I was just looking for her. I thought she might need help with something."

"If you are looking for something to do, perhaps you can help me," Zelandoni said, holding the drape open while she stepped back. Ayla's big, pleased smile made the older woman realize that was the real reason she had come.

"Is it all right for Wolf to come in?" Ayla said. "He won't disturb anything."

"I know he won't. I told you we understood each other," the donier said, holding back the drape to allow the animal in after Ayla. "The red ochre you collected for me needs to be ground into powder. There's the mortar," Zelandoni said, showing her a red-stained stone with a saucerlike depression formed by years of use, "and here's the rock for grinding. Jonokol will be here soon and will need it to assist me in making a post with Shevonar's abelan. He is my acolyte."

"I met a man named Jonokol at the welcoming feast, but he said he was an artist," Ayla said.

"Jonokol is an artist. He is also my acolyte. I think he is more artist than acolyte, though. He has no interest in healing, or even finding his way to the spirit world. He seems content to remain an acolyte, but he is young yet. Time will tell. He may yet feel the call. In the meantime, he is a fine artist, and he makes an excellent assistant," Zelandoni said, then added, "Most artists are also zelandonia. Jonokol has been since he was very young, when he first showed talent."

Ayla was glad to grind the red iron oxide into powder, it was a way to be of help without special training, but the repetitious physical activity left her mind free to think. She wondered about the zelandonia, and why artists, like Jonokol, would be brought into the group when they were so young; they couldn't possibly know anything about what it was or meant. Why would artists need to be part of the zelandonia?

While she was working, Jonokol came in. He looked at Ayla, and then the wolf with some surprise. Wolf lifted his head up, then glanced at Ayla, tensing to rise if she signaled. She motioned a sign that meant the man was welcome. The wolf relaxed, but continued to be watchful.

"Ayla came over to help, Jonokol," Zelandoni said. "I understand you have met."

"Yes, the first night she was here. Greetings, Ayla," Jonokol said.

Ayla finished grinding the red lumps into fine powder and gave the mortar, grinding stone, and the red powder to Zelandoni, hoping the woman would give her something else to do, but it soon became evident that they were both waiting for her to go. "Is there anything else you would like me to do?" she finally asked.

"Not right now," the donier said.

Ayla nodded, then signaled to Wolf and left. Marthona was still gone when she returned to the dwelling, and with Jondalar away, she didn't know what to do. I should have stayed and had tea with Proleva, she thought. Then she decided, Why not go back? Ayla wanted to get to know the accomplished and admired woman. After all, they were going to be related; she was the mate of Jondalar's brother. Maybe I could even bring a nice tea, Ayla thought, something with dried linden flowers to add a nice fragrance and a little sweetening. I wish I knew if a linden tree grew nearby.

15

The men were nearly finished digging the grave pit, and glad of it. The Zelandonia had invoked strong protection for them before they left to make the ground ready to receive the body of Shevonar, including pouring red powdered ochre over their hands, but each of them still had trembled privately when they crossed the invisible barrier marked by the carved and red-painted posts.

The four diggers wore large leather hides with no shaping and totally devoid of decoration, sort of a blanket with a hole through the middle for their heads. A face-covering hood went over their heads with holes cut out for their eyes but not their mouths or noseholes—bodily openings that invited the entry of a spirit.

The covering was intended to hide their identity from any spirits that might be lurking nearby looking for a living body to inhabit; there could be no abelans, no symbols or designs of any kind to announce who was encroaching upon the sacred ground and disturbing the spirits. They did not speak, for even the sound of their voices could give them away. Digging a grave trench was not a job that was easy to delegate, and Joharran had decided that since he was the one who was responsible for organizing the ill-fated hunt, he ought to be one of the diggers. He had chosen his two aides, Solaban and Rushemar, and his brother Jondalar, to assist him. Though the four men knew each other well, they sincerely hoped it was not apparent to any lingering elans.

It was hard work chopping up the hard ground with the stone mattocks. The sun was high overhead, and they were sweaty and hot. It was difficult to breathe inside the leather hoods, but not one of the strong, fearless hunters even considered removing them. Any one of them could face up to a charging rhinoceros and dodge aside at the last moment, but it took far more courage to brave the unseen dangers of the hallowed burial ground.

None of them wanted to stay in the enclosure haunted by spirits any longer than necessary, and they worked as fast as they could, scooping out the dirt loosened by the mattocks. The shovels they used were made of the large flat bones, scapulas or pelvises, of the bigger animals with one side tapered, then smoothed with a round stone and river sand to a fairly sharp edge to make shoveling easier. The opposite end was attached to a long branch. The dirt was placed on leather hides similar to the ones they wore, so it could be pulled away from the edge of the pit to make room for the many people who would be crowding close.

Joharran nodded to the others when the last few shovelfuls of loose earth were pitched out of the hole. It was deep enough. They gathered up the tools and quickly left. Still not speaking, they walked far away from the living areas to a place that had been selected earlier, one seldom frequented by people.

Joharran thrust the pick end of the mattock into the ground, then the diggers dug a second hole, smaller than the first, took off the hoods and coverings and threw them into it, then carefully filled the dirt back in. The digging tools would be returned to the special place they were kept, but the diggers were careful not to let any part of the tools touch any part of their own naked bodies, except for their ochre-reddened hands.

They went directly to a special small cave near the valley floor in the cave-pocked limestone cliffs. A carved post with the Zelandonii abelan and other markings was planted in the ground in front of it. They went in, replaced the burial digging tools, and quickly left, grasping the post with both hands and murmuring a few sounds under their breaths asking for the protection of the Mother as they went. Then they followed a snaking path to another cave in the highland, the one used primarily by the zelandonia for ceremonies involving men and boys.

The six Zelandonia of the Caves that took part in the tragic hunt were waiting for them outside the cave, along with several acolytes. They had water, heated almost to the boil with hot rocks, and several varieties of saponin-producing plants, generally referred to as soap-roots. The foamy lather turned red from the ochre powder used to protect their hands and feet. Hot water, almost too hot to stand, was poured over their stained appendages into a small hole dug in the earth. The ablution was performed a second time, making sure no trace of red remained. They even cleaned under their fingernails with small pointed sticks. Then they washed a third time. They were inspected and, if necessary, washed again, until each Zelandoni was satisfied.

Then each man took watertight baskets of warm water and more soaproots and washed his entire body, including his hair. Only when they were finally declared purified, and were allowed to don their own clothing, did they breathe easier. The One Who Was First gave each of them a cup of hot, bitter-tasting tea, instructing them to first rinse out their mouths, spit it out in a special hole, then drink the rest. They rinsed and swallowed hurriedly and left quickly, relieved that this part was over. None of them liked being so close to such powerful magic.

Jondalar and the other men walked into Joharran's home, talking softly, still conscious of their close contact with the world of the spirits.

"Ayla was here looking for you, Jondalar," Proleva said. "She left, then came back with some delicious tea. We talked a little, but then several people came to talk about the burial feast. She offered to help, but I told her next time. I'm sure Zelandoni has other plans for her. She left not long ago. I have to go, too. There's some food and hot tea for you in the cooking room."

"Did Ayla say where she was going?" Jondalar asked.

"To your mother's."

"Thank you. I'll go see what she wanted."

"Have a bite to eat first. That was hard work," Proleva said.

He ate quickly, washed it down with some tea, then started out. "Let me know when the zelandonia are ready, Joharran," Jondalar said as he left.

Everyone was sitting around the low table, drinking Marthona's wine, when he went into his mother's dwelling.

"Get your cup, Jondalar," she said. "I'll pour you some. This has been a difficult day, and it's not over yet. I thought we should all try to relax a little."

"You look all scrubbed and clean, Jondalar," Ayla said.

"Yes, and am I ever glad that's over. I want to do my part, but I hate digging in hallowed ground," Jondalar said, and felt a shudder.

"I know how you feel," Willamar said.

"If you were digging, why are you so clean?" Ayla asked.

"He was helping to dig the burial pit," Willamar explained, "and he had to be completely purified after digging in the sacred burial ground and disturbing the spirits. The zelandonia use hot water and lots of soaproot, and foam up several times."

"That reminds me of the hot pool of the Losadunai. Remember,

Jondalar?" Ayla said. She noticed that his expression had changed to a suggestive smile, and she recalled one pleasurable afternoon with him in the natural hot spring. She looked away, trying not to smile back. "Do you remember that cleansing foam they made using rendered fat and ashes?"

"Yes. It really foamed up and made things cleaner than anything I've ever seen," he said. "It even took all taste and smell away." His smile had grown, and she knew he was teasing her with double meanings. He had said then, when they shared Pleasures, that he couldn't even taste her. But it was an interesting experience to feel so clean.

"I was thinking," Ayla said, still avoiding Jondalar's amorous glances and trying to be serious, "that cleansing foam could be very good for purifying. Some Losadunai women showed me how to make it, but it can be tricky, and doesn't always work. Maybe I should try to make some to show Zelandoni."

"I can't imagine how fat and ashes can make someone clean," Folara said.

"I wouldn't believe it myself if I hadn't seen it," Ayla said, "but when you mix them together in a certain way, something happens and you don't have fat or ashes anymore, but something else. You have to add water to the ashes, cook it a while, then let it cool before you strain it. It becomes very strong, it can even give you blisters if you are not careful. It is like the part of fire that burns you, but without heat. Then you add melted fat to it, about the same amount of fat as there is liquid, but both the fat and the strained liquid must have the same feeling of heat as the skin at the inside of your wrist. If you've done everything right, when you mix it around, it makes a foam that can clean almost anything. You rinse the foam away, and it takes dirt with it. It can even take grease away."

"Why would someone decide to put fat and ash-water together in the first place?" Folara asked.

"The woman who told me about it said it was an accident the first time she did it," Ayla explained. "She'd been cooking or rendering some fat over a firepit when it started to rain very hard. She ran to get under cover. When she went back, she thought the fat was ruined. It had overflowed into the firepit that had been full of ashes and had filled up with rain. Then she saw the wooden spoon she'd been using to stir it. It had taken a long time to carve and was a favorite of hers, so she decided to retrieve it. She reached through a slippery foam that she thought was ruined fat to get the spoon, and when she went to clean the foam off, she discovered it not only rinsed away easily, but it left her hand and the spoon clean."

Ayla didn't know that the lye leached from wood ashes, when mixed with fat at a certain temperature, caused a chemical reaction that created soap. She didn't need to know why the process made a cleansing foam, she just knew that it did. It wasn't the first time, and it wouldn't be the last, that a discovery was made by accident.

"I'm sure Zelandoni would be interested," Marthona said. She had been aware of the byplay between her son and the young woman. Jondalar wasn't as subtle as he thought, and she was trying to help Ayla keep the discussion in a more serious vein. After all, they would be going to a funeral soon. It was hardly the time to be thinking about Pleasures. "I made a discovery like that once when I was making wine. Afterward, my wine always seemed to turn out well."

"Are you finally going to tell your secret, mother?" Jondalar said.

"What secret?"

"How you make wine that always turns out better than anyone else's wine, and never goes to vinegar," Jondalar said with a grin.

She nodded her head with a look of exasperation. "I don't think of it as a secret, Jondalar."

"But you never would tell anyone how you did it."

"That's because I was never sure if what I did really made a difference, or if it would work for anyone else," Marthona said. "I don't know why I did it the first time, but I watched Zelandoni do something similar with one of her medicinal drinks, and it seemed to give it a potent magic. I wondered if it might add some magic to my wine, too. It does seem to work," Marthona said.

"Well, tell us," Jondalar said. "I always knew you did something special."

"I watched Zelandoni chew some herbs when she made a certain medicine, so the next time I crushed the berries for wine, I chewed some and spat the juice into the mash before it began to ferment. I think it's strange that something like that should make a difference, but apparently it does."

"Iza taught me that there are some medicines and some special drinks that must be chewed with the mouth to make them work," Ayla said. "Perhaps mixing the berries for wine with a little of the juices from the mouth adds some special ingredient." She had never thought of it before, but it was possible.

"I ask Doni to help make the fruit juice into wine, too. Maybe that's the real secret," Marthona said. "If you don't ask for too much, sometimes the Mother will give you what you want. When you were little, it never used to fail for you, Jondalar. If you asked Doni for it, you always seemed to get what you really wanted. Is that still true?"

Jondalar reddened slightly. He didn't realize anyone else knew, but he should have guessed Marthona would. "Usually," he said, looking away from her direct stare.

"Has She ever *not* given you what you asked for?" his mother pressed.

"Once," he said, squirming with discomfort.

She watched him, then nodded. "Yes, I imagine that was too much even for the Great Earth Mother to let you have. I don't think you're sorry now, are you?"

Everyone looked puzzled by the rather cryptic conversation between mother and son. Jondalar was noticeably disconcerted. Ayla watched them, then it suddenly came to her that Marthona was talking about Zelandoni, or rather Zolena, the young woman she had been.

"Did you know digging in hallowed ground is one thing only men do, Ayla?" Willamar said, changing the subject to cloak the awkward moment. "It would be too dangerous to expose the Blessed of Doni to such dangerous forces."

"And I'm glad, too," Folara said. "It's bad enough to have to clean and dress a person whose spirit is gone. I hate having to do that! I was so happy when you asked me to look after Wolf earlier today, Ayla. I invited all my friends over, and told them to bring their little sisters and brothers. Wolf met a lot of people."

"No wonder he's so tired," Marthona said, glancing toward the wolf, who was in his sleeping place. "I'd go to sleep after a day like that."

"I don't think he's sleeping," Ayla said. She knew the difference between his resting and sleeping postures. "I'm sure you are right, though. He is tired. He does love little ones, but they wear him out."

They all turned with a start at a gentle knock on the panel beside the entrance, though they had been expecting it. "The zelandonia are ready." It was Joharran's voice. The five of them inside quickly swallowed the last of their wine and went out. Wolf followed them out, but Ayla tied him with the special rope to a firmly planted stake not far from Marthona's dwelling to keep him away from the burial ceremony that everyone would be attending.

Many people had already gathered around the burial shelter. There was a soft hum of conversation as people greeted each other and talked, but in low voices. The wall panels had been removed and Shevonar's body was exposed for all to see, lying on the grass-mat shroud and netted hammock that would be folded around him later to carry him to the burial place. But first he would be carried to the Gather Field, which was large enough for all the people from the six Caves in the region that had taken part in the hunt to come together.

Jondalar had gone off with his brother and several others shortly after they reached the area. Marthona and Willamar knew their parts in the forthcoming rituals and hurried to take their places. Ayla didn't know what to do and was feeling at a loss. She decided she would stay in the background and observe, and hope she wouldn't do anything that might embarrass her or Jondalar's family.

Folara introduced the foreign woman her brother had brought back to some of her friends, several young women, and two young men. Ayla was talking to them, or at least trying to. They had already heard so many stories about her, they were awestruck and either tongue-tied with shyness or babbling to overcompensate. She didn't hear her name being called at first.

"Ayla, I think they want you," Folara said when she noticed Zelandoni coming toward them.

"You'll have to excuse her," the donier said to Ayla's young admirers, a bit abruptly. "She needs to be in front with the zelandonia." Ayla followed the woman. Behind her, the young people were even more impressed. When they were out of hearing range of the youngsters, the woman spoke softly to Ayla. "The zelandonia don't eat at a burial. You will walk with us, but then you will join Jondalar and Marthona at the head of the line to get your food for the feast."

Ayla didn't question why she would be walking with the fasting zelandonia but eating with Jondalar's family, though she thought about it later. She had no idea what was expected of her. She could only follow when they started across the bridge up to Down River and continued on to the Gather Field.

The zelandonia did not eat because it was necessary to fast to communicate with the next world, which would be necessary during the burial. Afterward, the First planned to make an extended meta-physical excursion to contact the elan of Thonolan. It was always difficult to travel to the next world, but she was accustomed to it now and knew what she had to do. Fasting was a part of the life of the zelandonia, and she sometimes wondered why she continued to grow in size, when often she did not eat. Perhaps she made up for it the next day, but it did not seem to her that she ate more than others. She was aware that many people felt that her tremendous size contributed to her presence and her mystique. Her only objection was that she was beginning to find it more difficult to move comfortably. Bending over, climbing a slope, and sitting on the ground or, rather, getting up again were all harder, but the Mother seemed to want her to be substantial, and if it was Her wish, the donier was willing.

From the food being spread out near the high wall at the back, far away from the place where the body was placed, it was evident that many people had been working very hard to prepare it. "This is like a small Summer Meeting," Ayla heard someone say, and thought, If this is small, how big is a Zelandonii Summer Meeting? With something close to two hundred people from the Ninth Cave alone, plus the people from five other Caves, all of them rather populous, Ayla knew she would never be able to remember all of them. She didn't think there were even enough counting words for them all. She could only think of them as something like a herd of bison when they came together for mating or migrating.

When the six Zelandonia and the six leaders of the Caves arranged themselves around the burial shelter, which had been taken down, carried to the field, and erected again, people began to sit down on the ground and grow quiet. Someone had filled a large plate with choice portions from the feast, including a whole shank of bison. The One Who Was First picked it up and held it high for everyone to see. Then she placed it beside Shevonar's body.

"The Zelandonii hold this feast in your honor, Shevonar," she said, addressing the dead man. "Please join us in spirit so that we may wish your elan Good Journey as you travel to the next world."

Then the rest of the people lined up to take their portions. Most of the time, when there was a feast, people fell into line at random, but this was a formal public occasion, one of the few times when there was a specific order. People lined up according to their understood but seldom displayed status in order to announce their place in this world to the spirits of the next, and to assist the elan of Shevonar in making the difficult transition.

The grieving mate, Relona, and her two children were first, since it was Shevonar's funeral, followed by his brother, Ranokol. Joharran and Proleva and Jaradal filed behind them, then Marthona and Willamar along with Folara, Jondalar—the highest-ranking members of the Ninth Cave—and Ayla.

Ayla didn't know it, but she had presented quite a problem. As a foreigner, her status in the Cave should have been last. If she and Jondalar had been officially Promised in a recognized ceremony, it would have been easier to place her among Jondalar's high-ranking family, but their upcoming mating was only understood, and her acceptance into the Cave was not even formally sanctioned yet. When it came up, Jondalar made it clear that wherever Ayla was placed, he would stay with her. If she was placed last in line, then he would stand last in line.

A man's status originally came from his mother, until he mated. Then, it might change. Normally, before a mating was officially authorized, the families, and sometimes the leaders and the zelandonia, engaged in Matrimonial negotiations, which involved many aspects. For example, gift exchanges were agreed upon; whether the couple would live with his Cave, her Cave, or some other Cave; and the setting of a bride price since her status was considered the most valuable. One of the important aspects of the negotiations was the status of the new couple.

Marthona was convinced that if Jondalar stood at the end of the line, it could be misunderstood, not only by the Zelandonii, but by the spirits of the next world, to mean that he had lost status for some reason, or that Ayla's position was so low, his status could not be negotiated any higher. That was why Zelandoni insisted that she walk to the feast with the zelandonia. Even as a foreigner, if she was recognized as one of the metaphysical elite, it gave her prestige, ambiguous though it was. And though the zelandonia did not eat at a burial feast, she could be shifted into the line with Jondalar's family before anyone could object.

Though some people might realize that a subterfuge had been perpetrated, once it was done, her place was proclaimed to both this world and the next, and it would be a little late to change it. Ayla herself was completely unaware of the small deception exercised on behalf of Jondalar and her, and in fact, those who engaged in it felt it was an insignificant transgression. Both Marthona and Zelandoni, for different reasons, were convinced that Ayla was genuinely a person of high status. It was just a matter of making it known.

While the family was eating, Laramar came around and poured some barma into their cups. Ayla remembered him from the first night. She had come to understand that while the beverage he made might be appreciated, the man himself was often disparaged, and she wondered why. Ayla watched him as he poured liquid from a waterbag into Willamar's cup. She noticed that his clothing was decidedly dirty and frayed, worn through where it could have been patched.

"Can I pour some for you?" he said to her. She allowed him to fill her cup and, without staring directly, observed him more closely. He was an ordinary-looking man with light brown hair and beard, and blue eyes, not tall or short, and not fat or thin, though he did have a potbelly and generally a musculature that seemed softer, not as defined as that of most men. Then she saw that his neck was gray with grime, and she was sure that he seldom washed his hands.

It was easy enough to get dirty, particularly in winter when water often had to be melted from ice or snow, and using fuel for water to wash with was not always wise. But in summer, when water was available and soaproot plentiful, most people she knew preferred to be reasonably clean. It was unusual to see anyone quite so filthy.

"Thank you, Laramar," she said, smiled, and took a sip, though seeing the one who produced the brew made it less appetizing.

He smiled back. She had the feeling he didn't smile often and the distinct impression that this smile was insincere. She also noticed that his teeth were crooked. That wasn't his fault, she knew. Many people had crooked teeth, but it did add to his generally disagreeable appearance.

"I was looking forward to your company," Laramar said.

Ayla was puzzled. "Why were you expecting my company?"

"At a burial feast, strangers are always at the end of the line, after everyone who belongs to a Cave. But I noticed you were at the front," he said.

Marthona was annoyed for a moment, and Ayla caught the fleeting look on her face. "Yes, she probably should have been at the back near you, Laramar," the woman said, "but you know, Ayla will soon belong to the Ninth Cave."

"But she's not Zelandonii, yet," the man said. "She is foreign."

"She is Promised to Jondalar, and her status among her own people was quite high."

"Didn't she say she was raised by flatheads? I didn't know the status of flatheads counted for more than a Zelandonii," he said.

"To the Mamutoi she was a healer and a daughter of their Mamut, their Zelandoni," Marthona said. The former leader was becoming irritated. She did not like having to make explanations to the lowest-ranked man of the Cave . . . especially when he was right.

"She didn't do much to heal Shevonar, did she?" Laramar said.

"No one could have done more for him than Ayla did, not even the First," Joharran said, coming to her defense. "And she did help relieve his pain so he could hold on until his mate arrived."

Ayla noticed that Laramar's smile had become malicious. He was taking great pleasure in upsetting Jondalar's family and putting them on the defensive, and it had something to do with her. She wished she understood what it was about, and planned to ask Jondalar when they were alone, but she was beginning to understand why people spoke of Laramar with such reproach.

The zelandonia were beginning to gather around the burial shelter again, and people were taking their plates to a far corner of the Gather Field and scraping the remains onto a pile of leftovers. The midden would be left, and once the people were gone, the discarded meat and bones would be taken by various scavengers, while the vegetal matter would decay back into the ground. It was a common method of disposal. Laramar walked with Jondalar's family to the refuse heap, Ayla was sure it was to cause them a little more chagrin, then went his own way with a distinct swagger.

After people had gathered around the burial shelter again, the One Who Was First picked up the tightly woven basket of red ochre that Ayla had powdered. "There are Five Sacred Colors. All other colors are aspects of those primary colors. The first color is red," the large donier began. "It is the color of blood, the color of life. Some flowers and fruits show the true color of red, but they are ephemeral.

"Red seldom stays true for long. As blood dries it darkens, becomes brown. Brown is an aspect of red, sometimes called old red. The red ochres of the land are the dried blood of the Great Mother Earth, and though some can be almost as bright as new red, they are all old red.

"Covered with the red of blood from your mother's womb, you came into this world, Shevonar. Covered with the red earth of the Great Mother's womb, you shall return to her to be born again into the next world as you were born into this one," the First said as she sprinkled the body of Shevonar liberally from head to toe with the powdered red iron ore.

"The fifth primary color is dark, sometimes called black," Zelandoni said, making Ayla wonder what the second, third, and fourth Sacred Colors were. "Dark is the color of night, the color in deep caves, the color of charcoal, after fire has burned the life out of wood. Some say charcoal black is really the darkest shade of old red. It is the color that overcomes the color of life as it ages. Just as life becomes death, red becomes black, dark. Dark is the absence of life; it is the color of death. It does not even have an ephemeral life; there are no black flowers. Deep caves show the color in its true form.

"Shevonar, the body your elan inhabited has died and will go into the black under the ground, will return to the dark earth of the Mother, but your elan, your spirit, will go to the world of the spirits, will return to the Mother, the Original Source of Life. Take with you the spirit of this food we have given you to sustain you on your Journey to the spirit world." The large, impressive woman picked up the dish of food that had been left for him, held it up to show, then put it down beside him and sprinkled it with red ochre powder.

"Take with you your favorite spear to hunt the spirit animals for sustenance." The donier put his spear beside him and sprinkled it with red ochre. "Take with you your tools to make new spears for the hunters of the next world." She put his spear-shaft straightener under his hand, stiffened with rigor mortis, and sprinkled it with the red powder. "Do not forget the skills you learned in this world, make use of them in the next world. Do not grieve for your life here. Spirit of Shevonar, go freely, go confidently. Do not look back. Do not linger. Your next life awaits you."

The grave goods were arranged around him, the food in its containers was placed on his stomach, then the grass-mat shroud was wrapped around him and the cords that were threaded through the ends at head and foot were pulled tight, making it look like a cocoon. The long cords were then wrapped around him, which kept everything together and gave the body and its accoutrements a lumpy definition. The netting was pulled up and attached to either end of a pole, which had recently been a small, straight tree. The bark still on the tree helped to keep the hammock with its macabre bundle from sliding.

Then the same men who had dug a pit in the sacred burial

ground lifted the body of Shevonar and carried it between them. Joharran was at the front with the pole resting on his left shoulder, and Rushemar slightly behind him and on the other side rested it on his right. Solaban was at the rear on the same side as Joharran, but the pole rested on padding on his shoulder, since he was not as tall as Jondalar, who followed him.

The One Who Was First led the way toward the sacred burial ground. The men carrying the body followed her, and the rest of the Zelandonia placed themselves around the pallbearers. Relona with her two children and then Ranokol walked behind the swaying hammock. The rest of the people fell in behind in the same order they had assumed for the feast.

Ayla again walked with Marthona near the front. She noticed Laramar watching her as he headed toward the last of the people of the Ninth Cave, which put him in front of the leaders of the Third Cave. Although Manvelar tried to keep a slight distance behind the Ninth to create a gap that would separate the two Caves, Laramar, along with his tall, bony woman and her large brood of children, slowed down enough to keep the gap in front of him. Ayla became convinced that he did it on purpose to give the impression that he was the first of the Cave behind him rather than the last of the one ahead, though of course everyone knew his status and to which Cave he belonged.

The long line of people followed the path in single file as it narrowed in front of Big Rock, then used the few well-placed flattish stepping-stones to traverse Fish Creek, which ran down the middle of Little Valley. As the path closed in again in front of High Rock, they stayed in line until they reached the Crossing, but instead of continuing south after gaining the opposite bank, as they had done before to go to Two Rivers Rock, they turned left back toward the north and followed another trail.

No longer constrained by a narrow track between river and rock wall, they spread out and walked two or three abreast through the level field of the floodplain, then began to climb the slope of the rolling hills Ayla had seen across The River. The sun was descending in the west, nearing the tops of the cliffs behind when they came to an outcrop and a small, secluded, fairly level depression. The procession slowed and then stopped.

Ayla turned and looked back the way they had come. The view swept down a field of fresh summer green that stopped at the shadow cast by the sun setting behind the steep cliffs. The natural soft yellow of the limestone, streaked with the black wash of leached-out impurities, was darkening to deep purple, and a somber gloom cloaked the water flowing at the foot of the stone ramparts. It stretched across The River to shroud the row of brush and trees that lined its bank, though the tops of the tallest trees still threw an abbreviated silhouette beyond the creeping darkness.

Seen from this perspective, the wall of stone, fringed at the top with grass and an occasional bush, displayed a unified moody grandeur she hadn't expected, and she tried to identify the places whose names she had learned. Toward the south, crowding close to the water's edge, the sheer walls of High Rock and Big Rock straddled Little Valley. The cliffs that pulled back to create the recessed rear wall of the Gather Field led then to the sculptural relief of the shelters in the cliff of Down River and then, just as The River took a sharp turn to the east, the huge overhanging stone ledge that housed the Ninth Cave.

As they started to move again, Ayla noticed several people carrying torches. "Should I have brought a torch, Willamar?" she asked the man walking beside her. "It will probably be dark before we return."

"It's supposed to be dark," Marthona said; she was walking on the other side of Willamar, "and there will be many torches there. When people leave the burial ground, they will light torches to find their way, but they will not all go in the same direction. Some will go one way, some another, some will go down to The River, and some uphill toward a place we call Lookout. As Shevonar's elan and any other spirits that are near watch us go, they may try to follow us. We need to confuse them so that if they manage to get beyond the boundaries, they won't know which lights to follow."

As the procession approached the burial ground, Ayla noticed the moving light of flickering fire from behind the outcrop and an aromatic scent detectable from quite a distance away. They moved around the obstruction toward a circle of lit torches that produced as much smoke as light. Drawing closer, she saw the boundaries, a circle of carved poles just beyond the torches that surrounded and defined the sacred area.

"The torches have a very strong smell," she commented.

"Yes. The zelandonia make special torches for burials. It keeps the spirits contained so people can enter the burial ground without danger, or perhaps I should say without as much danger," Marthona explained. "And if there is a smell, the torches make it easier to bear."

The Zelandonia of the six Caves placed themselves at equidistant intervals around the inside of the circle, offering another layer of protection. The One Who Was First stood at the head of the grave pit, then the four pallbearers with their sad burden carried the hammock into the area encircled by the torchlight. The two men in front walked around the right side of the hole they had dug until they faced the First and stopped, leaving the other two men at the foot.

The four men waited silently, holding the body in the burial hammock hanging over the grave. Other family members and the leaders of Shevonar's Cave filled up the area within the torchlit circle, the rest of the people crowded around the outside of the boundaries created by the carved poles.

Then the Zelandoni of the Ninth Cave stepped forward. She paused, and for a moment all was still. Not a single sound was made by the entire throng. Into the silence came the distant roar of a cave lion, followed by the cackle of a hyena, which seemed to set the mood. The next sound she heard was eerie and high-pitched. Ayla was stunned. She felt a shiver down her back; she was not alone.

She had heard the otherworldly music of a flute before, but not for a long time. Manen had played the instrument at the Mamutoi Summer Meeting. She recalled that she had performed the traditional burial rituals of the Clan for Rydag, the boy who reminded her of her own son, because they would not allow the child of mixed spirits that Nezzie had adopted to have a Mamutoi burial. But Manen had played his flute in spite of them as she moved through the silent, formal sign language to implore the Great Cave Bear and her totem spirit to take Rydag to the next world of the Clan.

She found herself remembering Iza's burial, when Mog-ur had made those signs in his modified one-handed way over her grave. Then Ayla recalled his death. She had gone inside the cave after the earthquake and found him with his skull crushed by falling stones, lying on top of Iza's burial cairn. She made the signs for him, since no one else had dared to go into the cave with the earthquake still rumbling aftershocks.

But the flute evoked another memory. She had heard the instrument before she ever heard Manen play his flute. It was during the ritual Cave Bear Ceremony at the Clan Gathering. The mog-ur of another clan had played a similar instrument, though the high-pitched warbling sound that symbolized the spiritual voice of Ursus had a different tonal quality from the one Manen had played and the one she heard now.

She was distracted from her thoughts by the First, who began to speak in a rich, resonant voice: "Great Earth Mother, First Progenitor, You have called Your child back to You. He was called in sacrifice to the Spirit of Bison, and the Zelandonii, Your children who live in the southwest of this land, ask that this one life be enough. He was a brave hunter, a good mate, a maker of fine spears. He honored You well in this life. Guide him back to You safely, we beseech You. His mate grieves for him, her children loved him, the people respected him. He was called to serve You while in his prime. Let the Spirit of Bison be satisfied, O Doni, let this one be enough."

"Let it be enough, O Doni," the rest of the Zelandonia intoned. It was repeated again by the people of all the gathered Caves, more or less in unison.

The measured beat of something pounding on something began. The sound was slightly dulled—or at least not as crisp—because several instruments were playing together. The objects consisted of skins stretched very tight over one side of circular hoops, with a handle to hold it. The eerie sound of the flute joined in, weaving in and around the steady beat of the drums. The evocative tone seemed to encourage the emotional release of tears. Relona began to cry and keen her misery and grief once more. Soon all the people were wailing and keening, with tears in their eyes.

Then a voice joined in, a full sonorous contralto singing without words but fitting into the rhythm of the drums and blending with the flute, sounding almost like an instrument. The first time Ayla heard anyone sing was when she went to live with the Mamutoi. Most of the Lion Camp sang, at least along with a group. She had enjoyed listening to them and tried to join in, but singing was something she couldn't seem to do. She could hum in a kind of monotone, but she could not carry a tune. She recalled that some people were much better singers than others, and had admired them, but she had never before heard so rich and vibrant a voice. The voice belonged to Zelandoni, the One Who Was First, and Ayla was overwhelmed.

The two men who held the pole in front shifted around to face the two men behind, then they lifted the pole from their shoulders and began to lower the swaying burial hammock. The grave pit was not very deep, and the small tree pole was longer than its length. By the time both ends of it were on the ground, the body was already resting on the bottom of the hole. They untied the slack cords of the netting and dropped them in as well.

They dragged the hide upon which the earth from the grave had been piled closer to the hole again, and wedged the tree pole upright into the grave below the foot, using some of the loose dirt to support it. Another, shorter pole was placed at the head of the man, one that had been carved and painted with red ochre in the shape of Shevonar's abelan. His identifying mark would indicate the place where he was buried and act as a warning that his body was laid to rest there and that his elan might still be nearby.

Relona walked forward stiffly, trying to stay in control of herself. She went to the pile, then, almost angrily, grabbed some dirt in each hand and threw it into the grave. Two older women helped each of her two children to do the same, then picked up handfuls themselves and dropped it on the wrapped body. Then all the people came forward, each taking a couple of handfuls of earth and tossing it into the grave. By the time everyone had passed by, adding their dirt, the hole was filled in and loose earth was heaped into a mound.

A few went back to add a little more. Then, suddenly, Relona fell to her knees, and tears nearly blinding her, she threw herself on the soft earth over the grave, heaving great sobs. Her eldest child walked back to her and stood there crying, knuckling his eyes to wipe away tears. Then the youngest, looking lost and bewildered, ran to the grave and pulled on her mother's arm, trying to make her get up and comfort her.

Ayla wondered where the two older women were and why no one tried to help and console the children.

16

After a while, Ayla saw the mother begin to respond to the young child's fearful sobs. Relona pushed herself away from the grave and, without even brushing herself off, took her daughter into her arms. The older one sat down and wrapped his arms around his mother's neck. She put an arm around him, too, and all three sat there crying together.

But the sound of these sobs seemed to have a different tone, Ayla thought, not so much of despair, but of mutual sadness and comfort. Then, at a signal from the First, the zelandonia and several others, including Ranokol, Shevonar's brother, helped them all up and led them away from the grave.

Ranokol's pain at the loss of his brother had been as great as Relona's, but he expressed it differently. He kept wondering why Shevonar had to make the sacrifice and not him. His brother had a family, and he didn't even have a mate. Ranokol couldn't stop thinking about it, but he didn't want to talk about it. He would have avoided the burial ceremony altogether if he could have, and throwing himself on the grave was the last thing he wanted to do. He just wanted to leave as soon as he could.

"We have returned Shevonar of the Ninth Cave of the Zelandonii to Your breast, Great Mother Earth," Zelandoni intoned.

All the people who had gathered together for the burial of Shevonar stood surrounding the grave, and Ayla sensed an anticipation. They were expecting something to happen and were focusing on the great donier. The drums and flutes had continued to play, but the sound had become part of the environment and Ayla hadn't noticed it until the tone of the music changed, and Zelandoni began to sing again.

> "Out of the darkness, the chaos of time,
> The whirlwind gave birth to the Mother sublime.
> She woke to Herself knowing life had great worth,
> The dark empty void grieved the Great Mother Earth."

The people responded in unison, some singing, some just saying the words.

"The Mother was lonely. She was the only."

Then the One Who Was First sang alone again.

"From the dust of Her birth She created the other,
A pale shining friend, a companion, a brother.
They grew up together, learned to love and to care,
And when She was ready, they decided to pair."

And the people responded again, with the next line.

"Around Her he'd hover. Her pale shining lover."

Ayla realized this was a familiar and understood story song that everyone knew and had been waiting for. She was already caught up in it and wanted to hear more. She listened while Zelandoni continued to sing the first part and the people responded with the last line.

"She was happy at first with Her one counterpart.
Then the Mother grew restless, unsure in Her heart.
She loved Her fair friend, Her dear complement,
But something was missing, Her love was unspent."
"She was the Mother. She needed another."

"She dared the great void, the chaos, the dark,
To find the cold home of the life-giving spark.
The whirlwind was fearsome, the darkness complete.
Chaos was freezing, and reached out for Her heat."
"The Mother was brave. The danger was grave."

"She drew from cold chaos the creative source,
Then conceiving within, She fled with life-force.
She grew with the life that She carried inside.
And gave of Herself with love and with pride."
"The Mother was bearing. Her life She was sharing."

"The dark empty void and the vast barren Earth,
With anticipation, awaited the birth.
Life drank from Her blood, it breathed from Her bones.
It split Her skin open and sundered Her stones."
"The Mother was giving. Another was living."

> *"Her gushing birth waters filled rivers and seas,*
> *And flooded the land, giving rise to the trees.*
> *From each precious drop more grass and leaves grew,*
> *And lush verdant plants made all the Earth new."*
>> *"Her waters were flowing. New green was growing."*

> *"In violent labor spewing fire and strife,*
> *She struggled in pain to give birth to new life.*
> *Her dried clotted blood turned to red-ochred soil,*
> *But the radiant child made it all worth the toil."*
>> *"The Mother's great joy. A bright shining boy."*

Ayla's breath caught in her throat when she heard those words. They seemed to tell the story of her and her son, Durc. She remembered struggling in pain to give birth to him and afterward, how it was all worth it. Durc had been her great joy. Zelandoni continued in her magnificent voice.

> *"Mountains rose up spouting flames from their crests,*
> *She nurtured Her son from Her mountainous breasts.*
> *He suckled so hard, the sparks flew so high,*
> *The Mother's hot milk laid a path through the sky."*
>> *"His life had begun. She nourished Her son."*

This story seems so familiar, Ayla thought. She shook her head as though trying to make something fall into place. Jondalar, he told me some of this on our Journey here.

> *"He laughed and he played, and he grew big and bright.*
> *He lit up the darkness, the Mother's delight.*
> *She lavished Her love, he grew bright and strong,*
> *But soon he matured, not a child for long."*
>> *"Her son was near grown. His mind was his own."*

> *"She took from the source for the life She'd begun.*
> *Now the cold empty void was enticing Her son.*
> *The Mother gave love, but the youth longed for more,*
> *For knowledge, excitement, to travel, explore."*
>> *"Chaos was Her foe. But Her son yearned to go."*

Ayla's mind kept nagging at her. It's not just Jondalar, she thought. I feel as if I know this, or at least the essence of it. But where could I have learned it? Then something clicked. Losaduna! I memorized all kinds of things he taught me! There was one story like this about the Mother. Jondalar even recited parts of it during that ceremony. It wasn't exactly the same, and it was in their language, but Losadunai is close to Zelandonii. That's why I was able to understand what they said so fast! As she listened, she concentrated on bringing the memory of the Mother's story back and began to feel a sense of the similarities and differences.

> *"He stole from Her side as the Great Mother slept,*
> *While out of the dark swirling void chaos crept.*
> *With tempting inducements the darkness beguiled.*
> *Deceived by the whirlwind, chaos captured Her child."*
> *"The dark took Her son. The young brilliant one."*

> *"The Mother's bright child, at first overjoyed,*
> *Was soon overwhelmed by the bleak frigid void.*
> *Her unwary offspring, consumed with remorse,*
> *Could not escape the mysterious force."*
> *"Chaos would not free. Her rash progeny."*

> *"But just as the dark pulled him into the cold,*
> *The Mother woke up, reached out and caught hold.*
> *To help Her recover Her radiant son,*
> *The Mother appealed to the pale shining one."*
> *"The Mother held tight. And kept him in sight."*

Ayla began to smile as she started anticipating the next verse, or at least the essential meaning of it. The Mother Earth tells Her old friend, the Moon, the story of what happened to Her son next, Ayla thought.

> *"She welcomed him back, Her lover of old,*
> *With heartache and sorrow, Her story She told.*
> *Her dear friend agreed to join in the fight,*
> *To rescue Her child from his perilous plight."*

And now the listeners say it their way, Ayla said to herself. That's how the story is supposed to be told. First the Losaduna, or the Zelandoni, narrates it, then the listeners answer or repeat it another way.

> *"She told of Her grief. And the dark swirling thief."*

Then it's Zelandoni's turn again.

"The Mother was tired, She had to recover,
She loosened Her hold to Her luminous lover.
While She was sleeping, he fought the cold force,
And for a time drove it back to the source."
  "His spirit was strong. The encounter too long."

"Her fair shining friend struggled hard, gave his best,
The conflict was bitter, the battle hard pressed.
His vigilance waned as he closed his great eye.
Then darkness crept close, stole his light from the sky."
  "Her pale friend was tiring. His light was expiring."

"When darkness was total, She woke with a cry.
The tenebrious void hid the light from the sky.
She joined in the conflict, was quick to defend,
And drove the dark shadow away from Her friend."
  "But the pale face of night. Let Her son out of sight."

"Trapped by the whirlwind, Her bright fiery son,
Gave no warmth to the Earth, cold chaos had won.
The fertile green life was now ice and snow,
And a sharp piercing wind continued to blow."
  "The Earth was bereft. No green plants were left."

"The Mother was weary, grieving and worn,
But She reached out again for the life She had borne.
She couldn't give up, She needed to strive,
For the glorious light of Her son to survive."
  "She continued the fight. To bring back the light."

"And Her luminous friend was prepared to contest,
The thief who held captive the child of Her breast.
Together they fought for the son She adored.
Their efforts succeeded, his light was restored."
  "His energy burned. His brilliance returned."

The Great Mother Earth and the Moon have brought the Sun
back, but not all the way; Ayla was again anticipating.

"But the bleak frigid dark craved his bright glowing heat.
The Mother defended and would not retreat.
The whirlwind pulled hard, She refused to let go.
She fought to a draw with Her dark swirling foe."
  "She held darkness at bay. But Her son was away."

Was the Zelandonii version longer than the Losadunai story? Or did it just seem that way? Maybe singing the story makes it seem longer, but I really like the singing. I wish I understood it more. I think the songs change sometimes, the singing of some verses doesn't sound the same as other verses.

> *"When She fought the whirlwind and made chaos flee,*
> *The light from Her son glowed with vitality.*
> *When the Mother grew tired, the bleak void held sway,*
> *And darkness returned at the end of the day."*
>   *"She felt warmth from Her son. But neither had won."*

> *"The Great Mother lived with the pain in Her heart,*
> *That She and Her son were forever apart.*
> *She ached for the child that had been denied,*
> *So She quickened once more from the life-force inside."*
>   *"She was not reconciled. To the loss of Her child."*

> *"When She was ready, Her waters of birth,*
> *Brought back the green life to the cold barren Earth.*
> *And the tears of Her loss, abundantly spilled,*
> *Made dew drops that sparkled and rainbows that thrilled."*
>   *"Birth waters brought green. But Her tears could be seen."*

I really like this next part, but I wonder how Zelandoni will sing it, Ayla thought.

> *"With a thunderous roar Her stones split asunder,*
> *And from the great cave that opened deep under,*
> *She birthed once again from Her cavernous room,*
> *And brought forth the Children of Earth from Her womb."*
>   *"From the Mother forlorn, more children were born."*

> *"Each child was different, some were large and some small,*
> *Some could walk and some fly, some could swim and some crawl.*
> *But each form was perfect, each spirit complete,*
> *Each one was a model whose shape could repeat."*
>   *"The Mother was willing. The green earth was filling."*

> *"All the birds and the fish and the animals born,*
> *Would not leave the Mother, this time, to mourn.*
> *Each kind would live near the place of its birth,*

And share the expanse of the Great Mother Earth."
"Close to Her they would stay. They could not run away."

"They all were Her children, they filled Her with pride,
But they used up the life-force She carried inside.
She had enough left for a last innovation,
A child who'd remember Who made the creation."
"A child who'd respect. And learn to protect."

"First Woman was born full-grown and alive,
And given the Gifts she would need to survive.
Life was the First Gift, and like Mother Earth,
She woke to herself knowing life had great worth."
"First Woman defined. The first of her kind."

"Next was the Gift of Perception, of learning,
The desire to know, the Gift of Discerning.
First Woman was given the knowledge within,
That would help her to live, and pass on to her kin."
"First Woman would know. How to learn, how to grow."

"Her life-force near gone, The Mother was spent,
To pass on Life's Spirit had been Her intent.
She caused all of Her children to create life anew,
And Woman was blessed to bring forth life, too."
"But Woman was lonely. She was the only."

"The Mother remembered Her own loneliness,
The love of Her friend and his hovering caress.
With the last spark remaining, Her labor began,
To share life with Woman, She created First Man."
"Again She was giving. One more was living."

"To Woman and Man the Mother gave birth,
And then for their home, She gave them the Earth,
The water, the land, and all Her creation.
To use them with care was their obligation."
"It was their home to use. But not to abuse."

"For the Children of Earth the Mother provided,
The Gifts to survive, and then She decided,
To give them the Gift of Pleasure and sharing,

That honors the Mother with the joy of their pairing."
"The Gifts are well-earned. When honor's returned."

"The Mother was pleased with the pair She created,
She taught them to love and to care when they mated.
She made them desire to join with each other,
The Gift of their Pleasures came from the Mother."
"Before She was through. Her children loved too."
"Earth's Children were blessed. The Mother could rest."

Ayla waited for more, but when there was only silence, she realized the Mother's Song had come to an end.

People straggled back to their Caves in twos and threes. Some would not return to their homes until the middle of the night, some made plans to stay with friends or relatives. A few acolytes and Zelandonia remained behind at the gravesite, completing some of the more esoteric aspects of the ceremony, and would not be back until morning.

Several people went home with Relona and her children and stayed overnight in her dwelling, most sleeping on the floor. It was thought necessary for many people to surround her. The elans of deceased mates had been known to try to return to their homes before they understood that they no longer belonged to this world. The grieving mates were susceptible to invasion by the roaming spirits and needed the protection of many people to ward off malign influences. Older people in particular were sometimes tempted to follow their mates' elans to the next world shortly after one of them died. Fortunately, Relona was young yet and had young children who needed her.

Ayla was one of those who stayed with the new widow, and Relona seemed pleased that she did. Jondalar had planned to stay as well, but by the time he completed the last of his ceremonial duties, it was quite late, and when he looked inside the dwelling, there were so many people sprawled out, he couldn't see any room to squeeze in his large frame. Ayla waved at him from the other side of the room. Wolf was with her, and probably because of him, she had a little more room around her, but when he tried to step around people to reach her, he woke a few up. Marthona, who was closer to the entrance, told him to go home. He felt a bit guilty about it, but was grateful. Overnight vigils to ward off wandering spirits were not something he enjoyed. Besides, he'd had enough dealings with the spirit world for one day, and he was tired. He missed having Ayla beside him when he crawled into his sleeping roll, but he fell asleep quickly.

When she returned to the Ninth Cave, the One Who Was First went immediately into her dwelling. She would soon be making another Journey to the next world and wanted to meditate, to prepare for it. She took off her chest plaque and turned it around to the plain undecorated side. She did not want any interruptions. She would not only try to guide Shevonar's spirit to the world beyond, she planned to search for the elan of Thonolan as well, but for that she would need both Jondalar and Ayla.

Jondalar awoke with a strong urge to make some tools. Although he might not have expressed it as such, he was still feeling uneasy about all the arcane events he'd recently been involved with. Flint-knapping was not only his craft, it was something he enjoyed, and getting his hands on a solid piece of stone was a good way to forget about the ambiguous, intangible, and vaguely ominous spirit world.

He took out the pack of flint that he had quarried from the Lanzadoni flint mine. Dalanar had looked over the material that Jondalar had extracted from the outcrop, which contained the superior-quality flint that the Lanzadoni were known for. He made specific suggestions regarding what pieces to take with him and helped him trim away excess material, so that all he'd had to carry with him were workable blanks and cores. Horses could carry a great deal more than people, but flint was heavy. There was a limit to the amount of stone that could be taken, but when he examined the flint he had, he appreciated again just how fine it was.

He selected two of the trimmed stones and put the others back, then brought out his leather bundle of flint-working tools. He untied the cords and laid out several bone and antler hammers and retouchers, and his hammerstones, then picked up each tool and inspected it carefully. Then he wrapped them back up, along with the flint cores. By midmorning he was ready to find a place to work his flint, somewhat out of the way. Chips of flint were very sharp and could be quite erratic in the way they flew. Serious workers of the stone always chose to stay away from the areas where people regularly walked, especially away from the bare feet of running children and their often harried mothers or distracted caretakers.

Pushing aside the entrance drape, Jondalar walked out of his mother's dwelling. Looking toward the ledge, he noticed that the sky was overcast and gray. A dreary drizzle kept almost everyone under the rock shelter, and the large open area near the dwellings was in full use. There were no particular times for pursuing individual crafts and interests, but it was the kind of day that many chose to work on their various projects. Windbreaks of panels, or hides strung over cords, were put up to keep out wind and any rain it might blow in, and several fires provided additional light and warmth, though cold drafts made warm clothes essential.

He smiled when he saw Ayla coming toward him. When they met, he greeted her with a touching of cheeks and noticed her womanly scent. It made him remember that he hadn't slept with her the night before. He felt a sudden desire to take her back to bed and do more than sleep.

"I was just going to Marthona's to look for you," she said.

"I woke up with an urge to work the stone I got from Dalanar's flint mine, to make some new tools," he said, holding up his familiar leather bundle. "But it looks like everyone wanted to work on something this morning." He glanced toward the crowded and busy work space. "I don't think I'll stay here."

"Where will you go to work?" Ayla asked. "I thought I'd see to the horses, but I might come by later and watch."

"I think I'll go Down River. There are usually a lot of toolmakers there," he said. Then, thinking about it, he added, "Do you want me to help you with the horses?"

"Not unless you want to," Ayla said. "I'm just going to check on them. I don't think I'll ride today, but I may take Folara with me and see if she wants to try sitting on Whinney. I told her she could sometime, and she said she'd like to."

"It might be fun to see how she does, but I really would like to work on some tools today," Jondalar said.

They walked together as far as the working area, then Jondalar went on toward Down River, while Ayla and the wolf stopped to look for Folara. The drizzle had turned to a steady rain, and while she waited for it to let up, she found herself watching first one person and then another as they worked on their various projects. She had always been fascinated with different crafts and skills and was easily distracted. It was a busy but relaxed atmosphere. Certain aspects of every craft required intense concentration, but repetitive elements allowed time to chat and visit. Most people were pleased to answer her questions, show her their techniques, and explain their methods.

When Ayla saw Folara, she was in the middle of stringing a loom with Marthona and not able to come to a good stopping place easily, though she would have liked to go. Ayla wouldn't have minded staying to see how the stringing was done, but she felt the horses needed attention. She promised Folara they would visit the horses another time, and when the rain let up, she decided to go out before it started again.

Whinney and Racer were in fine fettle and delighted to see her and Wolf when she found them, quite a distance back in Wood River Valley. They had discovered a small green meadow in the middle of the forested glen, with a clear spring that had formed a pond and a place under some trees to stand when it rained. The red deer that were sharing it with them broke away at the sight of the woman and the wolf at the same time that the horses neighed and ran toward them.

Those deer have been hunted, Ayla thought. They might have stopped and eyed Wolf, but it's not likely that full-grown deer in their prime would run from a single wolf. The wind is taking my scent right to them, and I think they have found more to fear from human hunters.

The sun had come out, and she found some of the previous year's dried flower heads of teasel and used the prickly herb top to curry the horses' coats. When she was done, she noticed Wolf stalking. She reached for her sling, which was tucked into her waist thong, and a pebble from the rocky edge of the pond, and when he scared up a couple of hares, she got one of the large rabbits with her first try. She let Wolf get the other.

A cloud cast a shadow over the sun. She looked up and noticed the placement of the sun in the sky, and realized that the time had passed quickly. Things had been so busy the past few days, she felt good having no demands on her or her time. But when it started to sprinkle, she decided to ride Whinney back to the Ninth Cave. Racer and Wolf followed. She was glad she had when the rain came down in earnest just as she arrived at the shelter. She led the horses up to the stone front porch and walked them past the living area and down toward the more unused area.

She passed by some men sitting around a fire, and though she didn't recognize the game, from their actions, she guessed they were gambling. They stopped and watched her as she walked by. She thought they were very rude to stare at her the way they did, and she made a point of showing better manners by avoiding looking at them. But she did have the Clan woman's skill of glancing unobtrusively yet taking in a great deal of information with quick glimpses. She noticed that they were making comments to each other, and she thought she smelled barma.

Farther on, she saw some people in various stages of curing hides, both bison and deer. They probably found the usual work area too crowded, too, she thought. She brought the horses almost to the end of the ledge, near the small stream that separated the Ninth Cave from Down River, and thought that it could be a good place to build a shelter for them before winter. She'd have to talk to Jondalar about it. Then she showed them the trail that led down to the bank of The River and left them to see what they would decide to do. Wolf decided to go with the horses when they started down the trail. Raining or not, they preferred grazing near The River to staying up on the barren ledge just to keep dry.

She thought about going on to see Jondalar, then changed her mind and went back to where they were working on hides. People were glad for an excuse to take a break, and for some of them to talk to the woman that a wolf followed and from whom horses didn't run away. She noticed that Portula was there. The young woman smiled at Ayla, still trying to make friends. She seemed genuinely sorry for her part in Marona's trick.

Ayla had been wanting to make some clothing for Jondalar, herself, and the expected baby, and remembered that she had killed a young giant deer buck. She wondered where it was, but while she was here she decided she could at least skin the hare that was hanging from her waist thong to make something for the baby.

"If there's room, I'd like to skin this hare quickly," Ayla said to the group in general.

"There's plenty of room," Portula said. "And I'd be glad to let you use some of my tools, if you need them."

"I would, Portula, thank you for offering. I do have many tools, I live with Jondalar, after all," Ayla said with a wry smile. Several people smiled back knowingly. "But I don't have them with me."

Ayla liked the feeling of having people around her all busily engaged in tasks at which they were skilled. What a difference from the lonely days in her cave in the valley. This was more like her childhood in Brun's clan with everyone working together.

She quickly gutted and skinned the hare, then asked, "Do you mind if I leave these here for now? I need to go Down River. I'll pick them up on my way back."

"I'll watch them," Portula said. "If you want, I'll take them back with me when I go, if you're not back yet."

"That would be very nice of you," Ayla said. She was warming to the young woman, who was obviously trying hard to be friendly. "I'll be back later," Ayla said as she left.

After she walked up the log bridge that crossed the creek, she saw Jondalar with several others under the shelter of the first abri. The place had obviously been used to knap flint for a long time. The ground was thick with the sharp-edged chips and flakes left from the process of knapping flint. It would not be wise to walk there with bare feet.

"There you are," Jondalar said. "We were just getting ready to go back. Joharran was here and said Proleva has organized a meal using meat from one of the bison. She does that so well and so often, people are going to get too used to it, I'm afraid. But everybody has been busy today, and she decided it would be easier. You can walk back with us, Ayla."

"I didn't realize it was so close to midday," she said. As they started toward the Ninth Cave, Ayla saw Joharran ahead of them. She hadn't seen him coming this way. He must have passed by me when I was talking to Portula and the others, and skinning that hare, she thought. She noticed him heading toward the rude men who were sitting around the fire.

Joharran had seen Laramar and some others, gambling, when he was hurrying to tell the craftspeople at Down River about the meal that Proleva had arranged. He recalled thinking how lazy they were, gaming while everyone else was busy, probably using wood someone else had collected, but when he saw them on the way back, he decided he ought to tell them, too. They were members of the Ninth Cave, even if they didn't contribute much.

The men were deep in conversation when he approached and didn't see him coming. As he drew near, he overheard one of them saying, ". . . What can you expect from someone who says she learned how to heal from flatheads? What can those animals know about healing?"

"That woman is no healer. Shevonar died, didn't he?" Laramar agreed.

"You weren't there, Laramar!" Joharran interrupted, trying to keep his temper under control. "As usual, you couldn't be bothered to join the hunt."

"I was sick," the man said defensively.

"Sick from your own barma," Joharran said. "I'm telling you, no one could have saved Shevonar. Not Zelandoni, not the most skilled healer that ever lived. He had been trampled by a bison. What man can bear the full weight of a bison? If it hadn't been for Ayla, I doubt that he would have survived until Relona arrived. She found a way to ease his pain. Ayla did as much as anyone could. Why are you spreading malicious rumors about her? What has she ever done to you?" They stopped talking when Ayla and Jondalar and several others walked past.

"Why are you sneaking around listening to private conversations?" Laramar countered, still defensive.

"Walking up to you in full daylight is hardly sneaking, Laramar. I came here to tell you that Proleva and some of the others have prepared some food for everyone, so you could share it," Joharran answered. "What I heard was said out loud. I couldn't exactly close my ears." Then he directed his comments to the others. "Zelandoni is convinced that Ayla is a good healer, why not give her a chance? We should be glad to welcome a person with such good skills, you never know when you might need them yourselves. Now, why don't you all come and eat?" The leader looked at each man directly, letting them know that he recognized and would remember each one, then he walked away.

The tight little group broke up and followed him toward the other end of the ledge. Some of them agreed with Joharran, at least as far as giving Ayla a chance to prove herself, but a few didn't want to or could not overcome their prejudice. Laramar, though he had been agreeable with the man who had been talking loudly against her, really didn't care one way or the other. He tended to go along with whatever way was easiest.

As Ayla walked with the group from Down River toward the work area, staying under the protective overhanging shelf when it started raining harder again, she thought about all the different talents and abilities that people enjoyed exercising to occupy themselves. Many people liked to make things, although the choice of materials they worked with were quite varied. Some, like Jondalar, liked to work with flint to craft tools and hunting weapons, some liked working with wood, or ivory, or bone, some liked working with fibers, or hides. It came to her that some, like Joharran, enjoyed working with people.

As they got closer and her nose detected wonderful cooking odors, Ayla realized that cooking and working with food was also a task some people enjoyed. Proleva's penchant for organizing community gatherings was obviously something she enjoyed, which was probably the reason for this impromptu feast. Ayla thought about herself and what she liked to do best. She was interested in many things and enjoyed learning how to do things she had never done before, but more than anything else, she loved being a medicine woman, a healer.

The meal was being served near the large area where people were working on their projects, but as they approached, Ayla noticed that an adjacent area was being set up for a task that may not have been quite as enjoyable but needed to be done. Several nets for drying the meat they had hunted had been stretched out a couple of feet above the ground between upright posts. There was a layer of soil on the stone surface of the abri and its front porch, shallow in some areas, but deep enough to support posts in others. Some uprights were permanently wedged into cracks in the stone or supported by post holes dug into the soil. Piles of rocks were often added for additional bracing.

Other similar constructions, obviously made for the same purpose, were simply pegged and lashed together, making them essentially portable food drying racks. They could be lifted up and leaned against the back wall to get them out of the way when not in use. But when meat or vegetables needed to be dried, the portable frames could be placed anywhere on the floor they wanted. Occasionally meat was dried for preservation near the place it was killed, or on the grassy floodplain below, but when it rained, or just because people wanted to work closer to their homes, they developed ways to support drying cords or netting.

A few small tongue-shaped pieces of meat were already hanging on the drying racks, and small, rather smoky fires were burning nearby, to keep away insects and incidentally to add a flavor to the meat. Ayla thought that after they ate she would offer her help to cut up the meat to dry. She and Jondalar had just selected their food and were deciding where to eat when she saw Joharran stalking toward them with a rapid stride and a grim expression.

"Jondalar, does Joharran seem angry to you?" she asked.

The tall man turned to look at his approaching brother. "I think so," he said. "I wonder what happened?" He would ask later, he thought.

They glanced at each other, then strolled over to join Joharran, Proleva, her son, Jaradal, Marthona, and Willamar. They were greeted warmly, and a place was made for them. It did seem obvious that the leader was not happy about something, but he did not seem to want to talk about it, at least not with them. They all smiled in welcome when Zelandoni decided to join them, too. She had spent the morning in her dwelling, but came out when people gathered to eat.

"Can I get you something?" Proleva asked.

"I have been fasting and meditating today, preparing myself to search, and still limiting my food," Zelandoni said, and looked at Jondalar in a way that made him very uncomfortable. He was suddenly afraid that his association with other worlds was not over yet. "Mejera is getting something for me. I asked Folara to help her. Mejera is an acolyte of Zelandoni of the Fourteenth Cave, but she is not happy with her and wants to come here with me, to be my acolyte. I have to consider it, and of course, ask if you would be willing to accept her into the Ninth Cave, Joharran. She's quite shy and diffident, but definitely has some ability. I wouldn't mind training her, but you know I have to be particularly careful with the Fourteenth," Zelandoni said, then she looked at Ayla.

"She was expecting to be selected the First," the donier explained, "but the zelandonia chose me instead. She tried to stand up to me and force me to step down. It was my first real challenge, and even though she was the one who backed down, I don't think she has ever really accepted their choice, or forgiven me."

She addressed everyone again. "I know she will accuse me of luring her best acolyte away if I accept Mejera, but I have to consider what is right for everybody. If Mejera isn't getting the training she should have to develop her talents, I can't worry about someone's hurt feelings. On the other hand, if one of the other Zelandonia would be willing to train her and can form a bond with her, perhaps I can avoid another confrontation with the Fourteenth. I'd like to wait until after the Summer Meeting before making a decision."

"That seems wise," Marthona said just as Mejera and Folara joined them. The young acolyte was holding two bowls, and Jondalar's younger sister carried her bowl plus a waterbag. She had put some eating implements in her carrying pouch. Mejera gave a bowl of clear broth to the First, glanced gratefully at Folara, smiled timidly at Ayla and Jondalar, and then looked down at her food.

There was a moment of uneasy silence, then Zelandoni spoke. "I don't know how many of you know Mejera."

"I know your mother, and the man of your hearth," Willamar said. "You have some siblings, don't you?"

"Yes, a sister and a brother," Mejera said.

"How old are they?"

"My sister is a little younger than me, and my brother is about his age," Mejera said, indicating Proleva's son.

"My name is Jaradal. I am Jaradal of the Ninth Cave of the Zelandonii. Who are you?"

He said it with such careful precision, as he had obviously been taught, everyone had to smile, including the young woman. "I am Mejera of the Fourteenth Cave of the Zelandonii. I greet you, Jaradal of the Ninth Cave of the Zelandonii."

Jaradal smiled with self-importance. She obviously understands boys his age, Ayla thought.

"We are remiss. I think we should all make proper introductions," Willamar said. The introductions were made, and everyone greeted the shy young woman warmly.

"Did you know the mate of your mother wanted to be a trader before he met her, Mejera?" Willamar said. "He went on a few trips with me, then he decided he didn't want to spend so much time away from her, or you, after you were born."

"No, I didn't know that," she said, pleased to learn something about her mother and her mother's mate.

No wonder he's a good trader, Ayla thought. He has a way with people. He can make anyone feel comfortable. Mejera seemed a little more relaxed, but still a bit overwhelmed by all the attention. Ayla understood how she felt.

"Proleva, I saw some people starting to dry meat from the hunt," Ayla said. "I'm not sure how meat is divided, or who is supposed to preserve it, but I'd like to help if it's appropriate."

The woman smiled. "Of course you can help, if you want. It's a lot of work, we'd welcome your help."

"I know I would," Folara said. "It can be a long, tedious job, unless there are a lot of people working on it. Then it can be fun."

"The meat itself and half the fat is for everyone to use as they need," Proleva continued, "but the rest of the animal, the hide, horns, antlers, and all, belongs to the person who killed it. I think you and Jondalar each have a megaceros and a bison, Ayla. Jondalar killed the bison who sacrificed Shevonar, but that one was given back to the Mother. We buried it near his grave. The leaders decided to give both Jondalar and you another one. Animals are marked when they're butchered, usually with charcoal. By the way, they didn't know your abelan, and you were busy with Shevonar, so someone asked Zelandoni of the Third. He made a temporary one for you so your hides and other parts could be marked."

Jondalar smiled. "What does it look like?" He was always conscious of his own enigmatic abelan and curious about the name marks of others.

"I think he saw you as protective or sheltering, Ayla," Proleva said. "Here, I'll show you." She took a stick, smoothed the dirt, and drew a line straight down. Then she added a line starting near the top and slanting down somewhat on one side, and a third line matching it on the other side. "It reminds me of a tent or shelter of some kind, something to get under if it was raining."

"I think you're right," Jondalar said. "It's not a bad abelan for you, Ayla. You do tend to be protective and helpful, especially if someone is sick or hurt."

"I can draw my abelan," Jaradal said. Everyone smiled indulgently. The stick was given to him, and he was allowed to make the drawing. "Do you have one?" he said to Mejera.

"I'm sure she does, Jaradal, and she will probably be happy to show you. Later," Proleva said, gently reprimanding her son. A little attention was all right, but she didn't want him to get in the habit of demanding attention from the adults around him.

"What do you think of your abelan, Ayla?" Jondalar said. He wondered about her reaction to being assigned a Zelandonii symbol.

"Since I didn't get an elandon with an abelan marked on it when I was born, at least not that I can remember," Ayla said, "it's as good a mark as any. I don't mind using it as my abelan."

"Did you ever get any kind of mark from the Mamutoi?" Proleva asked, wondering if Ayla already had an abelan. It was always interesting to learn how other people did things.

"When I was adopted by the Mamutoi, Talut cut a mark on my arm to draw blood so he could make a mark with it on the plaque he wore on his chest during ceremonies," Ayla said.

"But it wasn't a special mark?" Joharran said.

"It was special to me. I still have the scar," she said, showing the mark on her arm. Then she added a thought that occurred to her: "It's interesting how people use different ways of showing who they are, and who they belong to. When I was adopted by the Clan, I was given my amulet bag with a piece of red ochre in it, and when they name a person, the mog-ur makes a line in red from the forehead to the end of the nose. That's when he tells everyone, especially the mother, what the baby's totem is, by making the totem mark with salve on the infant."

"Are you saying your people of the Clan have marks showing who they are?" Zelandoni said. "Like abelans?"

"I guess they are like abelans. When a boy becomes a man, the mog-ur cuts the mark of his totem on him, then rubs in a special ash to make it a tattoo. Girls are not usually cut on the skin, because when they grow up, they will bleed from the inside, but I was marked by the cave lion when he chose me. I have four marks from his claws on my leg. That's the Clan mark for a cave lion, and that's how Mog-ur knew he was my totem, even though it's not usually a female totem mark. It is a man's, given to a boy who is destined to be a strong hunter. When I was accepted as the Woman Who Hunts, Mog-ur made a cut here," she put her finger on her throat, just above the breastbone, "to draw blood and used it to mark over the scars on my leg." She showed the scars on her left thigh.

"Then you already have an abelan. That's your mark, those four lines," Willamar said.

"I think you are right," Ayla said. "I don't feel anything about the other mark, maybe because it's just a mark of convenience, so that people will know who to give some hides to. Even though my Clan totem mark is not a Zelandonii sign, it is a mark that is special to me. It meant that I was adopted, that I belonged. I would like to use it as my abelan."

Jondalar thought about what Ayla said about belonging. She had lost everything, she didn't know to whom she was born, or who her people were. Then she had lost the people who raised her. She had referred to herself as "Ayla of No People" when she'd met the Mamutoi. It made him realize how important belonging was to her.

17

There was an insistent tap on the panel beside the entrance drape. It woke Jondalar, but he lay in his sleeping roll, wondering why someone wasn't answering it. Then he realized that no one but him seemed to be home. He got up and called out, "Be there in a moment," while he was putting on a few clothes. He was surprised to see Jonokol, the artist who was Zelandoni's acolyte, only because the young man seldom paid a visit without his mentor. "Come in," he said.

"The Zelandoni of the Ninth Cave says it is time," Jonokol said.

Jondalar's brow creased. He didn't like the sound of that. He wasn't entirely sure he understood what Jonokol meant, but he had a good idea, and he wasn't looking forward to it. He'd had his share of the other world. He didn't really want to have to deal with that place again.

"Did Zelandoni say what it was time for?" Jondalar asked.

Jonokol smiled at the tall man's sudden nervousness. "She said you would know."

"I'm afraid I do," Jondalar said, resigning himself to the inevitable. "Can you wait until I find something to eat, Jonokol?"

"Zelandoni always says it's best if you don't."

"I suppose you're right," Jondalar said. "But I wouldn't mind a cup of tea to wash my mouth out with. I'm still tasting sleep."

"They may have some tea for you to drink," Jonokol said.

"I'll bet they do, but I don't think it's mint, and that's what I like first thing in the morning."

"Zelandoni's teas are often flavored with mint."

"Flavored, yes, but it's probably not the main ingredient."

Jonokol just smiled.

"All right," Jondalar said with a wry grin. "I'll come right away. I hope no one minds if I go to pass water first."

"It's not necessary to hold your water," the young acolyte said, "but bring something warm to wear."

When Jondalar came back, he was both surprised and pleased to see Ayla waiting with Jonokol, tying the sleeves of a warm tunic around her waist. Jonokol had probably told her to bring something warm, too. Watching her, it occurred to him that the night before last was the first time he had not slept with Ayla since he was captured by the S'Armunai on their Journey, and it left him feeling rather unsettled.

"Hello, woman," he whispered in her ear when he rubbed her cheek with his in greeting, then embraced her. "Where did you go this morning?"

"To empty the night basket," Ayla said. "When I came back I saw Jonokol and he said Zelandoni wanted us, so I went to ask Folara if she would keep Wolf. She said she'd find some children to keep him occupied. I went down to check on the horses earlier. I heard some other horses nearby. I wonder if we should build a surround of some kind to keep them."

"Perhaps," Jondalar said. "Especially when it's time for Whinney's Pleasures. I'd hate to have a herd try to capture her, Racer would probably try to follow her."

"She'll have her foal first," Ayla said.

Jonokol listened, interested in hearing about the horses. They had obviously gained knowledge in their association with them. Ayla and Jondalar left with Jonokol. When they reached the stone front porch of the Ninth Cave, Jondalar noticed that the sun was quite high.

"I didn't know it was so late," he said. "I wonder why someone didn't get me up sooner?"

"Zelandoni suggested that you be allowed to sleep since you may be up late tonight," Jonokol said.

Jondalar took a deep breath and blew it out of his mouth as he shook his head. "Where are we going, by the way?" he said as they walked beside the acolyte along the ledge toward Down River.

"To Fountain Rocks," Jonokol said.

Jondalar's eyes opened wide with surprise. Fountain Rocks—a cliff that featured two caves and the immediate area around it—was not the home of any particular Cave of Zelandonii; it was much more important than that. It was one of the most sacred places in the entire region. Though no one lived there regularly, if any group could call it home, it was the zelandonia, the Ones Who Served, for this was a place blessed and sanctified by the Great Earth Mother Herself.

"I am going to stop for a drink of water," Jondalar said emphatically as they approached the bridge over the creek of fresh spring water that divided the Ninth Cave from Down River. He wasn't going to let Jonokol talk him out of quenching his thirst, even if he had let the man dissuade him from having his morning cup of mint tea.

Near the streamlet a few feet from the bridge, a post had been pounded into the ground. A drinking cup made of cattail leaves torn into strips and woven watertight was attached to it with a cord; if it wasn't attached, it was often lost. The cup was changed periodically as it became worn, but as long as Jondalar could remember, one had been there. It had been learned long ago that the sight of the fresh sparkling water invariably inspired thirst, and while a person could bend over and reach in with hands to get a drink, it was much easier to have a cup handy.

They all had a drink, then continued along the well-used trail. They forded The River at the Crossing, and at Two Rivers Rock turned into Grass Valley, crossed the second river, then followed the path alongside it. People from other Caves waved and greeted them as they passed by, but made no attempt to delay them. All the zelandonia of the area, including the acolytes, had already gone to Fountain Rocks, and everyone had a good idea where the two people with Zelandoni's acolyte were going.

They also had some idea why. In the tight-knit community, word had gotten out that they had brought back something that might help the zelandonia to find the wandering spirit of Jondalar's dead brother, Thonolan. Though they knew it was important to help guide a newly liberated elan to its proper place in the world of the spirits, the idea of entering the next world before they were called by the Mother was not something most people wanted to do. It was fearful enough to think about helping Shevonar's elan, who had just passed on and was probably nearby, but to look for the spirit of someone who had died far away and a long time ago was something they didn't even want to contemplate.

Not many, except for the zelandonia—and not all of those— would have wanted to trade places with Jondalar or Ayla. Most people were happy to let the Ones Who Served The Mother deal with the world of the spirits. But no one else could do it; only they knew where Jondalar's brother had died. Even the One Who Was First knew this would be an exhausting day, though she was intrigued and wondered if they would be able to find Thonolan's roving spirit.

As Ayla, Jondalar, and Jonokol continued upstream, an imposing outcrop of rock loomed ahead on the left. The massive rock stood out with such prominence that it seemed almost a monolith, but a closer look revealed that it was only the first spur of a progression of cliffs that pulled back in a line at right angles to Grass River. The stately stone at the head of the cliffs reared up from the valley floor, rounded to a bulge in the middle, narrowed toward the top, then abruptly flared out into a flat-topped jaunty cap.

Moving around to the front and looking straight on at the rock that extended out ahead, one could, with a little imagination, envision in the cracks and rounded shapes, the cap as hair, a high forehead below the cap, a flattened nose, and two nearly closed eyes enigmatically looking over a slope of scree and brush. To those who knew how to look, the subtly anthropomorphic front view was understood to be a hidden face of the Mother, one of the few visages of Herself She ever chose to show, and even that was well disguised. No one could ever look directly upon the face of the Mother, not so much as a likeness of it, and even mysteriously disguised, Her face held unspeakable power.

The row of cliffs flanked a smaller valley with a creek down the middle that ran into Grass River. The source of the small stream was a spring that bubbled out of the ground with such energy, it created a small fountain with a deep pool surrounding it in the middle of a wooded glen. The common name was Fountain of the Deep, and the small waterway running from it was called Fountain Creek, but the zelandonia had other names for them, which most people also knew. The spring and pool were the Birth Waters of the Mother, and the creek was the Blessed Water. They were known to have great powers to heal and particularly to help women conceive, if used correctly.

A path over twelve hundred feet long climbed up the side of the stone wall well beyond the leading spur to a terrace not far from the top, with a small rock overhang that sheltered the mouths of two caves. The numerous cavities in this region of limestone cliffs were sometimes called "caves," but were thought of as hollowed-out spaces in the rock and often referred to as "hollows" as well. Conversely, an especially long or deep cave was sometimes referred to as a "deep." The opening to the left on the small terrace penetrated the rock only twenty feet or so, and was used as a living space for those who stayed there from time to time, usually zelandonia. It was generally known as Fountain Hollow, but some referred to it as Doni's Hollow.

310

The cave on the right led to a deep passage that went four hundred feet into the heart of the huge cliff, with chambers, alcoves, niches, and other passages leading off the main corridor. This was the place that was so sacred that its esoteric name was usually not even voiced. The site was so well-known, and so revered, it wasn't necessary to declare its sanctity and power to the mundane world. If anything, those who knew its true meaning preferred to understate it, not make an issue of it in ordinary existence. That was the reason people referred to the cliffs simply as Fountain Rocks, and why the cave was called the Deep Cave in Fountain Rocks or, sometimes, Doni's Deep.

It was not the only sacred site in the region. Most caves had some measure of sanctity attached to them, and some places outside of caves were also blessed, but the deep cave in Fountain Rocks was one of the most exalted. Jondalar knew of a few others that equaled Fountain Rocks, but none was more important. As they continued up the cliff with Jonokol, Jondalar felt a combination of excitement and dread and, as they approached the terrace, a frisson of fearful anticipation. This wasn't something he really wanted to do, but for all his apprehension, he did wonder if Zelandoni could find the free spirit of his brother, what would be expected of him, and how it would feel.

When they reached the high terrace in front of the caves, two more acolytes met them, a man and a woman. They had been waiting just inside the mouth of the deep cave on the right. Ayla paused for a moment and turned around to see where she had come from. The lofty stone porch overlooked Fountain Creek Valley and part of Grass Valley with its river, and the panorama was impressive, but somehow, when they entered the passage, the closer views within the dark cavity were more daunting.

Especially in daytime, stepping into the cave brought an immediate transformation, a shift in perspective from an open, expansive view to a close, narrow corridor, from stone-reflecting sunlight to disquieting dark. The change went beyond the physical or external. Especially to those who understood and accepted the inherent power of the place, it was a metamorphosis that went from easy familiarity to apprehensive fear, but also a transition into something rich and wondrous.

Only a few feet of the ingress could be seen from the light outside, but as eyes became accustomed to the diminished light at the entry, the rock walls of the constricted passage suggested the way into the shadowy interior. A small vestibule just beyond the opening held a lighted stone lamp resting on a projecting piece of the wall, and several unlit lamps. In a natural stone niche below it were torches. Jonokol and the other young man picked up a lamp, then a thin, dry stick, which they held to the flame of the burning lamp until it ignited. With it, they each lit the moss wicks that were resting against the edge of the bowl of a lamp, opposite the handle, soaking in the slightly congealed fat. The woman lit a torch and beckoned to them.

"Watch your footing," she said, holding the torch lower to show the uneven floor and the wet, glistening clay that filled in some of the spaces between the rocks that were jutting up. "It can be slippery."

When they started into the passage, picking their way carefully across the uneven floor, there was still a suggestion of light from the outside. It diminished quickly. After something more than a hundred feet the darkness was complete, held back only by the soft glow of small flames. A sigh of moving air strayed down from the stalactites suspended from the ceiling, bringing a chill of fear as the tiny lights of the lamps flickered. They knew that once into the depths, if the fire went out, a blackness more complete than the darkest night would obscure all vision. Only hands and feet on cold, damp rock could show the way, and might lead only to a dead-end passage rather than the way out.

A deeper black on the right, no longer reflecting the small flames off damp stone walls, indicated that the distance to that side had increased; perhaps a niche or another passageway. Behind them and ahead, the tenebrious gloom was palpable, the blackness almost suffocatingly thick. The wisp of air was the only manifestation of a corridor that led back to the outside. Ayla wished she could reach for Jondalar's hand.

As they proceeded, the lamps the acolytes carried were not the only light. Several shallow, bowl-shaped stone lamps had been placed on the floor at intervals along the dark corridor, casting a light that seemed amazingly bright in the darkness within the cave. A couple of them were sputtering, however. They either needed more fat to melt into the bowl or a new moss wick, and Ayla hoped someone would tend to them soon.

But the lamps gave Ayla an eerie sense that she had been in this place before, and an irrational fear that she would be again. She didn't want to follow the woman in front of her. She had not thought of herself as one who feared caves, but there was something about this one that made her want to turn around and run, or touch Jondalar for reassurance. Then she remembered walking the dark corridor of another cave, following the small fires of lamps and torches, and finding herself watching Creb and the other mog-urs. She shivered at the memory and suddenly realized that she was cold.

"You might want to stop and put on your warm clothing," the woman in front said, turning back and holding up the lamp for Ayla and Jondalar. "It's rather cold deep in a cave, especially in summer. In winter, when it's snowy and icy outside, it actually feels rather warm. The deep caves stay the same all year."

The stop for something as ordinary as putting on her long-sleeved tunic had steadied Ayla. Although she had been ready to turn around and run out of the cave, when the acolyte started walking again, Ayla took a deep breath and followed her.

Although the long passageway had seemed narrow and the temperature had become progressively colder, after another fifty feet the rocky corridor closed in even more. A greater humidity in the air was verified by a sheen of moisture reflected off the walls, the stalactite icicles projecting down from the ceiling, and their stalagmitic mates growing up from the floor. At slightly more than two hundred feet into the dark, damp, and chilly cave, the floor of the passageway ascended, not blocking the way, but making it difficult to proceed. It was tempting to turn back here, to think this was far enough, and many a faint-heart had. It tested determination to continue beyond this point.

Holding the torch, the woman in front climbed up the rocky incline to a small, constricted opening higher up. Ayla watched the wavering light as she climbed, then breathed deeply and started up over sharp stones until she reached the woman. She followed her through a narrow aperture, scrambling over more rocks to get through the opening that descended into the heart of the stone cliff.

The nearly subliminal passage of air in the first section was noticeable now only for its lack. After the confined gap, no movement of air could be detected at all. The first indication that someone had come this way before was three red dots painted on the left-hand wall. Not long afterward, Ayla saw something else in the flickering light of the torch the woman in front held. She couldn't quite believe her eyes and wished the acolyte would stop for a moment and hold the light closer to the left wall. She stopped and waited for the tall man behind her to catch up.

"Jondalar," she said in a quiet voice, "I think there is a mammoth on that wall!"

"Yes, there is, more than one," Jondalar said. "I think if there wasn't something that Zelandoni felt was more important to do right now, this cave would be shown to you with the proper ceremony. Most of us were brought in here when we were children. Not young children, old enough to understand, but still children. It's frightening, but wonderful, when you see this place for the first time, if it's done right. Even when you know it's all part of the ceremony, it's exciting."

"Why are we here, Jondalar?" she asked. "What is so important?"

The acolyte in front had turned around and come back when she noticed that she wasn't being followed anymore.

"Didn't anyone tell you?" she said.

"Jonokol just said Zelandoni wanted Jondalar and me," she said.

"I'm not absolutely certain," Jondalar said, "but I think we're here to help Zelandoni locate Thonolan's spirit and, if he needs it, to help him find his way. We're the only ones who saw the place where he died, and with the stone you wanted me to pick up—Zelandoni said that was a very good idea, by the way—she thinks we may," Jondalar said.

"What is this place?" Ayla asked.

"It has many names," the woman said. Jonokol and the other acolyte had caught up with them. "Most people refer to it as the Deep Cave in Fountain Rocks, or sometimes Doni's Deep. The zelandonia know its sacred name, and most people do, too, though it is seldom mentioned. This is the Entrance to the Womb of the Mother, or one of them. There are several others that are just as sacred."

"Everyone knows, of course, that entrance implies exit," Jonokol added. "That means the entrance to the womb is also the birth canal."

"So that means this is one of the birth canals of the Great Earth Mother," the young male acolyte said.

"Like the song Zelandoni sang at Shevonar's burial, this must be one of the places from which the Mother 'brought forth the Children of Earth,'" Ayla said.

"She understands," the woman said, nodding toward the other two acolytes. "You must know the Mother's Song well," she said to Ayla.

"The first time she heard it was at the burial," Jondalar said, smiling.

"That's not entirely true, Jondalar," Ayla said. "Don't you remember? The Losadunai have something like it, except they don't sing it. They just say the words. The Losaduna taught it to me in their language. It's not exactly the same, but it's similar."

"Maybe that's because Losaduna can't sing like Zelandoni," Jondalar said.

"Not all of us sing it," Jonokol said. "Many just say the words. I don't sing, and if you ever heard me, you'd know why."

"Some of the other Caves have different music, and some of the words are not exactly the same, either," the young male acolyte said. "I'd be interested in hearing the Losadunai version some time, especially if you can translate it for me, Ayla."

"I'd be glad to. Their language is very close to Zelandonii. You might be able to understand it, even without a translation," Ayla said.

For some reason, all three acolytes suddenly noticed her unfamiliar accent. The older woman had always thought of the Zelandonii—the language and those who used it—as special; they were the People, they were Earth's Children. It was hard to grasp the idea that this woman could think that people who lived all the way across the plateau glacier on the highland to the east could have a language that seemed similar to their own. The foreign woman must have heard many languages of people who lived far away that were very much different from Zelandonii to think so.

It struck them all how different the background of this foreign woman was from theirs, and how much she knew about other people that they didn't. Jondalar, too, had learned much on his Journey. In the few days since he had been back, he had already shown them many things. Perhaps that was the reason for Journeys, to learn new things.

Everyone knew about Journeys. Almost all young people talked about making one, but few actually did, and even fewer of those went very far, at least not that came back. But Jondalar was gone five years. He'd traveled far, had many adventures, but more important, he brought back knowledge that could benefit his people. He also brought ideas that could change things, and change wasn't always so desirable.

"I don't know if I should show you the painted walls as we pass by. It might spoil the special ceremony for you, but you are bound to see at least part of them, so I suppose I could hold up the light and let you see them a little better," the woman in front said.

"I would like to see them," Ayla said.

The acolyte in front held the torch up high so the woman Jondalar had brought home with him could see the paintings on the walls. The first one, the mammoth, was painted showing a side view, the way most portrayals of animals that she had seen were made. The hump on the head followed by a second hump high on the withers, but slightly lower down the sloping back made it easy to recognize. That configuration was the distinctive feature of the great woolly beast, even more than its curving tusks and long trunk. It was painted in red but shaded in reddish brown and black to show the contours and precise anatomical detail. It was facing the entrance and was so perfectly made that Ayla half expected the mammoth to walk out of the cave.

Ayla didn't quite understand why the painted animals looked so lifelike, or fully appreciate what it had required, but she couldn't resist looking closer to see how it was done. It was an elegant and accomplished technique. A flint tool had been used to cut a fine, distinct outline of the animal with exacting detail into the limestone wall of the cave, paralleled by a painted black line. Just outside of the engraved line, the wall had been scraped to show the light ivory-tan natural color of the stone. It highlighted the outline and the colors with which the mammoth had been painted, and contributed to the three-dimensional quality of the work.

But it was the paint within the outline that was so remarkable. Through observation and training from those who first conceived of the idea of taking a living animal and reproducing it on a two-dimensional surface, the artists who had painted the walls of the cave had gained a surprising and innovative knowledge of perspective. The techniques had been passed down, and though some artists were more skilled than others, most of them used shading to convey the sense of lifelike fullness.

As Ayla moved past the mammoth, she had the eerie sensation that the mammoth had also moved. She felt impelled to reach for the painted animal and touched the stone, then closed her eyes. It was cold, slightly damp, with the texture and feel of any limestone cave, but when she opened her eyes, she noticed that the artist had used the stone wall itself to advantage in the incredibly realistic creation. The mammoth had been placed on the wall in such a way that a rounded shape of the stone became the fullness of the belly, and a concretion of stalactite adhering to the wall that suggested a leg was painted as the back of a leg.

In the flickering light of the oil lamps, she noticed that when she moved, she saw the animal from a slightly different angle, which changed the way the natural relief of the stone appeared and threw shadows to a slightly different position. Even standing still, watching the reflections of the fire move on the stone, she had the impression that the animal painted on the wall was breathing. She understood then the reason that the mammoth had seemed to shift when she moved, and knew that if she hadn't examined it carefully, she could easily be convinced that it had.

She was reminded of the time at the Clan Gathering when she had to prepare the special drink Iza taught her to make for the mog-urs. The Mog-ur had shown her how to stand in the shadows so she would not be noticed, and told her exactly when to move out of them, which made it seem that she suddenly appeared. There was method to the magic of those who dealt with the world of the spirits, but there was magic, too.

She had felt something when she touched the wall, something that she couldn't quite explain or understand. It was a hint of that certain strangeness she had occasionally felt ever since she had inadvertently swallowed the leavings of the mog-urs' drink and followed them into the cave. From that time on, she occasionally experienced disturbing dreams and sometimes unsettling sensations even when she was awake.

She shook her head to rid herself of the feeling, then looked up and saw that the others were watching her. Smiling diffidently, she pulled her hand away from the stone wall quickly, afraid she had done something wrong, then looked toward the woman who held the torch. The acolyte said nothing as she turned to lead the way along the passage.

The lights from the small flames glinted faintly off damp walls with eerie hints of reflections as they moved quietly in single file along the corridor. There was a tingle of apprehension in the air. Ayla was sure they were going into the very heart of the steep limestone cliff and was glad to be with other people, sure she would get lost if she were alone. She trembled with a sudden flash of fear and foreboding, and a sense of what it might be like to be in a cave alone. She tried to shake off the feeling, but the chill in the dark, cool cave was not easy to dispel.

Not far beyond the first one there was another mammoth, then more mammoths, then two small horses, painted primarily in black. She stopped to look at them more closely. Again, a line perfectly defining the shape of a horse was engraved in the limestone, highlighted by a line painted in black. Within the line, the horses were painted black, but as with the rest of the paintings, the shading gave them a surprising realism.

Ayla noticed then that there were paintings on the right wall of the passage as well, some facing out and some in. Mammoths predominated; it seemed that a herd of mammoths was painted on the walls. Using the counting words, Ayla counted at least ten on both sides of the passage, and there may have been more. As she was continuing down the dark corridor, looking at the paintings momentarily lighted as she passed by, she was brought to a halt by the arresting scene of two reindeer greeting each other on the left wall. She had to see them better.

The first reindeer, facing into the cave, was male. He was painted in black, with the definitive shape and contours of the animal accurately rendered, including his huge antlers, though they were suggested by the arcing shapes rather than precisely painted with all their points. His head was lowered, and to Ayla's wonder and surprise, he was tenderly licking the forehead of a female. Unlike the majority of deer, female reindeer also had antlers, and in the painting as in life, hers were smaller. She was painted in red and her knees were bent so she could lower herself to accept his gentle caress.

The scene manifested a genuine sense of tenderness and caring, and it made Ayla think of Jondalar and herself. She had never thought of animals being in love before, but these seemed to be. It nearly brought her to tears, she was so moved. The acolyte guides allowed her to spend some time. They understood her reaction; they, too, were moved by this exquisite scene.

Jondalar was also staring in wonder at the painted reindeer. "That's a new one," he said. "I thought there was a mammoth there."

"There was. If you look closely at the female, you can still see some of the mammoth underneath," the young man in the rear explained.

"Jonokol made that," the woman in front said.

Both Jondalar and Ayla looked at the artist acolyte with new respect. "Now I understand why you are Zelandoni's acolyte," Jondalar said. "You are extraordinarily gifted."

Jonokol nodded to acknowledge Jondalar's comment. "We all have our Gifts. I am told you are an extraordinarily gifted flint-knapper. I look forward to seeing some of your work. In fact, there's a tool I've been trying to get someone to make for me, but I can't quite seem to explain it to any of the toolmakers so they understand. I was hoping Dalanar would be coming to the Summer Meeting so I could ask him."

"He is planning to come, but I'll be glad to give your idea a try, if you like," Jondalar said. "I enjoy a challenge."

"Perhaps we can talk tomorrow," Jonokol said.

"Can I ask you something, Jonokol?" Ayla said.

"Of course."

"Why did you paint the deer on top of the mammoth?"

"That wall, that place, drew me to it," Jonokol said. "It's where I had to put the reindeer. They were in the wall and wanted to come out."

"It is a special wall. It leads beyond," the woman said. "When the First sings there, or a flute is played, that wall answers. It echoes, resonates to the sound. Sometimes it tells you what it wants."

"Did all these walls tell someone to make paintings on them?" Ayla asked, indicating the paintings they had passed by.

"That's one reason this deep is so sacred. Most of the walls talk to you, if you know how to listen; they lead you places, if you are willing to go," the woman acolyte said.

"No one ever told me this before. Not in exactly this way. Why are you telling us now?" Jondalar asked.

"Because you will have to listen, and perhaps go through, if you are going to help the First find the elan of your brother, Jondalar," the woman said, then she added, "The zelandonia have been trying to understand why Jonokol was inspired to make these figures here. I'm beginning to get an idea." The woman smiled enigmatically at Jondalar and Ayla, then turned to walk deeper into the cave.

"Oh, before you go on," Ayla said to the woman, touching her arm to detain her. "I don't know what to call you, can I ask your name?"

"My name isn't important," she said. "When I become Zelandoni, I will be giving it up anyway. I am the First Acolyte to the Zelandoni of the Second Cave."

"Then, I suppose I could call you Acolyte of the Second," Ayla said.

"Yes, you could, although the Zelandoni of the Second has more than one acolyte. The other two are not here. They have gone ahead to the Summer Meeting."

"Then perhaps First Acolyte of the Second?"

"If it pleases you, I will respond to that name."

"What should I call you?" Ayla asked the young man who brought up the rear.

"I've only been an acolyte since the last Summer Meeting, and like Jonokol, I still use my own name most of the time. Perhaps I should give you a formal greeting and introduction." He held out both his hands. "I am Mikolan of the Fourteenth Cave of the Zelandonii, Second Acolyte of the Zelandoni of the Fourteenth Cave. And I welcome you," he said.

Ayla took his hands in hers. "I greet you, Mikolan of the Fourteenth Cave of the Zelandonii. I am Ayla of the Mamutoi, Member of the Lion Camp, Daughter of the Mammoth Hearth, Chosen by the Spirit of the Cave Lion, Protected by the Cave Bear, Friend of the horses, Whinney and Racer, and the hunter, Wolf."

"I seem to have heard that some people to the east refer to their zelandonia as the Mammoth Hearth?" the woman acolyte said.

"You are correct," Jondalar said. "They are the Mamutoi. Ayla and I lived with them for a year, but I'm surprised anyone here has heard about them. They live far away."

She looked at Ayla. "If you are a daughter of the Mammoth Hearth, that explains some things. You are zelandoni!"

"No, I am not," Ayla said. "The Mamut adopted me to the Mammoth Hearth. I wasn't called, but he was starting to teach me some things before I left with Jondalar."

The woman smiled. "You would not have been adopted if you were not meant to be. I am sure you will be called."

"I don't think I want to be," Ayla said.

"That may be," the First Acolyte of the Second said, then turned and continued leading them into the heart of Fountain Rocks.

Ahead, they began to see a glow, and as they approached, it grew almost brilliant. After the total darkness of the cave with only a few small lights, their eyes had adapted, and any greater illumination was all but dazzling. The corridor opened out and Ayla saw several people waiting in an enlarged area. It seemed almost crowded, and as she reached the area, and recognized people she had met, she realized that everyone there was zelandonia, except for Jondalar and her.

The large woman from the Ninth Cave was sitting on a seat someone had brought in for her. She got up and smiled. "We've been waiting for you," said the First. She gave both of them a hug that was held at a slight distance, and Ayla suddenly understood that it was a formal embrace, a greeting one gave to close associates in public.

One of the other Zelandonia nodded to Ayla. She responded with a nod to the short and slightly built man she identified as Zelandoni of the Eleventh, the one who had impressed her with his strong grip and self-confidence. An older man smiled at her, and she smiled back at Zelandoni of the Third, who had been so kind and supportive when she was trying to help Shevonar. She recognized most of the others only as people she had met and greeted.

A small fire had been made on top of some stones that had been brought in for the purpose—they would be taken back out when they left. A partially filled waterbag was on the ground beside a good-size wooden cooking bowl full of steaming water. Ayla watched a young woman use a pair of bentwood tongs to fish out a couple of cooking stones from the bottom of the cooking bowl, then add more from the fire. The steam billowed out as the hot rocks touched the water. When she looked up, Ayla recognized Mejera and smiled at her.

Then the One Who Was First added some material from a pouch. She's making a decoction, cooking it, not just steeping a tea, Ayla thought. There is probably some root or bark in that drink, something strong. The next time hot stones were added, the billowing steam filled the air with a strong aroma. The mint was easy to detect, but she smelled other odors and flavors, which she tried to identify, and suspected that the mint was there to cover the taste of something less pleasant.

A couple of people spread a heavy leather covering on the damp and rocky floor near the seat that the First had occupied. "Ayla, Jondalar, why don't you come over here and make yourselves comfortable," the large woman said, indicating the leather. "I have something for you to drink." The young woman who was tending the potion in the cooking bowl brought out four cups in preparation. "It's not quite ready yet, but you might as well relax."

"Ayla has been enjoying the wall paintings," Jonokol said. "I think she might like to see more of them. It might be more relaxing than sitting there waiting until that drink is ready."

"Yes, I would like to see more," Ayla added quickly. She found herself suddenly feeling rather anxious about drinking some unknown decoction that she knew was intended to help her find some other world. Her past experience with similar drinks had not been especially agreeable.

Zelandoni observed her closely for a while. She knew Jonokol well enough to understand that he would not have made the suggestion without good reason. He must have noted that the young woman was showing some distress, and she did seem to be agitated.

"Certainly, Jonokol. Why don't you show her the painted walls," the First said.

"I'd like to go with them," Jondalar said. He wasn't feeling very calm himself. "And maybe the torch carrier could come with us."

"Yes, of course," said the First Acolyte of the Second, picking up the torch she had put out. "I'll need to relight it."

"There is some fine work on the wall behind the zelandonia, but I don't want to bother them," Jonokol said. "Let me show you something interesting down this corridor."

He led them down a passageway that turned off to the right from the main one. Immediately on the left, he stopped in front of another panel of reindeer and a horse.

"Did you do these, too?" Ayla asked.

"No, my teacher did. She used to be Zelandoni of the Second, before Kimeran's sister. She was an exceptional painter," Jonokol said.

"She was good, but I think the student has outdone the teacher," Jondalar said.

"Well, for the zelandonia, it is not so much the quality, although it is appreciated. It is the experience. These paintings are not just for looking at, you know," the First Acolyte of the Second said.

"I'm sure that's true," Jondalar said with a wry smile, "but for me, I think I like the looking more. I must admit, I'm not exactly waiting eagerly for this ... ceremony. I'm willing, of course, and I think it may be interesting, but for the most part, I'm happy to let the zelandonia have the experience."

Jonokol grinned at his admission. "You are not alone in that feeling, Jondalar. Most people would rather stay firmly in this world. Come, let me show you something else before we have to get serious."

The artist acolyte led them to another area on the right side of the passage, where many more stalagmites and stalactites than usual had formed. The wall was covered with the calcareous formations, but on top of the concretions had been painted two horses that incorporated them to create the effect of a long shaggy winter coat. The one behind was leaping in a very animated way.

"These are very lively," Ayla said, quite intrigued. She had seen horses behave in similar ways.

"When boys first see it, they always say this one in back is 'leaping for Pleasure,'" Jondalar said.

"That is one interpretation," the woman acolyte said. "That could be a male attempting to mount the female in front, but I believe it is purposely ambiguous."

"Did your teacher paint these, Jonokol?" Ayla asked.

"No. I don't know who made them," Jonokol said. "No one does. They were done long ago, when the mammoths were painted. People say they were made by the ancestors, the forebears."

"There is something I want to show you, Ayla," the woman said.

"Are you going to show her the vulva?" Jonokol said with some surprise. "That is not usually shown on a first visit."

"I know, but I think we should make an exception for her," the other acolyte said, holding up the lamp and leading the way to a place not far from the horses. When she stopped, she lowered the torch to throw light down on a very unusual formation of rock that extended out from the wall and parallel to the floor, but raised up from it.

When Ayla first looked, she noticed an area of stone that had been enhanced with red, but it was only after looking carefully that she understood what it was, and then perhaps only because she had assisted more than one woman who was giving birth. A man might have recognized it before a woman. By accident—or supernatural design—the concretion had naturally formed an exact replica of a woman's sexual organ. The shape, the folds, even a depression that matched the entrance to her vagina, everything was there. Only the red color was added, to highlight it, to make sure they could find it easily.

"It is a woman!" Ayla said, astonished. "It is exactly like a woman! I have never seen anything like it."

"Now do you understand why this cave is so sacred? The Mother herself made this for us. It is proof that this cave is the Entrance to the Mother's Womb," said the woman who was training to serve the Great Earth Mother.

"Have you seen this before, Jondalar?" Ayla asked.

"Only once. Zelandoni showed it to me," he said. "It is remarkable. It is one thing for an artist like Jonokol to look at a cave wall, see the figure that is in it, and bring it to the surface for everyone to see. But this was here just as it is. The added color only makes it a little easier to see."

"There is one more place I want to show you," Jonokol said.

He went back the way they had come, and when they reached the enlarged area where everyone was waiting, he hurried past and turned right, back into the main corridor. At what appeared to be the end, on the left was a circular enclosure, and on the wall were concave depressions, the reverse of rounded-out bumps. In some of these, mammoths had been painted in a way that created an unusual illusion. At first glance, they didn't appear to be depressions; instead, they took on the characteristic of a mammoth's stomach, rounded outward. Ayla had to look twice, then reach to touch to convince herself that they actually were concave, not convex, dips and not bumps.

"They are remarkable!" Ayla said. "They are painted so that they seem to be opposite of what they are!"

"These are new, aren't they? I don't recall seeing them before," Jondalar said. "Did you paint them, Jonokol?"

"No, but I'm sure you'll meet the woman who did," he said.

"Everyone agrees, she is exceptional," the woman acolyte said. "As is Jonokol, of course. We are lucky to have two artists who are so talented."

"A few small figures are just beyond here," Jonokol said, looking at Ayla, "a woolly rhinoceros, a cave lion, an engraved horse, but it's a very narrow passage and hard to reach. A series of lines marks the end."

"They are probably ready for us. I think we should go back," the woman said.

As they turned around and were heading back, Ayla glanced up on the right wall, opposite the chapel-like enclosure with the mammoths and back along the corridor a short way. A strange feeling of uneasiness came over her. She was afraid she knew what was coming. She had felt it before. The first time was when she made the drink from the special roots for the mog-urs. Iza had told her it was too sacred to be wasted, so she wasn't allowed to practice making it.

She had already become disoriented, first from chewing the roots to soften them, then from the other preparations she had drunk during that night of special ceremony and celebration. When she noticed that there was some liquid left in the ancient bowl, she drank it so it wouldn't be wasted. The potent concoction had become stronger from soaking, and the effect on her was devastating. In her confused state, she had followed the light of the fires into the honeycombed depths of the cave, and when she'd come upon Creb and the other mog-urs, she hadn't been able to go back.

Creb was changed after that night, and she was never the same, either. That was when the mysterious dreams started and the waking moments of strange feelings and enigmatic visions that took her to some other place and sometimes came as warnings. They had been stronger and more prevalent on their Journey.

And now, as she stared up at the wall, the solid stone suddenly felt tenuous, as though she could see through it or into it. Instead of the firelights barely glinting off the hard surface, the wall was soft and deep and utterly black. And she was there, inside that menacing, nebulous space, and couldn't find her way out. She felt exhausted and weak, and she hurt deep inside. Then suddenly Wolf appeared. He was running through the tall grass, racing to meet her, coming to find her.

"Ayla! Ayla! Are you all right?" Jondalar said.

18

"Ayla!" Jondalar said, louder.

"What? Oh, Jondalar. I saw Wolf," she said, blinking her eyes and shaking her head to try to overcome her dazed confusion and vague sense of foreboding.

"What do you mean, you saw Wolf? He didn't come with us. Remember? You left him with Folara," Jondalar said, his forehead creased with fear and concern.

"I know, but he was there," she said, pointing to the wall. "He came for me when I needed him."

"He has before," Jondalar said. "He saved your life, more than once. Maybe you were remembering."

"Maybe," Ayla said, but she didn't really think that was it.

"Did you say you saw a wolf there, on that wall?" Jonokol said.

"Not exactly on it," Ayla said, "but Wolf was there."

"I do think we need to go back," the woman acolyte said, but she was staring at her with a speculative expression.

"There you are," Zelandoni of the Ninth said when they returned to the widened area of the corridor. "Are you feeling more relaxed now and ready to proceed?" She was smiling, but Ayla had the distinct impression that the large woman was impatient and not entirely pleased.

After her vivid memory of the time when she drank some liquid that altered her perceptions, and her moment of displacement when she saw Wolf in the wall, Ayla was, if anything, feeling less inclined to drink some kind of beverage that would put her into some other kind of reality, or next world; but she didn't feel that she had a choice.

"It's not easy to feel relaxed in a cave like this," Ayla said, "and it frightens me to think about drinking that tea, but if you think it is necessary, I am willing to do what you want."

The First smiled again, and this time it seemed genuine. "Your honesty is refreshing, Ayla. Of course it is not easy to relax here. That is not the purpose of this place, and you are probably right to have some fear of this tea. It is very powerful. I was going to explain to you that you will feel strange after you drink it, and its effects are not entirely predictable. The effects usually wear off in a day or so, and I don't know of anyone who has been harmed by it, but if you would rather not, no one will hold it against you."

Ayla frowned in thought, wondering if she should refuse, but though she was glad she had been given the choice, it made it harder to say no. "If you want me to, I am willing," she said.

"I'm sure your participation would be helpful, Ayla," said the donier. "Yours as well, Jondalar. But I hope you understand, you also have the right to refuse."

"You know I've always been uncomfortable with the spirit world, Zelandoni," Jondalar said, "and in the last couple of days, what with digging graves and everything, I've been much closer to that place than I want to be until the Mother calls me. But I was the one who asked you to help Thonolan, and I can do no less than help you in any way I can. In fact, I'll be just as glad to get it all over with."

"Then why don't you both come over here and sit down on this leather pad, and we'll proceed," said the First Among Those Who Served The Great Earth Mother.

When they sat down the young woman ladled the tea into cups. Ayla glanced at Mejera and smiled. She smiled back, shyly, and Ayla realized that she was quite young. She seemed nervous, and Ayla wondered if it was the first time for her to be participating in this kind of ceremony. Probably the zelandonia were using this occasion as a teaching experience.

"Take your time," they were told by Zelandoni of the Third, who was assisting the acolyte in handing them the cups. "It tastes strong, but with the mint, it's not too bad."

Ayla took a sip and thought "not too bad" was a matter of opinion. Under any other circumstances, she would have spit it out. The fire in the hearth was out, but the beverage was rather hot, and she thought that whatever else was in it actually made the mint taste bad. Besides, this wasn't really a tea. It had been boiled, not steeped, and boiling never did bring out the best qualities of mint. She wondered if there weren't other, more compatible, innocuous, or healing herbs that might blend with the primary ingredients in a pleasanter way. Licorice root, perhaps, or linden flowers added later, after it was boiled. In any case, it wasn't a taste to savor, and she finally just drank it down.

She saw that Jondalar had done the same, and so did the First. Then she noticed that Mejera, who had boiled the water and ladled the beverage, had also drunk a cup.

"Jondalar, is this the stone you brought with you from Thonolan's burial?" the First said, showing him the small, sharp-edged, ordinary-looking gray stone with one iridescent blue opal face.

"Yes, it is," he said. He would recognize that stone anywhere.

"Good. It is an unusual stone, and I'm sure it still carries a trace of your brother's elan. Take it in your hand, Jondalar, and then hold hands with Ayla so that the stone is held by both of you. Move close to my seat and with your other hand, take my hand. Now, Mejera, you move up close to me and take my hand, and Ayla, if you will come a little closer, you and Mejera can hold hands."

Mejera must be a new acolyte, Ayla thought. I wonder if it is her first time for something like this. It's my first time with the Zelandonii, although that time at the Clan Gathering with Creb was probably similar, and of course, what I did with Mamut was. She found herself recalling her last experience with the old man of the Lion Camp who interceded with the spirit world, and it did not make her feel better. When Mamut found out she'd had some of the special Clan roots that the mog-urs used, he wanted to try them, but he was unfamiliar with their properties and they were stronger than he had thought. They were both nearly lost to the deep void, and Mamut warned her against ever using them again. Though she did have more of those roots with her, she didn't plan to take them.

The four who had consumed the drink were now facing each other, holding hands, the First sitting on a low padded stool, the rest sitting on the leather mat on the ground. The Zelandoni of the Eleventh brought an oil lamp and placed it in the middle of them. Ayla had seen similar lamps but found herself quite intrigued by it. She was already beginning to feel some effects from the drink as she stared at the stone that held fire.

The lamp was made of limestone. The general shape, including the bowl-like section and the handle extension, had been pecked out with a much harder stone, like granite. Then it was smoothed with sandstone and decorated with symbolic markings etched in with a flint burin. Three wicks were resting against the side of the bowl opposite the handle at different angles, each with one end sticking out of the liquid fat, and the rest of the absorbent material soaking in it. One was quick-starting and hot-burning lichen that melted the fat, the second was dried moss twisted into a sort of cord that gave good light, and the third was made of a dried strip of a porous fungus that absorbed the liquefied fat so well, it kept burning even after the oil was gone. The animal fat that was used for the fuel had been rendered in boiling water so that the impurities fell to the bottom, leaving only pure white tallow floating on top after the water cooled. The flame burned clean, with no visible smoke or soot.

Ayla glanced around and noted, somewhat to her dismay, that a Zelandoni was putting out an oil lamp, and then she saw another going out. Soon all the lamps were out, except for the one in the center. Seeming to defy its diminutive size, the light from the single lamp spread out and lit the faces of the four people holding hands with a warm golden glow. But beyond the circle deep and utter darkness filled every cranny, every crack and hollow, with a black so complete, it felt thick and stifling. Ayla began to feel apprehensive, then she turned her head and caught the bare glimpse of a glow coming from the long corridor. Some of the lamps that had guided their way must still be lit, she thought, and let out a breath that she didn't know she was holding.

She was feeling very strange. The decoction was taking effect quickly. It seemed as though things around her were slowing down or that she was going faster. She looked at Jondalar and found him staring at her, and she had the strangest sense that she almost knew what he was thinking. Then she looked at Zelandoni and Mejera, and felt something, too, but it was not as strong as her feeling with Jondalar, and she wondered if she was imagining it.

She became conscious of hearing music, flutes, drums, and people singing, but not with words. She wasn't quite sure when or even from where it originated. Each singer maintained a single note, or series of repetitive notes, until he or she ran out of breath, and then would take a breath and start again. Most singers and the drummers repeated the same thing over and over, but a few exceptional singers varied their song, as did most of the flute players. Beginning and ending at each person's own choosing meant that no two people started or stopped at the same time. The effect was a continuous sound of interweaving tones that changed as new voices began and others ended, with an overlay of divergent melodies. It was sometimes atonal, sometimes closely harmonic, but overall a strangely wonderful, beautiful, and powerful fugue.

The other three people in her circle were singing as well. The First, with her beautiful, rich contralto, was one who varied her tones in a melodic way. Mejera had a pure, high voice, and a simple, repetitive set of tones. Jondalar also sang a repetition of tones, a chant he had obviously perfected and was happy with. Ayla had never really heard him sing before, but his voice was rich and true, and she liked the sound. She wondered why he didn't sing more.

Ayla felt that she should join in, but she had attempted to sing when she lived with the Mamutoi and knew she simply didn't know how to carry a tune. She never learned as a child, and it was a little late to learn now. Then she heard one of the men nearby who just crooned in a monotone. It reminded her of when she was living alone in her valley and used to hum a similar monotone at night while she rocked herself to sleep, the leather cloak that she had used to hold her son to her hip crumpled up into a ball and held close to her stomach.

Very softly, she began to hum her low-pitched monotone and found herself rocking very slightly. There was something soothing about the music. Her own humming relaxed her, and the sounds of the others gave her a comforting, protected feeling, as though they were supporting her and would be there for her if she needed them. It made it easier for her to give in to the effects of the drink, which was having a strong influence on her.

She became acutely aware of the hands she was holding. On her left, the hand of the young woman was cool, moist, and so softly compliant, the grip was slack. Ayla clasped Mejera's hand but felt almost no return hold; even her grasp was young and shy. In contrast, the hand on her right was warm, dry, and slightly callused from use. Jondalar held her hand with a firm grip, as she held his, and she was extremely conscious of the hard stone held between them, which was slightly disconcerting, but his hand made her feel secure.

Though she couldn't see it, she was sure the flat opal side was against her palm, which meant that the triangular ridge on the side opposite was in his. As she concentrated on it, the stone seemed to be warming, matching their body heat, adding to it, feeling as though it were becoming a part of them or they a part of it. She remembered the chill she'd felt when she first entered the cave, and that the cold intensified as they got farther into its depths, but at the moment, sitting on the padded leather and dressed in her warm clothes, she did not feel cold at all.

Her attention was caught by the fire in the lamp; it made her think of the pleasant heat of fire in a hearth. She stared at the small flickering flame, became fixated on the bit of incandescence to the exclusion of everything else. She watched the small yellow light as it fluttered and trembled. With every breath she took, she seemed to control the flame.

As she watched closely, she saw that the light wasn't entirely yellow. To keep it still while she studied it, she held her breath. The small fire was rounded in the middle, with the brightest yellow part starting near the end of the wick and tapering up to a point. Inside the yellow was a darker area that began below the end of the wick and narrowed into a cone as it rose up within the bit of fire. Below the yellow, at the bottom where the flame began, the fire had a hint of blue.

She had never looked at the fire of an oil lamp with such intensity before. When she started breathing again, the lambent fire seemed to be playing with the lamp, moving to the meter of the music. As it danced over the glossy surface of the melted tallow, its light reflecting from the fuel, the flame grew more radiant. It filled her eyes with its softly glowing luminescence until she could see nothing else.

It made her feel airy, weightless, carefree, as though she could have floated up into the warmth of the light. Everything was easy, effortless. She smiled, laughed softly, then found herself looking at Jondalar. She thought about the life that he had started growing inside her, and a sudden flood of intense love for him welled up and overflowed. He could not help but respond to her glowing smile; as she watched him begin to smile back, she felt happy, loved. Life was full of joy, and she wanted to share it.

She beamed at Mejera and was rewarded with a tentative smile in return, then turned to Zelandoni and included her in the beneficence of her happiness. In a dispassionate corner of her mind that seemed to have distanced itself from her, she seemed to be watching everything with a strange clarity.

"I am getting ready to call Shevonar's elan and direct him to the spirit world," the One Who Was First interrupted her singing to say. Her voice sounded far away, even to her own ears. "After we help him, I will try to find the elan of Thonolan. Jondalar and Ayla will have to help me. Think about how he died, and where his bones are resting."

To Ayla, the sound of her words was full of music that grew louder and more complex. She heard tones resonating from the walls all around her, and watched as the huge donier seemed to become a part of the reverberating chant she sang again, a part of the cave itself. She saw the woman's eyes close. When she opened them, she seemed to be seeing something that was far away. Then her eyes rolled back, showing only whites, and closed again as she slumped forward in her seat.

The young woman whose hand she was holding was shaking. Ayla wondered if it was from fear or if Mejera was simply overwhelmed. She turned to look at Jondalar again. He seemed to be looking at her and she started to smile, but then she realized that he, too, was staring into space, not seeing her at all but something far away inside his mind. Suddenly, she found herself back in the vicinity of her valley again.

Ayla heard something that chilled her blood and set her heart racing: the thundering roar of a cave lion—and a human scream. Jondalar was there with her, inside her, it seemed; she felt the pain of a leg being mauled by the lion, then he lost consciousness. *Ayla stopped, her blood pounding in her ears. It had been so long since she had heard a human sound, yet she knew it was human, and something else. She knew it was her kind of human. She was so stunned that she couldn't think. The scream pulled at her—it was a cry for help.*

With Jondalar's presence unconscious, no longer dominant, she could feel the others there. Zelandoni, distant but powerful; Mejera, closer but vague. Underlying everything was the music, voices and flutes, faint but supporting, comforting, and the drums, deep and resounding.

She heard the growling of the cave lion and saw its reddish mane. Then she realized Whinney had not been nervous, and she knew why. . . . "That's Baby! Whinney, that's Baby!"

There were two men. She pushed aside the lion she had raised and knelt to examine them. Her main concern was as a medicine woman, but she was astonished and curious as well. She knew they were men, though they were the first men of the Others she could remember seeing.

She knew immediately that the man with the darker hair was beyond hope. He lay in an unnatural position, his neck broken. The toothmarks on his throat proclaimed the cause. Though she had never seen him before, his death upset her. Tears of grief filled her eyes. It wasn't that she loved him, but that she felt she had lost something beyond value before she ever had a chance to appreciate it. She was devastated that the first time she saw people of her own kind, one was dead.

She wanted to acknowledge his humanity, to honor him with a burial, but a close look at the other man made her realize that it would be impossible. The man with the yellow hair still breathed, but his life was pumping out of him through a gash in his leg. His only hope was to get him back to the cave as quickly as possible so she could treat him. There was no time for a burial.

She didn't know what to do. She didn't want to leave the man there for the lions. . . . She noticed that the loose rock at the back of the blind canyon looked very unstable—much of it had piled up behind a larger boulder that was none too stable itself. She dragged the dead man to the back of the blind canyon near the slide of loose rock. . . .

When she finally got the other man wrapped into the travois, she returned to the stone ledge with a long sturdy Clan spear. She looked down at the dead man and felt sorrow for the fact of his death. With the formal silent motions of the Clan, she addressed the World of the Spirits.

She had watched Creb, the old Mog-ur, consign the spirit of Iza to the next world with his eloquent flowing movements. She had repeated the same gestures when she found Creb's body in the cave after the earthquake, though she had never known the full meaning of the holy gestures. That wasn't important—she knew the intent. . . .

Using the sturdy spear as a lever, in much the same way as she would have used a digging stick to turn over a log or extract a root, she prised free the large stone and jumped back out of the way as a cascade of loose rock covered the dead man. . . .

When they neared an opening between jagged rock walls, Ayla dismounted and examined the ground. It held no fresh spoor. There was no pain, now. It was a different time, much later. The leg was healed, a large scar was all that remained of the wound. They had been riding double on Whinney. Jondalar got down and followed her, but she knew he didn't really want to be there.

She led the way into a blind canyon, then climbed up on a rock that had split from the wall. She walked to a rockslide at the back.

"This is the place, Jondalar," she said, and, withdrawing a pouch from her tunic, gave it to him. He knew this place.

"What is this?" he asked, holding up the small leather bag.

"Red earth, Jondalar. For his grave."

He nodded, unable to speak. He felt the pressure of tears and made no effort to check them. He poured the red ochre into his hand and broadcast it on the rocks and gravel, then spread a second handful. She waited while he stared at the rocky slope with wet eyes, and when he turned to go, she made a gesture over Thonolan's grave.

They arrived at the blind canyon strewn with huge, sharp-angled boulders and started in, drawn to the slope of loose gravel at the far end. Time had passed again. They were living with the Mamutoi now, and the Lion Camp was going to adopt her. They had gone back to her valley, so Ayla could get some of the things she had made to give as gifts for her new people, and were returning. *Jondalar stood at the foot of the slope, wishing there was something he could do to acknowledge this burial place of his brother. Perhaps Doni had already found him, since She called him back to Her so young. But he knew Zelandoni would try to find this resting place of Thonolan's spirit and help guide him to the spirit world, if she could. But how could he tell her where this place was? He couldn't even have found it without Ayla.*

He noticed Ayla had a small leather pouch in her hand, one similar to the kind she wore around her neck. "You have told me his spirit should return to Doni," *she said.* "I don't know the ways of the Great Earth Mother, I only know of the Spirit World of the Clan totems. I asked my Cave Lion to guide him there. Maybe it is the same place, or maybe your Great Mother knows of that place, but the Cave Lion is a powerful totem and your brother is not without protection."

She held up the small pouch. "I made an amulet for you. You, too, were chosen by the Cave Lion. You don't have to wear it, but you should keep it with you. I put a piece of red ochre in it, so it can hold a piece of your spirit and a piece of your totem's, but I think your amulet should hold one more thing."

Jondalar was frowning. He didn't want to offend her, but he wasn't sure if he wanted this Clan totem amulet.

"I think you should take a piece of stone from your brother's grave. A piece of his spirit may stay with it, and you can carry it back in your amulet to your people."

The knots of consternation on his forehead deepened, then suddenly cleared. Of course! That might help Zelandoni find this place in a spirit trance. Maybe there was more to Clan totems than he realized. After all, didn't Doni create the spirits of all the animals? "Yes, I'll keep this and put a stone from Thonolan's grave into it," *he said.*

He looked at the loose, sharp-edged gravel sloping against the wall in a tenuous equilibrium. Suddenly a stone, giving way to the cosmic force of gravity, rolled down amid a spattering of other rocks and landed at Jondalar's feet. He picked it up. At first glance, it appeared to be the same as all the other innocuous little pieces of broken granite and sedimentary rock. But when he turned it over, he was surprised to see a shining opalescence where the stone had broken. Fiery red lights gleamed from the heart of the milky white stone, and shimmering streaks of blues and greens danced and sparkled in the sun as he turned it this way and that.

"Ayla, look at this," *he said, showing her the opal facet of the small rock he had picked up.* "You'd never guess it from the back. You'd think it was just an *ordinary stone, but look here, where it broke off. The colors seem to come from deep inside, and they're so bright, it almost seems alive."*

"Maybe it is, or maybe it is a piece of the spirit of your brother," she said.

Ayla became aware of Jondalar's warm hand and the stone pressing against her palm. Its heat increased, not enough to cause discomfort, but enough to make her notice it. Was it Thonolan's spirit that was trying to be noticed? She wished she'd had a chance to get to know the man. The things she'd heard about him since she arrived indicated that he had been well liked. It was a shame that he'd died so young. Jondalar had often said that Thonolan was the one who had wanted to travel. He had gone on the Journey only because his brother was going, and because he didn't really want to mate Marona.

"O Doni, Great Mother, help us to find our way to the other side, to your world, to the place beyond and yet within the unseen spaces of this world. As the dying old moon holds the new within its slender arms, the world of the spirits, of the unknown, holds this world of the tangible, of flesh and bone, grass and stone, within its unseen grasp. But with your help it can be seen, it can be known."

Ayla heard the plea, sung in a strange muted chant by the huge woman. She had noticed that she was getting dizzy, though that was not quite the word to describe her sensations. She closed her eyes and felt herself falling. When she opened them again, lights were flashing from within her eyes. Though she had not really paid attention to them when she was looking at the animals, she realized now that she had seen other things, signs and symbols marked on the walls of the cave, some of which matched the visions in her eyes. It didn't seem to matter now whether her eyes were open or closed. She felt that she was falling into a deep hole, a long dark tunnel, and she resisted the sensation, tried to keep control.

"Don't fight it, Ayla. Let go," the great donier said. "We are all here with you. We will support you, Doni will protect you. Let Her take you where She will. Listen to the music, let it help you, tell us what you see."

Ayla dove through the tunnel headfirst, as though she were swimming underwater. The walls of the tunnel, of the cave, began to shimmer, then seemed to dissolve. She was looking through them, seeing into them, beyond them to a grassland and, in the distance, many bison.

"I see bison, huge herds of bison on a large open plain," Ayla said. For a moment the walls solidified again, but the bison stayed. They covered the walls where the mammoths had been. "They are on the walls, painted on the walls, painted in reds and black, and shaped to fit. They're beautiful, perfect, so full of life, the way Jonokol makes them. Don't you see them? Look, over there."

The walls melted again. She could see into them, through them. "They're in a field again, a herd of them. Heading toward the surround." Suddenly Ayla screamed. "No, Shevonar! No! Don't go there, it's dangerous." Then, with sorrow and resignation, "It's too late. I'm sorry, I did everything I could, Shevonar."

"She wanted a sacrifice, to show respect, so people know that sometimes they, too, must give of their own," the First said. She was there with Ayla. "You cannot stay here anymore, Shevonar. You must return to Her now. I will help you. We will help you. We will show you the way. Come with us, Shevonar. Yes, it's dark, but see the light ahead? The bright, glowing light? Go that way. She waits for you there."

Ayla held Jondalar's warm hand. She could feel that the strong presence of Zelandoni was with them, and a fourth companion, the young woman with the limp hand, Mejera, but she was ambiguous, inconsistent. Occasionally she would manifest quite strongly, then would fade to uncertainty.

"Now is the time. Go to your brother, Jondalar," the large woman said. "Ayla can help you. She knows the way."

Ayla felt the stone they held between them and thought about the beautiful, blue-toned milky surface with fiery red highlights. It expanded, filling the space around her until she dove into it. She was swimming, not on top but through the water, underwater, so fast that it felt as if she were flying. She was flying, speeding over the landscape, seeing meadows and mountains, forests and rivers, great inland seas and vast grassy steppes, and the profusion of animals those habitats supported.

The others were with her, letting her lead. Jondalar was closest, and she felt him most strongly, but she sensed the proximity of the powerful donier as well. The other woman's presence was so faint, it was hardly noticed. Ayla took them directly to the blind canyon on the rugged steppes far to the east. "This is the place I saw him. I don't know where to go from here," she said.

"Think of Thonolan, call to his spirit, Jondalar," Zelandoni said. "Reach out to your brother's elan."

"Thonolan! Thonolan! I can feel him," Jondalar said. "I don't know where he is, but I can feel him." Ayla had a perception of Jondalar with someone else, though she could not discern who. Then she sensed other presences, at first just a few, then many, calling out to them. Out of the throng, two stood out . . . no, three. One of them carried an infant.

"Are you still traveling, still exploring, Thonolan?" Jondalar asked.

Ayla heard no answer, but sensed laughter. Then, she had the feeling of an infinity of space to travel and places to go.

"Is Jetamio with you? And her child?" Jondalar queried.

Again, Ayla sensed no words, but felt a surge of love radiating from the amorphous form.

"Thonolan, I know your love of travel and adventure." This time it was the First who spoke with her thoughts to the elan of the man. "But the woman with you wants to return to the Mother. She has followed you only out of love, but she is ready to go. If you love her, you should go and take her and her infant with you. It is time, Thonolan. The Great Earth Mother wants you."

Ayla discerned confusion, a sense of being lost.

"I will show you the way," the donier said. "Follow me."

Ayla perceived herself being drawn along with the rest, speeding rapidly over a landscape that might have been familiar if the details were not so blurred, and if it were not getting so dark. She held tight to the warm hand on her right and felt her left hand being fervently clutched. A brightness appeared before them in the distance that was like a great bonfire, but different. It grew more intense as they approached.

They slowed. "You can find your way from here," Zelandoni said.

Ayla sensed relief from the elans, and then separation. A somber darkness engulfed them, and with the absolute absence of light, a silence, pervasive and complete, surrounded them. Then, faintly, in the unearthly quiet, she heard music: a fluctuating fugue of flutes, voices, and drums. She felt movement. They were accelerating at a tremendous rate, but this time it seemed to come from the hand on the left. Mejera was clutching hard, in fear, determined to return as fast as possible and dragging everyone else along in her wake.

When they stopped, Ayla felt both hands holding hers. They were in the immediate presence of the music, back in the cave. Ayla opened her eyes, saw Jondalar, Zelandoni, and Mejera. The lamp in their midst was sputtering, the oil almost gone and only one wick burning. In the darkness beyond, she saw the small fire of a lamp move, seemingly by itself, and shivered. Another lamp was brought forward and exchanged for the dying light in the center. They were sitting on the leather pad, but now, even in her warm clothing, she felt chilled.

They let go of each other's hands, though Ayla and Jondalar held on for a beat or two longer than the rest, and began to shift positions. The One Who Was First joined in with the singers and brought the musical fugue to a close. More lamps were lit and people started moving around. Some stood up and stamped their feet.

"I want to ask you something, Ayla," the large woman said.

Ayla looked at her expectantly.

"Did you say you saw bison on the walls?"

"Yes, the mammoths had been covered over and made into bison, with the shape of the head and the hump on the back filled in and made to look like the large hump on a bison's withers, and then the walls seemed to disappear and they became real bison. There were some other animals, the horses, and the reindeer facing each other, but I saw this place as a bison cave," Ayla said.

"I think your vision is because of the recent bison hunt and the tragedy surrounding it. You were in the midst of it, and you treated Shevonar," the First said. "But I think there is a meaning to your vision beyond that. They came to you in great numbers in this place. Perhaps the Spirit of Bison is telling the Zelandonii that there has been too much hunting of bison and we need to suspend the hunting of them for the rest of the year to atone, to overcome the bad luck."

There were murmurs of assent. It made the zelandonia feel better to think they could do something to placate the Bison Spirit and remove the ill fortune the unexpected death presaged. They would inform their Caves of the ban on bison hunting, almost grateful to have a message to bring them.

The acolytes gathered up the things that were brought into the cave, then the lamps were all relit and used to light their way out. The zelandonia left the chamber and retraced their steps. When they reached the ledge outside the cave, the sun was setting in a brilliant display of fiery reds, golds, and yellows in the west. On the way back from Fountain Rocks, no one seemed inclined to talk much about their experiences in the deep cave. As the various zelandonia left the group to return to their respective Caves, Ayla wondered what the others had felt and if it was the same thing that she had, but she was reluctant to bring it up. Though she had many questions, she wasn't sure if it was appropriate to ask, or if she really wanted to know the answers.

Zelandoni asked Jondalar if he was satisfied that they had found his brother's spirit and helped his elan to find his way. Jondalar said he thought Thonolan was content, and therefore he was, but Ayla thought it was more that he was relieved. He had done what he could, though it hadn't been easy for him, now the burden of worrying about it was over. By the time Ayla, Jondalar, Zelandoni, and Jonokol reached the Ninth Cave, only the lonely flickering lights in the night sky and the small fires in their stone lamps and torches remained to light their way.

Ayla and Jondalar were both tired when they reached Marthona's dwelling. Wolf was nervously excited and very happy to see Ayla. After comforting the animal and exchanging greetings, they had a light meal and not long after went to bed. It had been a difficult few days.

"Can I help you cook this morning, Marthona?" Ayla asked. They were the first two awake and were enjoying a quiet cup of tea together while everyone else still slept. "I'd like to learn how you like food prepared, and where you keep things."

"I'd be happy to have your help, Ayla, but this morning we've all been invited to share a morning meal with Joharran and Proleva. Zelandoni has been invited, too. Proleva often cooks for her, and I think Joharran feels that he hasn't had much time to talk with his brother since he returned. He seems particularly interested in learning more about that new spear-throwing weapon," Marthona said.

Jondalar woke up remembering the discussion about abelans and how important it was to Ayla to feel that she belonged. Since she had no memory of her own people, and no longer had any connection with the people who had raised her, it was understandable. She had even left behind the Mamutoi, who had made her one of them, to go home with him. The thought preyed on his mind all through the meal with Joharran's family. Everyone there belonged to the Zelandonii, they were all his family, his Cave, his people. Only Ayla was not. It was true they would soon be mated, but she would still be "Ayla of the Mamutoi, mated to Jondalar of the Zelandonii."

After a discussion with Joharran about the spear-thrower, exchanging anecdotes with Willamar about traveling, and general conversation with everyone about the Summer Meeting, the talk turned to Jondalar and Ayla's mating at the First Matrimonial. Marthona was explaining to Ayla that there were two mating ceremonies each summer. The first, and usually the biggest one, was held as early as reasonably possible. Most people who would be joined then had been making the arrangements for some time. The second one was conducted shortly before they left and usually mated those who decided to tie the knot during the summer. There were also two womanhood ceremonies, one shortly after they arrived and the second just before the Summer Meeting ended.

Impulsively Jondalar interrupted her explanations. "I would like Ayla to belong, to become one of us. After we are mated, I would like her to be 'Ayla of the Ninth Cave of the Zelandonii,' not 'Ayla of the Mamutoi.' I know that is usually a decision that a person's mother, or the man of her hearth, makes when that person wants to change affiliation, along with the leaders and Zelandonia, but Mamut gave the choice to Ayla when she left. If she is willing, can I have your agreement, mother?"

Marthona was startled by the suddenness of his request and was caught off guard. "I would not refuse you, Jondalar," she said, feeling that her son had put her in an untenable position to ask such a thing in public without warning. "But it is not entirely up to me. I am happy to welcome Ayla to the Ninth Cave of the Zelandonii, but it is your brother, and Zelandoni, and others, including Ayla herself, who have a say in that decision."

Folara grinned, knowing that her mother did not like to be taken by surprise like that. It rather pleased her that Jondalar had caught her without warning, but she had to admit, Marthona had recovered well.

"Well, I for one would not hesitate to accept her," Willamar said. "I would even adopt her, but since I am mated to your mother, Jondalar, I'm afraid it would make her a sister, like Folara, an unmatable woman. I don't think you would want that."

"No, but I appreciate the thought," Jondalar said.

"Why do you bring it up now?" Marthona asked, still a little miffed.

"It seemed as good a time as any," Jondalar said. "We'll be leaving soon for the Summer Meeting, and I would like it settled before we go. I know we haven't been home very long, but most of you have gotten to know Ayla. I think she would be a valuable addition to the Ninth Cave."

Ayla was more than a little surprised, too, but she said nothing. Do I want to be adopted by the Zelandonii? she asked herself. Does it matter? If Jondalar and I are going to be mated, I will be the same as one, whether I have the name or not. He seems to want it. I'm not sure why, but maybe he has a good reason. He knows his people much better than I do.

"Perhaps I should tell you something, Jondalar," Joharran said. "I think to those of us who know her, Ayla would be a more than acceptable addition to our Cave, but not everyone feels that way. When I was walking back from Down River, I decided to tell Laramar and some others about the bison feast, and when I approached, I overheard them talking. I'm sorry to say, they were making disparaging remarks, in particular about her healing skills and treatment of Shevonar. They seem to feel that anyone who learned healing from . . . the Clan, could not know much. It's their prejudice talking, I'm afraid. I told them no one, not even Zelandoni, could have done more, and I must admit they made me angry. That's not always the best time to make a point."

So that's why he was so angry, Ayla thought. The knowledge gave her mixed feelings. She was upset by what those men said about Iza's healing abilities, but pleased that Joharran had spoken up for her.

"All the more reason to make her one of us now," Jondalar said. "You know those men. They do nothing but gamble and drink Laramar's barma. They haven't even bothered to learn a craft or a skill, unless you consider gambling one. They are not even decent hunters. They are lazy, worthless men who contribute nothing, unless they're shamed into it, and they have little shame. They will do anything to avoid making an effort toward helping the Cave, and everyone knows it. No one will pay attention to what they say if the ones people respect are willing to accept her and make her Zelandonii." He was obviously upset. He wanted Ayla to be accepted for herself, and this put a different character on it.

"That's not entirely true about Laramar, Jondalar," Proleva said. "He may be lazy about most things, and I don't think he likes to hunt much, but Laramar does have a skill. He can make a drinkable beverage out of almost anything that will ferment. I've known him to use grains, fruits, honey, birch sap, even some roots, and turn out a drink that most people like, and he makes it for almost every occasion when people get together. It's true, some people overdo it, but he's just the provider."

"I wish he was a provider," Marthona said with a scornful edge. "Then maybe the children of his hearth wouldn't have to beg for everything they need. Tell me, Joharran, how often is he too 'sick' in the mornings to join a hunting party?"

"I thought food was for everyone, as they need it," Ayla said.

"Food, yes. They won't starve, but for everything else, they have to depend on the goodwill and generosity of other people," the First said.

"But if, as Proleva says, he has the skill to make a very good drink that everyone likes, can't he exchange that for whatever his family needs?" Ayla said.

"He could, yes, but he doesn't," Proleva said.

"What about his mate? Can't she convince him to contribute to his family?" Ayla said.

"Tremeda? She's even worse than Laramar. All she does is drink his barma and produce more children that she doesn't take care of," Marthona said.

"What does Laramar do with all the drink he makes if he doesn't trade it for things for his family?" Ayla wanted to know.

"I'm not sure," Willamar said, "But he would have to trade some of it for ingredients to make more."

"It's true, he always manages to trade for what he wants, but he never has enough for his mate and her children," Proleva said. "It's a good thing that Tremeda doesn't seem to mind asking people to give her things for her 'poor children.'"

"And he does drink a lot of it himself," Joharran said. "Tremeda does, too. I think he gives a good measure away. There is always a bunch around him hoping for drinks. I think he likes to have them around. He probably thinks they're his friends, but I wonder how long they'd stay if he stopped giving them barma."

"Not long, I'd guess," Willamar said. "But I don't think Laramar and his friends are the ones to decide whether Ayla becomes Zelandonii."

"You are right, Trade Master. I think there's no question that we would have no problem accepting Ayla, but maybe we should let Ayla decide," Zelandoni said. "No one has asked her if she wants to be a woman of the Zelandonii."

All heads turned to look at her. Now she was the one who felt uncomfortable. It was a while before she said anything, which made Jondalar a bit nervous. Maybe he had misjudged her. Maybe she didn't want to become Zelandonii. Maybe he should have asked her first before he started this, but with all the talk about Matrimonials, it seemed an appropriate time. Finally Ayla spoke.

"When I decided to leave the Mamutoi and go with Jondalar back to his home, I knew how the Zelandonii felt about the Clan, the people who raised me, and I knew that you might not want me. I admit I was a little afraid to meet his family, his people." She stopped for a moment, trying to gather her thoughts and find the right words to say what she felt.

"I'm a stranger to you, a foreign woman, with strange ideas and ways. I brought animals that live with me and asked you to accept them. Horses are animals that are usually hunted, and I wanted you to make a place for them. I have just been thinking today that I would like to make a covered shelter for them at the south end of the Ninth Cave, not far from Down River. During the winter, the horses are used to having a refuge that is out of the weather. I also brought a wolf, a meat-eating hunter. Some of his kind have been known to attack people, and I asked you to allow me to bring him inside, to sleep in the same dwelling that I sleep in." She smiled at Jondalar's mother.

"You didn't hesitate, Marthona. You invited me and Wolf to share your home. And Joharran, you allowed the horses to stay nearby, and let me take them right up on the ledge in front of your dwellings. Brun, the leader of my clan, would not have. You all listened when I explained about the Clan, and you didn't turn me away. You were willing to consider that the ones you call flatheads might be people, perhaps a different kind of people, but not animals. I didn't expect that you would be so thoughtful, but I am grateful.

"It's true that not everyone has been kind, but many more of you have defended me, though you hardly know me. I've been here only a short time. It may be because of Jondalar, because you trust that he would not bring someone who would try to harm his people or that you could not accept." She stopped and closed her eyes for a moment, then continued.

"For all my fears about meeting Jondalar's family and his people, the Zelandonii, when I left I knew there would be no turning back. I didn't know how you would feel about me, but it didn't matter. I love Jondalar. I want to spend my life with him. I was willing to do whatever was needed, to put up with whatever I had to, to be with him. But you have welcomed me, and now you ask if I want to become

Zelandonii." She closed her eyes to maintain her control and tried to swallow the fullness in her throat.

"I have wanted that since I first saw Jondalar, and wasn't even sure if he would live. I grieved for his brother, not because I knew him, but because I recognized him. It troubled me that I would never have an opportunity to know one of the first people of my own kind that I could remember seeing. I don't know what language I spoke before the Clan found me and took me in. I learned to communicate the way the Clan does, but the first language I can remember speaking is Zelandonii. Even if I don't speak it quite right, I think of it as my language. But before we could even speak to each other, I wished that I was one of Jondalar's people so that I would be acceptable to him, so that someday he might consider me for his mate. Even if it was his second or third woman, it would have been enough.

"You ask me, do I want to be a Zelandonii woman? Oh, yes, I want to be a Zelandonii woman. With all my heart I want to be a Zelandonii woman. I want that more than I have ever wanted anything in my life," she said, her eyes sparkling with tears.

There was a stunned silence. Without even realizing how he got there, Jondalar had taken the few steps to reach her and take her in his arms. He felt so much for her, there were no words to convey it. He thought it was amazing that she could be so strong and yet so vulnerable. There wasn't a person there who wasn't moved. Even Jaradal had some understanding of what she said. Folara's cheeks were wet with tears, and several others were close to it. Marthona was the first to regain her composure.

"I, for one, am happy to welcome you to the Ninth Cave of the Zelandonii," she said, hugging her in a spontaneous gesture. "And I'll be glad to see Jondalar settle down with you, though there may be several women who would wish otherwise. Women have always loved him, but I sometimes doubted that he would find a woman he could love. I thought that he might not choose someone from among our people, but I didn't think he would have to travel so far. Now I know there must have been some reason that he did, because I understand why he loves you. You are a rare woman, Ayla."

They started talking about the Summer Meeting again, and when they would be leaving, and Zelandoni mentioned that they still had time to have a small ceremony to bring Ayla into the Ninth Cave and make her a Zelandonii woman.

Just then there was an urgent knocking on the panel next to the entrance, but before anyone could respond, a girl burst in and ran to Zelandoni, obviously very distressed. Ayla thought she could count perhaps ten years, but was surprised at how tattered, stained, and dirty her clothes were.

"Zelandoni," she said, "they told me you were here. I can't get Bologan up."

"Is he sick? Did he hurt himself?" Zelandoni asked.

"I don't know."

"Ayla, why don't you come with me. This is Tremeda's daughter, Lanoga. Bologan is her eldest brother," Zelandoni said.

"Isn't Tremeda Laramar's mate?" Ayla asked.

"Yes," Zelandoni said as they hurried off together.

19

As they neared Laramar and Tremeda's home, Ayla realized she had passed by it many times but hadn't paid attention. The stone shelter of Jondalar's people was so large, housed so many, and so much seemed to have happened since they arrived, it was difficult to take it in all at once. Maybe with so many people it was always this way, but it would take a while for her to become accustomed to it.

The dwelling was at the far end of the living sites, set apart from its neighbors, and farthest away from most Cave activities. The living structure itself was not large, but the family claimed a substantial amount of the surrounding area by spreading out in an untidy array, though it was difficult to distinguish between personal belongings and trash. Some distance away from the dwelling was the space Laramar appropriated to make his fermented brew, which might change in flavor depending upon his ingredients, but could always be counted on.

"Where is Bologan, Lanoga?" Zelandoni asked.

"Inside. He won't move," Lanoga said.

"Where's your mother?" the donier asked.

"I don't know."

When they moved aside the entrance drape, an unbelievably foul smell assaulted them. Except for one small lamp, the only light was the shadowed daylight reflecting off the stone above the roofless dwelling from the great overhanging shelf above the abri, and it was dark inside.

"Do you have any more lamps, Lanoga?" Zelandoni asked.

"Yes, but no oil," the girl said.

"We can tie back the drape for now. He's right here, just inside the entrance, blocking the way," Zelandoni said.

Ayla found the tieback attached to the drape and wrapped it around the post. When she looked inside, she was appalled at the filth. There were no paving stones and the dirt floor was muddy in places where liquid of some kind had found its way down. From the stench, she thought some of it was probably urine. It appeared that every piece of their household furnishings was strewn across the floor, tattered mats and baskets, pads with the stuffing half gone, piles of leather and woven material that might have been clothing.

Bones with most of the meat chewed off were scattered here and there. Flies buzzed around rotting food that was left out, she couldn't guess how many days before, on plates made of wooden slabs that were so rough, there were splinters in them. In the light she saw a rat's nest beside the entrance, containing several squirming, red, hairless newborn, their eyes still closed.

Just beyond the entrance, a skinny youth was sprawled on the ground. She had met him briefly before, but now she looked more closely. He could count perhaps twelve years, Ayla thought, and his belt indicated he was coming of age, but he was more boy than man. It was fairly obvious what had happened. Bologan was bruised and battered, and his head was covered with dried blood.

"He's been in a fight," Zelandoni said. "Someone dragged him home and left him here."

Ayla bent down to check his condition. She touched the pulse in his neck and noticed more blood, then put her cheek near his mouth. She not only felt his breath, she smelled it. "He's still breathing," she told Zelandoni, "but he's badly hurt, the pulsing is weak. His head is injured and he has lost a lot of blood, but I don't know if the bone is cracked. Someone must have hit him or he fell on something hard. That may be why he's not waking up, but he smells of barma, too."

"And I don't know if he should be moved, but I can't treat him here," Zelandoni said.

The girl walked toward the entrance, carrying on her hip a thin, lethargic baby of about six months, who looked as though she hadn't been washed since she was born. A toddler with snot running down his nose was hanging on her leg. Ayla thought she saw another child behind her, but wasn't sure. She seems to be more mother than her mother, Ayla thought.

"Bologan all right?" Lanoga said, a worried look on her face.

"He's alive, but he is injured. You did right to come and get me," the donier said. Zelandoni shook her head with exasperation and a feeling of anger toward Tremeda and Laramar. "I'll have to take care of him at my place," she said.

Normally, only the most serious maladies were attended to in the donier's dwelling; in a Cave as large as the Ninth, there wasn't room enough for all the people who were sick or injured at one time to move there. Someone with Bologan's injuries, as serious as they were, usually would be cared for in his own home, with Zelandoni going there to treat him. But there was no one at this home to take care of him, and Zelandoni couldn't bear the idea of even entering the place, much less spending any time there.

"Do you know where your mother is, Lanoga?"

"No."

"Where did she go?" Zelandoni said, rephrasing her question.

"Went to the burial," Lanoga said.

"Who is taking care of the children?"

"I am."

"But you're not able to feed that baby," Ayla said, shocked. "You can't nurse."

"I can feed her," Lanoga said, a defensive tone in her voice. "She eats food. The milk dried up."

"Which means Tremeda will have another baby within a year," Zelandoni said under her breath.

"I know babies that young can eat food if they have to," Ayla said, sympathetically, feeling a twinge of painful memory. "What do you feed her, Lanoga?"

"Mashed-up boiled roots," she said.

"Ayla, will you go tell Joharran what happened, and ask him to come here with something to carry Bologan to my dwelling? And some help to carry him?" Zelandoni said.

"Yes, of course. I'll be right back," Ayla said, hurrying away.

It was late in the afternoon when Ayla left Zelandoni's dwelling and hurried toward the leader's. She had been helping the Ninth Cave's healer and was going to tell Joharran that Bologan was awake and seemed to be coherent enough to talk.

Joharran had been waiting for her. After he left, Proleva said, "Would you like something to eat? You've been with Zelandoni all afternoon." Ayla shook her head and started to go. She opened her mouth to make apologies, but Proleva quickly added, "Or maybe a cup of tea? I have some tea ready. It's chamomile, lavender, and linden flower."

"Well, maybe a cup, but I need to get back soon," Ayla said. As she got out her drinking cup, she wondered if the mixture had been suggested by Zelandoni or whether Proleva realized that it was a good drink for pregnant women. It was innocuous, with only a mildly calming effect. She took a sip of the hot tea the woman ladled into her cup and savored the taste. It did have a nice flavor, and anybody could drink it, not just pregnant women.

"How is Bologan?" the leader's mate asked as she sat down beside Ayla with her own cup.

"I think he will be fine. He had a bad knock on the head, bled a lot. I was afraid the bone might have been cracked, but head wounds do tend to bleed heavily. We cleaned him and couldn't find any evidence of a break, but he does have a big swollen lump, and other injuries. He needs rest and care right now. It seems obvious that he was in a fight, and he was drinking barma."

"That's what Joharran wanted to talk to him about," Proleva said.

"The one that worries me even more is that baby," Ayla said. "She needs to be nursed. I'd think other nursing mothers could give a little of their milk to her. Women of the Clan did when . . ." she hesitated a moment ". . . a woman lost her milk early. She had been taking care of her mother, and grieved too much when she died." Ayla decided to refrain from mentioning that she was the woman who had lost her milk; she hadn't yet told anyone that she'd had a son when she was living with the Clan. "I asked Lanoga what she fed her. She said mashed-up roots. I know children that young can eat food, but all babies need milk, too. She won't grow right without it."

"You're right, Ayla. Babies do need milk. I'm afraid no one has been paying attention to Tremeda and her family. We know the children are not very well cared for, but they are Tremeda's children, and people don't like to interfere in other people's lives. It's hard to know what to do about them, so most of us just ignore them. I didn't even know she had lost her milk," Proleva said.

"Why didn't Laramar say something?" Ayla asked.

"I doubt that he even noticed. He doesn't pay any attention to the children, except Bologan, occasionally. I'm not sure he even knows how many there are," Proleva said. "He goes there only to eat and sleep and sometimes not even for that, which may be for the best. When they are together, Laramar and Tremeda argue all the time. It often leads to real fights, which invariably she gets the worst of."

"Why does she stay with him?" Ayla asked. "She could leave him if she wanted to, couldn't she?"

"Where would she go? Her mother is dead, and she never mated, so there never was a man at their hearth. Tremeda had an older brother, but he moved away before she grew up, first to another Cave, and then farther away. No one has heard anything about him in years," Proleva said.

"Couldn't she find another man?" Ayla asked.

"Who would have her? It's true, she manages to find some man to honor the Mother with her at a Mother Festival, usually someone who's had too much barma, or meadow mushrooms, or something else, but she's not exactly a prize. And she has six children that need to be provided for."

"Six children?" Ayla said. "I saw four, or possibly five. How many years can they count?"

"Bologan is the eldest. He can count twelve years," Proleva said.

"I guessed that," Ayla said.

"Lanoga can count ten years," Proleva continued. "Then, there's an eight-year, a six-year, a two-year, and the baby. She's only some moons, about a half-year. Tremeda had another one who would be a four-year, but he died."

"I'm afraid this baby will die. I examined her, she is not healthy. I know you said food is shared, but what about babies who need milk? Are Zelandonii women willing to share their milk?" Ayla asked.

"If it were anyone but Tremeda, I wouldn't hesitate to say yes," Proleva said.

"That baby is not Tremeda," Ayla said. "She's just a helpless infant. If my baby were here, I wouldn't hesitate to share my milk with her, but by the time mine is born, she may already be gone. Even by the time yours is born, it may be too late."

Proleva bowed her head and smiled self-consciously. "How did you know? I haven't told anyone yet."

It was Ayla's turn to feel self-conscious. She hadn't meant to presume. It was usually the mother's prerogative to announce that she was expecting a child. "I am a medicine woman, a healer," she explained. "I have helped women give birth and know the signs of pregnancy. I didn't mean to mention it until you were ready. I was just concerned about Tremeda's baby."

"I know. I don't mind, Ayla. I was getting ready to tell people anyway," Proleva said, "but I didn't know you were expecting. That means our babies will be born close together. I'm glad." She paused for a while, thinking, then she said, "I'll tell you what I think we should do. Let me get together the women who have young infants, or are almost ready to give birth. They're the ones whose milk hasn't yet adjusted to their own baby's needs and have extra. You and I can talk to them about helping to feed Tremeda's baby."

"If several of them share it, it won't be too much of a drain on any one of them," Ayla said, then she frowned. "The trouble is, that baby really needs more than milk. She needs better care. How could Tremeda leave an infant for so long with a girl who can count only ten years?" Ayla said. "Not to mention all the rest of the children. It's too much to expect of a ten-year."

"They probably get better care from Lanoga than from Tremeda," Proleva said.

"But that doesn't mean someone so young should have to do it," Ayla said. "What's wrong with Laramar? Why isn't he doing something to help? Tremeda is his mate, isn't she? They are the children of his hearth, aren't they?"

"Those are questions many of us have asked," Proleva said. "We don't have answers. Many people have spoken to Laramar, including Joharran and Marthona. It makes no difference. Laramar doesn't care what anyone says. He knows that no matter what he does, people will want that drink he makes. And Tremeda is just as bad in her own way. She is so often in a stupor from his barma, she hardly knows what goes on around her. Neither one of them seem to care about the children, I don't know why the Great Earth Mother keeps giving her more. No one really knows what to do." There was frustration and sadness in the voice of the tall, handsome woman who was the mate of the leader.

Ayla didn't have an answer, but she knew she had to do something.

"Well, there is one thing we can do. We can talk to the women and see about getting some milk for the baby. It's a start." She put her cup back in her carrying pouch and stood up. "I should be getting back now."

When Ayla left Proleva's, she didn't return directly to Zelandoni's place. She was concerned about Wolf and wanted to stop at Marthona's first. When she went in, the whole family was there, including Wolf. He rushed at her, so pleased to see her that Ayla was almost knocked down when the large wolf jumped up on his hind legs and landed with his paws in front of her shoulders. But she had seen him coming and managed to brace herself. She allowed him to give her the canine greeting to the leader of the pack, licking her neck and taking her jaw gently in his teeth. Then she held his head between both her hands by the thick fur of his ruff and gently bit his jaw. She looked into his adoring eyes and buried her face in his fur. She was glad to see him, too.

"It startles me when he does that to you, Ayla," Willamar said as he got up from a cushion on the floor.

"It used to scare me, too," Jondalar said. "I trust him now, I'm not afraid for Ayla anymore. I know he won't hurt her, and I've seen what he can do to someone else who might try, but I admit, that special greeting of his does surprise me sometimes."

When Willamar approached, they greeted each other with a quick touching of right cheeks. By now Ayla had learned that it was a customary informal greeting between family members or very close friends.

"I'm sorry I couldn't go with you to see the horses, Ayla," Folara said as they greeted each other the same way.

"There's time for you to get to know the horses," she said, then touched Marthona's cheek with hers. The greeting with Jondalar was similar, but more lingering and closer. More like an embrace.

"I have to go back and help Zelandoni," Ayla said, "but I was a little concerned about Wolf. I'm glad he returned here. It means he feels that this is his home, even if I'm not here."

"How is Bologan?" Marthona asked.

"He is awake and able to talk, finally. I just came to tell Joharran." Ayla wondered if she should mention her concerns about Tremeda's baby. She was a stranger still, and maybe it wasn't appropriate for her to bring it up. It could be construed as criticism of the Ninth Cave, but nobody else seemed to know about the situation, and if she didn't say something, who would? "I talked to Proleva about another thing that bothers me," she said.

There were looks of interest from Jondalar's family. "What?" Marthona asked.

"Did you know that Tremeda's milk has dried up? She hasn't been home since Shevonar's burial, and she left the baby and the rest of her children for Lanoga to care for and feed. That girl can count only ten years, she can't nurse. All that baby is eating is mashed-up roots. She needs milk. How can a baby grow right without milk? And where is Laramar? Doesn't he care at all?" Ayla said in a rush, blurting it all out at once.

Jondalar glanced around at everyone. Folara was aghast; Willamar looked a little stunned; and Marthona was caught off guard, which didn't please her at all. Jondalar had to hold back a smile at the expressions on their faces. He wasn't surprised at Ayla's response to someone who needed help, but Laramar, Tremeda, and family had long been an embarrassment to the Ninth Cave. Most people didn't talk about it, but Ayla had just brought it out into the open.

"Proleva said she didn't know that Tremeda's milk was gone," Ayla continued. "She's going to get the women together who can help, and we're going to talk to them, explain what the baby needs, and ask them to share some of their milk. She thought the new mothers, and the ones who are almost ready to give birth, would be the ones to ask. This is such a big cave, there must be many women who could help feed that baby."

Jondalar knew they could, but he wondered if they would, and he speculated about whose idea it was; he thought he knew. He was aware that women sometimes nursed children other than their own, but usually it was a sister or a close friend whose infant they were willing to share their milk with.

"That sounds like an admirable idea," Willamar said.

"If they're willing," Marthona said.

"Why wouldn't they be?" Ayla said. "Zelandonii women wouldn't let a baby die for lack of a little milk, would they? I did tell Lanoga I would go there tomorrow in the morning and teach her how to make more than mashed roots for the baby."

"What can a baby eat besides milk?" Folara asked.

"Many things," Ayla said. "If you scrape cooked meat, you get a soft substance that a baby can eat, and they can drink the liquid left after you boil meat. Nuts, ground to mush and mixed with some liquid, and grain that has been ground very fine and cooked, are good for them. Any vegetable can be cooked until it's soft, and some fruit just needs to be mashed, though the seeds have to be strained out. I always poured fruit juice through bunched-up fresh cleavers. They're full of prickles and stick together easily and catch the seeds. Babies can eat almost anything their mothers can eat, if it's smooth and fine enough."

"How do you know so much about food that babies can eat?" Folara asked.

Ayla stopped and flushed with dismay. She hadn't expected the question. She knew babies were not limited to nursing because Iza had taught her how to make food for Uba when the woman got sick and lost her milk. But Ayla's knowledge had expanded manyfold when Iza died, and Ayla was so devastated by the loss of the only mother she knew, her milk dried up. Though the other women in Brun's small clan who were nursing all fed Durc, she'd had to supplement with regular food to keep him satisfied and healthy.

But she wasn't ready to tell Jondalar's family about her son just yet. They had recently said they wanted to accept her into the Zelandonii, make her one of them, even though they knew she had been raised by the people they called flatheads and considered to be animals. She would never forget the pain she had felt at Jondalar's first reaction when she told him that she had a son who was a mixture of both, of mixed spirits. Because the spirit of one of those people he thought of as animals had mixed with hers to start a life growing inside her, he had looked at her as though she were a filthy hyena and called her an abomination. She was worse than the child, because she had produced him. Jondalar had learned more about the Clan since then, and he did not feel that way anymore, but what about his people, his family?

Her mind raced. What would his mother say if she knew that her son wanted to mate with a woman who was an abomination? Or Willamar, or Folara, or the rest of his family? Ayla looked at Jondalar, and though usually she could discern his feelings and know what he was thinking by interpreting his expression or his demeanor, this time she could not. She didn't know what he would wish her to say.

She had been raised with the understanding that she had to answer a direct question with a truthful answer. Ayla had since learned that unlike the Clan, the Others, her kind of people, could say things that were not true. They even had a word for it. It was called a lie. For a moment, she actually thought about saying a lie, but what could she say? She was sure they would know it if she tried; she didn't know how to lie. At most, she could refrain from mentioning, but it was hard not to reply when she was asked a direct question.

Ayla had always supposed that his people were bound to find out about Durc sometime. He was often in her thoughts, and she knew there would come a moment when she would forget or decide not to refrain from mentioning him. She didn't want to avoid talking about Durc forever. He was her son. But this was not the time.

"I know about making baby food, Folara, because after Uba was born, Iza lost her milk early and she taught me how to make food that Uba could eat. A baby can eat anything its mother can eat if you make it soft and easy to swallow," Ayla said. It was the truth, but it was not the whole truth. She refrained from mentioning her son.

"You do it like this, Lanoga," Ayla said. "You pull the scraper across the meat. It gets the essence out and leaves the fibrous part behind. See? Now you try it."

"What are you doing here?"

Ayla jumped with a start at the voice, then turned to face Laramar. "I'm showing Lanoga how to prepare some food that this baby can eat, since her mother has no more milk for her," she said. She was sure she detected a look of surprise flit across his face. So he didn't know, she thought.

"Why should you bother? I doubt that anyone else cares," Laramar said.

Not even you, she thought, but held her tongue. "People care. They just didn't know," she said. "We only found out when Lanoga came and got Zelandoni because Bologan was hurt."

"Bologan is hurt? What happened?"

This time there was concern in his voice. Proleva was right, Ayla thought. He does have some feelings for the eldest. "He drank your barma and . . ."

"Drank my barma! Where is he? I'll teach that boy to get into my barma!" Laramar stormed.

"You don't have to," Ayla said. "Someone already did. He got in a fight, someone hit him hard, or he fell and hit his head on a rock. He was brought back home and left. Lanoga found him unconscious and went to find Zelandoni. That's where he is now. He was badly hurt and lost a lot of blood, but with rest and care, he should be fine. But he won't tell Joharran who hit him."

"I'll take care of it, I know how to get it out of him," Laramar said.

"I haven't lived with this Cave very long, and it's not my place to say, but I think you should talk to Joharran first. He's very angry and wants to know who did it, and why. Bologan was lucky. It could have been much worse," Ayla said.

"You're right. It's not your place to say," Laramar said. "I'd rather take care of it myself."

Ayla said nothing. There was nothing she could do about it, except tell Joharran. She turned to the girl. "Come on, Lanoga. Get Lorala and we'll go," she said, picking up her Mamutoi haversack.

"Where are you going?" Laramar said.

"We're going to take a swim and clean up a little before we go to talk with some of the women who are nursing, or will be soon, and ask them if they will share some of their milk with Lorala," Ayla said. "Do you know where Tremeda is? She should come to this meeting, too."

"Isn't she here?" Laramar said.

"No. She left the children with Lanoga, and hasn't returned since she went to Shevonar's burial," Ayla said. "In case you're interested, the rest of the children are with Ramara, Salova, and Proleva right now." It was Proleva who had suggested that she get Lanoga and the baby cleaned up a little. Women with infants might not want to hold such a grimy baby for fear she might soil their own child.

As Lanoga picked up the baby, Ayla signaled Wolf, who had been lying down watching the activities, partly hidden by a log. Laramar hadn't seen the animal, and when Wolf stood up, his eyes widened with surprise as he became aware of what a large, powerful carnivore he actually was. The man backed off a few steps, then gave the foreign woman an insincere smile.

"That's a big animal. Are you sure it's safe to bring him around people, especially children?" he asked.

He doesn't care about children, Ayla thought, reading his subtle body language. He's talking about children and implying that I am doing something that might harm people to hide his own fear. Other people had voiced a similar concern without offending her, but she disapproved of Laramar because he had so little concern for the children for whom he should have been responsible. She didn't like the man, and his objections evoked a negative reaction in her.

"Wolf has never threatened a child. The only person he ever harmed was a woman who attacked me," Ayla said, looking directly into his eyes. Among the people of the Clan, such a direct glare would have been construed as a threat, and a subliminal impression of that was communicated. "Wolf killed the woman," she added. Laramar took another step back, grinning nervously.

That was not a smart thing to say, Ayla thought as she walked toward the front terrace with Lanoga, the baby, and Wolf. Why did I say it? She looked down at the animal trotting confidently beside her. I was acting almost like a wolf leader, making a lower-ranked pack member back down. But this is not a wolf pack, and I am not a leader. He's already talking against me, I might be making trouble for myself.

When they started down the path at the lower end of the terrace, Ayla offered to carry the baby for a while, but Lanoga said no and shifted Lorala on her hip. Wolf sniffed at the ground, and Ayla noticed hoofprints. The horses had come this way before. She was going to point them out to the girl, but changed her mind. Lanoga didn't talk much, and Ayla didn't want to pressure her into uncomfortable conversation.

They reached the edge of The River, and as they continued along the bank of waterway, Ayla stopped now and then to examine a plant. With a digging stick she carried pushed through her waist thong, she removed several plants with the roots. The girl watched her, and Ayla was going to show her the defining characteristics of the vegetation so she could find it herself, but decided to wait until after she understood their use.

The spring-fed creek that separated the Ninth Cave from Down River tumbled down from the stone porch in a narrow waterfall, then became a minor tributary of The River. Ayla stopped when they reached the water flowing out of the groove it had worn into the limestone and over the edge in a thin cascade of gurgling, foaming liquid. Somewhat beyond the falls, large stones had broken loose from the limestone wall and created a kind of dam with a small pond behind it. One of the stones had a natural basin with mosslike water plants lining it.

The water that filled it came primarily from rain and the back-splashing spray of the waterfall. In the summer, when there was less rain, the water level of the basin was lower and she thought the sun might have warmed it. She dipped her hand in. As she expected, it was tepid, a little cool, but warmer than the water in the pool, and the water plants made the bottom of the basin soft.

Ayla put down her carrying sack. "I brought some food, do you want to feed Lorala now or later?" she asked.

"Now," Lanoga said.

"All right, let's eat now," Ayla said. "I have some cooked grain, and that meat that we scraped for Lorala. I brought enough food for all of us. Even some meaty bones for Wolf. What do you use to feed the baby?"

"My hand," she said.

Ayla looked at her dirty hands. It didn't matter. She had fed the child with her dirty hands before, but the woman decided to show her anyway. She held up the plants she had collected on the way.

"Lanoga, I'm going to show you what these plants are for," Ayla said. The girl looked at them. "They are called soaproot. There are several different kinds, and some work better than others. First I will wash the dirt off of them in this little stream," she explained, showing Lanoga how to clean them. Then she looked for a round hard stone and a level place on one of the fallen boulders near the basin. "Next, you need to crush the roots. They will work if you just crush them, but soaking draws out more of the slippery juice." The girl watched closely, but said nothing.

Ayla got a small watertight woven basket out of the pack she carried over one shoulder and moved to the stone basin. "Water by itself doesn't always get dirt off very well. Soaproot makes it easier. The water in this basin is a little warmer than the water in the stream. Would you like to feel it?" Ayla said.

"I don't know," the girl said, looking at her as if she didn't quite understand.

"Lanoga, come here and put your hand in this water," Ayla said.

She came closer and put the hand that was not holding the baby in the water.

"It's warmer isn't it? Do you like how it feels?" Ayla said.

"I don't know," Lanoga said.

Ayla dipped a little of the tepid water into the basket, added the crushed soaproot, and mixed it around with her hand. Then she took out a little of the mashed plant and rubbed her hands together. "Lanoga, put the baby down, pick up some of this soaproot, and do what I am doing," the woman said.

The girl watched her, lifted the baby off her hip, put her down in the dirt near her feet, then slowly reached for the soaproot. She dipped it in the water and rubbed her hands together. A little foam started to form, and a brief expression of interest crossed Lanoga's face. The saponin-filled roots did not create an abundance of soapy lather, but it was enough to clean her hands.

"Good soaproot should be slippery and make some foam," Ayla said. "Now rinse it off, like this. See how much cleaner your hands are?" The girl dipped her hands in the water and then looked at them. Again an expression of interest crossed her face. "Let's eat now."

Ayla went back to where her haversack was and took out some packages. One was a carved wooden bowl with a lid, tied on with cordage wrapped around it. She untied the cords, removed the lid, and lightly touched the top of the contents. "It is still slightly warm," she said, showing her the congealed mass of finely ground cooked grains of different varieties. "I collected this grain last fall when Jondalar and I were on our Journey. There are some rye seeds and wheat seeds, and some oats. I added a little salt while it was cooking. The little black seeds come from a plant I call goosefoot, but it has a different Zelandonii name. The leaves are good to eat, too. I made this cereal for Lorala. I think there's enough for you and me, too, but why don't you see if she likes the meat we scraped first."

The meat was wrapped in some large plantain leaves. Ayla handed it to Lanoga and watched to see what she would do. She opened the package, took some of the mushy substance in her fingers, and put it in the baby's mouth while she was sitting on her hip. The child opened her mouth readily for her sister, but at the first taste, she looked surprised. She moved it around in her mouth, examining the taste and texture, and when she finally swallowed it, she opened her mouth for more. She reminded Ayla of a little bird.

Lanoga smiled, and Ayla realized it was the first time she had seen the girl smile. Lanoga fed her sister the rest of the meat, then started on the cereal. She took a taste herself first, then put some in the baby's mouth. They both watched her reaction to the new taste. With an expression of intense concentration, she examined it with her mouth, even chewing the somewhat gummy concoction. She seemed to think about it for a moment, then swallowed and opened her mouth for more. Ayla was amazed at how much the baby was able to eat, but only when she finally stopped opening her mouth did Lanoga put another taste in her own mouth.

"If you give her something to hold, does Lorala put it in her mouth?" Ayla asked.

"Yes," the girl said.

"I brought a little piece of marrow bone. I knew a boy who used to love them when he was a baby," Ayla said with a smile of fond remembrance and sorrow. "Give it to her and see if she likes it." Ayla handed her a small piece of deer leg bone, with a hole in the center filled with rich marrow. As soon as Lanoga gave her the bone, the baby put it in her mouth. Again there was that startled look as she stopped and examined the taste, but soon they could hear her making sucking sounds. "Put her down and eat something yourself, Lanoga."

Wolf had been watching the baby from the place a few feet away where Ayla had motioned him to stay. Making little yearning whines, he crept slowly toward the infant as she was sitting on a patch of grass. Lanoga watched him a moment, than turned toward Ayla with a look of concern. She hadn't even acknowledged the presence of the animal before.

"Wolf loves children," Ayla said. "He wants to play with her, but I think that marrow bone might distract him a little. If she drops it, he might think she is giving it to him and take it. I brought a bone with some meat on it for him. I'll give it to him over there by The River while we have our meal."

Ayla pulled a rather large, leather-wrapped package out of her haversack and opened it to reveal some pieces of cooked bison and one good-size raw bone with some hard, dry pieces of brownish meat clinging to it. She got up, signaled Wolf to follow her, and walked toward the large stream, then gave him the bone. He seemed content to settle down with it.

When she returned, she started taking several more things out of her carrying pack. She had brought a variety of foods. Besides the meat and cereal, she had several things left over from her Journey. There were some dried pieces of a starchy root; some roasted pine nuts from stone pines; some hazelnuts in their shells; and slices of small dried apples, tart and tasty.

As they were eating, Ayla talked to the girl. "Lanoga, I told you we were going to swim and clean up a little before we go to talk to the women, but I think I should tell you why. I know you've done the best you know how to feed Lorala, but she needs more than mashed roots to be healthy and grow properly. I showed you how to fix other things to feed her, like scraping the meat so she can eat it, even though she doesn't have teeth yet. But what she needs most is milk, at least some milk." The girl watched her while she ate, but did not say anything.

"Where I grew up, women always fed each other's babies, and if the milk of one of the mothers dried up, the other women would take turns feeding her baby. Proleva told me that Zelandonii women feed other babies, too, but usually only family or close kin. Your mother doesn't have any siblings or cousins who are nursing mothers, so I'm going to ask the women who are nursing, or will be soon, if they will help. But mothers get very protective of their own babies. They may not want to hold a baby who isn't clean and doesn't smell nice, and afterward hold their own.

"We need to clean Lorala so she will be fresh and appealing to the other mothers. We are going to use that soaproot we used on our hands. I will show you how to bathe her, because you will have to keep her clean, and since you will probably be the one who will have to bring her to the women to nurse her, you need to bathe, too. I brought something for you to wear. Proleva got it for me. It's been worn before, but it is clean. The girl who wore it got too big for it." Lanoga did not respond, and Ayla wondered why she said so little. "Do you understand?" she asked.

Lanoga nodded and kept on eating, now and then glancing at her sister, who was still working on the marrow bone. Ayla thought the baby was starving for foods that offered some of the nourishment she had been lacking. Boiled starchy roots weren't enough for a growing infant. By the time Lanoga had her fill, the baby seemed to be getting sleepy, and Ayla thought they should wash her now and let her sleep later. She put the containers away and stood up, then noticed a distinctive odor.

The girl noticed it, too. "She messed," Lanoga said.

"There's some moss by the little stream. Let's clean her off before we give her a bath," Ayla said. The girl just looked at her. The woman picked the baby up. She seemed surprised, but did not object. Ayla carried her to the runoff creek, knelt down near the edge, plucked a handful of moss growing on nearby stones, dipped it in the water, and, holding the baby over her arm, used it to wipe her bottom. With a second handful, she did it again. As she was examining her to make sure she was clean, the baby produced a warm stream. Ayla held her over the ground until she was done, washed her with moss again, then handed her to Lanoga.

"Bring the baby to the basin, Lanoga. It's time to get her cleaned up. Why don't you put Lorala in here," Ayla said, indicating the water-filled stone depression.

The girl gave her a puzzled look, but didn't move. Her brow wrinkled in thought, Ayla studied her. She didn't think the girl lacked intelligence, though she hardly spoke, but more that she didn't seem to understand what to do. Suddenly Ayla remembered a time, when she first lived with the Clan, that she hadn't known what to do, and it made her think. She had noticed that the girl seemed to respond best to direct statements.

"Lanoga, put the baby in this water," she said. It was not a conversational request, but a statement, almost a command.

Lanoga moved slowly toward the stone basin, started to lift the naked baby from her hip, but seemed a little reluctant to let go of her sister. Ayla picked Lorala up from the back, holding her under the arms so that she faced Lanoga, let her feet dangle, and slowly lowered her into a sitting position in the middle of the water in the stone depression.

The lukewarm water was a new sensation to the child and coaxed her to explore her surroundings. She reached into the water, then pulled her hand out and looked at it. She tested it again, this time accidentally splashing it a little, which caused her to look again, then she pulled her hand out and stuck her thumb in her mouth.

Well, she didn't cry, Ayla thought. It's a good start.

"Put your hand in this basket, Lanoga, and feel how slippery the water is because of the soaproot." The girl did as she was told. "Now, hold some in your hand and let's rub it on Lorala."

As both pairs of hands rubbed the slippery liquid with bits of root on the baby, she sat still, but with a little frown on her face. It was a new but not totally unpleasant sensation. "Now we need to wash her hair," Ayla said, thinking this might be more difficult. "We'll start by rubbing some soaproot on the back of her head. You can wash her ears and neck, too."

She watched the girl and noticed that she handled the baby with calm assurance and seemed to be getting more comfortable with the process of bathing her. Ayla stopped for a moment with a sudden realization. I wasn't much older than Lanoga when I had Durc! Perhaps I could count a year or two more, that's all. Of course, I had Iza to teach me how to take care of him, but I learned.

"Next, lay her on her back, support her with one hand, don't let her face get in the water, and wash the top of her hair with your other hand," Ayla told her. She helped Lanoga ease the baby back. Lorala resisted somewhat, but the girl's hands were sure now, and the child didn't object to the warmish water once she was in it, secure in her sister's arms. Ayla helped wash her hair, and then with her hands still soapy, she washed the baby's legs and bottom. They had been soaking in the water, which in itself was getting a bit slick.

"Now wash her face, very carefully, just using your hands and the water. Don't let anything get in her eyes. It won't hurt, but it may make her uncomfortable," Ayla said.

When they were through, they sat the baby up again. The woman pulled a very soft, pliable yellowish hide out of her pack, laid it out, lifted the baby out of the water, and wrapped her in it. She gave the baby to Lanoga. "Here she is, all clean and fresh." She noticed the girl rubbing the soft suede-leather of the drying blanket. "It is nice and soft, isn't it?"

"Yes," Lanoga said, looking up at the woman.

"That was given to me as a gift by some people I met on our Journey. They were called Sharamudoi, and they were known for making the skins of chamois soft like that. Chamois are animals that live in the mountains near their home. They are something like mountain goats, but they are smaller than ibex. Do you know if there are chamois around here, Lanoga?"

"Yes," the girl said. Ayla waited, smiling encouragingly. She had discovered that Lanoga responded to questions or direct commands, but didn't seem to know how to engage in conversation. She didn't know how to talk to people. Ayla kept smiling, waiting. Lanoga frowned, then finally said, "Some hunters brought one."

She can talk! She volunteered a statement, Ayla thought, feeling pleased. She just needed some encouragement. "You can keep that hide, if you want," she said.

Lanoga's face showed a range of expressions the woman didn't expect. First her eyes lit up, then showed doubt, and then fear. Then she frowned and shook her head. "No. Can't."

"Do you want the hide?"

The girl looked down. "Yes."

"Then why can't you keep it?"

"Can't keep it," the girl said, then hesitated. "Won't let me. Someone will take it."

Ayla began to understand. "All right, let's do it this way. You keep it for me. Then you will have it when you want to use it."

"Someone will take it," Lanoga repeated.

"Tell me if someone takes it, then I will go and take it back," Ayla said.

Lanoga started to smile, then frowned and shook her head again. "Someone will get mad."

Ayla nodded. "I understand. I will keep it, then, but remember, any time you want to use it, for Lorala or for you, you can come and borrow it. If someone wants to take it, tell them it belongs to me."

Lanoga took the soft hide off the baby and put her down on a patch of grass. She gave the hide to the woman. "She'll mess it," she said.

"That wouldn't be so bad. We'd just have to wash it. Let's put her on it. It's softer than the grass," Ayla said. She spread it out and laid the baby on it, noticing that it still retained a slight, but pleasant, smoky odor.

After a hide was cleaned and scraped, it was processed, often with the brains of the animal, then worked and stretched while it dried to a beautiful soft, napped finish. The nearly white hide was then tanned over a smoky fire. The wood and other fuel that was burned determined the color of the hide, usually tan with a brownish or yellowish hue, and, to a slight degree, the texture of the finished piece. The tanning wasn't done primarily for the color, however, it was done to maintain elasticity. While a hide might be soft before tanning, if it got wet and wasn't worked and stretched again, it would dry stiff and hard. But once the smoke coated the collagen fibers, a change took place that kept the leather soft even through a washing. Smoke tanning was what made animal hides truly usable.

Ayla noticed that Lorala's eyes were closing. Wolf had finished with his bone and had moved closer while they were washing the baby, too curious to stay away. Ayla had glanced up and seen him. Now she signaled him to come closer, and he ran toward them.

"It's our turn to bathe," Ayla said. She looked at the animal. "Wolf, watch Lorala, watch the baby." Her hand signals told him the same thing. It wasn't the first time the wolf had been left to guard a sleeping child. Lanoga had a slight frown of concern. "He'll stay right here and make sure nothing harms her, and he'll let us know if she wakes up. We will be right over there in that pond behind the stone dam. You will be able to see them. We're going to wash ourselves the same way we washed Lorala, but our water will be colder," Ayla added with a smile.

The woman picked up her haversack and the basket of soaking soaproot on their way to the pond. She took off her clothes and stepped in first. She demonstrated how to clean herself and helped Lanoga wash her hair, then took out two more pieces of the hide toweling and a long-toothed comb she had gotten from Marthona. After they dried, she worked the snarls and tangles out of Lanoga's hair and, with a second comb, did her own.

Then, from the bottom of the carrying pack, she took out a tunic. Though it had been used, it was not worn. It looked new and had a simple decoration of fringes and some beadwork. Lanoga looked at it with longing and then touched it softly. She smiled when Ayla told her to put it on.

"I want you to wear this when we go to see the women," Ayla said. Lanoga did not object, did not say a word, in fact, and did not hesitate to put it on. "We should go now. It is getting late. They are probably waiting for us."

They followed the path back up to the stone terrace and started toward the living section and Proleva's dwelling. Wolf fell back, and as Ayla turned to find him, she noticed he was looking back the way they had come. She followed his gaze and saw a woman and a man some distance behind. The woman weaved and stumbled as she walked. The man stayed beside her, but not very close, though one time he caught her when she almost fell down. When the woman turned toward Laramar's living space, Ayla realized she was Lanoga and Lorala's mother, Tremeda.

For a moment, Ayla wondered if she should try to bring her to the meeting with the women, but she decided against it. The women were likely to be much more sympathetic toward a pretty girl carrying a clean baby than they would be if a woman who had probably drunk too much barma was with them. Ayla started to go on, but her eye was caught by the man. He did not turn in with the woman, but kept on coming.

There was something about his shape and the way he moved that seemed familiar. He saw her and kept looking at her while he approached. As he drew closer, Ayla identified the man and, watching him, suddenly knew what she had recognized. The man was Brukeval, and though he might not like it, what Ayla saw was the sturdy shape and confident, effortless movement of a man of the Clan.

Brukeval smiled at her as though he was genuinely glad to see her, and she smiled back before she turned around and hurried Lanoga and the baby toward Proleva's dwelling. She glanced back for a moment and noticed that his smile had turned to a look of anger, as though she had done something to displease him, and she wondered what it was.

She saw me coming and then turned away, Brukeval thought. She couldn't even wait to exchange a greeting. I thought she would be different.

20

She's coming now," Proleva said. She had stepped out of her dwelling to look for Ayla and was glad to see her. She was afraid the women she had invited were getting bored and would soon be making excuses to leave, curious as they were. She had told them only that Ayla wanted to talk to them. The fact that the mate of the leader had asked them into her home was an added incentive. Proleva held the drape open and beckoned Ayla and the children in; Ayla signaled Wolf to go home, then urged Lanoga with the baby to go first.

There were nine women inside, making the dwelling feel rather small and cramped. Six of them held infants, all newborn or slightly older; three were in the late stages of pregnancy. In addition, two toddlers played on the floor. They all knew each other, more or less, some only in passing, though two were sisters, but conversation flowed easily. They compared babies and discussed the intimacies of birth, nursing, and learning to live with a new and often demanding individual in their households. They stopped talking and looked up at the new arrivals, showing various expressions of surprise.

"You all know who Ayla is, so I won't go through a long formal presentation," Proleva said. "You can introduce yourselves later."

"Who's the girl?" a woman said. She was older than most of the others, and one of the toddlers got up and walked to her at the sound of her voice.

"And the baby?" someone else asked.

Proleva looked at Ayla, who had felt rather overwhelmed by all the mothers when she first walked in, and it was obvious they were not shy, but their questions gave her a way to begin.

"This is Lanoga, Tremeda's oldest daughter. The baby is her youngest, Lorala," Ayla said, sure some of them should have known the children.

"Tremeda!" the older woman said. "Those are Tremeda's children?"

"Yes, they are. Don't you recognize them? They belong to the Ninth Cave," Ayla said. There was a murmur among the women as they spoke to each other under their breaths. Ayla caught comments both about her unusual accent and the children.

"Lanoga is her second child, Stelona," Proleva said. "You must remember when she was born, you helped. Lanoga, why don't you bring Lorala and sit down here, next to me." The women watched as the girl lifted the baby from her hip and walked toward the leader's mate, then sat down with Lorala on her lap. She would not look at the other women, but watched only Ayla, who smiled at her.

"Lanoga came to get Zelandoni because Bologan was hurt. He had been in a fight and had a head injury," Ayla began. "It was only then that we discovered a more serious problem. This baby can count only a few moons, and her mother's milk has dried up. Lanoga has been taking care of her, but she only knew how to feed her mashed-up cooked roots. I think you all know that no baby can live or grow if all she has to eat is cooked roots." Ayla noticed that the women hugged their infants to them more closely. It was a reaction almost anyone could interpret, and now they were beginning to get an idea of what Ayla was leading up to.

"I come from a place far from the land of the Zelandonii, but no matter where or with whom we are raised, there is one thing all people know: a baby needs milk. Among the people I grew up with, when a woman lost her milk, the other women helped to feed her baby." They all knew Ayla was talking about the ones that they called flatheads, considered to be animals by most Zelandonii. "Even those with older children, who didn't have much extra, would offer her breast to the baby now and then. Once, when a young woman lost her milk, another woman, who had more than enough for her own baby, treated the other baby almost as her own, and fed them as though they were two born together," Ayla said.

"What about a woman's own baby? What if she doesn't have enough milk left for her?" one of the pregnant women asked. She was quite young, and it was likely her first.

Ayla smiled at her, then looked at the other women and included them. "Isn't it wonderful how a mother's milk will increase with her need? The more she nurses, the more milk she makes."

"That's entirely correct, especially in the beginning," said a voice from the entrance that Ayla recognized. She turned and smiled at the tall, rotund woman coming in. "I'm sorry I couldn't get here sooner, Proleva. Laramar came to see Bologan and began questioning him. I didn't approve of his methods and went to get Joharran, but between them, they did finally get some answers out of that young man about what happened."

The women began an excited murmuring among themselves. They were very curious and hoped Zelandoni would say more, but knew it wouldn't do any good to ask. She would tell them only as much as she wished them to know. Proleva removed a tall watertight basket, half-full of tea, from a stone block off to the side and put a stuffed pad on it; it was Zelandoni's permanent seat in the leader's dwelling, put to other uses when she wasn't there. When the donier sat down, she was handed a cup of the beverage. She took it and smiled at everyone.

If the space had seemed crowded before, it felt absolutely crammed with the addition of the big woman, but no one seemed to mind. To be at a meeting with both the mate of the leader and the First Among Those Who Served The Mother made the women feel important. Ayla got a sense of their feeling, but she hadn't lived among them long enough to understand the full sense of the occasion for the women. She thought of Proleva and Zelandoni as a relative and a friend of Jondalar. The donier looked at Ayla, encouraging her to continue.

"Proleva told me that among the Zelandonii, all food is shared. I asked her if Zelandonii women would be willing to share their milk. She told me they often do with relatives and close friends, but Tremeda has no kin that anyone knows of, and definitely not a sister or cousin who is nursing," Ayla said, not even mentioning close friends. She beckoned to Lanoga, who got up and came slowly toward her, carrying the baby.

"Though a ten-year may be able to care for a baby, she can't nurse her. I have started to show Lanoga how to make other foods that a baby can eat besides mashed roots. She is quite capable, she just needs someone to teach her, but that's not enough." Ayla stopped and looked at each one of the women.

"Are you the one who cleaned them up, too?" Stelona, the older woman, asked.

"Yes. We went to The River and bathed, just as you do," Ayla said, then she added, "I have come to know that Tremeda is not always looked upon with favor, and perhaps with reason, but this baby is not Tremeda. She is just an infant who needs milk, at least some milk."

"I will tell you frankly," Stelona said. She had become, in effect, a spokeswoman for the group. "I wouldn't mind feeding her once in a while, but I do not want to go into that dwelling, and I'm not terribly interested in visiting with Tremeda."

Proleva turned aside to hide a smile. Ayla did it, she thought. She's got one commitment, the rest will come through, or at least most of them.

"You won't have to go to extra effort. I have already talked to Lanoga. She will carry her sister to you, we can work out a routine. With many to help, it won't be much drain on any one woman," Ayla said.

"Well, bring her here," the woman said. "Let's see if she still knows how to nurse. How long has it been?"

"Since sometime in spring," Ayla said. "Lanoga, take the baby to Stelona."

Lanoga avoided looking directly at the other women as she headed toward the older woman, who had given the baby sleeping in her lap to the pregnant woman beside her. With experienced ease, Stelona presented her breast to the baby. She nuzzled around for a while, seemingly eager, but no longer familiar with the position, but when Lorala opened her mouth, the woman put her nipple in. She mouthed it for a while, then finally began to suckle.

"Well, she took hold," Stelona said. There was a general sigh of relief and smiles all around.

"Thank you, Stelona," Ayla said.

"I suppose it's the least one can do. She does, after all, belong to the Ninth Cave," Stelona said.

"She didn't exactly shame them into it," Proleva said, "but she made them feel that if they didn't help, they would be worse than flatheads. Now, they can all feel virtuous about doing what is right."

Joharran got up on an elbow and looked at his mate. "Would you feed Tremeda's baby?" he asked.

Proleva rolled onto her side and pulled a cover up over her shoulder. "Of course I would," she said, "if someone asked, but I admit, I might not have thought of working out a routine for everyone to share the task, and I'm ashamed that I didn't know that Tremeda had gone dry. Ayla said Lanoga was capable, she just needs someone to teach her. Ayla's right, the girl is capable. She kept that baby going, and she is more mother to the rest of those children than their mother, but a girl who can count only ten years should not have to be mother to that brood. She hasn't even had her First Rites yet. The best thing would be if someone would adopt that baby. And maybe some of the other young ones, too," Proleva said.

"Maybe you can find someone who'll take them at the Summer Meeting," Joharran said.

"I thought I would try, but I don't think Tremeda is through having babies. The Mother tends to give more to those women who have had children, but She usually waits until a woman is through nursing one before giving her another. Now that she's not nursing, Zelandoni says Tremeda will probably be pregnant again within a year."

"Speaking of pregnant, how are you feeling?" Joharran asked, smiling at her with love and a look of delight.

"Good," she said. "I seem to be past the sickness, and I won't be too big during the heat of summer. I think I will start telling people. Ayla already guessed."

"I can't see any sign yet, except you're more beautiful," he said, "if that's possible."

Proleva smiled warmly at her mate. "Ayla apologized for mentioning it before I was ready to announce it—it was just a slip. She said she knew the signs because she's a medicine woman, which is what she sometimes calls a healer. She does seem to be a healer, but it's hard to believe she could have learned so much from . . ."

"I know," Joharran said. "Could the ones who raised her really be the same as the ones around here? If they are, it worries me. They have not been treated well, I wonder why they haven't retaliated? And what would happen if they should decide to strike back someday?"

"I don't think it's something we have to worry about now," Proleva said, "and I'm sure we'll learn more about them as we get to know Ayla better." She paused, turning her head toward Jaradal's sleeping place, and listened. She had heard a sound, but he was quiet now. Probably a dream, she thought, and turned back to her mate. "You know, they want to make her a Zelandonii woman before we leave, so it will be done before she and Jondalar are mated."

"Yes, I know. Don't you think it's a little too soon? It seems as though we've known her much longer than we have, but it wasn't that long ago that they arrived," Joharran said. "I don't usually mind doing what my mother proposes. She doesn't make suggestions often, for all that she's still a powerful woman, and when she does, it's generally something I hadn't thought of, but makes sense. When the leadership was turned over to me, I wondered if she could really give it up, but she wanted me to take it as much as the rest, and she has always been very careful not to interfere. But I can't see a good reason to acknowledge Ayla so quickly. She'll be considered one of us when she mates Jondalar anyway."

"But not in her own right, only as the mate of Jondalar," Proleva said. "Your mother is concerned about standing, Joharran. Remember Shevonar's burial? As an outsider, Ayla should have walked at the back, but Jondalar insisted he would walk with her, wherever she walked. Your mother did not want her son walking behind Laramar. It would give the impression that the woman he was mating had little status. Then Zelandoni said she belonged with the healers, that's why she was up front, but Laramar didn't like it and he embarrassed Marthona."

"I didn't know that," Joharran said.

"The problem is we don't know how to judge Ayla's rank," Proleva said. "Apparently she was adopted by high-ranking Mamutoi, but how much do we know about them? It's not like they're Lanzadonii, or even Losadunai. I never even heard of them before, though some people claim they have. And she was raised by flatheads! What kind of position does that give her? If a high rank isn't recognized for her, it could bring down Jondalar's status and that would affect all our 'names and ties,' Marthona's, yours, mine, all his kin."

"I hadn't thought of that," Joharran said.

"Zelandoni is pushing to get her recognized, too. She is treating Ayla as though she is zelandonia, and an equal. I'm not sure what her reasons are, but she also seems determined to have her seen as a woman of high standing." Proleva turned her head again in the direction of her son at a sound he was making. It was an automatic reaction that she hardly noticed. He must be having lively dreams, she thought.

Joharran was considering her comments, feeling rather pleased that his woman was both accomplished and astute. She was a real help to him, and he valued her talents. Just now it was her talent to clarify his mother's motivations that he appreciated. He was a good listener and communicator in his own way, that was one reason why he was a skillful leader, but he didn't have her innate sense of the repercussions and innuendos of a situation.

"Will it be enough to have just us declaring acceptance?" Marthona asked, leaning forward.

"Joharran is leader, you are former leader and adviser, Willamar is Trade Master . . ."

"And you are First," Marthona said, "but in spite of rank, we're all kin, except you, Zelandoni, and everybody knows that you are a friend."

"Who would object?"

"Laramar would." Marthona was still vexed and somewhat embarrassed that Laramar had caught her in a breach of etiquette, and her face showed her irritation. "He'd make an issue of it, just to make trouble. He did it at the burial," she said.

"I wasn't aware of that. What did he do?" the large woman said. The two women were in her dwelling, drinking tea and chatting quietly. The donier was glad her latest patient had finally gone home, giving her back her privacy, where she could meditate in solitude and speak privately.

"He let me know that Ayla should have been at the end of the procession."

"But she is a healer and belonged with the zelandonia," the donier said.

"She may be a healer, but she is not zelandonia, whether she belongs there or not, and he knows it."

"But what can he do?"

"He can bring it up, he is a member of the Ninth Cave. There may be others who feel as he does but would hesitate to mention it. If he does, those others may go along with him. I think we should get more people to agree to accept her," Marthona said with a note of finality.

"You may be right. Whom do you suggest?" Zelandoni said. She took a sip of tea and frowned in thought.

"Stelona and her family might be a good possibility," the former leader said. "According to Proleva, she was the first to agree to feeding Tremeda's baby. She's respected, well liked, and not related."

"Who will ask her?"

"Joharran can, or perhaps I should. Woman to woman. What do you think?" Marthona said.

Zelandoni put her cup down and her frown deepened. "I think you should talk to her first, feel her out," she said. "Then, if she seems agreeable, Joharran should ask her, but as a member of the family, not as leader. That way, it won't be as though he is making an official request, and bringing the pressure of his leadership to it. It will be more that he is asking a favor. . . ."

"Which he would be," Marthona said.

"Of course. But just the fact that it's the leader who is making the request brings the force of his position to it. We all know his rank. It doesn't need to be mentioned. And she might consider it a compliment that he would ask her. How well do you know her?" the First said.

"I know her, of course. Stelona is from a reliable family, but we haven't had occasion to associate on a personal level. Proleva knows her better. She's the one who asked her to come when Ayla wanted to talk about Tremeda's baby. I do know she has been very cooperative whenever there are gatherings to organize, or food to be prepared, and I always see her helping out when there's work to be done," the older woman said.

"Then you should include Proleva, and take her with you when you go to see Stelona," Zelandoni said. "Find out what she thinks would be the best way to approach her. If she likes to cooperate, and is willing to help, you might appeal to that side of her."

The two women were silent for a time, sipping their tea and thinking. Then Marthona asked, "Do you want to keep the acceptance ceremony simple or make it more dramatic?"

Zelandoni looked at her and realized the woman had a reason for raising the question. "Why do you ask?" she said.

"Ayla showed me something that I think could make quite an impact, if it was handled properly," Marthona said.

"What did she show you?"

"Have you ever seen her make fire?"

The large woman hesitated only a moment, then sat back and smiled. "Only the time she started one to get some water boiling for a calming drink for Willamar, when he came home and found out about Thonolan. She did say she was going to show me how she did it so fast, but I admit, it slipped my mind, what with the burial, and planning for the Summer Meeting, and everything else that's been going on."

"The fire was out when we got home one night, and she and Jondalar showed us. Willamar, Folara, and I have been making it her way ever since. It requires something she calls a firestone, and apparently they have found some nearby. I don't know how many, but enough to share with some of the others," Marthona said. "Why don't you come over this evening? I know they planned to show you, they could do it then. In fact, why don't you share a meal with us? I still have a little of that last batch of wine left."

"I'd enjoy that. Yes, I will come."

"As usual, Marthona, that was very good," Zelandoni said, putting an empty cup down beside a nearly clean bowl. They were sitting on cushions and stuffed pads around the low table. Jondalar had been glancing and smiling at everyone all through the meal, as though he were anticipating something especially delicious. The donier admitted to herself that it did make her curious, though she had no intention of showing it.

She had lingered over her meal, regaling them with stories and anecdotes, encouraging Jondalar and Ayla to talk about their Journey, and inducing Willamar to tell of his travel adventures. It had been a thoroughly enjoyable evening for everyone, except that Folara looked as if she would burst with anticipation, and Jondalar was so smug and pleased with himself, it made the woman want to smile.

Willamar and Marthona were more accustomed to waiting until the time was right; it was a tactic often used in trade negotiations and dealings with other Caves. Ayla also seemed content to wait, but it was hard for the One Who Was First to fathom her real feelings. She didn't know the foreign woman well enough yet, she was an enigma, but that made her intriguing.

"If you are finished, we'd like you to move closer to the hearth," Jondalar said with an eager smile.

The large woman hoisted herself up from the stack of pads upon which she was sitting and walked toward the cooking hearth. Jondalar rushed to pick up the pads and put them down near the fireplace, but Zelandoni remained standing.

"You might want to sit, Zelandoni," Jondalar said. "We're going to be putting all the fires out, and it will be as dark as a cave in here."

"If you prefer," she said, seating herself on the stack of pads.

Marthona and Willamar took their cushions with them and also sat while the younger people collected all the oil lamps and placed them around the hearth, including, Zelandoni was a little surprised to notice, the one from in front of the donii in the niche. Just bringing them all together made the rest of the dwelling much darker.

"Is everyone ready?" Jondalar said, and when the three who were waiting nodded, the others began to snuff out the small flames. No one spoke as each one went out. The shadows deepened until the encroaching darkness overtook every glimmer of light and permeated the entire space, creating an eerie sense of close, impenetrable thickness in the intangible air. It was as dark as a cave, but in the dwelling, which moments before had been filled with a warm golden glow, the effect was eerie, unnerving, and, curiously, more frightening than in the cold deeps. Darkness was expected there. It wasn't that fires did not go out inside a dwelling, but that all the illumination was not purposely put out. It felt as if they were tempting chance. The mystic impact was not lost on the First.

But as time passed and eyes adjusted to the darkness, Zelandoni noticed that the deep black was slightly less. She still could not see the shape of her own hand in front of her eyes, but above the roofless dwelling, on the underside of the overhanging shelf, the light from other fires was faintly reflected into neighboring spaces. It wasn't much, but it was not quite as dark as a cave. She would have to remember that, she thought.

Her thoughts were distracted by a light nearby that was startling to eyes grown accustomed to the profound dark. It held for a long moment, highlighting Ayla's face, then went out, but a moment later a small flame had started and was soon blazing.

"How did you do that?" she said.

"Do what?" Jondalar said, grinning widely.

"Start that fire so fast." Zelandoni could see that everyone was smiling now.

"It's the firestone!" Jondalar said, and held one out to show her. "When you strike it with flint, it makes a long-lasting, very hot spark, and with good dry tinder, if you aim it just right, it will catch and make a flame. Here, let me show you how it works."

He made up a tinder bundle with fireweed fuzz and some shaved pieces of wood held in dried grass. The First got up from her padded seat and sat down on the floor near the fireplace. She preferred to sit on raised seats or chairs because it was easier to get up, but that didn't mean she couldn't get down if she wanted to or felt it was important enough. And this fire-making trick was. Jondalar demonstrated, then gave the stones to her. She tried it a few times with no success, frowning deeper with each attempt.

"You'll get the technique," Marthona encouraged. "Ayla, why don't you show her."

Ayla took the flint and iron pyrite, set the fire bundle just so, and carefully showed the woman the position of her hands. Then she struck off a spark that landed on the tinder. It sent up a thin wisp of smoke, which she crushed out; then she gave the stones back to Zelandoni.

The woman held them in front of her and started to strike, but Ayla stopped her and changed the position of her hands. She tried again. This time she watched a hot spark land close to the tinder, and changed her own hand position slightly, and struck. This time the spark found the tinder. She knew what to do then. She picked up the bundle, held it close to her face, and blew. The tiny start turned bright red. The second breath of air turned the fireweed down into a small flame, and the third caught the shaved wood on fire. The donier put it down and started feeding it small pieces of wood and then larger ones. Then she sat back and smiled, pleased with her accomplishment.

Everyone else was smiling, too, and offering comments of approval all at once. "You caught on fast," Folara said. "I knew you could do it," Jondalar said. "I told you, it's just a matter of technique," Marthona said. "Well done!" Willamar said. "Now, try it again," Ayla said. "Yes, that's a good idea," Marthona said.

The One Who Was First Among Those Who Served The Mother dutifully did as she was directed. She made fire the second time, but then had trouble the third time until Ayla showed her that she wasn't drawing a good spark and how to strike the stones at a different angle. After the third successful try, she stopped, got up, and sat down again on her padded seat and looked at Ayla.

"I will work on this at home," she said. "The first time I do it in public, I want to be as sure as you. But tell me, where did you learn to do this?"

Ayla told how she had absentmindedly picked up a stone that was on the rocky beach of the valley where she lived, rather than the hammerstone she had been using to make a new tool to replace one that had broken. Since her fire had gone out, the hot spark and bit of smoke gave her the idea to try to relight her fire that way. To her surprise, it worked.

"And is it true there are some of those firestones around here?" the donier asked.

"Yes," Jondalar answered, full of excitement. "We collected all that we could find from her valley, and hoped to find more on our Journey. We never did, but Ayla stopped to get a drink at that small stream in Wood Valley and found some there. Not many, but where there are some, there must be more."

"That seems logical. I hope you are right," Zelandoni said.

"They would be exceptional for trading," Willamar said.

Zelandoni frowned slightly. She had been thinking more of the dramatic aspects for ceremonies, but that would require that they remain inaccessible to everyone except the zelandonia, and it was already too late for that. "You are probably right, Trade Master, but perhaps not right away," she said. "I would rather the knowledge of these stones be kept secret, for the time being."

"Why?" Ayla said.

"They could be useful for certain ceremonies," Zelandoni said.

Suddenly Ayla remembered the time Talut held a meeting to present the idea of the Mamutoi adopting her. To the surprise of both Talut and Tulie, the brother-sister headman and headwoman of the Lion Camp, since they had both sponsored her, one man had objected. It was only when they had made an impromptu, but dramatic, demonstration of fire-making with a firestone, and had promised to give him one, that Frebec relented.

"I suppose they could," she said.

"But when can I show my friends?" Folara implored. "Mother made me promise not to tell anyone yet, but I've been yearning to show them."

"Your mother was wise," Zelandoni said. "I promise you'll have a chance to show them, but not yet. This is too important and needs to be presented properly. It really would be better if you wait. Will you?"

"Of course, if you want me to, Zelandoni," Folara said.

"It seems like there have been more feasts and ceremonies and gathers in the few days since they came than in all of last winter," Solaban said.

"Proleva asked me to help, and you know I won't refuse her," Ramara said, "any more than you'd refuse Joharran. Jaradal always plays with Robenan anyway, I don't mind watching him."

"We'll be leaving for the Summer Meeting in a day or so, why can't it wait until we get there?" her mate complained. He had an array of objects spread out on the floor of their dwelling and was trying to decide what to take with him. He did not relish the job. It was the part of going to the Summer Meeting that he always put off until the last moment, and now that he'd finally gotten into it, he wanted to finish without children playing around and disturbing things.

"I think it has to do with their mating," Ramara said.

She thought about her own Matrimonial and glanced at her darkhaired mate. His hair was probably the darkest of anyone of the Ninth Cave, and when she met him, she liked the contrast he made with her own pale blond coloring. Solaban's hair was almost black, though his eyes were blue, and his skin was so pale that he often sunburned, especially early in the summer season. She also thought he was the most handsome of all the men of the Cave, even compared to Jondalar. She understood the appeal of the tall blond man with the extraordinary blue eyes, and when she was younger, like most women, she had been infatuated with him. But she learned what love was when she met Solaban. Jondalar didn't seem quite so attractive since his return, perhaps because he gave all his attention to Ayla. Besides, she rather liked the woman.

"Why can't they get mated just like everyone else?" Solaban said, obviously feeling grouchy.

"Well, they aren't just like everyone else. Jondalar just returned from a Journey that was so long, no one expected him to come back, and Ayla isn't even Zelandonii. But she really wants to be. At least that's what I heard," Ramara said.

"When she mates him, she'll be the same as Zelandonii anyway," Solaban said. "Why do they need to bother with an acceptance ceremony for her?"

"It's not the same. She wouldn't be Zelandonii. She'd be 'Ayla of the Mamutoi, mated to Jondalar of the Zelandonii.' Whenever she was introduced, everyone would know she was a foreigner," she said.

"She just has to open her mouth and everyone knows it anyway," he said. "Making her Zelandonii isn't going to change that."

"Yes, it will. She might talk like a stranger, but when people meet her, they would know that she isn't a foreigner anymore," Ramara said.

Ramara looked at the tools, weapons, and clothing covering every flat surface. She knew her mate and understood the real reason for his irritability, and it had nothing to do with Ayla or Jondalar. She smiled to herself and said, "If it wasn't raining out, I'd take the boys to Wood River Valley to watch the horses. All the children like to do that. They don't usually get a chance to see animals up close."

Solaban's frown deepened. "That means they'll have to stay here, I suppose."

Ramara flashed a teasing grin. "No, I don't think so. I thought I'd go to the other end of the shelter where everyone is cooking and getting things prepared, and help the women who are watching the children so their mothers can work. The boys can play with the others who are their age. When Proleva asked me to watch Jaradal, she meant she wanted me to be particularly aware of him. All the mothers do that. The watchers have to know who they are responsible for, especially when children get to be about Robenan's age. They get more independent and sometimes try to go off on their own," Ramara said, watching her mate's frown ease. "But you should get done before the ceremony. I may have to bring the boys here afterward."

Solaban looked around at the neatly organized assortment of his personal things, and the rows of antler, bone, and ivory trimmed to about the same size, then shook his head. He still didn't know precisely what to take with him, but it was this way every year. "I will," he said, "as soon as I get everything set out so I can see what I want to take to the Summer Meeting for myself, and what I want to take to trade." Besides being one of Joharran's close aides, Solaban was a maker of handles, especially knife handles.

"I think most everyone is here," Proleva said, "and it's stopped raining."

Joharran nodded, went out from under the overhang that had protected them from the cloudburst, and jumped up on the platform stone at the far end of the shelter. He looked at the people starting to gather around, then smiled at Ayla.

Ayla smiled back, but she was feeling nervous. She glanced up at Jondalar, who was looking at the crowd forming around the large raised stone.

"Weren't we here not very long ago?" Joharran said with an ironic smile. "When I first introduced her to you, we didn't know much about Ayla, except that she had traveled here with my brother Jondalar, and had an unusual way with animals. We have learned much more about Ayla of the Mamutoi in the short time that she's been here.

"I think we all suspected that Jondalar planned to mate the woman he brought home with him, and we were right. They will join at the First Matrimonial of the Summer Meeting. Once they are mated, they will live with us at the Ninth Cave, and I for one welcome them."

There were several comments of agreement from the assembly.

"But Ayla is not a Zelandonii. Whenever a Zelandonii mates someone who is not one of us, there are usually negotiations and other customs that need to be worked out between us and the other people. In Ayla's case, however, the Mamutoi live so far away, we'd have to travel a year just to meet her people, and to be honest, I'm getting too old to make such a long Journey."

Laughter and comments greeted his remark. "Getting long in the tooth, Joharran?" a young man called out.

"Wait until you've lived as many years as I have. Then you'll know what old is," a white-haired man said.

When things settled down, Joharran continued. "Once they are mated, most people will think of her as Ayla of the Ninth Cave of the Zelandonii, but Jondalar suggested that the Ninth Cave accept her as Zelandonii before the Matrimonial. In effect, he has asked that we adopt her. It would make the Matrimonial ceremonies easier and less confusing, and we wouldn't have to get special dispensations from everyone at the Summer Meeting if we do it before we go."

"What does she want?" a woman asked.

Everyone turned to look at her. Ayla swallowed hard, and then, concentrating on saying the words as correctly as she could, she said, "More than anything in this world, I want to be a Zelandonii woman, and mated to Jondalar."

Though she tried, she couldn't prevent the unusual quality of the way she spoke, and no one who heard her could mistake her foreign origins; but the simple statement, spoken with such sincere conviction, won most people over.

"She did travel a long way to get here." "She'll be the same as Zelandonii anyway."

"But what is her status?" Laramar asked.

"She will have the same status as Jondalar," Marthona said. She had expected him to make trouble, and this time she was ready.

"Jondalar has a high position in the Ninth Cave because you are his mother, but we don't know anything about her, except that she was raised by flatheads," Laramar said loudly.

"She was also adopted by the highest-ranked Mamut, which is what they call a Zelandoni. She would have been adopted by the leader if the Mamut hadn't spoken for her," Marthona said.

"Why does there always seem to be one who objects?" Ayla said to Jondalar in Mamutoi. "Are we going to have to make fire with a firestone and then give him one to persuade him, like Frebec at the Lion Camp?"

"Frebec turned out to be a good man; somehow I don't think Laramar will," Jondalar murmured back.

"That's what she says. How do we know?" Laramar said, continuing his loud objections.

"Because my son was there, and he says the same thing," Marthona replied. "The leader, Joharran, doesn't doubt them."

"Joharran is family. Of course Jondalar's brother isn't going to doubt her. She will be part of your family, and you all want her to have a high status," Laramar said.

"I don't know why you are objecting, Laramar," a voice from another quarter spoke out. People turned and were surprised to see that it was Stelona. "If it wasn't for Ayla, your mate's youngest daughter would probably have starved to death. You didn't tell us that Tremeda got sick and lost her milk, or that Lanoga was trying to keep her alive with mashed-up roots. Ayla did. I wonder if you even knew. Zelandonii don't let Zelandonii starve. Several of us mothers are feeding the baby, and Lorala is already getting stronger. I would be more than willing to sponsor Ayla, if she needs one. She is a woman the Zelandonii would be proud to claim."

Several other women spoke up, defending Ayla, all nursing mothers holding their infants. The story of Ayla and Tremeda's baby had started to spread, but not everyone knew, or knew the entire story. Most people understood what kind of "sickness" Tremeda had, but in any case her milk was gone, and they were glad the baby was being fed.

"Do you have any more objections, Laramar?" Joharran said. The man shook his head and backed away. "Does anyone else have any objections to accepting Ayla into the Ninth Cave of the Zelandonii?" There was a background murmur, but no one spoke up. He reached down and gave Ayla a hand to help her up onto the level stone, then they turned to face the people. "Since several people are willing to sponsor her, and there are no objections, let me introduce Ayla of the Ninth Cave of the Zelandonii, formerly a Member of the Lion Camp of the Mamutoi, Daughter of the Mammoth Hearth, Chosen by the Spirit of the Cave Lion, Protected by the Cave Bear, Friend of the horses, Whinney and Racer, and the four-legged hunter, Wolf." He had spoken to Jondalar to make sure he got her names and ties right, and memorized them. "And soon to be mated to Jondalar," he added. "Now, let's go eat!"

They both got down from the Speaking Stone, and as they made their way toward the food, they were stopped by people introducing themselves again, commenting on Tremeda's baby, and in general welcoming her.

But one person had no wish to welcome her. Laramar was not a man who was easily embarrassed, but he had been thoroughly chastened and was not happy about it. Before Laramar left the group, he glared at Ayla with a look so full of anger, it left her chilled. He didn't know Zelandoni had seen it, too. When they reached the place where the food was being served, they noticed that Laramar's barma was being offered, but the one who was pouring it was his mate's oldest son, Bologan.

As people were beginning to eat, it started raining again. They found places beneath the deep overhanging shelf to enjoy their food, some sitting on the ground, others on logs or blocks of stone that had been brought in at various times and left for future use. Zelandoni caught up with Ayla as she was walking toward Jondalar's family.

"I'm afraid you have an enemy in Laramar," she said.

"I'm sorry about that," Ayla said. "I didn't mean to cause problems for him."

"You didn't cause his problems. He was trying to cause you problems, or rather trying to humiliate Marthona and her family, and brought problems on himself instead. But now, I think he will blame you," Zelandoni said.

"Why should he want to make trouble for Marthona?"

"Because he is the lowest-ranked member of the Ninth Cave and she and Joharran are the highest, and he managed to catch her in a slight mistake the other day. As you may already know, that is hard to do. I think it may have given him a temporary illusion of triumph, and he liked it so well, he thought he'd try it again," the donier said.

Ayla's frown deepened as Zelandoni explained. "It may not be just Marthona he wanted to get the better of," Ayla said. "I think I made a mistake the other day, too."

"What do you mean?"

"The day I went there to show Lanoga how to make food for the baby and give her a bath, and clean herself, Laramar came home. I'm sure he didn't know the baby had no milk, he didn't even know about Bologan's injuries. It made me angry; I don't like him. Wolf was with me, and I know when Laramar saw him, he got scared. He tried to cover up his fear, and I found myself feeling like a wolf pack leader wanting to put a lower-ranked wolf in his place. I knew I shouldn't have done it. It just gave him bad feelings toward me," Ayla said.

"Do leaders of wolf packs really put lower-ranked wolves in their place?" Zelandoni said. "How do you know?"

"I learned to hunt meat-eaters before I learned to hunt meat," Ayla said. "I'd spend whole days watching them. That may be why Wolf can live with people. Their ways are not so different from ours."

"How amazing!" Zelandoni said. "And, I'm afraid you're right. You created some bad feelings, but it wasn't entirely your fault. At the burial, you were among the highest ranked of the Ninth Cave, which is where I thought you belonged; Marthona and I agreed. He wanted you in the place he thought you belonged, which was behind him. Traditionally, he was correct.

"At a burial, all the members of a Cave should go before anyone who is visiting. But you are not exactly a visitor. First you were with the zelandonia, because you are a healer, and they always go first. Then you were with Jondalar and his family, which is also where you belong, as everybody agreed today. But at the burial, he mentioned it to Marthona and caught her off guard. That's why he thought he'd triumphed. Then, without even knowing it, you put him in his place. He thought he could get back at both of you through Marthona, but he seriously underestimated her."

"There you are," Jondalar said. "We were just talking about Laramar."

"So were we," Ayla said, but she doubted that their conversation had brought out the same insights. Partly because of her own doing, and partly because of circumstances she wasn't aware of, she had created an enemy. Another one, she realized. She hadn't wanted to cause bad feelings in any of Jondalar's people, but in the short time she had been there, she had made two people angry at her. Marona hated her, too. She realized she hadn't seen the woman for some time and wondered where she was.

21

The people of the Ninth Cave had been making preparations for their annual trek to the Summer Meeting of the Zelandonii since they returned from the last one, but as the time of their departure drew near, activities and anticipation became more intense. There were final decisions about what to take with them and what to leave behind, but it was the process of closing down their dwellings for the summer that always made them aware that they were leaving and would not be back until cold winds blew.

A few people would stay behind for one reason or another: temporary or more serious illness, to finish a project, to wait for someone. Others would return occasionally to their winter home, but most would be gone all summer. Some people would stay close to the place that had been chosen for the Summer Meeting, but many would travel to different places for diverse reasons throughout the warm season.

There would be hunting trips, harvesting treks, visits to relatives, sojourns to group meetings of other Zelandonii, and travels to neighboring peoples. Some young people would venture farther afield and go on Journeys. Jondalar's return with new discoveries and inventions, a beautiful and exotic woman with rare talents, and exciting stories would encourage some of those who had been thinking about it to decide to go on a Journey of their own, and some mothers who knew that his brother had died far away would be unhappy that Jondalar had returned and caused such excitement.

The evening before they planned to leave, the entire Ninth Cave was eager and restless. When Ayla thought about the Summer Meeting, where she and Jondalar would be mated, she could hardly believe it was really true. Sometimes she would wake up and be almost afraid to open her eyes for fear that it might be just a wonderful dream and she would find herself back in the small cave in her lonely valley. She thought often of Iza, wishing that somehow the woman she regarded as her mother could know that she would soon have a mate, and that she had finally found her people, at least the ones she chose to be her people.

Ayla had long ago accepted the fact that she would never know the people to whom she was born, or even who they were, and realized that it didn't matter. When she was living with the Clan, she had wanted to be one of them, a woman of the Clan, which clan was not important. But when she finally understood that she was not Clan, and never would be, then the only distinction that mattered was that she was one of the Others, in her mind kin to all of the Others. She had been happy to be Mamutoi, the people who had adopted her, and she would have been content to be Sharamudoi, the people who had asked Jondalar and her to stay and live with them. She wanted to be Zelandonii only because they were Jondalar's people, not because they were any better than, or even very different from, any of the Others.

During the long winter, when most people stayed close to the Ninth Cave, many of them spent time making gifts they would be giving to people when they saw them again at the next Summer Meeting. When she heard people talking about gifts, Ayla decided to make some, too. Though she'd had only a short time to work on them, she made small tokens that she planned to give to those people who had been especially kind to her, and who she knew would be giving gifts to her and Jondalar for their Matrimonial. She had a surprise for Jondalar, too. She had brought it with her all the way from the Summer Meeting of the Mamutoi. It was the one thing she insisted on taking with her through all the adversities and hardships of their Journey.

Jondalar was planning a surprise of his own. He had discussed with Joharran the best place to establish a home for Ayla and himself within the abri of the Ninth Cave of the Zelandonii, and he wanted it to be ready for Ayla when they returned in the fall. To that end, he had been making arrangements. He talked with the fabricators of outside wall panels, and the people who were best at the construction of the lower stone walls, with those who were skilled at stone paving, and the ones who made interior room division panels, with the specialists in making all the components required to erect a dwelling.

Planning their future home involved some complicated trading and bargaining. First, Jondalar agreed to trade some good stone knives for fresh hides from several people, mostly from the recent megaceros and bison hunts. The blades of the knives would be knapped by him, but they would be hafted in finely made handles fabricated by Solaban, whose work Jondalar especially admired. In return for the handles, Jondalar had agreed to produce several burins—chisel-like flint carving tools—to the handle-maker's specific requirements. Long talks between the two men that included drawings made with charcoal on birch bark had created an understanding of what was wanted.

Some of the skins Jondalar acquired would be used to make the rawhide panels Jondalar needed for his dwelling, and some would compensate Shevola, the panel-maker, for her time and effort. He also promised to make her a couple of special leather-cutting knives, some hide-scrapers, and some woodcutting tools.

He made similar arrangements with Zelandoni's acolyte, the artist Jonokol, to paint the panels, which would incorporate Jonokol's own ideas of design and composition using basic symbols and animals that all Zelandonii were generally expected to use, along with some that Jondalar wanted. Jonokol also wanted some special tools. He had some ideas for sculpturing limestone in high relief, but he lacked the flint-knapping skill to convert the ideas he envisioned for a special kind of burin with a beaked nose into the tool he wanted. Burins and specialized flint tools were difficult to make in any case. It took a very experienced and skilled flint-knapper to make them well.

Once the materials and various components were ready, it would take relatively little time to actually construct the dwelling. Jondalar had already persuaded several of his relatives and friends to make a trek back with him to the Ninth Cave from the Summer Meeting, along with the skilled workers—but without Ayla—to help him build it. He smiled to himself every time he imagined how pleased she would be when they returned in the fall to find she had a home of her own.

Though it took several long afternoons for Jondalar to barter his skill at making flint tools with all the other people who could make the elements that would be needed for him to construct a place to live, the bargaining was often enjoyable. It usually started with pleasantries, then good-natured arguments that sometimes sounded like heated battles or insulting comments, but usually concluded in laughter over a cup of tea, or barma, or wine, or even a meal. Jondalar was careful to make sure Ayla was not present when he was bargaining for the dwelling, but that did not mean she wasn't exposed to the practice.

The first time she heard people bargaining, she didn't understand the nature of the loud, colorfully vilifying exchange. It was between Proleva and Salova, Rushemar's mate, who was a maker of baskets. Ayla thought they were really angry, and she hurried to get Jondalar, hoping he could do something to stop it.

"You say Proleva and Salova are having a terrible disagreement? What are they saying?" Jondalar asked.

"Proleva said Salova's baskets were ugly and poorly made, but it's not true. Her baskets are beautiful, and Proleva must think so, too. I've seen several in her dwelling. Why would she say such a thing to her?" Ayla said. "Can't you do something to stop them from fighting like that?"

Jondalar understood her genuine concern, but he was having trouble suppressing a smile. Finally he could not hold back any longer and laughed out loud. "Ayla, Ayla. They are not fighting, they are enjoying themselves. Proleva wants some of Salova's baskets, and that's the way it's done. They will come to an agreement, and both will be happy. It's called bargaining, and I can't stop it. If I could, they would feel cheated of their fun. Why don't you go back and watch them? You'll see. Before long, they will be smiling, each thinking she has made a good trade."

"Are you sure, Jondalar? They seem so angry," Ayla said. She could hardly believe Proleva just wanted some of Salova's baskets and that this was the way they went about it.

She went back and found a place to sit nearby to watch and listen. If this was the way things were done among Jondalar's people, she wanted to be able to bargain, too. After a few moments, she noticed that several other people were watching the confrontation, smiling and nodding to each other. She soon realized the two women were not really angry, but she doubted that she would ever be able to say something was so dreadful if she really believed it was beautiful. She shook her head in wonderment. What a strange way to behave!

When the bargaining was concluded, she went to find Jondalar. "Why do people enjoy saying such terrible things when they don't mean them? I'm not sure if I'll ever learn to 'bargain' like that."

"Ayla, both Proleva and Salova knew that each didn't really mean what the other said. They were playing a game with each other. As long as both of them know it's a game, there is no harm," Jondalar said.

Ayla thought about it. There is more to it than it seems, she thought, but she couldn't quite think what it was.

The night before they were to leave, after bundles had been packed, the tent checked and repaired, and traveling gear readied, everyone in Marthona's home was so excited, no one wanted to go to bed. Proleva stopped by with Jaradal to see if any help was needed. Marthona invited them to come in and sit for a while, and Ayla volunteered to make a nice tea. After a second tapping at the entrance, Folara admitted Joharran and Zelandoni. They had arrived together from different directions, both with offers and questions, but actually wanting to visit and talk. Ayla added more water and extra herbs to the tea.

"Did the traveling tent need repairs?" Proleva asked.

"Not many," Marthona said. "Ayla helped Folara with it. They used Ayla's new thread-puller."

The traveling tents that would be set up each evening were large enough to accommodate several people, and Marthona's family tent would be shared by all of them: Marthona, Willamar, and Folara; Joharran, Proleva, and Jaradal; and Jondalar and Ayla. Zelandoni would be traveling with them as well, Ayla was pleased to learn. She seemed like a member of the family, like an aunt without a mate. The tent would have one other occupant, the four-legged hunter Wolf, and the two horses would be nearby.

"Did you have any trouble getting poles?" Joharran asked.

"I broke an axe cutting them down," Willamar said.

"Could you resharpen it?" Joharran asked. Though tall straight trees had been cut for tent poles, they would still need wood for fires along the way and after they arrived at the site of the Summer Meeting, and axes to cut trees down, though unpolished stone axes had their own way of being used.

"It shattered. I couldn't sharpen it, I couldn't even get a blade out of it," Willamar said.

"It was a bad piece of flint," Jondalar said. "Full of small inclusions."

"Jondalar made a new axe, and resharpened the others," Willamar said. "It's good to have him back."

"Except now we're going to have to watch out for stray chips of flint again," Marthona said. Ayla noticed she was smiling and understood that she wasn't really complaining. She was glad he was home, too. "He did clean up the flakes he knocked off to sharpen the axes.

Not like when he was a boy. I didn't see a single sharp sliver of stone. Of course, I don't see as well anymore."

"The tea is ready," Ayla said. "Does anyone need a cup?"

"Jaradal doesn't have one. You should always remember to bring your own cup, Jaradal," Proleva said, reminding her young son.

"I don't need to bring my own cup here. Grandam has my own cup for me," Jaradal said.

"He's right," Marthona said. "Do you remember where it is, Jaradal?"

"Yes, 'Thona," he said, getting up and running to a low shelf and returning with a small cup shaped and hollowed out of wood. "Here it is." He held it high to show everyone, causing delighted smiles from the assembled group. Ayla noticed that Wolf had moved from his customary spot near the entrance and was wriggling on his belly toward the boy with his tail held high, every motion of his body expressing his yearning to reach the object of his desire. The boy spied the animal, drank down his tea in a few gulps, then announced, "I play with Wolf now," though he was watching Ayla to see what her reaction would be.

Jaradal reminded her so much of Durc, she couldn't help but smile. The boy headed toward the animal, who made a whining yelp as he got up to meet him, then started licking Jaradal's face. Ayla could tell that Wolf was beginning to feel comfortable with his new, though very large, pack, especially the child of the extended family and his friends. For Wolf's sake, she almost felt sorry that they would be leaving so soon. She knew it would be hard on him to be faced with the many new people they would meet. It would be hard on her, too. Her excitement about the Summer Meeting was tinged with trepidation.

"This is very good tea, Ayla," Zelandoni said. "You sweetened it with licorice root, didn't you?"

Ayla smiled. "Yes. It's calming for the stomach. Everyone is so excited about leaving, I thought I should make something calming."

"And it tastes good." Zelandoni paused, considering her words. "It occurs to me, since we are all here, that perhaps you should show Joharran and Proleva your way of making fire. I know I asked everyone not to tell anyone else about it yet, but we are all going to be traveling together and they will see it anyway."

Jondalar's brother and his mate glanced at the others with questioning looks, and then at each other.

Folara smiled. "Should I put the fire out?"

"Yes, why don't you," the donier said. "It is more impressive to see it that way the first time."

"I don't understand. What's this about fire?" Joharran said.

"Ayla discovered a new way to start a fire," Jondalar said, "but it's easier to show you."

"Why don't you show them, Jondalar?" Ayla said.

Jondalar asked his brother and Proleva to come to the cooking hearth, and after Folara smothered the fire, and other people put out the lamps that were near them, Jondalar used the firestone and flint and soon had a small fire started.

"How did you do that?" the leader asked. "I've never seen anything like it."

Jondalar held up the firestone. "Ayla discovered the magic in these stones," he said. "I've been meaning to tell you about them, but there's been so much going on, I haven't had time yet. We just showed Zelandoni, and not long ago Marthona, Willamar, and Folara."

"Are you saying anyone can do that?" Proleva said.

"Yes, with practice, anyone can do it," Marthona said.

"Yes, let me show you how the stones work," Jondalar said. He went through the process, and Joharran and Proleva were amazed.

"One of those stones is flint, what is the other one? And where does it come from?" Proleva said.

"Ayla calls it a firestone," Jondalar said, and explained how she happened to discover its properties. "We looked, but didn't see any on the way back. I was beginning to think they could be found only in the east, then Ayla found some not far from here. If there are some nearby, there should be more. We'll keep looking. We have enough for all of us, but they could be significant gifts, and Willamar thinks they would be good to trade."

"Jondalar, I think we're going to have to have some long talks. I wonder just what else you haven't told me. You go off on a Journey, and return with horses that carry you on their backs, a wolf that lets children pull his fur, powerful new throwing weapons, magic stones that make instant fire, stories about intelligent flatheads, and a beautiful woman who knows their language and learned healing from them. Are you sure there isn't something else you've forgotten to tell me?" Joharran said.

Jondalar smiled wryly. "Not that I can think of right now," he said. "When you put it all together like that, I guess it does sound rather unbelievable."

"'Rather unbelievable'? Listen to him!" Joharran said. "Jondalar, I have a feeling your 'rather unbelievable' Journey is going to be talked about for many years."

"He does have interesting stories to tell," Willamar admitted.

"It's all your fault, Willamar," Jondalar said with a grin, then looked at his brother. "Don't you remember staying up late listening to him telling stories about his travels and adventures, Joharran? I always thought he was better than many of the traveling Story-Tellers. Did you ever show Joharran the gift he just brought you, mother?"

"No, Joharran and Proleva haven't seen it yet," Marthona said. "I'll go get it." She went into her sleeping room and returned with a flat section of palmate antler and gave it to Joharran. It was carved with two streamlined animals apparently swimming. They were fishlike, but not fish. "What did you say these were, Willamar?"

"They're called seals," he said. "They live in the water, but they breathe air, and come to shore to give birth."

"This is remarkable," Proleva said.

"Yes, it is, isn't it?" Marthona said.

"We saw some animals like those on our Journey. They live in an inland sea far to the east," Jondalar said.

"Some people think they are spirits of the water," Ayla added.

"I saw another creature that lives in the Great Waters of the West that is thought of as a special spirit helper of the Mother by the people who live nearby," Willamar said. "They are even more fishlike than seals. They give birth in the sea, but it is said they breathe air and nurse their young. They can stand on top of the water on their tails—I saw one do it—and it's said they speak their own language. The people who live there call them dolphins, and some of them claim they can speak dolphin language. They made high squeaking sounds to show me.

"They tell many stories and legends about them," Willamar continued. "It's said they help people to fish by driving them into nets, and they have saved the lives of people whose boats have capsized far from shore, who would otherwise have drowned. Their Elder Legends say that all people once lived in the sea. Some of them returned to the land, but the ones who stayed behind became dolphins. Some call them cousins, and their Zelandoni says they are related to people. She's the one who gave this plaque to me. They venerate the dolphin almost as much as the Mother. Every family has a donii, but everyone also has some dolphin object, a carving like that, or a part of the animal, a bone or tooth. It is considered very lucky."

"And you said I had interesting stories to tell, Willamar," Jondalar said. "Fish that breathe air and stand on their tails on top of the water. It almost makes me want to go with you."

"Maybe next year when I go to trade for salt, you can come. It's not such a long Journey, especially compared to the one you made," Willamar said.

"I thought you said you didn't want to travel again, Jondalar," Marthona said, "and here you are, home only a short time and planning another trip. Have you developed a traveling urge? Like Willamar?"

"Well, trading missions aren't exactly Journeys," Jondalar said, "and I'm not ready to make a trip now, except to the Summer Meeting, but a year is a long way off."

Folara and Jaradal, curled up with Wolf on Folara's bed, tried to stay awake. They didn't want to miss anything, but with the wolf between them, listening to the stories and the soft buzz of conversation, they both fell asleep.

The next day dawned with a gray drizzle, but the summer shower didn't dampen the enthusiasm of the Cave for the impending trek. Despite staying up late the night before, the members of Marthona's household were up early. They made a morning meal of the food they had set out the night before and then finished packing. The rain eased up, and the sun tried to burn off the clouds, but moisture from the night's accumulation on leaves and in puddles made the air foggy, cool, and damp.

When everyone who was going had gathered on the front terrace, they started out. With Joharran leading the way, they headed north, walking down from the stone front porch to Wood River Valley. It was a large party, much larger, Ayla observed, than the group from the Lion Camp when they went to the Mamutoi Summer Meeting. There were still many people Ayla did not know very well, but by now she at least knew almost everyone's name.

Ayla was curious which way Joharran would go. From the ride they took on the horses, she knew that when they started, the floodplain valley on the right bank of The River—the Ninth Cave side—was broad. If they headed upstream along The River in its meandering but generally northeast direction, trees would be close to the water, and a wide expanse of grassy field separated The River from the highlands on both sides, and climbed up to the highlands in a gradual slope. However, after a short distance, water hugged steep cliffs on the other side, the left bank, which was on the right-hand side as one traveled toward the source. "Left bank" and "right bank" were terms that always referred to the sides of rivers when going downstream in the direction of the flowing current. They were traveling upstream.

Jondalar had told her that the next closest community of Zelandonii was only a few miles away, but that they would need a raft to complete the trip if they stayed close to The River because the course of the waterway changed. Farther upstream it curved in a more northerly direction, and the lay of the land forced the water to the wall of the cliff on the right bank, their side, with no space for even a narrow path after it turned north, and finally east again before the next abri was reached. The people of the Ninth Cave usually took an overland route to visit their nearest northern neighbors.

The leader turned up the path beside the Wood River tributary to the shallow crossing, then cut directly across Wood River Valley. Ayla noticed that they were not following the route she and Jondalar had taken with the horses shortly after they arrived. Instead of cutting across to the narrow valley with the steep, dry streambed, Joharran took a trail that was parallel to The River, leading to the flat lowlands of the right bank. They turned left through grass and brush and started up the gradual slope, then switchbacked in a zigzag up the face of the highland.

Ayla kept track of Wolf out of the corner of her eye as he ran ahead, following his nose. She recognized most of the plants she saw and registered in her mind their uses and where they were growing. There's a stand of black birch over there by The River, she thought, the bark can help prevent miscarriage, and here's some sweet rush, which can cause one. And it's always good to know where willow grows; a decoction of the bark is so good for headaches, and the aching bones of the elderly, and other pains. I didn't know there was marjoram around here. It makes a nice tea, adds a good flavor to meat, and it's good for headaches, too, and helps a baby's colic. I'll have to remember this for later. Durc didn't suffer from colic much, but some babies do.

The trail steepened as they reached the sharper incline near the top, then opened out to the high level field. When they reached the windy plateau, she walked a ways ahead to the edge, then stopped to rest and wait for Jondalar, who was having a little trouble leading Racer and his travois up the steep, rocky path with the abrupt turns. Whinney cropped a few blades of fresh grass while they waited. Ayla adjusted the mare's pole drag and checked the load she carried in panniers and on her back, then stroked her and talked to her in the special horse language. Ayla looked down at The River and its floodplain, and the long line of people, young and old, straggling up the trail, then the view beyond.

The elevated plateau offered an expansive panorama of the surrounding countryside, and a misty, illusionary scene below. A few wisps of fog were still tangled in the trees near the water, and a shroud of soft white concealed The River in places, but the veil was lifting, revealing shafts of light from the brilliant orb glinting from the surging stream. Across in the distance, the fog thickened and the limestone hills faded into a gray-white sky.

When Jondalar arrived with Racer, they started across the high plateau together. Walking with the tall man with whom she had Journeyed for so long, with the wolf at her heels and the horses pulling the pole drags following close behind, Ayla was euphoric. She was with the ones she loved most and could hardly believe the man beside her would soon be her mate. She remembered only too well her feelings during the similar trek they had made with the Lion Camp. Then, she had felt that every step she took brought her closer to an inevitable destiny she did not want. She had promised to mate a man she truly cared for, and might have been happy with, if she hadn't met and loved Jondalar first. But Jondalar had become distant, didn't seem to love her anymore, and there was no doubt that Ranec not only loved her, but wanted her desperately.

Ayla had no such adverse feelings now. She was so filled with happiness, she felt sure it overflowed and suffused the air around her, permeating the ground she walked upon. Jondalar was also remembering the trip to the Mamutoi Summer Meeting. The problem had been his jealousy and his fear of facing his people with a woman who might not be acceptable. He had resolved his problems and was no less full of joy than she. Then, he had been sure Ayla was lost to him forever, but here she was beside him, and every time he looked at her, she looked back at him with eyes full of love.

They followed the trail across the level highland that took them to another viewpoint at the cliff's edge, where they had stopped when they were there alone. Before they crossed the small stream, they paused to watch the thin waterfall dropping over the edge into The River directly below. The people of the Cave had spread out across the high field, some making their own trail. The walkers took with them only what they could carry, though packs could be heavy and some planned to go back to get a second load, usually of items they wanted to trade.

Ayla and Jondalar had talked to Joharran and offered to the Cave the hauling services of the two horses. The leader spoke to several people, but he decided to load up the horses with meat from the recent deer and bison hunts. When he originally planned the hunts, he had expected that several people would need to make an extra trip back to the Ninth Cave to bring the meat to the site of the Summer Meeting.

Using the horses saved them the trouble, and for the first time he realized that trained horses could be more than a novelty. They could be useful. Even the help they had provided on the hunt, and Jondalar's fast trip back to the Ninth Cave to tell Zelandoni and Shevonar's mate about the tragic accident, had not given him the full awareness of their potential benefit. He understood better when he and several others were saved a trek back to the Ninth Cave, but with the horses traveling so close, he also became aware that the animals required extra work.

Whinney was used to the pole drag, she had pulled a travois during most of their Journey. Racer was less accustomed to hauling a load and was more unmanageable. Joharran had seen that his brother had to work with the horse, especially turning on the trail where the poles restricted his movement. It required patience to keep the young stallion calm and lead him around obstacles while maintaining the load intact. At the Ninth Cave, Ayla and Jondalar had started out near the front of the group, but by the time they crossed the small stream and angled northwest again, they were closer to the middle.

They reached the place where Ayla and Jondalar had turned back before, where the path began to descend. This time they followed it as it twisted and turned along the easiest grade, winding through brush, open grassland, and, in a protected dip, trees. They reached a rock shelter that was so close to the water, part of it extended over the water. They had traveled just under two miles in actual distance, though the steep climbs made the journey longer.

The shelter had a front porch that was so close to the edge of The River, a person could dive into water from it. The shelter was called River Front and faced south. It extended from west to east all the way to a southward-turning meander of The River that swung back around on itself so close, it would have joined at the neck of the loop it formed if it hadn't been for the finger of highland between. Though it appeared to be a habitable shelter, no Cave lived there, though travelers, expecially those on rafts, sometimes stopped off. The water was a little too close, and it sometimes overflowed into the shelter when The River flooded.

The Ninth Cave didn't stop at River Front, but climbed back up the cliff behind the shelter. The trail continued north, then curved around toward the east. About a mile after leaving River Front, the trail headed down a fairly steep grade to the valley of a small stream that was usually dry in summer. After crossing the muddy streambed, Joharran stopped and everybody rested while he waited for Jondalar and Ayla. Several people made small fires to boil water for a hot tea. Some took out traveling food, especially those with children, and had a snack.

"We need to make a choice here, Jondalar," Joharran said. "Which way do you think we should go?"

Because The River meandered through its valley, crowding close to cliff walls on first one side and then the other, it was sometimes easier to travel between Caves across the highlands. To reach the next site, however, there was another possibility.

"From here there are two ways we can go," Jondalar said. "If we follow this trail across the top of the cliffs, we'll have to climb up this slope, go across the highland for about half the distance we've already come, then go down again until we come to another little stream. It usually has water, but it's shallow and easy to cross. Then we have another steep climb that traverses the front of the cliff overlooking The River, then down again. The River runs through the middle of a large grassy field there, the floodplain. We'll stop and visit with the Twenty-ninth Cave, probably overnight."

"But there's another way to go," Joharran said. "The Twenty-ninth Cave is called Three Rocks because they have three shelters, not right next to each other, but spaced around The River and the large floodplain. Two of them are on this side, the third is on the other side of The River."

Joharran pointed to the slope ahead. "Instead of climbing this, we can turn east to The River. It turns north ahead and you have to cross to the other side because the water runs right next to the cliffs on this side, but there's a long, shallow stretch that's easy to get across. And the Twenty-ninth Cave keeps stepping-stones there, as we do at the Crossing. We go along the other side for a while, then The River turns east again and crowds the cliffs on the other side, so you have to cross back over, but it spreads out and gets shallow again and that crossing also has stepping-stones. We can stop at two of the shelters on this side to visit, but we have to cross over again to get to the third and biggest one, because that is probably where we'll stay, especially if it rains."

"If we go that way, we have to climb; if we go this way, we have to cross running water," Jondalar finished for him. "What do you think would be the best way with the horses and the pole drags?"

"It's easy to cross rivers with the horses, but if it's very deep, the meat on the pole drags can get wet, which means it could spoil if it's not dried out again," Ayla said. "On our Journey, we had the poles attached to the bowl boat, so it always floated up when we had to cross rivers. But didn't you say we have to cross The River at least once anyway?"

Jondalar walked behind Racer's pole drag. "I was thinking, Joharran. If we can get a couple of people to walk back here behind the horses and lift up the ends of the poles just enough to keep them out of the water, I think we could get across without getting anything wet."

"I'm sure we could find people to do that. There are always a few young men who like to splash through the water whenever there's a crossing anyway. I'll go ask around," Joharran said. "I think most people would rather not climb any more than they have to, with the loads they're all carrying."

When Joharran left, Jondalar decided to check Racer's lead rope. He stroked the horse, gave him some grain that he had in a pouch. Ayla smiled at him; she was paying attention to Wolf, who came to see why they stopped. She felt the special bond she and Jondalar had formed on their Journey. Then it occurred to her that they had another. They were the only people who understood the connection that could develop between a person and an animal.

"There is another way to go upriver ... well, two more," Jondalar said while they were waiting. "One is to pole up by raft, but I don't think that would work too well with the horses. The other is to go along the top of the cliffs on the other side of The River. You have to take the Crossing, and it's actually easier to go all the way to the

Third Cave and start from there. They have a good path to the top of Two Rivers Rock that continues as a trail across the highland. It's more level than this side, only a few minor dips. There aren't as many tributaries on that side of The River, but if you plan to stop at the Twenty-ninth Cave, you have to come down and cross The River again. That's why Joharran decided to stay on this side."

While they rested, Ayla asked about the people they were going to visit. Jondalar described the unusual arrangement of the people of the Twenty-ninth Cave of the Zelandonii. Three Rocks consisted of three separate settlements of stone shelters in three separate cliffs that formed a triangle around the floodplain of the meandering river, all within a mile and a half of each other.

"The Histories say that they used to be separate Caves, numbered with earlier counting words, and there were more than three," Jondalar explained, "but they all had to share the same field and rivers, and they were always disputing rights, arguing about which Cave could use what, and when. I guess it got rather bitter, some men actually started fighting with each other. Then the Zelandoni of South Face got the idea to join together into one Cave, work together and share everything. If a herd of aurochs migrated through, it wouldn't be the hunters of all the different Caves going after them separately, but one hunting party from all the Caves working together."

Ayla thought for a while. "But the Ninth Cave works together with the neighboring Caves. On that last hunt, the hunters from the Eleventh, the Fourteenth, the Third, the Second, and a few people from the Seventh all hunted together and everyone shared the food."

"That's true, but all of our Caves don't have to share everything," Jondalar said. "The Ninth Cave has Wood River Valley, and animals sometimes move along The River right in front of the porch, the Fourteenth has Little Valley, the Eleventh can raft to a big field right across The River, the Third has Grass Valley, and the Second and Seventh share Sweet Valley—when we get back, we'll go and visit them. We can all work together when we want, but we don't have to. All the Caves that joined to become the Twenty-ninth had to share the same hunting area. They now call it Three Rocks Valley, but it is a part of The River Valley and North River Valley."

He explained that The River took an eastward turn, cutting through the middle of the large grassy floodplain. It was joined on the north by a healthy tributary and its valley. Two of the settlements were on the right bank of The River, the one to the west that could be reached overland from River Front and another to the north. A third massive cliff with several stories of rock shelters was to the south, across The River on the left bank. It was one of the few inhabited rock shelters with a north-facing front.

The western settlement, or the West Holding of the Twenty-ninth Cave of the Zelandonii, consisted of several small rock shelters in the side of a hill. Jondalar told her they also maintained a more or less permanent campsite of lean-tos, fireplaces, and drying racks and, in summer, tents and other temporary shelters near West Holding. It was at the opening of a sheltered valley of stone pines, whose pine-nut-filled cones were a source of vegetable oil so rich, it could be burned in lamps, though it was so delicious, it was seldom used for that purpose.

People from the entire community of Three Rocks, and others that were invited to help in return for a share, gathered for the pine-nut harvest. That was the primary purpose for the outdoor camp, but it was also near a very good fishing spot that lent itself to fish traps and weirs. It was used quite often by the community all through the warmer part of the year and usually not closed down until the freeze stilled The River for the winter. Though people lived in the various rock shelters of West Holding all year and the nut harvest, which was the original reason the campsite was established, was in autumn, the first tents went up at the beginning of the warm season to work the fish traps, and everyone always talked about going to "summer camp." The western settlement came to be known as Summer Camp.

"Their Zelandoni is a good artist," Jondalar said. "In one of the shelters, she has engraved animals on the walls, maybe we'll have time to visit her. She makes small carvings to carry, too. But we'll be back here for the nut harvest, anyway."

Joharran returned with three young men and one young woman who had volunteered to walk behind the travois and lift the poles out of the water when they crossed rivers. They all seemed rather pleased to have been chosen to perform the task. Joharran had no trouble finding people who were willing, the problem was making the selection. Many people wanted to get closer to the horses, and the wolf, and learn more about the foreign woman. It would give them something interesting to talk about at the Summer Meeting.

On the more level terrain, except during the actual water cross-ings, Jondalar and Ayla were able to walk side by side, leading the horses. Wolf, as usual, did not follow as closely. He liked to explore when he traveled, running ahead and falling behind, following his curiosity and the scents his sensitive nose detected. Jondalar used the opportunity to tell Ayla more about the people they would be staying with and their territory.

He talked about the large tributary coming down from the north, called North River, that joined The River on the right bank. The northern side of the grassy floodplain was enlarged by North River's valley as well as by the continually expanding upstream valley of The River itself. Jutting out between the valleys of the tributary and the primary was the oldest living site of the community, the northern settlement, formally the North Holding of the Twenty-ninth Cave of the Zelandonii, but referred to as South Face. To reach it from Summer Camp, he told her, they used a path that led to stepping-stones across the tributary, but now they were approaching it along The River.

Ahead, on a hill overlooking the open landscape, was a triangular-shaped cliff that held three south-facing terraces arranged like steps, one over the other. Though it was within a mile and a half of all the living sites that made up the Three Rocks community, several auxiliary sites were much closer and now considered themselves part of the North Holding of the Twenty-ninth Cave.

He explained that a well-used trail traversed easily up the hillside in two switchbacks to the middle level, which was the main living site of South Face. The upper small abri, which overlooked much of the large valley, was used as a lookout and was usually referred to as the South Face Overlook, or simply the Overlook. The lowest level was semisubterranean and used more for storage than everyday living. Among other food and supplies, the nuts collected at Summer Camp were kept there. Some of the other abris that were part of the South Face settlement complex had their own descriptive names, such as Long Rock, Deep Bank, and Good Spring, referring to the natural spring that welled up nearby.

"Even the storage area has a name," he said. "It's called Bare Rock. The old people tell the story that was told to them when they were young. It's part of the Histories. It's about a very hard winter and a cold, wet spring when they ran out of all their stored food— the lower rock storage area was Bare Rock. Then the last gasp of winter howled in with a driving blizzard. Everyone went hungry for a while. The only thing that saved them from starvation was a large cache of pine nuts stored by squirrels in the lower rock shelter that a

400

young girl happened to find. It's amazing how much those little nut chasers can pile up.

"But even when the weather cleared enough to hunt, the deer and horses they managed to kill had been starving, too," Jondalar continued. "The meat was lean and tough, and it was a long time before the first greens and roots of spring. The next fall, the whole community gathered many more of the nuts from the stone pines as a hedge against future hard winters and hungry springs, and started the tradition of collecting them."

The young people who had helped them keep the food dry while crossing rivers crowded in close so they could hear Jondalar as he talked about their closest neighbor to the north. They didn't know that much about them, either, and listened with interest.

About a mile and a half away, and across The River, they could see the South Holding of the Twenty-ninth Cave of the Zelandonii, the largest and most unusual cliff in the region. Though north-facing sites were seldom utilized as living places, this one on the south side of The River was too inviting to be ignored. The cliff face, a half mile in length, rose vertically two hundred fifty feet from The River in five levels and held nearly a hundred caves and cavities, plus over-hanging rock shelters and terraces.

Grand views of the valley could be seen from all the terraces, so a specific shelter or cave to use as a lookout was not needed. But the cliff did offer a different, unique view. In one section of a lower ter-race that projected over a quiet backwater of the moving stream, it was possible to look down and see one's reflection in the still water.

"It's not named for its size, as you might think," Jondalar said. "It's named for that unusual view. It is called Reflection Rock."

The cliff was so huge that most of the possible living sites were not even occupied—it would have been as crowded as a marmot mound if they had been. The natural resources of the surrounding area would not have supported so many people. They would have depleted whole herds and stripped the landscape of vegetation. But the huge cliff was an exceptional place, and those who lived there knew that the mere sight of their home left strangers and first-time visitors gaping with awe.

It could even dazzle those who were familiar with it, Jondalar realized as he looked at the extraordinary natural formation. The Ninth Cave, with its magnificent overhanging stone shelf sheltering a spacious and comfortable area, was certainly remarkable in its own right, and in most ways offered more livability—that it primarily faced south was a tremendous advantage—but he had to admit that the extensive and imposing cliff ahead was impressive.

But the people who were standing on the lowest-level terrace were feeling a touch of awe themselves at the sight that was approaching them. The welcoming gesture of the woman who was standing somewhat ahead of the others was more tentative than usual. She was holding her hand up with her palm facing her, but her beckoning motion was not very vigorous. She had heard of the return of Marthona's wandering second son and the foreign woman he brought back. She had even heard that they had horses and a wolf with them, but hearing it was not the same as seeing it, and seeing two horses walking calmly amid the people of the Ninth Cave, behind a wolf—a big wolf—a tall, blond, unfamiliar woman and the man she knew as Jondalar was unnerving, at the very least.

Joharran looked aside to cover up a smile he couldn't help making when he saw the woman's expression, though he understood entirely how she felt. It wasn't so long ago that he had experienced the same frisson of fear at the same uncanny sight. He was amazed, when he thought about it, how quickly he had gotten used to it. So quickly that he hadn't anticipated the reaction of his neighbors, and he knew he should have. He was glad they had stopped. It gave him a hint of the effect they would very likely have on people when they reached the Summer Meeting.

22

"If Joharran hadn't decided to set up the tent in the field, I think I would have stayed out anyway," Ayla said. "I want to be close to Whinney and Racer while we're traveling, and I didn't want to bring them up on that cliff. They wouldn't have liked it."

"I don't think Denanna would have like it much, either," Jondalar said. "She seemed exceptionally nervous around the animals."

They were riding upstream through the valley of the tributary called North River, giving the animals, and themselves, a break from the close association of so many people. They had gone through the formality of meeting all the leaders, and Ayla was still trying to sort them out. Denanna, who was the leader of Reflection Rock, the South Holding, was the acknowledged leader of the Twenty-ninth Cave, but Summer Camp and South Face, the West and North Holdings, also had leaders. Whenever there were decisions to make that concerned all of Three Rocks, the three leaders worked together to reach a consensus, but it was presented by Denanna, because the rest of the Zelandonii leaders insisted that if the Twenty-ninth Cave was going to call itself one Cave, they should have just one leader to speak for them.

The zelandonia had a slightly different set of requirements. West, North, and South Holdings each had their own Zelandoni, but the Zelandonia of the three holdings were assistants to a fourth donier, who was the Zelandoni of the Twenty-ninth. Because there was a great enough distance between the holdings, it was reasonable that each would want its own Zelandoni, and one who was a good healer, especially during the seasons of cold and stormy weather, but the primary relationship of any individual Zelandoni was to the zelandonia as a whole, although the Cave they served was of almost equal, and in some ways greater, importance.

The Zelandoni of Reflection Rock was such a good healer that even women during childbirth were glad to have him assist. The Zelandoni of the Twenty-ninth, who also lived at Reflection Rock to be close to the nominal leader, was not a particularly good healer, but she was a good mediator who could work diplomatically with the three other Zelandonia and the three leaders, and soothe the sometimes prickly feelings of all of them. Some people felt that if it were not for Zelandoni of the Twenty-ninth, the whole complex arrangement called the Twenty-ninth Cave would not hold together.

Ayla was happy to have the excuse of the horses needing care and attention to get away from the rest of the formal greetings, feasting, and other rituals. She had spoken to Joharran and Proleva before meeting their neighbors of the next Cave to the north, and told them it was essential for the well-being of Whinney and Racer that she and Jondalar tend to them. The leader said he would make their excuses, and the leader's mate promised to save some food for them.

Ayla was conscious of being watched while they unhitched the pole drags and removed the rest of the loads, and when she examined both horses carefully to make sure they had not sustained any injuries or developed any sores. They rubbed down and combed both animals, then Jondalar suggested that they take Whinney and Racer out and let them run after the day of slow and careful walking. Ayla's beautiful smile of gratitude made him glad he had. Wolf leaped ahead when he saw them heading out; he seemed pleased, too.

Joharran was among those who watched them with the horses. He had often seen them doing the same thing before, but this time he understood it as one more element of the care they required. Horses obviously didn't need that kind of attention when they were living with their herds, but when they did the work that people wanted, perhaps they did. Yes, the potential benefit of using horses to help in various ways was there, but was it worth the amount of work they required? It was a question he was pondering while he watched Ayla and his brother ride off.

Ayla felt herself relax almost as soon as they left. There was a sense of release, of freedom, to riding away by themselves. They had grown accustomed to traveling together with just the animals on their long Journey, and they both found respite in returning to their habit. When they reached North River Valley and saw the long open grassland ahead, they looked at each other simultaneously, grinned, then urged the horses on until they were galloping across the field full-tilt. They didn't notice when they passed a couple of people returning to the Twenty-ninth Cave from a quick trip to the site of the Summer Meeting, but the people noticed them. They stared with mouths agape at a sight they had never seen before and weren't sure they wanted to see again. People racing along on the backs of horses left them uneasy.

Ayla stopped beside a small creek, Jondalar pulled up at the next step. With tacit agreement, they both turned and followed it. The source was a spring-fed pool with a large willow hovering over it, as though protecting its birthright of water for itself and its offspring: a collection of smaller willows crowding close to the large, overflowing basin. They dismounted, took the riding blankets off the horses, and spread them out on the ground.

The horses drank from the creek, then both of them decided it was a good time for a roll. The young couple couldn't help laughing at the animals squirming on their backs with their legs in the air, feeling comfortable and safe enough to enjoy a good back scratch.

Suddenly Ayla reached for the sling wrapped around her head, unwrapped it quickly, and glanced down toward the pool for stones. She grabbed a couple of rounded pebbles, fit one into the pocket of the hurling weapon, and let fly. Without looking, she grabbed the leather strap again, pulled it through her hand to the end, brought both ends together, and had another stone ready to go just as a second bird was taking to the air. She brought it down, then went to retrieve her two willow ptarmigan.

"If it was just the two of us, and we were going to set up camp here, we'd have our evening meal," Ayla said, holding up her trophies.

"But it's not just the two of us, so what are you going to do with them?" Jondalar said.

"Well, the feathers of ptarmigan are the warmest and lightest, and the feather markings are rather nice this time of year. I could make something for the baby," she said. "But I'll have time to make baby things later. I think I'll give these to Denanna. After all, this is their territory, and she seems so anxious about Whinney and Racer, and Wolf, that I think she wishes we hadn't come. Maybe a gift will make her feel better."

"Where did you learn to be so wise, Ayla?" Jondalar said, looking at her with love and warmth.

"That's not wisdom, that's just sense, Jondalar." She looked up and felt herself become lost in the magic of his eyes. The only place she had ever seen such a rich blue color was in the deep pools of glaciers, but his eyes were not icy. They were warm and full of love.

He put his arms around her, and she dropped the brace of birds to reach up and kiss him. It seemed like a long time since he had held her like this, then she realized it had been a long time. Not since he had kissed her, but since they had been alone in an open field, with the horses grazing contentedly and Wolf poking his inquiring nose into every bush and hole in the ground, and no one else around. Soon they would have to go back and continue the trek to the Summer Meeting, and who knew when they would have a moment like this again? When Jondalar began nuzzling her neck, Ayla responded eagerly.

His warm breath and moist tongue sent shivers through her and she gave herself to them, letting the sensation overcome her. He blew in her ear and nibbled her lobe, then pulled his hands forward to hold the fullness of her breasts. Even more full now, he thought, reminding him that she was carrying new life inside her, new life that she said was as much his as hers. At the least, the life had to be of his spirit, of that he felt sure. For most of their Journey, he had been the only man around for the Mother to take an elan from.

She untied her waist thong, from which hung various objects and pouches that were secured by loops or strings, and laid it down beside the riding blanket, making sure all the things that were attached to it stayed in place. He sat down on the edge of the leather covering that smelled strongly, though not unpleasantly, of horse. It was a smell he was used to and that carried with it enjoyable associations. Quickly, he began untying and unwrapping the thongs of his foot coverings from around his legs, then stood up and untied the waistband that held closed the overlapping front of his leggings and pulled them off.

When he looked up, Ayla had done the same. He looked at her and liked what he saw. Her shape was more full, not only her breasts, but her stomach, which was rounder, starting to show the new life growing. He felt his manhood respond, snatched off his tunic, then helped Ayla with hers. He felt a cool breeze on his bare skin, saw chill bumps raise on hers, and took her in his arms, feeling her warmth and trying to keep her that way.

"I'm going to wash in the pool," she said.

He smiled, feeling that it was an invitation for him to Pleasure her the way he liked. "You don't have to," he said.

"I know, but I want to. All the walking and climbing made me sweaty," she said, walking toward the pond.

It was cold, but she usually washed in cold water and found the chill, tingling sensation stimulating, most of the time. In the mornings, it woke her up. It was a shallow pond except for the end near the spring. There, she found it dropped off quickly until her feet no longer touched the rocky, silty bottom. She treaded water, moving out of the deep part and back toward the stony bank.

Jondalar followed her in, though he liked cold water far less than she did. He was up to his thighs, and when she got close, he splashed her. She squealed and sloshed the water around, roiling it up, and with both hands splashed a wave toward him that caught him in the face and soaked him from the shoulders down.

"I wasn't ready for that," he said, sputtering with a sudden shiver, and slapped the water back at her. The horses looked up at the commotion they were making in the water. She grinned at him, he reached for her, and the noisy water play stopped as they stood together with arms entwined and lips pressed together.

"Maybe I should help you wash," he murmured in her ear as he reached between her legs and felt himself respond.

"Maybe I should help you," she said, reaching for his hard erect member, and with the water, she rubbed her hand up and down, exposing the head from the foreskin. The cold liquid ought to have cooled his ardor, he thought, but her cool hand on his warm organ was strangely, intensely stimulating. Then she knelt down and when she took the head of his manhood in her mouth, it felt hot. He moaned as she moved back and forth, working her tongue around the head, and he felt such urgency, it caught him by surprise. Suddenly, before he could control it, he felt his ardor rise and burst forth as waves of release washed through him.

He pushed her back. "Let's get out of this cold water," he said. She spit out his essence and rinsed her mouth, then smiled at him. Taking her hand, he led her out. When they reached the riding blanket, they sat down, then he pushed her back and lay down beside her, raising up on an arm to look at her. "You caught me by surprise," he said, feeling relaxed but slightly flustered. It had not turned out the way he had planned.

She smiled; it wasn't often that he gave up his essence so quickly, he was always the one who liked to maintain control. Her smile turned to a grin of delight. "You must have been more ready than you thought," she said.

"You don't have to look so pleased with yourself," he said.

"It's not often that I can surprise you," she said. "You are the one who knows me so well, it surprises me, and always makes me feel so Pleasured."

He couldn't help but smile back at her delight. He leaned over to kiss her, and she opened her mouth slightly, welcoming him. He enjoyed touching her, holding her, kissing her, in any case. He probed inside her mouth, gently, tentatively, and she did the same. Then he felt just the hint of an urge start to rise again and felt pleased. He might not be entirely spent yet, and there was no hurry to get back.

He spent time just kissing her, then running his tongue over her lips. He found her neck and her throat, nibbling and kissing them. It tickled and she had to restrain herself to keep from moving aside. She was already stimulated, and holding herself still added to the experience. When he started to move lower, kissing her shoulder and her inner arm all the way to the elbow, she could hardly stand it and wanted more at the same time. Without her realizing it, her breathing increased, which encouraged him. Then, suddenly, he took a nipple in his mouth, and she gasped as streaks of fire flashed inside to her inner place.

His manhood was growing again. He felt the roundness of her breast, then took the contracted, upright nipple of her other breast in his mouth and suckled hard. He reached for the first nipple with his hand, squeezing and manipulating it between his fingers. She pushed against him, feeling the intensity and wanting more. She did not hear the breeze in the willows or feel the coolness of the air, her entire attention was focused inside, on the sensations he caused her to feel.

He, too, was feeling the heat rise inside himself and his tumescent manhood. He moved lower, settled himself between her thighs, and, opening her folds, bent down for his first sample. She was still wet from the water, and he reveled in the cold and the wet and the warmth and the salt and the familiar taste of Ayla, his Ayla. He wanted all of her, all at once, and reached up for her nipples as he found her hard, pulsing nodule.

She moaned and cried out, arching up to him as he suckled and manipulated her with his tongue. She was not thinking, just feeling. Then, before she knew it, she was there, feeling the surge grow and expand until suddenly it washed over her, as he felt the wetness. Then she was reaching for him, making little cries of need, wanting to feel him inside her. He rose up, found her opening, and pushed himself in, then pulled his manhood out and pushed in again.

She was meeting him, pushing closer and pulling back, arching and turning her body to feel him just where she needed him. His urge was there, but not quite as demanding as it sometimes was. Rather than having to control, he just let it build, rocking with her, moving with her, feeling the tension grow, plunging deeply with joy and abandon. She was calling out, and her wordless sounds gained in pitch and intensity. Then it reached the peak, and with words and sounds increasing they felt a great release swell up and gush forth. They held for a moment, then pushed in and pulled out a few more times, and lay still, panting to catch their breath.

As she lay there with her eyes closed, Ayla heard the wind soughing through the trees and a bird calling to its mate, felt the cool breeze and the delicious feeling of his weight on her, smelled horse from the blanket, and the scent of their Pleasures, and remembered the taste of his skin and his kisses. When he finally pulled himself up and looked at her, she was smiling, a dreamy, half-dozing, warm smile of contentment.

When they finally got up, Ayla went back into the pond to clean herself as Iza had taught her long ago. Jondalar did, too. It seemed to him that if she did, he ought to, though it hadn't been his habit until he met her. He really didn't like cold water. As he was rinsing off, however, he thought if there were many more days like today, he could learn to like it.

On the way back to the South Holding of the Twenty-ninth Cave, Ayla found she was not looking forward to seeing the neighbors, which seemed somewhat inimical. Though she felt accepted by Jondalar's kin and the members of the Ninth Cave, she realized she wasn't especially eager to see them, either. As much as she had wanted their Journey to come to an end, and to have the company of other people around her, she had grown used to the patterns she and Jondalar had established while they were traveling, and she missed them. When they were with the Cave, there was always someone who wanted to talk to either Jondalar or her, or both. They were both glad for the close warmth of the people, but sometimes young lovers wanted to be alone.

In their sleeping rolls in the family tent that night, with everyone much closer together, Ayla was reminded of the sleeping arrangements within the Mamutoi earthlodge and found herself thinking about them. When she first saw it, she had been amazed at the semi-subterranean longhouse the Lion Camp had constructed. They used mammoth bones to support the thick walls of sod and thatch, covered by clay, which kept out the intense wind and winter cold of the midcontinental periglacial regions. She remembered thinking that it was as if they had built their own cave. In a sense they had, since there were no habitable caves in their region, and she was right to be amazed; it was a remarkable feat.

Though the families that lived in the longhouse of the Lion Camp had had separate living areas around hearths aligned in a row down the center, and drapes to close off their sleeping platforms, everyone shared the same shelter. They lived less than an arm's length away from the next family and had to pass through each other's living spaces to come and go. In order to live in such a confined space, they practiced a tacit courtesy that allowed privacy, and was learned as they grew up. Ayla hadn't thought the earthlodge was small when she lived there, only since she had begun sleeping in the Ninth Cave's huge shelter. She recalled that each family of the Clan had had separate hearths, too, but there were no walls, only a few stones to indicate boundaries. The people of the Clan also learned early to avoid looking into another family's living space. To them, privacy was a matter of convention and consideration.

Though the dwellings of the Zelandonii had walls, they did not keep out sounds, of course. Their homes did not have to be as sturdily built as the earthlodges of the Mamutoi; their natural shelters of stone protected them from most of the elements. Zelandonii structures primarily conserved heat inside and blocked winds that strayed under the overhanging cliff shelf. Walking through the living area under the abri, snatches of conversation could often be heard from inside each home, but the Zelandonii learned to ignore the voices of their neighbors. It was like the people of the Clan, who learned not to see into the neighboring hearth, and the unspoken courtesy of the Mamutoi. Thinking about it, Ayla realized that in the short time she had lived there, she had already learned not to hear people from the neighboring dwellings anymore . . . most of the time.

As the young couple were snuggling together, with Wolf beside them, hearing quiet murmurs from the other sleeping rolls, Ayla said, "I like the Zelandonii way of making a separate dwelling for each family, Jondalar, of having a home apart from others."

"I'm glad you do," he said, feeling even more pleased with himself for making arrangements to have a home ready for her when they returned from the Summer Meeting, and for keeping it a secret so he could surprise her with it.

As she closed her eyes, Ayla was thinking about having her own dwelling someday, with walls. To her, the walls of the Zelandonii dwelling afforded a measure of privacy unknown to the Clan, or even to the Mamutoi. The internal partitions enlarged on that privacy. Although she had been lonely, Ayla had learned to enjoy her solitude in her valley, and traveling alone with Jondalar had reinforced her desire to put something between herself and other people. But the closeness of the dwellings gave her the security of knowing that there was always someone nearby.

If she wanted to, she could still hear the comforting sounds of people settling down for the night, sounds she had heard all her life: low voices talking, a baby's cry, a couple making love. She had hungered for those sounds when she lived alone, but in the Ninth Cave there was also a place to get off by oneself. Once inside the thin walls of each dwelling, it was easy to forget that anyone else was around, but the undercurrent of background sounds gave her a fundamental feeling of security. She thought the way the Zelandonii lived was just right.

When they started out the next morning, Ayla noticed that their number had grown. Many people from the Twenty-ninth Cave had joined them, though not, she noticed, the people from Reflection Rock, or at least none she recognized. When she mentioned the increase to Joharran, he said most of Summer Camp, nearly half of South Face, and a few from Reflection Rock would be traveling with them. The rest would start out in the next day or so. She recalled that Jondalar had mentioned something about returning to Summer Camp to help with the pine-nut harvest and got the impression that the Ninth Cave had closer ties with West Holding than with the other Holdings of the Twenty-ninth Cave.

From Reflection Rock, if they proceeded along The River upstream, they would first head due north at the beginning of a broad bend that curved around to the east, then curved south and east again, making a second large loop that ended up going north again, making an extensive S curve. The waterway then continued with easier meandering curves toward the northeast. There were a few small stone shelters at the northern end of the first loop that were used as temporary stopping places when people were traveling or hunting, but the next settlement was at the southernmost end of the second loop, where a small stream joined The River through Old Valley, the home of the Fifth Cave of the Zelandonii.

Unless they were traveling by raft, which required poling upstream for almost ten miles, it was easier to reach Old Valley from Reflection Rock by going directly cross-country rather than following The River around the generous bend to the north and back again. Over land, the home of the Fifth Cave was only a little more than three miles east and somewhat north, though the trail itself, taking the easiest way across the hilly terrain, was not quite so direct.

When Joharran came to the head of the clearly marked trail, he veered away from The River and started up a path that traversed the side of a ridge, then crossed a rounded top, where it met the high trail coming from the Third Cave at Two Rivers Rock and went down the other side to the level of The River again. As they walked, Ayla was interested in learning more about the Fifth Cave and decided to try to encourage Jondalar to talk about them.

"If the Third Cave is known for its hunters, and the people of Fourteenth Cave are recognized as good fishers, what is the Fifth Cave known for, Jondalar?" she asked.

"I'd say the people of the Fifth Cave are known for being very self-sufficient," he said.

Ayla noticed that the four young people who had volunteered to lift the travois when they were crossing The River the day before were still traveling near them and crowded in closer when they heard her question. Though they had lived at the Ninth Cave all their lives, and knew the various neighboring Zelandonii Caves, they had never heard them described so that a stranger would understand them. They were interested in Jondalar's characterizations.

"They pride themselves on having skilled hunters, fishers, and experts in every craft," Jondalar continued. "They even make their own rafts, and say that they were the first Cave to make them, though the Eleventh Cave takes exception to that claim. Their Zelandonia and artists have always been well respected. There are deep carvings on the walls of several of their shelters, others have painted or carved plaques, mostly of bison and horses, because the Fifth Cave has a special connection with those animals."

"Why is this called Old Valley?" Ayla asked.

"Because people have lived here longer than most of the other settlements. Their counting number alone shows their age. Only the Second and Third Caves are older than the Fifth. The Histories of many Caves speak of ties to the Fifth Cave. Most of their wall carvings are so old, they don't really know who made them. One is of five animals that was carved by an ancestor so long ago, it is mentioned in the Elder Legends and is a symbol of their number," Jondalar said, "and the zelandonia say five is a very sacred number."

"What do they mean by sacred?"

"It has special meaning to the Mother. Ask Zelandoni to tell you about the number five sometime," Jondalar said.

"What happened to the First Cave," Ayla paused for a moment to mentally go through the counting words, "and the Fourth Cave?"

"There is a lot about the First Cave in the Histories and Elder Legends, you will probably hear more at the Summer Meeting, but nobody knows what happened to the Fourth. Most people think it was a tragedy of some kind. Some think an enemy used an evil Zelandoni to cause sickness that made them all die. Others think it might just have been an argument with a bad leader that made most of the people decide to leave and join another Cave. But when new people join a Cave, it usually becomes part of their History, and no Cave's History has any mention of the Fourth Cave, at least none that are around now," Jondalar said. "Some people think the number four is unlucky, but the First says it is not the number, only some of its associations that are unlucky."

After a walking distance of about four miles, they climbed a last rise and approached a narrow valley with a lively stream running down the middle and high cliffs rearing up on both sides that offered eight rock shelters of various sizes. As the big procession with Joharran in the lead started down a trail to the head of Old Valley, two men and a woman came up the same trail and met them. After the formality of greetings, they told the travelers that most of the Fifth Cave had already left for the Summer Meeting.

"You are welcome to stay, of course, but since it is barely midday, we thought you might want to continue," the woman said.

"Who is here?" Joharran asked.

"Two oldsters who can't make the trip—one can hardly get out of bed—and a woman who is close to giving birth. Zelandoni didn't think it was safe for her to travel, she's had trouble before. And, of course, these two hunters. They will stay until the moon is new."

"You are First Acolyte of Zelandoni of the Fifth, I believe," The One Who Was First said.

"Yes, I am. I stayed to help with the birth."

"I thought I recognized you. Is there anything we can do to help?"

"I don't think so. She's not ready yet. It will be several days, and her mother and aunt stayed, too. She should be fine."

Joharran called for a consultation with people from the Ninth Cave as well as from the Caves who had joined them. "The best places to set up camp may already be taken," he said. "I think we should keep going rather than stop over here." The others quickly agreed, and it was decided to push ahead.

The River's course straightened out somewhat after the big S curve as it veered toward the northeast. There were several shelters that were home to small Caves along the next stretch of river. All but one had already left for the Summer Meeting, and that one joined them, falling in behind the party of travelers. Joharran became even more concerned about finding a desirable location for his large Cave to settle for the summer.

It surprised Ayla that there were so many people in the region, and so close together. Like the Zelandonii, the people she grew up with foraged for all their needs. They gathered, hunted, and fished for their food and clothing, used natural shelters they found, or manufactured protection from the elements, along with their tools and hunting weapons, out of the materials at hand. She understood at a deep intuitive level that if more people lived in a region than its resources could support, there would not be enough for all. Some would either have to move or do without. She realized that the land of the Zelandonii had to be extremely rich to provide for so many, but in an analytical corner of her mind, she could not help but wonder what would happen to people if things changed.

It was the reason the Summer Meeting was held at a different place every year. Such a large concentration of people depleted the resources of the immediate area, and it would need several years to recover. The meeting this year was not far from the shelter of the Ninth Cave, perhaps twenty miles upstream if they followed The River closely, but they had saved some of that distance by going more directly cross-country from the Twenty-ninth Cave to the Fifth Cave.

The place they were heading was a little more than ten miles from Old Valley, and Joharran decided to try to make it without stopping overnight. He thought about calling a meeting to discuss it, to see if he could encourage them to hurry, but there were too many people, of different ages and abilities, and their pace was inevitably going to be as fast as the slowest of them could go. A meeting would just slow them down more. Instead, he thought he would try to push them a little more than usual without saying anything. If people started to complain, he would worry about stopping then. They did take a break for a midday meal, but when Joharran started out again, people fell in behind him.

It was not dark yet, but the sun was definitely going down, when The River angled right, close to a sloping hillside on the left bank— their right. They turned inland, away from the water, and ascended a moderate hill along a well-used path. As they climbed, a view of the surrounding countryside opened out, showing a wide panorama for some distance.

But when they reached the crest, Ayla caught her breath at the sight of a different view: an enormous horde of people in the valley below. She knew there were already more Zelandonii here than the total number who had attended the Mamutoi Summer Meeting, and not everyone had arrived yet. Even if she counted every person she had ever met, she was sure she had never seen so many people, much less all in one place. Though there were not as many, to her the only sight that came close were the tremendous herds of bison or reindeer that congregated in the thousands every year, but this was a teeming, seething herd of humanity.

The group that had started out from the Ninth Cave had enlarged considerably, but the ones who had joined them along the way quickly dispersed, looking for friends and relatives and a place to establish their camp. Zelandoni headed for the main camp area, where the zelandonia had their own special lodge in the center of everything. They always played a major role at the Summer Meeting. Ayla hoped that the Ninth Cave would find a place somewhat away from the major activities. It would be easier to take the animals out for exercise if they didn't have to be led through crowds of curious people.

Jondalar had already spoken to his brother about the needs of the animals and their nervousness around so many people. Joharran had nodded and said he would keep it in mind, but privately he felt that the needs of the people of the Ninth Cave were more important than those of the animals. He wanted to be close to the centers of activity, and he hoped to find a spot near a river so it would not be such a burden to carry water, perhaps close to a tree or two for shade, and not too far from the wooded area that would supply firewood. He knew, however, that the large woods near the encampment would be denuded before the end of the season. Everybody needed firewood.

But when he, Solaban, and Rushemar started looking, Joharran quickly realized that the good, close-in spots near the woods and water were already taken. The Ninth was a sizable Cave with more people than other Caves, they needed more space for their camp, and he wanted to find a place before it got too dark. It forced Joharran to inspect the periphery of the Summer Meeting area. The large waterway had narrowed around the turn of the last bend, and he'd noticed that the banks were steeper on the downriver side of the campsite, making it harder to reach the water.

The three men went back to The River and started walking upstream. After a short distance, they saw a small runoff creek that flowed through a grassy meadow and emptied into the main river, and they turned to follow it. Somewhat back from The River, they noticed an open stand of trees. As they neared they saw that the woodland was a gallery forest lining both sides of the small stream. They headed into the woods. As they walked along the little stream, Joharran became aware that the creek was curving around the base of a hill, and the wooded area was growing thicker, becoming an actual forest that was bigger and went deeper than it seemed at first.

After some time they came to the source of the creek, a small spring that bubbled up from underground, overhung with trailing branches of willow that were framed by birch, spruce, and a few larch. A deep pool fed by the same source was on the other side of the spring. The entire countryside was full of natural springs, and like many others, this one created a small tributary to The River. Behind the trees on the other side of the pool was a fairly steep, rock-strewn slope littered with stones of all sizes, from tiny pebbles to massive boulders. In front of the pool was a grassy glen that led to a small open beach of soil, fine sand, and smooth, water-rounded stones, with a screen of dense brush along the near side of the pool.

It was an agreeable place, and Joharran thought that if he were by himself or with just a few people, he would set up camp right there, but with the whole Cave, they not only needed more room, they needed to be closer to the main campsite. The three men headed back along the creek, and when they reached the meadow beside The River, Joharran stopped.

"What do you think?" he asked. "It's a little farther away from everything."

Rushemar dipped his hand in the creek and took a taste of the water. It was cool and fresh. "This will have good water all summer. You know that by the end of the season both the stream through the main campsite and The River in front of the camp and downstream will not be fresh and clean anymore."

"And everyone else will be using the big woods for firewood," Solaban said. "This area won't get as much use, and there's more here than it seems."

The Ninth Cave set up their camp on the grassy level meadow between the woods and The River close to the small stream. Most people agreed it was a good enough campsite. No other Cave was likely to set up their lodges upstream from them and muddy their water, it was too far from the center of activities. Their water would stay clean for their own swimming, bathing, and washing of clothes. The spring-fed stream would provide clear drinking water no matter how befouled The River might become after hundreds of people used it for their needs.

The woods offered shade and firewood, and it appeared small enough that it would not draw too many people in search of the same resources, at least not for a while. Most would head for the larger grove of trees farther downstream. The woods, along with the meadow, also provided wild vegetables—berries, nuts, roots, leaves—and small game. Fish were plentiful in The River, as were freshwater mollusks. The site had many advantages.

Its major disadvantage was the distance people would have to walk to reach the area where most of the activities would take place. Some people did think it was too far, primarily those who had family or close friends in other Caves that had already made their camp in places they thought were more desirable. Several of those decided to camp with others. In a way, Jondalar was glad. It would make room for Dalanar and the Lanzadonii when they arrived, if they wouldn't mind being somewhat out of the way.

To Ayla, it was perfect. The animals would have a place away from the thronging masses of people, with a meadow for them to graze in. The animals were already the objects of increased attention, which meant, of course, that Ayla was, too. She remembered how skittish Whinney, Racer, and Wolf had been when they had first arrived at the Mamutoi gathering, though they seemed to accept large numbers of people more easily now, perhaps even better than she did. People spoke out openly, and Ayla couldn't help hearing. They seemed to be especially astonished at how well the horses and the wolf tolerated each other—they actually appeared to be friends—and how well they all responded to the foreign woman and Marthona's son.

She and Jondalar rode up the stream and found the idyllic glen with its pond. It was exactly the sort of place they loved. It was so perfect for them, it made them feel it was theirs, though of course anyone could use it, but Jondalar doubted that it would be used much. Most people came to the Summer Meeting for the group activities and had less need for moments of solitude than Ayla, or the animals, or, he had to admit, himself. She was delighted to discover that the dense brush was mostly hazelnut shrubs, one of her most favorite foods. The nuts were not ripe yet, but it looked as if it would be a good crop, and Jondalar was already planning to come back to see if any of the rocks and stones on the slope on the far side of the pond were flint.

After the people settled in and began surveying their location, most thought it was a choice spot. Joharran was pleased to have arrived soon enough to lay claim to it. He felt it would have been chosen sooner had there not been a second and somewhat larger tributary that meandered through the middle of the large field that encompassed the Summer Meeting. Most of the earlier-arriving Caves had arranged themselves along the banks of that stream, knowing the waters of The River would soon become polluted from overuse. It was the area Joharran first tried, but he was pleased now that he had looked farther afield.

Jondalar thought that his conversation with his brother had made him consider looking for a place that would be comfortable for the horses and mentioned that he appreciated it. Joharran didn't correct him. He knew he had been concerned for the comfort of the people, but perhaps the comment about the animals had stayed in the back of his mind and helped him find the place. He couldn't say it wasn't true, and if it made his brother feel a little indebted to him, he didn't mind. It could be hard enough leading such a big Cave, and he never knew when he might have to call upon Jondalar for assistance.

Since it was so late, they decided to wait until morning to erect their summer lodges, and used their traveling tents that night. Once the camp was established, a few people went to the main area, seeking friends or relatives they had not seen since the last Summer Meeting and to see what was planned for the next day; but most people were tired and decided to stay close by. Many looked over the local area, deciding exactly where they wanted to situate their camp and their individual lodges and to locate where various vegetation grew, particularly the materials they would need to construct their summer residences.

Ayla and Jondalar tethered the horses near the woods and stream, feeling it would be best to keep them secured, more to protect them from people than to restrain them. They would have liked to give them more freedom, but perhaps, after the entire encampment was familiar with them and would not be tempted to hunt them, they could let them wander as they wished, as they did near the Ninth Cave.

In the morning, after they were sure the horses were settled down, Jondalar and Ayla accompanied Joharran as he went to the Summer Meeting's main area in search of other leaders. Decisions needed to be made about hunting, foraging, and sharing the products of those excursions, and to plan activities and ceremonies, including the first summer Matrimonial. Wolf paced alongside Ayla. Everyone had heard of the woman who had an uncanny control over animals, but hearing was not the same as seeing. As they threaded their way between campsites, stares of consternation followed them, and if a person didn't happen to see them approach and was suddenly confronted with the sight, the first response was shock and fear. Even people who knew Joharran and Jondalar gaped instead of calling out greetings.

They were walking behind some low bushes, which hid the wolf, when a man approached them. "Jondalar, I heard you were back from your Journey, and brought a woman with you," he called out, running up. "I'd like to meet her." His speech had a strange impediment that Ayla couldn't quite place, then she realized he spoke somewhat like a child, but with a man's voice. He had a lisp.

Jondalar looked up and frowned. The man was not someone he was particularly happy to see. In fact, it was the one person of all the Zelandonii that he hoped he would not see, and he did not like the assumed friendliness, but he felt he had no choice but to make the introduction.

"Ayla of the Mamutoi, this is Ladroman of the Ninth Cave," he said, not realizing that he had introduced her with her former status. His voice was as neutral as he could make it, but Ayla immediately detected the disapproving undertone and glanced at him. The tension of his jaw showed he was just short of gritting his teeth, and the stiff, unwelcoming posture gave her further clues that this was not someone he was pleased to see.

The man held out both hands and smiled, showing his two missing front teeth, as he moved toward her. She thought she knew who he might be, but the empty space in the front of his mouth confirmed it. This was the man Jondalar had fought with; Jondalar had hit this man and knocked out those two front teeth. As a result, Jondalar had had to leave the Ninth Cave and went to live with Dalanar for a while, which, as it turned out, was probably the best thing that could have happened. It gave him a chance to get to know the man of his hearth and to learn the skill he ultimately grew to love—knapping flint—from the one who was acknowledged the best.

Ayla had learned enough about the tattooed facial markings to realize that the man was an acolyte, training to become a Zelandoni. Then, to her surprise, she felt Wolf brush against her leg as he moved forward to put himself between her and the stranger, and she heard his low warning growl. The only time the wolf ever did that was when he felt she was threatened. Maybe he's sensing Jondalar's stiffness and rejection, she thought, but for some reason, Wolf did not like this man, either. The man hesitated, stepping back, his eyes opened wide with fear.

"Wolf! Stay back," she said in Mamutoi as she stepped ahead to respond to the formal greeting. "I grrreet you, Ladrrroman ob the Ninth Cave." She took both his hands. They were damp.

"It's not Ladroman anymore, or the Ninth Cave. I am Madroman of the Fifth Cave of the Zelandonii now, and an acolyte in the zelandonia. You are welcome here, Ayla of the . . . what was that name? Muh, Mutoni?" he said, watching the wolf, whose growl had increased in volume. He immediately let go of her hands. He had noticed her accent, but the wolf had so disconcerted him, he hardly paid attention.

"And she is not Ayla of the Mamutoi anymore, Madroman," Joharran corrected. "She is now Ayla of the Ninth Cave of the Zelandonii."

"You've been accepted by the Zelandonii already? Well, Mamuto or Zelandonii, I'm glad we happened to meet, but I have to go . . . to a meeting, now," he said, backing away as fast as he could. He turned around and almost ran back the way he had come. Ayla looked at the two brothers. They were grinning with almost identical smiles.

Joharran saw a group of the people he was looking for. Zelandoni was among them. She motioned the three over, but it was the fourth, Wolf, who got most of the attention. Ayla signaled him back while formal introductions were made. She didn't know if he would react to someone else the way he had to Madroman. Several people were surprised when the foreign woman with the strange accent was introduced as Zelandonii, formerly Mamutoi, but it was explained that since there was no question about where she would live after she and Jondalar were mated, the Ninth Cave had already accepted her.

The most important decision, other than deciding to mate, was whether the man would live with the woman's people or if the woman would go to live with his. In either case, acceptance by both Caves was necessary, but most especially by the people who would have a new member living with them. Because they knew where Jondalar and Ayla would live, the Ninth Cave's acceptance of her settled the matter.

Ayla kept the wolf close while she and Jondalar listened to the secular and spiritual leaders discuss plans. It was decided to have a ceremony the following night to find out the best direction to go for the first hunt. If all went well, the First Matrimonial would be held not long after. Ayla had learned that there were always two Matrimonials each summer. The first was to mate those couples, usually from the same region, who had decided to mate during the previous winter. The second was held shortly before they left in the fall. Most of those couples were from more widespread Caves who made their decision during the Summer Meeting, perhaps having met only that year or a season or two before.

"Speaking of the Matrimonial," Jondalar said, "I would like to make a request. Since Dalanar is the man of my hearth and he is planning to come, I would like to ask if the first ceremony can be delayed until he arrives. I would like to have him here for my mating."

"I wouldn't object to a delay of a few days, but what if Dalanar doesn't come until much later?" a Zelandoni asked.

"I would prefer to mate during the first ceremony, but if Dalanar is delayed too long, I would be willing to wait for the second. I would like him to be present when we are joined," Jondalar said.

"That's acceptable," the Zelandoni Who Was First said, "but I think we have to decide just how long we can hold off the First Matrimonial, and that depends on the others who want to mate now."

An older woman with Zelandoni markings on her face rushed to join them. "I understand Dalanar and the Lanzadonii will be joining us this season," she said to Joharran. "He sent a messenger to Zelandoni of the Nineteenth, since they are closest to the Summer Meeting campsite, to let everyone know. The daughter of his mate is to be joined this summer, and he wants a full Matrimonial for her. I understand that he would like to find a donier for his people. This could be a real opportunity for an experienced acolyte or new Zelandoni."

"Jondalar told us, Zelandoni of the Fourteenth," Joharran said.

"That's one reason he's bringing his Lanzadonii here this year," Jondalar explained. "They don't have a healer, although Jerika has some knowledge, and they don't have anyone to perform ceremonies for them. He doesn't feel they can hold a proper Matrimonial until they have a donier of their own. We visited on our way here. Joplaya promised while we were there. She is going to mate with Echozar . . ."

"Dalanar is going to allow Joplaya to mate a man whose mother was a flathead? A man of mixed spirits?" Zelandoni of the Fourteenth interrupted. "How could he do that? His own daughter! I know Dalanar has accepted some unusual people into his Cave, but how can he take in those animals?"

"They are not animals!" Ayla said, frowning in anger at the woman.

23

The woman turned to look at Ayla, surprised that the new-comer had spoken out, and even more that she had contradicted her so brazenly. "It is not your place to speak," she said. "It is not your concern what we say at this meeting. You are a visitor here, not even Zelandonii." She knew the foreign woman was supposed to become the mate of Jondalar, but she apparently needed to be corrected and to learn proper behavior.

"Forgive me, Zelandoni of the Fourteenth," the One Who Was First interjected. "Ayla was introduced to the others, I should have introduced you to her when you first came. Actually, Ayla is Zelandonii. The Ninth Cave accepted her before we left."

The woman turned toward the First, and her hostility was almost palpable. Ayla discerned that the animosity was of long standing, and she recalled something about a Zelandoni who had expected to be named First but was passed over in favor of Zelandoni of the Ninth. She guessed this was the one.

"Ayla and Jondalar tell us flatheads are people, not animals. I think it's something we need to talk about, and I planned to bring it up," Joharran said, stepping forward, trying to calm the situation. "But I don't know if this is the best time, we have other things to discuss first."

"I don't know why we have to talk about them at all," the woman retorted.

"I think it's important, if only for our own safety," Joharran said. "If they are intelligent people—and Ayla and Jondalar have nearly convinced me they are—and we have been treating them like animals, why haven't they objected?"

"Probably because they are animals," the woman said.

"Ayla says it's because they choose to avoid us," Joharran said, "and for the most part, we avoid them. But if we think of them only as animals, perhaps not hunting them, but claiming all the land as ours, as Zelandonii territory—hunting grounds, gathering fields, everything—what if they start resisting? And what should we do if they decide to change and start to claim some of it for themselves? I think we need to be prepared; at least we ought to talk about the possibility."

"I think you are making too much of it, Joharran. If flatheads haven't made claims to territory before, why should they start now?" Zelandoni of the Fourteenth said, dismissing the entire concept.

"But they do make claims to territory," Jondalar said. "On the other side of the glacier, the Losadunai understand that the land north of the Mother River is flathead country. They stay south, except for some young ruffians who have been stirring up trouble, and I'm afraid the Clan won't put up with it much longer, especially the younger ones."

"What makes you say that?" Joharran said. "You never mentioned this before."

"Shortly after we started out, when Thonolan and I got down off the other side of the glacier over the highland to the east, we met up with a band of flatheads—men of the Clan—probably a hunting party," Jondalar said, "and had a small confrontation."

"What kind of confrontation?" Joharran asked. Everyone else was paying close attention, too.

"A young one threw a stone at us, I think because we were on their side of the river, in their territory. Thonolan threw a spear back when he saw someone moving in the woods where they were hiding. Suddenly they all stepped forward and showed themselves. Two of us against several of them, the odds were not good. To tell you the truth, I don't think the odds would be good one on one. They may be short, but they are powerful. I wasn't at all sure how to get out of it, it was their leader who resolved it."

"How could you tell they had a leader? And even if they did, how do you know they weren't just a pack, like wolves?" another man asked. Jondalar thought he recognized him, but wasn't sure. He had been gone five years, after all.

"Now I know for sure, I've met others since, but even then it was obvious. He told the youngster who had thrown the stone to return Thonolan's spear and retrieve the stone, then they slipped back into the woods," Jondalar said. "He put everything back the way it was, and thought that settled it. Since no one was hurt, I guess it did."

"Told the youngster? Flatheads can't talk!" the man said.

"In fact, they can," Jondalar said. "They just don't talk like we do. They use hand signs, mostly. I've learned some of them, and I've communicated with them, but Ayla is much better. She knows their language."

"I find that hard to believe," Zelandoni of the Fourteenth said.

Jondalar smiled. "I did at first, too," he said. "I never saw one up close before that encounter. Have you?"

"No, I can't say that I have, and I have no desire to," the woman said. "I understand they rather resemble bears."

"They don't resemble bears, any more than we do. They look like people, a different kind of people, but there is no mistaking them. That hunting party was carrying spears and wearing clothes. Did you ever see bears do that?" Jondalar asked.

"So they are clever bears," she said.

"Don't underestimate them. They are not bears, or any other kind of animal. They are people, intelligent people," Jondalar said.

"You said you communicated with them? When?" asked the man Jondalar couldn't quite place.

"Once, when we were staying with the Sharamudoi, I got into trouble on the Great Mother River. The Sharamudoi live beside her, not too far from the end where she empties into Beran Sea. When you first get down off the glacier, the Mother is hardly a stream, but where they live she is huge, so wide in places, she almost looks like a lake. But though she can seem placid and smooth, she has a deceptively deep, swift, and strong current. By then so many other rivers, large and small, have flowed into her that when you see her from the home of the Sharamudoi, you know why she's called the Great Mother River." Jondalar was getting into Story-Telling mode, and people were listening with rapt attention.

"The Sharamudoi make excellent watercraft out of huge logs that are dug out and shaped to make a shell with pointed ends. I was practicing to control a small dugout boat using a paddle, when I lost control." Jondalar made a deprecating smile that showed his chagrin. "To be honest, I was showing off a little. They usually keep a line— with one end attached to the boat—and a hook with bait ready all the time in their boats, and I wanted to prove to them that I could catch a fish. The trouble is, fish in a river that big match its size, especially sturgeon. The River Men don't call it fishing when they go after the big ones; they say they are hunting sturgeon."

"I once saw a salmon nearly as big as a man," someone called out.

"Some sturgeon near the end of the Great Mother River are bigger than the length of three tall men," Jondalar said. "When I noticed the fishing gear, I threw out a line, but I was not lucky. I caught one! Or rather, a big sturgeon caught me. Because the line was fastened to the boat, when that fish started swimming, he took me with him. I lost the paddles and had no control. I reached for my knife to cut the line, but the boat hit something and knocked it out of my hand. The fish was strong and fast. He tried to dive and almost swamped me a couple of times. All I could do was hang on while that sturgeon pulled me upriver."

"What did you do?" "How far did you go?" "How did you stop it?" voices called out.

"It turned out that the hook did injure the fish and was causing it to bleed. It finally wore him out, but by then he had dragged me across a wide part of the river and quite a ways upstream. When he gave up the fight, we happened to be in the arm of a little backwater shoal. I got out and swam to land, grateful to feel something solid under my feet. . . ."

"It's a good story, Jondalar, but what does it have to do with flat-heads?" Zelandoni of the Fourteenth said.

He smiled at her, giving her all his attention. "I was just getting to that part. I was on land, but I was soaked and shivering with cold. I didn't have a knife to cut wood, I didn't have anything to make fire, most of the wood on the ground was wet, and I was really getting chilled. Suddenly, standing in front of me was this flathead. He had just the start of a beard, so he couldn't have been very old. He beckoned me to follow him, though I wasn't sure what he meant at first. Then I noticed smoke in the direction he was going, so I followed him and he led me to a fire," Jondalar said.

"Weren't you afraid to go with him? You didn't know what he might do," another voice called out. More people were joining them, Jondalar noticed. Ayla had been aware of the gathering crowd, too.

"By then, I was so cold, I didn't care. All I wanted was that fire. I squatted down, getting as close as I could to it, then I felt a fur being laid across my shoulders. I looked up and saw a woman. When she saw me, she ducked behind a bush and hid, and though I tried, I couldn't see her. From the glimpse I got of her, I think she was older, maybe the young man's mother.

"When I finally warmed up," Jondalar continued, "he led me back to the boat and the fish, belly up near the bank. It wasn't the biggest sturgeon I ever saw, but it wasn't small, at least the length of two men. The young Clan man took out a knife and cut that fish in half, *lengthwise*. He made some motions to me, which I didn't understand at the time, then wrapped up half that fish in a hide, flung it over his shoulder, and carried it off. Just about then, Thonolan and some River Men came paddling upstream and found me. They had seen me being pulled upriver and came looking for me. When I told them about the young flathead, just like you, Zelandoni of the Fourteenth, they didn't want to believe me, but then they saw the half fish that was left. Those men never stopped teasing me about going fishing and getting only half a fish, but it took three of them to drag the other half fish into the boat, and that young flathead picked it up and carried it away alone."

"Well, that's a good fish story, Jondalar," Zelandoni of the Fourteenth said.

Jondalar looked at her directly, with the full intensity of his amazing blue eyes. "I know it sounds like a fish story, but I promise you it is true. Every word," he said with earnest sincerity, then he shrugged and smiled, adding, "but I can't blame you for doubting.

"I got a bad cold after that dunking," he continued, "and while I was in bed staying warm by a fire, I had time to think about flatheads. That young man probably saved my life. At least he knew I was cold and needed warmth. He may have been just as afraid of me as I was of him, but he gave me what I needed and, in exchange, took half my fish. The first time I saw flatheads, I was surprised that they carried spears and wore clothes. After meeting that young man, and his mother, I knew they used fire and had sharp knives—and were very strong—but more than that, he was smart. He understood I was cold and he helped me, and for that, he thought he had a right to a share of my catch. I would have given him the whole thing, and I think he could have hauled it off, too, but he didn't take it all, he shared it."

"That is interesting," the woman said, smiling at Jondalar.

The unintentional charm and charisma of the decidedly handsome man was beginning to make an impression on the older woman, which was not lost on the One Who Was First. She would remember it for the future. If she could use Jondalar to ease her relationship with Zelandoni of the Fourteenth, she wouldn't hesitate. The woman had been like a canebrake of sharp thorns ever since she was selected to be First, impeding every decision and obstructing every policy she tried to make.

"I could tell you about the boy of mixed spirits that was adopted by the mate of the Mamutoi headman of the Lion Camp, because that was when I learned some of their signs," Jondalar continued, "but I think telling about the man and woman we met just before we started back across the glacier would be more significant, because they live close . . ."

"I think you should wait with that story, Jondalar," said Marthona, who had joined them. "It should be told to more people, and this meeting is to make decisions about the Matrimonial that is, if no one objects," she added, looking directly at Zelandoni of the Fourteenth Cave and smiling sweetly. She, too, had seen the effect her captivating son had on the older woman, and she was more than aware of the problems the Fourteenth had given the First. She had been a leader herself and understood.

"Unless you are really interested in hearing all the discussion and details," Joharran said to Jondalar and Ayla, "this might be a good time to look for a place to demonstrate your spear-thrower. I'd like you to do it before the first hunt."

Ayla wouldn't have minded staying. She wanted to learn as much as she could about Jondalar's—and now her—people, but he was eager to follow up on the suggestion. He wanted to share his new hunting weapon with all the Zelandonii. They explored the campsite of the Summer Meeting, Jondalar greeting friends and introducing Ayla. They found themselves the object of attention because of Wolf, but they expected it. Ayla wanted to get the initial disturbance over with as soon as possible. The sooner people started getting used to seeing the animals, the sooner they would begin to take them for granted.

They decided on an area that they thought would work for the spear-thrower demonstration, then they saw one of the young men who had helped hold up the travois when they crossed rivers to keep the goods they were transporting dry. He was from Three Rocks, the West Holding of the Twenty-ninth Cave, also known as Summer Camp, and had traveled with them the rest of the way. They chatted a while, then his mother came along and invited them to have a meal with them. The sun was already high, and they hadn't eaten since early in the day, and gratefully accepted. Even Wolf was given a bone with some meat on it. They were extended a special invitation to help with the pine-nut harvest in the fall.

On their way back to their camp, they passed by the large lodge of the zelandonia. The First was just coming out and stopped to tell them that all the people who were involved with the First Matrimonial that she had spoken with so far were willing to delay the ceremony until the arrival of Dalanar and the Lanzadonii. They were introduced to several of the other zelandonia, and the people from the Ninth Cave observed with interest their various reactions to the wolf.

By the time they started back to the camp of the Ninth Cave, the sun was dropping over the horizon in a blaze of gold coruscating in resplendent beams through red clouds. When they reached the bank of The River, flowing smoothly with hardly a ripple at that point, they continued upstream until they crossed the small creek that joined it. They stopped for a moment to watch the evening sky transform itself in a show of dazzling radiance as gold transmuted into shades of vermilion that waned into shimmering purple, then darkened to deep blue as the first glittering sky fires appeared. Soon the sooty black night became a backdrop to the multitude of blazing lights that filled the summer sky, with a concentrated accumulation wending its way like a path across the vault above. Ayla recalled the line from the Mother's Song, "The Mother's hot milk laid a path through the sky." Is that how it was made? she wondered as they turned toward the welcoming fires of their nearby camp.

When Ayla awoke the next morning, everyone else seemed to be up and gone already and she was feeling uncharacteristically lazy. Her eyes were accustomed to the dim light inside the dwelling, and she lay in her sleeping roll, looking at the designs carved and painted on the sturdy wooden center pole and the smudges of soot that already blackened the edges of the smoke hole, until she had to pass water—she felt the need even more often lately. She didn't know where the community waste trenches had been dug, so she used the night basket. She wasn't the only one who had used it, she noticed. I'll empty it later, she thought. It was one of the unpleasant chores that were shared by those who felt it was a duty and those who were shamed into it if it was noticed that they hadn't recently.

When she walked back to her sleeping roll to shake it out, she looked more closely around the inside of the summer camp shelter. She had been surprised at the structures that had been made while she and Jondalar were visiting the day before. Though she had noticed the lodges of the people who had set up their camps near the main area, she was still expecting to see the traveling tents, but most people did not use the tents they had traveled with at the Summer Meeting camp. During the warm season, the traveling tents would be used by various people for temporary treks to hunt, or gather produce, or visit as they ranged over their territory. The summer lodge was a more permanent structure, a circular, straight-sided, rather substantial dwelling. Though made differently, Ayla understood they were similar in purpose to the lodges used by the Mamutoi during their Summer Meetings.

Though it was dark inside—the only light came from the open entrance and an occasional sliver of sunlight that found its way through cracks in the wall where pieces joined—Ayla saw that, besides the center pole of pine, the dwelling had an interior wall of panels woven out of flattened bullrush stems and painted with designs and animals. They were attached to the inside of poles that encircled the center pole and provided a fairly large enclosed space that could be left open or divided into smaller areas with movable interior panels. The ground was covered with mats, which were made of bullrushes, tall phragmite reeds, cattail leaves, or grasses, and sleeping rolls were spread out around a slightly off-center fireplace. The smoke escaped through a hole above it, near the center pole. A smoke hole cover could be adjusted from the inside with short poles that were attached to it.

She was curious about how the rest of the structure was made and stepped outside. First she glanced around the camp, which was composed of several large circular lodges surrounding a central fireplace, and then she walked around the outside of the dwelling. Poles were lashed together in a way that was similar to the fence of the surround that was erected to capture animals, but instead of the freestanding flexible construction that could yield when an animal bumped or butted into it, the summer lodge fencing was attached to widely spaced anchoring poles of alder that were sunk into the ground.

A wall of sturdy vertical panels made of overlapped cattail leaves, which shed rain, was attached to the outside of the poles, leaving an air space between the outer and inner walls for extra insulation to make it cooler on hot days and, with a fire inside, warmer on cool nights. It also avoided accumulation of moisture condensation on the inside when it was cold out. The roof was a fairly thick thatch of overlapping reeds that sloped down from the center pole. The thatch was not particularly well made, but it kept the rain out and was required only for a season.

Parts of the lodge were brought with them, in particular the woven mats, panels, interior walls, and some of the poles. Generally, each person who was sharing a dwelling carried some sections or pieces, but much of the material was gathered fresh from the surrounding area each year. When they returned home in the fall, the structures were partially dismantled to retrieve the reusable parts but left standing. They seldom lasted through the heavy snows and winds of winter, and by the following summer, there were only collapsed ruins, which disintegrated back into the environment before the same location was used again for a Summer Meeting.

Ayla remembered that the Mamutoi had different names for their summer camps than they did for their winter dwellings. The Lion Camp, for example, was the Cattail Camp at the Summer Meeting, but the same people who lived at Lion Camp lived there. She asked Jondalar if the Ninth Cave had a different summer name. He explained that their location was just called the camp of the Ninth Cave, but living arrangements at Zelandonii Summer Meetings were not quite the same as they were in winter in the shelters of stone.

Each summer dwelling accommodated more people than usually shared the roomier, more permanent structures under the large overhang of the Ninth Cave. As a rule, family members, including those who had separate dwellings in winter, shared a lodge, but some people didn't even stay at the same camp. Instead, it was not uncommon for some to spend the summer with other relatives or friends. For example, young matrons who had moved to their mates' Caves often liked to take their children and spend the summer with their mothers, siblings, or childhood friends, and their mates usually accompanied them.

In addition, young women who would be having their First Rites that year lived together in a separate dwelling near the large central dwelling of the zelandonia, at least for the first part of the summer. Another dwelling nearby was set up for the women who chose to be donii-women that year, to be available for the young men who were approaching puberty.

Most young men who were past puberty—and some men not so young—often chose to band together separately away from their home camps and set up lodges of their own. They were required to be on the periphery of the camp, as far away as possible from the very desirable young women who were being prepared for First Rites. For the most part the men didn't mind. They would have liked to ogle the women, but they rather liked the privacy of being off by themselves, so no one could complain if they were a little loud or rowdy. As a consequence, the men's dwellings were called "the far lodges," usually shortened to fa'lodges. The men who stayed in a fa'lodge were usually unmated or between mates—or wished they were.

Since he didn't rush to greet her when she went out, Ayla assumed that Wolf was with Jondalar. There were not many people outside, most were probably somewhere around the central area, the main focus of the Summer Meeting, but she found some leftover tea near the camp's fireplace. She noticed that the fireplace was not shaped like a big round bonfire, but more like a trench. She had seen the evening before that more people could get closer to a fire if it was extended and longer logs and branches, cut down or deadfall, could be used without having to hack them into smaller pieces. While she was drinking the tea, Salova, Rushemar's mate, came out of her lodge, holding her baby daughter.

"Greetings, Ayla," she said, putting her baby down on a mat.

"Greetings, Salova," Ayla said, coming closer to see the baby. She held out a finger for the infant to grab and smiled at her.

Salova looked at Ayla, hesitated, then asked, "Would you mind watching Marsola for a while? I gathered some materials to make baskets and have some of them soaking in the creek. I'd like to get them and sort them out. I promised some people I would make baskets for them."

"I'd love to watch Marsola," Ayla said, smiling at her, then turned back to the baby.

Salova was a little anxious around the foreign woman and kept up a nervous chatter. "I just fed her, so she shouldn't be any trouble. I've got plenty of milk. Giving a little to Lorala isn't any trouble at all. Lanoga brought her around last night. She's getting nice and plump, and smiles now. She didn't used to smile at all. Oh, you haven't eaten yet, have you? I have some soup left over from last night with some good pieces of deer meat in it. You are welcome to it, if you want. It's what I ate this morning, it's probably still warm."

"Thank you. I think I will have a little soup," Ayla said.

"I'll be right back," she said, then hurried away.

Ayla found the soup in a large aurochs stomach container that had been mounted on a wood frame and placed over some hot coals at the edge of the long community fireplace to simmer—the coals had almost died, but the soup was still hot. A stack of odd bowls was nearby, some tightly woven, some carved out of wood, a couple of shallow ones shaped out of some large bone. A few used bowls were scattered around where people had left them. Ayla scooped out some soup with a ladle made of a curved sheep horn, then took out her eating knife. She saw that there were vegetables in it, too, though they were rather soft by now.

She sat on the mat beside the baby, who was lying on her back, kicking her feet into the air. Some deer dewclaws had been tied to one ankle, and they rattled whenever she kicked up her feet. Ayla finished her soup, then picked up the baby and, supporting her head with her hands, held her so that she was looking at her. When Salova came back with a wide, flat basket full of various fibrous vegetation, she saw Ayla talking to her baby and making her smile. It warmed the young mother's heart and made her feel more relaxed around the stranger.

"I really appreciate your watching her, Ayla. It gave me a chance to get this ready," Salova said.

"It was my pleasure, Salova. Marsola is a wonderful baby."

"Did you know that Proleva's younger sister, Levela, is getting mated at the First Matrimonial, just like you? You always feel a special tie to the people who mate at the same Matrimonial as you," Salova said. "Proleva wanted me to make some special baskets for her, as part of her Matrimonial gift."

"Would you mind if I watched you for a little while? I've made baskets, but I'd like to know how you make them," Ayla said.

"I don't mind at all. I'd like the company, and maybe you can show me how you do it. I always like to learn new ways," Salova said.

The two young women sat together, talking and comparing basket-making techniques, while the baby slept beside them. Ayla liked the way Salova used materials of different colors and actually wove pictures of animals and various designs into her containers. Salova thought Ayla's subtle techniques that created different textures gave a rich elegance to her seemingly simple baskets. Each gained an appreciation for the other's skill, and for each other.

After a while Ayla got up. "I'm going to have to use the trenches, can you tell me where they are? I should empty the night basket, too. And I might as well wash these bowls," she added, picking up the used ones that were scattered around. "And then I should go check on the horses."

"The trenches are over there," Salova said, pointing in a direction away from the creek and the camp, "and we've been washing the cooking and eating things at the end of the creek, where it empties into The River. There's some clean sand for scouring nearby. I don't have to tell you where the horses are." She smiled then. "I went to look at the horses yesterday with Rushemar. They made me nervous at first, but they seem gentle, and content. The mare ate some grass out of my hand." Her smile turned to a grin and then to a worried frown. "I hope that was all right. Rushemar said Jondalar told him it would be."

"Of course it's all right. It makes them more comfortable if they get to know the people around them," Ayla said.

She's not so strange, Salova thought as she watched Ayla go. She talks a little funny, but she's really nice. I wonder what ever made her think that she could make those animals do what she wanted them to? I never even imagined that one day I would feed a horse some grass out of my own hand.

After cleaning up the bowls and stacking them near the fire trench, Ayla thought it might be nice to clean herself up and go for a swim. She went back to their lodge, smiled at Salova and the baby, and slipped inside. She took the soft drying hide out of her traveling pack and then looked over her clothing. She didn't have much, but it was more than she came with. Though she had cleaned them, she did not want to wear the worn and stained clothes she had worn on her long Journey except as working clothes.

The clothes she had worn on the recent trek to the Summer Meeting were the ones she had saved to wear when she met Jondalar's people, but even they were well-worn and had their share of stains. She also had the boys' winter underwear that Marona and her friends had given her, but she knew that wouldn't be appropriate. Of course, she had her Matrimonial outfit, but that would be saved, as would the beautiful outfit that Marthona had given to her, for special occasions. What was left were a few things of theirs that Marthona and Folara had given her. They were unfamiliar to her, but she thought they might be suitable.

Before she left the lodge, she noticed her riding blanket folded up near her sleeping roll and decided to take it as well. Then she went to see the horses. Whinney and Racer were both glad to see her and crowded close to get her attention. Both wore halters with a long lead attached to a sturdy tree; she removed them and put them in her pack, then she tied the riding blanket on Whinney, mounted her, and started upstream.

The horses were in high spirits and broke out at a fast run, happy for the freedom. Their feeling was communicated to Ayla, who let them set their own pace. She was particularly pleased when she reached the meadow near the pool to see Wolf racing toward them. That had to mean Jondalar was nearby.

Sometime after Ayla left, Joharran came to the camp and asked Salova if she had seen Ayla.

"Yes, we were making baskets together," she said. "The last time I saw her, she was heading toward the horses. She said she needed to check on them."

"I'll go look for her, but if you see her, will you tell her Zelandoni wants to talk to her?"

"Of course," Salova said, wondering what the donier wanted. Then she shrugged. No one was likely to tell her what the First wanted.

Ayla saw Jondalar step out from behind some brush with a surprised grin on his face. She pulled to a stop, slid down, and raced into his arms.

"What are you doing here?" he asked after their warm embrace. "I didn't even tell anybody I was coming here. I was just walking upstream, and when I got this far, I remembered that scree slope behind the pool, and thought I'd check to see if there was any flint."

"Is there?"

"Yes, not the best quality, but serviceable. What made you decide to come here?"

"I woke up feeling lazy. Hardly anyone was around, except Salova and her baby. She asked me to watch Marsola when she went to get her materials to make baskets. She's such a wonderful baby, Jondalar. We talked for a while and did some basket-weaving, then I decided to come for a swim and take the horses for a run. And found you. What a nice surprise," she said, smiling.

"A nice surprise for me, too. Maybe I'll take a swim with you. I'm pretty dusty from hauling rocks around, but first I should get the stones I've found and bring them here. Then, we'll see," he said with an inviting grin. He gave her a slow, lingering kiss. "Maybe I can worry about those rocks later."

"Go ahead and get them, so you won't have to clean the dust off twice. I wanted to wash my hair, anyway. It was a long, sweaty trek getting here," Ayla said.

When Joharran reached the place where the horses had been, it was obvious they were gone. They've probably gone for one of their long rides, he thought, and Zelandoni really wanted to see Ayla. Willamar wanted to talk to them, too. Jondalar knows they'll have plenty of time to themselves after the Matrimonial, you'd think he would realize that there are important issues to settle at the beginning of a Summer Meeting, Joharran thought, a little irritated that he couldn't find them. He had not been all that pleased that he was the one the donier happened to see when she was looking for someone to send for them. After all, he had more important things to do than chase after his brother, but he didn't feel he could exactly refuse Zelandoni, at least not without a very good excuse.

He glanced down and saw the fresh tracks of the horses. He was too experienced a tracker not to notice the direction they had taken, and he knew they had not headed off away from camp. It looked as if they were following the creek upstream. He recalled the pleasing little glen at the head of the small waterway, with the spring-fed pond and the grassy meadow. That's probably where they went, he thought, smiling to himself. Since he had been sent on a mission to find them, he didn't like returning without them.

He followed the creek, checking the tracks as he went to make sure they hadn't veered off, and when he saw the horses ahead, grazing contentedly, he knew he'd found them. When he reached the screen of hazelnut shrubs, some as tall as trees, he peered through and, seeing only Ayla, wondered where his brother was. When he reached the sandy bank, she was just ducking under the water, and he called to her when she came up for air.

"Ayla, I've been looking for you."

Ayla pushed back her hair and rubbed her eyes. "Oh, Joharran, it's you," she said in a tone of voice he couldn't quite identify.

"Do you know where Jondalar is?"

"Yes, he was looking for flint in the rock pile behind the pond, and went to get the stones he found. Then he was going to come and bathe with me," Ayla said, seeming a little disconcerted.

"Zelandoni wants to see you, and Willamar wanted to talk to you both," Joharran said.

"Oh," she said, sounding rather disappointed.

Joharran had often seen women without clothes on. Most of them bathed in The River every morning in the summer and washed themselves in winter. Nakedness by itself was not considered especially suggestive. Women wore special clothing or accoutrements that were meant to be inviting when they wanted to show interest in a man, or behaved in certain ways, especially at a festival to honor the Mother. But as Ayla started out of the water, it occurred to him that she and his brother had had other plans, which he'd interrupted. The thought made him aware of her body as she approached him, walking out of the water.

She was tall, with shapely curves and well-defined muscles. Her large breasts still had the firmness of a young woman, and he'd always found a woman with a slightly rounded stomach appealing. Marona has always been considered the Beauty of the Bunch, he thought, no wonder she took such a dislike to Ayla from the beginning. She looked good in that winter underwear she got tricked into wearing, but that was nothing compared to really seeing her. Marona doesn't compare. My brother is a lucky man, he thought. Ayla is a fine-looking woman. But she is going to get a lot of attention at Mother Festivals, and I'm not sure how Jondalar will like that.

Ayla was looking at him with a puzzled expression, and it made Joharran realize that he'd been staring. He flushed slightly and looked away, and saw his brother coming, carrying a heavy load of stones. He went to help him.

"What are you doing here?" Jondalar said.

"Zelandoni wants to talk to Ayla, and Willamar would like to talk to both of you," Joharran said.

"What does Zelandoni want? Can't it wait?" Jondalar said.

"She didn't seem to think so. Chasing down my brother and his Promised is not the way I planned to spend the day, either. Don't worry, Jondalar," Joharran said with a conspiratorial grin. "You'll just have to wait a while. And she's worth waiting for, isn't she?"

Jondalar started to make protests and denials of his innuendos, then he relaxed and smiled. "I waited a long time to find her," he said. "Well, now that you're here, you can help me carry these stones back. I did want to take a swim and clean up a little."

"Why don't you leave the stones here for now. They won't go

away, then you'll have an excuse to come back later," Joharran said, "and I'm sure you'll have time for a swim . . . if that's all you do."

It was near midday by the time Ayla and Jondalar, and Wolf, found their way to the main camp area, and from their air of relaxed contentment, Joharran suspected they had found time for more than a quick swim after he left. He'd told Zelandoni he had found them and passed on her message, and he had encouraged his brother to hurry. It wasn't his fault if Jondalar dallied, not that he could blame him.

Several people from the Ninth Cave had gathered around the long cooking hearth near the zelandonia lodge, and just as Ayla was approaching the entrance to let the donier know she was there, the large woman who was First came out, followed by several others with the distinctive tattoos on their foreheads of Those Who Served The Mother.

"There you are, Ayla," Zelandoni said when she saw her. "I've been expecting you all morning."

"We were upstream from the camp when Joharran found us. There is a nice spring-fed pond there. I wanted to give the horses a run and brush their coats. They get nervous around so many people until they get used to them, and brushing calms them, and I wanted to take a swim and clean up after the trek here," Ayla said. Everything she said was entirely true, though it may not have included all of her activities.

The donier regarded her, clean and dressed in the Zelandonii clothing that Marthona had given to her; then she saw Jondalar, also looking fresh and clean, and raised her eyebrows in a knowing look. Joharran was watching the One Who Was First and the woman his brother had brought home with him and realized that Zelandoni had a pretty good idea what had delayed them, and that Ayla didn't seem to care that she hadn't rushed. The large woman had an authoritative bearing and he knew she intimidated many, but she didn't seem to daunt the stranger.

"We were just stopping for a meal," Zelandoni said, walking toward the large cooking hearth, compelling Ayla to fall in beside her. "Proleva has organized the preparation and just informed us it was ready. You might as well join us. It will give me a chance to talk to you. Do you have one of your firestones?"

"Yes. I always keep a fire-making kit with me," Ayla said.

"I would like you to demonstrate your new fire-making technique to the zelandonia. I think it should be introduced to the people, but it is important that it be shown in the right way, with appropriate ritual."

"I didn't need a ritual to show it to Marthona, or you. It's not that difficult once you see how it's done," Ayla said.

"No, it's not difficult, but it is a new and powerful technique, and that can be disturbing, especially for those people who don't accept change easily and resist it," the donier said. "You must know people like that."

Ayla thought of the Clan, with their lives based on tradition, their reluctance to change, and their inability to cope with new ideas. "Yes, I know people like that," she said. "But the people I've met recently seem to enjoy learning new things."

All the Others she had met seemed to adapt so easily to changes in their lives, to thrive on innovation. She hadn't realized that there might be some who were not comfortable with a different way of doing things, who actually resisted it. It gave her a sudden insight, and she frowned at the thought. That could explain certain attitudes and incidents that had puzzled her, such as why some people seemed so unwilling to accept the idea that the Clan were people. Like that Zelandoni, the one from the Fourteenth Cave, who kept calling them animals. Even after Jondalar explained, she acted as if she didn't believe him. I think she didn't want to change her opinion.

"It is true. Most people do like to learn a better or quicker way of doing something, but sometimes it depends upon how it is presented," the First said. "For example, Jondalar has been away for a long time. He matured while he was gone and learned many new things, but the people he knows weren't there to see it, so some of them still think of him the way he was when he left. Now he has returned and he's eager to share what he's learned and discovered, which is commendable, but he didn't learn everything all at once. Even his new weapon, which is a valuable tool for hunting, takes practice to use. Those who have been successful and are comfortable with the weapons they know may not be willing to put forth the effort it will take to learn the new one, though I have no doubt it will be used by all hunters one day."

"Yes, the spear-thrower does take practice," Ayla said. "We know it now, but in the beginning, we worked at it."

"And that is only one thing," the donier continued, while she picked up a plate made from the shoulder bone of a deer and put some slices of meat on it. "What kind of meat is it?" she asked a woman who was standing nearby.

"That's mammoth. Some hunters from the Nineteenth Cave went north on a hunting trek and got a mammoth. They decided to share some. I understand they got a woolly rhinoceros, too."

"I haven't had mammoth for a long time," Zelandoni said. "I'm going to relish this."

"Have you tasted mammoth?" the woman asked Ayla.

"Yes," she said. "The Mamutoi, the people I lived with before, are known as mammoth hunters, although they hunted other animals, too. But it's been some time since I've had any. I, too, will enjoy this."

Zelandoni thought about introducing Ayla to the woman, but once she started, there would be no end, and she still wanted to talk to her about a ceremony using the firestone. She turned back to Ayla while she added some round white roots, ground nuts, to her plate, and cooked greens, nettles, she thought, mixed with pieces of brown-capped, spongy, boletus mushroom.

"Jondalar also brought you, and your animals, Ayla. You must know how astonishing that is. People have hunted horses, and observed them with other horses, but they have never seen horses behave as yours do. It is frightening, at first, to see those horses go where you want them to, or that this wolf will walk through a camp full of people and do what you tell him," she said, specifically acknowledging Wolf for the first time, though she had certainly seen him. He yipped a small bark when she looked at him.

It was a custom the wolf and the woman had developed that rather surprised Ayla. Zelandoni didn't always acknowledge Wolf when she saw him, and he ignored her until she did, but when she did, he responded with a short yip. She seldom touched him, except for a pat on the head now and then, but on rare occasions, Wolf would take her hand in his teeth, never leaving any toothmarks. She always allowed it, saying only that they understood each other. It seemed to Ayla that they did, in their own way.

"I know you say that anyone could do it, if one starts with a young animal, and that may be true, but people don't know that. They can only see it as something not natural to this world, so it must come from another world, from the spirit world. I am frankly amazed at how well they have accepted the animals, but it is an uneasy acceptance. It will take time. And now we want to show them something else you have brought that no one has seen before. People don't know you yet, Ayla. I'm sure people will want to use the firestone, once they've seen how it works, but they may be afraid of it. I think it has to be seen as a Gift from the Mother, which can be done if it is first understood and accepted by the zelandonia, and presented with the proper ritual," the donier said.

The way she explained it seemed entirely logical, but in a quiet space in her own mind, it made Ayla realize how persuasive Zelandoni could be. "When you explain it like that, I understand," Ayla said. "Of course I will show the zelandonia how the firestone works, and help you with whatever ritual you feel is necessary."

They joined Jondalar's family and some of the people from the Ninth Cave who were sitting with a few people from other Caves. After the meal, Zelandoni took Ayla aside. "Can you leave the wolf outside the lodge for a while? I think it's important to concentrate on the fire-making, and I'm afraid Wolf would be a distraction," she said.

"I'm sure Jondalar won't mind keeping him," Ayla said, turning to look at him. He nodded, and when she got up to leave, she told Wolf to stay with him, making hand signs as well, though they were not noticed by most people. The midday sun had been bright, which made the inside of the zelandonia lodge seem dark even though many lamps were lit. Her eyes adjusted quickly, but when the First stood up to begin speaking, the Zelandoni of the Fourteenth Cave objected.

"Why is she here?" the Fourteenth said. "She may be a Zelandonii woman, but she is not zelandonia. She is an outsider and does not belong at this meeting."

24

The One Who Was First Among Those Who Served The Mother repressed a sigh of frustration. She was not going to make any obvious display of her irritation and let the tall, thin Zelandoni of the Fourteenth Cave have the satisfaction of knowing how much she annoyed her. But the question brought frowns and disapproving looks from some of the other Zelandonia, and a smirk from the acolyte of the Fifth Cave with the missing front teeth.

"You are right, Zelandoni of the Fourteenth," the First said. "Outsiders, those who are not part of the zelandonia, are not usually invited to these meetings. This is a gathering of those who have had some experience with the world of the spirits, the ones who have been called and the acolytes, who have shown promise and are in training. That's why I have invited Ayla. You know that she is a healer. She was a great help to Shevonar, the man who was trampled when that bison bolted during the last community hunt," the donier said.

"Shevonar died, and I don't know how much help she was, I didn't examine him," the Fourteenth said. "There are many who have some knowledge of certain medicinals. Almost everyone knows about willow bark and its ability to stop the pain of minor aches, for example."

"I assure you that she knows a great deal more than the uses of willow bark," the One Who Was First said. "One of her names and ties from her previous people is Daughter of the Mammoth Hearth. The Mammoth Hearth of the Mamutoi is the same as the zelandonia, they are Those Who Serve The Mother."

"Are you saying she's a Zelandoni of the Mamutoi? Where is her tattoo?" The question was asked by an elderly woman with white hair and intelligent eyes.

"Her tattoo, Zelandoni of the Nineteenth?" the large woman asked, and thought, what did the Nineteenth know that she didn't? She was an experienced and reliable Zelandoni, who had learned a great deal in her long life. It was a shame she'd been having so much trouble with arthritis during the past years. The time was drawing near when she would not be able to walk to the Summer Meetings. If this meeting were not near the Nineteenth Cave, she might not have made it this year.

"I know of the Mamutoi. Jerika of the Lanzadonii lived with them for a while when she was young and still traveling with her mother and the man of her hearth on their long journey. One summer, many years ago, when she was pregnant with Joplaya, she was having some trouble and I attended her. She told me about the Mamutoi. Their doniers are also marked with tattoos on their faces, though not quite like ours, but if Ayla is the same as a Zelandoni, where is her tattoo?"

"She was in training, but not fully trained when she left to come here with Jondalar. She is not the same as a Zelandoni, she is more like an acolyte, but with more knowledge of healing than most. In addition she was adopted to the Mammoth Hearth by the Mamut Who Was First, because he saw her potential," the First said.

"Are you sponsoring her to become an acolyte of the zelandonia?" the Nineteenth asked. Though they seldom spoke out, there were a few quiet murmurs from the acolytes in attendance.

"Not at this time. I haven't yet asked her if she wants to further her training," the First said.

Ayla felt a touch of consternation. Though she would not mind talking about healing with some of them, she had no desire to become a Zelandoni. She just wanted to mate with Jondalar and have children, and she noticed that few of the zelandonia had mates or children. It wasn't that they couldn't mate if they chose, but it seemed that there were so many other demands on their time and attention when they were in the service of the Great Earth Mother that they didn't have time to be mothers themselves.

"Then why is she here?" the Fourteenth asked. Her wispy gray hair had pulled loose from the small bun on the back of her head, more on one side than the other, giving her a careless, disheveled appearance. If someone were kind, they would tactfully suggest that she fix her hair before she went out, but the First wouldn't dream of it. The contentious Zelandoni would take anything she said as criticism.

"I asked her to come because I would like her to show you something that I think you will find very interesting."

"Is it about those animals she controls?" asked another donier.

The First smiled. At least someone was willing to admit that Ayla had some unusual skills that might be worthy of the zelandonia. "No, Zelandoni of the South Holding of the Twenty-ninth Cave. That might be cause for another meeting, but this time, she has something else for you to see." Though the South Holding Twenty-ninth was an assistant to the primary Zelandoni of the Twenty-ninth, it was only in terms of speaking for all of Three Rocks. He was a full-fledged Zelandoni in his own right, and the First knew him to be a good healer. He had the same right to speak out as any other donier.

Ayla noticed that the One Who Was First addressed the members of the zelandonia by their full titles, which were sometimes quite long, since they included the counting words of their Caves, but sounded very formal and important. Then it occurred to her that the only way to differentiate among them was by the counting words. They had given up their personal names and were all "Zelandoni." They had, she realized, exchanged their names for counting words.

When she lived in her valley, she had scratched a mark on a stick every day she was there. By the time Jondalar arrived, she had a bundle of sticks full of marks. When he used the counting words to tally the cut marks and was then able to tell her how long she had lived in her valley, it had seemed to her magic that was so powerful, it was almost frightening. When he taught them to her, she had sensed that counting words were very important and highly valued by the Zelandonii. Now she realized that, at least among Those Who Served The Mother, they were more important than names, and their use by the zelandonia gave them the essence of those powerful symbols.

The First beckoned to Jonokol. "First Acolyte of the Ninth Cave, will you use the sand I asked you to get and put out the fire? And First Acolyte of the Second Cave, will you put out all the lamps?"

Ayla recognized the two acolytes the First had called upon for assistance. They had guided her when she visited the deep cave with the animals painted on the walls at Fountain Rocks. She heard comments and questions of curiosity from the assembled group who knew the First was setting them up for something dramatic. Most of the older, experienced ones were preparing themselves to be critical. They knew and understood the techniques and impact of dramatic presentations and were determined not to be easily deluded by tricks or misdirection.

When all the fires had been put out, there was still enough light to see from the occasional beams of sunlight that filtered in here and there. The lodge was not completely dark. Ayla looked around and noticed light seeping in, particularly around the outline of the entrance, though it was closed, and around another less obvious access almost directly opposite it. Later, she thought, she might walk around the outside of the spacious zelandonia lodge to find out if she could see the second opening.

The First knew the demonstration would be much more impressive at night when the dark was total, but that didn't matter with the ones who were here. They would understand the possibilities immediately. "Would anyone like to come here and verify that the fire in this fireplace is completely out?" she said.

The Fourteenth quickly volunteered. She patted the sand carefully and dug her fingers in at a few warm spots, then stood up to announce, "The sand is dry, warm in a few places, but the fire is out and there are no hot coals."

"Ayla, will you tell me what you need to start a fire?" the First said.

"I have most of it here," she said, taking out the fire-starting kit that she had used so often on her Journey, "but tinder is necessary; almost anything that catches fire quickly will work, fireweed fuzz, or rotted wood from an old stump, if it's dry and especially if it's pitchy, for example. Then it's good to have some small kindling close by, and of course some larger pieces of wood."

There was a little buzz of noise, and the First picked up some words of irritation. They didn't need a lesson in fire-making, they were saying. Everyone knew how to make a fire from the time they were small children. Good, she thought, feeling rather pleased. Let them grumble. They only think they know all there is to making fire.

"Will you make a fire for us, Ayla?" the Zelandoni leader said.

Ayla had fluffed up a small mound of fuzzy fireweed tops as tinder and had a piece of iron pyrite in her left hand and a flint striker in her right, but it wasn't obvious. She struck the firestone, saw a good spark land in the fluff of fireweed, blew it into life, and added kindling. In less time than it took to explain it, she had a fire going.

There were some involuntary oohs and "How did she do that?"

comments, then the Zelandoni of the Third Cave said, "Can you do it again?"

Ayla smiled at the Third. The older man had been so kind and supportive when she was trying to help Shevonar, she was pleased to see him. She moved over to another spot nearby and lit another fire beside the first one within the circle of stones that defined the fireplace, and then, without being asked, she lit a third.

"All right, how does she do that?" a man asked the First. Ayla had not met him before.

"Zelandoni of the Fifth Cave, since she is the one who discovered it, Ayla will explain her technique," the First said.

Ayla realized this was the Zelandoni of the Cave that had already left for the Summer Meeting when they'd stopped at Old Valley. He was a younger, middle-aged man with brown hair and a round face, which characterized his body as well. There was a round softness about him, and the fleshiness of his face tended to make his eyes look small, but she sensed a shrewd cleverness to him. He could see there might be some benefit to her fire-making technique and wasn't too proud to ask. Then she recalled that the acolyte with the missing front teeth that Jondalar didn't like and Wolf had threatened was also from the Fifth Cave.

"First Acolyte of the Second, will you light the lamps again, and Ayla, would you demonstrate how you make fire to the zelandonia?" the large woman said, fighting to keep from gloating. She noticed that her acolyte, Jonokol, was grinning with delight. He loved to see his mentor outmaneuver the rest of the wise, canny, intelligent, strong-willed, and sometimes arrogant zelandonia.

"I use a firestone, like this, and strike it with a piece of flint." She held out both her hands and showed the iron pyrite in one and the flint in the other.

"I've seen those kinds of stones," Zelandoni of the Fourteenth said, pointing to the hand that held the iron pyrite.

"I hope you can remember where," the First said. "We don't know yet whether they are rare or plentiful."

"Where did you find stones like that?" the Fifth asked Ayla.

"I found the first ones in a valley far to the east of here. Jondalar and I looked for more on our way here. They might not have been where we looked, but I didn't find any until after we arrived here. A few days ago, I found a few near the Ninth Cave," Ayla explained.

"And you will show us how they work?" said a tall blond woman.

"That's what she came here to do, Zelandoni of the Second Cave," the First said.

Ayla knew she had not met the One Who Served The Mother from the Second Cave, but there was a familiarity about her. Then she remembered Jondalar's friend Kimeran, the age-mate with whom he shared a superficial resemblance because of their height and hair color. He was the leader of the Second Cave, and though the woman looked a little older, Ayla could definitely see the resemblance. With the brother as leader and the sister as spiritual leader, the arrangement was reminiscent of the brother-sister leadership customs of the Mamutoi—she smiled at the memory—except with them the leadership was shared and Mamut was their spiritual leader.

"I have only two firestones with me," Ayla said, "but we have more at camp. If Jondalar is nearby, perhaps he can bring some so several people can try it at once." The large woman nodded, and Ayla continued. "It's not hard to do, but it takes a little practice to get the knack of it. First make sure you have some good tinder nearby. Then, if you strike them together right, you can draw a long-lived spark that you can blow into a flame."

While Ayla demonstrated how to use the firestones to the crowd gathered around her, the One Who Was First sent Mikolan, the Second Acolyte of the Fourteenth Cave, to look for Jondalar. As the leader of the zelandonia watched, she noticed that no one held back. There were no more doubts or questions. This new technique for starting a fire was not a trick, it was a legitimate new way to make fire quickly, and they were all eager to learn, as she knew they would be. Fire was too important not to know everything they could about it.

To the people who lived in that cold, ancient, periglacial region, fire was essential, it was the difference between life and death. They needed to know how to start it, how to keep it going, and how to move it from place to place. Though it could be intensely cold, the broad expanse of territory surrounding the massive sheets of glacial ice stretching far south of polar regions was rich with life. The brutally frigid and dry winter conditions inhibited the growth of trees, but at the middle latitudes climate was still seasonal. It could even be hot during the summer, which fostered extensive grasslands that supported vast herds of a great variety of grazing and browsing animals. They, in turn, provided high-energy food to carnivorous and omnivorous animals.

All the species of animals that lived near the ice had adapted to the cold by growing dense, warm, furry coats—except for one. The bare-skinned, furless human animal was a tropical creature who could not live in the cold unassisted. Humans came later, drawn by the rich food supply, but only after they learned how to control fire. Using the fur of the animals they killed for food, they could survive for a while exposed to the elements, but to live, they needed fire, to keep them warm when they rested and slept, and to cook their food, both meat and vegetable, to make it more digestible. When materials to burn were available, they tended to take fire somewhat for granted, but they never forgot how indispensable it was, and when fuel was scarce, or the weather was wet or snowy, they knew how much they depended on fire.

After several people had used one of the two firestones to make a fire and passed it on to the next one waiting to try, Jondalar arrived with more of them. The First personally took the firestones from him at the entrance, counted them to herself, and brought them to Ayla. The training sessions went faster after that. Once all the Zelandonia had each made at least one fire, the acolytes were invited to learn the technique, the more confident doniers helping Ayla to teach their apprentices. It was the Zelandoni of the Fourteenth who brought up the question that everyone wanted to ask.

"What do you plan to do with all these firestones?" she asked.

"From the beginning, Jondalar talked about sharing them with his people," Ayla began. "Willamar has also talked about using them for trade. It depends on how many we find. I don't think it's for me alone to say."

"Of course, we can all look for some, but do you think there are enough so that each Cave at this Summer Meeting can have at least one?" the First Zelandoni asked. She had counted them and knew the answer.

"I don't know how many Caves are at this Summer Meeting, but I think there may be enough," Ayla said.

"If there's only one for each Cave, I think it should be entrusted to the Zelandoni of that Cave," the Fourteenth said.

"I agree, and I think we should keep this way of making fire with firestones to ourselves. If only we can make fire like that, imagine how awe-inspiring it would be. Think how a Cave will react to seeing instant fire created by a Zelandoni, especially if it's really dark," said Zelandoni of the Fifth Cave. His eyes were full of enthusiasm.

"We would command much more authority, and it could be a very effective way to make ceremonies more meaningful."

"You're right, Zelandoni of the Fifth," the Fourteenth said, adding her agreement. "That's a good idea."

"Or perhaps it should be entrusted to the Zelandoni and the leader jointly," the Eleventh said, "to avoid any possible conflict. I know Kareja would not like it if she didn't have some control over this new technique."

Ayla smiled at the small slender man who she recalled had a powerful grip and confident manner. He was loyal to his Cave's leader, which she thought was commendable.

"These firestones would be too useful to a Cave to be kept a secret," the First said. "We are here to Serve The Mother. We give up our personal names to become one with our people. We must always think first of the best interests of our Caves. It might be exciting for us if we could keep this firestone to ourselves, but the benefit to the entire Zelandonii outweighs our wishes. The stones of the earth are the bones of the Great Earth Mother. It is a Gift from Her, we cannot withhold it."

The One Who Was First stopped and looked searchingly at each member of the zelandonia in attendance. She knew the firestones could never be kept secret, even if they hadn't already been shared. There was some obvious disappointment and perhaps a little resistance from the doniers of some of the Caves. She was sure the Fourteenth was getting ready to object.

"You can't make them a secret," Ayla said with a frown.

"Why not?" said the Fourteenth. "I think that should be a decision for the zelandonia."

"I have already given some to Jondalar's family," Ayla said.

"That's too bad," the Fifth said, shaking his head, immediately acknowledging the uselessness of pursuing it, "but what's done is done."

"We have enough authority without them," Zelandoni Who Was First said, "and we can still use them in our own way. For one thing, we can make an exciting ceremony when we present the firestone to the Caves. I think it will be most effective if Ayla starts the ceremonial fire tomorrow."

"But will it be dark enough to see the spark that early in the evening? It might be best to let the fire go out and have her relight it," said Zelandoni of the Third.

"Then how will the people know it was started by the firestone and not by a live coal?" said an older man with light hair, though Ayla wasn't sure if it was blond or white. "No, I think we need a new hearth, one that has not been lit, but you're right about the darkness. There are too many distractions at twilight, when the ceremonial fire is lit. Only when it is totally dark can you draw the attention of everyone where you want it, when they can see nothing except what you want them to see."

"That's true, Zelandoni of the Seventh Cave," the First said.

Ayla noticed that he was sitting next to the tall blond woman of the Second Cave, and there was a close resemblance. He could have been the elder man of her hearth, perhaps the mate of her grandma or grandam. She recalled that Jondalar had told her that the Seventh and the Second Caves were related and were located on opposite sides of Grass River and its floodplain. She remembered well because while the Second Cave was the Elder Hearth, the Seventh was Horsehead Rock, and he promised to take her there for a visit when they returned in the autumn to show her the horse in the rock.

"We can start the ceremony without fire and light the hearth after it becomes dark," Zelandoni of the Twenty-ninth Cave volunteered. She was a pleasant-looking woman with a conciliatory smile, but Ayla's ability to read body language detected an underlying strength of character and forcefulness. She had met her briefly. This was the woman she had heard people say held the Three Rocks of the Twenty-ninth Cave together.

"But people would think it was strange if there is no ceremonial fire from the beginning, Zelandoni of the Twenty-ninth," the Zelandoni of the Third countered. "Perhaps it would be best to delay the beginning until darkness falls."

"Is there something else that can be done first? Some people start gathering early. They will get restless if we hold off too long," another added. She was a middle-aged woman, nearly as fat as the One Who Was First, but rather than tall, she was quite short. Where the size of the First, both height and weight, gave her a commanding presence, this woman looked warm and motherly.

"How about telling stories, Zelandoni of West Holding? The Story-Tellers are here," suggested a young man sitting beside her.

"Stories may detract from the seriousness of the ceremony, Zelandoni of North Holding," the Zelandoni of the Twenty-ninth said.

"Of course, you're right, Zelandoni of Three Rocks," the young man said quickly. He seemed rather deferential toward the primary Zelandoni of the Twenty-ninth Cave. Ayla realized that the four Zelandonia of the Twenty-ninth referred to each other by a name of their respective sites rather than their counting words. It made sense, since they were all Zelandonia of the Twenty-ninth Cave. What a confusing situation, she thought, but they seem to be making it work.

"Then have someone talk about a serious matter," said the Zelandoni of South Holding.

He was the one who had asked the First if Ayla was here about the animals, and the South Holding was Reflection Rock, which housed the Cave led by Denanna. She was the one that Ayla felt viewed her, or perhaps the horses and wolf, with some animosity, but his tone had not seemed unfriendly. She would wait and see.

"Joharran wants to bring up the matter of flatheads and whether or not they are people," Zelandoni of the Eleventh said. "That is a very serious matter."

"But some people won't like to hear such ideas, and are liable to get argumentative. We don't want to start this Summer Meeting with contentious feelings. That could make them quarrelsome about everything," Zelandoni Who Was First said. "We have to create a receptive mood before new ideas about flatheads are broached."

Ayla wondered if it was appropriate for her to comment. "Zelandoni," she finally said, "could I make a suggestion?" Everyone turned to look, and she didn't think all the zelandonia were pleased.

"Of course you can, Ayla," Zelandoni Who Was First said.

"Jondalar and I visited the Losadunai on our way here. We gave the Losaduna and his mate a few firestones . . . for the whole Cave . . . they were so kind and helpful . . ." Ayla hesitated.

"Yes?" Zelandoni encouraged.

"When they made a ceremony to introduce the firestones, they made two hearths," Ayla continued. "One was all set to light, but cold. The other was burning. They put that one out completely. It was suddenly so dark, you couldn't see the person sitting next to you, and it was easy to see that not a single coal in the first hearth gave even a hint of a glow. Then I lit the fire in the second hearth."

There was silence for only a moment. "Thank you, Ayla," Zelandoni said. "I think that's a good idea. Perhaps we can do something like it. It could be a very impressive demonstration."

"Yes, I like that," Zelandoni of the Third said. "That way we could have the ceremonial fire from the beginning."

"And a cold fireplace ready to be lit would make people curious. They'd wonder what it was for, and that would build up some anticipation," Zelandoni of the West Holding of the Twenty-ninth said.

"How should we put the fire out? Douse it with water and make a lot of steam?" the Eleventh said. "Or dump dirt on it and make it go out instantly?"

"Or dump mud on it?" one of the others, whom Ayla hadn't met, suggested. "Create a little steam, but kill the coals."

"I like the idea of using water and making lots of steam," said another one that Ayla didn't know. "That would be more impressive."

"No, I think putting it out instantly would be more impressive. Light one moment, dark the next."

She hadn't met all the Zelandonia who were there, and as the discussion became more animated, they didn't always address one another as formally, and she wasn't able to identify them. She'd had no idea how much planning and consultation went into a ceremony. She always thought that the events just happened spontaneously, that the zelandonia and others who dealt with the spirit world were just agents of those invisible forces. They spoke out freely, and she began to appreciate why some had objected to her presence, but as they discussed each little detail, Ayla's mind began to stray.

She wondered if the mog-urs of the Clan planned their ceremonies with as much detail, then realized that they probably did, but it would not have been quite the same. Clan ceremonies were ancient, and were always done the way they had always been done, or as close to it as possible. She understood a little more now what a dilemma it must have been when Creb, The Mog-ur, wanted her to take a significant part in one of their most sacred ceremonies.

She looked around the large round summer lodge of the zelandonia. The double-walled circular construction of vertical panels that enclosed the space was similar to the sleeping lodges at the camp of the Ninth Cave, but larger. The movable interior panels that divided the interior into separate areas had been stacked in between sleeping places near the outer walls, creating a single large room. She noticed that the sleeping places were clustered together in one location and that they were all raised, and she recalled that they were also raised in Zelandoni's lodge at the Ninth Cave. She wondered why, then thought that it was probably because when they were used by patients that had to be brought to the zelandonia lodge, it was easier to tend to them.

The ground was covered with mats, many of them woven with intricate and beautiful patterns, and various pads, pillows, and stools used for seating were scattered around near several low tables of various sizes. Most of them were graced with oil lamps usually made of sandstone or limestone that were, as a rule, lit day and night inside the windowless shelter, many with multiple wicks. Most of the lamps were carefully shaped, smoothed, and decorated, but like the lamps in Marthona's dwelling, some were crude stones with naturally formed or roughly pecked-out depressions for the melted tallow. Near many of the lamps she saw small carvings of women, propped up in woven bowls of sand. They were all similar, yet different. She had seen several like them and knew they were representations of the Great Earth Mother, what Jondalar called donii.

The donii ranged in size from about four inches to eight inches in height, but each one could be held in a hand. There was some abstraction and exaggeration. The arms and hands were barely suggested, and the legs tapered together with no real feet so the woman figure could be stuck into the ground, or a bowl of sand, and stand upright. It was not a carving of a particular person, there were no features to give identity, though the body may have been suggested by a woman known to the artist. She was not a high-breasted, nubile young woman, at the beginning of her adult life, nor was hers the lean figure of a woman who walked every day, a peripatetic wanderer constantly foraging for food.

A donii depicted a richly obese woman with some experience in living. She was not pregnant, but she had been. Her broad buttocks were matched by huge breasts that hung down over the large, somewhat drooping stomach of a woman who had given birth to and nurtured several children. She had the ample figure of an experienced older woman, a mother, but her shape suggested much more than the fertility of procreation. In order for a woman to be fat, food had to be plentiful and she had to lead a fairly sedentary life. The small carved figure was meant to look like a well-fed, successful mother who provided for her children; she was a symbol of plenty and generosity.

The reality was not too far off. Some years were worse than others, but most of the time, the Zelandonii managed fairly well. There were fat women in the community; the carver of the figures had to know how a fat woman looked to depict her in such faithful detail. Late spring, when the food stored for winter was nearly gone and the new plants had barely sprouted, could be a lean time. The same was true for animals; in spring, they were scrawny and thin, and their meat was stringy and tough with so little fat, even the marrow in their bones was depleted. Then, the people may have done without certain foods, but they did not starve, at least not usually.

To those who lived off the land, hunted and foraged for everything they required to survive, the earth was like a great mother who nourished her children. She gave them what they needed. They did not plant seeds, tend crops, cultivate or water the land, and they did not herd animals, protect them from predators, gather feed for them for winter. Everything was theirs for the taking, if they knew where to look and how to harvest. But they could not take it for granted, because sometimes it was withheld.

Each donii they carved was a receptacle for the spirit of the Great Earth Mother, and a manifest demonstration to inform the unseen forces that controlled their lives what they needed to survive. She was sympathetic magic, meant to show the Mother what they wanted, and therefore extract it from Her. The donii was a representation of the hope that edible plants would be profuse and easy to find and gather, that the animals would be abundant and easily hunted. She was a symbol of and a plea for an earth that was generous, a land that was rich, food that was plentiful, and life that was good. The donii was an idealized figure, an evocation of the conditions that they earnestly desired.

"I would like to thank Ayla . . ."

She was startled out of her daydreaming when she heard the sound of her name. She couldn't even remember what she was thinking about.

". . . for her willingness to show this new way of making fire to all the zelandonia, and for her patience with some of us who took a little longer to learn," the One Who Was First said.

There were many voices in agreement, even the Zelandoni of the Fourteenth Cave seemed to be genuine in her appreciation. Then they began to discuss the details of the rest of the ceremony to start off this year's Summer Meeting, and other ceremonial occasions coming up, particularly the mating ceremony known as the Matrimonial. Ayla wished they would talk more about that, but primarily they talked about when they would meet again to discuss it further. Then the focus of the meeting shifted to the acolytes.

454

Zelandoni Who Was First stood up. "It is the zelandonia who keep the History of the people." She looked at the zelandonia-in-training, the acolytes, but Ayla felt that Zelandoni seemed to make a special point of including her.

"Part of an acolyte's training is the memorization of the Elder Legends and the Histories. They explain who the Zelandonii are and where the People come from. Memorizing also helps one to learn, and there are many things an acolyte must learn. Let us finish this gather with Her Legend, the Mother's Song."

She paused and her eyes seemed to look inward, dredging up from the recesses of her own mind a story that she had committed to memory long ago. It was the most important of all the Elder Legends, because it was the one that told of the beginnings. To make the legends easy to remember, they were told in rhyme and meter, and to make the stories that were required to be memorized even easier to recall, melody was often added by those who had the talent to compose music, which other people enjoyed learning. Some of the songs were ancient and so familiar that the sound of the melody was often enough to recall the story.

Zelandoni Who Was First, however, had created a melody of her own composition for the Mother's Song, and many people were starting to learn it. She began to sing, a cappella, in a pure, strong, beautiful voice.

> *"Out of the darkness, the chaos of time,*
> *The whirlwind gave birth to the Mother sublime.*
> *She woke to Herself knowing life had great worth,*
> *The dark empty void grieved the Great Mother Earth."*
> *"The Mother was lonely. She was the only."*

Ayla felt a chill of recognition as the First began and joined in with the rest when they spoke or sang the last line in unison with the One Who Was First.

> *"From the dust of Her birth She created the other,*
> *A pale shining friend, a companion, a brother.*
> *They grew up together, learned to love and to care,*
> *And when She was ready, they decided to pair."*
> *"Around Her he'd hover. Her pale shining lover."*

Ayla remembered the last line of the second verse, too, and said it with the others, but then she listened through several more verses, trying to hear the words, saying what she remembered under her breath. She wanted to memorize it exactly because she loved this story, and she loved the way the First sang it. Just the sound of her voice almost brought tears to her eyes. Though she knew she would never learn to sing it, she wanted to learn the words. She had learned the Losadunai version on their Journey, but the language, the meter, and some of the story were different. She wanted to learn the story in Zelandonii and listened carefully.

> *"The dark empty void and the vast barren Earth,*
> *With anticipation, awaited the birth.*
> *Life drank from Her blood, it breathed from Her bones.*
> *It split Her skin open and sundered Her stones."*
> *"The Mother was giving. Another was living."*

Jondalar had repeated a few lines to her while they were traveling, but she had never heard anything like the resonance and full dramatic power with which the First Among Those Who Served The Mother brought to it. His words had not been exactly the same, either.

> *"Her gushing birth waters filled rivers and seas,*
> *And flooded the land, giving rise to the trees.*
> *From each precious drop more grass and leaves grew,*
> *And lush verdant plants made all the Earth new."*
> *"Her waters were flowing. New green was growing."*

> *"In violent labor spewing fire and strife,*
> *She struggled in pain to give birth to new life.*
> *Her dried clotted blood turned to red-ochred soil,*
> *But the radiant child made it all worth the toil."*
> *"The Mother's great joy. A bright shining boy."*

> *"Mountains rose up spouting flames from their crests,*
> *She nurtured Her son from her mountainous breasts.*
> *He suckled so hard, the sparks flew so high,*
> *The Mother's hot milk laid a path through the sky."*
> *"His life had begun. She nourished Her son."*

This was one of the parts she especially loved. It reminded her of her own experience, especially the part about it being all worth it because of her great joy, her wonderful boy.

> *"He stole from Her side as the Great Mother slept,*
> *While out of the dark swirling void chaos crept.*
> *With tempting inducements the darkness beguiled.*
> *Deceived by the whirlwind, chaos captured Her child."*
> *"The dark took Her son. The young brilliant one."*

Just as Broud had taken her son. Zelandoni told the story so well, Ayla found herself feeling anxious for both the Mother and Her son. She was leaning forward, not wanting to miss a word.

> *"And Her luminous friend was prepared to contest,*
> *The thief who held captive the child of Her breast.*
> *Together they fought for the son She adored.*
> *Their efforts succeeded, his light was restored."*
> *"His energy burned. His brilliance returned."*

Ayla let out a deep breath and looked around. She wasn't alone in being caught up in the story. Everyone's rapt attention was focused on the large woman.

> *"The Great Mother lived with the pain in Her heart,*
> *That She and Her son were forever apart.*
> *She ached for the child that had been denied,*
> *So She quickened once more from the life-force inside."*
> *"She was not reconciled. To the loss of Her child."*

Tears were running down Ayla's face, and she felt a sudden clenching ache for her own son that she had been forced to leave behind with the Clan, and a deep empathic sorrow for the Mother.

> *"When She was ready, Her waters of birth,*
> *Brought back the green life to the cold barren Earth.*
> *And the tears of Her loss, abundantly spilled,*
> *Made dew drops that sparkled and rainbows that thrilled."*
> *"Birth waters brought green. But Her tears could be seen."*

Ayla was sure she would never again be able to think of morning dew or rainbows the way she had before. From this time on, they would always remind her of the Mother's tears.

> *"With a thunderous roar Her stones split asunder,*
> *And from the great cave that opened deep under,*
> *She birthed once again from Her cavernous room,*
> *And brought forth the Children of Earth from Her womb."*
> *"From the Mother forlorn, more children were born."*

The next part was not so sad, but it was interesting. It explained how things were now, and why.

"They all were Her children, they filled Her with pride,
But they used up the life-force She carried inside.
She had enough left for a last innovation,
A child who'd remember Who made the creation."
    "A child who'd respect. And learn to protect."

"First Woman was born full-grown and alive,
And given the Gifts she would need to survive.
Life was the First Gift, and like Mother Earth,
She woke to herself knowing life had great worth."
    "First Woman defined. The first of her kind."

Ayla looked up and noticed Zelandoni watching her. She glanced at the other people around her and when she looked back, Zelandoni's gaze had shifted.

"The Mother remembered Her own loneliness,
The love of Her friend and his hovering caress.
With the last spark remaining, Her labor began,
To share life with Woman, She created First Man."
    "Again She was giving. One more was living."

"To Woman and Man the Mother gave birth,
And then for their home, She gave them the Earth,
The water, the land, and all Her creation.
To use them with care was their obligation."
    "It was their home to use. But not to abuse."

"For the Children of Earth the Mother provided,
The Gifts to survive, and then She decided,
To give them a Gift of Pleasure and sharing,
That honors the Mother with the joy of their pairing."
    "The Gifts are well-earned. When honor's returned."

"The Mother was pleased with the pair She created,
She taught them to love and to care when they mated.
She made them desire to join with each other,
The Gift of their Pleasures came from the Mother."
    "Before She was through. Her children loved too.
    Earth's Children were blessed. The Mother could rest."

Ayla felt a little confused about the two lines at the end. It broke the established pattern, and she wondered if something was wrong or missing. When she looked at Zelandoni, the woman was staring at her, which made her uncomfortable. She looked down, but when she glanced back up, Zelandoni was still watching her.

After the meeting broke up, Zelandoni fell into stride beside Ayla. "I have to go to the camp of the Ninth Cave, do you mind if I walk with you?" she said.

"No, of course not," Ayla said.

They walked in companionable silence at first. Ayla was still feeling overwhelmed by the legend, and Zelandoni was waiting to see what she would say.

"That was beautiful, Zelandoni," Ayla finally said. "When I lived at the Lion Camp, sometimes everyone would make music and sing, or dance, together, and some of them had beautiful voices, but none as beautiful as yours."

"It is a Gift of the Mother. I didn't do anything to make it happen, I was born with it. The Legend of the Mother is called the Mother's Song, because some people like to sing it," Zelandoni said.

"Jondalar told me a little of the Mother's Song while we were on our Journey. He said he couldn't remember it all, but some of his words were not exactly the same as yours," Ayla said.

"That's not unusual. There are slightly different versions. He learned from the old Zelandoni, I memorized my mentor's song. Some of the zelandonia make slight revisions. It's perfectly all right, as long as it doesn't change the meaning, and keeps the rhythm and rhyme. If they feel right, people tend to adopt them. If not, they are forgotten. I made up my own song because it pleased me, but there are other ways to sing it."

"I think most people sing the same song as you do, but what do the words 'rhythm and rhyme' mean? I don't think Jondalar ever explained them to me," Ayla said.

"I don't suppose he would. Singing and Story-Telling are not his greatest skills, though he has become much better at telling about his adventures."

"They are not mine, either. I can remember a story, but I don't know how to sing. I love to listen to it, though," Ayla said.

"Rhythm and rhyme help people to remember. Rhythm is the sense of movement. It carries you along as though you are walking at a steady pace. Rhymes are words that sound similar. They add to the rhythm, but they also help you remember the next words."

"The Losadunai have a similar Legend of the Mother, but it didn't make me feel the same way, when I memorized it," Ayla said.

Zelandoni stopped and looked at Ayla. "You memorized it? Losadunai is a different language."

"Yes, but it's so similar to Zelandonii, it's not difficult to learn."

"Yes, it is similar, but not the same, and some people find it quite difficult. How long did you spend with them?" Zelandoni asked.

"Not too long, less than a moon. Jondalar was in a hurry to get across the glacier before the spring melt made it more dangerous. As it is, the warm wind came on the last day, and we did have some trouble," Ayla explained.

"You learned their language in less than a moon?"

"Not perfectly. I still made a lot of mistakes, but I did memorize some of Losaduna's legends. I've been trying to learn the Legend of the Mother as the Mother's Song and say it the way you sing it."

Zelandoni looked at her a moment longer, then started walking back toward the campsite again. "I'll be happy to help you with it," she said.

As they continued, Ayla thought about the legend, especially the part that reminded her of Durc and herself. She was sure she understood how the Great Mother felt when She had to accept that Her son was gone from Her forever. She, too, ached to have her son at her side sometimes, and looked forward to the birth of her new child, Jondalar's child. She recalled some of the verses she had just heard and began to walk in time to the rhythm as she recited them to herself.

Zelandoni noticed a slight change in their pace. There was a familiar feeling to it. She glanced at Ayla and noted an expression of intense concentration. This young woman belongs in the zelandonia, she said to herself.

Just as they reached the campsite, Ayla stopped and asked a question. "Why are there two lines at the end, instead of just one?"

The woman studied her for a moment before answering. "It's a question that comes up now and then," she said. "I don't know the answer. That's the way it's always been. Most people think it's meant to give the legend a definite ending, once for the verse and once for the entire story."

Ayla nodded. Zelandoni wasn't sure if her nod meant acceptance of the explanation or simply comprehension of the statement. Most acolytes don't even discuss the finer points of the Mother's Song, she thought. This one definitely belongs in the zelandonia.

They walked a little farther. Ayla noticed the sun was lowering toward the western horizon. It would be getting dark soon.

"I thought the gather went well," Zelandoni said. "The zelandonia were impressed with your fire-making, and I do appreciate your willingness to show everyone. If we can find enough firestones, everyone will be making fire like that soon. If we can't find very many . . . I don't know. It will probably be best if they are used only to light special ceremonial fires."

Ayla frowned. "What about people who already have a firestone, or those who may find one? Can you tell them they can't use it?" she asked.

Zelandoni stopped and looked directly at Ayla. Then she sighed. "No, I can't. I can ask people to agree, but you're right. I can't make them, and there will always be those who will do what they want in any case. I suppose I was thinking out loud of an ideal situation, but in fact, it wouldn't work, not after everyone knows how to make fire that way." She made a wry expression. "When the Fifth and the Fourteenth were talking about keeping it a secret for the zelandonia, they were simply saying out loud what I think most of us wished, and I have to include myself. It would be an impressive tool for us, but we can't keep it from the people." She started walking again.

"We won't be planning the Matrimonial until after the first hunt. All the Caves will participate in that," Zelandoni said. "People get very anxious about it. They believe that if the first hunt is successful, it bodes well for the whole year, but if it's not, it portends bad luck. The zelandonia will be doing a Search for game. Sometimes that helps. If there are herds around, a good Searcher can help to locate them, but not even the best Searcher can find game if there are none to be found."

"I assisted Mamut on a Search. It was a surprise to me the first time, but we seemed to have an affinity, and I was caught up in his Search," Ayla said.

"You Searched with your Mamut?" Zelandoni said with surprise. "What was it like?"

"It's hard to explain, but something like a bird flying over the land, but there was no wind," Ayla said, "and the land didn't look the same, exactly."

"Would you be willing to assist the zelandonia? We have some Searchers, but it is always better if there are more," the donier said. She could see some reluctance.

"I'd like to help . . . but . . . I don't want to be a Zelandoni. I just want to mate with Jondalar and have children," Ayla said.

"If you don't want to, you don't have to. No one can force you, Ayla, but if a Search leads to a successful hunt, then the Matrimonial will be lucky, or so it is believed, and will produce long matings and successful hearths—families," the First said.

"Yes, well, I suppose I could try to help, but I don't know if I can," Ayla said.

"Don't worry. No one is ever sure. All anyone can do is try." Zelandoni felt pleased with herself. It was obvious that Ayla was reluctant and would try to resist becoming zelandonia, and this would be a way to get her started. She needs to be a part of the zelandonia, the First thought. She has too much talent, too many skills, and she asks questions that are too intelligent. She has to be brought into the fold or she might create dissension outside of it.

25

When they neared the camp, Wolf raced out to greet her. She saw him coming and braced herself, just in case he jumped up on her in his enthusiasm, but signaled him to stay down. He stopped, though it seemed it was all he could do to control himself. She hunkered down to his level and allowed him to lick her neck while she held him down until he composed himself. Then she stood up. He looked up at her with what seemed to her to be such a hopeful, yearning expression, she nodded her head and tapped the front of her shoulder. He jumped up, putting his paws where she had signaled and, with a low-rumbling growl, took her jaw in his teeth. She returned the gesture, and then she held his magnificent head in both her hands and looked into his gold-flecked eyes.

"I love you, too, Wolf, but sometimes I wonder why you love me so much. Is it just that I have become the leader of your pack, or is it something more?" Ayla said, touching her forehead to his, then signaled him down.

"You command love, Ayla," the First said, "and the love you invoke cannot be denied."

Ayla looked at her, thinking it was a strange comment. "I don't command anything," she said.

"You command that wolf. He is motivated to please you by the love he feels for you. It's not that you try to beguile or entice, but you draw it to you. And those who love you, love you profoundly. I see it in your animals. I see it in Jondalar. I know him. He has never loved anyone the way he loves you, and he never will. Perhaps it is because you give of yourself so fully and so openly, or perhaps it is a Gift from the Mother, to inspire love. You will always be loved with great fervor, but one must be wary of the Mother's Gifts."

"Why do people say that, Zelandoni?" Ayla asked. "Why should someone be concerned about a Gift from the Mother? Aren't Her Gifts a good thing?"

"Perhaps it's because Her Gifts are too good. Or because they are too powerful. How do you feel if someone gives you something of great value?" the donier asked.

"Iza taught me that a gift creates an obligation. You must give something of equal value back," Ayla said.

"The more I learn about the people who raised you, the more I grow to respect them," said the One Who Was First. "When the Great Earth Mother bestows a Gift, She may expect something in return, something of equal value. When much is given, much may be expected, but how can one know what that is until the time comes? So people are leery. Sometimes Her Gifts are too much, more than one wants, but they can't be given back. Too much doesn't necessarily bring any more happiness than not enough."

"Even too much love?" Ayla asked.

"The best example to answer that is Jondalar. He was definitely favored by the Mother," said the woman once known as Zolena, "too favored, he was given too much. He is so remarkably handsome and well made, he can't help but draw attention. Even his eyes are such an exceptional color, one can hardly keep from staring at him. He has a natural charm, people are drawn to him, but women in particular—I don't think there is a woman alive who could refuse him whatever he asked, not the Mother Herself—and he delights in pleasing women. He's intelligent, and exceptionally skilled at flint-knapping, and with it all he was given a caring heart, but he cares too much. He has too much love to give.

"Even his love for working the stone, for making tools, is for him a true passion. But the intensity of his feelings for whatever he loves is so strong, it can overwhelm him, and those he cares for. He fights to keep it under control, but it has occasionally gotten away from him. Ayla, I'm not sure you understand how powerful his feelings are. And all his Gifts didn't make him happy, at least not until now, they have often aroused more envy than love."

Ayla nodded with a thoughtful frown. "I have heard several people say Jondalar's brother Thonolan was a favorite of the Mother and that's why he was taken so young," Ayla said. "Was he exceptionally handsome, and given many Gifts?"

"He was a favorite of everyone, not only the Mother. Thonolan was a fine-looking man, but he didn't have the overwhelming . . . I'm tempted to say beauty—masculine beauty, to be sure—of Jondalar, but he had such a warm and open nature that wherever he went, people loved him, men and women alike. He made friends, easily and naturally, and no one resented him, or was envious of him," the woman said.

They had been standing and talking, with the wolf crouched at Ayla's feet. As they started walking again toward the campfire, Ayla still frowned, thinking about the donier's words.

"Now that Jondalar has brought you home, many men are even more envious, and many women are jealous of you, because he loves you," Zelandoni continued. "That was why Marona tried to make you look foolish. She was jealous, envious of both of you, I think, because you have found happiness in each other. Some people think she was given much, but all she ever had was an unusual beauty, and beauty alone is the most deceptive of Gifts. It doesn't last. She is an unpleasant woman, who seems to think of little besides herself, with few friends and no real talents. When Marona's beauty fades she will have nothing, I'm afraid, not even children, it seems."

They walked together a few steps, then Ayla stopped and turned toward the woman. "I haven't seen Marona lately, not for several days before we left and not on the trek here."

"She went back to the Fifth Cave with her friend and came here with them. She is staying at their camp," the donier said.

"I don't like Marona, but I am sorry for her if she can't have children. Iza knew some things that could be done to make a woman more receptive to the impregnating spirit," Ayla said.

"I know of a few, too, but she hasn't asked for help, and if she is really unable to conceive, nothing will help," the woman said.

Ayla heard the tone of sorrow in her voice. She would be sorry, too, if she couldn't have children. Then her frown was replaced by a radiant smile. "Did you know I am going to have a child?" she said.

Zelandoni smiled back. Her speculation about Ayla was confirmed. "I'm very happy for you, Ayla. Does Jondalar know your mating has been blessed?"

"Yes. I told him. He's very pleased."

"He should be. Have you told anyone else?"

"Only Marthona, and Proleva, and now you."

"If it's not generally known, we can surprise everyone at your Matrimonial and announce your good news, if you like," Zelandoni said. "There are special words that can be part of the ceremony if the woman is already Blessed."

"I think I would like that," Ayla said. "I've stopped marking my moon times, since my bleeding has stopped, but I'm wondering if I should start marking days again, to keep track of them until my baby is born. Jondalar taught me how to use the counting words, but I don't know how to count that far."

"Do you find the counting words difficult, Ayla?"

"Oh, no. I like using counting words," she said. "Jondalar surprised me the first time he used them, though. Just from the marks I made on my sticks every night, he knew how long I lived in the valley. He said it was easier because I cut an extra line above the marks on the days when my moon time started, so I would be prepared for it. I seemed to have more trouble hunting when I was bleeding. I think animals could smell me. After a while I noticed that my bleeding always came when the waning moon reached the same shape, so I didn't have to make the marks, but I made them anyway. You can't always see the moon if it's stormy or cloudy."

Zelandoni thought she was getting accustomed to the surprises Ayla could come up with in such an offhand way, as though it were nothing. But making counting marks when she bled and then making the connection to moon phases was rather astonishing for someone to make by herself.

"Would you like to learn more counting words, and different ways to use them, Ayla?" the woman said. "They can be used to know when seasons are ready to change, before the changes are apparent, for example, or to count the days until your baby is born."

"Yes, I would," Ayla said, smiling broadly. "I learned how to make marks from Creb, although I think it made him nervous when I did it. Most women of the Clan, or men, for that matter, couldn't count much past three. Creb could make counting marks because he was The Mog-ur, but he didn't have words for counting."

"I'll show you how to count larger numbers," the First said. "I think it's best that you are having your children now, when you are young. You may not want to worry about taking care of young children when you are older. There is no telling what you may decide to do."

"I'm not so young, Zelandoni. I can count nineteen years, if Iza was right about how many years I was when she found me," Ayla said.

"You certainly look younger than you are." A fleeting frown crossed Zelandoni's face. "But it shouldn't matter. You have a head start," she said almost to herself, and finished in her thoughts, She is already a skilled healer, she won't have to learn that before becoming a Zelandoni.

"A head start on what?" Ayla asked, puzzled.

"Uh . . . you have a head start on your family, since life has already begun," Zelandoni said. "But I hope you don't have too many children. You're in good health, but too many can drain a woman, age her more quickly."

Ayla got a strong impression that Zelandoni did not want her to know what she was thinking and quickly said something else because she wanted to keep from telling her. It was her right, Ayla thought. She could refrain from mentioning what she was thinking if she chose, but it did make her wonder.

Twilight had settled by the time they approached the campfire, and it was already getting hard to see. When they arrived at the fire trench, people greeted them and offered them food. Ayla realized she was hungry; it had been a full and busy afternoon. Zelandoni ate with them and planned to sleep at the camp of the Ninth Cave that night, then immediately got into a discussion with Marthona and Joharran about the upcoming hunt and the Search the zelandonia would make. She mentioned that Ayla would be joining them, which they seemed to think was entirely appropriate, but it made Ayla feel uneasy. She did not want to become one of Those Who Served The Mother, but circumstances seemed to be pulling her in that direction and she wasn't happy about it.

"We should get there early. I need to arrange to set up some targets and step off the distances," Jondalar said as they walked out of the lodge the next morning. He was holding the cup of mint tea Ayla had made for him and began chewing on the end of the wintergreen twig she had recently peeled, to prepare it for him to clean his teeth.

"I want to check on Whinney and Racer first. I hardly saw them at all yesterday. Why don't you go ahead and get things ready. I'll keep Wolf with me and meet you later," Ayla said.

"Don't take too long. People will be gathering early, and I'd really like you to show them what you can do. It's one thing for me to cast a spear a long way, but when they see that a woman, using the spear-thrower, can fling a spear farther than any of the men, that will make them interested," Jondalar said.

"I'll be there as soon as I can, but I want to brush them down, and check Racer's eye. It seemed red, like he got something in it. I may want to treat it," Ayla said.

"Do you think he's all right? Should I come with you?" he said, full of concern.

"It didn't look that bad. I'm sure he's fine. I just want to check it. You go on, I won't be long," she said.

Jondalar nodded as he scrubbed at his teeth, then swished out his mouth with the mint tea. He drank down the balance and smiled. "That always makes me feel better," he said.

"It does make your mouth feel clean, and wakes you up," Ayla said. She had made his tea and prepared his twig nearly every morning since shortly after she met him, and had begun to follow his morning ritual. "I noticed it especially when I was sick in the morning."

"Are you still having morning sickness?" he asked.

"No, not anymore, but I do notice that my stomach is getting bigger," she said.

He smiled. "I like your bigger stomach," he said, then reached over and put an arm around her shoulders and the other hand on her belly. "I especially like what's in it."

She smiled back. "I do, too," she said.

He kissed her with warmth and feeling. "The thing I miss most about traveling is that we could stop and share Pleasures whenever we felt like it. Now, it seems there is always something to do and it's not as easy to stop and do what we want whenever we want." He nuzzled her neck, felt the fullness of her breasts, and kissed her again. "Maybe I don't have to get to the spear-throwing range so early," he added with a huskiness in his voice.

"Yes, you do," she said with a laugh. "But if you want to stay . . ."

"No, you are right, but I'm going to look for you later."

Jondalar headed for the main camp and Ayla went back into the lodge. When she came out, she was carrying her backpack, the one with the holders for spears and spear-thrower, into which she had packed a few things. She whistled for Wolf and headed upstream along the small creek. Both horses knew she was coming and had strained to come toward her as far as their lead ropes would allow. Ayla noticed that the ropes had gotten caught in some of the vegetation. Besides the long grass that had twisted itself around both leads, Whinney's rope had an entire dry bush tangled in it, and Racer had pulled a living shrub out of the ground, roots and all. Maybe a surround would work better than those ropes, she thought.

Ayla removed both their halters and lead ropes, and while she was at it, she checked Racer's eye. It was a little red, but otherwise seemed fine. Racer and Wolf rubbed noses and then, so glad to be free of the restricting rope, Racer began running in a large circle, and Wolf chased after him. Ayla started brushing Whinney, and when she looked up, Racer was chasing Wolf. The next time she looked, Wolf was chasing Racer again. She stopped brushing for a while to watch them. As Wolf got close to Racer, the young stallion actually slowed down a bit until the wolf passed him and raced ahead. When they came full circle, Wolf slowed down and let Racer pass him.

At first, Ayla thought she was imagining that they were doing it on purpose, but as she continued to watch them, it soon became obvious that they were playing a game with each other, and enjoying it. Both young male animals, so full of life and energy, had discovered a way to run some of it off and have fun doing it. Ayla smiled and shook her head, wishing Jondalar were there to enjoy their antics with her, then went back to brushing the mare. Whinney, too, was beginning to show her pregnancy, but she appeared to be in good health.

When Ayla finished with her horse, she saw that Racer was grazing quietly and Wolf was nowhere in sight. Off exploring, she thought. She whistled the particular tones that Jondalar had developed to call his horse. He looked up and started toward her. He had nearly reached her when another whistle sounded, repeating the exact tones. They both looked for the whistler. Ayla thought it must be Jondalar, back for some reason, but when she looked up she saw a boy coming in her direction.

He was not familiar to her, and she wondered what he wanted and why he had imitated her particular whistle. When he neared, she thought he could count perhaps nine or ten years, then she noticed that one of his arms was somewhat stunted, shorter than the other, and hung a little awkwardly, as though he didn't have full control of it. The boy reminded her of Creb, whose arm had been amputated at the elbow when he was a boy, and she warmed to him immediately.

"Are you the one who whistled?"

"Yes."

"Why did you whistle like I did?" Ayla said.

"I never heard a whistle like that. I wanted to see if I could do it," he said.

"You did," she said. "Are you looking for someone?"

"No," he said.

"What are you doing here?"

"I'm just looking. Someone told me there were horses here, but I didn't know anyone had set up camp. He didn't tell me that. Everyone else is by Middle Creek," he said.

"We just recently arrived. How long have you been here?"

"I was born here."

"Oh, then you are of the Nineteenth Cave."

"Yes. Why do you talk funny?"

"I was not born here. I come from far away. I used to be Ayla of the Lion Camp of the Mamutoi, now I am Ayla of the Ninth Cave of the Zelandonii," she said, then stepped toward him, holding out both hands in the manner of a formal greeting.

He became a little flustered because he could not reach out well with his partially paralyzed arm. Ayla stretched a bit for his crippled limb and took both hands in hers as though it were perfectly normal, but she noted that his hand was smaller and misshapen, and the little finger was fused to the one next to it. She held his hands for a moment and smiled.

Then, as though he just remembered, the boy said, "I am Lanidar of the Nineteenth Cave of the Zelandonii." He was about to let go, but added, "The Nineteenth Cave welcomes you to the Summer Meeting, Ayla of the Ninth Cave of the Zelandonii."

"You whistle very well. Your whistle was a very good copy of mine. Do you like to whistle?" she asked when she let go.

"I guess so."

"Can I ask you not to make that whistle sound again?" she said.

"Why?" he asked.

"I use that sound to call the horse, this one, the stallion. If you whistle like that, I'm afraid he will think you are calling him and it will confuse him," Ayla explained. "If you like to whistle, I can teach you other sounds to whistle."

"Like what?"

Ayla looked around and noticed a chickadee perched on the limb of a nearby tree, singing the *chick-a-dee-dee-dee* sound that gave the bird its name. She listened for a moment, then repeated the sound. The boy looked startled, and the bird stopped singing for a moment, then started up again. Ayla repeated the sound. The black-capped bird sang again, looking around.

"How do you do that?" the boy said.

"I'll teach you if you like. You could learn, you're a good whistler," she said.

"Can you whistle like other birds, too?" he asked.

"Yes."

"Which ones?"

"Any one you want."

"How about a meadow lark?"

Ayla closed her eyes for a moment, then whistled a series of tones that sounded exactly like a lark that had soared high into the sky and swooped down, making its glorious melody.

"Can you really teach me to do that?" the boy asked, looking at her with wonder in his eyes.

"If you really want to learn," Ayla said.

"How did you learn?"

"I practiced. If you have patience, sometimes the bird will come to you when you whistle its song," the woman replied. Ayla remembered when she lived alone in her valley and taught herself to whistle and imitate the sounds of birds. Once she started feeding them, there were several that always came at her call and ate out of her hand.

"Can you whistle other things?" Lanidar asked, completely intrigued by the strange woman who talked funny and whistled so well.

Ayla thought for a moment, then perhaps because the boy reminded her of Creb, she began to whistle an eerie melody that sounded like a flute playing. He had heard flutes many times, but he had never heard anything like it. The haunting music was totally unfamiliar to him. It was the sound of the flute played by the mog-ur at the Clan Gathering she had gone to with Brun's clan when she still lived with them. Lanidar listened until she stopped.

"I never heard whistling like that," he said.

"Did you like it?" she asked.

"Yes, but it was a little scary, too. Like it came from a place far away," Lanidar said.

"It did," Ayla said, then she smiled and pierced the air with a sharp, commanding trill. Before long, Wolf came bounding out of the long grass of the field.

"It's a wolf!" the boy screamed with fear.

"It's all right," she said, holding Wolf close to her. "The wolf is my friend. I walked through the main camp with him yesterday. I thought you would know that he was here, along with the horses."

The boy calmed down, but still looked at Wolf with large round eyes full of apprehension.

"I went with my mother to pick raspberries yesterday. Nobody even told me you were here. They just said there were some horses in the Upper Meadow," Lanidar said. "Everybody was talking about some kind of spear-throwing thing some man wanted to show. I'm not good at throwing a spear, so I decided I'd look for the horses instead."

Ayla wondered if the omission was on purpose, if someone was trying to trick him the way Marona had tried to trick her. Then she realized that a boy of his age who went berry picking with his mother probably led a pretty lonely life. She got a sense that the boy with a crippled arm, who could not throw a spear, did not have many friends and that the other boys made fun of him and tried to trick him. But he did have one good arm. He could learn to throw a spear, especially using a spear-thrower.

"Why aren't you good at throwing a spear?" she asked.

"Can't you see?" he said, holding out his malformed arm and looking at it with loathing.

"But you have another arm that is perfectly good," she said.

"Everybody always holds their extra spears with their other arm. Besides, nobody wanted to teach me. They said I could never hit a target, anyway," the boy said.

"What about the man of your hearth?" Ayla asked.

"I live with my mother, and her mother. I guess there was a man of the hearth once, my mother pointed him out to me, but he left her a long time ago, and he doesn't want anything to do with me. He didn't like it when I tried to visit him. He seemed embarrassed. Sometimes a man will come and live with us for a while, but none of them bother with me much," the boy said.

"Would you like to see a spear-thrower? I have one with me," Ayla said.

"Where did you get one?" Lanidar asked.

"I know the man who made it. He's the man I'm going to mate. I'll be going to help him show his spear-thrower as soon as I finish with the horses."

"I guess I could look at it," the boy said.

Her backpack was on the ground nearby. She got her spear-thrower and a couple of spears and walked back.

"This is how it works," she said, taking a spear and laying it on top of the strange-looking implement. She made sure the hole carved into the butt end of the spear was up against the small hook at the back of the narrow board with the groove down the middle, then put her fingers through the loops attached to the front end. She sighted down the field, then launched the spear.

"That spear went a long way!" Lanidar said. "I don't think I've ever seen a man throw a spear that far."

"Probably not. That's what makes the spear-thrower such a good hunting weapon. I think you could throw a spear with this. Come here, I'll show you how to hold it."

Ayla could see that her spear-thrower was not made for someone of Lanidar's size, but it was good enough to demonstrate the principle of leverage behind it. It was his right arm that was deformed, which had forced him to develop his left arm. Whether he would naturally have been left-handed if his right arm had developed properly didn't matter. He was left-handed now, and he was strong on that side. She didn't worry about aiming for the moment, but she showed him how to pull back and cast the spear. Then she set it up and let him do it. The spear flew high and wide, but quite far, and the grin on Lanidar's face was ecstatic.

"I threw that spear. Look how far it went!" he nearly shouted. "Can you actually hit something with it?"

"If you practice," she said, smiling. She looked around the field, but didn't see anything. She turned to Wolf, who'd been lying on his belly with his head up, watching the whole thing. "Wolf, go find something for me," she said, although the hand signal she gave him said more.

He jumped up and raced into the meadow of full-grown grass turning from green to gold. Ayla followed behind slowly, and the boy walked behind her. Before long she saw movement of the grass ahead, then caught sight of a gray hare darting away from the wolf. She had the spear poised, watching carefully, and when she saw the direction it would likely bound the next time, she cast the small spear. It landed true, and when she reached it, the wolf was standing over it, looking up at her.

"I want that one, Wolf. You go catch one of your own now," she said to the carnivore, again signaling him at the same time. But the boy didn't really see the signals and was completely amazed at the way the huge wolf minded the woman. She picked up the hare and started back toward the horses.

"You should go and see the man demonstrate the spear-thrower he made. I think you might find it interesting, Lanidar, and just because you don't know how to throw a spear won't make any difference. No one else knows how to use a spear-thrower, either. Everybody will be learning from the beginning. If you want to wait a while, I'll walk over there with you," Ayla said.

Lanidar watched her brushing down the young stallion. "I've never seen a brown horse like that. Most horses look like the mare."

"I know," Ayla said, "but far to the east, beyond the end of the Great Mother River that starts on the other side of the glacier, some horses are brown like that. That's where these horses come from."

After a while the wolf returned. He found a spot, circled around it a few times, then lowered himself to his belly, panting and watching.

"Why do these animals stay around you, let you touch them, and do what you say?" Lanidar asked. "I've never seen animals do that."

"They are my friends. I was hunting and the mare's dam fell into my pit trap. I didn't know she was nursing until I saw the foal. A pack of hyenas saw the foal, too. I don't know why I chased them away. The foal couldn't have lived alone, but since I saved her, I raised her. I guess she grew up thinking I was her mother. Later we became friends, and learned to understand each other. She does things I ask her to do, because she wants to. I named her *Whinney*," Ayla said, but the way she said the name was the perfect copy of a horse's whinny. In the field, the dun-yellow mare raised her head and looked in their direction.

"That was you! How did you do that?" Lanidar said.

"I paid attention and practiced. That is her real name. To most people I usually say 'Whinney' because they understand it better, but that's not how I said it when I named her. This stallion is her son. I was there when he was born. So was Jondalar. He named this horse Racer, but that was later," Ayla explained.

"Racer can mean someone who likes to go fast, or someone who likes to be ahead of everyone else," the boy said.

"That's what Jondalar said. He named him that because Racer loves to run, and likes to get ahead, except when I put him on a rope. Then he will follow behind his dam," Ayla said, and went back to grooming the horse. She was nearly through.

"What about the wolf?" Lanidar asked.

"Almost the same thing. I raised Wolf from a baby. I killed his mother because she was stealing ermine from some traps I set. I didn't know she was nursing. It was in winter with snow on the ground, and she had whelped out of season. I followed her tracks back to her den. She was a lone wolf, with no other wolves to help her, and all but one of her cubs had died. I pulled Wolf out of the den when his eyes were barely open. He grew up with Mamutoi children, and thinks of people as his pack," she said.

"What is that name you call him?" Lanidar said.

"Wolf. It's the word for a wolf in Mamutoi," Ayla said. "Would you like to meet him?"

"What do you mean, 'meet him'? How can you meet a wolf?"

"Come here and I'll show you," she said. He approached with caution. "Give me your hand, and we'll let Wolf smell it, and get used to your scent, then you can rub his fur."

Lanidar was a little hesitant about putting his good hand so close to the mouth of the wolf, but he extended it slowly. Ayla brought it to Wolf's nose. He sniffed it, then licked it.

"That tickles!" the boy said with a nervous titter.

"You can touch his head, and he likes to be scratched," Ayla said, showing Lanidar how. The boy broke into a delighted grin when he touched the animal, but looked up when the young stallion nickered. "I think Racer would like a little attention, too. Would you like to pet him?"

"Can I?" Lanidar asked.

"Come here, Racer," she said, signaling him to come as well as saying it. The dark brown stallion with black mane, tail, and lower legs nickered again, took a few steps toward the woman and the boy, and lowered his head toward the youngster, making the boy move back a ways from the large animal. He may not have been a carnivore with a mouth full of sharp teeth, but that didn't mean he was without defenses. Ayla reached into the backpack at her feet.

"Move slowly, let him smell you, too. That's how animals get to know you, then you can pat his nose, or the side of his face," Ayla said.

The boy did as she said. "His nose is so soft!" Lanidar said. Suddenly, as if out of nowhere, Whinney was there, pushing Racer aside. The boy was startled. Ayla had seen Whinney approaching from the field, wanting to find out what was going on.

"Whinney likes attention, too," Ayla said. "Horses are very curious, and like to be noticed. Would you like to feed them?" He nodded. Ayla opened her hand and showed him two pieces of a white root that she knew the horses liked, fresh young wild carrot. "Is your right hand strong enough to hold something?"

"Yes," he said.

"Then you can feed them both at the same time," she said, putting a piece of root in each of his hands. "Hold one out to each horse, letting it rest on your open hand, so they can take it," she said. "They get jealous if you feed one and not the other, and Whinney will push Racer out of the way. She's his mother, she can tell him what to do."

"Even horse mothers can do that?" he said.

"Yes, even horse mothers." She stood up and got the halter with the ropes attached. "I think it's time to go, Lanidar. Jondalar is expecting me. I'm going to have to put their ropes back on. I'd rather not, but it's for their own safety. I don't want them wandering around loose until everybody at the Summer Meeting knows that these horses are not to be hunted. I was thinking a surround might be a better place for them, rather than using ropes that get tangled on bushes and grass."

The bush caught up in Racer's rope was so tangled, she dropped it and went to find her backpack. She thought she had put the small axe that Jondalar had made for her in it, though when they were traveling, she usually wore it with the hafted handle put through a loop attached to her waistband. It would be easier to untangle the rope if she could break up the woody bush first. She searched around the bottom of the pack and found it. After she made sure they were cleared of the debris they had picked up, Ayla put the ropes back on the horses and gathered up her backpack and the hare to give to whoever might be working around the camp of the Ninth Cave. Then she looked at the boy. "If I teach you how to whistle like birds and things, would you do something for me, Lanidar?"

"What?"

"Sometimes I have to be away almost all day. Would you come and check on the horses once in a while when I'm gone? You can call them with a whistle then, if you want. Make sure their ropes aren't tangled, and give them some attention? They like company. If there are any problems, come and find me. Do you think you could do that?"

The boy could hardly believe what she was asking. He never would have dreamed she would ask him to do something like that. "Can I feed them, too? I liked it when they ate off both my hands."

"Of course. You can always pick some fresh green grass, and they really like wild carrots, and some other roots I can show you. I have to go, do you want to come with me to watch Jondalar show his spear-thrower?"

"Yes," he said.

Ayla walked with the boy back to the camp, making a few bird whistles along the way.

When Ayla, Wolf, and Lanidar reached the site of the spear-throwing demonstration, Ayla was surprised to see several more of the hunting implements besides Jondalar's. Some people who had seen their earlier presentation to the Caves in their immediate region had made their own versions of the weapon, and they were showing their capabilities with varying degrees of success. Jondalar saw her coming and looked relieved. He hurried to meet them.

"What took you so long?" he started right in. "Several people tried to make spear-throwers after we showed them," he said, "but you know how much practice it takes to develop accuracy. So far, I'm the only one who's been able to hit what I aimed for, and I'm afraid people are beginning to think my skill is just a fluke, and that no one else will ever be able to hit anything using them. I didn't want to say anything about you. I thought that a showing of your skill would make a better impression. I'm glad you finally made it."

"I brushed the horses—Racer's eye is fine—and let them run for a while," she explained. "We need to think of something besides ropes that get caught on bushes and things. Maybe we could make a surround, or an enclosure of some kind. I've asked Lanidar to check on them when we're away from camp. He's met the horses and they like him."

"Who is Lanidar?" Jondalar asked rather impatiently.

She indicated the boy who was standing beside her, trying to edge around behind her, looking up at the tall man who seemed angry, which made the boy a little frightened. "This is Lanidar of the Nineteenth Cave, Jondalar. Someone told him there were horses in the field where we camped, and he came to see them."

Jondalar started to shrug him off, his mind on the demonstration that was not going as well as he'd hoped, then he noticed the deformed arm and a frown of concern on Ayla's face. She was trying to tell him something, and it was probably about the boy.

"I think he could be a big help," she said. "He's even learned the whistle we use to call the horses, but he's promised not to use it without a good reason."

"I'm glad to hear that," Jondalar said, turning his attention to the child, "and I'm sure we can use the help." Lanidar relaxed a little, and Ayla smiled at Jondalar.

"Lanidar came to see the demonstration, too. What targets do you have set up?" Ayla asked as they started walking back toward the crowd of mostly men who were watching them. A few of them looked as though they were getting ready to leave.

"Drawings of deer on a hide tied to a bundle of grass," he said.

Ayla pulled out a spear and her spear-thrower as they approached, and as soon as she saw the targets, she sighted and let fly. The solid *thunk* caught a few by surprise, they hadn't expected the woman to make a cast so quickly. She made a few more demonstrations, but unmoving targets seemed rather commonplace, and even if the spear did fly farther than anyone had ever seen a woman throw before, they had already watched Jondalar do that several times. It was no longer exceptional.

The boy seemed to understand that. He had walked along beside her because he wasn't sure if she wanted him to stay or go, and tapped her.

"Why don't you tell the wolf to find a rabbit or something?" Lanidar said.

The woman smiled at him, then made a silent signal to the wolf. The area was trampled by the many people milling around, and it was not likely that there were many animals left, but if any could be found, Wolf would find them. With a little trepidation, some people noticed the wolf dashing away from Ayla. They had started to become accustomed to seeing the meat-eater with the woman, but rushing off on his own was another thing.

Before Ayla arrived, a man had asked Jondalar how far he could cast a spear with one of those spear-throwers, but he said he had used up all his spears and needed to retrieve them before he could throw them again. Jondalar and a knot of men were just starting off together to gather them up when Ayla spied Wolf in a stance that signaled to her that he had found something. Suddenly a noisy willow grouse appeared out of a clump of trees halfway up a slope near the target course. Ayla had been waiting with a lightweight spear in the thrower, one she and Jondalar had started using for birds and small animals.

She hurled the weapon with a speed that was so practiced, it was almost instinctive. The bird squawked when it was hit, causing several people to look. They watched it fall from the sky. Suddenly there was renewed interest in the hunting weapon. "How far can she throw?" the man who had asked about distance wanted to know.

"Ask her," Jondalar said.

"Just throw, or hit the mark?" Ayla asked.

"Both," the man said.

"If you want to see how far a spear will go using a thrower, I have a better idea," she said, then turned to the boy. "Lanidar, would you show them how far you can throw a spear?"

He glanced around rather shyly, but she knew he hadn't been hesitant to speak out or answer questions when he first talked to her, and she thought he wouldn't mind the attention. He looked at Ayla and nodded.

"Do you think you can remember how you threw the spear before?" she asked.

He nodded again.

She gave him her spear-thrower and a projectile, another bird dart—she had only two lightweight spears left. He was a little awkward at getting the spear set on the spear-thrower with his shorter arm, but he did it himself. Then he walked to the middle of the practice course, pulled his good left arm back, and threw the spear the way he had done it before, letting the back of the thrower lift up and add the leverage that would give it more distance. It went less than half the distance down the course than either Ayla's or Jondalar's spears had gone, but it was still much farther than anyone expected a boy to cast a spear, especially one with his affliction.

More people started to crowd around, and no one seemed interested in leaving now. The man who had asked for the demonstration came forward. He looked at the boy, noticed the decorations on his tunic and the small necklace around his neck, and seemed surprised. "That boy is not Ninth Cave, he's Nineteenth. You just arrived, when did he learn to use that thing?"

"This morning," Ayla said.

"He threw a spear that far and he only learned this morning?" the man said.

Ayla nodded. "Yes. Of course, he hasn't learned how to hit what he aims for yet, but that will come with time, and practice." She glanced at the youngster.

Lanidar's grin was so full of pride, Ayla had to smile, too. He gave her the spear-thrower and she selected a light spear, set it on top of the thrower, and heaved it with all her might. People watched as it flew high and landed well beyond the targets Jondalar had set out. Everyone was so busy watching the spear, few noticed that she had selected a second spear and hurled it. It landed in one of the targets with a satisfying sound, and several people turned their heads in surprise to see the long dart sticking out of the neck of the painted deer.

The hubbub of voices grew, and when Ayla looked at Jondalar, his grin was as wide as Lanidar's had been. People crowded around them both, wanting to see the new implements, and several wanted to try them. But when they asked to use hers, Ayla directed them to Jondalar, making excuses about having to find Wolf. She found that while she didn't mind offering to let someone use her weapon, she didn't like it as well when people asked to use hers, though she was surprised at her reaction. She had never had much that she thought of as her own.

She was getting a little concerned about Wolf's whereabouts and looked for him. She saw him sitting beside Folara and Marthona on the side of the slope. The young woman noticed her looking at them and held up the willow grouse. Ayla headed in their direction.

A woman approached her as she left the target field, then she saw that Lanidar was with her, but hanging back a little. "I am Mardena of the Nineteenth Cave of the Zelandonii," said the woman, holding out both hands in greeting. "We are hosting this year. In the name of the Mother, I welcome you to this Summer Meeting." She was a small woman, and thin. Ayla could see a resemblance to Lanidar.

"I am Ayla, of the Ninth Cave of the Zelandonii, formerly of the Lion Camp of the Mamutoi. In the name of Doni, the Great Earth Mother, known also as Mut, I greet you," Ayla replied.

"I am Lanidar's mother," Mardena said.

"I thought you might be. There is a resemblance," Ayla said.

She noticed Ayla's strange accent and was slightly put off by it. "I'd like to ask how you know my son. I asked him, but he can be very closemouthed sometimes," his mother said, looking a bit exasperated.

"Boys are like that," Ayla said with a smile. "Someone told him there were horses at our camp. He came to see. I happened to be there at the time."

"I hope he didn't bother you," Mardena said.

"No, not at all. In fact, he could be a help to me. I am trying to keep the horses out of the way, for their own safety, until everyone gets used to them and knows they are not horses to be hunted. I plan to build an enclosure for them, but I haven't had time, so for now, I just have them on long ropes fastened to a tree. The ropes drag the ground and get caught in grass and brush, and then the horses can't move around as well. I've asked Lanidar if he would check on them when I have to be gone for some time, and come and tell me if there is a problem. I just want to make sure they are all right," Ayla said.

"He's just a boy, and horses are rather big, aren't they?" the boy's mother asked.

"Yes, they are, and if they are crowded, or in an unknown situation, they sometimes get frightened. Then they might rear or kick out, but they took to Lanidar quite well. They are very gentle with children and people they know. You are welcome to come and see for yourself. But if it troubles you, I'll find someone else," Ayla said.

"Don't say no, mother!" Lanidar implored, rushing up. "I want to do it. She let me touch them, and they ate out of my hands, both hands! And she showed me how to throw a spear with that spear-thrower. All the boys throw spears, and I never threw a spear before."

Mardena knew that her son longed to be like the other boys, but she felt that he had to learn that he never would be. It had hurt when the man who had been her mate left after Lanidar was born. She was sure that he was ashamed of the child, and she thought everyone felt the same way. In addition to the handicap, Lanidar was small for his age, and she tried to protect him. Spear-throwing didn't mean anything to her. She had come to watch the demonstration only because everyone else was and she thought Lanidar might enjoy watching. But when she looked for him, she couldn't find him. No one was more surprised than Lanidar's mother when the foreign woman called on him to demonstrate the new weapon, and she had to find out how Ayla came to know him.

Ayla could see her hesitation. "If you are not busy, why don't you come to the camp of the Ninth Cave tomorrow morning with Lanidar. You can see the boy with the horses and judge for yourself," Ayla said.

"Mother, I can do it. I know I can do it," Lanidar pleaded.

26

I need to think about it," Mardena said. "My son is not like other boys. He can't do the same things they do."

Ayla looked at the woman. "I'm not sure I understand."

"Certainly you can see that his arm limits him," the woman said.

"Somewhat, but many people learn to overcome those kinds of limitations," Ayla said.

"How much can he overcome? You must know he'll never be a hunter, and he can't make things with his hands. That doesn't leave much," Mardena said.

"Why can't he be a hunter or learn to make things?" Ayla said. "He's intelligent. He can see well. He has one perfectly good arm and some use of the other. He can walk, he can even run. I've seen far worse problems overcome. He just needs someone to teach him."

"Who would teach him?" Mardena said. "Even the man of his hearth didn't want to."

Ayla thought she was beginning to understand. "I would be happy to teach him, and I think Jondalar would be willing to help. Lanidar's left arm is strong. He might have to learn to compensate for the right arm, balance mostly, for accuracy, but I'm sure he could learn to throw a spear, especially with a spear-thrower."

"Why should you bother? We don't live at your Cave. You don't even know him," the woman said.

Ayla didn't think the woman would believe that she would do it because she liked the boy, though she had just met him. "I think we all have an obligation to teach children whatever we can," she said, "and I have just become Zelandonii. I need to make a contribution to my new people to show that I am worthy. Besides, if he helps me with the horses, I would owe him a debt, and I would want to give him something of like value in return. That is what I was taught when I was a girl."

"Even if you try to teach him, what if he can't learn to hunt? I hate to get his hopes up," the boy's mother said.

"He needs to learn some skills, Mardena. What will he do when he grows up, and you become too old to protect him? You don't want him to be a burden on the Zelandonii. Neither do I, no matter where he lives."

"He knows how to gather food with the women," Mardena said.

"Yes, and that is a worthwhile contribution, but he should learn some other skills. At least he should try," Ayla said.

"I suppose you're right, but what can he do? I'm not sure he could really hunt," Lanidar's mother said.

"You saw him throw a spear, didn't you? Even if he doesn't become an excellent hunter—though I think he could—if he learns to hunt, it could lead to other things."

"Like what?"

Ayla tried to think of something in a hurry. "He's a good whistler, Mardena. I've heard him," she said. "A person who knows how to whistle can often learn to imitate the sounds that animals make. If he can, then he could learn to be a Caller, and entice them to where the hunters are waiting. You don't need arms for that, but he would need to be where animals are so he could hear them, and learn how they sound."

"It's true, he is a good whistler," Mardena said, considering something she hadn't thought of. "Do you really think he could do something with that?"

Lanidar had been listening to the discussion with keen interest. "She whistles, mother. She can whistle like birds," he interjected. "And she whistles to call her horses, but she can imitate a horse, and she sounds just like one when she does."

"Is that true? Can you make the sound of a horse?" the mother asked.

"Why don't you and Lanidar come and visit the camp of the Ninth Cave tomorrow morning, Mardena," Ayla said. She was sure the woman was going to ask her to demonstrate, and she didn't really want to make a loud horse neigh with so many people around. They would all turn and stare at her.

"Can I bring my mother?" Mardena asked. "I'm sure she'll want to come."

"Of course. Why don't you all come and share a meal with us."

"All right. We'll come tomorrow morning," Mardena said.

Ayla watched the boy and his mother walk away together. Before she turned to join the women and Wolf, she saw Lanidar look back at her with an absolutely grateful smile.

"Here's your bird," Folara said as she approached, holding out the willow grouse with the small spear still sticking out of it. "What are you going to do with it?"

"Well, since I just invited some people to share a meal tomorrow morning, I think I will end up cooking it for them," Ayla said.

"Whom did you invite?" Marthona asked.

"That woman I was talking to," Ayla said.

"Mardena?" Folara said with surprise.

"And her son, and her mother."

"No one invites them, except to community feasts, of course," Folara said.

"Why not?" Ayla asked.

"Now that I think about it, I'm not really sure," Folara said. "Mardena keeps to herself. I think she blames herself, or thinks people blame her, for the boy's arm."

"Some people do," Marthona said, "and the boy may have trouble finding a mate. Mothers will be afraid that he'll bring crippling spirits with him to a mating."

"And she always drags her boy around wherever she goes," Folara said. "I think she's afraid the other boys will pick on him if she lets him go anywhere alone. They probably would. I don't think he has any friends. She doesn't give him any opportunities."

"I wondered about that," Ayla said. "She seemed very protective of him. Too much, I think. She thinks his crippled arm limits his abilities, but I think his biggest limitation is not his arm, it's his mother. She's afraid to let him try, but he has to grow up sometime."

"Why did you pick him to throw a spear, Ayla? It seemed like you knew him," Marthona asked.

"Someone told him there were horses where we're camped—the Upper Meadow, he called it—and he came to see them. I happened to be there when he came. I think he was trying to get away from the crowd, or his mother, but whoever told him didn't say anything about us camping there. I know Jondalar and Joharran have been passing the word for people to stay away from the horses. Maybe the 'someone' who told Lanidar about them thought he would get in trouble if he came looking for them. But I don't mind if people want to look, I just don't want anybody thinking about hunting them. They're too used to people. They wouldn't know to run away," Ayla explained.

"So of course, you let Lanidar touch the horses, and he got all excited, just like everyone does," Folara said, grinning.

Ayla smiled back. "Well, maybe not everyone, but I think if people have a chance to get to know them, they'll know they are special and won't be tempted to hunt them."

"You are probably right," Marthona said.

"The horses seemed to take to him, and he learned my whistle for them right away, so I asked Lanidar if he would check on the horses when I'm not around. I didn't think that his mother might object," Ayla said.

"Not many mothers would object to letting a son who will soon be able to count twelve years learn more about horses, or any animal," Marthona said.

"That many years? I would have thought he was a nine- or maybe a ten-year. He talked about Jondalar's spear-throwing demonstration, but he said he didn't want to go because he couldn't throw a spear. He seemed to think it was beyond him, but there is nothing wrong with his left arm, and I had my spear-thrower with me, so I showed him how to use it. After talking to Mardena, I know where he got the idea, but at his years he should be learning some skills besides picking berries with his mother." Ayla looked at both women. "There are so many people here, you can't know all of them. How do you know Lanidar and his mother?"

"Any time a baby is born with something wrong with him like that, everybody hears about it," Marthona said, "and they talk about it. Not necessarily in a bad way. They just wonder why it happened, and hope nothing like that ever happens to any of their children. So, of course, everyone knew when the man of his hearth left. Most people think it was because he was embarrassed to call Lanidar the son of his hearth, but I think at least part of it was Mardena. She didn't want anybody to see the baby, not even her mate. She tried to hide him, and kept his arm covered, and got very protective of him."

"That's his problem, she still is. When I told her that I asked him to check on the horses when I'm not there, Mardena didn't want to let him. I wasn't asking for something he couldn't do. I just want someone to make sure they are all right, and to come and get me if there is a problem," Ayla said. "That's why she's coming over tomorrow, so I can try to persuade her that the horses won't hurt him. And I've promised to teach him to hunt, or at least to throw a spear. I'm not sure how it all happened, but somehow the more she objected to him even trying to learn, the more determined I became to teach him."

Both women were smiling and nodding with understanding.

"Will you tell Proleva that we are having visitors in the morning?" Ayla said. "And that I'll cook this grouse?"

"Don't forget your hare," Marthona said. "Salova told me you got one this morning. Do you want help with your cooking?"

"Only if you think more people may decide to join us," Ayla said. "I think I'll dig a ground oven, put some hot rocks in it, and cook the grouse and the hare at the same time, overnight. Maybe add some herbs and vegetables, too."

"A morning feast coming out of a ground oven—food is always so tender when it's cooked that way," Folara said. "I can hardly wait."

"Folara, I think we'd better plan to help," Marthona said. "If Ayla is going to cook, I think everyone will be curious and want a taste. Oh, I nearly forgot. I was told to tell you, Ayla, there will be a gathering tomorrow in the afternoon of all the women who are to be mated, and their mothers, in the zelandonia lodge."

"I have no mother to bring," Ayla said, frowning. She didn't want to be the only one there without a mother, if one was expected.

"Generally it is not the place of the man's mother to go, but since the woman you were born to can't be here, if you want, I would be willing to go in her place," Jondalar's mother said.

"Would you really?" Ayla said, feeling overwhelmed by the offer. "I would be very grateful."

A meeting of the women who will be mating soon, Ayla thought. Soon I will be Jondalar's mate. How I wish Iza could be here. She's the mother who should be with me, not the woman I was born to. Since they are both walking in the next world, I am grateful that Marthona is willing to come, but Iza would have been so pleased. She was afraid I would never find a mate, and I might not have if I had stayed with the Clan. She was right to tell me to leave and find my own people, find my own mate, but I miss her, and Creb, and Durc. I need to stop thinking about them.

"If you are going back to camp, will you take the grouse with you?" Ayla asked. "Right now I'm going to look for something else to cook with the morning meal."

Behind and toward the right of the main Summer Meeting camp, the limestone hills formed the general shape of a large scooped-out shallow bowl curving around on the sides, but open in front. The base of the curved slopes converged to a small, relatively level field, which had been evened out with stones and packed earth over the many years the location had been used for meetings. The grass-covered hillsides within the partial bowl depression rose up in a gradual, irregular slope with dips and hills, less steep areas that had been made more level to provide places for family groups or even some entire Caves to sit together with a good view of the open space below. The sloped area was sufficiently large to hold the entire Summer Meeting camp of more than two thousand people.

In a wooded copse near the rugged crest of the slope, a spring rose that filled a small pool, then spilled down the middle of the bowl-shaped slope, through the flattened area at the bottom, and eventually into the larger stream of the camp. The spring-fed creek was so small that people stepped over it easily, but the clear, cold pool at the top provided a constant source of clean drinking water.

Ayla walked uphill toward the trees, along a path beside the shallow creek that painted a sheen of water over a bed of cobbled stones. She stopped to get a drink at the spring, then turned around. Her eyes were drawn by the glimmering creek trickling downhill. She observed it run into the stream, which flowed through the large crowded camp and on to The River and the valley beyond. It was a landscape contoured by the deep relief of high hills, limestone cliffs, and river-cut valleys.

Her attention was caught by the sound that funneled up the rounded incline from the camp. It was a sound unlike anything she had ever heard: the combined voices of a large camp full of people, talking, channeled into one sound. The merging of the babble of voices was like a muted roar punctuated by occasional outcries, calls, and whoops. It was not the same, but it reminded her of a large hive of bees or a bawling herd of aurochs in the distance, and she was rather glad to be alone for the moment.

Well, not entirely alone. She watched Wolf poking his nose into every little crack and cranny, and smiled. Ayla was glad he was with her. Although she was unaccustomed to so many people, especially all at one time and in one place, she didn't really want to be alone. She'd had her fill of that in the valley she found after she left the Clan, and she wasn't sure she could have stood it if she hadn't had Whinney and, later, Baby for company. Even with them it had been lonely, but she knew how to obtain food and make the things she needed, and she had learned the joy of utter freedom—and its consequences. For the first time, she could do whatever she wanted, even adopt a baby horse or lion. Living alone, dependent entirely on herself, had taught her that one person could live, for a while, in reasonable comfort if she was young, and healthy, and strong. It was only when she became seriously ill that she realized how completely vulnerable she was.

It was then that Ayla fully understood that she would not be alive if the Clan had not allowed an injured and weak little girl, orphaned by an earthquake, to live with them, though she had been born to the ones they knew as the Others. Later, when she and Jondalar lived with the Mamutoi, she came to realize that living with a group, any group, even one that believed the wishes and desires of individuals were important, limited individual freedom, because the needs of the community were equally important. Survival depended upon a cooperative unit, a Clan or a Camp or a Cave, a group who would work together and help each other. There was always a struggle between the individual and the group, and finding a workable balance was a constant challenge, but not without benefits.

The cooperation of the group provided more than essentials for individuals. It also granted leisure time to devote to more enjoyable tasks, which among the Others allowed an aesthetic sense to bloom. The art they created wasn't so much art for itself as it was an inherent part of living, part of their daily existence. Nearly every member of a Zelandonii Cave enjoyed pride of workmanship and, in varying degrees, appreciated the results of one another's skills. From the time they were young, each child was allowed to experiment to find the area in which they excelled, and practical crafts were not considered more important than artistic talents.

Ayla remembered that Shevonar, the man who died during the bison hunt, had been a spear-maker. He was not the only person of the Ninth Cave who could make a spear, but specialization of a craft developed greater skill, which gave status to the individual who made it, often economic status. Among the Zelandonii, and most other people she had met or lived with, food was shared, though the hunter or gatherer who supplied it gained standing for giving it. A man or woman could survive without ever foraging for food, but without some specialized craft or particular talent that gave a person prestige, no one could live well.

Though it was still a difficult concept for her, Ayla had been learning how goods and services were bartered by the Zelandonii. Nearly everything that was made or done had value, even though its practical worth was not always obvious. The value was generally agreed upon by consensus or individual bargaining. The result was that truly fine workmanship was rewarded over and above the ordinary, partly because people preferred it, which created demand, and partly because it often took longer to make or do something well. Both talent and workmanship were highly valued, and most members of a Cave had a well-developed aesthetic sense within their own canon.

A well-made spear that was beautifully decorated had more value than an equally well-made spear that was only functional, but that had infinitely more value than a poorly made spear. A basket that was clumsily woven might serve as well as a basket that was carefully made with subtle textures and patterns or colored in various tones, but it was not nearly as desirable. The barely serviceable one might be used for roots just dug from the ground, but once the roots were cleaned or dried, a more beautiful basket might be preferred to store them. Expedient tools and objects that served an immediate need were often made and then discarded, while one that was beautiful and well made was usually kept.

It wasn't only handicrafts that were valued. Entertainment was considered essential. Long, cold winters often kept people confined to their dwellings within the shelter for long periods of time, and they needed ways to alleviate the pressures of close quarters. Dancing and singing were enjoyed both as individual efforts and as community participation, and those who could play a flute well were as highly valued as those who made spears or baskets. Ayla had already learned that Story-Tellers were especially esteemed. Even the Clan had storytellers, Ayla recalled. They had particularly enjoyed the retelling of stories they knew.

The Others also liked hearing the stories retold, but they liked novelty, too. Riddles and word games were enthusiastically played by young and old alike. Visitors were welcomed, if only because they usually brought new stories. They were urged to tell about their lives and adventures, whether or not they had dramatic narration skills, because it added a measure of interest and gave people something to discuss for long hours as they sat around winter fires. Although almost anyone could weave an interesting tale, those who showed a real talent for it were urged, coaxed, and cajoled to pay visits to neighboring Caves, which was the impetus that gave rise to the traveling Story-Tellers. Some of them spent their lives, or at least several years, traveling from Cave to Cave, carrying news, bringing messages, and telling stories. No one was more welcomed.

Most people could be quickly identified by the designs on their clothing, and the necklaces and other jewelry they wore, but over time the Story-Tellers had adopted a distinctive style of clothing and design that announced their profession. Even young children knew when they arrived, and almost all other activities stopped when one or more of the traveling entertainers made an appearance. Even planned hunting trips were often canceled. It would be a time for spontaneous feasts, and although many could, no Story-Teller ever had to hunt or forage to survive. They were always given gifts as an encouragement to return, and when they grew too old or tired of traveling, they could settle down with any Cave they chose.

Sometimes several Story-Tellers traveled together, often with their families. Particularly talented groups might include singing and dancing or the playing of instruments: various kinds of percussions, rattles, rasps, flutes, and occasionally tightened strings that were struck or plucked. A local Cave's musicians, singers, dancers, and those who had stories to tell and liked to tell them often participated as well. Stories were often dramatized as well as narrated, but no matter how it was expressed, the story and the teller were always the focal point.

Stories could be anything: myths, legends, histories, personal adventures, or descriptions of far-off or imaginary places, people, or animals. A part of every Story-Teller's repertoire, because it was always in demand, were the personal happenings of neighboring Caves, gossip, whether funny, serious, sad, real, or invented. Everything and anything was fair game, as long as it was well told. The traveling Story-Tellers also carried private messages, from a person to a friend or relative, from a leader to a leader, from one Zelandoni to another, although such private communication could be very sensitive. A Story-Teller had to prove very trustworthy before being entrusted with particularly confidential or esoteric messages between leaders or the zelandonia, and not all were.

Beyond the crest, which was a high point of the area for some distance around, the land dropped down, then leveled out. Ayla climbed over the top ridge and started down, traversing at an angle along a faint trail that had been recently cleared through the hillside of dense brambles and a few scraggly pines. She veered away from the path at the bottom of the hill where the sloping canebrake of berry vines gave way to sparse grass. At an ancient dry streambed, whose tightly packed stones gave little space to establish new growth, she turned and followed it uphill.

Wolf seemed especially curious. It was new territory to him, too, and he was diverted by every pile and pocket of earth that offered his nose a new smell. They started up the rocky riverbed that had cut through the limestone in the days when water rushed along it, then he bounded ahead and disappeared behind a hill of rubble. Ayla expected him to reappear any moment, but after what seemed to be an unusually long time, she became concerned. She stood near the mound of rocks, looked all around, and finally whistled the sharp, distinctive tones that she had specifically developed to call the wolf. Then she waited. It was some time before she saw the overgrown brambles behind the mound moving and heard him scrabbling out from under the thorny briar.

"Where have you been, Wolf?" she said as she bent down to look into his eyes. "What is under all these berry vines that it took you so long to get here?"

She decided to try to find out and took off her pack to get out the small axe Jondalar had made for her. She found it at the bottom of the pack. It was not the most effective tool for hacking through the long woody stems full of thorns, but she managed to create an opening that allowed her to see, not the ground, as she had expected, but a dark, empty space. Now, she was curious.

She worked at the vines some more and enlarged the opening enough for her to force her way through it with only a few scratches. The ground sloped down into what was obviously a cave with a comfortably wide entrance. With daylight coming through the hole she had made, she continued down, using the counting words to name her steps. When she reached thirty-one, she noticed that the slope leveled out and the corridor had widened. Faint daylight still filtered into the cave from the entrance, and with eyes adjusted to the near darkness, she saw that she had entered a much larger area. She looked around, then made a decision and headed back outside.

"I wonder how many people know about this cave, Wolf?"

She used her axe to widen the opening a little more, then went out and scanned the area. A short distance away, but surrounded by prickly briars, was a pine tree with needles that were brown. It appeared to be dead. With the small stone axe, she hacked her way through the tough woody vines a short distance, then tested a low branch to see if it was brittle enough to break. Though she'd had to hang on it with all her weight, she finally managed to snap off a section of a branch. Her hand felt sticky, and she smiled when she looked at the branch and saw some dark blobs of pitch. The pitchy branch would make a good enough torch without additional materials, once she got it lit.

She collected some dry twigs and bark from the dead pine, then walked to the middle of the rocky dry streambed. She got her fire kit out of her backpack and, using the crushed bark and twigs as tinder, and her firestone and a striking flint, she soon had a little fire started. From it, she lit the pine branch torch. Wolf watched her, and when he saw her heading back toward the cave, he raced ahead over the pile of rocks and wriggled his way in as he had the first time, under the hole Ayla had cut through the tangle of blackberry vines. Long before, when the dry bed was the river that had created the cave, the roof had extended farther out, but it had since collapsed, creating the pile of rubble that was in front of the present opening in the side of the hill.

She climbed the rocky mound and eased through the opening she had made. With the light from the flickering torch, she proceeded down the rather slick ramp of moist sandy-clay soil, again naming her steps with the counting words. This time it took only twenty-eight steps before the ground leveled out; with a torch to show the way, her stride was longer. The wide entry gallery opened onto a large, roundish, U-shaped room. She held the torch high, looked up, and caught her breath.

The walls, glinting with crystallized calcite, were nearly white, a pure, clean, resplendent surface. As she moved slowly into the cave, the light from the flickering torch sent animated shadows of the natural relief chasing each other over the walls as though they were alive and breathing. She walked closer to the white walls, which started a little below her chin—about five feet up from ground level—with a rounded ledge of brownish stone, and extended up in a curve that arced inward to the roof. She would not have thought of it before her visit to the deep cave of Fountain Rocks, but she could imagine what an artist like Jonokol might do in a cave like this.

Ayla walked around the room next to the wall, very carefully. The floor was muddy and uneven, and slippery. At the bottom of the U, where it curved around there was a narrow entrance to another gallery. She held the torch up and looked inside. The upper walls were white and curved, but the lower area was a narrow twisting corridor and she decided not to enter. She continued around, and to the right of the entrance to the gallery at the back there was another passageway, but she only looked inside. She had already decided that she would have to tell Jondalar and some others and bring them back to this cave.

Ayla had seen many caves, most filled with beautiful stone icicles suspended from ceilings or stalactite draperies hanging down the walls and corresponding deposits of stalagmites growing to meet them from the floors, but she had never seen a cave like this. Although it was a limestone cave, a layer of impermeable marl had formed that blocked the calcium carbonate–saturated drops of water and kept them from seeping through to form stalactites and stalagmites. Instead the walls were covered with calcite crystals, which grow very little, leaving large panels of white covering the bumps and dips of the natural relief of the stone. It was a rare and beautiful place, the most beautiful cave she had ever seen.

She noticed the light of her torch dimming. It was building up an accumulation of charcoal near the end, stifling the flame. In most caves she would have simply knocked it against any wall to dislodge the burned wood and refresh the fire, but that usually left a black mark. In this place she felt constrained to be careful; she couldn't just knock off the charcoal and mar the unblemished white walls. She chose a place in the darker stone area, lower down. Some of the charcoal dropped on the ground when she rapped the torch against the stone, and she had a momentary urge to clean it up. There was a sacred quality to this place; it felt spiritual, otherworldly, and she didn't want to desecrate it in any way.

Then she shook her head. It's only a cave, she thought, even if it is special. A little charcoal on the ground won't hurt it. Besides, she noticed that the wolf didn't hesitate to mark the place. He had lifted his leg every few feet, proclaiming with his scent that this was his territory. But his scent marks didn't reach the white walls.

Ayla walked back to the camp of the Ninth Cave as quickly as she could, excited to tell people about the cave. It was only when she arrived, and noticed several people were hauling away dirt from a pit oven that had just been dug and several others were preparing food to go into it, that she remembered she had invited some people over the following morning. She had planned to forage for food to cook, to find an animal to hunt or some edible plant food, and in her excitement over the cave she had forgotten all about it. She noticed that Marthona, Folara, and Proleva had taken out an entire haunch of a bison from the cold storage pit.

The first day they arrived, most of the Ninth Cave had worked to dig the large pit all the way down to the level of the permafrost to preserve the part of the meat, which they had hunted before they left, that had not been dried. The land of the Zelandonii was close enough to the northern glacier for permafrost conditions to prevail, but that did not mean the ground was permanently frozen year-round. In winter the soil became as hard as ice, frozen solid all the way to the surface, but in summer a layer on top thawed to varying depths from a few inches to several feet depending on the surface cover and the amount of sun or shade it received. Storing meat in a hole that was dug down to the frost kept it fresh longer, though most people didn't mind if meat aged a little, and some people preferred the flavor of meat that was quite high.

"Marthona, I'm sorry," Ayla said when she reached the main hearth. "I went to find more food for tomorrow's morning meal, but I found a cave nearby and forgot all about it. It is the most beautiful cave I've ever seen, and I wanted to show it to you, and everyone."

"I never heard of any caves nearby," Folara said. "Certainly not any beautiful ones. How far is it?"

"It's just down the other side of that slope at the back of the main camp," Ayla explained.

"That's where we go to gather blackberries in late summer," Proleva said. "There is no cave there." Several other people had heard Ayla and had gathered around, Jondalar and Joharran among them.

"She's right," Joharran said. "I never heard of a cave there."

"It was hidden by the canebrake, and a big pile of rubble in front of it," Ayla said. "Wolf actually found it. He was sniffing around under the brambles and disappeared. When I whistled for him, it took him a long time to get back, so I wondered where he went. I hacked my way through and found a cave."

"It can't be very big, can it?" Jondalar asked.

"It's inside that hill, and it's a big cave, Jondalar, and very unusual."

"Can you show us?" he said.

"Of course. That's what I came here to do, but now I think I should help prepare the food for the meal tomorrow morning," Ayla said.

"We've just lit the fire in the pit oven," Proleva said, "and piled a lot of wood in it. It'll take a while for it to burn down and heat the rocks that line it. We were just going to put the food up on the high rack until we were ready for it, so there's no reason we can't go now."

"I invite people here to share a meal, and everyone else has done all the work. I should at least have helped dig the roasting pit," Ayla said, feeling embarrassed. It seemed to her that she had shirked the hard work.

"Don't worry about it, Ayla. We were going to dig one anyway," Proleva said. "And a lot of people were still here. Most of them have gone to the main camp now, but it's always easier when everybody does it together. This just gave us a reason."

"Let's go see your cave," Jondalar said.

"You know, if we all go there together, the whole camp will follow us," Willamar said.

"We could all go up separately, and meet at the spring," Rushemar said. He was one who had helped dig the roasting pit and was waiting for Salova to finish feeding Marsola before going to the main camp. Salova, who was nearby, smiled at him. Her mate was not one to say much, but when he did, it usually showed his intelligence, she thought. She looked around for Marsola, who was sitting on the ground nearby. She'd have to get the baby's carrying cloak if they were going to go hiking around, but it did sound exciting.

"That's a good idea, Rushemar, but I think I have a better one," Jondalar said. "We can get to the back of that slope by going up our little creek and around the back. That scree slope behind the pond is not very far from there. I climbed to the top of it, looking to see if there was any flint in that pile of rocks, and got a good look at the lay of the land."

"That's perfect! Let's go," Folara said.

"I would like to show it to Zelandoni and Jonokol, too," Ayla said.

"And since this is their territory, I think it would be appropriate to ask Tormaden, the leader of the Nineteenth Cave, to join us," Marthona added.

"You're right, of course, mother. By all rights, they should explore it first," Joharran said. "But since they never found it in all the time they've lived here, I think we can make it a joint adventure. I'll go ask Tormaden to come with us." The leader smiled. "But I won't tell him why. I'll just tell him Ayla found something and wants to show it to us."

"Why don't I come with you, Joharran, and stop by the zelandonia lodge and ask Zelandoni and Jonokol to join us," Ayla said.

"How many want to go?" Joharran asked. Everyone who was there indicated their interest, but since most of the two hundred or so people who belonged to the Ninth Cave were in the main camp area, it wasn't as huge a crowd as it might have been. Using the counting words, he estimated about twenty-five people and thought a group that size ought to be manageable, especially since they would be going another way. "All right, I'll go with Ayla to the main camp. Jondalar, you take everyone else the back way, and we will meet you on the down slope behind the spring."

"And take something to cut through those thorny stems, Jondalar, and some torches and your fire kit," Ayla said. "I only went into the first big room, but I noticed a couple of passageways leading off from it."

Zelandoni and several of the zelandonia, including some new acolytes, were in the middle of preparing for the meeting with the women who were about to be mated; The One Who Was First was always busy at Summer Meetings. But when Ayla asked to speak to her privately, she sensed from the young woman's demeanor that it could be important. Ayla told her about the cave and mentioned that several people from the Ninth Cave were going to be meeting behind the spring as soon as they could get there to go to see it. When the woman hesitated, Ayla insisted that Jonokol had to come, if no one else. That piqued the curiosity of the First, and she decided that perhaps she should go after all.

"Zelandoni of the Fourteenth, will you take charge of this gathering?" the First Donier said to the one who had always wanted to be First. "I have to attend to a Ninth Cave matter."

"Of course," the older woman said. She was curious—they all were—about what could be so important that the First would leave in the middle of a significant meeting, but she was also pleased that she had been called upon to fill in for her. Perhaps the First was beginning to appreciate her.

"Jonokol, come with me," Zelandoni of the Ninth said to her First Acolyte. That created even more curiosity, but no one would dream of asking, not even Jonokol, though he was glad that he might find out.

Joharran had a little trouble finding Tormaden, and then convincing him to drop everything and come, especially since the leader of the Ninth wouldn't tell him what it was about.

"Ayla found something that we think you should know about, since it's your territory," Joharran told him. "Several people from the Ninth Cave are already aware of it—they were there when she told me about it—but I think you should know before the whole Summer Meeting does. You know how fast word can get out."

"You really think it's that important?" Tormaden said.

"I wouldn't ask you if I didn't," Joharran said.

Going to see the cave Ayla found had become a Ninth Cave adventure, and some people wanted to bring food or gathering baskets as well as torches and make an outing of it. Most of them felt lucky that they had still been at their camp when Ayla came and told them about it, and were therefore able to get a first look at a new cave, one that the interesting woman that Jondalar had brought home with him claimed was so beautiful. They assumed the beauty would be in the stalactitic formations, that it would be another cave like the one named Pretty Hollow that was near the Ninth Cave.

It was some time later when they all finally met. Joharran and Tormaden were the last to arrive, but the ones who came first, the group from the Ninth Cave, waited behind the crest down the slope a ways. A crowd of people standing at the top of the ridge would have been noticed from the main camp, and they didn't want to be conspicuous. A little secrecy added to the excitement, but every so often someone would go up to the spring and, staying behind trees, check to see if Ayla and the two zelandonia were coming, or Joharran and the Nineteenth Cave's leader.

After short courtesy greetings were exchanged—Ayla had formally met Tormaden and the Nineteenth Cave soon after they arrived—she and Wolf started traversing down the trail through the hillside of blackberry vines full of ripening berries, leading the rest, with the wolf at her heel. She had signaled the animal to stay close, and he seemed to prefer it. With so many people, Wolf was feeling protective of her, and she didn't want the large carnivore to alarm anyone, although most of the Ninth Cave were getting quite used to him.

They loved the reaction he caused in the rest of the people at the Meeting, and the inevitable attention they received because of him.

At the bottom, she turned toward the dry streambed. When they arrived, they first saw the remains of her fire, but soon noticed the hole cut through the thick, woody, running vines. Rushemar, Solaban, and Tormaden immediately set to work enlarging the hole, while Jondalar quickly started a fire. They were all getting more curious about the cave, Jondalar in particular. Once they got a few torches lit, they all tromped toward the dark hole that had been cut through the greenery.

Tormaden was very surprised. He could see it was a cave, but he'd had no idea it was there. They only used the back hillside when the berries were ripe. It was a huge wild berry patch that covered the entire hill and had been there as long as anyone knew. Just picking from the path, which was renewed every year, and from around the edges provided more fruit than all of them could pick, even during a Summer Meeting. No one had bothered to hack their way in very far, or to cut through and find a cave.

"What made you decide to cut through the brambles here, Ayla?" Tormaden asked as they started into the dark hole.

"Wolf did," she said, looking down at him. "He is the one who found it. I was out looking for something for a morning meal tomorrow, perhaps a hare or a grouse. Wolf often helps me hunt, he has a good nose. He disappeared behind this pile of rubble and under the vines and was a long time coming out. I wondered what was there. I cut through and discovered it was a cave, then came out and lit a torch and went back in."

"I thought there had to be a reason," he said, aware of both her unusual way of speaking and her. She was a beautiful woman, especially when she smiled.

With Ayla and the wolf in the lead, and Tormaden behind her, each holding a torch, they started into the opening one at a time. Zelandoni and Jonokol were behind him, followed by Joharran, Marthona, and Jondalar. Ayla realized that the people had intuitively ranked themselves in the order that they used for very special or formal occasions, like a funeral, except that she had ended up in front, which made her a bit uneasy. She didn't think she deserved to be first in such a line.

She waited until everyone was in the cave. The last one in was Lanoga carrying Lorala, daughters of Laramar's mate, Tremeda, the family that was always last. She smiled at them and received a shy smile in return from Lanoga. Ayla was glad she had decided to come. Lorala was getting the rounded look that a baby her age should have, and becoming more of a handful for her surrogate mother, but Lanoga seemed very pleased about it. She had taken to sitting with the young mothers of the Cave and, hearing them brag about their babies, had begun to talk a little about Lorala's accomplishments.

"The floor is slippery, so be careful," Ayla said as she started out, leading the group underground. With several torches, it was easier to see that the entrance gallery widened as the floor sloped down. She became aware of the cool dampness of the cave, the earthy smell of wet clay, a muffled sound of dripping water, and the breathing of the people behind her, but no one really spoke. The cave seemed to inspire silence, an expectant hush even from the babies.

When she felt the floor level out, she slowed and lowered her torch. The others did the same, watching their feet and where they were going. When all of them had reached the level area, Ayla lifted her torch and held it high. As the rest of them did the same, first there were involuntary sounds of surprise, ooohs and aaahs, and then stunned silence as the people were truly overcome by the glorious white walls of crystallized calcite molded to the shape of the rock, shimmeringly alive in the torchlight. The beauty of the cave had nothing to do with stalactites, the cave had almost none, but the cave was beautiful, and more, it was filled with a powerful aura that was magical, supernatural, and spiritual.

"O Great Earth Mother!" said the Zelandoni Who Was First. "This is Her sanctuary. This is Her womb." Then she began to sing, in her own gloriously rich and vibrant voice:

> "Out of the darkness, the chaos of time,
> The whirlwind gave birth to the Mother sublime.
> She woke to Herself knowing life had great worth,
> The dark empty void grieved the Great Mother Earth."
> "The Mother was lonely. She was the only."

The walls resonated with her voice, creating a feeling of accompaniment. Then someone started playing a flute and actually did accompany her. Ayla looked to see who it was. A young man who was a stranger was making the music. Though he looked vaguely familiar, she knew he was not from the Ninth Cave. From his clothing she recognized that he was Third Cave, and then she knew why he seemed to be someone she knew. He resembled the leader of the Third Cave, Manvelar. She tried to recall if she had met him, and the name Morizan came to mind. He was standing beside Ramila, the plump, attractive, brown-haired young woman who was one of Folara's friends. He must have been visiting their camp and came along with them.

The people had joined in singing the Mother's Song, and they had reached a part that seemed especially profound:

> *"When She was ready, Her waters of birth,*
> *Brought back the green life to the cold barren Earth.*
> *And the tears of Her loss, abundantly spilled,*
> *Made dew drops that sparkled and rainbows that thrilled."*
> *"Birth waters brought green. But Her tears could be seen."*

> *"With a thunderous roar Her stones split asunder,*
> *And from the great cave that opened deep under,*
> *She birthed once again from Her cavernous room,*
> *And brought forth the Children of Earth from Her womb."*
> *"From the Mother forlorn, more children were born."*

> *"Each child was different, some were large and some small,*
> *Some could walk and some fly, some could swim and some crawl.*
> *But each form was perfect, each spirit complete,*
> *Each one was a model whose shape could repeat."*
> *"The Mother was willing. The green earth was filling."*

Suddenly Ayla perceived a feeling that she'd had before, but not for a long time: a sense of foreboding came over her. Ever since the Clan Gathering, where Creb had learned in some inexplicable way that she was different, she had sometimes felt this peculiar fear, this strange disorientation, as though he had changed her. She felt a tingling, a prickling, a goosebump-raising nausea and weakness, and she shivered as her memory of a darkness deeper than any cave became real. In the back of her throat she tasted the dark cool loam and growing fungus of ancient primeval forests.

An angry roar shattered the silence, and the watching people jumped back with fear. The huge cave bear pushed at the gate to the cage and sent it crashing to the ground. The maddened bear was loose! Broud was standing on his shoulders; two other men were clinging to his fur. Suddenly one was in the monstrous animal's grip, but his agonized scream was cut short when a powerful bear hug snapped his spine. The mog-urs picked up the body and, with solemn dignity, carried it into a cave. Creb, in his bearskin cloak, hobbled in the lead.

Ayla stared at a white liquid sloshing in a cracked wooden bowl. She felt an anxious worry, she had done something wrong. There wasn't supposed to be any liquid left in the bowl. She held it to her lips and drained it. Her perspective changed, a white light was inside her, and she seemed to be growing larger and looking down from high above at stars blazing a path. The stars changed to small flickering lights leading through a long endless cave. Then a red light at the end grew large, filling her vision, and with a sinking, sickening feeling, she saw the mog-urs sitting in a circle, half-hidden by stalagmite pillars.

She was sinking deeper into a black abyss, petrified with fear. Suddenly Creb was there with the flowing light inside her, helping her, supporting her, easing her fears. He guided her on a strange trip back to their mutual beginnings, through salt water and painful gulps of air, loamy earth, and high trees. Then they were on the ground, walking upright on two legs, walking a great distance, going west toward a great salty sea. They came to a steep wall that faced a river and a flat plain, with a deep recess under a large overhanging section; it was the cave of an ancient ancestor of his. But as they approached the cave, Creb began fading, leaving her.

The scene grew hazy, Creb was fading faster, was nearly gone. She scanned the landscape, searching desperately for him. Then she saw him at the top of the cliff, above his ancestor's cave, near a large boulder, a long, slightly flattened column of rock that tilted over the edge, as though frozen in place as it was about to fall. She called out, but he had faded into the rock. Ayla felt desolate; Creb was gone and she was alone. Then Jondalar appeared in his place.

She sensed herself moving with great speed over strange worlds and felt the terror of the black void again, but it was different this time. She was sharing it with Mamut, and the terror overcame both of them. Then faintly, from far away, she heard Jondalar's voice, full of agonized fear and love, calling to her, pulling her back and Mamut as well, by the sheer strength of his love and his need. In an instant she was back, feeling chilled to the bone.

"Ayla, are you all right?" Zelandoni said. "You're shivering."

27

I'm fine," Ayla said. "It's just cool in here. I should have brought something warmer." Wolf, who had been exploring the new cave, had appeared at her side and was pushing against her leg. She reached down and felt his head, then kneeled down and hugged him.

"It is cool, and you are pregnant. You feel things more," Zelandoni said, but she knew there was more to it than Ayla was saying. "You know about the meeting tomorrow, don't you?"

"Yes, Marthona told me. She will be coming with me, since I have no mother of my own to come," Ayla said.

"Do you want her to come?" Zelandoni asked.

"Oh, yes. I was grateful that she offered. I didn't want to be the only woman there without a mother, at least someone who is like a mother," Ayla said.

The First nodded. "Good."

People were getting over their first feelings of awe at the new cave and were beginning to move around in it. Ayla saw Jondalar walking the length of the large room with purposeful strides, and smiled. She knew that he used his body to measure, she had seen him do it before. The width of his clenched fist was one measurement, the length of his hand another. He used his open arms to gauge spaces, and he often paced off distances by naming his steps with the counting words. That was why she had started doing it. He looked into the gallery at the back, holding his torch high, but didn't enter.

A cluster of people were watching him. Tormaden, the leader of the Nineteenth Cave, was talking to Morizan, the young man from the Third Cave. They were the only two people who were not from the Ninth Cave. Willamar, Marthona, and Folara were standing next to Proleva and Joharran and his two closest advisers and their mates. Dark-haired Solaban and his pale blond mate, Ramara, were talking to Rushemar and Salova, who was holding little Marsola on her hip. Ayla noticed that neither Proleva's son, Jaradal, nor Ramara's son, Robenan, was with them and guessed that the two boys who played together had gone off to do something at the main camp. Jonokol was smiling at Ayla as she walked toward them with Zelandoni and the wolf. Jondalar came back and joined them.

"I would guess this room is the height of three tall men to the ceiling," he said, "and about the same or a little more across, about six of my strides. Probably the length is something short of three times that much, around sixteen steps, but I have a long stride. The darker stone of the lower part of the walls comes to about here," he held his hand about midchest height, "that's about five of my feet, one after another."

Jondalar had judged the distances fairly well. He was six feet six inches tall, and the white walls, which began at the middle of his chest, were around five feet up and went all the way to the nineteen-foot ceiling. The room was about twenty-two feet across and fifty-five feet in length, with some water pooled in the middle. The space was not large enough to hold everyone at the Summer Meeting, but more than enough to hold an entire Cave, except perhaps the Ninth, and certainly big enough for the entire zelandonia.

Jonokol walked to the middle of the room and stared up at the walls and ceiling with an entranced grin. He was in his element, lost in his imagination. He knew that these beautiful white walls hid something spectacular that wanted to come out. He wasn't in a hurry. Whatever was done with them had to be exactly right. He was beginning to get some ideas, but he needed to consult with the First, to meditate with the zelandonia, to reach inside those spaces and find the imprint of the other world that the Mother had left there. She had to tell him what was there.

"Should we explore those two passageways now, or come back later, Tormaden?" Joharran asked. He wanted to go farther now, but felt that he should defer to the leader within whose territory the cave was.

"I'm sure some people of the Nineteenth Cave would like to see this cave, and explore it deeper. Our Zelandoni probably can't do anything very strenuous, but I'm sure her First Acolyte would like to be involved. His kinship line has a wolf sign, and since it was a wolf that found this cave, he will be very interested," Tormaden said.

"Yes, the wolf found it, but if Ayla hadn't been curious enough to see where he had been, we still wouldn't know it was here," Joharran said.

"I'm sure he'd be interested in any case," Zelandoni said. "We all are, and all the Zelandonii will be. This is a rare and sacred cave.

The other world is very close here, I'm sure we all feel it. The Nineteenth Cave is very fortunate that it is so close to them, but I suspect that means you will be hosting more of the zelandonia, and others, of course, who will want to make a pilgrimage to this spiritual place," the First said. She was making it clear that no one Cave could lay claim to such a special find even if it was within their understood territory. This place belonged to all of Earth's Children. The Nineteenth Cave of the Zelandonii only held it in trust for the rest.

"I think that a closer look is necessary, but there is no hurry," Jonokol said. "Now that we know it is here, it won't go away. No one knows how much is here or how deep this cave is. Any explorations should be carefully planned, or we could wait until someone is called to it."

Zelandoni nodded slightly to herself. She understood, more than he did himself, that her First Acolyte, who had wanted only to be an artist and didn't care if he ever became Zelandoni, had found a reason to make the commitment. He wanted this cave. It claimed him. He wanted to know it, to explore it, to be called to it, and especially to paint it. He would find a way to move to the Nineteenth Cave so he could be closer to it, not that he would actually plan it, but he would work toward it because all his thoughts and dreams from now on would be of this cave.

Then another thought came to her mind. Ayla knew it! From the moment she saw it, she knew this cave belonged to Jonokol. That's why she insisted that he had to see it, even if I didn't. She knew it would be more important for him than anyone else. She is Zelandoni, whether she knows it or not, even whether she wants it or not. The old mamut knew. Perhaps the magician of the people she grew up with, the one she calls Mog-ur, recognized it. She cannot avoid it, she was born to it. And she could replace Jonokol as my acolyte. But as he says, there is no hurry. Let her have her mating, and her baby, then she can start her training.

"Of course, it would take some planning to explore all of it, but I'd like to take a closer look at that passageway at the back," Jondalar said. "Wouldn't you, Tormaden? A couple of us could go back there and see where it goes."

"And some people are ready to leave," Marthona said. "It's cool in here, and no one brought warm clothes. I think I'll take a torch and start out, though I'm sure I'll want to come back."

"I'll go, too," Zelandoni said, "and Ayla was shivering earlier."

"I'm fine now," Ayla said. "I'd like to see what's back there."

In the end Jondalar, Joharan, Tormaden, Jonokol, Morizan, and Ayla, six of them—and Wolf—stayed to look a little deeper into the new and wonderful cave.

The corridor at the back of the main room of the cave was almost directly opposite and along the axis of the entrance corridor. The entrance to the axial gallery was fairly symmetrical, wider and rounded at the top, narrowing down at the bottom. To Ayla, who had delivered babies and had examined many women, the opening was feminine, maternal, a wondrous evocation of the female organ. Though both were the same, it didn't so much put her in mind of the vagina, but the upper round part suggested the birth canal, narrowing to the lower extension of the anal region. She understood exactly what Zelandoni meant when she said this was the womb of the Mother, although all caves were considered an entrance to Her womb.

Once they went in, the winding passage continued to be narrow and difficult to negotiate, although the upper white walls widened out into a broadly curving archway. It wasn't very long, about the same length as the entrance gallery. When they reached the end, the walls opened out around a pillar of stone that gave the false impression that it supported something above, but in fact it was short of reaching the ground by more than twenty inches. The passage went around the large stone shaft on the right side, making a sharp turn to the left and meandering off a few more feet until it ended.

At the place where it turned around the column, the surface of the floor dropped down about three feet, but it was a wide horizontal space that extended up ten feet, making it one of the few really comfortable places to stand or sit and relax. Ayla took the opportunity and sat down to see how it looked from that position. She noticed that something could easily be stashed beneath the stone shaft, out of the way. She also observed a low hole in the wall opposite the pillar into which one could put small things, so they could be easily found again. She thought when she came again she would bring in something to sit on, even a bundle of grass would keep her off the cold floor.

After they worked their way back out of the gallery, they looked into the entrance of the other passageway that was to the right of it, but it was a smaller tunnel, which would require crawling up into it on hands and knees, and there were pools of water on the floor. They all decided to save exploring that place for another time.

As they left the cave, Wolf went ahead with Jondalar and the two leaders, Joharran and Tormaden. Jonokol walked beside Ayla and stopped her with a question. "Did you ask Zelandoni to invite me here?"

"After seeing what you did inside Fountain Rocks, I thought you ought to see this cave," she said, "or should it be called a deep?"

"Either one. When it gets named, it will be called a deep, but it's still a cave. Thank you for bringing me here, Ayla. I have never seen a more beautiful cave. I am overwhelmed," Jonokol said.

"Yes, I am, too. But I'm curious, how will this cave get named? Who will name it?" Ayla asked.

"It will name itself. People will start referring to it in whatever way best describes it or feels most appropriate to them. What would you call it if you wanted to talk about it to someone?" Jonokol asked.

"I'm not sure, maybe the cave with white walls," Ayla said.

"I'd guess the name will turn out to be close to that, at least one of the names, but we don't know much more about it yet, and the zelandonia will make their own name," Jonokol said.

Ayla and Jonokol were the last ones out of the cave. The sun seemed especially bright when they reached the entrance, after the dark cave lit only by a few torches. When her eyes adjusted, Ayla was surprised to see Marthona waiting, along with Jondalar and Wolf.

"Tormaden invited us for a meal," Marthona said. "He has hurried ahead to let them know to expect us. Actually, he invited you, but then he asked me to come, too, and all the rest of you who were in the cave just now. Including you, Jonokol. Everyone else has other things to do, most people are busy at Summer Meetings."

"I know Joharran is having a gather at our camp with people from all the other Caves to plan the hunt," Jondalar said. "In fact, Tormaden will be going, too, after he introduces you to his camp. I was going to go, but it will still be going on after the meal, and I'll go later. It's not that I would usually be included in the planning of these things, but since we returned, Joharran has been getting me involved in them."

"Why don't we all go to our camp?" Ayla said. "There is still a special meal to prepare for tomorrow morning, and I haven't helped at all."

"For one thing, when the leader of the host Cave at a Summer Meeting invites you for a meal, it's a courtesy to go, if you can."

"Why would he invite me?"

"It's not every day one finds a cave like that, Ayla. All of us are excited about it," Marthona said, "and it's close to the Nineteenth Cave, in their territory. They will probably become a more important Cave now."

"You'll be getting more attention, too," Jondalar said.

"I get too much attention as it is," she said. "I don't want all that attention. I just want to get mated, and have a baby, and be like everyone else."

Jondalar smiled at her and put his arm around her. "Give it some time," he said. "You're still new. When people get used to you, things will settle down."

"It's true, things will settle down, but you know you are never going to be like everyone else. For one thing, everyone else doesn't have horses and a wolf," Marthona said, looking down at the big carnivore with an ironic smile.

"Are you sure they know we're coming, Mardena?" the older woman said, stepping carefully across the small creek that emptied into The River.

"She invited us, mother. She said come and share a morning meal with them. Didn't she, Lanidar?"

"Yes, grandma, she did," the boy said.

"Why did they camp so far away?" the grandmother asked.

"I don't know, mother. Why don't you ask them when we get there?" Mardena said.

"Well, they are the biggest Cave and take a lot of room," the woman said. "A lot of people were already here and had set up camps."

"I think it's because of the horses," Lanidar said. "She has them in a special place so no one will think they are just regular horses and decide to hunt them. They would be easy to hunt. They don't run away."

"Everybody is talking about them, but we were out when they came. Is it true the horses let people sit on their backs?" the older woman asked. "Why would anyone want to sit on the back of a horse?"

"I didn't see that, but I don't doubt it," Lanidar said. "The horses let me touch them. I was touching the young stallion, and the mare came and wanted me to touch her, too. They ate off my hands, both of them. She said I should feed both horses at the same time, so they don't get jealous. She said the mare is the mother of the stallion, and she can tell him what to do."

Mardena slowed and knit her brow as they approached the campsite and watched people talking and smiling around the long trenchfire. There seemed to be a lot of people. Maybe she was mistaken, maybe they weren't expected.

"There you are! We've been waiting for you."

The two women and the boy turned at the sound of the voice and saw a tall, attractive young woman.

"You probably don't remember me. I'm Folara, daughter of Marthona."

"Yes, you look like her," the older woman said.

"I suppose I should offer a formal greeting, since I'm the first one to see you." She held out both her hands to the older woman. Mardena watched as her mother stepped forward and took the young woman's hands. "I am Folara of the Ninth Cave of the Zelandonii, Blessed of Doni, Daughter of Marthona, former Leader of the Ninth Cave of the Zelandonii, Daughter of the Hearth of Willamar, Master Trader of the Zelandonii, Sister of Joharran, the Leader of the Ninth Cave of the Zelandonii, Sister of Jondalar of the Ninth Cave of the Zelandonii, Master Flint-Knapper and Returned Traveler, who is soon to be mated to Ayla, of the Ninth Cave of the Zelandonii. She has a bunch of names and ties of her own, but the one I like best is 'Friend of horses and Wolf.' In the name of the Great Earth Mother, Doni, you are welcome to the camp of the Ninth Cave."

"In the name of Doni, the Great Mother, I greet you, Folara of the Ninth Cave of the Zelandonii. I am Denoda, of the Nineteenth Cave of the Zelandonii, Mother of Mardena of the Nineteenth Cave and Grandmother of Lanidar of the Nineteenth Cave, once mated to . . ."

Folara has a lot of important names and ties, Mardena thought as her mother began her recitation. She's not yet mated, I wonder what her kinship sign is? Then, as though her mother knew what she was thinking, as she finished her names and ties, the woman asked, "Wasn't Willamar, the man of your hearth, once of the Nineteenth Cave? I think we share a kinship sign. I am the Bison."

"Yes, Willamar is the Bison. Mother is the Horse, I am, too, of course."

Several people had gathered around in the course of the formal introduction. Ayla stepped forward and greeted Mardena and Lanidar, and then Willamar greeted Denoda in the name of the entire Ninth Cave. Names and ties could take all day if someone didn't cut it short. He finished by saying, "I remember you, Denoda. You were a friend of my older sister, weren't you."

"Yes," she said, smiling. "Do you ever see her? Since she moved so far away, I haven't seen her in years."

"Sometimes I visit her Cave when I go to the coast of the Great Waters of the West to trade for salt. She is a grandma. Her daughter has three children, and a grandam as well. Her son's mate has a boy."

A movement around Ayla's legs caught Mardena's attention. "That's the wolf!" she almost screamed in her fear.

"He won't hurt you, mother," Lanidar said, trying to calm her. He didn't want her to leave suddenly.

Ayla bent down and put her arm around him. "No, he won't hurt you. I promise," she said. She could see the fear in the woman's eyes.

Marthona stepped forward and greeted Denoda, much more informally, then said, "The wolf lives in our lodge with us, and he likes to be greeted, too. Would you like to meet a wolf, Denoda?" She had noticed that the older woman showed more interest than fear. She took her by the hand and led her toward Ayla and Wolf. "Ayla, why don't you introduce him to our guests."

"Wolves have good eyes, but they learn to recognize people with their noses. If you give him a chance to smell your hand, he will remember you later. That is his formal introduction," Ayla explained. The woman held out her hand and allowed the wolf to smell it. "If you'd like to greet him, he likes to be stroked on the head."

Wolf looked up at Denoda as she lightly stroked his head, with his mouth open and his tongue lolling out the side. She smiled at him. "He is a warm, living animal," she said. She turned to her daughter. "Come, Mardena. You should meet him, too. Very few people ever get to meet a wolf, and walk away to tell about it."

"Do I have to?" Mardena said.

It was obvious that Mardena was uncommonly frightened, and Ayla knew Wolf would smell it. She held him firmly. He didn't always respond well to such evident fear.

"Since they offered, it's the polite thing to do, Mardena. And you'll never be able to visit again if you don't. You will be too afraid. You don't need to fear this wolf. You can see that no one else does, not even me. So why should you?" Denoda said.

Mardena looked around and saw the large crowd watching her. She thought it was probably the whole Ninth Cave, and none of them seemed to be afraid. She felt as though she were on trial and was sure she'd be too humiliated to face any of them again if she didn't go close to that wolf. She looked at her son, the boy for whom she'd always felt mixed emotions. She loved him more than anything in her life, and she was embarrassed by him, by the fact that she gave birth to him.

"Go ahead, mother," he said. "I met him."

Finally, Mardena put one foot toward the woman and the wolf, and then another. When she reached them, Ayla took her hand and, holding it in hers, brought it to the wolf's nose. She could almost smell her fear, but the woman did overcome it and face the animal. Ayla thought Wolf probably smelled her own hand more than Mardena's. Then she took the hand and led her to touch the fur on his head.

"Wolf fur can be a little rough, but you'll notice how smooth it is on his head," Ayla said, letting go of her hand. Mardena kept it there a moment longer before pulling it away.

"See, that wasn't so bad, was it?" Denoda said. "Sometimes you make more of things than you need to, Mardena."

"Come and have some hot tea, it's a mixture that Ayla makes, and it's quite good," Marthona said. "We decided to make an occasion of your visit, and cooked everything in a roasting pit. We're almost ready to take it out."

Ayla was walking with Mardena and Lanidar. "That's a lot of work to go to for a morning meal," Mardena said. She wasn't used to being treated so generously.

"Everybody worked on it," Ayla said. "When I told them I had invited you and thought I'd dig a pit oven, they thought it would be a good time to dig a big roasting pit. They said they planned to do it anyway, but this gave them a reason. I cooked some of the things the way I learned when I was a girl. Try the willow grouse, it's the one I killed with the spear-thrower yesterday, but if the taste is not to your liking, please don't hesitate to have something else instead. I learned on our Journey that there are many ways of cooking things, and not everyone likes all of them."

"Welcome to the Ninth Cave, Mardena."

It was the First Among Those Who Served The Mother! Mardena didn't think she had ever spoken to her before, except in unison during a ceremony.

"Greetings, Zelandoni Who Is First," Mardena said, feeling a little nervous to be talking to the huge woman who was sitting on a raised stool. It was similar to the one she used in the zelandonia lodge, but it was left at the Camp for when she wanted to spend time with her Cave.

"And welcome to you, too, Lanidar," the First said. There was a warmth in her tone when the donier spoke to her son that Mardena had never heard from the powerful woman. "Though I understand you were here yesterday."

"Yes," he said. "Ayla showed me the horses."

"She tells me you can whistle very well," Zelandoni said.

"She taught me some birdsongs."

"Would you like to show me?"

"If you want. I've been practicing the meadow lark," he said, then proceeded to imitate the beautiful sound. Everyone turned to look, even his mother and grandmother.

"That's very good, young man," Jondalar said, beaming at the youngster. "It's nearly as good as Ayla's meadow lark."

"We're ready," Proleva called. "Come and eat."

Ayla led the three guests to the pile of bone-and-wood platters first and urged them to try everything. Then everyone else fell into line. Usually, those who shared a lodge had their morning meal together, but this had become the first of what would be many meals that would be shared, not only with their own Cave, but with other friends and relatives. There would even be a few occasions when the entire Summer Meeting would all feast together, but that would involve a great deal of organizing and planning. One of them would be the Matrimonial Feast.

When everyone was through eating, people started leaving for various other activities, but most of them stopped by to say a few words to their guests. Mardena was feeling a little flustered with all the attention, but she also felt a glow of warmth. She couldn't remember ever being treated so well. Proleva came to talk to them and said a few words to Mardena and Denoda, then turned to Ayla.

"We'll finish up here, Ayla. I think you have something you want to talk to Mardena about," she said.

"Yes. Would you and Lanidar, and Denoda if she wants, like to take a walk with me?"

"Where are we going?" Mardena said with a touch of edginess.

"To see some horses," Ayla said.

"Can I come along, Ayla?" Folara said. "If you don't want me to, just go ahead and say so, but I haven't seen the horses for a while."

Ayla smiled. "Of course you can," she said. It might actually make it easier to get Mardena to agree to let Lanidar watch them if someone so friendly and unafraid of them was there. She turned to look for the boy and saw him sitting next to Lanoga, who was holding Lorala, and they seemed to be talking easily. Tremeda's two-year boy was sitting on the ground nearby.

As they headed in their direction, Mardena asked, "Who is that girl? Or is she a woman? She seems very young to have a baby that age."

"Too young, for certain. She hasn't even had First Rites," Ayla said. "That's her sister, and the other one, the two-year, is her brother, but as far as the babies are concerned, Lanoga is their mother."

"I don't understand," Mardena said.

"I'm sure you've heard of Laramar? He's the one who makes the barma?" Folara said.

"Yes," Mardena said.

"Everyone has," Denoda said.

"Then perhaps you've heard of his mate, Tremeda. She does nothing but drink the barma he makes, and have children that she won't take care of," Folara said, full of derision.

"Or can't," Ayla said. "She can't seem to stop herself from drinking the barma, either."

"And Laramar is often drunk and just as irresponsible. He doesn't even care about the children of his hearth," Folara said with disgust. "Ayla found out that Tremeda had lost her milk, and Lanoga was trying to feed Lorala on nothing but mashed-up roots because that's all she knew how to make. Ayla got several of the new mothers to agree to nurse the baby, but Lanoga is still the one who takes care of her, and all the rest of Tremeda's children. Ayla showed her how to make other food that babies can eat, and she's the one who takes Lorala to the other mothers to nurse. She's really an amazing girl, and will be a wonderful mate and mother someday, but who knows if she'll ever find a mate? Laramar and Tremeda have the last-ranked hearth in our Cave. Who would be willing to mate the daughter of that hearth?"

Mardena and Denoda stared at the talkative young woman. Most people liked to gossip, but they were not usually so open about the ones who were an embarrassment to their own Cave. Denoda's rank had slipped since her daughter gave birth to Lanidar, and her mate had severed the knot. They weren't the lowest, but not far from it. Their Cave was much smaller, however. To be the last of such a large Cave was a low rank. But even if we were the first ranked, Lanidar will have trouble finding a mate, because of his affliction, Denoda thought.

"Would you like to go see some horses, Lanidar?" Ayla asked as they approached. "You can come, too, Lanoga."

"No, I can't. It's Stelona's turn to feed Lorala, and she's getting hungry. I didn't want to give her too much food until after she nurses."

"Maybe another time," Ayla said, smiling affectionately. "Are you ready, Lanidar?"

"Yes," he said, then he turned to the girl. "I have to go, Lanoga." She smiled shyly at him, and he smiled back.

As they passed by her lodge, Ayla said, "Lanidar, will you get that bowl over there? It has some horse food in it, pieces of wild carrot and some grains." He ran to get it.

Ayla noticed that he carried the bowl on his right side, supported against his body with his crippled arm, and she had an unexpected memory of Creb holding a bowl of red ochre paste against his body with the arm that had been amputated at the elbow, just before he named her son and accepted him into the clan. It brought a smile of joy and pain. Mardena was watching her and wondered. Denoda had noticed her expression, too, and wasn't as shy about mentioning it.

"You looked at Lanidar with such a strange smile," she said.

"He reminds me of someone I used to know," Ayla said. "A man who was missing the lower part of his arm. He had been attacked by a cave bear when he was a child. His grandmother was a healer, and she had to cut it off because it was poisoning his body. He would have died if she hadn't."

"What a terrible thing!" Denoda said.

"Yes, it was. He was blinded in one eye, too, by that attack, and his leg was hurt. He had to walk with a stick from then on."

"The poor boy. He had to be taken care of the rest of his life, I suppose," Mardena said.

"No," Ayla said. "He made a valuable contribution to his people."

"How did he manage? What did he do?"

"He became a great man, a mog-ur—that's like a Zelandoni— and he was recognized as the First. He and his sister were the ones who took care of me after my own family died. He was the man of my hearth, and I loved him very much," Ayla said.

Mardena was looking at her with jaw agape and her eyes open wide. She could hardly believe the woman, but why would someone lie about something like that?

As Ayla talked, Denoda became particularly conscious of her unusual accent, but the story made her understand why she seemed to have taken a liking to Lanidar. When she mates, she is going to be related to some very powerful people, and if she likes him, she could help him a lot. This woman might be the best thing that ever happened to the boy, she thought.

Lanidar had been listening, too. Maybe I could learn to hunt, he thought, even if I only have one good arm. Maybe I could learn to do something besides picking berries.

They were approaching a construction that was like a surround, except that it didn't seem particularly sturdy. It was made of long, thin, straight alder and willow poles lashed together in horizontal Xs with other poles across the top, attached to shorter, somewhat sturdier poles sunk into the ground. Bushes and tree branches, already drying out, loosely filled in the spaces between. If a herd of bison, for example, or even a large male—six feet six inches at the top of the hump on his shoulders, with long black horns—tried to break out, the enclosure would not have held. Even the horses could likely break it down, if they were determined.

"Do you remember how to whistle to call Racer, Lanidar?" Ayla asked.

"Yes, I think so," he said.

"Why don't you call him and see if he'll come?" she said.

The boy whistled the loud, piercing call. Very soon the two horses, the mare following the young stallion, appeared from behind some trees that lined the small waterway and came trotting toward them. They stopped at the enclosure fence and watched the humans approaching. Whinney snorted and Racer whickered at them. Ayla answered with the distinctive whinny that was the sound she had originally named her horse, and both horses neighed back.

"She does know how to make a sound like a horse," Mardena said.

"I told you she could, mother," Lanidar said.

Wolf raced ahead, easily slipping under the fence. He sat in front of the mare while she dropped her head in what appeared to be a gesture of greeting. Then Wolf approached the young stallion, dropped down on his chest and forepaws, with his hindquarters up in the air in a playful pose, and yipped at Racer. The stallion nickered back, then they touched noses. Ayla smiled at them as she ducked inside the fence. She hugged the mare around the neck, then turned and stroked the stallion, who was crowding in looking for attention, too.

"I hope you like this surround better than having to wear halters and ropes all the time. I wish I could let you run free, but I don't think it's safe when so many people are out hunting. I've brought some visitors today, and it's important for you to be very cooperative and gentle. I want the boy who whistles to check on you for me, and his mother is protective of him and nervous about you," Ayla said in the language she had invented when she lived alone in the valley.

It comprised certain sounds and gestures from the Clan, some of the nonsense sounds she and her son had made to each other when he was a baby and they were alone, and certain onomatopoeic sounds she had begun to make in imitation of the animals around her, including horse snorts and whickers. Only she knew what she meant, but she had always used her invented language when she talked to the horses. She doubted if they fully understood, though certain sounds and gestures had meaning for them, since she used them as signals and directions, but they knew it was her way of addressing them and they responded by paying attention.

"What's she doing?" Mardena said to Folara.

"She's talking to the horses," Folara said. "She often talks to them like that."

"What is she saying to them?" Mardena asked.

"You'll have to ask her," Folara said.

"Do they know what she's saying? It doesn't make any sense to me," Denoda said.

"I don't know, but they seem to listen," Folara said.

Lanidar had crowded up close to the fence and was watching her closely. She really did treat them like friends, more like family, actually, he thought, and they treated her the same way. But he wondered where the enclosure came from. It hadn't been there the day before.

When Ayla was through talking to the horses and turned around to face the people, Lanidar asked her, "Where did the surround come from? It wasn't here yesterday."

Ayla smiled. "A lot of people got together and built it yesterday afternoon," she said.

When Ayla returned from having a meal with the Nineteenth Cave, she mentioned to Joharran after his meeting that she wanted to build an enclosure for the horses, and explained why. Joharran stood up on Zelandoni's stool and talked about Ayla's desire to create a safe place for the horses. Most of the people who were at the meeting were still there, as well as many people from the Ninth Cave. Many questions were asked, including how strong it had to be, and several suggestions were made. Before long, most of them moved up the meadow and pitched in to build the corral. The ones who were not from the Ninth Cave were curious about the horses anyway, and most of those who were didn't want to see the horses accidentally hurt or killed. They were a novelty that brought added distinction to their Cave.

Ayla was so grateful, she didn't know what to say. She thanked them but didn't think that was near enough, and felt a debt to the Zelandonii that she didn't know how to repay. Working together brought people closer together, and she felt that she got to know some people better. Joharran had mentioned wanting to include the horses in the hunt, which was planned for the following morning. Both Ayla and Jondalar rode the horses and demonstrated their control of them, which made Joharran's suggestions much more acceptable. If the hunt was successful, the Matrimonial would normally take place the next day, but since Dalanar and the Lanzadonii had not yet arrived, they were prepared to wait a few days, though some people were getting anxious.

Ayla put halters on the horses and led them out of the enclosure through a gate that Tormaden of the Nineteenth Cave had devised. He dug a hole beside one of the support posts for the base of a pole to which the gate was attached and used a loop of rope to slip over the top. Rope loops also served as hinges. She was beginning to feel a closer tie to the Nineteenth Cave. When she brought the horses up close, Mardena backed away fast. They were so much bigger up close. Folara immediately stepped into her place.

"I haven't seen the horses nearly as much as I wanted to," she said, petting Whinney's face. "Everyone has been so busy what with that bison hunt where Shevonar died, and the burial, and getting ready to come. You said once you'd let me have a ride on a horse."

"Would you like to do it now?" Ayla said.

"Could I?" she said, her eyes glowing with pleasure.

"Let me get a riding blanket for Whinney," Ayla said. "Would you and Lanidar like to give them something to eat while I get it? He has some food they like in that bowl."

"I'm not sure if Lanidar should get so close," Mardena said.

"He's already close, Mardena," Denoda said.

"But she's there. . . ."

"Mother, I already fed them once. They know me, and you can see they know Folara," Lanidar said.

"They won't hurt him," Ayla said, "and I'm only going over there." She pointed to an arrangement of stones near the gate. It was a traveler's cairn that Kareja had made for her. Ayla only had to remove a few rocks to reach the space inside where she could keep a few things, like a leather riding blanket. The rocks were overlapped in such a way that rainwater would flow over the top and not seep inside. The leader of the Eleventh Cave showed her how to put them back to keep the inside dry. Similar cairns were placed along several well-used routes with emergency fire-making materials and often a warm cloak inside. Other cairns had dried food inside. Occasionally both would be in one cairn, but the food cairns were broken into more often, and bears, wolverines, or badgers, the most frequent offenders, usually vandalized and scattered everything.

Ayla left them with the horses. When she reached the cairn, she glanced back, making it very inconspicuous. Folara and Lanidar were letting the large herbivores eat out of their hands, while Mardena stayed back, acting nervous and looking concerned, and Denoda watched. Ayla walked back and casually tied the riding blanket on Whinney's back. Then she led the mare to a stone.

"Get up on the stone, Folara, then put your leg over her back and try to find a comfortable seat. You can hang on to her mane. I'll hold Whinney so she won't move," Ayla said.

Folara felt a little clumsy, especially when she recalled how smoothly Ayla mounted the horse, but she managed to get on, then sat there, grinning. "I'm sitting on a horse's back!" she said, feeling rather proud of herself.

Ayla noticed that Lanidar was watching her with a yearning look. Later, Ayla thought. Let's not press your mother too hard, yet. "Are you ready?" she said.

"Yes, I think so," Folara said.

"Just relax, you can hold her mane for support if you want, but you don't have to," Ayla said, then started off at a walk, leading the horse by the halter, though she knew Whinney would follow her without it.

At first Folara held the mane and sat up stiffly, bouncing with each step the horse made, but after a while she settled down, began to anticipate the gait and relax into it. Then she let go of the mane.

"Do you want to try it alone? I'll give you the lead rope."

"Do you think I can?"

"You can try it, and if you want to get off, just tell me. When you want Whinney to go faster, lean forward," Ayla explained, "hug her neck if you want. When you want her to slow down, start to sit up."

"All right. I think I will try," Folara said.

Mardena looked absolutely petrified when Ayla put the lead rope in Folara's hand. "Go ahead, Whinney," she said, signaling her to go slow.

The horse started walking across the meadow. She had given rides to several people and knew to go easy, especially the first time. When Folara leaned forward a little, Whinney increased her pace, but not by much. She leaned down a little farther, and Whinney shifted into a trot. She was an amazingly smooth-riding horse, but the trot jogged Folara a little more than she expected. She quickly sat back up, and Whinney slowed down. After they had gone out a ways, Ayla whistled to call her back. Folara got braver and leaned forward again, and this time she stayed with the trot until they returned and stopped. Ayla led the mare to the rock and held her until Folara got down.

"That was wonderful!" Folara said, her face flushed with excitement. Lanidar was smiling at her just because she looked so pleased.

"See, mother," the boy said. "You can ride on the back of these horses."

"Ayla, why don't you give Mardena and Denoda a demonstration of what they can really do," Folara said.

Ayla nodded, then quickly and smoothly leaped on the horse, guided her out toward the middle of the meadow at a fast trot, with Racer and Wolf at her heels. She signaled a gallop, and the horse raced at top speed across the field. She made a large circle, then headed back, slowing the horse as they got close, pulled to a stop, threw her leg over the horse, and jumped down. Both women and the boy were wide-eyed.

"Well, now I know why someone would want to ride on the back of a horse," Denoda said. "If I were younger, I'd like to try it."

"How do you have so much control over this animal?" Mardena said. "Is it some kind of magic?"

"No, not at all, Mardena. Anyone could do it, with practice."

"What made you decide to ride on a horse? How did you start?" Denoda asked.

"I killed Whinney's dam, for food, and only later discovered she was nursing a young filly," Ayla began. "When hyenas came after the foal, I couldn't stand to let them take her—I hate those filthy animals—so I chased them away, and then realized I would have to take care of her." She told them about saving the baby horse from hyenas and then raising her, and that because she had, they grew to know each other well. "One day I got up on her back, and when she started running, I held on. It was all I could do. When she finally slowed down and I got off, I could hardly believe what I had done. It was like flying with the wind in my face. I couldn't help doing it again, and though at first I had no control, after a while I learned how to direct her. She goes where I want because she wants to. She's my friend, and I think it pleases her to let me ride."

"Still, it was an unusual thing to do. Didn't anyone object?" Mardena said.

"There was no one to object. I was alone then," Ayla said.

"I would have been afraid to live alone, with no other people," Mardena said. She was full of curiosity and wanted to ask more questions, but before she had the chance, they heard a call and turned to see Jondalar coming.

"They're here!" he said. "Dalanar and the Lanzadonii have arrived!"

"Wonderful!" Folara said. "I can hardly wait to see them."

Ayla smiled with delight. "I am also anxious to see them." She turned back to her visitors. "We have to go back to camp. The man of Jondalar's hearth has arrived, in time for our Matrimonial."

"Of course," Mardena said. "We'll go right away."

"Well, I wouldn't mind greeting Dalanar before we leave, Mardena," Denoda said. "I used to know him."

"You should," Jondalar said. "I'm sure he'd be glad to see you."

"And before you go, I need to ask you if you will allow Lanidar to come and check on the horses for me when I'm busy, Mardena," Ayla said. "He doesn't have to do anything except make sure they are all right, and come and get me if he notices anything wrong. I would appreciate it very much. It would be such a relief if I didn't have to worry about them."

When they turned to look, the boy was petting the young stallion and feeding him pieces of wild carrot.

"I think you can see they won't hurt him," Ayla said.

"Well, I suppose he could," Mardena said.

"Oh, mother, thank you!" Lanidar said, grinning. Mardena had never seen such a pleased and happy expression on his face.

28

Where's that boy of yours, Marthona? The one that everyone says looks just like me . . . well, perhaps a little younger," said the tall man with long blond hair tied in a club in back. He held out both hands and smiled warmly in greeting. They knew each other too well for much formality.

"When he saw you coming, he ran to get Ayla," Marthona said, taking his hands in hers and leaning forward to rub cheeks. He may be getting older, she thought, but he's still handsome and as charming as ever. "They'll be here soon, Dalanar, you can be sure. He's been watching for you since we got here."

"And where's Willamar? I was very sorry to hear about Thonolan. I liked that young man. I want to express my sadness to you both," he said.

"Thank you, Dalanar," Marthona said. "Willamar is at the main camp, talking to some people about a trading mission. The news about Thonolan was especially hard on him. He always believed the son of his hearth would return. In all honesty, I doubted that either one of them would. When I first saw Jondalar, for a moment I thought it was you. I could hardly believe my son had come home. And what surprises he's brought back, not the least of which is Ayla and her animals."

"Yes, they are a shock. You knew they stopped off to visit on their way here?" said the woman at his side.

Marthona turned to the woman. Dalanar's mate was the most unusual person Marthona, or any of the Zelandonii, had ever seen. She was tiny, especially in comparison with her mate—if he held his arm out, she could walk beneath it without bending. Her straight long hair pulled back in a bun was as glossy and black as a raven's wing, though streaks of gray lightened the sides, but the most arresting aspect was her face. It was round with a little snub of a nose, high wide cheekbones, and dark eyes that appeared slanted because of the epicanthic fold of her eyelids. Her skin was fair, perhaps a shade darker than her mate's, though as the summer progressed both their faces would darken from the sun.

"Yes, they told us you planned to come to the Summer Meeting," Marthona said after she had greeted the woman. "I understand Joplaya will be mated, too. You've arrived just in time, Jerika. All the women who are mating, along with their mothers, are supposed to meet with the zelandonia this afternoon. I am going with Ayla, since her own mother isn't here to go. If you are not too tired, you and Joplaya should come."

"I think we can make it, Marthona," Jerika said. "Do we have time to put up our lodges first?"

"I don't see why not. Everyone will help," Joharran said, "if you don't mind setting up here, next to us."

"And you won't have to do any cooking. We had guests for a morning meal, and have plenty left over," Proleva said.

"We'll be glad to camp beside the Ninth Cave," Dalanar said, "but what made you decide to pick this place? You usually like to be in the thick of things, Joharran."

"By the time we arrived, all the best places in the main camp were taken, especially for a Cave as big as ours, and we didn't want to be crowded. We looked around and found this, and I like it better," Joharran said. "See those trees? That's just the beginning of a good-size grove with plenty of firewood. This creek starts up there, too, in a clear spring. Long after everyone else's water is muddy and churned up, we'll still have good water, and there's a nice pool. Jondalar and Ayla like it here, too, there's space for the horses. We made a place for them upstream. That's where Ayla went, with her guests. She's the one who invited them."

"Who are they?" Dalanar asked. He couldn't help but be curious about whom Ayla would invite.

"Do you remember that woman from the Nineteenth Cave who gave birth to the boy with the deformed arm? Mardena? Her mother is Denoda," Marthona said.

"Yes, I do," Dalanar said.

"The boy, Lanidar, can now count almost twelve years," she said. "I'm still not sure how it came about, but I think he came up here to get away from all the people and probably some teasing from the other boys. I guess someone told him there were horses here. Everyone is interested in them, of course, and the boy is no exception. Somehow Ayla met him and decided to ask him to keep an eye on the horses for her. She's concerned that with all the people here, someone, not realizing how special they are, might try to hunt them. It would be easy, they don't run away."

"That's true," Dalanar said. "Too bad we can't make all animals that docile."

"Ayla didn't think that the boy's mother might object, but it seems she's very protective," Marthona said. "She won't even let him learn to hunt, or doesn't think he can. So Ayla invited the boy and his mother and grandmother here to see the horses to try to convince her that they won't hurt him. And only one good arm or not, she's also decided that she's going to teach him to use Jondalar's new spear-thrower," she said.

"She does have a mind of her own," Jerika said. "I noticed that, but she's not unkind."

"No, she's not, and she's not afraid to stand up for herself, or to speak up for others," Proleva said.

"Here they come," Joharran said.

They saw a group of people, and a wolf, coming toward them, Jondalar in the lead, his sister close behind. They had all been walking at the pace of the slowest, but when he saw Dalanar and the others, Jondalar rushed ahead. The man of his hearth came toward him. They grabbed hands, then let go and hugged each other. The older man put his arm around the shoulders of the younger man as they walked back, side by side.

The similarity between the two men was uncanny; they could have been the same man at two different stages of his life. The older one was a tad thicker at the waist, his hair a little thinner on top, but the face was the same, though the brow of the younger was not as deeply etched, and the jowls of the older were getting soft. They matched each other in height, walked with the same step, and moved the same way; even their eyes were the same vivid shade of glacier blue.

"There is no doubt which man's spirit was chosen when the Mother created him," Mardena said quietly to her mother, nodding her head at Jondalar as the visitors neared the camp. Lanidar saw Lanoga and went to talk to her.

"Dalanar looked just like him when he was young, and he hasn't changed much," Denoda said. "He's still a most handsome man."

Mardena was watching with great interest as Ayla and Wolf were greeted by the new arrivals. It was obvious they all knew each other, but she couldn't help but stare at some of the people. The black-haired, tiny woman with the strange face seemed to be with the tall, blond older man who resembled Jondalar, perhaps as his mate.

"How do you know him, mother?" Mardena said.

"He was the man at my First Rites," Denoda said. "Afterward, I begged the Mother to bless me with the spirit of his child."

"Mother! You know that's too soon for a woman to have a baby," Mardena said.

"I didn't care," Denoda said. "I knew that sometimes a young woman got pregnant soon after First Rites, when she was finally a full woman and able to take in a man's spirit. I hoped it would make him pay more attention to me if he thought I was carrying a child of his spirit."

"You know a man is not allowed to get close to a woman he opens for at least a year after First Rites, mother." Mardena was almost shocked at her mother's confession. She had never talked like that to her before.

"I know, and he never tried to, though he didn't avoid me and was always kind when we saw each other, but I wanted more than that. For a long time, I couldn't think of anyone but him," Denoda said. "Then I met the man of your hearth. My greatest sorrow in life was that he died so young. I would have liked more children, but the Mother chose not to give me more, and it was probably for the best. Taking care of you by myself was hard enough. I didn't even have a mother to assist me, although some women from the Cave helped out when you were young."

"Why didn't you find another man to mate?" Mardena asked.

"Why didn't you?" her mother countered.

"You know why. I had Lanidar, who would be interested in me?"

"Don't blame it on Lanidar. That's what you always say, but you never tried, Mardena. You didn't want to get hurt again. It's still not too late," the older woman said.

They didn't notice the man approaching. "When Marthona told me the Ninth Cave had visitors this morning, I thought the name was familiar. How are you, Denoda?" Dalanar said, taking both her hands in his and leaning forward to rub cheeks as though she were a close friend.

Mardena saw a little color rise to her mother's face as she smiled at the tall, handsome man, and noticed that she seemed to hold her body differently. There was a womanly, sensual quality about her. Suddenly she was seeing her mother in a new light. Just because she was a grandmother didn't mean she was really so old. There were probably men who would find her attractive.

"This is my daughter, Mardena of the Nineteenth Cave of the Zelandonii," Denoda said, "and my grandson is around here someplace."

He offered his hands to the younger woman. She took them and looked up at him. "Greetings, Mardena of the Nineteenth Cave of the Zelandonii, Daughter of Denoda of the Nineteenth Cave. It is my pleasure to meet you. I am Dalanar, Leader of the First Cave of the Lanzadonii. In the name of the Great Earth Mother, Doni, please know that you are welcome to visit our camp anytime. And our Cave, too, for that matter."

Mardena was flustered at the warmth of his greeting. Though he was more than old enough to be the man of her hearth, she found herself drawn to him. She even thought she heard a certain emphasis on the word "pleasure" that made her think of the Mother's Gift of Pleasure. She never felt so overwhelmed by a man before.

Dalanar glanced around and saw a tall young woman. "Joplaya," he called, then turned and spoke to Denoda. "I'd like you to meet the daughter of my hearth," he said.

Mardena was astonished by the young woman who approached. She was not as completely foreign looking as the tiny woman, though there was a resemblance, which made her almost more unusual. Her hair was nearly as dark, but with lively highlights. Her cheekbones were high, but her face was neither as round nor as flat as the other woman's. Her nose resembled the man's, but was more delicate, and her black eyebrows were smooth and finely arched. Thick black lashes outlined eyes that were quite different from her mother's, though they were similar in shape, if not in color. Joplaya's eyes were as distinctly colored as the vivid blue eyes of the man beside her, but hers were a brilliant shade of green.

Mardena hadn't gone to the Summer Meeting when Dalanar's Cave came the last time. The man of her hearth had recently left, and she didn't want to face people. She had heard of Joplaya but hadn't met her. Now that she had, she felt a compelling urge to stare and struggled to control it. Joplaya was an exotically beautiful woman.

After Dalanar introduced Joplaya and greetings were exchanged, along with a few pleasantries, they left to talk to someone else. Mardena was still feeling the warmth of Dalanar's presence and began to understand why her mother had been so captivated by him. If he had been the man at her First Rites, she might have been as entranced. But his daughter, while unusually lovely, had an air of melancholy about her, a despondency that belied the joy of an impending mating. Mardena couldn't understand why someone who ought to be happy could seem so sad.

"We need to go, Mardena," Denoda said. "We don't want to overstay our welcome, not if we want to be invited back. The Lanzadonii are close to the Ninth Cave, and it's been many years since Dalanar and his Cave have come to a Summer Meeting. They need to renew their ties. Let's find Lanidar and thank Ayla for inviting us."

The camps of the Ninth Cave of the Zelandonii and the First Cave of the Lanzadonii were, ostensibly, two camps of two Caves of two different people, but actually it was one very large camp of close family and friends.

Walking through the main camp toward the zelandonia lodge, the four women were a compelling sight. People didn't even try not to stare. Marthona was always noticed wherever she went. She was a former leader of a major Cave and still powerful, not to mention an attractive older woman. Although some people had met or seen Jerika before, she was still such an unusual-looking woman, so unlike anyone they had seen before, people couldn't keep their eyes away. The fact that she was mated to Dalanar, and had co-founded with him not only a new Cave, but a new people, made her even more exceptional.

Jerika's daughter, Joplaya, the dark-haired melancholy beauty, who, it was rumored, planned to mate with a man of mixed spirits, was a woman of mystery and speculation. The beautiful blond woman that Jondalar brought back, who traveled with two docile horses and a wolf and was rumored to be an accomplished healer, was probably some kind of foreign zelandoni. She spoke their language clearly, if not perfectly, and she had recently found a new and beautiful cave right under the nose of the Nineteenth Cave. Together, the foursome brought more attention than usual, but Ayla was learning to ignore it and was glad for the company.

Many people had already arrived when they reached the zelandonia lodge. They were observed carefully at the entrance by several Zelandonia who were men, which made Ayla curious. As if Marthona knew what she was thinking, the woman explained.

"Men are not allowed at this meeting, unless they are zelandonia, but every year there are always a few young men, usually from the fa'lodges, who try to get close so they can listen," she said. "Some have even attempted to sneak in dressed up as women. The male zelandonia act as guards to keep them away." She noticed several more men who were zelandonia standing around the large structure, Madroman among them.

"What are fa'lodges?" Ayla asked.

"The far lodges, the men's lodges—people always slur it to fa'lodges. They are summer lodges built around the edges of the Summer Meeting camp by men, usually young men, who are past the need for a donii-woman but not yet mated," Marthona said. "Young men don't like to stay with their Caves, they'd rather be with friends their age—except when it's time for a meal." She smiled. "Their friends don't restrict their behavior the way their mothers and their mother's mates do. Unmated men, especially of that age, are absolutely forbidden to go anywhere near the young women who are getting ready for First Rites, but they always try, so the zelandonia keep a close watch on them when they are in camp.

"In their own lodges, if they construct them far enough away, they can be rowdy and loud, so long as they don't disturb other people. They can have gathers and invite other friends, and young women, of course. They become very good at badgering their mothers and her friends for extra food and they always try to get barma, or wine, or whatever. I think it becomes a competition to see which lodge can entice the prettiest young women to visit them.

"There are also fa'lodges of older men, usually those who have no mates for one reason or another, men who prefer other men, or men who are between mates, or who wished they were and want to get away from their Caves or families. Laramar spends more time at a fa'lodge during Summer Meetings than he does at his own lodge. It's where he trades for his barma, though I don't know what he does with his trades. He certainly doesn't bring anything home to his family. Men who are to be mated spend a day or more at a fa'lodge with the zelandonia before the Matrimonial. Jondalar will be going soon, I think."

When the four women first went in the zelandonia lodge, with only the light from a fire in the central hearth and a few lamps, it felt dark inside. But when her eyes adjusted, Marthona looked around and then led the others toward two women who were sitting on a mat on the floor near the wall on the right side of the open central area. The women smiled when they saw them coming and moved over to make room.

"I think it's about to start," Marthona said as they were sitting down on the mat. "We can do formal introductions later." She spoke to the ones who came with her. "This is Proleva's mother, Velima, and her sister, Levela. They are from Summer Camp, the West Holding of the Twenty-ninth Cave." Then to them, "This is Dalanar's mate, Jerika, and her daughter, Joplaya. The Lanzadonii just arrived this morning. And this is Ayla of the Ninth Cave, formerly Ayla of the Mamutoi, the woman Jondalar plans to mate."

The women smiled at each other, but before they could exchange many words, they noticed a hush settling over the assembly. The One Who Was First Among Those Who Served The Great Earth Mother and several other Zelandonia were standing in front of the group. Conversations stopped as the women became aware of them. When it was totally silent, the donier began.

"I am going to be speaking of very serious matters, and I want you to listen carefully. Women, you are the Blessed of Doni, the ones She created with the ability and privilege of bringing forth new life. To those of you who will soon be mated, there are some important things you must know." She ceased speaking and made a point of looking at everyone there. When she saw the women with Marthona, she stayed for a moment. There were two here she hadn't expected. Marthona and Zelandoni nodded to each other, then the One Who Was First continued.

"At this gather, we will be talking about womanly things, how you should treat the men who will be your mates and what you can expect from them, and about having children. We will also be talking about how not to have children and what to do if one starts that you are not ready for," the large donier said.

"Some of you may already be Blessed with the first stirrings of life. Yours is a special honor, but the honor carries with it a great responsibility as well. Some of what I will be telling you, you have heard before, especially at your Rites of First Pleasures. Listen carefully even if you think you already know what I am going to say.

"First, no girl should mate until she has become a woman, until she has started her bleeding and has had her First Rites. Notice the phase of the moon on the day your blood first starts. For most women, the next time the moon is at the same phase, your blood will flow again, but it may not always stay the same. If several women live in the same dwelling for some time, often their moon times will change until their blood courses together."

Some of the younger women looked around at their friends and relatives, especially those who didn't know of this phenomenon. Ayla had not been told of it, and she tried to recall if she had ever noticed it.

"The first indication that you have been Blessed by the Mother, that She has chosen a spirit to blend with yours to start a new life, will be when your blood does not flow at your phase of the moon. If it doesn't flow the following moon, you may begin to assume that you have been Blessed, but your moon time should be missed for at least three moons, and you should have other indications before you can be reasonably sure that a new life has begun. Does anyone have any questions about this?"

There were no questions. Except for being told that women who lived together tended to bleed at the same time, it was all repetition.

"I know most of you have been sharing the Mother's Gift of Pleasure with your Promised, and you should be enjoying it. If you aren't, talk to your Zelandoni. I know it can be hard to admit such a thing, but there are ways to help, and the zelandonia will always keep your secret, all your secrets. Except for young men just into their full maturity, it is wise to remember that few men can couple with a woman more than once or twice a day, and less as they get older.

"There is something you should be aware of. Sharing Pleasures with your mate is not required, if that is what you choose and your mate does not object, but most men will object. Most men will not stay with a woman who will not share Her Gift with them. Though you are preparing to tie the knot and may not imagine it now, the knot can also be severed, for many reasons. I'm sure you all know someone who severed the knot with a mate."

There was some shuffling, changing of positions, glancing around. Most everyone did know someone who had been mated to a person they were no longer with.

"It has been said that women can make use of the Mother's Gift to hold their mates by keeping them happy and content. There are those who claim it was given to Her children for that reason. That may be one reason, though not the only reason, I'm sure. But it is true that your mate will not be as tempted to look with Pleasure upon other women if you satisfy his desires. He will be happy to save those fleeting moments of interest in someone else for ceremonies that honor the Mother, when it is acceptable, and pleasing to Her when Pleasures are shared.

"But remember, though it can be a welcome diversion, anyone can accept, or reject, any offer to share the Mother's Gift. Sharing Pleasures with someone else is also not required. If you and your mate are happy and joyfully share Her Gift with just each other, the Mother is pleased. It is also not required to wait for a Mother Ceremony. Nothing about Pleasures is required. It is a Gift from the Mother, and all Her children are free to share it with whomever they like whenever they wish. Neither you nor your mate should be concerned by each other's passing diversions. Jealousy is far worse. Jealousy can have terrible repercussions. Jealousy can cause violence, and violence can lead to death. If someone gets killed, it can lead to revenge by the loved ones of the person who died, and more revenge in return until there is nothing left but fighting. Anything that threatens the well-being of the children of the Mother who were chosen to know Her is not acceptable.

"The Zelandonii are a strong people because they work together and help each other. The Great Earth Mother has provided everything that we need to live. Whatever is hunted or gathered is given to us by Doni and in turn should be shared by everyone. Because accepting what She offers can be hard work and even dangerous, those who give most gain the greatest respect. That is why the best providers and those who are willing to work for Her children have the highest status. That is why leaders are so respected. They are willing to help their people. If they were not, people would no longer turn to them and someone else would be acknowledged as the leader." She didn't add that it was also the reason that the zelandonia had such high status.

Zelandoni was a powerful speaker, and Ayla was listening with rapt attention. She wanted to learn as much as she could about the people of the man she was soon to mate, who were now her people, but when she thought about it, the Clan were not so different. They also shared everything, and no one went hungry, not even that woman she was told about who died in the earthquake. She had come from another clan, never had children, and after her mate died, she had to be taken as a second woman, always considered a burden. But although she had the lowest status of anyone in Brun's clan, she never went hungry and always had warm enough clothing.

The Clan knew all those things, they didn't have to express it with words. The people of the Clan were not as full of words as the Others. Mates were shared, too. They understood about relieving a man's needs. No Clan woman ever refused any man who gave her the signal. She didn't know anyone who even thought of refusing ... except her. But she knew now that what Broud wanted was not Pleasures. She even knew it then, though she couldn't express it. He didn't give her the signal because he wanted to share the Gift or to relieve his needs, he did it only because he knew she hated it.

"Remember," the donier was saying, "it is your mate who must help you and provide for you and your children, especially when you are heavy with child, or have just given birth and are nursing. If you care about him, if you have shared Pleasures with him often and kept him reasonably content, most men are more than happy to provide for their mates and her children. Perhaps some of you can't imagine why I should make this point so strongly. Ask your mothers. When you are busy and tired with many children, there may come a time when the Gift is not so easy to share. And there are times when it should not be shared, but I'll talk about that later.

"Doni is always more pleased and smiles with favor on those children who bear some resemblance to your mate. Mates, too, often feel closer to those children. If you want your children to resemble your mate, you must spend time together so it will be his spirit that will be the easiest to be selected. The ways of the spirits are willful. There is no way to tell when one will decide to allow itself to be chosen, or when the Mother will decide it is time to blend them. But if you enjoy each other and are pleased with each other, your mate will want to stay with you, and his spirit will be happy to join with yours. Does everyone understand so far? If you have questions, now is the time to speak of them," the First said, looking around and waiting.

"But, what if I get sick or something, and can't feel any Pleasure in the Gift?" a woman asked. Others turned to look to see who had asked.

"Your mate should be understanding of that, and it is always your choice in any case. There are some who are mated and seldom share the Gift with each other. If you are kind and understanding of your mate, he will usually be the same to you. Men are children of the Mother, too. They get sick, and usually it's their mates who care for them. Most mates will try to care for you when you are sick, too."

The young woman nodded and smiled rather tentatively.

"What I'm saying is that couples should have consideration and show kindness and respect for each other. The Gift of Pleasure can bring happiness to both of you and help to make your mate feel happy and contented, so the union will last. Any other questions?"

The First waited to see if anyone else had any more questions, then continued.

"But mating is more than two people choosing to live together. It involves your kin, your Cave, and the world of the spirits as well. That is why mothers and their mates consider carefully before they allow their children to mate. With whom will you live? Will you or your mate be a worthy addition to the Cave you live with? Your feelings for each other are also important. If you start without caring, the union may not last. If the union does not last, the responsibility for any children usually falls to the mother's kin and Cave, as it does if both of you should die."

Ayla was fascinated by the discussion. She almost asked a question about the blending of spirits starting life. She was more than ever convinced that it was the Gift of Pleasures itself that was necessary for life to begin, but she decided not to mention it here.

"Now," Zelandoni continued, "while most of you will be eagerly looking forward to your first baby, there may come a time when a life has started that should not have started. Until you have received the elandon for your infant from your Zelandoni, it has no spirit of its own, only the combined spirits that started it. At that time, the Great Earth Mother will accept the infant, separate the spirits, and give them back. But it is better to stop the continuation of life before it is ready to be born, best within the first three moons of pregnancy."

"Why would anyone want to stop a new life that has started?" a young woman asked. "Shouldn't all babies be welcomed?"

"Most babies are welcomed," the Zelandoni said, "but there may be reasons why a woman should not have another. Though it doesn't happen often, she may get pregnant again while she is still nursing, and give birth to another baby when she has one that is still very young. Most mothers cannot adequately care for another baby so soon. The one who is already here and named, particularly if it is healthy, must come first. Too many young ones die as it is, especially in their first year. It is unwise to risk the life of a child who is healthy and growing by forcing her from the breast too soon. After surviving the first year, weaning is the next most difficult time for a child. If a baby must be weaned too soon, less than three years, it can weaken the child, and the person they grow into. It is better to have one healthy child that will grow into a strong adult than two or three weak ones, who may not live long."

"Oh . . . I didn't think of that," the young woman said.

"Or, as another example, perhaps a woman has given birth to several seriously malformed children, who have died. Should she continue carrying full term and have to go through such sorrow each time? Not to mention weakening herself?"

"But what if she really wants a baby like everyone else?" said a young woman with tears in her eyes.

"All women do not have children," Zelandoni said. "Some choose not to. With others, life never starts. Some can't seem to carry full term, or have stillborn children or children that are so malformed, they don't live, or they shouldn't."

"But why?" the tearful woman asked.

"No one knows why. Perhaps someone who has something against her has cursed her. Perhaps an evil spirit found a way to harm the unborn baby. It even happens to animals. We've all seen malformed horses or deer. Some say that white animals are the result of an evil spirit that was thwarted, that's why they are lucky. People, too, are sometimes born white with pink eyes. Animals no doubt have stillborns and young that don't live as well, though I suspect carnivores take care of them so quickly, we don't see them. That's just the way it is," Zelandoni said.

The young woman was in tears, and Ayla wondered why the donier seemed so unemotional in her response.

"Her sister has had difficulties having a baby, and she's been pregnant two or three times," Velima said under her breath. "I think she's afraid the same thing will happen to her."

"It's wise of Zelandoni not to build up false hopes. Sometimes it runs in families," Marthona murmured in return. "And if she has a child, she'll be all the happier for it."

Ayla watched the young woman and was so moved, she couldn't resist speaking out. "On our way here . . . ," she began. Everyone turned to look in surprise at the newcomer who spoke out, and many noticed her speech difference. "Jondalar and I stopped at a Losadunai Cave. There was a woman there who had never been able to have children. A woman from a nearby Cave had died, leaving her mate with three young children. The woman who couldn't have any went to live with them to see if they could work out a compatible arrangement. If they could, she was going to adopt the children, and take the man for a mate."

There was silence for a time, then an undercurrent of conversation. "That's a very good example, Ayla," Zelandoni said. "It's true.

Women can adopt children. Did this childless woman have a mate of her own?"

"No, I don't think so," Ayla replied.

"Even if she had, she could have brought him with her, if the men were willing to accept each other as co-mates. An extra man to help provide for those children could be helpful. Ayla has made a good point. Women who are not able to give birth to their own children don't always have to remain childless," Zelandoni said, then she went on.

"There are other reasons a woman may choose to end a pregnancy. A mother may have too many children, making it difficult for her to care for them all, and for her, her mate, and her Cave to provide for them. Often women who are in that situation don't really want more, and wish the Mother wouldn't be quite so generous with them."

"I know a woman who kept having children," another young woman said. After Ayla spoke out, others weren't so hesitant about it. "She gave two to her sister, and one to a cousin to adopt."

"I know the one you mean. She seems to be a particularly strong and healthy woman who likes being pregnant and has little trouble giving birth. She is very fortunate. And she has done a great service for her sister, who was unable to have children, I believe because of an accident, and for her cousin who wanted another without carrying it herself," the large woman said, then turned the talk back to the subject.

"But not all women are as capable, or that lucky. Some women have such a difficult childbirth with one or more, another child may kill them and leave their living children without a mother. Everyone is different. Fortunately, most women are able to have children, but even they may not want, or should not bring every pregnancy to term.

"There are several things that can be done to stop a pregnancy. Some can be dangerous. A strong tea made from an entire tansy plant, root and all, can bring on bleeding, but it can be fatal. A shaved slippery elm stick inserted deeply into the opening from which the child is born can be very effective, but it is always best to talk to your donier, who will know how strong a tea to make or how to insert the stick. There are other measures. Your mothers or your Zelandonia will discuss them with you in greater detail if and when you want to know more.

"The same is true of childbirth. There are many medicines that can speed delivery, stop hemorrhaging, and ease the pain. There is almost always some pain with childbirth," the First said. "The Great Mother

Herself struggled in pain, but most women have little trouble and the pain is soon forgotten. Everyone must bear some pain in her life. It is a part of living, there is no escape from it. It is best to accept it."

Ayla was interested in the medicines Zelandoni talked about, although the ones she mentioned were relatively simple and well-known. Almost every woman she talked with about it had learned some way to end a pregnancy, though some seemed more dangerous to her than others. Men often didn't like the idea, and Iza and the other medicine women of the Clan had kept it secret from the men, or they would have forbidden it.

The donier had not talked about preventing life from getting started, and Ayla very much wanted to talk to her about that and perhaps compare notes. Ayla had been midwife at several births. It suddenly occurred to her that she would soon be giving birth herself again. Yes, Zelandoni was right. Pain was a part of living. She had endured great pain in giving birth to Durc, she had almost died, but like the Mother's great shining son, he had been worth it.

"There is more than physical pain in life," Zelandoni was saying. Ayla turned her attention back to the woman. "Some pain is worse than physical, but you must accept that, too. As a woman, you have a great responsibility, and a duty that may at times be difficult, but one that you may have to consider someday. There are times when the life you carry is very tenacious. When nothing is able to prevent the pregnancy from progressing, even though you may have decided the life should not have begun. It is always more difficult after the child is born to return it to the Mother, but there are times when it must be done.

"Remember, the ones who are already here must come first. If a second one is born too soon, or is greatly malformed, or other valid reasons, the infant should be returned to Doni. It is the mother's choice, always, but you must remember your responsibility, and it must be done quickly. As soon as you are able, you must take it outside and lay it on the breast of the Great Earth Mother, as far away as possible from your home, and never near a sacred burial ground or a wandering spirit may try to inhabit the body. Then the spirit will become confused and not be able to find its way to the next world. Such spirits can become evil. Is there anyone here who does not understand exactly what I just said?" This was always a very difficult moment in the pre-mating meeting, and Zelandoni allowed some time for the young women to comprehend the harsh revelation, but they had to understand it and accept it.

No one spoke. The young women had heard rumors and talked among themselves about the distressing duty they might be called upon to perform someday, but this was the first time it had been brought up to them directly. Each young woman there hoped fervently that they would never have to expose a baby to the cold breast of the Great Earth Mother to die. It was a somber thought.

A few of the older women sat tight-lipped with pain in their eyes because theirs had been that awful duty to preserve the life of one by giving up another. Though it was still not an easy decision, most women would far rather end a pregnancy early than lose a child to whom she had given birth, or worse, to have to do it herself.

Zelandoni's comments devastated Ayla. She would never be able to, she thought. Memories of Durc flooded back. He was supposed to have been exposed, and she had no say in it. She recalled with anguish the days spent hiding in the little cave to save his life. They had said he was deformed. But he wasn't. He was just a mixture, of her and Broud, although Broud was the first to condemn him. If Broud had known every time he forced me that Durc would be the result, Ayla thought, he would never have done it! Ayla was tempted to ask why life was not prevented from starting in the first place, but she didn't trust herself to speak.

Marthona was puzzled by the obvious distress Ayla was feeling. True, it was not an easy thought to bear, but Ayla's coming baby had little likelihood of having to be given back to the Mother. Maybe it's just that she's pregnant, she thought. She must be very sensitive.

There was not much more information to impart. Prohibitions on sharing the Gift of Pleasure when a woman was close to delivery, for a certain period of time afterward, and before, during, or after certain ceremonies. Other duties of a mated woman, the times when it was necessary to fast, other times when certain foods were not to be eaten.

There were also bans against mating with certain people, such as close cousins. Jondalar had explained about close cousins, and when it was mentioned, she had glanced at Joplaya in the unobtrusive, all but unseen way of Clan women. She knew the reason for the aura of sadness that shrouded the beautiful young woman. But she'd heard several people mention kinship signs since they arrived at the Summer Meeting, and she didn't know what they were talking about. What did it mean to have an incompatible kinship sign? The other women knew all about bans and prohibitions, and she didn't want to say anything in front of them. She decided to wait until most people left before she asked her question.

"There is one other thing," the First said, concluding. "Some of you may have already heard that a request was received to delay the Matrimonial a few days." There was a moan of regret from a few of the women. "Dalanar and his Cave of Lanzadonii planned to come to the Zelandonii Summer Meeting so the daughter of his mate could be mated at our First Matrimonial." There was whispering and murmuring from the assembly. "You may be pleased to know that no delay will be necessary. Joplaya is here with her mother, Jerika. Joplaya and Echozar will be mated with the rest of you.

"Remember everything that was spoken of here. It is important. The beginning hunt of this Summer Meeting will start tomorrow morning, and if all goes well, the Matrimonial will follow soon after. I will see you all then," said the One Who Was First.

As the meeting was breaking up, Ayla heard the word "flathead" a few times and "abomination" at least once. It did not please her, but it was obvious that many were eager to leave and tell someone else about the fact that Joplaya was promised to the half-flathead man Echozar.

Many of the women remembered him. He had come to their Summer Meeting once before, the last time that the Lanzadonii came. Marthona remembered that there had been some unpleasantness concerning Echozar and his mixed spirits at that meeting and she hoped it would not come up again. It reminded her of the other Summer Meeting that was unpleasant for her, the one that Jondalar had missed when he went on his Journey with his brother and left Marona waiting for a Matrimonial partner that did not arrive. She did mate that summer, at the Second Matrimonial, just before they went home, but it didn't last. Now, Marona was again available, but Jondalar had brought a woman home with him, a woman that was far better suited to her son for all her foreign ways, if only because she genuinely cared for him and he loved her.

Zelandoni had a passing thought of forbidding the women from talking about anything that was said at the meeting, but she knew there was no way to enforce such an edict. It was just too juicy a piece of news to expect people to keep it to themselves. The First noticed that Ayla and those with her did not seem to be in a hurry and were perhaps waiting to talk to her. She was still Zelandoni of the Ninth Cave. When nearly everyone except the zelandonia was gone, Ayla approached her.

"I have something I'd like to ask you, Zelandoni," she said.

"All right," the woman said.

"You were talking about certain bans and prohibitions, people that you could or could not mate. I know that someone can't mate a 'close cousin.' Jondalar told me that Joplaya is his close cousin—sometimes he says hearth cousin—because they were both born to the hearth of the same man," Ayla said. She avoided looking at Joplaya, but Marthona and Jerika glanced at each other.

"That's correct," Zelandoni of the Ninth said.

"Just since we arrived at the Summer Meeting, I've been hearing people talk about something else. You did, too. You said a person shouldn't mate someone with an incompatible kinship sign. What is a kinship sign?" Ayla asked.

The other zelandonia had listened for a while, but when it appeared that Ayla was just asking for information, they began talking quietly amongst themselves or going to their personal space within the lodge.

"That is a little more difficult to explain," Zelandoni said. "A person is born with a kinship sign. In a way, it's part of one's elan, one's life-force. People know their kinship signs almost from the time they are born, just as they know their elandon. Remember, all animals are children of the Mother. She birthed them, too, as it says in the Mother's Song:

> 'With a thunderous roar Her stones split asunder,
> And from the great cave that opened deep under,
> She birthed once again from Her cavernous room,
> And brought forth the Children of Earth from Her womb.
> 'From the Mother forlorn, more children were born.
>
> 'Each child was different, some were large and some small,
> Some could walk and some fly, some could swim and some crawl.
> But each form was perfect, each spirit complete,
> Each one was a model whose shape could repeat.
> 'The Mother was willing. The green earth was filling.'

"The kinship sign is symbolized by an animal, by the spirit of an animal," Zelandoni said.

"You mean like a totem?" Ayla interjected. "My totem is the Cave Lion. Everyone in the Clan has a totem."

"Perhaps," the First said, considering thoughtfully for a moment.

"But I think totems are something else. Not everybody has one, for one thing. They are important, but they are not quite as important as an elan, for example, though it is true that one must go through some trial or struggle to gain a totem. Usually you are chosen by a totem, but everyone has a kinship sign, and many people have the same sign. A totem can be any animal spirit, a cave lion, a golden eagle, a grasshopper, but certain animals have a kind of power. Their spirits have a force of a certain kind, like a life-force, but it's different. The zelandonia call them power animals, but they have more force in the next world than in this one. Sometimes we can draw upon that force for protection when we travel in the spirit world, or to cause certain things to happen," the One Who Was First said.

Ayla was frowning with concentration, trying to remember something. "The Mamut did that!" she said. "I remember at a ceremony, he made strange things happen. I think he took a piece of the spirit world and brought it into this one, but he had to fight to control it."

Zelandoni's expression showed her surprise and admiration. "I think I would have liked to know your Mamut," she said, then she continued. "Most people don't think too much about their kinship signs, except when they are thinking about mating. One should not mate with someone whose kinship sign is in opposition to theirs, which is probably why it's brought up more at Summer Meetings, where matings are planned and mating ceremonies, Matrimonials, take place. That's why the common name for one's power animal is a kinship sign. The name is misleading, but it's how most people think of it, because they don't deal with the spirit world, and the only time it has a bearing on their lives is when planning to mate."

"No one has asked me about kinship signs," Ayla said.

"It only has meaning for one who was born a Zelandonii. Those who are born elsewhere may have kinship signs or power animals, but they don't affiliate with Zelandonii power animals, as a rule. Once a person becomes a Zelandonii, a kinship sign may assert itself, but it will never be one that is in opposition to the mate she already has. The power animal of her mate won't let it."

Marthona, Jerika, and Joplaya were listening just as intently. Jerika had not been born Zelandonii, and she was curious about the customs and beliefs of her mate. "We are Lanzadonii, not Zelandonii. Does that mean if a Lanzadonii wants to mate with a Zelandonii, the kinship signs don't matter?"

"In time, they may not, but many of you, including Dalanar, were born Zelandonii. The ties are still close, so they do have to be considered," the First said.

"I was never a Zelandonii, but I am now Lanzadonii. So is Joplaya. Since Echozar was not born to either one, it doesn't matter, but doesn't a daughter get her kinship sign from her mother? What is Joplaya's kinship sign?" Jerika asked.

"Usually a daughter has the same kinship sign as her mother, but not always. I understand that you have requested a Zelandoni to move to your Cave and become your first Lanzadoni. I think it will be a wonderful opportunity for someone. Whoever it is will be well trained—I plan to make sure of that—and will be able to discover the kinship signs for all your people," the donier said.

"What is Jondalar's kinship sign, and how can I get one to give to my daughter, if I have one?" Ayla asked.

"If you want to find out, we can look into it. Jondalar's power animal is a horse, like Marthona, but though he has the same mother, Joharran's is different. His is a bison. Bison and horses are in opposition," Zelandoni said.

"But Jondalar and Joharran don't oppose each other. They get along well," Ayla said with a frown.

The big woman smiled. "For mating, Ayla. They are opposing kinship signs."

"Oh. I guess they're not likely to mate," she said, and smiled, too. "You said they are power animals. Since my totem is the Cave Lion, do you think that would be my power animal? He is powerful, and his spirit has protected me before."

"Things are different in the spirit world," the First said. "Power means different things. Meat-eaters are powerful, but they tend to keep to themselves, either alone or in small packs, and other animals stay away from them. When you enter the spirit world, it is usually because you need to learn something, to find something out. The animal that can reach farther, that has access to, maybe I should say that can communicate with, many other animals, has more power, or more useful power. It depends what you go there for. Sometimes you do want to seek out meat-eating animals because of their special qualities."

"Why are a bison and a horse opposing kinship signs?" Ayla asked.

"Probably because in this world they tend to cover the same ground at different times, so there is some overlap, some competition for food. Aurochs, on the other hand, eat the tender new greens, or just the green tops of the grasses, leaving behind the stalks and roughage, which horses seem to prefer, so they are compatible. The two most opposing power animals are bison and aurochs, but when you think about it, it is logical. Most plant-eaters tolerate each other, but bison and aurochs can't stand to be in the same meadow. They avoid each other and have been known to fight, especially when females come into the season of their Pleasures. They are too similar. Aurochs bulls are affected when they smell a bison female in heat, and bison bulls will occasionally go after a female aurochs. Someone with an aurochs kinship sign should never mate someone with a bison sign," Zelandoni said.

"What is your power animal, Zelandoni?" Ayla asked.

"You should almost be able to guess," the woman said, smiling. "I am a mammoth when I go into the spirit world. When you go, Ayla, you will not look the same as you do here. You will go as your power animal. That's when you will find out what it is."

Ayla wasn't sure she liked hearing Zelandoni talking about her going into the spirit world, but Marthona wondered why Zelandoni was being so forthcoming. She didn't usually go into such detailed and in-depth answers. Jondalar's mother had the distinct sense that Zelandoni was trying to tempt Ayla, to entice her with fascinating bits of knowledge that were available only to those in the zelandonia.

Then she understood. Ayla was already considered by most people to be some kind of zelandoni, and the First wanted her on the inside where she could exercise some control, not out of her reach where she could create problems. But Ayla had already declared that she wanted only to get mated and have children and be like everyone else. She didn't want to join the zelandonia, and knowing her son, Marthona realized that he wouldn't particularly want her to be zelandoni, either. But he did have a tendency to be attracted to women who were. It was going to be an interesting game to watch.

They were getting ready to go, but as they were leaving, Ayla turned back. "I have another question," she said. "When you were talking about babies, and causing miscarriages to end an unwanted pregnancy, why did you not say something about preventing the life from starting in the first place?"

"There is no way. Only Doni has the power to begin life, and only She can prevent it from starting," Zelandoni of the Fourteenth said. She had been standing nearby, listening to the conversation.

"But there is!" Ayla said.

29

The First gave the young woman a sharp look. Perhaps she should have spoken with Ayla earlier, in more depth. Was it possible she knew of a way to thwart the will of Doni? This was the wrong way to bring it up, but it was too late now. The zelandonia who were standing nearby were talking loudly and gesticulating among themselves, some were just as agitated as the Fourteenth. A few were saying it was wrong. The rest were coming back to the central area to find out what was going on. Ayla didn't know her statement would cause such a stir.

The three women with her were standing back and watching. Marthona looked on with sardonic amusement, though her expression remained neutral. Joplaya was astounded that the esteemed zelandonia could quarrel so ardently, but was just as shocked as they were. Jerika listened with great interest, but she had already decided to speak with Ayla in private. Her announcement to the zelandonia could be the solution to a serious problem that had been worrying the woman for some time.

When she first met him, Jerika had fallen completely and irrevocably in love with the handsome giant of a man who was so charmed by the exquisitely dainty yet fiercely independent young woman. He was a gentle man and consummate lover in spite of his size, and she reveled in their Pleasures. When he asked her to be his mate, she accepted without hesitation, and when she discovered that she was pregnant, she was delighted. But the baby she carried was too big for her tiny frame, and the delivery nearly killed her and her daughter. It damaged her internally, and she never became pregnant again, much to her regret, and relief.

Now her daughter had chosen a man who was, though not as tall, if anything more robust, with powerful muscles and huge bones. Though Joplaya was tall, she was thin and rather delicate with, Jerika had carefully noticed, narrow hips. From the time she realized who her daughter would probably end up choosing, and therefore be the one whose spirit would most likely be chosen by the Mother to start any children she might have, she worried that Joplaya would suffer her fate, or worse. She suspected that Joplaya was already pregnant, since she had started having violent bouts of morning sickness on the trip, but she refused her mother's suggestion to end the pregnancy.

Jerika knew there was nothing she could do about it. It was the Great Mother's decision. Joplaya would be Blessed or not, when She wished, and live or die at Her discretion, but Jerika suspected that with the man Joplaya had chosen, the chances were that her daughter would die young and painfully in childbirth, if not with the first, then later, with another one. Her only hope was that her daughter would live through this first one and, like herself, as painful as it was, be damaged so badly that she would never be able to get pregnant again . . . until she heard Ayla say that she knew how to prevent life from starting. She immediately decided that if her daughter had as much trouble as she did and managed to live through the birth of her first, to save her life, she would make sure Joplaya would not get pregnant again.

"Quiet, please," the One Who Was First said. The noise finally settled down. "Ayla, I want to make sure I understand you. Are you saying you know how to stop a pregnancy before it starts? That you know how to prevent life from beginning?" she asked.

"Yes. I thought you would know, too. I was using certain plants on my Journey from the east with Jondalar. I did not want to have a baby while we were traveling, I had no one to help me," she said.

"You told me that you were already Blessed by Doni. You said it has been three moons since your last bleeding. You were still traveling then," the donier said.

"I'm almost certain this baby was started after we crossed the glacier," Ayla said. "We brought only enough of the Losadunai burning stones to melt ice for water to drink for the horses and Wolf and the two of us. I did not even try to boil water for tea and did not prepare my usual morning drink. It was a very difficult crossing, and we almost didn't make it. When we reached this side and got down off the ice, we stayed and rested for a while, and I didn't bother to make the preparation. By that time, it didn't matter if life started. We were almost here. I was happy when I realized I was pregnant."

"Where did you learn about this medicine?" Zelandoni asked.

"From Iza, the medicine woman who raised me."

"How did she say it worked?" Zelandoni of the Fourteenth asked.

The First looked at her, trying to contain her annoyance. She was asking questions in a logical sequence. She didn't need help or interference, but Ayla answered anyway.

"The Clan believes that the spirit of a man's totem fights the spirit of a woman's totem, and that is why she bleeds. When the man's totem is stronger than a woman's, it defeats hers and begins the new life. Iza told me that certain plants could make a woman's totem strong and help her totem spirit fight off the man's," she explained.

"Primitive, but I'm surprised they have ideas about it at all," the Fourteenth said, and got a hard stare from the First.

Ayla heard the disdain in her tone and was glad now that she hadn't said anything earlier about a man starting a baby inside a woman. She didn't think it was a blending of spirits by Doni any more than it was a defeated totem, but she thought the Fourteenth or someone else would probably find her thoughts more worthy of criticism than consideration.

"You said you used the plants on your Journey. What made you think the medicine would work?" the First asked, taking control of the questions again.

"Men of the Clan put great value on the children of their mates, particularly if they are boys. When their mate has a child, it adds to their prestige. They believe it shows the vigor of their totem, which is in a sense their inner strength. Iza told me she used the plants herself for many years to keep from getting pregnant because she wanted to bring disgrace upon her mate. He was a cruel man who beat her to show his authority over a medicine woman of her rank, so she decided to show that his totem spirit wasn't strong enough to defeat hers," Ayla said.

"Why would she put up with such behavior?" the Fourteenth interjected again. "Why didn't she just sever the knot and find another mate?"

"Women of the Clan have no choice in whom they mate. It is decided by the leader and the other men," Ayla explained.

"No choice!" the Fourteenth sputtered.

"Under the circumstances, I'd say it showed a great deal of subtle intelligence on the part of the woman, what was her name, Iza?" the First said quickly, before the Fourteenth could butt in and ask another question. "Do all the women of the Clan know about these plants?"

"No, only medicine women, and I think this preparation was known only to women of Iza's line, but she gave the preparation to some of the other women if she thought they needed it. I don't know if she told them what it was, though. If any of the men had found out, they would have been very angry, but no one would ask Iza. A medicine woman's knowledge is not for men to know. It is passed down to her daughters, who would become medicine women themselves, if they showed the inclination. Iza thought of me as her daughter," Ayla said.

"I am very surprised at the sophistication of their medicine," Zelandoni said, knowing she was speaking for many of the others.

"Mamut of the Lion Camp understood how effective their medicine was. He went on a Journey when he was young, and broke his arm, quite badly. He stumbled into the cave of a clan, and the medicine woman there set his arm and nursed him back to health. We both believed it was the same clan as the one I lived with. The woman who healed him was Iza's grandmother."

There was total silence in the tent when Ayla finished. What she said was very difficult to believe. The zelandonia of the nearby Caves had heard Joharran and Jondalar talk to people about the flatheads, whom Ayla said called themselves the Clan, and were people, not animals. There had been much discussion about it the next few days, but most dismissed the idea. Flatheads might be a little more clever than most people thought, perhaps, but hardly human. Now this woman was saying that they had healed a man of the Mamutoi and had thought about how life began. She even implied that their medicinal practices might be more advanced than those of the Zelandonii.

The zelandonia started discussing these issues again, and the commotion inside the tent could be heard outside. The male zelandonia who had been guarding the women's meeting were dying of curiosity to find out what was causing the uproar, but were waiting to be invited back in. They knew there were still a few women inside, but it was most unusual for a women's meeting to become so heated.

The First had heard Ayla speak in depth of the Clan before and was quicker to grasp the implications and to extend them. She was now persuaded that they were people, and believed it was important for the Zelandonii to understand the possible consequences, but even she had not realized how advanced they were. Zelandoni had presumed a simpler, more primitive way of life and believed that their medicine was at a similar level. She felt that Ayla had gained some good basic instruction that she could develop. This called for a reevaluation.

Their own Histories harked back to a time when the Zelandonii lived a simpler life, but their comprehension of vegetable foods and medicines had been more advanced than other kinds of knowledge. She suspected that awareness of plants was older, went back further. If the Clan was as ancient as Ayla seemed to think, it was not beyond the realm of possibility that their knowledge could be quite developed. Especially if it was true, as Ayla had indicated, that they had some kind of special memory they could draw on. Zelandoni wished that she had spoken with Ayla before it was brought up to the zelandonia, but perhaps it was best this way. It might take just such a shock to make the zelandonia realize the full impact that the people Ayla knew as the Clan could have on them.

"Let's be quiet, please," Zelandoni said, trying to settle them down again. When order was finally restored, she made an announcement. "It appears that Ayla has brought us some information that may be very useful. The Mamutoi were very perceptive when they adopted her to the hearth of the Mammoth, which was, in effect, the same as being adopted by the zelandonia. We will speak with her in some depth later and explore the extent of her knowledge. If she does in truth know of ways to prevent the start of life, this could be a great benefit, and we should be grateful to have it."

"I should tell you that it doesn't always work," Ayla interjected. "Iza's mate died when an earthquake collapsed their cave, but she was pregnant when she found me. Her daughter, Uba, was born not long after. But Iza could count twenty years by then, very old for a woman of the Clan to have a first child. Their girls become women at eight or nine years. But the medicine worked for her for many years, and it worked for me for most of my Journey."

"Very little of the knowledge of medicine or healing is absolutely certain," Zelandoni said. "In the end, it is still the Great Mother who decides."

Jondalar was glad to see the women returning. He had been waiting for Ayla. He had stayed at their camp with Wolf when Dalanar went to the main camp with Joharran and had promised that he would meet them as soon as Ayla returned. Marthona had told Folara to have some hot tea and a little food ready for them, and invited Jerika and Joplaya to their lodge. Marthona and Jerika talked about mutual friends and relations, and Folara started telling Joplaya about some activities the younger people were planning.

Ayla joined them for a while, but after the rather contentious ending to the meeting in the zelandonia lodge, she felt a need to go off by herself. Saying that she wanted to check on the horses, she picked up her haversack and left with Wolf. She walked upstream along the creek, visited with the horses for a while, then continued on until she came to the pool. She was tempted to go for a swim, but decided to keep on walking instead. She proceeded along a newly developing path, and when she found herself near the new cave, she realized that she had gone the way that Jondalar and the others had come before.

As she approached the small hill that held the cave, she could see the mouth clearly and noticed that the obstructing brush had been cleared away. Dirt and stones around the opening had also been removed, which enlarged the entrance. It was likely that nearly every one of the people at the Summer Meeting of Zelandonii had been inside the new cave at least once by now, but there was little evidence to show for the visits. Because it was so beautiful, and so unusual with its nearly white stone walls, it was considered a very sacred place and rather inviolable. The zelandonia and Cave leaders were still getting accustomed to it, working out the appropriate times and ways to use it. Traditions hadn't been developed yet, it was too new.

The spot where she had made a small fire to light torches and left charcoal remains had become a fireplace with stones encircling it and a few partially burned torches nearby. She removed her fire-making kit from her pack, quickly kindled a fire and lit one of the torches, then walked to the entrance of the cave.

Holding the torch high, she stepped inside the dark space. The sunlight coming in through the entrance lit the soft dirt floor of the sloping entry corridor, which had acquired an accumulation of footprints of all sizes, both bare and in footwear. She saw an imprint of a long, narrow bare foot, probably of a tall man, another of average size and slightly wider, the foot of either a grown woman or a growing boy. There was the sole of a sandal woven of grass or reeds, near it the blurred outline of a leather moccasin, then a line of the widely spaced, rather unsteady, tiny footprints of a toddler just learning to walk. On top of them was the pawprint of a wolf. Ayla wondered what a tracker, unaware of the animal that walked ahead of her into the cave, would make of that.

She felt the air become cool and damp and the space darken as she proceeded underground. The cave did not require feats of agility to get into, at least to the large main room. This was a cave that whole families would use, but not as a living space. Underground caves were too dark and damp to live in, especially when the region was full of shelters open to daylight with level floors and overhanging stone ledges above to protect them from rain and snow. And this cave was so beautiful, it felt like a special sanctuary, an extraordinary entrance to the womb of the Mother.

She and Wolf walked along the left side of the large room with the white walls, then she went into the narrow gallery at the back with the walls that widened out as they rose and came together in the curved white ceiling. She stepped down into the widened area around the round column, which came down from the roof but didn't reach the floor. She was beginning to feel cold and reached into her pack to take out the soft leather hide of a giant deer and put it around her shoulders. It was from the deer that she had brought down with her spear-thrower before the bison hunt that killed Shevonar. So much had happened since then, it felt as though it was long ago. But it wasn't, she thought.

She walked to the end of the narrow corridor after it turned around the hanging pier, then came back and sat down. She liked the roominess of the space. Wolf came and rubbed his head against her free hand. "I think you want some attention," she said, shifting her torch to her left hand and scratching behind his ears. When he left to explore again, her mind wandered back to the meeting earlier with the other women who were going to be mated and the zelandonia, and the discussions after most of the other women left.

She thought about kinship signs and remembered that Marthona's was the horse and wondered what hers was. She found it interesting that in the spirit world horses and aurochs and bison were power animals that were more important than wolves or cave lions, or probably cave bears. It was a place where things were reversed, backward, maybe inside out, or upside down. As she sat there a feeling started to come over her, a feeling that she'd had before. She didn't like it and tried to fight it, but she had no control over it. She seemed to be remembering something, remembering her dreams, but it was more than memory and more than dreamlike, it was as though she were reliving her dreams and memories, with a vague sense of remembering things that hadn't happened.

She felt an anxious worry, she had done something wrong, and drained the liquid left in the bowl. She followed flickering lights through a long endless cave, then bathed in firelight she saw the mog-urs. She felt sickened and petrified with fear, she was falling into a black abyss. Suddenly Creb was helping her, supporting her, easing her fears. Creb was wise and kind. He understood the spirit world.

The scene changed. With a tawny flash, the feline sprang for the aurochs and wrestled the huge reddish-brown wild cow, bawling in terror, to the ground. Ayla gasped and tried to squeeze herself into the solid rock of the tiny cave. A cave lion roared, and a gigantic paw with claws outstretched reached in and raked her left thigh with four parallel gashes.

"Your totem is the Cave Lion," the old Mog-ur said.

It changed again. The line of fires showing the way down the corridor of a long, winding cave cast light upon beautiful draped and flowing formations. She saw one that resembled the long flowing tail of a horse. It turned into a dun-yellow mare who flowed into the herd. She nickered and swished her dark tail, seeming to beckon. Ayla looked to see where she was going and was startled to see Creb stepping out of the shadows. He motioned her on, urging her to hurry. She heard a horse whinny. The herd was galloping away toward the edge of the cliff. She was in a panic, ran after them. Her stomach churned into a knot of fear. She heard the sound of a horse screaming as it was falling over the edge, tumbling end over end, upside down.

She had two sons, brothers whom no one would guess were brothers. One was tall and blond like Jondalar, the other, older one, she knew was Durc, though his face was in shadow. The two brothers approached each other from opposite directions in the middle of an empty, desolate, windblown prairie. She felt great anxiety; something terrible was about to happen, something she had to prevent. Then, with a shock of terror, she knew one of her sons would kill the other. As they drew closer, she tried to reach them, but a thick viscous wall held her trapped. They were almost upon each other, arms raised as though to strike. She screamed.

"Wake up, child!" Mamut said. "It is only a symbol, a message."

"But one will die!" she cried.

"It is not what you think, Ayla," Mamut said. "You must find the real meaning. You have the Talent. Remember, the spirit world is not the same, it is reversed, upside down."

Ayla jerked when the torch dropped. She grabbed for it and picked it up before the fire died, then glanced up at the hanging pillar that looked as though it supported something, but didn't even reach the ground. It was reversed, upside down. She shivered. Then, for an instant, the pillar turned into a transparent, viscous wall. On the other side a horse was tumbling end over end, upside down, falling off the edge of a cliff.

Wolf was back, nosing at her and whining, running out, then coming back and whining again. Ayla stood up and watched the wolf, still trying to clear her head. "What do you want, Wolf? What are you trying to tell me? Do you want me to follow you? Is that it?"

She started out of the back gallery, and when she reached the opening, she saw another torch coming down the slope into the cave. The person carrying the torch obviously saw her, too, though her torch was starting to sputter and die. She hurried, but took only a few more steps before her light went out. She stopped, then noticed that the light coming toward her was moving faster. She felt relieved, but before the person reached her, her eyes began to adjust to the dark. She could see a little by the faint light that reached the back of the large chamber from outside, and thought she could probably find her way, if she had to, but she was glad someone was coming. She was surprised, however, when she saw who it was.

"It's you!" they both said together.

"I didn't know anyone was in here, I don't want to disturb you."

"I'm so glad to see you," Ayla said at the same time, then smiled. "I really am glad to see you, Brukeval. My torch died."

"I noticed," he said. "Why don't I walk you out? That is, if you are ready to go."

"I've been in here too long," she said. "I'm cold. I'll be glad to feel the sun. I should have paid attention."

"It's easy to get distracted in this cave. It's so beautiful, and feels so . . . I don't know, special," he said, holding the light high between them as they started out.

"It does, doesn't it?"

"It must have been exciting for you to be the first one to see it. We've been on these slopes so many times, I couldn't even say all the counting words, yet no one found it until you came," Brukeval said.

"Just to see it is exciting, being the first one doesn't matter. I think it must be just as exciting for anyone the first time they see it. Have you been here before?" Ayla asked.

"Yes. Everyone was talking about it, so before it got dark, I got a torch and came to see it. I didn't have time to see much, the sun was going down. Just enough to make me decide to come back today," Brukeval said.

"Well, I'm grateful you did," Ayla said as they started up the slope of the entranceway. "I probably could have gotten out, a little light reaches back there, and Wolf would have helped me, but I can't tell you how relieved I was to see your torch coming toward me."

Brukeval looked down and noticed the wolf. "Yes, I'm sure he would have. I didn't see him before. He's special, too, isn't he?"

"He is to me. Have you met him yet? There's a kind of formal introduction that I do with him. He understands then that you are a friend," Ayla said.

"I'd like to be your friend," Brukeval said.

The way he said it made Ayla look at him, quickly, in her unobtrusive Clan woman way. She felt a chill and a sense of foreboding. There seemed to be more in his statement than a wish for friendship. She sensed a yearning for her and then decided she didn't want to believe it. Why should Brukeval yearn for her? They hardly knew each other. She smiled at him, partly to cover her disquiet, as they walked out of the cave.

"Then let's introduce you to Wolf," she said.

She took Brukeval's hand and went through the process of giving Wolf his scent in the context of her approval.

"I don't think I ever told you how much I admired you that day you faced Marona down," he said when she was through. "She can be a cruel and vicious woman. I know, I lived with her when I was growing up. We're considered cousins, far cousins, but her mother was the closest relation to my mother after she died, who could nurse a baby, so she was stuck with me. She accepted the responsibility, but she didn't like it."

"I admit, I don't care much for Marona," Ayla said, "but some people think she may not be able to have children. If that is true, I feel sorry for her."

"I'm not sure if she can't, or just doesn't want to. Some think she just makes sure that she loses it whenever she's Blessed. She wouldn't make a decent mother anyway. She doesn't know how to think of anyone but herself," Brukeval said. "Not like Lanoga. She'll be a wonderful mother."

"She already is," Ayla said.

"And thanks to you, there's a good chance Lorala will live," he said. The way he was looking at her made Ayla uncomfortable again. She looked down and petted Wolf as a distraction.

"It's the mothers who are nursing her, not me," she said.

"But no one else bothered to find out that the baby wasn't getting any milk, or cared enough to get help for Lorala. I've seen how you are with Lanoga. You treat her like she's worth something."

"Of course she's worth something," Ayla said. "She's an admirable girl, and she's going to be a wonderful woman."

"Yes, she is, but she's still part of the lowest-ranked family in the Ninth Cave," Brukeval said. "I'd mate her and share my status with her, it doesn't do me any good, anyway, but I doubt if she'd want me. I'm too old for her, and too . . . well . . . no woman wants me. I do hope she finds someone worthy of her."

"So do I, Brukeval. But why do you think no woman wants you?" Ayla protested. "I understand you have a ranking in the Ninth Cave that is near the first, and Jondalar says that you are an excellent hunter who contributes a lot to the Cave. Jondalar thinks a lot of you, Brukeval. If I were a Zelandonii woman looking for a likely mate, and if I weren't going to mate Jondalar, I would consider you. You have so much to offer."

He watched her carefully, trying to make sure that she wasn't saying those things just so she could twist them around in her next breath into a condescending sarcasm the way Marona used to do. But Ayla seemed sincere and her feelings genuine.

"Well, you're not looking, I'm sorry to say," Brukeval said, "but if you ever decide to start, let me know." Then he smiled, trying to make it seem like a joke.

From the first moment he saw her, Brukeval knew she was the woman he had always dreamed of. The trouble was, she was going to mate Jondalar. What a lucky man, he thought, but then, he always was lucky. I hope he appreciates what he has, but if he doesn't, I would. I'd take her in a heartbeat, if she would have me.

They looked up when they heard the sound of voices and saw several people coming from the direction of the camp of the Ninth Cave. The two tall men who looked so much alike were immediately identifiable. Ayla waved and smiled at Jondalar and Dalanar. They all recognized her and waved back. The two tall young women with them couldn't have looked more different, and though they were considered cousins, it was far cousins, but they both had a close connection to Jondalar. The complex family ties of the Zelandonii had been explained to Ayla, and she thought about their relationships as she watched them approach.

Among the Zelandonii, only children of the same woman were

called brothers and sisters; children of the same man's hearth were considered cousins, not siblings. Folara and Jondalar were sister and brother because they shared the same mother, though the men of their hearths were different; Joplaya was his close cousin because although Dalanar was the man of the hearth to both of them, they had different mothers. But while a sibling relationship wasn't acknowledged, it was understood. Close cousins, especially the ones also called hearth cousins, were too close to mate with each other.

The last person who was with them was Echozar, Joplaya's Promised. He was as distinctive in his general shape and size as the tall men were, especially to Ayla. Joplaya and Echozar would be mated during the same Matrimonial as she and Jondalar, and couples who shared the same ceremony often developed strong friendships. She wished that could be true, but they lived far apart and it was not likely. As they got closer, Ayla noticed that Joplaya glanced at Jondalar now and then, and surprisingly, she didn't mind. She felt an empathetic sorrow for her. She understood Joplaya's melancholy. She, too, had once been Promised to the wrong man, but for Joplaya there would be no last-moment reprieve.

Close cousins were often raised together, or lived nearby and knew they were close kin and not available to be considered for mating. But when Jondalar went to live with the man of his hearth, after the fight in which he knocked out the two front teeth of the man now known as Madroman, he was already a teenager. The daughter of Dalanar's hearth, Joplaya, was a little younger, but neither had known each other while they were growing up.

Dalanar was delighted to have both his hearth children together and wanted them to get to know each other. He decided that one way was to train them both in the art of flint-knapping, which would give them something in common to talk about. It was, in fact, a very good idea, but he didn't know what effect the youngster who was so much like himself would have on Joplaya. She had always adored the man of her hearth, and when Jondalar came, it was all too easy to transfer that overpowering love to her close cousin. Jerika saw it, but both Dalanar and Jondalar were unaware of it. Joplaya always couched her feelings about him in terms of jokes, and they, knowing that close cousins couldn't mate, took it at face value and assumed that she was only teasing.

There were relatively few people in Dalanar's Cave of Lanzadonii, and none that offered much to a beautiful and intelligent young woman. After Jondalar left on his Journey, Jerika urged Dalanar to take the Lanzadonii Cave to Zelandonii Summer Meetings occasionally. They both hoped that Joplaya would find someone, and a great many young men were interested in her, but she felt different and self-conscious because people stared at her. And she could find no one with whom she was as comfortable as she had been with her cousin Jondalar.

She knew that occasionally some cousins did mate—far cousins, to be sure—but she chose to forget that and fantasized that on his Journey Jondalar would decide that he loved her as she loved him. She knew the dream was unlikely, but she passionately hoped that someday he would come home and claim her as his one true love. Instead, he returned with Ayla. She was devastated, but she saw the love he felt for the foreign woman and knew that her dream was shattered.

The one man with whom she had developed some affinity was a new member of Dalanar's Cave, a man who was also stared at wherever he went, Echozar, a man of mixed spirits. Joplaya was the one who helped him integrate into their Cave, made him understand that he was accepted by Dalanar and the Lanzadonii, and even helped him with his language skills. And she was the one who coaxed his story out of him.

His mother had been raped by a man of the Others, who also killed her mate. When she gave birth, she was cursed as a bad-luck woman because her mate had been killed and her son was deformed. She left her clan, ready to die, but was rescued by Andovan, an older man who had run away from a vicious leader of the S'Armunai. He had lived for a while with a Zelandonii Cave, but was not comfortable with people whose customs were so different from his own. He moved away and lived by himself until he found the Clan woman and her son. Together they raised him. Echozar learned the Clan language of signs from his mother, and spoken language from Andovan, though it was a mixture of his own language and the Zelandonii he had learned. But when he reached manhood, Andovan died. His mother couldn't stand to live alone and succumbed to the death curse that had been imposed on her. She died shortly after Andovan, leaving Echozar alone.

The young man didn't want to live alone. He tried to return to a clan, but they thought of him as deformed and refused to accept him. And though he could speak, he was rejected by the Caves as an abomination of mixed spirits. Out of desperation, he tried to kill himself, and woke up to Dalanar's smiling face, who found him injured, but not dead, and brought him back to his Cave. The Lanzadonii took him in, and he idolized the tall man, but it was Joplaya that he loved.

She had been kind to him, talked to him, listened to him, even made him a beautiful decorated tunic for his adoption ceremony into the Lanzadonii. He loved her so much, it hurt to think about it, but he didn't think he had a chance. He had struggled with himself for a long time to get up enough courage to ask if she would be his mate, and could hardly believe it when she finally accepted. It was after her hearth cousin Jondalar returned with Ayla, both of whom he liked immediately. They didn't treat him as though he were different.

Wherever Echozar went, people stared at him. The combined characteristics that he inherited from the Clan and the Others were not the most appealing. In height, he was as tall as an average man of the Others, but he retained the powerful, barrel-chested physique, relatively short, bowed legs, and hairy body of the Clan. His neck was long and he could speak, he even had a slight chin, like the Others, though it receded, making it look weak. His prominent nose and heavy browridges with unruly eyebrows that crossed his forehead in a single line were entirely Clan. His forehead was not. It rose up as straight and high as any man of the Others.

The combination seemed outlandish to many people, as though he didn't quite fit together, but not to Ayla. She had grown up with the Clan and had consequently adopted their standard of beauty. She had always thought of herself as big and ugly. She was too tall, and her face was too bland and flat. Though she may have thought the look of the mixture was attractive, to everyone else Echozar was extraordinarily ugly, except for his eyes. Liquid dark at night and sparkling with highlights of hazel in the sun, his large, deep brown eyes were profoundly intense, acutely compelling, and highly intelligent, and when he looked at her, they revealed his love for Joplaya.

Though she did not love him, Joplaya did feel a kind of kinship with Echozar and a genuine respect. Though people stared at her because of her exotic beauty, it still made her feel different, and she hated it as much as he did. She also felt comfortable with him, she could talk to him. She decided if she couldn't have the man she loved, she would mate the man who loved her, and she knew she would never find a man who loved her more than Echozar.

As the group from the camp drew near, Ayla noticed Brukeval

become tense. He was staring at Echozar, and there was no friendliness in his expression. It made her aware of the similarities and the differences between them. In Echozar's case, it was his mother who had given birth to a child that was mixed; with Brukeval, it was his grandmother. Echozar's Clan characteristics were definitely more pronounced, but to her—and to everyone there—the mixture was obvious in both. Brukeval did, however, resemble the Others more than Echozar.

Though she was learning to appreciate what was pleasing to the Others, she still found the strong Clan features attractive. She had meant it when she told Brukeval that she couldn't understand why he thought no woman would want him. She probably would consider him, if she weren't mating Jondalar and if she were a Zelandonii woman. But she knew she wasn't really a Zelandonii woman, at least not yet, and she personally wouldn't consider Brukeval at all. While she thought he was handsome, and that he did have a lot to offer, there was something about him that disturbed her. The member of the Clan that he reminded her of most was Broud, and the way he was looking at Echozar right now explained why.

"Greetings, Brukeval," Jondalar said, walking up to the man with a smile on his face. "I think you know Dalanar, the man of my hearth, but have you met my cousin Joplaya, and her Promised, Echozar?" Jondalar was prepared to do the formal introductions, and Echozar had raised his hands in readiness, but before he could begin, Brukeval interrupted.

"I have no desire to touch a flathead!" he said, putting his hands down to his sides, then he turned aside and stalked away.

Everyone was stunned. It was Folara who finally spoke.

"How could he be so rude!" she said. "I know he blames flatheads for his mother's death—I guess I should say the Clan now—but that was unforgivable. I know mother taught Brukeval better manners than that, if no one else did. She would be appalled."

"My mother may have been flathead or Clan. You can say it any way you want, but I am neither," Echozar said. "I am Lanzadonii."

"Yes, you are," Joplaya said, reaching for his hand. "And soon we will be mated."

"We know there is Clan in Brukeval's lineage, too," Dalanar said. "It's obvious. If he can't bear to touch someone with that background, how can he stand himself?"

"He can't. That's his problem," Jondalar said. "Brukeval hates himself. He was teased a lot when he was young, other children used to call him a flathead, and he always denied it."

"But he can't change what he is no matter how much he denies it," Ayla said.

No one had lowered their voices, and Brukeval had excellent hearing. He heard everything that was said. He had another characteristic of the Others that the Clan lacked, he cried tears, and as he walked away, tears filled his eyes. Even her, he said to himself after Ayla's comment. I thought she was different. I thought she meant it when she said she would consider me if Jondalar were gone, but she thinks I'm a flathead, too. She didn't mean it. She would never consider me. The more he thought about it, the more angry he became. It's not right for her to encourage a person when she doesn't mean it. I am not a flathead, no matter what she says, no matter what any of them say. I am not a flathead!

It was dark, but the sky had already changed from black to inky blue, with a hint of gold outlining the hills on the eastern horizon, when the group from the Ninth Cave of the Zelandonii and the First Cave of the Lanzadonii started from their camp. They used torches to make their way to the place where Jondalar had demonstrated the spear-thrower, and they were glad to see the bonfire burning in the middle of the open stretch of trampled ground that had once been a field of grass. Some hunters had already arrived. As the sky lightened, the cool morning mist rising from The River began filling the spaces between trees and brush on the periphery and mingling with the people standing around the fire.

The morning chorus of birds was in full throat, trilling, chirping, twittering, and calling over the low murmur of voices, highlighting the mood of anticipation. Holding Whinney's halter rope, Ayla knelt down and put an arm around Wolf, then smiled at Jondalar, who was stroking Racer to keep him calm. She looked around in wonder; it was the largest hunting party she had ever seen. There were far too many people for her to count. She recalled that Zelandoni had offered to teach her how to use the words to count larger numbers, and she decided to ask her. She would like to be able to say how many people were there milling around.

Women who were about to mate did not usually participate in the pre-Matrimonial hunt, there were usually certain restrictions and various other activities planned for them. The First did a cursory run-through with her so she could be excused. This hunt was going to be a test of using horses, and trying out Jondalar's spear-thrower, and they wanted her. Ayla was glad that she had been allowed to join the hunt, in spite of her upcoming Matrimonial. She had always enjoyed hunting. If she hadn't learned to hunt when she lived alone in her valley, she might not have survived, and it had given her a certain sense of self-reliance.

Though several of the women who were to be mated had hunted, only one of them cared about joining the hunt. Since an exception had been made for Ayla, she was also allowed to join them. When they were young, most girls loved to go hunting just like the boys. After they reached puberty, many of them still hunted, mostly because that's where the boys were. Several enjoyed hunting for itself, but once young women mated and began to have children, most were so busy, they were happy to let the men do it. That was when they began to develop other crafts and skills that added to their status and ability to trade and bargain for things they wanted and that wouldn't take them so far away from their children. But women who had hunted in their youth were looked upon as favorable mates. They could understand the challenges of the hunt, appreciate the successes and sympathize with the failures of their mates.

Ayla had gone to the Search ceremony arranged by the zelandonia the evening before, along with most of the leaders and some hunters, but she had only observed, not participated. Through the Search, it was determined that a large herd of aurochs were congregated in a nearby valley that was particularly good for hunting, and they planned to try there first, but nothing was guaranteed. Even though a zelandoni might metaphysically "see" animals during a Search, they might not still be where they were seen the next day. But the valley held a good meadow that attracted the wild cattle, and if the aurochs were gone, it was likely some other animals would be there. The hunters hoped to find aurochs, however, because the cattle were massing together in larger herds this time of year, and they provided tasty meat in very big packages.

When the food he thrived on was in abundance, a full-grown bull aurochs grew to six feet six inches at the shoulder and weighed nearly three thousand pounds, two and a half feet taller and more than twice the weight of his largest domesticated descendant. He looked like an ordinary bull but was so much bigger, he approached the size of a mammoth. The food preferred by aurochs was grass, fresh green grass, not mature stalks and not tree leaves. They favored clearings, edges of forests, meadows, and marshes rather than steppes. Although they would eat acorns and nuts in the fall, as well as grass seeds, to build up a reserve of fat, and in winter's hungry time they wouldn't disdain browsing on leaves and buds.

The bull's coat was usually black and long, with a light stripe down his back. He had a tight knot of curly hair on his forehead and two long, rather thin horns, whitish gray shading into black, forward-pointing tips. Cows were smaller and shorter, and their coats tended to be lighter in color, often with a reddish tone. Usually only the old or the very young fell to four-legged predators. The bull in his prime was unafraid of any hunter, including humans, and didn't bother to avoid them. Especially during the fall rutting season, but not limited to then, he was ready to fight and could charge in an uncontrolled rage, pick up a man or a wolf with his horns, and toss him in the air, and would gore and often disembowel even a cave lion. Aurochs were fast, strong, agile, and very dangerous.

The horde of hunters started out as soon as it was light enough to see. Walking fast, they sighted the herd of aurochs before the sun was very high; the valley was surprisingly close. One end of it led into a fairly large canyon that funneled to a narrow defile, then opened out again into a natural corral. It wasn't completely blind, it had a few narrow outlets, but the place had been used before, though generally no more than once per season. The smell of blood from a major hunt tended to keep animals away until the snows of winter washed it clean again. But in anticipation of future use, fencing had been constructed across the outlets, and several of the hunters circled around to check on them and choose a vantage point from which to throw their spears. A wolf howl, not too bad an impression, Ayla thought, was the signal that all was ready. She had been warned and kept her arm around Wolf to restrain him in case he was tempted to respond. The loud caw of a crow was the return signal.

The rest of the hunters had been edging around the herd, trying not to disturb it too much, a difficult task with so many people. Ayla and Jondalar had stayed quite a ways back, not wanting the scent of the wolf to precipitate anything. They mounted the horses at the signal and started forward at a gallop, Wolf running alongside. As fast and powerful as a bull could be, aurochs were still herd animals and there were young among them. The sound of whoops and yells and the sight of unknown things being flapped at them was enough to spook them, and when one started running, others soon followed. With two humans on horseback getting surprisingly close with their flapping and shouting, and the scent of Wolf, the herd was soon stampeding blindly into the canyon.

The narrow constriction slowed them down as they piled up behind it, trying to get through. Amidst the dust of the bawling, bellowing, roaring herd, some of them tried to break out and go another way, any other way. The people and the horses and the wolf were everywhere, turning them back, but finally, one determined old bull had had enough. He stood his ground, pawed the earth, lowered his horns, and was hit with two swift spears cast from spear-throwers. He dropped to his knees, then tumbled to his side. By then, most were through, and the fence was closed. Then the slaughter began.

Spears of every description were flung at the trapped beasts, flint-tipped, sharpened bone or ivory-tipped, long and short. The hunters had to rotate behind the narrow gates that protected them from massive horns and sharp hooves. Some were hurled with spear-throwers, not just from Ayla's and Jondalar's spear-throwers. A few adventurous souls had been practicing and tried them out here, where a few misses wouldn't hurt because the aurochs weren't going anywhere except back to the breast of the Great Earth Mother in the world of the spirits.

In one morning, enough meat had been secured to last the entire Summer Meeting for some time, and for a large Matrimonial Feast besides. A messenger was sent back to the camp when the aurochs were in the trap, and a second large party left to help, and by the time the last animal was down, they rushed in to begin the butchering and preserving and storing.

There were several means of storage. Because of the closeness of the glaciers, and the permanently frozen layer that existed at variable depths below the surface, the underlying permafrost could be utilized as ice cellars to store fresh meat simply by digging holes in the ground. Fresh meat could also be stored in deep ponds or lakes, or the quiet backwaters of streams or rivers. Weighted down with rocks, and marked with long poles so it could be found and recovered later, meat could last a year with surprisingly little deterioration. Meat could also be dried to last several years. The problem with drying was that early summer was the season of blowflies, which could quickly spoil meat that was set out to dry in the sun and wind. Very smoky fires would keep off the worst of the insects, but it required constant supervision and monitoring in an unpleasantly smoky environment. It was necessary, however, to dry some of the meat for traveling food.

In addition to the meat, hides were extremely important. They were used for many things from implements and containers to clothing and shelters. Fat would be rendered for heat and light and sustenance; hair for fibers and stuffing, and warm clothing; tendons for sinew to make cordage and lashings for various constructions. Horns would be used to make containers, various devices such as hinges on panels, and even jewelry. Teeth were used as often for jewelry as they were for tools. Intestines could be made into waterproof coverings and clothing and casings for sausage and fat.

Bones had many uses. They could be made into utensils and plates, carvings and weapons, cracked for their nutritious marrow, or burned in hearths for fuel. Nothing would be wasted. Even the hooves and scraps of hides would be boiled for glues and adhesives, which had many uses. In combination with sinew, for example, it would help attach points to spears, handles to knives, and join composite spear shafts. It would also be used to join tough soles to softer foot coverings.

But first the animals had to be skinned, the parts separated out, and the meat stored, and it had to be done quickly. Guards were posted to keep away the thieves, the other carnivores more than willing to share in the kill by whatever means they could. Such a large concentration of slaughtered aurochs brought every other meat-eating animal in the vicinity. The slinking hyenas were the first ones Ayla saw. She had her sling out and almost without thinking signaled Whinney to go after the pack.

She had to dismount and get more stones, but the speed with which she dispatched them was reason enough to make both her and Jondalar guards. Almost anyone could butcher, even youngsters helped, but keeping away the carnivores took some effort and skill with weaponry. The pack of wolves caught Wolf's attention. He was eager to drive off interlopers from the kill of his pack, but Ayla backed him up. The vicious, aggressive wolverines were worse. Two of them, probably male and female, together because it was their season, sprayed one cow with their musk glands. It smelled so bad that after they retrieved the spear to give credit to the hunter, several people hauled it off to let the wolverines fight over it between themselves and any other carnivore that wanted to try for it—no easy task, since wolverines were known to defend their kills against lions.

Ayla saw stoats, summer brown now, though come winter they would become ermines, entirely white weasels except for the black tips of their tails. She saw foxes and lynxes, and a spotted snow leopard, and at the periphery, casually observing it all, a pride of cave lions, the first she'd seen since she arrived. She paused to observe them. All cave lions were pale in color, usually light ivory, but these were almost white. At first she thought they were all females, but the behavior of one made her look twice. It was a male without a mane! When she asked Jondalar, he told her that cave lions in this region did not have manes; he'd been surprised by the eastern lions that did, though they were rather scraggly.

The skies above held their share of marauding meat-eaters waiting their chance to land or being chased away and flying off again. Vultures and eagles, expending little energy, floated on thermals, rising currents of warm air that supported their large outstretched wings. Kites and hawks and lammergeiers soared and dove, sometimes fighting with stately ravens and raucous crows. It was easier for small rodents and reptiles to scurry or slither in and hide from the humans, but the small predators were often prey themselves. Eventually, it would all be cleaned up by the smallest of them, the insects. But no matter how diligent the guards, all the meat-eaters would get a share before the aurochs could be completely butchered and stored, and though it wasn't their primary goal, they didn't mind that before they were through, they managed to secure a few distinctive furs as well.

A successful first hunt of the Summer Meeting was a lucky sign. It assured a good year for the Zelandonii and was considered especially fortunate for the couples who were about to be mated. The mating day would take place as soon as the meat and other products were brought back to camp and stashed so they would not spoil or be stolen by four-legged carnivores.

Once the excitement and work of the hunt were over, the attention of the Summer Meeting camp turned to the upcoming nuptials. Ayla could hardly wait, but she was also nervous. Jondalar felt the same way. They caught themselves looking at each other often, smiled almost shyly, and hoped that everything would go well.

30

Zelandoni tried to find a time to speak with Ayla privately about the medicine that would prevent conception, but something always seemed to interfere. There were demands on Ayla's time as well as hers. Because this was a community hunt that represented the entire Zelandonii, the First had to hold special ceremonies to make sure that the spirit of the aurochs would be appeased and major rituals to thank the Great Mother for the lives of all the animals who had sacrificed themselves so that the Zelandonii could live.

The hunt was almost too successful and it took longer than usual to accomplish everything that needed to be done. The meat was cut and the fat rendered and portioned out. Hides were either scraped and dried or rolled and stored in the underground ice cellars along with meat, bones and other parts, and most people helped, including the women who were to be mated. Mating could wait.

The First resigned herself to the delay, but she wished she had taken the time to talk with Ayla in more depth before they left the Ninth Cave, when it would have been easier to study the stranger and learn more about her. Who would have guessed that the young woman—at nineteen, still young, though Ayla seemed to think she was ancient—would possess so much knowledge? She had seemed so guileless, it made her seem inexperienced somehow. But Zelandoni was coming to understand that there was far more to Ayla than she realized. She knew that it was never wise to underestimate an unknown element, but she had not followed her own counsel.

And now the First was busy with another matter. The zelandonia decided to conduct First Rites before the Matrimonial, though generally it was afterward, for a very specific reason. Before their First Rites, all females were considered girls and were not supposed to share the Mother's Gift of Pleasures. The Rites of First Pleasures was the ceremony where, under strict and careful supervision, girls were physically opened and became able to receive the spirits that would start a new life. Not until then were they fully women. But

First Rites were always held during the Summer Meetings, and usually there was some period of time after their first moon time and before their First Rites when girls were in a kind of limbo. It was during this time that men found them incredibly appealing, probably because they were forbidden.

There was always a second ceremony at the end of the Summer Meeting for the girls who started their bleeding during the summer, but the long interval in between Meetings was difficult. Young men, and some not so young, were constantly after the pubescent girls, and festivals to honor the Mother during the year made the young women more aware of their own urges, especially those who reached menarche in autumn. No mother ever wanted her daughter to start her moon times then, with a whole winter of darkness and reduced outdoor activity ahead of them.

Though a stigma of shame was placed on those who did not wait until they had their First Rites, some girls, inevitably, did succumb to the persistent blandishments. But no matter how relentless the pressure, by yielding to it, the girls became ultimately less desirable as mates because it indicated a lack of sufficient self-control. To some, it seemed ultimately unfair to stigmatize a woman because as a girl she made what might have seemed at the time to be a naive transgression of accepted custom. But there were those who considered it to be an important test of basic character, of their inherent integrity, fortitude, and perseverance, which were considered important traits in women.

Mothers inevitably enlisted the aid of the zelandonia to try to conceal the indiscretion, and First Rites were conducted in any case because a young woman could not be mated without them. The zelandonia always tried to make sure that the men selected to "open" the young women who were already open would be discreet, so nothing would be divulged. But those who had yielded were known, not least to the zelandonia who were among those who privately believed the test to be revealing, and were at least suspected by many others.

This summer, however, a rare problem had arisen. One young woman, Janida of the South Holding of the Twenty-ninth Cave, who had not yet had her First Rites, was pregnant, and she wanted to mate the young man who had prematurely opened her. Peridal, also of the South Holding of the Twenty-ninth Cave, was not as anxious to mate her, though he had been inordinately persistent in pursuing her throughout the winter and had made extravagant promises.

Reflection Rock was so huge with so many levels, it was too easy to find secluded places for their trysts.

In his favor, it was said that Peridal was quite young. He wasn't sure he wanted to get mated yet, and his mother was not eager for her son to make such a commitment, particularly with a girl who had yielded. But the zelandonia were using all their persuasive pressure to encourage them to agree. While it was not essential for a woman to be mated when she gave birth, it was preferable for a child to be born to the hearth of some man, especially the first child.

The other side of the issue was that, generally, if a woman became pregnant before she was mated, she became more desirable, because she had already proven that she was capable of bringing children to a man's hearth, but the stigma of shame for not showing enough restraint to wait until First Rites was strong. Janida and her mother knew it, but they also knew that if Janida was already Blessed when she mated, it was considered lucky and she ought to be looked upon with favor. They hoped that one would compensate for the other.

Many people were talking about the girl, some feeling one way and some the other, but most agreed that it was an interesting situation, particularly the approach that was taken by Janida and her mother. Those who took the side of Peridal and his mother felt that he was too young to assume the responsibilities of mating; others felt that if the Mother had indeed chosen his spirit to Bless the girl, then She must feel that he was capable of being a man of the hearth. And in spite of her lack of restraint, perhaps Janida was lucky, and Peridal should be glad to mate her. A few men were even considering the idea of mating her themselves, shame or not, if the boy didn't want to. She must indeed be favored among the Blessed of Doni if she became pregnant so quickly.

The young women who were preparing for their Rites of First Pleasures were all housed in a special guarded lodge near the zelandonia lodge. It was decided that the young pregnant woman should stay with the other girls and go through the full ceremony, since she had to have First Rites before she could be mated anyway. It was felt that she needed to be taught what young women needed to know, but when she was moved in with the others, some of them objected.

"The Rites of First Pleasures is a ceremony to open a girl to make her a woman. If she's already open, why is Janida here? It's supposed to be for girls who wait, not girls who cheat," one of them said in a voice loud enough for all to hear.

Several agreed with her, but not all. One of them countered, "She's here because she wants to get mated at the First Matrimonial, and a girl can't get mated until she's had First Rites, and besides, the Mother has Blessed her."

Others, some of whom had started their moon times not long after the previous Summer Meeting and were rumored to have experimented with some private opening rites themselves, tried to be more welcoming, but most felt a need to be careful. They knew their good names were likely to be dependent on the discretion of the man who was chosen for them, and he could be related to one of the girls who had waited. They didn't want to offend anyone. They were more than aware that they could suffer a similar shame, and they were seeing the problems it could cause.

Janida smiled at the one who spoke up for her, but said nothing. She felt a little older and wiser than most of the girls in the lodge. At least she knew what to expect, not like the ones who waited and were both eager and worried, and she was gaining some courage for having faced up to all her detractors. Besides, she was pregnant, Blessed by Doni, no matter what anyone said, and she was at the stage in her pregnancy when she was awash with optimistic feelings. She didn't know that certain hormones in her body had been activated by her pregnancy, she only knew she was happy to be having a baby and feeling content.

Although the girls were supposed to be in seclusion and well guarded, somehow the comments that had been made when Janida joined them, especially the phrase that First Rites were supposed to be "for girls who wait, not girls who cheat," were reported all through the camp. When the First heard about it, she was furious. It had to be one of their own, the zelandonia, who had spread the word—no one else could have been that close—and she wished she knew who it was.

Ayla and Jondalar had been working on aurochs hides most of the day, first scraping off the fat and membranes from the inside, and the hair on the outside with flint-scrapers, then soaking them in a solution of the cow's brains that had been worked by hand into a puree and mixed with water, which gave the hides an amazingly soft elasticity. Then the hide was rolled up and twisted to squeeze out as much liquid as possible, often using two people, one at each end. Small holes were then pierced all around the edge, about three inches apart. A rectangular frame that was larger than the full hide had been constructed out of four poles, and the wet skin was attached to the frame with a cord tied through each hole and pulled tight. Then the hard work began.

With the frame anchored securely, resting against trees or a horizontal beam, the hides were straked. A pole with a flattened, but rounded end was used to poke the hides as far as they would stretch, up and down, side to side, over and over, until after half a day of work the hide was finally dry. At that stage it was nearly white, with a soft and supple suede finish. It could have been made into something and worn, but if it got wet again, it would have to be straked all over again or it would dry into hard rawhide. In order for the hide to retain its pliable velvety texture even after washing, it had to go through another process. There were several choices, depending on what finished product was wanted.

The simplest was to smoke it. One method was to use a small conical traveling tent, block the smoke hole, and build a smoky fire inside. Several hides could be hung near the top, and the entrance fastened shut. As the smoke filled the tent and enveloped the hides, it coated each of the collagen fibers within the skin. After smoking, even if it got wet or was washed, the leather stayed supple. Smoking also changed the color of the hide, and depending on the type of wood used, it could range from shades of yellow through tan and taupe to deep brown.

Another process was to mix powdered red ochre with tallow— fat rendered in simmering water—and rub the mixture into the hide. It not only gave the leather a red color, which could vary in shade from bright orangy red to deep maroon, it also acted as a water repellent. A smooth stick or bone could be used to rub the fatty substance in, crushing the surface, burnishing it to a harder, shiny finish, making it almost waterproof. Red ochre inhibited bacterial decay and was also an insect repellent, including the small parasitic insects that lived on warm-blooded animals like humans.

Yet another process, not as well known and requiring more work, was to make the almost white natural color of the hide pure white. It was somewhat prone to failure because it was difficult to keep the hide supple, but it was stunning when successful. Ayla had learned the process from Crozie, an old Mamutoi woman. It started with saving her urine, then letting it stand until through natural chemical processes it became ammonia, which was a bleaching agent. After scraping, the hide was soaked in ammonia, then washed with saponifying roots that made a soapy lather, then softened with the brain mixture and burnished with powdered kaolin, a fine white clay mixed in very pure tallow.

Ayla had made only one white garment, and Crozie had helped her, but she had noticed a lode of kaolin not far from the Third Cave and thought she might try it again. She wondered if the lather she had learned to make from the Losadunai out of fat and wood ashes would work better than soaproot.

While she was working, Ayla heard some of the discussions about Janida and found the situation interesting because it was a fascinating insight into the traditions and customs of the Zelandonii. There was no doubt in her mind that Peridal had started the baby growing inside Janida, since both of them had indicated that no other man had penetrated her and Ayla was convinced it was the essences of men's organs that started pregnancy. But as they were walking back to the camp of the Ninth Cave, tired after a day of working hides, she asked Jondalar about the Zelandonii insistence on First Rites before women were free to make their own choices.

"I don't understand what difference it makes whether the young man opened her last winter, or another man opens her here, so long as she wasn't forced," Ayla said. "It's not like Madenia of the Losadunai, who was forced by that band of young men before her First Rites. Janida is a little young to be pregnant, but so was I, and I didn't even know what First Rites were until you showed me."

Jondalar felt a great deal of empathy and compassion for the young woman. He had broken the accepted traditions of his people during his initiation into manhood, by falling in love and wanting to mate his donii-woman. When he found out that Ladroman ... Madroman ... had been eavesdropping on them, that he had actually hidden and watched them, then told everyone that they planned to mate, Jondalar went into a rage and hit him repeatedly, breaking his teeth. Madroman had also wanted Zolena for his donii-woman— everyone did—but she chose Jondalar and never Madroman.

Jondalar thought he understood why Ayla felt the way she did. She wasn't born here and didn't quite appreciate how the Zelandonii felt about the customs they had lived with all their lives, or how difficult it could be to go against the traditions you knew. He didn't fully understand that she had broken Clan traditions and had paid dire consequences; she nearly died for it, but she no longer feared to question anyone's traditions.

"People can be more tolerant of those who come from another place," Jondalar said, "but Janida knew what was expected. I hope the young man does join with her and that they will be happy together, but even if he doesn't, I hear there are some men who would gladly mate her."

"I should think so. She's a young, attractive woman who is going to have a baby that she can bring to a man's hearth, if he's worthy of her," Ayla said.

They walked in silence for a pace, then Jondalar said, "I think this Summer Meeting's Matrimonial will be remembered for a long time. There's Janida and Peridal, who will probably be among the youngest to ever mate if they decide to do it, even without her early pregnancy. And I've just come back from a long Journey, and you come from a great distance away, so people will talk about that, but I don't think anyone here understands how far it really was. Then there's Joplaya and Echozar. They both have a background and kinship line unlike anyone else's. I just hope that those few people who object don't make it troublesome. I could hardly believe what Brukeval did. I thought he had more manners than that, in spite of how he feels."

"Echozar was right when he said he isn't Clan," Ayla said. "His mother was, but he wasn't raised by them. Even if they had taken him back, I think he would have found it difficult to live with them. He knows their signs, more or less, but he doesn't even know that he's using women's signs."

"Women's signs? You never mentioned anything about that before," Jondalar said.

"It's subtle, but there is a difference. The first signs that all babies learn are from their mothers, but when they get older the girls stay with their mothers and continue to learn from them. The boys start doing more with the men, and begin to learn their ways," Ayla said.

"What did you teach me, and the Lion Camp?" Jondalar said.

Ayla smiled. "Baby talk," she said.

"You mean, when I was talking to Guban, I was talking baby talk?" Jondalar said, appalled.

"Even less than that, to be honest, but he understood. Just the fact that you knew something, that you tried to speak the correct way, impressed him," Ayla said.

"The correct way? Guban thought his way was the correct way to talk?" Jondalar said.

"Of course. Don't you?"

"I suppose so," he said, then smiled. "What do you think is the correct way?"

"The correct way is always whatever way you're used to. Right now, the Clan way, Mamutoi, and Zelandonii are all correct, but after a while, when all I have spoken is Zelandonii for a long time, I will no doubt think that is the correct way, even if I don't speak it correctly, and I probably never will. The only one I will ever know perfectly is the Clan language, but only of the clan I grew up with, and that's not quite the same as the way they do it around here," Ayla said.

As they reached the small stream, Ayla noticed the sun was going down and was caught up again by a glorious blaze of color in the sky. They both stopped to watch for a while.

"Zelandoni asked me if I wanted to be chosen for First Rites tomorrow, probably for Janida," Jondalar said.

"She told you that?" Ayla said. "Marthona said the men are never told who they will be with, and they are never supposed to tell."

"She didn't exactly tell me. She said she wanted someone who would be not only discreet, but caring. She said she knew you were pregnant, and she thought I would know how to treat someone who might need the same kind of concern. Who else could it be?" he said.

"Are you going to do it?" Ayla said.

"I thought about it. There was a time when I would have been more than willing, eager, but I said I didn't think so," he said.

"Why?" she asked.

"Because of you," he said.

"Me? Did you think I would object?"

"Would you?"

"I understand it is a custom of your people, and other men who are mated do it," Ayla said.

"And you'd agree to it, whether you liked it or not, wouldn't you?"

"I suppose," she said.

"The reason I declined wasn't because I thought you would object, although I probably wouldn't like it if you decided to become a donii-woman for a season. It's because I don't think I could give her the attention she deserves. I'd be thinking about you, comparing her to you, and that would be unfair to her. I've always had more size than many, and I'd be withholding and trying to be careful and gentle, so I wouldn't hurt her, and wishing all the time I was with you instead," he said. "I don't mind being caring and gentle, but we fit together. I don't have to worry about hurting you, at least not now. As you get further along, I don't know, but we can work something out then."

She hadn't realized how pleased she would be that he had refused. She had heard how attractive most men found those young women, and she wondered if she was feeling jealous. She didn't want to be, she had heard what Zelandoni said at the women's meeting, and she would not have objected if he had accepted the offer, but she was happy that he had not. Ayla couldn't help but smile, a big radiant smile that almost matched the sunset, which gave Jondalar a warm glow.

All the couples who were to be mated met with the zelandonia the day following the Rites of First Pleasures ceremony. Most were young, but some were middle-aged, and a few were quite old, well over fifty years. Regardless of age, they were excited and looking forward to the event, and most were friendly to each other, the start of the special bond between people who were mated at the same Mating Ceremonial. Many lifelong friendships were established then.

Ayla left Wolf with Marthona, who said she would be willing to stay with him, though Ayla had to tie him down with a restraining rope to keep him from following her. Before she left, she noticed that Marthona was indeed a calming influence and he seemed more relaxed when she was with him.

When they arrived at the zelandonia lodge, Ayla saw Levela and a man she had not met. Levela waved them over and introduced everyone to Jondecam, a man of medium height with a red beard, a pleasant smile, and mischievous eyes.

"So you're from Elder Hearth," Jondalar said. "Kimeran and I are old friends. We got our manhood belts together. I saw him during the bison hunt. I didn't realize he had become the leader of the Second Cave."

"He's my uncle, my mother's younger brother," Jondecam said.

"Uncle? You seem closer to age-mates," Ayla said.

"He's only a few years older than I am, more like an older brother. My mother was about the age of a girl during First Rites when her brother was born," Jondecam said. "She was always like a second mother to him, even then. When his mother, my grandmother, died, my mother took care of him. She was pretty young when she mated, but her mate died early. I'm her firstborn, and I have a younger sister, but I hardly remember the man of my hearth. She was called to the zelandonia, and didn't mate again."

"I remember embarrassing myself," Jondalar said. "I saw Kimeran's mother and made some typical comment about the young attractive woman standing with the mothers, and wondering what baby was completing his manhood rites," he smiled. "You can imagine how I felt when he said she was there for him. He was as big as I was! Then he told me she was actually his sister."

After they had been there for a while and it appeared that the zelandonia were getting ready to begin, two more people arrived, the youngsters Janida and Peridal. The couple stood at the entrance looking nervous and a little scared, and for a moment seemed ready to bolt. Suddenly Levela left the group and walked quickly toward them.

"Greetings, I am Levela of the West Holding of the Twenty-ninth Cave. You are Janida and Peridal, aren't you? I think I met you, Janida, when you came to harvest pine nuts at Summer Camp a year or two ago. I'm with Ayla and Jondalar. She's the one with the animals, and he's the brother of my sister's mate. Come and meet them," she said, and started leading them back. They seemed at a loss for words.

"She *is* Proleva's sister, isn't she?" Joplaya said quietly.

"Yes, I can see Proleva welcoming someone like that," Ayla said.

"Joplaya and Echozar are here, too, they're the Lanzadonii couple who came to be mated with us," Levela was saying as they approached. "And here's my Promised. Jondecam of the Second Cave of the Zelandonii, meet Janida and Peridal, both of the South Holding of the Twenty-ninth Cave." Looking at the young couple, "That's right, isn't it?"

"Yes," Janida said, smiling nervously and frowning worriedly at the same time.

Jondecam held out his hands to Peridal. "Greetings," he said with a broad smile.

"Greetings," Peridal responded, taking his hands, though his grip was rather limp and he didn't seem to know what else to say.

"Greetings, Peridal," Jondalar said in turn, also holding out his hands. "Did I see you at the hunt?"

"I was there," the young man said. "I saw you . . . on a horse."

"Yes, and Ayla, too, I imagine."

Peridal looked uncomfortable and at a loss for words.

"Did you have much luck?" Jondecam asked.

"Yes," Peridal said.

"He killed two cows," Janida said for him, "and one had a calf inside."

"Did you know the skin of that calf will make wonderful baby clothes?" Levela said. "It's so fine and soft."

"That's what my mother said," Janida replied.

"We haven't met," Ayla said. She held out both hands. "I am Ayla, formerly of the Lion Camp of the Mamutoi, but now of the Ninth Cave of the Zelandonii. In the name of the Great Earth Mother, Mut, also known as Doni, I greet you."

Janida was a little shocked. She had never heard anyone speak so differently. There was a rather uncomfortable silence for a moment. Then, as though remembering her manners, she said, "I am Janida of the South Holding of the Twenty-ninth Cave of the Zelandonii. In the name of Doni, I greet you, Ayla of the Ninth Cave of the Zelandonii."

Joplaya then stepped forward and held out her hands to the young woman. "I am Joplaya of the First Cave of the Lanzadonii, Daughter of the hearth of Dalanar, Founder and Leader of the Lanzadonii. In the name of the Great Mother, I greet you, Janida. This is my Promised, Echozar of the First Cave of the Lanzadonii."

Janida looked directly at the couple, her mouth literally hanging open as she stared. She was not the first to look surprised, but she seemed less able to control it than most. Then, as though she suddenly realized what she was doing, she closed her mouth and flushed deep red.

"I'm . . . I am sorry. My mother would be so angry if she knew how rude I was, but I couldn't help it. You both look so different, but you are beautiful and he is . . . not," she said, then flushed again. "I'm sorry. I mean . . . I didn't mean that . . . I just . . ."

"What you mean is she's so beautiful, and he's so ugly," Jondecam said with a twinkle in his eye. He looked at them both and grinned. "It is true, isn't it?" There was a moment of awkward silence, then Echozar spoke.

"You are right, Jondecam. I am ugly. I can't imagine why this beautiful woman would want me, but I'm not going to question my luck," Echozar said, then he smiled, and it lit his eyes.

Seeing a smile on a Clan face always startled Ayla. People of the

Clan didn't smile. To them an expression that bared the teeth was seen as a threat or a nervous display of subservience. But somehow the expression changed the configuration of Echozar's face, eased the strong Clan features and made him seem much more approachable.

"Actually, I'm glad you're here, Echozar," Jondecam said. "Next to this big brute," he pointed to Jondalar, "everyone looks bad, but you make me and this youngster look good! The women, on the other hand, are all beautiful."

Jondecam was so ingenuous, he made everyone smile and relax. Levela looked at him with love in her eyes. "Why, thank you, Jondecam," she said. "You have to admit, though, that Echozar's eyes are as unusual as Jondalar's, and no less striking. I have never seen such beautiful dark eyes, and the way he looks at Joplaya makes me understand why they are mating. If he looked at me that way, it would be hard to turn him down."

"I like the way Echozar looks," Ayla said, "but yes, his eyes are his best feature."

"If we're all going to say what we think, and get it out in the open," Jondecam said, "you have an unusual way of speaking, Ayla. It takes a little getting used to, but I like it. It makes people take notice and listen. You must come from very far away, though."

"Farther away than you can imagine," Jondalar said.

"And I want to ask one more thing," Jondecam added. "Where is that wolf? Other people have talked about meeting him, and I was hoping to meet him."

Ayla smiled at the man. He was so straightforward and honest, she couldn't help but like him, and so relaxed and comfortable with himself, he made everyone else feel the same way. "Wolf is with Marthona. I thought it might be easier on him and everyone else if he stayed away. But if you stop by the Ninth Cave's camp, I'll be happy to introduce him to you, and I have a feeling he will like you, too," she said. "All of you are welcome," she said, looking at everyone, including the young couple, who were actually smiling in a natural and relaxed way.

"Yes, by all means," Jondalar added. He liked these couples that they had met, but particularly Levela, who was an outgoing and caring young woman, and Jondecam, who reminded him of his brother Thonolan.

They noticed that the First was standing in the center of the lodge, silently waiting for everyone's attention. When she had it, she spoke to them all, telling them of the seriousness of the commitment they were making, repeating some of the things she had said to the women earlier, and giving them some instructions on what was expected of them at the Matrimonial. Then some of the other zelandonia told them where they were supposed to stand and explained where to walk and what to say. They went through a rehearsal of the steps and movements.

Before they left, the First spoke to them again. "Most of you know this, but I want to say it now so it is clear. After the Matrimonial, for a period of half of a moon's cycle—approximately fourteen days using the counting words—the newly mated couples are not allowed to speak to anyone except each other. Only in the case of dire emergency are you to communicate with anyone else, and then only to a donier, who will decide if it was important enough to break the ban. I want you to understand why this is done. It is a way of forcing a couple together to see if they can really live with each other. At the end of the time, if they decide that their mating is incompatible, any couple can decide to break the tie with no consequences. It would be as if they had never mated."

The Zelandoni Who Was First knew most of the couples looked forward to the ban, delighted with the idea of spending time together totally involved with only each other. But at the end, she knew, there would likely be one or two couples who would quietly decide to go their separate ways. She looked carefully at each person trying to judge which couples might last. She was also trying to assess which of the couples would not last even fourteen days. Then she wished them all well and told them the Matrimonial would be the following evening.

Ayla and Jondalar were not concerned that their time alone would prove their union incompatible. They had already spent the better part of a year with only each other for company, except for the brief stops at a few Caves along the route of their Journey. They both looked forward to their period of forced intimacy, especially since there would be no pressures to keep traveling.

After leaving the lodge, the four couples walked together toward their camps. Janida and Peridal turned off first. Before they left, Janida held out both hands to Levela. "I want to thank you," she said, "for including us and making us welcome. When we walked in, it felt like everybody was staring at us, and I didn't know what to do. But I noticed when we left, that people were looking at Joplaya and Echozar, and Ayla and Jondalar, and even you and Jondecam. Maybe everyone was staring at everyone else, but you were the one who made me feel a part of something, not separate and outside of it." She leaned forward and brushed Levela's cheek with hers.

"Janida is an intelligent young woman," Jondalar said after they continued on. "Peridal is lucky to get her, and I hope he appreciates her."

"There does seem to be some real affection between them," Levela said. "I wonder why he was resisting the mating?"

"I would guess the resistance was more from his mother than from him," Jondecam said.

"I think you are right," Ayla said. "Peridal is very young. His mother still has a lot of influence on him. But so is Janida. How many years can each of them count?"

"I think both can count thirteen years. She just barely, he is some moons older, closer to a fourteen-year," Levela said.

"I am an old man next to him," Jondalar said. "I can count a double handful more, twenty-three years. Peridal hasn't even had a chance to live in a fa'lodge yet."

"And I am an old woman," Ayla said. "I can count nineteen years."

"That's not so old, Ayla. I can count twenty years," Joplaya said.

"What about you, Echozar?" Jondecam said. "How many years can you count?"

"I have no idea," he said. "No one ever told me, or even kept track, as far as I know."

"Have you ever tried to think back and remember each year?" Levela asked.

"I have a good memory, but childhood to me is a blur, each season just fading into the next," Echozar said.

"I can count seventeen years," Levela said.

"I'm a twenty-year," Jondecam volunteered. "And here's our camp. We will see you tomorrow." They waved farewell with the beckoning come-back-to-see-us-again motion to the four who continued toward the combined camp of Zelandonii and Lanzadonii.

Ayla woke early on the day she and Jondalar were to be mated. The faint light that preceded the rising sun glimmered feebly through the cracks between the nearly opaque panels of the lodge, highlighting the seams and outlining the opening. She lay still, trying to distinguish details in the shadowy shapes silhouetted against the walls.

She could hear Jondalar's regular breathing. She raised up quietly and looked at the face of the man sleeping beside her in the dim light. The fine straight nose, the square jaw, the high forehead. She remembered the first time she had studied his face while he slept, in the cave of her valley. He was the first man of her own kind she had seen, that she could recall, and he had been badly wounded. She didn't know if he would live, but she thought then that he was beautiful.

She thought so still, although she had learned since that men were not usually called beautiful. Her love for the man swelled to fill her whole being. It was almost more than she could bear, almost painful, excruciatingly full, wonderfully warm. She could hardly contain herself. She got up quietly, dressed quickly, and slipped outside.

She looked out over the camp. From the slightly higher elevation of their campsite she could see The River Valley spread out before her. In the near darkness, the lodges appeared as black mounds rising out of the shadowy earth, each round structure with its center pole supporting the multidwelling units. The camp was still now, so different from the bustling, noisy, boisterous place it would be later.

Ayla turned toward the small creek and followed it upstream. It was growing perceptibly lighter, blotting out more of the twinkling sparks in the sky. The horses in their fenced-in enclosure noticed her approach and nickered softly in greeting. She veered toward them, ducking under the poles strung between posts that defined their area. She put her arm around the hay-colored mare's neck.

"Today is the day Jondalar and I will be mated, Whinney. It seems so long ago that you brought him bleeding and almost dead to the cave. We've come such a long way since then. We'll never see that valley again," Ayla said to the horse.

Racer nudged her, wanting his share of attention. Ayla patted him, then hugged the strong, thick neck of the brown stallion. Wolf appeared from out of the woods, returning from his nightly hunting foray. He loped toward the young woman surrounded by the horses.

"There you are, Wolf," she said. "Where have you been? You were gone this morning." She caught a blur of movement among the trees out of the corner of her eye. She looked up just in time to see a second wolf, a dark one, dodge behind the thick underbrush. She bent over and cupped Wolf's head between both her hands, massaging his furry jowls. "Have you found yourself a mate, or a friend?" she said. "Do you want to go back to the wild like Baby did? I would miss you, but I wouldn't want to keep you from a mate of your own." The wolf growled softly in contentment as Ayla continued rubbing him. He seemed to have no inclination at the moment to return to the shadowy figure in the woods.

The top edge of the sun appeared on the horizon. Ayla smelled the smoke of morning campfires and looked downstream. A few early risers were moving about now. The camp was coming to life.

She saw Jondalar coming toward her in long strides. His brow was wrinkled in concern. The expression was familiar. He is a worrier, she thought. She had become familiar with every line and movement of his face. She often watched him surreptitiously, her eyes always seeking him out wherever he was or whatever he was doing. He knotted his brow the same way when he was concentrating on a new piece of flint, as though trying to see the minute particles in the homogeneous material so he would know in advance which way it would shear. She loved all his expressions, but most of all she loved to see him smiling in his gentle teasing way, or looking at her with his eyes dilated, full of love and desire.

"I woke up and you were gone, Ayla," Jondalar said as he approached.

"I woke up early and couldn't go back to sleep," Ayla said, "so I came outside. I think Wolf has a mate hiding in the woods. That's why he was gone this morning."

"That's a good reason to be gone. If I had a mate, I wouldn't mind running off with her to the woods," he said, a smile erasing the worried frown. He put his arms around her and pulled her close to him, and looked down at her. Her hair was still tousled from sleep, falling loosely down her shoulders and framing her face in a mass of thick, dark blond waves. She had begun to wear her hair coiled neatly around her head in the manner of the women of his Cave, but he still loved it best when it was loose and free, the way it was the first time he saw her standing naked in the bright sunlight on the ledge in front of her cave in the valley, after she had bathed in the river below.

"You'll have one before this day is through," she said. "Where would you like to run off with her?"

"To the end of my life, Ayla," he said as he kissed her.

"There you are! Remember, this is your mating day. No Pleasures until after the ceremony." It was Joharran. "Marthona wants you, Ayla. She asked me to look for you."

Ayla went back to the tent. Marthona had a cup of tea waiting for her. "This will have to do for your breakfast, Ayla. You are supposed to fast today."

"This is fine. I don't think I could eat today anyway. Thank you, Marthona." She watched Jondalar leave with Joharran carrying several bundles and packs.

Jondalar saw Joharran signal to him from across a field as he was about to go into the lodge that he was sharing with several of the men who were going to be mated that night. Most of them had some relational tie with each other, and all of them had one or two of their closest friends or relatives with them. He had just taken all of the things that he would need for the fourteen-day trial period to a small tent that he had set up away from the Summer Meeting camps, near the back of the hill where the new cave was. Although he felt he could have brought the things Ayla would need as well, someone else would bring them later, as was customary.

He waited for his brother just outside the entrance to the lodge. The place was not much different from the bachelor fa'lodges he had often shared with young men at Summer Meetings, young men who wanted to get away from the watchful eyes of their mothers, mothers' mates, and other people in authority. Jondalar recalled the summers spent in such a place with rowdy friends and often, temporarily, by various young women. There was usually good-natured rivalry between the lodges and the young men within them over who could entice the most young women to stay with them. The goal seemed to be for each man to have a different woman every night, except for the nights when they reserved it for the men only.

On those nights, no one slept until dawn. They drank barma, and wine, when they could get it. Some brought various parts of certain plants that were more usually reserved for ceremonial usage. The young men spent the night singing, dancing, telling stories, and gaming, usually mixed with a lot of laughter. On the nights when they invited women, the gatherings usually broke up sooner as couples or mixed groups left the party early for more private entertainment.

The men who were about to be mated were always subjected to jokes and comments from the others in bachelor fa'lodges, something Jondalar took in good humor—he had doled out his share—but the lodge he stayed in now was quieter and the men more serious. They were all facing the same event, and it wasn't quite the joking matter that it was to the young men who were still uncommitted.

All the men who were mating had been banned from the zelandonia lodge where the women were staying, the couples were prohibited from contact with each other until the Matrimonial. While the men were also in lodges away from their camps, they had more freedom. They were not restricted from moving about, except to stay away from the women to whom they were Promised. The men stayed in several smaller dwellings, but all the women, and their close friends and relatives, shared the one lodge. Though the zelandonia lodge was bigger than all the others, it was more crowded than the men's lodges, but the spontaneous outbursts and laughter that emanated from it always made the men curious.

"Jondalar!" Joharran called out to him as he neared. "Marthona wants to see you. At the zelandonia lodge, where the women are."

Jondalar was surprised at the summons, but he hurried, wondering what his mother wanted. He tapped at the post outside the entrance of the lodge, and when the flap moved aside, he couldn't resist craning his neck, trying to see in, hoping to catch a glimpse of Ayla. But Marthona was careful to close the opening behind her. She had a package in her hands, a package that was very familiar to him. It was the one that Ayla had so adamantly insisted on carrying with her on their entire long Journey. He recognized the covering of thin hides tied with cords. He had often been curious about it, but she had always evaded his questions.

"Ayla insisted that I give this to you," Marthona said, shoving the package at him. "You know you are not supposed to have any contact with each other until the ceremony, not even indirectly, but Ayla said she would have given it to you earlier if she had known. She was very upset, almost in tears, and ready to break the prohibition herself if I didn't give it to you. She told me to tell you it is for the Matrimonial."

"Thank you, mother," Jondalar said.

Marthona closed the opening before he could say another word. He walked away, looking at the package as he returned to the lodge. He hefted it to judge the weight, wondering what it could be. It was soft, but seemed rather bulky. That was one reason he couldn't understand why she insisted on keeping it whenever they needed to lighten their load and make more room. Had Ayla carried this the entire way just to give it to him for their Matrimonial? he thought. It seemed too important to casually open it out in the open. He wanted to find a more private place.

Jondalar was glad the lodge was empty when he went in with Ayla's mysterious package. He fumbled for a while, trying to untie the cord, but the knots resisted his efforts and he finally cut it with his knife. He peeled back the protective layers, then looked. It was white. He lifted it out and held it up. It was a beautiful, pure white leather tunic, decorated only with the black-tipped white tails of ermines. She said it was for the Matrimonial. Had she made him a Matrimonial tunic?

He had been offered several outfits to wear and had selected one that was elaborately decorated in the Zelandonii style. But this one was entirely different. The white tunic was cut more in the style of the Mamutoi, but their clothing was usually quite intricately decorated, too, often with beads of ivory, shells, and various other materials. This one had no decoration at all, except for a few ermine tails, but it was genuinely outstanding because of its color. The tunic was a pure, shining white, the most difficult of all shades to color leather, and stunning in its simplicity, because there was no decoration to detract from the purity of the color.

When did she make this? he thought. It could not have been made while they were traveling. There was no time, and besides, she had carried that package with her from the beginning. She must have made it the winter they were living with the Mamutoi, with the Lion Camp. But that was the winter she had Promised to mate with Ranec. Jondalar held the tunic up to himself. It was definitely his size, it would have been much too big for Ranec, who was a shorter man with a more compact body.

Why had she made a tunic for him, especially such a beautiful one, if she was planning to stay with the Mamutoi and live with Ranec? Jondalar clutched the tunic while his mind raced. It was so soft and supple. Her leather always had that quality, but how long had she spent working the leather to make it so soft? And the color. Where had she learned to make white leather? From Nezzie, perhaps? Then he remembered seeing Crozie, the old woman from the Crane hearth, wearing a white outfit at one of the ceremonies when everyone wore their finest clothing. Could Ayla have learned it from her? He couldn't recall ever seeing her working on white leather, but then, maybe he just hadn't been paying attention.

He pulled the silky ermine tails through his fingers. Where had she gotten ermine tails? Then he remembered that she had returned with some ermines the same day she brought the tiny living wolf cub back to the earthlodge. He smiled, remembering what a commotion that had caused. But they had argued—well, he had argued, it was his fault—and he had already moved to the cooking hearth by then. She was visiting Ranec's hearth at night. They were almost Promised. Yet she had probably spent many, many days making this soft, beautiful white tunic for him. Did she love him so much even then?

Jondalar's eyes misted, he was near tears. He knew he had been the one who had treated her coldly. It was his jealousy and, more than that, his fear of what his people would say if they knew who had raised her. He had driven her into the arms of another man, yet she had still spent long days making this garment for him, and then she'd carried it all the way here just to give it to him for their Matrimonial. No wonder she was upset and ready to defy the ban against seeing him to make sure he got it.

He looked at it again. It was not even wrinkled. She must have found some place to straighten it, steam it, after they arrived. He held the tunic to himself, feeling its softness, and almost felt that he was holding her, so much of her went into the making of it. He would have been happy to wear it even if it wasn't so beautiful.

But it was beautiful. The clothes he had chosen to wear for his Matrimonial, for all their decoration, now seemed drab by comparison. Jondalar wore clothes well, and he knew it. He had always secretly prided himself on it, and on his choice of clothing. It was a small vanity that he had learned at his mother's knee, and no one was more gracefully elegant than Marthona. He wondered if she had seen the tunic. Somehow he doubted it. She would have appreciated its stunning subtlety, with the ermine tails giving it just the right touch, and she would have given him some look, some hint.

He looked up as Joharran came into the tent. "There you are, Jondalar. I seem to be spending this day looking for you. You are needed for some special instructions." He noticed the white garment. "What do you have there?" he asked.

"Ayla made me a Matrimonial tunic. That's why mother wanted to see me, to give me this." He held it up in front of himself.

"Jondalar! That is exceptional!" his brother said. "I don't know if I've ever seen white leather so well made. You always have liked to dress well, but in that, you are really going to stand out. There is going to be more than one woman who will wish she were in Ayla's place. But there is more than one man who wouldn't mind being in yours, your big brother included—if it weren't for Proleva, of course."

"I am lucky. You don't even know how lucky, Joharran."

"Well, I want to say, I wish both of you much happiness. I haven't really had the opportunity to tell you before. I used to worry about you sometimes. Especially after that . . . problem you had, when you were sent away. When you came back, you always had women, but I wondered if you would ever find a woman that you would be happy with. You would have mated eventually, I'm sure, but I didn't know if you would ever find the kind of happiness you can have with a good mate like Proleva. I never did think Marona was the right kind of woman for you," Joharran said. Jondalar was moved.

"I know I'm supposed to be making jokes about how sorry you'll be now that you've tied yourself to the responsibilities of a hearth," Joharran continued, "but I will tell you truthfully, Proleva has made my life very happy, and her son brings a special warmth you can get no other way. Did you know she is expecting another?"

"No, I didn't. Ayla is expecting, too. Our mates will have children who are close to the same age, they will be like hearth cousins," Jondalar said with a big grin.

"I feel certain that Proleva's son is the result of my spirit, and I hope the one she is carrying will be, but even if they aren't, the children of his hearth can give a man such pleasure, such a special feeling, it's hard to describe. Looking at Jaradal fills me with such pride and joy."

The two men clasped each other by the shoulders, then hugged. "All this confessing of deep feelings from my big brother," Jondalar said to the slightly shorter man, smiling. Then his expression became more serious. "I'll tell you truthfully, Joharran. I have often envied your happiness, even before I left, before there were any children. I knew then Proleva would be a good woman for you. She makes your hearth a warm and welcome place. And just in the short time since I've returned, I have come to enjoy that little one of hers. And Jaradal looks like you."

"You'd better go, Jondalar. I was told to hurry you along."

Jondalar folded the white tunic, wrapped it loosely in its soft leather covering, and laid it carefully on his bedroll, then he left with his brother, but he looked back over his shoulder at the package, eager to try the white tunic on, the tunic he would wear when he and Ayla were mated.

31

I didn't know I would be so restricted today, or I would have made arrangements," Ayla said. "I need to make sure the horses are all right, and Wolf needs to be able to come and go. He gets upset if he can't check on me."

"This problem has never come up before," Zelandoni of the Fourteenth said. "You are supposed to be in seclusion before the ceremony on the day of your mating. The Histories tell of a time when women had to be in seclusion for an entire moon!"

"That was long ago, when matings were often in the winter, before they were done together in one Matrimonial," the First said. "There were fewer Zelandonii then, and they didn't have gathers the way we do now. For a single Cave to have one or two women restricted for a moon in the middle of winter is one thing, but to have many of them unable to contribute for that long in the hunting and harvesting season during a Summer Meeting is something else entirely. We'd still be trying to get the aurochs stored if the women who are mating had not helped."

"Well, that may be," the older Zelandoni said, "but one day shouldn't be too much."

"And normally it isn't, but the animals make it an exceptional situation," the First donier said. "I'm sure we can work something out."

"Do you object to the wolf coming and going as he chooses?" Marthona said. "The women don't seem to mind him. We only need to allow the lower part of the entrance drape to stay unfastened."

"I don't suppose that would be a problem," the Fourteenth said.

The Fourteenth had been pleasantly surprised when she met the four-legged hunter. He had licked her hand and seemed to warm to her, and she rather liked petting the fur of the living animal. After some questions, Ayla told the story of how she brought the baby wolf cub home and rescued the little filly from the hyenas. She had insisted that if they were young enough when you found them, many animals could probably become friendly with people. The

Fourteenth had noticed how much attention and prestige Wolf brought to the foreign woman and wondered how difficult it would be to befriend an animal, but perhaps a smaller one. The size didn't matter, any animal that would voluntarily stay in close contact with a person would bring attention.

"Then, it's just a matter of the horses. Can't Jondalar attend to them?" Marthona asked.

"Of course he can, but I need to tell him that he should. I'm the one who has been doing it since we arrived at the Summer Meeting because he's been busy with other things," Ayla said.

"She's not allowed to communicate with him," the Fourteenth insisted. "She can't tell him anything!"

"But someone else can," Marthona said.

"Not someone involved with the ceremony, I'm afraid. Not anyone who is related," the Zelandoni of the Nineteenth said. "The Fourteenth is right, of course, and because women no longer stay in seclusion as long, it is even more important that we adhere to the day of seclusion strictly." The white-haired woman may have been nearly crippled from her arthritis, but it did not limit her strength of character. Ayla had seen that before.

Marthona was glad she hadn't mentioned that she had given Jondalar the package from Ayla. The zelandonia would have been quite annoyed with her. They could get very adamant about complying with proper customs and behavior during important ceremonies, and while the former leader generally went along with them, privately she felt that exceptions could always be made. Leaders had to learn when to stand fast and when to bend a little.

"Can someone who is not involved with the ceremony be told?" Ayla asked.

"Who do you know that is absolutely not related to either you or your Promised?" the Fourteenth asked.

Ayla thought for a moment. "What about Lanidar? Marthona, is he related to Jondalar in any way?" she asked.

"No . . . no, he is not. I know that I am not, and Dalanar just mentioned to me on the morning they visited that he had been selected for the boy's grandmother's First Rites," Marthona said. "So he's not."

"That's true," the Nineteenth said. "I remember that Denoda was quite . . . overwhelmed by Dalanar. It took her some time to get over him. He handled it well. He was tactful, considerate, but kept his distance. I was impressed."

"Always," Marthona said, almost under her breath, and finished in her thoughts, he always was entirely correct, did exactly the right thing.

The Nineteenth wasn't going to let it go. "Always what? Tactful? Considerate? Impressive?" she asked.

Marthona smiled. "All of them," she said.

"And Jondalar is the child of his hearth," the First said.

"Yes," Marthona said, "but there are differences. The boy doesn't have quite the tact of the man, but perhaps more heart."

"No matter what man's spirit started him, the child always has something of the mother, too," the Zelandoni Who Was First said.

Ayla listened carefully to the rather oblique conversation, especially after Jondalar was mentioned, and detected the mannerisms of voice and body that communicated even more than words. She understood that the Nineteenth's comment about Denoda was less than complimentary, and sensed that the older Zelandoni had been quite attracted to Dalanar. There was also an implication that Marthona's son had not shown the same refinement as her former mate—they all knew about his youthful indiscretions, of course. Marthona was aware of the old woman's feeling toward both of them, and let her know that she knew Dalanar better and wasn't quite as impressed with him.

The First told them that she also knew both men and suggested that Jondalar was just like Dalanar and had the same attractive qualities, not less. She also paid an implied compliment to Marthona because Dalanar's spirit and the Mother had chosen her to make the child of his hearth. Ayla was becoming aware that a woman who was chosen to have children by spirit of the man to whom she was mated was held in higher esteem. Marthona made it clear to the zelandonia, especially to the Zelandoni of the Nineteenth, that while her son might not have all of Dalanar's fine qualities, he had some that were better. The First not only agreed with her, but said that his better qualities came from his mother. It was obvious that the former leader and the Zelandoni of the Ninth Cave had a close personal relationship and great respect for each other.

There were subtleties within subtleties that added meaning to the sign language of the Clan, including the understanding of facial expressions and postures as well as gestures and even some words, but the language that employed every nuance of voice, tone, and inflection as well as facial expressions, unconscious postures, and ancillary gestures conveyed even more, if one could grasp it. Ayla was very familiar with the unconscious signals of body language and was learning how they were expressed by the Others, but she was also becoming more consciously aware of spoken words and the manner in which they were used.

"Can someone find Lanidar," Ayla said, "so I can ask him to find Jondalar?"

"No, you can't ask him, Ayla," Marthona said. "But I will," she looked at the zelandonia who were gathered in the lodge that had become the mating women's lodge, "if someone will go and look for him."

"Of course," the First said. She looked around to see who was available and signaled Mejera, now an acolyte of the Zelandoni of the Third Cave. She was with them when they had gone to search for Thonolan's elan in the Deep of Fountain Rocks. She had been with the Fourteenth Cave then, but unhappy there. Ayla recognized her and smiled.

"I have an errand for you," the First said. "Marthona will explain."

"Do you know the boy Lanidar of the Nineteenth Cave?" Marthona started. There was no nod of recognition. "He's the son of Mardena, her mother is Denoda." Mejera shook her head in negation.

"He can count about twelve years, but he looks younger," Ayla added, "and his right arm is deformed."

A smile of affirmation creased Mejera's face. "Yes, of course. He threw a spear at the demonstration."

"That's the one," Marthona said. "You need to find him, and when you do, tell him to find Jondalar and give him a message from me. Tell Lanidar to tell Jondalar that Ayla is concerned about the horses, and he needs to see to them before the Matrimonial tonight. Do you understand?"

"Wouldn't it be easier if I went and told Jondalar?" Mejera said.

"It would be far easier, but you have a role in the Matrimonial this evening, and therefore you cannot give a message to Jondalar until afterward, certainly not from Ayla, even through me. However, if you cannot find Lanidar, I understand it would be acceptable for you to tell anyone else who is not related to him to give him the message. Do you understand?"

"Yes, I'll do it. Don't worry about them, Ayla, I'll make sure he knows," Mejera said, then hurried out.

"I suppose the zelandonia would find something objectionable about Mejera talking to you about it, so I don't think we have to explain in detail," Marthona said. "And we don't have to mention the package you wanted to give him."

"I think we can refrain from mentioning anything," Ayla said.

"Now, it's time for you to start getting ready," Marthona said.

"But it's just past noon. It's a long time until nightfall," Ayla said. "It won't take that long to put on the tunic Nezzie made for me."

"There's more to it than that. We will all be going to The River so the women who are to be mated can bathe. They are even boiling water to purify it for the ritual. Not to mention, hot water is very nice for washing with. That's one of the nicest parts of the pre-mating rituals. Jondalar and the men will be doing the same thing, in a different place, of course," Marthona explained.

"I love hot water," Ayla said. "The Losadunai have a hot-water spring near their shelter. You can't imagine how wonderful it feels to bathe in it."

"Yes, I can. I took a trip north once or twice. Not far from the source of The River, there are pools of hot water in the ground," Marthona said.

"I think I know the place, or one like it. We stopped there on our way here," Ayla said. "There is one thing I wanted to ask. I meant to ask earlier, and I don't know if it's too late, but I was hoping to get my ears pierced. I have those two matched ambers that were given to me by Tulie, the headwoman of the Lion Camp, and I wanted to wear them, if I can find some way to hang them from my ears. That's how she said I should wear them."

"I think that can be arranged," the woman said. "I'm sure one of the zelandonia will be happy to do it for you."

"What do you think, Folara, this way? Or this way?" Mejera said as she held a section of Ayla's hair in her hand and showed the young woman two alternatives. Folara had joined them when they returned to the zelandonia lodge, after their cleansing rituals. Though many lamps had been lit, it was still much darker inside than out in the bright sun, and Ayla wished she were out rather than sitting there while someone did things with her hair.

"I like the first way better," Folara said.

"Mejera, why don't you finish telling us where you finally found them," Marthona said. It was obvious that Ayla was uncomfortable. She was not used to having someone fixing her hair, and the young acolyte seemed quite adept at talking while she was working. Marthona thought it might distract her.

"Well, as I was saying, I asked everyone. No one seemed to know where either one of them was. Finally someone at your camp, I think it was the mate of one of Joharran's close friends, Solaban or Rushemar, the one who has a baby. She was making a basket . . ."

"That's Rushemar's mate, Salova," Marthona said.

"She said that one or the other might be with the horses, so I followed the creek upstream and that's where I found both of them. Lanidar said his mother told him that you would be with the women all day, Ayla, so he decided he should check on the horses, like you asked. And Jondalar said the same thing, more or less. He knew you'd be with the women in seclusion all day and decided to see how the horses were doing. He found Lanidar there and was showing him how to use that spear-thrower thing," Mejera explained.

"It turned out that I wasn't the only one who was looking for Jondalar. Joharran came a little later. He looked a little angry, or maybe just irritated. He'd been looking all over for Jondalar, to tell him that he was supposed to go to The River for his ritual purification with the rest of the men. Jondalar told me to tell you that the horses are fine, and that you were right, Wolf may have found a mate or a friend. He saw them together."

"Thank you, Mejera, it relieves my mind to know that Whinney and Racer are all right. I can't tell you how much I appreciate all your time and effort to find Lanidar and Jondalar," Ayla said.

She was glad to know that the horses were fine, and pleased that Lanidar had seen to them on his own. She normally would have expected it of Jondalar, but he was going to be mated, too, after all, and she had just wanted to make sure that he hadn't been distracted, or prevented, from checking on them. But she was a little worried about Wolf. Part of her wanted him to find a mate and be happy, but another part dreaded the thought of losing him, and she was concerned for him.

Wolf never lived with other wolves, she had probably spent more time around them when she was teaching herself to hunt than he ever did. She knew that while wolves were extremely loyal to their own pack, they defended their territory against other wolves fiercely. If Wolf had found a female lone wolf, or a low-ranked female from a nearby pack, and decided to live like a wolf, he would have to fight to make a territory of his own. While Wolf was a strong, healthy animal, bigger than most wolves, he hadn't been raised in a pack where he play-fought with siblings from the time he was a puppy. He wasn't used to fighting wolves.

"Thank you, Mejera. Ayla looks very nice. I didn't know you were so skilled at arranging hair," Marthona said.

Ayla reached up with both hands and gingerly felt her hair, gently touching the rolls and other shapes into which it had been coaxed and pinned. She had seen some of the other young women with what she was sure were similar arrangements, so she had some idea of how it looked.

"Let me get a reflector, so you can see it," Mejera said.

The dim image in the reflector showed a young woman with her hair fixed in a way that was similar to that of most of the other young women in the lodge. It just wasn't anyone she recognized as herself. She wasn't even sure Jondalar would.

"Let's put the matched ambers in your ears," Folara said. "You should start getting dressed."

The acolyte who had pierced Ayla's ears had left a sliver of bone through each of the holes. She had also wrapped some sinew around the front and back and both sides of the ambers and left loops that attached to the bones that pierced the lower fleshy part of her ears. Mejera helped Folara to attach the ambers to Ayla's ears.

Then Ayla put on her special mating outfit. Mejera was dazzled. "I have never seen anything like that," she breathed.

And Folara was delighted. "Ayla, that is so beautiful, and so unusual. Everyone is going to want one like it. Where did you get it?"

"I brought it with me. Nezzie made it for me. She's the mate of the headman of the Lion Camp. This is how it should be worn for the ceremony," Ayla explained as she opened the front to expose her breasts, even fuller now with her advancing pregnancy, then retied the sash. "Nezzie said a Mamutoi woman should proudly display her breasts when she is mated. Now I want to put on the necklace you gave me, Marthona."

"There is a problem with that, Ayla," Marthona said. "The necklace would look beautiful with the big piece of amber nestled between your breasts, but not with that leather pouch that you wear around your neck. The necklace won't show. I know it means something to you, but I think you should remove it."

"She's right, Ayla," Folara said.

"Let me show you in the reflector," Mejera said. She held up the piece of sanded, blackened, and oiled wood so Ayla could see.

It was the same strange woman that she had seen before, but this time Ayla saw the ambers dangling from her ears, and her worn amulet bag, lumpy with the objects it contained, hanging from a frayed cord.

"What is that pouch?" Mejera asked. "It looks full of things."

"It's my amulet, and the objects inside are all gifts from my totem, the Spirit of the Cave Lion. Most of them confirmed important decisions in my life. It holds my life spirit, too, in a sense."

"It's something like an elandon, then," Marthona said.

"The Mog-ur told me that if I ever lose my amulet, I will die," Ayla said. She grasped her amulet and felt the familiar lumps and bulges, and a kaleidoscope of memories of her life with the Clan rushed back.

"Then we need to keep it in a very special place," Marthona said. "Perhaps near a donii so the Mother can watch over it. But you don't have a donii, do you? Usually a woman gets one at her First Rites. I don't suppose you ever had a ceremony like that?"

"Well, yes, in fact I did. Jondalar taught me the Mother's Gift of Pleasure, and the first time, he made a ceremony of it and gave me a donii figure that he made himself. I have it in my backpack," Ayla said.

"Well, I suspect if anyone could make a proper First Rites ceremony for you, he could. He's had enough experience at it," Marthona said. "Why don't you let me take care of that amulet for you now, and when you and Jondalar leave to begin your trial period, I'll give it back to you so you can take it with you." The woman saw Ayla hesitate, then finally nod her head in agreement, but when she started to slip the leather bag off over her head, the leather cord got caught up in her new hairstyle.

"That's all right, Ayla. I can fix it," Mejera said.

Ayla held the familiar leather bag in her hand, reluctant to give it up. They were right, it didn't look good with her Matrimonial finery, but she hadn't been without it since Iza gave it to her, not long after she was found by the Clan. It had been a part of her for so long, it was hard to let it go. More than hard, she was afraid to let it go. It seemed the amulet itself had clung to her, grabbing at her hair when she took it off. Maybe her totem was trying to tell her something, maybe she shouldn't try to be only one of the Others on this day of her mating, with her Mamutoi clothes and her Zelandonii necklace. She had been hardly more than a woman of the Clan when she met Jondalar, maybe she ought to keep something of that time, too.

"Thank you, Mejera, but I think I've changed my mind. I'm going to wear my hair down and loose. Jondalar likes it that way," Ayla said. She held the amulet a moment longer, then handed it to Marthona. She let the woman fasten around her neck the necklace that had been given by Dalanar's mother and saved for her, before she started taking out the pins and ties that held her hair in the elegant Zelandonii style.

Mejera hated to see all her effort taken apart, but it was Ayla's choice, not hers. "Let me comb it for you," she said, acceding gracefully, which impressed Marthona. I think this young acolyte is going to be a fine Zelandoni someday, she thought.

When Jondalar and the rest of the men who were going to be mated started walking toward the zelandonia lodge near the foot of the slope where the ceremony was to be held, he suddenly felt nervous. He wasn't alone. The women had moved, leaving the big lodge empty. With the help of several of the zelandonia, the men arranged themselves in the order they had practiced, first according to the counting word of the Cave where they would live, and then by their rank within the Cave. Since all counting words were powerful—only the zelandonia knew the enigmatic differences among them—they did not designate rank, it was simply an ordering, a way to line up. The unnumbered and often unmentioned but perfectly understood ranking within the Cave was another story, although it wasn't hard and fast.

A person's status could change, and the position of many would, as a result of their upcoming matings. It was one of the many agreements that were negotiated prior to the ceremony. The rank of some would be higher, some lower than they had been before, because the status of the hearth was a combination of what both brought to the union, which also determined the status of any children. It was understood that the resulting hearth belonged to the man, but was tended by the woman; children that were born to the woman were also born to the hearth of the man. They and their families both wanted the status of the new hearth to be as high as possible for the sake of the children, and for the names and ties of those related to them, but a certain number of other Cave leaders and zelandonia had to agree. It could sometimes be a contentious negotiation.

Ayla hadn't been much involved in the negotiations for the status of her and Jondalar's new hearth, she wouldn't have understood the nuances anyway, but Marthona did. The oblique conversation that Marthona had had earlier with some of the zelandonia, including Zelandoni of the Nineteenth, that Ayla was beginning to understand, had been an element of those negotiations. The Nineteenth had been trying to use Jondalar's youthful indiscretions to bring down his status partly because Ayla had discovered the exceptional new cave within the territory of the Nineteenth Cave. The find had brought her status up considerably, even though she was foreign born, but it had embarrassed Zelandoni of the Nineteenth somewhat. If they had found the cave, they could have kept it private and limited who used it, giving them significant prestige. But the fact that it was found by a foreign woman during a Summer Meeting immediately opened it up to everyone, a point that was made clear by the First.

Jondalar's ranking was among the highest, with his mother as a former leader and his brother as the present leader of the largest Cave of the Zelandonii, not to mention his own contributions, some of which he brought back from his travels. Increased skill at flint-knapping, a complex talent that had to be attested to by respected and knowledgeable flint-knappers from other Caves, and the new, publicly demonstrated spear-thrower contributed, but determining Ayla's status had presented a problem. Foreigners always had the lowest status, which would normally bring the ranking of the new hearth down, but Marthona and several others were fighting it by claiming that her status among her own people was very high, and she had many attributes of her own. The animals were an ambiguous factor, with some saying they lowered her status and others saying they raised it. The ultimate ranking of the new hearth was still not fully resolved, though it did not prevent the mating. The Ninth Cave had accepted her, and that's where they would be living.

The women had moved to another lodge nearby. Until recently, it had housed the young women preparing for their First Rites, but was now empty and could be put to other uses. Someone had suggested that the men could have waited there so the women would not have to move, but the idea of going from housing girls during their transition into womanhood, to men about to be mated made the zelandonia and others uncomfortable. There were always lingering manifestations of spiritual forces whenever transcendent activities were involved, especially with a sizable group, and the significant vitalities of men and women were sometimes in opposition. It was decided to move the women who were to be mated there instead, since it was the next logical step for the girls who had previously occupied the dwelling.

The women were no less nervous than the men. Ayla wondered if Jondalar would decide to wear the tunic she had made for him, and wished she had known that she would not be allowed to talk to him today so she could have given it to him herself the day before. Then she would know if he thought it was appropriate and if he liked it. Now, she would not know until they came together for the Matrimonial.

The women were arranged in order, too, the same order as the men so they would match up properly. Ayla smiled at Levela, who was ahead of her. She would have liked to stand next to Proleva's sister while she was waiting, but she was of the Ninth Cave, and there were several women who stood between her and the young woman, who would be going to live at the Second Cave with Jondecam. Their rankings were similar since they came from the families of leaders and founders, those with the highest status, so the position of their combined hearth did not change much. Jondecam's status was a shade higher than Levela's, but the minor benefit could be accrued only if they lived at his Cave.

The Zelandoni of the Cave where the couple would ultimately live conducted the ceremony for each individual couple, with others acting as assistants. The mothers of the young people and their mates were also part of the ceremony, and often close family, who were in the front part of the audience, waiting until they would be asked to play their role. With older couples for whom it was not a first mating, but who wanted to declare a formal arrangement, no parents were necessary. They needed only the agreement of the Cave they would be living with, but they often included friends and relatives in their ceremony.

Ayla noticed Janida toward the rear, since she was of the South Holding of the Twenty-ninth Cave, and smiled at her when she glanced up in Ayla's direction. At the very back she saw Joplaya, also a foreign woman, a Lanzadonii, though the man of her hearth had once been a first-ranked Zelandonii. Though her position was last here, she was among the first of the Lanzadonii, and that was all that counted. Ayla looked around at all the women who were going to be mated tonight. There were still so many she didn't recognize, and Caves from which she hadn't met a single person, except during general introductions. She had overheard someone say she was of the

Twenty-fourth Cave, and someone else said she was from Bear Hill, a part of New Home on the Little Grass River.

To Ayla, the waiting seemed interminable. What could be taking so long? she wondered. They had to hurry to get in order, now they were just standing around. Maybe they were still waiting for the men. Maybe one of them changed his mind. What if Jondalar changed his mind? No. He wouldn't! Why should he? But, what if he did?

Inside the zelandonia lodge, the First moved aside the drape that covered the concealed private access at the rear of the large dwelling, directly across from the regular entrance, and pushed the screen aside. She peeked out and scanned the assembly area that came down from the hillside behind and opened out onto the camp. People had been gathering all afternoon and it was nearly full. It was time.

The men filed out first. When Jondalar looked up the slope, he was sure that every person who possibly could be there was in attendance. The murmuring hum of the crowd increased, and he thought he heard the word "white" more than once. He kept his eyes on the back of the man in front of him, but he knew the white leather tunic was making an impression. In fact, it was more than the white tunic. The tall, incredibly handsome, fair-haired man with the captivating eyes would have stood out anyway, but when his blond hair was clean it was nearly white, and bathed and freshly shaved, wearing the pure, shining white tunic, he was stunning.

"If I could imagine Doni's lover, Lumi, come to earth in human form, there he stands," said Jondecam's mother, the tall blond Zelandoni of the Second Cave to her younger brother, Kimeran, the leader of the Second Cave.

"I wonder where he got that white tunic. I wouldn't mind one like it," Kimeran said.

"I think every man here must feel that way, though I think you'd be one of the few who might wear it as well, Kimeran," she said. In her opinion, her brother was not only as tall and fair as his friend Jondalar, he was as handsome, or nearly so. "Jondecam looks wonderful, too. I'm glad he kept his beard this summer. He looks so good in it."

After the men lined up, forming a semicircle around one side of the huge bonfire, it was the women's turn. Ayla strained to see out when the entrance drape was finally opened. It was almost evening. The sun, not quite set, overwhelmed the large ceremonial fire with its coruscating brilliance and made indistinct the torches that had been placed around the area. They would be welcome enough later. She could see several people near the fire. The large figure with her back to her had to be Zelandoni. A signal was given and the women came out.

The moment Ayla stepped outside the lodge, she saw the tall figure in the white leather. As they formed a semicircle opposite the men, she said to herself, He's wearing it! He's wearing my tunic. Everyone was dressed in his finest, but no one else was wearing white, and he stood out from all the rest. In her mind, he was by far the most beautiful ... no, the most handsome man there. Most agreed with her. She saw him looking at her across the intervening distance, well lighted by the large fire, and he was staring as though he couldn't look anyplace else.

She is so beautiful, he thought. She had never looked so beautiful. The deep straw-colored, dark golden-yellow tunic Nezzie had made for her, with pale ivory highlights of decorative beads, almost perfectly matched her hair, which tumbled down loosely, the way he liked it best.

Her only jewelry were the amber earrings in her newly pierced ears—the matched ambers from Tulie, he remembered—and the amber-and-shell necklace Marthona had given to her. The brilliant yellow-orange stones picked up highlights from the setting sun and shone resplendently between her bare breasts. The tunic, open in front but cinched at the waist, was unlike any of the others, but it suited Ayla perfectly.

Marthona, watching from the front of the audience, was pleasantly surprised when her son appeared in the white tunic. She knew the garment he had originally chosen, and it wasn't hard to conclude that the white tunic was in the package she had delivered to Jondalar. The lack of decoration enhanced the simple purity of the color, which was embellishment enough. It didn't need any more, although the ermine tails were a nice touch. She had seen the few bowls and implements Ayla used and noticed her penchant for simple but well-made objects. The white tunic was an outstanding example of that. There was something to be said for letting quality be its own adornment.

The simplicity of his outfit also made a striking contrast to hers. Marthona was certain that attempts would be made to copy Ayla's outfit by more than one of the women watching, though probably none would get it quite right. She had examined it carefully when Ayla first showed it to her and knew the exquisite quality of the workmanship. Her outfit displayed wealth in the only way that had meaning for the Zelandonii: the time it took to make it. From the quality of the leather to the amber and the shells and the teeth, to the several thousand individually hand-carved ivory beads, this mating outfit was going to prove her case for Ayla's high status. Her son's hearth would be among the first.

Jondalar had eyes for no one but Ayla. Her eyes were bright, her mouth partly open to help fill her lungs, heaving with excitement. It was the look she wore when she was awed by something beautiful, or excited by the hunt, and Jondalar felt the blood draw to his loins. She is a golden woman, Jondalar thought. Golden like the sun. He wanted her, and he could hardly believe that this sensuously beautiful woman was going to be his mate. His mate . . . he liked the sound of that. She would share the home he planned to surprise her with. Would the ceremony ever begin? Would it ever end? He didn't want to wait, he wanted to run over to her, pick her up, and carry her off.

The zelandonia had gathered around, and the First began a haunting chant. Then another Zelandoni joined in with a steady tone, and then a third. Each donier chose a sound, a tone with a pitch and timbre that sometimes varied in a repetitive melody, but that each was comfortable with sustaining. As the Zelandoni who would join the first couple began to speak, a whole chorus was maintaining a soft, continuous chant in the background, each one making a distinct tone. The combination might or might not be harmonic, it didn't matter. Before the first one got out of breath, another voice would join in, and then another, and another at random intervals. The result was a droning, interweaving fugue of tones that could go on indefinitely, if there were enough people to provide sufficient rest for those people who had to stop for a while.

Though it was only in the background, the pleasant drone filled his mind as Jondalar stared, entranced, at the woman he loved. He hardly heard the words spoken by the zelandonia for the first few couples. Then he felt a slight poke from the man behind him, and jumped. They were saying his name. He walked toward the massive figure of Zelandoni, watching Ayla coming to meet him. They stood facing each other on opposite sides of the donier.

Zelandoni looked approvingly at both of them. Jondalar was the tallest of the men, and she had always thought he was by far the most attractive man she had ever seen. Though he was hardly more than a boy those many years ago, it was one reason she had chosen to teach him Doni's Gift of Pleasure when it was his time to learn. And he had learned well, almost too well. He had almost convinced her not to follow her calling.

She was glad now that circumstances had intervened, but looking at him in that spectacular white tunic, she knew again why he had almost persuaded her. She wondered where he had gotten the white tunic, no doubt on his Journey. The color, of course, immediately caught the eye, but it was also unusual in design, and its very lack of decoration made it exotic. He matched the woman he had chosen. She turned to look at Ayla.

And she matched him. No, she surpassed him, and that was not easy, Zelandoni thought. The donier would have been disappointed had he chosen someone not up to her opinion of him, but Zelandoni had to admit he had not only found a woman who was his equal, he had gone one better. She knew they were the center of attention, for many reasons. Everyone knew them, or knew who they were, they had been the talk of the Summer Meeting, and they were by far the handsomest couple there.

It was right, fitting, that she, First Among Those Who Served The Mother, should conduct the ceremony and be the one to tie the knot for the most outstanding pair. Zelandoni herself was a presence to be reckoned with. The tattooed design on her forehead had been reinforced with stronger colors, her hair was carefully, if somewhat outlandishly, styled, which appeared to make the tall woman even taller, and the heavily decorated long tunic was a work of art that almost needed a person of her size to be displayed adequately. All eyes were drawn to the trio, and Zelandoni paused to heighten the dramatic impact.

Marthona had stepped forward to stand beside her son, with her present mate, Willamar, on her right and a pace behind. On her left was Dalanar, and just behind him was Jerika. They would have to wait until the very end before her daughter, Joplaya, and Echozar would be mated. Arrayed beside Willamar were Folara and Joharran, Jondalar's sister and brother. Near Joharran was Proleva and her son, Jaradal. Many other friends and relatives were in the audience nearby in a place set aside for the use of the couple during their ceremony. Zelandoni looked at them all, then up at the large crowd on the slope before she began.

"All Caves of the Zelandonii," the donier said in a solemn resonant voice. "You are called upon to share in witnessing the joining of a woman and a man. Doni, Great Earth Mother, First Creator, the

Mother of All, She Who gave birth to Bali, who lights the sky, and She Whose mate and friend, Lumi, shines down upon us this night in witness with Her. She is honored by the sacred joining of Her children."

Ayla glanced up at the moon. It was gibbous, slightly more than half-full, and she suddenly realized it was dark out. The sun had set some time before, but the huge bonfire and many torches made it seem almost bright as day.

"The two standing here have pleased the Great Earth Mother by choosing to join together. Jondalar of the Ninth Cave of the Zelandonii, Son of Marthona, former Leader of the Ninth Cave, now mated to Willamar, Trading Master of the Zelandonii, born to the Hearth of Dalanar, Founder and Leader of the Lanzadonii, Brother of Joharran, Leader of the Ninth Cave of the Zelandonii . . ."

Ayla's mind couldn't help but wander as Zelandoni continued with the long, full recitation of Jondalar's names and ties, most of whom she didn't know. This was one of the few times when all his connections would be stated. Her attention was caught again when the donier's tone changed after the long litany.

". . . do you choose Ayla of the Ninth Cave of the Zelandonii, Blessed of Doni, and Honored by Her Blessing . . ." There was an undercurrent of murmuring. It was a lucky mating. She was already pregnant. ". . . formerly Ayla of the Mamutoi, Member of the Lion Camp, Daughter of the Mammoth Hearth, Chosen by the Spirit of the Cave Lion, Protected by the Cave Bear, Friend of the horses named Whinney and Racer, and the four-legged hunter, Wolf."

Ayla wondered where Wolf was. He'd been gone all afternoon and evening, and she was disappointed. She knew it wouldn't mean much to him, but she had hoped he would be there for her mating.

". . . Accepted by Joharran, Brother of Jondalar and Leader of the Ninth Cave of the Zelandonii, and by Marthona, Mother of Jondalar and former Leader of the Ninth Cave, Approved by Dalanar, Founder and Leader of the Lanzadonii, man of the hearth at Jondalar's birth . . ."

Zelandonii continued naming most of Jondalar's kin. Ayla didn't realize she was gaining so many new ties with this mating, but Zelandoni wished there were more. She had had to think long and hard to come up with enough legitimate ties to make the ritual appropriate. Ayla brought so few with her.

"I choose her," Jondalar was responding, facing Ayla.

"Will you respect her, care for her when she is sick, provide for her when she is with child, and help provide for all of the children born to your hearth while you are living together?" Zelandoni intoned.

"I will respect her, care for her, provide for her and her children," Jondalar said.

"And Ayla of the Ninth Cave of the Zelandonii, formerly Ayla of the Mamutoi, Member of the Lion Camp, Daughter of the Mammoth Hearth, Chosen by the Spirit of the Cave Lion, Protected by the Cave Bear, Accepted by the Ninth Cave of the Zelandonii, do you choose Jondalar of the Ninth Cave of the Zelandonii, Son of Marthona, former Leader of the Ninth Cave, now mated to Willamar, Trading Master of the Zelandonii, born to the Hearth of Dalanar, Founder and Leader of the Lanzadonii." Zelandonii had decided to name only the essential ties, rather than making a second recitation of all of them. Ayla was relieved—along with most of the people there.

"I choose him," Ayla said, looking at Jondalar. Her words resounded in her head. I choose him. I choose him. I chose him a long time ago, now I can finally choose him.

"Will you respect him, care for him when he is sick, teach your children to respect him as befits your mate and their provider, including the one Doni has already Blessed you with?" Zelandoni continued.

"I will respect him, care for him, and teach my children to respect him," Ayla said.

Zelandoni made a signal. "Who has the authority to approve the joining of this man to this woman?"

Marthona took a few steps forward. "I, Marthona, former Leader of the Ninth Cave of the Zelandonii, have the authority. I agree to the mating of my son, Jondalar, with Ayla of the Ninth Cave of the Zelandonii," she said.

Then Willamar stepped forward. "I, Willamar, Master Trader of the Zelandonii, mated to Marthona, former Leader of the Ninth Cave, also agree to this mating." Willamar's agreement wasn't essential, but his inclusion in the ceremony added approval to the mating of his mate's son to a foreign woman and made it easier to include Marthona's former mate, who was taking a step forward.

"I, Dalanar, Founder and Leader of the Lanzadonii, man of the hearth at Jondalar's birth, also agree to this mating of Jondalar, the son of my former mate, with Ayla of the Ninth Cave of the Zelandonii, formerly Ayla of the Mamutoi."

Dalanar gave Ayla a look of appreciation that was so much like Jondalar's, she almost smiled as she felt her body respond the same way. It was not the first time. Dalanar and Jondalar not only looked alike, except for the age difference, to Ayla they felt alike. Then she couldn't resist and smiled at the older man, one of her radiant smiles that seemed to beam like a light from within, and for just a moment, he almost wished he could trade places with the son of his mate. Then he looked at Jondalar and saw a smirking grin. That boy knew just what he was feeling and couldn't wait to tease him about it! He almost laughed out loud.

"I approve without question!" Dalanar added.

"Who has the authority to approve the joining of this woman with this man?" Zelandoni asked.

"I, Ayla of the Ninth Cave of the Zelandonii, formerly Ayla of the Mamutoi, Member of the Lion Camp and Daughter of the Mammoth Hearth, have the authority to speak on my own behalf. The authority was given to me by the Mamut of the Mammoth Hearth, eldest and most respected of all the mamuti, by Talut, headman of the Lion Camp, and by his sister, Tulie, headwoman of the Lion Camp. In their name, I agree to this mating with Jondalar of the Ninth Cave of the Zelandonii," Ayla said. That had been the part she was most nervous about, to memorize and repeat the words she was supposed to say.

"Mamut of the Mammoth Hearth, the One Who Serves The Mother for the Mamutoi," Zelandoni said, "gave the Daughter of his Hearth the freedom to decide for herself. As One Who Serves The Mother for the Zelandonii, I can also speak for Mamut. Ayla has chosen to mate with Jondalar, therefore her decision is the same as Mamut's agreement." Then Zelandoni said, throwing her voice so all could hear, "Who speaks for this couple?"

"I, Joharran, Leader of the Ninth Cave of the Zelandonii, speak for this couple, and welcome Jondalar and Ayla to the Ninth Cave of the Zelandonii," Jondalar's older brother said. Then he turned to face the people gathered behind him in the audience.

"We of the Ninth Cave of the Zelandonii welcome them," they said in unison.

Then Zelandoni held out both her arms, as though trying to embrace everyone there. "All the Caves of the Zelandonii," she said, her tone commanding attention. "Jondalar and Ayla have chosen each other. It has been agreed, and they have been accepted by the Ninth Cave. What do you say to this joining?"

There was a roar of approval. If anyone had disagreed, the objection would have been drowned out. The donier waited for the noise to subside, then she said, "Doni, the Great Earth Mother approves this joining of Her children. By Blessing Ayla, She has smiled on this union." At her signal, Ayla and Jondalar held hands and extended them toward the Zelandoni Who Was First. She took a simple leather thong, wrapped it around their joined hands, and tied it with a knot. When they returned from their trial period, they would return the thong whole, not cut, and in exchange they would be given matched necklaces, a gift from the zelandonia. That would be the signal that their joining was sanctioned and other gifts could now be given.

"The knot has been tied. You are mated. May Doni always smile on you." The young couple circled around to face outward toward the people, and Zelandoni announced, "They are now Jondalar and Ayla of the Ninth Cave of the Zelandonii."

They all stepped away together, including the One Who Was First To Serve The Great Earth Mother, to make room for the next couple. While everyone else moved back farther into the audience to make room for the family of the next couple, Ayla and Jondalar walked to where the other couples who had thongs tied around their wrists were waiting. They were not quite through.

Though most people watching enjoyed the spectacle of seeing this pair who had been so favored make their commitments and have their wrists bound, there were a few for whom the mating brought out other feelings entirely. One was a beautiful woman with nearly white hair, very fair skin, and gray eyes that were so dark, they were nearly black. Most men looked at Marona approvingly, until they saw her disagreeable frown, but she ignored them.

Marona was not smiling with approval at the lovely couple. She was glaring with pure hatred at the foreign woman and the man who had once Promised himself to her. She was supposed to have been the center of attention that year, but instead he went on a Journey and left her stranded with no man to mate. To make it worse, his close cousin had come, that strange-looking black-haired woman that everyone said was so beautiful—who was going to mate the ugliest man she had ever seen—and she got all the attention. Yes, she had found a reasonably acceptable man to mate before the summer was over, but he wasn't Jondalar, the man everyone wanted and she was supposed to get. They were both happy to sever the knot a few years later. It had been the worst Summer Meeting Marona had ever endured, until now.

This year, Jondalar had finally returned, but with a foreign woman, who insisted on having animals around her and didn't even care if she wore boys' underwear. Now they were mated, and she was pregnant, already Blessed. It wasn't fair. And where did she get that outfit she was wearing, open, and showing off her breasts? Marona wouldn't have hesitated to wear an outfit like that, if she had thought of it first, but she never would now, even if all the other women did, and she knew they would. Someday, Marona said to herself. Someday I'll find a way to show them. Someday he'll be sorry, they'll both be sorry. Someday.

There were others who were not particularly pleased with the pairing. Laramar just didn't like either one of them. Jondalar always looked at him with disdain, even when he was drinking his barma, and that woman Ayla, with that wolf, who made such an issue about Tremeda's youngest and had Lanoga thinking she was so wonderful. Lanoga wasn't even there to fix him a meal half the time anymore. Instead she was sitting around with those other women just like that baby was hers, and she wasn't even a woman yet, but she was getting there. She might even turn out to be a decent-looking woman some-day, a lot better looking than that slovenly old woman who was her mother. I just wish that Ayla would stay away from my lodge, Lara-mar thought. Then he smirked, unless she wants some honoring. I wonder what she'd be like full of barma at a Mother Festival? Who knows? Someday.

There was another person who was watching that wished the couple less than happiness. My name is Madroman now, the acolyte thought, and I wish they'd remember, especially Jondalar. Look at him, so smug, all dressed up in that white tunic, making all those newly mated women smile. He was surprised when he found out I am part of the zelandonia now. He never expected it, he didn't think I could do it, but I'm a lot smarter than he thinks. And I will become Zelandoni, in spite of that fat woman who's been playing up to Jondalar's foreign woman like she's already Zelandoni.

She is beautiful, though. I could have found someone like that if he hadn't knocked my teeth out. He had no reason to hit me like that. All I did was tell the truth. He wanted to mate Zolena, and she would have agreed if I hadn't let them know. I should have let them mate, then that smiling face would be mated to a fat old woman instead of that foreigner he brought back. She plays at being a Zelandoni, but she isn't. She's not even an acolyte, and she can't even talk right. I wonder how many women would think he was so wonderful if someone knocked his teeth out? That would be something to see. I'd really like to see that, someday.

A fourth pair of eyes had watched the mating of the favored pair with less than pleasant feelings of goodwill. Brukeval couldn't stop looking at the golden woman with her hair tumbling around her shoulders and her large, beautiful breasts exposed. She was pregnant, they were a mother's breasts, and he wanted more than anything to reach out and touch them, fondle them, suckle them. They were so perfect, he began to feel that she was flaunting those perfect breasts, taunting him on purpose with their fullness, their hard pink nipples begging to be sucked.

Jondalar is going to touch those breasts, hold them, take those nipples in his mouth and suck them. Always Jondalar, always the favored one, always the lucky one. He even had the best mother. Marona's mother never cared about me, but Marthona was always there when I couldn't stand it anymore. She would always talk to me, explain things to me, let me stay with them for a while. She was always kind. Jondalar wasn't so bad, but that was because he felt sorry for me, because I didn't have his mother. Now he is mating a mother, a woman golden as Bali, the great golden son of the Mother, with beautiful breasts, who is going to be a mother.

She had been so happy to see him coming for her with his torch to lead her out of that cave, and she had said if it weren't for Jondalar, she would consider him, but she didn't mean it. When Jondalar and that flathead came, she made it known that she thought he was a flathead just like that one from the Lanzadonii. I don't know how Dalanar could even allow that flathead to look at the daughter of his mate, much less to mate her. That's wrong. He is an abomination, half animal, half human. It shouldn't be allowed. Joplaya seemed like a decent young woman, she was quiet, and she'd always been nice to him, but how could she consider mating that flathead? It's just not right. Someone should stop it, Brukeval thought.

Maybe I should. If Ayla thought about it, she would know I was doing the right thing. It might make her appreciate me. I wonder if she really would consider me if something happened, if Jondalar wasn't there anymore? If something happened to Jondalar, I wonder, would she consider me, someday?

32

Levela and Jondecam held up their joined hands in welcome when Ayla and Jondalar arrived at the waiting area. "Did she say you were already Blessed, Ayla?" Levela said, rushing toward her.

Ayla nodded, a little too overcome with emotion to trust herself to talk.

"Oh, Ayla! That's wonderful! Why didn't you tell me? Did Jondalar know? You are so lucky!" she said, not giving Ayla time to answer and trying to give her a hug. But she forgot for a moment about the hand to which she was tied and got tangled up with Jondecam's arm. They all laughed, including some who were nearby, and Levela ended up giving Ayla a one-arm hug.

"And your outfit is so beautiful, Ayla. I've never seen anything like it. It has so many ivory beads and ambers, in places it almost seems to be made out of ivory and amber. The leather is the perfect shade of yellow to go with it. And I love the way you wear it, open like that, especially since you are going to be a mother soon. It must be heavy, though. Where did you get it?" Levela said. She was so excited, Ayla had to smile.

"Yes, it is heavy, but I'm used to it. I carried it a long way. Nezzie gave this to me when she thought I was going to be mating a Mamutoi man, and she told me how to wear it. She was the mate of the headman of the Lion Camp. When I decided to leave with Jondalar instead, she told me to take it and wear it when I mated him. She liked him, they all did. They wanted him to stay and become Mamutoi, but he said he needed to go home. I think I understand why," Ayla said. Several people were crowded around, listening. They wanted to be able to tell people what the foreign woman said about her richly made clothes.

"Jondalar looks wonderful, too," Levela said. "Your outfit is exquisite because of the beadwork and decorations, the whole thing. Jondalar's is a perfect contrast, stunning just because of the color."

"That's right," Jondecam said. "All of us are wearing our best clothes," he indicated his own clothing, "which usually means decorated, though no one has anything as incredible as your outfit, Ayla, but when Jondalar came out wearing that, everybody noticed. His tunic is simple elegance, especially on him. I know how these things work. All the women are going to want an outfit like yours, and all the men will want something white like his. Did someone give that to you, Jondalar?"

"Ayla did," Jondalar said.

"Ayla! Did you make that?" Levela said, surprised.

"A Mamutoi woman taught me how to make white leather," Ayla said. People were turning around, facing the next Zelandoni.

"We better stop talking, they are getting started," Levela said.

After they quieted so the ceremony for the next couple could begin, Ayla thought about why the mating ritual included tying the wrists of the couples together with a thong that would be difficult to untie. The tangle of arms when Levela, in her excitement, rushed to hug her made her understand that being tied together forced one to consider the other before rushing ahead without thinking. Not a bad first lesson to learn about being mated.

"I wish they'd hurry," one of the other newly mated men said under his breath. "I'm starving. With all this fasting today, I'm sure they could hear my stomach growling all the way in the back."

Ayla was rather glad for the Zelandoni's long recitation of the names and ties, it gave her time to think and be alone with her own thoughts. She was mated. Jondalar was her mate. Maybe now she could begin to feel that she really was Ayla of the Ninth Cave of the Zelandonii, although she was glad that Ayla of the Mamutoi was a part of her names. Just because they were going to be living with the Ninth Cave didn't mean she was a different person. She just had new names and ties to add to her list of connections and relations. She hadn't lost her Clan totem, either.

Her mind wandered back to the time when she was a girl living with the Clan. When they mated, they had no such knot-tying customs, but they didn't need them. From the time they were young, women of the Clan were taught always to be aware of the men of the Clan, particularly the one to whom they were mated. A good Clan woman was expected to anticipate the requirements and wishes of her mate, because a man of the Clan learned from an early age never to be aware of, or at least not to show that he was aware of, his own needs, discomfort, or pain. He could never ask for her help, she had to know when it was needed.

Broud didn't need her help when he asked, but he made demands all the time. He invented things for her to do just because he could make her do them—bring him a drink of water, tie on his leg coverings. He could claim that she was just a girl and had to learn, but he didn't care if she learned, and it didn't make any difference when she tried to please him. He wanted to show his power over her because she had resisted him, and women of the Clan did not willfully disobey men. She had made him feel less than a man and he hated her for it, or perhaps at some instinctual level he knew that her kind were different. It had not been an easy lesson for her to learn, but she had learned, and it was Broud, with his constant demands, who taught her, but Jondalar was the recipient. She was always aware of him, and it occurred to her that was why she was always uncomfortable when she didn't know where he was. She was that way about her animals, too.

Suddenly, as though thinking about him had made him appear, Wolf was there. It was her right hand and Jondalar's left that were tied together, and she stooped down and hugged him with her left. She looked up at Jondalar.

"I've been worried about him, wondering where he was," Ayla said, "but he seems rather pleased with himself."

"Maybe he has reason," Jondalar said with a grin.

"When Baby found a mate, he left. He came back to visit once in a while, but he lived with his own kind. If Wolf has a mate, do you think he'll decide to leave and live with her?"

"I don't know. You've said before that he thinks of people as his pack, but if he's going to mate, it has to be with his own kind," he said.

"I want him to be happy, but I would miss him so much if he never came back," Ayla said, standing. Most of the people around her were watching her with the wolf, especially those who didn't know her well. She signaled him to stay close to her.

"He's a very big wolf, isn't he," one of the women said, edging back a little.

"Yes, he is," Levela said, "but people who know him say he has never threatened people."

At that moment a flea decided to annoy the wolf. He sat down, hunched himself around, and started scratching. The woman tittered nervously. "That certainly doesn't look very threatening," she said.

"Except to the bug that's bothering him," Levela said.

Suddenly he stopped, cocked his head as though he was hearing or smelling or perceiving something, then stood up and looked up at Ayla.

"Go ahead, Wolf," Ayla said, signaling his release. "If you want to go, go ahead."

He raced off, weaving his way around people, some of whom looked rather startled when they caught sight of him.

The next joining was not of a couple, but of a triple. One man was mating identical twin sisters. They did not want to separate, and it was not uncommon for twins, or just sisters who were close, to become co-mates, although it could be difficult for one young man to try to provide for two women and their children. In this case the man was a little older, well established, with a good reputation and high status. Even so, the chances were that they would bring in a second man someday, although one never knew.

By the time the final couple was reached, people were getting bored with the inevitable repetition, especially when the ceremony was for someone they didn't know, but the last ones brought some interest again. When Joplaya and Echozar came forward, there was a collective gasp from the people watching and then a buzz of conversation. Though neither one of the two had the usual appearance of the Zelandonii, and the audience knew that they were in fact not Zelandonii but Lanzadonii, they were still a shocking sight for some of the people there.

They saw a tall, slender, exotically appealing woman with dark hair and an ethereal beauty that was hard to describe. The man beside her could not have looked more different. He was slightly shorter, with such strong and unusual features, most people saw them as ugly. His thick browridges, accented by heavy, unruly eyebrows, protruded like a shelf over his dark, deep-set eyes. His nose was prominent, partly because the front of his rather long and broad face jutted forward, and partly because his nose, sharply defined and shaped rather like the beak of an eagle, though not as narrow, was enormous, yet it was in proportion to the size of his face. Like many men, he usually let his beard grow in the winter, because it helped to keep his face warm, but he shaved it in summer. He had recently shaved and his heavy jaw was clearly defined, but like the people of the Clan, he lacked a chin— almost. He had the hint of one, but with his nose protruding out so far, he appeared to have a weak, receding chin.

Echozar's face was the face of the Clan, except for his forehead. The definitive, pushed-back, and flattened look of the sloping foreheads of the Clan was missing; he was not a flathead. Above Echozar's bony browridges, his forehead rose as high and round as any man's there. And while the people of the Clan were rather short, he was as tall as many of the men there, but with a stocky, robust frame and a big, rounded chest typical of the Clan. Like theirs, his legs were short in proportion and slightly bowed, but as muscular as his arms. There was no question that he was a strong man.

And there was no doubt that he was a man of mixed spirits, to some an abomination, half man and half animal. There were those who believed that he should not be allowed to mate the woman who was standing beside him. No matter how foreign she looked, it was undeniable that she was human, one of them, not one of those flathead animals. The Zelandonii should be discouraging them, not recognizing them or aiding in such a joining.

Since the Lanzadonii had no donier of their own yet, the One Who Was First stepped forward again. She was not only First, but the Zelandoni of the Ninth Cave, and Dalanar had once lived with the Ninth Cave. He still had closer ties with them than with any other Cave, and Joplaya was the daughter of his hearth.

As the First took her place, she thought, smiling to herself, that Echozar looked so strong, not many people would be willing to challenge him one on one in an individual competition. Since they were the last couple to be mated, the First was thinking ahead to the contests. And, she thought, after they are mated might be a good time to announce that the First Acolyte of the Second Cave of the Zelandonii had been called, and after examination has proved to be Zelandoni. She has decided to return with Dalanar and his Cave and become the First Lanzadoni to Serve The Great Earth Mother, a good fit, and a good place for her to start out.

The donier looked at the people gathering around. Dalanar, standing there full of pride. It was amazing how much Jondalar looked like him, but the First was aware of some minor differences, probably because she had once been so intimate with the younger one. Jondalar, still tied to Ayla, had moved out of the group of newly joined and into the family circle. Joplaya was his close cousin, after all. Beside Dalanar was Jerika, Joplaya's mother, and standing behind her was Hochaman, the man of Jerika's hearth. He was leaning heavily on a young man who was unfamiliar to the First. She guessed he was originally a Zelandonii either from a far Cave or from some more distant people, perhaps the Losadunai, but the designs on his clothing and jewelry declared him as Lanzadonii.

Hochaman was an ancient, wizened little man with a face like Jerika's, but he could hardly stand, much less walk. Dalanar and Echozar had carried him on their backs the whole way to the Summer Meeting. He told people he used up his legs on his Journey, but no one had ever walked as far. He had traveled all the way from the Endless Seas of the East to the Great Waters of the West, and spent most of his life doing it. He knew how to tell a good story, had many to tell, didn't mind repeating them, and would probably be in demand after the ceremonies were over and the games and contests and Story-Telling could begin. The newly mated couples would have to forgo those events this year; they would be in the silence of their two-week trial period. The zelandonia chose that time on purpose. If a couple wasn't serious enough about their mating to give up a few games and Story-Tellings, then they probably shouldn't be getting mated.

The chanters were still maintaining their fugue, though it was an entirely different set of them now, as the First began the ceremony. "All Caves of the Zelandonii," the donier's voice was still resonant. "You are called upon to share in witnessing the joining of a woman and a man. Doni, Great Earth Mother, First Creator, the Mother of All, She Who gave birth to Bali, who lights the sky, and She Whose mate and friend, Lumi, shines down upon us this night in witness with Her. She is honored by the sacred joining of Her children.

"The two standing here have pleased the Great Earth Mother by choosing to join together." The sound level from the audience rose with background comments. The ceremony went somewhat faster than the others, there weren't as many names and ties; Echozar had almost none. He was Echozar of the First Cave of the Lanzadonii, Son of Woman, Blessed of Doni, accepted by Dalanar and Jerika of the First Cave of the Lanzadonii. Joplaya had a longer list of names and ties, mostly through Dalanar to the Zelandonii. Jondalar and Ayla were mentioned. Through her mother, only the names of Jerika's mother, Ahnlay, who walked the spirit world, and the man of her hearth, Hochaman.

"I, Dalanar, Leader of the First Cave of the Lanzadonii, speak for this couple, and I am pleased that Joplaya and Echozar will continue to live at the First Cave of the Lanzadonii," the leader said at the end, "and I welcome them." Then he turned to face the people gathered behind him in the audience, the rest of the Lanzadonii who had come all the way to the Zelandonii Summer Meeting to help sanction the mating.

"We of the First Cave of the Lanzadonii welcome them," they said in unison.

Then the Zelandoni Who Was First Among Those Who Served The Mother held out both her arms, as though trying to embrace everyone there. "All the Caves of the Zelandonii and the Lanzadonii," she said, "Joplaya and Echozar have chosen each other. It has been agreed, and they have been accepted by the First Cave of the Lanzadonii. What do you say to this joining?"

There was a sizable number of the people there who replied, "Yes," but also a segment that said, "No."

Zelandoni was shocked and, for a heartbeat, at a loss. She had never officiated at a mating ceremony that was not seconded by all the people. If there were any objections, they had always been worked out beforehand. This was the first time she had ever heard a "no" from anyone. Dalanar and Jerika were both frowning, and many of the Lanzadonii people were looking around. Most appeared uncomfortable, some angry. The First decided to ignore the "no" and continue as if she hadn't heard it.

"Doni, the Great Earth Mother, approves this joining of Her children. She has smiled on this union. She has already Blessed Joplaya," she said. She signaled them to extend their hands. There was a moment of hesitation, then Joplaya and Echozar held hands and offered them to the Zelandoni Who Was First. She wrapped a leather thong around their joined hands and tied it with a knot.

"The knot has been tied. You are mated. May Doni always smile on you." They turned around to face the people, and Zelandoni announced, "They are now Joplaya and Echozar of the First Cave of the Lanzadonii."

"No!" came a shout from the audience. "They shouldn't be. It's wrong. He's an abomination."

Several people recognized the voice. It was Brukeval! The First again tried to ignore him, but another voice joined his.

"He's right. They shouldn't be mated. He's half animal!" Marona said.

I can understand Brukeval, Zelandoni of the Ninth thought, but Marona doesn't care. She's just trying to cause trouble. Is she trying to get back at Jondalar and Ayla by humiliating his close cousin?

Then another voice joined in, from the area where the Fifth Cave was sitting. "They're right. The Zelandonii should not be approving this mating." It was a man who had tried to join the zelandonia but had been turned down. Malcontents seemed to be joining in just to make trouble.

A few others voiced a similar opinion, including Laramar. She recognized his voice, too. Why is he making a fuss? she wondered. Some of those who objected have strong feelings about it, but he doesn't care about anything.

"Maybe you should reconsider this mating, Zelandoni," another voice called out. It was Denanna, the leader of all three holdings of the Twenty-ninth Cave.

I have to put a stop to this, the First thought. "Why would you suggest such a thing, Denanna? These two young people have made their choice and it has been accepted by their people. I don't understand your objections."

"But you are asking us to accept it, not just their own people," Denanna said.

"And most of the Zelandonii have. I know individually each person who has made an objection to this mating." She looked up at the slope full of people, and though she couldn't see much in the dark, the ones who objected had the distinct impression that she could, and that she was looking directly at them. "Most have their own reasons, which have nothing to do with this couple. Only a few genuinely hold strong feelings on this issue. I can see no reason why those few should disrupt this ceremony, offend the Lanzadonii, and embarrass the Zelandonii. Joplaya and Echozar are mated. When they have finished their trial period, their mating will be sanctified. There is no more to be said about it. It is now time for the procession, and the feast."

She signaled the zelandonia, who organized the newly mated couples and led them around the fire, which was starting to die down. When they had slowly made five full circuits, they were led toward the area where food was being served to begin the feast and the celebration, but the joyous feeling of the Matrimonial had been dampened.

The ones who had been delegated began carving the massive haunches of aurochs that had been turned on spits, cooking over hot coals all day. Other, sometimes tougher cuts had been buried in pits lined with hot rocks, along with certain root vegetables. A soup thickened with daylily flowers, which also contained buds and small new roots from the plant, plus ground nuts, greens, fern fiddleheads, and onions, and was seasoned with herbs, was called "green soup." It was traditional at the First Matrimonial feast of the season. The matured roots of daylilies and cattails, pounded to remove the fibrous material, were mixed with the first of the wild oat and black pigweed seeds, parched, pounded into flour, then baked into a kind of hard, flat bread and served with the soup.

The tiny red heart-shaped berries that grew close to the ground, and were covered with tiny seeds, were familiar to Ayla; she was delighted to see strawberries, piled fresh into bowls. Some that were picked earlier and were getting soft had been cooked into a sauce along with several other fruits and a plant with reddish-colored thick stalks, whose large leaves were always cut off and disposed of. The tart stalks added a pleasant tang to the berries and fruits, but the leaves could make one sick. There were also steamed young fireweed stalks, seasoned with salt from the Great Waters of the West, and watertight baskets of Laramar's fermented barma.

As the festivities progressed and more fermented brew was consumed, the tension eased. Jondalar thanked Dalanar warmly, his eyes glistening, for coming so far to attend his mating.

"I would have come just for you, but we also came for Joplaya and Echozar. I'm sorry that it became unpleasant. I'm afraid it spoiled their mating, and maybe everyone else's," Dalanar said.

"There are always those few who try to spoil things for other people, but we won't have to worry about coming back to Zelandonii Summer Meetings for our young people to get mated. We now have our own Lanzadoni," Jerika said.

"That's wonderful, but I hope you'll come back once in a while anyway," Jondalar said. "Who is it?"

"Lanzadoni. You know that," Dalanar said, then smiled. "They are supposed to give up their individuality and become one with their people, but I notice they use the counting words to name themselves instead, and counting words have more power than ordinary names. She was the First Acolyte of the Zelandoni of the Second Cave. She will now be called the Lanzadoni of the First Cave of the Lanzadonii."

"I know who that is," Ayla said. "She was one of the acolytes who guided us into the Deep of Fountain Rocks when we went to help Zelandoni find the spirit of your brother. Do you remember, Jondalar?"

"Yes, I do. I think she will be a good Lanzadoni for you. She is very dedicated, and a good healer, I'm told," Jondalar said.

As the evening grew late, the newly mated couples spoke the last words they would say to friends and relatives for fourteen counted days. To some it felt strange, like saying good-bye without leaving. Smaller feasts would be held by the individual Caves when the couples returned to the fold after the trial period of exclusion. Then they would be given gifts to start out their new lives together. The matings were not fully recognized until after the trial period, since they would be free to separate then, if they wished. Though the couples usually left early, for others the festivities would continue until the first streaks of dawn.

As Ayla and Jondalar left, they were hazed with crude comments and general banter by several hecklers who followed for a ways, mostly young men who had been indulging in Laramar's barma. But many of them didn't know Jondalar, except by reputation. He had been gone when they were growing up. Most of the friends his age were past the stage of harassing couples who had just made a commitment. They were already mated, with a child or more at their own hearths.

Jondalar got one of the torches that had been used to light the area of the ceremony to find their way and to light a fire when they arrived. They walked up the slope beside the small stream and stopped at the spring for a drink. Ayla didn't know where they were going, but she knew when they arrived. The tent she saw was the same one they had used all during their long Journey, and she felt a pang of nostalgia at seeing it set up again. She was glad their long trip was over, but she would never forget it, either. She heard a nicker of welcome and smiled at Jondalar.

"You brought the horses!" she said, smiling with delight.

"I thought we might go for a ride in the morning," he said, holding up the torch so she could see them.

The fireplace had been set and ready, and he lit the fire with the torch, then walked with her to greet the mare and the stallion. They were used to working together, with each doing separate tasks. Having their hands tied together made it more difficult even to handle the horses, and they found themselves in each other's way.

"Let's go get these thongs off," Jondalar said. "I was glad enough to have them tied on, but now I'll be glad to remove them."

"Yes, but they are a good reminder to pay attention to each other," she said.

"I don't need a reminder to pay attention to you, certainly not on this night," Jondalar said.

Ayla crawled inside the familiar shelter, holding her hand up and back so Jondalar could follow behind. He lighted a stone lamp with the torch, then tossed it into the fireplace outside. When he looked back in, Ayla was sitting on the sleeping furs that had been spread out on the ground over a leather padding that he had carefully stuffed with dry grass. He stopped for a moment and looked at the woman who had just become his mate.

The soft light of the lamp made her shadow dance behind her, and her hair gleamed with highlights from the small flame. He saw the yellowish tunic, open in front to reveal her full, taut breasts, with the beautiful amber pendant of the necklace nestled between them. But something was missing. Then he realized what it was.

"Where is your amulet?" he asked, drawing closer to her.

"I took it off," she said. "I wanted to wear this outfit that Nezzie gave me and the necklace from your mother, and it didn't look right with them. Marthona gave me a small packet made out of rawhide with no decoration for the amulet. It seemed appropriate. She brought it back to the lodge with her. She suggested that tomorrow we bring back the clothes we wore tonight, rather than carry them around with us. She did ask if I would mind if she showed my outfit to some people. I told her I wouldn't mind at all, probably Nezzie would be pleased that she wanted to. I'll get my amulet then. I have never been without it since I was first adopted into the Clan, and it does feel strange not to have it."

"But you don't belong to the Clan anymore," Jondalar said.

"I know, and I never will again. I was cursed with death and can never go back, but the Clan will always be a part of me, and I will never forget them," she said. "Iza made my first amulet and then asked me to choose a piece of red ochre to put in it. . . . I wish she could have been here. She would have been so happy for me. All of the things in my amulet are important to me, they mark important moments in my life. They were given to me by my totem, the Spirit of the Cave Lion, who has always protected me. If I ever lost my amulet, I would die," she said with absolute surety.

It made Jondalar realize how important the amulet was to her, and how much her mating meant for her to take it off, but he didn't like the idea that she believed she would die if she ever lost it. "Isn't that just superstition? The superstition of the Clan?"

"No more than your elandon, Jondalar. Marthona recognized that. The amulet holds my spirit, that's how my totem can find me. When I was adopted by the Lion Camp, it didn't take away my life with the Clan. It added to it. That's why Mamut added my totem to my formal name. Now that I have become a member of the Ninth Cave, it hasn't changed the fact that I'm still Ayla of the Mamutoi. It just made my name longer," she said, then she smiled. "Ayla of the Ninth Cave of the Zelandonii, formerly of the Lion Camp of the Mamutoi, Daughter of the Mammoth Hearth, Chosen by the Spirit of the Cave Lion, Protected by the Cave Bear, Friend of horses and Wolf . . . and mated to Jondalar of the Ninth Cave of the Zelandonii. If my name gets much longer, I won't be able to remember it all."

"Just so long as you remember the last part, mated to Jondalar of the Ninth Cave of the Zelandonii," he said, reaching over and gently fondling a nipple, watching it draw together and harden in response to his touch. She felt a tingle of pleasure.

"Let's get these thongs off," Jondalar said. "They are getting in my way."

Ayla bent over their wrists and tried to pick apart the knots, but only her left hand was free, and she was right-handed and felt clumsy trying to pull apart knots with only one hand, and her left one at that.

"You are going to have to help me, Jondalar," she said. "I'm not very good at untying knots with just my left hand. It would be much easier to cut it."

"Don't even say that!" Jondalar said. "I never want to sever the knot from you. I want to be tied to you for the rest of my life."

"I already am, and will always be, thong or not," Ayla said, "but you're right. I think this is meant to be a challenge. Let me see that knot again." She studied it for a while, then said, "Look, if you will hold this, I will pull that, and I think it will come undone. It's that kind of knot."

He did as she said, she pulled, and the knot came apart.

"How did you know it would do that? I know something about knots and it wasn't obvious," Jondalar said.

"You've seen my medicine bag," she said. He nodded. "You know all the pouches inside are tied with knots. The kind of knot and how many there are tell me something about what is inside the pouch. Sometimes those pouches need to be opened fast. I can't be fumbling with trying to open knots when someone needs attention right away. I know about knots, Iza taught me long ago."

"Well, I'm glad you do," he said, holding up the long, slender thong. "I am going to put this in my pack so it doesn't get lost. We have to show that it wasn't cut, and exchange it for our zelandonia necklaces when we go back." He rolled it up, tucked it away, and then turned his attention entirely to Ayla. "This is the way I like to hold you when I kiss you," he said, putting both arms around her and filling them with her.

"That's the way I like it, too," she said.

He kissed her mouth, opening hers with his tongue, and reached for a breast. Then he pushed her back onto the furs and bent over to take the nipple into his mouth. She felt herself respond instantly, and the intensity of the sensations increased as he sucked and lightly bit on one nipple and caressed the other with his fingers.

She pushed him back and started pulling up the white tunic she had made for him. "What are you going to do when the baby comes, Jondalar? They'll be so full of milk."

"I promise not to steal too much, but you can be sure I'm going to taste it," he said, smiling, then he pulled his tunic off over his head. "You've had one child. Does it feel the same when a baby sucks?"

She thought about it. "No, not exactly," she said. "It's pleasurable to nurse a baby, after the first few days. The baby sucks so hard, it makes the nipples sore at first, before they get used to it. But I didn't get the same feelings deep inside me when I nursed a baby that I do when you suck. Sometimes when you just touch, I can feel it all the way down. That never happens with a baby."

"I can feel it down inside me just looking at you sometimes," he said. He took off the belt cinched around her waist, then opened her tunic and rubbed her slightly rounded stomach and caressed her inner thighs. He liked just touching her. He helped her slip out of her open tunic. She untied the thongs from around her waist and removed the rest of her clothes, then helped him untie his tightly wrapped foot coverings.

"I was so happy to see you wearing the tunic I made for you, Jondalar," Ayla said.

He picked up the tunic that he had dropped on his bedroll, turned it inside out, and, folding it together, laid it carefully on top of his back frame before he began to unwrap his leggings. Ayla took off her amber-and-shell necklace and removed her earrings—her ears were still a little sore from the recent piercing—and put the jewelry away in her pack. She did not want to lose it. When she turned around, she noticed that Jondalar, who couldn't stand in the tent, was stooping on one foot, pulling off his leggings, but his swollen member was more than ready. She couldn't resist reaching for it, which unbalanced him. He fell over on the furs, both of them laughing.

"How am I supposed to get these off with you so eager?" he said, pushing off the remaining legging with his other foot and kicking them out of the way. Then he stretched out beside her on the sleeping furs. "When did you make that tunic for me?" he asked, raising up on one elbow so he could look at her. His deep, rich blue eyes were dark, with only hints of blue in the single flame, dilated and glowing as he looked at her with love and longing.

"When we were staying with the Lion Camp," she said.

"But you were Promised to Ranec that winter. Why were you making a tunic for me?"

"I'm not sure," she said. "I think I was hoping. And then I got a strange idea. I remembered that you said you wanted to capture my spirit when you made that little carving of me in the valley, and I was hoping that I could somehow capture your spirit if I made something for you. That time everyone was talking about black animals and white animals, you said that white was special to you. So when Crozie agreed to teach me how to make white leather, I decided to make something for you. Whenever I worked on it, I thought of you. I think I was happiest that winter when I was working on it. I even imagined seeing you wearing it at a mating ceremony. Making it kept my hope alive. That's why I carried it with me on the Journey back."

He almost felt his eyes grow moist.

"I'm sorry it isn't decorated. I was never very good at sewing on beads and things. I started to do it a few times, but I always seemed to get interrupted. I did get some ermine tails on it. I wanted to get more, but never got back to do it that winter. Maybe next winter I can go out and find some more," she said.

"It was perfect, Ayla. Just the white color was decoration enough. Everyone thought you left it undecorated on purpose, and they were so impressed. Marthona told me she liked the way you were not afraid to let quality and good workmanship be its own decoration. I think you are going to be seeing some white tunics around," he said.

"When Marthona said I wouldn't be able to see you or talk to you until after the ceremony, I was ready to break every Zelandonii custom there was just to give it to you. That's when Marthona said she would do it, although I think she thought even that was too much contact. But I didn't know if you liked it, and I didn't know if you would understand why I wanted you to wear it."

"How could I have been so stupid and blind that winter? I loved you so much. I wanted you so much. Every time you went to Ranec's bed, I couldn't stand it. I couldn't sleep, I'd hear every sound. That's why I took you that day out on the steppe when we went out to train Racer. I could feel every movement of your body when we rode out together on Whinney. Can you ever forgive me for forcing you like that?"

"I kept trying to tell you, but you never would listen. You didn't force me, Jondalar. Couldn't you tell how quickly I responded? How could you think you forced me? That was my happiest day all winter. I dreamed about it afterward for days. Every time I closed my eyes I could feel you and want you again, but you wouldn't come back."

He kissed her then, suddenly hungry for her. Then he couldn't wait. He was on top of her, pushing her legs apart, finding her warm, moist well and thrusting deep, feeling her warmth caressing his manhood. She was ready for him. She felt him penetrate and strained to meet him, and moaned as she felt his fullness inside her own engorged depths. He pulled back and entered again and again. As the pace quickened, she arched to force the pressure where she wanted it. There. That was right. She was so ready. So was he. Jondalar felt that he would burst with his fullness, and then, every nerve straining, aware of nothing else, the wondrous waves of Pleasure engulfed them both, bursting forth in glorious release. He thrust again a few more times, then collapsed on top of her.

"I love you, Ayla. I don't know what I'd do if I ever lost you. I will always love you, only you," he said, holding her tight, his voice sounding strained with the intensity of his feeling.

"Oh, Jondalar. I love you, too. I always have." There were tears in the corners of her eyes, partly from the fullness of her love for him, partly from the tension so quickly mounted and so suddenly released.

They lay quietly for a while in the light of the flickering lamp, then he raised up and slowly extracted his spent organ and rolled over to his side. He put his hand on her stomach again.

"I thought I might be too heavy for you. I don't think I should put too much weight on you now," he said.

"You are not heavy yet," she said. "Later we can worry about finding ways to make it easier, when the baby starts to grow more."

"Is it true that you can feel the life moving inside you?"

"Not yet, but before long I will. You will be able to feel it, too. You just have to put your hand on my stomach like that."

"I think I'm glad you've already had one child. You know what to expect."

"But it's not exactly the same. I was really sick when I was carrying Durc, almost all the time."

"How are you feeling now?" he asked, his worry frown evident.

"I feel wonderful. Even in the beginning I hardly had any sickness at all, and now that is gone."

They were quiet then for a long time. Jondalar wondered if she had fallen asleep. He was just feeling like beginning again, taking more time, but if she was sleeping . . .

"I wonder how he is?" she suddenly said. "My son."

"Do you miss him?"

"Sometimes I miss him so much, I don't know what to do. At the meeting of the zelandonia, Zelandoni sang the Mother's Song. I love that story. Whenever I hear it, I feel like crying when they come to the part about the Great Mother not being able to have Her son at Her side, how they are forever apart. I think I know how She felt. Even if I never see him again, I just wish I knew how he was, if he's all right. How Broud and the others have treated him," Ayla said. She was quiet again.

Her words set Jondalar thinking. "In the song it says the Great Mother struggled in pain to give birth. Is it very painful?"

"He was hard to deliver. I don't like to think about it. But, like the Mother's Song says, he was worth it."

"Are you afraid, Ayla? Afraid to give birth again?" he asked.

"A little. But I feel so good this time, maybe this delivery won't be so bad, either."

"I don't know how women do it."

"We do it because it's worth it, Jondalar. I wanted Durc so much, and then they told me he was deformed, that I couldn't keep him." She started to cry. Jondalar held her. "It was so awful. I just couldn't do it. At least with the Zelandonii, the mother has the choice. No one will ever try to force me."

They heard wolves howling in the distance, and another answering that was close by, but that howl was familiar. Wolf was nearby, but not in the tent with them. "I wonder if he will leave me, too," she said.

She buried her head in his shoulder. Jondalar held her, comforted her. It is difficult being the honored of Doni, he thought. A blessing, but still . . . He tried to imagine what it would feel like to have a life growing inside him, but it was beyond him. Men did not have babies. Why did Doni make men, anyway? If there were no men, the women would be able to take care of themselves. Women are not all pregnant at the same time. Some of them could hunt and some could help the others when their bellies were big or their babies were small. Women always help each other when they give birth. They could probably survive even without hunting. Gathering is easier for a woman with small children anyway.

He had asked himself that question before, and wondered if other men ever asked themselves the same question. If they did, it was not something they ever mentioned out loud. Doni must have had some reason for making two kinds of people. There always seemed to be logic in what She did. The world was orderly. The sun rose every day, the moon went through its phases regularly, the seasons followed each other the same way every year.

Could Ayla be right? Was a man necessary for life to begin? Is that why there are both men and women? Jondalar struggled with his thoughts as he held the woman in his arms. He wanted there to be a reason for his existence, a real reason. Not just to enjoy Pleasures, not just to provide or help or support. He wanted his life to be necessary, his gender to be necessary. He wanted to believe that there would be no new life without men, that without men there would be no more children, that all of Earth's Children would no longer exist.

He was so deep in thought, he didn't notice when Ayla's sobs ceased. He looked at her and smiled. She was breathing quietly, sound asleep. It had been a long day, she had gotten up early. He eased his arm out from under her, flexed it to restore circulation, and yawned widely. He was tired himself. He got up to extinguish the moss-wick flame of the oil lamp and felt his way in the darkness back to the sleeping woman and crawled in beside her.

In the morning, when Jondalar opened his eyes, it took him a moment to orient himself. He had grown accustomed to sleeping in the lodge at the camp; the inside of the tent was much closer. But the tent was even more familiar. They had slept in it together for a year. Then he remembered. They were mated last night. Ayla was his mate. He reached to his side, but she was gone. Then he smelled something cooking on the fire outside. He sat up and, without thinking about it, reached for his cup and was surprised to find it there, full of hot mint tea. He took a sip. It was just the temperature he liked, and beside the cup was a freshly peeled wintergreen twig. She had done it again, anticipated what he liked in the morning and had it ready for him. He still didn't know how she did it.

He took another drink, then pushed back the sleeping furs and got up. Ayla was with the horses, and Wolf was there, too. He swished out his mouth, chewed on the end of the twig and used it to clean his teeth, and swished his mouth once more, then swallowed the last of the tea. He reached for his clothes, then decided it didn't matter, no one else was around, and walked to her naked. She smiled at him and glanced at his organ. That was all it took, it started to grow. Her smile became a mischievous grin. He just smiled back.

"It's a beautiful day," he said as he approached her with his proud manhood jutting out in front of him.

"I was thinking that I'd like to go swimming with you this morning," she said, watching him approach. "That pool that is upstream of the camp is not far from here, if we go the back way."

"When do you want to go?" he said. "I smelled something cooking."

She smiled slyly. "We could go now. I can move the food off the fire," she said.

"Let's do it, woman," he said, taking her in his arms and giving her a kiss. "I'll get some clothes, we can ride the horses there." Then he smiled. "We can get there faster that way."

Ayla took her pack, but they rode bareback. Within a few moments they reached the pool and left the horses free to graze. They spread a hide on the ground, then ran for the water, laughing. Wolf ran with them, but as they splashed into the pool, he followed another interest.

"This feels so good, so refreshing," Ayla said, ducking down, then standing up again.

Jondalar ducked down, too. They swam across the pool, then back again. When they started out, he reached for her. "You feel good, too," he said, "and I think you might taste good, too." He picked her up and carried her out of the water and put her down on the hide. "Yesterday was too busy, today we have time," he said, looking down at her with his amazing blue eyes. Then he bent down to kiss her, slowly, sweetly, pressing close to her, feeling their skin cool from the water and the body heat from within. He nibbled on her ear, kissed her throat, then reached for her breast and found her nipple. It was what he wanted, what she wanted.

He spent time, touching, squeezing, rubbing one between his fingers, sucking and nibbling on the other, and felt himself fill and get ready. To her, his touching and caressing gave her feelings through her body that felt like lightning, reaching into her parts of Pleasure. He rubbed her rounded belly and loved the feel of its swelling, knowing that inside a baby was growing, then he reached lower, for her rising mound, and the slit at the top.

She pushed herself toward him, and he found the small knob. The sharp pulses of feeling grew stronger inside her. Then he got up and moved around and positioned himself between her thighs. He opened her rose-colored folds and just looked for a moment. Then he closed his eyes and let his tongue find her taste. This was the woman he wanted, the one who tasted like her. This was his Ayla.

She held herself still, let him explore, find all the warm places, then he found the knob again and with his tongue began to play with it, moving it, rubbing it, sucking it. She began to moan, her mind in some other place, a place where Jondalar knew how to put her. She pushed up against him as he moved faster, and the moans escaping from her increased in pitch and intensity.

He could feel himself growing so full, and he ached to feel her envelop him, but first, he needed to feel her peak. It kept getting closer, the feeling that was ready to overcome her, and then, suddenly, it was there, bursting over the crest in rising and rising waves of Pleasure. And then she wanted to feel him inside her.

She pulled him up and helped him enter, and waited for the first satisfying push. He pulled back and pushed in again, and filled her again. He felt her warm folds embrace him as he plunged in deeply, completely. They fit together so well. This was the woman he wanted. She could hold all of him, he didn't have to worry about his size. He pulled out almost all the way, then plunged in again, and then again, and each time she felt him, the sensation grew stronger, her breath expelled with a rising tone to match the feeling growing inside.

And then the pulsing grew until it flooded over him. He released as she reached her peak. He pulled out and pushed in again a few times, and then let himself go and relaxed on top of her. She didn't want him to move. She loved the feeling of him on top of her like that. She wanted to savor the Pleasures and relax, too.

They went swimming again, but this time when they got out, Ayla took their soft drying skins out of her pack. They whistled for the horses and rode back to their campsite. Wolf was there, pacing around their tent, growling at something, and the horses seemed nervous.

"There's something out there," Ayla said. "Wolf doesn't like it, and it's making the horses nervous. Those wolves we heard last night, do you think it could be them?"

"I don't know, but after we eat, why don't we pack up the tent and go for a long ride," Jondalar said. "Maybe spend tonight some other place."

"That's a good idea," Ayla said. "We can stop by the lodge and leave our mating outfits, get the rest of our traveling things, and explore the area around here. When we come back, we can set up our tent near the pool. Hardly anyone goes there. And let's take Wolf with us. Some pack might think he's in their territory, and wolves will fight to defend their territory against other wolves."

33

When they rode to the camp of the Ninth Cave and dismounted near their lodge, the people ignored them as though they weren't there, walking past and averting their eyes or looking beyond them. Ayla felt a chill of uneasy recognition; it felt like the death curse of the Clan. She knew what it meant when people she loved shunned her, refused to see her though she stood in front of them waving her arms and shouting.

Then she saw Folara glancing at them and trying to hide a smile, and Ayla relaxed. There was no ill will. It was their trial period and they weren't supposed to talk to anyone but each other, but she noticed several others glancing in their direction and trying not to smile at them. It was obvious that everybody was very much aware of their presence. They went into the lodge just as Marthona was coming out. They sidestepped each other as they passed by without saying a word, but the older woman looked directly at them and smiled. She didn't think it was necessary to go through all the elaborate avoidance schemes, neither speaking to them nor encouraging them to talk was enough.

They put their mating outfits on the grass-stuffed underpads of their bare sleeping place and packed some additional traveling gear, then they walked to Marthona and Willamar's place. She had placed the rawhide packet with Ayla's amulet in it on her bed, and put some food she had packed up for them beside it. Ayla almost thanked her out loud, but caught herself, then with a quick smile she made the Clan hand signs for "I am grateful for your kindness, mother of my mate."

Marthona didn't understand the signs, but she guessed it was a gesture of appreciation of some kind and smiled at the young woman who was now the mate of her son. It might be valuable to learn some of those signs, she thought. It could be interesting to communicate without speaking, and without anyone else knowing what you were saying. When they left, Marthona walked over to their place and looked at the clothing they had worn the previous night.

Jondalar's white tunic had made him stand out, but then he usually did, and while it was stunning and displayed an advanced technique for working with leather, it was still Ayla's entire outfit that had made the real impression, just as Marthona hoped it would. It had already caused some people to reconsider the status they were willing to grant her. Marthona had invited some people over for a taste of some bilberry wine, which she had recently started serving—it had been stored for two years in a dark, dry corner of her dwelling in the well-washed and securely stoppered stomach of an elk. She decided she would place a few lamps around the inside of the lodge so they could see better in the dim interior space. She bent over and straightened the tunic and leggings, rearranging them slightly to show off a particular area of intricate beadwork that had been covered by a fold.

Ayla and Jondalar loved their days of nominal separation from the Zelandonii. It was like a return to their Journey, but without the pressure of having to keep traveling. They spent the long summer days hunting, fishing, and gathering just for their own needs, swimming and taking long rides on the horses, but with Wolf only a sometime companion, and Ayla missed him when he was gone. It was as though he couldn't quite make up his mind whether to stay with the humans he adored or return to whatever it was he found so fascinating in the wild. He always found them, no matter where they camped, and every time he made an appearance at the tent, Ayla was delighted. She paid attention to the animal, stroked and petted him, talked to him, hunted with him. Her attention usually encouraged him to stay with them for a while, but eventually he would go again and often stay away through the night or several.

They explored the hills and valleys of the surrounding area. As well as Jondalar thought he knew the countryside of his birth, because they were riding on horses and able to cover so much more territory, he was able to see it on a broader scale and from a different perspective. He gained an insight he hadn't had before, and it gave them an appreciation for the richness of the region. Sometimes in herds, and sometimes in fleeting glimpses, they saw a tremendous number and remarkable variety of animals that inhabited the land of the Zelandonii.

Most grazing and browsing creatures placidly shared the same fields, meadows, and open woodlands, and the two horses were usually ignored along with the humans who were riding them. As a result, they were able to get quite close. Ayla liked to sit quietly on Whinney's back while the mare grazed and study the other animals, and Jondalar often joined her, though he also spent time doing other things. He was working on spears and a spear-thrower for Lanidar more appropriate to his size, and with an adaptation he hoped would make it easier for him to use with one arm. Jondalar was with her when they came upon a herd of bison one afternoon.

Although many bison and aurochs had been hunted, it was hardly noticed; their numbers were insignificant in comparison with the vast numbers of animals that roamed the open landscape. But the two distinct bovines were never seen together. They avoided each other. Though Ayla and Jondalar had killed and helped to butcher their share of bison recently, observing them as they moved through their environment was enlightening. The grazers had lost their thick, dark, woolly fur during the spring molt and were wearing their lighter-colored summer coats. Ayla especially enjoyed watching the lively, playful calves, still quite young—the cows calved in late spring and early summer. The young developed rather slowly and required close, attentive care, but still fell prey to bears, wolves, lynxes, hyenas, leopards, the occasional cave lion—and humans.

Deer of various species were abundant and came in all sizes, from huge giant deer to tiny roe deer. Jondalar and Ayla saw a small bachelor herd of megaceros with their delicate sharp noses, and marveled at their fantastic antlers. They were shaped like a hand with outstretched fingers, and though they could span twelve feet and weigh one hundred sixty pounds or more, these were younger animals, slimmer, with smaller appendages. They had not yet developed the huge muscular necks of the mature deer, though they all sported humps on their withers, where the tendons to support their future massive antlers were attached.

Even young megaceros avoided woods where their antlers could get caught in tree branches. The spotted fallow deer was the woodland variety. In a marshy area, they saw a single deer of another kind, tall and gangly, with smaller, though still quite substantial, palmate antlers, standing in the middle of the water, dipping his head under and pulling out a mouth full of dripping, green water plants, but this deer had a huge overhanging nose. It was called moose in some countries, but the name given to it in Jondalar's region was elk.

Far more prevalent were the variety of elk known in this land as red deer. They also grew large antlers, but of the branching variety. Red deer were primarily grazers and could live in a broad range of open country, from mountains to steppes. Nimble and fearless, steep hills and rough country didn't deter them, nor did narrow ledges above the treeline if there was grass to tempt them. Forests with enough spaces between trees to allow an undergrowth of grasses and ferns or interspersed with sunny glens were acceptable habitats, as were heather-covered hills and open steppes.

Red deer didn't like to run, but their long-legged walk or lively trot covered ground with celerity, and if chased, they could run for miles, leap a forty-foot distance, and jump to a height of eight feet. They were also excellent swimmers. Though they preferred to eat grass, they could feed on leaves, buds, berries, mushrooms, herbs, heathers, bark, acorns, nuts, and beechnut mast. Red deer congregated in small herds at this time of year, and in a meadow beside a stream, Ayla and Jondalar saw several of the deer and stopped to observe them. The grass was just turning from green to gold, and a few fully leafed-out, luxuriant beech trees lined the bank, but on the other side was a substantial gallery forest.

It was a male herd of various ages, and their antlers were in full velvet. Antlers began when the males were about a year old with single spikes. They were cast off in early spring, but they started to grow new ones almost immediately. Each year a new tine was added, and by early summer even the biggest were fully grown, encased in velvet, a soft skin full of blood vessels, which carried the nutrients that allowed their antlers to grow so quickly. By mid- to late summer, the velvet dried and became very itchy, causing the deer to scratch against trees and rocks to rub it off, but the bloody skin often hung in tatters until it was gone.

They counted twelve points on the biggest, which weighed around eight hundred pounds. Though they were called red deer, the color of the coat of the twelve-point buck was a black gray brown; others in the herd were a light brownish-red color, some shading toward taupe, and one was blond. A young one with just the hint of spikes still showed faintly the white spots of a fawn. Although Jondalar was tempted, he decided not to go after the one with the huge rack, though he was sure he could bring it down with his spearthrower.

"That big one is in his prime," he said. "I'd like to come back and watch him later, they often come back to the same places. In his season of Pleasures, he'll fight for as many females as he can, though many times just displaying that rack is enough to discourage competitors. But they fight hard and will go at it all day. It makes so much noise when they run into each other with those antlers, you can hear them from very far away, and they will even get up on their hind legs and fight with their front legs. As big as he is, he must be a very good, aggressive fighter."

"I've heard them fight, but I've never seen them," Ayla said.

"Once, when I was living with Dalanar, we saw a couple of them locked together with their antlers intertwined. They couldn't get apart no matter how they tried. We had to cut the antlers to separate them so we could use them. They were an easy kill, but Dalanar said we were doing them a favor, they would have died anyway of hunger and thirst."

"I think that big stag has had a brush with people before," Ayla said, signaling Whinney to move back. "The wind just shifted and must have given him our scent, he's getting edgy. You can see he's starting to walk away. They will all go if he goes."

"He does look nervous," Jondalar said, backing off, too.

Suddenly, a lynx that had been lying in wait, unseen, in one of the beech trees, dropped down onto the back of the youngest when he walked underneath. The faintly spotted deer leaped forward, trying to dislodge the wildcat, but the short-tailed feline with the tufted ears held on to the deer's shoulders and bit down, opening his veins. The other deer raced away, but the young cervid with the cat on his back ran in a large arc and circled around. As they watched the panicky animal heading back, both Ayla and Jondalar readied their spear-throwers for protection, just in case, but the lynx had been drinking his blood and the deer was showing signs of exhaustion. He stumbled, the lynx took a new grip, and more blood spurted. The deer took a few more steps, stumbled again, then dropped to the ground. The lynx bit open the head of the young animal and started feeding on the brains.

It was over quickly, but the horses were nervous and the humans were both ready to leave. "That's why he looked nervous," Ayla said. "It wasn't our scent at all."

"That deer was young," Jondalar said. "You could still see his spots. I wonder if his dam died early and left him alone a little too young. He found the male herd, but it didn't matter. Young animals are always vulnerable."

"When I was a little girl, I once tried to kill a lynx with my sling," Ayla said, urging Whinney to a walk.

"With a sling? How old were you?" Jondalar asked.

She thought for a moment, trying to remember. "I think I could count eight or nine years," she said.

"You could have been killed as easily as that deer," Jondalar said.

"I know. He moved and the stone just bounced off. It just irritated him and he sprang at me. I managed to roll aside and found a piece of wood and hit him with it, and he went away," she said.

"Great Mother! That was a close call, Ayla," he said, leaning back on his horse, which caused Racer to slow down.

"I was afraid to go out alone for a while afterward, but that was when I got the idea to throw two stones. I thought if I had had another one ready, I could have hit him a second time before he came for me. I wasn't sure if it could be done, but I practiced and worked it out. Still, it wasn't until I killed a hyena that I felt confident to go hunting again," she said.

Jondalar just shook his head. When he thought about it, it was amazing that she was still alive. On the way back to their current camp, they saw a herd of animals that made Whinney and Racer pay attention: a horselike animal called an onager, which appeared to be a cross between a horse and donkey, but were a viable species of their own. Whinney stopped to smell their droppings, and Racer nickered at them. The whole herd stopped grazing and looked at the horses. The sound they returned was closer to a bray, but both animals seemed to be aware of their similarity.

They also saw a female saiga antelope with two young. Saiga were goatlike animals with overhanging noses who preferred plains or steppes, no matter how barren, to hills or mountains. Ayla remembered that the saiga antelope was Iza's totem. The following day they saw another herd of animals that bothered Ayla more than she wanted to admit: horses. Both Whinney and Racer were drawn to them.

Ayla and Jondalar studied them and noticed some differences between the wild herd and the animals they had brought with them from the east. Rather than Whinney's dun-yellow color, which was most common all over, or even the rare dark brown of Racer's coat, most of the horses in this herd were a bluish-gray color with a white belly. They all, their two included, had similar stand-up brushlike black manes and black tails, black stripes down their backbones, and black lower legs, with some suggestion of striping on their lower haunches. They were generally small horses, broad backed with rounded bellies, but the herd animals seemed to stand a fraction higher and had slightly shorter muzzles.

The herd was watching Whinney and Racer with as much intensity as the two were watching the herd, but this time Racer's nicker brought a ringing neigh of challenge in return. She and Jondalar looked at each other when they heard the call and saw a large stallion coming toward them from the back of the herd. By tacit agreement, Ayla and Jondalar rode their horses in another direction as fast as they could. Jondalar did not want Racer to be drawn into a fight with the herd stallion, and with Wolf being gone so much of the time, Ayla was afraid the horses, too, might be tempted to leave her and decide to live with their own kind.

In the next few days, Wolf spent some time with them, which made Ayla feel as though her family were back together. They made a point of staying away from a big wild boar digging for truffles, laughed at a pair of otters playing in a pond that was formed by a dam built by a reclusive beaver that had quickly dived into the water when he saw them. They saw the wallow of a bear and some of his hair caught in the bark of a tree, but not the animal itself, and smelled the distinctive musk of a wolverine. They watched a spotted leopard gracefully leap down from a high ledge, and some ibex, wild mountain goats, nimbly vault up the face of an almost perpendicular cliff.

Several female ibex and their young, their tight wool making them seem round and shapeless, with sticks for legs, had come down from the highlands to fatten up on the rich lowland growth. They had long horns that curved over their backs, very wide-set eyes, a hump behind their heads, and hooves that were hard and strong around the edges, with soft, spongy, flexible soles that gripped the hard stone.

Jondalar saw Ayla close her eyes as though concentrating, turning her head back and forth to better hear something. "I think mammoths are coming this way," she said.

"How do you know? I can't see anything."

"I can hear them," she said, "especially the big male."

"I can't hear anything," Jondalar said.

"It's a deep, deep rumbling sound," she said, straining to listen again. "Look, Jondalar! Over there!" she called out, full of excitement, when she saw a herd of mammoths in the distance coming in their direction. Ayla was detecting the long-distance bellow of a male mammoth in musth, which was below the auditory range normally heard by humans, but could be heard by a female mammoth in heat for up to five miles because such low-level sounds did not attenuate as easily over distance. Though Ayla couldn't exactly hear it, she could sense the deep call.

The herd was essentially female and their young, but since one of the young females was in heat, several males were crowding around the edges, always hopeful, though the dominant bull of the region was already in consort with her. She had refused the persistent advances of the lesser males until he arrived. Now he kept the others away, since none of them dared to challenge him, which allowed her to eat and nurse her first young calf in between mating sessions.

The thick coat of the woolly mammoth covered the huge animal completely, from the toes to the end of its long nose, including the small ears. As they came closer, the various shades of their fur became more apparent. The little ones had the lightest-colored hair, the females shaded from bright chestnut in the younger ones to the dark brown of the old matriarch. The males became almost black as they aged. The coat had a very dense underfur out of which grew fairly long, straight hairs that kept them very warm even in the coldest of the winters, especially after consuming the sometimes icy water or eating snow or ice. That's when their bodies tended to become chilled.

"It's early in the season for mammoths," he said. "We never used to see them until fall, late fall. Mammoths, rhinos, musk oxen, and reindeer, those are the winter animals."

On the last day of their isolation, Ayla and Jondalar rose early. They had spent the previous few days exploring the region to the west of The River near a second river that ran nearly parallel to it. They packed all their belongings but wanted to make one more long ride before they went back to the Summer Meeting with all its people and social interactions, which put demands on their time and attention, but brought rewards, satisfaction, and pleasure as well. They had enjoyed the respite, but they were ready to return and looking forward to seeing the people they cared about. They had spent nearly a year with only each other and the animals for company and were familiar with both the joys and the sorrows of solitude.

They took food and water with them, but they were in no hurry and had no particular destination in mind. Wolf had left them two days before, which saddened Ayla. He had been eager to stay with them on their Journey, but he was little more than a puppy then. He was still young. Although it seemed much longer, they could count only one year and about two seasons since the winter they lived with the Mamutoi, when Ayla brought back a fuzzy little wolf who had been born no more than a moon before. For all of Wolf's great size, he was still a juvenile.

Ayla didn't know how long wolves lived, but she suspected that the length of their lives was far less than that of most humans, and she thought of Wolf as an adolescent—considered by most mothers and their mates as the most troubling years. Those were the years of exuberant energy and little experience when youngsters, full of life and convinced it would last forever, took chances that endangered their lives. If they lived, they usually gained some background and knowledge that would help them to survive longer. She thought it was probably not much different for wolves, and she couldn't help worrying.

It had been a cool summer, and drier than Jondalar recalled. On the open plains mini-whirlwinds of dust blew up, spun around for a while, then died, and they were happy to see a small lake ahead. They stopped beside it and shared Pleasures in the shade of a weeping willow, extravagantly full of small lanceolate leaves on boughs that bent to the water's surface, then rested and talked before going for a swim.

After splashing into the water, Ayla shouted, "I'll race you across," and immediately reached out with long, sure strokes. Jondalar followed quickly, slowly gaining on her with his longer arms and powerful muscles, but it was an effort. She looked back, saw him drawing near, and renewed her efforts in a fresh burst of speed. They reached the other side in a dead heat.

"You had a head start, so I won," Jondalar said as they reached the opposite shore of the small lake and flopped to the ground, breathing hard.

"You should have challenged me first," Ayla answered, laughing. "We both won."

They swam at a more leisurely pace back to the other side as the sun passed its zenith and was starting its descent, signaling the last half of the day. They were a little sad as they repacked their things, knowing their idyllic respite was nearly over. They mounted the horses and headed in the direction of the Summer Meeting camp, but Ayla missed Wolf and wished he was with them.

They were approaching the campsite, perhaps a few miles away, when they heard shouts amid clouds of dust rising from the dry earth of the plains. Riding closer, they saw several young men who probably shared one of the bachelor fa'lodges, and from the glimpse of decoration on their clothing, Jondalar thought they were mostly from the Fifth Cave. Each one held a spear, and they were spaced out in a rough circle, in the middle of which was a beast with a long shaggy coat and two huge horns protruding from his snout.

It was a woolly rhinoceros, a massive creature, eleven and a half feet in length and five feet high. He was a ponderous beast, with short, thick, stubby legs to support his immense bulk. He ate huge quantities of the grasses, herbs, and brush of the steppes, as well as the twigs and branches of evergreens and willows that lined the banks of the rivers. His nostrils were partitioned, and his eyes were on the sides of his head. He could not see well, especially in front, but his senses of smell and hearing were particularly acute and discerning to make up for his poor eyesight.

The front one of his two horns was more than a yard long, heavy and vicious looking as it swept the ground in an arc from side to side. In winter he could use it to sweep snow away and expose the dried, recumbent steppe grasses that lay underneath. A thick, woolly, light grayish-brown fleece covered his body, with longer outer hair hanging down, nearly brushing the ground. A wide distinctive band of fur around the middle of the rhino was a shade darker and looked, Ayla thought, as though someone had covered him with a saddle blanket, not that anyone would dream of riding such a tremendously powerful, unpredictable, sometimes malicious, and very dangerous animal.

The woolly rhinoceros pawed the ground, turning his head from side to side, trying to see the young man that his sensitive nose told him was there. Suddenly he charged. The man stood his ground until, at the very last moment, he dodged aside, and the long, forward-pointing horn of the rhinoceros barely missed him.

"That looks dangerous," Ayla said as they pulled up the horses a safe distance away.

"That's why they're doing it," Jondalar said. "Woolly rhinos are difficult to hunt under any circumstances. They are mean tempered and unpredictable."

"Like Broud," Ayla said. "The woolly rhino was his totem. The

Clan men hunted them, but I never watched them. What are they doing?"

"They're baiting him, see? Each man tries to get his attention to make him charge, then they dodge away when he comes near. They are making a sport of wearing him down, trying to see who can let the rhino come closest before they jump aside. The bravest is the one who can feel the beast brush past as he charges. It's usually young men who like to hunt rhinoceros like that," Jondalar explained.

"If they kill one, they give the meat to the Cave, and get lots of praise for it. Then they share the other parts, but the one who gets credited with the kill gets first choice. He will usually take the horn. The horns are prized, they say, for making tools, knife handles, and such, but more likely it's for other reasons. Probably because its shape resembles a man in heat for Pleasures, there are rumors that grinding up the horn and secretly giving it to a woman will make her more passionate for the man who gave it to her," Jondalar said with a smile.

"The meat is not bad, and there's a lot of fat under that heavy coat," Ayla said. "It's rare to see one, though."

"Especially this time of year," Jondalar said. "Woolly rhinos are solitary animals most of the time, and usually scarce around here in summer. They like it colder, even though they shed the soft fur under the long outer hair every spring. It gets caught in bushes before they leaf out, and people like to go out and collect it, particularly weavers and basket-makers. I used to go with my mother. We did it several times a year. She knows when all the animals shed, ibex and mouflon, musk-ox, even horses and lions, and of course, mammoths and woolly rhinos."

"Have you ever baited a rhinoceros, Jondalar?"

The man laughed. "Yes, most men do, especially when they are young. They bait lots of animals like that, aurochs bulls and bison, but they like to bait rhinos best. Some women do, too. Jetamio did, the time I showed them how to hunt a rhino. She was the Sharamudoi woman who became Thonolan's mate. She was good at it. They didn't usually hunt rhinos. They hunted the huge sturgeon of the Great Mother River from those boats they showed you, and ibex and chamois up high in the mountains, which are very hard to hunt, but they didn't know the techniques to hunt woolly rhinos." He paused and looked sad. "It was because of a rhino that we met the Sharamudoi. Thonolan had gotten gored by one, and they saved his life."

They watched as the young men played their dangerous game.

One man, standing out in the open shouting and waving his arms, was trying to make the rhino charge. The animal's usually keen sense of smell was confused by so many men arrayed around him. When he finally detected movement with his small, nearsighted eyes, he started in that direction, gaining speed as he drew closer to his antagonist. For all his short legs, the animal could move remarkably fast. He lowered his head a bit as he neared, preparing to ram his massive horn into a resistive mass. It encountered air instead as the man deftly spun around and moved aside. It took a moment for the beast to realize his charge had been in vain and slow to a halt.

The rhino was baffled and getting tired and angry. He pawed the ground as the men quickly deployed in a new circle around him. Another man stepped out, shouting and waving to draw the huge brute's attention. The rhino turned and charged again, and the man darted away. The next time it took longer to entice him to charge. They seemed to be succeeding in tiring the rhino. The exhausting, infuriating bursts of energy were taking their toll.

The great beast stood still, head drooping, breathing heavily. The men tightened the circle, closing in for the kill. The man whose turn it was to draw the beast out moved in cautiously, spear held in readiness. The rhino appeared not to notice. As the man drew near, the unpredictable beast caught the movement with his weak eyes. His flagging strength, revived by the short rest, was goaded by the fury that filled his primordial brain.

Without warning, the rhino charged again. It happened so fast that the man was unprepared. The huge woolly beast finally succeeded in thrusting his massive horn into something more solid than air. They heard an agonized scream and the man was down. When Ayla heard it, without thinking she urged her horse forward.

"Ayla! Wait! It's too dangerous!" Jondalar called after her, prodding his own mount as he readied his spear-thrower.

The other men were hurling their spears even as Jondalar spoke. When Ayla jumped off her still-moving horse and ran toward the wounded man, the huge beast lay crumpled in a heap; several spears, a couple from a spear-thrower, were sticking out of his body in every direction, like the quills of some enormous grotesque porcupine. But the kill was too late. The enraged beast had had his satisfaction.

Several young men, looking scared and lost, were ranged around the fallen man, who was crumpled, unconscious where he dropped. As Ayla approached them with Jondalar close behind, they appeared surprised to see her, and it seemed for a moment that one was going to bar her way or ask who she was, but she ignored him. She turned him over and checked his breathing, and pulled out her knife to cut away blood-soaked leggings from his leg, her hands already colored from the task. There was a smear of red on her face where she had unconsciously pushed aside a strand of hair. She didn't have any Zelandoni marks on her face, yet she seemed to know what she was doing. The young man backed away.

When she exposed the leg, the damage was obvious. The calf of his right leg was bent backward where there was no knee. The huge pointed horn had gored the man in the calf and broken both bones. The muscle was torn open, the jagged end of a bone was showing, and blood was pouring out of the gash and pooling on the ground.

She looked up at Jondalar. "Help me straighten him out while he's unconscious, it's going to hurt to move him when he wakes up. Then get me some soft hides, our toweling hides will work. I need to apply pressure to stop the bleeding, then I'll need help to splint the leg." The tall man hurried off, and she turned to one of the young men who were standing around, gaping.

"He'll need to be carried back. Do you know how to make a stretcher?" He looked blank, as though he hadn't heard or understood her. "We need something for him to lie on while he's carried."

He nodded. "A stretcher," he said.

He was really only a boy, she realized. "Jondalar will help you," she said as the man returned with the hides.

They laid him out on his back. He moaned from the movement, but didn't wake up. She checked him again; he might have sustained a head injury from the fall, but she didn't see anything obvious. Then, leaning hard on his leg above the knee, she tried to slow the bleeding. She thought about a tourniquet, but if she could get the bone straightened and wrap the leg, she might not need it. Pressure on the wound itself should be enough. He was still bleeding, but she had seen worse.

She turned to Jondalar. "We need splints, some straight wood about the length of his leg, break some of those spears if you need to."

Jondalar brought her two splints, broken lengths of spears. She quickly cut strips out of one of the hides, and other pieces to wrap around the splints for padding, to get them ready. Then, grasping the foot of the broken leg by holding the toes with one hand and his heel with her other hand, she gently pulled it straight, feeling where it resisted and easing it through. He spasmed a few times, and noises escaped his mouth; he'd been close to waking. She reached into the bleeding gash and tried to feel if the bones were aligned.

"Jondalar, hold his thigh for me," she said. "I need to set this leg before he wakes up, and while he's still bleeding. The blood will help keep the wound clean." Then she looked up at the young men—boys—who were standing around watching with looks of horror and amazement on their faces. "You, and you," she said, looking directly at two of them. "I'm going to lift his leg and pull to align the bones so they will heal straight. If I don't, he'll never walk on that leg again. I want you to get those splints and put them underneath his leg, so when I lower it, the leg will be right between them. Can you do that?"

They nodded and hurried to get the wrapped spears. When everybody was ready, Ayla grasped the foot by the toes and heel again with both hands and gently but firmly lifted his leg. With Jondalar holding the thigh, she pulled, exerting strong pressure carefully. It was not the first time he had seen her set bones, but now she was trying to set two of them. He could see the concentration on her face as she pulled, trying to sense by the feel of his leg in her hands if the bones were lining up. Even he felt what seemed to be a slight jerk and a settling, as though a bone had found its place. She lowered the leg gently, then examined it critically. It looked straight to Jondalar, but what did he know? At least it wasn't bent backward at a place it had no right to be.

She signaled that he could let go and turned her attention to the bleeding wound. Pressing it together as best she could, with Jondalar's help to lift it, she wrapped it up, splints and all, then tied everything together with the strips of leather she had cut. Then she sat back on her heels.

It was then that Jondalar noticed the blood. It was everywhere, the wrappings, the splints, Ayla, himself, the young men who had helped. The young man on the ground had lost a lot of blood. "I think we have to get him back soon," Jondalar said.

A fleeting thought passed through his mind. The prohibition against talking was not quite over, and the ritual releasing the newly mated couple from it had not been performed, but Ayla hadn't even considered it, and Jondalar dismissed it as soon as he thought about it. This was an emergency, and there was no Zelandoni around to ask.

"You will need to make the stretcher," she said to the young men standing around, seeming to be in more shock than the one on the ground.

They looked at each other, shuffled their feet. They were all young and inexperienced. Several had only recently reached manhood, a few had made their first kill during the massive bison hunt that marked the beginning of the summer hunting season, and that had been an easy hunt, hardly more than target practice. The rhino baiting had been at the instigation of one of them who had watched his brother at similar sport a few years before, and a couple of the others who had heard about it, but primarily it was a spur-of-the-moment decision because they happened to see the beast. They all knew that they should have brought in some experienced older hunters before they attempted to bring down the huge animal, but they could only think of the glory of doing it themselves, the envy of the other bachelor fa'lodges, and the admiration of the whole Summer Meeting when it was brought it in. Now one of them was badly hurt.

Jondalar quickly assessed the situation. "What Cave does he belong to?" he asked.

"The Fifth," came the reply.

"You run ahead and tell them what happened," Jondalar said. The young man to whom he had spoken sprinted off. He thought that he could have ridden in to tell them on Racer faster than a boy could run, but someone needed to supervise the construction of the stretcher. The boys were still scared and in shock, and having a grown man around to direct them right now was exactly what they needed. "We'll need three or four of you to help carry him in. The rest of you should stay here and gut that animal. It could bloat up fast. I'll send some people back to help you. There's no point in wasting the meat, the cost was too high."

"He's my cousin. I'd like to help carry him back," one young man said.

"Fine. Pick three more, that should be enough to get him back. The rest can stay," Jondalar said. Then he noticed that the youngster seemed almost overcome and was trying to hold back tears. "What is your cousin's name?" he asked.

"Matagan. He is Matagan of the Fifth Cave of the Zelandonii."

"I know you must care about Matagan, and this has been very hard on you," Jondalar said. "He was very seriously hurt, but I will tell you the truth, he is very lucky that Ayla happened to be here. I can't promise, but I think he will be all right, and may even walk again. Ayla is a very good healer. I know. I was mauled by a cave lion, and would have died on the steppes far to the east, but Ayla found me, treated my wounds, and saved my life. If anybody can save Matagan, Ayla will."

The young man let out a sob of relief and then tried to control himself again.

"Now, get me some spears so we can carry your cousin home," Jondalar said. "We'll need at least four, two for each side." Under his guidance, they soon had the spears tied together with thongs to make two sturdy supports, and spare pieces of clothing laced between them. Ayla checked the wounded young man, then several of them lifted him onto the makeshift stretcher.

They were not too far from the camp. Ayla and Jondalar signaled Whinney and Racer to follow, and they walked beside the wounded young man. She watched him with worried concentration, and when they stopped to change bearers, she checked his breathing and felt for the beat in his wrist. It was faint, but definite.

They were nearest the upstream end of the camp, close to the encampment of the Ninth Cave. News of the accident had spread rapidly, and several people had followed the young man back to meet them. Joharran was among them and spotted them in the distance. When they joined up, the two who were bearing the litter were relieved of their place, and the pace back to the large Meeting place quickened.

"Marthona went to tell someone to get Zelandoni, and Zelandoni of the Fifth," Joharran said. "They were at the other end of the camp at some Zelandonia meeting. Should we take him to our camp, or to his own?" he asked Ayla.

"I want to change those wrappings, and get a poultice on that wound, I don't want it to fester," Ayla said. She thought for a moment. "I haven't had much time to replenish all my medicines, but I'm sure Zelandoni has enough, and I want her to look at him. Let's take him to the zelandonia lodge."

"That's a good idea. It would take her a while to get here, we can probably get there faster. Zelandoni doesn't run the way she used to," Joharran said, somewhat diplomatically referring to her great size. "The Fifth's Zelandoni will probably want to see him, but healing was never his greatest talent, I'm told."

When they arrived at the zelandonia lodge, the First met them at the entrance. A place had already been made ready, and Ayla wondered if someone had gone ahead and told her that she had decided not to keep the man at the camp of the Ninth Cave, or if the woman had just assumed that the injured man would be brought there. Several people who had seen them coming were already talking about all the blood. Though several of the zelandonia were outside, no one else was inside the lodge.

"Put him down over there," the First said, showing them one of the raised beds at the far side, opposite the entrance. The men carried him there, then moved him to the bed. Most of the men left, but Joharran and Jondalar stayed.

Ayla made sure the leg was straight, then started to remove the wrappings. "It needs a poultice so it won't fester," she said.

"He will keep for a moment. Tell me what happened," the First said.

Both Ayla and Jondalar quickly explained the circumstances, then Ayla finished, "Both lower legbones in that leg are broken, the calf was bent backward at the break. I knew if they weren't set straight, he would never walk on that leg again, and he's a young man. I decided to set the leg right there, while he was unconscious and before it started to swell up, and make it harder to work with the bones. I had to feel around inside, and pull hard to get the bones aligned again, but I think they are. He was making some noises on the way here, he may wake up soon. I'm sure he will be in pain."

"It's obvious that you know something about it, but I need to ask you some questions. First, I presume you have set bones before," the First said.

Jondalar answered for her. "A Sharamudoi woman, a good friend that I cared for very much, the mate of a leader, had fallen down a cliff and broken her arm. Their healer had died, and they hadn't been able to get word to another one, and the bone was healing together wrong, and very painfully. I watched Ayla rebreak it and set it right. I also watched her set a badly broken leg of a man of the Clan. He had jumped off a very high rock to protect his mate from some young Losadunai men who had been attacking Clan women. If there is one thing Ayla knows about, it's broken bones and open wounds."

"Where did you learn, Ayla?" she asked.

"Clan people have very sturdy bones, but the men of the Clan often break them when they are hunting. They don't usually throw spears, they chase after an animal to stab him with a spear or sometimes jump on him. Or they do what those boys were doing, get an animal to chase several of them until the beast is so tired, they can get close enough to spear him. It's very strenuous. Women break bones, too, but mostly it's the men. I first learned about broken bones from Iza. The people of Brun's clan would break a bone sometimes, but it was the summer that we went to the Clan Gathering that I really learned, from the other Clan medicine women, how to set broken bones and treat wounds," Ayla said.

"I think this young man is very lucky that you happened to be there, Ayla," the One Who Was First said. "Not every Zelandoni would have known what to do with a leg that badly broken. There will be some more questions, the Fifth will want to talk to you, I'm sure, and the boy's mother, of course, but you did well. What kind of poultice were you going to put on this leg?"

"I dug some roots that I saw on the way here. I think you call it anemone," Ayla said. "The wound was bleeding while I was handling it, and a person's own blood is sometimes the best thing to clean out a wound, but now that the blood is drying, I was going to mash the root and boil it to make a wash to clean the wound, and then add some fresh to the mash and use it with some other roots in a poultice. In my medicine bag, I have some powdered geranium root, to clot the blood, and spores of club moss to absorb fluid, and then I was going to ask if you had certain things or knew where they grow."

"All right, ask me."

"There is a root, when I described it to Jondalar he thought you might call it comfrey. It is very good for healing, inside and out. It's good for bruises, in a salve made with fat, but it's very good on fresh wounds and cuts. A fresh poultice can keep the swelling down when a bone is broken, and it helps broken bones to grow back together," Ayla said.

"Yes, I have some powdered, and I know a place nearby where it grows, and I would describe its properties the same way," the First said.

"I would also use the bright pretty flowers that I think are called marigolds. They are especially good for open wounds, also for wounds and sores that won't heal. I like to squeeze the juice out of fresh flowers, or boil the dried petals to put on open wounds, then keep it wet. It helps prevent the smelly bad festering, and I'm afraid this boy will need that. I'm sorry, I don't know his name," Ayla said.

"Matagan," Jondalar said. "His cousin told me he is Matagan of the Fifth Cave."

"What else would you use if you had it?" Zelandoni asked.

For an instant, Ayla had a fleeting image of Iza testing her knowledge. "Crushed juniper berries for a bleeding wound, or the mushroom that is round, puffball. That can stop bleeding of wounds. A dry powder of goldenseal is also good, and . . ."

"That's enough. I'm convinced that you know what to do. The treatment you suggest is very appropriate," the First said, "but right now, Jondalar, I want you to take her someplace where she can clean up, both of you, in fact. That boy's blood is all over you, and that will upset his mother more than anything. Leave the anemone roots with me, I will send someone to get fresh comfrey. We'll take care of him for now. You can come back when you are clean and rested. Why don't you go to your camp the back way, so you don't have to walk through the whole Summer Meeting camp again. I'm sure there is a crowd waiting outside. Use the other entrance, it'll be faster, and you may avoid those who'll want to detain you. Before you go, though, I think you need to be released from your ban against talking. It seems your isolation ended a day early."

"Oh! I forgot," Ayla said. "I didn't even think about that!"

"I did," Jondalar put in, "but didn't have time to worry about it."

"You were right. This was certainly emergency enough," Zelandoni said, "but I must ask you formally. You have completed your trial period, Jondalar and Ayla, have you decided that you want to stay mated, or would you rather end this now and try to find someone else with whom you would be more compatible?"

The two looked at her, then looked at each other, and then a grin stole over Jondalar's face that transferred to a smile from Ayla.

"If I'm not compatible with Ayla, who on earth would I ever be compatible with?" Jondalar said. "This may have been our Matrimonial, but in my heart, we have been mated for a long time."

"That is true. We even said words like that before we crossed the glacier, right after we left Guban and Yorga. We knew we were mated then, but Jondalar wanted you to tie the knot for us, Zelandoni."

"Do you want to become unmated, Ayla? Jondalar?" she asked.

"No, I don't," Ayla said, smiling at Jondalar. "Do you?"

"Not for a heartbeat, woman," he said. "I waited long enough, I'm not about to end it now."

"Then you are released from the prohibition against talking to others and you can declare to all that Jondalar and Ayla of the Ninth

Cave of the Zelandonii are mated. Ayla, any children born to you are born to the hearth of Jondalar. It will be the responsibility of both of you to care for them until they are grown. Do you have your leather thong?" While they retrieved the long strip of leather, Zelandoni got two necklaces from a nearby table. She took back the thong and tied a simple necklace around each of their necks. "I wish you both a long and happy life together," the One Who Was First Among Those Who Served The Great Earth Mother concluded.

They slipped out the back entrance and hurried around the back way. Some people saw them leaving and called after them, but they kept on going. When they reached the spring-fed pool, Ayla walked into the water fully dressed. Jondalar followed her in. Once Zelandoni had brought it to their attention, they could feel and smell the blood on them, and they wanted to get it off. If the bloodstains were going to come out at all, Ayla thought, it would have to be in cold water. If not, she would probably just dispose of the clothing and make herself some new. After the major hunts, she now owned several hides and various other parts of animals that she ought to be able to use.

They left the horses at the pasture near the Ninth Cave's camp on their way to the zelandonia lodge, and the animals found their own way to their enclosure. The smell of blood was always a little unsettling for them, and both the rhinoceros and the young man had bled profusely. The fenced-in place had a feeling of security to it. Jondalar had wrapped his wet clothing back around him and ran toward the camp, hoping he would find the horses and extra clothing from the pack baskets.

He was surprised to see Lanidar there comforting the horses, but the boy seemed upset and said he wanted to talk to Ayla. Jondalar told him as soon as he brought her some clothes, she would come. He did take the time to take the baskets and blankets and bridles off the horses. He told Ayla about Lanidar, and when she saw him, she could tell from his posture, even from a distance, that he was very unhappy. She wondered if for some reason his mother had forbidden him to care for the horses anymore.

"What's wrong, Lanidar?" she asked as soon as she reached him.

"It's Lanoga," he said. "She's been crying all day."

"But why?" Ayla said.

"The baby. They are taking Lorala away from her."

34

Who is going to take the baby away from her?" Ayla asked.

"Proleva, and some women," he said. "They say they have found a mother for Lorala, someone who can nurse her all the time."

"Let's go see what this is all about," Ayla said. "We'll come back and take care of the horses later."

When they got to the camp, Ayla was glad to see Proleva there. She saw them coming and smiled. "Well, is it affirmed? Are you mated? Can we have the feast and get out the gifts? You don't have to answer. I see your necklaces."

Ayla had to smile back. "Yes, we are mated," she said.

"Zelandoni just affirmed it," Jondalar said.

"I need to talk to you about something else, Proleva," Ayla said with a serious frown.

"What?" The woman knew from Ayla's expression that she was concerned about something.

"Lanidar said that you are taking the baby away from Lanoga," Ayla said.

"I wouldn't put it that way. I thought you would be pleased that we had found a home for Lorala. A woman from the Twenty-fourth Cave lost her baby. He was born with a serious deformity and died. She's full of milk, and said she'd be willing to take Lorala, even if she is older. She really wants a child, and I get the impression she has miscarried before. I thought it would be a perfect match," Proleva said.

"It does seem like it ought to be. Do the women who are nursing Lorala now want to stop?" Ayla asked.

"Actually, no. I was rather surprised. When I mentioned it to a couple of them, they seemed a little upset. Even Stelona said the Twenty-fourth Cave is so far away, she would be sorry if she couldn't continue to watch Lorala growing strong and healthy," Proleva said.

"I know you were thinking of what is best for Lorala, but did you ask Lanoga?" Ayla said.

"No, not really. I asked Tremeda. I thought Lanoga might like to be free of the responsibility. She's so young to have to worry about taking care of a baby all the time. There will be time enough when she has her own to mother," Proleva said.

"Lanidar says Lanoga has been crying all day."

"I know she's upset, but I thought she'd get over it. After all, she's not nursing Lorala, she's not even a woman yet. She can only count eleven years."

Ayla remembered that she could count less than twelve years when she gave birth to Durc, and she couldn't give him up then. She would rather have died than give him up. When she lost her milk, the women of the Clan had nursed Durc, but that didn't mean she was any less his mother. She was sorry still that she had to leave him behind when she was forced out of the Clan. She had wanted to take him. It was only her fear about what would happen to him if something happened to her that persuaded her to leave her three-year son behind. It didn't matter that she knew Uba would take care of him and love him as her own. It still hurt when she thought about him. She never got over him, and she didn't want Lanoga to suffer that kind of pain.

"It isn't nursing that makes a mother, Proleva. And it certainly isn't age," Ayla said. "Look at Janida. She's not much older, but no one would dream of taking her baby away from her."

"Janida has a mate, and a good one with some status, and her baby will be born to his hearth. He'll always be responsible, and even if the mating doesn't last, there are already several men who have made it known they would be willing to mate her. She has high status, she's attractive, and she's pregnant. I just hope Peridal realizes what a favored woman she is, his mother is already making trouble. She actually found them during their trial period and tried to get him to give up the mating." Proleva stopped. Time enough later to tell Ayla about that. "But Lanoga is not Janida."

"No, Lanoga is not a favored young woman, but she ought to be. You don't spend nearly a year taking care of a baby and not grow to love her. Lorala is Lanoga's baby now, not Tremeda's. She may be young, but she has been a good mother," Ayla said.

"Yes, of course she's been a good mother. That's just it. She's a wonderful girl and she'll be a wonderful mother someday," Proleva said, "if she ever has the chance. But when she gets old enough to mate, what man will be willing to take her and a little sister, not as a second woman, but as a child he would have to be responsible for that wasn't even born to his hearth? Lanoga has enough going against her, considering the hearth she and Lorala were born to. I'm afraid the only one willing to take her will be someone like Laramar, no matter who recommends her. I'd like to see her have a chance for a better life."

Ayla was sure that Proleva was absolutely right, and it was obvious that she really cared about the girl and would do whatever she could to help her, but she knew how Lanoga would feel if she lost Lorala.

"Lanoga doesn't have to worry about finding a mate," Lanidar said.

Ayla and Proleva had almost forgotten he was still there. Jondalar was surprised, too. He had been listening to the debate between the two women and could see both sides.

"I am going to learn how to hunt, and I am going to learn how to be a Caller, and when I grow up, I am going to mate Lanoga and help her take care of Lorala, and all the rest of her brothers and sisters, if she wants. I already asked her, and she agreed. She's the only girl I ever met who doesn't care about my arm, and I don't think her mother will care, either."

Ayla and Proleva both gaped at Lanidar, then they looked at each other as though to be sure that they had heard the same thing, and that both of them were thinking the same thing. In fact, it wouldn't be a bad match, especially if the idea really encouraged Lanidar to learn some skills to better himself. They were both decent children, and surprisingly grown-up for their ages. Of course, they were young, and they could easily change their minds, but on the other hand, who else would there be for either one?

"So don't give Lanoga's baby away to some other woman. I don't like to see her crying," Lanidar said.

"She really does love that child," Ayla said, "and the Ninth Cave has been willing to help her. Why not just let things be the way they are?"

"What will I tell the woman who was going to take her?" Proleva said.

"Just tell her Lorala's mother didn't want to give her up. It's true. Tremeda isn't really her mother, Lanoga is. If that woman really wants a baby, she'll get one, either one of her own or another baby that needs a mother, maybe even one who is younger. The Zelandonii have many Caves and a lot of people. Things are happening all the time," Ayla said. "I've never seen things change so much."

Nearly everyone from both the Ninth Cave of the Zelandonii and the First Cave of the Lanzadonii came to the big celebration held jointly to celebrate the Matrimonials of the brother of the leader of one and the daughter of the hearth of the leader of the other, who were also related to each other. It turned out that two other people from the Ninth Cave had also mated at the same time to people from other Caves. Proleva learned about them and made sure they were also included. A young woman named Tishona had joined with Marsheval of the Fourteenth Cave, and she would be going to live with him. And another, somewhat older woman, Dynoda, had moved away and had a son, but she severed the knot from her former mate and formed a new relationship with Jacsoman of the Seventh Cave. They were moving back to the Ninth Cave. Dynoda's mother was ill, and she wanted to be closer to her.

During the course of the day, other people came to offer their good wishes as well. Levela and Jondecam, and her mother, Velima, who was also Proleva's mother, spent most of the day with them, which pleased Ayla and Jondalar, and Joplaya and Echozar. They all enjoyed each other's company. Jondecam's mother and uncle also came for a while.

Ayla and Jondalar were pleased to see Kimeran, who was now distantly related through his nephew's mate, who was the sister of Jondalar's brother's mate. Ayla got lost in some of the convoluted relationships, but she was particularly pleased to see Jondecam's mother, Zelandoni of the Second Cave. She had met the woman, but hadn't realized who she was. For some reason, Ayla was particularly glad to meet a Zelandoni who had children, especially a son who was as friendly and confident as Jondecam.

Janida and Peridal also spent most of the day at the Ninth Cave, conspicuously without Peridal's mother. They wanted to move away from the Twenty-ninth Cave and were talking to both Kimeran and Joharran, to see if either the Second Cave or the Ninth Cave would accept them. Jondalar was certain that one or the other would. The First had already spoken to the leaders and the Zelandoni of the Second about it. She felt it would be wise to separate the young couple from Peridal's mother, at least for a while. The First had been quite angry with the woman for forcing herself on them during their trial period of isolation.

Toward evening as things started to quiet down, Marthona made tea for several relatives and friends who were still there. Proleva, Ayla, Joplaya, and Folara helped pass cups around. A young man, who had recently been accepted as an acolyte of the Zelandoni of the Fifth Cave, was also there, staying only because it was the first time that he was a part of such august company and couldn't bear to leave. He was especially in awe of the First.

"I'm sure he'd never walk again if someone hadn't been there who knew what to do," said the acolyte. He had directed his comment to the company at large, but he was really trying to impress the great donier.

"I think you are entirely correct, Fourth Acolyte of Zelandoni of the Fifth. You are very perceptive," the woman said. "The rest is up to the Great Mother now, and the young man's powers of recovery."

The young man swelled with pride that she had responded, hardly able to contain his pleasure at Zelandoni's compliment. He was enjoying the fact that he was included in this informal conversation with the One Who Was First.

"Since you are an acolyte now, will you be taking a turn at watching Matagan? He is of your Cave, isn't he?" the First said. "Of course, it's difficult to stay up through the night, but he does need to have someone with him all the time, right now. I presume your Zelandoni has asked for your help. If not, you could volunteer. The Fifth would no doubt appreciate it."

"Yes, of course I'll take a turn," he said, getting up. "Thank you for the tea. I must go now. I have my responsibilities," he said, trying to sound dignified. He squared his shoulders and pulled his face into a serious frown as he headed toward the main camp.

After the young acolyte had gone, several of those who were there finally gave in to the smile they had been struggling to keep from making. "You have made that young man very happy, Zelandoni," Jondalar said. "He was almost glowing with pleasure. Do all the zelandonia hold you in such awe?"

"Only the young ones," Zelandoni replied. "The way the rest argue with me, I sometimes wonder why they continue to name me First. Perhaps because I'm more portentous than they are," she said, and smiled. She meant it as a pun on her rather portly size.

Jondalar smiled back, getting the joke. Marthona just gave her a meaningful glance with arched eyebrows. Ayla noticed the exchange and thought she understood, but wasn't certain. The subtleties that came from deep understanding of someone known for a long time were still beyond her here.

"I think I'd rather have the arguing, though," Zelandoni continued. "It can be a little trying to have every word you speak treated as if it came straight from the mouth of Doni Herself. It makes me feel that I have to be careful about everything I say."

"Who does decide which one of the zelandonia is First Among Those Who Serve The Mother?" Jondalar asked. "Is it like the leader of a Cave? Does each Zelandoni just say who they think it should be? Does everyone have to agree, or most of them, or just certain ones?"

"The choices of the individual zelandonia are part of it, but it's not as simple as that. Many things are considered. A gift for healing is one, and no one judges that more severely than zelandonia healers. A person may be able to cover up some ineptitude to people in general, but you can't deceive someone who knows. But healing is not absolutely essential. There have been Firsts who had only a rudimentary knowledge of healing, but it was more than compensated for by ability in other areas. Some have natural gifts or other attributes."

"We only hear about the First. Is there a Second, or a Third? Someone who can step in if something happens to the First? And is there a Last?" Jondalar asked, warming to the subject. Everyone was interested. Zelandoni wasn't often so forthcoming about the inner workings of the zelandonia, but she was noticing Ayla's interest and had her reasons for being so uncommonly candid.

"The order does not descend individually. There are ranks. It would be difficult for a Cave to accept a donier who was Last Among Those Who Serve, wouldn't it? The acolytes are the lowest rank, of course, but there are ranks within the acolytes, too, sometimes depending on particular skills. You may have guessed that the young man who is the Fourth Acolyte of the Zelandoni of the Fifth Cave was just recently accepted. He is a novice, the lowest rank, but he has potential or he would not have been accepted. Some don't want to go beyond acolyte. They don't want to take on the full burden of responsibility, they only want to exercise their skill, and can do it best within the zelandonia.

"After the acolytes, the next lowest rank are the new doniers. Every Zelandoni must feel they have personally been called, and more than that, they must convince the rest of the zelandonia that it was a true calling. Some never get beyond the rank of acolyte, even though they may want to. Sometimes acolytes want to be a Zelandoni so much, they try to claim a false call or even feign one, but they are invariably rejected. One who has been through the ordeal knows the difference. It has made some acolytes—and former acolytes—very bitter."

"What else is required to become a Zelandoni," Jondalar pressed, "and what is especially needed to be the One Who Is First?" The rest were happy to let him do the asking. Though some of them, such as Marthona, who was once an acolyte herself, knew most of the requirements, few of the others who were there had ever had their questions to Zelandoni answered so directly.

"To become one of the zelandonia, one must memorize all the Histories and Elder Legends, and have a good comprehension of their meaning. One must know the counting words and how to use them, the coming of the seasons, the phases of the moon, and some things that are only for the zelandonia to know. But perhaps most important, one must be able to visit the world of the spirits," Zelandoni said. "That is why one must truly be called. Most zelandonia know from the beginning who will be First, and who is most likely to be the next one. The first time one feels the call to venture into the spirit world, it may be revealed. Being First is also a calling, and not a calling every Zelandoni wants."

"What is it like, the spirit world? Is it frightening? Are you afraid when you have to go there?" he asked next.

"Jondalar, no one can describe the spirit world to one who has never been there. And yes, it is frightening, especially the first time. It never entirely ceases to be frightening, but with meditation and preparation, it can be controlled, along with the knowledge that the zelandonia, and particularly the Cave, is there to help. Without the help of the people of one's Cave, it could be difficult to return," she explained.

"But if it's frightening, why do you do it?" Jondalar asked.

"There is no way to refuse it."

Ayla suddenly felt a chilling cold, and shuddered.

"Many try to fight it, and some succeed for a while," the donier continued, "but in the end the Mother will have Her way. It is best to go prepared. The dangers are never kept from one who may think to venture in that direction, that is why the initiation can be so grueling. The test on the other side is even worse. You may feel that you are torn apart, scattered to the whirlwind and the dark unknown. Some go and never return to their body. Some who do return leave part of themselves behind, and they are never quite right afterward. But no one can go and remain unchanged.

"And once you get the call, you must accept it, and the duties and responsibilities along with it. I think that's why so few of the zelandonia are mated. There are no restrictions on mating, or having children, but it is much like being a leader. It can be difficult to find a mate who is willing to live with someone who has so many demands made on them. Isn't that right, Marthona?" Zelandoni asked.

"Yes, Zelandoni," she answered, then she smiled at Dalanar before turning to her son. "Why do you think Dalanar and I severed the knot, Jondalar? We talked about it the day after your mating. It was more than his urge to travel—Willamar has that, too. In many ways, Dalanar and I were too much alike. He's happy now that he's leader of his own Cave—his own people, really—but it took him a while to understand that was what he really wanted. He fought the responsibility for a long time, but I think that was why he was drawn to me in the first place. Joconan had died and I was already leader when we mated. We were very happy at first. But he became restless. It was for the best that we parted. Jerika is the right woman for him. She is strong willed, and he needs a strong woman, but Dalanar is leader." The two she mentioned looked at each other and smiled, then Dalanar reached for Jerika's hand.

"Losaduna is the One Who Serves for the people who live on the other side of the glacier. He has a mate, and his mate has four children. She seems very happy," Ayla interjected. She had been listening to Zelandoni with a fascination that was akin to fear.

"Losaduna is fortunate to have found a woman like her. Just as I was fortunate to find Willamar," Marthona said. "I was very reluctant to mate again, but I'm glad he persisted." She turned to smile at him. "I suppose that's one reason I finally passed on the leadership. I was leader for many years with Willamar beside me, and we never had a problem over it, but I grew tired of the demands. I wanted some time to myself, and I wanted to have some time to share with Willamar. After Folara came along, I wanted to be a mother again. Joharran seemed to have the potential, so I started to prepare him, and when he was old enough, I was glad to pass the responsibility on to him. He is very much like Joconan, I'm sure he's the son of Joconan's spirit." She smiled at her eldest son. "I still keep a hand in. Joharran often consults with me, though I think he does it for my sake, not his."

"That's not true, mother. I value your advice," Joharran said.

"Did you love Dalanar very much, mother?" Jondalar asked. "You know there are songs and stories about your love." He had heard them, but he'd often wondered, if it was really so strong, how could they have parted?

"Yes, I loved him, Jondalar. A small part of me still does. It is not easy to forget someone you have loved that much, and I'm glad we are still friends. I think we are better friends now than when we were mated." She noticed her elder son. "I still love Joconan, too. His memory remains with me and reminds me of when I was a young woman and in love for the first time, even though it took him a while to decide what he wanted," she added rather cryptically.

Jondalar remembered the story he had heard about his mother on his Journey. "You mean between you and Bodoa or both?" he asked.

"Bodoa! I haven't heard that name in a long time," Zelandoni said. "Isn't she the foreign woman who was being trained by the zelandonia? From some eastern people, what were they called? Zar . . . Sard . . . something."

"S'Armunai," Jondalar said.

"That's it. I was still young when she left, but it's said she was quite skilled," Zelandoni said.

"She is S'Armuna now. Ayla and I met her on our Journey. The S'Armunai Wolf Women captured me, and Ayla followed their trail and came after me. We were lucky to get away from them alive. If it hadn't been for Wolf, I don't think either one of us would be here. You can imagine how surprised I was to find someone among those people who not only knew how to speak Zelandonii, but knew my mother!"

"What happened?" several people asked.

Jondalar briefly related the story of the cruel woman Attaroa and the S'Armunai Camp she had perverted. "Although S'Armuna helped Attaroa in the beginning, she regretted it and finally decided to help her people and try to correct the problems Attaroa caused." Everyone shook their heads in wonder.

"That's the most outlandish story I've ever heard," Zelandoni said, "but it shows what can happen when a donier becomes warped. I think Bodoa could have gone far if she hadn't abused her power. It's lucky for her that she finally came to her senses. It is said One Who Serves The Mother will pay in the next world if they misuse their power in this one. That's one reason the zelandonia are so careful about whom they accept. There is no turning back. It's one way we are different from leaders of a Cave. A Zelandoni is a Zelandoni for life. Even if we may sometimes want to, we cannot drop the burden."

Everyone was quiet for a while, thinking about the story Jondalar had told. They looked up when Ramara came by. "I'm supposed to let you know, Joharran, that they brought the rhino in. Jondalar gets credit, it was his spear that killed him."

"I'm glad to hear that, thank you, Ramara."

Ramara would have liked to stay and hear what everyone was talking about, but she did have other things to do, and she wasn't specifically invited, although no one would have told her go.

"You have first choice, Jondalar," Joharran said after she left. "Are you going to take the horn?"

"I don't think so. I'd rather have the fur."

"Tell me what happened out there with that rhino," Joharran asked.

Jondalar told how they happened to see the young men baiting the woolly rhinoceros and stopped to watch. "I didn't realize how young they were until after the accident. I don't think they wanted the rhino as much as they wanted admiration and praise, and to be the envy of their friends."

"None of them had any experience with rhinos, and not much with hunting. They shouldn't have tried to get one on their own. This was a hard way for them to learn that hunting rhinos, or any animal, is not really a game," Joharran said.

"But it is true that if they had brought in that woolly rhinoceros by themselves, they would have been highly praised, and the envy of their friends," Marthona said. "In one sense, this accident, terrible as it was, may help prevent future attempts and even worse tragedies. Think how many youngsters would be trying the same thing if they had succeeded. This way, it may make others think again before they attempt such a game, at least for a while. The mother of this young man may suffer and worry, but it may spare other mothers even more grief. I just hope Matagan survives without severe crippling."

"As soon as Ayla saw the rhino gore him, she raced to help," Jondalar said. "It's not the first time she's rushed into a dangerous situation when someone is hurt, but she worries me sometimes."

"He was very lucky that she was there. I'm sure he would be crippled for life, or worse, if someone hadn't been there who knew what to do," Zelandoni said, then to Ayla: "Exactly what did you do first?"

Ayla explained in general. Zelandoni drew her out for more detail, and her reasoning. In the guise of interested conversation, Zelandoni was examining Ayla's knowledge of the healing arts. Though she hadn't mentioned it yet, the One Who Was First was trying to arrange a formal meeting of the zelandonia so they could learn the extent of Ayla's training, but she was glad for this opportunity to question her alone first. It was unfortunate for poor Matagan, but Zelandoni was glad for this demonstration of her skills to the whole Summer Meeting. It gave her this opportunity to begin to approach the zelandonia with the idea of her entering into their alliance.

Zelandoni had already reevaluated her first impression several times, but now she looked at the young woman in an entirely new light. Ayla was no novice. She was an equal, a true colleague. It was entirely possible that Zelandoni might learn a few things from her. Those club moss spores, for example. That was an application Zelandoni had not used, but upon reflection, it was probably a good procedure. She was anxious to talk to Ayla alone, to compare ideas and knowledge, and it would be good to have someone to talk with at the Ninth Cave.

Zelandoni did work with the other zelandonia in the region and discussed professional matters with colleagues during the Summer Meetings. She had a couple of acolytes, of course, though she had no serious acolyte interested in healing. To have a true healer within her own Cave, especially one who brought new knowledge, that could be very worthwhile.

"Ayla," Zelandoni said, "it might be a good idea to talk to Matagan's family."

"I'm not sure I know what to say to them," Ayla said.

"They must be worried, and I think they might like to know what happened. I'm sure it would help if you reassure them."

"How can I reassure them?" Ayla said.

"You can say that it is up to the Mother now, but there is a chance that he will be all right. Isn't that your opinion? It's mine," Zelandoni said. "I think Doni smiled on that young man, because you happened to be there."

Jondalar stifled a big yawn as he took off his tunic, a new one he had received from his mother at their mating party, woven of threads of the flax plant that she had prepared and woven. She had arranged for someone else to decorate it with some embroidery and beads, but not too much. It was very lightweight and comfortable. She had given a similar one to Ayla, made very full and loose so she could wear it as her pregnancy progressed. Jondalar had put his on immediately, but Ayla was saving hers for later.

"I've never heard Zelandoni speak so openly about the zelandonia," he said as he prepared to get into their sleeping roll. "It was interesting. I never realized how difficult it could be, but I remember her saying, whenever she had some test to endure, that it had its compensations. I wonder what they are? She didn't talk about it that much."

They lay together in silence for a while. Ayla was tired, she realized. So tired that she could hardly think. Between the rhino hunting accident yesterday, and staying at the zelandonia lodge until late, and the mating celebration today, she had slept very little and had been under some strain. She was feeling some pain around her temples and considered getting up and making some willow bark tea for it, but she was too tired to bother.

"And mother," Jondalar continued, almost as a verbal continuation of his thoughts. "I always thought she and Dalanar just decided to separate. I never knew why. I guess you don't always think of your mother as anything but your mother. Someone who loves you and takes care of you."

"I don't think the separation was easy for her. I think she loved Dalanar very much," Ayla said. "I can understand why. You are very much like him."

"Not in all ways. I never wanted to be a leader. I still don't. I would miss the feel of stone in my hands. There is nothing so satisfying as seeing a perfect blade flake off, one that turned out just the way you planned," Jondalar said.

"Dalanar is a flint-knapper, too, Jondalar," Ayla said.

"Yes, the best, but he doesn't get the chance to work at it much anymore. The only one who could match him is Wymez, and he's still back at the Lion Camp, making beautiful blades for the spears of the Mammoth Hunters. It's a shame they will never meet. They would have enjoyed learning from each other."

"But you've met them both. And you understand the stone as well as anyone. Can't you show Dalanar what you learned from Wymez?" Ayla said.

"Yes, I have already begun," Jondalar said. "Dalanar is as interested as I was. I'm so glad they delayed the Matrimonial until the Lanzadonii could get here. And I'm pleased that Joplaya and Echozar shared our Matrimonial. It's a special tie. I've always felt a deep affection for my cousin, and this brings us closer. I think Joplaya was pleased, too."

"I'm sure Joplaya was pleased to share a Matrimonial with you,

Jondalar. I think it's something she's always wanted." And this was as close as she could get to what she really wanted, Ayla added in her own mind. She did feel sorry for Joplaya, but she had to admit, she was glad of the prohibition against close cousins mating. "Echozar seems very happy."

"I think he still couldn't quite believe it. There were a few others who felt the same way, for different reasons," Jondalar said, putting his arm around her and nuzzling her neck.

"Echozar loves her almost beyond reason. Such love can compensate for a lot," Ayla said, fighting to stay awake.

"He really isn't so ugly when you get used to him. He just looks different, but you can see the Clan in him," Jondalar said.

"I don't think he's ugly at all. He reminds me of Rydag, and Durc," Ayla said. "I think they are handsome people, the Clan."

"I know you do, and you're right. They are handsome people, in their way. You are pretty handsome yourself, woman." He nuzzled her neck, then kissed her, and could feel his need for her beginning, but he could see she was almost asleep. He knew she wouldn't refuse him if he pressed her, she never did, but this wasn't the time. It would be better when she was rested, anyway.

"I hope Matagan is going to be all right," Jondalar said as Ayla rolled over and he snuggled against her back. He wasn't all that tired himself, but he didn't mind holding her.

"That reminds me, Jondalar." She rolled back over to look at him. "Zelandoni, and the Fifth's donier, and I were talking to his mother. We had to tell her that he could have problems. He may be able to walk again, but no one can say for sure."

"It would be a shame if he couldn't. He's so young."

"We just don't know, of course, but even if he does walk, he may be lame," Ayla said. "Zelandoni asked his mother if he had shown any interest in any skill or craft. The only thing that came to her mind, besides hunting, was that he made his own points for his spears. It made me think of those S'Armunai boys that Attaroa crippled. You were teaching one of them how to knap flint so he could make a life for himself. I told his mother that if it was something he wanted to do, I would ask you if you'd be willing to teach him."

"He's from the Fifth Cave, isn't he?" Jondalar said, thinking over the idea.

"Yes, but maybe he could come and live at the Ninth Cave for a while. Didn't Danug live at a different Mamutoi Camp for a year or so to learn more about flint?" Ayla said. "Maybe we could do the same for Matagan."

"That's true. Danug had just returned from a year of living with a Camp of flint miners, so he could learn about the stone at the source. Just as I learned at Dalanar's mine. He couldn't have had a better teacher than Wymez when it came to learning how to work it, but a good knapper needs to know the stone, too." Jondalar's forehead wrinkled as he pondered the implications. "I don't know. I'd be happy to teach him, but I'd have to talk to Joharran about him coming to the Ninth Cave. The boy would have to have a place to live. Joharran would have to work it out with the Fifth Cave, that is, if Matagan wants to learn. He may have been making points because he couldn't find anyone else to make them for him, and he wanted to hunt. We'll see, Ayla. It's a possibility. If he was hurt that badly, he will need to learn some craft."

They both settled down in the furs, but as tired as Ayla was, sleep did not come immediately. She found herself thinking about her future, and that of the baby she was carrying. What if it was a boy and he wanted to bait rhinos? What if something else happened? And where was Wolf? He was almost like a son to her, too, but she hadn't seen him for several days. When she finally went to sleep, she dreamed about babies, and wolves, and earthquakes. She hated earthquakes. They more than frightened her, they were like a personal harbinger of bad news.

"I can't believe some people are still objecting to Joplaya and Echozar getting mated here," Zelandoni said. "It's done. They were mated. They've been through their isolation trial, they're affirmed. It's over with. They've even had their mating party. There is nothing more to be said." The First was having a last cup of tea before returning to the zelandonia lodge after spending the night at the camp of the Ninth Cave. Several others were sitting around a large trenchfire, finishing their morning meal before the busy activities of the day began.

"They are talking about going home early," Marthona said.

"That would be a shame after coming so far," Jondalar said.

"They have what they came for, Joplaya and Echozar are officially mated, and they have their Zelandoni, or rather, Lanzadoni," Willamar said.

"I was hoping to spend some time with them. I don't think we'll be seeing them again for a while," Jondalar said.

"I was hoping the same," Joharran said. "I've been talking to Dalanar about why he decided to establish the Lanzadonii as a separate group. It's more than the fact that they live a good distance away. He has some interesting ideas."

"He always did," Marthona said.

"Echozar and Joplaya don't even like to go to the main camp area because they say people stare at them, and the looks are not especially friendly," Folara said.

"They may be feeling a little sensitive since the objections during the Matrimonial," Proleva said.

"I've looked into every one. None of those objections has merit. It was all started by Brukeval, of all people, but everyone knows what his problem is," the First said. "And Marona is just trying to make trouble because the Lanzadonii are related to Jondalar, and she still wants to get back at him and anyone around him."

"That woman seems to be training herself in the craft of carrying a grudge," Proleva said. "She needs something to do. Maybe if she had a child it would give her something else to think about."

"I wouldn't wish her as a mother on any child," Salova said.

"Doni may agree with you," Ramara said. "She's never been Blessed as far as anyone knows."

"Isn't she related to you, Ramara? You both have the same pale blond hair," Folara said.

"She's a cousin, but not a close one," Ramara said.

"I think Proleva is right," Marthona said. "Marona does need something to do, but it doesn't mean she has to have a baby. She should learn a craft of some kind, something to devote herself to that would be worthwhile, and that would take her thoughts away from making trouble for people just because her life hasn't turned out the way she wanted. I think all people should have some craft or skill, something that they enjoy, are naturally drawn to, and do well. If she doesn't, she will just continue to make trouble to get attention."

"Even that may not be enough," Solaban said. "Laramar has a skill, one he's recognized, and even admired for. He makes good barma, but he's been making all kinds of trouble. He sides with Brukeval about Joplaya and Echozar, and he's getting attention for it, too. I heard him say to some people of the Fifth Cave that Jondalar's hearth shouldn't be among the First anymore because he mated a foreign woman, and she has the least status. I think he's still resentful that Ayla wasn't behind him at Shevonar's burial. He pretends to ignore it, but I think he doesn't like being last."

"Then he should do something about it," Proleva said angrily, "like take care of the children of his hearth!"

"Jondalar's hearth is exactly where it should be," Marthona said with a slight smile of satisfaction. "It was an exceptional situation, and it was decided by the leaders and the zelandonia, as it should have been. It's not for someone like Laramar to say."

"Perhaps that's the thing to do," the First said. "I think I'll talk to Dalanar about having the zelandonia and the leaders gather and talk about this problem over Joplaya and Echozar, bring it out in the open and perhaps give those people who feel some objections an opportunity to air their feelings."

"That might be a time for Jondalar and Ayla to talk about their experiences with flatheads . . . the Clan, as she calls them," Joharran said. "I've been wanting to have a talk with the other leaders about them anyway."

"Perhaps we can go over and talk to him now," Zelandoni said. "I need to get back to the lodge. I've got a problem. Someone from among the zelandonia is passing around information that is supposed to be kept private. Some of it is very personal information about certain people, and some is knowledge that shouldn't be talked about outside the zelandonia. I need to find out who it is, or at the least put a stop to it."

Ayla had been listening very carefully to all that was said, and she thought about it as everyone got up and went in various directions. The people of the Zelandonii made her think of a river. While the surface might appear calm and smooth, there could be many undercurrents at many different levels. She thought that probably Marthona and Zelandoni knew more about what was going on under the surface than most, but she guessed that even they didn't know all of it, not even about each other. She had noted certain expressions, postures, tones of voice, that gave her clues about what might be deeper, but as with Zelandoni's problem with someone telling things, even after that problem was resolved, there would be something else. The deep currents would shift and slide, leave little ripples on the surface and eddies around the sides. It would never come to an end as long as there were people.

"I'm going to go see to the horses," she said to Jondalar. "Are you coming, or do you have something else to do?"

"I'll come with you, but wait a moment," Jondalar said. "I want to get the spear-thrower and spears I'm making for Lanidar. I'm almost finished with them and I'd like to test them out, but I'm too big. I was hoping you might be able to do it. I know they will be small for you, too, but maybe you can get a sense if they will work for him."

"I'm sure they'll be fine, but I'll try them," she said. "The best one to know will be Lanidar himself, and he won't even know until he gains some real skill. This will give him something to practice with, and I'm sure he'll be pleased. I have a feeling you are going to make that boy very happy."

The sun was approaching its zenith when they started gathering up their things. They had brushed the horses, and Ayla checked them over carefully. When the season warmed, flying insects often tried to lay eggs in the moist, warm corners of the eyes of various ruminants, deer and horses in particular. Iza had taught her about the clear fluid from the bluish-white plant that was like a dead thing and that grew in shaded woods. It drew its nourishment from decaying wood since it lacked the living green chlorophyll of other plants, and its waxy surface turned black when touched, but there was no better treatment for sore or inflamed eyes than the cool liquid that oozed from a broken stem.

She had tried out the small spear-thrower and decided it would work just fine for Lanidar. Jondalar had finished the spears he was working on, but decided to make a few more when he saw a small stand of straight young alders with slender trunks, just the right diameter for small spears. He cut down several. Ayla wasn't sure what it was that made her want to go into the woods beside the creek beyond the horse enclosure.

"Where are you going, Ayla?" Jondalar asked. "We should be heading back. I need to go to the main camp this afternoon."

"I won't be long," she said.

Jondalar could see her moving through the screen of trees and wondered if she had seen something moving back there. Maybe something that could be a danger to the horses. Maybe he should go with her, he was thinking when he heard her cry out in a loud scream.

"No! Oh, no!"

The man raced as fast as his long legs could go toward the sound, crashing through brush and bruising himself banging into a tree. When he reached her, he cried out a denial, too, and dropped to his knees.

660

35

In the mud at the edge of the small stream, Jondalar bent over Ayla. She was lying almost flat beside the large wolf, who was down on his side, holding his head in her hands. A torn bloody ear was staining the back of her hand. He tried to lick her face.

"It's Wolf! He's hurt!" Ayla said. The tears streaming down her face left white streaks through a muddy smudge on her cheek.

"What do you think happened to him?" Jondalar asked.

"I don't know, but we've got to help him," she said, sitting up. "We need to make a stretcher to carry him to camp." Wolf tried to get up when she did, but fell back.

"Stay with him, Ayla. I'll make a stretcher from those spear shafts I just cut," Jondalar said.

When she and Jondalar brought him in, several people hurried over to see if they could help. It made Ayla understand how many people had come to care about the wolf.

"I'll make a place for him in the lodge," Marthona said, going in ahead of them.

"Is there anything I can do?" Joharran said. He had just returned to the camp.

"You can find out if Zelandoni has any comfrey left from Matagan's injuries, also marigold petals. I think Wolf's been in a fight with other wolves, and wounds from bites can be bad. They need strong medicine, and they have to be well cleaned," Ayla said.

"Will you need to boil some water?" Willamar asked. She nodded. "I'll get a fire going. It's a good thing we just brought in a load of wood."

When Joharran came back from the zelandonia lodge, Folara and Proleva were with him, and Zelandoni had said she would come by shortly. Before long the entire Summer Meeting knew that Ayla's wolf was hurt, and most people were concerned.

Jondalar stayed with her while she examined the wolf and knew from her expression that his wounds were serious. She was sure he had been attacked by an entire pack, and she was surprised that he was still alive. She asked Proleva for a piece of aurochs meat, scraped it the way she did for baby food, then mixed it with ground datura and put it down his throat to help him relax and make him sleep.

"Jondalar, will you get some of that skin from the unborn calf of the aurochs I killed? I need soft absorbent hides to clean his wounds," Ayla said.

Marthona watched her put roots and powders into various bowls of hot water, then handed her some material. "Zelandoni likes to use this," she said.

Ayla looked at it. The soft material was not made from hides. It looked more like the finely woven material that the long tunic Marthona had given her was made of. She dipped it in the water of one of the bowls. The fabric absorbed it quickly. "This will do, very well, in fact. Thank you," Ayla said.

Zelandoni arrived about the time that Jondalar and Joharran were helping her turn the wolf over so she could work on his other side. The First worked with Ayla to clean a particularly bad wound, then Ayla surprised several people when she threaded a thin piece of sinew through the small hole in her thread-puller and used it to sew the worst of the wounds together with some strategically placed knots. She had shown the ingenious device to several people, but no one had ever seen it used to sew living skin. She even sewed his torn ear, though it would still have a jagged edge.

"So that's what you did to me," Jondalar said with a grim smile.

"It does seem to help to hold the wound together so it can heal properly," Zelandoni said. "Is that something you learned from your Clan medicine woman, too? To sew skin together?"

"No. Iza never did this. They don't exactly sew, but they do knot things together. They like to use that sharp little bone that is in the lower foreleg of a deer as an awl to pierce holes in skins, and sinew after it's partially dried and hard at the ends to poke through the holes, and then they tie it into knots. They make birch bark containers that way, too. It was when Jondalar's wounds kept sliding apart and opening up even when I tried to wrap it tight to hold everything together that I wondered if I could make some knots that would keep his skin and muscles in the right place. So I tried it. It seemed to work, but I wasn't sure how soon to take them out. I didn't want the wounds to tear apart, but I didn't want the knots to heal into his skin, either. I might have waited a little too long before I finally cut them.

It probably hurt a little more than it should have when I pulled them out," Ayla said.

"You mean that was the first time you sewed someone's wound together?" Jondalar said. "You didn't know if it would work, but you tried it out on me?" He laughed. "I'm glad you did. Except for the scars, you would hardly know I was mauled by that lion."

"So you invented this technique to sew wounds," Zelandoni said. "Only someone very skilled and with a natural aptitude for healing and medicine would think of something like that. Ayla, you belong in the zelandonia."

Ayla looked unhappy. "But I don't want to be in the zelandonia," she said. "I . . . I appreciate . . . I mean . . . please don't misunderstand me, I feel honored, but I just want to be mated to Jondalar and have his baby, and be a good Zelandonii woman." She avoided looking at the donier.

"Please, don't you misunderstand me," the woman said. "It wasn't an offhand offer, made lightly with only a moment's thought, like a casual invitation to a meal. I said you belong in the zelandonia. I have thought so for some time. A person with your skill needs to associate with others who have a similar level of knowledge. You like being a healer, don't you?"

"I am a medicine woman. I cannot change that," Ayla said.

"Of course you are, that's not the issue," the First said. "But among the Zelandonii only those who belong to the zelandonia are healers. People would not be comfortable with a healer who is not. You would not be called upon when a healer is needed if you are not in the zelandonia. You would not be able to be a medicine woman, as you call it. Why do you resist the zelandonia?"

"You've talked about all that must be learned, and the time that it takes. How can I be a good mate to Jondalar and take care of my children if I have to spend so much time learning to be a Zelandoni?" Ayla said.

"There are Those Who Serve The Mother who are mated and have children. You yourself told me about the one across the glacier with a mate and several children, and you have met Zelandoni of the Second Cave," the woman said. "There are others."

"But not very many," Ayla said.

The First observed the young woman closely and was convinced there was more to it than Ayla was saying. Her reasons weren't in character. She was an excellent healer, and she was curious, learned quickly, and obviously enjoyed it. She wouldn't neglect a mate and children, and if there were times that she had to be away, there would always be someone who would help her. If anything, she was almost too attentive. Look how much time she devoted to those animals, but she was usually available and always willing to help whenever anything needed to be done, and she took on more than was required.

The First had been impressed with the way she got everyone involved in helping Lanoga to care for her youngest sister and the other children. And the way she was helping the boy with the deformed arm. Those were the kinds of things that a good Zelandoni did. She had naturally assumed the role. The donier decided that she was going to have to discover her real problem, because one way or another, the First was determined that Ayla was going to be One Who Served The Great Earth Mother. She had to be brought in, it could pose too great a threat to the stability of the zelandonia to have someone with her knowledge and innate skills outside of their influence.

People smiled when they saw the wolf with bandages tied on him, made of Marthona's fiber material and soft hides, as he walked beside Ayla through the main camp. It made Wolf almost seem to be dressed in human clothing, and he seemed to be a caricature of a fierce, wild meat-eater. Many stopped to ask how he was, or to offer the opinion that he was looking good. But he stayed very close to Ayla. He was so unhappy the first time she left him behind that he howled, then broke loose and found her. Some of the Story-Tellers had already begun to weave tales about the wolf who loved the woman.

She had to train him all over again to stay where she told him. He finally did begin to feel comfortable staying with Jondalar, or Marthona, or Folara, but he also felt defensive about the territory of the camp of the Ninth Cave, and she had to retrain him not to threaten visitors. People, especially those who were close to her, were amazed at Ayla's seemingly unlimited patience with the animal, but they also saw the results. Many of them had thought that it might be interesting to have a wolf that obeyed commands, but they weren't sure it was worth the time and effort. It did make them understand, though, that her control of her animals wasn't magic.

Ayla was beginning to relax, thinking that he was finally getting comfortable with casual visitors again, until a young man—she heard him introduced as Palidar of the Eleventh Cave—came to visit Willamar's apprentice trader, Tivonan. When Wolf got close to him, he began to growl and bare his fangs with real menace. She had to hold him to keep him down, and even then, he growled under his breath. The young man backed away in fear, and she apologized profusely. Willamar, Tivonan, and several others who were standing around watching were surprised.

"I don't know what's wrong with him. I thought he was over being defensive about his territory. Wolf doesn't usually behave like this, but he's had some trouble and he is still getting over it," Ayla said.

"I heard he was hurt," the young man said.

Then she noticed that he wore a necklace of wolf teeth and carried a pack decorated with wolf fur. "Can I ask where you got the wolf fur?" she asked.

"Well . . . most people think I went out and hunted wolf, but I'll tell you the truth. I found it. I actually found two wolves, and they must have been in a big fight because they were really torn up. One was a black female, the other, a normal gray wolf, was male. I took the teeth first, and then decided to salvage some of the fur."

"And you've got the gray male on your pack," Ayla said. "Now I think I understand. Wolf must have been in that same fight, that's how he got hurt. I knew that he'd found a friend, probably the black female. He's still young, and I don't think he was actually mating yet. He cannot yet count two years, but they were getting to know each other. She was either the lowest-ranked female of the local pack or a lone wolf from another pack."

"How do you know that?" Tivonan asked. Several more people were now gathered around them, listening.

"Wolves like wolves to look like wolves. I think they can read each other's expressions better if they have normal wolf coloring. Wolves that are out of the ordinary, all black, or all white, or spotted, are not accepted as well—except I was told by some Mamutoi friends that where there is a lot of snow all year long, white wolves are more normal. But the odd one, like that black wolf, is often the lowest ranked in a pack, so she probably left them and became a lone wolf. Lone wolves usually move on the fringes in between other wolves' territories, looking for a place of their own, and if they find another lone wolf, they may try to establish their own pack. My guess is that the wolves of this region were defending their territory against the two new ones," Ayla said. "And though he's big, Wolf was at a disadvantage. He only knows people. He was not raised around wolves. He would know some things, just because he is a wolf, but he never had brothers and sisters, or aunts and uncles, other wolves to teach him what wolves learn from each other."

"How do you know all that?" Palidar asked.

"I watched wolves for many years. When I was learning to hunt, I only hunted meat-eaters, not food animals. I'd like to ask you a favor, Palidar," Ayla said. "Can I trade with you for that wolf fur? I think the reason Wolf is growling and threatening you is that he smells the wolf he fought with, at least one of them, and he likely killed that one. But they also killed his friend and almost killed him. It could be a danger for you to wear it around him. You should never come here with it because I don't know what Wolf would do."

"Why don't I just give it to you," the young man said. "It's only a scrap of fur sewn on my pack loosely. I don't want to go down in songs and stories as the man who was attacked by the wolf who loved the woman. Is it all right if I keep the teeth? They have some value."

"Yes, keep the teeth, but I'd suggest that you soak them in a light-colored strong tea for a few days. And would you show me where you found the wolves?"

After the young man gave Ayla the offending piece of wolf fur, she gave it to Wolf. He attacked it, pounced on it, grabbed it with his teeth, and shook it, trying to tear it apart. It would have been funny if the people watching hadn't been aware of how seriously he had been injured, and that his friend or potential mate had been killed. Instead they sympathized with the wolf, attributing to him the feelings they would have experienced in a similar situation.

"I'm glad I'm not still attached to that," Palidar said.

He and Ayla made arrangements to go to the place where he found the wolves later, they both had other plans at the moment. She wasn't sure what she expected to find, scavengers would have disposed of everything by now, but as hurt as he was, she wondered how far Wolf had traveled to find her. After Palidar left, she thought about the songs and stories he had mentioned about the wolf who loved the woman.

She had visited the camp of the Story-Tellers and Musicians. It was a lively, colorful place, even their clothing seemed to have brighter hues. They were not all from one place, they had no stone shelter of their own, only their traveling tents and lodges. They traveled from place to place, staying for a while with one Cave and then with another, but it was obvious that they all knew one another and felt a kinship. There always seemed to be children at their place. Just as they did during the rest of the year, they visited the various Caves, but at their Summer Meeting camps rather than their shelters. They also gave general performances on the level area where the Matrimonial had been held, while people watched from the slope.

She knew the Story-Tellers had begun to tell stories about the animals at the Ninth Cave. Sometimes they were about how useful the animals could be, such as how the horses could carry heavy loads, or about Wolf helping her hunt by flushing out animals like the bird during the spear-thrower demonstration. There was a new story about how he helped her to find the new cave, but the stories of the Story-Tellers tended to have some supernatural or magical element in them. In their stories, Wolf hunted not because she had trained him, but because they had a special understanding, which was true, they did, but that wasn't why they hunted together. The story about the wolf who loved the woman had already become one of a man who became a wolf when he visited the spirit world, then forgot to change back into a man when he returned to this world.

The stories had already been told and retold many times and were on their way to being incorporated into the lore and legends of the people. Some Story-Tellers invented other stories about animals that were kept by people, or sometimes turned them about so that people were kept by animals. They sometimes became animal spirits, who helped people. They would, in all likelihood, be passed down for generations to come, keeping alive the idea that animals could be trained, or tamed, or kept, and not just hunted.

"Wolf will be fine with Folara," Jondalar said. "He's fine with visitors, and visitors are becoming more careful, making sure someone from the Ninth Cave knows they are coming. He won't suddenly turn on someone, we know why he was so aggressive toward Palidar. He's been through a difficult time, and it's bound to change him, but he's still basically the same Wolf that you have loved and trained since he was a tiny pup. I don't think we should take him to the meeting, though. You know how people get excited, and it could get rancorous. Wolf would not like to see people shouting or carrying on, especially if you are there and he thinks you are being threatened."

"Who will be there?" Ayla asked.

"Mostly the leaders and the zelandonia, and those people who have spoken out against Echozar," Joharran said.

"That means Brukeval, Laramar, and Marona," Ayla said. "None of them are friends."

"It gets worse," Jondalar said. "The Zelandoni of the Fifth Cave, and Madroman, his acolyte, who is certainly not my best friend, will also be there. And Denanna of the Twenty-ninth Cave, though I'm not sure why she made complaints."

"I don't think she likes the idea of animals living around people. You remember when we stopped there on the way here, she did not want the animals to come up to her shelter," Ayla said, "though I was just as glad to camp down on the field."

When they arrived at the zelandonia lodge, the drape was opened before they could announce their presence and they were ushered in. In a passing thought, Ayla wondered how they always seemed to know when she was coming, whether she was expected or not.

"Have you met the new member of the Ninth Cave?" Zelandoni said. She was speaking to the pleasant-looking woman with a conciliatory smile, but whom Ayla sensed had an underlying strength.

"I was at the introduction, of course, and the Matrimonial, but I haven't met her personally," the woman said.

"This is Ayla of the Ninth Cave of the Zelandonii, mated to Jondalar of the Ninth Cave of the Zelandonii, Son of Marthona, former Leader of the Ninth Cave, formerly Ayla of the Mamutoi, Member of the Lion Camp, Daughter of the Mammoth Hearth, Chosen by the Spirit of the Cave Lion, and Protected by the Cave Bear," Zelandoni said, making the formal introduction.

"Ayla, this is Zelandoni of the Twenty-ninth Cave."

She greeted the woman, but it came as a surprise to hear such a short formal introduction. It was, however, all that was necessary. As Zelandoni, she had given up her personal identity and had become the embodiment of the Twenty-ninth Cave of the Zelandonii, although if she had wished, the introduction could have included the person she formerly was, including her original name and all her previous ties. It just seemed unnecessary most of the time, since she was no longer that person.

Ayla thought about her most recent acquisition of names and ties. She liked the way Zelandoni had introduced her. She had become Ayla of the Zelandonii, and Jondalar's mate, and that came first, but she had been Ayla of the Mamutoi, she hadn't lost her connections to them, ties that meant so much to her. And she was still "Chosen by the Spirit of the Cave Lion, and Protected by the Cave Bear." It pleased her that even her totem and her Clan connections were included.

When she first arrived and heard the long recitations of names and ties in the formal Zelandonii introductions, Ayla wondered, very privately and only to herself, why they made such extended, almost interminable introductions, full of unknown names and connections. Why not simplify it and just say the names that people were usually called—Jondalar, Marthona, Proleva. But she had been so pleased to hear her familiar connections mentioned, she was glad now for the Zelandonii way of including past references. She had once thought of herself as Ayla of No People, alone with only a horse and a lion for company. Now she had ties to many people, and she was mated and expecting a child.

She had one more passing thought as she turned her attention back to the people at the meeting. She wished she could include "Mother of Durc of the Clan" in her names and ties, but considering the reason for this meeting, and recalling the night of their mating, and the disruptions that Echozar's appearance had made, she wasn't sure if she could ever tell the Zelandonii about her son, Durc.

When the First moved to the center of the lodge, it soon became quiet. "I will begin by saying that this meeting will not change anything. Joplaya and Echozar are mated, and only they can change that. But there seems to be an undercurrent of nasty rumors and general ill will toward them, which I think is shameful. It makes me less than proud to be a Zelandoni of people who could be so heartless to two young people who are just beginning their lives together. Dalanar, the man of Joplaya's hearth, and I decided to bring this matter out in the open. If some people have sincere complaints, this is the time to make them known," the donier said.

There was some shuffling around and avoidance of looking directly at people. It was clear that there was some embarrassment, especially among those who had listened avidly and perhaps passed on some item of malicious gossip. Even temporal and spiritual leaders were not above such human failings. No one seemed to want to broach the matter, as though it were too foolish to even bring up, and the First was ready to go on to the next reason for the meeting.

Laramar could see the moment he had been agitating for was

slipping away, and he had been one of the primary instigators of the discontent. "It is true, isn't it, that Echozar's mother was a flathead," he said.

The look the First gave him was a combination of disdain and irritation. "He has never denied it," she said.

"That means he's a child of mixed spirits, and a child of mixed spirits is an abomination. That makes him an abomination," Laramar said.

"Who told you that a child of mixed spirits is an abomination?" the Zelandoni Who Was First asked.

Laramar frowned and looked around. "Everybody knows that."

"How do they know that?" the First asked.

"Because people say so," he said.

"What people say so?" she pressed.

"Everybody," he said.

"If everybody said the sun will not rise tomorrow morning, would that make it so?" the donier asked.

"Well, no. But people have always said so," Laramar said.

"I think I remember hearing it from the zelandonia," one of the onlookers said.

The First glanced around to look at the person who had spoken; she had recognized the voice. "Are you saying it is a teaching of the zelandonia that a child of mixed spirits is an abomination, Marona?"

"Well, yes," she said defiantly. "I'm sure I heard it from the zelandonia."

"Marona, did you know that even a beautiful woman can look ugly when she lies?" the First said.

Marona flushed and glared at the First with a malicious look. Several people turned to stare at her to see if what the First said was true, and some of them agreed that the spiteful expression on the young woman's face did detract from her recognized beauty. She looked away, but mumbled under her breath, "How would you know, you fat old woman!"

Several people nearby heard her and gasped at the insult to the First Among Those Who Served The Great Earth Mother. Ayla, who was on the other side of the large room, caught her breath, too, but her hearing was almost supernaturally acute. A few others had heard Marona, among them the First, whose hearing was rather good as well.

"Look closely at this fat old woman, Marona, and remember that, like you, I was once considered the most beautiful woman at the Summer Meeting. Beauty is at most a fleeting Gift. Use it wisely while you have it, young woman, because when it's gone, you will be very unhappy if you don't have something else. I have never regretted the loss of beauty, because what I have gained in knowledge and experience is much more satisfying," the One Who Was First said.

Then she continued to the rest of the group, "Marona has said, and Laramar has implied, that it is taught by the zelandonia that children who are born as the result of the blending of the spirits of one of us with one of those whom we call flatheads are abominations. In the past few days, I have gone into deep meditation and recalled all the Histories and Elder Legends, and all the lore that is known only to the zelandonia, to try to find out where this idea came from, because Laramar is right in one respect. It is something that 'everybody' thinks they know." She paused and looked around the gathering. "That idea has never been a teaching of the zelandonia."

The zelandonia had been very quiet when they saw her meditating in solitude with her chest plaque turned around so that the carvings and decorations were hidden and only the plain side showed, meaning she did not want to be interrupted. Now they knew why.

There was an undercurrent of conversation. "But they're animals." "They aren't even human." "They are related to bears."

The Zelandoni of the Fourteenth Cave spoke out. "The Mother is appalled by such a mixture."

"They are an abomination," Denanna, the leader of the Twenty-ninth Cave, said. "We've always known that."

Madroman whispered to the Zelandoni of the Fifth Cave, "Denanna is right. They are half human, half animal."

The First waited until things quieted down. "Think about where you heard those things. Try to recall even one instance in the lore of the zelandonia, or the Histories and Elder Legends of the Zelandonii, where it specifically mentions that the children of mixed spirits are abominations, or even that the flatheads are animals. I am not talking about innuendos or suggestions, but specific references," she said.

She let them think for a while, then continued. "In fact, if you think about it clearly, you would know that the Mother would never be appalled, or want us to think of them as abominations. They are children of the Mother, just as we are. After all, who is it that selects a man's spirit to blend with the spirit of a woman? It doesn't happen often, we don't associate much with flatheads, but if the Mother sometimes decides to create a new life by blending the elan of a flathead with the elan of a Zelandonii, that is Her choice. It is not for Her children to disparage those offspring. The Great Earth Mother decided to create them, perhaps for a special reason. Echozar is not an abomination. Echozar is born of woman, as we all are. The fact that his mother was a woman of the Clan doesn't make him less a child of the Great Mother. If he and Joplaya have chosen each other, then Doni is pleased, and we should be, too."

There was another commotion, but the First heard no actual denials and decided to move on. "The other reason for having this gather is that Joharran wants to talk about the ones we call flatheads, but first I think you should learn more about them from someone who can speak from experience. Ayla was raised by the ones we know as flatheads, but that she knows as people of the Clan. Ayla, will you come here and tell us about them."

Ayla got up and walked toward the First. Her stomach was queasy and her mouth felt dry. She wasn't used to speaking formally to a group of people and she didn't know where to start, so she just began where her memories began.

"I was a five-year, I think, as close as I can guess, when I lost the family I was born to. I don't remember most of this very well, but I think it was an earthquake that took them. I dream about it sometimes. I guess I wandered alone for a while, I'm sure I didn't know where to go or what to do. I don't know how long I had been alone when I was chased by a cave lion. I think I hid in a small cave, very small, because a cave lion reached in to try to get me and scratched my leg. I still have the scars, four lines from his claws on my leg. My earliest real memory is opening my eyes and seeing Iza, a woman of those you would call flatheads. I remember screaming at the sight of her. Her response was to hold me in her arms until I quieted."

People were immediately caught up in the story of an orphaned girl who could count only five years. She explained that the home of the clan that found her had been destroyed by the same earthquake, and they were looking for a new one when they came across her. She told them that they knew that she was not Clan, but one of the Others, the word they used for people like her, and she talked about being adopted by the medicine woman of Brun's clan, and her brother, Creb, who was a great mog-ur, which was like a Zelandoni. As she continued, she forgot her nervousness and just spoke naturally, with all of the emotion and genuine feelings about her life with the people who called themselves the Clan of the Cave Bear.

She didn't hold back anything, not the difficulties she had with Broud, who was the son of the mate of the leader, Brun, or her joy in learning medicine from Iza. She talked about her love for Creb and Iza, and her Clan sister, Uba, and about her curiosity when she picked up the sling for the first time. She told how she taught herself to use it, and several years later, the consequences for doing so. She hesitated only when it came to talking about her son. For all the First's logical and high-minded argument about the Clan being children of the Mother, too, she could tell from the expressions and body language of several people, especially those who had made objections to Echozar mating Joplaya, that their feelings had not changed. They had just decided that it might be best to keep them to themselves for the time being. Ayla thought it might be best to refrain from mentioning, too.

She told them about being forced to leave the Clan when Broud became leader, and though she tried to explain what a death curse was, she didn't think they fully understood the real power of its coercive force. It did literally cause the death of individual members of the Clan if they had no place to go and no one, not even their dearest loved ones, would acknowledge that they even existed. She spoke only briefly about her time in the valley, but talked in more detail about Rydag, the mixed child that was adopted by Nezzie, the mate of the headman of the Lion Camp.

"Unlike Echozar, he did not have the strength of the Clan, and he was weak internally, but like the Clan, he could not make certain sounds. I taught him and Nezzie, and then the rest of the Lion Camp, and Jondalar, to communicate with hand signs. It made Nezzie very happy the first time he called her 'mother,'" Ayla ended.

Then Jondalar came forward and told the story of how he and his brother Thonolan met some men of the Clan shortly after they got across the plateau glacier on the highland to the east. Then he told the funny story on himself about catching only half a fish because he shared the other half with a young man of the Clan. He also explained the circumstances that led to their spending a few nights with the Clan couple Guban and Yorga, and of "talking" to them in the sign language Ayla had taught him.

"If there is one thing I learned on my Journey," Jondalar said, "it is that the ones we have always called flatheads are people, intelligent people. They are no more animals than you or me. Their ways may be different, their intelligence may even be different, but it is not less. It is just different. There are some things we can do that they can't, but there are also some things they can do that we can't."

Then Joharran stood up and talked about his concerns and working out new ways to deal with them. Finally, Willamar talked about the possibility of trading with them. Afterward there were many questions, and the discussion went on for a long time. It was a revelation to the zelandonia and the Zelandonii leaders. Some found it difficult to believe, but most listened with an open mind. It seemed obvious that Ayla's story was true; not even the best Story-Teller could have made up a tale that was so convincing. And it revealed the Clan as humane, even if some didn't want to believe they were human. Nothing was resolved, but it gave everyone something to think about.

The First stood then to end the meeting. "I think we have all learned some things of importance," she said. "I appreciate Ayla's willingness to come here and talk to us so freely about her unusual experiences. She has given us a rare insight into the life of people who may be strange, but who were willing to take in a child they knew was different and treat her as one of their own. Some of us have felt fear if we happened to see a flathead when we were out hunting or collecting something. It seems that fear is misplaced if they were willing to take in someone who is lost and alone."

"Do you think that means that they took in that woman from the Ninth Cave who was lost some time ago?" said the white-haired Zelandoni of the Nineteenth Cave. "If I recall correctly, she was pregnant when she returned. The Mother may have decided to Bless her when she was with the flatheads, and used the spirit of one of them to—"

"No! That's not true! My mother was not an abomination!" Brukeval cried out.

"That's right. Your mother was not an abomination," Ayla said. "That's what we've been trying to say. None of those with mixed spirits is an abomination."

"My mother was not of mixed spirits," he said. "That's why she was not an abomination." He looked at her with such loathing, Ayla had to turn her head aside to avoid the force of his glare. Then he stalked out.

There were no more discussions. People got up and started leaving. On the way out, the One Who Was First noticed Marona looking at her in a rude and insolent way, then she overheard Laramar talking with Zelandoni of the Fifth Cave and his acolyte, Madroman.

"How can Jondalar's hearth be among the first?" he asked. "The excuse was that she had such a high ranking among the Mamutoi, the people she supposedly came from, that it shouldn't be lowered here, but she doesn't even know what people she was actually born to. If she was raised by flatheads, then she's more flathead than Mamutoi. Tell me what rank a flathead has? She should have been last, but now she's among the first. I don't think it's right."

After the long and grueling session, which ended with such a vehement outburst, Ayla felt wrung out. She supposed it must be disturbing for people to suddenly learn that creatures they had thought of as animals were actually thinking, caring people. It was a radical change, and change never came easy, but Brukeval's reaction was irrational, and his glare so full of malice, he scared her.

Jondalar suggested they get the horses and go for a ride to get away from everyone and relax after the unsettling events that ended the meeting. Ayla was happy to see Wolf loping along beside them again and no longer wearing bandages, though he wasn't entirely healed yet.

"I tried not to show it, but I was so angry at those people who objected to their mating because Echozar's mother was Clan," Ayla said. "And though Zelandoni and Dalanar asked for a special meeting, I don't think anything was settled. At the Matrimonial, I think the only reason some of them agreed was because they were not Zelandonii. They call themselves 'Lanzadonii,' but I can't see any difference. What is the difference, Jondalar?"

"In one sense, Zelandonii just means us, the People, the children of the Great Earth Mother, but so does Lanzadonii. The actual meaning of Zelandonii would be Earth's Children of the Southwest, and Lanzadonii, Earth's Children of the Northeast," Jondalar explained.

"Why didn't Dalanar just continue to call himself Zelandonii and make his people another Cave with the next higher counting word?" Ayla asked.

"I don't know. I never asked him. Maybe because they live so far away. It's not like you can get there in an afternoon, or even in a day or two. I think he knows that while there may always be ties, someday they will be different people. Now that he has his own Zelandoni, or rather, Lanzadoni, he has even less reason to make the long trip to our Summer Meetings. Probably their doniers will still be trained by the zelandonia for quite a while, but as they continue to grow, they will begin to train their own."

"They will be like the Losadunai," Ayla said. "The language, and ways, are so close to Zelandonii, they must have been the same people once."

"I think you're right, and that may be why we are still such good friends with them. We don't count them in our names and ties, but there may have been a time when we did," Jondalar said.

"I wonder how long it has been. There are many differences now, even in the words of their Mother's Song," Ayla said. They rode a little farther. "If the Zelandonii and the Lanzadonii are the same people, why did the ones who objected to Joplaya mating Echozar finally go along with it? Just because their name says they live in the northeast? It's not reasonable. But then, their objection was not reasonable in the first place."

"Look who was behind it," Jondalar said. "Laramar! Why is he trying to stir up trouble? You've done nothing but try to help his family. Lanoga adores you, and I doubt if Lorala would even be alive today if you hadn't stepped in. I wonder if he really cares or just likes the attention. I don't think he has ever been invited to a special meeting like that with all high-status people, several of them, including the First, presenting the case to him and the few others who were making an issue out of it. Now that Laramar has a taste of it, I'm afraid he is going to keep on making problems, just to keep getting attention. But I still don't understand Brukeval, of all people. He knows Dalanar and Joplaya, he's even kin."

"Did you know that Matagan's mother told me Brukeval was at the camp of the Fifth Cave trying to convince some people to make an objection to Joplaya's mating before the Matrimonial?" Ayla said. "He has a strong feeling against the Clan, but seeing him and Echozar together, you can see the resemblance. There is a cast to his features that is definitely Clan, not as strong as Echozar's, but it is there. I think he hates me now because I said his mother was born of mixed spirits, but I was just trying to say that people who are mixed are not bad, not abominations."

"He must still think they are. That's why he tries so hard to deny it. It must be terrible to hate what you are," Jondalar said. "You can't change that. It's funny. Echozar hates the Clan, too. Why do they hate the people that they are a part of?"

"Maybe it's because other people hurt them because of who they are, and they can't hide it because they actually do look different," Ayla said. "But the way Brukeval glared at me before he left was so full of hate, he frightens me. He reminds me a little of Attaroa, as though there is something not right with him. As though there is something wrong or deformed about him, like Lanidar with his arm, but on the inside."

"Maybe some evil spirit has gotten inside of him, or his elan is twisted," Jondalar said. "I don't know, but perhaps you should watch out for Brukeval, Ayla. He may try to make more trouble for you."

36

The summer waxed, and the days became hotter. The grasses of the fields grew tall and turned golden, their heads nodding with the weight of their seed—the promise of new life. Ayla's body grew heavy, too, filled with the new life of her unborn child. She was working beside Jondalar, pulling seeds from wild oats, when she felt movement for the first time. She stopped and pressed her hand to her bulging middle. Jondalar saw the motion.

"What's wrong, Ayla?" he asked with a worried frown.

"I just felt the baby move. It's the first time I've felt life!" she said. She seemed to be smiling inwardly. "Here," she said, taking the winnowing stone from Jondalar's large hand and placing his hand on her stomach. "Maybe the baby will move again."

He waited expectantly, but felt nothing. "I don't feel anything," he finally said. Just then there was a small movement under his hand, barely a ripple. "I felt it! I felt the baby!" he said.

"The movement will get stronger later," Ayla said. "Isn't it wonderful, Jondalar? What would you like the baby to be? A boy or a girl?"

"It doesn't matter. I just want the baby to be healthy, and I want you to have an easy birthing. What do you want your baby to be?" he asked.

"I think I'd like a girl, but I'd be just as happy with a boy. It doesn't really matter. I just want a baby, your baby. It is your baby, too."

"Hey, you two. The Fifth Cave is sure to win if you keep loafing like that." They turned to watch a young man approaching. He was average height, with a compact, wiry build. He walked with a crutch under one arm, carrying a skin of water with his other. "Would you like some water?" he said.

"Hello, Matagan! It's hot, this water is welcome," Jondalar said, taking the bag, lifting it over his head, and letting the water pour from the spout into his mouth. "How is the leg?" he said, handing the waterbag to Ayla.

"Getting stronger all the time. I may be able to throw this stick away before long," he answered, smiling. "I'm only supposed to be carrying water for the Fifth Cave, but I saw my favorite healer and thought I'd cheat a little. How are you feeling, Ayla?"

"I'm fine. I felt life for the first time a little while ago. The baby is growing," she said. "Who do you think is ahead?"

"It's hard to say. The Fourteenth has several basketfuls already, but the Third just located a new large stand."

"How about the Ninth?" Jondalar asked.

"I think they have a chance, but I'll wager on the Fifth," the young man replied.

"You're biased. You just want the prizes." Jondalar laughed. "What did the Fifth Cave donate this year?"

"The dried meat from two aurochs killed at the first hunt, a dozen spears, and a large wooden bowl carved by our best carver. What about the Ninth?"

"A large skin of Marthona's wine, five birch spear-throwers with carvings, five firestones, and two of Salova's large baskets, one filled with hazelnuts, the other with tart apples," Jondalar replied.

"It's Marthona's wine I'm going to try for, if the Fifth wins. I hope the bones are lucky for me. Once I can get rid of this stick," he lifted the crutch, "I'm going to move back into the men's tent. I think I could move back now, stick or not, but my mother doesn't want me to go yet. She has been wonderful, no one could have cared more, but now I'm getting a little too much mothering. You'd think I was five years old ever since the accident," he said.

"You can't blame her," Ayla said.

"I don't blame her. I understand. I just want to get back to the men's tent. I'd even invite you to the party we'd have with the wine, if you weren't mated, Jondalar."

"Thanks anyway, but I've had enough of men's tents. Someday, when you're older, you'll find out that being mated isn't as bad as you think," Jondalar said.

"But you've already got the woman I want," the young man said, casting a teasing glance at Ayla. "If I had her, I'd be willing to move out of the men's tent, too. When I saw her at your Matrimonial, I thought she was the most beautiful woman I ever saw. I could hardly believe my eyes. I think every man thought so and wished he were in your place, Jondalar."

Though in the beginning Matagan was shy around Ayla, he lost his uneasiness after getting to know her during the many days she went to the zelandonia lodge to assist in his care. Then his natural outgoing friendliness and developing easy charm began to express themselves.

"Listen to him," Ayla said, smiling and patting her protruding middle. "Some 'beautiful.' An old woman with a belly full."

"That makes you more beautiful than ever. And I like older women. I may mate one someday, if I can find one like you," Matagan said.

Jondalar smiled at the young man, who reminded him of Thonolan. It was obvious he was infatuated with Ayla, but he was going to be a charmer someday, and he might need it if he ended up being permanently lame. Jondalar didn't mind if he practiced a little on Ayla. He had once been in love with an older woman, too.

"And you are my favorite healer." His eyes turned more serious. "I woke up a few times when I was being carried on the stretcher, and I thought I was dreaming when saw you. I thought you were a beautiful donii come to take me to the Great Mother. I'm sure you saved my life, Ayla, and I don't think I'd be walking at all if it weren't for you."

"I just happened to be there, and did what I could," Ayla said.

"That may be, but you know, if there is ever anything you need . . ." He looked down, his face flushed with embarrassment. He was having trouble saying what he wanted to say. He looked at her again. "If there is ever anything I can do for you, you only have to ask."

"I remember a time when I thought Ayla was a donii," Jondalar said to ease his distress. "Did you know she sewed my skin together? On our Journey, I can remember a time when an entire S'Armunai Camp thought she was the Mother Herself, a living donii come to help Her children. For all I know, maybe she is, the way men fall in love with her."

"Jondalar! Don't fill him full of such nonsense," Ayla said. "And we'd better get back to work, or the Ninth Cave will lose. Not only that, but I want to keep some of this grain for a couple of horses, and maybe for a new foal. I'm glad we collected so much rye when it ripened, but the horses like oats better."

She looked into the basket, which was hanging around her neck so her hands would be free, to see how many seeds were in it, then positioned the stone in her hand and set to work. With one hand she held together a few stalks of ripe wild grains, with the other she grasped the stalks so that the round stone was pressed against them a

680

little below the seed heads. Then, in a smooth motion, she pulled the stalks through her hand in one motion so that the hard stone stripped the seeds off into her hand. She emptied them into the basket and reached for the next few stalks.

It was slow, meticulous work, but not difficult once you got into the rhythm of it. Using a stone helped to strip the stalks more efficiently, and therefore faster. When Ayla asked, no one could remember where the idea came from, they'd been doing it that way for as long as anyone could remember.

As Matagan limped away, Ayla and Jondalar were both stripping grain seeds into their baskets. "You have a devoted admirer in the Fifth Cave, Ayla," Jondalar said. "Many others feel that way. You've made friends at this Meeting. Most people think of you as a Zelandoni. They are not used to a healer who is not a donier."

"Matagan is a nice young man," Ayla said, "and the fur-lined parka with the hood that his mother insisted on giving to me is beautiful, and roomy enough that I will be able to wear it this winter. She asked me to visit them after we return this autumn. Wasn't the home of the Fifth Cave the place we passed by on our way here?"

"Yes, it's upstream on a small tributary of The River. Maybe we'll stop on our way back. By the way, I'm going hunting with Joharran and several others in a few days. We may be gone a while," Jondalar said, trying to make it sound like a normal activity.

"I don't suppose I could go?" Ayla said wistfully.

"I'm afraid you're going to have to give up hunting for a while. You know, and Matagan's accident has made it plain, that hunting can be dangerous, especially if you are not quite as fast on your feet as you used to be. And after the baby is born, you'll be busy nursing and caring for it," Jondalar said.

"I hunted after Durc was born. One of the other women nursed him for me if I didn't get back in time to feed him."

"But you weren't gone for several days at a time."

"No, I just hunted small animals with my sling," she admitted.

"Well, you may be able to do that again, but you shouldn't go out with hunting parties for days at a time. Anyway, I'm your mate now. It's my job to take care of you and your children. That's what I promised when we mated. If a man can't provide for his mate and her children, what use is he? What's a man's purpose if women have children and provide for them, too?" Jondalar said.

Ayla had never heard Jondalar talk that way before. Did all men feel that way? she wondered. Did men need to find a purpose for their existence because they could not have children? She tried to imagine how it would feel if it were the other way around, if she could never have a baby and believed her only contribution was to help provide for them. She turned to face him.

"This baby would not be inside me if it were not for you, Jondalar," she said, putting her hands on the bulge below her breasts. "This baby is as much yours as mine. It's just growing inside me for a while. Without your essence, it would not have gotten started."

"You don't know that for sure," he said. "You may think so, but no one else does, not even Zelandoni."

The two stood facing each other in the middle of the open field, not antagonistic, but with conflicting beliefs. Jondalar noticed strands of sun-bleached blond hair had escaped from the restraining leather band and were whipping across her face in the wind. She was barefoot, and her tanned arms and breasts were exposed above the simple leather garment wrapped around her expanding middle and hanging loosely down to her knees to protect her body from the scratchy dry grasses they were gathering. Her eyes were determined, resolute, almost angrily defiant, but she looked so vulnerable. His look softened.

"It doesn't matter anyway. I love you, Ayla. I just want to take care of you and your baby," he said. He reached to enfold her in his arms.

"Our baby, Jondalar. Our baby," she said, putting her arms around him and clinging to his bare chest. He felt her bare breasts and the bulge of her stomach, and was glad for both.

"All right, Ayla. Our baby," he said. He wanted to believe it.

There was a noticeable nip in the air as they stepped out of the lodge. The leaves on the trees in the small woods were turning shades of yellow and an occasional red, and the grasses and herbs that were not trampled into dust around the encampment were brown and shriveled. Every bit of fallen wood or dry brush in the area had long since been burned, and the woods had been thinned out considerably.

Jondalar picked up the packs that had been lying on the ground near the opening of the lodge. "The horses with the pole drags are going to be a big help carrying back the winter food stores. It's been a good season."

Wolf raced up to them, his tongue lolling out of the side of his mouth. One ear drooped slightly and had a ragged edge, giving him a raffish air. "I think he knows we're leaving," Ayla said. "I'm so glad he came back and stayed with us, even if he was hurt. I would have missed him. I'm looking forward to returning to the Ninth Cave, but I'll always remember this Summer Meeting. This is the Meeting we were mated."

"I enjoyed this Summer Meeting, too, I haven't been to one in so long, but now that we're leaving, I'm anxious to get back," Jondalar said, then smiled. He was thinking of the surprise that he knew was waiting for Ayla. She noticed a difference in his expression. His smile was more a delighted grin, and he projected a sense of expectation. She had a feeling there was something he wasn't telling her, but she had no idea what it could be.

"I'm glad the Lanzadonii came. It's a long way for them to travel, but Dalanar got the donier he wanted," he continued, "and Joplaya and Echozar are properly mated. The Lanzadonii are a small people yet, but it won't be long before there's a second Cave. They have a lot of young ones, and they've been lucky. Most have survived."

"I'm pleased that Joplaya is pregnant," Ayla said. "She was Blessed before they were joined, but I don't think many people heard that during the Matrimonial."

"Some people had other things on their minds, but I'm glad for them. Joplaya seems different, somehow, sadder. Maybe all she needs is a baby," Jondalar said.

"We'd better hurry. Joharran said he wanted to leave early," Ayla said.

She didn't want to talk about Joplaya's sadness because she knew the reason, and she didn't want to mention the long conversation she'd had with Jerika. Joplaya's mother had wanted some specific information from her. She told Ayla about her own difficulty in giving birth and wanted to know everything Ayla could tell her that might make a potentially difficult delivery easier. She also wanted to know about her medicine that could prevent conception, and ways to bring on a miscarriage if that didn't work. She feared for the life of her only child and would have been satisfied with no grandchildren rather than lose her daughter. But since she was already pregnant, and determined to have this baby, if she survived the delivery, Jerika was determined to make sure there would be no more pregnancies.

The Eleventh Cave had brought all their rafts upriver, and Joharran arranged to send some things back that way, but River Place only had so many rafts and all the Caves wanted to use them. The Ninth

Cave loaded as many rawhide packages of dried meat and baskets of gathered foods on the travoises and the backs of Whinney and Racer as they could. The lodges that had been their homes for the summer were taken down, and the parts that could be salvaged and reused were also loaded on the horses. Each person also carried a full backpack, and some people, seeing the pole drags of the horses, fashioned a similar device for themselves to drag. Ayla thought about making one for Wolf, but she hadn't trained him to pull one yet. Perhaps next year he would have a load, too.

Joharran was all over the campsite, urging people to hurry, offering suggestions, making sure everything was in readiness. When he was sure the Ninth Cave was packed and ready to go, he started out ahead of the rest, his spear held loosely, but it was more symbolic than necessary. They were traveling in the daytime with a large group, and as long as they stayed together, no four-legged hunter would come near them. Nonetheless, at the first sign of danger, Joharran could have his spear mounted in his spear-thrower and ready to fling in an instant. He had practiced with the weapon over the summer, and had gained some skill with it. There were half a dozen others designated to guard the flanks, with Solaban and Rushemar bringing up the rear. The job of guarding would be rotated among several others, who were, at the moment, helping to carry a rich summer bounty back to the Ninth Cave.

Ayla looked out over the camp of the Summer Meeting one last time before they left. Piles of bones and trash littered the small valley. Several of the Caves had already departed, leaving large empty spaces between the campsites of those that remained, with poles and log frames left standing, and black circles and rectangles that showed where sustaining fires had been. A tent that was too worn for further use had been left behind, and a torn edge of leather no longer attached to a pole was flapping in the wind, which was also blowing an old basket around. As she watched, another Cave's lodges were being torn down. The Summer Meeting camp had a desolate, abandoned look to it.

But the litter was of the earth and would soon decompose. By the next spring there would be little evidence remaining of the Caves that had summered here. The earth would heal from the invasion.

The trip back was arduous. The heavily loaded people trudged under their burdens and dropped into their beds exhausted at night.

Joharran set a brisk pace in the beginning, but slowed as they progressed to enable the weakest to keep up. But they all looked forward to going home and their spirits were high. The loads they carried represented survival during the harsh winter months ahead.

As they neared the abri of the Ninth Cave, the familiar landscape encouraged the people to hurry. They were eager to reach the shelter under the overhanging ledge of stone, and they pushed themselves so they would not have to spend another night outside. The first evening stars were winking on in the sky as the familiar cliff with the Falling Stone came into view. They crossed Wood River on the stepping-stones with some difficulty under the failing light with their cumbersome loads, then followed the path up to the front porch of their abri. When they finally reached the stone porch in front of the opening under the protecting shelf, it was nearly dark.

It was Joharran's job to make the first fire and light a torch to carry into the abri, and he was glad for the firestones. The fire was quickly started and the torch lit, then people waited impatiently while Zelandoni removed the small female figurine that had been set in front of their shelter to protect it. After they thanked the Great Mother for watching over their home in their absence, several more torches were lit. The Cave formed a procession behind the large woman as she put the donii back in its place behind the large hearth at the rear of the protected space, then everyone scattered to their own dwellings to gratefully drop off their loads.

The inevitable first chore was to inspect any damage that might have been wrought by marauding creatures while they were gone. There were a few animal droppings, some hearthstones had been disturbed, a basket or two had been knocked over, but the damage was minimal. Fires were lighted in the hearths inside, and provisions and stores were brought in. Sleeping furs were spread out on familiar sleeping benches. The Ninth Cave of the Zelandonii had returned home.

Ayla started toward Marthona's home, but Jondalar led her off in a different direction. Wolf followed. Holding a torch in one hand and her hand with the other, he guided her farther back into the abri toward another structure, one she didn't remember being there. Jondalar stopped in front of it, pulled aside the flap that covered the entrance, and motioned to her to go inside. "You sleep in your own dwelling tonight, Ayla," he said.

"My own dwelling?" she said, so overwhelmed that she could

hardly speak. As she entered the dark interior, the wolf slipped in with her. Jondalar followed, holding up a torch so she could see.

"Do you like it?" he asked.

Ayla looked around. The inside was essentially bare, but there were shelves against one wall adjacent to the entrance and a platform built up at one end for sleeping furs. The floor was paved with smooth, flat sections of limestone from the nearby cliff, with hardened river clay between the spaces. A hearth was set up, and the niche directly opposite the entrance held a small fat female figure.

"My own home." She twirled around in the middle of the empty structure, her eyes sparkling. "A dwelling just for the two of us?" The wolf sat on his haunches and looked at her. This was a new place, but wherever Ayla was was home to him.

Jondalar's face was split by a ridiculous grin. "Or maybe the three of us," he said, patting her belly. "This place is still sort of empty."

"I love it. I just love it. It's beautiful, Jondalar."

He was so pleased by her delight, he felt tears welling up and had to do something to fend them off. He handed her the torch he still held. "Then you have to light the lamp, Ayla. It means you accept it. I have some rendered fat here. I carried it all the way from our last camp."

He reached under his tunic and withdrew a small pouch, warmed by his body heat, made of the cured bladder of a deer, encased in a slightly larger pouch made of its hide, with the fur side in. The bladder was nearly waterproof, although it did seep slightly over time, especially when warm. The second pouch was to absorb the minimal seepage, the fur adding an extra layer to soak up any grease that might permeate. The top of the bladder had been tied with sinew from a leg tendon around a vertebra from the spine of the deer, shaved of extraneous bone to a circular shape. The natural hole, which had once held a spinal cord, served as a pouring hole. It was stoppered by a leather thong tied several times into a knot that fit the hole.

Jondalar pulled the end of the thong to release the knot and poured some of the liquefied fat into a new stone lamp. He dipped one end of an absorbent wick made of lichen taken from the branches of trees at the Summer Meeting camp and placed it into the oil, then held a torch to it. It flared up instantly. When the fat was fully melted and hot, he took out a leaf-wrapped package of wicks that came from a porous fungus that had been cut into strips and dried. He liked using fungus wicks, with their capacity to burn longer and warmer illumination. He laid the wick from the middle of the shallow bowl to the rim and extended it a bit farther over the edge. Then he added a second and a third wick to the same lamp, so that one lamp could give the light of three.

Then he filled a second lamp and gave the torch to Ayla. She held the fire to the wick. It caught, sputtered, then settled down into a glowing light. He carried the lamp to the niche that held the donii and placed it front of the female figure. Ayla followed him. When he turned around, she looked up at the tall man.

"This dwelling is now yours, Ayla. If you allow me to light my hearth within it," Jondalar said, "any children born here will be born to my hearth. Will you allow it?"

"Yes. Of course," she said.

He took the torch from her and strode to the fireplace area, which was outlined with a circle of stones. Within it, wood had been set up, ready to light. He held the torch to the kindling and watched until the small wood set the larger pieces aflame. He did not want to take any chances that the fire would go out before it was well established. When he looked up, Ayla was looking at him with love in her eyes. He stood up and took her in his arms.

"Jondalar, I'm so happy," she said, her voice cracking as tears filled her eyes.

"Then why are you crying?"

"Because I'm so happy," she said, clinging to him. "I never dreamed I would ever be so happy. I am going to live in this beautiful home, and the Zelandonii are my people, and I'm going to have a baby, and I'm mated to you. Mostly because I'm mated to you. I love you, Jondalar. I love you so much."

"I love you, too, Ayla. That's why I built this dwelling for you," he said, bending his head to reach her lips, which were straining to reach his. He tasted the salt from her tears.

"But, when did you do it?" she asked when they finally parted. "How? We were at the Meeting all summer."

"Do you remember that hunting trip I went on with Joharran and the rest? It wasn't only a hunting trip. We came back here and built this," Jondalar said.

"You came all the way back here to build a dwelling? Why didn't you tell me?" she said.

"I wanted to surprise you. You are not the only one who can plan surprises," Jondalar said, still pleased at her happily shocked response.

"It's the best surprise I ever had," she said, tears threatening to well up again.

"You know, Ayla," he said, suddenly looking serious, "if you ever throw out the stones of my hearth, I will have to return to my mother's dwelling, or go someplace else. It would mean that you want to sever the knot of our joining."

"How can you even say that, Jondalar? I would never want to do that!" she said, looking appalled.

"If you had been born a Zelandonii, I wouldn't have to say it. You would know. I just want to make sure you understand. This dwelling is yours, and your children's, Ayla. Only the hearth is mine," Jondalar explained.

"But you were the one who made it. How can it be mine?"

"If I want your children to be born to my hearth, it is my responsibility to provide a place for you and your children to live. A place that will be yours no matter what happens," he said.

"You mean you were required to make a dwelling for me?" she asked.

"Not exactly. I am required to make sure you have a place to live, but I wanted to give you your own home. We could have stayed with my mother. It's not unusual when young men are first mated. Or if you were Zelandonii, we could have arranged to stay with your mother, or some other of your kin, until I could provide you with a place of your own. In that case, I would be obligated to your kin, of course."

"I didn't understand that you would be taking on so much obligation for me when we joined," Ayla said.

"It's not just for a woman, it's for the children. They can't take care of themselves, they must be provided for. Some people live with kin all their lives, often with a woman's mother. When the mother dies, her home belongs to her children, but if one has been living with her, that one has first claim. If a mother's home becomes her daughter's, her mate doesn't have to provide one, but he may be obligated to his mate's siblings. If the home becomes a son's, he may owe his own siblings."

"I think I still have a lot to learn about the Zelandonii," Ayla said, frowning at the thought.

"And I still have a lot to learn about you, Ayla," he said, reaching for her again. She was more than willing. He could feel himself wanting her as they kissed and could sense her responding to him.

"Wait here," he said.

He went out and returned with their sleeping furs. He untied the rolls and spread them out on the platform. Wolf watched from the middle of the empty main room, then lifted his head and howled.

"I think he's feeling unsettled. He wants to know where he is supposed to sleep," Ayla said.

"I think I'd better go to my mother's dwelling and get his bedding. Don't go away," Jondalar said, smiling at her. He returned quickly and set Ayla's old clothing that was Wolf's bedding and his feeding bowl by the entrance. The wolf sniffed at them, then circled around and curled up on them.

Jondalar went to the woman who was still waiting by the fire, picked her up and carried her to the sleeping platform, and put her down on top of the furs. He began to slowly undress her, and she started to untie a cord to help.

"No. I want to do it, Ayla. It would please me," he said.

She put her hand down. He continued undressing her slowly, tenderly, then removed his own clothing and crawled in beside her. And gently, with exquisite tenderness, he made love to her half the night.

The Cave quickly settled down into their usual routine. It was a glorious autumn. The grasses of the fields rippled in golden waves in the brisk wind, and trees near The River blazed with brilliant shades of yellows and reds. Bushes were heavy with ripe berries, apples were rosy but tart, waiting for the first frost to turn sweet, nuts were dropping from the trees. While the weather held, the days were filled with gathering the season's bounty of fruits, nuts, berries, roots, and herbs. After the temperatures at night dropped below freezing, hunting parties went out regularly to stock up on a supply of fresh meat to supplement the dried meat from the summer hunting.

During the warm days shortly after their return, storage pits were checked and new ones dug into the summer-softened soil so that they would be below the usual permafrost level, and lined with stones. The meat of fresh kills was cut up and left out overnight high on platforms, and away from prowling animals, to freeze. In the mornings it was put into the deep pits, which kept it from thawing out as the day warmed. Several such cold cellars were located near the Ninth Cave. Shallower root cellars, which kept fruit and vegetables cold but not frozen during the early part of the season, were dug as well. Later, as the freezing glacial winter progressed and the ground froze solid, the produce would be moved to the back of the abri.

Salmon, making their way upstream, were netted and smoke-dried or frozen, as well as other varieties of fish caught by a method new to Ayla: the fish traps of the Fourteenth Cave. She had visited Little Valley while the fish were running, and Brameval had explained how the woven traps, which were weighted down, allowed fish to easily swim in them, but not back out. He had always been very friendly and pleasant to her. She was pleased to see Tishona and Marsheval, too. Though she hadn't had the chance to get to know them as well during the Matrimonial, they still felt the tie of having mated at the same time.

Some people were also fishing with a gorge. Brameval gave her one of the small pieces of bone, sharpened at both ends and attached in the middle to a thin but strong cord, and told her to catch herself a meal. Tishona and Marsheval joined her, partly to see if she needed help, but also for her company. Jondalar had shown her how to use a gorge. She had both worms and small pieces of fish as bait, and started by threading a worm onto the bone. They were standing on the bank of The River, and she cast her line in. When she felt a pull, indicating that a fish had swallowed the baited gorge, she gave the line a sharp tug, hoping that the sharpened bone would lodge horizontally across its gullet, with both ends piercing the sides. She smiled when she pulled a fish from the water.

When she stopped at the Eleventh Cave on the way back, Kareja happened to be gone, but she saw the donier of the Eleventh with Marolan, his tall, handsome friend, and stopped to talk to them. She had seen them together at the Summer Meeting several times and understood he was more than a friend, more like a mate, though they didn't have a Matrimonial. But the official mating ceremony was primarily for the sake of potential children. Many people chose to live together without a mating ceremony besides those who were interested in those of the same gender, especially older couples who were past having children, and some women who had children without having a mate and later decided to live with a friend or two.

Ayla often accompanied Jondalar when he went out with a hunting party as they were starting out. But when the hunters of big game went farther afield, she stayed closer to the cave and used her sling or practiced with the throwing stick. Ptarmigan inhabited the plains across The River, as well as grouse. She knew she could have caught them with her sling, but she wanted to learn to use a throwing stick with equal skill. She also wanted to learn to make them. It was difficult to separate thinner pieces from logs, usually done with wedges, and then it took time to shape and smooth them. Even more difficult was learning to throw them with a special twist so that they spun horizontally through the air. She had once seen a Mamutoi woman use one of similar design. She could throw it at a flock of low-flying birds and often knock down three or four of them. Ayla always did enjoy hunting with weapons that took skill.

It made her feel less left out to have a new hunting weapon to practice with, and she was getting proficient with the throwing stick. She seldom came home without a bird or two. She always took her sling with her, too, and often had a hare or a hamster to add to the pot. It also gave her a certain economic independence. Though she was already pleased with the way her home was beginning to look—many of the gifts she had received when she and Jondalar were joined found good use—she was learning to trade and often exchanged bird feathers, and sometimes the meat, for things she wanted to furnish her new home with. Even the hollow bird bones could be cut into beads or small musical instruments, flutes with high-pitched tones. Bird bones could also be used as parts of various tools or implements.

But many of the hides of rabbits and hares that she hunted with her sling, or the thin, soft skins of birds, she saved for herself. She planned to use the soft furs and skins to make clothes for the baby when the weather got cold and she was bound to the shelter.

On a cool, crisp day late in the season, Ayla was rearranging her things, making a space for the baby and baby things. She picked up the boy's winter underwear that Marona had given to her and held the tunic up to herself. She had long since outgrown it, though she still planned to wear it later. It was a comfortable outfit. Perhaps I ought to make another one for myself with a little roomier top, she thought. She had some extra deerskins. She folded it and put it away.

She had promised to visit Lanoga that afternoon and decided to get some food to take with her. She had developed a real affection for the girl and the baby, and visited them often, even though it meant seeing and talking with Laramar and Tremeda more than she wanted. She also got to know the other children somewhat, especially Bologan, though it was a rather stilted acquaintance.

She saw Bologan when she arrived at Tremeda's dwelling. He had started learning how to make barma from the man of his hearth. Ayla had mixed feelings about it. It was right for a man to teach the children of his hearth, but the men who were always around drinking Laramar's barma were not those she thought Bologan ought to associate with, though it certainly wasn't for her to say.

"Greetings, Bologan," she said. "Is Lanoga here?"

Though she had greeted him several times since their return to the Ninth Cave, he still seemed surprised when she did, and always seemed at a loss for words.

"Greetings, Ayla. She's inside," he said, then turned to go.

Probably because she had been putting away her clothes, Ayla suddenly remembered a promise she had made to him. "Did you have any luck this summer?" she asked.

"Luck? What do you mean, 'luck'?" he asked, looking puzzled.

"Several young men your age made their first major kill at the Summer Meeting. I wondered if you had any luck hunting," she said.

"Some. I killed two aurochs in the first hunt," he said.

"Do you still have the hides?"

"I traded one for barma makings. Why?"

"I promised I'd make you some winter underclothing, if you would help me," Ayla said. "I wonder if you would like to use your aurochs hide, though I think deer hides would be better. Maybe you could trade it."

"I was going to trade it, for more barma makings. I thought you forgot about that," Bologan said. "You said it a long time ago, when you first came here."

"It was a long time ago, but I was thinking about some other things I wanted to make, and thought I'd make your outfit at the same time," she said. "I have some extra deer hides, but you'd have to come over and let me take measurements."

He looked at her for some time with a strange, almost speculative expression. "You have been helping Lorala a lot. Lanoga, too. Why?"

She thought for a moment. "At first, it was just that Lorala was a baby and she needed help. People want to help babies, that's why the women started nursing her, once they found out her mother had no more milk. But I've grown fond of her, and Lanoga, too."

Bologan was quiet for a while, then he looked at her. "All right," he said. "If you really want to make something, I have a deer hide, too."

Jondalar was on an extended hunting trip, along with Joharran, Solaban, Rushemar, and Jacsoman, who had recently moved to the Ninth Cave from the Seventh, along with his new mate, Dynoda. They were on a mission to find reindeer, not so much to hunt them just yet, but to find out where they were and when they might be migrating closer to their region, so they could arrange a major drive. Ayla was feeling restless. She had started out with the hunters early, then turned back. Wolf had scared up a couple of ptarmigan, not quite fully white yet, but getting close, and she dispatched them quickly.

Willamar was also gone, on what would likely be his last trading trip of the season. He had gone west, specifically to get salt from the people who lived near the Great Waters of the West. Ayla invited Marthona, Folara, and Zelandoni to share a meal and help her eat the ptarmigan. She told them she would cook it the way she used to for Creb when she lived with the Clan. She had dug a small pit in Wood River Valley at the foot of the sloping path to the ledge, lined it with rocks, and built up a good fire inside it. While it was burning down, she plucked the birds, including their snowshoe-feathered feet, then gathered an armload of hay to wrap them in.

If she had found eggs, she would have stuffed them in the cavities of the birds, but it was not the season for eggs. Birds didn't try to raise chicks when they were heading into winter. Instead she picked a few handfuls of flavorful herbs, and Marthona had offered her some of the last of her salt, for which Ayla was grateful. The ptarmigan were cooking, along with some ground nuts, in the pit oven, and she had spent time grooming the horses, and now she was looking for something else to do while she waited for the birds to cook.

She decided to stop off and see if she could do anything for Zelandoni. The donier said she was in need of some ground red ochre, and Ayla said she would be happy to get some for her. She went back down to Wood River Valley, whistled for Wolf, whom she had left exploring interesting new mounds and holes, and walked toward The River. She dug up the red-colored iron ore and found a nice river-rounded stone that she could use as a pestle to grind the ochre with. Then she whistled for Wolf again as she headed up the slope, not really paying much attention to who else was on the path.

It came as a shock when she almost bumped into Brukeval. He had actively avoided her since the meeting in the zelandonia lodge about Echozar and the Clan, though he constantly watched her from a distance. He observed her advancing pregnancy with pleasure, knowing she would soon be a mother, and actively imagined that the child she carried was of his spirit. Any man could fancy that any pregnant woman was carrying the child of his spirit, and most of them occasionally wondered if a particular woman might be, but Brukeval's dream was an obsession. He would sometimes lie awake at night envisioning an entire life with Ayla, most of it mimicking what he surreptitiously saw her doing with Jondalar, but when confronted by her on the path, he didn't know what to say. There was no way to avoid her now.

"Brukeval," she said, attempting to smile. "I've been wanting to talk to you."

"Well, here we are," he said.

She hurried ahead. "I just wanted you to know that I didn't mean to insult you at that meeting. Jondalar told me that you were teased before about flatheads, until you made people stop. I admire the fact that you stood up for yourself and made people stop calling you that. You are not a flathead . . . one of the Clan. No one should ever have called you that. You couldn't begin to live with them. You are one of the Others just like all the Zelandonii. That's how they would see you."

His expression seemed to soften. "I'm glad you recognize that," he said.

"But you must realize, to me, they are people," she hurried on. "They couldn't be animals. I have never thought of them any other way. They found me alone and injured, and they took me in and cared for me, raised me. I wouldn't be alive today if it wasn't for them. I find them to be admirable people. I didn't realize you would consider it an insult to suggest that your grandmother may have lived with them when she was lost and gone for so long, that they might have taken care of her, too."

"Well, I guess you couldn't know," he said, smiling.

She smiled back, feeling relieved, and tried to make her explanation more clear. "It's just that you remind me of some people that I care about. That's why I was drawn to you from the beginning.

There was a little boy I knew, who I loved, and you remind me of him . . ."

"Wait! Are you still saying that you think they are a part of me? I thought you said that I was not a flathead," Brukeval said.

"You aren't. Not even Echozar is. Just because his mother was Clan doesn't mean that he is. He wasn't raised by them, and you weren't, either . . ."

"But you still think my mother was an abomination. I told you, she was not! Neither my mother nor my grandmother had anything to do with them. None of those dirty animals had anything to do with me, do you hear me?" He was shouting and his face had turned an angry red. "I am not a flathead! Just because you were raised by those animals, don't think you can drag me down."

Wolf was growling at the excited man, ready to spring to Ayla's defense. The man looked as if he might want to hurt her. "Wolf! No!" she commanded. She had done it again. Why couldn't she have stopped when he was smiling? But he didn't have to call her Clan "dirty animals," because they weren't.

"I suppose you think that wolf is human, too," Brukeval sneered. "You don't even know the difference between people and animals. It's unnatural for a wolf to act the way he does around people." He was unaware just how close he was to Wolf's fangs with his shouting, but it probably wouldn't have mattered. Brukeval was beside himself. "Let me tell you something, if it hadn't been for those animals attacking my grandmother, she would not have been so frightened that she gave birth to a weak woman, and my mother would have lived to take care of me, love me. Those filthy flatheads killed my grandmother and my mother, too. As far as I'm concerned, they are no use to anyone. They should all be dead, like my mother. Don't you dare tell me they have anything to do with me. If it were up to me, I'd kill them all myself."

He was advancing on Ayla as he screamed, backing her down the path. She held Wolf by the fur on his neck to keep him from attacking the raging man. Finally he brushed past her, knocking her aside, and stormed down. He had never been so angry. Not only because she imputed flatheads to his lineage, but because in his rage, he had blurted out his innermost feelings. He had wanted more than anything else to have had a mother to run to when the others teased him. But the woman who inherited Brukeval along with his mother's possessions had no love for the baby she reluctantly nursed. He was a burden on her, and she considered him repulsive. She had several children of her own, including Marona, making it even easier to ignore him. But she wasn't much of a mother even to her own, and Marona had learned her callous, unfeeling ways from her mother.

Ayla was shaking. Now she had really done it. She tried to collect herself as she stumbled her way up the path and into Zelandoni's dwelling. The woman looked up as Ayla came through the entrance and immediately recognized that something was gravely wrong.

"Ayla, what is it? You look as if you've just seen an evil spirit," she said.

"Oh, Zelandoni, I think I have. I just saw Brukeval," she cried. "I tried to tell him I didn't mean to insult him at that meeting, but I always seem to say the wrong thing to him."

"Sit down, tell me about it," Zelandoni said.

She explained what had happened during her encounter on the path. Zelandoni was quiet after Ayla told her, then she fixed the young woman a cup of tea. Ayla settled down; talking about it had helped.

"I've watched Brukeval for a long time," Zelandoni said after a while. "There's a fury inside him. He wants to strike out at the world that has given him so much hurt. He has decided to lay the blame on the flatheads, the Clan. He sees them as the root of his pain. He hates everything about them, and anyone associated with them. The worst thing you could have done was to imply that he himself might be related in some way to them. It's unfortunate, Ayla, but I fear you have made an enemy. It can't be helped, now."

"I know it. I could tell. Why do people hate them so much? What's so terrible about them?" Ayla asked.

The woman looked at her, considering, then made up her mind. "When I said at that meeting that I had gone into deep meditation to recall all the Histories and Elder Legends, that was entirely true. I used every prompt and memory aid I know to bring out everything I ever memorized. It is probably something that should be done more often, it's enlightening. I think the problem, Ayla, is that we moved into their lands. In the beginning, it wasn't so bad. There was a lot of room, many empty shelters. It wasn't hard to share the land with them. They tended to keep to themselves, and we avoided them. We didn't call them animals then, just flatheads. The term was more descriptive than derogatory," she said.

"But as time went on, and more children were born, we needed more space. Some people began taking their shelters, sometimes fighting with them, sometimes killing them, sometimes being killed. By then, we had lived here for a long time, and this was our home, too. The flatheads may have been here first, but we needed places to live, so we took theirs.

"When people treat others badly, they have to rationalize it so they can go on living with themselves. We give ourselves excuses. The excuse we used was that the Great Mother gave us the earth for our home, 'the water, the land, and all Her creation.' That means all Her plants and animals are ours to use. Then we convinced ourselves that flatheads were animals, and if they were animals, we could take their shelters for ourselves," Zelandoni said.

"But they are not animals, they are people," Ayla said.

"Yes. You are right, but we conveniently forgot that. She also said the Earth is our 'home to use, but not to abuse.' The flatheads are also Earth's Children. That was the other thing I learned from my meditation. If She mixes their spirits with ours, they must be people, too. But I don't think it would have made much difference if we thought they were people or not. I think we would have done it anyway. Doni has made it easier for other living creatures that kill, so they can live. I don't think your wolf there worries about the rabbits he kills to survive, or the deer that a pack of them may hunt down. He was born to kill them. Without them he would not live, and Doni has given every living thing the desire to continue living," the donier said.

"But humans have been given the ability to think. That is what makes us learn and grow. It is also what gives us the knowledge that cooperation and understanding are necessary for our own survival, and that has led to empathy and compassion, but there's another side to those kind of feelings. The empathy and compassion we feel for our own kind is sometimes extended to the rest of the living things on the earth. If we allowed it to keep us from killing a deer, or other animals, we would not live long. The desire to live is the stronger feeling, so we learn to be compassionate selectively. We find ways to close our minds. We limit our sense of empathy." Ayla was listening closely, fascinated.

"The problem is knowing how much to stop those feelings without perverting them. In my opinion, I think that is really at the bottom of Joharran's concern over the knowledge you have brought us,

Ayla. As long as most people believed your Clan were only animals, we could kill them without thinking about it. It's harder to kill people. The empathy is so much stronger that the mind must invent new reasons. But, if we can somehow link it to our own survival, the mind will make the devious twists and turns necessary to rationalize it. We're very good at that. But it changes people. They learn to hate. Your wolf doesn't need to hate what he kills. It would be easier if we could kill without compunction, like your wolf does, but then, we wouldn't be human."

Ayla thought for a time about what Zelandoni said. "Now I know why you are First Among Those Who Serve The Mother. It is hard to kill. I know how hard it is. I remember the first animal I killed with my sling. It was a porcupine. I felt so bad, I didn't hunt again for a long time, and then I had to find a reason. I decided to kill only carnivores because they sometimes stole the meat from the hunters, and because they killed the same animals the Clan needed for food."

"That is truly the loss of innocence, Ayla, when we understand what we must do in order to live. That is why a young hunter's kill is so important. It is not only changes in the physical body that make a person an adult. The first hunt is the most difficult, and it is more than overcoming fear. A man and a woman must show that they can survive, that they can do what must be done to live. That is also the reason we have certain ceremonies to honor the spirits of the animals we kill. It is one way we show honor to Doni. We need to remember and appreciate that their life is given so that we may live. If we don't, humans can become too hardened, and that can turn against us.

"We must always show appreciation for what we take, we need to honor the spirits of the trees and grass and other foods that grow, too. We must treat all Her Gifts with respect. She can become angered if we ignore Her, and She can take back the life She has given us. If we ever forget our Great Earth Mother, She will no longer provide for us, and if the Great Mother should decide to turn Her back on Her children, we will no longer have a home."

"Zelandoni, you remind me of Creb in many ways. He was kind and I loved him, but more than that, he understood people. I could always go to him. I hope that doesn't insult you. It's not meant to," Ayla said.

Zelandoni smiled. "No, of course I'm not insulted. I would like to have known him. And, Ayla, I hope you know, you can always come to me."

Ayla thought about her conversation with the First as she prepared to grind the red ore. But when she began the hard work of crushing the lumps of iron ore with the roundish rock against a flat, saucer-shaped stone, she tried to bury herself in the job to forget about the incident with Brukeval. The exertion did help to wear off tension, but the repetitive physical activity left her mind free to think, and Zelandoni had given her much to think about. She is right, Ayla thought. I think I have made an enemy of Brukeval. But what can I do about it now? It's done. I don't think there was ever anything I could have done about it. He will think what he wants to think, no matter what I do or say.

It didn't occur to Ayla to lie and tell him that she didn't really think he had the look of the Clan. It wasn't true. She did think he was a mix. She began to wonder about his grandmother. The woman had been lost. When she was found again, she talked about being attacked by animals, but the animals she referred to must have been the ones she called flatheads. They must have found her, how else had she survived? But if they took her in, fed her, they would have expected her to work, like their own women. And any man of the Clan would then feel he could use her to relieve his needs. If she objected, someone may have forced her, the same way Broud had forced her. It was unthinkable for a woman of the Clan to resist. She would have been put in her place.

Ayla tried to imagine how a woman born a Zelandonii would respond in a situation like that. To the Zelandonii, it was the Gift of Pleasure from the Great Earth Mother, and it was never supposed to be forced. It was for sharing, but only when both the man and the woman wanted to share it. Without doubt, Brukeval's grandmother would have considered it an attack. How would it feel to be assaulted by someone you thought of as an animal? To be forced to share the Gift of Pleasure with such a creature? Would it be enough to affect the mind? Perhaps. Zelandonii women were not used to being ordered around. They were independent, as independent as the men.

Ayla stopped grinding the red stone. It had to be true that a man of the Clan had forced Brukeval's grandmother to couple with him, because she was pregnant, and that was what started the life growing inside her. And Brukeval's mother was born as a result. She was weak, Jondalar said. Rydag was weak, too. Perhaps there is something about the mixture that sometimes produces weakness in the offspring.

Her Durc was not weak, though, and Echozar was not weak. Neither were the S'Armunai. They were not weak, and many of them had the look of the Clan. Perhaps the weak ones died young, like Rydag, and only the strong ones lived. Could the S'Armunai be the result of such a mixture that began long ago? They were not so upset about mixtures, perhaps because they were more used to them. They seemed to be ordinary people, but they did have some Clan characteristics.

Was that why Attaroa's mate tried to dominate the women before she killed him? Was something about the way men of the Clan thought about women passed down, like some of their looks? Or was it just something he learned when he lived with them? But there was much that was good about the S'Armunai. Bodoa, the S'Armuna, had discovered how to take clay from a river and burn it into stone, and her acolyte was a fine carver. And Echozar, he is really very special. The Lanzadonii, just like the Zelandonii, think it was the mixing of spirits that gave him the look of both kinds of people, but his mother had been attacked by one of the Others.

Ayla began grinding stone again. How ironic, she thought. Brukeval hates the people who started the life that gave birth to him. It is men who start life growing inside a woman, I'm sure of it. It needs both. No wonder that Cave of S'Armunai were dying out when Attaroa was their leader. She couldn't force the spirits of women to blend to make life. The only women who had babies were those who sneaked in at night to visit their men.

Ayla thought about the life growing inside her. It would be Jondalar's baby as much as hers. She was sure it started when they got off the glacier. She hadn't made her special tea, and she was sure that was what kept life from starting inside her during their long Journey. The last time she had bled was shortly before she and Jondalar started across the glacier. She was glad she hadn't been sick much this time. Not like when she was pregnant with Durc. Children who were mixtures seemed to be harder on women, and on some of the babies. This time she felt wonderful, most of the time, but would she have a girl or a boy? And what would Whinney have?

37

The Ninth Cave built a refuge for the horses under the abri in the lesser-used section to the south near the bridge up to Down River. Ayla had asked Joharran if anyone would object if she and Jondalar constructed something to protect the animals. She had expected to make something simple that would just keep rain and snow from blowing in on them. Instead, when Joharran held a meeting at the Speaking Stone to see how people felt about it, they decided to pitch in and make a real dwelling for them, with low stone walls and panels above to keep out the wind. But there were no drapes at the entrance and no fence to keep them penned in.

The horses had always been free to come and go as they chose. Whinney had shared Ayla's cave in the valley, and both horses had grown accustomed to the horse shelter the people of the Lion Camp had built onto their longhouse for them. Once Ayla showed Whinney and Racer the place, fed them dried grass and oats, and gave them water, they seemed to know it was theirs. At least, they returned often, using the more direct route from the edge of The River that was nearby. They seldom used the path from Wood River Valley and across the busy ledge in front of the dwelling area, unless Ayla led them.

After the horse shelter was built, Ayla and Jondalar decided to make a watering trough out of wood, a kerfed square box made in the style of the Sharamudoi containers, and when they started, everyone was interested. It took several days, even though they had many helpers—and even more observers. First, they had to find the proper tree, and settled on a tall pine from the middle of a thick stand. The closeness of the other trees caused each one to grow tall to reach the sunlight, with few lower branches, which avoided knots.

The tree had to be cut down with flint axes, no small chore in itself. A flint axe did not bite deep. Instead, they started high, removing many chips and thin slivers as they worked through the trunk at a shallow angle. The remaining stump looked as though it had been chewed by a beaver. The tree had to be cut through again, just below the lowest branches. The top of the tree would not go to waste; carvers and toolmakers were already eyeing the wealth of wood, and any scraps would be used to feed fires. A feeding trough for the horses was made from the same tree. Following the tradition of the Sharamudoi, pinecone seeds were planted near the fallen tree, in thanks to the Great Mother. Zelandoni was quite impressed with the simple ceremony.

Next, they demonstrated how to extract planks out of the log using wedges and mauls. The resulting wooden boards, tapering to a thin edge from the outside toward the center, found many uses, including as shelves. The kerfed boxes were an ingenious idea. Using a flint burin, or similar chisel-like tool, they carved through a plank to cut off a long section with straight ends. The cut ends were then tapered at an angle along the edge. At three measured distances, they cut a kerf across the wooden board, a wedge-shaped groove that was not cut all the way through. With the help of steam, the plank was bent along the grooves with the uncut side out, allowing the tapered edges of the groove to meet inside to form a rectangular box. With a flint borer, several holes were hand-drilled into the tapering ends. Rubbing with sand and stones gave the plank a smooth finish.

For the bottom, another piece of plank was evened and shaped with knives and sanding stones to fit inside, and eased into a groove cut all the way around the inside lower edge of the box. When it was all shaped and maneuvered together, the tapered edges of the fourth corner of the box were fastened together with pegs that were pounded through the pre-drilled holes. Although it leaked at first, when soaked in water, the wood swelled, making the box waterproof, which made it a good storage container for liquids or fats and, using hot stones, an effective cooking vessel. They were also good containers to hold water and feed for horses. It was likely that more boxes would be made in the future.

Marthona watched Ayla, cheeks red and exhaling steam with every cold breath, climbing up the path. She wore thick-soled moccasins with attached uppers that wrapped around the calf over her fur leggings, and the fur-lined parka Matagan's mother had given to her. It did not conceal her obvious pregnancy, especially with her belt, worn rather high, from which her knife and some pouches were dangling. The hood was thrown back and her hair was caught up in a serviceable bun, but loose strands were whipping around in the wind.

She still used her Mamutoi carrying bag rather than one in the Zelandonii style, but it was full of something. She had gotten used to the haversack, the pack that was worn over one shoulder, and usually wore it when she went on short trips. It left a shoulder free to carry back her catch. At the moment, three white ptarmigan, tied together by their feathered feet, hung down her back over the other shoulder, balanced by two good-size white hares down the front.

Wolf followed behind her. She usually took him when she went out. He was not only good at flushing out birds or small animals, he could show her where the white birds or hares had fallen in the white snow.

"I don't know how you do it Ayla," Marthona said, falling in step beside her when she reached the stone porch. "When I was as far along as you are, I felt so big and awkward, I didn't even consider hunting anymore, but you are still going out, and nearly always bring something back."

Ayla smiled. "I feel big and awkward, but it doesn't take much to throw a stick or sling a stone, and Wolf helps me more than you know. I'll have to stay home soon enough."

Marthona smiled down at the animal padding along between them. Though she had been worried about him when he was attacked by the other wolves, she rather liked his slightly drooping ear. For one thing, it made him much easier to recognize. They waited while Ayla dropped off the game in front of her dwelling area on a block of limestone that was used sometimes as a place to put things and sometimes as a seat.

"I never was much good at hunting smaller animals," Marthona said, "except with a snare or a trap. But there was a time when I enjoyed going out with a group on a big hunt. It's been so long since I've hunted, I think I've forgotten how, but I used to have a fair eye for tracking. I don't see that well anymore."

"Look what else I found," Ayla said, taking off her bulging carrying bag to show Marthona. "Apples!" She had found an apple tree, bare of leaves but still decorated with small, shiny red apples, less hard and tart now after freezing, and had filled her haversack with them.

The two women walked toward the horse shelter. Ayla didn't expect to find the horses there in the middle of the day, but she checked the container that held their water. In winter, when it was below freezing for long periods of time, she would melt water for them, though horses in the wild fended for themselves just fine. She put several apples in the kerfed feeding trough.

Then she walked to the edge of the stone ledge and looked down at The River, bordered by trees and brush. She didn't see the horses, but she whistled the distinctive signal that the horses had been trained to answer, hoping they were close enough to hear. Before long she saw Whinney climbing the steep path, followed by Racer. Wolf rubbed noses with Whinney when she reached the ledge in a greeting that seemed almost formal. Racer nickered at him and received a playful yip and a nose rub in return.

When she was confronted with such direct evidence of Ayla's control over the animals, Marthona still found it hard to believe. She had gotten used to Wolf, who was always around people, and who responded to her. But the horses were more skittish, not as friendly, and seemed less tame, except around Ayla and Jondalar, more like the native wild animals she had once hunted.

The young woman was making the sounds that Marthona had heard her use before around the horses as she stroked and scratched the animals, then led them to the shelter. She thought of it as Ayla's horse language. Ayla picked out an apple for each one, and they ate from her hand as she continued talking to them in her strange way. Marthona tried to discern the sounds Ayla made. It was not quite a language, she thought. Although there was a similar feel to some of the words Ayla used when she demonstrated the language of the flatheads.

"You're getting a big belly, Whinney," Ayla was saying, patting her round stomach, "just like I am. You'll probably give birth in spring, maybe late spring, after it warms up a bit. By then, I should already have my baby. I'd love to go for a ride, but I guess I'm too far along. Zelandoni said it might not be good for the baby. I feel fine, but I don't want to take chances. Jondalar will ride you, Racer, when he gets back."

That was what she meant to say to the horses, and what she did say in her mind, although the combination of Clan signals and words and the other sounds of her private language would not have translated quite the same—if someone could have translated it. It didn't matter. The horses understood the welcoming voice, the warm touch, and certain sounds and signals.

Winter came unexpectedly. Small white flakes started to fall late in the afternoon. They turned big and fat, and by evening it was a swirling blizzard. The whole Cave breathed a sigh of relief when the hunters who had gone out in the morning stomped onto the stone ledge before dark, empty-handed but safe.

"Joharran decided to turn back when we saw the mammoths heading north as fast as they could," Jondalar said after greeting Ayla. "You've heard the saying 'Never go forth when mammoths go north.' It usually means snow is on the way, and they head north, where it's colder but drier and the snow doesn't pile up as deep. They get mired in deep, wet snow. He didn't want to take chances, but those storm clouds blew up so fast, even the mammoths may get caught in it. The wind shifted north, and before we knew it, the snow was blowing so hard that we could hardly see. It's halfway up to the knees out there already. We had to use snowshoes before we got back."

The blizzard lasted through the night, the following day, and the next night. Nothing could be seen except the moving curtain of white, not even just across The River. At times the snow, caught in a crosscurrent of moving air buffeting the high cliff and finding no outlet, rebounded against the primary direction of the prevailing winds in a vortex of swirling flakes. At other times, when the driving winds died down, snow fell heavily straight down in a constant hypnotic motion.

Ayla was glad for the protective overhang of the abri that extended all the way to the horses' area, though during the first night she was concerned, not knowing whether they had found their way to the shelter before the snows became too deep. If her horses had found some other shelter, she was afraid she would have been cut off from contact with them and they would be isolated, imprisoned, by the thick white mantle of snow.

She was relieved to hear a nicker when she approached their shelter early the next morning, and breathed a deep sigh when she saw both horses, but as she greeted them, she could tell they were nervous. They were not familiar with such deep snow, either. She decided to spend some time with the horses and groom them with teasel brushes, which usually comforted them and relaxed her.

But when she found them safe in their shelter, she wondered where the wild horses were. Had they migrated to the colder, drier region to the north and east, where the snow would not be as deep and would not cover the dry, standing hay that was their winter feed?

She was glad now that they had collected piles of grass for the horses, not just grains, to supplement their forage. It had been Jondalar's idea. He had known how deep the snow could get, she had not. Now she wondered if they had collected enough. The horses were adapted to the cold, she wasn't worried about that. Their coats had grown in thick and full, both the downy underlayer and the shaggy outer coat protected their stocky, compact bodies, but would they have enough grass?

Winters in the land where Jondalar's people lived were cold, but not dry. Their main feature was snow, heavy, air-choking, high-drifting snow. She hadn't seen so much snow since she lived with the Clan. She had become more used to the dry, frozen loess steppes that leached moisture from the atmosphere, farther inland around her valley and the territory of the Mammoth Hunters. Here, where the climate was subject to the maritime influences of the Great Waters of the West, the landscape was known as continental steppes. Winter was wetter and snowier, resembling somewhat the climate of the place where she grew up, the mountainous tip of a peninsula jutting into an inland sea far to the east.

The heavy snow piled up on the front ledge filled the lower half of the opening under the overhang with a solid barrier of soft snow that gleamed at night in the golden reflection of the fires inside the abri. Now Ayla knew why stout logs were used to support the many crosspieces covered with hides for the protected passageway leading to the exterior enclosure that was used instead of the trenches for wastes during the winter.

The second morning after the snow began, Ayla woke to the smiling face of Jondalar standing beside the sleeping platform, shaking her gently. His cheeks were red with cold, and his heavy outer clothing still bore traces of unmelted snow. He had a hot cup of tea in his hand.

"Come on, sleepy, get up. I remember when you used to be up long before me. There's still some food left. The snow has stopped. Dress warmly and come outside," he said. "Maybe you should wear those undergarments you got from Marona and friends."

"Have you been out already?" she asked, sitting up and taking a drink of the hot tea. "I do seem to need more sleep lately." Jondalar waited while she freshened up, had a quick morning meal, and began to dress, trying to refrain from urging her too much.

"Jondalar, I can't close these pants over my stomach. And that top will never fit. Are you sure you want me to wear this outfit? I don't want to stretch them out."

"The pants are most important. It won't matter if you can't close them all the way. Do the best you can. You'll be wearing your other clothes over them. Here are your boots. Where is your parka?" Jondalar said.

As they headed out of the abri, Ayla could see the radiant blue sky and the glowing sunlight streaming down on the ledge. Several people had obviously been up early. The path down to Wood River had been cleared of the accumulation of snow, and limestone gravel from underneath the abri had been strewn on the downslope to make it less slippery. On either side the walls of snow were chest high, but as she looked out over the countryside, she caught her breath.

The landscape was transformed. The glistening white blanket had softened the contours of the land, and the sky seemed even bluer in contrast with a white so brilliant, it hurt the eyes. It was cold; the snow crunched beneath her feet and her breath steamed. She saw several people on the flat floodplain across The River.

"Careful when you go down the path. It can be dangerous. Let me take your hand," Jondalar said. They reached the bottom and crossed the small frozen river. Some of the people who saw them coming waved and started toward them.

"I didn't think you were ever going to get up, Ayla," Folara said. "There's a place we usually go every year, but it takes half the morning to get there. I asked Jondalar if we could take you, but he said it was too far for you right now. When the snow gets packed down a little more, we can build a seat on a sledge and take turns pulling you. Most of the time sledges are used to pull wood or meat or something. But when they're not needed for that, we can use them." She was full of excitement.

"Slow down, Folara," Jondalar said.

The snow was so deep that when Ayla tried to walk through it, she floundered, lost her balance, and grabbed for Jondalar, pulling him over with her. They both sat covered with snow, laughing so hard that they couldn't get up. Folara was laughing, too.

"Don't just stand there," Jondalar called out. "Come and help me get Ayla up." Between them both, they got her back on her feet.

A round white missile flew through the air and landed with a splat on Jondalar's arm. After looking up and seeing Matagan laughing at him, Jondalar grabbed a handful of snow with both hands and began shaping it into a round ball. He heaved it toward the young man, whom he was considering taking on as an apprentice. Matagan ran away with a limp, but some speed, and the snowball fell short.

"I think that's enough for today," Jondalar said.

Ayla had a snowball hidden from view, and as Jondalar approached, she threw it at him. It landed on his chest and snow exploded into his face.

"So you want to play games," he said, picking up a handful of snow and trying to put it inside the back of her parka. She struggled to get away, and soon both were rolling around in the snow, laughing and trying to get snow into each other's necks. When they finally sat up, they were both covered from head to foot with the wet white stuff.

They went to the edge of the frozen river, crossed over, and climbed back to the ledge. They passed Marthona's dwelling on the way to their own, and she had heard them coming.

"Do you really think you should have taken Ayla out there and gotten her wet with snow in her condition, Jondalar?" his mother said. "What if she had fallen down and it started the baby coming early?"

Jondalar looked stricken. He hadn't thought about that.

"It's all right, Marthona," Ayla said. "The snow was soft, and I didn't hurt myself or overdo. And I never knew snow could be so much fun!" Her eyes were still sparkling with excitement. "Jondalar helped me down the path, and up again. I feel fine."

"But she's right, Ayla," Jondalar said, full of contrition. "You could have hurt yourself. I wasn't thinking. I should have been more careful. You're going to be a mother soon."

Jondalar was so solicitous after that, Ayla almost felt confined. He didn't want her to leave the area of the abri or go down the path. She occasionally stood at the top and looked down rather wistfully, but after she grew so big that she could not see her own feet when she looked down, and found herself leaning back when she walked to compensate for the load in front, she had little desire to leave the security of the Ninth Cave's shelter of stone for the cold ice and snow outside.

She was happy to stay near a fire, often with friends, in her dwelling or theirs, or in the busy central work space under the protective roof of the massive overhang, busily making things for the coming baby. She was acutely conscious of the life growing within her. Her attention was turned inward, not exactly self-centered, but her area of interest had contracted to a smaller sphere.

She visited with the horses every day, groomed and pampered them, and made sure they had adequate provisions and water. They were more inactive, too, although they did go down to The River, frozen solid, and across to the meadow beyond. Horses could dig down through snow to find fodder, though not as efficiently as reindeer, and their digestive systems were accustomed to rough feed: the straw of frozen yellow grass stems, bark from birch and other thin-skinned trees, and twigs of brush. But under the insulating snow near the dead-seeming stems of herbs, they often found the basal stems and beginning buds of new growth just waiting to start. The horses managed to find enough food to fill their stomachs, but the grains and grass Ayla provided kept them healthy.

Wolf was out more than the horses. The season that was so hard on those that ate vegetation was often a boon to the meat-eaters. He roamed far, and sometimes was gone all day, but he always returned at night to sleep in the pile of Ayla's old clothes. She moved his bed to the floor beside the sleeping platform and worried each evening until he returned, which sometimes was quite late. Some days he did not go at all, but stayed close to Ayla, resting or, to his great delight, playing with the children.

The Cave's leisure time during the relatively inactive winter months was filled with the pursuit of each person's individual crafts. Though they sometimes went hunting, looking particularly for rein-deer for their rich sources of fat stored even within the bones of the cold-adapted animal, there was sufficient food stored to sustain them and a more than adequate supply of wood to keep them warm, give them light, and cook their food. Throughout the year various materi-als they needed for their work were collected and saved for this time. It was the time to cure hides, work them soft, dye them for color, and burnish them for a shine or a waterproof finish, the time to fab-ricate clothes, then bead and embroider them. Belts and boots were fashioned, fastenings were made and often decorated with carvings. It was also the time to learn a new craft or perfect a skill.

Ayla had been fascinated with the process of weaving. She watched and listened carefully when Marthona talked about it. The fibers from animals that shed in spring had been collected from thorny bushes or barren ground and saved until winter, when there was time to make things. A great many kinds of fibers were avail-able, such as wool from mouflon, the great-horned wild sheep, and ibex, the mountain-climbing wild goat, which could be matted into felt. The warm downy underhair grown each fall close to the skin beneath the shaggy outer hair of several animals, including mam-moths, rhinos, and musk oxen, were favorites because of their soft-ness. The long, coarser hair from animals was a more permanent growth and collected only after they were killed, the outer hair of the woolly animals, for example, and the long horse tails. Fibers from plants of many varieties were also utilized. The fibers were made into cords, ropes, and fine threads, which could be left natural or dyed, then woven and made into clothing or mats, rugs, and wall hangings to keep out drafts and cover cold, rocky walls.

Bowls were gouged out of wood, then shaped, polished, painted, and carved with designs. Baskets of all shapes and sizes were woven. Jewelry was made from shaped ivory beads, animal teeth, shells, and unique stones. Ivory, bone, antler, and horn were shaped and carved, and made into plates and platters, handles for knives, points for spears, needles for sewing, and many other tools, implements, and decorative objects. Animal figures were carved with loving attention to detail by themselves or to decorate other things that were made of anything carvable, wood or bone, ivory or stone. Female figurines, donii, were also carved. Even the walls of the abri were carved and painted.

Winter was also the time to practice talents and to play. Musical instruments, especially interesting-sounding percussion instruments and melodic flutes, were crafted and played. Dances were practiced, songs sung, stories told. Certain more sedentary sports such as wrestling and target practice of various kinds were enjoyed by some, and gambling and wagering of all kinds were indulged by many.

The young were taught certain necessary basic skills, and for those who had an inclination or showed an aptitude for some special-ized activity, someone was always willing to show them. There was a well-worn path between the Ninth Cave and Down River, and many of the craftspeople who made the trek from their own homes to spend some time there often spent a few nights at the Ninth Cave.

Zelandoni taught counting words to those who wished to know them, and the Histories and Legends of the people, but she was sel-dom with free time on her hands. People caught colds, had headaches, earaches, bellyaches, and toothaches; the aches and pains of arthritis and rheumatism were always more difficult during the cold season; and there were other serious diseases. Some people died, and their bodies were placed in cold front passages of certain caves in the winter, where they would keep until spring, since snow and frozen ground prevented burial in the outdoor graveyards. Some-times, though rarely, they were left there.

And some were born. The winter solstice had passed. Zelandoni had explained to Ayla the position where the sun set over the horizon was at its farthest left and stayed there for several days before the position of its setting moved imperceptibly back to the right. It had been the occasion for a feast, ceremony, and festival to mark the turning point and to add some excitement to the quiet days.

The sun's setting from that time on would continue to the right with each passing day until the summer solstice, when it reached its farthest right position and seemed to stay there for some days. The place midway between the two marked the equinoxes, the beginning of spring, and, on its way back, the beginning of autumn. Zelandoni pointed to a dip in the hills on the horizon that marked the midpoints. She had used countings words and marked a gouge on a flat piece of antler, and Ayla found the information fascinating. She liked to learn those kinds of things.

In the deep of winter, the coldest, bitterest, harshest time of year, the snow no longer attracted playful excursions. Even short trips outside to get frozen meat or to bring in wood could be an ordeal. The cairn of rocks on top of caches and ice cellars often froze together, making it necessary to break them apart. The vegetables and fruits in root cellars had long since been transferred to stone-lined pits at the back of the abri, but it took a watchful eye and many snares and traps to keep the small animals from taking too large a share. Small rodents in particular survived quite well from the hard work of humans and always managed to share their cave.

One of the games children played was to throw stones at the swift little creatures. It was encouraged by the adults. A hard-flung stone could kill one. Not only did it provide one more element in the continuing battle against the voracious pests, but it gave the children some experience in developing the accuracy they would need to become proficient hunters, and some of the youngsters developed quite an aim. Ayla began using her sling to that purpose and before long was teaching the children how to use her favorite weapon. Wolf also proved to be a valuable asset in keeping down the rodent population.

The outside root cellars seemed to be freer of such vermin, and the food was stored in them as long as possible. But when the deep freeze of winter threatened to destroy the fresh quality, they were brought in. Once frozen, most vegetable foods were used only in cooking, as were most dried foods.

Ayla had experienced a sudden surge of energy the past few days. She had become increasingly uncomfortable as she grew larger and was occasionally given to fits of crying and other emotional outbursts that dismayed Jondalar. The active baby sometimes woke her at night, and she found it difficult to get up gracefully from her normal cross-legged sitting position, and she had always been able to get up from the floor gracefully. As she neared her time, her fears of delivery had grown, but recently she was getting so anxious to have the baby, she was even willing to face the delivery.

Zelandoni felt sure her time would be soon. She had told Ayla, "The Great Earth Mother, in Her wisdom, made the final days of pregnancy uncomfortable on purpose, so that women would be able to face their fear of delivery just to get it over with."

Ayla had finished straightening and rearranging everything for the baby, and then everything else in her home once again, and had decided to cook a special dinner for Jondalar when he came looking for her. She told him all the vegetables she wanted from her storage place at the back of the abri, and what meat she wanted. When he came back with everything, she hadn't moved, and she had a strange expression on her face: a combination of joy and dread.

"What is it, Ayla?" he said, dropping his basket of vegetables.

"I think the baby is getting ready to be born," she said.

"Right now? Ayla, you better lie down. I'll get Zelandoni. Maybe I better get mother, too. Don't do anything until I get Zelandoni," Jondalar said, suddenly nervous.

"Not right now. Relax, Jondalar. It will be a while yet. Let's wait before you get Zelandoni, to be sure," she said, picking up the basket of vegetables. She went to her cooking area and started to take them out of the basket.

"Let me do that. Shouldn't you be resting? Are you sure you don't want me to get Zelandoni?"

"Jondalar, you've seen babies born before, haven't you? You don't have to be so worried."

"Who says I'm worried?" he said, trying to appear calm. She stood still and held her hand to her stomach. "Ayla, don't you think I'd better go tell Zelandoni?" His forehead was pinched together with anxious worry.

"All right, Jondalar. You can go tell her, but only if you promise to say it is just beginning. There's no hurry," she said.

Jondalar dashed out. He came back almost dragging Zelandoni behind him.

"I told you to tell her there was no hurry, Jondalar," Ayla said, then looked at the donier. "I'm sorry he dragged you over here so soon. It's barely started."

"I think it may be better if Jondalar went to visit Joharran for a while, and tell Proleva I may need her later. I'm not busy. I'll stay and keep you company, Ayla. Do you have a little tea?" Zelandoni asked.

"I can have some ready soon," Ayla said. "I think Zelandoni's right, Jondalar. Why don't you go visit Joharran?"

"On your way, you can stop off and tell Marthona, but don't go dragging her back here," Zelandoni said. Jondalar rushed out. "He stood there the whole time when Folara was born, as calm as you please. But it's always different when it's a man's own mate."

Ayla stopped again, waiting for the contraction to pass, then she started to prepare some tea. Zelandoni watched her, noting how long she waited. Then she sat on a large stool that Ayla had made especially for Zelandoni's visits, knowing she did not like to sit on the ground or on cushions if she could help it. Ayla had been using it herself recently.

After they drank some tea and made some inconsequential conversation while Ayla had a few more contractions, Zelandoni suggested that she lie down so the donier could examine her. Ayla complied. Zelandoni waited for the next contraction and felt Ayla's stomach.

"It may not be too long after all," the healer said.

Ayla got up, thought about sitting down on a floor cushion, changed her mind and walked to her cooking area, had a sip of tea, and felt another contraction. She wondered if she should lie down again. This seemed to be happening faster than she expected.

Zelandoni checked her again, giving her a closer examination, then she looked at the young woman keenly. "This is not your first baby, is it?"

Ayla waited until a spasm passed before she answered. "No, it's not my first. I had a son," she said quietly.

Zelandoni wondered why he wasn't with her. Had he died? If he was stillborn, or if he died shortly after birth, that would be important to know. "What happened to him?" she asked.

"I had to leave him behind. I gave him to my sister, Uba. He still lives with the Clan, at least I hope he does."

"The delivery was very difficult, wasn't it?"

"Yes. I almost died giving birth to him," Ayla said in a flat, controlled tone, trying not to show any emotion about it, but the donier detected fear in her eyes.

"How old is he, Ayla? Or rather, how old were you when you had him?" Zelandoni wanted to know.

"I could not yet count my twelfth year," Ayla said, going into another labor pain. They were coming faster now.

"And now?" Zelandoni asked when it was over.

"Now I can count nineteen, twenty after this winter. I'm old to be having babies."

"No, you're not, but you were very young when you had your first. Too young. No wonder you had such a difficult time of it. You say you left him with your clan." She paused, thinking about how to ask the next question. "Your son, is he one of 'mixed spirits'?" the woman finally inquired.

Ayla didn't answer at first. She looked at Zelandoni and received as direct a look back, then suddenly she almost doubled up with a contraction. "Yes," she said when it was over, looking scared.

"I think that also contributed to your difficulty. From what I understand, children of mixed spirits can be very difficult for women to deliver. It's something about their heads, I'm told. They are shaped differently, and too big. They don't give as much," Zelandoni said. "This baby may not be as hard for you, Ayla. You're doing fine, you know."

The donier had seen her tense up with the last pain. Tensing up like that will only make it worse, she thought, but I'm afraid she's remembering a terrible delivery with her first. I wish she'd told me. I might have been able to help her. I wish Marthona would come. I think she needs someone paying close attention to her right now, but I would like to make something to help her relax. Maybe talking would take her mind off her fear. "Would you tell me about your son?"

"At first they thought he was deformed, and would be a burden to the clan," Ayla began. "He couldn't even hold his own head up in the beginning, but he grew strong. Everyone came to love him. Grod even made him a spear of his own, just his size. And he could run so fast, even as young as he was."

Ayla was smiling with tears in her eyes at the memory, and it gave the donier a surprising insight. She suddenly understood how much Ayla had loved the child, how proud she was of him, mixed spirits or not. When she said she had given him away to her "sister,"

Zelandoni thought it might have been a relief to find someone who would take him.

Some of the zelandonia still talked about Brukeval's grandmother. Though it was never mentioned in public, most of them felt certain that the daughter to whom she gave birth was a child of mixed spirits. No one really wanted to take her after her mother died, and Brukeval suffered the same fate. He had the look of his mother, perhaps not as strong, but he was mixed, too, Zelandoni was convinced, though she would never admit to it aloud, especially not to him.

Was it possible that Ayla would be prone to attracting their spirits since she was raised by them? Could this one be mixed, too? And if it was, what then? The wisest course might be to quietly end its life before it began. It would be easy enough, and no one would know it wasn't stillborn. It would probably save everyone heartache, even the baby. It would be a shame to have another child in the Cave who was unwanted and unloved, like Brukeval and his mother.

But, the donier thought, if Ayla loved her first child, wouldn't she love this one, too? It's amazing to see her around Echozar, I think she genuinely likes him, and he's very comfortable around her. Maybe it would work out, it would depend on Jondalar.

"Jondalar told me your labor had begun, Ayla," Marthona said, coming into the dwelling. "He took pains to say that it was just beginning and I shouldn't hurry, but he almost pushed me out, he was so eager for me to come."

"It's just as well that you did, Marthona. I'd like to make something for her," Zelandoni said.

"To hasten delivery?" Marthona asked. "First ones can be so long in coming." She smiled at Ayla.

"No," Zelandoni said, pausing thoughtfully before she continued. "Just something to help her relax. She's progressing quite well, faster than I thought she would, but she's very tense, apprehensive about this birth, I believe."

Ayla noticed that the healer did not correct Marthona's assumption that this was her first child. From the beginning, she had sensed that Zelandoni knew many things, many secrets that she kept to herself. Maybe it would still be best if she kept the knowledge of her son to herself, except for Zelandoni. She could talk to her about him.

There was a tap at the entrance, but Proleva came in without waiting. "Jondalar said Ayla was in labor. Can I be of help?" she said. She was supporting a young infant on her back with a carrying blanket.

"Yes, you can," Zelandoni said. She had assumed the right to allow access or not into the dwelling, and Ayla was grateful that she did. As she felt another pain coming on, the last thing she wanted to think about was who should be there. The healer noticed Ayla tensing up, beginning to fight the pain. It was obvious that she didn't want to cry out, either. "You can sit with Ayla while Marthona gets some water boiling. I need to go get some special medicine."

Zelandoni quickly left. She could move quite fast, in spite of her size, when she was so inclined. Folara was just approaching as the woman let the drape fall behind her.

"Can I go in, Zelandoni? I'd like to help, if I can," she said.

The donier paused only a moment. "Yes, go ahead. You can help Proleva try to keep her calm," she said, and hurried on.

When she returned, Ayla was thrashing around rather wildly, in the throes of another contraction, but she was still not crying out. Marthona and Proleva were on either side of her, holding a hand, looking worried. Folara was adding another hot stone to the water that had been heated, to keep it hot. Her expression matched her mother's. There was fear in Ayla's eyes, and relief at seeing the healer.

She hurried to the young woman. "It will be all right, Ayla. You are doing just fine, you just need to relax a little. I'm going to fix something for you, to help you get more comfortable," Zelandoni said.

"What's in it?" Ayla asked as the pain subsided.

Zelandoni looked at her closely. The question was asked not out of dread, but out of interest. It actually seemed to take her mind off her worry for a moment.

"Willow bark and raspberry leaf, primarily," she said, hurrying to see if the water was boiling. "Plus a few linden flowers, and a very little thorn apple."

Ayla was nodding. "Willow bark is a mild painkiller, raspberry leaf is especially relaxing during labor, linden flowers are a sweetener, and thorn apple—I think it's what I call datura—it can stop pain and make you sleep, but might possibly stop the contractions. Just a little might be helpful, though," she said.

"That's what I thought," the donier said.

As she hurried to add the herbs and barks to the hot water Folara was tending, Zelandoni could see that letting Ayla get involved in her own treatment might be just as helpful as the medicines in getting her to relax, but considering how much she knew about medications, it would be foolish to try to keep anything from her. It took some time to let the medicinal tea steep, during which time Ayla had several more labor pains. When she finally brought it to her, Ayla was more than ready to take it, but she sat up and tasted the tea first, concentrating with her eyes closed. She nodded, then drank it.

"More raspberry leaf than willow bark, and just enough linden to cover the bitter taste of the datura . . . thorn apple," Ayla said, lying back down to wait for the next paroxysm of labor.

For just an instant, Zelandoni felt a retort come to her mind, a sarcastic "Well, do you approve?" but she caught herself and then was surprised that she'd even thought of it. The experienced woman wasn't used to having someone testing and commenting on her medicine, but wouldn't she do the same? The young woman had not been criticizing, she was testing herself, Zelandoni realized. As the donier watched, she smiled inwardly, sure that she knew precisely what Ayla was doing, because she would do the same. Ayla was using herself to test the medicine, quietly checking her own responses, waiting to see how long the medication would take to work and how much effect it would have. And as the healer had guessed, that in itself was taking her mind off her fear and helping her to relax.

They all waited, speaking quietly. The birthing seemed to be going a little better for the young woman. Zelandoni didn't know if it was because of the medicine or the lessening of her fear, probably both, but she was not thrashing around anymore. Instead Ayla was concentrating on exactly what she was feeling, mentally comparing this birth with her previous one, and realizing that this one did seem to be easier. She was following the course that she had observed in other women who were having a normal delivery. She had been there when Proleva gave birth, and now she smiled when the woman nursed her baby girl.

"Marthona, do you know where her birthing blanket is? I think she's getting close," Zelandoni said.

"So soon? I didn't think it would go so quickly, especially since she seemed to be having so much trouble in the beginning," Proleva said, putting her infant down to sleep on her blanket.

"But she does seem to have it under control now," Marthona said. "I'll get the birthing blanket. Is it where you showed me before, Ayla?"

"Yes," she answered quickly, feeling another muscle-clenching, all-encompassing convulsion coming on. When it was over, Zelandoni directed Proleva and Folara to spread the leather birthing blanket, marked with drawings and symbols, on the floor, then beckoned to Marthona.

"It's time to help her up," she said. Then to Ayla, "You need to get up and let the pull of the Great Earth Mother help the baby out. Can you get up?"

"Yes," she said between panting breaths. She had been bearing down hard with each pain, and felt an urge to push again, but was trying to hold back for a moment. "I think so."

They all helped Ayla to her feet and led her to the birthing blanket. Proleva showed her the squatting position to take, then she got on one side of her while Folara supported her other side. Marthona was in front, smiling and offering moral support. Zelandoni got behind her and clasped the young woman to her massive breast, wrapping her arms around her, above the bulge of her stomach.

Ayla felt enveloped by the softness and warmth of the huge woman; it was comforting to lean back on her. She felt like Mother, like all mothers combined in one, like the soft bosom of the Earth itself. But there was something else, too. Enormous strength lay hidden underneath the mounds of flesh. Ayla felt sure this woman could display every mood of Mother Earth Herself, from the gentleness of a warm summer day to the fury of a driving blizzard. If she felt so moved, she could lash out with the devastating power of a raging storm, or comfort and nourish like a soft mist.

"Now, at the next pain, I want you to push," Zelandoni said. The two women on either side of her were each holding a hand, giving her something to grip.

"I feel it coming," Ayla said.

"Then push!" Zelandoni said.

Ayla took a deep breath and bore down as hard as she could. She felt the donier helping her, pushing down on the baby with her. A gush of warm water spilled on the blanket.

"Good. I was waiting for that," Zelandoni said.

"I wondered when her waters were going to break," Proleva said. "Mine seem to break so early, I'm almost dry by the time the baby comes. This is better. Here she goes again."

"Now, again, push, Ayla," Zelandoni said.

Ayla bore down again and felt movement.

"I can see the head," Marthona said. "I'm ready to catch the baby." She knelt down closer to Ayla, just as another strong contraction started. As Ayla took a deep breath and pushed.

"Here it comes!" Marthona said.

Ayla felt the passage of the head. The rest was easy. As the baby slid out, Marthona reached out and caught it.

Ayla looked down and saw the wet infant in Marthona's arms, and smiled. Zelandoni smiled, too.

"One last push, Ayla, to get out the afterbirth," Zelandoni said, helping her again. She pushed and watched a mass of bloody tissue fall on the birthing blanket.

Zelandoni let go of her and moved around to the front of the new mother. Proleva and Folara supported Ayla while Zelandoni took the baby, turned it over, and patted the tiny back. There were little hiccuping sounds. Zelandoni thumped the baby's feet and watched the infant expel breath in a startle response, then breathe in the first gulp of life-giving air. There was a small crying sound, hardly more than a mewling at first, but it grew as the lungs became accustomed to sustaining life.

Marthona held the infant while the donier cleaned Ayla up a little, wiping away blood and fluid, then Proleva and Folara helped her back to the bed. Zelandoni tied a piece of sinew around the baby's navel cord—at Ayla's request it had been dyed red with ochre—to pinch it off and prevent bleeding from the still engorged tube. With a sharp flint blade she cut the cord between the tie and the afterbirth, separating the infant from the placenta that had provided nourishment and a place to grow until birth. Ayla's infant was a separate entity, a unique and individual human being.

Marthona and Zelandoni cleaned the baby with a velvety soft rabbitskin that Ayla had made for the purpose. Marthona had a small blanket ready, again velvety soft, and so smooth, it felt like the baby's skin. It was made from the hide of a nearly full-term deer foetus. Zelandoni had told Jondalar that it would be especially lucky for the child born to his hearth if he could secure such a hide for the birth, and he and his brother had gone out near the end of winter looking for a pregnant deer.

Ayla had helped him make the foetal deerskin into the supple leather blanket. He had always been amazed at the softness of her leathers, a skill he knew she had learned from the Clan. After working with her on one, he understood how much effort it took, even starting with a tender foetal skin. Zelandoni laid the baby on the blanket, then Marthona wrapped the newborn in it and brought the child to Ayla.

38

You should be pleased. She's a perfect little girl," Marthona said, giving the tiny bundle to her mother.

Ayla looked at the tiny likeness of herself. "She's so beautiful!" She unwrapped the swaddling of soft skins and carefully examined her new daughter, half-fearful in spite of the reassuring words that she would find some deformity. "She is perfect. Did you ever see such a beautiful baby, Marthona?"

The woman just smiled. Of course she had. Her own babies, but this one, the daughter of her son's hearth, was no less beautiful than her own had been.

"The delivery wasn't very hard at all, Zelandoni," Ayla said when the donier came and looked at them both. "You helped a lot, but it wasn't really so hard. I'm so glad she's a girl. Look, she's trying to find my breast." Ayla helped her, with the ease of experience, Zelandoni thought. "Can Jondalar come and see her? I think she looks a lot like him, don't you, Marthona?"

"He can come soon," Zelandoni said as she examined Ayla and wrapped some fresh absorbent leather between her legs. "There was no tearing, Ayla, no damage. Only the bleeding to cleanse. It was a good delivery. Do you have a name for her?"

"Yes, I've been thinking about it ever since you told me I would have to choose the name for my baby," Ayla said.

"Good. Tell me the name. I will make a symbol for it on this stone, and exchange it for this," she said, picking up the birthing blanket wrapped into a bundle around the afterbirth. "Then I will take this out and bury it, before the spirit life still remaining in the afterbirth tries to seek a home close to the life it once held. I must do it quickly, then I will tell Jondalar to come in."

"I've decided to call her . . ." Ayla began.

"No! Don't say it out loud, just whisper it to me," Zelandoni said.

As the donier bent close, Ayla whispered in her ear. Then she left quickly. Marthona, Folara, and Proleva sat beside the new mother, admiring the baby and talking quietly. Ayla was feeling tired, but happy and relaxed, not at all as she had after Durc was born. Then she had been exhausted and in pain. She dozed off a little and was awakened when Zelandoni returned and gave her the small stone that now held enigmatic marks in red and black paint.

"Put this in a safe place, perhaps in the niche behind your donii," Zelandoni said.

Ayla nodded, then saw another head appear. "Jondalar!" she said. He knelt down beside the sleeping platform to get closer.

"How are you, Ayla?"

"I'm fine. It was not a bad delivery, Jondalar. Much easier than I thought it would be. And see the baby?" she said as she unwrapped the blanket so he could see. "She's perfect!"

"You got the girl you wanted," he said, looking at the tiny newborn and feeling a little awed. "She's so little. And look, she even has tiny fingernails." The thought of a woman giving birth to a complete new human being suddenly overwhelmed him. "What have you named your daughter, Ayla?"

She looked at Zelandoni. "Can I tell him?"

"Yes, it's safe now," she said.

"I've named our daughter Jonayla, after both you and me, Jondalar, because she came from both of us. She is your daughter, too."

"Jonayla. I like that name. Jonayla," he said.

Marthona liked the name, too. She and Proleva smiled indulgently at Ayla. It was not uncommon for new mothers to try to reassure their mates that their children came from their spirits. Although Ayla had not said "spirit," they were sure they understood what she meant. Zelandoni wasn't as sure. Ayla tended to say exactly what she meant. Jondalar had no doubt. He knew exactly what she meant.

It would be nice if it was true, he thought as he looked at the tiny little girl. Exposed to the cool air without her covers, she was beginning to wake up.

"She is beautiful. She's going to look just like you, Ayla. I can see it already," he said.

"She looks like you, too, Jondalar. Would you like to hold her?"

"I don't know," he said, backing off a bit. "She's so small."

"Not too small for you to hold, Jondalar," Zelandoni said. "Here, I'll help you. Sit down comfortably." She quickly wrapped the baby back up in her blanket, picked her up, and placed her in Jondalar's arms, showing him how to hold her.

The infant had her eyes open and seemed to be looking at him. Are you my daughter? he wondered. You are so tiny, you will need someone to watch over you, and help take care of you until you grow up. He held her a little closer, feeling protective. Then, to his surprise, he felt a sudden and completely unexpected flush of warmth and a protective love for the infant. Jonayla, he thought. My daughter, Jonayla.

The next day Zelandoni stopped to see Ayla. She had been waiting and watching for a time when she was alone. Ayla was sitting on a cushion on the floor, nursing her baby, and Zelandoni lowered herself to a cushion on the floor beside her.

"Why don't you use the stool, Zelandoni," Ayla said.

"This is fine, Ayla. It isn't that I can't sit on the floor, it's just that there are times when I prefer not to. How is Jonayla?"

"She's fine. She's a good baby. She woke me up last night, but she sleeps most of the time," Ayla said.

"I wanted to tell you that she will be named as a Zelandonii to Jondalar's hearth on the day after next, and her name given to the Cave," the woman said.

"Good," Ayla said. "I'll be glad when she's Zelandonii, and named to Jondalar's hearth. It will make everything complete."

"Have you heard about Relona? The mate of Shevonar, the man who was trampled on by the bison shortly after you arrived?" Zelandoni asked, sounding as though she were making friendly conversation.

"No, what about her?"

"She and Ranokol, Shevonar's brother, are going to mate next summer. He started out by helping her to compensate for the loss of her mate, and then they grew to care for each other. I think it may be a good pairing," the older woman said.

"I'm glad to hear that. He was so upset when Shevonar died. It was almost as though he blamed himself. I think he thought he should have died instead," Ayla said. There was a silence then, but she felt a sense of expectancy. She wondered if the First had come for a reason that she hadn't yet said.

"There is something else I want to talk to you about," Zelandoni said. "I'd like to know more about your son. I understand why you never mentioned him, especially after all that trouble about Echozar, but if you wouldn't mind talking about him, there are some things I would like to know."

"I don't mind talking about him. Sometimes I ache to talk about him," Ayla said.

She talked at length to the donier about the son she had when she lived with the Clan, the one of mixed spirits, about her morning sickness that lasted all day and almost for her entire pregnancy, and about her bone-wrenching delivery. She had already forgotten whatever discomfort she had felt giving birth to Jonayla, but she still remembered the pain of giving birth to Durc. She told her about his deformity in the eyes of the Clan, her flight to her small cave to save his life, and her return though she thought she would still lose him. She spoke of her joy at his acceptance, and the name Creb picked out for him, Durc, and the legend of Durc, where his name came from. She talked about their life together, his laughter and her delight that he could make sounds the way she could, and the language they started to make up together, and she talked about leaving him behind with the Clan when she was forced to go. Toward the end of her story, she was finding it difficult to talk for the tears.

"Zelandoni," Ayla said, looking at the large, motherly woman, "I had an idea when I was hiding in the small cave with him, and the more I have thought about it since, the more I believe it is true. It's about the way life begins. I don't think it is the blending of spirits that starts new life. I think life begins when a man and a woman couple. I think men start life to grow inside women."

It was a startling idea coming from the young woman, especially since no one had ever said anything like it to Zelandoni before, but it wasn't an entirely unfamiliar idea, though the only person she knew of who had ever thought of such a thing was herself.

"I have thought about it for a long time since then, and I am now even more convinced that life begins when a man puts his member inside a woman, into the place that a baby comes from, and leaves his essence. I think that is what starts a new life, not the mixing of spirits," Ayla said.

"You mean when they share the Gift of Pleasure from the Great Earth Mother," Zelandoni said.

"Yes," Ayla said.

"Let me ask you some questions. A man and a woman share Doni's Gift many times. There are not that many children born. If a life was started every time they shared Pleasures, there would be many, many more children," Zelandoni said.

"I have thought of that. It's clear that a life doesn't start every time they share Pleasures, so there must be something else besides Pleasures. Maybe they must share Pleasures many times, or maybe at special times, or maybe the Great Mother decides when life will start and when it won't. But it isn't their spirits that She blends, it's the man's essence, and maybe a special essence of the woman, too. I'm certain Jonayla was started right after Jondalar and I got down from the glacier, that first morning when we woke up and shared Pleasures."

"You say you thought about it for a long time. What made you think of it in the first place?" Zelandoni asked.

"I first thought about it when I was in my small cave hiding with Durc," Ayla said.

"They told me I had to take him outside and leave him because he was deformed," tears threatened as Ayla said it, "but I looked at him carefully and he wasn't deformed. He didn't look like them and he didn't look like me. He looked like the Clan and like me. His head was long and big in the back, and he had big browridges like theirs, but he had a high forehead like mine in front. He looked something like Echozar, except I think his body will be more like ours when he grows up. He was never as thick or as stocky as Clan boys, and his legs were long and straight, not bowed like Echozar's. He was a mixture, but he was strong and healthy."

"Echozar is mixed, but his mother was Clan. When would she have shared Pleasures with a man like us? Why would a man like us want to share Pleasures with a flathead woman?" Zelandoni asked.

"Echozar told me his mother had been cursed with death because her mate had been killed when he tried to protect her from a man of the Others. When they found out she was pregnant, they let her stay, until Echozar was born," Ayla said. Jonayla had let go of the nipple and was fussing a bit. Ayla put her over her shoulder and patted her back.

"You mean a man like us forced his mother? I suppose such things happen, but I can't understand them," Zelandoni said.

"It happened to one of the women I met at the Clan Gathering. She had a daughter who was mixed. She said she was forced by some men of the Others, men who looked like me, she said. Her own daughter was killed when one of the men grabbed her and her daughter fell from her arms. When she found that she was pregnant again, she wished for another girl, which made her mate angry. Clan women are only supposed to wish for boys, but many women secretly wish for girls anyway. When the girl was born deformed, he made her keep the girl to teach her a lesson."

"What a sad story, to be so badly treated by her mate after being attacked and suffering such a loss," the donier said.

"She asked me to talk to Brun, the leader of my clan, to arrange a mating between her daughter, Ura, and my Durc. She was afraid her daughter would never find a mate otherwise. I thought it was a good idea. Durc was deformed in the eyes of the Clan, too, and would have just as much trouble finding a mate. Brun agreed. Now Ura is promised to Durc. After the next Clan Gathering, she is supposed to move to Brun's clan . . . no, it's Broud's clan now. She must be there by now. I don't think Broud will be very kind to her." Ayla paused, thinking about Ura having to move to a strange clan. "It will be hard for her to leave her clan, and her mother who loves her, and move to a clan where she might not be very welcome. I hope Durc turns out to be the kind of man who will help her." Ayla shook her head, then the baby let out a little burp, and she smiled. She left her propped up on her shoulder for a while longer, still patting her back.

"Jondalar and I heard several other stories on our Journey about young men of the Others forcing women of the Clan. I think it's something they like to dare each other to do, but the people of the Clan don't like it."

"I suspect you're right, Ayla, much as the thought distresses me. Some young men seem to enjoy doing whatever they are not supposed to. But to force a woman, even a Clan woman, that bothers me even more," the One Who Was First said.

"I'm not sure all the mixed children are the result of some man of the Others forcing a woman of the Clan, or the other way around. Rydag was mixed," Ayla said.

"That's the child who was taken in by the mate of the leader of the Mamutoi people you lived with, isn't it?" Zelandoni asked.

"Yes. His mother was Clan, and like them, he couldn't really speak, except for a few sounds that no one could understand very well. He was a weak child. That's why he died. Nezzie said Rydag's mother was alone, and followed them. That's not like women of the Clan. She must have been cursed for some reason, or she would not have been alone, especially not so far along in her pregnancy. And she must have known someone of the Others, someone who treated her kindly, or she would have hid from the Mamutoi, not followed them. Perhaps it was the man who started Rydag."

"Perhaps," was all Zelandoni said. But thinking about those who were mixed, she wondered if Ayla knew any more about Echozar. She was more interested in him, since he had been accepted by Dalanar's people and allowed to mate Jerika's daughter. "What about Echozar's mother? You said she was cursed? I'm not sure what that means."

"She was shunned, ostracized. She was considered a 'bad luck' woman, because her mate was killed when she was attacked, and especially after she gave birth to a 'deformed' child. The Clan doesn't like mixed children, either. A man named Andovan found her alone, ready to die with her baby after she was turned out of her clan. Echozar said he was an older man, living alone for some reason, but he took her and her baby in. I think he was S'Armunai, but he was living on the edge of Zelandonii territory, and he knew how to speak Zelandonii. I think he may have escaped from Attaroa. He raised Echozar, taught him to speak Zelandonii and some S'Armunai. His mother taught him the Clan signs. Andovan had to learn them, too, because she couldn't speak his language. But Echozar could. He was like Durc."

She paused again, her eyes getting misty. "Durc could have learned to talk, if he'd had somebody to teach him. He talked a little before I left, and he could laugh. How could they think Durc would look like the Clan if he was my baby? Born to me? But he didn't look like me, either, not like Jonayla does, and he wouldn't, if it was Broud that started him."

"Who is this Broud?"

"He was Ebra's son, she was Brun's mate. Brun was the leader of the clan. He was a good leader. Broud was the one who made me leave the clan when he became leader. I grew up with him hating me. He always hated me," Ayla said.

"But you say he was the one who started the child you had? And you think that comes from sharing Pleasures. Why did he want to share Pleasures with you if he hated you?" Zelandoni asked.

"There was no sharing of Pleasures with him. No Pleasure in it for me. Broud forced me. I don't know why he did it the first time, but it was horrible. He hurt me. I hated it and I hated him for doing it. He knew I hated it, that's why he did it. Maybe he knew in the beginning that I would hate it, but I know that's why he kept doing it."

"And your clan allowed it!" Zelandoni said.

"Women of the Clan must couple whenever a man wishes, whenever he gives her the signal. That's what they are taught."

"I can't understand that," the donier said. "Why would a man even want a woman if she didn't want him?"

"I don't think Clan women minded too much. They even had

little ways to encourage a man to give them the signal. Iza told me about them, but I never wanted to use them. Certainly not with Broud. I hated it so much, I couldn't eat, I didn't want to get up in the morning, I didn't want to leave Creb's hearth. But when I found out I was going to have a baby, I was so happy, I didn't even care about Broud anymore. I just put up with him, and ignored him. He stopped after that. It wasn't fun for him if I didn't resist, if he couldn't force me against my will."

"You said you could only count eleven years when your child was born? You were very young, Ayla. Most girls are not even women yet, at that age. A few may become women that young, but not most."

"I was old for the Clan, though. Some girls of the Clan become women at seven years, and by the time they can count ten years, most girls have become women. Some of Brun's clan thought I would never become a woman. They thought I would never have children, because my totem was too strong for a woman," Ayla said.

"But obviously you did."

Ayla paused, thinking. "Only women can give birth. But if women get pregnant by a mixing of spirits, why did Doni create men? Just for company, just for Pleasures? I think there has to be some other reason. Women can be company for each other, they can support each other, take care of each other, they can even give each other Pleasures.

"Attaroa of the S'Armunai hated men. She kept them locked up. She would not allow them to share the Gift of Pleasure with women. The women shared their homes with other women. Attaroa thought if she did away with men, the spirits of women would be forced to blend and they would have only girls, but it wasn't working. Some of the women shared Pleasures, but they could not couple, they could not mix their essences. Very few children were born."

"But some children were born?" Zelandoni asked.

"Some, but they weren't all girls—Attaroa crippled two of the boys. Most of the women did not feel the way Attaroa did. Some of them sneaked in to visit their men, some of the women Attaroa used to guard the men helped them. The women with children were the ones who had a man to share their fires the first night the men were free. They were the ones who were mated, or wanted to be. I think the only reason they had children was because they visited a man. It wasn't that they shared a hearth and were together long enough for a man to show he was worthy so his spirit would be chosen. They saw their men seldom, and only for a little while, barely long enough to couple. It was dangerous, Attaroa would have had them killed if she found out. I think it was the coupling that made the women pregnant."

Zelandoni nodded. "Your reasoning is interesting, Ayla. We are taught that it is a mixing of spirits, and that seems to answer most questions about how life begins. But most people don't question it, they just accept it. Your childhood was different, you are more ready to question, but I would be careful about whom you discuss this idea with. There are some who would be quite upset. I have wondered sometimes why Doni made men. It is true that women could take care of themselves and each other if they had to. I have even wondered why she made male animals. Mother animals often take care of their young alone, and the males and females don't spend much time together, only at certain times of the year when they share Pleasures."

Ayla felt encouraged to press her point. "When I lived with the Mamutoi, there was a man of the Lion Camp. His name was Ranec and he lived with Wymez, the flint-knapper."

"The one Jondalar talks about?"

"Yes. Wymez went on a very long Journey when he was a young man, he could count ten more years before he returned. Wymez traveled south of the Great Sea, around the eastern end of it, and then west again. He mated a woman he met there, and was trying to bring her and her son back to the Mamutoi, but she died on the way. He brought only the son of his mate with him when he returned. He told me his mate had skin almost as black as night, all of her people did. She had Ranec after they were mated and Wymez said he looked different from all the other children because he was so light, but he looked very dark to me. His skin was brown, he was nearly as dark as Racer, and his hair was tight black curls," Ayla said.

"You think that this man was brown because his mother was almost black, and her mate was light? That could be caused by a mixing of spirits, too," Zelandoni said.

"It could," Ayla admitted. "It's what the Mamutoi believed, but if everyone else there was black except Wymez, wouldn't there be many more black spirits for his mother's spirit to mix with? They were mated, they must have shared Pleasures." She looked at her baby, then at Zelandoni again. "It would have been interesting to see what our children would have looked like if I had joined with Ranec."

"That's who you were going to mate?"

Ayla smiled. "He had laughing eyes, and smiling white teeth. He was clever and funny, he made me laugh, and he was the best carver I have ever seen. He made a special donii for me, and a carving of Whinney. He loved me. He said he wanted to join with me more than anything he ever wanted in his life. He looked like no one I have ever seen, before or since. He was so different, even his features were different. I was fascinated by him. If I hadn't already loved Jondalar, I could have loved Ranec."

"If he was all that, I don't blame you," Zelandoni said, smiling back. "It's interesting, there are rumors about some dark-skinned people living with a Cave to the south, beyond the mountains on the shore of the Great Sea. A young man and his mother, it was said. I never really believed it, you never know how much truth there is in such stories, and it seemed so incredible. Now, I'm not so sure."

"Ranec did resemble Wymez, in spite of the difference in skin color and features. They were the same size, had the same-shaped body, and they walked exactly alike," Ayla said.

"You don't have to go that far afield to find resemblances," Zelandoni said. "Many children bear a similarity to the mate of the mother, but there are some who look like other men of the Cave, some who hardly know the mother at all."

"It could have happened during a festival or ceremony to honor the Mother. Don't many women share Pleasures with men who are not their mates then?" Ayla asked.

Zelandoni was quiet, thinking. "Ayla, this idea of yours will require deep thought, and consideration. I don't know if you understand the implications. If it is true, it would cause changes that neither you nor I can even imagine. Such a revelation could only come from the zelandonia, Ayla. No one would accept such an idea unless they believed it came from one who speaks for the Great Earth Mother Herself. Who have you talked to about this?"

"Only Jondalar, and now you," Ayla said.

"I suggest that you say nothing to anyone else just yet. I will talk to Jondalar and impress upon him the necessity of speaking to no one, either." They both sat quietly, immersed in their own thoughts.

"Zelandoni," Ayla said, "do you ever wonder what it would feel like to be a man?"

"That's a strange thing to wonder about."

"I was thinking about something Jondalar said. It was when I wanted to go hunting, and he didn't want me to go. I know that part of the reason was that he was planning to come back here and build our home, but there was more to it than that. He said something about wanting a purpose. 'What's a man's purpose if women have children and provide for them, too?' That's how he said it. I never thought about a purpose for living before. What would it feel like to think my life had no meaning?"

"You can carry that a step further, Ayla. You know part of your purpose is to bring forth the next generation, but what is the purpose of having another generation? What is the purpose of life?"

"I don't know. What is the purpose of life?" Ayla asked.

Zelandoni laughed. "If I could answer that, I'd be equal to the Great Mother Herself, Ayla. Only She can answer that question. There are many who claim our purpose is to honor Her. Perhaps our purpose is just to live, and to care for the next generation so that they may live. That may be the best way to honor Her. The Mother's Song says She made us because She was lonely, that She wanted to be remembered, and acknowledged. But there are those who say there is no purpose. I doubt if that question can be answered in this world, Ayla. I'm not sure if it can be answered in the next."

"But at least women know they are necessary for there to be a next generation. How must it feel not to have even that much purpose?" Ayla said. "How would it feel to think life would go on just the same whether you were here or not, whether your kind, your gender, was here or not?"

"Ayla, I have never had any children. Should I feel my life has no purpose?" Zelandoni asked.

"It's not the same. Perhaps you could have had children, and if you could not, you are still a woman. You still belong to the gender that brings forth life," Ayla said.

"But we are all human. Including men. We're all just people. Both men and women continue on to the next generation. Women have boys as often as they have girls," the donier said.

"That's just it. Women have boys as often as girls. What do the men have to do with it? If you felt that you and all of your kind had no part in creating that next generation, would you feel as human? Or would you feel less important? Something added on at the last moment, something unnecessary?" Ayla was leaning forward, strongly making her points, passionate in her feelings about them.

Zelandoni pondered the question, then looked at the serious face of the young woman with the sleeping baby in her arms. "You belong to the zelandonia, Ayla. You argue as well as any of them," she said.

Ayla pulled back. "I don't want to be a Zelandoni," she said.

The heavy woman eyed her with speculation. "Why not?"

"I just want to be a mother, and Jondalar's mate," Ayla said.

"Don't you want to be a healer anymore? You are as skilled as anyone, including me," the donier said.

Ayla frowned. "Well, yes, I want to keep on being a healer, too."

"You said you assisted your Mamut a few times in some of his other duties, didn't you find it interesting?" said the One Who Was First.

"It was interesting," Ayla conceded, "especially learning things I didn't know, but it was frightening, too."

"How much more frightening would it have been if you had been alone and unprepared? Ayla, you are a daughter of the Mammoth Hearth. Mamut had a reason for adopting you. I can see it, I think you can, too. Look inside yourself. Have you ever been frightened by something strange and unfamiliar when you were alone?"

Ayla refused to look at Zelandoni, looking away, and then down, but she nodded just slightly.

"You know there is something different about you, something few people have, don't you? You try to ignore it, put it out of your mind, but it's difficult sometimes, isn't it?"

Ayla glanced up. Zelandoni was staring at her, forcing her to look back, holding her eyes the way she had done the first time they met. Ayla struggled to look away, but couldn't quite do it. "Yes," she said softly. "It is difficult sometimes." Zelandoni released her hold, and Ayla looked down again.

"No one becomes Zelandoni unless they feel the call, Ayla," the woman said gently. "But what if you should feel the call and not be prepared? Don't you think it would be better to have some training, just in case? The possibility is there, no matter how much you may want to deny it to yourself."

"But doesn't the preparation in itself make it more likely?" Ayla asked.

"Yes. It does. But it can be interesting. I'll be honest with you. I want an acolyte. I don't have too many years left. I want the one who follows me to be trained by me. This is my Cave. I want the best for it. I am First Among Those Who Serve The Great Earth Mother. I don't say this often, but I am not First without reason. If a person is gifted, no one could train her better than I can. You are gifted, Ayla.

You are, perhaps, more gifted than I am. You could be First," Zelandoni said.

"What about Jonokol?" Ayla asked.

"You should know the answer to that. Jonokol is an excellent artist. He was happy to remain an acolyte. He never wanted to become a Zelandoni, until you showed him that cave. You know he'll be gone by next summer. He will move to the Nineteenth Cave as soon as he can get the Zelandoni of the Nineteenth to accept him, and find an excuse to leave me. He wants that Cave, Ayla, and I think he should have it. He will not only make it beautiful, in that cave, he will bring to life the world of the spirits," Zelandoni said.

"Look at this, Ayla!" Jondalar said, holding a flint point. He was full of excitement. "I heated the flint the way Wymez does, very hot. I knew I had it right when it cooled because it felt shiny and slick, almost as if it had been oiled. Then I retouched it bifacially, using the pressure techniques he developed. It still isn't up to his quality, but I think with practice, I may get close. I can see all kinds of possibilities. I can remove those long thin flakes, now. That means I can make points almost as thin as I want, and get a long straight edge for a knife or a spear, without the curve that you always get when you start with a blade detached from a core. I can even straighten those blades more easily with careful retouching on the inner side of both ends of a curved blade. I can make any kind of notch I want. I can make shouldered points with a tang for hafting. You can't believe the control it gives me. I can do anything I want. It's almost like bending the stone to your will. That Wymez is a genius!"

Ayla smiled at him going on and on. "Wymez may be a genius, Jondalar, but you are just as good," she said.

"I only wish I were. Remember, he developed the process. I'm only trying to copy it. It's too bad he lives so far away. But I am grateful for the time I had with him. I wish Dalanar were here. He said he was going to experiment this winter, too, and I'd really like to discuss it with him."

Jondalar examined the blade again, looking it over critically. Then he looked up and smiled at her. "I almost forgot to tell you. I am definitely going to be taking on Matagan as an apprentice for more than this winter. Since he came to visit, I've been able to judge, and I think he does have talent and ability with the stone. I had a long talk with his mother and her mate, and Joharran is agreeable."

"I like Matagan," Ayla said. "I'm glad you will be teaching him your craft. You have so much patience, and you are the best flint-knapper of the Ninth Cave, probably of all the Zelandoni."

Jondalar smiled at her words. One's mate always made favorable comparisons, he said to himself, but at a deeper level, he thought it might be true. "Would it be all right if he stays with us all the time?"

"I think I would like that. We have so much room in the main room, we can take part of it to make him a sleeping room," she said. "I hope the baby doesn't disturb him. Jonayla still wakes up at night."

"Young men tend to be sound sleepers. I don't think he even hears her."

"I have been meaning to talk to you about something Zelandoni said," Ayla said.

Jondalar thought she looked a bit troubled. It was probably his imagination.

"Zelandoni asked me to be her acolyte. She wants to train me," Ayla blurted out.

Jondalar's head snapped up. "I didn't know you were interested in becoming a Zelandoni, Ayla."

"I didn't think I was, and I still don't know if I am. She has said before that she thought I belonged in the zelandonia, but the first time she asked me to be her acolyte was right after Jonayla was born. She says she really needs someone, and I already know something about healing. Just because I'm an acolyte doesn't mean I will neces-sarily become a Zelandoni. Jonokol has been an acolyte for a long time," Ayla said, looking down at the vegetables she was cutting.

Jondalar walked over to her and lifted her chin to look directly at her. Her eyes did look troubled. "Ayla, everyone knows the only rea-son Jonokol is Zelandoni's acolyte is because he's such a good artist, he captures the spirit of animals with great skill, and Zelandoni needs him for the ceremonies. He will never be a donier."

"He might. Zelandoni says he wants to move to the Nineteenth Cave," Ayla said.

"It's that new cave you found, isn't it?" Jondalar said. "Well, he'd be the right person for it. But if you become an acolyte, you would become a Zelandoni, wouldn't you?"

Ayla still could not refuse to answer a direct question or tell a lie. "Yes, Jondalar," she said. "I think someday I would be Zelandoni, if I join the zelandonia, but not right away."

"Is it what you want to do? Or has Zelandoni talked you into it because you are a healer?" Jondalar wanted to know.

"She says I already am Zelandoni, in a way. Maybe she's right, I don't know. She says I should be trained for my own protection. It could be very dangerous for me if I feel a call and I'm not prepared for it," Ayla said. She had never told him about the strange things that happened to her, and it felt like a lie, not telling him. Even in the Clan one could refrain from mentioning. It bothered her, but she still didn't tell him.

It was Jondalar's turn to look troubled. "There isn't much I can say about it, one way or another. It's your choice. It probably is best to be prepared. You don't know how you scared me when you and Mamut made that strange Journey. I thought you were dead, and I begged the Great Mother to bring you back. I don't think I ever begged for anything so hard in my life, Ayla. I hope you never do anything like that again."

"I thought it was you, not at first, but later. Mamut said someone called us back, called with such force, it could not be denied. I thought I saw you there when I came back to myself, but then I didn't see you," Ayla said.

"You were promised to Ranec. I didn't want to be in the way," Jondalar said, vividly recalling that terrible night.

"But you loved me. If you hadn't loved me so much, my spirit might still be lost in that empty void. Mamut said he would never go there again like that, and he told me that if I ever take that Journey again, I should make sure I have strong protection, or I might not return." Suddenly she reached for him. "Why me, Jondalar?" she cried. "Why do I have to be a Zelandoni?"

Jondalar held her. Yes, he thought, Why her? He recalled the donier talking about the responsibilities and the dangers. Now he understood why she had been so open. She had been trying to prepare them. She must have known all along, from the first day they arrived, just like Mamut seemed to know. That's why he adopted her to his hearth. Can I be the mate of a Zelandoni? He thought about his mother and Dalanar. She said he had not been able to stay with her because she was the leader. The demands on a Zelandoni are even greater.

Everyone said he was just like Dalanar, there was no doubt he was the son of Dalanar's spirit. But Ayla says it was not just spirits. She says Jonayla is my daughter. If she is right, then I must be Dalanar's son! The thought stunned him. Could he be as much Dalanar's son as he was Marthona's? If he was, would he be so much like him that he would not be able to live with a woman whose duties were so important? It was a very disturbing idea.

He felt Ayla shaking in his arms and looked at her. "What's wrong, Ayla?"

"I'm afraid, Jondalar. That's why I don't want to do it. I'm afraid to be Zelandoni," she sobbed. She quieted down and pulled away. "The reason I'm so afraid, Jondalar, is that things have happened to me that I never told you."

"What kind of things?" he asked, his forehead wrinkled in a frown.

"I never told you because I didn't know how to explain. I'm still not sure that I can, but I'll try. When I lived with Brun's clan, you know I went with them to a Clan Gathering. Iza was too sick to go—she died soon after we returned," Ayla's eyes started to fill at the memory. "Iza was the medicine woman, it was she that was supposed to prepare the special drink for the mog-urs. No one else knew how. Uba was too young, not a woman yet, and it had to be prepared by a woman. Iza explained it to me before we left. I didn't think the mog-urs would allow me to make it—they said I wasn't Clan—but then Creb came and told me to prepare myself. It was the same drink I made for Mamut and me when we took our strange Journey.

"But I didn't know how to do it right, and I ended up drinking some of it, too. I didn't even know where I was going when I followed the mog-urs back into the cave. The drink was so powerful, I may have already been in the Spirit World. When I saw the mog-urs I hid and watched, but Creb knew I was there. I told you Creb was a powerful magician. He was like Zelandoni, First, The Mog-ur. He was directing everything, and somehow my mind joined with theirs. I went back with them, back to the beginnings. I can't explain it, but I was there. As we came back to the present, we came to this place. Creb blocked out the others, they didn't know I was with them, but then he left them and followed me. I know it was this place, I recognized the Falling Stone. The Clan lived here for generations, I can't tell you how long."

In spite of himself, Jondalar was fascinated.

"Long ago we started from the same people," Ayla continued, "but then we changed. The Clan was left behind when we went ahead. As powerful as he was, Creb couldn't follow me, but he saw something, or felt something. Then he told me to leave, get out of the cave. It was like I heard him inside me, inside my head, as though he were talking to me. The other mog-urs never knew I was there, and he never told them. They would have killed me. Women were not allowed to participate in those ceremonies.

"Creb changed after that. He was never the same again. He began to lose his power, I think he didn't like directing the minds anymore. I don't know how, but somehow I hurt him, I wish I had never done it, but he did something to me, too. I've been different since then, my dreams feel different, and sometimes I feel strange, as though I go away someplace else, and—I don't know how to say it, but it's like I know what people are thinking sometimes. No, that's not quite it, either, it's more like I know what they are feeling, but that's not exactly right, either. What they are, I don't know the right words, Jondalar. I block it out most of the time anyway, but sometimes things get through, especially when there are very strong emotions, like Brukeval's."

Jondalar was looking at her strangely. "Do you know what I am thinking, what thoughts are in my head?"

"No, I never know thoughts, exactly. But I know that you love me." She watched his expression change. "It bothers you, doesn't it? Maybe I shouldn't have said anything," she mumbled, feeling Jondalar's emotions like a weight. She was always particularly perceptive to Jondalar. She put her head down, her shoulders slumped.

He could see her dejection, and suddenly his uneasy feeling evaporated. He took both her shoulders and made her look up, then looked into her eyes. They had that incredibly ancient look he had seen occasionally before, and a sadness, a deep, ineffable melancholy.

"I have nothing to hide from you, Ayla. I don't care if you know what I'm thinking or feeling. I love you. I'll never stop loving you."

Tears spilled out of her eyes, as much from relief as from love. She reached up to kiss him as he bent his head toward her. He held her tightly, wanting to protect her from anything that might cause her pain. And she held him. As long as she had Jondalar, nothing else really mattered, did it? Just then Jonayla started to cry.

"I just want to be a mother, and be mated to you, Jondalar, I don't really want to be a Zelandoni," Ayla said as she went to pick her up.

She is really scared, he thought, but who wouldn't be? I don't even like getting near a burial ground, much less think about visiting the world of the spirits. He watched her come back to him with the baby in her arms, tears still in her eyes, and felt a sudden surge of love and protectiveness for the woman and the baby. So what if she became Zelandoni? She would still be Ayla to him, and she would still need him.

"It will be all right, Ayla," he said, taking the baby from her and cradling her in his arms. He had never been happier than he had been since they were mated, and especially since Jonayla was born. He looked down at the infant and smiled. I believe she is my daughter, too, he thought.

"It's up to you, Ayla," he said. "You are right, even if you join the zelandonia, it doesn't mean you will have to be a Zelandoni, but if you do, that will be all right, too. I always knew I was mating someone special. Not only a beautiful woman, but one with a rare Gift. You were chosen by the Mother, that's an honor, and she showed it by honoring you at our mating. And now you have a beautiful daughter. No, we have a beautiful daughter. You said she's my daughter, too, right?" he said, trying to calm her fears.

Her tears spilled again, but she smiled through them. "Yes. Jonayla is your daughter and my daughter," she said, then broke out in new sobs. He reached out for her with his other arm and held them both. "If you ever stopped loving me, Jondalar, I don't know what I would do. Please never stop loving me."

"Of course I'll never stop loving you. I will always love you. Nothing can ever make me stop," Jondalar said, feeling it deep in his heart and hoping that it would always be true.

Winter finally came to an end. The drifts of snow, dirty from dust blowing on the wind, melted, and the first crocuses poked their purple-and-white flowers through the last vestiges of it. The icicles dripped until they disappeared, and the first green buds appeared. Ayla was spending a great deal of time with Whinney. With her baby held close to her in a carrying cloak, she walked with the mare or rode her slowly. Racer was feeling more frisky, and even Jondalar had some trouble controlling him, but he rather enjoyed the challenge.

Whinney whickered at the sight of her, and she patted and hugged her affectionately. She planned to meet Jondalar and several people at a small abri downstream. They wanted to tap a few birch trees, part of which would be boiled down into a rich syrup, and another part of which would be allowed to ferment to make a light alcoholic beverage. It wasn't far, but she had decided to take Whinney for a ride, mostly because she wanted to stay close to her. She was almost there when it started to rain. She urged Whinney faster and noticed that the mare seemed to be breathing hard. Ayla felt her rounded sides just as the mare had another contraction.

"Whinney!" she said aloud. "Your time has come, hasn't it. I wonder how close you are to giving birth. We are not far from the abri where I'm supposed to meet everyone. I hope you won't be too bothered by having other people around you."

When she reached the camp, she asked Joharran if she could bring Whinney under the abri. The mare was about to give birth. He was quick to agree, and a wave of excitement spread among the group. This would be an experience. None of them had ever been close to a horse giving birth. She led Whinney under the overhanging upper ledge.

Jondalar rushed over and asked if she needed any help. "I don't think Whinney needs my help, but I want to be close to her," Ayla said. "If you would watch Jonayla, it would help me. I just nursed her. She should be all right for a while." He reached for Jonayla. She saw his face and gave him a big, delighted smile. She had only recently started smiling and had begun to greet the man of her hearth with that sign of recognition.

"You have your mother's smile, Jonayla," he said as he picked her up, looking directly at her and smiling back. The baby focused on his face, made a soft cooing sound, and smiled again. It melted his heart. He tucked Jonayla into the crook of his arm and walked back toward the people at the other end of the small shelter.

Whinney seemed happy to be out of the wet weather. Ayla rubbed the mare down and led her to an area of dry soil as far away from the people as she could. They seemed to sense that Ayla wanted them to keep some distance away, but the space was small, and they had no trouble seeing. Jondalar turned around to watch with them. It was not the first time he had seen Whinney give birth, but the idea was no less exciting. Familiarity with the process of birth did not diminish the sense of awe at the new life about to make an appearance. Human or animal, it was still Doni's greatest Gift. They all waited quietly.

After a while, when it seemed that Whinney was not quite ready but as comfortable as she could be, Ayla walked to the fire where the people were waiting, to get a drink of water. She was offered hot tea, and she returned for it after bringing some water to the horse.

"Ayla, I don't think I've ever heard you tell how you found your horses," Dynoda said. "What makes them unafraid of people?"

Ayla smiled. She was getting used to telling stories, and she didn't mind talking about her horses. She quickly told how she had trapped and killed the horse that had been Whinney's dam, then noticed the young foal and the hyenas. She explained that she brought the baby horse to her cave, fed her, and raised her. She warmed to the tale, and without realizing it, the skill she had developed in the course of living with the people of the Clan of showing meaning by expression and gesture crept into her narration.

With half her mind on the mare, she unconsciously dramatized the events, and the people, several from the other nearby Caves, were captivated. Her exotic accent and her uncanny ability to mimic the sounds of animals added an interesting element to her unusual story. Even Jondalar was entranced, although he knew the circumstances. He had not heard her tell the whole story quite like that. More questions were asked, and she began to describe her life in the valley, but when she told about finding and raising a cave lion, there were expressions of disbelief. Jondalar was quick to back her up. Whether they entirely believed her or not, the story of a lion, a horse, and a woman all living together in a cave in a secluded valley was an enjoyable one. A sound from the mare stopped her from continuing.

Ayla jumped up and went to Whinney, who was by then lying on her side. A membrane-encased head of a foal began to emerge. For the second time she played midwife to the mare. Before the hindquarters were fully out, the wet newborn foal was trying to stand. Whinney looked back to see what she had done and nickered softly at her new baby. Still on the ground, the baby started squirming toward Whinney's head, stopping for a moment to try to nurse before either was on their feet. When she reached her dam, the mare immediately started washing her with her tongue. Within moments the tiny horse was trying to stand. She fell over on her nose, but by the second try she was on her feet, only several moments after foaling. A very strong little horse, Ayla thought.

As soon as the baby was standing, Whinney got up, and the moment she was on her feet, the foal was nuzzling her, again trying to nurse, ducking under at first, not quite able to find the right place. After a second pass under her hind legs, Whinney gave the baby a little nip to point the foal in the right direction. That was all it took. Whinney had been perfectly capable, without any assistance, to give birth to her spindly-legged foal.

The people had watched silently, seeing for the first time the knowledge that the Great Earth Mother had given to Her wild creatures about how to take care of their newborn. The only way the young of Whinney's species could survive, and most of the other animals that grazed the vast steppes in great numbers, was for the young to be able to stand on their own legs, and to run nearly as fast as an adult shortly after birth. Without that, they would have been such easy prey to predators, they could not have lived. With her baby nursing, Whinney seemed content.

The birth of the horse was rare entertainment for the people who were watching, and a story that would be told and retold in the future by everyone who had witnessed it. Several people had questions and comments for Ayla once both horses were comfortable and Ayla returned.

"I didn't realize that the babies of horses can walk almost from the time they are born. It takes at least a year for a human baby to walk. Do they grow faster, too?"

"Yes," Ayla replied. "Racer was born the day after I found Jondalar. He's a full-grown stallion now and he only counts three years of life."

"You are going to have to think of a name for the young one, Ayla," Jondalar said.

"Yes, but I will have to think about it," Ayla said.

Jondalar was quick to catch her implication. It was true that the hay-colored mare had given birth to a horse of a different color. It was also true that among the horses on the eastern steppes, near the region of the Mamutoi, there were some that were shades of dark brown, like Racer. He wasn't sure what color the little filly would be, but it didn't seem that she would have her mother's coloring.

Wolf found them shortly after. As though he instinctively knew to approach the new family carefully, he first went to Whinney. Despite her instincts, she had learned that this was not a carnivore to be feared. Ayla joined them, and after she satisfied herself that this wolf was the exception, especially since the woman was around, she allowed him to sniff her new baby and let the baby learn his smell.

The young horse was a gray filly. "I think I'm going to call her Gray," she said to Jondalar, "and she should be Jonayla's horse. But we'll have to teach them both." He grinned with delight at the prospect.

The next day, when they were back at the horse area on the ledge, Racer welcomed his new little sister with avid curiosity, but under the strict supervision of Whinney. Ayla happened to be looking toward the dwelling area when she saw Zelandoni coming. She was surprised to see the donier coming to see the new foal, she seldom made any special effort to see the animals. Other people had found occasions to take peeks and Ayla asked that they not go too close at first, but the donier got a personal introduction to Gray.

"Jonokol has told me he will be leaving the Ninth Cave when we go to the Summer Meeting," the donier announced after she had examined the foal.

"Well, you expected it," Ayla said, feeling edgy.

"Have you decided yet if you are going to be my new acolyte?" she asked directly, not hesitating.

Ayla looked down, then back at the woman.

Zelandoni waited, then looked into Ayla's eyes. "I think you have no choice. You know you will feel the call one day, perhaps sooner than you think. I would hate to see your potential destroyed, even if you were able to survive it without support and training."

Ayla struggled to break away from the commanding stare. Then, from the depths of her being, or the pathways in her brain, she found a resource. She felt a power rising within her, and knew that she was no longer constrained by the donier, but instead felt that she had dominion over the One Who Was First, and held her gaze. It gave her a sense of something indescribable, a feeling of strength, of mastery, of authority, that she had never consciously felt before.

When she released the woman, Zelandoni glanced away for an instant. When she looked back, the feeling of tremendous power that had held her was gone, but Ayla was looking at her with a knowing smile. The infant in her arms began to move as though something was bothering her, and Ayla's attention went back to her child.

Zelandoni was shaken, but she controlled it quickly. She turned to leave, but turned back and studied Ayla again, not with the gaze that engendered the contest of wills, but with a straightforward, piercing look. "Tell me now you are not Zelandoni, Ayla," she said quietly.

Ayla flushed and glanced around with uncertainty, as though trying to find some escape. When she looked back at the large woman, Zelandoni was the commanding presence she had always known.

"I will tell Jondalar," she said, then quickly looked down at the baby.

The Mother's Song

Out of the darkness, the chaos of time,
The whirlwind gave birth to the Mother sublime.
She woke to Herself knowing life had great worth,
The dark empty void grieved the Great Mother Earth.
    The Mother was lonely. She was the only.

From the dust of Her birth She created the other,
A pale shining friend, a companion, a brother.
They grew up together, learned to love and to care,
And when She was ready, they decided to pair.
    Around Her he'd hover. Her pale shining lover.

She was happy at first with Her one counterpart.
Then the Mother grew restless, unsure in Her heart.
She loved Her fair friend, Her dear complement,
But something was missing, Her love was unspent.
    She was the Mother. She needed another.

She dared the great void, the chaos, the dark,
To find the cold home of the life-giving spark.
The whirlwind was fearsome, the darkness complete.
Chaos was freezing, and reached out for Her heat.
    The Mother was brave. The danger was grave.

She drew from cold chaos the creative source,
Then conceiving within, She fled with life-force.
She grew with the life that She carried inside.
And gave of Herself with love and with pride.
    The Mother was bearing. Her life She was sharing.

The dark empty void and the vast barren Earth,
With anticipation, awaited the birth.
Life drank from Her blood, it breathed from Her bones.
It split Her skin open and sundered Her stones.

   The Mother was giving. Another was living.

Her gushing birth waters filled rivers and seas,
And flooded the land, giving rise to the trees.
From each precious drop new grass and leaves grew,
And lush verdant plants made all the Earth new.

   Her waters were flowing. New green was growing.

In violent labor spewing fire and strife,
She struggled in pain to give birth to new life.
Her dried clotted blood turned to red-ochred soil,
But the radiant child made it all worth the toil.

   The Mother's great joy. A bright shining boy.

Mountains rose up spouting flames from their crests,
She nurtured Her son from Her mountainous breasts.
He suckled so hard, the sparks flew so high,
The Mother's hot milk laid a path through the sky.

   His life had begun. She nourished Her son.

He laughed and he played, and he grew big and bright.
He lit up the darkness, the Mother's delight.
She lavished Her love, he grew bright and strong,
But soon he matured, not a child for long.

   Her son was near grown. His mind was his own.

She took from the source for the life She'd begun.
Now the cold empty void was enticing Her son.
The Mother gave love, but the youth longed for more,
For knowledge, excitement, to travel, explore.

   Chaos was Her foe. But Her son yearned to go.

He stole from Her side as the Great Mother slept,
While out of the dark swirling void chaos crept.
With tempting inducements the darkness beguiled,
Deceived by the whirlwind, chaos captured Her child.

    The dark took Her son. The young brilliant one.

The Mother's bright child, at first overjoyed,
Was soon overwhelmed by the bleak frigid void.
Her unwary offspring, consumed with remorse,
Could not escape the mysterious force.

    Chaos would not free. Her rash progeny.

But just as the dark pulled him into the cold,
The Mother woke up, reached out and caught hold.
To help Her recover Her radiant son,
The Mother appealed to the pale shining one.

    The Mother held tight. And kept him in sight.

She welcomed him back, Her lover of old,
With heartache and sorrow, Her story She told.
Her dear friend agreed to join in the fight,
To rescue Her child from his perilous plight.

    She told of her grief. And the dark swirling thief.

The Mother was tired, She had to recover,
She loosened Her hold to Her luminous lover.
While She was sleeping, he fought the cold force,
And for a time drove it back to the source.

    His spirit was strong. The encounter too long.

Her fair shining friend struggled hard, gave his best,
The conflict was bitter, the struggle hard pressed.
His vigilance waned as he closed his great eye,
Then darkness crept close, stole his light from the sky.

    Her pale friend was tiring. His light was expiring.

When darkness was total, She woke with a cry.
The tenebrious void hid the light from the sky.
She joined in the conflict, was quick to defend,
And drove the dark shadow away from Her friend.

But the pale face of night. Let Her son out of sight.

Trapped by the whirlwind, Her bright fiery son,
Gave no warmth to the Earth, cold chaos had won.
The fertile green life was now ice and snow,
And a sharp piercing wind continued to blow.

The Earth was bereft. No green plants were left.

The Mother was weary, grieving and worn,
But She reached out again for the life She had borne.
She couldn't give up, She needed to strive,
For the glorious light of Her son to survive.

She continued the fight. To bring back the light.

And Her luminous friend was prepared to contest,
The thief who held captive the child of Her breast.
Together they fought for the son She adored.
Their efforts succeeded, his light was restored.

His energy burned. His brilliance returned.

But the bleak frigid dark craved his bright glowing heat.
The Mother defended and would not retreat.
The whirlwind pulled hard, She refused to let go,
She fought to a draw with Her dark swirling foe.

She held darkness at bay. But Her son was away.

When She fought the whirlwind and made chaos flee,
The light from Her son glowed with vitality.
When the Mother grew tired, the bleak void held sway,
And darkness returned at the end of the day.

She felt warmth from Her son. But neither had won.

The Great Mother lived with the pain in Her heart,
That She and Her son were forever apart.
She ached for the child that had been denied,
So She quickened once more from the life-force inside.

　　She was not reconciled. To the loss of Her child.

When She was ready, Her waters of birth,
Brought back the green life to the cold barren Earth.
And the tears of Her loss, abundantly spilled,
Made dew drops that sparkled and rainbows that thrilled.

　　Birth waters brought green. But Her tears could be seen.

With a thunderous roar Her stones split asunder,
And from the great cave that opened deep under,
She birthed once again from Her cavernous room,
And brought forth the Children of Earth from Her womb.

　　From the Mother forlorn, more children were born.

Each child was different, some were large and some small,
Some could walk and some fly, some could swim and some crawl.
But each form was perfect, each spirit complete,
Each one was a model whose shape could repeat.

　　The Mother was willing. The green earth was filling.

All the birds and the fish and the animals born,
Would not leave the Mother, this time, to mourn.
Each kind would live near the place of its birth,
And share the expanse of the Great Mother Earth.

　　Close to Her they would stay. They could not run away.

They all were Her children, they filled Her with pride,
But they used up the life-force She carried inside.
She had enough left for a last innovation,
A child who'd remember Who made the creation.

　　A child who'd respect. And learn to protect.

First Woman was born full-grown and alive,
And given the Gifts she would need to survive.
Life was the First Gift, and like Mother Earth,
She woke to herself knowing life had great worth.

First Woman defined. The first of her kind.

Next was the Gift of Perception, of learning,
The desire to know, the Gift of Discerning,
First Woman was given the knowledge within,
That would help her to live, and pass on to her kin.

First Woman would know. How to learn, how to grow.

Her life-force near gone, The Mother was spent,
To pass on Life's Spirit had been Her intent.
She caused all of Her children to create life anew,
And Woman was blessed to bring forth life, too.

But Woman was lonely. She was the only.

The Mother remembered Her own loneliness,
The love of Her friend and his hovering caress.
With the last spark remaining, Her labor began,
To share life with Woman, She created First Man.

Again She was giving. One more was living.

To Woman and Man the Mother gave birth,
And then for their home, She gave them the Earth,
The water, the land, and all Her creation.
To use them with care was their obligation.

It was their home to use. But not to abuse.

For the Children of Earth the Mother provided,
The Gifts to survive, and then She decided,
To give them the Gift of Pleasure and sharing,
That honors the Mother with the joy of their pairing.

The Gifts are well-earned. When honor's returned.

The Mother was pleased with the pair She created,
She taught them to love and to care when they mated.
She made them desire to join with each other,
The Gift of their Pleasures came from the Mother.

    Before She was through. Her children loved too.
    Earth's Children were blessed. The Mother could rest.

LIST OF CHARACTERS

Ayla—of the Ninth Cave of the Zelandonii, formerly Ayla of the Lion Camp of the Mamutoi, Daughter of the Mammoth Hearth, Chosen by the Spirit of the Cave Lion, Protected by the Cave Bear, Friend of the horses, Whinney and Racer, and the four-legged hunter, Wolf

Jondalar—of the Ninth Cave of the Zelandonii, Ayla's intended, son of former leader, brother of leader; called Jondé by his sister Folara

Zelandoni (Zolena)—Current Zelandoni, former lover of Jondalar

Thonolan/d—Jondalar's younger brother, killed on Journey

Folara—Jondalar's younger sister

Marthona—Jondalar's mother, former leader, also mother of Joharran, Folara

Willamar—Marthona's mate, Trade Master, Traveler

Tivonan—Willamar's apprentice trader

Joconan/d—Marthona's first mate, dead, man of Joharran's hearth

Joharran—Jondalar's older brother, leader of Ninth Cave

Proleva—Joharran's mate

Jaradal—Proleva's son, Joharran's hearth child

Levela—Proleva's younger sister, Jondecam's mate

Jondecam—Levela's mate, nephew of Kimeran and son of Zelandoni of the Second Cave

Velima—mother of Proleva and Levela

Solaban—Hunter, adviser, and friend of Joharran

Ramara—Solaban's mate

Robenan—Ramara's son

Rushemar—Hunter, adviser, and friend of Joharran

Salova—Rushemar's mate

Marsola—Salova's daughter

Marona—Jondalar's former girlfriend

Wylopa—Marona's cousin

Portula—Marona's friend

Lorava—Portula's younger sister

Ramila—Folara's friend

Galeya—Folara's friend

Charezal—New member of Ninth Cave, stranger to Jondalar

Shevonar/d—Man who dies while hunting

Relona—Shevonar's mate

Ranokol—Shevonar's brother

Brukeval—Jondalar's distant cousin (part Clan)

Madroman—Formerly called Ladroman, acolyte of Fifth Cave

Laramar—Man who makes barma

Tremeda—Laramar's mate

Bologan—son of Tremeda, eldest, twelve

Lanoga—daughter of Tremeda, ten

Lorala—daughter of Tremeda, about six months

Stelona—Older woman who nurses Lorala

Thefona—Third Cave's best lookout, best vision

Thevola—Maker of rawhide panels

Lanidar—Boy of the Nineteenth Cave with deformed right arm, twelve

Mardena—Lanidar's mother

Denoda—Mardena's mother

Janida—Peridal's mate

Peridal—Janida's mate

Matagan—Young man who was gored by a woolly rhinoceros

Tishona—Marsheval's mate

Marsheval—Tishona's mate

Palidar—Tivonan's friend

Whinney—Ayla's horse, dun-yellow mare, Przwalski horse

Racer—Jondalar's horse, bay (brown) stallion, Cherski horse (rare)

Wolf—Ayla's wolf

LEADERS

Manvelar—Leader of Third Cave, Two Rivers Rock

Morizan—Son of Manvelar's mate, son of his hearth

Kareja—Leader of Eleventh Cave, River Place

Dorova—Kareja's mother

Brameval—Leader of Fourteenth Cave, Little Valley

Kimeran—Leader of Second Cave of the Zelandonii, Elder Hearth, brother of Zelandoni of the Second Cave, uncle of Jondecam

Denanna—Leader of the three holdings of the Twenty-ninth Cave, Three Rocks, and specifically of the South Holding, Reflection Rock

Tormaden—Leader of the Nineteenth Cave of the Zelandonii

ZELANDONIA

Zelandoni—of the Eleventh Cave, River Place, homosexual man

Marolan—man who is the Eleventh's friend and mate

Zelandoni—of the Third Cave, Two Rivers Rock, older man

Zelandoni—of the Fourteenth Cave, Little Valley, middle-aged woman

Zelandoni—of the Second Cave, Elder Hearth, older sister of Kimeran, mother of Jondecam

Zelandoni—of the Seventh Cave, Horsehead Rock, white-haired grandfather of Zelandoni Second, and Kimeran

Zelandoni—of the Nineteenth Cave, white-haired older woman

Zelandoni—of the Fifth Cave, Old Valley, middle-aged man

Zelandoni—of the Twenty-ninth Cave, Three Rocks, and mediator between the three assistant zelandonia and three leaders of the three separate locations of the Twenty-ninth Cave

Assistant Zelandoni of the Twenty-ninth Cave, Zelandoni of Reflection Rock (South Holding), middle-aged man

Assistant Zelandoni of the Twenty-ninth Cave, Zelandoni of South Face (North Holding), young man

Assistant Zelandoni of the Twenty-ninth Cave, Zelandoni of Summer Camp (West Holding), middle-aged woman

First Acolyte of the Second Cave (almost Zelandoni), young woman

Jonokol—First Acolyte of the Ninth Cave, artist, young man

Mikolan—Second Acolyte of the Fourteenth Cave, very young man

Mejera—Acolyte of the Third Cave (formerly Fourteenth Cave), very young woman

Madroman—Acolyte of the Fifth Cave (formerly Ladroman of the Ninth Cave), young man

FIRST CAVE OF THE LANZADONII
(DALANAR'S CAVE)

Dalanar—Man of Jondalar's hearth, Marthona's former mate, founder of the Lanzadonii

Jerika—Dalanar's mate, co-founder of Lanzadonii

Ahnlay/d—Jerika's mother, died

Hochaman—Man of Jerika's hearth—Great Traveler

Joplaya—Jerika's daughter, daughter of Dalanar's hearth

Echozar—Joplaya's half-Clan mate

Andovan/d—Man who helped raise Echozar

Yoma/d—Echozar's mother, Clan woman

THE SHELTERS OF STONE

JEAN M. AUEL

A Reader's Guide

A Conversation with Jean M. Auel

Question: While your novels focus on a civilization of the past, there is a very modern theme that runs throughout, of Ayla struggling to achieve equality with her peers. When you first created this dynamic character, how much thought did you put into giving her modern sensibilities?

Jean M. Auel: The reason there is a modern sensibility to my characters is that those Cro-Magnon "cavemen" were modern people, the first modern humans in Europe. I researched my characters as much as every other aspect of this early culture. My information is based on the knowledge of today's scientists, not the antiquarians of the nineteenth century whose views, unfortunately, are still held by too many. I have traveled to many of the locations where those early humans lived and have become acquainted with many professionals who study them, some of whom have shown me remarkable sites, including extraordinary painted and engraved caves.

Those early modern humans called Cro-Magnon were the first people who not only had skeletons like ours but were like us in many other ways, which can be convincingly demonstrated by the archaeological record. They were our many-times-great-grandparents; whatever qualities we claim for ourselves, we must grant them. They had the same range of intelligence that we do, the same emotional responses and psychological reactions, the same ease and facility with language, the same talents, skills, and abilities. And they had a remarkable creative impulse. I've seen it, and it certainly convinced me. Neanderthals are still unknowns, but they were far more advanced than most of us imagine; they were also human with brains larger than the average today. There were differences between us, but they were our close cousins. Once I learned this, I knew I could write the story of a young Cro-Magnon woman raised by a clan of Neanderthals who then finds her way back to her own kind of people. Ayla's struggle creates tension and conflict, but it is not a modern theme. It is a universal theme. It's natural, part of the human condition, to want to be accepted. People understand this and always have.

Q: Your research is praised throughout the world for its accuracy and detail. Can you tell us a bit about your process?

JA: Most of the information comes from reading and library research, but I have also learned a great deal from asking questions, taking classes, and traveling. For example, I took a class from an expert in arctic survival, where we spent a night on the snowy slopes of a nearby mountain to learn how to live in cold conditions. From a class in aboriginal life skills, I learned how people live off the land, and how to brain-tan a deer hide into wearable buckskin. I've taken plant identification classes and classes on how to cook wild foods. Ayla's medicine-woman skills come from a combination of first-aid books, books on herbal medicines, and asking questions of doctors and other skilled health practitioners like nurses and paramedics. I have visited many of the sites I write about to get a feel for them, even though conditions are most likely different now. I even worked for a short time at an archaeological dig so I could understand where information comes from and how scientists find it.

Q: How much in your books is based on fact, and how much is fiction? That is, do you fill in the gaps left by history?

JA: My books are entirely fiction, based on as much factual information as I could find on their subjects. They take place 30,000 years ago, and the only things left from that time are hard objects—things made of stone and bone, such as stone tools, carved items, animal and human skeletal remains—and, as it turns out, microscopic residues. Pollen has been found in Neanderthal graves. Hair from various animals and DNA traces of animal blood from stones and knives add information. Inference fills in a certain amount. For example, if the skeleton of an old Neanderthal man shows that from a young age he had been blind in one eye, had had an arm amputated, and walked with a limp, it is fair to surmise that he was not hunting woolly mammoths, which raises interesting questions: Who amputated his arm? Who stopped the bleeding? Who treated the shock? How did he live to be an old man? Obviously someone took care of him; the question is why? Could it have been because they loved him? Or that his culture took care of their weak and wounded? Perhaps "red in tooth and claw" is not an appropriate way to describe those enigmatic human cousins.

Q: The Earth's Children® series is an epic adventure spanning many years. Have you always known where the story is going, or has each book been planned separately?

JA: When I started, my question was "I wonder if I could write a short story." Then I got into the research and got all fired up, and I realized I was writing a book. At the time, I was calling it *Earth's Children*, and as it grew, I thought it would be one big saga that fell easily into six parts. I wrote about 450,000 words, and thought I would cut when I rewrote it. But when I started to reread it, I realized that I didn't know how to write fiction, so I read books about how to write a novel. When I went back and began rewriting the book, instead of editing and cutting down, I found that putting in the dialogue and the scenes to make a story made it grow. It was with some surprise and trepidation that I came to realize that each of the separate parts was a complete story, and that I had a six-book series. I have been working from that original rough draft as an outline for the series, so I have always known, more or less, where the story is going.

Q: Your own books have a great heroine in Ayla. Who is your favorite literary heroine?

JA: I don't really have one. It may once have been the princess in the fairy tale "East of the Sun and West of the Moon," which my favorite sixth-grade teacher read to the class. Though I didn't realize it at the time, I think the reason is that in this fairy tale, the man is captured and the princess has to perform feats of skill to save him. That was the trouble with so many of the books I read when I was young. The ones I liked were full of action and adventure, but it was always the men who were acting and adventuring. I never identified with the heroine that was sitting around waiting to be rescued. I was with the hero, *snick-snick*ing with the sword, or whatever. I still identify with the one actively making the story happen, and I enjoy both male and female protagonists. I don't think it was a conscious decision, but when I started writing, I wanted to write about a woman who did interesting things. I guess that's why she is a heroine.

Q: What advice would you give to an aspiring writer?

JA: You learn to write by writing, and by reading and thinking about how writers have created their characters and invented their stories. If you are not a reader, don't even think about being a writer. If you want to write, don't say you want to do it someday, don't wait until the spirit moves you: Sit down and do it every day, or at least on some kind of regular basis. But I would warn those who aspire to it that writing fiction is the hardest work I have ever done. Sometimes words don't want to come. For me, the way to get past writer's block, or whatever those periods are called, is to sit and put down one word after another. I may not even keep that work, though often I do. It doesn't matter. I need to get something written. Inspiration happens when you are working at it. At other times I can be so completely immersed in the story that I don't know where the time has gone, but when I get up, I'm drained. I have poured everything I have into the work—and sometimes I find myself finding ways to stall before I sit down to work the next time. But for all the effort, it's what I want to do for the rest of my life.

*Turn the page to read an exciting preview
from Jean M. Auel's latest novel,
and the sixth in the*

EARTH'S CHILDREN®

series:

THE
LAND
OF
PAINTED
CAVES

**AVAILABLE SPRING 2011
FROM CROWN PUBLISHERS**

I

The band of travelers walked along the path between the clear sparkling water of Grass River and the black-streaked white limestone cliff, following the trail that paralleled the right bank. They went single file around the bend where the stone wall jutted out closer to the water's edge. Ahead a smaller path split off at an angle toward the crossing place, where the flowing water spread out and became shallower, bubbling around exposed rocks.

Before they reached the fork in the trail, a young woman near the front suddenly stopped, her eyes opening wide as she stood perfectly still, staring ahead. She pointed with her chin, not wanting to move. "Look! Over there!" she said in a hissing whisper of fear. "Lions!"

Joharran, the leader, lifted his arm, signaling the band to a halt. Just beyond the place where the trail diverged, they now saw pale-tawny cave lions moving around in the grass. The grass was such effective camouflage, however, that they might not have noticed them until they were much closer, if it hadn't been for the sharp eyes of Thefona. The young woman from the Third Cave had exceptionally good vision, and though she was quite young, she was noted for her ability to see far and well. Her innate talent had been recognized early and they had begun training her when she was a small girl; she was their best lookout.

Near the back of the group, walking in front of three horses, Ayla and Jondalar looked up to see what was causing the delay. "I wonder why we've stopped," Jondalar said, a familiar frown of worry wrinkling his forehead.

Ayla observed the leader and the people around him closely, and instinctively moved her hand to shield the warm bundle that she carried in the soft leather blanket tied to her chest. Jonayla had recently nursed and was sleeping, but moved slightly at her mother's touch. Ayla had an uncanny ability to interpret meaning from body language, learned young when she lived with the Clan. She knew Joharran was alarmed and Thefona was frightened.

Ayla, too, had extraordinarily sharp vision. She could also pick up sounds above the range of normal hearing and feel the deep tones of those that were below. Her sense of smell and taste were also keen, but she had never compared herself with anyone, and didn't realize how extraordinary her perceptions were. She was born with heightened acuity in all her senses, which no doubt contributed to her survival after losing her parents and everything she knew at five years. Her only training had come from herself. She had developed her natural abilities during the years she studied animals, chiefly carnivores, when she was teaching herself to hunt.

In the stillness, she discerned the faint but familiar rumblings of lions, detected their distinctive scent on a slight breeze, and noticed that several people in front of the group were gazing ahead. When she looked, she saw something move. Suddenly the cats hidden by the grass seemed to jump into clear focus. She could make out two young and three or four adult cave lions. As she started moving forward, she reached with one hand for her spear-thrower, fastened to a carrying loop on her belt, and with the other for a spear from the holder hanging on her back.

"Where are you going?" Jondalar asked.

She stopped. "There are lions up ahead just beyond the split in the trail," she said under her breath.

Jondalar turned to look, and noticed movement that he interpreted as lions now that he knew what to look for. He reached for his weapons as well. "You should stay here with Jonayla. I'll go."

Ayla glanced down at her sleeping baby, then looked up at him. "You're good with the spear-thrower, Jondalar, but there are at least two cubs and three grown lions, probably more. If the lions think the cubs are in danger and decide to attack, you'll need help, someone to back you up, and you know I'm better than anyone, except you."

His brow furrowed again as he paused to think, looking at her. Then he nodded. "All right...but stay behind me." He detected movement out of the corner of his eye and glanced back. "What about the horses?"

"They know lions are near. Look at them," Ayla said.

Jondalar looked. All three horses, including the new young filly, were staring ahead, obviously aware of the huge felines. Jondalar frowned again. "Will they be all right? Especially little Gray?"

"They know to stay out of the way of those lions, but I don't see Wolf," Ayla said. "I'd better whistle for him."

"You don't have to," Jondalar said, pointing in a different direction. "He must sense something, too. Look at him coming."

Ayla turned and saw a wolf racing toward her. The canine was a magnificent animal, larger than most, but an injury from a fight with other wolves that left him with a bent ear gave him a rakish look. She made the special signal that she used when they hunted together. He knew it meant to stay near and pay close attention to her. They ducked around people as they hurried toward the front, trying not to cause any undo commotion, and to remain as inconspicuous as possible.

"I'm glad you're here," Joharran said softly when he saw his brother and Ayla with the wolf quietly appear with their spear-throwers in hand.

"Do you know how many there are?" Ayla asked.

"More than I thought," Thefona said, trying to seem calm and not let her fear show. "When I first saw them, I thought there were maybe three or four, but they are moving around in the grass, and now I think there may be ten or more. It's a big pride."

"And they are feeling confident," Joharran said.

"How do you know that?" Thefona asked.

"They're ignoring us."

Jondalar knew his mate was very familiar with the huge felines. "Ayla knows cave lions," he said. "Perhaps we should ask her what she thinks." Joharran nodded in her direction, asking the question silently.

"Joharran is right. They know we're here. And they know how many they are and how many we are," Ayla said, then added, "they may see us as something like a herd of horses or aurochs and think they may be able to single out a weak one. I think they are new to this region."

"What makes you think so?" Joharran said. He was always surprised at Ayla's wealth of knowledge of four-legged hunters, but for some reason it was also at times like this that he noticed her unusual accent more.

"They don't know us, that's why they're so confident," Ayla continued. "If they were a resident pride that lived around people and had been chased or hunted a few times, I don't think they would be so unconcerned."

"Well, maybe we should give them something to be concerned about," Jondalar said.

Joharran's brow wrinkled in a way that was so much like his taller though younger brother's, it made Ayla want to smile, but it usually showed at a time when smiling would be inappropriate. "Perhaps it would be wiser to just avoid them," the dark-haired leader said.

"I don't think so," Ayla said, bowing her head and looking down. It was still difficult for her to disagree with a man in public, especially a leader. Though she knew it was perfectly acceptable among the Zelandonii—after all, some leaders were women, including, at one time, Joharran's and Jondalar's mother—such behavior from a woman would not have been tolerated in the Clan, the ones who raised her.

"Why not?" Joharran asked, his frown turning into a scowl.

"Those lions are resting too close to the home of the Third Cave," Ayla said quietly. "There will always be lions around, but if they are comfortable here, they might think of it as a place to return when they want to rest, and would see any people who come near as prey, especially children or elders. They could be a danger to the people who live at Two Rivers Rock, and the other nearby Caves, including the Ninth."

Joharran took a deep breath, then looked at his fair-haired brother. "Your mate is right, and you as well, Jondalar. Perhaps now is the time to let those lions know they are not welcome to settle down so close to our homes."

"This would be a good time to use spear-throwers so we can hunt from a safer distance. Several hunters here have been practicing," Jondalar said. It was for just this sort of thing that he had wanted to come home and show everyone the weapon he had developed. "We may not even have to kill one, just injure a couple to teach them to stay away."

"Jondalar," Ayla said, softly. Now she was getting ready to differ with him, or at least to make a point that he should consider. She looked down again, then raised her eyes and looked directly at him. She wasn't afraid to speak her mind to him, but she wanted to be respectful. "It's true that a spear-thrower is a very good weapon. With it, a spear can be thrown from a much greater distance than one thrown by hand, and that makes it safer. But safer is not safe. A wounded animal is unpredictable. And one with the strength and speed of a cave lion, hurt and wild with pain, could do anything. If you decide to use these weapons against those lions, they should not be used to injure, but to kill."

"She's right, Jondalar," Joharran said.

Jondalar frowned at his brother, then grinned sheepishly. "Yes she is, but, as dangerous as they are, I always hate to kill a cave lion if I don't have to. They are so beautiful, so lithe and graceful in the way they move. Cave lions don't have much to be afraid of. Their strength gives them confidence." He glanced at Ayla with a glint of pride and love. "I always thought Ayla's Cave Lion totem was right for her." Discomfited by showing his strong inner feelings for her, a hint of a flush colored his cheeks. "But I do think this is a time when spear-throwers could be very useful."

Joharran noticed that most of the travelers had crowded closer. "How many are with us that can use one?" he asked his brother.

"Well, there's you, and me, and Ayla, of course," Jondalar said, looking at the group. "Rushemar has been practicing a lot and is getting pretty good. Solaban's been busy making some ivory handles for tools for some of us and hasn't been working at it as much, but he's got the basics."

"I've tried a spear-thrower a few times, Joharran. I don't have one of my own, and I'm not very good at it," Thefona said, "but I can throw a spear without one."

"Thank you, Thefona, for reminding me," Joharran said. "Nearly everyone can handle a spear without a spear-thrower, including women. We shouldn't forget that." Then he directed his comments to the group at large. "We need to let those lions know that this is not a good place for them. Whoever wants to go after them, using a spear by hand or with the thrower, come over here."

Ayla started to loosen her baby's carrying blanket. "Folara, would you watch Jonayla for me?" she said, approaching Jondalar's younger sister. "Unless you'd rather stay and hunt cave lions."

"I've gone out on drives, but I was never very good with a spear, and I don't seem to be much better with the thrower," Folara said. "I'll take Jonayla." The infant was now thoroughly awake, and when the young woman held out her arms for the baby, she willingly went to her aunt.

"I'll help her," Proleva said to Ayla. Joharran's mate also had a baby girl in a carrying blanket, just a few days older than Jonayla, and an active boy who could count six years to watch out for as well. "I think we should take all the children away from here, perhaps back behind the jutting rock, or up to the Third Cave."

"That's a very good idea," Joharran said. "Hunters stay here. The rest of you go back, but go slowly. No sudden moves. We want those cave lions to think we are just milling around, like a herd of aurochs. And when we pair off, each group keep together. They will probably go after anyone alone."

Ayla turned back toward the four-legged hunters and saw many lion faces looking in their direction, very alert. She watched the animals move around, and began to see some distinguishing characteristics, helping her to count them. She watched a big female casually turn around—no, a male, she realized when she saw his male parts from the backside. She'd forgotten for a moment that the males here didn't have manes. The male cave lions near her valley to the east, including one that she knew quite well, did have some hair around the head and neck, but it was sparse. This is a big pride, she thought, more than two handsful of counting words, possibly as many as three, including the young ones.

While she watched, the big lion took a few more steps into the field, then disappeared into the grass. It was surprising how well the tall thin stalks could hide animals that were so huge.

Though the bones and teeth of cave lions—felines that liked to den in caves, which preserved the bones they left behind—were the same shape as their descendants that would someday roam the distant lands of the continent far to the south, they were more than half again, some nearly twice as large. In winter they grew a thick fur that was so pale it was almost white, practical concealment in snow for predators who hunted all year long. Their summer coat, though still pale, was more tawny, and some of the cats were still shedding, giving them a rather tattered, mottled look.

Ayla watched the group of mostly women and children break off from the hunters and head back to the cliff they had passed, along with a few young men and women with spears held in readiness whom Joharran had assigned to guard them. Then she noticed that the horses seemed particularly nervous, and thought she should try to calm them. She signaled Wolf to come with her as she walked toward the horses.

Whinney seemed glad to see both her and Wolf when they approached. The horse had no fear of the big canine predator. She had watched Wolf grow up from a tiny little ball of fuzzy fur, had helped to raise him. Ayla had a concern, though. She wanted the horses to go back behind the stone wall with the women and children. She could give Whinney many commands with words and signals, but she wasn't sure how to tell the mare to go with the others and not follow her.

Racer whinnied when she neared; he seemed especially agitated. She greeted the brown stallion affectionately and patted and scratched the young gray filly; then she hugged the sturdy neck of the dun-yellow mare that had been her only friend during the first lonely years after she left the Clan.

Whinney leaned against the young woman with her head over Ayla's shoulder in a familiar position of mutual support. She talked to the mare with a combination of Clan hand signs and words, and animal sounds that she imitated—the special language she had developed with Whinney when she was a foal, before Jondalar taught her to speak his language. Ayla told the mare to go with Folara and Proleva. Whether the horse understood, or just knew that it would be safer for her and her foal, Ayla was glad to see her retreat to the cliff with the other mothers when she pointed her in that direction.

But Racer was nervous and edgy, more so after the mare started walking away. Even grown, the young stallion was accustomed to following his dam, especially when Ayla and Jondalar were riding together, but this time he did not immediately go with her. He pranced and tossed his head and neighed. Jondalar heard him, looked over at the stallion and the woman, then joined them. The young horse nickered at the man as he approached. With two females in his small "herd," Jondalar wondered if Racer's protective stallion instincts were beginning to make themselves felt. The man talked to him, stroked and scratched his favorite places to settle him, then told him to go with Whinney and slapped him on the rump. It was enough to get him started in the right direction.

Ayla and Jondalar walked back to the hunters. Joharran and his two closest friends and advisers, Solaban and Rushemar, were standing together in the middle of the group that was left. It seemed much smaller now.

"We've been discussing the best way to hunt them," Joharran said when the couple returned. "I'm not sure what strategy to use. Should we try to surround them? Or drive them in a certain direction? I will tell you, I know how to hunt for meat: deer, or bison, or aurochs, even mammoth. I've killed a lion or two that were too close to a camp, with the help of other hunters, but lions are not animals I usually hunt, especially not a whole pride."

"Since Ayla knows lions," Thefona said, "let's ask her."

Everyone turned to look at Ayla. Most of them had heard about the injured lion cub she had taken in and raised until he was full grown. When Jondalar told them the lion did what she told him the way the wolf did, they believed it.

"What do you think, Ayla?" Joharran asked.

"Do you see how the lions are watching us? It's the same way we're looking at them. They think of themselves as the hunters. It might surprise them to be prey for a change," Ayla said, then paused. "I think we should stay together in a group and walk toward them, shouting and talking loudly perhaps, and see if they back off. But keep our spears ready, in case one or more come after us before we decide to go after them."

"Just approach them head-on?" Rushemar asked, with a frown.

"It might work," Solaban said. "And if we stay together, we can watch out for one another."

"It seems like a good plan, Joharran," Jondalar said.

"I suppose it's as good as any, and I like the idea of staying together and watching out for one another," the leader said.

"I'll go first," Jondalar said. He held up his spear, already on his spear-thrower and ready to launch. "I can get a spear off fast with this."

"I'm sure you can, but let's wait until we get closer so we can all feel comfortable with our aim," Joharran said.

"Of course," Jondalar said. "And Ayla is going to be a backup for me in case something unexpected happens."

"That's good," Joharran said. "We all need a partner, someone to be a backup for the ones who throw first, in case they miss and those lions come at us instead of running away. The partners can decide who will cast first, but it will cause less confusion if everyone waits for a signal before anyone throws."

"What kind of signal?" Rushemar asked.

Joharran paused, then said, "Watch Jondalar. Wait until he throws. That can be our signal."

"I'll be your partner, Joharran," Rushemar volunteered.

The leader nodded.

"I need a backup," Morizan said. He was the son of Manvelar's mate, Ayla recalled. "I'm not sure how good I am, but I have been working at it."

"I can be your partner. I've been practicing with the spear-thrower."

Ayla turned at the sound of the feminine voice and saw that it was Folara's red-haired friend, Galeya, who had spoken.

Jondalar turned to look, too. That's one way to get close to the son of a leader's mate, he thought, and glanced at Ayla, wondering if she had caught the implication.

"I can partner with Thefona, if she would like," Solaban said, "since I'll be using a spear like her, not a spear-thrower."

The young woman smiled at him, glad to have a more mature and experienced hunter close by.

"I've been practicing with a spear-thrower," Palidar said. He was a friend of Tivonan, the apprentice of Willamar, the Trade Master.

"We can be partners, Palidar," Tivonan said, "but I can only use a spear."

"I haven't really practiced much with that thrower either," Palidar said.

Ayla smiled at the young men. As Willamar's apprentice trader, Tivonan would no doubt become the Ninth Cave's next Trade Master. His friend, Palidar, had come back with Tivonan when he went to visit his Cave on a short trading mission, and Palidar was the one who had found the place where Wolf had gotten into the terrible fight with the other wolves, and took her to it. She thought of him as a good friend.

"I haven't done much with that thrower, but I can handle a spear."

It's Mejera, the acolyte of Zelandoni of the Third, Ayla said to herself, remembering that the young woman was with them the first time Ayla went into the Deep of Fountain Rocks to look for the life force of Jondalar's younger brother when they tried to help his elan find its way to the spirit world.

"Everyone has already picked a partner, so I guess we're left. Not only have I not practiced with the spear-thrower, I have hardly ever seen it used," said Jalodan, Morizan's cousin, the son of Manvelar's sister, who was visiting the Third Cave. He was planning to travel with them to the Summer Meeting to meet up with his Cave.

That was it. The twelve men and women who were going to hunt a similar number of lions—animals with greater speed, strength, and ferocity that lived by hunting weaker prey. Ayla began having feelings of doubt and a shiver of fear gave her a chill. She rubbed her arms and felt an eruption of bumps. How could twelve frail humans even think of attacking a pride of lions? She caught sight of the other carnivore, the one she knew, and signaled the animal to stay with her, thinking, twelve people—and Wolf.

"All right, let's go," Joharran said, "but keep together."

The twelve hunters from the Third Cave and the Ninth Cave of the Zelandonii started out together walking directly toward the pride of massive felines. They were armed with spears, tipped with sharpened flint, or bone or ivory sanded to a smooth, round, sharp point. Some had spear-throwers that could propel a spear much farther and with more power and speed than one thrown by hand, but lions had been killed with just spears before. This might be a test of Jondalar's weapon, but it would test the courage of the ones who were hunting even more.

"Go away!" Ayla shouted as they started out. "We don't want you here!"

Several others picked up the refrain, with variations, shouting and yelling at the animals as they approached, telling them to go away.

At first the cats, young and old, just watched them come. Then some began to move around, back into the grass that hid them so well, and out again, as though they weren't sure what to do. The ones who retreated with cubs returned without them.

"They don't seem to know what to make of us," Thefona said from the middle of the advancing hunters, feeling a little more secure than when they started, but when the big male suddenly snarled at them, everyone jumped with a start, and stopped in their tracks.

"This is not the time to stop," Joharran said, forging ahead.

They started out again, their formation a little more ragged at first, but they pulled together again as they continued on. All the lions started moving around, some turning their backs and disappearing into the tall grass, but the big male snarled again, then rumbled the beginning of a roar as he stood his ground. Several of the other big cats were arrayed behind him. Ayla was picking up the scent of fear from the human hunters; she was sure the lions were, too. She was afraid herself, but fear was something that people could overcome.

"I think we'd better get ready," Jondalar said. "That male doesn't look happy, and he has reinforcements."

"Can't you get him from here?" Ayla asked. She heard the series of grunts that was usually a precursor to a lion's roar.

"Probably," Jondalar said, "but I'd rather be closer, so I can be more sure of my aim."

"And I'm not sure how good my aim would be from this distance. We do need to be closer," Joharran said, continuing to march forward.

The people bunched together and kept going, still shouting, though Ayla thought their sound was more tentative as they drew closer. The cave lions became still and seemed tense as they watched the approach of the strange herd that didn't behave like prey animals.

Then, suddenly, everything happened at once.

The big male lion roared, a staggering, deafening sound, especially from such close range. He started toward them at a run. As he closed in, poised to spring, Jondalar hurled his spear at him.

Ayla had been watching the female on his right. About the time that Jondalar made his cast, the lioness bounded forward running, then vaulted to pounce.

Ayla pulled back and took aim. She felt the back of the spear-thrower with the spear mounted on it rise up almost without her knowing it as she hurled her spear. It was so natural for her, it didn't feel like a deliberate move. She and Jondalar had used the weapon during their entire year-long journey back to the Zelandonii and she was so skilled, it was second nature.

The lioness soared into her leap, but Ayla's spear met her more than halfway. It found its mark from beneath the big cat, and lodged firmly in her throat in a sudden fatal slash. Blood spurted out as the lioness collapsed to the ground.

Ayla quickly grabbed another spear from her holder, and slapped it down on her spear-thrower, looking around to see what else was happening. She saw Joharran's spear fly, and a heartbeat later another spear followed. She noticed that Rushemar was in the stance of one who had just thrown a spear. She saw another large female lion fall. A second spear found the beast before she landed. Another lioness was still coming. Ayla cast a spear, and saw that someone else had, too, just a moment before her.

She reached for another spear, making sure it was seated right—that the point, which was affixed to a short length of tapering shaft made to detach from the main spear shaft, was firmly in place and the hole in the butt of the long spear shaft was engaging the hook at the back of the spear-thrower. Then she looked around again. The huge male was down, but moving, bleeding but not dead. Her female was also bleeding, but not moving.

The lions were disappearing into the grass as fast as they could, at least one leaving a trail of blood. The human hunters were gathering themselves together, looking around and beginning to smile at one another.

"I think we did it," Palidar said, a huge grin starting.

He had barely gotten the words out when Wolf's menacing growl caught Ayla's attention. The wolf bounded away from the human hunters with Ayla on his heels. The heavily bleeding male lion was up and coming at them again. With a roar, he sprang toward them. Ayla could almost feel his anger, and she didn't really blame him.

Just as Wolf reached the lion and leaped up to attack, keeping himself between Ayla and the big cat, she flung her spear as hard as she could. Her eye caught another one hurled at the same time. They landed almost simultaneously with an audible *thunk*, and *thunk*. Both the lion and the wolf crumpled in a heap. Ayla gasped when she saw them fall, swathed in blood, afraid that Wolf was hurt.

ABOUT THE AUTHOR

JEAN M. AUEL is an international phenomenon. Her Earth's Children® series has sold more than 45 million copies worldwide and includes *The Clan of the Cave Bear*, *The Valley of Horses*, *The Mammoth Hunters*, *The Plains of Passage*, *The Shelters of Stone*, and *The Land of Painted Caves*. Her extensive research has earned her the respect of archaeologists and anthropologists around the world. She has honorary degrees from four universities and was named an Officer in the Order of Arts and Letters by the French government's Ministry of Culture. She lives with her husband, Ray, in Oregon.

Include Me Out

My Life from Goldwyn to Broadway

FARLEY GRANGER

WITH

ROBERT CALHOUN

 St. Martin's Griffin 📖 New York

www.stmartins.com

Frontispiece photograph courtesy of Farley Granger

Library of Congress Cataloging-in-Publication Data

Granger, Farley.
 Include me out : my life from Goldwyn to Broadway / Farley Granger with Robert Calhoun.
  p. cm.
 Includes index.
 ISBN-13: 978-0-312-35774-0
 ISBN-10: 0-312-35774-5
 1. Granger, Farley. 2. Actors—United States—Biography. I. Title.

PN2287.G669 A3 2007
791.4302'8092—dc22
[B]

                  2006050194

First St. Martin's Griffin Edition: May 2008

10 9 8 7 6 5 4 3 2 1

In memory of my beloved Ethyl

There is only one success . . . to be able to spend your life in your own way.

CHRISTOPHER MORLEY

Currently embroiled in my own "Golden Age," I've done my best to assemble the facts of my private and professional life accurately. If at one time or another, the wrong person shows up at the wrong party, forgive me. Everyone mentioned was with me at one party or another, at one time or another. It's my movie and it changes with every passing day.

FARLEY GRANGER

CONTENTS

Acknowledgments   xv

Prologue   I

Act I

Discovered   7

Meeting Mr. Goldwyn   9

Indentured   13

Childhood Memories   13

Hello, Hollywood   15

Adolescence   15

A Player   17

The Gorgons   18

Millie   20

The New York Premiere   24

Turning Eighteen   25

A Real Movie Studio!   26

Actor Aweigh   29

At Sea   32

Hawaii   34

Sex, Sex, Sex, Sex . . .   37

VJ Day   41

My Escape   43

Act II

Picking Up the Pieces   47

A Gauntlet for Mr. G.   51

Getting a Life 52

Chomping at the Bit 56

Nick Ray vs. Howard Hughes 57

The Bel Air Circuit 59

Nick Ray 60

The Big Apple 61

Star Power 64

On the Boardwalk 65

Hitchcock 66

Rope 67

The Most Beautiful Woman in the World 71

The Little Tramp and Big Bill 73

Disenchantment 76

Shelley 77

Shooting *Roseanna* 79

Solo 83

Lenny 84

MGM 88

Changes 90

Two Turkeys 91

Frances Takes a Turn 91

Out of America by 1950 93

1950 93

Paris 96

London 100

Farley Granger on Broadway . . . Twice! 102

Italy 103

The Little Tramp 105

Hitchcock Number II 107

A New Year's Eve to Remember 111

Ava 112

Finding the Method 114

The Dog Stole the Movie 118

The Grand Tour 119

Life on the A-List 129

Contents · xi

"The Gift of the Magi"	131
Hans Christian Andersen	134
Suspended Again	137
Shelley	139
An A-List Diva	141
Senso	143
Venice	145
Il Conte	153
La Fenice	154
A Sad Little Jolly	159
Cats	167
Mambo	171
The Turkey	172
The Shiner	173
Hollywood Ending	176

Act III

The East Coast	183
Just Off Broadway	186
The Tube's Golden Age	188
Jane Austen Hits Broadway!	193
Out of Town	195
On Broadway	198
If at First You Don't Succeed . . .	200
Rita & Bertolt	202
R & H & I	204
On the Road	206
Home Again	208
NRT	209
Le G	212
Four Parts in Three Plays in Twelve Cities	213
Tragedy Intrudes	215
Washington	217
Liberated	219
NRT—Second Tour	221

Just a Long Weekend 222
The Princess 224
The State Department 225
Italy Again 228
Hollywood or New York 229
New York, 1977 230
Two Strikes 232
The Right Part 234
Sailing 236
Talley & Son 237
Giving It Another Try 239
The Obie 242
Epilogue 244
Index 245

Special Acknowledgment

To Lawrence Malkin, whose generosity of spirit, intelligence, good humor, and willingness to share his expertise as a professional writer made this collaboration possible.

Acknowledgments

To Diane Reverand, our editor, who missed nothing: our excess of, or lack of, information, opinion, style, continuity, and taste.
To Philip Spitzer, our agent, who patiently resumed his efforts on our behalf after a twelve-year hiatus and found, with his usual dispatch, the right people.
To Jay Julien, our lawyer/manager, who has been our rock and the repository of our trust for thirty years.
To Frederick Kaufman, whose personal and professional opinion has been cheerfully given, eagerly sought, and happily received.
To Shirley Kaplan, who has never wavered in her enthusiastic support for this project.
To Linda and Patrick Pleven, who assisted on every how-to problem, willingly, cheerfully, and lovingly, every time we called upon them.
To Neila Smith Kennedy, who has been there with and for us from day one, twelve years ago.
To Eddie Muller and the San Francisco Film Noir Festival.
To Regina Scarpa, our associate editor, whose unflappable good humor and good sense saved many fraught moments from descending into disaster.

Special Thanks

To Samuel Goldwyn, Jr.
To Jane Klane and the Museum of Television and Radio; to the New York Public Library for the Performing Arts and its staff at Lincoln Center; and to the Academy of Motion Picture Arts and Sciences.

Include Me Out

Prologue

In December 2004, I was invited to a Visconti retrospective to see a newly restored print of his 1954 film *Senso,* at the Brooklyn Academy of Music, one of New York City's most respected arts organizations. The print included some scenes that had been cut from the film. As the house lights dimmed, I felt a hint of the familiar tightness in my stomach that always accompanied viewing myself on screen. The film opens with a scene from Verdi's *Il Trovatore* being performed on the stage of La Fenice, Venice's jewel box of an opera house. Italian partisans stealthily infiltrate the audience composed of groups of officers from the occupying Austrian Army, Venetian aristocrats, and ordinary citizens to pass out materials for a public anti-Austrian demonstration. I was so swept up by the beauty and drama of the moment that I didn't even notice my character's first appearance. I continued to be that absorbed by the film up to the final scene of the Countess running like a broken bird through crowds of drunken Austrian soldiers in the streets of Verona at night after she has had her lover, Franz, executed. As the audience applauded at the film's conclusion, I found myself applauding with them. Not only had I enjoyed *Senso* as much as they had, but I was also proud of the performance of that young actor playing Franz Mahler.

I had only seen a version of the film that had been butchered to fit into a ninety-minute television format, released in the United States in 1968 as *The Wanton Contessa.* For the first time in my life, I realized that in the time I had spent making films between my first movie, *The North Star,* in 1944, and *Senso,* in 1954, I had become an actor.

Seeing *Senso* that evening in Brooklyn flooded my mind with memories of my days as a film actor. I realized how important those years had been, how they had helped mold whatever talent I was able to develop. I'd been lucky enough to work with some legendary directors and to appear in several classic films. It was a fascinating time in film history. The more I thought about it, the more I realized how important those days were to all of us. They were the foundation of my life as an actor, and they also represented a time that shaped an entire generation of post–World War II Americans.

I never liked looking at myself on screen. I found it disquieting in the same way as hearing your voice on an answering machine for the first time. It doesn't sound the same as you hear yourself and therefore seems disconnected from you. When watching a performance of mine, I've never been able to relax and enjoy it as a member of the audience, because my focus was always on the choices I or he, the character, made for the scene. For example, in a confrontational scene, was I too controlled, which could seem calculating, or too aggressive, which could seem out of control? In a love scene, was I too eager, which could come across as needy and immature, or too smooth and relaxed, which could be interpreted as narcissistic and self-absorbed? No matter what the demands of a scene—comic or tragic, naturalistic or operatic—watching myself just gave me another chance to worry that maybe I'd missed the acting choice that could have made the scene deeper, more moving, more exciting, more fun, or simply more honest. I was never satisfied with what I saw. It was painful to see my performance blown up on screen, so much larger than life.

Interviewers would sometimes ask me if I didn't feel lucky because of my looks. I never thought about my looks at all. They were a given, neither an accomplishment nor something I could work on to get better parts. At times how I looked felt like a handicap in terms of casting. Leading men are much more liable to be typecast. Character actors get to play a wider range of parts, which is more challenging and more fun.

One of the benefits of getting older, aside from the experience and technique acquired along the way, is that now it is easier for me to look objectively at that young actor up there on the screen. I have become a much less demanding self-critic. Since I am frequently requested to attend events honoring Alfred Hitchcock, I most often see my younger self as Guy, the tennis pro in the 1951 classic *Strangers on a Train*. This film, which after several flops reestablished Hitchcock as Hollywood's master of suspense, is so good that after many years and viewings, I can finally sit back and appreciate my contribution to it.

I have only made two other films that inspire the same sense of pride. One is Nicholas Ray's *They Live by Night*; the other is Luchino Visconti's *Senso*. Nick's film is a small, tight story of two doomed young lovers on the run in small-town middle America during the Depression.

Visconti's film is a lush, sprawling epic in which two doomed lovers play out their fate against the backdrop of the Risorgimento, Italy's struggle for independence and political unification in the mid-nineteenth century. The locations were Venice; a Palladio villa in Vicenza, a small town in the mountains north of Venice; and a sound stage in Rome. Making *Senso* was a unique and sometimes thrilling experience for me, but not always an enjoyable one.

I had not been happy making films in Hollywood. I wanted to move to New York, learn how to act, and work in the theater. Mr. Goldwyn had refused to—

using his own malapropism—include me out of the last two years of my seven-year contract. He finally agreed, provided I pay him a sum based on what he got for me when he loaned me out to other studios. This was approximately ten times what he paid me. I paid. I was free. I was broke.

My agent got me the deal to make *Senso* in Italy. The salary was what Goldwyn got for me on loanout. If the film did not finish in three months, it doubled. I was making good money, but I got frustrated when we hit the eight-month point with no end in sight. It seemed as if I was never going to get to New York and the theater.

Act I

Discovered

It was 1943. America was at war. I was a healthy seventeen-year-old high school student, halfway through my senior year. My future was clear: I would graduate and when I turned eighteen in July, I would join whatever branch of the armed forces most of my buddies were choosing. That's exactly what happened, with one exception: I became a movie star first.

As a clerk in the unemployment office in North Hollywood, my dad was used to seeing actors when they came in every week to collect their checks. There was the occasional grand one like Adolphe Menjou, who arrived in a chauffeured limousine each week to pick up his check, but most of them were just ordinary out-of-work actors waiting for their next paying job to come along. Dad became friendly with an actor who was far from ordinary. It was Harry Langdon, who had been one of the "Big Four," Hollywood's most beloved stars during the silent film era, along with Harold Lloyd, Buster Keaton, and Charlie Chaplin. Chaplin was the only one of the four who survived the transition to talkies. The others had fallen on differing degrees of hard times. Keaton and Lloyd eventually survived more successfully than Mr. Langdon. My dad had great admiration for his new friend, and eventually felt free enough with him to ask his advice about my dream of becoming an actor.

After mulling it over for several weeks, Langdon told Dad about a small showcase theater on Highland Avenue in Hollywood that was run by Mary Stewart, a little-known actress with a lot of money and some talent. There was no permanent company, no set schedule. Each production that Miss Stewart managed to put on consisted of a pickup group of actors, most of them amateurs who would work for nothing in order to get the experience, and the credit, not to mention an opportunity to live the dream of being discovered.

She was currently seeing young actors for *The Wookie*, an English play about Londoners during the blitz in World War II. At dinner that evening, my dad told us about it, and my mom agreed to take time off from her job at the five-and-ten-cent store to drive me to the theater the next day to find out how to go about trying out for a part.

The next afternoon, Mom got off early and picked me up at school, and off we went. The theater was a nondescript auditorium with folding chairs, much like many of today's Off-Broadway theaters. Lucky for me, they were having an open audition, one to which amateurs, actors who were not yet members of Actors' Equity, were welcomed. The stage manager gave me some pages from different scenes and told me to go study them and come back in an hour. I returned to read for Miss Stewart and the director using a Cockney accent, which had to be awful, because it was something I'd just made up after reading the scenes. I had no frame of reference for the accent other than the few English movies I'd seen. There was a long silence after I finished, and then what sounded like a whispered argument between Miss Stewart and the director. After what seemed like an eternity, Miss Stewart came to the edge of the stage to congratulate me on getting the part. Even though in my naïveté I had felt since childhood that it was my destiny to be an actor one day, I was in a state of shock when it happened.

At our first read-through of *The Wookie*, I met the rest of the cast, including Percival Vivian, our English director, who was also playing the leading man. We all, with the exception of Miss Stewart and Mr. Vivian, had to double and triple parts. Three of the actors were old-timers who had been extras in the movies for years and regulars in Mary Stewart's productions. There was a young boy who was a brand-new member of Actors' Equity. The last two members of the company, a pretty young redhead named Connie Cornwall and I, had never set foot on a real stage before.

Miss Stewart was grand, but she could not have been nicer to everyone. Percy, the director, often seemed as if he had it in for me. I had no idea why. Since he said he had been in London during the blitz, I hung on his every word as if they were graven in stone.

After three weeks of rehearsing scenes, it was time to add the costumes, lighting, and sound effects. Technical rehearsals were very exciting, with the sounds of bombs going off and sirens and shouting all over the place. I had to run on and off, change coats, and return to the stage as someone else. It was exhilarating. After the final tech rehearsal, Percy called me over and said, "Good show, young man. Be at the dress rehearsal tomorrow a wee bit early, would you?" Before I could reply, he turned and walked off. I was so pleased by his compliment that I didn't ask why. I couldn't wait to comply.

At the call for the dress rehearsal, I was in my costume, waiting outside his dressing room, when he arrived. He said he wanted to show me how to make up. I was very excited to get this chance to learn something professional. He did a full character makeup with heavy lines for age and big dark circles under my eyes. I thought I looked just terrific. He had turned me into a character man! My favorite actors were always people like Frank Morgan and Bert Lahr in *The Wizard of Oz*, never the young leading men. After thanking him profusely, I ran back to my dressing room so that everyone could admire the new me. No one even looked up.

The dress rehearsal went reasonably well except for a number of explosions in the wrong place, lots of collisions in the wings and backstage as we all tore on and off, and people forgetting their lines and or entrances. I, with my greasepaint, was letter- and traffic-pattern perfect. After we staged the curtain calls, Miss Stuart grabbed me by the hand and marched me back to her dressing room. She closed the door, turned to me, and, with a surprising lack of grandness, said, "Who put all that crap on your face!?" I told her that Percy had taught me how to do my makeup. She shook her head for a minute and started to laugh, "You tell that son of a bitch that if he ever lays another one of his dainty fingers on your face again, I'll cut them all off at the wrist! He just doesn't want anyone to be prettier than he is onstage. Now, go and scrub it all off. Do not wear *any* makeup tomorrow night. The last thing I want you to do is hide that face."

Backstage the following evening, I thought I saw Percy scowling at me. When I went over to apologize to him for not wearing makeup, he gave me a pat on the back and a tight little smile as he said, "Break a leg, laddie." The house was filled with friends and admirers of Miss Stewart, and of all of us in the cast. What nobody knew was that an up-and-coming young talent agent named Phil Gersh was there with Bob McIntyre, the casting director for Samuel Goldwyn.

Meeting Mr. Goldwyn

My father had already left for work when our phone rang the next morning. It was Phil Gersh. After explaining who he was, he asked me if I could come in and see him as soon as possible about a movie. I thanked him and said of course I could. I was fairly calm about it, because I knew (same old naïveté) that it was fate in action, but my mother was hysterical. She called my father, who had just arrived at work, and insisted that he come home immediately. Somehow he managed to get away from work. After I finished cleaning up and dressed in my best blazer, shirt, and good-luck tie, we headed for Mr. Gersh's office at the Goldstone Agency in Hollywood. My father told me to just keep quiet and listen. He would do all the talking.

Mr. Gersh's secretary buzzed us into his office. He made us comfortable and got right to the point. He told us that he and the casting director for Sam Goldwyn had seen me in *The Wookie*, and thought I might be right for a part in a new movie that Mr. Goldwyn was producing. Would I be interested in trying out for it? "I sure would!" popped out of my mouth before my father could speak.

Mr. Gersh laughed, and my father said, "We would certainly be interested in talking about it, Mr Gersh." They excused my mother and me, and a short time later came out beaming.

Mr. Gersh said; "Welcome to the fold, Farley. I'm sure we'll be doing great things together." He then apologized for having another appointment and not being able to come with us. He promised that Mr. McIntyre would take good care of us at the studio, and that he would see us again soon.

When we were out of earshot, I turned to my father. "What was he talking about? What studio? Where are we going? What did you talk about in there?"

"I think he's a good man, Sonny, so I signed with him to be our agent." I resented the "our" and not having been a part of the conversation even more than I resented that nickname, something he had known for years, but I was too excited to spoil the event with an argument.

We arrived at the Goldwyn Studio, and my name was at the gate. The guard directed us to the casting office. The studios were disappointingly drab and industrial-looking, mostly two-story gray stucco buildings with signs indicating what was inside. We found the casting office with no problem. There the secretary had me take a seat and politely told my eager stage parents that they would have to wait outside, which secretly delighted me. Bob McIntyre came out and took me into his office. He was a nice-looking older man, dressed like Robert Donat in *Goodbye, Mr. Chips*.

After we sat down, he talked about seeing me in *The Wookie* the night before and how good he thought I was. When he asked me if I would like to act in a movie, I said, "You bet!"

He smiled and asked me how old I was. When I told him seventeen, he said that the movie was about the life of a boy my age during the last forty-eight hours of peace and the first forty-eight hours of World War II in a Russian village called North Star. He gave me a couple of pages of a script and told me to go into the outer office and read it over. The part I was reading for was Damian. The scene was a very emotional one in which Damian was saying goodbye to the girl he loved because he was going off to fight with the resistance. She understood his decision, but was afraid he would be killed. After about ten minutes, Mr. McIntyre came out and asked if I was ready. I took a breath and nodded. He said we were going to a conference room to meet the three people I was going to read for: Mr. Goldwyn; Lillian Hellman, the writer of the movie; and Lewis Milestone, the director. By the time we got there, I was no longer calm.

We entered a big room with nothing in it other than a long table with a lot of chairs around it. Three people were seated at the far end of the long table.

Mr. McIntyre introduced me and quietly left. Mr. Goldwyn was tall, ramrod-straight, and healthy-looking, impeccably dressed in a steel-gray suit. He was bald with black eyebrows and ball-bearing eyes. He stood, nodded, and, in an incongruously thin, high-pitched voice said, "Mr. Granger." Miss Hellman, an ugly little lady wreathed in clouds of cigarette smoke, said nothing. Mr. Milestone, a friendly-looking, stocky middle-aged man, smiled at me and winked. He asked if I had any questions about the scene. I was afraid to ask anything, so I said, "No."

As if on cue, a pretty young girl around my age appeared to read with me. Mr. Milestone introduced us and asked us to begin. We finished and no one said a word except Mr. Milestone, who came over, shook my hand, and thanked me for a job well done.

I went back to Mr. McIntyre's office to find out what to do next, but he was in a meeting. His secretary told me, "Don't call us, we'll call you," and showed me the door. I was thrilled. They said they would call me, which echoed over and over in my head as I ran down the hall and out the door to inform my waiting parents, "They're going to call me!"

More than a month, and a mild case of scarlatina, went by as my discouraged parents began to give up hope. I never doubted that the call would come, and thought the fact that it was taking so long was fate providing me with time to get over my rash. How was I to know that Lillian Hellman had spent that entire month trying to talk Montgomery Clift into leaving a Broadway play for the part of Damian in *The North Star*? Luckily for me, Monty was very happy on Broadway, and now the movie was ready to go into production. They had to have someone for the part. My call did come.

I was back in the same conference room. The same three people were there along with another man introduced to me as Benno Schneider, an acting teacher from New York. He was the dialogue director for the film. He asked me to sit down with him to read the scene. I pulled out my tattered pages and we began.

Something was wrong—our lines didn't fit together. Miss Hellman jumped up waving her cigarette and yelled, "Stop, stop! That's not the new script, goddammit! Get him the right script and let him go look at it." They did, and told me to come back to Mr. Schneider's office in an hour.

I took it to a nearby drugstore, ordered an ice cream soda, and studied the new script. It was confusing because I had worked so hard on the other lines, and although some lines were the same, many of the others were a little bit different. When I returned, the guard directed me to Mr. Schneider's office. He was waiting for me. Mr. Schneider was a small middle-aged man with a slight European accent. He was courteous and very soft-spoken. He was also patient and kind.

He asked me if I knew anything about the story of *The North Star* or the character of Damian. I said, "No, nobody told me anything." He filled me in on all of it and asked me just to sit and read the scene with him. The scene was a rewritten version of the one from my first audition, in which I explained to my girl why I had to go and fight with the partisans. After we finished, he said, "Come with me."

We went to Bob McIntyre's office and Mr. Schneider said to him, "This is the boy." Mr. McIntyre replied, "Don't tell me, I'm the one who saw him in that play."

We went back to the conference room and I read the scene again with Mr. Schneider for Mr. Goldwyn, Mr. Milestone, and Miss Hellman. When we finished, Mr. Goldwyn said, "Do a screen test on this boy as soon as possible."

The next day I was walking into a soundstage on the Goldwyn lot when a voice from somewhere yelled out, "Hey, Farley, what the hell are you doing here?" I looked around and spotted Glen Lambert's father up on the seat of a boom microphone. Glen was my best friend and a member of The Daredevils, an adventure club that Glen and I and four of our friends had founded. His father was a sound man in movies. I yelled back, "I'm here to test for a part in the *The North Star* movie, Mr. Lambert." Just as he burst out with "No shit!," Mr. Milestone walked over to me with a glamorous young woman who was going to do the test with me. Her name was Constance Dowling. She was a contract player at the Goldwyn Studio whose career never took off.

The girl I had read with the first time was sweet and pretty, but she didn't look at me much during the scene, which made it hard for me to feel anything about her. When Connie looked at me and spoke, I felt as if I had known her all my life, and what a difference that made. To read the scene with someone who could act and was able to feel it emotionally helped me to feel it, too. We ended up crying in each other's arms.

This was the first time I was aware of what actors need to do for one another when working together. That, combined with what Mr. Schneider had told me about the story and the boy's life, made it possible for me to imagine that I really was Damian.

Phil Gersh called that same evening. Mr. Goldwyn wanted me for the part in *The North Star*. Mr. Gersh explained how happy he was to be representing me. Since I would be eighteen before too long, he wondered if I would mind signing the agreement, too. I was giddy with excitement, but managed to sound calm, because I didn't want to say anything stupid. I knew that my destiny had finally arrived and that Mr. Gersh was a part of it. I said I was very happy he would be representing me, and I would be glad to sign the agreement for myself. At this point my father demanded that I hand him the phone while my mother smothered me with a huge hug.

Indentured

The next morning, dressed once again in my Sunday best, we drove first to Mr. Gersh's office, where my father and I both signed an agreement. From there, we all drove to the Goldwyn Studio to sign a seven-year contract for $100 a week. The seven years did not include any time I spent in the armed forces. That would automatically be added on to my contract. It never occurred to my parents or me to have a lawyer look at anything we eagerly signed that day.

Mr. Goldwyn's office was much fancier than anything else I had seen at the studio. It was wood-paneled with windows and big bookcases. His desk seemed almost as big as the conference table in the room where I had read for him. He was warm and courteous to my father and me, calling me "my boy," and he was absolutely courtly with my mother. We learned that my mother had to be with me on the set every day because I was still only seventeen. They asked me to wait in the outer office for a few minutes.

I was sitting there thinking about my mother accompanying me to the set every day. This development had taken the edge off my excitement. I wasn't a child anymore, damnit! A chirpy voice penetrated my thoughts and wiped the frown off my face. "I said, aren't you excited, Farley?" It was Mr. Goldwyn's secretary. "Yes, I'm very happy," I said quickly and then added, with little false bravado, "but I always knew it was going to happen." And I did, ever since I was five.

Childhood Memories

One of my happiest childhood memories was of a Christmas play at the Mariposa School, a progressive private school that I attended as a child in my hometown, San Jose, California. In the first and third acts, I played an elf in Santa's workshop at the North Pole. The second act was set in an imaginary classroom. On the night of our performance, I was drafted to go on as a pupil in the second act, a last-minute replacement for a mumps victim. Not only was I letter-perfect in my own lines, but I also remembered all of my stricken classmate's lines. Truth be told, I think I knew every line in the play. My proud parents stood and led the bravos. I was so happy that I refused to remove my costume after the show. I lived in it for two days until my patient mother finally coaxed me out of it for a well-needed bath. From that moment on, I knew as a certainty that it was my destiny to be an actor.

The other memories of my early childhood were also happy ones. My father was well off, and he and my mother were social leaders in San Jose, California. We had a lovely new house on the edge of town as well as a beach house in the nearby seaside town, Capitola. I was an only child, born after thirteen difficult years of miscarriages. My parents lived for my every whim.

My father's beloved world-traveling sister, Edith Pomtag, lived with her husband, their only son, Jack, and her three daughters from an earlier marriage in a beautifully restored farmhouse on hundreds of acres in the countryside near San Jose. Jackie, who was a year younger than I to the day, was my closest friend and companion. They had a beach house next to ours in Capitola where Jackie and I and our dogs Mick and Beau spent magical, sun-drenched, waterlogged summers.

In 1929 my father lost everything in the crash. He had to sell the beach house and the house in town. He turned the second floor of his Willys-Overland regional automobile dealership in downtown San Jose into a large apartment where we lived for the next two years as he struggled to stay afloat. My parents' busy social life was replaced by their increasingly heavy drinking at home.

Unhappy cooped up in our new apartment, I would sneak down to the showroom, where I had a grand time meeting people. My dad didn't seem to mind. In fact, I think he enjoyed showing me off. When my mother realized what was going on, she raised the roof. She had always been very protective, but now that we lived in town, she was becoming obsessive about not letting me out of her sight.

My first really frightening memory is of the night when, locked in my bedroom, I heard everything that we owned being auctioned off in the main part of our apartment. I didn't understand what was going on, but I knew it wasn't good.

I now realize what shame and humiliation my parents must have felt when they bundled me into the back seat of the last car my father salvaged from his dealership in order to sneak off in the middle of the night. I felt that I must have done something very bad. I drifted in and out of sleep as we drove all night to Los Angeles. Neither of them ever explained why we left San Jose. It was never mentioned again.

Hello, Hollywood

We lived in a small courtyard apartment in a run-down area of Hollywood. I attended the closest public school, and my folks took various temporary jobs to keep food on the table and booze in the cupboard. Their drinking, which inevitably led to fighting, had become a part of our lives. Now I am able to appreciate how difficult this time must have been for them. As a child, after the freedom of my young life in San Jose and Capitola, I just felt isolated, frightened, and trapped.

When she had time between temporary jobs, my mother got busy chasing our dream. She had never forgotten how carried away I had been by my childhood stage triumph as Santa's elf, which explains her well-intentioned effort (along with untold thousands of other mothers in the heyday of Shirley Temple) to turn me into a tap dancer. She enrolled me as a member of the Meglin Kiddies, a popular performing group of the moment. After school, she would drive me to tap class two afternoons a week. I hated it! But she loved sitting around and talking with all the other would-be stage mothers and hearing all the latest show business gossip. Our reward for completing the course was a public performance at the Shrine Auditorium in downtown Los Angeles. The dream was that "people in the business" would be there to discover a new star. The Shrine was a mammoth theater, and the audience barely filled the front and center part of the orchestra. I felt like an ant with two left feet on that huge stage, but we all got through the program without anyone being knocked down. Considering the bumpy rehearsal, that was a triumph. My mother called the school for weeks to see if any scouts or agents had called to ask about me. Much to her chagrin, no one ever did. The dream was dropped for a while.

Adolescence

After several years, good luck arrived on our doorstep in the form of a long-overdue government bonus check for veterans of "The War to End All Wars." My father, who had enlisted and had risen through the ranks to become a captain in World War I, had been injured in the trenches in France and discharged.

At almost the same time as the veterans' bonus arrived, Dad got a permanent job as a clerk in the North Hollywood branch of the California Department of Unemployment.

This unexpected windfall enabled him to put a down payment on a small house in Studio City, an outpost of the urban sprawl that was creeping into the orange groves of the San Fernando Valley. The house was simple but nice, and the area was beautiful, with big old pepper trees, and an open-air vegetable stand at the nearby intersection of Laurel Canyon and Ventura Boulevard. As we made a real home, my parent's drinking and fighting tapered off a bit. My folks enrolled me in nearby North Hollywood Junior High and gave me a bicycle. That was the happiest moment of my life. In California, with its wide-open spaces, a bike meant I finally had some freedom. Things were looking up.

Our next-door neighbors were a big raucous Irish family of circus performers turned vaudevillians, the O'Connors. One of their sons was my age and already a movie star. Donald and I became friends, but I didn't see a lot of him because he was always working and went to the school at whatever studio he was working for at the time. He was an incredibly talented young man who had appeared in a string of low-budget musical films for Universal Studios in the early 1940s. Donald went on to star for MGM in what many, including me, consider to be one of the best films made during Hollywood's Golden Age of Musicals, *Singin' in the Rain.*

Once we had settled into our new life, my parents and I found something we could enjoy doing together as a family—going to the movies. There was a big movie theater in nearby Sherman Oaks. Best of all, we were close enough to Hollywood to go to the grandest movie palaces of them all—Grauman's Chinese, the Egyptian, and the Pantages. The Chinese was a real treat, not only because it was the most colorful, with a starry sky as the ceiling, but also because it had the handprints and footprints of all the big movie stars in cement out front and I could put my hands and feet in the impressions made by my favorite stars.

Sometimes I would get on my bike and head for Sherman Oaks to see a double feature in the afternoon. After an early supper, at which I would act out all the best parts for my parents, we would all get in the car and drive to Hollywood to see another movie in the evening. The parts I loved acting out were never the hero or the leading man; I much preferred the villains and the character men like Peter Lorre, Eric Blore, and Sydney Greenstreet, to name just a few of my favorites.

A Player

As soon as my seven-year contract with Mr. Goldwyn was signed, I was taken out of school and handed over to the studio machine—wardrobe, makeup, and publicity. My contract was for seven years, at one hundred dollars a week, exclusive of any years spent in military service. The studio provided a private tutor who was in touch with my teachers at North Hollywood High. Since I was in the last quarter of my senior year, my studies were not at all demanding. It was easy to schedule sessions with the tutor around preproduction for *The North Star*.

The publicity department wanted me to change my name. They were afraid people might mix me up with the British actor Stewart Granger, whose real name was Jimmy Stewart. They gave me a list from which to choose. The names were all interchangeable, like Gordon Gregory and Gregory Gordon. I didn't want to change my name. I liked Farley Granger. It was my father's name, and his grandfather's name. They kept bringing me new combinations, and finally I offered to change it to Kent Clark. I was the only one who thought that was funny. They just increased the pressure. I went to tell Mr. McIntyre about my dilemma and to seek his advice. He asked if Mr. Goldwyn had said anything about my name. I told him, "Not that I know of, just the people in the publicity department." He suggested that I lay off the jokes and quietly keep promising to make up my mind by tomorrow. Publicity had to go out very soon, and suddenly it would be too late for any name change. He liked my real name, too.

He was right. Three days later, the studio put out a story that Sam Goldwyn had placed an ad in the paper looking for a young man for his next production, *The North Star*. Farley Granger, a senior at North Hollywood High School, had answered the ad and been discovered. Even though I was delighted about my name, I thought that was a really dumb story. The truth was much more interesting.

The Gorgons

The studio publicity department called to tell me that I had been summoned to audiences with the two reigning Queens of Hollywood, Louella Parsons and Hedda Hopper, bitter rivals on rival newspapers. Their patronage in their daily columns could make or break careers. They were in league with the heads of the studios, who did not hesitate to use them to keep their actors in line, a tactic used on me in the early 1950s when my fights with Mr. Goldwyn increased in intensity.

My first appointment was with the thrice-married Miss Parsons, whose column was syndicated in Hearst newspapers, with which she had an unprecedented, unexplained lifetime contract. The rumor was that as a guest aboard Hearst's yacht in 1924, she had witnessed the shooting of Thomas Ince, a pioneering mogul of silent films. When Hearst caught his mistress, Marion Davies, kissing Charlie Chaplin, he had tried to shoot Chaplin, but missed and instead killed Ince . . . hence, Louella's lifetime contract.

She was known to be a tippler, along with her current husband, "Docky," a urologist and studio physician for MGM. Tippler may be too mild a word to describe this man's use or misuse of booze. Infamous as "clap (STD) doctor to the stars," Docky could be trusted by the studio heads to keep their stars' afflictions a dark secret.

They lived in a big Spanish house in Beverly Hills. When I rang the bell, a nondescript young man, her assistant, answered the door. He showed me into the living room. It was crammed with silver picture frames, cigarette boxes and lighters, porcelain figurines, crystal vases, radios, designer handbags, and cases of wine and Jack Daniel's, said to be her favorite. I learned later that this was all swag given to her at Christmastime by actors, producers, agents, and studio executives, anyone who had benefited or hoped to benefit from a positive mention in her column. After a few minutes she swayed into the room, a pudgy, middle-aged woman.

She plopped down on the sofa next to me, enveloping me in an overpowering cloud of perfume and alcohol, and spoke in a slow sighing manner, smiling vaguely all the while. "Young man, you must tell me all about yourself. Now, who are you?" Her assistant whispered in her ear and she sighed, "Oh yes. You're Sam's new boy. Now tell me everything. There wasn't any want ad, was there?"

I told her everything about my life, which was a very short story, but still long enough for her eyes to glaze over. She hauled herself up from the sofa, still smiling, and moved off, saying to no one in particular, "Oh dear ... the Niven party tonight, or is it the Rathbones'?"

"The Colmans'," her assistant sang out. She was almost out of the room when she turned to give me a final hazy smile. "Nappy time," she sighed and was gone.

My boss, Mr. Goldwyn, supposedly said of her: "Louella Parsons is stronger than Samson. He needed two columns to bring the house down. She can do it with one."

Hedda Hopper called her home in Beverly Hills "The House That Fear Built." She was very different from her rival; younger, and completely focused, she had a reputation for being sadistic. Married only once, to the actor DeWolf Hopper, she had started as an actress and still played small parts in films on occasion. She was tall, and imposingly attractive. Her penchant for wearing wild hats made her seem even taller and more formidable. The one she was wearing the day of my interview looked like a chef's toque with feathers. "So, you're Sam's new boy," she said from behind the desk of her small Hollywood office. "Take off your jacket and sit down. I want to hear all about *The North Star*. Christ, it's hot in here!" she exclaimed.

Before I could say anything, she whipped off her blouse, revealing her naked shoulders and a white bra. I had never heard a woman, except my mother, swear before, especially one in her bra, with a hat like that, sitting behind a desk. "What the hell is Sam doing making a damn Commie movie?!!" she suddenly shouted at me.

I glued my eyes on the ceiling while trying to get out something about the Russians being our allies, but she would have none of it. I sat silently, sweating, looking out the window, while she went on at length about the evils of sex, drink, smoking, "going Hollywood," and, of course, communism. Then I was dismissed. I stood, eyes on the floor, turned, and headed for the door. She stopped me by shouting, "Tell Sam that want-ad story was the goddamned dumbest thing I ever read!" I looked back at her and laughed as I scooted out the door.

When their columns came out, they were both very flattering, but reading them was like reading about someone I didn't know. Louella Parsons was sugary sweet about the wonderful Sam Goldwyn's latest discovery. Hedda Hopper's approach was a little less respectful, and she made a crack about the discovery story being both untrue and unimaginative.

Millie

As a youngster with no real acting experience, I had no way of knowing how lucky I was to have the great Lewis Milestone direct me and shape my performance in my first two movies. Milestone had won his first Oscar in 1927 for best comedy direction of *Two Arabian Knights*. In 1930 he scored again, winning the best director Oscar for his film about the futility of war, *All Quiet on the Western Front*. That was immediately followed by another Oscar nomination for directing *The Front Page*. In the thirties his superb work continued with *The General Dies at Dawn* and *Of Mice and Men*.

A director's vision not only can make a good film, it can make the difference between a good performance and a bad one.

The North Star, Goldwyn's first film after Pearl Harbor, was a big movie about the horrors of Hitler's invasion of a small town in Russia. In the winter of 1942, when the news from the Russian front was very bad indeed, Goldwyn received a message from President Roosevelt through Lowell Mellett, the chief of the Bureau of Motion Pictures of the Office of War Information, that America needed a film about our Russian allies. As soon as he was able to assemble the creative team of Lillian Hellman as writer and Lewis Milestone as director, with Aaron Copland composing the score, Goldwyn rushed *The North Star* into production. The ensemble cast was led by Dana Andrews, who may best be remembered as the detective in *Laura;* Teresa Wright, who had just won an Oscar as Greer Garson's daughter in *Mrs. Miniver;* Walter Brennan, a three-time Oscar winner; Walter Huston, a superb actor and father of John Huston; Ann Harding, Ruth Nelson, the great Erich von Stroheim, Jane Withers, and me. Although some of these names may now be forgotten, they were all terrific actors drawn from the pool of regulars developed by each of the major studios in the golden age. These character actors were appreciated by moviegoers with almost as much pleasure as the stars. Some of them, Humphrey Bogart and Jimmy Cagney, for example, went on to become big stars in their own right.

I was starting my film career in the very best company. Each actor had his own beautifully honed technique, and every one offered something from which I could learn. Before each scene, Mr. Milestone, or Millie as everyone called him, would explain to those involved what was happening and how he expected them to react. He would then shoot the scene as many times as he had to in order to get a finished product that satisfied him. For the first few days, I went up to him after every scene to find out how I was doing. After the third time he took me aside and explained that I didn't need to check with him after each scene. He would let me know when he wanted me to do anything different. Up until now he was very happy with my work. I was pleased as could be, but I also got the message not to bother him.

During my first day on the set of *The North Star*, a tall, spectacled gentleman with a raspy voice came up to me and introduced himself. "I'm Aaron Copland, and I just saw your screen test. I think you will be wonderful in the film." I thanked him and asked if he was working on the film. When he said that he was, I asked, "Doing what?" He said, "Oh, Ira Gershwin and I are writing a few songs for it." I recognized Gershwin's name, but, as a not very sophisticated seventeen-year-old, I hadn't a clue who Aaron Copland was. I said, "That's nice," and a call to the set for rehearsal saved me from putting my other foot into my mouth.

A couple of days later I found a record of "El Salon Mexico" in my dressing room with a note from Mr. Copland wishing me luck. I took it home that night, listened to it on the phonograph I had bought with my first paycheck, and was overwhelmed by the vitality and splendor of the music. I did not see Aaron Copland again until right after I finished the film. As I was leaving Bob McIntyre's office, I ran into Mr. Copland in the hall. I told him how much I loved the record he had given me. He asked if I had time to listen to some of the music he had composed for the film. I said, "You bet!" He laughed, and we went down the hall to his studio, where he spent about a half-hour playing music that he had composed and explaining how it worked in the film. I felt privileged to be exposed to that part of the process of putting a film together.

Who needed a dressing room to wait in? I never left the set. I was intrigued by everything: how the cameras worked; how special effects made bomb explosions look real; what fake blood was made of; where and how Milestone put the cameras and what he saw through the lens. I was a kid, and it was my first movie. In truth, everything was an adventure.

I was like a puppy trying to be liked by everyone. Two of the people I tried hardest with were Anne Baxter and Dana Andrews. Anne, who was Frank Lloyd Wright's granddaughter and an up-and-coming young actress at 20th Century-Fox, was a last-minute replacement for Teresa Wright, whose pregnancy got her out of the film. I had been looking forward to working with Teresa, but one look at Anne and I was a goner.

When a picture of the two of us became the cover of *Look* magazine, I was convinced that we were destined to be together. The fact that she was a couple of years older than I and had experience on the New York stage made her even more glamorous in my eyes. She was fun, she was sexy, she was great to work with, and she was very sweet to me, but my crush went nowhere. She treated me like a kid brother—something Dana never did even though I was playing his kid brother.

I tried my best to become friends with Dana, but it was not easy. He was taciturn by nature. Early each morning, when we were all in wardrobe and makeup, he was downright grumpy. On set he was always line-perfect and always there for me, but I never felt a connection to him as I would with a brother who loved me. Of course, I thought that it was my fault.

The great character actor Walter Brennan had been under contract to Goldwyn since 1935. This was his thirty-fifth picture under that contract, but only his sixth for Goldwyn, who rarely made more than one movie a year. The other twenty-nine films had been made on loanout to other studios for large fees. This made a great deal of money for Goldwyn, who only had to pay Walter his contractual wage.

Walter was warm and supportive and had become a sort of mentor to me. When I asked him what I was doing wrong with Dana, he said, "Nothing, kid, and stop worrying about it. You're doing fine. Dana's just hungover and trying to get it together each morning, and it don't help that you're the good-looking new kid on the lot, either." That made me feel a little better, because there was nothing I could do about either of those things.

One memory from *The North Star* that still tickles me is a trick Walter played for my benefit. He got a kick out of making me laugh, and he knew I was a pushover. One afternoon in his dressing room, he picked up his phone and, in a pitch-perfect imitation of Goldwyn, commenced firing people at the studio—the head of accounting, the motor pool chief, and the entire makeup department. Before too much chaos spread, he called back with outrageous explanations and rehired everyone. His practical joke was cruel, but his performance was very funny.

My mother was thrilled with her new role in show business. There were a lot of young children in the film, so there were plenty of stage mothers present. Mom bonded instantly with Jane Withers's mother. Jane, who was about my age, had become a popular child star in the 1930s as the brat everyone loved to hate. Her mother knew all the tricks of the stage mother's trade, which she generously shared with my mother. I liked Jane. I did not like the fact that my mom was embracing stage motherhood so enthusiastically. I intended to exercise my right to be free of parental supervision on my approaching eighteenth birthday, and knew the fight would be epic.

Late in the film, we had gone on location to the Fox ranch in Malibu Canyon to shoot a battle scene with lots of horses and extras that was too big for the soundstage. Milestone had only finished one setup when it clouded over. We stopped. After waiting an hour or so for the sun to return, we broke for lunch. Jane and I got permission to take two of the horses for a ride after lunch. We were instructed not to go far, and to come back immediately if the sun came out. By midafternoon, with still no sign of sun, we returned to find everyone packing up to go. I saw my mother sitting and laughing with some of the grips. When she headed toward me, I knew that my worst fears had come true. She'd been drinking.

We shared a car back to the studio with Dana and Anne. My mother was far too garrulous, going on about her life in San Jose society, her golf trophies, and how smart she had been to enroll me as one of the Meglin Kiddies. No one else could get a word in, not that anyone tried. Teenagers are always easily embarrassed by their parents. I felt like I was trapped in the longest ride of my life.

During the last few days of work on *The North Star*, I began to experience the onset of a chronic malady that is a part of every actor's life: the "will I ever work again syndrome." In my case it was compounded by the fact that in a month I would turn eighteen. My country was at war, and I wanted to do my part. On the last day of shooting, Mr. Milestone pulled me aside to say how proud he was of the work I had done, and then told me something I had to keep secret. His next film was being done at Fox and there was a part in it that he wanted me to do. Dana was going to be in it, because he had a split contract between Goldwyn and Fox, but Milestone needed to convince both studios in order for me to be cast. I was very proud that he wanted to use me again. It meant he liked my work. When I reminded him that I was soon to be eighteen and anxious to enlist, he assured me that the studio could get me a temporary deferment until the film was finished, because the film he wanted me for, *The Purple Heart*, was also important to the war effort.

At first Mr. Goldwyn refused to loan me out to 20th Century-Fox. He had never been happy about Dana's split contract, and since I was an unknown, he could not get a lot of money for me. He would have preferred to be the first to exploit his new discovery, but he had no projects ready for me to work on, and he was aware of my impending military service. Fox was not eager to cast me, either. The studio had its own stable of juveniles under contract and was not keen on paying for and promoting anyone under exclusive contract to the tight-fisted Sam Goldwyn.

Happily, Milestone got his way. As a celebrated director of such war movies as *All Quiet on the Western Front*, still one of the greatest antiwar movies ever made, his special talent was essential to the studio bosses' role in Hollywood's war effort. It was wise to defer to his wishes. Later, in 1945, he directed *A Walk in the Sun*, one of the most honest and penetrating studio films ever made about GIs in combat.

The New York Premiere

Goldwyn had arranged a gala premiere opening in New York for *The North Star*. Never one to leave anything to the whims of fate when he could take charge, he decided to call in a few paybacks in order to stack the critical odds in his new film's favor. This gambit was not entirely successful. As soon as *The North Star* opened, it became the center of a controversy that involved William Randolph Hearst, Henry Luce of Time-Life Inc., Sam Goldwyn, and various other members of the press on both sides of the political spectrum. Hearst was such a rabid anticommunist that the most Goldwyn had gotten from him was an agreement not to prejudge the film. Henry Luce was much more amenable. After its lavish opening, he called the film a "Cinemilestone!" Hearst's major New York paper, the *New York Journal-American*, came out on the morning after the premiere with a very positive and enthusiastic review. Goldwyn and everyone else connected with *The North Star* were thrilled. Hearst was decidedly not. That morning's review had slipped by him. He made sure that the next edition of the *Journal-American* reversed its positive review. It also made the outrageous suggestion that the film was not only Red propaganda but Nazi propaganda. Hearst's evening tabloid headlined its review, "UNADULTERATED SOVIET PROPAGANDA." Other reviews across the country were mixed except in the Hearst papers, where they were unanimously bad.

Despite an extensive advertising campaign, the picture never made its money back. Some years later, after it had been sold to television in the early 1950s, in an effort not to catch the attention of any Red-baiters gearing up for the high times of the McCarthy era, its name was changed to *Armored Attack*. Any indications that the film was about Russia were erased as completely as possible, including most of Aaron Copland's wonderful score, into which he had incorporated some stirring Russian folk songs. The new promotional material said that the whole movie took place in Hungary.

Turning Eighteen

My second film was the first that Darryl F. Zanuck produced for 20th Century-Fox after his discharge from the Army Signal Corps. *The Purple Heart* was a small film about the first American plane shot down over Japan in World War II. The crew was captured, tortured, tried, and executed by the Japanese. Aside from the Asian-American actors playing the Japanese, the cast consisted solely of the seven members of the bomber's crew, featuring Dana Andrews; Richard Conte, a brooding Italian-American leading man of the 1940s and 1950s; Sam Levene, a marvelous Jewish character actor from New York, who was equally at home onstage and before the cameras, and me. I was the kid—a sort of mascot—on the film. I had turned eighteen shortly after the film started shooting, which meant that I would be enlisting in the armed forces as soon as we wrapped. Although no one ever mentioned it, I'm sure everyone was aware of it.

Millie felt that it was important for us to bond as a group. When he arranged for us all to share one large dressing room adjacent to the sound-stage, no one complained even though a few wary looks were exchanged. Every actor cherishes his own private bit of space. It was fine with me. I was eager to bond with anyone. Again, I made a concerted effort with Dana. He warmed up a bit more on this, our second film together, particularly as the day wore on. As usual, Millie was right. We quickly became a band of brothers. I was the youngest. Sam Levene became my father and Dana Andrews my big brother.

Halfway into the film, my Japanese captors cut out my tongue—remember, this was a wartime film, with every propaganda stop pulled out. Whenever I started to speak or ask a question after this barbaric incident, I was shushed by both Millie and/or the other actors. Frustrating, yes, but they made sure I got into my character's head and stayed there.

A Real Movie Studio!

Working at 20th Century-Fox was far more exciting than working at my studio, because Goldwyn only did one film at a time, and often no more than one a year. At 20th they turned out pictures like products on an assembly line, so a whole cast of great Hollywood characters paraded before my wide and inexperienced eyes. While we were filming *The Purple Heart* on the Fox lot, Betty Grable, who along with Rita Hayworth was every GI's favorite pinup during World War II, was shooting *Pin Up Girl*. Roddy McDowall (*How Green Was My Valley*, *Lassie Come Home*, *The White Cliffs of Dover*) was finishing *My Friend Flicka*; Orson Welles and Joan Fontaine, who was so good in Alfred Hitchcock's *Rebecca*, were working on *Jane Eyre*, which included a young and very beautiful Elizabeth Taylor and a wonderful young actress, Peggy Ann Garner. Dana was getting ready to start *Laura* with Gene Tierney as soon as we finished our film.

It was an adventure just having lunch in a commissary filled with actors and extras decked out in splendid costumes, a bit like eating at a spectacular masquerade ball. Betty Grable, usually in feathers or sequins or both, may have been the studio's biggest star, but she came equipped with the soul of a chorus girl who relished a good dirty joke. She supposedly had it stipulated in her contract that Freddy Ney, an outrageously funny chorus boy from New York, was always directly behind her in big musical numbers. His filthy, stage-whispered running commentary kept a big smile on her face at all times. Elizabeth Taylor looked like a perfect porcelain doll in her mid-nineteenth-century costume from *Jane Eyre*, but even at that early age she was an earthy, no-nonsense young lady. Gene Tierney in modern dress was breathtakingly lovely and equally warm and gracious. The young and then trim Orson Welles was an overpowering presence. With his piercing gaze and a voice that reverberated throughout the dining room, I found him too intimidating to approach.

The first star I met in the commissary was "The Brazilian Bombshell," Carmen Miranda. Even in her ten-inch wedgies, she was tiny, a dynamo with a great big laugh, dressed like an oversized fruit salad. She was constantly in motion. With all her baubles, bangles, and beads, you could hear her coming a block away. It was easy to see how she almost stole every Betty Grable movie in which she appeared doing her "Souse American" song and dance numbers.

I particularly loved the 20th Century-Fox musicals, because their colors seemed brighter than those of the other studios and because nobody aged in them. In *Alexander's Ragtime Band*, Don Ameche, Tyrone Power, and Alice Faye looked just as young at the end of the movie, when they were all supposed to have aged forty years, as they did at the beginning. The same youth and beauty principle held fast for Betty Grable, June Haver, and John Payne in *The Dolly Sisters*. Maybe the women had their hair in pigtails at the beginning of the movie and in a bun at the end, and maybe the men's sideburns got a touch of gray as they aged, but that was about it. Perhaps we should lay the blame for America's obsession with youth and beauty at the feet of Darryl F. Zanuck.

At every major studio there was always a next-in-line being groomed to replace a star who got too big for the ruling mogul's comfort. For example, at MGM, Louis B. Mayer had Deborah Kerr ready to step into Greer Garson's lovely pumps; at Columbia, Harry Cohn began grooming Kim Novak when Rita Hayworth seemed irreplaceable; and at Fox, Betty Grable was brought in to be ready when Alice Faye decided she had had enough. The situation was the same for the men, just not as obvious.

Except for some sporadic dating in high school, I'd never had a real social life. During my first week at 20th, I met June Haver, a very pretty little blonde whom I liked and dated for a while. That word still signified a very chaste encounter in 1943. June, who was being groomed by the studio to replace Betty Grable if or when that became necessary, although lovely and talented, did not possess the wattage of Betty's star power. She later quit movies and became a nun. Later still, she left the convent, married an older actor, Fred MacMurray, and never returned to films.

I liked June, but dating her exposed me to the hyped-up world of the studio publicity machine that manufactured fake love lives of their young hopefuls for the fan magazines. They went into overdrive for us. Everywhere we went we were met by and pursued by photographers. We were featured in every fan magazine and every gossip column in Hollywood. YOUNG LOVE BLOSSOMS AT 20TH!, or FARLEY & JUNE MEANT FOR EACH OTHER!, or HOLLYWOOD'S NEWEST YOUNG LOVERS! the gossip columns and fan magazines shouted on a very false note. It didn't matter that we didn't even know each other that well. June had already done several movies and was not surprised by the commotion, but I was in shock. I don't think she liked it any more than I did, but she was not caught off guard the way I was. I hated it and never learned how to be comfortable with it.

There was a schoolhouse on the lot and any actors under eighteen were required to attend classes whenever we were not being used on set. The actors in our group included Elizabeth, Roddy, Peggy Ann, and several other young girls and guys whose names I don't remember. One name that none of the boys could ever forget was Linda Darnell. She was making a movie called *Summer Storm*. Whenever she appeared in class in her costumes, which emphasized every traffic-stopping curve, lessons went right out the window for the guys. I don't think Linda realized the effect she had. She was as shy and sweet as she was voluptuous. School on the lot was so much fun that I continued there even after I turned eighteen.

Before starting work at 20th, I had informed my mother that she would no longer be driving me to the studio and staying on set with me as my chaperone. Since I was about to be eighteen, I no longer needed to be accompanied at work by a parent. That was an unexpected blow for her and a furious fight ensued, but I refused to back down.

Neither she nor my father was happy with what they considered my premature declaration of independence, but my salary was easing our financial worries, and that helped me get my way. The only negative was that I would have to drive the funny family car. The beige Willys Overland with aquamarine fenders was all that remained of a more prosperous time in San Jose. I never saw another car like it. Early in the war, Willys had stopped making cars and started making Jeeps. Our car looked so odd that people pointed and cracked jokes. I was mortified. Looking back, I can see what an ungrateful, insecure, self-absorbed kid I was . . . in other words, a typical teenager.

Aside from a crash landing in a rice field, our scenes in *The Purple Heart* were staged in a studio mockup of a Japanese courtroom. Sam Levene took me under his wing and taught me some tricks of the trade. For example, he explained how not to fall into the inexperienced film actor's trap of listening only when you are also speaking in a scene. Listening intently to everyone at all times put you in the moment in every scene.

When I got home at night, all I talked about was how much fun the studio was, and how funny, kind, patient, and helpful Sam was. I must have carried on about him a bit too much, because one night at dinner, my father suddenly shouted, "At least you could get a white man for a friend!" At first, I didn't know what he meant, and then I got it.

In a flash of anger, I threw my water in his face and stormed out. With the drinking, the fighting, and the neighbors calling the police, things were spinning out of control on Maxwellton Road. The truth was, my parents had never accepted the comedown from their grand life in San Jose, were unable to make any real friends in Los Angeles, and, like so many who are forced to stare failure in the face and are ashamed to do so, turned to mutual recrimination, arguments, and alcohol.

Roddy McDowall and I became friends at the studio. He was a few years younger than I and a smart, decent kid. He invited me to his home for dinner one night, and I accepted gladly.

Roddy's family had moved to Hollywood from England before the war and lived in a big old house near the Fox studio, where Roddy was under contract. His father was off to war in the Royal Navy, his sister in high school in Beverly Hills. His mom, a large, warm, enveloping type, welcomed me as family. At dinner, we all laughed a lot, and when she asked if I would like to spend the night I jumped at the invitation, because the whole experience was so different from the drinking and fighting during meals at my house. I called my parents and asked permission to stay at Roddy's. I told them we both had early calls, and that I was practically next door to the studio, which would save my mother from getting up at 5:00 A.M. to make my breakfast. Roddy's mother got on the phone and confirmed the arrangement. This was the first of many nights of fun and laughter there while I was shooting *The Purple Heart*.

I had turned eighteen before the film finished, and my temporary deferment expired as soon as we wrapped. It was time for me to really say goodbye. I said my farewells to everyone on the set at 20th. Dana could not have been warmer. Hardest of all was saying goodbye to Millie, because I felt he had put himself on the line for me. When I went to talk with Sam, he said, "Forget it, kid. You ain't getting rid of me that easy. You call me and let me know what day you're leaving because Roddy and I are coming to see you off." I gave him a big hug and got out of there before he could see my tears.

The next day I went to tell everyone at my studio that I was going to enlist. I couldn't get in to see Mr. Goldwyn, so I just said goodbye through his secretary. Then I cleared out my dressing room and went to find Mr. McIntyre. He wasn't there. There was nothing filming at the studio, so I was not surprised to find it somewhat deserted. I walked through the soundstage where I had done my first movie. It was empty and dark. I couldn't even conjure any ghosts of the small Russian town of North Star. It was disconcerting to leave the studio to which I was under contract with no real farewell. I felt as if I was just fading away.

Actor Aweigh

I went downtown to the induction center with a couple of my high school buddies. We'd decided to join the Navy because they heard that it was the best branch of the service. We were herded upstairs for physicals, and then I was sent before the chief petty officer in charge. I gave him my papers. He asked, "You want regular Navy?"

Unaware that there was any other kind, I said, "Sure." He stamped my papers, gave me a copy, and sent me downstairs to rejoin my friends. One asked what I'd signed up for. "Regular Navy," I said.

"Are you crazy? Things are finally starting to go our way. The regular Navy is six years. You should have just signed for the duration. With any luck, we will get out a lot sooner than that."

I raced back upstairs, arriving just as the petty officer was covering his typewriter. I grabbed him. "Please, please, I've just made a terrible mistake!" He was understanding, thank goodness, and changed my papers.

I received a call from the studio publicity department at 20th. They had obtained a two-week extension for me to do publicity on *The Purple Heart* before I had to report for duty. This meant that my high school friends shipped out before I did. That made me a little apprehensive. I would be taking this next step in my life all alone.

Two weeks later, when I said goodbye to my parents, my mother, through her tears, promised hand-on-heart that they would stop drinking and fighting and would make a happy home for me when I returned. I knew my dad was angry because I told him Sam Levene and Roddy were driving me to Union Station to see me off. Even in the short time I knew them, I felt closer to them than to my parents. It seemed forever until my train arrived, but Sam managed to keep Roddy and me in stitches while we waited. I finally made them leave, but watching them disappear through the crowd was the loneliest moment of my life.

I don't know how much time passed before the loudspeaker summoned us aboard. I woke up later in a bunk still in my clothes. I had no idea how I got there. Suddenly a voice announced: "Lights out, NOW!" Someone in a nearby bunk began to strum a guitar and sing softly. For the next couple of days, I felt lost in a strange world. I supposed everyone else felt the same way. I made no effort to make any friends. I just stared out the window watching the countryside pass by. I'm not sure how many days it took to reach boot camp in Farragut, Idaho, landlocked in the desolate white-and-gray landscape near the western Canadian border.

When the train finally jerked to a stop, we dry-land sailors were herded into a single line that stretched as far as the eye could see. In an hour or so, I entered a small cafeteria, picked up a metal tray, and went down the line without knowing or caring what was being dumped into its compartments. When I emerged, I just kept going. I must have bumped into somebody or something. When my loaded tray hit the floor, I still just kept going. I followed the flow to a big building that looked like a soundstage. Inside men from the train were setting up cots to sleep on. I set one up, fell on it, and had my own lights out.

I was awakened by all kinds of loud noises—loudspeakers, people yelling, and bright lights. Everyone was running outside even though it was pitch black, like some crazy jailbreak. I followed the others and came to a mess hall. I had no idea what I was served, but it was hot, I ate it, and I felt a little better. An announcement blared over the loudspeakers for all new recruits to assemble on the parade ground "ON THE DOUBLE!!!" It was just getting light as we ran outside, milling around in confusion until several petty officers formed us into some rough sort of order. We were then sent off in alphabetical order to a supply tent where they issued our gear and sent us off to our barracks, where we were then assigned bunks.

I sat on my bunk wondering what was going to happen to me next. Three sailors whose stripes meant they were already more than recruits introduced themselves to me. They were obviously friends and obviously gay. They recognized me from *The North Star* and enthusiastically offered to look after me, show me the ropes. One of them worked in the barbershop, and the others were in the medical department. They said that anytime I needed anything, I should look them up and I would be taken care of. They had connections. Everything they said seemed loaded with innuendo. I didn't know what to say or do. I was a pretty green eighteen-year-old. I stammered my thanks and got very busy stowing my gear. With effusive goodbyes and don't-forget-to-look-us-ups, they disappeared into the crowd. I looked around to see if anyone had taken any notice, but everyone seemed to be too busy trying to figure out what to put where. As it turned out, those guys were always there to help me through the rigors of boot camp and sought no favors in return, sexual or otherwise.

As new recruits, we were a mixed crew, fresh-faced eighteen-year-olds like me and family men of forty. Washington had extended the draft age because of the desperate need for replacements as the war dragged on. Not only were we a strange assortment, so was our equipment. We had no guns. We marched in the snow with brooms. Just beyond the barracks was a large lake where we practiced launching lifeboats. It seemed like an exercise in futility, since the lake was frozen solid, but we slid around launching our boats, trying not to let them collide and to avoid hurting each other. The base was windy and bitterly cold. In some perverse way I enjoyed it. It was so different from everything in my native California. The surrounding snow-covered mountains were beautiful. I kept to myself, and made no real friends. There was even a showing of *Purple Heart*, but most of my dry-land shipmates gave me a wide berth. I think they were too shy, or maybe they just didn't know what to say. The exception of course was my three gay buddies. They thought the movie was fabulous and wanted to know all about Dana Andrews. They thought he was fabulous as well.

Finally it was time for graduation, a sorry affair that had us marching with our broomsticks to strains of "Anchors Aweigh" piped in on loudspeakers in the midst of a blinding snowstorm. We stumbled through it and received orders for our next assignment and a bus ticket for our last leave. I had a ten-day layover in Los Angeles before I was supposed to ship out, so I decided to splurge and bought a first-class air ticket. At the airport a young ensign behind me said, "Aren't you in the wrong line, swabbie?" I looked him straight in the eye, smiled, took a long beat, and replied, "Don't worry about me—SIR. I can afford it—SIR." It was my first trip on an airplane.

Back home my parents were on their best behavior—only one drink before dinner—and the hateful fighting had diminished to minor bickering. My mom thought I was much too skinny and cooked up a storm. I spent some time with Roddy and his family and saw some of my high school pals and of course Sam Levene—this time with no comment from my father.

I went to the studio, but Mr. Goldwyn was again in conference, too busy to be seen. I went to the casting office and found Bob McIntyre, who couldn't get over the fact that I was in uniform and ready to ship out. He made me promise to stay in touch and told me that great things were going to happen when I got back from the war. If I hadn't seen him, it would have been as if my being in the movies had never happened.

At Sea

When my leave was up, I reported to the naval base in Long Beach at the crack of dawn. This time, at my request, no one saw me off. I was put on a bus for San Francisco with a middle-aged father. It seemed strange, only the two of us, but just before we left Long Beach, we stopped at the brig to pick up about twenty prisoners. I guess the Navy was really getting desperate. Instead of being punished for whatever they had done, the detainees were being released back to active duty—and did they ever raise hell on that bus!

The sun was setting when we arrived at Treasure Island, where the cruiser that was to serve as our troopship was docked. We were ordered up the gangway, checked in, and directed down to the cargo deck, a big empty space with no lights containing a freestanding upright piano, a bunch of burlap sacks lashed to the bulkhead, and a lot of unassembled cots piled in the center of the hold. Somehow, with the help of a few flashlights and a lot of cooperation, we managed to assemble our cots in the darkness. I tossed my seabag on mine, and made my way back up topside. The officer on deck said that we could have one last night free before setting sail for Hawaii, but that we had to be back on board no later than 6:00 A.M. I was down the gangway like a shot to grab a cab and head straight for the USO in downtown San Francisco. I found the entertainment desk, asked what was going on in town, and the hostess gave me a ticket to the ballet. I must have looked skeptical, because she smiled sweetly and told me to give it a try, I might like it. In any case, it was the only free ticket she had left. So I found my way to the San Francisco opera house, an impressive place, and saw my first ballet.

The first half of the evening's program was *Rodeo*, with music by Aaron Copland and choreography by Agnes de Mille. Not only did I love it because I knew Copland and thought his music was great, but I had never seen dancing like this. I had expected girls in tutus and men in tights—no way. The cowboys on the stage were masculine and athletic, and their dancing was spectacular. No other world existed for me at that moment. I didn't want it to end. When it did, I found myself cheering and whistling as if the home team had just won the football championship. It seemed impossible to top that—until the second half. *Fancy Free* is a tale of three sailors on their last night's leave in New York before shipping out. Their adventures on this final night, their mishaps and mixups, their search for love and their heartaches, were set in dance by Jerome Robbins to a wonderfully jazzy score by Leonard Bernstein. It was as if they were doing my story. This was also *my* last night before shipping out. I was so involved with what was going on onstage that I didn't even let it get me down that, unlike the sailors in the ballet, I had no buddies with me on the town, and no beautiful girl to kiss goodbye. I practically danced all the way back to the USO. At 5:00 A.M. everyone who had slept there was awakened and herded onto a bus to the Navy Yard and our ship . . . dreams over, back to reality.

I went below to find my bunk and some shuteye, but I couldn't sleep and I felt starved of air. Somehow I made it topside and gulped in some cool air. As I looked around, I realized quite a number of sailors from our bus seemed to be missing. Half the men from brig seemed to have jumped ship. I did find the middle-aged father, and we talked. He had five kids and not a lot of money. The call-up was hard on him and his family, but it was 1943 and we were fighting on two fronts. Everybody was being called up.

With a shudder, the ship began to move. It wasn't long before we passed under the Golden Gate Bridge. I walked forward. My mind was a jumble: Where was I going? Would I come back? Would my parents continue their good behavior, or would they eventually destroy each other? Would anyone ever want me to make another movie? Would I ever get laid?

I felt lightheaded and threw up all over the deck. I just walked away from it. I had no idea how to get back to my bunk and was too dizzy to search around, so I just lay down on the deck and curled up. I don't know how much time passed before I felt a gentle kick. A chief petty officer told me I couldn't sleep there but had to go below to my assigned quarters with the others. I explained my predicament, and he guided me to the right hatch with instructions to proceed to sick bay if I didn't feel better in a few hours. I thanked him and went below, where I stumbled around in the dark until I found the cot with my seabag on it.

I was out again until I heard the call for chow; even the thought of food made me queasy. I returned to the deck for fresh air, and after my stomach calmed a bit, I tried to find the doctor. As soon as I went below I was sick again. Throwing up combined with the dry heaves continued sporadically for the rest of the voyage, which took seventeen days because of the ship's evasive antisubmarine maneuvers. I never found the sick bay, and I was never able to keep down more than a little clear broth and that only on calm days.

In heavy seas one night, the burlap sacks broke loose from the bulkheads, spilling clouds of white flour that dusted us all. The piano broke loose, sailors were run over, and half a dozen had bones broken. Somehow I stayed in one piece during that hellish night, but when we finally docked at Honolulu, I had to be carried off the ship. I had lost twenty-three pounds during our seventeen days at sea. The receiving officer took one look and sent me straight to the hospital. After several days of rehydration, the Navy decided that my war would best be spent on shore duty in Hawaii.

Hawaii

I was assigned to the cleanup crew at an enlisted men's club, a Quonset hut with an open-air bar at the end of Waikiki Beach. About eight men served there, plus a small band. We also doubled as the short-order cooks. We served soft drinks, 3.2 beer—the infamous low-alcohol beverage served by the military at enlisted men's clubs—hamburgers, and hot dogs. The band played evenings to entertain the troops. There was a dance floor but no girls. After enough 3.2 beer, some of the sailors would clown around and jitterbug with each other. Every now and then a couple of WAVES, the Navy's name for female sailors, would show up, and we all would trip over each other trying to dance with them, but that was it. The beer ended up being the only boost to troop morale, and some of the drunken brawls were terrific.

One part of my job was magical. It was being in charge of the garbage detail. Every day or two, we would load up the garbage truck, and I would drive it through pineapple fields to the dump. It was my quiet time, the only time I was totally on my own, and it was when I fell completely in love with the beauty of Hawaii. It rained every afternoon. If I was able to time it correctly, I would see two beautiful rainbows sparkle to life over Diamond Head just as the sun reappeared. My buddies at the club called me a nutcase for being so enthusiastic about the garbage run, but I preferred to take the heat rather than risk competition for my own private rainbow detail.

After about six months, I was reassigned to a unit in Honolulu that worked with Army Special Services. Almost immediately, I managed to get myself out of the Navy barracks I had been assigned to and into one assigned to the musicians. They were the most fun, in part because they paid the least attention to the rules and regulations—what the enlisted men call "chickenshit." I'd gotten to know some of them at the enlisted men's club in Waikiki, so I had a couple of friends. Those guys knew every out-of-the-way bar and club in Honolulu. If you felt like a good steak or a pair of silk stockings for a special date, they knew where to go, and they were also experts on where the prettiest girls hung out. Even better, their barracks was filled with music all the time. They had records of all the latest Broadway shows as well as classics and the best jazz and popular music. It was there that I heard Mozart for first time, and Dinah Shore singing with the Lower Basin Street Society, and Benny Goodman recorded live at Carnegie Hall. It was also the first time I ever heard a recording of a Broadway show, Rodgers and Hammerstein's *Carousel.* I was so caught up by its lyrical beauty and emotional power that I didn't know whether to laugh or cry. I think I did a little of both. The nice thing was that I didn't have to hide my reactions from the musicians. Even the most hard-boiled of them understood that kind of reaction to a terrific piece of music.

The Army Special Services Unit was under the command of the great classical actor Maurice Evans, who put together and arranged entertainment for all the troops in the Pacific. These entertainments varied from comedians like Bob Hope, who toured with a band, a girl singer, and sometimes Bing Crosby, to pinup girls like Rita Hayworth and Betty Grable or glamour queens like Marlene Dietrich and Hedy Lamarr. They, like other great patriotic stars, some of whom came from Broadway with a complete cast, would tour just behind the battlefronts.

The Navy had no Special Services unit of its own, so were completely dependent upon the Army. On the other hand, the Army had to depend on us to help coordinate the movement and scheduling of these entertainments. That was where my superior and I came in.

Our unit consisted of a resentful Navy lieutenant, Chuck Garvin, and me. We shared an office that had been set up in a small Quonset hut down the hill from the much larger Army Special Services Unit. Scheduling these shows wasn't made any easier by my mucho macho boss. He thought what we were doing was a big waste of his and the Navy's time and energy. He didn't believe that "a bunch of fags prancing around on a stage" had anything to do with morale-building, and he especially hated taking orders from Maurice Evans, "a fucking Army actor, no less!" Garvin told me, "When you have to go up there to the fucking Army, just do what you have to and get out of there like your ass is on fire! They are all fucking pansies up there, and I don't want any of that rubbing off on you." In all my work with Evans's unit—and I was up there several times a day—no one ever said or did anything remotely suggestive, although I have to admit that the sergeant serving as Major Evans's private secretary did wear a lot of makeup.

Maurice Evans—Major Evans, as he then was—had some great talent working for him. One with whom I became friendly was Carl Reiner. Carl was only a couple of years older than I. He was then still just a performer, but his wonderfully skewed take on life indicated a talent that would go far. He did not disappoint. From the mid-1950s to the mid-1960s he won eight Emmy Awards as writer, performer, and producer. One of his best productions is his gifted son, Rob.

I recently saw Carl for the first time since those days in Hawaii, and he was still as warm and funny as I remembered. It was at the opening of *Mr. Goldwyn*, a one-man show in New York featuring the comic legend Alan King playing my old boss. It had a running bit with Goldwyn's secretary buzzing him repeatedly in the course of the evening to say: "Mr. Goldwyn, Farley Granger is on the phone again. He says he wants out of his contract." Alan, with perfect comic timing, built Goldwyn's reactions from annoyance to exasperation to an explosion that brought the house down. I was there on opening night and somehow he got word that I was in the audience. During his curtain calls he called for the spotlight to find me and introduced me to the audience as "my co-star—who has finally gotten out of his contract!" Later, at a cast party at the Lambs' Club that was attended by everyone from Billy Crystal to Walter Cronkite, I saw Carl again and we were able to reminisce a bit more about Hawaii.

I kept busy in my little hut working, scheduling, and watching the scorpions skitter by. After an endless nine months, Lieutenant Garvin was transferred and replaced by Lieutenant Bill Militich. He was a good man who thought we were doing important work, but his real passion was golf. He left all of the scheduling details up to me, which I didn't mind, but paperwork and details were not my strong points, resulting in several near-disasters. I once put an extra day on the calendar in November ("Thirty days hath September, April, June, and . . . ???"). I booked three shows in different areas of the Pacific on November 31st. I caught my mistake just in time. Militich even left the golf course and jumped in to help. Aside from a few other similar last-minute near-misses, it was mostly tedious and lonely in my little hut with just me and the scorpions.

My dream of getting away from my desk job by somehow getting myself officially involved as an actor with any of the performers or troupes passing through
didn't look like it was going to happen.

Gertrude Lawrence had toured the South Pacific in her one-woman show
singing Nöel Coward songs. She was a unique performer best known in her native England as a farceur and light comedienne, but she was not that well
known in the United States. Her strong point was a brittle sophistication,
which had lot to do with British class distinction and nothing to do with sex
appeal—all in all, not the best choice for the troops. Coward's songs are charming, but I don't think there was a soldier, sailor, or marine in the entire Pacific
who gave a rat's ass whether or not "Mad Dogs and Englishmen Go Out in the
Noonday Sun." Gertie bombed, but Miss Lawrence was not stupid. She quickly
realized her mistake and regrouped. She came back to Hawaii and decided to
put on Noël Coward's brilliant comedy *Blithe Spirit* for a short run in Honolulu.
Major Evans brought in most of the cast who had performed it on Broadway to
support her, and gave it a smashing production. The troops loved it, and she
was redeemed. Evans's crew, against all advice, then put on a modern version of
The Mikado. Much to everyone's surprise, it was a huge success. Seeing the troops
forget the miseries of their wartime existence for a few hours, hearing them
laugh and cheer, confirmed my feelings about what a wrongheaded jerk Lieutenant Garvin had been.

Sex, Sex, Sex, Sex . . .

I was thinking about sex all the time. I was twenty and still a virgin. My hormones had long ago gone ballistic, and I was ready to join them. Something
had to be done soon! One of the musicians, Ray, the horn player, seemed to
know everyone in Honolulu. A young, single man, he was sympathetic to my
situation and knew of an estate on the outskirts of town that was being run by
the domestic staff as a private club catering to a select few for "special entertainment." Ray said it was a beautiful place, far off the beaten path, a well-kept
secret and therefore very safe. The girls were all well educated, spoke English,
and were also under the supervision of a Navy M.D. It was frequented mostly
by officers and a few well-placed civilians. No questions were asked as long as
you could pay the bill and behaved like a gentleman. The wealthy owners had
returned to the safety of the continental United States, and their trusted staff
remained to care for the estate. The staff was doing its job and at the same time

putting the manicured property to patriotic good use. Only a few customers were allowed every evening, because the man in charge wanted to keep the operation very low-key for obvious reasons. It was a perfect setup: many bedrooms, an open bar, and a pool house with bar.

All I had to do was pick the night, said Ray, and he would make all the arrangements for me. He recommended the pool house, because I could enter through a garden gate at the back of the estate, which would help narrow the chances that I would run into anyone who would recognize me.

The big night finally arrived. I headed out by taxi to become a man at last! Even in the bright moonlight, I could see nothing from the road except tropical foliage and a gated driveway. I walked around to what looked like a service road and continued several hundred yards until I saw an archway. A Hawaiian dressed like a houseman stood in the shadows under the oleander. I approached him and identified myself, and he politely asked me for "the membership dues." I paid him, in cash as Ray had instructed me, and he led me down the garden path to the pool house. He pointed out the fully stocked bar, showed me where to change, told me that my hostess would be down from the house in a few minutes, and disappeared into the night.

I looked around for a bathing suit, but all I could find were several clean thick terrycloth robes. I was beginning to feel a little nervous, but I got out of my uniform, put on one of the robes, which felt and smelled great, and walked past the bar out to the pool. The moonlight sparkling on the water made it look very inviting. I decided it would be a good idea to work off some of my nervous energy with a quick swim. I dropped the robe and dove in. The water felt great and smelled as if it had been scented with sandalwood. I swam several quick laps, then turned on my back and floated for a few minutes, feeling like a million. Then I swam back toward the pool house and climbed out. My robe was gone.

I was looking for it when a soft voice from the shadows called out, "I have it here, Mr. Farley." Walking toward me and holding out my robe was an absolutely ravishing young Hawaiian woman. She had on a simple white silk dress, and her skin looked like pale golden brown velvet. I was speechless. I instinctively covered my nakedness with my hands. She laughed softly, instructed me to turn around, draped the robe over my shoulders, and whispered into my ear, "You must not be so bashful, Mr. Farley. Here in Hawaii we are very comfortable with our bodies, and yours is very beautiful." I stammered out my thanks for this compliment. She laughed again and said, "Why don't we go have a drink?" She turned and walked to the bar while I quickly tied on my robe and followed her. As she walked behind the bar she asked, "What would you like, Mr. Farley?" I said that I would like her to call me Farley and that I would have whatever she was having.

"All right, Farley," she replied, "then you must call me Liana, and I will make us a rum and Coke." She did, and we just sat and talked through a couple of drinks.

She came from an old island family, was well educated, and had no idea who I was. Maybe it was the rum, maybe it was Liana, probably it was both, but suddenly I felt quite relaxed. She must have sensed this, because she stood up, took my hand, and said, "Come with me." I went with her into the bedroom.

I was only in a robe, and her silk dress was little more than a slip, so I was ready to tear into action. Liana stopped me before I could do anything. She made me remove her clothes, one article at a time, very slowly; first her shoes, then her belt, then her dress, one shoulder strap at a time until the whole thing slid off her. It was incredibly erotic. She did the same with my robe, one shoulder at a time, then the belt, and it dropped off. I slipped off her panties and pulled her down on the bed with me. We kissed, then I rolled her over and underneath me, ready for my big moment. She made me stop and slow down to follow her instructions.

That night, in the several hours I was with her, this beautiful Hawaiian girl taught me a great deal about women and about how to make love to them. I did not absorb it all at once, but the first time was wonderful for me, and I hoped the second time was wonderful for us both. She said it was.

After we made love the second time, I fell asleep in her arms. When I woke up about an hour or so later, Liana was gone. I decided on another swim before going back to the base. Robeless and proud of myself, I walked out to the pool and dove in. I felt as if I could swim back to California. Finally I climbed out and walked toward the pool house to get dressed. As I neared the veranda, I saw the glow of a cigarette. A deep voice said, "Mr. Granger, I think you are out of uniform." That stopped me for a moment. Then I walked closer, resisting the impulse to cover up again. A very handsome lieutenant commander stood up in the shadows and held out his hand. His shirt collar was opened, his tie was loosened, and his white jacket was draped over the back of his chair. He looked so much like the actor Sterling Hayden that I must have done a double take. He mistook my confusion and grinned, "Yes, I know, so am I—out of uniform, that is—but you've sure got me beat." I stood frozen in place, not knowing what to do. He grinned and said: "Why don't you get your robe and a drink. It might make introductions a little easier." I went inside, put on my robe, and, following orders, came back out with a drink. He stood again. As we shook hands, he said, "I'm Archie. I know who you are, Farley; I've seen your films. You are a very talented young man." I must have blushed. I had no idea how to answer Archie, whoever he was. He grinned again and said, "You'd better get used to compliments if you intend to stay in movies, because you are growing up very nicely." I think I just stood there in silence until he said, "Why don't you sit down and try to relax." I did, and after we had talked for a while, I actually did begin to relax for the second time that night.

He knew all about Lillian Hellman, Aaron Copland, Lewis Milestone, and *The North Star*. He knew a great deal about the movie business and the arts in general. He was a graduate of the Naval Academy and had been serving as a flight instructor at Edwards Air Force base in Washington, D.C. His request for a transfer to active duty had finally been granted. This was his last night in Hawaii. He was off the next day to take command of a fighter squadron in the South Pacific. When he asked, I told him how I got a contract with Goldwyn and what it had been like making the films. We talked about my last night in San Francisco seeing *Fancy Free* and *Rodeo* and how excited I had been. He said that he had seen them in D.C. and felt exactly the same, but he had been there with some friends who might not have understood if he danced home.

With a nervous laugh, I rose to fix another drink. It was after 1:00 A.M. and I realized it would be hard to find a cab to get back to base. Reluctantly, I said that I'd better get dressed and leave. He asked why I was going so soon, and I told him. Not to worry—he had a car and would drive me to his downtown hotel, where I could always get a cab. I agreed happily and went to make drinks. He followed me, and we continued talking. I mixed two drinks, put his down on the bar in front of him, and started out with mine. He grabbed my arm, took the drink out of my hand, looked into my eyes, and pulled me into his arms. After the first instant of shock and surprise, I struggled for a moment to pull away. Then I realized how excited I was. Before I knew it, we were in the bedroom and out of our clothes. The next three hours passed in what seemed like three minutes. It was almost 5:00 A.M. We scrambled back into uniform, ran out to Archie's car, and sped downtown. He stopped behind his hotel, took me in his arms, and said, "Take care of yourself, kid, because, I promise, I will find you when this mess is over." For a very long time after the war ended, I hoped he would reappear in my life, but I never saw or heard from him again.

It was a while before I was able to sort through my new experiences. I lost my virginity twice in one night. Maybe it was good that I had waited so long. Otherwise, how would I have had the stamina? The way I have lived my life ever since was set on that fateful night in Hawaii. I knew that what had happened between Liana and me was wonderful and right. I was confused by the fact that what had happened between Archie and me felt just as wonderful and just as right. I know most people would not see it that way, but try as I did, I could not feel any sense of guilt. Liana and I had pleasured each other, which made us both happy and had harmed no one. Archie and I had brought each other happiness and pleasure, and we also had harmed no one. What had passed between us was no one's business but ours. I finally came to the conclusion that for me, everything I had done that night was as natural and good as it had felt. The fact that I had to be secretive about Archie was a question of public perception and military policy, not of morals. I didn't care what

others might feel or think, but I wasn't stupid. I knew discretion was important then, but I looked forward to the time when I could be myself. And that's
how I have lived and still continue to live my life. Fortunately, it has been
many years since I felt the need to be secretive.

After several visits to see Liana again, she asked if we could meet in Honolulu like any other couple. Her feelings for me were too real for her to go on
accepting payment for us to be together. I felt the same way, and we spent many
wonderful nights in her tiny flat in downtown Honolulu before the war ended
and I shipped out.

I thought about Archie all the time. I knew his assignment was dangerous,
and all I could do was hope that he survived. Although I was still somewhat
naïve, I was not stupid. I was in the Navy. I never sought or responded to the
opportunity for that kind of male companionship again. At that time, "discretion is the better part of valor" was much more than a cliché, it was a necessity.
Now, I am a strong supporter of the Servicemembers Legal Defense Network.
The government policy of "don't ask, don't tell" has proven itself to be as un-
just as it is unnecessary. And I still wonder why my country, which I was as
proud to serve as I am proud to be a part of, is the last major power in the
Western world to address this particular social injustice.

I never have felt the need to belong to any exclusive, self-defining, or special
group. I find it difficult to answer questions about "gay life" in Hollywood
when I was living and working there. There were, of course, gay cliques, but I
had no close friends who belonged to any of them, and I had no desire to become involved with any of them.

I was never ashamed, and I never felt the need to explain or apologize for my
relationships to anyone. I had many gay friends, but more of my friends were
straight and most married with families. The ratio of my gay to straight friends
was probably in direct proportion to that of gay to straight people in all aspects
of the film business and society in general. I have loved men. I have loved women.
I will talk with affection and without guilt or remorse about both in this book.

V-J Day

Franklin D. Roosevelt died suddenly in April 1945. Our president, our
commander in chief, was gone. I don't think anyone imagined that could ever
happen. I know I thought he would always be there to lead us. The sense of
grief was palpable. Harry Truman was sworn in. After FDR, his speeches

seemed flat and uninspiring. I wondered if the war would ever end. Then, once again, everything suddenly changed. The atom bombs were dropped on Hiroshima and Nagasaki. Almost immediately, the war in the Pacific ended. We were all elated, but I couldn't avoid also feeling uneasy that now we could destroy an entire city and its inhabitants so easily.

After all the V-J Day celebrations, life on the base remained chaotic because of the heavy transport of troops returning from the South Pacific. I kept hoping that Archie would appear, but there was no sign of him. We opened our last production in Hawaii under the auspices of Evans's unit. Lieutenant Militich, who had come to the end of his tour of duty, was ordered to close down our office.

Our last production was Tennessee Williams's *The Glass Menagerie*, starring Kay Medford. Kay was in her early twenties, only two years older than I, but skilled enough to be playing the part of Amanda, a mother of two grown children, Tom and Laura. Years later, in my mid-thirties, I played Tom in a Broadway revival of the play with Jo Van Fleet, a rather tough Amanda; Hal Holbrook, the best Gentleman Caller I've ever seen; and Carol Rossen, a sweetly vulnerable Laura, whose father was the film writer and director Robert Rossen.

Kay was the first actor from the New York theater I got to know well. We spent all our spare time together, because we found so much in common to talk and laugh about. During the last week of the play's run in Hawaii, the manager and cast were called up to Evans's office. They had expected to go on to perform for troops in the Pacific, but he told them that unless they had any objections, they were being sent to Japan to perform for the occupation troops. None of them refused. I thought, What a great opportunity . . . I've got to get on that tour.

I found Lieutenant Militich all packed and getting ready to leave for his stateside discharge. I begged him as a last act of kindness to send me to Japan with the troupe. He told me to simmer down and come with him to the personnel office. He had a hunch about something. When I started to ask what, he shut me up again and said to bear with him. When we got there, he asked them for my records. I started to say something, and he shushed me again. After what seemed like an eternity, he smiled, waved the papers in my face, and said, "Tokyo, are you crazy? You have enough points to go home—now! Pack your seabag tonight and get down to the transport center first thing in the morning." He promised that one of his golfing buddies, Lieutenant Tom Morrow, who was in charge, would put me on a flight to California for discharge as soon as possible. I stood there dumbfounded and conflicted. I was going home! But I was missing the trip of a lifetime.

Militich clapped me on the back and said, "Wake up! You are legal. Now get the hell out of here or I'll miss *my* plane." He smiled and held out his hand. We shook, and he was out the door. Halfway down the path he turned back to shout, "And look me up sometime; I've got a job teaching English at Beverly Hills High School." By the time I did, a few years later, he was the school's principal.

I ran back to my quarters, packed, and called Lieutenant Morrow, who told me to report first thing in the morning, 8:00 A.M. *sharp!* Then I went to find Kay to tell her why I would not be going to Japan. Reacting to my mixed feelings, she told me to stop being crazy. She understood completely. She promised to see me in Hollywood soon, and I promised to look her up as soon as I visited New York.

I still had one more call to make. Liana didn't hesitate. She wanted me to spend my last night with her as much as I wanted to be with her. It was a wonderful, bittersweet parting. After a quiet dinner, we walked along the beach for hours and talked about our plans for the future. She had already applied to the University of Hawaii and was planning to go into medical research. I promised that we would see each other again, but I think we both knew that the odds were not with us. At dawn, she got me up. I showered, and she had hot strong coffee and fresh pineapple ready for me. We held each other as if we could freeze time by not letting go. When I walked down the path from her cottage, I couldn't look back.

My Escape

I went to the transport center and found it a mob scene. No one knew where Lieutenant Morrow was. No one knew about any travel orders for me, either. I waited for hours with no luck. He didn't show up, and I didn't know what to do. Lieutenant Militich was gone, and I convinced myself that if I went back to the base, I would never get away. I couldn't go back to Liana's after our goodbye. I had no clue which way to turn. Suddenly I remembered my musician friend Ray's girlfriend, Sarah. Maybe she could find out something for me. Sarah, a Navy nurse, had been stationed in Hawaii for the whole war, and she really knew her way around. I hunted her down. She assured me that she would locate my missing transport officer tomorrow. Meanwhile, she would fix us something to eat, and I was to try to get a good night's sleep on her sofa. I tossed, eyes wide open, all night long, but I must have fallen asleep just before daylight. When I did wake up it was almost 11:00 A.M. There was a note from Sarah to stay calm, and to fix myself some breakfast. She would be back as soon as she found out something. I showered and had something to eat, feeling almost normal for a short time.

It was almost 3:00 P.M. when Sarah returned, and I had worked myself back into an anxious lather all over again. She had a mile-wide smile on her face. She had tracked down Lieutenant Morrow. He had almost been run down in the parking lot outside his quarters the day before on his way to work, and in his effort to get out of the way, he had fallen and broken his ankle. He was in the hospital. She told me to phone him—"now!" He said, "Get here to the hospital ASAP." I did and went to his room. It was a nasty break and he was going to be out of commission for a while, but he had my papers with him. He told me to go to the base airport at Pearl immediately. He had cleared me for the evening flight to San Francisco. When I arrived, I was to tell them that I had priority clearance for a connecting flight to San Pedro outside Los Angeles. He said, "Make sure you get on that flight. When you arrive, do not let them send you to Treasure Island under any circumstances. Troopships from all over the Pacific are docking there, and it could be weeks before they get around to processing you. Now get out of here. You have less than ninety minutes to make your flight!" I thanked him and tore out of there.

I made it. The flight was endless. When we finally landed in San Francisco, I found another mob scene. It seemed like everyone was being herded on buses to Treasure Island. I hung back until the crowd thinned out a bit and I spotted a CPO who looked like he was in charge. I showed him my papers, and he pointed out where I should go to wait for the interairport bus outside the hanger. He warned me that most of the buses were for Treasure Island, and not to get on one of them by mistake. I had plenty of time, since the flight for the base in San Pedro was not leaving until the next morning. I thanked him and got out of there.

I sat on my seabag in the shadows and fell asleep. I woke up, dazed and confused, just as it was getting light out. I was afraid that I had missed my bus but saw some other sailors nearby and found out that they were waiting for the same bus. It finally came, and I was off to make the connecting flight to San Pedro. After a couple of days at the center, I got my honorable discharge and was free. It was a great feeling to know that I was home, that the war was over, and that I could pick up my life where I left off with all my newfound knowledge of the ways of the world.

Act II

Picking Up the Pieces

My mom and dad were overjoyed to have me home. Things seemed to be going fairly well between them. There were none of the awful fights I remembered, and they were not drinking as much. My dad would ask occasional questions about the war, but more often than not he would use my answers to segue into his own memories of World War I. I could still remember him showing me his treasured scrapbook from that war when I was a boy. A picture of three young German soldiers hanging by their necks gave me nightmares for months. I could also remember him taking out his violin and playing "The Roses of Picardy" over and over on those evenings when he had too much to drink.

My mom didn't seem to want to accept that I was now a man. She waited up for me when I had a date, no matter how late I got home. Then she would come into my room after I got in bed to "kiss me good night, and tuck me in" so tightly that I felt a bit like a mummy. To this day I'm not sure what she was trying to accomplish. I guess the simplest explanation was to keep me safe and to keep me there. I determined to find my own place as soon as I got back to work.

After I had settled in and spent my discharge bonus on some new clothes, I checked in at the studio. When Mr. Goldwyn heard I was back, he sent for me immediately. His greeting was warm and effusive. He even got up and came from behind his vast desk to welcome me. He was still a formidable figure of a man. Tall and impeccably dressed, he even seemed to move formally. His thin, high-pitched voice, so at odds with his imposing presence, never failed to take me by surprise. He said that I was like a son to him. It gave me a nice feeling to hear him say that, since my departure from the studio had gone so unnoticed. The problem, I was soon to find out, was that he only felt that way when I was doing exactly what he wanted me to do. When I was not, which became more frequent in the years to come, he referred to me as "that boy," as in "GET THAT BOY IN HERE!"

He told me that he had the part of the young soldier who lost his hands in the war in *The Best Years of Our Lives* written for me, but that they couldn't hold up production until my discharge. Maybe that was true, but I thought that if he had planned for me to be in that film, he must have known when I was due to get out of the Navy. It was nice of him to say it...I guess. Anyway, no one could have been better in the part than Harold Russell, a young man who actually had lost his hands in the war. What experience he lacked as an actor was more than compensated for by his life experience.

Mr. Goldwyn said that he had all his people looking for a property that was just right for me, and that they were very close to finding it. Meanwhile he was giving me a one-hundred-dollar weekly raise and starting my salary from the date of my discharge. He wanted me to come in to the studio the next day, because he had a special surprise for me. I thanked him and left his office feeling great. I was now making two hundred dollars a week.

I went down to the mailroom to see if anything was waiting for me, and they welcomed me like a long-lost friend. They told me that while I was away in the Navy, I received more fan mail than anyone else under contract. They also told me that my father had come by periodically to pick it up. I wondered why he had not mentioned it to me.

That evening at dinner I asked my father why he had not told me about picking up my fan mail. After an uncomfortably long pause, I looked at my mother, who avoided my eyes, and Dad finally blustered, "Well, Sonny," that nickname again, which I had asked him not to use for as long as I could remember, "I was just waiting until you got all settled in, and then I planned to surprise you." He went on to explain how proud he was that I received so much more mail than any other actor at the studio. He hated my fans to be disappointed, so he had been answering my fan mail for me. He said that he would not mind continuing to do it if I would like. I was touched by his offer, and since I hated the idea of dealing with fan mail, I agreed. A few years later, on a publicity tour for *Roseanna McCoy*, I learned what a mistake that had been. It seems that he had really gotten into the correspondence with some of my more fervent young female fans. One morning at about 2:00 A.M. in Indianapolis, there was a knock on my hotel room door. I opened it to a young woman. She threw herself into my pajama-clad arms, declared her undying love, and said she knew from my letters that I felt the same way. It took me a few sleepy minutes to figure out what was going on, and a few more wide-awake ones to get rid of her. The next morning, I called to tell my father to cease and desist with the fan mail. As soon as I got back to Hollywood, I arranged for a part-time secretary to handle my fan mail at the studio. My father then started keeping scrapbooks into which he pasted anything he could find that even mentioned my name. I couldn't stay mad at my dad for what he had done. It was just a little sad that he had not made more of his own life after San Jose.

I went into the studio the next day and reported to Mr. Goldwyn's office as directed. His secretary said that he was in a meeting, but that the studio now had an acting coach on staff, and he wanted me to set up a schedule with her. She asked me to check back in after that had been done. I tracked down the acting coach, whose name I can never remember, probably because I never thought she was any good. In her office, I met the young actress who was to be my next leading lady, Cathy O'Donnell.

Cathy was very different from anyone I had ever met. She was lovely, shy, wistful, and ethereal. I felt an instant urge to protect her. We hit it off right away and set up a schedule to work together with the coach.

That accomplished, I dropped in to see Bob McIntyre, the casting director who had been responsible for getting me started at Goldwyn. He had heard I was back and was delighted that I had come to see him. I don't think he was impressed by the acting coach, either, but he was happy that I was going to be doing scene work with Cathy, who he thought was unusually talented. He believed that Cathy and I had a lot of potential as a team and he wanted to see us do some scenes together. We talked about what was currently going on around town, and he suggested that I stop by Republic Studios to say hello to Lewis Milestone, who was shooting *The Red Pony* there. Bob and I made plans for lunch later in the week, and I headed back to Goldwyn's office. He came out this time and boomed, "My boy, you are like a son to me. I am happy to have you back and want you to be happy, too. Now go see the surprise waiting for you at the front gate. Go and enjoy and work hard and we are going to find a great film for you!" Then, shouting orders to his secretary, he strode back to his inner sanctum before I had a chance to say anything. I had a pretty good idea what the surprise was, since Mr. Goldwyn often gave his contract players new cars. That prospect, with all the advantages of independence it offered, made me as happy as I had been when I got my first bicycle in junior high. I hurried to the front gate where Gus, the P.M. guard, presented me with a set of keys to a not-so-new 1940 Ford Coupe. Oh, well, it was wheels, it worked; it set me free—I couldn't complain.

I called Millie at home that evening to tell him I was back. He asked me to come to Republic to have lunch with him the next day.

After straightening out the registration and insurance for the car the next morning, I headed over to Republic to have lunch with Millie. It was great to see him again. I'd forgotten how much he liked to laugh and what a great sense of humor he had. People who didn't know Millie always expected him to be somber and very serious, probably because so many of his films, like *All Quiet on the Western Front*, *Of Mice and Men*, and *A Walk in the Sun*, dealt with such serious subjects, but he had also done *The Strange Love of Martha Ivers*, *Anything Goes*, and *The Red Pony* along with dozens of other superb films. The Millie I knew was a charmer who loved life and a good story or joke. Although I never worked with him again, we remained good friends through the years. He and his wife, Kendall, gave an annual Christmas party that was one of the season's social events I actually enjoyed. It was also a prized invitation for many of Hollywood's movers and shakers—until he was blacklisted, a shameful injustice from which he never recovered.

As we were finishing lunch that day, Millie told me that Aaron Copland was in town doing the music for his film. He said that Aaron had heard that I was back, and wanted to see me. Millie gave me his number, and I promised to give him a call.

That night when I called him we arranged to meet at a Chinese restaurant in the valley owned by James Wong Howe. Jimmy, one of the most respected cameramen in Hollywood, had also worked on *The North Star* It would be like old times seeing them both again. The next evening, I put on one of my two new suits, a shirt, and a tie, got into my new car, and, feeling quite the man of the world, set off to meet Aaron.

Jimmy greeted me like a long-lost friend and took me to a booth where Aaron was already seated. He rose to greet me with a big grin. We shook hands, and Jimmy insisted on buying the first round as a welcome-home drink. Aaron ordered a seltzer, and I ordered a vodka martini, extra dry, with a twist, no olive. Then I took out a pack of cigarettes and offered him one, which he declined. I lit up and sat back expansively.

He asked me what the Navy had been like. I told him, and I also told him about seeing *Rodeo* and *Fancy Free* in San Francisco, and how much I loved the productions and his music. He thanked me and asked how I felt about the music for *Fancy Free*. I said that I liked the music and the ballet so much that I had practically danced my way back to the ship. It had been my last night in San Francisco before shipping out to Hawaii, and I had felt like it was my life being danced onstage. He said that was a great compliment and he would love to tell the composer, Leonard Bernstein, a protégé and friend of his, about my reaction, if I had no objection. I was delighted. I ordered another martini and lit up again. Then I asked Aaron if he thought that Shostakovich would ever make it in this country. He gave me a quizzical look, and I said, "You know, will he ever be as popular as someone like, uh, Prokofiev or Stravinsky."

There was a long pause, and he burst out laughing. After a moment, so did I. I was showing off, drinking and smoking and throwing Russian composers' names around. I was trying to show him that I was no longer a kid. He knew what I was up to, and I knew he did. Jimmy came over to recommend dinner and contributed his bit of teasing about my newfound sophistication.

A Gauntlet for Mr. G.

Two days later I was called into the studio to see Mr. Goldwyn. His secretary ushered me into his office immediately. This time, Mr. Goldwyn remained seated behind his vast desk, inscrutable and silent, his ball-bearing eyes hooded and his arms crossed. One of his vice presidents, a twitchy little man with wispy hair whom I had never met, asked me to take a seat. I thought maybe they were going to tell me that they had found that wonderful project Mr. Goldwyn had promised to me. Was I in for a surprise.

The vice president said, "It has come to our attention that you were seen having dinner with Aaron Copland the other evening."

"That's right . . . so?" I said.

He stole a glance at Goldwyn, who was still looking inscrutable, and continued, "Well, I'm afraid that just won't do."

I didn't know what the hell he was talking about. "What won't do?"

He pulled a chair up next to me, sat down, and almost whispered, "Aaron Copland is a known homosexual."

I started to laugh, "So what! He's a very nice man, and I met him for dinner at Jimmy Wong Howe's restaurant. It was great seeing him again. I'm honored that he wanted to see me."

"Don't you see, Farley," he continued, "it's bad for your reputation and the studio's for you to be seen in public with people like that."

I felt the same way I had when my father made his anti-Semitic crack about Sam Levene. I stood up, turned to Goldwyn, and said, "He's talking about one of the most important composers in America, a gentleman I met at this studio when you hired him to do the score for *The North Star*. I'm not going to be told by him"—I pointed to the vice president—"or anybody else, who I can or cannot see in my private life!" With that, I turned and walked out. As I was cooling off, it dawned on me that Goldwyn had not said one word. Even though this was the prelude to many fights I was to have with Sam Goldwyn, he never mentioned this particular incident again.

Getting a Life

I was trying to get a social life going again. I had called and seen most of my old friends. Sam Levene was back in New York working in the theater, and Roddy was working nonstop at 20th. Now that I was twenty-one and had been in the Navy, the discrepancy in our ages was more of a gulf between us than when we were teens. I got a call from Jane Withers, whom I had not seen since we worked together. I didn't get to know Jane all that well during the filming, because my huge, unrequited crush on Anne Baxter dominated all thoughts of the opposite sex. Jane said that she had heard I was back and thought I might like to meet some young people in the business. She invited me to an afternoon party at her home in Beverly Hills.

Jane, who had been cast over and over as Hollywood's obnoxious brat as opposed to Shirley Temple's plucky and adorable child star, had almost grown up. Now she was being cast as the obnoxious, smart-aleck teen as opposed to Deanna Durbin's or Judy Garland's plucky and adorable adolescent.

Jane had a famous doll collection, and now that she had grown up some, she had acquired a soda fountain as well. Her afternoon parties were the subject of many a fan magazine spread. In an effort to get back in the social swim, I went.

Jane hadn't changed a bit, but I had. There were a few pretty girls there, plus a lot of handsome juvenile types who I suspected were mostly gay, not a scene that interested me. Jane carried on about her doll collection endlessly. It didn't take long for me to realize that, sweet as Jane was, this was not the social life that I was looking for; I was ready for a new group of friends.

The next time I saw Jane was in 1990 at a star-studded bash in Hollywood that Shelley Winters talked me into attending. The evening was in honor of Elizabeth Taylor and Michael Jackson, an odd couple, I thought, but as usual the lure of press coverage had hooked Shelley. One of the first people we ran into was Jane Withers. When Jane began carrying on about some crisis that had to do with her doll collection, the feeling of déjà vu was so sharp that I found it hard to keep a straight face.

Meanwhile, back at the soda fountain party, I finally broke away from the doll collection discussion and went behind the soda fountain to search, in vain, for a real drink. A voice nearby chuckled, "Give up. I've already tried." I looked up and standing at the bar was a tall, good-looking guy who was probably a few years older than I. He introduced himself as Ted Reed, an actor currently working at Columbia. We talked for a while. When I agreed that this was a pretty dull excuse for a party, he asked if I wanted to go to an open house that some friends of his regularly threw. They were musicians. The host was a musical director on staff at Columbia, and his wife, a terrific pianist, was a funny, wise, and wonderful person. Musicians had been my salvation in Hawaii, so without hesitation I said, "Let's go." I followed his car to a funny, crumbling old house on Orange Grove Avenue in Hollywood. It looked like one of those castles at the bottom of a fish bowl in Woolworth's.

The family who lived inside this enchanted castle were Ethyl and Saul Chaplin, their young daughter, Judy, and Ethyl's mother and father, Rose and Sam. There was minimal furniture in the living room and a big, gaping hole in the floor in one corner. On the other side of the room was a grand piano. That proved to be more than enough. Ethyl's mother was a great cook, and there was a breakfast nook in the kitchen into which everyone crowded for meals. It was inset into the walls, which were painted black, and the table and benches were fixed. I later nicknamed that nook "the Black Hole of Calcutta." After one evening I knew that this was the home I had wanted all my life, a home filled with laughter, joy, and music, music, music. I loved Ethyl from the first time we talked, and have never stopped. She was beautiful, talented, opinionated, and in every way an original. Saul had a great sense of humor and a mind that seemed to race in at least six directions at all times. I never saw him express a tentative reaction to anything. His opinions, either negative or positive, were all bubbling over the top. His whole world was music, and his knowledge and talent in that world were prodigious. Ethyl welcomed me into their world with breathtaking generosity. She became my mentor, my confidante, my big sister, and my best friend.

Aside from their love for Judy, music was the glue that held everything together on Orange Grove. Their door was always open to friends, and a constant parade of musical talent from New York as well as Hollywood passed through. I spent every spare minute there. Through Saul and Ethyl, I learned about Gilbert and Sullivan, Puccini, Kurt Weill, Rodgers and Hart, Harold Arlen, and countless others, including George and Ira Gershwin.

As a teenager, I was so taken by *Porgy and Bess* and George Gershwin that I had spent my meager salary from the local market on a recording of it as well as one of *An American in Paris*. The only hitch was that we did not own a record player. My parents gave me one that Christmas, but it was on an installment plan and had to go back after the first week. I had read everything I could get my hands on about George Gershwin, and had learned of his tragic death in his thirties. In one of my moments of teen madness, I decided I had to be like Gershwin, to create a masterpiece and die young. I had abandoned that high-minded ambition by the time I met the Chaplins, but it thrilled me to be in the company of people who not only knew him and Ira, but probably knew every note George had ever written. I spent so much of my time at the Chaplin house that my mother got jealous, but it was where I had to be.

Saul and Ethyl's house was not only a magnet for me; everyone connected with any musical aspect of show business in New York showed up there when in Hollywood. At their home I met Betty Comden and Adolph Green, Jerry Robbins, Judy Holliday, Oscar Levant, Phil Silvers, and Leonard Bernstein. These people were savvy, quick, and exciting to be with. They all loved to perform, especially Betty and Adolph. Everyone also loved to play The Game, as charades was then called in Hollywood. If we were not playing that, Saul and Ethyl might be performing Schubert for four hands for Lenny or something else with him. Oscar pounded out George Gershwin's more serious compositions whenever he got his hands on the keyboard. Phil would grab any opportunity to work out some of his special material at the piano with Saul. Frequently, Betty, Adolph, and Saul would work on material for a Broadway musical, *Bonanza Bound*, that they were writing, based on the Alaskan gold rush. Any and every activity was creative and stimulating. I had never been happier.

Saul was working on a musical at Columbia called *Cover Girl*, starring Rita Hayworth and Gene Kelly. Phil Silvers was featured as Gene's sidekick. In those days, we worked six days a week. Saturday was the one night when everyone could get together and blow off some steam. The "old guard," meaning the older established stars and the moguls, had dinner parties that were relatively staid events at which a film was almost always screened. Sometimes, when people were allowed to comment on the film they were viewing, it could be bitchy good fun. But usually everyone had to sit and enjoy or endure the screening in respectful and solemn silence. At a screening of some now-forgotten feature at Jack Warner's house, Van Johnson's wife, Edie, and I got the giggles. Later, as we were leaving, we were taken aside by one of the Warner Brothers executives and scolded for our childish behavior.

Edie had been married to Keenan Wynn. Van was not only their closest friend, but he lived with them. I had gotten to know them all at Gene and Betsy Kelly's house, and we had all become friends. Van had been involved in a terrible automobile accident in 1942 that left him with a steel plate in his head. It also left him untouched by the draft. He became that rare commodity during the war, a clean-cut young leading man. He worked nonstop and soon became the darling of the bobby-soxers, in a series of hit movies made by MGM.

Louis B. Mayer put pressure on Van, who was homosexual, to get married in order to protect his all-American image. I will never understand exactly what happened or how it happened, but Keenan and Edie divorced, she married Van, and they all remained a close as ever. Louis B. must have had his publicity department in overdrive at that time, because all of the people involved came out of that experience relatively unscathed, at least in the gossip columns.

The fun place to be for the younger crowd, especially the musical group, was the weekly Saturday night and Sunday afternoon open house at Gene and Betsy Kelly's. Saul and Ethyl first took me there, and I became a regular. Saul was inexhaustible at the piano and a peerless accompanist. Everyone got up and performed just for the joy of it: Judy Garland, Phil Silvers, Lena Horne, Frank Sinatra, Betty Garrett, Johnny Mercer, Harold Arlen . . . whoever happened to be there on any given Saturday evening. Everyone participated in The Game and in improvised musical skits. Gene's competitiveness in any game was so fierce that it belied the charming grin that was his trademark. Most of the time people managed to laugh it off, but sometimes his aggressiveness got a bit off-putting, particularly at the Sunday volleyball matches. Regardless, he and Betsy were generous and gregarious hosts. Performing was a part of relaxing on these Saturday nights, and everyone took part willingly and enthusiastically. This was not necessarily true at all Hollywood gatherings.

The first time I was invited to Sunday lunch at Lee and Ira Gershwin's, I went upstairs to the bathroom at one point, and as I headed back downstairs, I overheard Judy and Lena talking in one of the bedrooms nearby. They were discussing what songs to do when "she" asked them to sing for their supper, or lunch, as was the case on this afternoon. I don't think you could find anyone in Hollywood who did not think that Ira was as sweet as he was talented, and his wife, Lee, was considered to be one of Hollywood's premier hostesses, but performing when requested is very different from doing it spontaneously. I particularly loved going there because the house was filled with paintings by my teen idol, George. I thought he was a terrific painter, and there was one self-portrait I coveted.

Another regular in the Kelly household was his close longtime friend, Stanley Donen. Stanley's presence in their house was such a given, everyone thought he lived there. Along with Van Johnson, Stanley had been in the chorus of *Pal Joey*, the Rodgers and Hart Broadway musical that made Gene a star. Stanley had come to Hollywood as Gene's sidekick and assistant. He co-choreographed many of Gene's early movie musical successes, including *Cover Girl* with Rita Hayworth and *Take Me Out to the Ball Game* with Frank Sinatra. His first co-directorial credit with Gene was *On the Town*; his most successful was the movie musical milestone *Singin' in the Rain*. He then went on to direct some very good films on his own, including *Seven Brides for Seven Brothers*, *Funny Face*, *Charade*, and *Two for the Road*.

Recently at a restaurant in the theater district in New York, I felt a tap on my shoulder. It was Stanley Donen, whom I had not seen in over fifty years. He sat for a drink, and we started reminiscing about the old days, laughing and trading stories. He concluded with a comment that has stayed with me. "You know, Farley, we didn't realize it at the time, but we were there right in the middle of what really were the best of the last of the golden days."

Chomping at the Bit

In 1947, those golden days were looking a little tarnished for me at the Goldwyn Studio. I went in for my scheduled scene work with Cathy. From bits and pieces of information I picked up around the studio, I realized that Mr. Goldwyn had no prospects at all in the pipeline for me. I was certainly less naïve than I had been before the war, but it was never a part of my nature to be in touch with all the behind-the-scenes machinations in Hollywood. What I later realized with the wisdom of hindsight was that after his triumph with the superb *The Best Years of Our Lives*, Sam Goldwyn went into a creative slump from which he never recovered. It began with the departure of his best director, William Wyler, and was accelerated by the death of his superb cameraman, Gregg Toland, in 1948, the same year that, as Goldwyn's youngest contract player, I was ready and chomping at the bit to resume what many thought, and I hoped would be, a promising career.

With William Wyler off in the Army, the fact that the Goldwyn Studio flourished during the war years was an accomplishment for which a former borscht belt comedian, Danny Kaye, should be given most of the credit. His first film for Goldwyn, *Up in Arms*, was a mediocre remake of Eddie Cantor's 1930 hit *Whoopee!* The film was a big moneymaker for Goldwyn, and made an instant star of Danny Kaye. In 1948, Goldwyn was in danger of losing Danny, who was unhappy with the rehashed scripts he was being asked to do, particularly *A Song Is Born*, a dismal remake of *Ball of Fire*, a wonderful film Goldwyn had produced only seven years earlier starring Barbara Stanwyck and Gary Cooper. Goldwyn was smart enough to leave Danny alone, but he forced Virginia Mayo to watch Stanwyck's performance in the original over and over. Used correctly, as Wyler used her in *The Best Years of Our Lives*, Virginia could be very effective, but she could never replicate Barbara Stanwyck, who was one of the most unique talents in the history of film. *A Song Is Born* not only didn't work, but it brought Goldwyn the worst reviews of his career. Danny was unhappy. His contract was coming to an end, and he was being wooed by Warner Brothers. Goldwyn was scrambling to find suitable material for his biggest star of the moment. That, and other developments within the industry, namely a growing alliance between the newly formed Motion Picture Alliance for the Preservation of American Ideals and the House Committee on Un-American Activities, HUAC, kept Mr. Goldwyn too busy to attend to the development of his youngest contract player's career.

Nick Ray vs. Howard Hughes

One evening at the Chaplins', Ethyl said that she wanted me to meet a new arrival from New York, a director named Nick Ray. He had recently directed a musical in New York for John Houseman that was a critical success but had flopped. I knew Houseman's name from the Mercury Theater and also as the producer of *Citizen Kane*. When Ethyl told me that Nick Ray had worked as Elia Kazan's assistant on the movie *A Tree Grows in Brooklyn*, I was suitably impressed. He was currently preparing to direct his first movie for John Houseman at RKO.

When we were introduced, I tried to make conversation but failed miserably. Nick was either shy, or inhibited, or taciturn, or all of the above. After a while, I gave up trying to communicate with him and went to get a drink and enjoy the evening.

Years later, Ethyl broke me up by saying she always knew when it was Nick calling because when she answered the phone, there would be silence on the other end of the line.

That night, and the next few times I was there, Nick spent the whole evening sitting in a corner with his drink watching me. I finally went to Ethyl and said, "This guy is giving me the creeps. All he does is stare at me."

Ethyl said, "Farley, he's just observing you. He thinks you could be terrific as the lead in his movie, and I think he is going to offer you a test. Now, just act natural. Relax and enjoy yourself."

I think we both had a laugh at "Relax." She knew exactly how I would react to what she had just told me. I headed straight for the bar.

The next day my studio called and told me to go to RKO for a meeting with John Houseman and Nick Ray. Nick was completely articulate when he talked to me about the part and what he thought I could bring to it. John Houseman was charming and, as I was to learn, more than articulate about everything. *Thieves Like Us* was the story of a young fugitive, the getaway driver for a couple of small-time bank robbers, who falls in love with the niece of one of the robbers. The lovers break away from the rest of the gang and, after a hasty marriage, hide out in a mountain cabin hoping to escape the law and her family.

They wanted me for the part of Bowie, the young driver, and gave me the screenplay to take home to read.

John explained that despite the fact that they wanted me, the odds were against my getting the part. Dore Schary, the head of RKO, had his own young contract players like Rory Calhoun and Guy Madison. He would resist borrowing me from Goldwyn, who was a tough negotiator. When Nick asked me if there was an actress with whom I would feel comfortable for the test, I mentioned Cathy O'Donnell, and Nick said he would make the arrangements.

The test was set for Monday morning. Cathy and I spent Sunday afternoon going over the script together and working on the emotional arc of the relationship between Bowie and Keechie, from their first meeting to falling in love. That evening at home I worked out my own backstory for Bowie, starting as a small boy and ending with his going to prison.

On Monday morning we worked with Nick and did the screen test. Before I knew it, everything was all set. Not only had Nick and John fought Schary to get me, they had also liked Cathy so much that they fought to use her as well. It was a great confidence-builder to know they had liked my work enough to fight for me. We went into production the following week. John Houseman, a very canny man, probably let the final casting go until the eleventh hour in order to be able to put that extra bit of pressure on Dore Schary.

Cathy and I had a wonderful group of character actors to work with. Howard Da Silva, who specialized in mean, heavy roles both on Broadway and in films, played Keechie's uncle, the one-eyed half-breed Chicamaw. J. C. Flippen, a Broadway musical actor who switched to films after the war, played his tough partner, T-Dub. The first day of shooting involved a helicopter shot that Nick had planned. I'm certain it was the first time one had ever been used in a feature film. The film opens after our escape from prison, and the camera follows from the air the old convertible we are escaping in until it has a flat and pulls off the dirt road and into a field. Our big problem was that Howard's toupee kept getting blown off by the downdraft from the rotor blades. Reshooting that setup took an enormous amount of time because of the helicopter, but Nick persevered and so, finally, did the glue on the hairpiece.

The next setup was of the three of us running across fields to a small highway. On the last take, my foot caught in a gopher hole and down I went with a badly sprained ankle. Fortunately, it worked in the following scene, in which the guys leave me hiding behind a roadside billboard while they go off to get some money. By the time we finished for the day, my foot had swollen so badly that my shoe had to be cut off. Howard refused to let me try to walk. He insisted on carrying me. He threw me over his shoulder in a fireman's carry. It was a long way to the car.

We were almost through shooting the film when we learned that Howard Hughes was taking over RKO and Dore Schary was going to MGM. I don't know if Nick had any idea of what this would mean for us. None of us did. It turned out that it meant a lot, none of it good.

Howard Hughes had made his name in movies in the late 1920s. In 1930, as the producer-director of *Hell's Angels*, he spent an unheard-of $3.8 million of his personal fortune to perfect the aerial sequences. It was a smash hit. He then produced the hit *Scarface* in 1932. His subsequent claim to Hollywood fame was the number of beautiful Hollywood stars he squired around town. In 1932, he left Hollywood in order to pursue his passion for aviation. His return to film-making in 1941 was to produce and direct *The Outlaw*, starring Jane Russell and her cleavage. The film was bad enough to disappear quickly but in a rare moment of Hollywood self-censorship, it was condemned by the Hays Office and withdrawn by Hughes. That action and Hughes's subsequent reaction, a well-publicized, protracted fight to have it released in 1946 and then again in 1950, made a star of the entertainer Bob Hope once introduced as "the two and only Miss Jane Russell," and a moneymaker out of a dismal movie.

Nick was afraid that our film would not be appreciated by Hughes. The first sign that he might be right was when Hughes insisted on changing the title because he thought people would think it meant *Thieves Like Us*. The title came from a line in the film when Chicamaw refers to bank owners as being "thieves like us." The next thing we knew the film was being called *The Twisted Road*, and then it became *Your Red Wagon*, the title of a song sung in a roadhouse in one scene in the film. Neither of these changes made any of us feel secure about Howard Hughes's understanding of the kind of film Nick was making.

I don't think anyone was terribly surprised several months later to open *Daily Variety* one morning and read that Howard Hughes had shelved Nicholas Ray's film starring Cathy O'Donnell and Farley Granger.

The Bel Air Circuit

Every major producer in Hollywood had his own private screening room in his house where they viewed old films, new films, and particularly films that were being made by rival studios. As soon as our film was finished, it played the "Bel Air Circuit," as the moguls' home screening rooms were called. For this reason, none of the actors felt that the shelving of *Thieves Like Us* had done serious damage to our future prospects. Goldwyn, who had viewed *They Live by Night* (its eventual new title), was so taken by Cathy and me in the film that he declared us his new Romeo and Juliet in a major publicity campaign that promised great things for us.

Quality work was hard to come by. To have his first film put aside by a man whose most recent claim to filmmaking fame was as tacky as *The Outlaw* was a lousy break for Nick.

Two years or so later, English good taste saved our film from oblivion. It opened with little fanfare in a small London art house, and the English critics loved it. Soon after that RKO released it in the States, where it received excellent reviews for Nick, Cathy, and me.

By 1954, under Hughes's sporadic management, RKO had lost $40 million. Although hardly a drop in today's Hollywood bucket, it was a lot of money back then. Hughes then bought all the outstanding stock from the studio's shareholders at bargain-basement prices and sold the studio for a ten-million-dollar profit.

Nick Ray

Nick Ray was one of the best and most sensitive directors I've ever worked with. For a man who was socially inarticulate, he was the complete opposite when working. If he wanted something special from any of the actors in a scene, he would put his arm around your shoulder and walk you away to talk privately about the situation and the character, even if it was for something as simple as wanting me to react differently to the sound of a car approaching. He made each actor feel as if he or she were getting special treatment. It took me fifteen years to encounter another director who worked that intimately. It was Eva Le Gallienne who was directing me in Chekhov on the stage.

I always wished I'd had the chance to work with Nick again. He did some cleanup work for Goldwyn on *Roseanna McCoy*, a film I was in a few years later, but the principal photography had already been finished, and there was very little he could do to improve the film. Beyond our initial warm hello, I couldn't get him to have a conversation with me. It was almost as if he were ashamed to be working as a cleanup director on a lost cause for Goldwyn. I still wonder about what might have been if Nick had been on the film from the beginning, with the original script.

Years later, he talked to me about playing Jesus in *King of Kings*. I did not feel that his heart was in it, and I knew that it was not a good idea for me. I tried to laugh it off by saying, "Nick, if I do that, I'll never work again."

He ended up using Jeff Hunter, a good-looking young man with bright blue eyes, and I think it did end his career. Now it seems as if that particular curse has been broken. Willem Dafoe's career survived playing the title role in Martin Scorsese's *The Last Temptation of Christ*. It also seems as if Jim Caviezel's career, though hardly taking off, was not been completely stalled by being flayed for twenty minutes as Jesus in Mel Gibson's *The Passion of the Christ*.

Much has been written about Nick's tendency to become emotionally and physically involved with his young leading actors, particularly James Dean, Natalie Wood, and Sal Mineo, the three stars of *Rebel Without a Cause*, but I never had any sense that he wanted our relationship to be anything other than professional. Certainly Nick's life was not exactly conventional. His second wife was Gloria Grahame, film noir's quintessential bad girl. Years later his son Tony by his first marriage, married Gloria. Nick was also plagued by substance abuse, both liquor and drugs, throughout his life, which partially accounts for the fact that such a talented director only sporadically lived up to his promise.

I did not see Nick again until 1979, when I returned to New York from Los Angeles after spending almost five years in Italy. I picked up *The New York Times* one morning and read that he was gravely ill and hospitalized. I tracked him down and went to see him. He was in a small ward with maybe half a dozen other terminal patients. He could not have been more surprised or more delighted to see me. I was surprised how happy I was to see him, even under these circumstances. Always taciturn, Nick now had an excuse not to say much. He was dying of smoking-related cancer, and it was difficult for him to talk. We reminisced a bit, and then I had to leave because he tired so easily. Before I could return for another visit, he died at age sixty-seven.

Nick is still considered one of America's film visionaries by students of the cinema all over the world. His reputation is based on three films: *They Live by Night*, *Rebel Without a Cause*, and *Johnny Guitar*. His other work in the 1940s, 1950s, and 1960s was not good. His personal life, the booze, the drugs, and the complicated relationships obviously kept this artist from realizing his great potential. I mourned him.

The Big Apple

Since Mr. Goldwyn had raised my salary to $250 a week when I started work on *Thieves Like Us*, I began to think about looking for a place of my own. This was still a relatively paltry salary at the time, but I had been away from the screen for almost four years while in the Navy, and I was insecure about having to prove myself again.

During this period, my love life was pretty barren. Just after I began the film, I met a young actress from New York named Patricia Neal. She had done wonderful work on the New York stage and was not a typical Hollywood ingenue, but she radiated star appeal. Pat was tall, with a throaty, cultured voice, a hearty laugh, and a quick wide smile. I really fell for her. We spent as much time together as we could, which was not nearly as much as I would have liked, since we were both busy working. Pat was filming *The Fountainhead* with Gary Cooper. Unfortunately for me and eventually even more so for Pat, she and Coop fell madly in love while making that film. In the end, he could not leave his wife, and the affair ended painfully for all concerned. Coop had a difficult time trying to paste the pieces of his marriage back together, and Pat suffered a much too well publicized nervous breakdown.

Harry Cohn, who ran Columbia, had the reputation of being a cheapskate, and it was a reputation that no one ever disputed. At the same time that I started working at RKO, Saul Chaplin left Columbia and went to MGM. It was a nice move upward for Saul, who had been overused and underpaid at Columbia. At Metro, for a very nice salary, he would be responsible for one film at a time. At Columbia he had been responsible for as many as five films at one time while having to deal with the crass and despotic Cohn. Saul and Ethyl celebrated by buying a new house on Doheny Drive in Beverly Hills. Their new living room could accommodate two baby grand pianos, and their new home continued to be a gathering place for the New York musical crowd.

About two weeks after I finished Nick's film, Ethyl called to tell me that Saul, Betty Comden, and Adolph Green had gotten the financing to put on their musical, *Bonanza Bound*. They had rented their new house and were leaving for New York immediately. She urged me to come to New York while they were there. While Saul was busy working, she and I could play together. Goldwyn had still not found "that great project" for me. I had never been to New York, and this was my chance to see it with good friends. Helen Craig, who had been in *They Live by Night* and went immediately into another movie, offered me her New York apartment at 55th Street and Sixth Avenue. She said it was a perfect location for going to the theater. I told my parents and the studio where to find me, packed a bag, and got on the first flight I could book for New York.

I treated myself to a first-class ticket on Pan Am. My seat was luxurious, comfortable enough to curl up and sleep in. The only problem was that I was much too excited to sleep. Flying may be a lot faster now, but it has gone downhill as far as comfort is concerned. In those days, when flying coast to coast, there was a stop in Chicago either to refuel or to change planes. When we landed in Chicago, I ran into the airport to call Ethyl with my latest brainstorm. Rather than go to a strange apartment on my first night in the big city, I asked her to get me a room in one of the best hotels in town. I must have sounded like an eight-year-old because she couldn't stop laughing, but she promised to take care of everything for me.

We got into La Guardia at about 8:30 P.M., and Ethyl and Saul were there at the gate. They were each holding up signs. Saul's said WELCOME TO NEW YORK, and Ethyl's said IT'S A HELLUVA TOWN! It was getting dark as we drove into the city. Los Angeles, which I had just come from, is a sprawling city with no one center. H. L. Mencken called it "six suburbs in search of a city." Manhattan seemed to be all in front of me in one magnificent vista. The setting sun back-lit that glorious skyline in shades of crimson and copper. It so surpassed any expectations I had formed from movies and newsreels that the effect on me was visceral.

The evening was hot and humid. After we crossed the 59th Street Bridge into the city, I couldn't get over the fact that steam was coming up through manhole covers in the streets. With that, and the neon lights reflecting off parked cars and the pavement, I felt as if we were driving on top of Dante's Inferno. It was spooky and thrilling. I still feel that way whenever I return to the city at night.

We went straight to Betty Comden's apartment on East 55th Street, only two blocks from where I would be staying. Betty and Adolph were there, as well as Betty's husband, Steve Kyle. Adolph's wife, Allyn Ann McLerie, who was performing in *Where's Charley?* on Broadway, was joining us after the show. I was almost as impressed by Betty's apartment as I was with the steam coming up from the streets. It was all black, the walls, the furniture, everything but one bright green ottoman. I thought, This is it. This is bohemian. This is for me.

The champagne popped, and everyone was talking at once. I felt like an insider, hearing all the latest Broadway gossip as well as the plans for *Bonanza Bound*. We were high and happy and hungry by the time Allyn Ann got home from her show. Betty and Ethyl had set out a terrific spread from the nearby Carnegie Delicatessen that introduced me to some great New York tastes. There was chopped liver, pastrami, corned beef, noodle kugel, new pickles, and other deli delights. After supper, we gathered around the piano to hear the new numbers they had written for *Bonanza Bound*. After one number, the change in time zones and the energy I had expended in excitement caught up with me. I had to go to bed. We hugged good nights all around, and Ethyl took me to the Essex House, my hotel on Central Park South. I was so tired, I didn't take in the lobby or anything. I just went up to my room and passed out on the bed.

When I woke the next morning and pulled open the drapes, my breath was taken away once again. I was on the twenty-first floor, and all of Central Park stretched out before me. It was summer, and everything was in bloom and green, green, green. The phone rang. Adolph was downstairs in the lobby. He said, "Hurry down. I want to show you New York." I jumped in the shower and was in the lobby in no time. We went to a coffee shop where I had my first bagel with cream cheese—a schmear—and lox. Even breakfast was new and exotic. Adolph was as good as a professional guide. It seemed as if he knew everything there was to know about New York. We went from Radio City down Fifth Avenue to the Empire State Building and then to Broadway, where we had lunch at a wonderful place called Dinty Moore's. It was all brass and white tiles, with bentwood chairs and coatracks. Jerry Robbins, the great choreographer, came in, and Adolph hailed him over to join us. I had been a huge Robbins fan ever since seeing *Fancy Free* in San Francisco. Adolph and I had been talking about which Broadway show should be my first. After much good-natured bickering about what was worth seeing, the name Ethel Merman came up, and they said in unison, *Annie Get Your Gun.* Adolph had to go to work, so Jerry said he would walk me to the Imperial Theatre to make sure I got a good seat. He insisted that the only place to see a musical was from dead center in the first row of the mezzanine. I'm not sure directors or set designers agree with him, but lighting designers and choreographers all do.

Star Power

I had never seen a Broadway show, much less a Broadway musical. Even though I knew that Ethel Merman was a big star, I had never seen any of her films, so I didn't know what to expect. She was extraordinary! She was magnificent! I was transported! I was blown away! I was in love! Thank God I got to know her some years later to tell her how I felt. She was a knockout off the stage as well, with a vocabulary that could make the Army, Navy, and Marines blush.

There is a famous story, possibly apocryphal, about her first trip to Hollywood, and a visit to the set of a movie starring Loretta Young, a world-class Catholic who kept a "swear box" on the set into which everyone had to make a deposit for their naughty words. Merman saw it, turned to Loretta, and said, "What the hell is this?"

Loretta smiled sweetly and said, "Oh, Ethel, I'm afraid now you have to put twenty-five cents into the swear box."

Ethel gave her a look and grinned as she said, "How much will it cost me to tell you to go fuck yourself?"

That's my Merman.

I couldn't get enough of the theater. I saw *Brigadoon* with its marvelous dances by Agnes de Mille, featuring the superb dancer James Mitchell. A few years later James came to Hollywood under contract to Warner Brothers and became a very close friend. Many years later, he played Captain Wickham in *First Impressions*, my first Broadway show. I saw *Mister Roberts*, starring the great Henry Fonda, a wonderful comedy that I would do in stock years later. There was *Where's Charley?* with Ray Bolger and Adolph's wife, Allyn Ann McLerie. David Wayne was a captivating leprechaun in search of a pot of gold in *Finian's Rainbow*. I was lucky enough to see those peerless actors the Lunts in *O Mistress Mine*. Last, but in no way least, I saw Elia Kazan's ground-breaking production of *A Streetcar Named Desire* starring Marlon Brando and Jessica Tandy. Everyone in it was wonderful, but I couldn't take my eyes off Brando. He made me think about acting in a whole new way.

Now I knew what my destiny was. I was going to be up there on the stage someday. I had done three movies, all with good directors, but I had never experienced the feeling of electricity generated by the connection between audience and actor at a live performance. It was something I had to be a part of. I was going to come to New York.

On the Boardwalk

Adolph told me that Nancy Walker, a comic actress I had met in Hollywood, was doing *On the Town* in a theater at the end of the Steel Pier in Atlantic City. On Allyn Ann's day off, she and I decided to go see it. I thought Atlantic City was just somewhere across the Hudson river in nearby New Jersey, and Allyn Ann didn't have a clue where it was. We just hailed a cab and I asked the driver to take us to the Steel Pier in Atlantic City. He turned and gave me a funny look, then shrugged and said, "Anything you say, buddy," and we took off. A couple of hours later, and many dollars lighter, we finally arrived.

We were about twenty minutes late, but the show had still not started. The audience was clapping in unison and obviously getting restless. Allyn Ann protected our seats while I went back to Nancy's dressing room to find out if she was okay. It wasn't hard to find. As soon as I got backstage, I could hear Nancy raising hell with someone. I followed her voice to her dressing room. All five feet of Nancy had the theater manager backed into a corner, saying she would do the first act, but there would be no second act until she had the cash in her hands. As the manager backed out of her dressing room, she spotted me, blew me a kiss, and said with a big smile, "Come back after the show, Farfel, and we'll get something to eat." I made my way back to my seat thinking, This is all much more glamorous than working in movies.

Hitchcock

I had come to New York for two weeks, which had stretched to four. I was having such a great time that I completely forgot my commitments in Hollywood. The studio reminded me. They called to tell me that I had to come back immediately. Mr. Goldwyn had loaned me out to Warner Brothers to do Alfred Hitchcock's new film, *Rope*. Even though I never wanted to leave New York again, the idea of working with Hitchcock was intriguing. I loved his films, particularly *Rebecca* and *Shadow of a Doubt*, and I was sure I could learn a lot from a director as good as he was.

Ethyl and Saul felt this was a major opportunity for me. I made arrangements to leave the next day. Ethyl asked me to do her a favor. She had rented their house in Hollywood to a beautiful Broadway dancer named Sono Osato, who had played Miss Turnstiles in *On the Town*. She made me promise to stop by, introduce myself, and check on her cat. "Keedy" was an outdoor cat that lived in the alley behind her house. He was a little feral and a little crazy, but she loved him and fed him. She wanted me to make sure that Sono was remembering to feed him. I promised to check.

The next day I got an early-morning flight for L.A. that arrived early in the evening. I got a cab from the airport and went by Doheny Drive on my way home. I rang the bell and instead of a gorgeous dancer named Sono, a short, energetic man with a ready grin answered. When I asked for Sono Osato, he told me that she had to go back to New York and that he had arranged to take her place. We introduced ourselves. His name, Arthur Laurents, meant nothing to me. I told him why I was there, and we went into the kitchen and opened the door to the alley. Sure enough, Keedy came when called. He looked fine, just as ratty as ever. Sono had shown Arthur all about feeding the cat, and he wanted me to tell Ethyl not to worry. Then he said he was sure I must have some more questions. Was there anything I wanted to ask him? I had no idea what he meant, so I shrugged no, said goodbye, and left.

Rope

After an early breakfast, over which I regaled my parents with stories about New York, I called the studio to tell them I was back. I was told to go straight to Hitchcock's office at Warner Brothers to meet him and get a script of *Rope*. He was expecting me.

When I walked into Mr. Hitchcock's office, I was bowled over. Every wall was covered by eight-by-ten-inch drawings from ceiling to floor. I was completely absorbed in this visualization of the script when that famous voice spoke out behind me: "Won't you come in, Mr. Granger, and I will tell you all about *Rope*."

I was caught completely off guard and don't remember what I said, something clever like "This is terrific," or "You're terrific," or "Wow," and followed him into his office. He sat down with a mischievous smile and told me the story of *Rope* and how he planned to shoot it.

The movie was based on a play, *Rope's End*, by the British playwright Patrick Hamilton, which had been inspired by a famous murder case that took place in Chicago in 1924. Two college students, Leopold and Loeb, just for kicks, and because they believed that their intellectual superiority entitled them, brutally strangled a young boy just to prove they were smart enough to get away with it.

In the movie, they hide the body in a chest in their New York City apartment and serve hors d'oeuvres off this chest to the dead man's parents and fiancée, who come for cocktails a short while later. Their college housemaster, Rupert, played by Jimmy Stewart, is both the inspiration for this sociopathic behavior and the person responsible for their undoing.

Hitchcock said he had screened a rough cut of *They Live by Night* and liked the film and my performance in it. He wanted me to play Phillip in *Rope*. My partner in crime, Brandon, was to be played by a New York theater actor, John Dall, who had had a success in his first film as Bette Davis's young protégé in *The Corn Is Green*. Hitchcock explained that all of *Rope* takes place in New York between 7:00 and 8:40 on a specific evening.

He planned to shoot the film in ten or twelve camera setups, each lasting ten minutes. This was the amount of time you got from each reel of film on the color cameras. The setups would be continuous, with no cutting away from the action. The set, the furniture, and the lighting would all be on wheels so that everything could be pulled away for tracking shots as we walked through the rooms of the apartment, which consisted of the hallway and front door, the living room, the bathroom, and the kitchen. Outside the huge living room windows was a skyline of New York that would gradually change from day to night. Mr. Hitchcock loved telling stories. He could make the phone book sound intriguing. Imagine how great *Rope* sounded. We were to start shooting in two weeks.

I asked my parents not to disturb me and settled down in my room to read *Rope*. On the title page I saw "Screenplay by Arthur Laurents." The name was familiar, but it took me a minute to place it. "Oh, that's that little guy I met at Ethyl's! No wonder he wanted to know if I had any questions." I would call him after I finished the screenplay.

The next morning, Arthur's call woke me up. I apologized for not knowing who he was when we met. He said not to worry and asked if I would like to get together to talk about the character. When I said that I would love to, he invited me to dinner.

I arrived at Ethyl's house at the appointed time. Arthur and I had several vodka tonics. Since I had not eaten lunch, I was getting a little sloshed and suggested we go for dinner. Arthur said, "Oh, I'm a great cook, I've got some chops. Is it okay if we eat here?" I said sure and followed him into the kitchen, where we continued to talk about *Rope* as he fixed dinner.

Arthur was very smart, with a bitchy sense of humor that made him an amusing storyteller and gossip. He knew a lot about the theater, a world I wanted very much to become a part of someday. After dinner and some brandy, always a mistake, I got up to leave. He had made a few remarks in the course of the evening that made it no surprise when he suggested that I spend the night. I thanked him and politely declined.

He called to invite me for dinner again several days later, and again we spent the evening talking, mostly about *Rope* and the theater. That night I did not decline his invitation to stay. In fact, I stayed with him every night until we went into rehearsal the following week. We discussed the text and subtext, the unspoken homoerotic bond between Phillip and Brandon, and Rupert's influence on them both. Arthur was attractive, fun, and great company. Being this close to the writer of the script I was going to work on was an extremely valuable learning experience.

Bonanza Bound, Saul's musical, never made it to Broadway. It closed out of town in Philadelphia. Ethyl and Saul were coming home sooner than they had hoped and Arthur had to find another place. He saw a house he liked on Lookout Mountain off Laurel Canyon and wanted me to come by to check it out.

We went over to the house on Sunday afternoon. He had already signed a lease and planned to move in as soon as he could. He made an obvious allusion as to what a great space it was for two people and how convenient it was to Warner's, where *Rope* was being shot, but I didn't bite.

When I went home, my parents lit into me. They were angry that I had stayed away from home for the last several nights without discussing it with them. The fact that I had called, that I was over twenty-one and was already looking to find my own place, did not slow them down a bit. I finally shouted that unless they wanted me to move out of their lives that minute, they had better lay off. I was going into rehearsal the next morning, and I needed to be rested and prepared. I knew I had not heard the end of it and that I needed to do something, and soon.

Rehearsals began the next morning, and went on for fifteen days. The filming was completed in twenty-one days. Everyone on the soundstage, from Jimmy Stewart to the prop men, called Mr. Hitchcock "Hitch." He liked it, and smiled when I did likewise. The rehearsals were grueling. Since there were no cuts, as one walked through the apartment, walls had to be pulled out of the way, lights had to follow and/or precede you, and furniture had to be removed and replaced, and this activity had to be silent because of the sound recording. The Technicolor cameras were almost as big as modern refrigerators. There were many opportunities for technical problems, and they all happened. We had to shoot a number of the ten-minute reels over. Even after all went well on the set, when Hitch watched the rushes the next morning, he would see that the color didn't match because of lighting differences from one take to another. At the end of each take or reel, Hitch would end with the camera on someone's back or an inanimate object that he could match with the first shot on the next take. After a couple of days of what felt like total chaos, throughout which Hitch was imperturbable, things settled down a bit, and the mistakes became fewer. At the end of the first week, everyone was exhausted with the exception of Constance Collier and Sir Cedric Hardwicke, the old theater pros. They were having a ball. The constant swirl of activity was so different from the stage that they went along with it like kids on a roller coaster. Fortunately, I was once close enough to catch Connie when she trustingly started to sit on a chair that the prop man had not yet managed to get in place.

To this day, reporters and film aficionados still ask about the actors' discussions with Hitchcock about the implied homosexual relationship between the two young men in *Rope*, and how Jimmy Stewart fit into those discussions. My answer is always disappointing to them: "What discussions? It was 1948."

Arthur made sure that I was aware of what he felt was going on between the characters, and, of course, John Dall and I discussed the subtext of our scenes together. We knew that Hitch knew what he was doing and had built sexual ambiguity into his presentation of the material. Jimmy Stewart must have known that the film was based on Leopold and Loeb, but I'm sure he felt that as far as his character was concerned, any implied sexual relationship between his students was strictly their business.

Jimmy was a gentleman, the real thing, and one of the nicest actors I've ever worked with. I have wondered quite often if this quality interfered with his realizing the darker side of Rupert. After all, the character is partially responsible for what happened, and is the person who pushes those buttons in the boys. It might have been interesting to see what an actor like James Mason, with his quirky, dark quality, would have brought to the part.

After the first week's work, I was too beat to go to any parties on Saturday, or to get into a deep discussion with Arthur about his script, so I headed home. That was a mistake. My father had been drinking. As soon as I walked in the door, he started in on me. I went straight to my room, packed a bag, and left. I hugged my mother, who was crying, and said, "It will be better this way, Mom, you'll see. I'll get the rest of my stuff as soon as I can." I got in my car, headed for Arthur's, and never looked back.

Arthur didn't seem surprised to see me when he answered the door. To this day, I'm not sure if this was what he was hoping would happen. In any case, he did not object, which I assumed to mean that we were taking the next step in our relationship. This next step lasted for about a year. It turned out to be a very busy year, with Arthur going back to New York to have his new play produced on Broadway and my doing two films almost back to back.

We had a constant stream of visitors on the set of *Rope*. Hitch loved showing off. Whether it was the press, old friends, or other celebrities, he obviously relished having them there. He loved publicity. If you think about it, in the 1940s and 1950s the average filmgoer neither knew nor cared who directed the film they were seeing. One went to the new Clark Gable movie, the latest Judy Garland movie, or Dean Martin and Jerry Lewis's new comedy. The few exceptions like Cecil B. De Mille and Hitchcock had mastered the art of self-promotion. Hitch made a cameo appearance in each of his films. It became a game for the public. They loved spotting him. His friends, who visited the set, were always interesting people to meet. One day it would be Cary Grant, the next Ingrid Bergman. A high point was when Noël Coward dropped by for lunch. He knew Sir Cedric and Connie from their years in the English theater. Hitch invited John and me to join them. Noël Coward was charming, amusing, and a great raconteur. His clipped, flat delivery made his stories seem even funnier. One only has to listen to the recording of Sir Noël and his frequent stage partner and lifelong friend, Gertrude Lawrence, doing a scene from his play *Private Lives* to understand what I mean. Hitch asked him how Gertrude Lawrence was. Coward responded that he had just seen her on the stage in London. "She was wonderful." Then he took a slight pause and with a twinkle confided, "One has to be terribly careful onstage with Gertie, you know . . . give her a phone or a box of chocolates . . . you're in serious trouble . . . and a scarf . . . *disaster!*" He mimed her actions as he spoke and you could see Gertie upstaging him. Even Hitch laughed.

As time passed, even though they never completely disappeared, the problems with the filming of *Rope* had settled down. There were so many difficult technical demands that uninterrupted or good takes were the exception rather than the rule. For actors it was always rewarding to have that much rehearsal before each setup, but the focus of these rehearsals had to be on things like hitting your marks on time and not getting run over while doing it. The novelty had worn off. It began to get frustrating. Hitch was incredibly patient. Though it was obvious that he loved the various challenges, I'd bet that he, too, was getting weary of the restrictions within which he had to work. The storytelling limitations imposed by not being able to be honest about the real relationship between Phillip, Brandon, and Rupert only made it feel more constricted. *Rope* was an interesting technical experiment that I was lucky and happy to be a part of, but I don't think it was one of Hitchcock's better films. It's interesting to speculate on what the film would have been like had he shot it normally. It's equally interesting to think about what kind of film he would have made if he had not had to worry about censorship.

The Most Beautiful Woman in the World

Since Arthur had never met Ethyl and Saul, we decided to throw a homecoming/housewarming party for them at their house on Doheny. They were due back on a Wednesday, and we decided that by Saturday they would be rested up and ready. Our plan was to take Ethyl and Saul to their favorite restaurant for an early dinner while Judy was greeting the arriving guests. I thought it might be fun to have a few new faces among the regulars. We invited some musician friends of Saul's from MGM; Betty Garrett, whom Metro was grooming for musical stardom, and her husband, Larry Parks, who had played Al Jolson at Columbia; Anita Ellis, a wonderful singer from New York, who had such bad stage fright that she could not sing in public, but had dubbed Rita Hayworth's sexy singing voice in *Gilda, Down to Earth,* and a number of other films; Gary

Merrill, who was making *All About Eve* with Bette Davis; and Nick Ray and his wife, Gloria Grahame, who later won an Oscar as the bad girl in *The Bad and the Beautiful*. I invited everyone to arrive after 7:30, which was when Arthur had booked a table at The Players. The surprise party would be in full swing when we got back after dinner.

By the time we got to the Chaplins' home, everyone was having a swell time, and the boisterous chorus of "SURPRISE!" was heartfelt. Saul immediately sat down at the piano, and what was already a good party just got better. A musician friend of Saul's arrived with Hedy Lamarr, whom none of us had ever met. MGM had built Miss Lamarr up as "The Most Beautiful Woman in the World," and she was that. She was also so shy and withdrawn that when she sat on the floor against one wall, it seemed as if she wanted to disappear . . . she almost did.

Some time later Ethyl joined Saul at the second piano to play and sing Kurt Weill's *Threepenny Opera*. Hedy came immediately to life. She jumped up and hurried to the piano to sing with them. The transformation was amazing. She joined in with complete animated abandon. If she had only been able to bring some of that joy to her screen roles, there would have been no stopping her.

I went to the bar, and Gary Merrill came over to confide in me. I later learned that he confided in everyone that night. He was madly in love. He was sorry, he could not say with whom, but he had never been so crazy about anyone. She was a fantastic lady, brilliantly talented, beautiful and smart, with a great sense of humor. He couldn't wait for me to meet her. Of course, we all knew who he was talking about. The affair he was having with Bette Davis was not the best-kept secret in town. I just wished that he had brought her to the party. Bette, a two-time Academy Award winner, was always in trouble or on suspension at Warner Brothers. Whenever she felt that a film was not right for her or was junk, she had no hesitation about refusing to do it and marching unannounced into Jack Warner's office to tell him exactly how she felt. She was my hero. When I did meet her at Jack Warner's house, I told her that and how much I loved her singing "They're Either Too Young or Too Old" in *Hollywood Canteen*. The next morning a messenger rang my doorbell and delivered a recording of Bette singing the song. I realized that she was everything Gary had said and more. Later, when I got to know her better, I realized that she was as down-to-earth as they come, and couldn't bear pretentiousness in anyone.

Ethyl and Saul had finished playing Kurt Weill, and Saul was now accompanying Betty Garrett as she sang some of the songs from a new film she was working on at MGM with Gene Kelly and Frank Sinatra, *Take Me Out to the Ball Game*. I spotted Hedy making her way to the bar and went over to introduce myself. Obviously relaxed now, she was open and completely at ease. She said that she had seen *They Live by Night* at a screening at Louis B. Mayer's house, and had thought it was very good. She also thought Cathy and I were wonderful together. I asked her what it had been like making films in Austria before the war. We found a seat, and she explained that she had only been a bit player until that stupid Czech film *Ecstasy* came along and made such a commotion. She had appeared nude in that film in 1933, and it became a worldwide sensation. By today's standards, her chaste little nude swim would most likely not even get a PG-13, but back then it caused an international furor.

She told me that after that film, she had turned down a Hollywood offer in order to marry a wealthy Austrian industrialist and had retired from acting. Her husband then spent the next five years trying in vain to buy up all the existing copies of *Ecstasy*. She gave me a wicked smile. "He had no more luck with that than he did turning me into the contented mistress of his fancy country mansion."

He had ensconced her on his estate in the beautiful Austrian countryside while he was off wheeling and dealing all over Europe. For a while she enjoyed playing house, but then boredom began to creep into her new world. One day she decided to entertain herself by taking all sixteen toilet seats from the house out on the lawn that swept down to the lake to paint them in the sun. As she was beginning the last one, she spotted a long line of black Mercedes limos in the distance coming up the long drive to the house. Her husband had not bothered to call to warn her that he was bringing important guests for the weekend. Hedy laughed. "I took one look at his thundercloud of a face when he got out of the lead car and knew that I was going to revive that Hollywood offer." It is just too bad that Metro never learned how to use her, because "The Most Beautiful Woman in the World" was a lot more than an unforgettable face, she was a delightful dame.

The Little Tramp and Big Bill

One morning Arthur asked me if I liked to play tennis. I told him I loved to, especially when I could get the ball over the net. He laughed and said, "I've got a perfect solution. Charlie Chaplin called me yesterday. Bill Tilden is going to be giving lessons up at Charlie's house. He's down on his luck, and Charlie is helping him out by letting him use his courts to give lessons. Charlie's also calling a lot of his friends to encourage them to take advantage of this opportunity. What do you think?" I said I thought it was a great idea. Who wouldn't want to take lessons from the greatest tennis player in the world?

Bill Tilden, also known as "Big Bill," began playing tennis at the late age of twenty-seven. Before long, he began winning championships, eventually leading the United States team to seven consecutive Davis Cup victories, a record that has never been equaled. He was known for his cannonball serve, which enabled him to serve aces at will. From 1920 to 1925 he was considered the greatest player who ever lived. During the Roaring Twenties, he, boxer Jack Dempsey, baseball player Babe Ruth, footballer Red Grange, and golfer Bobby Jones dominated American sports. In need of money, Tilden turned professional in 1931. Ten years later, at the age of forty-eight, he was still playing professionally against players like Don Budge, the twenty-five-year-old world champion . . . and still occasionally winning.

His downfall started in 1946 when he was arrested for soliciting an underage male prostitute. Three years later, after a second arrest for a similar offense, he was being banned from teaching at tennis clubs and public courts. He was quickly down and out. Charlie Chaplin had been Tilden's friend before these problems and remained his friend after them. By making his courts available to Tilden and encouraging friends and acquaintances in the movie colony to avail themselves of the opportunity to improve their game by taking lessons from a champion, he helped Tilden during a very rough patch for the tennis champ.

I loved taking lessons from him, and it proved tremendously helpful when I played a tennis champion in *Strangers on a Train*, but I never really got to know him. Everything was strictly business on the tennis court, and after a lesson was over, Bill always left immediately.

Charlie's house was a lovely Spanish-style home in Beverly Hills above Sunset Boulevard. It was large, light, and airy, and beautifully furnished in a comfortable lived-in way. When you drove through the gates the first structure you arrived at was the tennis court. The house was above that. I do not remember a pool. Charlie was warm and open, and not only a world-class clown, but also a world-class intellect, which was quite an achievement in light of his growing up with his brother as hungry urchins in the streets of London. Charlie was married to his fourth wife, Oona, the daughter of America's greatest playwright, Eugene O'Neill. They had married in 1943 when she was eighteen and he was fifty-four, despite her father's objections. I have never met a happier couple. Oona was warm, gracious, and a perfect hostess. She made me feel completely at home and at ease. I liked her immediately.

Several years after this, I got a call from Jerry Robbins, who was coming to Los Angeles the following week to discuss re-creating his brilliant ballet, *The Small House of Uncle Thomas*, for 20th Century-Fox's film version of *The King and I*. The ballet was the highlight of the stage show and would be in the film as well. In it Jerry used traditional Siamese dance to portray an incident from

Harriet Beecher Stowe's ground-breaking novel, *Uncle Tom's Cabin*: Eliza's escape from Simon Legree over a partially frozen river.

I invited Jerry to stay, but he said he was getting the first-class treatment with a suite at the Hotel Bel-Air. I couldn't beat that, so I invited him to dinner and asked if there was anyone he would like to meet. Without a beat he said, "Yes. Charlie Chaplin. Do you know him?" I admitted that I'd gotten to know him slightly playing tennis at his house. Jerry jumped in before I could tell him about Big Bill and told me he could only be here for three days. He said he would call back later to check on which night I'd made the arrangements . . . and hung up. Not being the most experienced host in town, I needed a couple of minutes to screw up my courage to call the Chaplins. Oona answered. After beating around the bush for a couple of minutes I finally blurted out, "I'm having a small dinner party next Thursday and I was wondering if by any chance you and Charlie might happen to be free because a friend of mine . . ."

She interrupted me, "Farley, how nice, we'd love to come." Then she called out, "Charlie. . . . It's Farley Granger on the phone . . . He's inviting us for dinner next Thursday. . . . Good, that's what I said. . . . Farley, what time would you like us?"

It was that easy. Maybe it was too easy. I started to worry again. I called to invite Ethyl and Buddy, Arthur, and Millard and Lorry Kaufman. Millard was a screenwriter who was to write the classic *Bad Day at Black Rock*. His wife, Lorry, on whom I'd had a crush from the first moment I saw her, was a brilliant anthropologist. The group was set. Now I just had to plan everything. After probably my sixth call to Ethyl, she said, "Farfel, get a caterer and a bartender and stop driving us both crazy. OK?" I did. It worked.

Everyone was on time and, judging from the amount of chatter and laughter and cross-talk over drinks, getting along famously. Dinner was cold watercress soup, a superb rack of lamb with flageolets, and a Bibb lettuce with camembert salad, all served with a nice California red wine, and this was when everyone thought California wine came from someone's backyard in earthenware jugs. Dessert was a Grand Marnier soufflé. Everyone was impressed by "my" dinner, especially me.

After dinner, we went back to the living room for coffee, drinks, and games. Still working at being a good host, I suggested that we play The Game. Everyone got right into it, expecting wonderful things from Charlie. It took a while for it to dawn on all of us that ironically, for one of cinema's great silent film stars, he was really terrible at charades. Ethyl whispered, "Put on some music fast, this is getting really uncomfortable."

I interrupted to take coffee and after-dinner drink orders and put on a record. Everyone relaxed as the conversation got lively again. At one point late in the evening Charlie asked Jerry about a specific dance step. Jerry stood up to demonstrate and suddenly Chaplin was up and dancing with him. They danced together doing a variety of routines for a blissfully long time. Charlie was as quick and light on his feet as any professional. Being there was a rare treat for us all.

Disenchantment

Not too long after we finished *Rope*, the studio called to tell me that Cathy and I were going to be in Mr. Goldwyn's new film, *Enchantment*, along with Teresa Wright and David Niven. At last, I thought, the big project! We were all to report to the studio on the following Monday morning for a read-through of the script with the director, Irving Reis. The studio messengered a copy of the script to me to read over the weekend. It was not only bad, but my part was insignificant. By the time I got in my car to go to the studio on Monday, I had convinced myself that it would all work out. After all, the cast was terrific, and sometimes an inventive director could work wonders with inferior material. When I got to the rehearsal hall, no one was there except a production assistant, who told me that the rehearsal had been cancelled. When I asked him why, he said he didn't know. The studio would call me later.

Then Cathy ran in. Her face was ashen, and she had obviously been crying. She said, "Please, Farley, I've got to talk to you." I took her in my arms and said, "Sure, come on, let's go to my dressing room." As soon as the door was closed, Cathy started sobbing as if her heart would break. When she finally calmed down a bit, the story came out between great shuddering intakes of breath. Soon after *The Best Years of Our Lives*, William Wyler, who had directed the film, and most of the other movies responsible for the studio's classy reputation, promoted as "the Goldwyn Touch," left to form his own production company. Goldwyn, who wanted everyone who worked for him to treat him like a benevolent patriarch instead of the wily dictator he really was, took his departure as a personal betrayal and never forgave him. Wyler and Goldwyn went on to fight for years over Wyler's share of the profits from *The Best Years of Our Lives*.

The week before we were to begin work on *Enchantment*, Cathy had very privately and quietly married Wyler's brother, a man much older than she. Goldwyn did not hear about it until Monday morning just before we were to begin the rehearsal for *Enchantment*. He went ballistic. He called Cathy into his office and screamed at her that William Wyler had put his brother up to marrying her to get even with him. Cathy either would get the marriage annulled or she was fired, and he would see to it that she never worked in Hollywood again. She tried to reason with him, but he never stopped yelling, and finally told her to get out! She was "fired and finished in movies."

The next thing I knew, Evelyn Keyes, who had played Scarlett O'Hara's younger sister, was playing Cathy's part. Evelyn, who was about ten years older than Cathy, was a good actress and could not have been easier to work with, but she was in the middle of a stormy divorce from John Huston and was obviously not getting a lot of sleep at the time. She was not looking her best. They put a skinny mustache on me to make me look older. Instead, it made me look like a kid with a fake mustache.

Irving Reis was a far cry from the inventive director I'd imagined before rehearsal. He was no help at all. Even the considerable charms and talents of Teresa Wright and David Niven could not help. Nothing was going to make this turkey fly. "Just About the Most Wonderful Love Story Ever Made," as our ridiculous ad campaign trumpeted in all the publicity for *Enchantment*, was just about the year's biggest flop . . . so much for my first postwar movie at the Goldwyn Studio. Almost immediately after we completed filming, our cameraman, Gregg Toland, died. He had done most of Wyler's great films for Goldwyn as well as *Citizen Kane* for Orson Welles. He had worked for Goldwyn for many years and had perfected the technique of deep focus, which allowed the director to keep an actor in the background as well as the actor in the foreground in sharp focus. If Wyler's departure signaled the beginning of the end of "the Goldwyn touch," Toland's death was certainly another nail in its coffin.

Shelley

I can't even remember when or where we first met, but as long as I'd known her, Shelley Winters was important to me. She has been the love of my life and the bane of my existence. We have laughed and cried together and fallen into each other's arms. We have fought and not spoken for years. We have been friends, there for each other through the worst of all possible disasters and the best of all possible triumphs. You name it, we've been it . . . sometimes exhilarating, sometimes depressing, always surprising . . . I wouldn't have had it any other way.

Preston Sturges, the brilliant director of screwball comedies like *The Lady Eve* and *The Palm Beach Story*, owned a restaurant on the Sunset Strip called The Players. It served the best Caesar salad I have ever had. I liked his restaurant so much that I went whenever possible. Sturges was there every evening. One night with Ethyl, Saul, and Arthur, I spotted Shelley Winters, alone and crying, in a booth nearby. I had met Shelley several times and thought she was smart, sweet, and a little zany. I went over to ask her what was wrong. She told me that she hated the movie that they were making her do at Universal. She was having awful problems with the producer. And it was her birthday, and she was all alone, and nobody loved her. It only took a minute to talk her into joining us. After introductions all around, we sat down and she launched into her litany of woes again for the whole table.

I excused myself, found Preston Sturges, and asked him if he could have a lit candle in a cupcake brought to our table by a couple of waiters who could sing "Happy Birthday" to Shelley. He was delighted to help and said, "Just give me a few minutes; I'll take care of everything." I thanked him and headed back to our table, where things were looking up. Shelley had stopped crying and was the center of attention. Soon the waiters arrived, not only with the cupcake and the song, but also with a bottle of fine Champagne, "Compliments of Mr. Sturges."

Shelley blew out her candle as we all sang "Happy Birthday." As they were pouring the champagne, she burst into tears all over again and began wailing that nobody loved her. Ethyl took her hand and said, "Cheer up, Shelley. We all love you." The real Shelley surfaced and replied, "Yes, I know, but you're not producers."

My dating Shelley did not make Mr. Goldwyn happy. He wanted me to be seen in public with someone squeaky-clean like Ann Blyth, who in real life was the exact opposite of the bad girl she played in *Mildred Pierce*. Ann was quiet and serious, a very nice girl ... with no sense of humor. She was lovely and proper and no fun. Shelley was totally unpredictable, a wise-cracking blonde who loved the spotlight. I was uncomfortable being a celebrity, but she loved being one. Faced with screaming fans at premieres, Shelley blossomed, while I turned to stone. She always had a crack or a quip ready for the press. I always mumbled incoherently. In a way, her public persona made it very hard for her to be taken seriously as an actress. I constantly tried to get her to calm down but soon realized that was impossible. Her pizzazz was one of the things that made her so attractive, and she did have a sense of humor, and we did have fun. What a paradox she was, though. She didn't smoke, she kept her drinks to a minimum, she never swore, and she didn't like it when I did. A blond bombshell in public, she was Miss Priss in private. She could be hell on wheels when she was being serious about acting. We never stopped talking and arguing about acting, or bitching about what we had to deal with as contract players.

Shelley had been involved in politics since she worked at a five-and-dime as a teen and became a union organizer. She was much more politically aware than I was, and she never stopped working to enlighten me. As everyone stood around the piano singing Rodgers and Hart or Cole Porter at the Kellys' she would be under it waiting for her chance to belt out a few old union songs. She was an original. We were a classic example of opposites who definitely attract. Shortly after I met Shelley, I ended the relationship with Arthur. I tried to make it amicable since we had so many good friends in common. Shelley knew all about him. We had no secrets from each other.

Shooting *Roseanna*

Through a writer friend who knew John Collier, I got a copy of an early draft of a screenplay that Collier was working on for Mr. Goldwyn. The script, as yet untitled, was based on a novel by Alberta Hannum about two feuding mountain clans, the Hatfields and the McCoys. Goldwyn had originally commissioned it as a vehicle for Cathy and me. It was Romeo and Juliet as southern hill folk, and it was flat-out wonderful. Collier, best known as a writer of fantasy fiction, was an inspired choice. He had enriched the tale with undercurrents of superstition and witchcraft. He set most of the tale at night, with coyotes howling in the hills and owls capturing helpless creatures by shadowy moonlight. I loved it and could not wait for work to begin. I was hurt by what Goldwyn had done to Cathy, and deeply disappointed that I'd be doing the movie without her. She would have made an enchanting Juliet.

The studio called to tell me not to leave town. A new film that I was to star in was about to go into production very soon. I innocently asked what it was, and was told the title, *Roseanna McCoy*. That is all anyone would tell me about the film. I asked who was playing Roseanna; no one knew. I asked who the director was; no one knew. They did tell me that the rest of the cast was terrific and included Richard Basehart, Charles Bickford, Raymond Massey, Aline MacMahon, and Hope Emerson. That was an impressive group of actors. With Collier's script and the right girl, I felt this could be a very special movie. Under threat of death if she blabbed to anyone, Shelley had wormed the information about *Roseanna McCoy* out of me. She was really happy for me even though her way of showing it consisted of constant moaning that she was destined to be cast in *Frenchie* parts, hookers with gumption and a heart of gold parts, for the rest of her life. As soon as I got the official call to report to the studio for work, I took her to Chasen's, the best restaurant in town, to celebrate.

The reality that hit like a sledgehammer on the following Monday is still hard to talk about. I walked into the studio where we all were to meet. The first person to greet me was Irving Reis, the highly neurotic and lackluster director of *Enchantment*. He introduced me to a kid named Joan Evans. She was the girl Goldwyn had picked as his new ingénue after a national talent search. Her first effort was to be replacing Cathy. She was a sweet, pretty fifteen-year-old who still had some baby fat, but no meaningful acting experience. I think her parents were Hollywood writers, and she was Joan Crawford's goddaughter. When I met her again, many years later, she admitted that she was really only fourteen when she started on the film. Perhaps that has something to do with the complete lack of sexual tension between our Romeo and Juliet. Her parents had added two years to her age in order to be able to say she was sixteen when the film was released. Unfortunately, a star was not born.

I was busy introducing myself to the other actors when the assistant director started rounding us up. The bus was there to take us to a train to the small town up in the Sierra Madre where we were to begin shooting the next day. The seasoned pros soon started to ask questions about the script, like where was it? We were told that the director was going to take care of that on the train. Irving, who had been driven to the station by one of Goldwyn's vice presidents, was the last one to hop onboard just as the train was pulling out. Once we were smoothly under way, the actors, who by now sensed that something was up, pinned him down and demanded some answers. He told us that Mr. Goldwyn had not been happy with the script and had thrown the whole thing out. He assured us that rewrites were already under way, and we could expect the first of them tomorrow after he had done some establishing shots. Irving's ability to lie convincingly was pretty much on a par with his ability to direct imaginatively. No one believed him. The empty feeling in the pit of my stomach spread. I could not tell anyone that I had read a bootlegged copy of the script, that it was wonderful, and that it had probably been thrown out because Goldwyn didn't understand it. I wondered if anyone else had seen it, but no one said a word.

The mountains were very beautiful. The town consisted of a hotel glued onto a small movie house, a post office, a bar, and a drugstore/general store/gas station. There were some wonderful ramshackle houses, and two sets built on opposite mountain ridges outside of town as the homes of the Hatfields and the McCoys, We all stayed in that one hotel. The rooms were clean and claustrophobic. We all ate at that one hotel. The food was all fried all the time. Everyone kept very much to him or herself. No friendships were forged, no sense of camaraderie surfaced at any time during the lengthy shoot of a film that should have been wonderful.

The entire first day was spent by the director and crew shooting establishing shots of the clan's two homes and the surrounding countryside. No pages arrived from the studio. The next day was a repeat of the first. For the next two weeks, we still had no script. Irving did all he could. He shot people standing outside the houses, entering the houses, and exiting the houses—the interiors were back at the studio. He shot me on a horse going from camera left to camera right, from camera right to camera left, up the hill, down the hill, on the ridge in the distance, on the ridge nearby, mounting the horse, dismounting the horse, with Joan on the horse with me, at a walk, at a canter, at a gallop, and just about anything you could imagine doing with a horse. Then he shot me walking with Joan, holding hands with Joan, chasing Joan through a field, and so on. This went on for two weeks and still no pages arrived from the studio. We were all beginning to feel a little crazed. Even the poor director was looking crazed. Suddenly we packed everything up and went back to Hollywood, where we were laid off for a week.

After our week of R&R, we reported to the studio anxious to get this impending disaster over with. Goldwyn had hired a writer named Phil Yordan to fix the script. Phil, who would not be miscast on *The Sopranos*, was a very funny man who had written some good screenplays. He had a reputation as the speediest script doctor in Hollywood. The rumor was that he had rotating platoons of writing students from UCLA chained to typewriters in his basement.

As the pages dribbled in, we went to work on the soundstage. The art department had built, along with the interiors, woods, creeks, and bridges to replicate the High Sierras. On some days we got a whole scene to shoot, on others we just got a page or two. Other times we would get different pages of the same scene. It was all very confusing. It's a testimonial to the professionalism of the cast that everyone worked hard and stayed cool. Joan and I had a scene riding together on a horse through the woods in which I was to sing a lovely song to her that Frank Loesser had written called "More I Cannot Wish You." This melody was intended to underscore all our scenes. Goldwyn hated it. He threw it out as soon as he heard it and had Loesser write a banal title song, "Roseanna."

Goldwyn took to appearing on the set every day. Someone always called down to warn the crew that he was coming. By the time he arrived, everyone would be extremely busy. When he was angry, which was often, his voice got even higher. This anger was usually directed at the director, whose tics just got worse. It took almost two chaotic months to finish this section of the filming. Then we were all laid off again.

It was several weeks before everyone was called and told that we were going back to the location in order to shoot some new scenes. Irving Reis was gone. When we got to the location, the first person I saw was Nick Ray. No one was ever told the why or wherefore of Irving's departure. When I saw Nick, I had a momentary surge of hope, but then I realized that it was too late for him to make any significant improvement. Nick must have realized it, too, because after a warm hello, he refused to talk about *Roseanna*. That night it started raining, and it did not stop for two weeks. Every morning at 4:00 A.M. we got up, got into makeup and costume, and drove up to the location. There we sat in our cars all day, waiting for the rain to stop. Then, every afternoon at 5:00 P.M., the cars would turn around and take us back to the hotel for a fried dinner.

Doris Day, one of the outstanding band singers of the war years, became a movie star in 1948. Her first film, *Romance on the High Seas*, was the beginning of a film career that flourished into the mid-1960s when she went on to become an equally big TV star. Miss Day has never had a bigger fan than me. I love her singing, her acting, her looks, her animal rights activism, and just about everything about her. For those two weeks in the mountains Doris Day drove me crazy. The little hotel we were in was attached to the movie theater in town, and my room had to be adjacent to the part of the movie house where the speakers were placed. Miss Day's first movie was playing. If I never hear the words "It's Magic" sung again, it will be way too soon. Believe me, it quickly ceased being magic to me. By the end of the first week, the crew and a few of the actors—to this day I don't know why, as I wasn't one of them—succumbed to cabin fever and began drinking, gambling, and fighting the nights away. Finally, we were called back to Hollywood to wait for the rain to stop. In a week it did, and we were hustled back up into the mountains. We began work the next morning.

The first setup we had to do was Roseanna and I walking along a mountain path on a steep slope. Suddenly her brother, my sworn enemy, played by Richard Basehart, appears on a ridge across from and slightly above us and takes a shot at me. For protection, I pull her down behind some bushes along the path. While he is reloading, I stand up to shoot back at him. Nick had us rehearse the scene with no blanks in the guns and was very happy with the way it went. So we loaded the guns and got ready to do the take. When Nick called "Action!" Richard fired at me, and I pulled Roseanna down behind the bushes. As I stood to shoot at Richard, the ground, which had absorbed weeks of rain, gave way under my feet. I slid downhill, falling flat on my face. At the same instant, there was an ear-splitting bang in my right ear. After a second or so, when I was able to look up, I was horrified. Joan was squirming in the grass like a snake, covered in blood, her hands over her face. She must have been screaming, but I couldn't hear anything. It was a terrible slow-motion moment during which I thought, "Oh my God, I've shot Roseanna!"

I'm sure it was only minutes, but it seemed like hours before we sorted out what had happened. The blank charge had only hit Joan in the wrist, thank God. The range was not close enough for any permanent damage, but it was close enough to penetrate her skin and cause a lot of bleeding. She was justifiably hysterical and needed to be taken to a hospital. We wrapped in the mountains and went back to Hollywood.

On the train back, one wag accused me of doing it on purpose to get us all out of the mountains. Another one said, "We don't know how we'll ever be able to repay you." Nick did his best to improve the quality of what was left of *Roseanna McCoy*, but too much damage had already been done. At least John Collier, Frank Loesser, and I knew what might have been. I wish Mr. Goldwyn did.

Solo

During one of the endless days waiting for the rain to stop layoffs that I had while making *Roseanna*, I got home unexpectedly early one afternoon and walked in on Arthur being a little bit too friendly with a delivery boy. I turned around, walked out, and found my first apartment. I was twenty-four and more than ready. It was in a small complex owned by the actor/designer/director Mitch Leisen. If I remember correctly, there were three separate buildings in a beautifully landscaped compound. Each building had four apartments. I lived over Mitch Leisen, and a nice middle-aged couple lived next door to me. We shared a terrace that was separated by a wrought-iron fence. Mitch directed a number of reliably good films in the 1930s and 1940s: *To Each His Own, Hold Back the Dawn*, and *Frenchman's Creek* are just three of many. He had begun his career as a costume designer and art director for Cecil B. De Mille. Needless to say, he had superb taste. All the apartments were decorated with antiques, gorgeous carpeting, and great paintings. I rented mine when I was still traveling back and forth to the High Sierra location, so I did not spend much time there. As soon as we finished the film, I got a dog, a great poodle mutt whom I named Gaby after the sailor in *Fancy Free*, and settled in.

Evelyn Keyes and Paulette Goddard shared an apartment identical to the one I had in one of the other buildings. They had me over for a welcome dinner soon after I arrived. Evelyn was over the trauma of her divorce from John Huston and looking terrific. Paulette was an irrepressibly delightful dame who as a young starlet had become Charlie Chaplin's third wife and starred in his films *Modern Times* and *The Great Dictator*. I had a great time with them at dinner and for the short time we were neighbors.

My tenure as a tenant was not destined to last. Neither, for that matter, was Evelyn's or Paulette's. In fact, they were the first to go. John Huston, in an effort to remain on good terms with Evelyn, returned from a safari in Africa with a present for her. It was an adorable adolescent chimpanzee. She loved it . . . for about forty-eight hours. Then the chimp had a tantrum, and it does not take too much imagination to guess what literally hit the fan. He wrecked their apartment and its antiques. I could hear the shouts and screams and chimpanzee sounds all the way over at my place. Mitch threw them all out the next morning.

It took another couple of weeks before he got to me. I really loved my dog, Gaby. I thought he was the smartest and best dog in the world. I was surprised every day by what great bowel and bladder control he had. After a long day at the studio or an afternoon of tennis lessons up at Charlie Chaplin's house, I would get home afraid of what I'd find because his morning walk had been so long ago. He never had an accident in the apartment. I was so proud. Then Mitch informed me that my neighbors had complained about me. They had been away in Mexico for a month and had returned late the previous night. When they opened the doors to their terrace they were greeted by mountains of dog doo, and plants that were yellowed and dead from dog pee. Gaby, in order not to soil his own nest, had obviously wriggled his way through the wrought-iron balcony divider and taken care of his needs next door. I think it was the fact that I was so proud of Gaby's smarts that upset Mitch the most. At least he gave me to the end of the week to clear out. Actually, I was not too upset. Mitch and his boyfriend, who lived directly below me, had all-too-frequent fights. The screaming, accompanied by smashing plates and slamming doors, was as loud as Evelyn's chimp. Also, I had never been completely comfortable in these chic surroundings.

The next day I found an apartment below the Sunset Strip in a complex that surrounded a swimming pool and was reassuringly ordinary. While I was packing the following evening, my doorbell rang. It was Arthur. He had heard what had happened from Ethyl, and had come to ask me to move back in with him. It wasn't until that moment that I fully realized how happy I was to be solo, completely on my own. I told him that and said that although I always would care for him, I had no desire to attempt to recapture something that was over.

Lenny

No sooner had I settled into my new digs when the studio called to say that Goldwyn had loaned me out to MGM for a film called Side Street. When I learned the particulars of the film, I was not unhappy to do it even though the script was ordinary and predictable. A big plus was that Cathy O'Donnell was to be my co-star. Louis B. Mayer, most likely in a move calculated to annoy

Goldwyn, had put her under contract shortly after Goldwyn fired her. The director, Anthony Mann, whose other films include *Winchester '73*, *Bend of the River*, and *The Far Country*, all with Jimmy Stewart, planned to shoot much of the film on location in New York. Location shooting was becoming more common even if it was more expensive. The post–World War II audience no longer accepted painted backdrops and studio streets as reality. Shortly before I heard about being loaned out, I'd found out that Shelley was having an affair with the very married Burt Lancaster while we were still together. The blowup that followed that discovery made New York seem even more attractive. I boarded Gaby with my parents, and left for New York ten days before we were scheduled to begin shooting there.

The Essex House was booked, but they arranged accommodations for me at the Plaza. I had a beautiful corner room that looked out on the park and east across Fifth Avenue into the sunrise. I felt as if I'd come home and slept better than I had since the last time I was in the city. After breakfast and a shower the next morning, I called Adolph Green to tell him I would be in town for almost a month doing a film for Metro. He said not to make any plans for that evening, because he had tickets to see Lenny Bernstein conduct the New York Philharmonic in an all-Stravinsky program. He had an extra ticket and was sure Lenny would love to see me.

I had gotten to know Leonard Bernstein at Ethyl and Saul's house in Hollywood. He was as attractive as he was articulate and passionate about music. He had expanded my favorite ballet, *Fancy Free*, into one of my favorite Broadway musicals, *On the Town*. At MGM, Arthur Freed had adapted the Broadway show into a hit movie musical of the same name, starring Gene Kelly, Frank Sinatra, Betty Garrett, Vera-Ellen, and Ann Miller, but he had inexplicably thrown out almost all of Bernstein's songs. The opening number, "New York, New York" survived Freed's error in judgment and is probably the one song that everyone remembers from the movie. Frank Sinatra was angry when he discovered that the lovely ballad "Lonely Town" had been cut, and Gene was equally upset to lose "Some Other Time." The experience had made Lenny wary of Hollywood. He protected himself much more successfully when they made the TV movie of *Wonderful Town* a few years later.

Lenny had recently been appointed assistant conductor for the New York Philharmonic. It was obvious from the way the musicians reacted to his conducting during the concert that they loved him almost as much as the audience did. When it was over, we went back to his dressing room, which was crowded with fans and well-wishers. Lenny spent time with each and every one of them, clearly enjoying himself. It seemed like hours before he was able to close the door on the last of his fans and get ready to go out with us.

Still high on the energy of the concert, we went to a tavern around the corner to eat, drink, and catch up on one another's lives for the next two hours. Adolph was the first to fade. He had to get home in time to see Allyn Ann, who was in previews with Irving Berlin's new musical, *Miss Liberty*. I was the next one to lose steam. I wasn't on New York time yet. Lenny, I'm sure, could have partied all night, but he took sympathy on me. We got a cab, and he dropped me off at the Plaza with a promise to call soon.

I got another perfect night of dreamless sleep and woke up early to a beautiful sunny day. The phone rang at 9:00 A.M. It was Lenny. He was driving up along the Hudson River to meet a young violinist. It was a beautiful day. Would I like to join him? It sounded like a great idea. We agreed that he would pick me up at 10:30.

As we crossed the George Washington Bridge, I was impressed by the beauty and size of the Hudson River. I had the same reaction to the lush greenery along the Palisades Parkway. Sure, Hawaii had plenty of lush, verdant vistas, but that was the tropics. This was only thirty minutes from Broadway. After another thirty minutes or so, we passed a sign that said Sneden's Landing and turned off the highway. We were on a road that ran along the top of a ridge that looked down to the river. We turned into a tree-lined driveway that went halfway down the hill to a big old shingled house in a grove of trees, surrounded by a green lawn that sloped past the house down to the river. We walked up to the front door. Lenny rang the doorbell. When the door opened, there stood Aaron Copland. I hadn't seen Aaron since our dinner at Jimmy Wong Howe's restaurant in Los Angeles just after I got out of the Navy two years earlier. He was grinning from ear to ear. Lenny had set the whole lunch up as a surprise for me.

Lunch on a flagstone patio overlooking the river was wonderful. I remember cold gazpacho, cold chicken, hot new potato salad, gorgonzola, and pears, all washed down with cool white Bordeaux. It was superb. After some great conversation and strong espresso, we went in to the sunroom, where Aaron and Lenny sat down at twin grand pianos and played nonstop selections from Haydn to Prokofiev. They played and stopped to discuss and replay passages and made musical puns as they played and joked—it was exhilarating. Time flew. What I've never forgotten about watching them was how happy they were just to be playing together. I didn't have to understand what was happening musically, because their joy was contagious. Years later, I watched a late-night television show about Yo-Yo Ma teaching at Tanglewood. The same joy passed between him and his students when they communicated musically and between him and the wonderful classical pianist Emmanuel Ax during their duets. After I die, if I have the choice of what to be in my next reincarnation, it will be a musician of that caliber. Before any of us realized it, it was almost 5:00 P.M. Lenny had a concert that evening and we had to leave.

In the late 1950s, I had another musical experience with Lenny and Aaron. At Tanglewood, Lenny was conducting a performance of Aaron's *Appalachian Spring* with the New York Philharmonic. Aaron and I were sitting together in the back of the tent, and he whispered a running commentary on tempi and interpretation throughout the piece. His remarks were basic enough for me to understand and not *too* bitchy. It was the best time I've ever had at a concert.

Lenny knew I was going to the theater that evening. He asked if I would meet him later at his place for a midnight supper. I did, and it could not have seemed more right when he asked me to stay. I did. We had a couple of glorious days and nights together. He was as passionate and enthusiastic a lover as he was a conductor. Then real life intruded. I started work on *Side Street*. That meant that I was up at six A.M. and worked all day, and Leonard was rehearsing in the afternoons and conducting every evening. Carving out time to be together became more complicated, but we managed. It was very easy to be completely caught up with Leonard Bernstein. Charisma was not a word in vogue at that time, but it could have been coined for Lenny.

One night during my second week of filming, Lenny surprised me with a ticket to accompany him on his South American tour, which was to begin at the end of the month. He also told me that he had decided to put his engagement to Felicia Montealegre, the Chilean pianist and actress, on hold. Both pieces of information came as a complete surprise to me. Nothing about any engagement had ever been mentioned, nor had we ever discussed our relationship as lasting beyond the present while I was working in New York. We had never been clandestine about being together. I'd assumed that Lenny and I were living completely in the now without a worry about the future.

I tried to explain why I couldn't go with him to South America—my film, which was not finished, my contract to Goldwyn, which was far from finished. . . .

"Don't you want to come? It will be terribly exciting. Think of all the beautiful places we can visit together, all the new people we will meet. We'll be the toast of South America."

"But, Lenny, it's just not possible. I have a contract, and I'm in the middle of a film. It would be like you walking out on the New York Philharmonic in the middle of a concert."

A man of his talent and powers of persuasion didn't get where he was by ever accepting "It's just not possible" as an answer. He got there by refusing to accept the impossible, but he eventually agreed that he had been hoping to postpone the inevitable.

I returned to Hollywood to finish the film at MGM, and Lenny left for South America. Shortly after his tour ended, he and Felicia were married. Our paths continued to cross for a number of years, and those occasions were always warm and affectionate. Our moment in time is one that will always stay with me..

Shooting so much of *Side Street* on location in New York was a good experience. Tony Mann knew how to take full advantage of the city as part of the
texture of the film. Hollywood was just beginning to break loose from the
shackles of the soundstages, and there were not many directors who had mastered this new technique. For its time, *Side Street* was a good-looking, well-
made film that was not able to rise above the banality of its story. Cathy, still
affected by what Goldwyn had done to her, was very subdued. She and her
husband spent all of her off-screen time keeping very much to themselves.

The movie introduced a young theater actress who had been Judy Holliday's
understudy in *Born Yesterday*, Jean Hagen. Jean and I became pals. She went on to
give a wickedly funny performance as Lina Lamont, the silent screen vamp, in
Singin' in the Rain. Aside from that musical, and her performance in *The Asphalt
Jungle*, Hollywood didn't really know how to take advantage of this unique
comedienne's talent any more than they knew how to use the gifted Judy Holliday other than in the film versions of her Broadway shows. Ironically, both actresses died young after cancer had curtailed their promising careers.

MGM

We finished the interiors of *Side Street* at MGM. Louis B. Mayer always
claimed to have "more stars than there are in the heavens," and damned if his
claim didn't seem true at lunch in the commissary. Everyone was there, from
Clark Gable and Greer Garson to Ginger Rogers and Fred Astaire. I had matured some during my four years in the Navy, but I was still able to feel
starstruck. Metro was the biggest and most glamorous lot in Hollywood. I
loved just wandering around the other soundstages whenever I wasn't being
used on the set of *Side Street*.

One morning on a break, I headed over to the Arthur Freed musical unit,
where I knew so many of the people from parties at Gene Kelly's house. They
had recently started production on *Annie Get Your Gun* starring Judy Garland
and Howard Keel, directed by Busby Berkeley. I'd heard that they had been having some problems with Judy, and I wanted to see how she was. There were a lot
of people in costume hanging around, but nothing was happening. I spotted
Keenan Wynn and went over to ask him if Judy was working that day. Keenan,
the son of the famous vaudeville and Broadway comic headliner Ed Wynn, was

one of Hollywood's most versatile character actors of the 1940s, 1950s, and 1960s. Things were not going well. Judy had not shown up on the set yet, which had been happening a lot lately. The whole company was just waiting around for her, and Busby Berkeley, not a patient man, was steaming. Trouble was brewing. I had to get back to my set, so I asked him to hug Judy for me. I'd come back later when I had another break.

As I was leaving, I ran into Judy on her way to the set. She looked beautiful, and slimmer than I had ever seen her. She was dressed in white buckskins. With her long ponytail, she reminded me of a high-strung young colt. We hugged, and I asked how everything was going. She grabbed my hand and looked at me with panic in those huge brown eyes: "Everything is wonderful, just wonderful! Why shouldn't it be? I'm on my own set with all my own people, and they all love me, Everything is wonderful."

As she was saying this, she gripped my hand so tightly that her nails dug into my palm. An assistant came over to say that they were ready to shoot and needed her at once on set. I promised to come back to see her after I finished my scene. It was almost three hours before I was able to get back. When I arrived, the lights were off and the set was deserted. I finally found a guard who told me that Miss Garland had had a complete breakdown. "They" had taken her away and the movie was closed down.

Louis B. Mayer's next move was to offer the part to Betty Garrett, who, after *Neptune's Daughter, Take Me Out to the Ball Game,* and *On the Town,* was a rising star in the musical unit at Metro. Betty's manager, obviously thinking he had Mayer in a corner, demanded more money for her to step into the part, a mistake that was as stupid as it was big. Louis B. fired her instead, and borrowed Betty Hutton from Paramount. The terrible irony of that manager's mistake was that not only would *Annie Get Your Gun* have made a big star of Betty Garrett, it might have saved her husband's career as well. Larry Parks of *The Jolson Story* fame was making a movie at Metro with Elizabeth Taylor at approximately the same time as *Annie Get Your Gun* was released. He was subpoenaed by HUAC. Even though he named names, his career was finished. If his wife had been in Metro's big musical of the year, the studio would have gone to any lengths to quash that subpoena, and two careers would most likely have been saved.

The tense and frightened young woman who made my hand bleed that morning was a different person from the Judy Garland I knew who loved to laugh. It was as if the inner fears we all have about life and work had overtaken the real person. The uppers and downers and diet pills the studio had kept her on for years didn't help. The job of maintaining or living up to her MGM star image must have become overwhelming. Walking back to the soundstage where *Side Street* was being shot, I grimly resolved never to let Goldwyn or the system do that to me.

Many years later, in the mid-1970s, while working on a totally forgettable TV movie at Metro, I wandered through the back lot one afternoon remembering the New York streets, Welsh mining towns, Western towns, and various rural areas that had been the backdrops for so many terrific films. It was now a wasteland. I headed for some treetops I saw in the distance and came upon a perfectly preserved block of Victorian houses. I stopped, enchanted, in front of a familiar one. The lawn was lush and verdant; the flowers and shrubs were in bloom and perfectly manicured. With a sudden pang I remembered it as the house from *Meet Me in St. Louis*, arguably Judy Garland's greatest film.

Changes

As soon as we finished *Side Street* at MGM I decided it was time to find a nice place to live. Everyone I cared about seemed to be going through difficult times. Ethyl had met someone who was devoted to her. George (Buddy) Tyne was a loveable bear of a man and a good character actor. He worshiped her, which was exactly what Ethyl needed, and eventually even Saul accepted that. But getting there was not easy. It was messy and painful for all concerned, particularly for their daughter, Judy, who although wise beyond her years was still an adolescent. This time must have been hell for her. Meanwhile Shelley, still depressed over Burt Lancaster and also upset at the choices Universal was offering her, was not exactly good company.

I found a terrific house to rent high above the Sunset Strip. It sat on a point of land from which I had a panoramic view from the ocean to downtown L.A. The pool extended out on the point, and the house sat behind the pool. I could jump into the pool from the deck outside my bedroom on the second floor. I reclaimed my dog Gaby from my parents and moved into my first house. Every morning I would whip open the drapes that covered the sliding doors to my bedroom and walk out on the deck to greet the day. It was a new feeling for me to be in charge of my own domain. I could play music as late and as loud as I wanted to and pick out my own sheets and furniture. I really loved the feeling of having my own domain.

One morning, standing on my deck, I couldn't help noticing that the TV antennas were proliferating. It was obvious that this new form of entertainment could no longer be shrugged off as a passing fancy. It was here to stay and needed to be recognized and dealt with as a major challenge to the film industry. Another thing that caught my attention was a line in the sky that looked almost painted in. It extended as far as the eye could see from the Pacific to downtown L.A. Above it the sky was its usual beautiful clear blue; below it everything was a little hazy. As the months went by, the line got higher and less distinct, and below it the haze got thicker and more impenetrable. Smog, never heard of in California, oozed its way into being a Los Angeles fact of life.

Two Turkeys

In 1949 I did two more films for Goldwyn, who along with the rest of Hollywood was finally waking up to realize that the growing threat called television should be taken seriously. Confusion over what to do about it was the problem. Goldwyn decided to make *Our Very Own*, a film that ironically would lead the way for television sitcoms of the future like *Father Knows Best* and *The Donna Reed Show*. It was an attempt to return to the simple family values portrayed by the Andy Hardy series at MGM ten years earlier. I was the boy next door to Ann Blyth's pretty, perky teenager. Unfortunately, nothing about our charmless effort lived up to the joyful innocence of the Hardy films. The script by F. Hugh Herbert was pointless and meandering. After reading it, I referred to him as F. U. Herbert, to the delight of all the other actors except Ann, who had a gaggle of nuns on the set almost daily. My part was amorphous and Ann was as sweet as an overdose of saccharine. The director, David Miller, a perfectly nice man, was no help to anybody. Struggling through *Our Very Own* and *Edge of Doom*, my next film for Goldwyn, made it apparent to me how little I knew about acting. With good material and a good director I could relax and just let the performance happen. With bad-to-ordinary material and inadequate-to-unimaginative direction, I hadn't yet developed the resources to solve those problems on my own.

Frances Takes a Turn

My next film was Mrs. Goldwyn's idea. I read in Louella Parsons's column one sunny morning that "Frances Goldwyn has purchased the rights to a new book, *Edge of Doom*, for the studio's rising young star, Farley Granger." I had always felt that as the only young man under contract to Goldwyn I suffered from his inability to develop the right kind of material to build a young man's career. That is why the only good films I made while under contract were done at other studios on loanout.

Once again excited, I raced out to the closest bookstore to buy the book. It was a slight book, and I got through it quickly. The story was about a young man who, when denied what he thinks is a proper funeral for his mother by a mean older parish priest, picks up a crucifix from the priest's desk and clubs him to death with it. A sympathetic younger priest, played in the film by Dana Andrews, manipulates me into admitting my crime . . . THE END. The book had a little more to it than that, but not much. Even taking her well-known Catholicism into consideration, I couldn't understand why Frances Goldwyn had been so eager to buy the book any more than I could understand how it could be translated into a film.

Obviously, neither could Phil Yordan, the same writer whom Goldwyn had hired to remove all the magic from the original script of *Roseanna McCoy*. The script was barely coherent. Yordan managed to reduce what little substance there was in the book to what Walter Winchell later described as "raw meat." Our director, Mark Robson, a talented man, had directed the movie *Champion* and made a star of Kirk Douglas. But as the saying goes, "You can't breathe life into a stiff."

At the sneak previews in California, the audiences responded as negatively as I had. Mark edited and reedited for months, to no avail. Goldwyn decided my character needed a love interest. Even though young Joan Evans was already in the film, he hired another ingénue of the moment, Mala Powers, to play my girlfriend. Several scenes were added for us, but they came across as what they were—unnecessary afterthoughts that had nothing to do with advancing the plot. After the film opened in New York, the critics gave it the same kind of beating that I had given the priest. In a practically unprecedented move, Goldwyn pulled the film out of distribution and hired Charles Brackett and Ben Hecht to come up with a way to save it. No matter what was done to it, it remained a stiff. It was another bad experience for me. Instead of it being the big project, I felt that with *Edge of Doom* I had exceeded the three-strike limit. It was time for a meaningful change.

Out of America by 1950

George Coulouris, who had played the lawyer in *Citizen Kane*, was a balding character actor of British/Greek parentage who generally played menacing characters, superbly. In life, he was the quintessential curmudgeon, and my hero. Whenever he railed about someone we both knew, whom I would unfailingly try to defend by saying, "Come on, George, he's not that bad. He's nice," George would look up to heaven, pull at his remaining hair, and rant, "Nice ... nice ... What is nice!?" Then he would fix me with a piercing gaze and say, "You have to hate to be really alive!"

Of course, this was all an act ... which I fell for every time. Despite his ferocity, George was shy and actually kind. Whenever his dramatic moments got too over the top, such as erupting at dinner when one of his children, who were then one and three years old, interrupted him—"Will I ever be free from the tyranny of children!"—Louise, his ever-patient wife, would just shake her head, sigh, and murmur, "Oh George ..."

Trained on the British stage, his movie career took off after *Citizen Kane* and *Watch on the Rhine*. We became friends when he was working in Saul Chaplin's Broadway musical, *Bonanza Bound*. George's rallying cry, which tickled all his friends, was "Out of America by 1950!" We all knew that George was eccentric. We never knew he was prescient.

1950

Hand in hand with the arrival of smog and the sprouting of TV aerials came the Internal Security Act of 1950. I will leave it up to you to draw any parallels you choose with the Patriot Act of 2003. I happen to agree with one of our country's founding fathers, Benjamin Franklin, who said, "They that can give up essential liberty to obtain temporary safety deserve neither liberty nor safety."

Hollywood was shaken to its core by the blacklist. It affected almost everyone I knew and cared about. While I had been struggling through my D-quality double-header for Goldwyn, many of my dearest friends had been engaged in a different and much more deadly struggle. Senator Joe McCarthy had successfully used the Cold War to make a name for himself by whipping up fear and hysteria across the country and in Congress. The activities of the House Committee on Un-American Activities, dubbed HUAC, spawned the blacklist in the entertainment industry. It was particularly virulent in Hollywood and killed the careers of many innocent people by branding any support for antifascist activities during the Spanish Civil War in the late 1930s or any exploration of a postrevolutionary Communist ideal as treason. Despite the fact that Stalin was a despot and a monster, Russia's importance to us as an ally in World War II, fighting Hitler, seemed to slip the minds of the ambitious senator from Wisconsin and his allies in the halls of Congress. Hollywood was in turmoil and split down the middle. Ten of the foremost writers, producers, and directors in the film industry were summoned to Washington to appear before HUAC. They became known as "The Hollywood Ten." Rather than name names of others who might have been involved in various left-of-center fringe groups in their youth, they went to jail. They were also called "The Unfriendly Ten." Probably the best known of them were Dalton Trumbo and Ring Lardner Jr.

Most of Hollywood's known names, predominantly actors, directors, and producers, were friendly witnesses, also known as volunteers of information. Samuel Goldwyn was one of more than forty influential people from Hollywood subpoenaed to appear before the committee. Fed up after waiting to be called for over a month, Goldwyn finally released his statement to the press. It included the sentence, "The most un-American activity which I have observed with the hearings has been the activity of the Committee itself." I was proud of him.

Shelley and I had become close again, despite or perhaps because of a traumatic evening during which Burt Lancaster and I both came to her rescue when she had too much to drink and inadvertently almost overdosed on her mounting supply of medications. Several weeks after that evening, we went to a major fundraiser for the Hollywood Ten. That same evening we had a dinner date with Janet Leigh and my friend Arthur Loew, son of Marcus Loew, owner of Loew's Inc., the parent company of MGM and the Goldwyn Company. We first went to the fundraiser, which was held at Gene Kelly's house. Everyone in Hollywood who was not an extreme conservative was there. One impassioned speaker was a skinny young writer whom we both knew and liked, Norman Mailer. Norman was politically savvier than we were. Unbeknownst to us, he probably saved Shelley and me from bringing our careers to an early end. The writer of *The Naked and the Dead* was hoping to have many of the most important people in Hollywood sign an *amicus curiae*—friend of the court—brief, which could be presented with an appeal to the Supreme Court before the Hollywood Ten were put in jail like common criminals by HUAC. His speech was wonderful, and everyone in the room was shoving money at him. Shelley and I each gave him a check for $100 and ran to get the car because we were late for dinner.

After an exhaustive campaign, Shelley finally succeeded in getting George Stevens to give her a screen test for *A Place in the Sun*. She called Norman the night before the test and asked if they could have dinner. She desperately needed to pick his brains because she had not done her homework. She had not read Dreiser's *An American Tragedy*, on which the movie was based. Her justification for this laziness was that an important American writer could give her insights that she might overlook on her own. She went to Norman's house, and they spent the evening discussing the story and her character. Whatever he told her must have helped, because she got the part. As she was leaving Norman's, he gave her back the checks we had written at the Kellys' and told her he had torn up the brief. He had wanted to get some blockbuster names that evening, but she and I were the only ones who signed it. He didn't deposit our checks, either. Everyone else had donated cash. The blacklist was mushrooming into such an ugly mess, he was afraid that our signed checks could have been used against us. Norman proved himself to be not only a terrific writer but also a good friend.

Ethyl Chaplin had barely had time to let the fallout from her breakup with Saul settle when a pamphlet called *Red Channels* appeared branding 151 entertainment industry professionals as "Red Fascist" sympathizers. This meant that Buddy Tyne, who at one time during his unemployed idealistic youth had been a member of some club that could have been affiliated with the Communist Party in sympathy with the antifascist forces in the Spanish Civil War, was in danger of having his passport restricted. He and Ethyl, with Saul's permission, decided to take Judy and leave immediately for Paris.

I was still licking my wounds from the last two films I had done for Goldwyn and determined not to do any more crap. When he tried to loan me out to Universal for a second-rate flying carpet opus, I flatly refused. Goldwyn called me in to tell me loudly and at length what a no-good, ungrateful, bad son I was, and then he put me on suspension for the first time. This meant that my salary was suspended for the entire time it took to make the film at Universal, and that time was automatically added onto my contract. The suspension was meant to teach me a lesson. I felt liberated! The next step was easy. I went to Europe.

I decided to lend my friends moral support, two helping hands, and a few laughs as they settled in. The irony of how we had all laughed and imitated George Coulouris's rallying cry, "Out of America by 1950!" was lost on none of us.

Ethyl, Buddy, and Judy went to New York to deal with family business and then planned to travel to France by ship. I would fly ahead to Paris, and be there to meet them at Le Havre. Ethyl called after they arrived in New York to say that

Arthur Laurents, who was having his own blacklist troubles, would be coming along. Did I mind? Undaunted, I said, "Not a problem." I was taking my first baby steps of independence from Goldwyn. I was up to and ready for anything.

Arthur had been very meaningful to me as a young actor starting again in Hollywood just after the war. I met wonderful people through him and with him. He was older than I and he was very knowledgeable about the theater and the arts in general. I learned a lot from him and we had some wonderful times together. He had a sharp sense of humor that was as funny as it was cutting. We have remained on-and-off friends through the years, and Arthur has always been generous with his advice. Age hasn't mellowed Arthur. It has concentrated his ego and sharpened his defenses. Perhaps it's because, despite Arthur's brilliant creative solution to the early problems with the book of *Gypsy*, Jerry Robbins, Jule Styne, and Stephen Sondheim are the ones most often remembered as the creative geniuses behind that show, just as Leonard Bernstein, Jerry, and Steve are the ones remembered for *West Side Story*. Perhaps it's because he has never been considered one of our best playwrights. Whatever the reason, remaining a friend to Arthur has never been easy, but this was an earlier time and he needed all his friends.

Paris

There are many beautiful cities in this world, quite a few of them here in the United States. Anyone who has ever been to Savannah or San Francisco, not to mention New York, can attest to that. In Italy you can't avoid beauty. But there are reasons why so many love songs have been written about Paris. It only took me one day to know why. Many places fail to live up to one's expectations. Paris exceeded all of mine.

In the taxi from the airport to the center of Paris, I was too excited to be upset by the churlish behavior of the driver, who had disdainfully not even tried to understand my attempts to tell him where I was going. I finally handed him a piece of paper on which I'd written the hotel's name. This was typical Parisian cabdriver behavior. They made an average New York cabbie at the time seem like St. Christopher. After checking in at L'Hôtel Mayfair and leaving my passport, which I was sure I'd never see again, at the tiny front desk, I took the even tinier lift up five flights and walked another half floor to my room. It was a two-room apartment on the top floor that looked out on the rooftops. When I opened my curtains, it was as if the music from *La Bohème* flooded in with the late-afternoon sunlight. I filled the bath, took a long soak, and tried to rest. I was too excited. I dressed and went down to the lobby to find out where I could go for dinner nearby.

I was at the desk when the elevator opened and out came two familiar Hollywood faces, Peter and Jigee Viertel. Peter, a would-be screenwriter, had written his first successful book at age eighteen. His mother, Salka Viertel, who had purportedly been Garbo's lover as well as her writer, held sway over an Old World–style intellectual salon at her home in Santa Monica. Jigee, sharp, witty, and mercurial, was a really smashing lady. I'd always thought that she could have been the model for Lady Brett in Hemingway's *The Sun Also Rises*. Her first husband, Budd Schulberg, wrote *What Makes Sammy Run?* They had been friends of Ernest Hemingway's for years. Jigee insisted I come along with them to a cellar on the Left Bank where they were meeting war photographer Bob Capa and his current girlfriend for dinner. Capa was world-famous for his photos of death, carnage, and devastation during the Civil War in Spain, as well as World War II. I joined them. The food and wine at my first meal in Paris, accompanied by blue-gray clouds of Gauloise cigarette smoke, was terrific, but my adrenaline high was wearing off and travel lag was taking over. A lot of the conversation was in French, but I even had a hard time keeping up with the English part. As the evening wore on, all talk turned to Poppa. I had to ask to find out that they were talking about Hemingway. After a half-hour or so of obsessive Poppa talk, I decided to walk home. Jigee gave me directions back to the hotel, and with hugs all around, I left to get some much needed air.

The night sky was clear and hung with a bright full moon. Walking along the Seine, with its lovely bridges and quiet nighttime river traffic, I became acutely aware of how much more the world had to offer than I had ever imagined. When I saw Notre Dame silhouetted against the night sky, it was almost overkill. I was a willing victim, completely, hopelessly in love. No Hollywood movie could have prepared me for the reality that was Paris. This was the moment in which my unquenchable thirst for travel was born.

Back at the hotel, I enjoyed twelve hours of the deepest, best sleep ever. When I woke I found a note that Jigee had slipped under my door. She and Peter had checked out and were off to Africa with Capa to meet Poppa. Since Ethyl, Buddy, Judy, and Arthur were not arriving until the following week, I was on my own. I spent the day in the Louvre. After seeing enough paintings to bring on an acute attack of Stendahl's Syndrome, I ended up lost in the maze of sarcophagi and pieces of ancient Egypt that seemed to go on for miles in the lower reaches of the museum.

That evening I chose a perfect change of pace by seeing *Annie du Far West*. It seemed ideal symmetry that my first Broadway musical was also my first theater experience in Paris. What a difference there was. This production not only had horses onstage, it also had camels and elephants. Annie sang "You Can't Get a

Man with a Gun" as a tragic love ballad à la Edith Piaf. The production was so wildly off the mark and so uniquely French that it was impossible not to be enchanted by it.

The next day while wandering through Les Halles, the incredible marketplace that once fed the bellies of Paris, I bumped into Uta Hagen. I had met Uta in New York and of course knew her by reputation, but we were merely acquaintances. She was alone in Paris, I was alone, it was a beautiful summer day, and we had a wonderful lunch at a little bistro on the Île St. Louis in the middle of the Seine near Notre Dame. After our lunch, which included many carafes of *vin ordinaire*, we browsed through the bookstalls along the Seine. I spent two memorable days and nights seeing the city with this terrific lady, who went on to become one of the great acting teachers of our time as well as one of our greatest actresses.

We went to the ballet to see Zizi Jeanmaire dance an incredibly sensual *Carmen* that her husband, Roland Petit, had choreographed for her. After the performance, we went backstage to introduce ourselves and they invited us to have a late supper with them. I was completely captivated by Zizi, a feeling that was obviously mutual. We communicated like old friends even though she did not speak any more English than I did French. Two years later Zizi was, for me, the only good thing about *Hans Christian Andersen*, a film we did for Goldwyn together with Danny Kaye.

Uta and I walked home that night along the bank of the Seine, stopping to sit under all the bridges we passed, where we tried to outproject each other with lines from plays and movies. We wanted to find out which bridge had the best echo in Paris.

In the late 1990s, I went backstage to see Uta after a performance of *Mrs. Klein*, one of the last plays she did in New York. As we said good night, she smiled and said, "Remember how good our projection was in Paris?" She also asked if I had seen Arthur recently. When I said, "Not for some time, I'm angry with him," she laughed and commented, "Who isn't?"

At one of Gene and Betsy Kelly's open houses, I had met François and Patrice Pleven, a pair of French brothers who were hoping to become film producers. I had promised to call them when I came to Paris. Since I still had a couple of days before Ethyl and the others arrived, I kept my promise and was invited to go with Patrice, the younger brother, that very evening to a dinner party at a château on the outskirts of Paris. The château was magnificent, with formal gardens that seemed to go on forever in the early-evening light. The dinner party numbered about a dozen people, most of whom spoke charming English when we were introduced and not another word for the rest of the evening, with one face-saving exception. I wandered off into a galleria, and there on the walls was an amazing collection of French Impressionist paintings dominated by Cézanne. I had recently seen several of his paintings in the Louvre and had been very taken with them. Now here were a half-dozen of them on a wall in front of me in someone's home. I would have happily spent the rest of the evening right there if a butler tinkling a bell hadn't come through calling the French equivalent of "Soup's on." At the table our hostess seated everyone as skillfully as a world-class conductor, but my friend Patrice was at the other end. I was on my own. Soup was served and I was staring helplessly at the array of silverware choices when my dinner companion on my right, a lovely older woman, leaned in and whispered in flawless English, "Just start from the outside and work your way in." After a "soup to nuts" dinner during which I used every utensil, we had moved to the living room for coffee and brandy when Richard Rodgers and Oscar Hammerstein arrived from London, where *Carousel* had recently opened to triumphant reviews. R & H were both obviously very high on their London success. Without hesitation, everyone trotted out his English.

Mr. Hammerstein was a big, friendly bear of a man. Mr. Rodgers was compact, quick, and didn't miss a trick. At one point, after we were introduced, I asked him about a song called "Fair" that he had written with Lorenz Hart. I told him I'd forgotten what show it was from. He thought for a moment and with obvious surprise said, "Damned if I can remember, either." It was almost ten years to the day before I saw R & H again. Barbara Cook and I were appearing in the first revival of *The King and I* at City Center in New York. R & H attended the dress rehearsal and came backstage immediately afterward. Hammerstein grabbed me in a giant hug to say how much he had loved what we had done with the parts. Rodgers walked purposefully over to me, pointed a finger, and said, "*Babes in Arms,* but it was cut."

Waiting on the platform at the station when the boat train from Le Havre arrived, I heard Judy Chaplin yelling my name. She jumped into my arms. I was so happy to see her and Ethyl and Buddy, I didn't even mind that Arthur had tagged along. In fact, I was even glad to see him.

We got all the baggage and went back to get everyone settled at L'Hôtel Mayfair. Then we spent two weeks enjoying Paris as if none of us had a care in the world. Ethyl and Buddy looked for a place to live, but we also explored the city, its artistic treasures and the differences of its arrondissements. At the innumerable bistros, for a few francs we enjoyed food that was better than any we had ever had before, accompanied by inexpensive liters of *vin ordinaire.* We also set out to explore the nightlife.

Arthur ran into Jimmy Lipton, whom he had known in New York. Lipton, then an out-of-work actor picking up odd jobs in Paris, is now known as the TV host of *Inside the Actors Studio.* He convinced Arthur that we had to see an "exhibition"; "It's as much a part of Paris as the Eiffel Tower or the Louvre." If we gave him the money, he would take care of all the arrangements. Arthur was sure he was getting a commission. Ethyl was game, so several nights later we went to a tacky brothel in Montmartre, where we were taken upstairs to a bed-room with nothing in it other than a large bed and some chairs grouped nearby. A few minutes after we settled down, a rather ordinary-looking thirtyish nude couple in towels entered and took a very formal bow. When they whipped off their towels Ethyl looked at me in such a way that I knew I would lose it if I looked at her again. Our "actors" then proceeded to demonstrate lovemaking styles from around the world: very formal and stiff as the British; frisky and ju-venile as the Americans; harsh and militaristic as the Germans; exaggeratedly passionate as the Italians. None of this was erotic. By the time they got to "and now the Russian way," the woman spread-eagled on the bed and the man launching himself at her from the far side of the room, Ethyl and I were laugh-ing so hard that we had to help each other from the room. We went downstairs to a little bar where we sat drinking and talking with all the prostitutes who were not otherwise engaged. Buddy and Arthur soon joined us. It was the high-light of the evening.

Harold Clurman and his then ex (but still beloved) wife, Stella Adler, were also in Paris, and we saw as much of them as possible. One night Arthur and I took them to Le Grand Véfour, perhaps the finest restaurant in Paris at the time. As soon as we were seated, I excused myself. As I was coming back into the dining room I heard Harold's voice. He was explaining to the maitre d', "You see, in America she is one of our most famous stage actresses, so we would appreciate it if you could extend all possible courtesies to her." The sweet man was making sure that his ex-wife got special treatment. Stella later played an important part in my life when I moved to New York and studied for the theater. She was the best teacher I ever had.

London

Before leaving New York, Ethyl and Buddy had run into Jerry Robbins, who told them that he was coming to London for the first time with the New York City Ballet to present one of his works. Since he had no friends there, he invited them to come over from Paris for his opening. He was on the outs with Arthur, a familiar position for many of Arthur's friends through the years, but he asked Ethyl to try to talk me into coming over with them. I liked Jerry as much as I admired him, and Buddy needed to check out the opportunities for work in London. Arthur was delighted to be on his own in Paris. Off we went.

We were not prepared for the devastation from the war that was still evident in that great city. Most of the rubble had been cleared, but there were still vast areas that had been leveled by firebombing where only a few skeletons of buildings remained. Rationing was still in effect, and it was next to impossible to get a decent meal, but the Brits carried on cheerfully and efficiently, with no complaints. Hotel rooms were impossible to find, but Jerry got Ethyl and Buddy a room in the small shabby hotel where his company was staying, and I managed to talk the manager of the Savoy into giving me his "special room," the one held for last-minute emergencies. The room was big and gorgeous, and overlooked the Thames. Seeing the river through the fog in the morning light prepared me for my first Turner paintings. The room was not only large enough for two; it was very close to Jerry's theater near Covent Garden. Since our schedules conveniently dovetailed, I invited him to stay.

I didn't know Jerry well, but I had been a fan since that night in San Francisco when I had seen *Fancy Free* before shipping out for Hawaii. He had a fearsome reputation among dancers as one of the most demanding and difficult-to-please taskmasters in the business. He was of medium height, with a tight athletic build, quite nice-looking in a balding, ordinary way. His smile was infrequent but could light up a room. He was quick and smart and I really enjoyed his company. As friendly as he was, Jerry was hard to read. I sensed that in some part of himself that he kept carefully guarded, he was not happy. Maybe it was his work. Agnes de Mille wrote in *The Book of the Dance*, "There is no single work of Robbins' in which he has not felt soul-crushing disappointment and that it was a mistake to start. He longs to just get out and escape. That he does not is merely a matter of spiritual discipline. His doubts and disappointments are thunderous, his group testifies, and his disciplines are applied to others besides himself. Rehearsals are sometimes inspiring and sometimes hell." He also could have been feeling the growing pressure from HUAC, which led him to name names, or "rat on his friends," not too long after his London triumph.

Unfortunately, I hardly ever saw him because he almost never got back from rehearsal until I had already gone out for the evening.

We were all low on funds, so we did most of our drinking and eating at the Savoy, where I could sign for everything. I was still waiting for the money my new business manager was supposed to send me via American Express. I went every day, but nothing arrived. Meanwhile my tab grew alarmingly. Since no money had changed hands, management was beginning to look politely askance. Ethyl, Buddy, and I were getting nervous about the subterfuges our lack of cash drove us to, such as hiding in the bathroom like teenagers with the shower on to avoid tipping when room service arrived, shouting, "Just leave the check there, I'll sign it later!"

We spent an evening with George and Louise Coulouris over dinner in their little sixteenth-century thatched-roof cottage on the Vale of Health overlooking Hampstead Heath. George looked at me like I was out of my mind when I shouted, "Well, we did it, George!... out of America by 1950!" Maybe he wasn't aware of how many times we had all used his line.

The ever-resourceful studio managed to track me down. Both *Our Very Own* and *Edge of Doom* were opening on Broadway in the same week, one at the Astor Theater and the other a block away at the Victoria Theater. Goldwyn was desperate for me to come back in order to do appearances and publicity for the event. If I agreed, "All would be forgiven." Sure, right, I thought. Let's spell that out. I called my agent and agreed to do it if I was immediately taken off suspension and put back on salary. I suggested doing a *Times* of London interview before I left if the studio took care of my current bill at the Savoy. They agreed and set up the interview. We were off the hook.

On a roll, I checked American Express one last time. I discovered that I had been going to the wrong department to check for my money transfer. It had been there the whole time. To celebrate, on my last night I took us all to a Greek restaurant that I had heard about from the concierge at the Savoy. The White Tower somehow managed to serve delicious food at this time when rationing seemed to affect every other restaurant in London. The mention of "potted shrimp" still transports me back to that evening.

Farley Granger on Broadway . . . Twice!

Back in New York, I was put to work immediately. After what seemed like a lifetime of newspaper, radio, and television interviews as well as public appearances all over the greater New York area and as far away as Boston and Philadelphia, the movies were about to open back to back. I was starring in two films on Broadway simultaneously, and I was only twenty-five years old. An actor's dream come true? You would think so, but I was filled with foreboding. I knew both films were bad, and I felt as if I were about to be doubly exposed as a charlatan. The first to open was *Our Very Own*, which the critics merely dismissed as ineffective fluff. My favorite quote for this one was from Hedda Hopper: "The kind of picture America has been screaming for!!!" *Edge of Doom* was a different matter. Dana Andrews and I somehow emerged unscathed, but the critics unanimously hated the movie. Their reviews differed only as to how much. The defining quote for this turkey was Walter Winchell's "It's raw meat!" What salvaged that trip for me was seeing Ethel Merman in *Call Me Madam* while I was in Boston making publicity appearances. Also while in New York, I saw *Guys and Dolls,* which to this day I think elevated musical theater to an art form. The brilliant music and lyrics were by Frank Loesser and the superb direction was by Abe Burrows, who directed my Broadway musical debut in 1959 with much less auspicious results. They say composers never throw away a good song. Frank didn't. Imagine how I felt when I heard "More I Cannot Wish You," my song from *Roseanna McCoy* which Goldwyn had cut, being sung to Sarah Brown, the Salvation Army doll, by her father at the top of Act II.

Goldwyn contacted me to say that he was canceling the nationwide openings of *Edge of Doom* in order for Charlie Brackett and Ben Hecht to do a rewrite. The plan was for Dana to narrate a wraparound, a new scene to begin the movie and another to end it that would explain the story of my character and change the focus from the bad boy to the good priest. It was not a good idea, since the film was about the boy, not the young priest. Meanwhile, Goldwyn expected me to go on a nationwide PR tour for the film. I'll never understand why he flogged that dead horse for as long as he did, but I wanted nothing more to do with it. I refused to do any more promotional appearances. After yet another tirade on what an ingrate I was, back on suspension I went . . . and back to Europe to join my friends, who were now in Rome.

A. Scott Berg, in his definitive biography of Goldwyn, writes of *Edge of Doom*: "Goldwyn was chewing out his staff one day for not creating a successful advertising campaign for the film: 'I don't know what's the matter with you. This is a simple story about a boy who wants a fine funeral for his mother, so he kills a priest.' Upon hearing his own words, he suddenly grasped the fundamental problem with the movie. With his next breath he said, 'Let's not spend another dime.' "

Italy

I had been captivated by the romance and literary world of expats in Paris. I had been impressed by the bravery and humor of the Brits. Now I was about to be introduced to Italy. It was the start of a love affair that still burns brightly. No matter where you go, from every city to every town, from the Italian Alps to Sicily, it is beautiful. The people are gorgeous, funny, and totally cynical. Maybe centuries of being marched over and conquered by one country after the other has made them more resilient than most. On the surface, nothing seems to bother the Italians except paying taxes and losing at football (soccer). But I don't mean to imply that they are superficial. Nothing could be further from the truth. It could be that since they have had to adjust to so many different peoples wielding power over them through the centuries, they have developed a fine sense of welcoming wariness with strangers and an immediate distrust for anyone in authority. They trust only their own families. Once they come to know and like you, they are the warmest and most generous people I know. You become part of the family and are treated and protected as such. On a less sociological level, there is the food. You can eat pasta 365 days a year and it can be different and delicious every time, and that is only the first course! I still go back every chance I get.

When I checked in to the Hotel de la Ville in Rome, Arthur was waiting for me, but Ethyl and Buddy were gone. Arthur had gotten Buddy a job on *Decision Before Dawn*, a film that Anatole Litvak was about to begin shooting in Munich. Knowing the depth of Ethyl's feelings about what the Jews had suffered at German hands during the war, I knew how much they must have needed that job to agree to go to Germany. Arthur had bought a little Hillman Minx convertible and wanted to see Florence and Venice after we had finished exploring Rome. I agreed to travel with him. We often went our own ways in the cities, but the joy of being in Italy overcame any strain between us. By the time we left Florence to head toward Venice, I had seen so many beautiful things—paintings, churches, tombs, squares, and hillside towns—that my brain was on overload. We parked the car in a big garage near the train station in the Piazza Roma on the outskirts of Venice and took a water taxi into the city. When we rounded a curve into the Grand Canal, I felt I had passed through a portal into another world. The beauty of Venice made everything else I'd ever seen pale by comparison. It still has the same effect on me, but this first time was overwhelming. We got off at the stop for the Grand Hotel, where we were given two rooms overlooking the canal. The Venice Biennale was in full swing, and the first person we ran into was Stella Adler, who was staying at a hotel over on the Lido. When Arthur was otherwise engaged, Stella introduced me to two people who played an important role in my life a few years later when I was making *Senso* for Luchino Visconti. One was a British art dealer who owned a beautiful house in Venice, which I rented while working on the Venice portion of *Senso;* the other was Peggy Guggenheim, who became a good friend and whose companionship warmed my winter during that same period.

The Little Tramp

It was time to visit Ethyl and Buddy. *Decision Before Dawn*, which Buddy was working on, had begun shooting in Munich. It starred Richard Basehart, at whom I had been aiming my rifle in *Roseanna McCoy* when I slipped and shot Joan Evans, and a superb young German actor, Oskar Werner, who was nominated for an Academy Award for *Ship of Fools* and became an international star in 1961 in Truffaut's *Jules et Jim*.

Leaving Italy was not easy because I never wanted to leave. I had already decided I would be very happy to live there. Spending money in Rome, Florence, and Venice had been worth every lira, but I was on suspension again. I had to resolve something before I went broke.

Arthur and I got his car out of Venice's parking garage, and we headed over the Dolomites into Austria.

Salzburg was our first stop, a baroque gem of a small city. It had sustained appreciable bomb damage toward the end of the war, but the industrious Austrians had cleaned up the center of town and all around were signs of reconstruction.

Wilhelm Furtwängler was conducting Richard Strauss at the music festival the night we were there. After discussing whether or not to try for tickets, Arthur and I decided not to attend what could have been a memorable concert. Our decision was based on the fact that both the composer and the conductor were thought to have been Nazi sympathizers, and we felt that we had to draw a line somewhere, no matter how great the music might have been.

Vienna had been devastated by the war. While driving through the rubble of what had once been the musical capital of the world and one of its loveliest old cities, I felt the same mixture of anger and sadness that I had felt in London. Vienna at the time was occupied by the four powers: the United States, England, France, and Russia. It was uniquely exciting and chaotic. On our last night in Vienna, we went to a little restaurant where a pianist played popular American songs. I went over to him at one point to request that he play some Gershwin. He looked at me and said, "I was about to play some selections from *Porgy and Bess.*" Then he looked down at his piano and said softly, "That is, if you don't mind." Guessing what he was implying, I snapped, "What do you mean by that?" He looked up and, still softly, said, "Some Americans do, you know." I held his gaze until he looked down and I said, "Well, I'm not one of them," and stuffed some Austrian schillings into the glass on his piano. Back at the table, before I could tell Arthur what had happened, the pianist had launched into one of the most beautifully played medleys of *Porgy and Bess* I've ever heard. It took me right back to my adolescent worship of George Gershwin.

As I was paying the check, he came over to our table, introduced himself, and invited us to his flat for coffee with him and his wife. Arthur looked skeptical, but I was curious enough to accept immediately. We got into our car, which was parked nearby, and followed his motorbike, maneuvering our way with some difficulty through the rubble that had been Vienna until we arrived at a building that was only partially destroyed. Hugging the wall, we climbed a staircase that, like a fire escape, was completely exposed to the elements where the outside wall had been blown away. It was like a scene out of *The Third Man*, Carol Reed's brilliant postwar film with Orson Welles, Joseph Cotten, and Alida Valli. We entered his tiny fourth-floor flat and met his wife. They were a pale young Jewish couple whose family had managed to send them to Israel before the Nazi purge. They had recently returned to search for family survivors. There were none.

Over coffee, when we mentioned that we had come from Salzburg, he asked if we had seen Furtwängler conduct. I told him no, we had decided that we had to draw the line somewhere. He gave me a sad, penetrating look and said very softly, "Mr. Granger, if you have any lines to draw, you should never have come to Vienna."

The next morning we left for Munich. The drive was uneventful, but we could tell when we reached the city limits how much destruction there was ahead. I felt numb. I was getting used to rubble. What we had to do to win the war was absolutely necessary, but I couldn't help feeling how wonderful it would be when mankind evolved to the point where war and killing became unnecessary.

It wasn't easy finding our hotel because the façade had been destroyed, but once we found it and passed through the temporary entrance, the big and rather plain lobby was undamaged. We were on our way to the elevator after checking in when a familiar voice boomed out, "Farley!" It was Orson Welles, seated at a table nearby with the chanteuse Eartha Kitt. He had seen *They Live by Night* in London and wanted to tell me how much he thought I'd grown as an actor. What a great compliment from the man I had been too intimidated to meet in the commissary at Fox at seventeen. As soon as I got to my room and was able to get a telephone line, I called Ethyl. She invited us to dinner with Oskar Werner and his girlfriend. Oskar, who was no barrel of laughs, was as smart as he was talented. It was wonderful to see Ethyl and Buddy again.

Back at the hotel, I found that my ever-resourceful studio had tracked me down. Alfred Hitchcock wanted to see me about his upcoming film. Without hesitation, I left on the next plane available. On my way to the airport the next day, in a particularly leveled area of the city, I saw the outline of a familiar figure standing alone in the rubble. I asked the driver to stop, got out, and picked my way a block or so to the figure. As I got close, I realized that it was an undamaged life-size cutout of Charlie Chaplin as the Little Tramp, jauntily surveying the destruction around him. I'll never figure out how or why it got there, but I'll always treasure the image of one of cinema's most famous Jewish entertainers, the man who had lampooned Hitler so accurately in *The Great Dictator*, surveying the ruins of the city that had played such a major part in Hitler's rise to power.

Hitchcock Number II

Many connections later I was back in L.A. After a weekend of rest, the studio set up a meeting for me with Hitch at his home in Bel Air Monday afternoon. When I arrived, he seemed genuinely happy to see me. We went out on his terrace, which overlooked the vast green expanse of the Bel Air Country Club. Over tea he told me the story of *Strangers on a Train*, playing all the parts with great relish. Hearing a story told by Hitch was almost as good as seeing the film. I was enthralled. When he asked me if I liked it, I said, "I think it's great!" He said, "Good, because you're playing Guy." I almost jumped out of my skin. Then he asked who I thought should play Bruno. I hadn't a clue. He leaned in with one of his inimitable smiles and said, "What would you think about Robert Walker?"

Bob Walker, a fine actor, had been typecast at MGM as the boy next door in films like *See Here, Private Hargrove* and *The Clock* with Judy Garland. His wife, Jennifer Jones, was already romantically linked with David O. Selznick in 1944 when Bob co-starred with her in *Since You Went Away*, a Selznick production. She and Bob were divorced in 1945. The whole affair took a heavy toll on Walker. He began drinking heavily and suffered several nervous breakdowns, accompanied by some unfortunate tabloid publicity. After a six-week marriage to John Ford's daughter, Barbara, was annulled, Bob was arrested for drunken driving and institutionalized for almost a year. This would be his first major role following his release.

I remembered Hitch's *Shadow of a Doubt*, in which he cast Joseph Cotten, an actor who almost always played honest and trustworthy characters, as the murderous Uncle Charlie. It was masterful surprise casting, and so was this. I said to him, "What a terrific idea!" Then he leaned in with that same grin and said, "Wouldn't it be interesting if something happened on our film?" I knew he was trying to shock me, so I just said something stupid like, "Oh, Hitch . . ."

Next thing I knew, Bob and I were in Washington, D.C., preparing to shoot the opening of the movie in Union Station. We spent our first day there walking all around the city, visiting the tourist spots and getting to know each other. We hit it off well, and I was looking forward to working with him. That first night, after a well-fueled dinner with Hitch, he announced that we had been invited to the home of the *Washington Post*'s drama critic, Richard Coe, for after-dinner brandies and coffee. Off we went. After one drink, Hitch announced that it was past his bedtime. He was leaving, but he urged us to stay. We were both feeling no pain, and Coe was both knowledgeable and interesting, so we remained. An hour or so later, Bob was getting a little slurry, so I asked Richard to call us a cab. We went back to our hotel, where I helped him to his room. He flopped down on his bed. I got him out of his shoes and jacket. Then, as I turned to go, he grabbed my arm and, in a panic, said, "Please, please, don't leave me alone!"

He broke down about Jennifer and how she had betrayed him with that son of a bitch Selznick, who was twice her age, just because he promised to make her a big star, and about how deeply he had always loved her and depended upon her, and what a struggle it was trying to go on without her. I knew he had the first call next morning, so I sat down on the other bed and stayed to lend him some kind of support.

The next thing I knew, the phone was ringing. The driver of Bob's car was calling from the lobby. I stalled him for a half-hour and called the assistant director. I explained that Bob had had a rough night, and if they could switch the schedule to use me first, it would give Bob a few more hours' sleep. I could be ready in a half-hour. He said he was sure it would be no problem, since they were just doing walking shots of our feet at Union Station. I raced back to my room, showered, and got to the lobby in a half-hour. When I showed up at the station, Hitch did not say a word to me about the switch. When Bob showed up around noon, he didn't say a word to me, either. In fact, he never again mentioned that first evening.

Despite Hitch's morbidly mischievous speculation, after that first day, Bob was a consummate professional, always on time and always creatively prepared. We became good friends during the course of the film, and it ended with us both promising to keep in touch. Despite those good intentions, it was a month or so before I saw Bob again. He was busy filming *My Son John* at Paramount with Helen Hayes and Van Heflin. We were both excited about the advance word that was spreading around town regarding *Strangers*, and promised to get together for dinner as soon as he had some free time. Two days later, Bob was dead. He had suffered a severe panic attack at home after some heavy drinking, and his housekeeper had called his psychiatrist, Dr. Frederick Hacker. The good doctor administered a heavy sedative, which, interacting with the alcohol in his system, killed Bob. All of this happened just a short time before *Strangers* opened to unanimous raves, particularly for Bob. He got the kind of reviews that could have made him one of the most sought-after leading men in Hollywood, despite those bad years after Jennifer Jones left him. Flashing back to Hitch's now almost prescient remark on the day he read me the script—"Wouldn't it be interesting if something happened on our film?"—gave me a very strange feeling.

While making the film, I became friendly with Hitch's daughter, Pat, the generous and steady-handed bartender in the Hitchcock household. Pat, who was in her early twenties at most, was very good and quite funny as the younger sister of my love interest, Ruth Roman. Warner Brothers was producing *Strangers*, and Ruth was under contract to them. Hitch had wanted the then-little-known young actress Grace Kelly for the part, but Warners had refused. Since they had to pay MGM to use Bob and Goldwyn to use me, they insisted that he use Ruth, who was really not right for the part. Hitch did not like his artistic wishes thwarted. As a result, he was cold and sometimes cruel to Ruth, which was unfair because as a contract player she was just doing what her studio told her to do. But Hitch was right, she was wrong for the part.

All in all, working on *Strangers on a Train* was my happiest filmmaking experience. Often on many of the films I had done, the director would arrive on set without a clue as to how he planned to shoot the scene. He would go to the cameraman or cinematographer, explain what he wanted to shoot, then ask where should the camera be placed and what lens should be used and so on. The underrated and overworked cinematographer, who often did most of the visual creative work on a film, would then tell the director how to shoot the scene. That was never the case with Hitch. He knew exactly what he wanted and how to get it. He had an assistant art director seated on a high stool next to the camera who was in charge of a very thick binder that contained every setup and shot for the entire film. These were the drawings I had seen pinned to all the walls of his office. After he finished a setup, he would walk to the assistant, who would turn over a page. Hitch would look at it and say, The camera goes here, here, and there; the lenses are this, this, and that; the action takes place from here to there. Then he would relax while the crew got things ready. They respected and trusted him because he was able to be precise about what he wanted. He never had to peer through a lens finder to see how a shot looked. Since all his shots were so well planned, his film was practically pre-edited. One afternoon early in the shoot, I noticed Hitch slumped unhappily in his chair between takes. I approached him, and when he looked up, I asked if he was OK. He looked at me for a moment and then said, "Oh, I'm just bored." It took me a while to take that at face value. He *was* bored. He had already done all the creative work in his head and was now merely transferring it from paper to film. Today, in a world of instant playback, a video monitor monopolizes everyone's attention on a film set.

After the film, I began to receive dinner invitations to Hitch's home. They were always small dinner parties that included regulars like Ingrid Bergman and Cary Grant. His wife, Alma Reville, had already been established as one of England's foremost screenwriters and film editors when she met and married the upcoming young director after a two-year courtship in 1926. Hitch trusted her completely and depended on her opinion of his final cut. Alma also happened to be a natural hostess, and their daughter, Pat, poured those drinks that always guaranteed a smooth takeoff.

One memorable evening, the dinner party consisted of Ingrid Bergman, her then-husband, Dr. Peter Lindstrom, Pat, and me. After a typically English dinner of roast prime rib and Yorkshire pudding washed down by liters of very good burgundy, Hitch decided that we would all go out on the town to see the Katherine Dunham Dancers at Ciro's. This took everyone by surprise, because he usually wanted nothing to do with the Hollywood social scene, but we were all feeling no pain, and it sounded like a great idea.

When we got to Ciro's, the place was packed, but for the maestro two tables were placed next to each other front and center, almost abutting the stage. We were spread out side by side, kind of like a mini–Last Supper across the front of the stage. I was in between Hitch and Ingrid, and on the other side of Hitch, Peter sat between Pat and Alma. Drinks were ordered and brought to the table.

The lights began to dim, and the drums began to throb. As the lights came up, the dancers burst onto the stage gyrating wildly in their colorful costumes. Hitch promptly fell sound asleep. Head down, arms folded contentedly across his belly, he began to snore loudly. Ingrid and I had to suppress our giggles. Suddenly Ingrid began to cry, softly at first but then in a torrent. I tried to comfort her and find out what was wrong, but it took a while before she could talk about it. She was filming *Joan of Arc* for director Victor Fleming and was being burnt at the stake the following morning. She had not figured out how to do the scene and was upset about it. I said that I didn't think I could help her, and between sobs she got out, "Don't worry. I'll think of something . . . or they'll just have to burn me." I started to laugh again, and so did she. With Hitch's snoring, Ingrid's sobbing, and my laughing, it's a wonder we weren't all tossed out, or at least attacked by the Dunham Dancers, who had every right to throw their bongos at us.

A New Year's Eve to Remember

Goldwyn himself called me into his office. He said that he had found his next *Best Years of Our Lives*. It was called *I Want You* and would be for the Korean War what *Best Years* was for World War II. I wasn't sure what he meant by that, but his enthusiasm was contagious. He said the parts for Dana Andrews and me were the best he'd ever seen. He had borrowed Dorothy McGuire from Selznick, and he had a new, beautiful leading lady for me, Peggy Dow, "Not another puny girl." By that I assumed he meant pudgy and was referring to Joan Evans, with whom he knew I'd been unhappy. The writer was going to be the Pulitzer Prize–winning dramatist Robert Sherwood, who had won an Academy Award for the screenplay of *The Best Years of Our Lives*. Goldwyn wanted it to go into production soon after the first of the year, and he was almost ready to sign a first-class director for the film. He clapped me on the shoulder before I could ask any questions, and walked me to the door. "Everything is first-class, my boy, no more of that New York old-country business of yours!" I promised to stay in town. He told me he was very proud of my work in *Strangers on a Train* and said this was going to be my big year.

It was Christmas, 1950, time to forgive and forget and to party. I made peace with Shelley, and before long we were back having endless discussions about acting and our careers; many squabbles, mostly about her insatiable lust for publicity; and many laughs. She was still justifiably high about her work in *A Place in the Sun*, and I was high on *Strangers* and Goldwyn's promises. We were ready to enjoy life.

We went to Lewis Milestone's big annual Christmas party together. He and his wife always went all-out, and it was the most festive and traditional party in town. Their large entry hall was two stories high and accommodated an enormous Christmas tree, which was decorated in a traditional fashion. The part of the evening everyone loved the most came just after dark, when the children's choir from the local church arrived. Millie would dim the lights as they filed in holding candles and surrounded the tree to sing carols from around the world. With only the Christmas tree lights and the candlelight on the children's faces as they sang, the experience was very moving.

Later that evening, long after the children had gone and after much good cheer had been consumed, I met one of my screen idols, Humphrey Bogart. His young wife, Lauren Bacall, was a knockout. Tall and slender, she was a quintessential New Yorker whose presence was felt the minute she walked into a room. She was very much a man's woman: tough, completely direct, and without artifice. All of these qualities are still very much a part of my neighbor, Betty Bacall. Bogie, on the other hand, was nothing like his hard-boiled screen persona. Quiet, a little shy and soft-spoken, and something of an intellectual, he was every inch a gentleman. At one point we were standing at the bar deep in conversation when Bogart, his back to the wall, slowly began to slide down to the floor. He neither missed a beat of conversation nor spilled a drop of his drink. I decided the best thing to do was slowly sink down to the floor with him.

There was a French actor in the bar whose name I forget, but whose claim to fame I cannot. He ate glasses. When Bogart heard that, he was off the floor in a flash, urging the Frenchman to do it. He did, and Bogie was determined to learn how to do it. Before we realized what was happening, he had herded the rest of us out of the bar and locked the door. A few minutes later Betty came looking for her husband. When she heard what was going on in the bar, she started pounding on the door and yelling at Bogie to "get out here now!" The door finally opened, and out he came sporting a big, bloody grin.

A week later I went to pick Shelley up for the newly traditional New Year's Eve bash given by the international producer Sam Spiegel. She kept me waiting for almost two hours while she talked on the phone to her press agent in between changing dresses. Needless to say, we fought all the way to the party and went our separate ways as soon as we got there, a separation I've never regretted. That was the night I met Ava Gardner.

Ava

Ava and Burt Lancaster had been discovered by the public in 1946 in the screen adaptation of Hemingway's short story *The Killers*. She has always been considered one of the screen's great beauties, but film didn't really do her justice. She had an animal magnetism that heated any room she was in. She moved like a panther and laughed like a man. That night she had come with Howard Duff. They had arrived fighting like Shelley and me and also had gone their separate ways. I was standing alone near the piano next to the bar when she came over to get a drink. After trading a few glances across the Steinway, I smiled at her, put my drink down, went over, and introduced myself. She laughed and said, "I thought you'd never come over." We drank for a while and made small talk until she said, "Honey, do you want to get out of here?" I nodded enthusiastically and took her hand.

Off we went without a word to Howard or Shelley, whom we had determined deserved each other, to a club where Nat King Cole and his trio were appearing. We celebrated with Nat at midnight, and ended up at my place. It was a memorable New Year's Eve. We both loved Nat Cole and went back to that little club many times during our short-lived but long-remembered affair. Ava was smart, honest, unpretentious, and outspoken, with a bawdy sense of humor. Ava hated all the demeaning, pretentious games actors had to play while working to learn our craft and hoping for a good role in a decent film to apply that knowledge. She was practical about her looks without being remotely vain. She felt they were a mixed blessing, because even though they opened a lot of the right doors, they were also responsible for getting her into sticky situations with the wrong people. Good looks tended to get an actor typecast, playing the same kind of part again and again. People took you at face value with never a thought about what more you might have to offer as an actor. Ava loved her work when the material warranted it, but she wasn't remotely driven by ego or ambition. She was also ahead of her time in terms of equality for women. Ava felt that for a man to be admired when he played the field while a woman was called a slut for doing the same thing was "bullshit, honey!"

I knew what we had going was not a lasting thing, but it certainly was a good thing. Ava was involved in a well-publicized on-again, off-again marriage to Frank Sinatra. She had first been married to Mickey Rooney, and then to the "intellectual bandleader" Artie Shaw. In between them, she had a serious relationship with Howard Hughes. She was not at all bitter about her experiences with men. Her life force was too strong to waste that kind of time. I think she really loved Frank, but the tempestuousness of their marriage had worn her down. All she wanted to do was have some fun without any hassles. I had not figured out how I really felt about Shelley, but the opportunity to spend time with this terrific lady was too tempting to walk away from.

Ava came from a small town in North Carolina and had never gotten time to see the real beauty of California. We took long nighttime drives up the coast to explore Big Sur and climbed down steep paths to get to lonely beaches. We went to San Simeon on a foggy day when the place was deserted and loved that it was all ours. I showed her the small beach town of Capitola where I spent summers as a child. The press had not discovered that we were spending time together, and we went to some effort to keep it that way.

After about a month, our real world intruded and our time alone ended. Ava got the part of Julie, the beautiful black girl who was passing for white, in MGM's upcoming remake of Jerome Kern's ground-breaking Broadway musical *Show Boat*. The film had started with Judy Garland in the part, but Judy's mental and physical collapse had shut it down. Ava always felt that the part should have gone to her good friend Lena Horne, but it was 1951, and Louis B. Mayer was not exactly interested in righting racial injustice. He was interested in adding to the bottom line. It had been easy enough for Metro to plan their all-star musical extravaganzas so that the ravishingly black Lena's solo numbers could be excised in the South in order to maximize box office potential, but the part of Julie could not be messed about with in that way. It was as integral to the piece as the young lovers, Gaylord and Magnolia. Mayer took the easiest or smartest way out, depending on your point of view, and cast his most Southern white beauty in the part.

Ava talked to Lena, who told her not to be a fool, but grab the part. Ava did after Louis B. promised her that she could sing Julie's songs. Her life got very busy. She took intensive singing lessons and was swamped with period costume fittings and everything else involved in the preparation for a big Metro musical. Not surprisingly, Louis B. didn't live up to his promise, and her songs ended up being dubbed. Recordings that surfaced many years later proved that her husky voice was not only very appealing, it would have worked perfectly for the part.

Finding the Method

There was a slight delay before *I Want You* could begin production, and Goldwyn said I could go to New York if I promised to stay in touch and get myself back to Los Angeles the minute he needed me. Shelley heard that I was going. Even though she was still angry about Ava, I had been somewhat understanding about Burt Lancaster, and she wanted to go to New York, so she buried her hatchet elsewhere.

We were both aware of a new kind of acting that was having a major impact on movie audiences, particularly the younger members. It was exemplified by Montgomery Clift in *The Search, Red River,* and *The Heiress* and by Marlon Brando in *The Men* and *A Streetcar Named Desire.* We knew that we wanted and needed the kind of training they had experienced before they made any films. The only place to get that training was in New York and in the theater. Our problem was that we were both under contract in Hollywood, and nothing comparable existed on the West Coast. The teachers employed by the studios ranged from inept to incompetent.

Shelley and I went to New York to explore the acting scene, or more accurately, the teaching scene. Because of its growing reputation, the first place we observed at was the Actors Studio. What I remember most about that day is a young actor who came onstage to do a scene, stood for a long time in seemingly frustrated silence, then looked at Lee Strasberg and said, "I'm not ready yet. I need a little more time to prepare." Lee nodded. The actor left the stage. We waited . . . and waited . . . for more than twenty minutes. The actor returned, stood silently for a few minutes more, turned back to Lee, said, "I'm sorry I just can't get there," and walked offstage to Strasberg's assurances that they would try again.

When an audience is in their seats or a camera is ready to roll, an actor who just can't get there is going to be in big trouble. In the course of that day, other things were said that I could not grasp, for example, that inner truth was even more important than the text.

That evening Shelley and I had our first fight about "the method." She had loved everything she heard that day, particularly the idea of developing a way to get at the inner truth in her acting. I agreed that inner truth was necessary, but felt that an actor had to be able to get to it through the text, not through his personal experiences. Chekhov, Shaw, and Shakespeare used words to lead an actor to the truth. One had to be faithful to the text, not adapt it to some personal sense memory in order to play a character truthfully. I knew that the actor I admired most, Monty Clift, had been involved with the Actors Studio, but he also had been a member of Alfred Lunt and Lynn Fontanne's company. They along with Eva Le Gallienne were considered America's finest stage actors of the 1920s, 1930s, and 1940s, and they did the classics as well as contemporary plays. I'm sure none of them ever said that a personal truth was more important than the truth of the text. And I know from my own experience that they would never put up with actors who just couldn't get there.

Marlon had come to fame with Elia Kazan, one of the founders of the Actors Studio, as his director in *A Streetcar Named Desire*. Kazan also directed two of Brando's other most successful films, *Viva Zapata!* and *On the Waterfront*. Even though Marlon's name has always been linked with "The Studio," he never studied there. His only teacher, and the one to whom he always gave complete credit, was Stella Adler. Stella was not a fan of the Actors Studio or the Method. She had gone to Paris in 1934 to meet with and study with Stanislavsky for five intense weeks. When she arrived back in New York, it was to explain to Lee Strasberg that he had gotten "it" all wrong. He paid no attention to her, and she went on to become one of our greatest acting teachers.

I went to the Neighborhood Playhouse to observe and met Sandy Meisner, another teacher with an excellent reputation. After his class, which made great sense to me, I went to his office to meet him. I was babbling on about acting when he interrupted with a simple question. "What do you want to study with me for? You're already a movie star."

"I want to learn how to act," I replied.

After a beat he shook my hand and said, "You're on. I teach a class for professionals. As soon as you settle in New York, I'll fit you in."

Many years later, in the early 1980s, I went back to the Actors Studio one day because Shelley was teaching there. Lee's class on comedy was in progress when we arrived, so we sat in to listen for a bit. He was still talking the same old nonsense about truth being more important than text when a pretty young girl asked him how that applied when doing Noël Coward. After a long pause he said, "Well ... with Noël Coward you have to do the words as written or it just won't work."

Now that Shelley and I had figured out where we wanted to study, figuring how to do it was the big problem. That was temporarily postponed when reality in the form of Hollywood interrupted our New York odyssey.

Universal had a project for Shelley called *Frenchie* and needed her back yesterday. The film turned out to be a mediocre remake of *Destry Rides Again* with Shelley as the Western saloon owner memorably created by Marlene Dietrich in the original. Goldwyn also wanted me back immediately. He was ready to go with *I Want You*. He seemed genuinely excited about it. His previous six films had been failures, and he needed this one to be a success. It was based on an idea that had come to him when his only son, Sammy, had been called up from inactive duty in the Army Reserves during the "police action" in Korea. Goldwyn wanted to tell a story about how an average American family was affected by America's involvement in another war just as the country was getting back on its feet after World War II. His first choice to write it had been Robert Sherwood. Sherwood liked the idea and told Goldwyn so but had to turn him down because of other commitments. Goldwyn then got Irwin Shaw, who had been writing undistinguished screenplays since 1936, but was now hot from the success of his first novel, *The Young Lions*, to do the screenplay. He then hired Mark Robson, the competent director whom he had saddled with *Edge of Doom*.

I felt that the screenplay was not only dull, but felt dated. Even though the part wasn't bad, I wasn't looking forward to playing a character who was self-involved to the point of indifference about his country. On the positive side, I was going to work with good actors. Dana was once again playing my older brother. Dorothy McGuire, always a particular favorite of mine, was playing my sister-in-law. My love interest was a talented newcomer, Peggy Dow. Peggy was a tall, leggy blonde with a husky voice who never took Hollywood seriously. This was to be her fourth and last film. She fell in love with a tall, handsome Oklahoma oil man and left the business without a backward glance. They had three tall, handsome sons who married three tall, gorgeous blondes. I met them all many years later when I was appearing in a play in Kansas City in the late 1970s. They all came backstage after the curtain, and Peggy could not have been more radiantly happy.

On the first day of rehearsal, I showed up on the soundstage where we were supposed to rehearse, and no one was there. Memories of *Roseanna McCoy* flooded back, and I thought, Oh Lord, not again. I don't think I can make it through another one.

Then Dorothy walked in, looking like a million bucks in a simple white dress. We introduced ourselves and sat down, and I asked her about her time in New York acting in the theater. We were deep in conversation when a secretary from Mark Robson's office came to apologize that they had not reached us at home before we left for the studio. There was no problem, just a slight change in the rehearsal schedule. The company call had been pushed ahead to 2:00 P.M. that afternoon. We were free until then. It was not quite 11:00 A.M., so Dottie and I decided to go for a relaxed early lunch.

The only reasonably decent restaurant near the Goldwyn Studio was a dingy Chinese place, the Formosa Café. They were not open yet, so Dottie suggested we go back to her place, where she would fix us "a little something." We did, but the cupboard was bare, and the only little something in the fridge was a bottle of very good champagne. She gave me a mischievous look and said, "Do we dare?" We did and before we knew it, it was time to get back to the studio. We arrived on time; slightly giddy and light-headed, and thankful for the ubiquitous coffee and Danish. The reading went smoothly, except that Dorothy and I got the giggles during a confrontation scene around the dinner table. We could never get through that scene again without losing it. Neither of us wanted to; in fact, we were ashamed of ourselves and tried desperately not to let it happen, but the harder we tried, the harder we laughed.

The day we filmed it was hell. Remote, taciturn Dana finally blew his top, turned to Dottie, and yelled, "For god's sake, Dorothy, pull yourself together! Farley is just a Hollywood kid, but you're from the theater! You should know better!!"

She looked at me and up we went again . . . helpless. Somehow we finally got that scene in the can and the rest of the film went smoothly.

I Want You, which turned out to be as tepid and old-fashioned as I had feared, had the additional misfortune to open just as the cease-fire negotiations with Korea began, so it was no longer even topical. Goldwyn pulled out all the promotional stops for his latest release, but it had neither the style nor the impact of *Best Years*. His losing streak remained unbroken.

The film that won the Academy Award that year was MGM's lavish musical

An American in Paris, a movie as different from Goldwyn's *Saturday Evening Post* cover take on American life as Toulouse-Lautrec's art was from Norman Rockwell's. Goldwyn then tried again to loan me out again to Universal for a piece of junk like *Son of Ali Baba.* I refused and was put on suspension.

The Dog Stole the Movie

The title of my next film, also starring Shelley Winters, embodied the one thing that she never learned how to do, *Behave Yourself.* I was on suspension, and she had finished something she knew was terrible for Universal. We were planning to go back to New York to work on our growth as actors when my agent, Charlie Feldman, called me to say that he had a good script that he wanted me to read. It was a screwball comedy owned by RKO, still run by Howard Hughes. It had great parts for Shelley and me and a wonderful cast of supporting actors. My agent was right. It was funny, well-written, and very different from anything either of us had ever done. Shelley and I played happy-go-lucky young marrieds who, along with our beloved dog, get involved with the mob in a series of smuggling misadventures. We both thought it would be great for our careers as a change of pace as well a lot of fun to do. Our agents arranged loan deals for us. A director had not been set, and we were hoping for someone with comedy experience. Timing is all-important in this kind of near-farce, not just in the performances, but also in the cutting room. When we got word that Hughes, whose involvement with production at the time was half-hearted at best, had given in to the writer's demand to direct his own script, Shelley and I were devastated. There have been a few genius comedy writers who can direct their own material. Preston Sturges and Billy Wilder spring to mind. Our writer/director, George Beck, was not only way out of their class, he was an untried novice . . . with bad instincts. He was clueless with actors. Faced with Shelley's horrendously bad behavior during the entire shoot, he was also helpless.

Shelley's short time observing at the Actors Studio on our New York trip had a deeper effect than I realized. She proved to be a superlative example of the cliché "A little knowledge can be a dangerous thing." Before she would shoot any close-ups, she would vanish into her dressing room and listen to *Madama Butterfly* to get in character. I could never figure out which sense memory she was trying to get to, or how Puccini could help prepare her for a screwball comedy about a couple who were a ripoff of Nick and Nora Charles of the *Thin Man* comedies. One day, when she was holding things up even longer than usual, the director asked me to help get her on the set. When she wouldn't answer the door to her dressing room, I charged in, and there she sat, *Butterfly* blasting, stuffing herself with jelly donuts ... and it was many years before *The Poseidon Adventure.*

On another occasion, the first setup of the day was a walking two-shot. Shelley accused our cameraman, Jimmy Wong Howe, of favoring me because we had worked together before. Nothing would convince her otherwise, and she walked off the set, refusing to come back until the next day when she could see the rushes. Of course, they proved her wrong, and without so much as a "sorry," we went back to work. She may have been angry because RKO insisted on my getting top billing. We eventually flailed our way to the finish. When I saw the edited version, all of my fears proved to be well founded. The only funny thing about the film was that the dog stole the movie. That my affection for Shelley managed to survive this first time working together is miraculous.

Fortunately for me, *Strangers on a Train* had recently opened and was a triumph. It revived Hitch's then-flagging career. It demonstrated Bob Walker's amazing versatility, and it moved me to Hollywood's A-list of young leading men.

The Grand Tour

Shelley obviously decided that there were fences to mend, because after enough time for me to cool down had passed, she invited me to dinner at Chasen's, then one of the top restaurants in Hollywood. After a long evening of inarticulate efforts to apologize, she finally said, "Will you forgive me if I get us a free trip to Europe and Israel?"

I asked how she intended to do that. She arched her brows. Gesturing grandly, she had a phone brought to our table. Then she rummaged through the yard sale interior of her purse and came up with a scrap of paper that had a phone number on it. She dialed the number and after a short pause said, "Howard ... hi, it's me, Shelley."

I knew at once what she had done. She had gotten Howard Hughes on the phone ... in Chasens! ... and proceeded to convince him to give us a free first-class trip on TWA around the world.

Hughes had entered that time in his life when he was becoming a recluse, and none of us had seen him during the film. Given his reputation as a womanizer, I wasn't too surprised that she had his number, but that she got him on the phone so easily and accomplished what she did so quickly astonished me. I was too taken with her chutzpah to stay mad at her, even though the trip was not without strings. She promised him that we would do "a little" publicity for *Behave Yourself*.

Ten days later, the night before we were to leave, I gave her a friendship ring, which she proceeded to tell the press that mobbed our departure was an engagement ring. I realized at the airport that "a little" publicity was probably going to be a lot more than I had bargained for. I forget which of the two gorgons, Hedda or Louella, outraged by the fact that Shelley and I were publicly traveling together and not married, headlined her column: "First to disgrace Hollywood worldwide, there was Ingrid Bergman and Roberto Rossellini, then Rita Hayworth and Aly Khan, now it's Shelley and Farley!" That was meant as a major slap on our wrists, but we were delighted to be in such glamorous company.

Unfortunately, just before we boarded the plane, a friend of Shelley's, probably Doris Dowling, an actress known mostly for her excellent performance with Ray Milland in *The Lost Weekend*, told her that she should have a tiny freckle on her upper lip looked at, because it might be "serious." After going through an endless photo session that began at the TWA desk, moved to the TWA limo that took us to the plane, then to the top of the gangway that was next to the TWA logo on the plane, then to an interior shot of us being greeted by the TWA captain, and finally to us being seated and served champagne by two comely TWA stewardesses, the press was herded off the plane, and we strapped ourselves in for takeoff. As soon as we were airborne, Shelley started to cry. After a minute or so, she told me that someone had told her that a freckle on her upper lip looked cancerous. No matter how I tried to comfort her, the drama played us to Chicago, where we stopped to refuel. By the time we were preparing to land at Idlewild, as New York's JFK Airport was then called, Shelley had cheered up and applied fresh full-glamour makeup, which made me realize the press was waiting for us. We were met on the runway by John Springer, a young publicist RKO had arranged to chaperone us through our press commitments in New York and London. In a roped-off area inside the terminal, the entire New York press corps was ready to spring. After that concluded, we were grateful for the police-escorted limousine that whisked us to the front entrance of the Plaza. Fans in front of the hotel and in the lobby screamed our names and tried to get at us for autographs. John and a couple of New York's finest got us through the mob and the lobby unscathed and up to our grand top-floor suite, with two bedrooms for propriety's sake. The enormous living room was filled with flowers, fruit, cheeses, liquor, and chilled champagne from Howard Hughes, Universal, RKO, the Theatre Guild, and the management of the Plaza. We could have thrown one helluva party, but we would have slept through anything, we were so tired. John handed us two single-spaced pages of a grueling publicity schedule for the rest of the week. I wanted to let Shelley have it about the price we were paying for our "free trip," but she was too tired, and so was I.

The next morning I had at John instead, and he eliminated some of the less important newspaper interviews and most of the personal appearances. John Springer was doing his job well, because he saw to it that there were featured items about us in the papers every day, topped off by several important television interviews.

I wanted to carve out some time to take Shelley to see the major museums and a couple of shows. I made her buy a pair of comfortable shoes, but after I had dragged her around the Metropolitan and the Museum of Modern Art, it was clear that she probably would have been happier doing interviews. The Broadway shows were another matter.

We saw and were completely captivated by Rodgers and Hammerstein's masterpiece *The King and I*, with Jerry Robbins's stunning ballet, *The Small House of Uncle Thomas*. We also saw a brand-new musical, *Flahooley*, which was a complete dog, except for a golden-voiced ingénue who lit up the stage. I believe it was Barbara Cook's first Broadway show. Nine years later, Barbara and I starred in the first revival of *The King and I* at New York's City Center to smashing reviews. During our hectic time in Manhattan, Shelley also managed to find two Park Avenue specialists who told her that her freckle was just that, nothing more, but she was not really convinced by their diagnoses.

As the time for us to leave for Europe got closer, Shell started acting up and out. She blamed me, rather than room service, for the fact that she had put on enough weight to need her girdle in public. When John told us that he had planned an official party in the Palm Court downstairs to announce our engagement to the press before we left for the airport, it came as a complete surprise. I did not know if I was ready to take such a public step. What I was ready for was a little acting up myself. John must have sensed that, because he headed me off at the pass by telling us that while he was off in London to set up a few press things for us to do there, he wanted us to go ahead to Paris where we could both relax and enjoy life, because he knew how tired we must be. Our TWA Clipper was to leave from Idlewild Sunday evening at nine, and after a stop for refueling in Ireland would arrive at Gatwick Airport outside of London. He would get off there, and we would continue on to Paris alone! We were so grateful at the thought of being on our own that we promised to be on our best behavior at the big party.

At 4:00 P.M. Sunday afternoon chaos reigned at the Plaza. John, as usual, had done his job well. It seemed as if every reporter and photographer in the greater New York area was crammed into the Palm Court. It was past our time to leave when John, with the help of two policemen, extricated us from the mob. They cleared a path for us. I took Shelley by the hand and ran for the waiting limo. As we started to pull out, Shelley screamed, "Stop! We forgot my girdle!" At one point during the melee, she had gone to the ladies' room and taken it off, because it was killing her. When she came back out, she had tried to get me to stick it under my coat. I dumped it into a potted palm. It seems that it was her favorite and "also very expensive," so she wouldn't leave it, even though we were in danger of being late for our plane. I had had enough for one day and flatly refused to go back into that mob to search for a girdle in some palm in a court full of potted palms. John went with her, and they finally emerged triumphant.

Though the stewardess found me an empty row to stretch out in, I just couldn't sleep. The whole situation, which had started out innocently enough with a friendship ring, had taken on a life of its own that I was not comfortable with. I really did love Shelley, but we were polar opposites who fought as much as we agreed, especially about life in our chosen profession. She adored being a star. I hated it. Now I felt as if we were somehow on a runaway train with no way off, and it scared me.

It was early afternoon when we arrived at Gatwick and said goodbye to John and responsibilities for a couple of weeks. We were both feeling strangely melancholy on the flight to Paris. When I asked Shell if she was okay, she said she was just worried about the possible cancer on her upper lip, but I thought it was more than that. By the time we got to Paris, she had sublimated all her other misgivings by focusing on that damn freckle again and convincing herself that she was at death's door. In the cab on the way to our hotel, I could not get her to look out the window at the beauty of the city. She said the Champs-Elysées looked just like the Grand Concourse in the Bronx. In fact, the entire time we were in Paris, all she really looked at was a little card that tabulated the conversion of dollars to francs. She did have two close brushes with death in Paris: at the hotel when she tried to get a better room by slowly and loudly explaining to a rather grand desk clerk, in her best pigeon French, "me no likee" about her current room; and at Le Grand Véfour, when she used the same tone with the maître d' to order a Coke. It took twenty-five minutes to arrive and was presented on a silver tray in a bottle that had not been dusted since before the Germans marched into Paris.

Ethyl and Buddy had a pretty walkup apartment, and we spent a couple of evenings with them. I bought a little Hillman Minx convertible that first week and proceeded to spend way too much time ferrying Shelley from doctor to doctor, none of whom she believed when they told her she did not have skin cancer. I finally refused to continue to be her chauffeur and told her to use taxis. After two days of dealing with Parisian cabdrivers and not finding a compliant doctor to remove her "tumor," she begged me to take her to London. I gave in, knowing that I would not have a minute of peace until she had exhausted all possibilities. We called John to tell him that we were coming to London sooner that expected and asked him to arrange a suite for us at the Savoy. Even though he had not arranged our press schedule yet, he managed to have as many photographers and reporters waiting for us at Gatwick as he had had in New York. London was still shaking off the ashes of World War II, and like the rest of Europe was not yet a PR destination for American film junkets. Since *A Place in the Sun* and *Strangers on a Train* had already been released in Great Britain, we got the real celebrity treatment.

In London Shelley finally found a sympathetic M.D. with an impressive Sir attached to his name who agreed to remove her worry and have it examined in his laboratory. Peggy Mailey, an old friend of Shelley's, showed up at the Savoy. When Shelley, caught up in the drama of her impending surgery, decided she was too weak to attend the Festival of Britain, to which we had been invited, I took Peggy. We went into one exhibition that was televised, and when we were introduced as Farley Granger and Shelley Winters, we just smiled and waved and played movie stars. When Shelley saw that on the TV news, she was ready for therapy as well as freckle removal. The next night, on "preop eve," I had to get out for a little quality time alone, so I convinced Shelley that she should stay in bed and prepare for the big event. I was going out to explore the city for the evening: "Don't wait up for me." Covent Garden was close to the hotel, so I wandered into the opera house and impulsively bought a ticket to see *Peter Grimes*, which was playing that evening. I knew nothing about it or Benjamin Britten. It was stirring, grand, and moving in a way I never expected. My knowledge of opera up to that point was mostly limited to the Puccini of Saul and Ethyl's four hands. Mr. Britten was a whole new world. At intermission, I was in the bar when a gorgeous couple came over to introduce themselves and to "pick me up," as they put it. I liked them at once. Peter and Mary Noble quickly became two of my most cherished friends. He was then a struggling young reporter, and she was a struggling young actress. They invited me to their adorable mews house for lunch the next day while Shelley was under the knife, having her freckle-ectomy. The other guests at lunch were Dolores Gray and her mother. Dolores was a Broadway musical star with a knockout voice and an equally knockout figure. Dolores, who did all of Ethel Merman's parts in London because Merman would not fly, was a bigger star here than she was in New York. They were dressed in identical blue-and-white gingham pinafores and, for a lady with a reputation as one extremely tough cookie, Dolores acted as demurely as she was dressed. She also never said a word, which was completely at odds with her reputation. Her mother, on the other hand, more than made up for both of them. She never shut up, and her conversation was punctuated with lots of, "Well, we told Cole that Dolores just had to have . . ." and, "We said to

Irving, that number is all right, but don't you think . . ." Lunch was an uninter-rupted mama-logue. Promptly at 3:00 P.M. the two little girls in blue got up and daintily departed so Dolores could get her beauty nap for the evening per-formance of *Call Me Madam*. The door closed and the three of us fell about laughing at the incongruity of it all.

A few days later, when her Band-Aid was small enough for her to be seen in public, and after she had gotten the news that her freckle was benign, I took Shelley to meet Peter and Mary. It was love at first sight all around, just as it had been for me. We decided to drive to Stratford-on-Avon together to see a young actor named Richard Burton, who was being hailed as the new Olivier. I rented a car the following day, and off we went. On the drive to Stratford I was concentrating so hard on keeping to the left that I had not looked at the gas gauge. In the lush, verdant countryside of the Cotswolds, with no sign of civi-lization as far as the eye could see, we ran out of gas. We had no option except to sit and wait on the narrow road for a car to come our way that we could flag down for help. We were at the bottom of a long steep hill, and the road ahead curved gently to the right. Shelley was the first to spot eight or ten cyclists headed in our direction. She got out of the car, yelling for us not to worry, she would get help. She huffed energetically up the center of the road toward them waving her arms and screaming, "STOP!!! . . . STOP!!!" As they got closer to her, they peeled off, as neatly as a formation of dive bombers, into a ditch on their side of the road. We watched in stunned silence as they picked themselves up one by one. Fortunately none of them was seriously injured, and one of them was even gallant enough to go back to the nearest petrol stop to get us enough gas for us to make it to Stratford. Shelley fussed and doctored and charmed the rest of the cyclists until our man of the hour returned with the petrol. In no time we were back on the road.

We got rooms at the Stratford Arms, and purchased our tickets to see *Ham-let* that evening and *Henry V* the next afternoon. I have seen a lot of *Hamlet*s in my life, including the one that Burton later did on Broadway early on during his marriage to Elizabeth Taylor, but never one as good as I saw that evening. It fairly crackled with energy. I swore to Shelley that I could smell the fuse burn-ing in this time bomb of a young Danish prince. And the way he sang the lan-guage swept us along with him. The scene where he rages at his mother for sleeping with his father's brother had such searing sexual energy that it was al-most painful to watch. We all went backstage to see him after the performance. His first wife, Sybil, was there, and before we could get a word out about his performance, Richard said he was a big fan of our work in films. Peter and Mary jumped in with their compliments on his performance, thank heaven, be-cause Shelley and I were like two stagestruck inarticulate kids mumbling ours. He grinned like a teenager when we praised him and accepted immediately when I invited him and Sybil to join us for supper. He and I sat up drinking Irish whiskey and talking about acting long after all the others had crept off to bed. He could not understand why I wanted to leave movies for the theater. He wanted the exact opposite. The next afternoon I could hardly drag my hungover self out of bed for some sustenance before the matinee. I didn't envy Richard having to go on as *Henry V*. But he performed splendidly and looked terrific. His rallying speech to the troops before the battle of Agincourt was so rousing that I would have followed him anywhere.

That evening, two friends richer, we drove back to London with Peter and Mary, who remained friends for life. A short time later, the Nobles, with their daughter Katina, moved to a big house in St. John's Wood, where they had their second daughter, Kara. They had more space in their new home on Abbey Road, and were able to expand their famous dinner parties. I have met more fascinating people at their home than I can remember, from the Beatles, whose studio was just down the road, to Sean Connery to a prime minister. For a countless number of famous actors, directors, painters, opera singers, and their many lesser known but equally wonderful friends, 46 Abbey Road was an open door. Shelley, through the years, would stay with them whenever she was in London. That must have been a mixed blessing, since Shell could never have enough heat, and their beautiful Edwardian house had plenty of cool drafts.

Shelley's surgery and convalescence complete, we contacted John, did a few more interviews, and then got on with our world tour, next stop Rome. Shelley had the name of a lady who made inexpensive ripoffs of couture dresses. No sooner had we checked into the Excelsior than, without even unpacking, she took off to get herself a bunch. I thought, Who knows how long that shopping spree will last? and, breathing freely, set out to walk around Rome. Half a block down the Via Veneto, I ran into Humphrey Bogart and Betty Bacall. We went to a Tuscan restaurant nearby for a great lunch, one of the world's best grilled veal chops, with liters of good wine. They told about their experience making *The African Queen* deep in the Congo with Kate Hepburn and John Huston. Hepburn, who was there all on her own with no friend or companion, was a consummate trooper who adapted to everything and anything cheerfully. John Huston segued from director to great white hunter effortlessly. In fact, it had often seemed as if he preferred the hunter to the director. Betty, who was trying to keep all of them in balance, said Huston took off to hunt whenever it rained. This infuriated Bogie, who hated the experience of roughing it and wanted Huston to get them all back to civilization quickly, if not yesterday. This meant that these two old pals had more than one memorable shout-up.

Bogie mentioned that Errol Flynn was living in Rome and said that we should look him up because life at his villa was a nonstop party. He gave me the number and, as Shelley knew and adored him, we did call a few days later and were invited over the next evening. I had never met him but had always been a fan, so we were both looking forward to it. We arrived at around 9:00 P.M., cocktail time in Rome. There was plenty to drink, but no sign of any dinner to come. Flynn, a little drunk and a lot out of focus, was dressed in a white and gold Tunisian robe. He could not have been more welcoming, and he was very flattering about our work in a vague sort of way. In truth, I had a feeling that he was just being nice and had never seen anything either of us had done. After a few glasses of champagne, we were not feeling comfortable with the fawning bevy of young female and male beauties that were very much in evidence. We left after a respectful couple of drinks and went to a restaurant in Rome's ghetto where we had my first *carciofi alla giudea,* Jewish-style baby artichokes deep fried until they open into a crispy dark gold flower. They tasted even better than they looked.

Shelley, having finished the fittings for her new wardrobe, was anxious to go to Israel. No attempt to persuade her to see the wonders of Rome worked. I should have realized in Paris when she told me that the Champs-Elysées reminded her of the Grand Concourse in the Bronx that she was no world-class traveler.

On the flight to Tel Aviv she said to me gleefully, "Now you'll see how it feels to be in the minority." I had to laugh. "Shelley, you know that almost everyone I love is Jewish," but she just gave me a little self-satisfied smile and repeated, "You'll see." A delegation met us at the airport, and on the way into town we passed the main movie theater. *They Live by Night* was playing. When we got out at the hotel, everyone recognized and made a big fuss over me and no one paid any attention to her. She didn't speak to me for two blissful days.

That night I went to the theater alone to see a good production of *Death of a Salesman.* At intermission I met a young Israeli journalist named Yuval Elizur. After the show I joined him and his girlfriend for a drink. We spent hours talking politics and show business. It was very late when we reluctantly decided it was time to say good night. He said that if I would like to see the real Israel, he and his girl would be delighted to show it to me and Shelley when she emerged from her funk. He had roared with laughter when I told him why she was sulking. I jumped on his invitation.

Shelley called the next morning and sheepishly admitted that she had not been at her best the day before. I told her about Yuval and his offer, and she was thrilled. The next day the four of us went to Jerusalem in a little car Yuval had rented. We stayed at a small, luxurious hotel that was partially bombed out and was located opposite the Wailing Wall. To touch that wall, which was all that remained of the ancient temple that existed in the time of Christ, stirred feelings in me that I didn't know were there. In the true sense of the word, it was awesome. We traveled all around Israel, from Haifa to the Dead Sea, and spent the night in several kibbutzes, all of which were in varying stages of being carved out of the harsh, rocky terrain. The spirit, hospitality, and courage of the settlers was inspiring. Dotted all over the place were spindly saplings that were so loved and cared for that you absolutely accepted that they would one day be mighty trees.

On our last night back in Tel Aviv, Shelley and I went to a large restaurant with a courtyard where a wedding party was in progress. The people in the wedding party were dark-skinned and not dressed in modern clothes as most of the rest of the people in the restaurant were. I leaned over to ask a man at an adjacent table what that signified, and he said with a smile, in a heavily accented stage whisper, "Oh, they are Yemenites . . . they are our niggers."

The blood drained from Shelley's face. I thought she was going to be sick. She ran out of the restaurant while I paid the bill. I found her outside shaking and just held her. She had been so excited and moved by the spirit of the people we had met that she wasn't ready to deal with the awful truth that the evil of prejudice could exist here in this land of promise, just as it has through the ages in the rest of the world.

It was time to go. Shelley booked a plane to Rome in order to pick up her dresses, and I went ahead to Paris to spend time with Ethyl and Buddy. Shell planned to join me as soon as possible to return to L.A.

Jerry Robbins was in Paris when I arrived. That night we all went to the Lido, a chic nightclub on the Champs-Elysées, because Jerry wanted to introduce us to two American dancers, Forrest Bonshire and Joe Milan, who were in the show there along with the famous "Bluebell Girls." These showgirls, all English, were known for their beauty, their stature, at least five feet eleven inches, and for the fact that they were all required to have classical ballet training. After the show, Jerry took us backstage and introduced us to Forrest and Joe. After the last show, sometime after 3:00 A.M., we all ended up in Les Halles having café au lait and fresh-baked croissants. None of us kept track of the time because Forrest kept us laughing constantly. He was one of the funniest guys I've ever met and reminded me of Freddy Ney, Betty Grable's favorite chorus boy. I went back to the Lido several times, and Forrest and Joe, along with as many girls as could pile into my little Hillman Minx, would party into the wee small hours. Shelley called several times postponing her arrival—"dress problems," she said. Jerry also introduced me to Ned Rorem, the young American composer who was living in Paris. Ned, knowing how taken I was by modern French painting, took me to lunch at the home of a countess who had a marvelous collection of contemporary art. Her apartment was a triplex on Boulevard Montparnasse that included a 1,500-square-meter garden. It was a bit like having your own park. The whole place was Art Deco and if it had been in black-and-white, I would have known that I'd stumbled into a Fred Astaire and Ginger

Rogers movie. The countess was a chic beauty of indeterminate middle age who spoke flawless English. Her collection included several American artists, including one Whistler that I coveted and a Milton Avery that I could have happily spent the rest of my life looking at. She offered to introduce me to the best small galleries in Paris, and I could not pass up the opportunity. At one of the galleries, I fell in love with two paintings. One was a small modern still life and the other was of Les Halles. I couldn't afford them both, so I chose one and bought it on the spot . . . my first real painting. The gallery owner promised to wrap it carefully so that I could carry it on the plane with me back to L.A. When I went back to pick it up, there were two paintings wrapped and waiting for me. I protested that there must be some mistake. I had only purchased one. The owner assured me that there was no mistake; the second one was a gift from the countess. Completely flustered, I stammered that I could not possibly accept it and made him redo the package. I was not able to reach her before I left Paris, so after much deliberation I wrote what I hoped was a graceful note of thanks for her extravagant gesture.

It was forty-five years before I saw Ned again. Patricia Highsmith, the author of the book on which Hitch had based *Strangers on a Train,* had died, leaving her estate to Yaddo, a well-known retreat for artists and writers. The event was celebrated by cocktails, dinner, and a showing of the film at the Museum of Modern Art. I was talking to some people before the dinner when I spotted a vaguely familiar face across the room smiling at me. As he started over, I realized it was Ned. We hugged, and before he could speak, I said, "I know what you're going to say." He laughed and said, "It's probably still there waiting for you."

Nick Ray contacted Buddy to ask him to work on a costume epic that Nick was preparing in Spain, so Buddy and Ethyl were getting ready to leave Paris. Jerry Robbins had already left, and I decided it was time for me to get home and deal with my life. Shelley finally called from Rome to give me the number of the flight she would be on when connecting to L.A. through Paris. I told her I would get a ticket and meet her on the plane. She was very subdued and a little vague about why she had stayed in Rome so long. Sitting on a secret was not something she was ever successful at, and soon it all came out. Somewhere over the Atlantic she dropped an ultimatum: "Are you going to marry me? . . . Because either you marry me or I am going to marry this Italian actor I met in Rome." I was shocked, since we had been apart for such a short time. I said, "Shelley, what actor? What the hell are you talking about? We've only been apart for three weeks. You just met this guy. You just want to get married, and you don't care who it is." "He's very nice," she said. "He's a very talented actor, and he's half Jewish."

I realized then that however much we enjoyed being with each other, we weren't really in love. We had gotten caught up acting out our publicity. I wanted nothing but happiness for Shelley, but I worried that this precipitous leap into what she considered respectability was a very tricky maneuver. Her Italian actor was Vittorio Gassman, who turned out to be extremely talented, extremely nice, and a good match for Shelley in the self-absorption category. He was tall and handsome with classic aquiline features and was a big star in Italy, both onstage and in films. Best known in the U.S. for his films *Big Deal on Madonna Street* and *The Easy Life*, he, along with Marcello Mastroianni, was a regular in the group of actors used in stage productions by Luchino Visconti. He eventually formed his own theater company in his native Genoa.

Vittorio came back to Hollywood with Shelley, where she managed to get him a contract at MGM. They settled down in Beverly Hills and had a beautiful little girl named Vittoria, or Tori for short.

Life on the A-List

I had let my rented house go before Shelley and I left on our grand tour. I was living at the Hotel Bel-Air until I found a new place to rent. Word had gotten around town that Shelley and I were no longer a couple, and the success of *Strangers* apparently opened a new set of social doors to me.

Gary Cooper called to invite me to a dinner party he was giving for Clark Gable at his house. When I accepted and he asked if I would mind picking up Barbara Stanwyck, I was delighted. I had always thought she was one of the greatest. *The Lady Eve* and *Double Indemnity* are two of my favorite films and feature two of the many terrific performances she gave through the years.

I arrived at her door promptly at 6:30 P.M., a huge bouquet of pink peonies in hand. The maid said she would be right down, took the flowers, and offered me a glass of champagne. Barbara came down a few minutes later, looking terrific in something silver and slinky. She carried on about the flowers as the maid brought them in and joined me for some champagne. I was anxious to get things off to a good start with the right kind of small talk, but unfortunately I was out of touch with the latest gossip. I asked how and where her husband was. An expletive told me how she felt about her husband: "That son of a bitch ran off with some kraut starlet."

As I struggled to pull my foot out of my mouth, she started to laugh and said, "Don't worry about it, baby, he's not worth sweating over," and the rest of the evening went like gangbusters.

We arrived at 7:30 on the dot and were met at the door by Rocky, Mrs. Gary

Cooper, who hugged Barbara and said, "He's going to be so glad to see you." Cooper and Stanwyck had made a couple of great films together, *Meet John Doe* and *Ball of Fire*, the latter for Sam Goldwyn, whom she liked even though she referred to him as "that tough old bastard." Rocky sent Barbara out to the garden to see Coop, took my arm, and showed me around their lovely home. As we walked into the garden, I spotted him laughing with Barbara. Rocky took me over to meet him. He was tall, lean, warm, and friendly. The thing I remember most about him is the twinkle in his deep blue eyes, which were framed by thick dark lashes. He was a movie star.

The group that evening turned out to be almost a who's who of Hollywood royalty, many of whom were Brits and all of whom could not have been kinder to this new kid on the block. Some of the people I remember meeting were: Greer Garson; Ronald Colman; David Niven, who had also been under contract to Goldwyn, and who was the best raconteur I have ever met; Myrna Loy; Ray Milland, with whom I later worked in *The Girl in the Red Velvet Swing*; and James Mason, who never seemed to be in the moment. It was as if he was off in his own secret places. Meeting him confirmed what I'd always suspected: he would have been terrific as Rupert in *Rope*.

Barbara and I had arrived early, so I got to admire everyone's entrance. We were seated at tables around a dance floor that had been set up on the lawn behind the house. Barbara and I shared a table with Deborah Kerr and her husband. Deborah, a lovely English redhead, had been brought to Hollywood to play opposite Clark Gable in *The Hucksters*. Louis B. Mayer needed a cool, refined beauty to replace the enormously popular redhead, Greer Garson, who had married a wealthy oil magnate and retired from the screen in the mid-fifties. Deborah, like her predecessor, had an ultra-ladylike air about her that was misleading. In fact, she was quick, sharp, and very funny. She and Barbara got along like old school chums.

Jimmy Stewart was also there with his wife. It was the first time I'd seen him since we'd worked for Hitchcock. It was a treat talking to him, and I felt closer to him than I ever did on the set of *Rope*. He was so genuinely happy for my success in *Strangers on a Train* that I was quite moved.

Clark Gable arrived late, and it was a star entrance to remember. He stopped for a moment at the top of the steps that led down to the garden. He was alone, tanned, and wearing a white suit. He radiated charisma. He really was the King.

The party was elegant. Hot Polynesian hors d'oeuvres were passed around during drinks. Dinner was very French, with consommé madrilène as a first course followed by cold poached salmon and asparagus hollandaise. During dessert, a lemon soufflé, and coffee, the cocktail pianist by the pool, who had been playing through dinner, was discreetly augmented by a rhythm section, and they became a small combo for dancing. The dance floor was set up on the lawn near an open bar, and the whole garden glowed with colored paper lanterns.

Later in the evening, I managed a subdued jitterbug with Deborah Kerr, who was much livelier than her cool on-screen image. She had not yet done *From Here to Eternity*, in which she and Burt Lancaster steamed up the screen with their love scene in the surf.

I was, of course, extremely impressed to be there with Hollywood royalty that evening, but as far as parties go, I realized that I had a lot more fun at Gene Kelly's open houses.

I took Miss Stanwyck home and had a great time listening to her dish the party and everyone there. We went in for a nightcap, and I ended up spending the night. We enjoyed each other's company to the fullest.

The next day I resolved not to fall into the trap of becoming the new, available young stud about town for the unattached A-list ladies. Other young actors I knew, like Peter Lawford, had been there and done that, and never ended up any better for the wear.

"The Gift of the Magi"

Goldwyn loaned me out to 20th again, and I took the opportunity to make another pitch to have my contract split with Fox, but Goldwyn refused to listen. The movie was *O. Henry's Full House*, a film version of five of O. Henry's short stories with an all-star cast that included Charles Laughton, Marilyn Monroe, Richard Widmark, Anne Baxter, Jean Peters, Fred Allen, Oscar Levant, Jeanne Crain, and me. Jeanne and I were appearing in "The Gift of the Magi," perhaps O. Henry's most beloved short story. Our director was Henry King, an old-timer with a solid reputation. It was a delightful change of pace for me. I had always enjoyed working at 20th, and Jeanne was not only beautiful, she was a delight to work with. It was a particularly good experience.

In the commissary on my first day there, Tyrone Power joined me for lunch. In person he was even more handsome than he was on screen. He was also devoid of pretension, easygoing, and friendly. I felt at ease with him right away. When he heard that I was living at the Hotel Bel-Air, he insisted that I stay with him and his wife, Linda Christian. They had a big hacienda-style home in Bel

Air with a large guest apartment over their garage, where I could stay until I found a place of my own. He was so genuinely welcoming that I accepted without hesitation.

When I got to their house the next day, Linda was there to greet me and help me settle in. Linda, who was born in Mexico, the daughter of a rich Dutch oilman, had grown up all over the world. She was gorgeous and charming, but I sensed something a bit calculating behind that lovely exterior. Their living room was dominated by a large portrait of her painted by Diego Rivera. In it she was naked from the waist up and surrounded by calla lilies, which were very much "in bloom again." She was justifiably proud of the portrait. It was very beautiful. A studio car came for Ty and me each morning. Since 20th was so close, my staying there was pleasant and convenient . . . until Linda stopped by one evening to be sure I had everything I wanted. Over a glass of wine, she smiled and asked whom I preferred, her or Ty? I managed to stammer out something intelligible about what an ideal couple they were and how much I liked them both while resolving to light a fire under my real estate agent. She let it slide and asked if I would come to a big party that she and Ty were giving next weekend. "Everyone is going to be here, and we will be disappointed if you don't come." I, of course, accepted. As Linda was leaving, she turned to add sweetly, "Shelley and Vittorio are coming. I hope that won't be a problem for you." I said, "Not at all, it sounds like fun."

I wasn't sure about the fun part, but actually I was looking forward to seeing how Shelley would behave. The day of the party, Ty asked me if I would do him a favor and pick up Hildegard Knef, a German actress whom David O. Selznick had just put under contract. I said that I would. A stunning German blonde with turquoise eyes set off by luxuriant dark lashes, Hildegard had a deep throaty voice, and a fascinating past. She was wearing a dark green strapless satin gown that showed off the most beautiful back I can ever remember seeing. She was already fighting with Selznick, who wanted to change her name to Gilda Christian and her nationality to Austrian. I liked her at once. She never made it in Hollywood, but in the mid-fifties she was a big success as the leading lady of *Silk Stockings*, a Broadway musical version of the classic Greta Garbo film *Ninotchka*. She wrote a refreshingly blunt and forthright bestselling autobiography in 1971 titled *The Gift Horse*. It detailed her growing up in wartime Germany under Hitler.

It rained heavily the evening of the party and the tent leaked, so everyone crowded into the living room. Hedda and Louella were there gathering scraps for their columns, and salivating for trouble between Shelley and me. When the Gassmans arrived, I went up to them. Shelley was obviously a nervous wreck, but Vittorio just clapped an arm around my shoulder and said, "*Ciao, Farley, an-*

diamo al bar per un po' di vino. Let's go to the bar for a little wine." And we walked off, leaving Shelley dumbstruck for the first and probably only time in her life. Vittorio and I talked about how much he already missed Italy. He couldn't get over the fact that there was no street life in Los Angeles. He compared his life here to "being in a cocoon with four wheels all the time," and this was before there were any traffic problems.

A couple of weeks later, I received an invitation to a party at Jack Warner's home. I took Hildegard, knowing that it would be a good thing for her to meet the Warner Brothers crowd. She was excited, and I was happy to have a chance to see her again. It was also when I saw the last of my top three favorite Hollywood portraits. The first had been George Gershwin's self-portrait, which I still coveted. The second was Diego Rivera's painting of Linda Christian with the calla lilies in bloom. This third one was priceless. As we walked into Jack Warner's large entry hall with its three-story atrium ceiling, two well-lit portraits dominated the area from alcoves on either side of the hall. Ann Warner's was fairly straightforward, as I recall, but Dalí had portrayed Jack Warner as a particularly venal-looking tycoon standing in a great pile of golden coins. Hildegard and I were at a loss for words standing in front of it when a familiar raspy voice behind us said, "It's perfect, isn't it . . . and he loves it." Then he winked at us and, with that famous emphysemic laugh, walked off. It was Sydney Greenstreet, the great (both in terms of girth and talent) character actor from *The Maltese Falcon.* Bette Davis was also there that evening. As soon as I spotted her, I went over to say hello. This was the evening when we had the conversation about how much I loved her singing "They're Either Too Young or Too Old" in the film *Hollywood Canteen.*

It has always confounded me that a man as tightfisted with money and as reactionary as Jack Warner, who, when he was introduced to Mme. Chiang Kai-shek, supposedly said, "I forgot my laundry," had not only a superb roster of actors, but perhaps the most politically liberal group of actors in Hollywood. The list included Edward G. Robinson, Humphrey Bogart, Lauren Bacall, Bette Davis, Errol Flynn, Peter Lorre, Sydney Greenstreet, and Olivia de Havilland, to name just a few. In the early 1940s Miss de H. took Warner Brothers to court and won the suit that set the limit of contract players at seven years, including suspensions. It was the beginning of fair and equitable treatment of contract players in Hollywood. The next step was residuals for actors. Unfortunately, I didn't benefit from that one.

Not too long after the party at Jack Warner's, I found a small, very private house above the Sunset Strip and bought it on the spot. I can't remember why I chose to buy at this time in my life, since I was thinking all the time about New

York and how I could spend time there studying acting. I must have been deluding myself by thinking I could straddle both worlds, film and theater, in the kind of bicoastal way that really didn't become practical until the 1970s with improved air travel.

Hans Christian Andersen

The emperor has no clothes, and this movie has no plot, was my reaction to the script for *Hans Christian Andersen*. Not only was it a shapeless mess, the story boiled down to boy meets girl, boy loses girl, boy gets boy. My character did not even appear until about halfway into the film, and then I had very little to do other than yell at my wife. Unwilling to play ball after my last three disasters for Goldwyn, I told him I wanted no part of it. He went ballistic and threatened me with suspension for the rest of my life.

Danny Kaye had made five pictures under contract to Goldwyn, who let him go after his last one flopped. The flop was not Danny's fault, it was Goldwyn's. The movie was *A Song Is Born*, a lugubrious remake of a superb movie that Goldwyn had made only seven years earlier. The original, *Ball of Fire*, written by Billy Wilder and Charlie Brackett, was directed by Howard Hawks. It starred Barbara Stanwyck and Gary Cooper at the top of their form and had been a huge hit. The remake with Danny and Virginia Mayo was a paste imitation of a real gem. It deserved to fail. Danny landed on his feet with a five-picture deal at Warner Brothers. Now, at great expense to Goldwyn, he was coming back to his old studio to play the Danish storyteller Hans Christian Andersen. My part was the ballet master of the Copenhagen Ballet. Moira Shearer, the red-headed Scottish dancer who had a huge artistic success in Michael Powell's ballet film *The Red Shoes*, was to play my wife, the prima ballerina of the company. Erik Bruhn, the famous Danish dancer, was to be her partner. The great George Balanchine was choreographing the ballet sequences, and Frank Loesser had come back from New York to write the score. Moss Hart, author of *Lady in the Dark*, the Broadway musical that made Danny a star, was writing the screenplay. Goldwyn already owned some thirty-odd treatments of the story. It took Hart and Loesser close to five months to cobble together a treatment that was heavily indebted to the original 1938 version, which told the story using Andersen's fairy tales rather than his actual life. He was not a happy man and is said to have been a closeted homosexual. He was also not a very nice man. Some wags about town called this typecasting. I had great admiration for Moss, but even though this film remains popular, with a defining role for Danny, it is a mess. The best thing about it is the enchanting score by Frank Loesser.

At the last minute, Miss Shearer said she was pregnant and pulled out of the film, and was replaced by Zizi Jeanmaire. When I heard that, I agreed to do the part, much to Goldwyn's surprise. I had felt such chemistry with Zizi when we met in Paris that I knew we would have fun working together, and it would keep me off suspension. Zizi had become an international sensation when she danced Carmen in Paris in the ballet of the same name choreographed by her husband, Roland Petit. It was the first time that carnality had been so openly expressed in the world of ballet, where love was most often poetic. *Life* magazine had done a big story on her, and Goldwyn obviously hoped that this would help the box office. Unfortunately, with his schedule now in conflict, Balanchine, a true genius, pulled out of the film. He was replaced by Zizi's husband.

Zizi's English had not gotten any better since I last saw her, so Goldwyn sent me to New York for two weeks to work with her and Moss on our scenes. Roland went ahead to Hollywood to work out some details of Zizi's contract. We were both as happy as naughty kids to be on our own. It gave us time for me to show Zizi my New York. At the end of two weeks of Moss's coaching, not only was she wonderful in the part, her English had improved dramatically, although you would never know it by the way Danny behaved on set when we got to Hollywood.

I had originally met Danny on the set of his first film for Goldwyn, *Up in Arms*. He was very nervous about his lack of experience in front of a camera. I respected what I knew about his reputation as a performer and told him that I would be delighted to show him the ins and outs of the studio if he wanted. He seemed extremely grateful and promised to call if he needed any advice. I stayed on the set to watch Dinah Shore do a number. Danny never called, but I never really expected him to. After that, I ran into him at the studio a few times, always with his wife, Sylvia, and he was always friendly.

I saw him onstage once at a Hollywood benefit at Ciro's. A number of well-known performers were appearing that evening, including the inimitable Kay Thompson. Kay was the vocal arranger for the Arthur Freed unit at MGM. She, along with the musical director Roger Edens, was responsible for all the great Judy Garland production numbers like "The Trolley Song" in *Meet Me in St. Louis* and "On the Atchison, Topeka, and the Santa Fe" in *The Harvey Girls*. In 1957 she appeared in Stanley Donen's film *Funny Face* and effortlessly stole the movie from its two stars, Fred Astaire and Audrey Hepburn. In it she played a Diana Vreeland–like editor of a famous fashion magazine. Her opening number, "Think Pink" is a classic. She was not pretty, but she was the epitome of chic. She also had her own nightclub act with the Williams Brothers before

Andy Williams became a solo singing star. The benefit was sold out. When the house lights dimmed and the curtain came up, Kay was onstage alone in a skin-tight white gown, with the four Williams Brothers behind her in silhouette. She began singing Cole Porter's "It Was Just One of Those Things," accompanied only by bongo drums. She must have been almost halfway through the song when the lights changed. At that moment I realized that is wasn't the Williams Brothers. It was Van Johnson, George Burns, and two other comedians whose names I can't remember. At that same moment I realized that it wasn't Kay Thompson, it was Danny Kaye. He was fabulous.

On our film, I was never able to figure him out. It was as if he were two different people. Sometimes he was unnervingly cozy with me, and other times he cut me dead. He treated Zizi either with insufferable rudeness or as if she didn't exist, which made me begin to dislike him. When he demanded that the duet Frank Loesser had written for Zizi and me, "No Two People," be given to him, I was flabbergasted. Who was he going to sing it with? The young boy who was always with him in the film, although his presence was never explained? When Goldwyn gave in to this demand, I was beyond angry. It gave Danny every song in the picture. My determination to get out of my contract at any cost was fired up with a vengeance. When Danny walked off the set with a caustic crack to the director that he would come back when and if anyone could understand Zizi, I don't know who I wanted to punch most, Danny or Charlie Vidor, our impotent director, who just shrugged hopelessly and let him get away with it. As a matter of fact, Zizi's English had improved so much since we began the film that Vidor reshot most of our scenes to take advantage of this improvement. A day or so later Danny sidled up to me, caressed my shirt, and whined, "How come you get to wear all these beautiful clothes and I have to wear rags?" I came dangerously close to telling him what I and a lot of other people on the film really thought of him.

When the film wrapped, at my insistence, my agent, Charles Feldman, and I met with Goldwyn to discuss my increasing unhappiness with my contract and how much I wanted to be released in order to move east to study and work in the theater. After a long pause that indicated he was thinking it over, Goldwyn made me an offer. After my twelve-city personal appearance tour to promote *Hans Christian Andersen,* he would give me two years off to do whatever I wanted: go to New York and study, work in the theater, whatever I wanted to do except movies. After that, I would come back to him for two additional years at the old terms. He smiled benevolently and sat back. I stood up calmly, said, "Thanks a lot, but no thanks!" and walked out.

Suspended Again

Shortly after that, I was told to report for another B picture at Universal. Some B pictures were the best things being made in Hollywood. In this case B merely stood for bad. When I said, "Not a chance," I was once again put on suspension. I went to see Charlie and told him that if Goldwyn continued to refuse to split my contract with 20th the way he had with Dana's, Charlie had to find a way to get me out of it. If he couldn't, I would just walk out and move to New York. He made me promise to be patient for a little while longer, because he had two good projects in the works for me at MGM. If they came through, it would buy him a little more time to work on Goldwyn. I told him that I'd do my best to hang in a bit longer, but I wouldn't make any promises. One morning the following week I got a call from Columbia. I had an appointment that afternoon with Harry Cohn, the head of Columbia Pictures.

Cohn, a short, dark, balding, barrel-chested specimen, had a reputation as the most vulgar, most despotic, most feared producer in Hollywood. The writer Ben Hecht dubbed him "White Fang," a name that fit perfectly. A well-known anecdote about Cohn tells how most actors, writers, directors, and producers in town felt about him. Almost every name in Hollywood attended Cohn's funeral. It was a huge turnout. As the service was about to begin, Red Skelton, the beloved comedian, turned to the person next to him and was overheard saying; "Well, it only proves what they always say . . . Give the public something they want to see, and they'll show up every time." Even Hedda Hopper had something to contribute. Her comment was, "You had to stand in line to hate him."

I called Goldwyn to find out why I was going to Columbia, but could not get through to him, and his secretary knew nothing about my appointment. Then I called Charlie, but he was not in his office. At the appointed time I went to Columbia and was ushered into Cohn's presence. Jerry Wald, who had produced *Behave Yourself* at RKO, was now head of production at Columbia, He was waiting for me in Cohn's outer office and greeted me warmly. When we entered the office, Harry Cohn stayed seated behind his desk. After an uncomfortable pause during which he gave me the once-over, Cohn finally spoke: "Sit down, kid." I did, and after another pause he said; "Okay, kid, what am I gonna do with you?"

This took me completely by surprise. So it was a minute before I said, "I don't know what you're talking about."

"I won you from Sam in a poker game last night," he said. "Now what kind of movies do you wanna do?"

I felt as if someone had hit me in the chest with a shovel.

Jerry jumped in with the title of something they had in development, and Cohn snarled at him, "Not that, you asshole. He's all wrong for that. What the fuck do I pay you for, anyway?"

He then had Jerry give him other ideas and with each suggestion continued to belittle him. I finally got up and without a word walked out.

I went straight to my agent's office to raise hell. When I stopped for breath, he jumped in to tell me to relax, no court in the land would accept the poker game as a legal transfer of contract, it was probably Goldwyn's idea of a joke to teach me to behave. When I started in with "Well, that bastard can shove . . ." Charlie cut me off by saying that he had just gotten word that Vincente Minnelli wanted me for his upcoming film at Metro. That shut me up. Minnelli was a wonderful director. I still think his film *Meet Me in St. Louis* is the best musical film ever made. Vincente wanted me to be in "Mademoiselle," one of three short films that made up *The Story of Three Loves*. The other actors in our segment were Leslie Caron, Ethel Barrymore, and a newcomer, Zsa Zsa Gabor. The story was a champagne bubble. It concerned a boy, played by Ricky Nelson before he became a teen idol, who hates his French lessons, and his tutor, played by Leslie Caron. One evening, in a secluded glade on the grounds of the hotel they are staying in, he meets a mysterious old lady in a wheelchair, Ethel Barrymore. The boy is fascinated by her and has a long conversation with her about his troubles. She wisely counsels him not to be so impatient, because things are not always as they seem to be. Later that evening, while dressing for dinner, Ricky looks in the mirror to tie his tie and reflected back at him is me. He has magically transformed into a young man. Now grown up, I walk into the bar to sit down and to order a drink. In comes a ravishing blonde in a scarlet dress that emphasizes her milky white cleavage. She has a captivating smile and a killer Hungarian accent. It is, of course, Zsa Zsa, in one of her first movie appearances. She comes on to me with charming but alarming speed. I manage an escape to the garden, where, wandering in the moonlight, I suddenly bump into my tutor, Leslie, whom I, of course, see in a whole new way. As we get to know each other, she confides her unhappiness at what she feels is her failure to be a good tutor to her young charge, who she thinks hates her. We fall deeply in love on this enchanted night. The script was mysterious and magical. Many years later, in a much less subtle version, the same idea was recycled as the award-winning *Big*. Tom Hanks, an actor who can do no wrong in my opinion, was wonderful in it, as was Elizabeth Perkins, but the film was beer, not champagne.

Unfortunately, the producer of *The Story of Three Loves*, Gottfried Reinhardt, also directed the other two segments. Reinhardt cut "Mademoiselle" mercilessly to make more time for his two episodes. Aside from the joy of working with Miss Barrymore, Leslie, and Vincente, despite the fact that he stood next to the camera mouthing and miming every word of every take, my most vivid memory of this film was Zsa Zsa's first day on the set. The part she played of the woman who flirted with me at the bar may have been small, but when Zsa Zsa was called to the set, she arrived with the entire hair, makeup, and wardrobe departments in tow, fussing over her as if she was royalty. She made a very big entrance.

Some time after this, Oliver Smith, who was then Broadway's leading set designer and one of the formative forces behind American Ballet Theatre, and I were invited to Vincente's home for dinner. His latest film, *Brigadoon*, was opening that same evening on Broadway. During drinks an adorable seven-year-old Liza Minnelli kept appearing in different, perfectly executed costumes with wigs and makeup to match. She would enter and curtsy as Marie Antoinette, then a while later as Little Bo Peep, then as the Wicked Witch of the West. While this was happening, Vincente kept getting called to the phone to hear the New York reviews of the film, which were not good. Needless to say, everyone's focus was fractured. Oliver and I were trying to appreciate Liza; eavesdrop on Vincente's calls, to one of which we heard him say: "It was that bad!?"; and keep sober. We accomplished the first two efforts, but the third wasn't easy.

Liza was dear that evening, doing something that could have been obnoxious. I loved both Judy Garland and Vincente, and I know that they both worshiped Liza, but childhood and growing up cannot have been easy for her. The last time I had a chance to sit and talk with her was after a performance in *Best Foot Forward*, her first New York show. She was such a combination of talent, intelligence, and humor, all fueled by a fierce desire to please, that it made my heart hurt.

Shelley

Out of sheer chutzpah, Shelley had gotten a contract for Vittorio at MGM, where he made several films that he did not think were any good. He was right. He came home from the studio one afternoon and announced to his wife that she should pack up, they were going home. She said, "But darling, we are home." He replied, "Italy is home. Pack!" By this time in her career *A Place in the Sun* had given Shelley recognition as a serious actress. That and the birth of her daughter had given her the respectability she had always wanted. She was not about to walk away from Hollywood to become Signora Gassman in Italy any more than

Vittorio was about to remain in Hollywood as Mr. Winters. The result was that he went home, and she stayed home. They tried to put a good face on things for several years. Their daughter, Tori, who bore the brunt of the separation, was secondary to their work schedules and was shuttled between them whenever it could work out. The final blowup took place in Italy in a much too public way, when I just happened to be making a film there.

Much to the confusion of the Hollywood gossips, Shelley and I started seeing each other again. She was unhappy and needed a friend. As her friend, I wanted to be there for her. I think we made much better friends than lovers, and we both felt, "To hell with people who don't understand our relationship, it is what it is, and it works for us."

Charlie Feldman had been busy. He had gotten me the lead in a musical, *Small Town Girl*, for the Joe Pasternak unit at Metro. The most prestigious musical unit at the studio was headed by Arthur Freed, but Pasternak had done his share of good and successful films. This was a remake of an old Janet Gaynor/Robert Taylor movie about a rich playboy and a small-town girl. I was the playboy who, while having an affair with a jazzy showgirl played by Ann Miller, gets a speeding ticket driving through a small town and is put in jail, where I meet and fall for an all-American girl played by Jane Powell. My mother was played by Billie Burke. S. Z. (Cuddles) Sakall and a terrific young dancer, Bobby Van, were also in the film. Pasternak had assigned his brother-in-law, whose name was Lazlo Kardos, Americanized to Leslie Kardos, as the director. The cameraman was Joe Ruttenberg, one of the most highly esteemed cinematographers in town. The famous, or infamous, choreographer Busby Berkeley did Ann's dance numbers. I adored Billie Burke and could listen to her stories about her husband, "Mr. Ziegfeld," as she always called him, and the Broadway stage for hours on end. Annie Miller and I got along like two kindred souls. She wore a fake nose, the result of a bad nose job, and she would always say to me, "Don't make me laugh or I'll flip my nose!" At around 5:00 or 6:00 P.M. every afternoon, when the ravages of a long day began to show on everyone's makeup, Annie would touch her loosening nose and say; "Oh, oh . . . Shangri-la time." I could barely get through any scenes with S. Z. "Cuddles" Sakall. His endless repertoire of Viennese shtick never failed to bring me to the point of breaking up. I never felt that Jane Powell and I connected on the film. She was pregnant and having a difficult time. We could never lock in the shooting schedule since we never knew if she was going to show up.

Annie had two wonderful dance numbers, one of which, "I've Gotta Hear That Beat," became a classic, and Bobby also had two terrific numbers. In retrospect, they should have been the stars of the movie. One morning when we were almost finished, the director failed to show up. Nobody was ever told why. I think he had a nervous breakdown. He had been getting a little twitchy. Nobody knew what to do, and nobody from the front office knew what we were to do. Since the remaining scenes involved just Ann and me, and we had spent a lot of time working on them, I went to Joe and told him that Annie and I had them down cold. I suggested we just shoot them and finish the film so we could all go home. With no fanfare that's what we did and no member of management ever said a word.

An A-List Diva

I got a call one evening from Joan Crawford's press agent. Miss Crawford wanted to meet me and would be most pleased if I would agree to have dinner with her one evening next week. I was surprised and intrigued. She was a major star, up there with Garbo and Gable. What could she want with me? Maybe she was planning a movie with a good part in it for me. I said of course I would like to have dinner with Miss Crawford. We set it up for 7:00 P.M. the following Tuesday at Don the Beachcomber's, a Polynesian restaurant that was then Hollywood's answer to Trader Vic's. I was there on the dot, but Miss Crawford had not yet arrived. The maitre d' showed me into a private dining room, and I ordered a Navy Grog, a large drink with the least fruit, the most rum, and no umbrella. It was more than an hour and two more Navy Grogs later when she swept in with a PR man and a secretary in tow. She asked if I'd had anything yet, and I answered, "Just a couple of drinks." She said, "Then I'll order a drink and some appetizers," which she did. While issuing orders to her PR man and her secretary, she'd toss an occasional question my way, like, "Do you know so-and-so?" I'd say, "Yes," and she'd say, "Aren't they mahvelous?" or "Don't you just love him, her, or it?" and I'd say yes or no. This went on for a while before I realized she wasn't even listening. The result was that my answers got more contrary. Finally she turned to me and with a high-voltage smile said, "There. I'm done." I stood and smiled back and said, "So am I," and walked out. I hope to this day that I didn't stagger. In the cab on my way home, I wondered what project it was that she had in mind.

The next day, when I told Charlie Feldman the story, he roared with laughter and said that it was probably a very personal project that she had in mind. I then told him that I was going to New York to find a place to live and that he could tell Sam in his own misspoken words to please, please "include me out." I knew he would not appreciate me using one of his most well-known malapropisms against him; in fact, I was hoping it would make him angry enough to throw me off the lot. I repeated to Charlie what he already knew about how determined I was to get out, but for the first time I added the words "at any cost." He was neither happy about that choice nor optimistic about it happening.

It was 1953. I found an apartment on the Upper East Side in Manhattan that was just around the corner from Bloomingdale's, which to my Los Angeles eyes was the chicest store I had ever been in, and the Third Avenue El, an elevated subway line that is long gone. Riding on it made me feel as if I was in some film noir where when I looked into someone's apartment, I might discover some terrible secret that could change the course of my life forever. My old pal Roddy McDowall and also Monty Clift lived on the same block. That helped me to feel like I was in the right place at the right time in my life.

I went back to the coast ready to pick up and pack out, but Charlie did not have good news for me. Goldwyn would not budge. There was no way he was going to let "that boy" out of his contract. He then had gone on about how he had loved me more than his own son and what it had cost him to make a star of me and here I was turning on him like a viper, plunging a knife into his heart and on and on and on. He finally said that he wouldn't let me go even if I was to pay him every penny of the salary that would come to me in the remaining two years of my contract. Charlie said, "I knew the moment he said it that was the only way Goldwyn would let you go." I told him, "Do it. You know I don't care what it costs!" He did it, and it cost me every penny I had.

I went in to Charlie's office to sign all the papers and to say goodbye. He said to me. "Farley, you can't go to New York, you can't go anywhere. You just bought out your contract. You have no money!" I told him I had already rented an apartment, and I had to go. I think I was indulging in some romantic dream about being a starving artist in the big city who works and slaves to become a great actor.

Charlie repeated, with less patience, "Farley, listen to me! You have no money!!!" Before I could say anything else, he said, "But I think I have a solution. Marlon Brando has just turned down a film in Italy for a very interesting Italian director named Luchino Visconti. Although he is not yet known in this country, he has a terrific reputation as a genuine artist in Europe."

I said that I'd never heard of Luchino Visconti, and in any case I didn't want to go to Italy, I wanted to go to New York to begin studying and working in the theater. Before I could repeat my mantra, he said that I was their next choice and that he had negotiated a sweetheart deal for me. For a three-month commitment, I would be paid the equivalent of the top dollar Goldwyn had gotten for me on my last loanouts to Metro, a goodly sum. If the film went over schedule, that amount would double.

As I started to shake my head no, he jumped in with "And the English dialogue is being written by Tennessee Williams and Paul Bowles."

Tennessee's name stopped my objections. Here was a chance to work with one of the most talented theater writers of our time. How could I pass that up if I was going to be a theater actor?

Senso

Two weeks later, on a hot summer evening in late August, I arrived at Leonardo da Vinci Airport on the outskirts of Rome. I breezed through passport control, then barely a formality for anyone with an American passport, and could not even find a customs control checkpoint. I went outside to get a cab only to find a chauffeur holding a sign with my name on it. Lux Films, which was producing and distributing *Senso* for Visconti, had sent a car to meet me. My bags and I were gathered, and I was taken directly to an unpretentious trattoria in Trastevere (which means "across the Tiber"), where in my jet-lagged state I met what seemed like dozens of people.

Count Luchino Visconti was a striking presence, darkly handsome, with a leonine head, chiseled features, and piercing dark eyes. He spoke not one word of English. His assistant directors, Francesco Rosi and Franco Zeffirelli, were there along with his principal writer, Suso Cecchi D'Amico. Also present were the English dialogue writers, Tennessee Williams and Paul Bowles, as well as various other members of the film company and representatives from Lux Films. Only Tennessee, Paul, and Franco spoke English. Platters of wonderful food never stopped arriving, and wineglasses were magically always full. It was festive. It was a feast. It was overwhelming. The din of excited Italian drowned out the few English voices in the crowded little restaurant. I was never able to get into any kind of meaningful conversation with Tennessee. When I was about to collapse from exhaustion, after endless hugs and kisses and *ciao bellos*, I was taken to the Hotel de la Ville, at the top of the Spanish Steps. I crashed for twelve hours. The next morning I found out that everyone had left Rome. It was a month before I was able to see or speak to or even locate any of them again, including the representatives from Lux Films responsible for providing my per diem.

The next morning, I had a luxurious bath, fresh blood-red Sicilian orange juice, a double cappuccino, and a tray of flaky Italian breakfast pastries. It was that morning that I developed a lifelong love of the pastry that Italians call *ventaglios*, the French *palmiers*, and New Yorkers elephant ears. I called Lux Films to see about collecting some per diem. I reached a secretary who spoke no English and responded to each name I mentioned with a cheerful "*Scusi, signore, ma non l'ho capito. Excuse me, sir, but I don't understand you.*" Fortunately, I'd brought along enough cash and traveler's checks to carry me for a while.

That afternoon, after lunch in the atrium of the hotel, I went to the front desk to check for messages. The clerk who spoke a little English told me no messages, *niente*, nothing. Of course, he knew who the count was. He even knew who Francesco Rosi was, but Lux Films drew a blank stare. He was very sorry but it was Ferragosto, the last two weeks in August. No one was in Rome. Everything was closed. Everyone was in the mountains or by the sea. He was very sorry, but there was nothing he could do to help me. I wandered around Rome for two days, certain that someone from the film company would be contacting me. The Eternal City was glorious but deserted and shut down aside from a few tourists and me. I was ill at ease at having been abandoned like this. I had to do something. Before leaving Hollywood, Shelley had called to say good-bye and had given me the phone number of a friend of hers in New York who she said spoke fluent Italian and would make a great secretary for me in Italy. I'd met Janet Wolf several times with Shelley and found her a bit flaky. Besides, I had no intention of hiring a secretary. Why on earth would I ever need a secretary?

Two days later Janet arrived. Helping her check in, I soon realized that her grasp of the Italian language was basic at best. After dinner and a lot of laughs, I also realized how good it was for me to have someone around who spoke English. The next day at the office of Lux Films, after many "*Non capisco's*"—I don't understand—from the gorgeous young Italian woman who seemed to be the only person who worked there, I had my third realization: Janet's Italian was less than basic, it was *pochino*, very little. We walked over to the Via Veneto for some lunch and people-watching, but it was too hot to eat, and there were only a few tourists wandering by. As I was paying the check, Janet lit up: "I know what we can do!" "What?" I asked her. "Let's go to Capri!" said Janet. "Okay," said I. We went back to the hotel and asked the concierge to find us two rooms in Capri. He was not very hopeful at this late date in August with everyone at the resorts. We refused to bow to his pessimism and were in our rooms packing when he called me to say that my name had worked "*un miracolo*." A miracle. He had gotten us two rooms at the Hotel Quisiana e Grande, the best hotel on Capri. I called Janet, and, excited as two kids, we raced down to the lobby, left a message for Lux Films telling them where we would be, tipped our concierge handsomely, and left for the train station. We hopped a train for Naples and arrived several hours later. As we were entering the main station, I realized that I

My father, Captain Farley E. Granger, returns to his wife, Eva Mae, after World War I with a Silver Star and a Purple Heart.

Me in 1927, as a two-year-old gaucho, in front of my father's dealership in San Jose. I have no idea who the fellow on the high-wheeler is.

Me in 1926.

My parents and me in 1943, outside the studio the day I signed my exclusive seven-year contract for $100 a week with Samuel Goldwyn.

The North Star, the first movie I made for Mr. Goldwyn, 1943, put Anne Baxter and me on *Look* magazine's cover. *(Courtesy of the Academy of Motion Picture Arts and Sciences and the Samuel Goldwyn Foundation)*

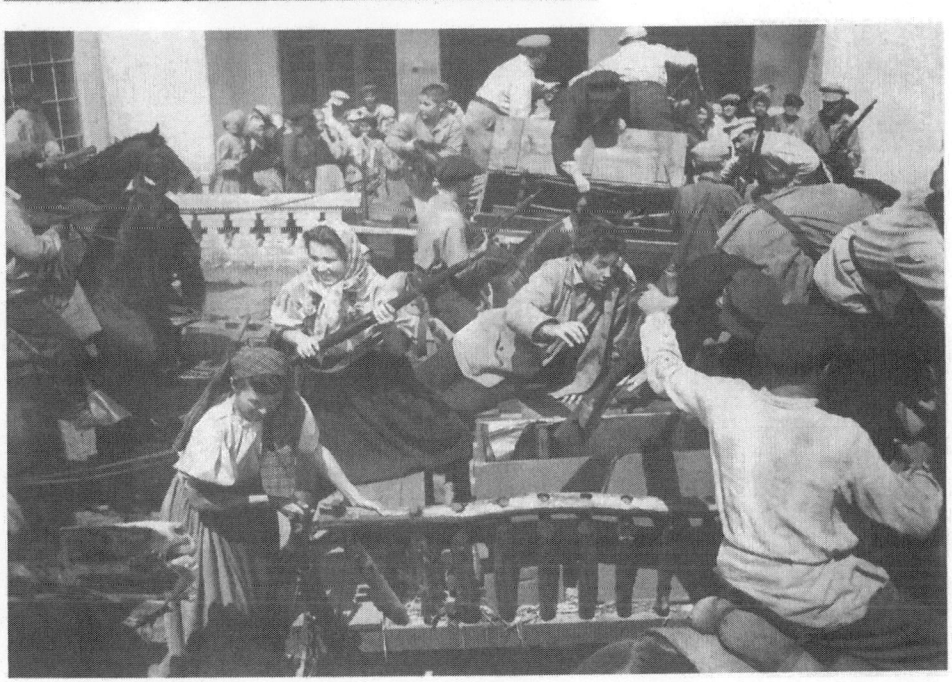

The North Star. Escaping after I had been blinded by the German troops invading our small Russian town. *(Courtesy of the Samuel Goldwyn Foundation)*

The Purple Heart, 1944. As crew members of the first American bomber to crash in Japan in World War II, Sam Levene and Dana Andrews stand trial with me in Tokyo, after my tongue had been cut out by our captors.

Saying good-bye to my pal Roddy McDowell after I had enlisted in the U.S. Navy and was shipping out. I had turned eighteen in July 1943.

Boot camp in Farragut, Idaho.

My first film after being discharged from the Navy in 1947 was Nicholas Ray's *They Live by Night*, co-starring Cathy O'Donnell. Thanks to Howard Hughes, it almost didn't get released. It is one of three favorite films that I made.

Three of My Least Favorite Films

Riding back and forth and forth and back with young Joan Evans while awaiting script rewrites for *Roseanna McCoy*, 1949. *(Courtesy of the Samuel Goldwyn Foundation)*

Frances Goldwyn bought this property for me. It was a bad idea. *(Courtesy of the Samuel Goldwyn Foundation)*

Our Very Own, 1950, sizzled only in this frame. It was really a tepid little film. *(Courtesy of the Samuel Goldwyn Foundation)*

Alfred Hitchcock

Strangers on a Train, 1951, was one of Hitch's great films. *(Photofest)*

Rope, 1948, with John Dall and James Stewart. Working with Hitch was always fun, even when the film turned out to be just an interesting experiment in technique. *(Photofest)*

Strangers on a Train has a great performance by Robert Walker, who died just before the film was released.

Hitch loved to make a surprise appearance in each of his films. *(©Sunset Boulevard/Corbis)*

My Favorite Leading Ladies

Cathy O'Donnell in *They Live by Night*, 1948; a unique talent whose career was badly damaged by Mr. Goldwyn.

Dorothy McGuire in *I Want You*, 1951; a classy lady with whom I shared a bottle of good Champagne before our first rehearsal. We giggled our way through our big scene from that day on. *(Courtesy of the Samuel Goldwyn Foundation)*

Jeanne Crain in "The Gift of the Magi" from *O. Henry's Full House*, 1952. She was as sweet as she was lovely and talented. *(Billy Rose Theatre Division, The New York Public Library for the Performing Arts, Astor, Lenox and Tilden Foundations)*

Zizi Jeanmaire in *Hans Christian Andersen*, 1952. This was the delicious French ballerina's first English-language movie, and my last movie for Goldwyn. *(Courtesy of the Samuel Goldwyn Foundation)*

Leslie Caron in "Mademoiselle" from *The Story of Three Loves*, 1953; two French knockouts in a row.

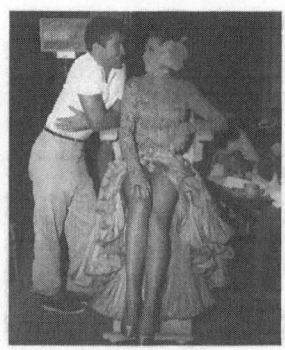

Ann Miller in *Small Town Girl*, 1953. Annie was a hoot. I laughed every minute we worked together. *(Photofest)*

Joan Collins in *The Girl in the Red Velvet Swing*, 1955. Joan was a raven-haired British stunner with a wonderfully bawdy sense of humor. *(Photofest)*

Shelley and me in an unguarded moment. *(Photofest)*

Behave Yourself, 1951. During the shoot Shelley didn't, and I wanted to kill her.

The real Shelley, whom I always loved, at my sixty-fifth birthday party. *(Photo by Valerie Brea Ross)*

Luchino Visconti

The opening sequence in Luchino Visconti's *Senso*, 1954, at La Fenice, the beautiful little opera house in Venice, shows the Italians demonstrating against the Austrian occupation. (© *Paul Ronald/Archivio Storico del Cinema/AFE Roma*)

As Franz Mahler, the amoral Austrian officer in *Senso*.

Talking over a scene with Luchino. (*Photofest*)

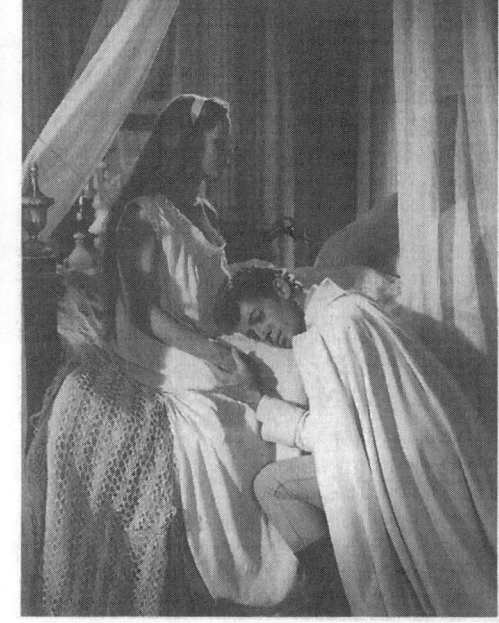

With Alida Valli, as the obsessed Countess Serpieri in *Senso*. (© *Paul Ronald/Archivio Storico del Cinema/AFE Roma*)

With Anne Bancroft in *The Naked Street* (1955), my last Hollywood film before I moved permanently to New York. *(Photofest)*

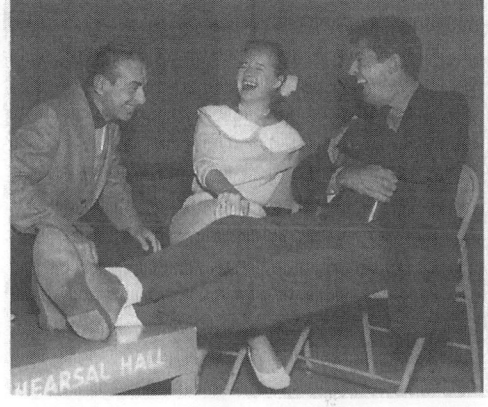

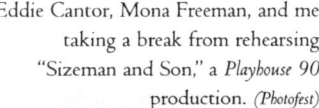

Eddie Cantor, Mona Freeman, and me taking a break from rehearsing "Sizeman and Son," a *Playhouse 90* production. *(Photofest)*

Ten-year-old Ricky Nelson went to bed as an unhappy boy and woke up as a very surprised me in Vincente Minnelli's *The Story of Three Loves*.

New York

First Impressions, 1959. My first Broadway show was an adaptation of Jane Austen's *Pride and Prejudice*, with Polly Bergen and Hermione Gingold, who never spoke to each other off stage. (*© Bettmann/Corbis*)

With Julie Harris in a television adaptation of *The Heiress*. (*Photofest*)

"Shall We Dance?" from the 1960 City Center revival of *The King and I*, with Barbara Cook. Everything about this experience was glorious, especially Barbara. (*Billy Rose Theatre Division, The New York Public Library for the Performing Arts, Astor, Lenox and Tilden Foundations*)

First rehearsal of *The Warm Peninsula*, 1959, with Ruth White, Larry Hagman, June Havoc, and Julie Harris. (*Billy Rose Theatre Division, The New York Public Library for the Performing Arts, Astor, Lenox and Tilden Foundations*)

The National Repertory Theatre

Frances Ann Dougherty; one of the National Repertory Theatre producers was a North Carolina beauty who had been JFK's first sweetheart. She was dynamic and passionate about her work.

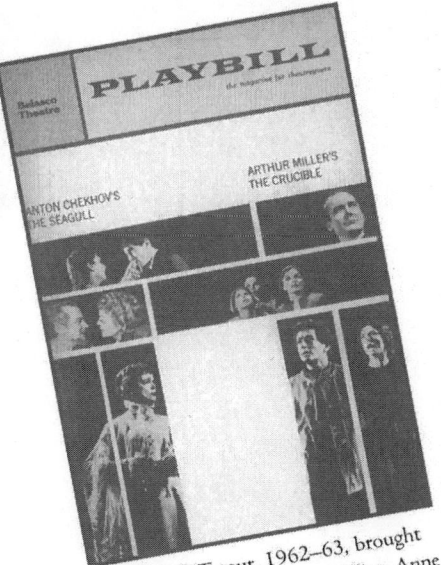

My first NRT tour, 1962–63, brought Eva Le Gallienne, Denholm Elliot, Anne Meacham, and me to New York in Arthur Miller's *The Crucible* and Anton Chekhov's *The Seagull.*

My second NRT tour, 1963–64, starred Signe Hasso and me. The plays on the program cover, in descending order, are: Oliver Goldsmith's *She Stoops to Conquer,* Henrik Ibsen's *Hedda Gabler,* and Ferenc Molnár's *Liliom.*

With Eva Le Gallienne in Jean Anouilh's *Ring Round the Moon*. I got to play identical twins in this French farce. *(Photo by Van Williams; Billy Rose Theatre Division, The New York Public Library for the Performing Arts, Astor, Lenox and Tilden Foundations)*

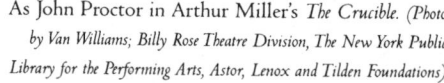

As John Proctor in Arthur Miller's *The Crucible*. *(Photo by Van Williams; Billy Rose Theatre Division, The New York Public Library for the Performing Arts, Astor, Lenox and Tilden Foundations)*

With Eva Le Gallienne in Anton Chekhov's *The Seagull*. *(Photo by Van Williams)*

With Princess Lee Radziwill in
a remake of *Laura* (1968),
adapted especially for her by
Truman Capote.
(© Bettmann/Corbis)

At our house in Malibu in 1968.

Molly, me, Luke, and Bob in
Rome in 1972.

With Marian Seldes as my trusting wife and Steve Bassett as my scheming lover in *Deathtrap*, 1981. *(Billy Rose Theatre Division, The New York Public Library for the Performing Arts, Astor, Lenox and Tilden Foundations)*

Al Hirschfeld's drawing of me in *Talley & Son*, the play for which I won an Obie Award in 1986. Staged by Marshall Mason at the Circle Repertory, the Lanford Wilson play also featured Edward Seamon *(foreground)* and *(from left)* Julie Bargeron, Steve Decker, Laura Hughes, and Joyce Reehling Christopher. *(© Al Hirschfeld. Reproduced by arrangement with Hirschfeld's exclusive representative, The Margo Feiden Galleries, Ltd., New York. www.alhirschfeld.com)*

had left my passport on the train with a book. Janet turned, raced back to the train, and a few minutes later, as it began pulling out for Reggio Calabria, jumped off triumphantly waving my passport and book. She had more than earned her salary that day.

We fought our way through the chaos that was Naples and made it onto a late-afternoon ferry for Capri, where we spent two lazy weeks that carried us into early September. The crowds on Capri started thinning out, which was a sure sign that Italy was getting ready to go back to work. Even though no one from Lux Films had called, we decided it might be best to return to Rome.

Venice

Waiting for us at the Hotel de la Ville was a message from Lux Films. The Venice Film Festival was about to start, and they were expecting me to be there for interviews and other public relations work. A room had been booked for me at the Hotel Danieli on the Grand Canal just off the Piazza San Marco. Before we left for Venice, I had to go to an address in Rome for a costume fitting. Janet, still acting out her Italian translator fantasy, came along to help me communicate. Taking our bags with us, we went to the address and into a large building that looked like a big empty church. Splendid costumes that had been designed for *Senso* by the great Marcel Escoffier were everywhere, stored on rolling racks in lofts, hanging on double-tiered racks placed against the walls, draped over clothing dummies, and spread out on worktables, where seamstresses attended to minute details of buttons, jeweled bodices, and lace inserts. The fabrics were luminous silks and velvets, rich brocades, the finest linen, and transparent cotton. The colors ranged from deep-stained glass jewel tones to brilliant yellows, pinks, and lavenders, and everywhere the white capes, tunics, and trousers of the Austrian officers. I was overwhelmed by the beauty of it all.

I was soon to learn that Visconti was not only fanatical about historical accuracy, but that his attention to the detail of costumes, props, and set décor as well as to the sets themselves was scrupulous and never-ending. The man executing the costumes for Escoffier, a talented designer in his own right, was Piero Tosi. He spoke no English, which was not a problem because by using the clothes he was able to communicate perfectly. Aside from the dressing gown I wore in one scene near the end of the film, my only other costume was the white uniform of an Austrian lieutenant.

Janet was seated nearby and I was standing on a small platform surrounded by a three-sided mirror. As we were finishing, Piero asked me something that I couldn't understand. I looked to Janet, who just gave me her best Italian shrug. Piero gestured toward my crotch with his right hand and then his left hand and finally with both hands. I still didn't understand. Janet got it and burst into raucous laughter. She finally contained herself enough to explain, "He needs to know what side you dress on, dummy!" I didn't know what that meant.. By then everyone in the workshop was trying to hide or stifle giggles. When Janet blurted out what he needed to know in basic Anglo-Saxon, I turned crimson. Piero then lost it as well. I guess my secretary/linguist earned her salary again that day.

As soon as the fitting was completed, Piero called us a cab. We went to the train station, where I bought our tickets to Venice. There was a short wait, just time enough to get some coffee before they posted the next express train for Venice. After several hours, which we passed having a marvelous lunch, the train pulled into the ugly 1930s modern train station in Cannaregio, Venice. A porter helped us with the bags, and I splurged on a gondola to take us directly to our hotel, which was located on the Grand Canal just past the Piazza San Marco. I thought I would be prepared for Venice this time, but I don't think anyone who doesn't live there can ever be really prepared for that splendid city. It was a crystal-clear evening, and the setting sun turned the water to molten copper as the gondola slipped under the first bridge past the station. Every time I have been there, and I go to Venice whenever I can, it casts the same magical spell all over again.

The lobby of the Danieli was beautiful, with a stained-glass atrium several stories high, all very Art Nouveau. Our rooms were like two little cells in which we would have felt like prisoners had we stayed. Back at the front desk, the manager swore that he had nothing better to offer because of the Biennale and the upcoming Regatta. I asked him to get the Grand on the phone for my secretary and told Janet that I had stayed there the last time I was in Venice. "Make it work."

They remembered me! Within the hour, we were being escorted into the most luxurious suite that I had ever seen. The foyer was all white marble with a chandelier, and was as big as most hotel rooms. It opened into a sitting room of white marble with four big Venetian glass chandeliers over four sitting areas, each with a jewel-toned silk damask couch, four armchairs, and an appropriately sized coffee table artfully arranged on huge silk oriental rugs. There were also many well-placed, ornate, gilded-framed paintings and two huge mirrors. The manager opened the doors at the far end of the sitting room, and we entered a beautifully appointed antechamber off of which there were two large bedrooms, each with its own splendid bathroom. My bedroom was all deep red, with silk damask on the walls and a gilded fourposter bed on a dais. Janet had a slightly smaller but just as lavish pale green and gold bedroom at the other end of the antechamber. The manager said that if everything met with my approval, he would send for our bags. I murmured a *grazie*. He handed me the keys, bowed, and left the suite. Neither of us spoke or moved for a long minute. Then I moved silently around the room picking up things and looking at them. By the time I got back to Janet she said to me quietly, "What are you going to do?" I told her to call room service and order some champagne and caviar, and we would worry about how to pay for all this tomorrow.

In the morning, I was awakened by a phone call from a Lux Films press representative, who had tracked me down through the Danieli. They were expecting me to give an interview that afternoon at the Venice Film Festival, which was in progress out on the Lido, a smaller island that had a number of the city's best hotels as well as its famous beach. I was to meet him in the lobby of the Grand at 4:00 P.M., and he would take us there. Janet and I went for a light lunch to the Taverna Fenice, a restaurant next to Venice's exquisite little opera house, La Fenice, where months later Visconti shot the brilliant opening sequence of *Senso*. We met the press agent later that afternoon and were taken to the Lido. I made my dutiful appearance at the film festival, after which I informed him that I was not available for any more press until I received the per diem that was coming to me. He was sympathetic and understanding and promised to contact the producers about my problem. Feeling a little bit more hopeful, Janet and I went off to the Excelsior, the oldest luxury hotel on the Lido, to have a cool drink. As we walked into the lobby, I spotted Stella Adler and her daughter Ellen. Stella was staying there, and Ellen, who lived in Paris at the time, had come to Italy to visit her. I'm sure she really was there because Marlon Brando and Billy Redfield were cycling into Venice from Paris, and Ellen always had a thing for Stella's star pupil, Marlon. They joined us in the bar, and we were soon all laughing at my predicament of no per diem, little money, and lots of hotel suite.

Stella said, "Darling, there's only one thing to do . . . throw a party!"

I laughed along with the rest before realizing that she not only was serious, she was right. It's better to go out with a bang than a fizzle. "But I don't know anyone in Venice," I hesitated.

"Not to worry, cookie, I do. So all we have to do is pick a date," said Stella.

We decided on the afternoon before the last day of the film festival.

The next morning I received a phone call from a Countess Marina Cicognia. Visconti had called to tell her parents that I was in Venice and asked them if she would look after me. I met her for tea that afternoon. She was a young woman, around my age, who spoke excellent English and turned out to be a good friend for the remaining weeks I was there as well as later, in November and December, when we were shooting the rest of the Venice sequences. She told me that

Luchino was, as usual, behind schedule shooting the battle sequences in Custoza, and he wanted to be sure that I was enjoying myself while waiting for them to arrive in Venice for the opera house sequences. Since I had known nothing about the progress of the film, this at least was a welcome sign that I wasn't totally forgotten. Marina asked if I was planning to attend the Volpi Ball that was held at the end of the film festival. The press agent had given me an invitation, but since I didn't know what it was, I was not planning to attend. She insisted, "But you must, it marks the end of the Biennale, and is the beginning of the Venetian social season." She explained that Count Giuseppe Volpi di Misurata, who had founded the Venice Film Festival in 1932, planned the ball as an event to thank all his friends who had helped make the festival a success. It was also a prelude to the Regatta, which was coming up. Giovanni, the present Count Volpi, was still very involved and the ball was a must. The best families from all over Italy would be there. She asked if I would do her the honor of escorting her and I, of course, said that it would be my pleasure.

That evening I went with Stella to dinner at the home of a British art and antiques dealer whom she knew. It was a gem of a house on a side canal not too far from my hotel. There were only eight people there, and I was seated next to Peggy Guggenheim. Yes, that Peggy Guggenheim, whose father, Benjamin, went down with the *Titanic*. She inherited a small fortune when she turned twenty-one. It was small only in comparison with her father's siblings' riches, particularly her Uncle Solomon's. The Solomon R. Guggenheim Foundation owns and administrates some of the finest museums in the world. Before, during, and after World War I I, Peggy Guggenheim acquired one of the most important collections of modern art in private hands in the world. It was and is housed in her home, the Palazzo Venier dei Leoni in Venice. Upon her death, she willed it to her Uncle Solomon's foundation with the stipulation that it always be kept in Venice, but maintained by the foundation. The Venetians venerate her.

Not only did she match me drink for drink before and during dinner, she introduced me to a fiery new one called Grappa after. At one point, I asked her how she got to know so much about modern art. She thought for a moment and said, "When I first realized how little I knew about early twentieth-century art, I decided the best way to learn was to buy a painting a week . . . and I did."

After dinner that evening, as I walked Stella back through the Piazza San Marco, I told her about Marina and the Volpi Ball. I could tell by her wistful tone of voice that she would love to go to the ball, but had not been invited. I determined to see if I could do something about that.

The next day Janet made arrangements with the hotel for our cocktail party. When they asked how many people we were expecting, she said expansively, "Oh, at least sixty or seventy." Then, when they asked how long we were planning to stay, she said grandly, "Oh, at least through the Regatta." That seemed to make them happy, and they did not ask about money, which made us happy.

I got a call from the press agent. He had talked to Lux Films, and they promised that there was no problem with my per diem. "The problem is, I don't have it!" I barked. Nonplussed, he went right on to ask if I would attend the early screening of *The Bad and the Beautiful*. Kirk Douglas and Lana Turner would be there along with the director, Vincente Minnelli. I liked the idea of surprising Vincente, so I agreed, as long as the press agent arranged for us to have a private motor launch for the evening. He did, and later, just as Janet and I were leaving for the Lido, Ellen Adler rushed in. Marlon had just called her from the Piazza Roma. He and Billy had parked in the public garage there near the station. They were on their way in to meet her at a cafe in the Piazza San Marco and needed a place to clean up before they tried to get a room. She wanted to know if they could use my suite at the Grand. Her room was so tiny and we had two huge bathrooms . . . I said of course and gave her my keys. We arranged to meet for dinner at 10:00 P.M. at La Columba, a restaurant that was then well off the beaten path and was full of paintings by local artists. It also had great food.

The press agent was there to meet us when we arrived, and he ushered us immediately into the grand salon at the Excelsior. Vincente was surprised and delighted that I was there. He said that he was very proud of this film. He had every right to be. It was not only very good, it was also a wickedly truthful look at the underbelly of the film industry. He got excellent performances out of everyone. Both Kirk Douglas and Lana Turner displayed more range than they ever had before, and Gloria Grahame won a Best Supporting Actress Oscar for her work.

We finally broke away from the festival and made it to the restaurant by around 10:30. Marlon and Billy were having a great time polishing off a liter of white wine. We ordered another and dove in. Marlon told us that as they were finishing their baths that evening, an assistant manager barged in on them. He said they were not guests in the hotel and told them to leave at once. Marlon got out of the tub and agreed to leave . . . as he was, dripping wet and stark naked. That had scared the overzealous young man off, so they had time to finish their clean up. I was mortified that I had forgotten to tell the front desk, but Marlon had enjoyed the whole situation. He had us all laughing by the time Ellen arrived. It took a while to get her to join in the general high spirits of the group. She was a bit miffed about her Marlon having been disrespected by my hotel.

Stella came over early the next afternoon to help me plan for the rapidly approaching party. The very thought of making the arrangements had been too daunting for me. She took care of everything with a few brief instructions to the manager: "Have the bar stocked with your best champagne and plenty of good liquor, and be ready for fifty or sixty people to begin arriving at five P.M. As for food, nothing too difficult, no dinner plates or silverware, plenty of Beluga, and make sure that your most attractive young men are serving." She gave him her best smile, turned to me, and said, "Now, where shall we have lunch, cookie?"

Over a couple of Bellinis and carpaccio of Chiana beef filet at Harry's Bar, Stella showed me an invitation that had been delivered to her hotel that morning. It was to the Volpi Ball. She was beaming. God bless Marina.

Two days later my party went off without a hitch . . . if you don't count the fact that I hadn't a clue as to how I would pay for it. As a matter of fact, until around 6:30 P.M. it looked as if it was going off without people as well. Then an assortment of fabulous Italians began to arrive. I recognized no one until Rex Harrison and his wife, Lilli Palmer, made an appearance. Sexy Rexy, as he had been dubbed by the entertainment press, had married the lovely German actress in 1943, and as a team they became stars of the English stage and film. In 1945 he came to Hollywood to do *Anna and the King of Siam*, which made him an international star. Even though he had a reputation for being demanding and difficult, I was always a big admirer. Ellen arrived looking lovely but lonely without Marlon and Billy, who had decided to take off for Rome that morning. Stella came late, entering with her usual flair and with a very attractive gentleman, Mike Todd. By that time, the place was packed. In the course of the evening Mike Todd pulled me aside to ask how long I would be in Venice. I said, "I'm not sure, but at least for several weeks." He said, "Good! I'll see you soon," and was off in the crowd before I could ask what he meant. This was four years before he and Elizabeth Taylor met and married.

At about 9:00 P.M., Marina stopped by with her parents, who were gracious in that way that seems unique to Italian aristocrats. I made sure that they met Stella, knowing that even though she was socially the most secure person I'd ever met, it would be nice if she knew some titled Italians at the Volpi Ball the next evening.

Janet finally rousted me out of bed around noon the next day. When I went out into the sitting room, it was perfectly restored and filled with flowers. It was as if last night's party never happened. I knew I was going to have to pay for it somehow, but at that moment I didn't care. I was so grateful it had all been taken care of so effortlessly that it was worth whatever price I was going to pay. After I rented dinner clothes for the evening, we went out to the Lido to find Stella, but she was having her hair done, so, avoiding the festival crowd as much as possible, we relaxed on the beach and got some sun.

That evening Stella and I went with Marina in her family's gondola to the

Volpi Palace on the Grand Canal. The gondola glided over the submerged entrance steps into a torchlit entrance hall with a marble floor that we could see underwater. Servants assisted us out of the gondola at the foot of the grand staircase and took the ladies' wraps when we reached the top. Marina looked lovely in a yellow chiffon ball gown, and Stella was radiant in a black and white satin with long white matching gloves. Her entrance drew every eye in the room as we were escorted to meet the Count and Countess Volpi. The yellow and white ballroom itself was magnificent, with huge windows that looked out onto the canal. The Venetian glass chandeliers were all ablaze, an orchestra played at one side of the ballroom, and a magnificent buffet of Venetian seafood delicacies was set up on the other side. Waiters circulated with hors d'oeuvres. It was not a sitdown dinner, but there were little ballroom tables and chairs placed around the perimeter of the ballroom, in the rooms off the ballroom, and on the terraces for those who wished to take a plate and sit. Titled and upper-class Italians as well as all the important names connected to the Biennale and quite a few Italian film stars, none of whom I recognized, made up the majority of the people at the ball. I felt as if I had stepped back in time to a more gracious age, albeit a decidedly snobby one. Later in the evening, Stella whispered to me in passing that Marina and I should not worry about seeing her home, as she'd met friends going back to the Lido who would take her. Sometime later, as Marina and I were leaving, I looked back and Stella was still in full swing waltzing with Rex Harrison.

Two mornings later my phone rang at around 9:00 A.M., and the manager said that the mayor was on his way up with several other gentlemen. I said, "What are you talking about? What mayor?" And on cue the bell rang. Janet opened the door and in came Mike Todd with two assistants and a small elderly man who turned out to be the mayor of Venice. Again on cue, the phones in both bedrooms began to ring. Mike said, "Don't bother, they're for me," and motioned his two guys to get them. Janet and I just stood there as he turned back to the mayor, took him over to the window, and demanded as they looked out on the canal: "Now you gotta promise me it won't rain on the Regatta! . . . OK? . . . Promise!"

The mayor just wrung his hands and said, *"Va bene, va bene, Dottore. Non fa piovere* (Okay, okay, sir. It won't rain.) . . . *se Dio vuole."* The last three words, "if God's willing," were said under his breath as he looked up to God and back at us.

Mike then clapped his arm around the mayor's shoulders, walked him to the door while saying, "Good, good. I'm depending on you now, okay?" and gave him a hearty handshake and a *grazie.*

As the little mayor backed out the door, trailing a string of *va bene*s behind him, Mike walked back to us saying, "Farley, sit down, I've got a proposition for you." We all sat down as he told me about a very special promo in Todd-AO that he was shooting for his next film, *Around the World in 80 Days*. He was traveling around the world himself, filming special events in every city that he visited. He was here to film the Venice Regatta, which was taking place this week. He would then intercut the events with nonspeaking surprise appearances by top-name celebrities from all over the world. When Stella told him I was in Venice, he thought I'd make a perfect surprise gondolier.

I thanked him and told him I was flattered, but I was under contract to do a film in Italy and I didn't think it would be legal for me to do anything else. "Farley, relax," he said. "This isn't a film. It isn't even a speaking part. There won't be any contract. It won't interfere with anything else you're doing. It'll only take a few minutes. Come on, what do you say?"

I was tempted but still pondering the legalities involved when he said, "I'll give you a thousand dollars in lire, and there'll be no record of it."

Janet poked me in the ribs, hard, and Mike laughed when I said, "Ouch!" "She's right," he said. "Let's go get this over with."

Fifteen minutes later we were standing in front of the Danieli Hotel on the Grand Canal, where he had four young gondoliers my size lined up. I stood back to back against each of them, and Mike picked one. We went into the men's room in the lobby of the hotel, where I put on the gondolier's outfit. Back on the canal Mike had an attractive young Danish couple waiting. The camera and its operator were already in place in one of the other gondolas, and they shot over my shoulder as I helped the couple into my gondola. Then he had them put the camera on land, and cut to the reverse shot of me smiling at the couple as they sat. That was all there was to it. I then went back into the men's room to change clothes. When I got back outside, Janet waved a thick envelope at me. Mike gave me a bear hug and said he hoped we would work together for real sometime soon. Then he and his crew were off into the crowd. When he was killed so unexpectedly in 1958, a year after he and Elizabeth married and had a little girl, the world lost one of the most dynamic entrepreneurs I've ever met.

The day of the Regatta arrived, and it was perfect. I started out with Marina at her family's palace, which was on the canal almost directly opposite my hotel. The Grand Canal was jammed with small boats that had to leave room in the center for the procession of the fantastically decorated longboats. I think the largest of them had eighteen or twenty oarsmen. The procession started in Castello near the gardens where the Biennale took place, entered the Grand Canal after passing San Marco, and proceeded up the canal as far as the Rialto Bridge. It was majestic and outrageously colorful. The palaces along the canal all held open house for fellow Venetians and their friends.

Marina and I only made it from her palace to Peggy Guggenheim's not too far up the canal. Everyone had spreads of food that varied from assorted cheeses to cold cuts, a much more enticing assortment of cold meats than that name usually signifies, accompanied by an unending supply of *prosecco*, the Venetian equivalent of everyday champagne. Peggy had tables out in her garden on the canal, which was overseen by a Marino Marini statue of a young man on a horse. Naked, his arms raised to heaven, the young man sported an impressive erection.

When I walked over to it, Peggy followed. "Are you scandalized?" she asked impishly.

"Not a bit." I laughed.

She explained that the erect member could be unscrewed and taken off when she was having guests who might be.

"And who would they be?" I asked her.

"I haven't the foggiest," she answered, "and if I did, I'd never invite them."

Marina showed me a Venice that the average tourist never gets to see: struggling painters' one-room studios; tiny trattorias that only neighborhood Venetians knew about; off the beaten track little churches with frescos and paintings that were priceless treasures. I felt she might have liked our relationship to move to another level, but as much as we enjoyed each other's company, and as much as I liked her . . . *like* remained the operative word. Aside from Marina, my free time in Venice was spent seeing Stella, until she left after the Biennale. Through no conscious effort of mine, my sex life was an uneventful bore. Then, the movie company and Visconti arrived in town.

Il Conte

Working within Hollywood's studio system had not prepared me for Luchino Visconti. This scion of the family that had ruled the duchy of Milan for two centuries knew only one way to work—his way. An aristocrat who was also an avowed Communist and openly homosexual, he was accustomed to having crates of fine leather gloves or handmade cashmere scarves or other luxuries sent to him to pick and choose from wherever he was. On *Senso* his first assistant director was the renowned Francesco Rosi, whose films include *Salvatore Giuliano* and *Moment of Truth*, and his second was Franco Zeffirelli, whose first two movies, *The Taming of the Shrew* and the exquisite *Romeo and Juliet*, were still a decade away. Franco was also Luchino's lover at the time, a relationship that was as much in the open as it was tumultuous. As a filmmaker, Visconti was a perfectionist who rarely got more than two or three setups finished in a day. He refused to be rushed by anyone or anything. At that rate, it was inevitable that my three-month contract would go on for over seven months. It would have been even longer had I been able to return to Italy when Luchino finally decided how he wanted the film to end.

My co-star Alida Valli was multilingual. We did our scenes in English, and she did her scenes with Massimo Girotti, who played her cousin, in Italian, and her scenes with Heinz Moog, the Austrian actor who played her husband, in German. Whenever producers showed up on the set hoping to speed up the process, Luchino treated them to impressive displays of artistic temperament that sent them scurrying. When we finished shooting the opening sequence of the film in La Fenice, Venice's breathtaking little opera house, the company moved to Vicenza to shoot in a Palladio villa that was used as the country home of the Count and Countess Serpieri, the parts played by Heinz Moog and Alida.

Vicenza is a small mountainside town about an hour north of Venice where many wealthy Venetians summered in order to escape the heat and stench of La Serenissima in the summer months. The incestuous life of our merry band of players living together in the small postwar Jolly Hotel outside Vicenza for three months nearly drove me mad. But the results are splendid and I am very proud of my work in *Senso*.

La Fenice

The company was staying at the hotel La Fenice et Des Artistes across the square from the opera house, but since I was finally receiving my per diem, I decided to splurge and remain in our luxurious digs at the Grand. I swore Janet to secrecy, always a chancy thing to try, because I didn't want to be perceived as the ugly American, above staying in a normal hotel room like the rest of the company. As soon as the stagehands had begun work at the opera house, Franco Zeffirelli called me to meet him at a little beauty parlor that all the opera singers used not far from the theater. I assumed it was to get a haircut and to discuss how to let it grow for the period. When I arrived, he surprised me by saying that since I was playing an Austrian, Luchino was hoping that I would agree to have my hair bleached blond, "like Laurence Olivier in *Hamlet*" was the line meant to bait the hook. Today, actors change hair color as readily as people change hats, but in 1953 it was still a big deal for a man. After mulling it over for a few minutes, I thought, What the hell, I can dye it back when we finish the movie, and agreed. Franco was delighted. After conferring with the hairdresser, he left to tell Luchino the good news. They sat me down, covered me up, and applied some thick malodorous gunk to my head. I closed my eyes and relaxed.

I don't know how much time had passed when my scalp began to sting. I bore that in silence for a bit, but when it got too painful I started yelling at them to get the stuff out of my hair. I didn't have to speak Italian to get my point across. They understood something was wrong. While the lady was rinsing my hair I heard her yell at someone to get Signor Zeffirelli. By the time Franco arrived, I was trying my best to deal with the fact that my hair was the color of strawberry sherbet.

Franco took one look, said *"O Dio mio!"* and launched into an excited exchange in Italian with the hairdresser and her assistants. That took a while. I was beginning to be aware that each moment is lived to its fullest in Italy. A bit later, as we walked to the theater, he explained that my scalp was obviously very sensitive to the compound that the hairdresser was using to strip the color from my hair. If she had left it on any longer, I could have been burned. I asked why they didn't just color it now to a dirty blond or light brown. He said that they were afraid my hair could fall out if they messed with it anymore. We went backstage to talk with Alberto, the head of the makeup department on the film, whom everyone adored. While he and Franco were talking, Luchino walked into the room. He stopped dead in his tracks and looked at me without batting an eye for a moment, then walked over to give me a warm welcoming hug, as he said, *"Caro* Farley, *finalmente, benvenuto* . . . Finally, welcome." He then pulled Franco aside and began an intense one-sided conversation that grew slightly in volume until he stalked out. At the door he turned to throw a *"Ciao, bello. Ci vediamo a presto* . . . see you soon," over his shoulder as he left giving Franco a final glare.

I had to press Franco to tell me what had been said. He finally gave a tight laugh and said, "He told me to get you fixed, and to do it soon and do it well, because you looked like a goddamned lollipop."

Alberto, who spoke a little English, clapped an arm around my shoulder and told me not to worry. He had a solution that would make this just a bad memory in no time at all. He had a way with him, because I really did start to relax. He also gave me a cap to wear as Franco took me into the theater.

We went through the door into one of the boxes for my first look at the opera house. La Fenice was breathtaking. Aside from my one time at Covent Garden, my only other frame of reference for opera houses was the old Metropolitan Opera in New York, which seemed like a vast unlovely barn compared to this little blue and gold jewel box. Many of the seats in the orchestra had been removed in order to be true to the period of the movie, which was 1866, when the young available men stood in groups or milled about the orchestra preening and flirting with the young women in the boxes. In our case, this group in the orchestra would consist of a potentially combustible combination of Austrian officers and upper-class Italians. As I stood there drinking it all in,

Visconti strode in from the lobby down to the center of the orchestra, shouting in Italian. He was followed by a protesting older man, the theater manager. Franco whispered that Luchino was demanding that the big Venetian glass and crystal chandelier be lowered to the floor in order for them to change it to candlelight, which was authentic for the period. The manager was trying to convince him that it was too dangerous. The chandelier had not been lowered since its conversion to electricity decades earlier. He was not sure that the old mechanism would even still work, much less support the weight of taking it up again. Visconti's tirade built to epic proportions as he somehow managed to compare the importance of this event with Italy's victory over the Austrian occupier at the time of *Senso*. The manager manger eventually gave in, and almost on cue, all work in the theater stopped. Heads appeared everywhere to watch as the chandelier was fitfully lowered. A big cheer, which Luchino gracefully acknowledged, went up as it finally settled. Franco said softly, "That was a good lesson to learn, Farley. He always gets what he wants, and he is almost always right."

We only had two weeks to complete the scenes at the opera house in Venice, because their season was about to begin. It seemed to be going slowly, but I was not yet used to the Italian way of working, much less Visconti's way of working. The scenes in La Fenice included most of the main characters and a full house of extras, as well as a full Verdian orchestra in the pit and a stage filled with opera singers, chorus and principals.

The staging was complicated and difficult and began with all the principals' entrances. I enter the orchestra to stand with a group of young Austrian officers; the Count and Countess Serpieri, Alida and Heinz, enter and settle in their box; and finally Massimo Girotti, who played Alida's cousin Roberto, a wanted Garibaldi partisan, appears in the midst of the crowd of Italians in the orchestra. All this is happening as the theater fills up with spectators and the orchestra enters, opens their scores, and tunes up. Finally, the chandelier is lit and hoisted as the house lights dim, and *Il Trovatore* begins. In the end, this scene was not used in the movie.

It begins instead close to the end of Act III of the opera as we see leaflets and red, white, and green rosettes, the colors of the new Italy, being silently passed from hand to hand in the upper reaches of the opera house, which is largely occupied by standees. As the tenor and chorus thunder out the call to arms, *"All'armi, all'armi!,"* a young girl's voice rings out from the gallery, "Foreigners, get out of Venice!" From the top of the theater a shower of red, white, and green streamers, rosettes, and leaflets rain down on the Austrian officers as the audience erupts. During the general chaos, Roberto and I have an encounter that results in a challenge to a duel. The plot is set in motion.

I arrived for my first morning of filming and went right to Alberto, who had something approximately the size of a deodorant stick with gooey black stuff in it that he applied to my hair. After he was through combing it in, it looked surprisingly natural, although it was hell washing it out each day. As Alberto had assured me, it also seemed to hasten the process of my hair darkening to its natural color. Janet took great delight in calling me Pinky for those two weeks, but the Italians were too polite to mention it.

Visconti was passionate about perfection in every area. No detail was too insignificant for his attention. The amount of food on a plate, or a partially consumed glass of wine, or the degree to which a candle had burned down all had to be absolutely right for the time frame of the scene. The angle of the sun's rays coming through a partially covered window had to be exact for the time of day in the story. If I sat on the floor at Alida's feet with my head in her lap, he wanted her loosened hair to fall over her shoulder just so. He was concerned with the fold of my cape and how much of my leg it covered. He knew exactly how he wanted her hand to be placed on my cheek and how much of the moonlight or sheet covered our bodies in bed. Every frame was a painting.

He orchestrated the emotions he wanted with the same precision. There was no leeway. On what word did a slap take place and with what hand? Where in the shadows did I place her in order to shield her from seeing too much of the dead body of an Austrian soldier along the canal? He felt so passionately about all of these things that I found it contagious. Luchino was very specific about what he wanted from me in each scene, emotionally and physically. After a few days, Franco was able to stop interpreting, because I instinctively understood what Luchino wanted even though he was demonstrating in Italian. I was used to working in a much faster way in Hollywood, and his specificity not only didn't hinder me, I got to like the challenge of it. In the course of the film, he was sometimes stern and unyielding with me, but I never was on the receiving end of his legendary temper. He was often curt, sometimes cruel, and occasionally lost his temper with Alida. He never lost his temper with her in front of me, but all film locations are rife with gossip, and in Italy this was as much a sport as a way of life. Sooner rather than later, everyone heard everything.

With the exception of the opening in the opera house, every scene I had in the film was with Alida. Even in the several scenes that included a third person, she was my focus. Alida was a professional and, as a good actor must be, she was always there in the moment. Off camera, she was remote to the point of coldness, and I've always felt her performance reflected that aloofness. Her passion always seemed more cerebral than visceral. I often wondered how the film would have turned out had I been able to play the love scenes with Ingrid Bergman, who had been Visconti's first choice for the part.

We finished at the opera house and were preparing to move to the next location, the Palladio villa near Vicenza, when Janet dropped the bomb that she was leaving. She had been corresponding with an ex-husband, and she wanted to go home to see if it was worth trying to rekindle something. Janet may not have been a good secretary or interpreter, but she was a fellow American, and we did have a good time together. After working all day with people who spoke next to no English, it was a huge relief for me to be able to relax and laugh with Janet. Franco spoke excellent English, but he also had a complex relationship with Visconti. I felt it would be unwise to rely on him off the set for anything other than group social activities. I asked if she could just come to Vicenza and help me get settled, but she had already booked a flight home and was taking a morning train to Rome. "Thanks for the notice," I snapped at her as I walked out the door.

I was walking off my anger along the Grand Canal when a voice called out, "*Farley, che fai?*" . . . *Dove vai?* What's up? . . . Where are you going?" It was Franco. He fell into step beside me. I told him I was walking off a head of steam because Janet had quit with no notice. When he asked why, I told him. He wryly observed that I shouldn't begrudge her a chance at getting back with the right man. I snapped, "The right man! He's her third ex! And they were only married for six weeks!" He started to laugh, and I finally joined him.

He told me that he was on his way to meet Francesco at a place nearby that was like a working man's private club. It was a hangout for the Venetian gondoliers, who were like one big family. The food and wine were fresh, inexpensive, and delicious. It was for men only and no tourists were allowed, but he was sure they would honor me as a special guest. At some point in the evening, different men or groups of men would spontaneously sing opera. Luchino, one of Italy's most important opera directors, had introduced him and Francesco to the place. Would I like to join them? I said, "You bet," and we plunged off into the dark side alleys of Venice.

We were less than ten minutes away from the Piazza San Marco when we crossed a small bridge and walked under it to an unmarked heavy double door. Inside we were greeted with the din of happy male voices mixed with the smell of cigarette smoke and good food. We entered a vast room containing long tables loaded with food and liters of wine, flanked by benches filled with men of every size, age, and shape. By the time the owner made his way over to us to welcome Franco, I spotted Francesco on the far side of the room, and we made our way over to his table. Waiters threaded their way through the crowd balancing trays of glasses and silverware, pitchers of wine, and baskets of bread. There were also platters of different pastas, delicately fried *frutti di mare*, and assorted vegetables. After we finished our first and second courses, out came trays of cheeses and fruits and more wine. We were having a great time as the two Francos tried to top each other with stories about Visconti at his most outrageous, when without warning the singing began. It started at the other end of our table. A sweet-voiced young tenor climbed up on it and sang the duke's aria, *"La donna è mobile,"* from *Rigoletto.* The room quieted immediately. A couple of accordions at different places in the room joined the aria. Next, two men at different tables across the room climbed up and sang Rodolfo and Marcello's fourth act duet from *La Bohème.* The singing went on for at least ninety blissful minutes, with duets, solos, quartets, and sextets from Italian operas being sung from everywhere in the hall, some in groups and some scattered about. Being a part of this evening made me feel as if I had become one of the group, an honorary Italian, and I think my ability to understand and to speak the language started to improve.

Janet's departure, which left me without an English-speaking buffer, was the beginning of my really bonding with Franco and Francesco on the film. They began to treat me like one of them. It was a good feeling.

A Sad Little Jolly

The Jolly Hotels were a chain that sprung up all over Italy shortly after the war. They were modern and functional but charmless, rather like a vertical Italian version of the Howard Johnson motels that sprang up across America in the 1950s. There were a number of *pensioni*, small B & B's, in town, where some of the crew stayed, but our Jolly was the only real hotel in Vicenza, and the only one within a half-hour's drive from our location, the Palladio villa. Luchino, his assistants, and the department heads stayed in the hotel along with all the principal cast members and their significant others. There is a lovely Italian word, *accogliente*, which means warm, inviting, cozy, and welcoming. Our sad little Jolly was none of the above. It was at odds with everything we associate with Italy: warmth, earth tones, classic taste. A five-story-high cement block structure with white stucco walls, white marble floors, and harsh modern lighting, it had all the modern conveniences in rooms that were small and cell-like. This was home for the next month and a half.

Dinner was served promptly at nine each evening, and the food was not too bad. Our long table consisted of Luchino, the two Francos, Massimo Girotti and his wife, and Rina Morelli, a wonderful character actress whom Luchino used whenever he could. In *Senso* she played Alida's companion. Rina spoke some English and had a wicked, bitchy sense of humor. She loved to gossip, and took great delight in shocking me. From Rina I learned why Alida never appeared at dinner. She supposedly was having an affair with Giancarlo Zagni,

Luchino's third assistant, "and since Luchino fancied him as well...," she let it trail off with an amused shrug. In the course of our stay there, I learned enough about Alida, and everyone else in the company, from Rina to write a book, and it would have made a great read.

Alida studied acting at a motion picture academy that Mussolini had set up in Rome just before the war. She became a star in the escapist *telefono bianco* (white telephone) films popular during the war. Her first love was an Italian Air Force pilot who was shot down over Africa by the British. She was married to Oscar de Mejo, an Italian painter/jazz pianist, when David O. Selznick discovered her and brought her to Hollywood in 1946. She almost did not get her visa to go with Selznick because of a rumor that she had an affair with Goebbels, Hitler's minister of propaganda. After her marriage to de Mejo, she had gone into hiding for two years rather than make fascist propaganda films for the Italian government. Her husband was a bigger success in Hollywood than she was when he wrote the song "All I Want for Christmas Is My Two Front Teeth." She fell madly in unrequited love with Frank Sinatra when they made the flop *The Miracle of the Bells*. Now she was betraying Visconti by having this affair with his third assistant. But after all, Luchino was still fooling around with Massimo Girotti behind his wife's back, and also behind Franco's back. The gossip was like a stream of consciousness that picked up again each evening exactly where it had ended the previous evening. The penance I paid for being plugged into all this company gossip was that "Fritzie," Rina's aging, corpulent, and flatulent dachshund, was always seated on a chair between us at dinner. Fritzie was so overweight that he resembled a bratwurst with feet, but he always managed to heave himself into a sitting position to drool and beg for my food.

Visconti's work process at the villa was as extravagant as the most voluptuous images in his films. At La Fenice, the schedule had been dictated by the time left before the opera season began, but there were no time constraints at Villa Godi Malinverni. He did not decide what scenes to do each day until inspiration struck in the early morning. Every area in which we might work had to be freshly dressed, set up, and ready to go each day. That included food, fresh flowers, and the myriad things that make a set ready, except lighting. That always had to be set up after the location was chosen because we only had a limited number of lighting instruments.

My first call to work at the villa was also a dangerously close call. Alida and I had a long tracking shot to do when she takes me from her bedroom to hide me in the granary. As we were passing a massive antique table, I heard a loud snap and instinctively pulled her aside with me. We just missed being hit by a pipe hung with lights that split the table in two when it hit. Shooting ended for that day.

After two days, I realized that since my work at the villa was limited to a couple of scenes in the countess's boudoir and a love scene in the granary, I was going to spend a lot of time just sitting around doing nothing. As lovely as the bedroom assigned to me as a dressing room was, I had no intention of just hanging out there while the rest of the film was being so painstakingly shot. I knew Visconti wanted that, but what I wanted was a car and the freedom it would give me. I told Franco how strongly I felt and he promised to speak to Luchino about it.

That evening, Luchino, Franco, and I had a summit before dinner. Luchino spoke first. Through Franco, he explained dramatically that it would make him very happy if I did not go driving around the countryside by myself. Driving in Italy was not like driving in America. The country roads were dangerously curvy and rough, and the highways were paved with the blood of young Italian men because they all thought they were racing driver champions. The cities were no better. There everyone drove like they were in a bumper car ride in an amusement park and paid no attention to stop signs or red lights. He loved me too much to see my life ended at this early age when he foresaw so many good things for me in the future.

I was 25 percent bamboozled, 25 percent flattered, and 50 percent still determined to have a car. I pleaded my case. Growing up in California meant that I had learned to drive almost as soon as I got out of the eighth grade. Since the time of my first movie, I had always had my own car, which I drove along the dangerously curvy and narrow Mulholland Drive, which connected the studios via the treacherous, twisty canyon roads. During the rainy season, there were mudslides around every other curve and produce trucks from the San Fernando Valley coming at me like a train if I missed the boulders on the roads. Franco gave me a "not bad" look, but Luchino just sat there glowering, so I forged ahead. "And besides, just a couple of years ago, I drove all through Italy, Austria, Germany, France, Spain, and England in a little Hillman Minx. I went over the Alps, over the Pyrenées, and never even got a scratch. I also . . ." "*Va bene, va bene* . . . okay, okay," he interrupted me curtly as he got up. "*Ci pensi tu, Franco* . . . Franco will see to it," and he stalked off.

Franco grinned at me wickedly and said "Good work" when Luchino was out of earshot. I asked him to get me a little red sportscar like the one that Aldo, our cameraman, drove. He raised his eyebrows at me; "I would not push my luck, Farley." Several days later, he gave me the keys to a car that had arrived from Milan. I raced out to see my car. There sat a big, black, vintage Buick sedan, out of a 1930s gangster film. At lunchtime, I drove it up to the dirt-floor tavern in the countryside near the villa where the company ate each afternoon, literally scraping the walls of the houses on both sides of the road as I went through the nearby little village. The whole company was waiting for me outside the tavern when I pulled up. I backed in smoothly next to Aldo's red Alfa and got bravos.

Luchino and Franco both had huge grins when I walked over to them. I admitted to Luchino that it was a great joke and asked when my real car was arriving. His grin vanished as he said firmly that this was it. It was too dangerous for me to have a speedy little Italian car that trucks could squash like a bug, and this was the only solid American car he could find, and that was that. *"Basta! È finito!*... Enough! It's finished!" He turned and walked into the tavern. I started after him when Franco grabbed my arm and said, "It won't change, Farley. Don't press him." Reluctantly, I gave in, and after I got used to maneuvering along the country roads I started to have fun with the car. It guaranteed me a big welcome wherever I went while exploring the countryside in search of the many other Palladio villas near Vicenza. I became something of a celebrity in our little village, because one day while scraping my way through, a ritual that the locals now came out for either to shout encouragement or to watch potential disasters take place, I came to a nose-to-nose standoff with a government oil truck. When he gestured at me to back up, I shook my head no. I had become pretty deft at getting through the town without incident, but I was not about to try it backward. The two of us got out of our vehicles. I had learned by now never to utter a word of Italian in situations like this. You win much more quickly by sticking to your point in English. After much shouting and gesticulating in English and in Italian, accompanied by loud partisan encouragement for me from the delighted bystanders (Italians will always side against the government in a private squabble), I finally forced him to back up to the outskirts of the town where the road widened and I could get by. From that day on, I was a local hero.

Dinners at the Jolly may have been mediocre but the lunches at that little country taverna were incredible. I don't know how the sweet older couple who ran it managed, although I'm sure the daily presence of the count inspired them. In the entire time we were there, we never had the same meal twice. The antipasti were always freshly homemade surprises; the primi piatti were a new kind of pasta with a different sauce every day or different hearty soups; the *contorni*, vegetables, were prepared in such a variety of ways that it seemed to be something different each time; the main courses ranged from whole roast suckling pig—I still dream of the cracklin'—to the chickens that pecked underfoot the day before, to trout caught that morning from a nearby stream. For dessert there was always a platter of superb local cheeses and fresh fruit. All of this was washed down by uncomplicated homemade wines that were perfect with the food, followed by strong caffè to jolt us awake enough to return to work sated and invigorated. The meals were such that I did everything I could to get back for them each day, even when I wasn't working. She was missing out on some terrific meals, but Alida still never ate with the company.

One afternoon, after a particularly satisfying meal, Franco told me that

Luchino was thinking about changing the afternoon schedule. Would I come back to the villa to be there in case he needed me? I did, of course, and fell sound asleep in my dressing room. I woke up sitting in a chair outside in the rain with our makeup man slapping my face. Alberto had come to my room to tell me that I was not going to be used, and he smelled gas as he came down the hall. He raced in to find me unconscious and not breathing, and scooped me up to carry me outside, where he administered some kind of CPR that probably saved my life. Apparently a draft had extinguished the flame on the heater in my room, and the room had filled with gas. Except for a lingering headache, I felt fine almost immediately after I regained consciousness.

That night at the Jolly, Luchino asked if I would like to take a long weekend off and go to Paris for a change of scenery. I jumped at his suggestion. He arranged cars and tickets for me and booked me a room in his favorite little hotel, the Lancaster, on the Right Bank near the Étoile. It was a gem, furnished with exquisite antiques. I couldn't have felt more privilaged. After checking in, I tried to get in touch with Ethyl and Buddy, with no success. As I started to unpack, thinking that I should have called before leaving Italy, and wondering what I would do if they were not here, there was a knock on the door. I opened it to one of France's most popular and admired leading men of the 1940s and 1950s, Jean Marais. After he introduced himself, I guess I just stood there looking stupid because he said, "May I?" gesturing into the room.

"Of course," I said, jumping out of the way. I closed the door, followed him in, shook his hand, and introduced myself.

He laughed as he said, "I know who you are, Farley. I've seen your Hitchcock films, and also the one directed by Nick Ray. You are a good actor." His English was on a par with my French, so this entire exchange was much more awkward for both of us than I've made it sound. He went on to say, "Luchino has made me promise to help make your stay in Paris a great success. What would you like to do?"

The lightbulb finally went on. Luchino! He must have known Marais through Cocteau. As a young theater director, Luchino had done several of Cocteau's plays in Rome, and Marais's early career had been guided by Jean Cocteau, who wrote both plays and screenplays for the sensationally handsome young actor. My thoughts raced for a moment. I was not eager to be a part of one of Luchino's manipulations, but I also didn't want to be rude to Jean Marais. Finally, because I couldn't think of what to say and the silence was awkward, I finally blurted, "Do you know Zizi Jeanmaire?" He said no, but he certainly knew who she was. I asked if he thought he could help me find her, since I had no idea of how to begin and I would really love to see her. He said that he would make a few calls and be back in an hour or so after I had finished settling in. "Would that be okay?" I assured him that it would, and he left. After I had finished unpacking and tried Ethyl and Buddy again with no luck, I sat there wondering if Luchino had an ulterior motive for having set this up. Before I could come to any conclusion, Jean Marais was back with an address on the Rue Ravignan, and off we went.

Next thing I knew, we were knocking on an apartment door in Montmartre. The door was opened by Zizi, who did a classic double-take, then jumped into my arms squealing, "Oh, my good thing!" I introduced her to Jean, whom she had recognized on sight, and she led us into the living room where she introduced us to Paul, a young dancer with whom she was obviously involved. Paul went to get some glasses and a bottle of wine. Several glasses of wine later, we went out to a little place nearby for something to eat. We had escargot, steak frites, and a salad of frisée with lardons, accompanied by liters of good house wine and baskets full of peerless Parisian bread. With Zizi's help, or it may have been the wine, the language barrier seemed to melt away long before the evening was over. From there, Zizi took us up to tiny little club up near Sacré-Coeur, the white church that sits at the top of Montmartre and stands out as one of the landmarks of Paris. An old Russian guitar player who had been a legend in Paris since the Russian Revolution was performing there. He was as much a landmark as the church, and supposedly could give Segovia a strum for his money. Jean knew of him, but had never seen him. So we were all up for the idea. The guitarist did not disappoint. He was a big grizzled bear of a man with a full beard and a wild head of hair that somewhat resembled the untrimmed tops of his guitar strings. He played classical music and Russian folk songs so beautifully it brought tears to my eyes. He came over to envelop Zizi in an enormous hug, and politely bowed as we were introduced, but we could not talk him into sitting down for a glass of wine.

The owner of the club, who also sang there, was a woman named Genette Auger, also known as Geneviève. She became a semi-star on late-night TV in this country, along with the British music hall favorite Hermione Gingold, as a regular guest on the *Tonight Show* with Jack Paar in the late 1950s.

The next day, the smell of *café filtre* and hot croissants woke me at noon. Jean put the coffee down next to the bed and opened the curtains, and I realized that we were on his luxurious houseboat on the Seine. I didn't remember all the details of the night before, but I remembered enough to know he had been caring and very sweet. I decided that getting us together had not been a self-serving manipulation on Luchino's part. It had been a successful attempt to bring together two people he cared about. After I had showered and dressed, I joined Jean in the main cabin for more coffee, and we sat and talked for hours. He told me how he had always hated the in-crowd and the social scene in Paris, which was why he lived on a houseboat. It afforded him more privacy. We talked about his early career and how it wasn't until he became involved with Jean Cocteau both personally and professionally that he was able to tap into the talent that made him so successful. As a director, Cocteau had managed to break through the self-protective barriers that many good-looking actors build to hide behind. Before that Jean had felt that the only thing that he brought to his work was his looks, and he had not liked that feeling.

At one point, I called Ethyl and Buddy again, and Ethyl answered! When she heard I was in Paris for a long weekend she said, "You get over here right now!" I told her I was having lunch with Jean Marais. She said, "Oh my . . . come to dinner, then, and by all means, please invite him. I've been in love with him ever since I saw *Beauty and the Beast*." I promised to try. But Jean had plans to attend the opera with friends that evening. Too bad; I think he would have lived up to Ethyl's fantasy.

I spent that evening and the next day and evening with them as we caught up on one another's lives and just enjoyed being in Paris together. I had to get back to work. As I was packing to leave for the airport, there was a knock on the door. It was Jean. He had come to say goodbye and to tell me that he had talked to Luchino to tell him how lucky he was to have me in his film. We promised to stay in touch.

Back in Vicenza that evening, Luchino said that I looked rested and that he hoped I had enjoyed myself. I said that it had been a wonderful break and thanked him for introducing me to such a lovely little hotel. I had decided to let him be the one to bring up Jean's name. He didn't, so neither did I.

Two days later, it was late Friday afternoon, and Alida and I were finishing a scene in her boudoir, when three representatives in black suits from Lux Films appeared on the set. Luchino called a break. As I headed for my dressing room, Franco pulled me off to the side and said, "Stay. You will enjoy this."

I watched the tight little huddle on the set for a couple of minutes, and then Luchino's voice and gestures started getting louder and more dramatic. He wheeled and strode off through the bedroom we were shooting in, threw open the doors, marched down to an unlit alcove off the antechamber, grabbed the armful of flowers out of a large vase on a table in front of a mirror, marched all the way back to the executives, and dashed the now-wilting flowers to the ground at their feet. He then proceeded to jump up and down on the flowers while bellowing at the executives: "*Merde, merde, merde!!!* How do you expect me to work like this? I am an artist, not a banker!" This slightly paraphrased line I recognized from Chekhov's play *The Seagull*. The executives were trying to get their "*Scusi, Contes*" in as they backed out of the room stumbling over one another in an effort to escape his wrath. As soon as the doors closed behind them, he yelled to no one in particular, "We will resume work in ten minutes after this mess is cleaned up." None of us knew it at the time, but *Senso* was to bankrupt Lux Films.

One morning I arrived on the set to see Luchino walking back and forth in deep conversation with a man who for one crazy moment I thought was Erich von Stroheim. Then I realized that the bald head, the jodhpurs, the boots, and the riding crop were what had fooled me. I sat down ready to work, and Franco sat down quietly next to me. He said, "Farley, it might be a good idea for you to wait in your dressing room. I'll come get you when Luchino is ready." When I asked him why, he leaned in and whispered, "The man Luchino is talking to is Palmiro Togliatti, the head of the Italian Communist party. He might want to have a picture taken with you. That would not make your Senator McCarthy happy if he happened to see it, right?" He was absolutely right, and I slipped away to avoid any potentially embarrassing moments.

It was November, and we were nearing the completion of our work at the villa when I had a brainstorm. In order to avoid any repeat of the Jolly Hotel togetherness experience, I would rent a house in Venice when we returned to resume shooting there. I called Stella in New York and got the name of the art dealer at whose house we had dinner the evening I met Peggy Guggenheim. She gave me his number in London, and I called. Not only was he in, he said that he would be delighted to rent me his house as long as I had no objection to the two servants, Marco and Maria, who lived there full-time. They both spoke reasonably intelligible English, and Maria was a wonderful cook. I had no objections. It sounded ideal. I was delighted. We made a deal, and it was done. He would tell Marco and Maria of our arrangement, and I would call to let them know when to expect me. When I asked Franco to let Luchino know, he said he would.

At our last dinner at the Jolly, it may have been my imagination, but everyone seemed more lighthearted than usual. Luchino stood to thank us all for our good work and to say how much he looked forward to finishing the sequences in Venice before we returned to Rome. He then looked at me and said, "Unfortunately, we will not have the pleasure of Farley's company as much as we did here, since he has rented himself a house in Venice." It was obvious that he was not thrilled by what I had done, and would have preferred to have me more under his control as I had been in Vicenza.

I thought quickly and said that one of my reasons for renting a house was so that I could invite them all to help me celebrate one of our most important American holidays, Thanksgiving. Luchino gave me a level look and said, "I'm not so sure that discovering America was a good thing."

Next to me Franco murmured under his breath, "Capitalism."

I quickly improvised a little speech about what kind of a holiday Thanksgiving was. It had nothing to do with the discovery of America. It was a holiday in memory of a time when the early settlers invited the Indians to share the bounty of their first major harvest. Everyone sat down together like brothers for a communal feast in celebration of times to come.

Luchino absorbed the translation of that and finally smiled as he said he would be pleased to come. That night, drifting off to sleep, I was jolted wide awake by the thought, "Where the hell am I going to find cranberry sauce in Venice?"

Cats

Sunday evening, as I got off the train in Venice, I spotted a distinguished middle-aged man waiting in the fog at the end of the platform, holding up a sign with my name on it. I had called the house to tell Marco and Maria when I would be arriving, and much to my surprise he was there to meet me. He insisted on carrying my bags to a boat he had waiting, and we were off. We arrived, and they showed me to my bedroom on the second floor. It was a lovely big room, all windows on one end that looked out onto a pretty walled garden. There was a very large adjoining bathroom at the opposite end next to the bed. One wall was all books and the other was filled with Venetian lithographs surrounding a fireplace. I could not have designed a place in which I would be more at home. Upon my arrival, Maria had asked what I would like for dinner, and I had asked her to please make it something very simple. I was not as hungry as I was tired.

After I had settled in, there was a soft knock at the door, and Marco entered with a glass of *prosecco* and told me that supper would be ready in about twenty minutes. When I went downstairs I was greeted by a lovely meal of *risotto ai frutti di mare*, cold chicken, green salad, and assorted cheeses. It was perfect.

I was awakened the next morning by Marco when he brought in my breakfast. He set it down on a table by the windows and opened the drapes. Then a scene appeared that I could happily wake up to every morning for the rest of my life. Dozens of cats of every size, shape, and color, or mixture of colors, had managed to squeeze onto the ledge and were pressed against my windows. They obviously slept there for the warmth of the house that passed through the panes of glass, and they took the drawing of my curtains as their clue to begin the day. Watching them get up to yawn, stretch, and groom themselves and one another before jumping down to the top of the garden walls was a start to my day that I have never been able to equal. Marco and Maria were gems, and their English was far superior to my Italian. I convinced Marco that I was not a breakfast-in-bed type. All I wanted was a glass of juice outside my door. When the glass vanished, I was up. I would take my juice, draw the curtains, and sit to enjoy my cats before showering. After dressing, I would go down to the dining room.

I discovered that Marco was an avid movie fan, and I loved talking movies with him as I breakfasted. One morning I mentioned what a brilliant actress I thought Anna Magnani was. He would have no part of it. He hated the whole neorealistic trend in Italian films. "It was all too ugly and dirty!" I was scoring a pretty good point in my pro argument when he cut me off by unexpectedly clearing my breakfast dishes. As he turned to back out the pantry door, he declared with great finality, "Well, she's no Lana Turner!" I had to laugh even though I understood the feelings that shaped his sensibility. Italy went through some bad times before, during, and after the war, and he missed the days of their escapist films in the 1930s and early 1940s. *Telefono Bianco*—White Telephone— was what the genre was called. It was pure escapism, comparable to the Astaire and Rogers series in America during the Great Depression.

I only had one scene to shoot this time around, so I wasn't surprised that more than a week passed before I heard from anyone connected to the company. During those days I discovered the enchantments of Venice in the winter. It was almost devoid of tourists, and the constant fog gave the city a new layer of mystery. Saints and gargoyles would suddenly and spookily materialize as I approached. At night, the colors from a lit flower shop across a square appeared, first as a faint glow of colors that as you got closer, would brighten and slowly swim into focus.

On several mornings, I got up early to go to the market with Maria. It was a unique spectacle, with boats arriving from the mainland piled high with fruits, vegetables, meats, and every other kind of supplies imaginable that had to be off-loaded to individual vendors from Venice's market. The various vendors all knew Maria by name, and God forbid that any one of them tried to sell her anything that did not live up to her standards. She was capable of a performance that Magnani would envy. Shopping with her helped me to understand the Italian joy of fully participating in all the interactions of life.

After over a week with no word from the company, I called Franco at his hotel. He apologized at once for not contacting me, but something terrible had happened and shooting had been delayed. Aldo, our cinematographer, whose red sportscar I had coveted, had been killed in a car crash while driving down from Vicenza to Venice. He had been with Luchino ever since his first film. Luchino was beside himself with grief and having a very difficult time deciding how to replace Aldo. Franco promised to contact me as soon as they had a replacement.

Possibly because I had been fortunate enough to work with several of Hollywood's legendary cinematographers, Gregg Toland, James Wong Howe, and Joe Ruttenberg to name three of them, I knew what an essential part they played in the realization of a director's vision. Aldo had been with Visconti for so long that he had developed the ability to anticipate the Maestro's wishes and needs. Not only that, an unspoken love had grown out of their mutual respect. There is no way to forge that kind of bond instantly. It can only grow out of working together in a variety of circumstances both good and bad.

I was also terribly upset, possibly because I was aware of how much cinematographers contributed to the quality of a film, but also because he was such a sweet and caring man. In the short time I had known Aldo, I had come to care about him as much as everyone else did. Not only did he know how to make beautiful pictures, he knew how to say the right thing to everyone. When I did a scene, he would say, "Farley, when you speak it is like Shakespeare."

With more unexpected time on my hands, I took a chance and gave Peggy Guggenheim a call. Much to my surprise, she was listed in the phone book. She also just happened to be in Venice and answered the phone herself. She invited me over to dinner the next evening. It turned out to be the first of many evenings that she and I and her beloved pack of Lhasa apsos spent together that cold and foggy November. The dogs originated in Tibet and were believed to receive the souls of their masters when they died. Peggy and her doggies lived together in one big room, the only one with heat in the palazzo. The rest of the rooms were closed down for the winter. It was there that Peggy reminded me about the restorative or at least warming quality of Italian grappa, which in those days was more like marc, the shot of liquid fire made from the dregs of grape pressings, that many a French workingman uses to kick-start his day. Now grappa has been refined to the level of a French *eau de vie* and is quite fashionable.

I never tired of hearing stories about how, at age thirty-eight, she began collecting artists and their works. She also told me about the time when she and her second husband, Max Ernst, the Dadaist/Surrealist painter, were hanging her first show in Paris as the German troops marched into France. Peggy had had shows in New York and in London, but Paris was then the center of the art world, and she was damned if any war was going to ruin her first chance to show there. She and Max ignored all the unofficial and official warnings to leave until the highest government officials remaining in Paris appeared at her gallery one morning and ordered them to leave. The German army would be in Paris within forty-eight hours, and France could not be responsible for her or Max's safety, much less the safety of the paintings. She and Max finally heard the warning. They packed all the paintings into the back of an old truck and fled just hours ahead of the Germans' triumphant entry into Paris. They were heading for Portugal via northern Spain. Somewhere near Bordeaux, they admitted to themselves that they could not risk entering Fascist Spain with the paintings and struck a deal with a French farmer to bury them under the floor in his dilapidated old barn. She went back after the war when Americans were very welcome all over France. The old farmer and her paintings were still there and still in great shape.

One morning while exploring the city, I came upon the restaurant that Franco Zeffirelli had taken me to, where the gondolieri hung out and sang opera. I tried the door, and it opened. The owner, who was working at a table near the front door, recognized me and got up to greet me. After a minute, I asked him if he ever made an exception to the no women rule. He frowned and started to shake his head, but I kept on going and said that I was only asking because I was wondering if perhaps one evening I could bring a Signora Peggy Guggenheim who owned an important...he interrupted me excitedly. Of course he knew who la Signora Guggenheim was, and she was not just a woman, she was "una vera padrona...a patron saint" to the people of Venice. He would be honored to have her in his place, and...now it was my turn to interrupt. I thanked him and promised to call before bringing her. He was overjoyed at the prospect.

It was the first time I was aware of what esteem Peggy was held in by the people of Venice. This only grew through the years. When I next saw her in the early 1970s, she had been made the Venetian equivalent of a Dame. I can only imagine how they revered her when, upon her death, she left her entire collection to the Solomon Guggenheim Foundation with the stipulation that it be maintained in perpetuity in Venice. She had a ball being the only woman there the night we joined the gondolieri for food, wine, and song. I think she was particularly pleased and flattered when the same handsome young tenor whom I had heard with the Francos came over, knelt, and dedicated "La donna è mobile" to her.

Ever since I felt comfortable enough to do it, I had started pestering Luchino about getting me a copy of *Ossessione* to see. I was not only curious to see his first movie, but I was eager to see how he had translated *The Postman Always Rings Twice* into an Italian subject. It had been the film that initiated Neorealism and anticipated the rebirth of Italian cinema after the war. What we were doing now was so epic, I just had to see that first film. I knew how busy he was, so I had not pestered him for a while. One morning on the set, he asked if I had plans for the evening. When I said that I didn't, he said, "Good. Tonight you will see *Ossessione*."

I thought that meant that he had gotten a 16-millimeter copy of it to project in one of the public rooms in his hotel. No way. He had commandeered the local movie house for the evening and screened it for me, and of course any other members of the company who wished to see it, which was everyone except Alida. It was a terrific movie. All I had loved about the Hollywood version was wiped out by the raw intensity of this version, with the possible exception of John Garfield's superb performance. Massimo Girotti was equally superb in the Garfield part, and Visconti had stripped Clara Calamai, in the Lana Turner part, of any of the glamorous crutches that had been Miss Turner's trademark. The other changes that he made to transfer the action from California to the Po Valley only seemed to intensify the tragic inevitability of the story. The movie's style was as far removed from what he was now doing with *Senso* as an MGM musical was from a Warner Brothers gangster movie.

Mambo

Visconti had engaged the services of Robert Krasker, the British cinematographer whose work on Laurence Olivier's film of Shakespeare's *Henry V* was so impressive. Krasker was on his way, and we would be ready to resume work as soon as he and Visconti were able to screen the footage that had already been shot. I was home expecting that call when one came from Robert Rossen, a well-known American screenwriter (*The Strange Love of Martha Ivers, Blues in the Night,* and *The Treasure of Sierra Madre*) and director (*Body and Soul, The Brave Bulls,* and *All the King's Men*). As a result of the blacklist, he was now working exclusively in Europe. He had a project pending and wanted to know if I had a free day in my schedule to meet him for lunch at Harry's Bar.

We met the next day for what turned into a very long lunch that began at 1:30 P.M. and lasted until 6:00 P.M. He was doing a film in Italy called *Mambo*. It was to star Shelley Winters, Vittorio Gassman, Silvana Mangano, and, he hoped . . . me. I haven't given you the slow buildup he gave me that day, which included the story, my great part in it, and all the rest, which had kept me interested through the first two Bellinis. I've cut to the punch line, his naming the actors, which was delivered with the third drink. "You've got to be kidding," was my answer.

He wouldn't give up and went on about how right we all were for the parts and what terrific actors we were, and soon he capped it with "Think of the great press we will get!" My response was: "That's exactly what I am thinking about! What are you, crazy?"

Rossen was a good screenwriter and a good director who understood the frustration I had felt at being typecast by Goldwyn as the sensitive, tortured young man. He assured me that his film would go a long way toward changing that perception of me. But his idea was just too perverse. Shelley and Vittorio had separated, and she was revving up for a divorce. God only knows what publicity stunts she was planning. I was a former lover and still her friend. Vittorio, a notoriously temperamental womanizer, was about to be her ex-husband. *Bitter Rice* had made Silvana Mangano the hottest new sex symbol in the Italian cinema. The ravenous Italian gossip press, for which the word *paparazzi* was coined, would hound us mercilessly. I could see why it appealed to Rossen as great publicity for the film, but all the Bellinis in Italy would not be enough to convince me to be a part of that particular three-ring circus.

The Turkey

The jellied cranberry sauce and mincemeat that I had ordered from New York arrived along with a recipe for a Thanksgiving dinner. I shopped with Maria, who figured out how to substitute Italian products like squash for yams. The problem was the turkey . . . *il tacchino*. In 1954, it was impossible to find a plump, well-fed turkey in Venice. All one could find was a scrawny bird that had much more in common with a scrawny oversized chicken than it did with a Butterball or its 1954 equivalent. Then I had a brainstorm. There was an American air base near Venice. I rented a car the day before Thanksgiving, found my way to the base, and talked my way into a meeting with the CO. He heard me out and finally agreed to help me in my effort to confront Count Luchino Visconti with the fruits of capitalism. He called his commissary, and within a half-hour presented me with a bona fide American turkey. I handed it to an astonished Maria late that afternoon She and Marco outdid themselves with *il tacchone*, as they christened our bird . . . -*one* is the Italian suffix that means very big. So our *tacchino* became a *tacchone*.

Luchino and the Jolly Hotel contingent arrived as a group. After they entered, Luchino grandly but benevolently announced that even though he disapproved of capitalism, their great love for me brought them here today. He explained to all that it was a holiday commemorating the one time that the early American settlers had treated the Native American people like equals. It seemed best simply to accept his benediction and go into the sitting room for drinks.

After several glasses of champagne, someone suggested that we play the Truth Game, something I'd managed to wriggle out of whenever it took place in Vicenza. But this was my house, and I was trapped. This is the Italian version of Truth or Dare, which the Italians, or at least this group, played for much higher stakes than we do. It started off innocently enough, but when it was her turn, Massimo Girotti's wife upped the stakes. She smiled at Luchino and asked him sweetly, "When did you last have sex, Luchino?"

He smiled back just as sweetly and replied, "Yesterday afternoon with your husband, my dear."

Marco, who was standing nearby with champagne, jumped in with, "*Signori e signore*, Thanksgiving dinner is served."

Other than a little too much truth, and the fact that no one could understand the concept of either jellied cranberry sauce or mince pie except the Brit Bob Krasker and me, Thanksgiving Day was a smash. Maria's dressing, which bore a close resemblance to polenta, was a particular triumph.

The following week Alida and I filmed the one scene we had left to do in Venice. It was a love scene that took place in a cheap rented room near the Austrian Army barracks in the city. In the film the scene was meant to illustrate Livia's willingness to abandon caution and to risk her good name, despite her aristocratic upbringing, because of her growing obsession with Franz.

The company prepared to move to Rome to shoot the end of the film. Alida and I had one more scene together. It was our most important and emotionally complex scene in the film.

The Shiner

I had barely settled into my room at the Hassler, which overlooked Rome from the top of the Spanish Steps, when someone started pounding on my door. I opened it . . . and in fell a hysterical Shelley. She was sporting a perfect bull's-eye of a shiner. I called room service to order a raw steak and went to work calming her down. It took a while, but after I got her resting on my bed with the steak draped over her eye, she finally slowed down enough to get her story out.

She'd come to Italy to do Robert Rossen's movie *Mambo*, in part because it gave her a chance to tie up some loose ends with Vittorio. Even though their relationship was amicable, she felt that the marriage needed to be ended formally so they could get on with their lives. In other words, she wanted a divorce. He was performing *Hamlet* in Genoa with his company, and she had gone there to see him in it as a surprise. The only problem was that she had hated both the production and his performance. She went backstage after the show with the good intention of keeping her mouth shut, a difficult goal for Shelley. When he asked her what she thought about his performance, she told him, "It was terrible." He responded by presenting her with a black eye. She had come straight to Rome and checked into the Excelsior, where she heard that I was in town and tracked me down. I got her moved into the Hassler, but aside from dinner that first night, the only other time I got to see her was when she heard that Gassman was doing a telephone interview about his separation from her with *Il Tempo*, one of Italy's major newspapers. She made a deal with the reporter doing the interview: she would be present when his interview with Gassman took place, and she would comment on everything Vittorio said. The reporter jumped at the opportunity to get this two-sided interview. Of course, she had not told me about her plan of journalistic one-upmanship. She just told me that she needed my moral support because she was doing an interview that could affect her divorce.

Wanting to help, I agreed. During the interview, when Vittorio got dramatic about how much he missed his fourteen-month-old baby daughter, Vittoria, Shelley added: "If he misses her so much, how come he doesn't know that she's eighteen months old?" She had a topper ready for everything he said about their relationship and separation. The press ate it up, and she came out of the interview looking like the poor little wronged woman. In this case, it was true that she was somewhat wronged. But poor? . . . little? . . . Never!

Shelley could still not understand why I refused to do *Mambo*. She kept begging me to change my mind, saying, "Think of the publicity we will get. You just can't buy that kind of publicity. They'll be reading about us all over the world! Besides, I'll feel so much safer with you there with me." I tried to explain how happy I was being involved in a quality project with a wonderful director. I didn't want to follow it by being involved in a project that was destined to become a press-feeding frenzy. As usual, publicity always trumped common sense with Shelley, and I could not get through to her. I'll never understand how she and Vittorio survived the film together without bloodshed. It turned out to be a pretty bad movie. Even though I was irritated with her that day at *Il Tempo* for tricking me into her planned effort to one-up Vittorio, I had to admire her chutzpah.

While reading the newspaper that afternoon, I found out that Ava Gardner was in Rome shooting *The Barefoot Contessa* with Humphrey Bogart and Rossano Brazzi. Before I had a chance to call her, she called the Hassler to say that she'd just found out that I was in town and invited me over to a Sunday-afternoon party in her suite at the Excelsior. As soon as I got there, she dragged me away from the crowd into her bedroom to talk. She was as funny and gorgeous as I remembered her. She was in the middle of complaining about what a piece of crap the film was, and how lucky Rita Hayworth was because she turned it down, and how difficult Sinatra was being over their split-up, when the phone rang. It was Frank. She listened for a bit, then said, "Frank, I can't talk anymore right now, call me later . . . I said not now, later! Because I'm with Farley! That's why!" She banged down the phone, looked at me, and started to laugh. "Come on, honey, let's go get you a drink." We went out into the living room, found the bar, and there, of course, was Bogart. I think Betty was making a film back in Hollywood. Bogie was even more colorfully outspoken with his opinion of the film than Ava had been. The only one who came out of the film well was Brazzi. It made him a viable Hollywood star.

Luchino did not get to the big scene between Alida and me until after

Christmas. So I flew to London to get away from all the craziness in Rome and to see some theater. But most of all, I wanted to spend a little sane time with Peter and Mary, who always had a real old-fashioned English Christmas, complete with roast goose and Christmas pudding, for family and stray friends. It was a wonderful restorative. In no time at all, I felt grounded again and back in the real world.

On Twelfth Night, I got the call I'd been waiting for. Luchino was ready to shoot my final scene in *Senso*. The scene, which took place in Verona, was shot in a gorgeous little movie studio that was built into one of the ancient walls that surrounded the city of Rome. At the time, I thought, Leave it to the Italians to have a romantic movie studio. I had been brought up on the industrial-looking soundstages of Hollywood, where nothing was real except anxiety, insecurity, and fear.

The final scene was the most emotionally complex one I had in the movie. In it, the countess leaves the villa during the battle and undertakes a dangerous and stifling carriage ride to Verona in search of Franz. The city streets are filled with drunken Austrian troops celebrating their victory over the Italian army at Custoza. When Livia locates Franz, he is living in luxurious squalor with a young prostitute on the partisan funds meant for Garibaldi that Livia had given him to bribe his way out of the Austrian army. These funds had been entrusted to her to deliver to her cousin Roberto to be used to arm the Italian partisan troops. Franz is drunk and filled with feelings of self-loathing as well as anger at Livia. He lashes out, forcing her to pour wine for the prostitute, and demands that she recognize him for the useless coward that he is.

Luchino told me in detail what he wanted in this scene. I assumed that he had done the same with Alida. I also assumed that it would take several days to complete. We rehearsed it in the morning and did two takes in the afternoon. When we finished, Alida departed without so much as a fare-thee-well. As soon as Franco had checked both takes and declared them a buy, I got a big cheer and a prolonged round of applause from everyone else on the set. Luchino swept me into a major hug and asked me to have lunch with him the next day. He said that Franco and Francesco wanted to take me to dinner that evening, but he would have me all to himself the next afternoon.

That evening the two Francos took me back to the trattoria in Trastevere where we had all first met. Alberto and the other members of the crew with whom I'd become close were there. Even though I was more than happy to finish the film and get on with my life, I had pangs of separation anxiety at the thought of saying goodbye. These fellows had become my *cari amici* . . . my dear friends. I was going to miss them. The Italians don't say *miss*. They say, We will feel your absence, which covers it beautifully.

The next day Luchino took me to lunch at Ranieri, which at that time was the best restaurant in Rome. Over lunch, he told me about some of the problems he had been having with the Italian government censors over *Senso*. They were being extremely difficult, and he was worried that if they had their way, our beautiful film would be ruined. I must have looked stricken, because he hurried to assure me that they were not talking about my scenes, it was mostly the battle sequences and the scenes that concerned them that he was worried about. I said I was worried about his film, not just my scenes, and asked him if the battle wasn't, in effect, the framework of the movie? He looked at me for a long moment before saying, "Thank you, Farley."

We then talked about the ending of the film. He had not decided if Franz's execution should be seen. His plan was to show Livia's final descent into madness after she turns Franz in to be shot as a deserter. He would end the film on the countess running through the streets of Verona, colliding with drunken Austrian soldiers and their prostitutes, screaming Franz's name over and over. I loved that idea. It was the perfect ending.

Three months later I got a call from Lux Films to come back to Italy in order to do the execution scene. I was filming *The Girl in the Red Velvet Swing* at 20th Century-Fox, and they could not give me the time off to go to Italy. As a result, Franz's execution, which was shot against the blood-soaked walls of the Castel Sant'Angelo in Rome, where countless executions had taken place through history, had to be done in a long shot. This particular sequence has often been singled out by critics because of the dramatic effect Visconti achieved by not showing Franz's face. That scene and Livia's carriage ride to Verona where she discovers Franz and his prostitute were shot by Giuseppe Rotunno, Aldo's assistant cameraman. After our work in Venice at Thanksgiving, Visconti and Robert Krasker had a falling-out, and Krasker did not finish the film.

Hollywood Ending

I arrived back in Hollywood exhilarated and exhausted from my nearly nine-month experience on *Senso*. I felt ten years older, but in all the right ways. Obviously, I had grown up during those months in Italy. My agent, Charlie Feldman, asked me to meet him for lunch as soon as I was rested. He wanted to hear everything about working for Visconti. More good films were being made in Italy by a whole new crop of talented directors, and he felt it was inevitable that more American actors would be receiving offers to work there. Over lunch, he asked how Tennessee had behaved on the production. I had completely forgotten that Tennessee was even involved. I told Charlie that I had met him on my first night in Rome, and then I never saw or heard about him again. The only writer that I heard mentioned during the filming was Suso Cecchi D'Amico. We both laughed at the irony, because it was Williams's name that had sold me on the whole project in the first place. Then over coffee he dropped the news that Darryl Zanuck had a two-picture deal for me at Fox, and he was willing to pay me very handsomely to do them. Charlie felt that if I still intended to leave for New York, it would be good for me to go with two big American films coming out rather than hoping for the best from a foreign film that might not ever be released in the United States. I warily asked what these two films were. He told me that *The Girl in the Red Velvet Swing* was going to be a lavish production based on a real-life murder/sex triangle that involved the famous architect Stanford White and the young millionaire Harry K. Thaw, who shoots White over Evelyn Nesbit, a sixteen-year-old model who became the Gibson Girl. Ray Milland, who won an Academy Award for *The Lost Weekend*, was playing the architect, and a young English actress who was getting "the build-up" as the next Elizabeth Taylor was playing Evelyn Nesbit. "Who?" I asked. "Her name is Joan Collins. This will be her first major American film, and she really is a great beauty," he told me. The scriptwriter, Charlie Brackett, was an old pro, and the director, Richard Fleischer, was solid and dependable. My part, Harry K. Thaw, was the psychotic millionaire who marries the girl and kills her former lover, Stanford White. It sounded intriguing.

"What is the other one?"

"It's a mystery. I don't know much about it yet, but you'll get top billing and the other featured actors in it are Anthony Quinn and a young actress named Anne Bancroft, who I hear is very good. She studied at the Actors Studio in New York."

Charlie always knew how to bait my hook, and I had always been a fan of Tony Quinn's work. I said I'd think about it. I then did some research on the actual case of the murder of Stanford White and decided that it would be a happy change for me to play an obsessed madman after all the sensitive-young-man parts I had been stuck with while under contract to Goldwyn.

My first day on the set I discovered that Cornelia Otis Skinner was playing my mother. While in Rome, I had stumbled on a tiny English bookshop run by two British matrons and their pug dog. Coincidentally, I'd bought a book there to read on my flight home about two innocent American girls abroad called *Our Hearts Were Young and Gay*. Miss Skinner had written it with her friend Emily Kimbrough. A renaissance woman, she was a successful playwright and author of numerous essays and collections of light verse. She was a unique comic talent and a gifted character actress. She toured all over America in the late 1920s performing a one-woman show of short character sketches she had written. I headed straight for her dressing room to introduce myself. She was a dignified middle-aged lady with a sly sense of humor. I liked her at once and grew to like her even more as the movie went on. I couldn't bring myself to call her Cornelia, and Miss Skinner seemed too impersonal. At the end of our first day working together, without planning it, I said, "See you tomorrow, Miss Skinner, sir." She did a slight take and gave me a little smile and that was it . . . Miss Skinner, sir.

Joan Collins was a very different cup of tea. A gorgeous girl with raven hair, a peaches-and-cream complexion, and dazzling blue-green eyes, she had both stage and screen experience in England and was in no way intimidated by the Hollywood buildup the studio was putting her through. I don't know whether or not she enjoyed it, but she was smart enough to embrace it for what it was worth and not let anything go to her head. I liked her enormously. How could I not? She was beautiful, talented, grounded, and loved a good dirty joke.

I had very little to do with Ray Milland in the movie except shoot him in the face three times at point-blank range. I wish we had had some scenes together. He was a very good actor as well as very much a gentleman. I would have enjoyed the chance to work with him.

I've never seen *The Girl in the Red Velvet Swing*, so I have no idea of how good or bad it is. However, up there with *Strangers on a Train*, it was one of my more enjoyable filmmaking experiences in Hollywood. No one behaved like a prima donna, there were no mishaps with guns on the set, and my hair had grown back to its natural color. Richard Fleischer didn't deviate from his shooting schedule; and all the actors liked one another and working together.

By the time we had finished, *The Naked Street* was ready to begin. All I have to say about my final movie at 20th Century-Fox is, "Thank God for Tony Quinn and Anne Bancroft." The writer, Maxwell Shane, was not very good and was an even worse director. Tony was a unique actor, as was Anne, and we all struggled to inject some kind of drama into a script that was preachy, trite, and pedestrian.

Anne and I would spend our lunches talking about the theater and life in New York. This was her tenth film, and she was not happy about any of them. I felt that she was too special and too good for Hollywood to ever figure out how to use her well and suggested that she go back to the theater. Perhaps I was projecting my own intentions, but in any case, she did return to New York and was soon to win a Tony for her work in *Two for the Seesaw*, followed by another one for *The Miracle Worker*.

When Anne did go back to Hollywood in 1961, it was to re-create her role as Annie Sullivan in the film version of *The Miracle Worker*. For that, she had the play's Broadway director, Arthur Penn, to thank. United Artists had hired Penn to direct the film version of his stage success. He wanted Anne and Patty

Duke to repeat their roles. U.A. offered Penn a lavish two-million-dollar budget for the small, black-and-white film if he would use either Elizabeth Taylor or Audrey Hepburn as Annie Sullivan, but Penn, backed by author William Gibson, turned them down. The film won Academy Award nominations for Penn and Gibson. Anne and Patty took home Oscars for their performances. Anne was now a movie star. Shortly after that, she married the great Mel Brooks. Anne became a film icon for her performance as Mrs. Robinson in Mike Nichols's decade-defining hit, *The Graduate*.

Tony Quinn continued to do good work in all mediums. When he and *Zorba the Greek* found each other, he became famous the world over. On the set of our movie together, going over our lines one afternoon in Tony's dressing room, I noticed a terrific photograph of him. His head shot in profile looked as if it belonged on a Mayan or Aztec frieze. I asked him, "Do you have any copies of this?" He said he did, and I asked if I could have one. "Are you sure you want one?" He was obviously flattered and a little flustered.

Tony went on to play Stanley to Uta Hagen's Blanche in the national company of *A Streetcar Named Desire*. I heard so many good things about their production that I flew to Chicago to see it. They were very different from Marlon Brando and Jessica Tandy in the Broadway production, but they were spectacular. It's a testament to the strength of the Tennessee Williams play that different actors can make it an equally exciting and involving experience. After that, Tony made some of the biggest films in his career both here and in Italy in the late 1950s and the 1960s. His parts were all based on his masculine earthiness, which was used to great advantage in *Zorba*. There was no one else quite like him, and he always did his thing with great style and panache.

Act III

The East Coast

The film was over. I was done. It was finally time for me to go to New York and begin my new life. Shelley was already bicoastal and had gotten a lovely apartment in an old prewar building on Central Park to complement her house in Beverly Hills. One way or another, our paths would continue to cross. I said goodbye to my parents and the other people who were near and dear to me and finally moved to New York. At last my apartment in the East Sixties, which I had rented before *Senso*, was going to be occupied.

I had barely settled in and started to work out a schedule of classes when Charlie called from Hollywood. Marlon Brando had just turned down a script at Twentieth, *The Egyptian*. I was Zanuck's next choice. This time I said no. I had made a clean break, and I was sticking to my plan. Two hours later he called again. Zanuck had upped the money and carried on about what a big movie this was going to be, starring Jean Simmons, Gene Tierney, and Victor Mature. The director was Michael Curtiz, an old pro with dozens of films to his credit and a great track record for success. After several more calls and a lot more pressure, I agreed to think about it and asked for a copy of the script. The script was undergoing rewrites, and they had nothing to send at the moment, but the cast had to be set so they could begin publicity as soon as possible. "Hmmmm, not a good sign," I thought as I went out to buy the book on which the film was based. It was a quick read, perhaps because I didn't think it was any good. I knew at once that I wanted no part of it, and told Charlie so. Next thing I knew, several of the producers involved started calling, and each time I said no, each of them said in disbelief, "But it's a Darryl F. Zanuck production!" I told each of them that I was suitably impressed and properly grateful but not interested. It took many more calls for it to sink in, but they finally gave up.

A handsome British newcomer, Edmund Purdom, had stepped in at the last minute to mouth Mario Lanza's singing in *The Student Prince* when Metro decided that Mario was too fat to be seen. Operettas had not been in fashion since the late 1930s, when Nelson Eddy and Jeanette MacDonald were dubbed "America's Sweethearts." Mr. Purdom went right from that into the part I had been offered in the "Darryl F. Zanuck production," *The Egyptian*. Neither film worked to launch his career. A couple of years and several other sumptuous costume epics later, his Hollywood career faded as quickly as his one-year marriage to Tyrone Power's ex, Linda Christian. Miss Christian never made it as an actress in Hollywood, either. She surprised everyone in 1964 with her performance in an Italian/Spanish co-production, *The Moment of Truth*. That film, which many consider the definitive film about bullfighting, was directed by Francesco Rosi, Luchino's first assistant on *Senso*.

In almost every way, life in New York exceeded all my expectations. I loved the freedom of being in a city where I could walk everywhere, from Central Park to the Garment District to Wall Street. It was like being able to walk to different countries. I had an infinite variety of behavior to observe and learn from.

Shortly after I settled in, the actress Geraldine Brooks called me about a party she was arranging to introduce Anna Magnani to the New York theater crowd. I'd dated Gerry in Hollywood when we were both living there, and we had remained good friends. In 1950 she had gone to Italy to play Magnani's younger sister in a film called *Volcano*, and they had become friends. Magnani was coming to New York for a week on her way to Hollywood to make her first American film, *The Rose Tattoo*. Gerry said that Anna was very nervous about having to do a film in English, and she wanted to spend some time just hearing the language before she had to begin filming. The party was being hosted by some wealthy friends of Gerry's father, who was a well-known costume manufacturer and designer. Gerry knew how much I loved Italy and Visconti, and Anna had done a couple of films for Luchino. In the hope of putting Magnani at ease, she invited me over early the night of the party. Magnani was everything I hoped she would be: warm, funny, volatile, and definitely larger than life. Having Visconti in common helped us to feel comfortable with each other almost from the moment we met. She and Gerry had decided that when the party started, she would stay in the bedroom and Gerry would bring in the people who wanted to meet her, a few at a time, so that Anna, with her limited English, wouldn't feel overwhelmed.

Everybody in the New York theater showed up. The place was jammed beyond all expectations. I was at the bar talking to Julie Harris a while later when Gerry came over to pull me aside, "Farley, you have to help me. Anna needs to see you. She hurried me through several rooms, past an endless line of people, to the bedroom. We stopped outside the door for a moment where she whispered, "She wants to go back to her hotel, and wants you to take her," and pulled me into the room after her. Anna and her manager were standing there at the ready. She grabbed my arm, Gerry opened the bedroom door, and out we went, followed by her manager past the endless line of startled actors and other theater luminaries. The private elevator near the entry hall was waiting, and as we scuttled in, Gerry hissed, "Her limo is downstairs." As the doors closed, I could see the mob moving in on Gerry.

I climbed in the backseat with Anna, and her manager got in front with the driver. As we pulled away from the curb, I heard him say, "Plaza Hotel" to the driver. Then Magnani erupted. She leaned over, and while cuffing her poor manager about the head, she berated him for getting her stuck in that mess, sitting on the bed like some English queen receiving people. It was a splendid Italian tirade. When she wound down, she looked over at me and caught me grinning in appreciation. I thought I was in for it, but she suddenly laughed and slapped me on the knee. "Farley, you come and we watch TV, okay? In the lobby at the Plaza, she told her manager to call Gerry and give her four names to bring over to meet. *"Nessun' altro!* (Nobody else!)" I remember Julie Harris and Danny Kaye were two of the names. We went up to her suite, where she immediately turned on the TV and pulled a chair right up to it, fascinated.

In the mid-1950s, summer stock was still the place where apprentice actors went to learn their craft; established actors went to expand their abilities in roles they might not normally be chosen to do, and stars went to keep themselves in the public eye. In the 1960s, stock began its painful decline under the onslaught of prepackaged musical dinner theater. I decided that the best way for me to learn about theater was to get onstage. Summer stock was a place where my name assured easy entry, as opposed to Broadway, where a young movie star with no stage experience ranked pretty low on the list of desirables. All I needed was the right play, the right co-star, and a good director.

In Hollywood I had gotten to know a talented composer named Sol Kaplan. His wife, Frances Heflin, was actor Van Heflin's sister. Fra, as she was known by all who loved her, cut her acting teeth on Broadway in plays that include *I Remember Mama*, in which she played one of the children, and *The Skin of Our Teeth*, directed by Elia Kazan, starring Tallulah Bankhead, Frederic March, and Florence Eldridge, with Montgomery Clift and Fra playing the children. Fra may also be remembered as Mona, mother of the oft-nominated Emmy Award–winning actress Susan Lucci, on *All My Children.*

Sol and Fra had moved to New York from Hollywood when Sol's rising career as a film composer was cut off by the blacklist. They, along with their two young children, Jonathan and Nora, became my New York family. And their big, warm apartment on West End Avenue became my second home for many love-filled years. Jonathan, who is a very talented and successful film and TV director/producer, lives in Los Angeles. Nora and Mady, the youngest, are both terrific actresses who wisely left the business for less precarious careers. They are still my family.

That first summer in New York, Fra and I decided to tour the East Coast summer stock circuit in *The Hasty Heart,* a sentimental World War II comedy/drama by John Patrick. We piled Jonathan and Nora into the car and took off for our first engagement. I loved traveling with Fra and the kids. Just driving through the lush green eastern countryside, playing word games with the kids, was great. The beauty of New England, with its pristine small towns clustered around their white steepled churches, made an instant East Coast convert of me. Our demand to share a dressing room shocked many an uptight theater manager. Not only were we not married, we had children in there with us. The tour was a great success, and we played to packed houses with appreciative audiences. The first time I got a laugh onstage, I knew what live acting was all about. Having that many people connected to you, sharing your emotions, is an exhilarating experience. The only thing we were not happy about was that we had to perform with a different group of actors at each theater with no time to rehearse. We barely had time enough to do a walkthrough so that we wouldn't trip over the furniture. Sometimes we had good actors, and sometimes they were so bad that Fra and I didn't dare look at each other for fear of losing it. One memorable night, we were so distracted by one actor's outrageous antics that Fra transposed the words "cocked" and "cap" in a line she had about me, saying, "You walked in and just stood there with your cock capped over one eye." It wasn't easy getting through the rest of that performance. We decided that next summer would be different, and it was. We assembled our own company for *The Rainmaker,* and had the sets designed to our specifications.

Just Off Broadway

Fresh from having toured in stock, I was eager to get started at the Neighborhood Playhouse to begin studying with Sandy Meisner. He put me in his "professional" class, which was quite small. I was in diverse company: Bob Fosse, who went on to Broadway and Hollywood acclaim as a director/choreographer; Gloria Vanderbilt, a multitalented lady who painted and designed fabrics; Jimmy Kirkwood, a comedian who went on to write a number of funny books and plays and eventually co-wrote *A Chorus Line;* and Tom Tryon, a handsome guy but a wooden actor who starred in the movie *The Cardinal,* and went on to write bestsellers. I had no sooner settled into class when I got a call from my agent. The producers of the Phoenix Theatre had offered me a leading part in a new play they were presenting called *The Carefree Tree*.

The Phoenix Theatre on Second Avenue at 12th Street was a leader in the off-Broadway movement that took root in the mid-1950s. Its founders, T. Edward Hambleton and Norris Houghton, were dedicated to presenting challenging new productions of high artistic quality at affordable prices. The Phoenix Theatre was in a Broadway-size house of about 1,200 seats. Such notable directors as Tyrone Guthrie, Michael Redgrave, and Jack Landau, co-founder along with John Houseman of the American Shakespeare Festival and Theatre, worked there in the formative years of the company.

The Carefree Tree was a Chinese fantasy of a play that was to be directed by Jack Landau, who had also designed the scenery. Alvin Colt, Broadway's best and busiest costume designer, did the costumes. A number of well-known theater actors were to be in the play, and the billing was alphabetical. The actress who played my love interest was Janice Rule, who first captured Broadway theatergoers with her beauty as well as her talent in *Picnic* in 1953. Everything about the project sounded good. I said yes.

Our rehearsal studios were over a famous dairy delicatessen near the Phoenix on lower Second Avenue in what used to be the heart of the Yiddish art theater district. I loved the neighborhood with its unique theater history, and the deli with its ancient waiters whose hands shook so much that the delivery of every bowl of borscht was a real-life drama. The rehearsal process, a three-to-four-week period during which we and the director explored the play and the life and direction of our characters, involves the actors laying themselves bare in order to get inside the skin of the character they are playing. Ideally the actors are guided, helped, and supported by the director, who has an overall vision of the play. With very rare exceptions, which is almost always the case when the director is from the theater, there is no comparable process in film. Instead, the film actor has to arrive with a fully developed character that, with a few instant adjustments, he hopes will integrate into the story. There are occasional exceptions; Robert Altman springs to mind, but his process is unique in big-budget films. Rather than rehearse a written script, he depends largely on his actors' ability to improvise their performances within a given framework. Most often his results are wonderful, spiced with some deliciously chaotic moments.

I fell in love with Janice. She was an exquisite redhead with the long-limbed, long-waisted figure of a dancer, which is how she had started in the business. One of a large "lace curtain" Irish family from New Jersey, she was feisty and competitive, with a deep throaty laugh. We were both smitten. Our play did not get great reviews, but we loved doing it and found each other. Janice's divorce from the playwright N. Richard Nash was soon to become final. It is ironic that Dick had written the play my company was to do in summer stock the subsequent summer, *The Rainmaker*.

When the "Chinese Boo Boo," our affectionate name for *The Carefree Tree*, closed, Janice moved in with me, and before long we were making wedding plans. In the few months it took us to reach the wedding invitation stage, we had also begun to reach a firsthand understanding of the Cole Porter lyric "our love affair was too hot not to cool down." It was a gradual awareness of the fact that it had been great, but it was time to move on with our lives and careers, not with married life. It's a fact of theatrical life that actors, when playing people in love onstage, frequently fall in love offstage. Later in her career, Janice gave up acting to study psychoanalysis. Her specialty was actors and the various emotional entanglements that ensue when the characters they are playing are emotionally involved. Since we remained friends always, we managed to share many a good laugh over what coulda, shoulda, woulda been.

The Tube's Golden Age

I had bought out my contract with Sam Goldwyn during the twilight of the Golden Age of Hollywood. That twilight coincided with the full flowering of the golden age of live television. It was fortunate for me because that first tour in summer stock and that first role in a prestigious Phoenix Theatre production had not opened any doors for me to Broadway's movers and shakers. They still thought of me as a movie star, not as a serious actor. My agent suggested that he look into television, where they could never get their fill of movie names. I'm glad I listened to him, because during the next five years I did approximately thirty live television shows with wonderful directors like Alex Segal and Sidney Lumet.

Live television was the most exhilarating, adrenalized experience I'd had to date as an actor. We rehearsed in sequence for several weeks. Then, after a dress and technical rehearsal, we performed it on air. There were no such things as TelePrompTers, tape stops, reshoots, fixes in editing . . . none of the technical advantages that are taken for granted today. When you got on that thirty-, sixty-, or ninety-minute express train, there was no getting off until it reached its destination. If you or another actor went up (forgot the line) or didn't make the entrance, you had to keep going until, one way or another, everything got back on track. If the show was under, they could fill time with a commercial. It could not be over. It had to end on time. Some of the shows were bad, many of them were good, and some of them were superb. All of them were fun to do. I worked with some of the most talented actors and directors in the business.

Janice called me one morning. She and Roddy McDowall, who lived right down the street from me, had had dinner with a director friend of theirs, Alex Segal, the night before. He was starting rehearsal for a live telecast the next day with a show about Sigmund Freud as a young man and had lost his leading man. They had convinced him that I was perfect for the part, and he was going to call me. I got off the phone and waited. Not more than a half-hour passed before Alex called. He and the producers would be overjoyed if I agreed to do the part. They were messengering the script to me, and would appreciate it if I could read it right away and let them know my answer. I read it, liked it a lot, called him back to accept, and spent the rest of the evening reading it over and over.

The next morning I arrived at rehearsal, met Alex and the cast, and was measured on the spot by the costume designer for my clothes. That done, I expected we would sit down for a read-through. Alex said, "No way, I want you all on your feet." This isn't going to be easy, I thought as I took my script and joined the others on the taped-out demarcation of the set. Alex yelled out, "No scripts, Farley."

"But I just got it last night, I don't know anything yet," I said with more than a touch of desperation.

"Don't worry about that, my assistant will cue you," he said. Cue me she did, every line, for days.

For several days all I could worry about were words. I didn't have a brain cell free to worry about blocking or motivation or anything else. In the second week, as the words began to fall into place, it seemed like everything else began to fall into place with them. I wasn't plagued by any of the usual uncertainty about my character's motivation or his relationship with the other characters.

As a director, Alex had a reputation as a yeller, but that didn't bother me at all. I was so happy about the ease with which I got inside the skin of young Freud that I completely forgot the agony of those first few days. I loved working with Alex, and I think that the feeling was mutual, because I did several more shows with him.

As Apollodorus, the emissary who smuggles Cleopatra into Caesar's quarters wrapped in an oriental rug and unrolls her at his feet in the *DuPont Show of the Month* production of George Bernard Shaw's *Caesar and Cleopatra*, I was in the company of some of theater's heavy hitters. My fellow cast members included Sir Cedric Hardwicke, Claire Bloom, Jack Hawkins, Cyril Ritchard, and Dame Judith Anderson.

The only problem I had was with wardrobe. My costume was a short white tunic and a big enveloping hooded cloak. The tunic narrowed and gathered on the left side to drape over my shoulder. At the dress and tech rehearsals I had trouble with that damned tunic. It kept slipping off my shoulder, a bit like Rita Hayworth's lace nightgown strap in the famous World War II *Life* magazine pinup. I got little sympathy, and worse, no help from the costumer, who was too busy with other problems to worry about my shoulder. My character appeared in only one act of the play, and I was damned if my costume was going to distract me or the viewing audience. Before we went on air, I borrowed scissors from wardrobe, cut off the entire top off my costume, and had makeup do my chest and back. When I whipped off my cloak, and climbed onto the railing around the terrace to dive into the harbor of Alexandria, I was topless. The costumer had a fit, but when the show was over, I got applause from the stagehands, congratulations from my fellow players, and excellent reviews.

I played Eddie Cantor's son in the *Playhouse 90* production "Seidman and Son." I had been told my father was going to be played by Lee J. Cobb. Eddie, whose films had helped to keep the Goldwyn Studio afloat during the Depression, was now an old-timer, but definitely a trooper, and very much a presence. At times I had to guide him around a bit, but he did a great job and was very sweet, thanking me for my help when we finished. My girlfriend was played by Mona Freeman, who was excellent as one of the young women in the film adaptation of *Our Hearts Were Young and Gay* by Cornelia Otis Skinner. She loved "Miss Skinner, sir" as much as I did, so we bonded immediately. Peter Lorre, one of Warner Brothers' outstanding character actors, was also in it. He had rocketed to fame in 1931 playing a psychopathic child murderer in *M*, director Fritz Lang's first talking film. I had lunch with Peter whenever possible. I listened avidly to his stories of the old days at UFA in Germany for as long as he was willing to tell them. He used to sneak up on me during rehearsal and, in that inimitable voice, whisper in my ear, "What are the creeps doing now?" I would always lose it, no matter how serious the moment.

I played twins, with twenty costume changes, in *Playhouse 90's* production "The Clouded Image," which was based on Josephine Tey's mystery novel *Brat Farrar*. Our director was Franklin Schaffner and the rest of the cast included John Williams, Vincent Price, and Dame Judith Anderson. To everyone's horror, I took to calling the diminutive Australian actress "Big Judy." She loved it and invited me to her Santa Barbara home for a weekend when we finished. Unfortunately, this was one of a five-show back-to-back marathon that necessitated flying from New York to California for *Playhouse 90* and immediately back to New York to begin the next show.

Alex Segal directed me again in the title role in a ninety-minute adaptation of the Sinclair Lewis novel *Arrowsmith*, produced by David Susskind for *DuPont Show of the Month*. This time I was prepared for the way Alex worked. He could yell all he wanted; when things fell into place, they did so with amazing clarity. I thought Alex was one of the best directors I ever worked with.

I had the good fortune to be cast as Morris Townsend opposite the wonderful Julie Harris in *The Heiress*. Julie, with whom I was later to do a Broadway show, was absolute perfection in the part. We became good friends, and some years later she wrote a very flattering introductory piece about me for National Repertory Theatre's souvenir program.

In my next live TV show, *The Prisoner of Zenda*, directed by Alex Segal for David Susskind and DuPont, as Rupert of Hentzau I dueled with Chris Plummer with heavy broadswords until my arms felt dead, then threw my sword at him and dove out of a castle window into the moat. I was beginning to become a pro at diving from high places into bodies of water. At least this time I had no shoulder strap to worry about.

I also played Peter Ilich Tchaikovsky to Helen Hayes's Madame von Meck. I was intimidated at the prospect of working with Miss Hayes, whom many considered the finest actress in the American theater. We, along with the New York City Ballet and a Philharmonic-sized orchestra, were working at NBC's new state-of-the-art color television studio in Brooklyn. NBC had erected two enormous soundstages on the site of a former silent film studio at Avenue M in Midwood. We were in Studio 1, and next to us in Studio 2, Mary Martin was doing *Peter Pan*. As we finished our first day of rehearsal, Helen said to me, "They've given me a big limo, and I go through New York on my way home to Nyack, may I drop you?" I said, "That would be very nice if you're sure that I'm not taking you out of your way." She assured me that it would not. When she dropped me off at my apartment, she said, "Since we both have to be there in the morning, why don't I pick you up?" From that day on, we drove together to and from the studio. She was great company and confided in me that she found working in movies very difficult because nothing was ever done in continuity, and she hated having to summon up emotions in such a haphazard way.

One morning on the way to Brooklyn she asked if I would like to meet Mary Martin. "I'd love to!" I said. Mary Martin was up there along with Ethel Merman as one of Broadway's musical comedy greats, and her biggest hit, *The Sound of Music*, was still to come. That afternoon, when we broke for lunch, Helen took my arm and we went through a pass door to a loading area between the two studios. It was deserted except for a huge amount of crates and scenery from both shows. We stopped, and Helen listened for a moment before calling out in a child's voice that would have reached the last row of the balcony, "Where are you? ... Where is my little fella? ... I know you're hiding here someplace ... Come on out!"

A disembodied voice rang out from a pile of crates: "I'll come out if you promise me that you believe!"

"I believe, I believe!"

"You have to clap if you believe!"

Helen started to clap, and from nowhere out popped Peter Pan. Two great ladies of the American stage collapsed into each other's arms giggling like schoolgirls. I hope it didn't show, but for a brief moment I was completely unnerved.

That evening, after Helen dropped me off, the phone started to ring as I was coming up the stairs to my brownstone apartment. I took the stairs two at a time, threw my groceries down in the hall, fumbled for my keys, got in, ran for the phone, and shouted "Yes" into the receiver.

A voice at the other end asked quietly, "Is Farley Granger there?"

"This is Farley Granger, who's this?"

"This is Noël."

"Noël who?" I asked impatiently.

There was a brief pause, then a burst of laughter, and the voice said, "Noël Coward."

"Oh my God, I didn't dream . . . I mean I never thought . . ."

He laughed again. "Don't be silly, dear boy, how could you possibly have known. I called at the last minute to see if there was a chance that you might be free for dinner. They are doing a play of mine on television, and I'd like to talk to you about doing one of the parts."

I said that I'd be delighted. I had only met him that one time on *Rope*, but it was very good to see him again. After we ordered a drink and got through the usual small talk, he said with a smile, "You must know, Farley, that I find you terribly attractive. I would like very much to go to bed with you."

I took that in for a long moment, and then told him carefully that although I was very flattered, I was involved with someone, which wasn't true, but I wanted very much not to hurt his feelings.

He let out a theatrical sigh and said, "Thank God that's out of the way. Now we can relax and enjoy ourselves." We spent a great evening together. We also talked about his play, which I knew, and I told him that I wasn't really right for the part. He agreed with me. It was the part of the young man in *Present Laughter*. I have no memory of who played it on television, but Nathan Lane was nominated for a Tony in George C. Scott's 1983 Broadway production of this play, and he deserved it.

I had also been getting a lot of the stage experience I needed at this time in my life because whenever I was not involved in a major television project, I kept busy doing plays in a year-round stock company in New Jersey run by Robert Ludlum and his wife. Their company was close to New York, just across the Hudson River in New Jersey. This was years before he became one of the leading mystery/spy novelists of our time. I got to do a wide variety of roles for him, including the leads in *Mister Roberts*, *Sweet Bird of Youth*, and *Picnic*, with Sandra Church doing the part in the last that Janice Rule had done on Broadway.

Sandra and I became friends. She was a lovely redhead and a very talented young lady. Not too long after this I took her to the opening night of Betty Comden and Adolph Green's off-Broadway show, and at the after-party she met Jule Styne, who was instantly smitten. Their subsequent relationship led to her getting the title role in Jule's great musical *Gypsy*.

Sidney Lumet, another fine director I worked with in live television, went on to become one of our best film directors. He was then married to Gloria Vanderbilt, who had become a friend when we were in class together at the Neighborhood Playhouse. Gloria confided in me a few years later that Sidney had tried his best to get me for a film he did with Sophia Loren. Unfortunately, he didn't have the same kind of clout that Hitch had with the studio. When Warner Brothers insisted on using one of their contract players in the part, he had to go along with them. In the late 1960s, Sidney and I talked about my playing Nicky Arnstein in *Funny Girl* with Streisand, but when he opted out of that one, my chance of working with Barbra went with him.

I met an amazingly talented diversity of wonderful actors and directors in those days of live television. Along with doing stock and studying with Sandy Meisner and Stella Adler, it was the best kind of training that an actor could get. When my Broadway break arrived, I was ready for it.

Jane Austen Hits Broadway!

My agents called to say that I had gotten an offer to play Fitzwilliam Darcy in a musical adaptation of Jane Austen's *Pride and Predudice* on Broadway. The show was to be called *First Impressions*, the initial title of Miss Austen's book. The producers included the composer Jule Styne. Our set designer was Broadway's current golden boy, Peter Larkin, and the costumes were being done by Alvin Colt. Abe Burrows, one of the forces responsible for the classic American musical comedy *Guys and Dolls*, and who in the intervening eight years had had almost as many hits, had adapted the book and was directing. Gisele MacKenzie, a name I knew only as the star of *Your Hit Parade* on television, was playing Elizabeth. Hermione Gingold, the eccentric star of dozens of British music hall revues, was playing Mrs. Bennett, the desperate mother of five unmarried daughters, who was portrayed so brilliantly by Mary Boland in the MGM movie. That excellent film starred the lovely Greer Garson as Elizabeth, and gave Laurence Olivier his third big hit in this country as Fitzwilliam Darcy. Those were pretty big shoes to presume to fill, but the idea was too good to resist. The huge success of *My Fair Lady* had proven that good period material, well cast and well presented, definitely had a place on Broadway. One of my best friends from Hollywood, James Mitchell, a marvelous dancer who had done the dream ballet in the film of *Oklahoma!* and was the lead dancer in *Brigadoon* on Broadway, was playing the cad, Mr. Wickham. So I would have a friend in the company.

One evening a week or so before we were scheduled to begin rehearsal, I got a panicked call from Hermione. "Gisele has dropped out of the show because she is pregnant, and the producers replaced her with that @#%$*+^#$%* Polly Bergen!!! I will never work with that @#$% again. She drove everybody crazy in *Almanac*, even Harry [Belafonte] couldn't stand her, and you know how sweet he is."

Hermione and Polly Bergen had done a show together called *John Murray Anderson's Almanac*. I never found out precisely what had caused these two women to dislike each other so vehemently, but Polly's reputation was not a secret. The fact that Polly was currently married to Freddie Fields, one of the top agents in one of Hollywood's most important talent agencies, gave her a sense of power that she did not work too hard to disguise. Hermione felt that she had either strong-armed John Murray Anderson or worked her wiles on him to get several additional numbers. And that it had been done at the expense of others.

I just let her babble on, knowing that at this rate she would exhaust herself. Soon enough, she stopped, and I could just hear panting. Finally she said, "Well, I'm quitting! What are you going to do?"

"Hermione, haven't you signed a contract? I did."

There was a long pause and then a wail, "OOOH, daahling . . . What are we going to do?" And she hung up.

I didn't know much more about Polly Bergen than I did about Gisele MacKenzie. In *Who's Who* Polly is listed as a business executive first and an actress second, which is curious for a performer of her repute. Of course, I had seen her on numerous television variety shows and knew that she had gorgeous eyes and a nice throaty voice, but she came across as more 1950 American nightclub than 1813 English landed gentry. I felt that an ideal Elizabeth should have the pure exuberant soprano of a Barbara Cook or Julie Andrews, but with Jule Styne and Abe Burrows at the helm, who was I to question their choice? I was too preoccupied about what was going to come out of my mouth when I did open it for my first try at singing on stage. Thank the gods for Rex Harrison, who so brilliantly broke ground for the song/speak style of delivering a number, although he set a standard that was every bit as daunting for me as Olivier's performance in the film.

We rehearsed at the Variety Arts Studios, which were in Midtown in the theater district. In the beginning, the book or scene rehearsals were in one studio, the musical and singing rehearsals in another, and the dance rehearsals in yet another. At various times in the rehearsal period, the director would combine these elements until he felt it was time to bring the whole thing together. Polly and Hermione, as mother and daughter, had many scenes together. But from the first day of rehearsal until Polly left the show, neither one of them ever spoke one word to the other that wasn't scripted.

Hermione always swept grandly into rehearsal with her little dog, Mr. Poodle, in her arms and would throw her ratty mink on the floor in the corner for the little fella to sleep on. He would then spend what seemed like hours at a time happily humping her coat. We principals had all gotten used to it, but as Abe began to integrate the singers and dancers, it was a daily treat to watch the newcomers' reactions. I'll never forget the efforts of the dancers to focus on their movement without stumbling over each other or breaking up when they first tried to ignore Mr. Poodle in action.

Out of Town

Our first opening out of town at the Shubert Theater in New Haven was chaotic, to put it mildly. Abe and Jonathan Lucas, the choreographer, had obviously asked for the moon, scenically, and Peter Larkin had tried to give it to them. There was much too much scenery to fit into the theater. One of the sets, a ballroom for which Lucas had done elaborate choreography that included the dancers weaving in and out of numerous standing columns, was a painted backdrop. I overheard Abe say to Jonathan, "I guess Peter really screwed us on this one." I wanted to ask, "Did either of you ever talk to him?" Whenever the unwieldy beast that is a Broadway musical succeeds, it has to reflect good communication between the disparate elements that make up the whole, and the director, the boss, is the one responsible. Often that doesn't happen until disaster strikes.

New Haven was a disaster for us. There was one magnificent set that got thrown out immediately, which probably saved many a dancer from injury. Abe and Jonathan had set one dance number in a harborfront tavern, which, to give the illusion of being at water level, was entered from above. On this set, the dancers had a number in which they had to balance themselves with their arms and legs fully extended inside oversized barrels and roll head over heels in choreographed patterns. During the rehearsals at Variety Arts Studios in New York, one of the most daunting challenges was to try to concentrate on rehearsing the scenes with the sound of barrels crashing and injured dancers screaming coming from the studio above us. Many a brave young male dancer had been taken to the hospital with broken bones while rehearsing this mayhem. In New Haven, no tears were shed when this number was cut from the show.

Another moment in the show that did not work on opening night in New Haven was a scene in which Darcy and Elizabeth competed at archery. Peter had ingeniously rigged the targets to partially expel an arrow after we drew and released the strings of our bows. That visual with an accompanying sound effect was to give the impression of actual arrows hitting the target. With the luck of the draw, I was to shoot the first arrow. The arrow popped out of the target before my bow was fully drawn. There were sniggers from the audience, but I soldiered on. After several more increasingly out-of-sync tries, I had the audience rolling in the aisles. That number joined the barrels in the tavern, out of the show. It was too bad. With the correct allotment of rehearsal time, which was by now in very short supply, that bit could have worked and been a lovely moment of one-upmanship for Elizabeth.

Everyone looked gorgeous. Alvin Colt's costumes were superb. Outside of the theater, I saw less and less of my friend Jimmy Mitchell. His "big number" had, so far, failed to materialize, and he was retreating into a major funk.

Our show curtain, a lovely example of Peter's ingenuity, was a huge open lace fan on which was painted, in silhouette, two men running from the figure of a woman pulling five young women after her. As the overture, orchestrated by Hershey Kay in the style of the period, harpsichord and all, finished, the curtain opened, which resulted in the fan closing, and the play began. Behind the curtain were two twelve-foot-high boxwood hedges on tracks. When closed, they overlapped, leaving an exit between the overlap. They were used to create an "in-one" or limited downstage area with a painted drop behind, for intimate numbers that were done while the scenery upstage of it was being changed. The problem we had was that the crew had not yet had enough technical rehearsal time to master their operation. Sometimes the hedges came on too slowly or jerkily and jammed, and sometimes they came on with a speed that terrified anyone near them. The dancers, who had much of the in-one action, were the most vulnerable to being hit by a runaway hedge.

Our reviews in New Haven were mixed. The critics there were used to bumpy opening nights and were somewhat forgiving of technical mishaps. Even our negative reviews were along the line of "Promising" and/or "With a lot of work and a little luck . . ." The creative powers that be met after the show and worked and argued and tinkered all night long, every night. I think it was Neil Simon who said, "Hell is being out of town with a Broadway musical." By the end of our run in New Haven, Jimmy still had not gotten his promised number and Jonathan Lucas, our choreographer, was gone. Jimmy fared no better with three subsequent choreographers. The rest of us could barely keep up with the daily changes in the show.

Our next and last out-of-town booking was the Forrest Theatre in Philadelphia. The Forrest was a lovely theater with one minor problem: when it was built, they forgot dressing rooms. They acquired space for them in a building across the alley from the theater. In order to get there, we had to go down to the basement, cross under the alley, and take an elevator up to the dressing rooms. I imagine that wasn't too much to ask of actors in a settled touring play, but we were a musical in a state of . . . flux. Consequently, everyone claimed the basement as home base. The wardrobe, hair, and makeup departments that usually had it to themselves had to share the space with the cast, some fifty-odd people. Some of the more sensitive souls tried to rig sheets for privacy's sake, but most of us threw caution to the alley and just got on with it. The basement was bedlam, definitely not a place to prepare calmly for a new running order each evening. We also rehearsed every afternoon in the theater.

In midweek I arrived at the theater to find that Hiram (Chubby) Sherman, who was not only wonderful as Mr. Collins but the only one who had gotten unanimous praise from the New Haven critics, had been fired. Abe had replaced him with a friend of Hermione's who had been hanging around since our rehearsals in New York. He was a vulgar and campy performer, no more suited to the subtleties of Jane Austen than his patroness. Chubby's performance had been so good and he was so well loved that most of the company was outraged at this change. That evening I heard a new overture for the first time. In an effort to sound more contemporary, Abe had thrown out Hershey Kay's lovely period arrangements, and had tarted up our overture to no good effect. I love a good, jazzy overture. *Gypsy's* thrills me every time I hear it, but Gypsy Rose Lee and Jane Austen . . . well, there's no comparison. That night, at the end of the new overture, the fan closed and a dancer got stuck onstage and was nearly crushed by our lovely hedges, at which point he turned upstage and started to scream while beating on the scenery. The stage manager dimmed the lights and helped the dancer offstage, and the men in white came to take him away.

The Philadelphia reviews were slightly better than those in New Haven. This encouraged a false sense of security in those who thought our show was getting better. I didn't and decided to get into it with Abe before the next rehearsal. Since we could not have our conversation in the basement, where we would have an all-too-attentive built-in audience, he and I went into the men's room downstairs at the back of the theater to talk. We were soon "talking" at the top of our lungs. I held nothing back, and when I stomped up into the theater, I was startled by a solid round of applause. A large contingent sitting at the back of the darkened theater waiting for a dance rehearsal to begin, had heard every word.

My only pals in the cast, since Jimmy had understandably become a black cloud, were Donald Madden, who played Mr. Bingley, Darcy's best friend, and Marti Stevens, who played his sister, Caroline. Marti was a Schenck, the behind-the-scenes royalty of the movie business. Her father, Nicholas, and his brother Joe were two of the richest men in America in the 1930s. They ran United Artists, Metro-Goldwyn-Mayer, and Loews Inc. Marti grew up in a family that dominated the movie business, but when she decided that she wanted to be an actress, her father disinherited her. She just wanted to be on the stage, as I did. Devastated but undeterred, she pursued her dream. Fortunately, her Uncle Joe supported her dream. Marti and I became friends soon after we met.

Marti knew about an elegant little hotel off Rittenhouse Square in Philadelphia. Since no one else in the company was staying there, we three moved there in order to distance ourselves from the constant creative chaos that was going on nightly at the theater and also to be able to drown our sorrows and commiserate about a good idea that was being painfully dragged in all the wrong directions.

On Broadway

Ready or not, it was time. We moved to New York to prepare for our Broadway opening at the Alvin Theatre. The theatre had approximately 1,300 seats, a perfect size for a musical. It took a couple of days to load the production in, set up the scenery, and get everything in working order. Of course, I went down there early on Monday morning to check the place out. Several days later, the company received its official first call. More than getting the show in, up, and working had happened since Monday morning.

My geographical memory of the dressing room layout may be a bit hazy, but what had been done to them still shines brightly in my mind's eye. Polly Bergen was then married to Freddie Fields, an agent I had known in Hollywood, who had always called me "Kirk Baby." Freddie, also a successful producer, was with MCA, one of the most powerful agencies in show business. Possibly that gave Polly a little extra clout with our producers. In any case, she had taken over what had always been the chorus dressing room downstage left. The room was meant to accommodate eighteen or more people. It had been converted to a suite for one, carpeted and decorated all in white, with gorgeous period antique furniture that included a white-tiled Swedish stove. Everything had an MCA sticker on it. A red carpet ran from the stage door, past Hermione's small dressing room on stage right, all the way across the back of the stage up to Polly's dressing room door on stage left.

The first number that Polly and I did together in the show, "A Perfect Evening," took place at the Assembly Dance, where my character and Mr. Bingley, the other desirably wealthy newcomer, played by Donald Madden, are introduced to Mrs. Bennet and her five daughters. Elizabeth and Darcy were dancing at the moment when we began to sing; we were downstage center, arm in arm, facing the audience. On musical cues we could link arms to circle around to come to a stop facing in opposite directions. When Polly sang out to the audience confiding how she really felt about Darcy, I faced upstage, and then we reversed positions for me to sing privately to the audience. Polly had the first line in the song, and on opening night, she quite clearly and loudly sang "A Poifect Evening." When we reversed for me to sing my line to the audience, she hissed in my ear, "Did you hear what I said!?" I not only heard her, the conductor was looking up in shock and there were a couple of titters from the audience. I almost choked on my reply, "Ah, yes."

Our reviews, two favorable, one mixed, three unfavorable, and one pan, did not lead to long lines at the box office. I came off well, but the show was judged to be a failed attempt to repeat the success of *My Fair Lady*. Aside from unanimous criticism of a weak score, it was Hermione who received the hardest knocks. Richard Watts Jr. in the *New York Post*, then a serious and well-respected newspaper, wrote: "In a recent interview, Hermione Gingold said she was no admirer of Jane Austen, and it saddens me to report that she proved it last night." That sentence was merely a jumping-off point for his criticism.

For some reason, Abe Burrows took to hanging out in my dressing room. I remember him sitting there shaking his head and saying, "I don't know what happened . . . I thought she [Hermione] was the critics' darling."

Almost immediately after we opened, Polly began to complain about vocal problems. From that moment on, we hardly ever performed the same show twice running. We all had to check the call board before each performance to see which of Polly's numbers was being cut for that show.

A week later, at a matinee performance, I noticed the ensemble was paying less attention to the conductor during their numbers than usual. For the most part, they all seemed to be focused on someone in the theater. After one of our exits, I grabbed a dancer and said, "Who the hell is out there?"

She answered breathlessly, "Don't you know? Marlene Dietrich is in the audience."

I'd never met Miss Dietrich, but knew that she and Marti Stevens were friends, so it made sense that she would come to see our show. I sneaked a quick peek the next time I was onstage, but I couldn't spot her, so I forgot all about it.

Back in my dressing room after the show, I had gotten out of my costume and was cleaning off my makeup when my dresser burst into the room hyperventilating. I turned to ask him what was wrong as he blurted out, "Miss Marlene Dietrich is outside and she wants to see you." I finished cleaning up and told him to show her in.

As I stood up, in she came, looking very glamorous. I held out my hand, but she walked into my arms and gave me a big warm hug. Then she held me back at arm's length, looked deep into my eyes, and said, "Oh, Fahley, Fahley, where did you get those twousers? Your twousers are wonderful! I must know where to get them!"

She walked over to where they were hanging on a costume rack and proceeded to caress them. At one point she held them to her cheek. I explained that they had been designed by Alvin Colt and made by Madame Karinska, the world-famous costumer. She thanked me and backed out of the room still looking longingly at the twousers. She never mentioned a word about my performance or the show.

I was telling Marti about it sometime later when the lightbulb went on. Miss Dietrich was getting ready to make her first appearance in Las Vegas, and at one point in the show she appeared in top hat, tails, and . . . you guessed it.

That evening a notice on the board said that Polly was out of the show . . . permanently. I ran up the two flights of stairs to Ellen Hanley's dressing room. Ellen had been playing the part of Charlotte Lucas and was Polly's understudy. Even though we had not had a chance to rehearse, I knew that she was going to be a lovely Elizabeth. I wanted as much as possible, under the circumstances, to put her mind at ease and let her know how happy I was about the prospect of working with her. The rest of the company felt the same way and were incredibly supportive. That evening everything clicked, and the audience response was terrific. The show just got better for the rest of our run. We closed at the end of two and a half months.

If at First You Don't Succeed . . .

I was convinced I'd never work again, but not too many months later I received a call from a director named Warren Enters. Warren was directing a new play by Joe Masteroff called *The Warm Peninsula*. It was a comedy/drama about the comings and goings and entanglements of four young vacationers all staying at the same boardinghouse in Miami Beach.

The play was being produced for Julie Harris by her husband, Manning

Gurian. It had been touring the provinces for seven months, undergoing rewrites and tune-ups until he decided it was in good enough shape to bring to New York. When it closed out of town, Manning decided that he wanted an all-star cast. He fired the three leads with the obvious exception of Julie, and I was brought in along with June Havoc and Larry Hagman. He also brought in Ruth White, one of Broadway's most beloved character actresses, to take over the part of the landlady.

I was very happy about the prospect of working with Julie again. I had not seen her since *The Heiress*. In some ways, working in the theater is like playing a one-on-one sport: the better your opponent, the better you perform. Working with Julie in television had been both a challenge and a thrill. I couldn't wait to begin the rehearsal process with her in a play. She pulled me aside after our first few days of rehearsal and said, "You've obviously been working hard, Farley. I'm very impressed by how much you've grown."

That was a big compliment coming from Julie, who took her acting very seriously and is one of the most nominated and award-winning actresses of our time.

June Havoc was a multitalented artist, a good actress, a good writer, and, along with her sister, Gypsy Rose Lee, a survivor of a life that began in vaudeville under the iron fist of the quintessential stage mother, portrayed by Ethel Merman in *Gypsy*. Larry was also a theater brat. His mom, Mary Martin, who created leading roles in *Lute Song, One Touch of Venus, South Pacific, Peter Pan*, and *The Sound of Music*, was well on her way to becoming a musical theater legend. Larry played June's love interest in our play, and Julie and I were the other lovers. One evening Larry confided that June was driving him crazy in one of their scenes by being a little too hands-on. She was fussing with him, arranging his tie, fixing his hair, and brushing imaginary lint off his suit. He wanted to stop it without saying anything that might hurt her feelings. I had a wonderful, wise, and funny dresser who came up with the perfect solution when I mentioned this to him. Just before the scene, he put a spool of white thread in the breast pocket of Larry's jacket and just barely pulled the end of it through his lapel buttonhole. Larry worried that she might miss it, but we reassured him. June went for it like a trout for the right fly. In their scene, she gave it a little pull and then a bigger one. The more she pulled, the more it kept coming. Finally she cracked up and ran offstage. She never fussed with him again for the rest of our run.

We were playing at the original Helen Hayes Theatre, which became the center of controversy in 1982 when hundreds of New Yorkers, led by prominent members of the acting community, fought in vain to save it from the real estate developer's wrecking ball. While we were there, Mary Martin, opened across Forty-sixth Street at the Lunt-Fontanne Theatre in *The Sound of Music*. When their show loaded into the theater, Larry took me over to say hello to his mom.

She was seated on her dressing room floor surrounded by a huge pile of black lace-up boots from which she had to choose the correct ones for the show. She held her arms out to Larry, who leaned over for a hug and kiss, and welcomed me before he could make any introductions. Miss Martin remembered meeting me with Helen Hayes when she was playing *Peter Pan* for NBC in Brooklyn. She apologized to us for not having seen our show, but we all knew how hectic it was opening a Broadway musical. Larry and his mother seemed to have a nice easygoing relationship, so I don't want to imply that having his mom, one of the biggest stars of the musical theater, playing across the street made Larry nervous, but his intake of one preshow martini increased to an icy shaker-full by the time she opened. I still wish I had taken the opportunity of our proximity to get to know her better. Another image of *The Sound of Music* that I will always carry with me is walking past the Lunt-Fontanne's stage door and seeing nuns from the chorus hanging around with their skirts hiked up, smoking cigarettes and flirting with the guys passing by.

We opened on October 20, 1959, to fair reviews. The critics were kind to the four young lovers, unkind to the play, and unanimously in love with Ruth White, who deserved every rave. After two and a half months, we closed on New Year's Day. This was my second Broadway show and they both had almost identical two-and-a-half-month runs. I was developing a case of short-run paranoia.

Rita & Bertolt

With the decline of the anticommunist fever of the early 1950s, Buddy and Ethyl had decided to come home from Europe. Buddy was still in Spain working on a film, and Ethyl was in New York looking for an apartment for them. We had already seen each other several times when she called me one afternoon. Rita Hayworth was in town, knew no one, and Ethyl thought it would be nice if we took her out that evening for dinner and maybe the theater. I had only met Miss Hayworth one time briefly at Gene Kelly's after they had made *Cover Girl* together. She had seemed to be rather shy and very sweet.

Her screen persona, which had been set forever by *Gilda* and *Down to Earth*, was that of a screen siren who was improbably good beneath her veneer of dangerously seductive beauty. In *Gilda*, she immortalized the black satin strapless dress forever when she sang "Put the Blame on Mame" to torture her confused lover, Glenn Ford. In *Down to Earth*, she played the goddess Terpsichore, who danced her way into a Broadway musical. She was quickly baptized "America's

Goddess of Love" by the press. The men aboard the *Enola Gay*, the plane that dropped the atom bomb on Hiroshima to hasten the end of World War II, are said to have taped Rita's famous *Life* magazine wartime pinup to the bomb.

Ethyl got three tickets to an off-Broadway production of Bertolt Brecht's *The Good Soldier Schweik*. It was a great choice for Ethyl, who had worked in Germany and knew all about Brecht and his unusual technique of using alienating effects to encourage audiences to think rather than become emotionally involved. I was not too sure it was a great choice for either Rita or me. It was about a soldier who obeyed orders so scrupulously that he messed up everything with which he was involved.

I arrived at Rita's hotel in time to pick her up to meet Ethyl at Sardi's for a drink before the theater. She came out of the elevator looking gorgeous in a dark green satin dress with a white mink stole. I don't think Rita had any awareness of the effect she had on people. As she crossed the lobby to meet me, everyone stopped dead in their tracks to follow her with their eyes. She gave me a warm and friendly hug, and I was a goner.

We met Ethyl in the small downstairs bar at Sardi's and left for the theater after a couple of quick drinks. Rita had the same effect on the customers and also on the actors that she had everywhere: she took focus.

I remember nothing about the play, how good it was, whether or not I got it, nothing at all. Rita, on the other hand, had a swell time and at the curtain calls cheered the cast with lusty *olé*'s.

From there, we went off to the St. Regis for supper and lots of Champagne. After not too long, Ethyl begged off because she was meeting apartment brokers early in the morning. Rita wanted to dance, and that we did for what seemed like hours. At first I felt like a klutz, but she was such a feather, I soon relaxed, and started feeling like a pro. Rita was indefatigable. After an hour or so, the wine, which was going to her head, was going to my feet. I was getting tired, and she was tipsy. I paid the check and escorted her back to her hotel, where it took a few minutes for me to assure a suspicious room clerk that I was just seeing Miss Hayworth to her room. In the elevator she began to fold. I got her into her bedroom and on the bed. She did not want me to go. I slipped off her shoes and her dress and got her under the covers. She was like a lost little girl who was afraid to be left alone. I sat with her, holding her in my arms, until she went to sleep.

Ten years later, in Hollywood, Ethyl called to ask if I would mind picking Rita up for a dinner party she and Buddy were having. I had not seen her in the intervening years, and I said I would be delighted. I called for her at her new house behind the Beverly Hills Hotel. She was slightly heavier, but in her late forties she was still very beautiful. The house had an unlived-in air about it. What little furniture there was seemed to have been placed at random with no thought as to how it functioned. Even though Rita had been there for a while, there were a number of unpacked boxes and unhung pictures scattered about. She took me out by the pool so that she could point out Glenn Ford's house in the near distance. Ford had been her leading man in *Gilda*, the film that made her a superstar in 1946. He also co-starred with her in *The Loves of Carmen* in 1948, and in *Affair in Trinidad* in 1952 after her four-year marriage to Aly Khan broke up.

In the course of that evening, Rita's moods shifted unpredictably and swiftly from sweet to angry to frightened. At the time, we all thought that her behavior reflected the toll taken by disappointments in her personal life, as well as those exacted by her life as a contract player for one of the crassest of the old-time moguls, Harry Cohn. It was years before the world became aware that Rita was beginning to suffer the cruel ravages of Alzheimer's disease.

R & H & I

Not too much time passed before I got another call about a musical from my agent. A director named John Fearnley wanted to meet with me to discuss an upcoming project. We met in Charley's, a long-gone unpretentious bar in the theater district, and hit it off at once. He wanted me to play the king in a revival of *The King and I* that was opening the spring season at City Center. I was flattered, but not sure that I was old enough, or right enough, or anything enough for this part. He assured me that I was exactly who he wanted for the part. Barbara Cook was playing Anna, and he saw the king and Anna as a young couple whose sexual chemistry the audience could buy into. That sold me. I'd seen Barbara in *Plain and Fancy* and *Candide*. I thought she was delicious, a charming actress and the best soprano voice in the American musical theater. Gertrude Lawrence, who played Anna in the original production, had been very ill when she did it on Broadway and had neither the strength nor the voice to do the lovely songs justice.

It turned out to be one of the happiest productions in my life. Barbara was trying to make her failing marriage to David LeGrand work for the sake of their young son, Adam, so we never took our relationship to the next level, but oh, did we love each other, as well as working together and working with John and the superb cast. Barbara and I also fell in love with the twelve adorable kids who played the king's children. I've never had a more joyous experience on the stage.

At our final dress rehearsal John came back to tell us that Rodgers and Hammerstein would be in the house. It was one of those rehearsals when, magically, since we were on such a tight schedule, everything clicked and the invited audience was on its feet for the curtain calls.

When the knock came on the dressing room door. I jumped up to say "Come in," and John entered with R & H. Hammerstein came over to me, swept me up in a great bear hug, and said, "Thank you. You were wonderful." As he released me, Rodgers stepped in, pointed a finger and said, "*Babes in Arms!*" I was totally thrown for a moment, then I remembered that night I met them in Paris. Somehow their reactions backstage summed up the difference between the two men for me. Hammerstein was warm, loving, and totally open. Rodgers was smart, always on his game, and a bit guarded.

On opening night, I had a drink with Hal Prince and Mary Rodgers, Richard Rodgers's daughter, after the show. Mary went on about how much more her father loved our production than the original. I think it must have been because he had never heard his songs sung as beautifully as Barbara did them. I was on cloud nine. I picked up Barbara and we went off to a party that two old friends, Tom Morrow and A. T. Hannett, threw for me in their spectacular old wooden Federal house on Ninety-second Street. The reviews came out, and they were excellent. The party was full of the contagious high spirits that a hit show or a major sports event win can engender. It went on till dawn.

Each night the week after we opened, well-known Broadway producers started showing up at City Center. We all knew what that meant: we might be transferred to Broadway. The only dark cloud threatening what might be was an impasse between Actors' Equity Association and the League of Broadway Producers over contributions to an actors' pension and welfare fund. We were all confident, despite producer David Merrick's "war-like posturing," that the problem would be resolved. We were held over for two additional weeks, and it looked as if Rodgers and Hammerstein themselves were going to move us to a Broadway theater. Then, contrary to all expectations, the actors' strike struck. The lockout went on for several weeks before it was settled by Mayor Wagner. By then the momentum to move us to Broadway was gone. We discovered that Oscar Hammerstein was seriously ill. There is no way I can describe how devastated Barbara and I were by how quickly our high hopes were crushed. We had been ready to move to a Broadway house and open in a week.

Shortly after the lockout ended, we received an offer to do *The King and I* for a month, and for very good money, at the Carter Barron Amphitheater in Washington, D.C. John Fearnley kept as many of the City Center cast as possible, actually most of it, and, hoping to recapture some of the joy we had felt while performing in New York, Barbara and I agreed to do it.

The Carter Barron is a 3,700-seat amphitheater in a beautiful part of Rock Creek Park in D.C. On clear, moonlit, starry nights it could be magical, despite its overadequate size. We were rained on or out for almost the entire run. After a week straight of hot, steamy wet weather, there was nothing left to do but laugh and try to slosh through it when possible. The hardest hit—it seems they always are—were the poor dancers. If it was too wet, we cut the ballet *The Small House of Uncle Thomas*. It was just too dangerous for the dancers to try to maneuver on that vast stage. As miserable as ·the performance situation was, Barbara and I pulled out of our respective New York funks and managed to have a good time together.

We were invited for tea to Margaret Landon's house. Miss Landon wrote the book *Anna and the King of Siam*, on which a movie of the same name starring Rex Harrison, Irene Dunne, and Linda Darnell was based in 1946. She told us fascinating stories of being in Siam before World War II. While there, she heard rumors about an Anna Leonowens, an English governess at the Siamese court in the early nineteenth century, but every time she asked about her, she ran into a stone wall of silence. No one would speak about her. It was as if the woman had never existed.

When World War II broke out, she and her husband were sent back home to Washington, D.C. One afternoon, while browsing through a secondhand bookshop in Georgetown, she came across a book, *The English Governess at the Siamese Court*, by Anna Leonowens. She told us that she felt that if she picked up that book, her life would change forever. She did. It did.

As soon as I got back to New York, I wrote Rodgers and Hammerstein a short note explaining how much doing their show meant to me and how much I respected them. I had it hand-delivered to Mr. Rodgers. The next day, he called to say he had gotten the note and how much he appreciated it. He also said that he was going to read it to Oscar that evening. I was so pleased by his reaction that the implication of what he said didn't really register. That evening, after dinner with some friends, I came home, turned on the radio, and heard that Oscar Hammerstein had died. Even though it did not come as a complete surprise, a loss of that magnitude takes time to sink in. All I could think of was how much I hoped that Rodgers had been able to read my note to him.

On the Road

Actors did revivals at City Center for love, and for the opportunity to do parts that might not usually be offered to them. The pay was Actors' Equity minimum, which just about covered cab fares and food. Aside from the Carter Barron fiasco, which was short-lived, I had not been making a lot of money. Foolishly, since I was too naïve to understand what a bus-and-truck tour entailed, I allowed myself to be talked into going on one for the money.

Advise and Consent was the play. It was to star Chester Morris, a well-respected older actor, and me, and was being produced by a boyish entrepreneur named Martin Tahse who was a protégé of Maurice Evans. I felt that it might not be smart to leave town for eight months so soon after the success of *The King and I*, but I allowed myself to be talked into it by my agent, who not only got me a handsome salary but a percentage of the take as well. Financially it was a very good deal. It took almost no time at all for me to realize what a mistake it was.

The cast was a group of older, not-well-paid character actors playing senators and not doing it well. For the first couple of months, I was too depressed to leave my hotel room except to perform. I got a lot of worthwhile reading done. The original Broadway producers of the play were Fryer and Carr. Word must have gotten back to them about how unhappy I was, because Bobby Fryer came to see me in Cincinnati. He brought with him an extremely good-looking young man and suggested I might have a better time if I kept him, even though he behaved erratically every once in a while. I couldn't speak. I just got up, held the door to my dressing room open, and gestured at them to get out. I slammed it so hard, it splintered the door frame.

When I was in Detroit with this tour, I saw that Bette Davis was in town in a pre-Broadway tryout of Tennessee Williams's *The Night of the Iguana*. I stopped by her theater to say hello. As I expected, they were rehearsing, and she was there. She seemed delighted to see me and suggested that we get together for dinner after our respective shows. There was a wonderful roadhouse outside the city limits that she and Gary Merrill had discovered. Our curtain came down first, so I walked over to her theater to pick her up. She had a stretch limo waiting, and we took off into the night. Her co-star in the show was an English actress, Margaret Leighton, who, although a critic's darling, had a reputation as cold and technical with her fellow players. Bette mixed us both a drink, sat back in her seat, a drink in one hand and a cigarette in the other, and lit into Maggie: "She's impossible!" *(puff)* "I can't take it!" *(puff ... puff)* "She's nothing but a *(puff)* technician!" *(puff ... puff)*

All of this was delivered in her own inimitable technical fashion. Although I fought the impulse with every fiber of my being, I finally started to laugh, and for a moment I thought I was in serious trouble. She just stared at me with those enormous eyes, and then she started to laugh along with me.

Several months later, after we had opened in San Diego, Martin Tahse, our boyish, deceptively innocent-looking producer, came to pay us a visit. He asked me to have breakfast with him the next morning. First, he went on at length about how good he thought I was in the show. Then he talked about how important it was to keep the show running and how difficult it was with the payroll for such a large company. Then he waxed tragic about the fate of so many older actors if we had to close. Then he asked me if I would give up my percentage in order for him to be able to keep us going.

Now, even though math had never been my strong point, I knew full houses from empty houses, and I had been periodically checking the weekly take as we went along. We had been doing consistently good business all along, a fact that could be attributed to my movie name. I refused to take a cut and told him that if he wanted to replace me in the part I would be very happy to let him off the hook, but he would have to continue to pay me until the show closed. His true colors showed when he hit the roof. He said that he would go back to New York and spread the word to all of Broadway about how I refused to help the show, and I would never work again. I said, "Feel free," threw a couple of bucks down on the table, "for my coffee," and walked out.

Later, I asked Chester Morris if Tahse had asked him to cut his salary. He looked at me as if I'd lost a few marbles and said, "Of course not. Why on earth would I do that?" That confirmed my instinct that Tahse had hoped I would not know any better. We went on to a very successful engagement in San Francisco and another one in Los Angeles, and at last we closed.

Home Again

I returned to New York and fired my agents. I signed with Milton Goldman, who handled a number of English actors and had a reputation for doing first-rate things. I settled down and started enjoying life in New York again. I vividly remember the first big theater party I attended back in the city. It was at Ethel Merman's spacious East Side apartment during the run of *Gypsy*. It was a Monday evening, when all the Broadway theaters were dark, so just about everyone in the theater would be there to pay tribute to Merman. Marti Stevens knew her well and had asked me to accompany her. In the cab on the way we were discussing what a perfect show *Gypsy* was and what a high point it was in Merman's great career. She said that Ethel was having a great time doing it, with one exception; for some reason she couldn't stand Sandra Church, who was playing Gypsy. "Uh-oh," I said. "I wonder if she knows that I was the one who introduced her to Jule, which indirectly got her the part." Marti gave me a deadpan look and then laughed as she said, "For your sake, I hope not." We got there and the place was jammed. The entrance to her sunken living room was several steps up. As we came in, it was as if we were being presented. I spotted Ethel surrounded by a crowd of celebrities across the room just as she spotted us and waved. "Get over here, Farl," she sang out in that voice that could bounce off the back wall of Broadway's largest theater, "I wanna talk to you about that cunt!" We became great pals that evening. She was every bit as much larger than life in real life as she was on the stage.

I went to all the theater, opera, and ballet that I could cram in. I went to Stella Adler's master class and began to feel good about myself again. There I met an actor named Steve Hill. Steve will now most likely be remembered as the original D.A. on the television series *Law & Order*, but those of us who had the good fortune to see him onstage will always remember him as an actor of immense depth and range. Steve was directing his own adaptation of a Dostoyevsky short story at the Bucks County Playhouse, a prestigious summer theater with enough ties to Manhattan to be thought of almost as we think of off-Broadway today. Steve asked me to be in his play, and I gladly accepted his offer.

Unfortunately, the play didn't work. It was long, and the more Steve worked on it, the longer it got. Somewhere near the end of the third act, I had a scene in which I fought with my mother's lover, knocking him through the living room window. I then sank to the floor, head in hands, and cried out, "Oh, my God! What have I done. . . . What have I done?" One unforgettable evening, a deep voice boomed out from the back of the house: "You've kept us up till eleven-thirty . . . That's what you've done!"

NRT

Milton called me to say that two young producers, Michael Dewell and Frances Ann Dougherty, were starting a national repertory theater and wanted me to be a member of the company along with Eva Le Gallienne, Denholm Elliott, and possibly Julie Harris. The plays to be performed were Chekhov's *The Seagull*, Arthur Miller's *The Crucible*, and a third play yet to be chosen. I was intrigued, but when Milton told me that it would mean touring for nine months before coming to Broadway, I said, "No way!" Milton asked me to at least meet with the producers, and I finally agreed.

I went to meet them at Frances Ann's townhouse on Beekman Place. Michael Dewell was a graduate of Yale's renowned drama school. He was passionate, articulate, and obviously the driving force behind the company. Frances Ann Cannon Dougherty was a smart Southern beauty who had been engaged briefly to Jack Kennedy in the late 1930s. Her father, James W. Cannon, had nixed the marriage because no daughter of his, pampered and brought up at White Oaks in Charlotte, North Carolina, was going to marry a Yankee Catholic whose father was a bootlegger. Of course, it didn't occur to him that as a nouveau rich textile baron who founded and owned Cannon Mills, he and young Jack's father probably had a lot in common. She eventually married the writer John Hersey, but always had wonderful memories of her time with Jack, and they had remained friends. She had recently divorced Hersey, and as a member of the board of Theatre Inc., which was the governing body of the Phoenix Theatre, set out to satisfy her creative needs in the world of theater. Enter Michael Dewell, who had the passion, the ego, and a solid scholastic background in theater. A partnership was born. He had push and a driving need to get ahead, and she had ties to the social, literary, and political worlds that would prove invaluable for the creation of a national theater.

In 1959, Michael and Frances Ann became partners and formed the National Phoenix Theatre to send out touring companies of the Phoenix Theatre's more successful productions. Everyone thought they were crazy that first season to send to the provinces a company performing Friedrich Schiller's *Mary Stuart*, directed by Tyrone Guthrie and starring Eva Le Gallienne as Elizabeth I and Signe Hasso as Mary Stuart. It was conventional wisdom in the theater community that one did not tour the classics. It was hard enough to get an audience for them in New York. Everyone was proven wrong. The tour played to packed houses in San Francisco, Los Angeles, St. Louis, Chicago, Boston, Philadelphia, and Washington, D.C., plus a handful of smaller cities sprinkled in as connective stops. It opened in Los Angeles, where the *Los Angeles Times* critic said, "The fires that burned on the stage of the Biltmore Theatre last night were brighter than those of the brush fires in the canyons that threaten to engulf the city." From there, it went on to get unanimous rave reviews all across the country. Now, two years later, they formed a new company, the National Repertory Theatre, which was no longer affiliated with the Phoenix. They were in the process of assembling an acting company to tour with three plays in rotating repertory. Michael said that a friend of mine, Julie Harris, was seriously considering joining them.

I admired their ambitious plans to the extent that I said I would be both flattered and pleased to be a part of their company at some point, but I was still convinced that it was too soon for me to be away from New York for another Broadway season. They begged me not to rule anything out until I had met and talked with Miss Le Gallienne.

I had seen Le Gallienne on the stage at the Phoenix Theatre in their production of Schiller's *Mary Stuart* in 1958. It was a lean new adaptation of the 1801 play, and it had been directed by one of the theater's greatest men of the twentieth century, Tyrone Guthrie. Miss Le Gallienne had played Elizabeth I to Irene Worth's Mary of Scotland. The production was jet-fueled. Once started, it roared to its conclusion without giving the audience time to relax and breathe.

Irene Worth was a beautiful and moving Mary Queen of Scots, and Eva Le Gallienne gave the most riveting and complex performance I've ever seen on a stage.

I agreed to go up to Wilton, Connecticut, where Frances Ann lived, to meet her, but first I called Julie Harris. Julie invited me over for drinks. I knew she had apprenticed with Le Gallienne, and I also knew that, like stage stars of earlier generations, Julie felt strongly about the importance of touring. I wanted to know if she was seriously considering joining NRT.

She was. She adored Le G, as she called her, and thought that acting with her in a repertory of good plays, as well as being directed by her, would be the best of all possible worlds. That was why she had thought it over for so long, but she had decided she had to stay in New York just then. She and Manning Gurian had been going through some difficult times in their marriage, and she felt that it was very important, particularly for their young son, Peter, that she not leave New York. She understood my hesitation to leave New York for two seasons in a row, but felt that the opportunity to work with one of the major talents in the American theater was one I had to consider very seriously.

Just then, Manning came home. We all had a drink and a few laughs about the trials and tribulations of *The Warm Peninsula*. Manning then brought up June Havoc and told Julie that June was working on a play based on her memoirs, *Early Havoc*. She was interested in Julie playing the lead. We all knew that June had not been happy with the way she was portrayed by her sister, Gypsy Rose Lee, in the musical smash *Gypsy*. It sounded as if she was preparing to set the record straight. Julie asked if June had sent him anything to read. He said she hadn't, but she would if the idea appealed to Julie. She had read and liked the book and said she would love to see June's dramatization. She did the play on Broadway the following year and it was a very interesting flop.

When I left, Julie walked me to the door, where we stopped as she gave me a warm hug and whispered in the Irish lilt that crept in when she was being intensely serious, "Artists should never marry, Farley."

Le G

Eva Le Gallienne was born in England in 1899. Her father, Richard, was a renowned poet, and her mother, Julie Norregard, was a well-known Danish journalist and feminist. After three years, her parents divorced, and Eva spent half her time in London with her handsome, man-about-town father, and the other half in Paris with her pioneering feminist mother. Le G, as her friends called her, was fluent in Danish, Norwegian, French, and English. She and her mother sailed for America in 1915, where Eva pursued her ambitions as an actress. In 1921, she became an overnight star on Broadway playing Julie to Joseph Schildkraut's Liliom in the Hungarian playwright Ferenc Molnar's play of the same name. Many years later, in one of the rare instances when an adaptation outshone the original, Rodgers and Hammerstein based *Carousel* on *Liliom*.

She once told me that Pepe—her pet name for Schildkraut, whom she truly loved—could be very naughty and was always trying to break her up onstage. During a scene in *Liliom* where she had a heartbreaking monologue over Liliom's dead body, he kept tickling her breast with his upstage hand. She begged him to stop. When he didn't, she issued one last warning and threatened to make him pay if he did it again. He didn't. So the next time he "tickled her tittie," she lifted his hand to her lips as if to kiss it and bit through to the bone. She roared with laughter as she said, "He never tried *that* again."

Molnar was so enchanted by the young actress playing Julie in *Liliom* that he wrote his next play, *The Swan*, for her. In 1923 she was the toast of Broadway. Rather than following the path that most young actors would have taken to capitalize on her success, she turned her back on Broadway and founded her own theater company, the Civic Repertory Theatre, at 14th Street and Sixth Avenue, in 1926. There she gathered a group of dedicated actors and proceeded to introduce the classics and new plays in rotating repertory at prices that the general public could afford. The top-price ticket at the Civic Rep was one dollar. The productions were fully realized and first-class. The actors included some of the top names in the theater. She introduced the great European playwrights Ibsen and Goldoni to America. She was not the first one to present Chekhov in this country, but she was the first to popularize him. She also did most of her own translations of these plays, specializing in those of Ibsen and Chekhov.

Although she was an outspoken lesbian, she had tempestuous affairs with the actors Joseph Schildkraut and Basil Rathbone and managed to remain close to them throughout her life. In 1927 she had an affair with the married actress Josephine Hutchinson. When Hutchinson's husband sued for divorce, he named Le Gallienne as co-respondent, which was quite the public scandal, one she faced with her usual fearlessness.

During the Great Depression, President Roosevelt offered her the directorship of the Theatre Division of the WPA. She turned him down and struggled to keep the Civic Rep afloat. Her theatre closed in 1932, a victim of the Depression. Shortly after that, a gas furnace in her Connecticut home blew up in her face. Her hands, which she had instinctively held up in front of her face, were seriously disfigured, and her facial burns were bad. Years of painful plastic surgery followed.

In 1946, she and the English director Margaret Webster founded the American Repertory Theatre in an effort to revive Miss Le Gallienne's original idea. It lasted only two years. Now, in 1962, Michael and Frances Ann were trying it again with Le Gallienne as their figurative leader.

The producers of NRT drove me up to Miss Le Gallienne's home in Weston, Connecticut, the next afternoon. It did not take long for me to fall under her spell. The stories were true. Her passion for the theater and particularly for repertory theater was contagious. She convinced me that an actor had not lived until he had done repertory, where the creative juices stirred by one play spilled over to enrich the work in the others. She infused me with her enthusiasm for the benefits to an actor of being able to do great works rather than having to be limited to potentially successful commercial works. We also talked about some ideas for the third play. I remembered a comedy by Jean Anouilh that I saw in London with Claire Bloom called *Ring Round the Moon*. I suggested it as a play that might bring a nice balance to the other two more serious plays. She loved the idea, and said that Claire Bloom might be an ideal leading lady for the company. I realized that I had just committed myself to another tour.

Four Parts in Three Plays in Twelve Cities

Claire Bloom was interested but had conflicting film dates. The producers were also talking to Anne Meacham, who had impressed the Broadway critics that season in *A Passage to India*. Anne and an ingenue fresh out of Carnegie Tech, Kelly Jean Peters, were the last two pieces to fall into place. We began rehearsal in September in New York on *The Crucible*, directed by Jack Sydow, and *The Seagull*, directed by Miss Le Gallienne. After three weeks, the entire company moved to the University of North Carolina at Greensboro, where we continued rehearsing for three more weeks, adding *Ring Round the Moon*, also directed by Jack, to the other two plays.

Including a week of performances, we were there for four weeks as part of a program for drama students who observed the entire process. We lectured to classes and rehearsed each day. The schedule was exhausting. The sheer bulk of the lines that had to be memorized sometimes seemed overwhelming. In the Anouilh, I was playing two parts, the twins Hugo and Frederick, along with Konstantine in the Chekhov and John Proctor in the Miller play. In the same order of plays, Denholm was playing Patrice, Trigoran, and Reverend Hale; and Anne was playing Lady India, Nina, and Goody Proctor. Miss Le Gallienne urged us to drop thinking about one play when we moved to another. She always said the first would cook in our subconscious like a pot of soup on the back of the stove. Sometimes I could not avoid giving in to the jumble in my head. When that happened, I started to get agonizing cluster headaches.

The company and the producers stayed in a hotel in downtown Greensboro. The directors, the technicians, the designers, and the production staff all stayed at a motel adjacent to the campus in order to be closer to the theater. Their rooms were enormous, with multiple beds, probably to accommodate visiting families of students. They also had kitchens. Bob Calhoun, the production supervisor, and I had become friends in the course of rehearsal in New York. He was very good at what he did. We shared a love of the same kind of movies, music, dance, and theater, as well as tennis, sailing, and being beach bums. When the headaches hit, he suggested that I use his room nearby to lie down, in the dark, and relax till they passed. It was easier than getting a car downtown to the hotel and seemed to help the bouts pass more quickly. We were aware of a growing mutual attraction. Not only did we not act on it, but we didn't even speak about it. I guess we were trying to keep things simple, but like all the best-laid plans . . .

At the end of the three weeks, we began performing the first two plays to paying audiences. At the end of the third week, we added the Anouilh. By the time we had all three plays on their feet, the headaches were slowly replaced by a feeling of overwhelming elation. By no means did everyone feel that we were on top of things, but wow! we were doing it. The tour began.

After getting wonderful reviews in our first two cities, Cincinnati and Cleveland, Frances Ann decided to contact President Kennedy about the National Repertory Theatre and the great success it was having, and to ask if he could do anything to help establish NRT officially. After some thought and deliberation, he agreed to attend opening night at the National Theatre in Washington, D.C., and the gala afterward. He was going to anoint NRT as America's national theater and have it read into the *Congressional Record*. Needless to say, Frances Ann, Michael, and all of us involved were ecstatic.

Tragedy Intrudes

A number of weeks and several cities later, at the beginning of November, we opened to rave reviews in Philadelphia. I was flying high. This was theater! Le G, which she had finally asked me to call her, was a joy to work with, as was Kelly Jean, and I had as much fun with Denholm onstage as I had with him and his lovely young wife, Susan, offstage. Anne Meacham, who played my wife in one play and the unrequited love of my life in another, could be standoffish and neurotic offstage, but she was a consummate professional and rock-solid on stage. We were all having a wonderful time in Philadelphia and looking forward to our big opening night in Washington, D.C.

One Wednesday matinee of *The Crucible* was filled with inner-city high school kids whose admission had been free thanks to NRT and a local arts organization. At first the actors were a little nervous. This was not your usual polite "ladies who lunch" audience, but a bunch of rowdy teenagers who were not used to attending any theater, much less theater with a capital T. The auditorium was bedlam, but as the house lights dimmed and the curtain went up, they settled down very quickly and got with us. Soon you could have heard a pin drop. They didn't hesitate to interact with the characters: to warn their favorites of what they could see coming, to tell the ones they hated what they thought of them, to whistle, or to boo and hiss. They broke every conventional rule of audience behavior, and it was thrilling. The curtain calls were not accompanied by applause or standing ovations or bravos. We were met with pure sound, screams and whistles or boos and hisses. I hope we touched the hearts and souls of those kids the way they touched ours.

The Girl Who Came to Supper, a musical comedy version of Terence Rattigan's play *The Prince and the Showgirl* was the other big show in town. Noël Coward had written the music for it, and I was looking forward to seeing him again. The philanthropist and art collector Henry McIlhenny threw a party for both companies at his gorgeous mansion on Rittenhouse Square. Bob and I arrived late to the party because he had taken me to do a television interview after our show. We arrived at the mansion, and I was standing in the foyer admiring a Degas bronze ballerina when a familiar voice behind me said, "Mr. Granger, it's Noël."

Without turning, I said, "Noël who?" and he burst into laughter.

He pulled me off into a quiet corner where we sat and talked about the theater for a long time. He had read our reviews and told me how proud he was of what I was doing, which made me feel very good indeed. He knew Le G and admired her greatly. He also knew Denholm, who had acted in the great British wartime movie that Coward had written and co-directed with David Lean, *In Which We Serve*. We went in to join our host and the rest of the guests, and in no time at all Noël was as captivated by Denholm's wife, Susan, as everyone else always was. As the party began to slow down he pulled Bob, Susan, Denholm, and me aside to invite us back to a late-night party on an English battleship that was at anchor in Philadelphia. It seems that the admiral was a great pal of his. I'm not sure who the killjoy was who had the good sense to turn that one down. It probably was Bob, allowing the cautious and sensible side of his stage manager's nature to overrule our party instincts.

It was our last weekend in Philadelphia. Denholm, Susan, and I had arranged to go to see the Barnes Collection on Friday. It was a half-hour drive outside the city, so we got a cab. After spending at least two hours at the spectacular art collection, we decided to go back downtown for lunch. We got another cab and took off. After a few minutes, the driver said, "Did you hear the President's been shot."

We waited. "Okay," said Susan, "what's the punch line?" The driver said, "No punch line, that's it."

"Well, that certainly isn't very funny," I said.

"Another cabbie told me," he said. "That's all I know."

We didn't know what to think, so we just sat in silence. As we began to get into the center of the city, we saw people spilling out of the buildings. Around City Hall right in the center of the city, traffic jammed up. "I think I have to get out of this cab," I said. Denholm and Susan agreed.

The streets were now becoming filled with people. We paid the driver, got out of the cab, and began to run toward the hotel. I got to my room just as word was announced that John Fitzgerald Kennedy had been pronounced dead. I sat on the bed trying to comprehend what had happened. The phone rang. It was Bob calling from the theater. Had I heard the news? The show would be canceled tonight. He would see me as soon as he could get away. I didn't know what to do. I just lay on the bed and watched the news over and over.

The president was dead. John Kennedy was dead. How could that be? He was so young, so popular. He and his beautiful young wife and "Camelot" had brought so much promise to us all. Bob called again. Things were crazy at the theater. No one knew what to do about Saturday's two performances.

Bob and I met later for dinner in some famous old restaurant, I can't remember its name. I do remember running into Harry Kurnitz there with a contingent from his show, *The Girl Who Came to Supper*, which included José Ferrer, Florence Henderson, and, of course, Noël Coward. They were trying to figure out how to write a new opening for their show, which opened with an attempted assassination of the prince. They invited us to join them, but we knew they had work to do and we did not want company that evening.

Bob and I had something to eat and plenty to drink, although we both remained dead sober. We left the restaurant and walked in silence in the bitter cold for hours through the historical part of the city that was the first capital of the United States. We stopped at Independence Hall and the Liberty Bell, at Congress Hall and Declaration House. We walked until we were too tired and cold to walk anymore. We went back to my hotel. That night that he and I moved past our resolution to keep our friendship uncomplicated and became lovers.

The next morning I woke to an empty bed. Bob had gone off to the theater early to deal with performance and transportation schedules. I turned on the TV and watched the shock and dismay of the entire world reacting to the news. Bob called from the theater. Saturday's performances had definitely been canceled, and the company was leaving today for D.C. We were opening in Washington, D.C., on Monday. Oh, God!

Le G had been asked to read one of John Kennedy's favorite poems by Robert Frost in a memorial program that was to be televised live from Independence Hall on Sunday morning, and she wanted me to be there with her. Bob agreed to stay behind and drive us Washington after the ceremony on Sunday.

Bob was at his hotel packing, and I was doing the same. Both of us had our TV sets on, as I imagine most of the country did. We were watching in stunned disbelief as Jack Ruby shot Lee Harvey Oswald on camera. It felt as if the entire world as we knew it had gone mad.

Sunday morning was very cold and windy. I sat alone in Independence Hall. Four large TV monitors were there, and I watched as JFK's casket was taken to lie in state at the Capitol rotunda. Suddenly there was a flurry of activity as the dignitaries arrived, and the camera crews prepared for the ceremony. Bob came in with Le G and we took our seats on the platform.

Washington

After the ceremony in Philadelphia, we left as quickly as possible and sat lost in our own reflections for most of the two-and-a-half-hour drive. We dropped Le G and her companion off at the Willard and went to the Jefferson, where we, the Elliotts, and Michael and Frances Ann were staying. At the desk there was a note from Denholm and Susan asking us to meet them at an Italian restaurant downtown. We dumped our bags and left immediately. We needed friends. When we got there, it was like a reunion. We ate some pasta and drank a lot of wine. How on earth were we going to open the next night at the National Theatre with *The Crucible,* a play about senseless hysterical violence? It was almost midnight when we got up to leave. Outside the restaurant Denholm stopped, turned to us, and said, "Let's go." We knew what he meant and left immediately for the Capitol.

We walked there and got in a line that seemed to snake for miles to the rotunda. It was bitterly cold and brilliantly clear. The bright white Capitol dome looked two-dimensional, almost like marzipan, against the night sky. There was no wind, which was merciful, since so many of the people in line had children and infants with them. We were struck by how silent it was. Even with all those children and infants, there was no noise, no crying, just thousands of people waiting patiently in cold silence. About thirty minutes later, a guard who recognized me came up and said, "Mr. Granger, by the time you get to the Rotunda, the President will be gone. The line is too long, and they are removing his body to St. Matthew's Church at six A.M." We thanked him, and we left after a few minutes.

We had to open as scheduled on Monday with *The Crucible.* It was too late to cancel the party that had been planned for after the show. The theater was more than half empty. Of the many who had accepted the invitation, the only government dignitary in attendance was an elderly Supreme Court justice and his very young wife. Our gala, in the lobby of the National Theatre, was even more sparsely attended than the performance. This was a very difficult time for our producers, Michael and Frances Ann. They could feel their dream of launching a national theater slipping away from them as well as experiencing the grief we all felt at the loss of our young president. In Frances Ann's case, all those feelings were compounded by the fact that John F. Kennedy had been her first young love.

On Tuesday morning, the funeral mass for JFK was held in St. Matthew's Church, which was only a block away from our hotel.

Our reviews were very good, but under the circumstances that was small comfort. For the entire run in Washington, we played to half-empty houses. The assassination had pulled the rug from under what could have been the defining moment for the establishment of a national theater company. We were too involved with the common grief shared by the country at the time to think about this, but in the subsequent years, NRT slowly lost its impetus. It lasted for only three more years, when an attempt to establish it as the resident company at Ford's Theatre in Washington, D.C., succumbed to political infighting.

Liberated

Christmas was rapidly approaching when we finally closed in D.C. and left for Boston. We felt so liberated to be out of Washington that some of us actually kissed the ground when we got off the plane. We were booked there for a month. We received great reviews and got back to the joy of performing on-stage. The company stayed at a turn-of-the-century hotel, the Touraine, which was in the center of Boston's small theater district. Unfortunately, like so many of the older buildings that gave character to our cities, it has since been torn down and replaced with a bland postmodern cube.

I had a corner suite, which overlooked the Boston Garden and the Common. My living room had a large bowed window, which was a perfect place for a Christmas tree. Bob and I walked to the old Faneuil Hall public market and bought a ten-foot tree, which we carried back to the hotel through the snow. Exchanging Christmas greetings with smiling Bostonians along the way was almost like an antidote to the pain that was still with us from Washington. I threw a Christmas party and invited the company, suggesting that everyone bring ornaments to dress the tree. Everyone came, even Le G, who usually stayed away from any and all company social activities. The director in her came out as people began decorating the tree. She stayed until the last ornament was placed to her satisfaction.

Kelly Jean was convinced that she was being stalked by the Boston Strangler. She had received several strange phone calls, and suspicious notes were being left for her at the hotel. The police took this very seriously and security was placed at the hotel and at the theater. Fortunately, nothing happened before we closed and left for New Haven, where Kelly Jean did have a problem.

One of the major plot points in *Ring Round the Moon* involved a ball gown worn by Kelly's character, Isobel, in the second act. It was an elaborately draped pink and blue chiffon gown that accomplished its purpose admirably by turning the plain young girl into the princess with whom Hugo and Frederick, the twins I played, fell in love. The night after *Ring* opened, the Shubert Theatre in New Haven was broken into. All that was missing was the dress. A scramble to find a replacement took place the next day because there was no time to make another one. Kelly took the train to New York and she and Frances Ann found a flowing pale green and blue chiffon gown at Bergdorf's that looked even better on her than the original. The New Haven police did their best to track down the original, but came up with no answers.

Also playing in Boston while we were there was *Funny Girl* in its out-of-town tryout. My old pal from my Navy days, Kay Medford, was playing Fanny Brice's mother. This was the first time I had seen Kay since we were in Hawaii when World War II ended. She said that their show was a mess but that the girl playing Fanny Brice, although she could be a major pain, was also a major talent. Everyone was working furiously to pull it together. The work paid off. When the musical opened in New York in March, it was a huge hit, and Barbra Streisand was on her way to megastardom. Kay and I laughed about the fact that she seemed doomed to play mothers: Amanda in *The Glass Menagerie* in Hawaii and Japan in her early twenties, Dick Van Dyke's mother in *Bye Bye Birdie* in her early thirties, and Streisand's mother in *Funny Girl* before she hit forty.

Our tour continued to be a great success, and we ended it by coming to New York for several months. Once again, the reviews were excellent ... but only for *The Crucible* and *The Seagull*. We were not able to put on *Ring Round the Moon* because it had been optioned to be adapted into a musical and could not be performed anywhere within a fifty-mile radius of New York City. Its absence hurt us because it was the light comedy in our repertory of three plays, and it helped to display the diversity of styles we were able to handle.

Incidentally, Kelly's stolen ball gown was found in use at a rowdy New Haven party just before we opened in New York. The party was a drag ball, and the gown was again serving its purpose, this time turning a young man into a princess.

A high point of our Broadway run was when Bob came backstage after a matinee of *The Crucible* to tell me that Arthur Miller had been in the audience and wanted to meet me. He came to my dressing room, and we talked for at least ten minutes. He said to me, "This is what I always wanted my play to be." I think he felt the original Broadway version had been overproduced. He then said he would like to meet the rest of the company.

I went to find Bob, who, anticipating the moment, had assembled everyone onstage. Mr. Miller shook hands with each person and thanked them for the way they had fulfilled his expectations. Jack Sydow, who had directed *The Crucible*, was also there that afternoon. Mr. Miller told him that he was extremely impressed with the clarity of our production. A taciturn man, Arthur Miller had a reputation for not being easy to please. We were all aware of that, which made his praise very important to all of us.

NRT—Second Tour

Out of loyalty, I stayed with NRT for another season, which kept me out of New York for the third season in as many years. We did Ibsen's *Hedda Gabler* with the Swedish actress Signe Hasso in the title role; Sheridan's *She Stoops to Conquer*, and Molnar's *Liliom* with me in the title role. The tour was successful, but it was not as good as the first one, and did not come into New York. If I had worries about being absent from Broadway for two years in a row before the first tour, going on the road again made very little sense. It was a combination of several things that made me decide to do it: Bob had been made associate producer and would be traveling with the company in order to try and set up committees to support NRT in each city; my loyalty to Frances Ann had no limits; and Le Gallienne would be directing me in two of her signature plays, *Liliom* and *Hedda Gabler*. I had never done Restoration comedy and this might be my only chance, with Jack directing *She Stoops to Conquer*. After seven months, when we were preparing to close in Chicago, my agent suggested that I think about going to Hollywood to explore the opportunities presented by television, which was now almost exclusively shot on the West Coast. I promised I would think about it.

Once back in New York I could not resist the lure of Broadway. Hal Holbrook, Carol Rossen (Robert Rossen's daughter), Jo Van Fleet, and I were offered the parts in *The Glass Menagerie*. It had been opened with Maureen Stapleton as Amanda. When Maureen had to leave, the producers decided to put in a whole new cast. The only problem was that there was almost no time for rehearsal. The director did his best in the little time he had, but it was learn as you go. As a result, Hal, Carol, and I bonded quickly and became fast friends. I must admit that Hal stole the show. He was the best Gentleman Caller I have ever seen. Jo Van Fleet could be a wonderful actress in the right part, but her lack of whimsy did not help her interpretation of Amanda.

Just a Long Weekend

Not too long after *Menagerie* closed, Bob and I were having dinner with Tharon Musser, Broadway's top lighting designer, who also did the lighting for NRT. Tharon's partner, Dina, was on tour with the national company of *Funny Girl* in the Kay Medford part. Bob had finished a season with the Dallas Civic Opera and I had no new show in sight, so we all spontaneously decided to go to Los Angeles, surprise Dina, and see *Funny Girl.* We planned to stay for about a week, but for Bob and me, it turned into four years.

Shortly after we got to L.A., my West Coast agents called to say that I had been offered a guest shot on the popular series *Run for Your Life* starring Ben Gazzara. Bob had been observing at NBC on a brand-new daytime series called *Days of Our Lives* when he was offered a job as production supervisor for a new theater that was opening in the Los Angeles answer to New York's Lincoln Center, the L.A. Music Center. A friend of his, Gordon Davidson, had been hired to run the Mark Taper Forum, which was the Music Center's equivalent of the Vivian Beaumont at Lincoln Center in New York. He in turn hired Bob to help him get it up and running. So we rented a great house in Malibu, got two Airedales and two cats, and went to work.

My part on the TV series was that of a movie star who had seen and done it all and wanted to experience the thrill of fighting a bull. There were two Mexican matadors there to coach me with the bullfighting moves. When the day for my big scene arrived, we were on the back lot of Universal where they had set up a small bullring. A large van arrived and they unloaded several bulls. They were light gray with large humps on their backs. There was a moment of dead silence, then everyone roared with laughter. Everyone, that is, except the Mexican matadors. One of them went up to the stunned director and said in Spanish the equivalent of "I ain't going in no ring with that animal." With that, he gestured to his pal and they walked off the set. The director sent all the actors home with instructions to report back the next morning. The next day I got into costume and makeup and reported for duty. There in the ring was a large black bull with a large black hump. They had taken one of the Brahma bulls and somehow spray-painted it black. I was about to repeat the Mexican matador's phrase when the director hurried over to tell me there was nothing to worry about because the bull and I would never have to be in the ring at the same time. He would shoot us separately and cut it so it looked like we were. That was my first experience back in Hollywood.

For the next three years Bob was kept very busy at the Mark Taper Forum, while I did a variety of guest-starring roles on episodic television. It was nothing at all like the live television experience I had grown to love so much in New York. The material rarely rose above mediocre. There was never enough time to discuss anything with the director or fellow actors. The focus on the set was always on the technical, never on the performances. The work was usually done in the midst of chaos. I had grown up on quiet soundstages, gone on to quiet TV studios in live television, and graduated to theater, where rehearsals and performances were organized and focused experiences. This was a new way of doing things, and not only could I not get comfortable with it, I quickly grew to loathe it.

Our life in Malibu was idyllic. The dogs took to the ocean like seals. The cats littered the entire living room with fish one moonlit night when the grunion were running. We had friends over for weekends and beach barbecues. Except for the fact that Bob was off at work all the time, it was perfect and I was miserable.

At one Hollywood party or social gathering or another, I ran into some of the movie directors I had known and worked with in the early 1950s. They were all delighted to see me, all happy that I was back, all saying that I looked better than ever, but none of them ever called to ask me to do a film.

My close friend Alex North, the film composer who had introduced jazz to movies in *A Streetcar Named Desire* and had scored such memorable films as *Viva Zapata!*, *Cleopatra*, *The Rose Tattoo*, *Spartacus*, *The Long Hot Summer*, *Unchained*, *Who's Afraid of Virginia Woolf?*, and countless others, lived two houses down the beach from us. When I was talking to him about my predicament one evening, he said, "Farley, when you bought out your contract, Goldwyn put out the word not to use you. Zanuck didn't care about anything Goldwyn wanted, so he did use you. But when you refused to do one of his biggest productions . . ."

I interrupted him: "Alex, *The Egyptian* was a world-class stinker!"

"You don't have to convince me," he explained. "I've been there. I also know times have changed, but a lot of the old prejudices still exist. Some of the hardliners out here probably feel that since you turned your back on Hollywood, they are not going to let you back into the club that easily." I knew he was making sense, and I had expected some of this, but from people I had considered friends it hurt, and it made me angry.

The Princess

During the 1950s a number of the live TV shows I had acted in were produced by David Susskind. Now, in 1966, he called to offer me a part in a TV version of *Laura*. It was a new adaptation by Truman Capote, who had written it for his friend Princess Lee Radziwill, Jackie Kennedy's sister. The other people cast in it were Robert Stack, George Sanders, and Arlene Francis, and it was to rehearse and shoot in London.

I accepted.

We gathered in London for the first reading in a studio in the Duke of York's Barracks, where each morning we had to pause while the Queen's Guard piped whatever it was they were piping. George, Arlene, and I hit it off immediately, as we all realized that we were stuck in an archetypical vanity production. I'd hesitate to call Robert Stack dumb, but he had no sense of humor. George used to bait him mercilessly. Most of the time, it went right over Bob's head. The actors all lunched together most days at a little Italian restaurant nearby on Kings Road. Stack never failed to ask us if we needed our receipts...every day. George observed wryly that the poor chap may have had tax problems.

One day at lunch George leaned over to me and whispered, "Farley, Ray Milland is over there in the corner booth. I think he would appreciate if you went over and said hello." Ray had played Stanford White in *The Girl in the Red Velvet Swing* with me. I had not noticed him when we came in, but I knew that Ray had not worked in a while. I went over to say hello, and he seemed quite touched. That was the real George Sanders, thoughtful, caring, and considerate.

Arlene Francis was my closest friend, my drinking buddy, and my salvation during this entire production. She was warm without being gushy, sharp without being bitchy, and a trooper who never let any of the daily trials and tribulations that we all went through, trying to make a princess look like an actress, get her down. After rehearsal we usually went to a nearby pub to unwind and recap the day's events, a process that almost always began with "Did you see what she did when..." I asked George to come with us several times, but he confided that his wife, Benita Hume, was quite ill and he needed to spend as much time with her as possible. As difficult as that must have been for him, he never let any of it show at work.

Arlene and I spent as many evenings as possible going to the theater. We saw *Rosencrantz and Guildenstern Are Dead*, which heralded the amazing talent of Tom

Stoppard. We saw Laurence Olivier in Strindberg's *Dance of Death* at the National Theatre after hearing the rumor that he was gravely ill with cancer. Not only was his performance magnificent, but he beat the cancer!

One day at rehearsal, Lee came up to me and said, "You take Arlene out all the time. How come you never ask me to do anything?"

So, like a good boy, I asked her out. We went to the theater and had supper afterward at a nearby seafood restaurant. Lee spent the whole evening complaining about the script and how Truman had done her in by not showing up. Two martinis, two Dover soles, and some very good white Bordeaux later, we poured ourselves into a cab and went back to her house in Chelsea for a nightcap. When we got there, I had a brainstorm. "Why don't we call Truman?" I suggested. She loved the idea and had a bunch of numbers for him. The hunt was on, but he was nowhere to be found. Knowing Truman, I would not be a bit surprised if he had heard that things on *Laura* were not going well and was avoiding this particular phone call. After an hour or so we gave up, and I went home. *Laura* turned out to be no one's finest hour, but at least I had the good fortune to get to know George and Arlene. George's wife died shortly after our production, and two years later, after a brief fourth marriage to Zsa Zsa Gabor's sister Magda, George killed himself, leaving a note that said, "I am leaving because I am bored. I feel I have lived long enough. I am leaving you with your worries in this sweet cesspool. Good luck."

The State Department

Bob and Eddie Parone, a talented New York director who helped launch Edward Albee's career, had gotten a Rockefeller Foundation grant to produce a program called *New Theatre for Now* at the Taper. It was a big success and the State Department had approached Gordon Davidson about sending two evenings of new American plays to India, Iran, and the capitals of Eastern Europe. Davidson had agreed to do it and had submitted the plays for approval. As is always the case, this bureaucratic decision was taking a very long time. Bob had never been to Europe, and I thought this was the perfect time. He needed a vacation and at least he would have some of his shots and a passport if his tour came through. Selfishly, I would have the pleasure of introducing him to places I loved, most of them in Italy.

We went first to Munich to spend some time with Alex North and his young German wife, Anna. There we rented a car and drove to a small town called Fussen to visit Ethyl and Buddy. Ethyl's daughter, Judy, had married Hal Prince, who was directing a film there. His studio was an inflated dome in a field at the foot of the mountain peak that mad King Ludwig's fairytale castle, Neuschwanstein, perched on. Coming upon the site for the first time was as surreal an experience as rounding a corner today in Bilbao and seeing Frank Gehry's titanium-sheathed Guggenheim Museum.

After a couple of days, we left for Italy, crossing the Alps via the Brenner Pass. We arrived in Verona in the middle of the night. The next morning over *caffè latte* and pastries in the main square, Bob fell in love with Italy. Our next stop was *La Serenissima*, Venice. We stayed in La Fenice et des Artistes, the small hotel next to the opera house. The first thing I did was look in the phone book for my old friend and drinking buddy, Peggy Guggenheim. She was there and invited us to come over for lunch. We did. It had been fourteen years since I had seen her, and she was every bit as lively as I remembered. After lunch she asked if I would like anything else. I said I was perfectly content. She raised her eyebrows and said, "Have you forgotten?"

I still didn't get it. She said, "Not even a little grappa?"

Then I laughed. We had ended many cold winter evenings with "just a little grappa." Then she took us through the museum to show me the improvements that had taken place in the fourteen years since I had last been there, including a small downstairs gallery devoted to the paintings of her daughter, Pegeen, who had killed herself in 1967 after a number of attempts. A couple of days later, we met for dinner at the Taverna La Fenice and spent a marvelous last evening in Venice with the woman the Venetians called "the Last Duchess."

The following morning we headed for Rome. After checking in at the Hotel de la Ville, we ran into Mickey Knox in the bar. I'd known Mickey slightly in Hollywood during his acting days. After becoming one of the early victims of the blacklist, he had moved to Paris and now lived in Rome. He was married to Joan Morales, whose sister Adele had been stabbed with a pen knife by her husband, Norman Mailer, during their tempestuous marriage. Adele, who was not critically wounded, had refused to press charges. The sisters had a Cuban mother and a Peruvian father. Joanie was a completely down-to-earth young woman whose Brooklyn accent could be cut with a knife. She was crazy-funny, and one of the most beautiful women I've ever seen. She, Bob, and I bonded immediately. Through Mickey, who was working nonstop as a dialogue director in the Italian film world, I met Roger Beaumont, the representative in Italy for Creative Management Associates, one of Hollywood's most prestigious talent agencies at the time. Roger and Mickey began trying to convince me to remain in Italy because of all the film work still going on there.

Meanwhile, Bob received a telegram from the Mark Taper Forum. Two one-act plays that he had directed had been chosen as part of a two-evening program of new plays to be sent to India, Iran, and the capitals of Eastern Europe. He had to return immediately for casting and rehearsals. I decided to stay in Rome and explore the film possibilities about which Roger seemed so positive.

I settled into a small hotel in the heart of Rome. The two people who best helped keep my loneliness at bay were Joanie and Gore Vidal, who had an apartment in Rome as well as his mountaintop villa on the Amalfi coast. He invited me to dinner and then on a weekly basis to his Sunday gatherings, where he would collect a few of the most interesting people in town at that moment for drinks and dinner.

Bob was in rehearsal back in Los Angeles, and our phone bills began to mount. Franco Zefferelli heard I was in town and called to invite me to a party he was giving at his villa on the Appian Way. He said that Luchino would be there, and it would be just like old times. I arrived and didn't know a soul. The hit of the evening was Franco's new ice-making machine. It was sitting front and center in the living room like an honored guest.

After Franco and I hugged, I was left on my own feeling like an out-of-place wallflower. Then Monica Vitti came over to talk with me and changed all that. She knew and loved every frame of *Senso* and was also a big Hitchcock fan. She could not have been more gracious. I had only known her, as most Americans do, as the glacial, elusive leading lady in Antonioni films like *L'Avventura* and *Red Desert*. In the 1960s she was the only female star in Italy whose name would guarantee the money for a film. She was also their number-one comedienne, and after seeing several of her other films, I knew why. She was an Italian combination of Carole Lombard and Carol Burnett, equally at home doing high style or low comedy. If you ever get a chance to see her in *Dramma della Gelosia*, or *The Pizza Triangle*, as it is called here, along with Marcello Mastroianni and Giancarlo Giannini, or *Polvere di Stelle*, a k a *Stardust*, with Alberto Sordi, you will see what I mean.

Late in the evening, Visconti made his grand entrance with his latest find, Helmut Berger, in tow. I was concerned that he might still be angry because I had been unable to return for the execution scene in *Senso*. But he seemed as genuinely glad to see me as I was to see him. Helmut Berger, not a very good actor, was perfect as Ingrid Thulin's decadent son in Visconti's disturbing film about pre–World War II Germany, *The Damned*. Luchino went on to make one more cinematic masterpiece in 1971. It was his film of Thomas Mann's famous novella, *Death in Venice*, starring Dirk Bogarde in an unforgettable portrayal of Gustav von Aschenbach. Visconti's last major film, *Ludwig*, in 1972, starred Hemut Berger as the mad king of Bavaria. Berger was merely adequate opposite the delicious Austrian actress Romy Schneider as Empress Elisabeth of Austria. One of Ludwig's follies was building my favorite castle, Neuschwanstein.

The next day I got two job offers. Roger had gotten me the lead in an Italian film that was being shot in Egypt, and my agent in Hollywood called to say I had been offered a leading role in a prestigious film being made for TV. The cast included Uta Hagen, Marty Balsam, Cloris Leachman, and Johnny Rubenstein as my son. I stalled them both and called Bob.

He told me that the United States Information Agency had finally read the plays that had been submitted for the tour months ago. They did not approve of their political content and had canceled the State Department tour, citing unrest in the Middle East as their reason. Bob urged me to come back and do the TV film in L.A. Then we would pack up the Malibu house, take the dogs and cats, and move to Rome. It was a plan.

I was delighted to be in rehearsal again. I had worked with the director, Paul Bogard, before and thought he was top-notch. Uta was as much fun to work with as she had been to play with in Paris. Marty was a rock-solid old pro. Johnny Rubenstein, the great pianist's son, was a gifted young actor who was obviously going places. Cloris Leachman was playing my wife. She had put her career on hold to raise a family and be supportive of her husband, the director George Englund. Since she was playing my wife, we sat together for the first reading. All she did that day was complain about how old she looked and how tired she was. Obviously Paul was not appreciative of her lack of focus on the part or the script. The next day she was not there. A couple of years later Cloris won an Oscar for *The Last Picture Show* and appeared on *The Mary Tyler Moore Show* and her own spinoff, *Phyllis*. Our star-studded TV movie, from which she was fired on the first day, played to good reviews and sank without a trace. This is an example of the crapshoot that is show business.

Soon it was Christmas. Bob and I gave a party to say good-bye to all our friends. The lease was up on the beach house on January 1, so we packed up, put everything in storage, took Luke and Molly, our two Airedales, and the two cats, and left for Rome right after the first of the year in 1970.

Italy Again

After a month at the Cavalieri Hilton, which had grounds where the dogs could run, we rented a beautiful rooftop apartment with a terrace in a fifteenth-century building in the heart of old Rome. It soon became obvious that Roger, my agent, and Mickey, my friend, had exaggerated the amount of quality work available in the early 1970s. I was offered a lot of projects but, especially since I had done a film with Visconti, none of them was remotely interesting or challenging. In the four years we spent in Rome, I averaged two films a year, none of which were worth writing home about. One of them, *Lo Chiamavano Trinità* or *They Call Him Trinity*, a comic book of a movie, was one of the highest-grossing films ever made in Italy.

In 1975 the bottom fell out of the Italian film industry and film production came almost to a complete halt. Also, Watergate and its repercussions were looming large in America. It was time to go home. We packed up the dogs and cats, gave away the furniture, and left for New York and then California.

Hollywood or New York

My friends Ethyl and Buddy were going to Mallorca to spend a month with Judy, Hal, and their grandchildren at Hal's mountaintop villa in Pollensa. They suggested that Bob and I use their house in Beverly Hills while we were deciding whether or not to stay in L.A. To complicate this decision, things were not going well between Bob and me.

I began accepting guest-starring roles on episodic TV again. There were a lot more opportunities, but if anything, the quality of the material and the lack of time for preparation had gotten worse. I was not happy. My agent knew how I felt and called to say that I had been offered a lot of money to do a soap opera in New York. He said that many respectable New York theater actors worked in soaps in order to make enough money to live decently in New York and to be available to work in the theater whenever the right part came along. I said that I needed time to think about it and accepted an offer from the Seattle Repertory Theatre to play one of the leads in Noël Coward's *Private Lives*.

The production was a smash hit with both the public and the critics, and I had the time of my life playing Elyot. When it closed, I returned to Hollywood and episodic television, which seemed even more banal after Noël Coward. When my agent said that the soap, *One Life to Live*, in New York was still interested in me and had upped the money, I returned to New York. Bob stayed in California.

New York, 1977

Back in my favorite city, I stayed with Shelley, who was in a big prewar apartment on Riverside Drive. We sat up until the wee small hours having the same old discussions about acting and planning things that we could do together in the theater. I found an apartment with a magnificent view looking east across Central Park. At sunset, all the windows of the East Side high-rises turned a brilliant shiny copper. It was just a short walk to the ABC studio where I worked. When Shelley saw my apartment, she fell in love with it. Never warm enough, even in the dog days of summer, she said that the winter winds coming down the Hudson River were killing her over on Riverside Drive. She called Jay Julien, our trusted mutual lawyer and business manager, and he was able to get her an apartment in my building, four floors below me.

Shelley had her apartment redesigned, making the master bedroom and living room into one large space with wall-to-wall windows on two sides. The views were spectacular, but seeing all that expanse of Central Park made her cold, so she covered them with heavy insulated drapes that were always drawn. When that didn't work well enough for her, she bought several of the largest portable electric heaters that could be found, plugged them all in at the same time, and plunged her wing of the building into complete blackness. After that was sorted out, she purchased a lot of cheap mattresses and leaned them over the drapes as another layer of insulation. The end result was that it was impossible to visit her for too long a time because it was like being in a sauna.

I thought I disliked episodic TV, but the soap was worse. Soap acting requires certain skills that I have never been able to develop: the ability to be a very fast study, the ability to concentrate in the middle of complete chaos, the ability to learn material that is the same but slightly different each day, and always, the need for instant acting with little or no rehearsal or preparation time. I have nothing but admiration for the many fine actors who have mastered these skills. For young actors it is an invaluable technique to acquire for a limited period of time. I couldn't master any of these necessary abilities. It took me many painful years and two additional tries to realize this.

At the time I thought, maybe my mind is going. Maybe my ability to memorize lines has deserted me. I was able to memorize three plays simultaneously for repertory and couldn't remember three scenes for a soap. Maybe I had early-onset Alzheimer's. I went to doctors, to hypnotists, to acupuncturists, to people who supposedly knew how to teach acting technique for soaps. Nothing worked. I developed a spastic colon. My gut had always spoken for me when I was unhappy and felt unable to do anything about it. I had memories of it speaking out in meetings with Mr. Goldwyn, or at formal dinner parties in my young movie star days, but this was getting more serious. I was in danger of perforating my intestine.

One day, in an effort to stop the mental and physical pain, I just walked off the set, went to my dressing room, got my things, and left the studio. I didn't go back. I didn't answer my phone for days. I just slept. When I started to feel a little better, I went to see Jay Julien. Jay handled everything. My colon stopped complaining, and I began to feel whole again. I needed to work in order to prove to myself that I could work.

I went into a bad dinner-theater production of *The Sound of Music* and had no problem at all memorizing the lines, which erased a huge worry. It paid very well, but I quickly realized that dinner theater was not for me. I then toured summer stock in a bad production of "the original" *Dracula*. At one theater a handsome young apprentice came up and introduced himself to me. He said, "Hi, Farley, I'm Sam Goldwyn's grandson, Tony." I was taken completely by surprise. I'd liked and felt a certain kinship with his father, Sammy Jr. Even though life with my father was far from ideal, I knew that Sammy's was no day at the beach either. I felt an almost personal sense of pride about the good things Sammy had been doing in the movie business. Tony has distinguished himself in both theater and in films as a triple threat: actor, director, and producer.

Shelley and I finally got to do a play together. We were offered two of the parts in a limited run of *Kennedy's Children* in Chicago. The play consisted of six actors in a bar doing long intersecting monologues that define them as children of the 1960s. Once again, I proved to myself that learning lines was not a problem for me. Shelley did have an occasional problem with her lines. I'll never know whether or not it had to do with her love of improvisation, but I always knew she was up when she would pause for a moment and say, "I remember when I first met Eleanor Roosevelt..." The estimable wife of FDR had never been mentioned in the play by the author. The original production had not been a success in New York, but the subject matter had enough appeal for enough people, including me, that it continued to be performed all over the country for several years. It's a hard piece to pull off and we didn't fare any better than most. The only person in our company who came off well, and deservedly so, was the talented and too infrequently seen actor Al Freeman Jr.

Bob and I had kept in touch. He came to New York for a monthlong trial run to explore producing and directing for a soap. It would mean a significant increase in income, and he decided that if he received an offer to direct he would accept. The offer was tendered, he did accept, and he moved, with the

Airedales, Luke and Molly, into an apartment across the hall from me. At the time, it was the best of all possible worlds.

The next project I worked on was with a close friend, Shirley Kaplan. Shirley is a very talented director who just happens to also be a superb painter. She was involved in developing projects at Playwrights Horizons. She was working with Carol Hall, who had composed the music and lyrics for *The Best Little Whorehouse in Texas*. This project was tentatively titled *Sweet Main Street*. It was an effort to create the *Saturday Evening Post*, Norman Rockwell world of pre–World War II small-town America. Shirley was designing the sets as well as directing. We worked on it for almost a month. It was a good idea that never came together. But we all had fun trying to make it happen. Frances Ann, my producer with NRT, loved it and tried to get the funding that would enable Shirley to continue developing *Sweet Main Street*, but that never happened.

Two Strikes

Michael Kahn was a member of the McCarter Theatre Company in Princeton, New Jersey. He had been artistic director of the American Shakespeare Festival in Stratford, Connecticut, and he is currently the artistic director of the American Shakespeare Festival in Washington, D.C. Michael asked if I would be interested in coming to the McCarter to be in the classic comedy about amateur theater, George Kelly's *The Torch Bearers*. Some of the other actors in it were Peggy Cass, Dina Merrill, and, last but never least, Tovah Feldshuh. Tovah was young, talented, and defined the tasty Yiddish word *chutzpah*. I've watched her grow through the years into a very accomplished actress and singer. I don't know how good our production was, but I had fun, especially with Peggy, whose tart Boston Irish sense of humor kept everything in perspective.

While performing in Princeton, I was invited to Mel Gussow's house for an after-theater Christmas party. Mel was a drama critic with *The New York Times*. He had been a major force in the evolution of off-Broadway, and he had also written many superb books with and about the most important playwrights in modern theater. It had been a long snowy drive back to New York from Princeton, and like most actors after a performance, I was starving. I jumped out of the car in front of the Gussows' town house in Greenwich Village, hoping there would be some food left. As I started up the steps, the front door burst open and out came a sobbing Jessica Tandy followed quickly by her husband, Hume Cronyn. Jessie rushed down the steps, and Hume sputtered out a "Merry

Christmas, Farley" as he rushed after her. Inside, in front of the fireplace, nose to nose, stood Joe Papp, the artistic director of the Public Theater, and Edward Albee, one of America's foremost playwrights, screaming obscene insults at each other. I felt a hand on my arm and turned. Mel's wife, Ann, was standing there. She said sweetly, "Welcome, Farley. I'm so glad you could come. Why don't we go downstairs and get you something to eat." With a quiet smile she took me down to the kitchen and got me a drink and some food. As she sat down with me, we heard the front door slam with such force that it shook the house. She gave me a nonplussed look and shrugged. As I was taking my first bite, I heard heavy, determined footsteps coming down the stairs behind me. I glanced at Ann, whose look had become mildly apprehensive. Edward plunked down beside me and glowered at me. I took another bite and looked at him. He was still glowering and narrowed his eyes slightly. As he started to say something, I said quietly and slowly, "Go away."

He looked a little surprised but continued to stare. So I repeated, a little louder and very slowly, "Go away!" He did. And as I heard him clumping up the stairs, Ann stood and said, "May I freshen your drink?"

I've gotten to know Edward through the years, and every time we meet, he is warm, friendly, and a complete gentleman.

About a month after *The Torch Bearers*, Michael Kahn called again. He was directing Turgenev's *A Month in the Country* for the Roundabout, now one of the most important theater companies in New York. Then it was a relatively low-profile group with a large theater or two down in Chelsea. I loved the play and Michael was assembling a first-rate cast that included Tammy Grimes, Jerome Kilty, Phil Bosco, Boyd Gaines, and Amanda Plummer. I had liked working with Michael, so I jumped at the chance.

The read-through went very well, but after several days of rehearsal, a dangerous pattern began to emerge. Tammy was monopolizing the rehearsal time. A director always has to head off this possibility at the pass, but Michael went along with Tammy's never-ending need to discuss her character's motivation and purpose. The days were slipping away, and a lot of the other scenes and people were not getting the attention they needed. The part I was playing, her lover, was a bit of a wimp, but with a little help from the director I had hoped to make a choice that could change that, for the good of the play. As it turned out, I was barely given enough time to discuss my blocking, much less my character. At one point, quite close to the opening, I discovered that Michael and Tammy had done *A Month in the Country* together before. I was furious. It is the director's responsibility to guide all of the actors into a cohesive whole to realize a particular vision of a play. Indulging one performer's need for attention while neglecting the rest of the cast can produce very uneven results. I was not good in the play when it opened. By the time we were several weeks into the run I had pulled together a relatively decent performance, but that was several weeks too late.

Next I appeared in an off-Broadway revival of *Outward Bound*, directed by an old pro who lived across the street from me, Harold F. Kennedy. Through the years we had run into each other frequently and had often talked about working together. Harold called one evening to ask if I would be interested in his newest project. He had put together an interesting cast, which included two comic geniuses, Imogene Coca and Henry Morgan. The result was disappointing, but the people were fascinating. Imogene, who came to fame as Sid Caesar's sublimely funny partner on television's *Your Show of Shows* in the 1950s, was actually one of the most painfully shy and insecure performers I have ever known. Henry Morgan, one of radio's last big stars during the same period, was known for being snide, sarcastic, and just plain mean. He was actually one of the most polite and pleasant people with whom I've ever worked. The show did not fare as well as I did with the critics. *The New York Times* called it "a leaky dramatic vessel." Of me they said, "Mr. Granger skillfully follows his predecessors, Alfred Lunt and Leslie Howard, in the central role as a self-destructive prodigal with a strong sense of decency."

Harold Kennedy, our director, also just happened to write the funniest book I've ever read about summer theater. If you ever come across it in some used-book bin, buy it. The title is *No Pickle, No Performance*. If it doesn't make you laugh out loud, I will buy it from you. I can never find enough copies to give my friends.

The Right Part

I went into the long-running Ira Levin play *Deathtrap*. It had been on Broadway for four years, and four different actors had played the leading part of Sidney Bruhl. Two members of the original cast had remained the same: Marian Seldes as my wife, Myra, and Elizabeth Parrish, a protégée of Stella Adler's, as the psychic, Helga ten Dorp. William LeMassena, who been a member of the Lunts' company, played Porter, my lawyer. The other new member of the cast, who had been there for a few months, was Steve Bassett, a young actor fresh from Juilliard. Steve played Clifford, the ambitious and unscrupulous young writer who was my lover. They were all rock solid and extremely good. The producers were Alfred de Liagre Jr. and Roger Stevens, both men with good reputations. I only saw de Liagre, and I assumed he was now running the show since Roger Stevens was the head of the Kennedy Center in Washington, D.C. I also assumed that de Liagre was obviously not prepared to spend any more money than necessary to keep *Deathtrap* alive. Perhaps he thought it had run its course. He said he would pay for only two weeks' rehearsal. My character never left the stage and never stopped talking. The amount of tricky stage business was mind-boggling. If ever a play demanded a full rehearsal period, this was it. I loved the play and I knew what fun I could have with the part. I agreed to do it.

We began rehearsal, just the stage manager and I. By the time we finished that first day, I knew I was in deep trouble. He was not the original stage manager, and therefore had not been a part of the original creative process, when a cast and director find the truth that works for them. He was going to be no help at all. He wanted a robot, or an unquestioning understudy who would mimic the actor currently playing the lead. He could not deal with the fact that I had ideas about the part. I asked him when the director was coming in to work with me. He said, "Oh, he's too busy. He won't be coming in."

I don't know which reaction was stronger, anger or the sinking feeling in the pit of my stomach. In any case, I held them both in check and went to the theater to talk to the assistant stage manager. He was an intelligent young man who without saying a word against his boss let me know that he understood my dilemma. We made a plan for him to come to my apartment and work with me on the QT. I don't know that I would have gotten through this period without his help. In the second week of rehearsal, he let a little bit of information slip that saved my life. It seems that another name actor had turned the part down before it was offered to me. He had told them that he would not consider doing this part with less than three weeks' rehearsal. That was all I needed to hear. I told the stage manager to notify the producer that I would not go on unless I had another week of rehearsal. Mr. de Liagre did not come in from East Hampton, but Jay Julien's phone was very busy for a few hours. Jay stuck to my guns and got my third week.

Business began to pick up as soon as I went into the show. A short time later the play was re-reviewed in *The New York Times*. The review was excellent for me and the show. Sales picked up even more, and we ran for almost another year and a half. At one point during our run, Mr. de Liagre received a special award for his contribution to the the theater. There was a ceremony at Sardi's across the street, and we were all encouraged to attend. When I entered the private dining room upstairs, Mr. de Liagre came up to me and said, "Who did you have to pay to get that review?"

I smiled and moved on. Then the director, Robert Moore, whom I had never met, came up to me and said, "Hi, I'm Bob Moore. I hear you're in a hit." I bit my tongue, smiled, and moved on.

I enjoyed doing *Deathtrap* so much that when it was time for a two-week vacation, I only took one week. Bob took a week at the same time, and we flew to London. We went to the theater every night, and met Susan Elliott after the curtain every night. Susan and Denholm had gotten a large apartment on Abbey Road just down the street from where we were staying with our friends Peter and Mary Noble. We never got home before 6:00 A.M. After this week of round-the-clock reveling, we flew back to New York on Sunday, and were back at work on Monday. We both felt as renewed and refreshed as if we'd spent a month on a deserted beach.

Sailing

I met Betsy Crawford when she was working as Shelley Winters's assistant in New York on theater-related projects. For years, Betsy had been involved in various aspects of the theater. She was currently involved with a small off-Broadway company that was struggling to stay alive and had come up with two one-act plays. Louise Lasser, Woody Allen's second wife, was still hot as a result of the cult hit TV series *Mary Hartman, Mary Hartman*. She had agreed to star in the one-acts. Betsy sent me the plays to read and I loved one of them. *Sailing* was written by Michael Shurtleff, one of Broadway's most important casting directors. It was a two-character play about an older well-to-do couple at their summer home on a bluff overlooking a beautiful bay. The husband, an avid sailor, is a cynical, overly articulate curmudgeon who never stops complaining about the decline of civility and manners in today's society. His wife has long ago learned to tune him out and concern herself mainly with the trivia of their existence. Their marriage has little substance left, and they no longer communicate on any meaningful level, but they are stuck with each other.

The companion piece was an outrageous sex farce. After the first company read-through, I realized two things: I was wrong for the farce, and Louise was wrong for *Sailing*. Louise was a unique talent, and I would have loved to work with her, but these two plays were not the right vehicles for us to co-star in. I went to Betsy, and she confided that both directors agreed. Happily, she was able to talk the producers into making the change. Louise got a new leading man, and I got a new leading lady. Together we got great reviews, and our little theater was packed every night, mostly with theater people.

Talley & Son

Almost immediately after *Sailing* closed, I received a call from Marshall Mason, the head of the Circle Repertory company. He was a longtime collaborator of Lanford Wilson, one of contemporary theater's more original voices. Marshall wanted to send me Lanford's new script to read. Would I be interested? I said, "Yes."

I read the play as soon as I received it, and called Marshall immediately. I knew at first reading that the play, the man, and the words were as right for me as I was for them. Now all I had to worry about was the audition.

Although some rare and courageous actors love the process of auditioning, most of us hate it and feel that we come off badly. The number of choices for the approach to any material are so numerous that we always worry that whatever we choose may be different from what the director wants and will scuttle our chance at getting the part. I know that I'm not putting enough faith in the director's imagination, but it is the only plausible reason I can come up with to explain the number of really talented actors who do not work nearly enough.

When I called Marshall with my reaction to Lanford's play, he said, "Good. Then you've got the part."

"When do you want me to audition?"

"Farley, we saw you in *Sailing*. You don't have to audition."

Talley & Son is the third play in Lanford's trilogy about the Talley family, which includes *The Fifth of July* and *Talley's Folly*. It takes place in 1944, during World War II, in the Talley house at the same time that *Talley's Folly* is taking place down at the dock. *The Fifth of July* is set in 1977, after the Vietnam War.

Our company was rehearsing and opening in Saratoga, a beautiful town in upstate New York, famous for its racetrack. The theater there was an old proscenium house. Our award-winning set designer, John Lee Beatty, had designed the set so that it would only have to be reconfigured slightly when we moved into the Circle Rep's much smaller multipurpose space in the heart of Greenwich Village.

My wife was being played by Helen Stenborg, a member of the Circle Rep and a superb actress, who was married to actor Barney Hughes. There was a small college near the theater that had donated two dorms for the company to use. After a couple of nights in the men's dorm, I decided that it might be a little quieter and more conducive to learning lines if I stayed with the women. So I moved to their dorm. The women were worse than the men. I went back to where I had been assigned . . . with earplugs.

After the first read-through of the play, Marshall told us how he planned to rehearse. I didn't like his idea at all. He wanted us up on our feet at once and planned to go though the play sequentially, a specific number of pages at a time. He would spend several days on each section until we were all comfortable and starting to absorb both movement and words, then he would move on to the next section. After two days, it felt like the most natural way to learn the material and was a method of rehearsal that I quickly grew to love. Instead of stopping repeatedly to discuss problematic moments, we let the momentum carry us through them. By the time we got to the end of the section, most of our questions had answered themselves. Lanford's words had a unique rhythm that was tasty and inevitable. I had not felt this comfortable with any text since doing Chekhov.

We opened to full houses and appreciative audiences, and settled in happily for our two-week pre–New York City run. Helen had a car with her, so we explored Saratoga and its environs. She took me to visit Yaddo, a community for artists on a beautiful 400-acre estate in nearby Saratoga Springs. One of Yaddo's alumni was Patricia Highsmith, whose first novel was *Strangers on a Train.*

We also passed a few peaceful hours at the Saratoga racetrack watching the horses work out. All in all, breaking in the play was not the usual hectic effort to get the rewrites in, up, and working. It was, instead, a rewarding time during which we polished and deepened the material before opening in New York.

We moved into the Circle Rep's home on Sheridan Square, and within a short period of adjusting to a different stage and a much more intimate theater, we were ready to open in New York. Our reviews were generally good, but some critics preferred the other two plays in the trilogy. Happily, my reviews were excellent. Even the potentially caustic John Simon was complimentary. I know a lot of actors say that they don't read reviews. I can't make that claim, but I don't seek them out. The good ones make me feel good and the bad ones make me feel bad. Touring the country's major cities with the National Repertory Theatre helped me put reviews in perspective. When you open in ten cities in three plays over a number of months and are reviewed by critics in at least two papers in each of those cities, there are so many different points of view to choose from, quite often in direct contradiction to each other, that the easiest thing to do is enjoy the good reviews and forget the bad ones. In my lifetime there have been a few critics I've read to learn from. Elliot Norton in Boston was one, and Mel Gussow in *The New York Times* was another. Their intelligence and their wealth of theater knowledge, as well as their ability to be objective, made their criticism helpful. Otherwise, I feel that it is easiest to let the reviews fall where they may.

Giving It Another Try

During this time, Bob had progressed from director and line producer on two NBC daytime shows to executive producer at CBS on his fourth soap, *As the World Turns*. It took him nine grueling months, but he finally met the head writer with whom he could transform the eighth-ranked show into a winner. Within six months, he and Doug Marland had moved the show into first place, and it went on to win a Best Show Emmy Award for the first time in its thirty-five-year history.

Against Bob's instincts and, even though I was tempted to take on the challenge of mastering a technique which had up to this time eluded me, against mine, Doug persuaded him to persuade me into signing me for the show. Immediately after signing a three-year contract with mutual out clauses for *As the World Turns*, I was offered a part in a movie, *The Whoopie Boys*, that would reunite me with my old friend Denholm Elliott, as well as Carole Shelley, Michael O'Keefe, and a host of other good actors. We discussed the shooting dates with Douglas, and it looked as if I could finish the film before I was needed to begin on the soap. The movie company kept changing its start date, and Bob finally had to exercise his right to say no to the movie since I had signed with him first. When they got around to making the movie, it was a disaster. For some strange reason I still get credited with being in it. The soap is another story.

Eileen Fulton, whose singing still continues to charm supper club patrons in Manhattan, has played Lisa, the resident vixen on *As the World Turns*, since shortly after the show went on the air. She was chosen to be my love interest on the show. Eileen was helpful, caring, a consummate professional, and in general a delight to work with. Lisa also happened to own the one restaurant/club in Oakdale, the fictitious Midwestern city somewhere near Chicago in which the show took place. Doug Marland was a master at writing scenes at this restaurant/club, the Mona Lisa, where a large number of the show's leading characters supped, drank, plotted, and crossed paths. In this way, he was able to spread information quickly, and dramatically illustrate its effect on the various people involved. The technique worked wonderfully, but these scenes were the most difficult and time-consuming to stage, rehearse, and tape. Whenever the cast saw a heavy day scheduled in the Mona Lisa, we knew that we would be lucky to finish before midnight.

On my first day of work, I had an early-morning call for some of the intimate scenes that introduced my character to Oakdale as well as an afternoon call to play a number of see-and-be-seen scenes at the Mona Lisa. The morning scenes were finished by around 11:00 A.M. I went back to my dressing room, where I sat until my next call at ten-thirty that evening. It was complete chaos in the studio, and everyone was tired. I could not remember one word.

I tried, oh, Lord, I tried. I had a recliner put in my dressing room, kept to myself, and studied my ass off. By the time I was called to the set, I always knew my lines perfectly. The moment I hit the studio, even for the simplest of scenes, the normal noise and chaos of daytime television—sets being changed, last-minute lighting adjustments, the cameras and boom microphone platforms working out traffic problems—blew my concentration. I would tense up and the words would desert me.

There were not enough hours in most days to allow the actors a quiet run-through or two on the set. Whenever we were able to have one, I could remember lines and come up with a performance. But those opportunities were extremely rare. More often than not, the dress would be taped in hopes of getting something good enough. The producers, the directors, the technical staff, and almost all of the other actors could not have been more supportive and encouraging, but it wasn't enough. I still couldn't master the technique of tuning out the surroundings. I knew it and everyone else did, too. I was miserable. By this time in my life, I knew I was a good actor, but that knowledge also made it possible for me know how bad I was in this particular situation. I kept trying for over a year, partially out of loyalty, partially out of stubbornness, but my health began to suffer. I tried new diets, meditation, acupuncture, hypnosis, and whatever else anyone recommended. Nothing helped. Things did not improve. After a few more months, old reliable, my colon, started to act up for the second time since my battle to get out of my contract with Sam Goldwyn.

I was diagnosed with spastic colitis brought on by stress. I asked what I could do about it because it was obviously the soap and I had eighteen months left on my contract. My doctor's answer was, "You have no time left. A perforated colon is an extremely serious problem. It is also one you will be facing soon, if you do not stop what is causing your colitis."

I went to Bob the next day. He said that he knew how unhappy I had been, but had no idea that it was making me sick.. He called Doug immediately, and they discussed replacing me with another actor or writing me out of the show in a way that would be dramatic and serve the plot.

Within two days, Doug Marland had figured out how to write me out of the show, but he needed a month. He agreed to keep my performance schedule as light as he could without damaging the story line. As soon as I heard that, I started to shed some of the tension that was making me ill. After several days, people at the studio started complimenting me on how well the scenes were going. Bob called me into his office and said, "Do you have any idea of how much better you've gotten since we agreed to release you from your contract?" I said that I hadn't, but I did acknowledge that the scenes seemed to be getting a little easier to do. At that point he said, "Maybe you won't have to leave the show." As I quickly turned to leave his office, he yelled after me, "Just kidding."

I got a call from Marshall asking me if I would accept being made a permanent member of the Circle Repertory Company. I was pleased and flattered and said yes. A week later, I received a notification in the mail that I had been nominated for a *Village Voice* Obie Award for my performance in *Talley & Son*. I was pleased, of course, but I knew very little about the award. In fact, I was scheduled to be working at the studio in one of our Mona Lisa marathons on the afternoon of the award ceremony, so I put it aside and forgot about it.

Shirley Kaplan, who had directed me in *Sweet Main Street*, was the first of my friends to call to congratulate me on the Obie nomination. In the course of our conversation, I mentioned that I didn't think that I would be able to make it to the ceremony. She started in about how important it was, but I told her that I had no time to discuss it, because I was studying my lines for the next day's taping. Within the hour I got a call from Mel Gussow. Mel was a very polite and soft-spoken gentleman. I could tell that he was upset. "Farley, Shirley called to tell me that you are thinking of not attending the Obie Award ceremony. Is that true?"

I explained that I would be working at the studio that afternoon, and I was sure that we would go late into the evening. He asked if I'd talked to Bob about getting out early.

"No." I didn't say that I knew nothing about the awards, but he must have sensed a lack of enthusiasm on my part, because he went on to tell me about them.

The Village Voice, the alternative to New York's mainstream papers, had founded the Obie Awards in 1956 under the direction of theater critic Jerry Tallmer. Through the years, they had grown in importance as off-Broadway had grown in importance. Mel, one of the strongest supporters of off-Broadway, felt that the Obies were every bit as important to the theater as the Tonys. For one thing, they represented the world of theater that was there for a younger and broader audience who could not afford Broadway prices. For another, they represented that aspect of New York's theater world where chances could be taken on new writers, actors, directors, and experimental work. It was not nearly as dependent on commercial success. In essence, off-Broadway was the future. Of course, I knew this was true; I had just been preoccupied with my own problem of getting through the last few days on the soap. Mel said, "Farley, please try to attend."

"Yes. Of course I will," I responded.

At the studio the next day, I stopped by the office of the associate producer in charge of arranging the rehearsal and taping schedules. We did not rehearse or tape in sequence. It was done out of order depending upon which sets were standing and which had to be replaced for the next day. When I told her about the Obie Award nomination, Susan Strickler chided me gently for not coming to her sooner about such an important thing and agreed immediately to re-arrange the shooting schedule in order to get me out early. When I said that I hadn't wanted to bother her, because everyone was constantly pestering her for early outs, she laughed, "Farley, bothering me is trying to get out early for a party or a ball game. This is something that really is important. Most of the good things I see in theater are off-Broadway. You will be finished in the A.M. session. Go win an award." She waved me out of her office as I tried to thank her.

The Obie

I was impressed by everyone's enthusiasm about my nomination, and feeling a bit stupid about my lack of knowledge of the award, since I had worked off-Broadway several times and loved it. I called Janice Rule, with whom I'd done my first off-Broadway play, and asked if she would attend with me.

We arrived at the downtown club where the awards were being held. It was small and dark, with a bar and a somewhat central raised performance space. Not knowing anyone officially associated with the Obies, Janice and I headed for the bar. Drinks in hand, I spotted Helen Stenborg and her husband, Barney Hughes, waving at us from a small table. Helen, who played my wife in *Talley & Son*, was also nominated for an acting award. We threaded our way through the crowded space, saying our hellos to the actors each of us recognized, and joined Barney and Helen. Shortly after we got seated, the lights brightened on the performing area and the ceremony began. It was all very informal and relaxed.

I was getting up to get us another drink when I heard my name being called out. This was so unexpected that I just stood there frozen until Janice took the glasses out of my hands and pushed me toward the stage. I made my way through the applauding crowd to the lighted area where I was presented with a plaque signed by six critics as Best Actor of the Year for my performance in *Tal-*

ley & Son. I was still in a state of shock when I made it back to our table and a barrage of hugs and kisses. When I heard them call out Helen's name as Best Actress, my happiness for her brought everything back into focus. I had never won anything in my whole life. Now, at a moment in time when my self-esteem needed it most, I had been publicly honored for my work in a play that I had loved doing.

After the awards had all been handed out and after meeting and thanking the critics who had voted for me, Janice and I slipped away to a small Italian restaurant we both knew in the Village and digested the evening along with some terrific pasta.

We reminisced about working together at the Phoenix, which had been my first onstage appearance in New York. After that, she had married Ben Gazzara, whom she had met in a play produced by Ben's and my lawyer and business manager, Jay Julien. They kept an apartment in New York, but moved to Beverly Hills to make it in the movies. Instead, she had become a highly respected psychoanalyst who left the Coast when their marriage fell apart. I, too, had bounced back and forth, including a four-year stint in Italy. But unlike Janice, the only times I had been really happy in my work was when I was onstage.

I had realized my ambition to become a real actor, and had been lucky enough to do some extremely good things in each of the three golden ages I worked my way through: movies, live television, and theater. The Obie Award was much more to me than an affirmation of work well done, it was proof that the world I fell in love with when I saw Ethel Merman hold an audience in the palm of her hand during my first trip to New York was where I belonged.

Epilogue

I never thought that one of Goldwyn's most famous malapropisms would apply to me so accurately that I would one day quote it as the title for my memoir.

I'm sure he was smart enough to realize that celebrity and talent are not necessarily one and the same. I don't know if he was sensitive enough to realize *I* was smart enough to have figured this out from the beginning. I wanted to develop my talent. I had no interest in becoming a household name or in playing by the rules of the game to become a movie star. When I bought out my contract, Goldwyn thought I was escalating my rebellion to a crazy level for some ulterior motive. I was following my heart and doing what I had to do.

It worked. To this day I cannot forget the thrill of getting my first laugh onstage, the joy of dancing and singing "Shall We Dance?" onstage with Barbara Cook, the sense of accomplishment when the curtain came down on the plays with the National Repertory Theatre. I loved the excitement of creating a character in a new play with the playwright's collaboration, and I will never forget the pride and happiness I felt for receiving an award for doing something I enjoyed so much.

I owe Sam Goldwyn for creating the circumstances that forced me to include myself out. Thanks, Mr. G.

INDEX

FG stands for Farley Granger.

acting schools, 114–15
Actors' Equity Association, 205
Actors Studio, 115–16
Adler, Ellen, 147, 149, 150
Adler, Stella, 100, 104, 115, 147–51, 166, 193, 209, 234
Advise and Consent (play), 206–8
African Queen, The (film), 125
Albee, Edward, 233
Alberto (makeup man), 155, 156, 163, 175
Aldo (cameraman), 161, 168–69, 176
Alexander's Ragtime Band, 27
All About Eve (film), 72
Allen, Fred, 131
Allen, Woody, 236
All Quiet on the Western Front (film), 20, 23, 49
Altman, Robert, 187
Aly Khan, 120, 204
Ameche, Don, 27
American in Paris, An (film), 118
American in Paris, An (composition), 53
American Repertory Theatre, 213
American Shakespeare Festival, 187
American Tragedy, An (book), 95
Anderson, John Murray, 194
Anderson, Dame Judith, 189–90
Andrews, Dana, 20, 21, 22, 23, 25, 26, 92, 102–3, 111
Andrews, Julie, 194
Andy Hardy series, 91
Ann, Peggy, 27
Anna and the King of Siam (book and film), 206
Annie du Far West (musical), 97–98
Annie Get Your Gun (film), 88–89
Annie Get Your Gun (musical), 64
Anouilh, Jean, 213
Antonioni, Michelangelo, 227
Anything Goes (film), 49
Appalachian Spring (composition), 87
"Archie" (FG's second lover), 39–40
Arlen, Harold, 53, 55

Armored Attack (adaptation of *North Star*), 24
Army Special Services Unit, 35
Around the World in 80 Days (film), 152
Arrowsmith (TV play), 190
Asphalt Jungle, The (film), 88
Astaire, Fred, 88, 135, 168
As the World Turns (soap), 239–41
auditioning, 237
Auger, Genette, 164
Ax, Emmanuel, 86

Babes in Arms (musical), 99
Bacall, Lauren (Betty), 112, 125, 133, 174
Bad and the Beautiful, The (film), 72, 149
Bad Day at Black Rock (film), 75
Balanchine, George, 134–35
Ball of Fire (film), 56, 134
Balsam, Marty, 228
Bancroft, Anne, 177, 178–79
Barefoot Contessa, The (film), 174
Barrymore, Ethyl, 138–39
Basehart, Richard, 79, 82, 105
Bassett, Steve, 234
Baxter, Anne, 21–22, 52, 131
Beatles, the, 125
Beatty, John Lee, 237
Beau (dog), 14
Beaumont, Roger, 226–28
Beck, George, 118
Behave Yourself (film), 118–19
Belafonte, Harry, 194
"Bel Air Circuit," 59
Bergen, Polly, 194–95, 198–200
Berger, Helmut, 227
Bergman, Ingrid, 70, 110, 120, 157
Berkeley, Busby, 88–89, 140
Berlin, Irving, 86
Bernstein, Leonard, 33, 50, 54, 85–87, 96
Best Years of Our Lives, The (film), 47–48, 56, 76, 111
Bickford, Charles, 79

Big (film), 138
blacklist, the, 93–95, 171, 185
Blithe Spirit (play), 37
Bloom, Claire, 189, 213
Blore, Eric, 16
Bluebell Girls, 127
Blyth, Ann, 78, 91
Bogard, Paul, 228
Bogarde, Dirk, 227
Bogart, Humphrey, 20, 111–12, 125, 133, 174
Boland, Mary, 193
Bolger, Ray, 65
Bonanza Bound (musical), 54, 62, 63, 68, 93
Bonshire, Forrest, 127
Bosco, Phil, 233
Boston, 219
Bowles, Paul, 143
Brackett, Charles, 92, 103, 134, 177
Brando, Marlon, 65, 114–15, 142, 147, 149, 150, 179, 183
Brazzi, Rossano, 174
Brecht, Bertolt, 203
Brennan, Walter, 20, 22
Brigadoon (film), 139
Brigadoon (musical), 65
Britten, Benjamin, 123
Broadway theater, 188
Brooks, Geraldine, 184–85
Brooks, Mel, 179
Brown, Sarah (character in *Guys and Dolls*), 103
Bruhn, Erik, 134
Bucks County Playhouse, 209
Budge, Don, 74
Burke, Billie, 140
Burns, George, 136
Burrows, Abe, 103, 193–95, 197–99
Burton, Richard, 124–25
Burton, Sybil, 124–25
bus-and-truck tours, 206

Caesar, Sid, 234
Caesar and Cleopatra (TV show), 189–90
Cagney, Jimmy, 20
Calamai, Clara, 170
Calhoun, Bob, 214, 216–17, 219–23, 225–29, 231–32, 236, 239–41
Calhoun, Rory, 58
Call Me Madam (musical), 103, 124
Cannon, James W., 209
Cantor, Eddie, 56, 190
Capa, Bob, 97
Capote, Truman, 224–25
Capri, 144–45
Carefree Tree, The (play), 187–88
Caron, Leslie, 138–39
Carousel (musical), 35, 99, 212

Carr (producer), 207
Carter Barron amphitheater, 205–6
Cass, Peggy, 232
Caviezel, Jim, 61
Chaplin, Charlie, 7, 18, 73–76, 83, 107
Chaplin, Ethyl, 53–55, 57, 62–63, 66, 71–72, 75, 78, 85, 90, 95, 99–102, 104–6, 122, 127, 128, 163, 165, 202–3, 226, 229
Chaplin, Judy, 53, 90, 95, 99, 226, 229
Chaplin, Saul, 53–55, 62–63, 66, 68, 71–72, 78, 85, 90, 95
Christian, Linda, 131–32, 184
Church, Sandra, 192–93, 208–9
Cicognia, Marina, 147–53
cinematographers, 168
Circle Repertory Company, 237, 241
Citizen Kane (film), 57, 77, 93
City Center, 204, 206
Civic Repertory Theatre, 212
Clift, Montgomery, 11, 114–15, 142
"Clouded Image, The" (TV play), 190
Clurman, Harold, 100
Cobb, Lee J., 190
Coca, Imogene, 234
Cocteau, Jean, 163–65
Coe, Richard, 108
Cohn, Harry, 27, 62, 137–38, 204
Cole, Nat King, 113
Collier, Constance, 69
Collier, John, 79, 83
Collins, Joan, 177–78
Colman, Ronald, 130
Colt, Alvin, 187, 193, 196, 200
Columbia Pictures, 27, 62, 137
Comden, Betty, 54, 62, 63, 193
Connery, Sean, 125
Conte, Richard, 25
Cook, Barbara, 99, 121, 194, 204–5
Cooper, Gary, 56, 62, 129–30, 134
Cooper, Mrs. Gary (Rocky), 129–30
Copland, Aaron, 20, 21, 33, 50, 51, 86–87
Corn Is Green, The (film), 67
Cornwall, Connie, 8
Cotten, Joseph, 106, 107–8
Coulouris, George, 93, 95, 102
Coulouris, Louise, 93, 102
Cover Girl (film), 54
Coward, Noël, 37, 70–71, 116, 192, 215–17, 229
Craig, Helen, 62
Crain, Jeanne, 131
Crawford, Betsy, 236
Crawford, Joan, 80, 141
Creative Management Associates, 226
critics, 238
Cronyn, Hume, 232–33

Crosby, Bing, 35
Crucible, The (play), 213, 215, 218, 220
Curtiz, Michael, 183

Dafoe, Willem, 61
Dalí, Salvador, 133
Dall, John, 67, 69
Damian (movie part), 10, 12
D'Amico, Suso Cecchi, 143, 177
Damned, The (film), 227
Dance of Death (play), 225
Daredevils, The (club), 12
Darnell, Linda, 27–28, 206
Da Silva, Howard, 58
Davidson, Gordon, 222, 225
Davies, Marion, 18
Davis, Bette, 67, 72, 133, 207
Day, Doris, 82
Dean, James, 61
Death in Venice (film), 227
Deathtrap (play), 234–36
Decision Before Dawn (film), 104, 105
de Havilland, Olivia, 133
de Liagre, Alfred, Jr., 235
de Mejo, Oscar, 160
de Mille, Agnes, 33, 65, 101
De Mille, Cecil B., 70, 83
Dempsey, Jack, 74
Destry Rides Again (film), 116
Dewell, Michael, 209–10, 211–13, 214, 217–18
Dietrich, Marlene, 35, 116, 199–200
Dina (lighting designer), 222
dinner theater, 231
Dolly Sisters, The, 27
Donen, Stanley, 55–56, 135
Donna Reed Show, The (sitcom), 91
Double Indemnity (film), 129
Dougherty, Frances Ann, 209–13, 214, 217–18, 219–21, 232
Douglas, Kirk, 92, 149
Dow, Peggy, 111, 116–17
Dowling, Constance, 12
Dowling, Doris, 120
Down to Earth (film), 71, 202–3
Dracula (play), 231
Duff, Howard, 112
Duke, Patty, 178–79
Dunham, Katherine, 110
Dunne, Irene, 206
Dupont Show of the Month, 189, 190
Durbin, Deanna, 52

Ecstasy (film), 73
Eddy, Nelson, 183
Edens, Roger, 135
Edge of Doom, 91–92, 102–3

Egyptian, The (film), 183–84, 223
Egyptian (movie theater), 16
Elizur, Yuval, 126–27
Elliott, Denholm, 209, 214–18, 236, 239
Elliott, Susan, 215, 217–18, 236
Ellis, Anita, 71
Emerson, Hope, 79
Enchantment (film), 76–77
Englund, George, 228
Enola Gay (bomber), 203
Enters, Warren, 200
Ernst, Max, 169
Escoffier, Marcel, 145
Evans, Joan, 80–81, 92, 105, 111
Evans, Maurice, 35, 36, 207

Fancy Free (ballet), 33, 50, 64, 85, 101
fan mail, 48
Father Knows Best (sitcom), 91
Faye, Alice, 27
Fearnley, John, 204–5
Feldman, Charlie, 118, 136–38, 140, 141–42, 176–77, 183–84, 204
Feldshuh, Tovah, 232
Ferrer, José, 216
Fields, Freddie, 194, 198
Finian's Rainbow (musical), 65
First Impressions (musical), 65, 193–200
Flahooley (musical), 121
Fleischer, Richard, 177–78
Fleming, Victor, 110
Flippen, J. C., 58
Flynn, Errol, 125–26, 133
Fonda, Henry, 65
Fontaine, Joan, 26
Fontanne, Lynn, 115
Ford, Barbara, 107
Ford, Glenn, 202, 204
Fosse, Bob, 186
Fountainhead, The, 62
Francis, Arlene, 224–25
Franklin, Benjamin, 93
Freed, Arthur, 85, 88, 135, 140
Freeman, Al, Jr., 231
Freeman, Mona, 190
Frenchie (film), 116
Front Page, The (film), 20
Fryer, Bobby, 207
Fulton, Eileen, 239
Funny Girl (musical), 193, 220, 222
Fürtwangler, Wilhelm, 105, 106

Gable, Clark, 88, 129, 130
Gabor, Zsa Zsa, 138–39
Gaby (dog), 83, 84, 85, 90
Gaines, Boyd, 233

Garbo, Greta, 97
Gardner, Ava, 112–14, 174
Garfield, John, 170
Garland, Judy, 52, 55, 88–89, 90, 107, 113, 135, 139
Garner, Peggy Ann, 26
Garrett, Betty, 55, 71, 72, 85, 89
Garson, Greer, 27, 88, 130, 193
Garvin, Chuck, 35–37
Gassman, Vittoria (Tori), 129, 140, 174
Gassman, Vittorio, 129, 132–33, 139–40, 171, 173–74
gays
    in Hollywood film, 69–70
    in the military, 31, 36, 41
Gazzara, Ben, 222, 243
General Dies at Dawn, The (film), 20
Gersh, Phil, 9–10, 12–13
Gershwin, George, 53–54, 55, 105–6, 133
Gershwin, Ira, 21, 53–54, 55
Gershwin, Lee, 55
Giannini, Giancarlo, 227
Gibson, Mel, 61
Gibson, William, 179
Gilbert and Sullivan, 53
Gilda (film), 71, 202
Gingold, Hermione, 164, 193–95, 197, 199–200
Girl in the Red Velvet Swing, The (film), 130, 176, 177–78, 224
Girl Who Came to Supper (musical), 215–17
Girotti, Massimo, 154, 156, 159, 160, 170, 172
Glass Menagerie, The (play), 42, 221
Goddard, Paulette, 83
Golden Age of Hollywood, 188
Goldman, Milton, 208, 209
Goldwyn, Frances, 91–92
Goldwyn, Samuel
    casting FG, 9–12
    contract signed with, 13
    FG called into his office, 51
    FG wants to get out of contract with, 136–38, 141–42, 223
    film-making style, 60, 81
    heroic testimony at HUAC hearings, 94
    "include me out" saying, 141–42, 244
    loans FG to other studios, 23, 66, 84–85, 131
    looking for a hit, 80, 91–92, 102, 103, 116, 117–18
    neglects FG's career, 56–57
    patriotic movie making in World War II, 20, 24
    promotes FG's career, 59, 111
    reputation in the film industry, 130
    said to have blacklisted FG after contract break, 223
    says FG is like a son to him, 47–48, 49
    son and grandson of, in the business, 231
    tries to control FG's life, 51, 76–79, 114
    tyrannical behavior of, toward actors, 76–77, 79
Goldwyn, Samuel, Jr., 231
Goldwyn, Tony, 231
Goldwyn Studio, 10, 56–57, 94
Goodman, Benny, 35
Good Soldier Schweik, The (play), 203
gossip columnists, 18–19, 27
Grable, Betty, 26, 27, 35
Graduate, The (film), 179
Grahame, Gloria, 61, 72, 149
Grange, Red, 74
Granger, Eva Mae (FG's mother), 22–23, 47, 67, 70, 183
Granger, Farley E. (FG's father), 28, 47, 51, 67, 70, 85, 90, 183
Granger, Farley Earle, II (author)
    in Army Special Services as entertainer, 35–37
    casting of, 9–12
    childhood, 13–14
    contracted with Samuel Goldwyn, 9–11, 13
    early days in Hollywood, 7–29
    first acting as teen, 8–9
    first Broadway shows attended, 64–65
    first screen work, 11–12, 17, 19–29
    Goldwyn's contract and control of career, 23, 47–49, 51, 56–57, 59, 66, 78, 84–85, 111, 114, 131, 223
    joins Navy and goes to war, 29–35
    keeps real name, 17
    loses virginity twice, 37–41
    sex relationships and attitudes, 41
    in soap operas, 239
    stage acting, 186
    in television, 188
    tries to break contract with Goldwyn, 136–38, 141–42, 223
    viewing own movies, 1–2
    wins Obie Award, 241–43
Granger, Stewart (real name Jimmy Stewart), 17
Grant, Cary, 70, 110
Grauman's Chinese (movie theater), 16
Gray, Dolores, 123–24
Great Dictator, The (film), 107
Green, Adolph, 54, 62, 63, 64, 85–86, 193
Greenstreet, Sydney, 16, 133
Grimes, Tammy, 233
Guggenheim, Pegeen, 226
Guggenheim, Peggy, 104, 148, 152–53, 169–70, 226
Guggenheim, Solomon R., 148
Gurian, Manning, 200–201, 211
Gurian, Peter, 211

Gus (MGM guard), 49
Gussow, Ann, 233
Gussow, Mel, 232–33, 238, 241
Guthrie, Tyrone, 187, 210
Guys and Dolls (musical), 103
Gypsy (musical), 96, 193, 197, 201, 208, 211

Hacker, Dr. Frederick, 109
Hagen, Jean, 88
Hagen, Uta, 98, 228
Hagman, Larry, 201–2
Hall, Carol, 232
Hambleton, T. Edward, 187
Hamilton, Patrick, 67
Hammerstein, Oscar, 99, 121, 204–6, 212
Hanks, Tom, 138
Hanley, Ellen, 200
Hannett, A. T., 205
Hannum, Alberta, 79
Hans Christian Andersen (film), 98, 134–36
Harding, Ann, 20
Hardwicke, Sir Cedric, 69, 189
Harris, Julie, 184–85, 191, 200–201, 209–11
Harrison, Rex, 150, 151, 194, 206
Hart, Lorenz, 53, 99
Hart, Moss, 134–35
Hasso, Signe, 210, 221
Hasty Heart, The (play), 186
Haver, June, 27
Havoc, June, 201, 211
Hawkins, Jack, 189
Hawks, Howard, 134
Hayes, Helen, 108, 191–92, 202
Hayworth, Rita, 26, 27, 35, 54, 55, 71, 120,
    174, 189, 202–4
Hearst, William Randolph, 18, 24
Hecht, Ben, 92, 103, 137
Hedda Gabler (play), 221
Heflin, Frances, 185–86
Heflin, Van, 108, 185
Heiress, The (TV show), 191, 201
Helen Hayes Theatre, 201
Hellman, Lillian, 10–11, 12, 20
Hell's Angels (film), 59
Hemingway, Ernest, 97
Henderson, Florence, 216
Hepburn, Audrey, 135, 179
Hepburn, Katharine, 125
Herbert, F. Hugh, 91
Hersey, John, 210
Highsmith, Patricia, 128, 238
Hill, Steve, 209
Hitchcock, Alfred, 66, 67, 106–10, 119
    genius of, 109–10
Hitchcock, Pat, 109, 110
Holbrook, Hal, 42, 221

Holliday, Judy, 54, 88
Hollywood
    the blacklist, 93–95, 171, 185
    Golden Age of, 188
    gossip magazines, 27
    public appearances of stars, 78
    publicity and columnists, 18–19
    stage mothers, 22–23
    studio system, 78
    young actors' school, 27–28
Hollywood Canteen (film), 72
Hollywood Ten, the, 94–95
Hope, Bob, 35, 59
Hopper, DeWolf, 19
Hopper, Hedda, 18, 19, 102, 120, 132, 137
Horne, Lena, 55, 114
Houghton, Norris, 187
House Committee on Un-American Activities
    (HUAC), 57, 89, 93–94, 101
Houseman, John, 57–59, 187
Howard, Leslie, 234
Howe, James Wong, 50, 119, 168
Hughes, Barney, 237, 242
Hughes, Howard, 58–59, 60, 113, 118, 119
Hume, Benita, 224–25
Hunter, Jeff, 60
Huston, John, 20, 77, 83, 125
Huston, Walter, 20
Hutchinson, Josephine, 213
Hutton, Betty, 89

Ibsen, Henrik, 221
Ince, Thomas, 18
"include me out" saying, 141–42, 244
Internal Security Act of 1950, 93
In Which We Serve (film), 216
Israel, 126–27
Italy, 103
I Want You (film), 111, 114, 116–17

Jackson, Michael, 52
Jeanmaire, Zizi, 98, 135–36, 163–64
Joan of Arc (film), 110
Johnson, Edie, 54
Johnson, Van, 54–55, 136
Jones, Bobby, 74
Jones, Jennifer, 107–8
Julien, Jay, 230, 231, 235, 243

Kahn, Michael, 232–33
Kai-shek, Mme. Chiang, 133
Kaplan, Jonathan, 185
Kaplan, Mady, 185
Kaplan, Nora, 185
Kaplan, Shirley, 232, 241
Kaplan, Sol, 185

Kardos, Lesie, 140–41
Karinska, Madame, 200
Kaufman, Lorry, 75
Kaufman, Millard, 75
Kay, Hershey, 196, 197
Kaye, Danny, 56, 98, 134–36, 185
Kaye, Sylvia, 135
Kazan, Elia, 57, 65, 115
Keaton, Buster, 7
Keel, Howard, 88
Kelly, Betsy, 54, 55, 98
Kelly, Gene, 54, 55, 72, 85, 88, 94, 98, 131, 202
Kelly, George, 232
Kelly, Grace, 109
Kennedy, Harold F., 234
Kennedy, John F., 209–10, 214, 216–18
Kennedy's Children (play), 231
Kerr, Deborah, 27, 130, 131
Keyes, Evelyn, 77, 83–84
Killers, The (film), 112
Kilty, Jerome, 233
Kimbrough, Emily, 177
King, Alan, 36
King, Henry, 131
King and I, The (film), 74
King and I, The (musical), 99, 121, 204–6
King of Kings (film), 60
Kirkwood, James, 186
Kitt, Eartha, 106
Knef, Hildegard, 132
Knox, Mickey, 226, 228
Krasker, Robert, 171, 173, 176
Kurnitz, Harry, 216
Kyle, Steven, 63

Lady Eve, The (film), 77, 129
Lahr, Bert, 8
Lamarr, Hedy, 35, 72–73
Lambert, Glen, 12
Lambs' Club, 36
L.A. Music Center, 222
Lancaster, Burt, 85, 90, 94, 112, 114, 131
Landau, Jack, 187
Landon, Margaret, 206
Lane, Nathan, 192
Lang, Fritz, 190
Langdon, Harry, 7
Lanza, Mario, 183
Lardner, Ring, Jr., 94
Larkin, Peter, 193, 195
Lasser, Louise, 236
Last Temptation of Christ, The (film), 61
Laughton, Charles, 131
Laura (TV play), 224–25
Laurents, Arthur, 66, 75, 78
  in Europe, 98–101, 104–6

as friend and mentor, 73, 79, 83, 84, 95–96
  as writer, 69–70
Lawrence, Gertrude, 37, 70–71, 204
Leachman, Cloris, 228
League of Broadway Producers, 205
Lean, David, 216
Lee, Gypsy Rose, 197, 201, 211
Le Gallienne, Eva, 60, 115, 209–17, 219, 221
LeGrand, Adam, 204
LeGrand, David, 204
Leigh, Janet, 94
Leighton Margaret, 207
Leisen, Mitch, 83–84
LeMassena, William, 234
Leopold and Loeb case, 67
Levant, Oscar, 54, 131
Levene, Sam, 25, 28, 30, 32, 51, 52
Levin, Ira, 234
"Liana" (FG's first lover), 38–39, 43
Liliom (play), 212, 221
Lindstrom, Peter, 110
Lipton, Jimmy, 99–100
Litvak, Anatole, 104
Lloyd, Harold, 7
Lo Chiamavano Trinità (film), 229
Loesser, Frank, 81, 83, 103, 134–36
Loew, Arthur, 94
Loew, Marcus, 94
Loews Inc., 198
Loren, Sophia, 193
Lorre, Peter, 16, 133, 190
Los Angeles, 91, 222
Loy, Myrna, 130
Lucas, Jonathan, 195, 196
Luce, Henry, 24
Ludlum, Robert, 192
Ludwig (film), 227
Lumet, Sidney, 188, 193
Lunt, Alfred, 65, 115, 234
Lux Films, 143–46, 149, 165

Ma, Yo-Yo, 86
MacDonald, Jeanette, 183
MacKenzie, Giselle, 193–94
MacMahon, Aline, 79
MacMurray, Fred, 27
Madden, Donald, 198, 199
"Mademoiselle" (segment of *The Story of Three Loves*), 138–39
Madison, Guy, 58
Magnani, Anna, 168, 184–85
Mailer, Norman, 94–95, 226
Mailey, Peggy, 123
Malibu, 223
Mambo, 171, 173–74
Mangano, Silvana, 171

Mann, Anthony, 85, 88
Marais, Jean, 163–65
Marco and Maria (servants), 166–68, 172–73
Mariposa School, San Jose, Calif., 13–14
Mark Taper Forum, 222–23, 226
Marland, Doug, 239–40
Martin, Mary, 191–92, 201–2
Mary Stuart (play), 210–11
Mason, James, 70, 130
Mason, Marshall, 237–38, 241
Massey, Raymond, 79
Masteroff, Joe, 200
Mastroianni, Marcello, 129, 227
Mature, Victor, 183
Mayer, Louis B., 27, 54–55, 84–85, 88, 89, 114, 130
Mayo, Virginia, 56, 134
MCA, 198–99
McCarter Theatre Company, 232
McCarthy, Joe, 94, 166
McDowall, Roddy, 26, 27, 28–29, 30, 32, 52, 142, 189
McGuire, Dorothy, 111, 116–17
McIlhenny, Henry, 215
McIntyre, Bob, 9, 10–11, 12, 17, 29, 32, 49
McLerie, Allyn Ann, 63, 65, 86
Meacham, Anne, 213–14, 215
Medford, Kay, 42, 43, 220
Meet Me in St. Louis (film), 90, 138
Meglin Kiddies, 15
Meisner, Sanford, 115–16, 186, 193
Mellett, Lowell, 20
memorizing lines, 230–31, 240
Mencken, H. L., 63
Menjou, Adolphe, 7
Mercer, Johnny, 55
Mercury Theatre, 57
Merman, Ethel, 64–65, 103, 123, 191, 201, 208–9, 243
Merrick, David, 205
Merrill, Dina, 232
Merrill, Gary, 71–72, 207
Metro-Goldwyn-Mayer (MGM), 27, 58, 62, 84–85, 94, 135, 139, 140, 198
Mick (dog), 14
Mikado, The (modernized opera), 37
Milan, Joe, 127
Mildred Pierce (film), 78
Milestone, Kendall, 49
Milestone, Lewis, 10–12, 20–21, 23–25, 49–50, 111
Militich, Bill, 36, 42–43
Milland, Ray, 130, 177–78, 224
Miller, Ann, 85, 140–41
Miller, Arthur, 220
Miller, David, 91

Mineo, Sal, 61
Minnelli, Lisa, 139
Minnelli, Vincente, 138–39, 149
Miracle Worker, The (film), 178–79
Miranda, Carmen, 26
Miss Liberty (musical), 86
Mister Roberts (play), 65, 192
Mitchell, James, 65, 194, 196–98
Molnar, Ferenc, 212, 221
Moment of Truth, The (film), 184
Monroe, Marilyn, 131
Montealegre, Felicia, 87
Month in the Country, A (play), 233–34
Moog, Heinz, 154, 156
Moore, Robert, 235
Morales, Adele, 226
Morales, Joan, 226–27
"More I Cannot Wish You" (song), 81, 103
Morelli, Rina, 159
Morgan, Frank, 8
Morgan, Henry, 234
Morris, Chester, 206–8
Morrow, Tom, 42, 43, 44, 205
Motion Picture Alliance for the Preservation of American Ideals, 57
Mozart, W. A., 35
Mr. Goldwyn (one-man show), 36
Mrs. Klein (play), 98
Musser, Tharon, 222
My Fair Lady (musical), 194

Naked Street, The (film), 178
Nash, N. Richard, 187
National Phoenix Theatre, 210
National Repertory Theatre, 210–21, 238
NBC television, 191
Neal, Patricia, 62
Neighborhood Playhouse, 115, 186
Nelson, Ricky, 138
Nelson, Ruth, 20
New Haven, 219–20
New Theatre for Now program, 225
New York, 64, 183–84, 220
Ney, Freddy, 26, 127
Nichols, Mike, 179
Night of the Iguana, The (play), 207
Niven, David, 76, 77, 130
Noble, Kara, 125
Noble, Katrina, 125
Noble, Mary, 123–25, 175, 236
Noble, Peter, 123–25, 175, 236
No Pickle, No Performance (book), 234
Norregard, Julie, 212
North, Alex, 223, 225
North, Anna, 225
North Hollywood Junior High, 16

North Star, The (film), 11–12, 20–24, 50, 51
Norton, Elliot, 238
Novak, Kim, 27

Obie Award, 241–43
O'Connor, Donald, 16
O'Donnell, Cathy, 49, 58, 60, 73, 76, 79, 84, 88
off-Broadway, 186–87, 241–43
Of Mice and Men (film), 20, 49
O. Henry's Full House (film), 131
O'Keefe, Michael, 239
Olivier, Laurence, 171, 193, 225
O Mistress Mine (play), 65
O'Neill, Eugene, 74
O'Neill, Oona, 74, 75
One Life to Live (soap), 229
On the Town (film), 66, 85
On the Town (musical), 65, 85
Osato, Sono, 66
Ossessione (film), 170
Our Very Own (film), 91, 102
Outlaw, The (film), 59
Outward Bound (play), 234

Paar, Jack, 164
Pal Joey (musical), 55
Palm Beach Story, The (film), 77
Palmer, Lilli, 150
Pantages (movie theater), 16
Papp, Joe, 233
Paris, 96
Parks, Larry, 71, 89
Parone, Eddie, 225
Parrish, Elizabeth, 234
Parsons, "Docky," 18
Parsons, Louella, 18–19, 91, 120, 132
party games, 75, 172
Passion of the Christ, The (film), 61
Pasternak, Joe, 140–41
Patrick, John, 186
Paul (dancer), 164
Payne, John, 27
Penn, Arthur, 178–79
Perkins, Elizabeth, 138
Peter Grimes (opera), 123
Peters, Jean, 131
Peters, Kelly Jean, 213, 215, 219–20
Petit, Roland, 98, 135
Philadelphia, 215
Phoenix Theatre, 187, 210
Picnic (play), 192
Pin Up Girl (film), 26
Place in the Sun, A (film), 95, 111, 123, 139
Players, The (restaurant), 77–78
Playhouse 90, 190
Playwrights Horizons, 232

Pleven, François and Patrice, 98–99
Plummer, Amanda, 233
Plummer, Chris, 191
Pomtag, Edith, 14
Pomtag, Jackie, 14
Porgy and Bess (opera), 53, 105–6
Porter, Cole, 136
Postman Always Rings Twice, The (film), 170
Powell, Jane, 140
Powell, Michael, 134
Power, Tyrone, 27, 131–32
Powers, Mala, 92
Present Laughter (play), 192
Price, Vincent, 190
Prince, Hal, 205, 226, 229
Prisoner of Zenda, The (TV show), 191
Private Lives (play), 70, 229
Puccini, Giacomo, 53
Purdom, Edmund, 183–84
Purple Heart, The (film), 23, 25, 28–29, 30, 31

Quinn, Anthony, 177, 178

Radziwill, Lee, 224–25
Rainmaker, The (play), 186
Rathbone, Basil, 213
Rattigan, Terence, 215
Ray, Nicholas, 57–59, 60–61, 72, 81–82, 128
  genius of, 60–61
Ray, Tony, 61
Ray (musician in army), 37
Rebecca (film), 66
Rebel Without a Cause, 61
Red Channels (pamphlet), 95
Redfield, Billy, 147, 149, 150
Redgrave, Michael, 187
Red Pony, The (film), 49
Reed, Carol, 106
Reed, Ted, 52–53
Reiner, Carl, 36
Reinhardt, Gottfried, 138–39
Reis, Irving, 76–77, 80–81
repertory theater, 213
Republic Studios, 49
reviews, 238
Reville, Alma, 110
Ring Round the Moon (play), 213–14, 219–20
Ritchard, Cyril, 189
Rivera, Diego, 132, 133
RKO, 57–58, 60, 62, 118, 119–20
Robbins, Jerry, 33, 54, 64, 74–76, 96, 100–101,
  121, 127–28
Robinson, Edward G., 133
Robson, Mark, 92, 116–17
Rodeo (ballet), 33, 50
Rodgers, Mary, 205

Rodgers, Richard, 53, 99, 121, 204–6, 212
Rogers, Ginger, 88, 168
Roman, Ruth, 109
Romance on the High Seas (film), 82
Rome, 226
Rooney, Mickey, 113
Roosevelt, Eleanor, name thrown in when lines
    are forgotten, 231
Roosevelt, Franklin D., 20, 41, 213
Rope (film), 66, 67, 130
Rope's End (play), 67
Rorem, Ned, 127–28
Roseanna McCoy (film), 48, 60, 79–83, 92, 103,
    105
Rosencrantz and Guildenstern Are Dead (play), 224
Rosi, Francesco, 143, 144, 153, 158–59, 175,
    184
Rossellini, Roberto, 120
Rossen, Carol, 42, 221
Rossen, Robert, 42, 171, 173
Rotunno, Giuseppe, 176
Rubenstein, Johnny, 228
Rule, Janice, 187–89, 242
Run for Your Life (TV series), 222
Russell, Harold, 48
Russell, Jane, 59
Ruth, Babe, 74
Ruttenberg, Joe, 140, 168

Sailing (play), 236
Sakall, S. Z. (Cuddles), 140
Sanders, George, 224–25
Sarah (Navy nurse), 43–44
Scarface (film), 59
Schaffner, Franklin, 190
Schary, Dore, 58
Schenck, Joe, 198
Schenck, Nicholas, 198
Schildkraut, Joseph, 212–13
Schiller, Friedrich, 210
Schneider, Benno, 11–12
Schneider, Romy, 227
Schulberg, Budd, 97
Scorsese, Martin, 61
Seagull, The (play), 213, 220
Seattle Repertory Theatre, 229
Segal, Alex, 188, 189, 190, 191
"Seidman and Son" (TV play), 190
Seldes, Marian, 234
Selznick, David O., 107–8, 111, 132, 160
Senso (film), 1, 2–3, 104, 143–46, 148, 153–76,
    227
Servicemembers Legal Defense Network, 41
Shadow of a Doubt (film), 66, 107–8
Shane, Maxwell, 178
Shaw, Artie, 113

Shaw, Irwin, 116
Shearer, Moira, 134–35
Shelley, Carole, 239
Sheridan, Richard, 221
Sherman, Hiram (Chubby), 197
Sherwood, Robert, 111, 116
She Stoops to Conquer (play), 221
Shore, Dinah, 35, 135
Shostakovich, Dmitri, 50
Show Boat (film), 113
Show Boat (musical), 113
Shurtleff, Michael, 236
Side Street (film), 84, 87–88
Silk Stockings (musical), 132
Silvers, Phil, 54, 55
Simmons, Jean, 183
Simon, John, 238
Simon, Neil, 196
Sinatra, Frank, 55, 72, 85, 113, 160, 174
Singin' in the Rain (film), 16, 88
Skelton, Red, 137
Skinner, Cornelia Otis, 177–78, 190
Small House of Uncle Thomas, The (ballet), 74, 121
Small Town Girl (film), 140
Smith, Oliver, 139
soap operas, 229–31, 239–41
Sondheim, Stephen, 96
Song Is Born, A (film), 56, 134
Son of Ali Baba (film), 118
Sordi, Alberto, 227
Sound of Music, The (musical), 201–2, 231
Spiegel, Sam, 112
Springer, John, 120–23
Stack, Robert, 224
Stalin, 94
Stanislavsky method, 115
Stanwyck, Barbara, 56, 129–31, 134
Stapleton, Maureen, 221
Stenborg, Helen, 237–38, 242–43
Stevens, George, 95, 235
Stevens, Marti, 198, 199, 208
Stewart, Jimmy, 67, 69–70, 85, 130
Stewart, Mary, 7–9
Stoppard, Tom, 224–25
Story of Three Loves, The (film), 138–39
Stowe, Harriet Beecher, 75
Strange Love of Martha Ivers, The (film), 49
Strangers on a Train (film), 2, 74, 107–10, 111,
    123, 128, 129, 130, 178
Strasberg, Lee, 115–16
Streetcar Named Desire, A (play), 65, 179
Streisand, Barbra, 193, 220
Strickler, Susan, 242
Strindberg, August, 225
Student Prince, The (operetta), 183
Sturges, Preston, 77–78, 118

Styne, Jule, 96, 193–94, 208
summer stock, 185–86
Summer Storm, 27
Susskind, David, 190, 191, 224
Sweet Bird of Youth (play), 192
Sweet Main Street project, 232
Sydow, Jack, 213–14, 220, 221

Tahse, Martin, 207–8
Take Me Out to the Ball Game (film), 72
Talley & Son (play), 237–38, 241, 242–43
Tallmer, Jerry, 241
Tandy, Jessica, 65, 179, 232–33
Taylor, Elizabeth, 26, 27, 52, 89, 124, 152, 179
Telefono Bianco films, 168
television, 90–91
    episodic, 223, 229
    live, 188–93
Temple, Shirley, 52
Tey, Josephine, 190
They Call Him Trinity (film), 229
They Live by Night (film), 2, 59, 61, 67, 72–73, 106, 126
Thieves Like Us (original title for *They Live by Night*), 57–59
Thin Man comedies, 118–19
Third Man, The (film), 106
Thompson, Kay, 135–36
Threepenny Opera, The (musical), 72
Tierney, Gene, 26, 183
Tilden, Bill, 73–74
Todd, Mike, 150, 151–52
Togliatti, Palmiro, 166
Toland, Gregg, 56, 77, 168
Torch Bearers, The (play), 232
Tosi, Piero, 145–46
Tree Grows in Brooklyn, A (film), 57
Truman, Harry, 41–42
Trumbo, Dalton, 94
Tryon, Tom, 186
Turgenev, Ivan, 233
Turner, Lana, 149, 168, 170
TWA, 119–20
20th Century-Fox, 23, 25, 27, 131, 137, 178
Twisted Road, The (title considered for *They Live by Night*), 59
Two Arabian Knights (film), 20
Tyne, George (Buddy), 75, 90, 95, 99–100, 101–2, 104, 105, 106, 122, 127, 128, 163, 202, 203, 226, 229
typecasting, 109

UFA, 190
Uncle Tom's Cabin (novel), 75

United Artists, 198
United States Information Agency, 228
Up in Arms (film), 56

Valli, Alida, 106, 154, 156, 157, 159–60, 162–63, 165, 173, 174–75
Van, Bobby, 140
Vanderbilt, Gloria, 186, 193
Van Fleet, Jo, 42, 221
Venice, 104, 146, 168, 226
Vera-Ellen, 85
Vidal, Gore, 227
Vidor, Charlie, 136
Vienna, 105
Viertel, Jigee, 97
Viertel, Peter, 97
Viertel, Salka, 97
Village Voice, The (newspaper), 241
Visconti, Luchino, 104, 129, 142–46, 148, 153–76, 184, 227
    genius of, 153–54, 157
Vitti, Monica, 227
Vivian, Percival, 8–9
Volpi, Giovanni, 148, 151
von Stroheim, Erich, 20

Wagner, Mayor Robert, 205
Wald, Jerry, 137–38
Walker, Nancy, 65–66
Walker, Robert, 107–9, 119
Walk in the Sun, A (film), 24, 49
Warm Peninsula, The (play), 200–202
Warner, Ann, 133
Warner, Jack, 54, 72, 133
Warner Brothers, 56, 66, 109, 133, 134, 190, 193
Washington, D.C., 217
Watch on the Rhine (film), 93
Watts, Richard, Jr., 199
Wayne, David, 65
Webster, Margaret, 213
Weill, Kurt, 53
Welles, Orson, 26, 77, 106
Werner, Oskar, 105, 106
West Side Story (musical), 96
Where's Charley? (musical), 63, 65
White, Ruth, 201–2
Whoopee! (film), 56
Whoopie Boys, The (film), 239
Widmark, Richard, 131
Wilder, Billy, 118, 134
Williams, Andy, 136
Williams, John, 190
Williams, Tennessee, 42, 143, 176–77, 207
Williams Brothers, 135
Wilson, Lanford, 237–38

Winchell, Walter, 92, 103
Winters, Shelley, 52, 77–79, 85, 90, 94–95,
    111–12, 114–16, 118–29, 132–33,
    139–40, 144, 171, 173–74, 183, 230,
    231, 236
Withers, Jane, 20, 22–23, 52
Wolf, Janet, 144–52, 154, 157–59
Wonderful Town (TV film), 85
Wood, Natalie, 61
Wookie (English play), 7–9
World War II, 94, 105
Worth, Irene, 210–11
Wright, Teresa, 20, 21, 76, 77
Wyler, William, 56, 76–77

Wynn, Ed, 88
Wynn, Keenan, 54–55, 88–89

Yaddo, 238
Yordan, Phil, 81, 92
Young, Loretta, 64
Your Red Wagon (title considered for They Live by
    Night), 59

Zagni, Giancarlo, 159–60
Zanuck, Darryl F., 25, 27, 177, 183, 223
Zeffirelli, Franco, 143, 153, 154–62, 166, 168,
    175, 227
Zorba the Greek (film), 179

Made in the USA
San Bernardino, CA
05 November 2013